Hollywood Wives
&
Hollywood Husbands

Jackie Collins brings the wild and sexy world of superstardom alive. Her phenomenally successful novels have made her as famous as the movers and shakers, power-brokers and superstars she writes about with an insider's knowledge. With 200 million copies of her books sold in more than forty countries, Jackie Collins is one of the world's top-selling writers. In a series of sensational best-sellers, she has blown the lid off Hollywood life and loves. 'It's all true,' she says. 'I write about real people in disguise. If anything, my characters are toned down – the real thing is much more bizarre.'

There have been many imitators, but only Jackie Collins can tell you what *really* goes on in the fastest lane of all. From Beverly Hills bedrooms to a raunchy prowl along the streets of Hollywood. From glittering rock parties and concerts to stretch limos and the mansions of the power-brokers – Jackie Collins chronicles the *real* truth.

Jackie Collins

Hollywood Wives
&
Hollywood Husbands

PAN BOOKS

Hollywood Wives first published 1983 by William Collins & Sons Ltd.
First published by Pan Books 1984
Hollywood Husbands first published 1986 by William Heinemann Ltd.
First published by Pan Books 1987

This omnibus edition published 2004 by Pan Books
an imprint of Pan Macmillan Ltd
Pan Macmillan, 20 New Wharf Road, London N1 9RR
Basingstoke and Oxford
Associated companies throughout the world
www.panmacmillan.com

ISBN 0 330 43931 6

1 3 5 7 9 8 6 4 2

A CIP catalogue record for this book is available from
the British Library.

Printed and bound in Great Britain by
Mackays of Chatham plc, Chatham, Kent

Hollywood Wives

For Tracy, Tiffany, and Rory
with all my love.

Nobody is allowed to fail within a two-mile radius
of the Beverley Hills Hotel

Gore Vidal

prologue

He stood in the living room of the small house in Philadelphia. He stood and stared at the three of them. Three pigs. Three laughing faces. Teeth and eyes and hair. Three pigs.

There was a black rage within him. A rage which beat at his head from the inside.

The television was on in the room. Archie Bunker mouthing futile jokes. Canned studio laughter.

And more laughter. In the room with him. More inane laughter.

His mother. Mousy wisps of brown hair. A sagging body and a sagging mind

His father. Balding. Skinny. False teeth that clicked in and out at will.

Joey. He had thought she was different.

Three pigs.

He walked to the television set and raised the sound.

They took no notice. They were too busy laughing. At him. Yes. They were laughing at him.

The rage was in his head, but outwardly he was calm. He knew how to make them stop. He knew . . .

Fast and fluid. Before they had time to stop laughing and start thinking . . .

Fast and fluid. The machete swung in a lethal circle.

Fast and fluid as the blood spurted. His mother and father felled with the first lethal sweep.

But Joey. Swifter, younger. Her eyes bulging with horror as, clutching at her wounded arm, she staggered towards the door.

You've stopped laughing now, Joey. You've stopped laughing now.

He swung the machete again, felling her before she could progress further.

They did not scream. Not one of them.

He had taken them by surprise, just like soldiers were trained to do. Only he wasn't a soldier was he? He wasn't a soldier . . .

Sobs began to shake him violently. Strange silent sobs which convulsed his body as he wielded the machete. Dealing with all three of them equally. Indulging in a frenzy of grisly death blows.

The television drowned out the sounds of the carnage. Archie Bunker. Canned laughter.

And the machete continued to whirl and slash as if powered by some demonic force.

book one

1

Elaine Conti awoke in her luxurious bed in her luxurious Beverly Hills mansion, pressed a button to open the electrically controlled drapes, and was confronted by the sight of a young man clad in a white T-shirt and dirty jeans pissing a perfect arc into her mosaic tiled swimming pool.

She struggled to sit up, buzzing for Lina, her Mexican maid, and at the same time flinging on a marabou trimmed silk robe and pressing her feet into dusty pink mules.

The young man completed his task, zipped up his jeans and strolled casually out to view.

'Lina!' Elaine screamed. 'Where *are* you?'

The maid appeared, inscrutable, calm, oblivious to her mistress's screams.

'There's an intruder out by the pool,' Elaine snapped excitedly. 'Get Miguel. Call the police. And make sure all the doors are locked.'

Unperturbed, Lina began to collect the debris of clutter from Elaine's bedside table. Dirty Kleenex, a half-finished glass of wine, a rifled box of chocolates.

'Lina!' Elaine yelled.

'No get excited, Señora,' the maid said stoically. 'No intruder. Just boy Miguel sent to do pool. Miguel sick. No come this week.'

Elaine flushed angrily. 'Well why the hell didn't you tell me before?' She flung herself into her bathroom, slamming the door so hard that a framed print sprang off the wall and crashed to the floor, the glass shattering. Stupid maid. Dumb ass woman. It was impossible to get good help anymore. They came. They went. They did not give a damn if you were raped and ravaged in your own home.

And this *would* have to happen while Ross was away on location. Miguel would *never* have dared to pretend to be sick if Ross was in town.

Elaine flung off her robe, slipped out of her nightgown, and stepped under the invigorating sharpness of an ice cold shower. She gritted her teeth. Cold water was best for the skin, tightened everything up – and God knows – even with the gym and the yoga and the modern dance class it still all needed tightening.

Not that she was fat. No way. Not a surplus piece of flesh on her entire body. Pretty good for thirty-nine years of age. Pretty damn good.

When I was thirteen I was the fattest girl in school. Etta the Elephant they called me. And I deserved the nickname. Only how could a kid of thirteen know about nutrition and diet and exercise and all that stuff? How could a kid of thirteen help it when Grandma Steinberg stuffed her with cakes and latkes, lox and bagels, strudle and chicken dumplings. Constantly.

Elaine smiled grimly. Etta the Elephant, late of the Bronx, had shown them all. Etta the Elephant, former secretary in New York City, was now slim and svelte. She was called Elaine Conti, and lived in a six bedroomed, seven bathroomed, goddamn Beverly Hills palace. On the flats too. Not stuck up in the hills or all the way over in Brentwood. On the flats. Prime real estate.

Etta the Elephant no longer had a sharp nose, mousy hair, gapped teeth, wire rimmed glasses and flat tits.

Over the years she had changed. The nose was now retroussé, cute. A perfect Brooke Shields in fact. The mousy hair was a rich brown, cut short and tipped with golden streaks. Her skin was alabaster white and smooth, thanks to regular facials. Her teeth were capped. White and even. A credit to Charlie's Angels. The unbecoming glasses had long been replaced with soft blue contact lenses; without them her eyes were slate grey and she had to squint to read. Not that she did a lot of reading. Magazines of course. 'Vogue', 'People', 'Us'. She skimmed the trades, 'Variety' and 'Hollywood Reporter', concentrating on Army Archerd and Hank Grant. She devoured 'Women's Wear Daily', but was not really into what she termed hard news. The day Ronald Reagan was elected President was the only day she gave a passing thought to politics. If Ronald Reagan could do it how about Ross?

The tits, while being nowhere in the Raquel Welch class, were a perfect 36B, thanks to the ministrations of her first husband, Dr. John Saltwood. They stuck defiantly forward, no pull of gravity would ever harm *them*. And if it did, well . . . back to good old Johnny. She had found him in New York, wasting himself doing

14

plastic surgery for a city hospital. They met at a party and she recognized a plain lonely man not unlike herself. They married a month later, and she had her nose and tits fixed within the year. Then she talked him into going to Beverly Hills and setting up in private practice.

Three years later he was *the* tit man, and she had divorced him and become Mrs. Ross Conti. Funny how things worked out.

Ross Conti. Husband. Movie star. First class shit.

And she should know. After all they had been married ten long years and it hadn't all been easy and it wasn't getting any easier and she knew things about Ross Conti that would curl the toes of the little old ladies who still loved him because after all he was hitting fifty and his fans were not exactly teenagers and as each year crept by it was getting more and more difficult and God knows financially things were not as good as they had been and each film could be his last and . . .

'Señora.' Lina hammered on the bathroom door. 'The boy, he go now. He want pay.'

Elaine stepped out of the shower. She was outraged. He wanted paying – for what? Pissing in her pool?

She wrapped herself in a fluffy terrycloth robe and opened the bathroom door. 'Tell him,' she said grandly, 'to piss off.'

Lina stared blankly. 'Twenny dollar, Meesus Conti. He do it again in three day.'

Ross Conti swore silently to himself. Jesus H. Christ. What was happening to him? He couldn't remember his frigging lines. Eight takes and still he was screwing up.

'Just take it easy, Ross,' said the director calmly, placing a conde-scending hand on his shoulder.

Some frigging director. Twenty-three if he was a day. Hair hanging down his back like a witch at Halloween. Levis so tight the outline of his schlong was like a frigging beacon.

Ross shook the offending hand off. 'I'm taking it easy. It's the crowd – they keep on distracting me.'

'Sure,' soothed Chip, signalling to the first assistant. 'Calm them down for crissakes, they're background – not auditioning for Chorus Line.'

The first assistant nodded, then made an announcement through his loud speaker.

'Ready to go again?' questioned Chip. Ross nodded. The director turned to a suntanned blonde. 'Again, Sharon, sorry babe.'

Ross burned. *Sorry babe. What the little prick really means is sorry babe but we gotta humour this old fart because this old fart used to be the biggest thing in Hollywood.*

Sharon smiled. 'Right on, Chip.'

Sure. Right on, Chip. We'll humour the old schmuck. My mother used to love him. She saw all his movies. Creamed her panties every time.

'Make-up,' Ross demanded, then added, his voice heavy with sarcasm, 'That's if nobody minds.'

'Of course not. Anything you want.'

Yeah. Anything I want. Because this so-called hotshot needs Ross Conti in his film. Ross Conti means plenty at the box office. Who would line up to see Sharon Richman? Who has even heard of Sharon Richman except a couple of million television freaks who tune in to see some schlock programme about girl water ski instructors. Glossy crap. Sharon Richman – a hank of hair and a mouthful of teeth. I wouldn't even fuck her if she crawled to my trailer on her hands and knees and begged for it. Well . . . maybe if she begged.

The make-up girl attended to his needs. Now *she* was all right. She *knew* who the star was on this picture. Busily she fussed around him, blotting out the shine of sweat around his nose with an outsize powder puff, touching up his eyebrows with a small comb.

He gave her a perfunctory pinch on the ass. She smiled appreciatively. *Come to my trailer later, baby, and I'll show you how to give a star head.*

'Right,' said Chip the creep. 'Are we ready, Ross?'

We are ready asshole. He nodded.

'Okay. Let's go then.'

The scene began all right. It was a simple bit of business which involved Ross saying three lines to Sharon's six, then strolling nonchalantly out of shot. The trouble was Sharon. She stared blankly, making him blow his second line every time.

Bitch. She's doing it purposely. Trying to make me look bad.

'Jesus H. Christ!' Chip finally blew. 'It's not the fucking soliloquy from Hamlet.'

Right. That's it. Talking to me like some nothing bit player. Ross turned and stalked from the location without a backward glance.

Chip grimaced at Sharon. 'That's what happens when you're dealing with no talent.'

'My mommy used to love him,' she simpered.

'Then your mommy is an even bigger moron than her daughter.'

She giggled. Chip's insults did not bother her. In bed she had him under control, and that was where it *really* mattered.

Elaine Conti drove her pale blue Mercedes slowly down La Cienega Boulevard. She drove slowly so as not to spoil her nails which she had just had done at a senational new nail clinic called The Nail Kiss of Life. Wonderful place. They had wrapped her broken thumb nail so well that even *she* couldn't tell. Elaine loved discovering new places, it gave her a tiny shot of power. She pushed in a Streisand tape and wondered – as she had wondered countless times before – why dear Barbra had never had her nose fixed. In a town so dedicated to the perfect face . . . And God knows she had the money . . . Still . . . It certainly had not harmed her career . . . nor her love life for that matter.

Elaine frowned and thought about her own love life. Ross hadn't ventured near her in months. Bastard. Just because *he* didn't feel in the mood . . .

Elaine had indulged in two affairs during the course of her marriage. Both of them unsatisfactory. She hated affairs, they were so time consuming. The highs and the lows. The ups and the downs. Was it all worth it? She had decided no, but now she was beginning to wonder.

The last one had taken place over two years previously. She blushed when she thought about it. What absurd risks she had taken. And with a man who could do her absolutely no good at all except fix her teeth, and they were already perfect. Milton Langley, her dentist – and probably everyone else's with money in Beverly Hills. How indiscreet of her to have picked him. But really he had picked her. He had sent his nurse scurrying off on an errand one day, climbed aboard the chair, and made fast and furious love to her. She remembered the day well, because he had climaxed all over her new Sonia Rykiel skirt.

Elaine giggled aloud at the thought, although she hadn't giggled at the time. Milton had poured mouthwash over the damaged garment, and when his nurse returned sent her over to Saks to purchase a replacement. After that they had met twice a week in some dreadful motel on Santa Monica for two hot months. One day Elaine had just decided not to go. End of *that* little episode.

The other one wasn't even worth thinking about. An actor on one of Ross's films. She had slept with him twice and regretted both times.

Whenever she mentioned their lack of a sex life to Ross he flew into a rage. 'What the frig do you think I am? A machine?' he would snarl. 'I'll get it up when *I* want to – not just because you've read some crap sex magazine that says you should have ten orgasms a day.'

Chance would be a fine thing. She was lucky if she got ten a year. If it wasn't for her trusty vibrator she would be climbing walls.

Maybe his erection would return if the movie he was doing turned out to be a hit.

Yes. That was what Ross needed – a massive shot of success. It would be good for both of them. There was nothing like success for putting the hard-on back in a man's life.

Carefully she made a left on Melrose. Lunch at Ma Maison was a must on Fridays. Anybody who was anybody and in town invariably showed up. Elaine had a permanent booking.

She made a right into the small parking lot, and left her car in the hands of a parking jockey.

Patrick Terrail, the owner of Ma Maison, greeted her at the entrance to the small outdoor restaurant. She accepted a kiss on each cheek, and followed a waiter to her table, keeping an eagle eye out for anyone she should acknowledge.

Maralee Gray, one of her closest friends, was already waiting. She nursed a spritzer and a sour expression. At thirty-seven Maralee maintained more than a shadow of her past prettiness. In her time she had been voted the most popular girl in high school *and* Miss Hot Rod 1962. That was before she had met, married and divorced Neil Gray – the film director. Her father – now retired – owned Sanderson Studios. Money had never been Maralee's problem. Only men.

'Darling. I'm not late am I?' Elaine asked anxiously, brushing cheeks with her friend.

'Not at all. I think *I* was early.' They exchanged 'You look wonderfuls', admired each other's outfits, and cast their eyes around the restaurant.

'And how's Ross making out on location?' Maralee inquired, extracting a long black cigarillo from a wafer thin gold case.

'You know Ross – he makes out wherever he is.'

They both laughed. Ross's reputation as a cocksman was an old Hollywood joke.

'Actually he hates everything,' she confided. 'The script, the director, the crew, the food, the climate – the whole bug-ridden set-up as he so charmingly puts it. But Maralee, believe me –' She

18

leaned confidentially towards her friend, 'He's going to be dynamite in this movie. The old Ross Conti – full force.'

'I can believe it,' Maralee murmured. 'I've never counted him out, you know that.'

Elaine nodded. Maralee was a true friend, there weren't many of them around. In Hollywood you were only as hot as your last hit – and it had been a long time between hits.

'I'm going to have my eyes done,' Maralee announced dramatically. 'I'm only telling you, and you mustn't mention it to anyone.'

'As if I would!' Elaine replied, quite affronted. 'Who's going to do it?'

Maralee laughed. 'The Palm Springs connection, of course. I'll spend a couple of weeks there – after all I have the house – then I'll come back and nobody will know the difference. They'll just think I was vacationing.'

'Wonderful idea,' Elaine said, thinking to herself was Maralee stupid or what? Nobody took a vacation in Palm Springs – even if they did have a house there. They either weekended or retired. 'When?' she asked, her eyes flicking restlessly round the restaurant.

Maralee shrugged. 'As soon as possible. Next week if he can fit me in. He's so busy.'

They both stopped talking to observe the entrance of Sylvester Stallone. Elaine threw him a perfunctory wave but he did not appear to notice her. 'Probably needs glasses,' she sniffed. 'I met him at a party only last week.'

Maralee produced a small gold compact and inspected her face. 'He won't last,' she remarked dismissively, removing a smudge of lipstick from her teeth. 'Let's face it – Clark Gable he's not.'

'Oh yeah, that's it . . . Don't stop . . . don't ever stop. Oh yeah, yeah . . . Just keep on going, sweetheart, keep right on going.'

Ross Conti listened to the words pouring from his mouth and wondered how many times he had uttered them before. Plenty. That was for sure.

On her knees, Stella, the make-up girl, worked diligently on his weak erection. She sucked at him like he was a water pump. Her technique could do with some improvement. But then – in his time – Ross had had some of the best little cocksuckers in the business. Starlets, whose very livelihood depended on doing a good job. Hookers, who specialized. Bored Beverly Hills housewives who had elevated cocksucking to an art.

He felt his erection begin to deflate, and he dug his fingers hard into the girl's scalp. She yelped with pain and stopped what she was doing.

He wasn't sorry. Quick as a flash he tucked himself out of sight and firmly zipped up. 'That was great!'

She stared at him in amazement. 'But you didn't come.'

He could hardly lie. 'Sometimes it's better this way,' he mumbled mysteriously, reaching for a bottle of tequila on the side table in his hotel room.

'It is?' She continued to stare.

'Sure. Keeps all the juices inside. Keeps me buzzing. That's the way I like it when I'm working.' If she believed that she'd believe anything.

'I think I know what you mean,' she began enthusiastically. 'Sort of like a boxer before a fight – you mustn't release that precious energy. Instead you have to make it work for you.'

'Right! You got it!' He smiled, took a slug of tequila straight from the bottle, and wished she would go.

'Would you like me to . . . do anything?' she questioned expectantly, hoping that he would ask her to undress and stay.

'There's a million things I'd like you to do,' he replied. 'But the star has got to get some sleep. You understand, don't you?'

'Of course, Mr. Con . . . Ross.'

He hadn't said she could call him by his first name. Mr. Conti would do nicely. Women. Give them nine inches and they frigging moved in. 'Goodnight, Sheila.'

'It's Stella.'

'Right.'

She finally left, and he switched on the television set. Just in time for The Tonight Show. He knew that he should call Elaine in L.A. but he couldn't be bothered. She would be furious when she heard he had blown his lines and walked off the set. Elaine thought he was on the way out. She was always nagging him about keeping up with what the public wanted. He had done his last movie against her advice, and it had bombed at the box office. God, that had pissed him off. A fine love story with a veteran director and a New York stage actress as his leading lady. 'Old fashioned garbage,' Elaine had announced baldly. 'Sex, violence and comedy, that's what sells tickets today. And you've got to get in on the act, Ross, before it's too late.'

She was right of course. He did have to get in on the act because he was no longer Mr. Box Office, not even in the frigging top ten. He

20

was on the slide, and in Hollywood they could smell it.

Johnny Carson was interviewing Angie Dickinson. She was flirting, crossing long legs and looking seductive.

Abruptly Ross picked up the phone. 'Get me the bell captain,' he snapped.

Chip had come grovelling to his trailer after his walk-out earlier. 'Nothing we can't sort out, Ross. If you want to quit today we can schedule to reshoot the scene first thing in the morning.'

He had agreed. At least they knew they were dealing with a star now, and not some nothing has-been.

'Yes, Mr. Conti. This is the bell captain. How may I help you?'

Ross balanced the phone under his chin and reached for the tequila bottle. 'Can you be discreet?'

'Of course, sir. It's my job.'

'I want a broad.'

'Certainly Mr. Conti. Blond? Brunette? Redhead?'

'Multi-coloured for all I care. Just make sure she's got big tits – and I *mean* big ones.'

'Yes *sir!*'

'Oh – and you can charge her to my account. Mark it down as room service.' Why should *he* pay. Let the film company pick up the tab. He replaced the receiver and walked to the mirror. Fifty. He was soon going to be fifty. And it hurt. Badly.

Ross Conti had lived in Hollywood for thirty years. And for twenty-five of those years he had been a star. Arriving in town in 1953, it had not taken long before he was discovered hauling boxes in a food market on Sunset Boulevard by an ageing agent's young wife. She was entranced by his blond good looks, and set about persuading her husband to handle him. In the meantime she was handling him herself – twice a day – and loving every minute.

Her husband discovered their affair on the day Universal decided to sign his young client. In a fit of fury the old agent negotiated the worst deal he possibly could, waited until it was signed, then dropped Ross, and badmouthed him as an untalented stud all over town.

Ross didn't care. He had grown up in the Bronx. Spent three years kicking around New York grabbing bit parts here and there, and a Hollywood contract seemed just perfect to him, whatever the terms.

Women adored him. For two years he worked his way through the studio, eventually picking on the pretty mistress of a studio executive, who promptly saw to it that Ross's contract was dropped.

21

Two years, and all he had done were a few small parts in a series of beach party movies. Then suddenly – no contract, no prospects, no money.

One day, lounging around Schwabs drugstore on the strip he got talking to a girl called Sadie La Salle, a hard working secretary with the most enormous knockers he had ever seen. She was not a pretty girl. Overweight, suspicions of a moustache, short of leg. But oh those magnificent tits! After talking for a while he surprised himself by asking her for a date. She accepted readily, and they went to the Aware Inn, ate health burgers and talked about him. He loved every minute of it. How many girls were prepared to discuss him and only him for five solid hours?

Sadie was very smart – a quality Ross had not encountered in a woman before. She refused to go to bed with him on their first date, slapped his hands away when he went after the magic tits, gave him sound advice about his career, and on their second date cooked him the best meal he had ever had.

For six months they had a platonic relationship. Seeing each other a couple of times a week, speaking on the phone daily. Ross loved talking to her, she had an answer for every problem. And oh boy, did he ever have problems! He told her about the girls he was screwing, the trouble he was having finding work. Going on interview after interview and getting nowhere was depressing, not to mention terrible for his ego. Sadie was a wonderful listener, plus she cooked him two great meals a week and did his washing.

One night he had a narrow escape while visiting a nubile girlfriend. Her out-of-town husband returned home sooner than expected, and Ross was forced to drop out of her bedroom window desperately clutching his pants. He decided to pay Sadie an unexpected visit and tell her the story, sure that she would love it.

When he arrived at her small apartment on Olive Drive he was shocked to discover her entertaining a man, the two of them sitting at her candlelit dining table finishing off a delicious smelling pot roast. There was wine on the table, fresh cut flowers and her best cutlery. Sadie was wearing a low cut dress and looked flustered to see him.

It had never occurred to him before that she had boyfriends, and for some unknown reason he was extremely pissed off.

'Ross, I want you to meet Bernard Leftcovitz,' she said primly, eyeing Ross's crumpled clothes and mussed hair with distaste.

He flung himself familiarly into a chair and threw a brief silent nod in Bernard Leftcovitz's direction. 'Get me a drink, hon,' he said to

Sadie, reaching out to slap her on the ass. 'Scotch, plenty of ice.'

She glared, but did as he asked. Then he outsat Mr. Leftcovitz who finally left an hour later.

'Thanks a lot!' Sadie exploded, as soon as the door shut behind him.

Ross grinned. 'Wassamatter?'

'You know what's the matter. Walking in here like you own the place, treating me like one of your . . . your . . . goddamn women!' She was spluttering with anger. 'I hate you, Ross, you know that? I really hate you! You think you're such a big deal. Well, let me tell you—'

He grabbed her fast. Moved in for the kill – for he knew that's what it would be – a killer scene, all thighs and heat and those amazing mountainous tits enveloping him.

She pushed him away. 'Ross –' she began to object.

He wasn't about to listen to any reason why they shouldn't. Sadie La Salle was going to be his and only his – screw the Bernard Leftcovitzes of this world.

She was a virgin. Twenty-four years old. A resident of Hollywood and a virgin.

Ross could not believe it. He was delighted. Ten years of solid fucking and she was his first.

The next day he packed up his things and moved in with her. He was two months overdue with the rent on his apartment anyway, and money was becoming a definite problem. Moving in with Sadie seemed like a great idea, plus she loved having him in her life. She said goodbye to Bernie without a second thought and devoted all her time to taking very good care of Ross indeed. 'We have to find you an agent,' she fretted, because she knew his failure to land a part in a movie was upsetting him more than he cared to admit. Unfortunately all the agents he visited seemed to have got the message – Ross Conti equals bad news.

One day she made a major decision. 'I'll be your agent,' she stated quite seriously.

'You'll what?' he roared.

'I'll be your agent. It's a good idea. You'll see.'

The next week she gave up her job, withdrew her savings from the bank, and soon found a tiny little room in a seedy building on Hollywood Boulevard. She stuck a notice on the door – Sadie la Salle – Agent to the Stars. Then she had a phone installed, and was in business.

23

Ross found the whole thing hysterically funny. What the hell did Sadie know about being an agent?

What she didn't know she soon found out. For six years she had worked as a secretary in a large law firm which specialized in show business work. Sadie had the legalities down pat. And the rest wasn't difficult. She had a product. Ross Conti. And when the women of America got a good look at him they were going to want to buy.

'I have a great idea,' she told him one day, 'and I don't even want your opinion of it because it'll work. I know it's going to work.'

As it happened he loved her idea – although it was a little crazy, and very expensive. She borrowed the money she needed from her former boss, an uptight jerk named Jeremy Mead who Ross suspected wanted to ball her. Then she had Ross photographed by the Pacific Ocean in just faded Levi cut-offs and a smile. And she had the picture blown up and placed on as many billboards as she could afford all across America, with just the words – 'WHO IS ROSS CONTI?'

It was magic time. Within weeks everyone was asking, 'Who is Ross Conti?' Johnny Carson began making cracks on his show. Letters started to arrive by the sackload, addressed to Ross Conti, Hollywood. (Sadie had prudently informed the post office where to forward them.) Ross was stopped in the street, mobbed by adoring women, recognized wherever he went. The whole thing took off like a rocket just as Sadie had predicted it would.

At the peak of it all Sadie flew with her now famous client to New York, where he had been invited to do a guest appearance on The Tonight Show. They were both ecstatic. New York gave Ross the feel of what it would be like to be a star. Sadie was thrilled that it was she who had done it for him.

He was marvellous on the show – funny, sexy, and magnetically attractive. By the time they got back to Hollywood the offers were piling up. Sadie sifted through them and finally negotiated an ace three picture deal for him with Paramount. He never looked back. Success as a movie star was instantaneous.

Six months later he dumped her, signed with a big agency and married Wendy Warren, a rising young star with impressive thirty-nine inch breasts. They lived together in much photographed luxury on top of Mulholland Drive, five minutes from Marlon Brando's retreat. Their marriage lasted only two years and was childless. After that Ross became the Hollywood bachelor. Wild stories, wild pranks, wild parties.

Everyone was delighted when in 1964 he married again. This time to

24

a Swedish starlet of seventeen with, of course, wonderful tits. The marriage was stormy. Lasted six months. She divorced him claiming mental cruelty and half his money. Ross shrugged the whole thing off.

At that time his star was at its peak. Every movie he appeared in was a winner. Until 1969, when he made two disastrous films in a row.

A lot of people were not sorry to observe his fall from superstardom. Sadie La Salle for one. After his defection from her loving care she had faded from sight for a while, but then she had resurfaced and slowly but surely built herself an empire.

Ross met Elaine when he went for a consultation with her husband. At thirty-nine he thought that maybe he needed a little face work. He never got the surgery, but he did get Elaine. She moved in on him without hesitation, and she was just what he needed at that time in his life.

He found her sympathetic, supportive and an excellent listener. The tits were nothing to get excited about, but in bed she was accommodating and warm, and after the aggression of the usual Hollywood starlet he liked that. He decided that marriage to Elaine was just what he needed. It did not take a lot of persuasion for her to divorce her husband. They married a week later in Mexico, and his career took a sharp upwards swing. It stayed up for five years, then slowly, gradually, it began to slip. And so did their marriage.

Forty-nine. Heading full speed towards fifty. And he didn't look a day over forty-two. The blond boyish good looks had aged nicely. Although he could do without the greying hair that had to be carefully bleached, and the deep indentations under his piercing blue eyes.

Still . . . he was in excellent shape. The body was almost as good as new. He stared at his reflection, hardly hearing the discreet knock on the door.

'Yes?' he called out, when the knock was repeated.

'Room service,' crooned a feminine voice.

Room service was twenty-five and stacked. Ross made a mental note to tip the bell captain royally.

25

2

'He was never a normal boy, Deke Andrews wasn't, always a strange one.'

'Yeah? How so?'

'You know . . . Not interested in television, movies or girls. Not like the other kids round this street – even when he was growin' up.'

'What *was* he interested in?'

'Cars. First job he got he went right out and put a down payment on an old Mustang. Loved that car. Polished it, tuned it, worked on that old jalopy for hours on end.'

'What happened to it?'

'Got sold. Don't know why. He never did get another one.'

'You sure about that?'

'Sure about what?'

'That he never got another car.'

' 'Course I'm sure. I know everything goes on in Friendship Street. I've sat lookin' out this same window for thirty years. Did I tell you 'bout my accident? Had heavy machinery collapse on my legs. I ain't never walked a step since. Compensation? You think I got money? I got *nothing* for all the stinkin' time I put in at that lousy plant. Have you any idea . . .' The old man went red in the face as his voice rose and shook with anger.

Detective Leon Rosemont rubbed the bridge of his large nose and stared at a cheap framed print on the wall. Who could ever figure people out? This old man was more interested in what had happened to him thirty years previously than what had happened only hours before in the house across the street. As a witness he was useless. He had heard nothing. Seen nothing. Knew nothing.

Soon the newspapers would be screaming their banner headlines. SAVAGE TRIPLE KILLING. MURDER HORROR IN SUB-URBIA. BLOOD MASSACRE. How the press loved a good juicy mass murder. Three people brutally murdered in a small house on

26

Friendship Street in a respectable suburb of Philadelphia. Jesus! How he wished he could wipe the morning's carnage from his mind. Bile rose in his throat, and he swallowed it down sharply.

Detective first grade Leon Rosemont. A heavy-set man in his early fifties, broad shouldered and powerfully built, with a mass of thick grey hair, shaggy eyebrows, and sharp, kindly brown eyes. He looked like an out-of-condition football star. And that's exactly what he had been in college – the hero of the field. He had been twenty-nine years on the force. Twenty-nine years of mutilations, sex killings and vicious slayings.

How he hated all the shit that came his way.

They gave all the pretty ones to him, but this was the prettiest in a long while. Three people hacked to pieces for no apparent reason. No sexual assault. No robbery. No nothing. And not a good god-damn thing to go on. Except maybe Deke Andrews, the son of the household who seemed to be missing.

So – was this just another nice old-fashioned family murder?

Deke Andrews wasn't around to tell. But then perhaps he was away on a trip, staying with friends, or shacked up with some girl. After all, it was only Saturday afternoon, and according to forensic the killings could have taken place any time between 11 p.m. Friday and 4 a.m. Saturday.

Deke Andrews. Twenty-six years old. A loner who kept to himself.

But then how many people had been questioned about him? Four? Five? The investigation hadn't even started yet. These were early days.

'Niggers!' the old man stated fiercely. 'They're causin' trouble all over.'

'What?'

'It's these niggers moved in down the street. I wouldn't be surprised if they did it,' he snorted. 'I keep my doors locked now – not like the old days – why I can remember when you didn't hafta *have* locks.'

Detective Rosemont nodded curtly. There was a sour taste in his mouth, and the memory of the early morning tableau danced horrifically before his eyes. His head ached, his lips were parched and his eyes felt sunken and dry. He wished he was at home in bed with his wife, sweet black Millie, and wouldn't *that* give this old bigot something to think about.

'They should stay on South Street where they belong,' muttered

27

the old man ominously. 'Comin' to live among decent folk. It ain't right, there should be a law . . .'

Detective Rosemont pushed himself heavily out of the overstuffed armchair he was sitting in and headed towards the door. Screw it. He was beginning to feel suffocated. 'Thank you, Mr. Bullen,' he said tightly. 'We'll be needing a formal statement of course. One of my men will be back later –'

'Niggers!' screeched the old man hysterically, warming to his subject. 'They shoulda been left in Africa runnin' around naked. That's what I think. That's what all decent folk think.'

Angrily Leon Rosemont let himself out of the small house. It was raining, a bleak relentless drizzle. The television trucks were blocking the end of the street, and some ghoulish sightseers huddled in a group behind a police barricade. What did they come for? What was so exciting about the outside of a house where violent deaths had occurred? *Just what the hell did they expect to see?*

He shook his head. People. He would never understand them.

Grimly he pulled up the collar of his old English raincoat and hurried across the street.

In all his years of hard grind service he had never had to deal with a murder case where he knew one of the victims. This was a horrible sickening first. And in a chilling way he wondered if any of the guilt was his . . .

3

Montana Gray gazed at her husband, Neil, as he studied himself in the dressing room mirror of their Coldwater Canyon house. His obsession with his appearance whenever he wore a suit amused her. She waited patiently for the inevitable question.

He did not disappoint. 'Do I look alright?' he asked, quite secure in the fact that he looked fine, but anxious for her approval anyhow.

She grinned. 'How come you're always so insecure when you know you look terrific?'

'Me? Insecure. Never,' he replied, sounding more like Richard Burton than the original article. 'I merely enjoy your praise.'

She loved his English accent, it had always been a turn-on.

'Hmmm . . .' She regarded him quizzically. 'Later – in bed – I'll praise you 'til your hair stands on end.'

'Only my hair?' he mocked.

'And anything else you can think of.'

'Oh, I'll think of something.'

She laughed. 'I'm sure you will, not only are you the greatest movie director around, but your imagination ain't bad either!'

He grabbed her and they began to kiss.

Montana was twenty-nine. Neil fifty-four. During a year of living together and four years of marriage the twenty-five year age gap had never bothered either of them, although it still bothered a lot of other people. Neil's ex-wife, Maralee. Some of his friends, and *all* of their wives.

'Hey.' Gently she pushed him away. 'We have a whole bunch of guests anxiously awaiting our illustrious presence at the Bistro. We'd better shift ass.'

He sighed theatrically.

'Don't go giving *me* any heavies about tonight. This whole celebration bit was *your* idea, Neil.'

He mock bowed and ushered her to the door. 'Well madam, in that case let us – as you so succinctly put it – shift ass!'

Montana. Five feet ten inches tall. Waist length black hair. Direct gold-flecked tiger eyes. A wide sensual mouth. An unusual and striking beauty.

Montana. Named for the state she was born in by parents who were unconventional to say the least. Her father was a geologist. Her mother a folk singer. They both loved to travel, and by the time Montana was fifteen she had been around the world twice, had two short affairs, spoke fluent French and Italian, could water ski, snow ski and ride horses like a cowboy.

Her parents were strong, independent people who instilled in their only child a fun sense of confidence and self-worth. 'Believe in yourself and you can do anything,' her mother often said.

'Never be frightened in life,' was her father's motto. 'Face whatever comes your way with dignity and strength.'

It was alright for them, they had each other, and although they loved her very much, she often felt like an intruder, so when they finally decided to settle down on a ranch in Arizona, she knew the time had come to move out into the world on her own. She took off with their blessing and a small amount of money to keep her going. It was 1971,

29

she was seventeen years old and filled with all the energy and enthusiasm of extreme youth.

First she went to stay with an older cousin in San Francisco. He gave her pointers on sex, drugs and rock 'n' roll and left her to her own devices. She was inquisitive and anxious to learn, trying out a series of jobs – everything from waitressing to making silver jewelry and selling it on the street.

This kept her busy until she met a rock musician who talked her into India and meditation. They ended up in Poona, sitting at the feet of the celebrated guru, Rajneesh. She tired of this sooner than her companion, and travelled on to London alone, where she stayed with friends in Chelsea, mixing with photographers, models and writers. She tried a little of everything until eventually she moved to New York with a radical journalist and began to do what she had decided really interested her most of all – writing. The pieces she turned out were both cynical and stylish, and it wasn't long before she developed a name for herself, and a regular page in 'Worldly', an avant garde magazine. It was on a working trip to Paris that she first met Neil.

A party on the Left Bank. Crowded. Noisy. Montana arrived with a sometime boyfriend – Lenny. Neil was already there, stoned on a mixture of Jack Daniels and Acapulco Gold. A wasted looking man with intense eyes, a well lived in face, and a mass of unruly greying hair, he was sitting in a corner holding court while a group of admirers hung on to his every word.

'You know – I really want to meet that guy,' Lenny said. 'He's better than Altman.'

'Nobody's better than Altman,' she replied dismissively, heading in the direction of friends.

It was hours later when she finally wandered over to the group still gathered around Neil Gray. Lenny introduced her.

By this time Neil was so drunk he could hardly speak. But he did manage, 'What kind of a bullshit name is Montana?'

She ignored him, smiled sweetly at Lenny and said, 'Let's split.'

Two days later, while browsing magazines in the American Drug Store on the Champs Elysées, a voice said, 'Montana. What kind of a bullshit name is that?'

She turned, and for a moment did not remember him. Then he breathed whisky fumes in her face and she recalled the party.

'Want to have a drink?' he asked.

'Not particularly.'

Their eyes locked and for a brief moment something sparked. She

30

was intrigued enough to change her mind, although older men had never been her scene.

He took her to a bar where he was obviously a regular patron, and proceeded to get totally smashed. Before doing this he impressed her with sharp, knowledgeable and witty conversation, and she began to wonder why he had this need to obliterate the present.

She took the trouble to find out more about him. He was a complex man bent on self-destruction. A talented director, he had alienated many people along the way with his drinking and erratic behaviour, and he was now reduced to shooting television commercials for large sums of money which he used to support his ex-wife, Maralee, who lived in great style in Beverly Hills.

In Paris he seemed to enjoy his celebrity, starting off each day sober, but by early afternoon becoming hopelessly drunk.

Montana postponed her return to New York and began spending more and more time with him. Neil Gray was a challenge, and that excited her. Her father would have said she had the hots for him. Sex had always been a very open subject when she was growing up, and the only advice her parents had ever given her on the subject was to do whatever she felt was right. Something told her that Neil Gray was right, although he made no move to get her into bed, which intrigued her even more. She finally invited herself, and to his drunken amusement he couldn't get it up.

Montana did not find this funny. She thought that maybe the time had come to do something about Mister Neil Gray, so she hired a car, borrowed a friend's chateau in the country, and persuaded him to spend the weekend. He agreed, expecting a two day binge of booze and fun.

The chateau was isolated and empty, Montana had made sure it housed no spirits. She hid the keys of the car, pulled the connection on the phone, and kept him there for three delirious weeks. Well, after the first few days it was delirious, when she calmed him, stopped his furious ravings, and finally got him into bed in a sober state. He was a devastating lover when he didn't have alcohol slowing him down. No young stud, but a man who she felt very comfortable with indeed.

By the time they returned to Paris they had both decided together-ness was the name of the game. They stayed in Paris for only a few months. By that time Montana managed to convince Neil he was wasting his talent, and he finally agreed to return to America. Word was out he was sober and straight, and by the end of their first year together, he was back in action shooting a low-budget thriller movie on

31

the streets of New York. The film was a mild hit, and once more Hollywood beckoned. They headed west. 'You'll hate Beverly Hills,' he warned her. 'There's more shit per square inch than a sewage plant.'

She grinned and busied herself with her own projects. She had an idea for a television series, and there was a book she wanted to write about Hollywood in the thirties. Neil encouraged her all the way. He also insisted that they get married. She would have been happy leaving things the way they were, but he was not prepared to risk losing her. She was special. She had dried him out, got him working again, and given him a whole new outlook on life.

They got married in Hawaii, and from then on commuted between a permanent suite at the Beverly Wilshire Hotel and a New York apartment.

Montana wrote her television series – which was quite successful. She collaborated on the book about Hollywood, and drawn towards the movies, she wrote, produced and directed on offbeat, short film about children in the Watts area of Los Angeles. It won two awards.

Neil was proud of her accomplishments, he had more than encouraged her on the next project she became involved in – a gritty screenplay titled 'Street People' which she wrote in six weeks flat. When he first read the script he was thrilled. As a director he felt it had the potential to be an exciting and important movie. And he knew at once that he wanted to do it. He was hot again due to the fact that his previous two movies had made money, and several studios were ready to back anything he cared to do. But he wanted control, so after discussing it with Montana, he took the script to Oliver Easterne Productions. Oliver was a snake, but Neil knew he would give them the deal they were after.

Now everything was agreed, and as of that very morning contracts were signed.

It was an excellent deal. Total artistic control – which meant that no one could mess with Montana's script or with what Neil planned on putting up there on the screen. As long as they stayed under budget and on schedule, no interference from anyone. They were both delighted.

Final cut. Total control. Magic words, and now a special dinner to announce the project to their friends.

Montana stared moodily out of the car window as three hours later they drove home. As far as she was concerned, the entire evening had been one big waste of time. Friends. She could manage quite nicely without them thank you very much. As long as she had Neil of course, because *he* didn't give a damn about anybody, and she admired that quality in a town full of ass kissers. In fact it was one of the qualities that had attracted her to him in the first place.

'Cigarette?' He shook one out of the pack while he guided his red Maserati across Santa Monica, up Beverly towards Sunset.

She accepted it without a word, and thought yet again about the reaction to their news from Neil's so-called friends. They had all said, 'Wonderful!' 'Congratulations!' Then one by one they got their little digs in.

Bibi Sutton, *the* social pacesetter of Beverly Hills. Chic, French wife of one of filmland's biggest stars, Adam Sutton. 'Sweetie? Neil? He *really* do film *you* wrote?' Her obvious amazement was hardly disguised.

Chet Barnes, a talented screen writer with two Oscars to prove it. 'Writing for movies is a very specialized art, Montana. It's not like hacking it out for T.V.' *And fuck you too, Mr. Barnes.*

Gina Germaine, thirtyish sex symbol trying to be taken seriously and looking like an overgrown Barbie Doll. 'Did you have a ghost writer, Montana? You can confide in me, I won't tell. As a matter of fact I do a little writing myself . . .'

And so on and so on. One crack after another. People were just plain jealous, and that was the truth. Good looking women had roles in life and they were supposed to stick to them. They could be movie stars, models, housewives, hookers, but God forbid they should skirt onto what was strictly regarded as Big Boy's Territory. Writing a major movie for a major director was Big Boy's Territory. And in their own pretty little way everyone wanted to let her know that. She felt soured by their jealousy. But then, what had she expected?

'Sometimes I hate people!' she exploded.

Neil laughed. 'Don't waste your energy, my love.'

'But they were all so –'

'Envious.'

'You noticed it too?'

'I could hardly help it. Karen Lancaster kept on asking me to admit that I wrote the bloody movie myself.'

'That spoiled bitch!'

'And then Chet insisted on telling me I'd ruin my career. Oh, and even Adam Sutton wanted to know why I was helping you this way.'

'Christ! Friends!'

He took his hand from the steering wheel and patted her on the knee. 'I told you when I first brought you here never to take any of them seriously. Hollywood's a funny town with funny rules. You break them all.'

'I do, huh?'

'Most certainly.'

'How?'

'Well . . . let's see now. You don't shop on Rodeo Drive. You don't give catered parties. You don't lunch with the girls. You don't employ a maid. You don't have impeccable fingernails. You don't gossip. You don't spend my money at a speed faster than sound. You don't –'

She held up her hand, still laughing. 'Enough already! Let's go home and make out.'

'*And* you don't wait to be asked.'

Her hand slid across the gear lever and settled on his crotch. 'Aren't *you* the lucky one.'

The Maserati swerved across the street. 'Who, my love, is arguing?'

Montana slept soundly as Neil crept quietly from their bed early in the morning. He found that the older he got the less sleep he needed, so he showered, did a few half-hearted push ups, then walked out to the patio and admired the view. When the smog wasn't in action you could see for miles, sometimes as far as the ocean. It was one of the main reasons they had purchased the house several months previously. A lot of people put Los Angeles down – but Neil had a genuine love for the city. Born and raised in England, he found he never missed the place. America was his home, and had been for over twenty years.

Neil Gray first came to Hollywood in 1958. He was a young brash director who thought he knew it all. The studio who brought him over after his first big English film treated him royally. A bungalow at the Beverly Hills Hotel, a parade of beautiful starlets, and an endless expense account.

The movie he made for them died at the box office. A woman slapped him with a paternity suit which he hotly denied, and, suitably chastised, he fled back to England.

However, American fever was in his blood, he wanted more, and early in the sixties he returned to Hollywood – this time with no studio to back him. He rented a room at the Chateau Marmont, a modest old-fashioned hotel above the Strip. There he tried to get a script he had optioned off the ground. The going was hard, until one day, round the pool, he quite literally bumped into Maralee Sanderson. She was a pretty, spoiled teenager whose mother had died when she was fourteen, and who had been raised by her father, Tyrone, the founder of Sanderson Studios. At the time Maralee was having an affair with a New York method actor, but she took an immediate fancy to Neil and switched affections. He had no choice. What Maralee wanted – she got. Besides, he was flattered. She was young, gorgeous and rich. And daddy owned a studio. What more could an out-of-work film director want?

'Daddy'll put up the money for your movie,' she remarked casually one day. 'If I ask him, that is.'

'What the hell are you waiting for?' he yelled.

'A little thing called marriage,' she replied innocently.

Marriage. The very word scared him. He had tried it once at nineteen and found it sadly lacking. But now . . . seventeen years later . . . many women later . . . much booze later . . .

Marriage. He thought about it for a week. Then decided why not? It was about time he took the big step again, and besides, it seemed to be the only surefire way to get his movie off the ground.

An inner voice nagged him constantly: 'What about integrity? Making it on your own? Love?'

Fuck it – he thought. I want to make this film. I want a little clout in this town. Fuck it.

'Yes,' he told Maralee.

'Good,' she replied. 'Daddy wants to meet you.'

Tyrone Sanderson had not got where he was by charm. He was short and thick set. He smoked outsize cigars and favoured starlets with outsize attributes. He was desperate to marry his daughter off. She had bedded half of Hollywood but Neil Gray was the first man she had shown any permanent interest in.

'You wanna do a movie – do it,' *Tyrone growled at their first meeting.*

'I have a script for you to read –'

'Who reads? Do it.'

'Aren't you interested in what it's about?'

'I'm interested in you marrying my daughter. Period.'

Maralee and he were married on the terrace of Tyrone's Bel Air estate two weeks later. Most of the big names in Hollywood attended the wedding. They honeymooned in Acapulco, and returned to live on

35

Rodeo Drive in the house daddy bought them as a wedding present. Neil went straight to work.

His first film was a success, both artistically and financially. From being referred to as just 'the son-in-law' he became the new wonder kid in town. Every studio was after him, and since Tyrone Sanderson had not signed him to a contract he was free to do whatever he wanted.

'You have to stick with daddy,' Maralee insisted. 'He gave you your first chance.'

'Screw daddy,' Neil replied. 'I took my first chance, he never gave me anything.'

Neil made a succession of hot movies, while Maralee indulged in a succession of hot affairs. Neil drank, Maralee spent money.

Then came the flops. Suddenly Neil was bad news. He took off for Europe after a major fight with Maralee which ended when she summoned her father to the house. 'If you bring him into our life it's over,' he threatened.

'So goodbye,' she snapped. 'You no-talent-pain-in-the-ass-English-has-been!'

Montana turned up at just the right moment.

Divorcing Maralee had not been easy. Although she didn't want him, she didn't want to not have him either.

The divorce was messy and expensive. But worth every cent.

Neil gazed out at the sweeping view and thought about Montana. She was strong, intelligent and sensual. And he had been faithful to her for longer than he had ever thought possible. But in the last year he had disgusted himself with the occasional bird brain he took to bed. Fluffy blondes with low I.Q.s.

If Montana ever found out she would walk, just like that. He knew his wife.

So why did he do it? He honestly didn't know. Maybe the risk element was exciting. Or the fact that sometimes he felt the need to have a woman underneath him who wasn't his equal. A full breasted piece – who was just that – a piece. No conversation. No intellectual meeting of the minds. Just a lay.

Not that Montana wasn't the best. In bed she was as stimulating as ever. But she was always his equal and sometimes he felt this burning desire to bed a woman who wasn't. Sometimes all he wanted was a hot impersonal uninvolved fuck. He was fifty-four years old. Life goes on and you never learn a goddamn thing.

He left the patio and went indoors to the kitchen where he fixed himself a cup of tea and a dish of cereal.

Gina Germaine. Fluffy. Blonde. Dumb. And worse. A movie star.

He had bedded her twice and was going back for more. It was madness, but he couldn't help himself.

4

Getting lost in the city of New York was no problem for Deke. Burying his anger in a small room in the Village. Thinking. Brooding. Working things out.

Got a job. Changed his name.

No sweat.

Altered his appearance. It was easy. A pair of scissors was all it took to cut off his shoulder length hair. A barber finished the job, shearing his scalp until all that remained was a light sprouting – less than a crew cut – more like a delousing.

Could not do anything about the eyes. They burned black and angry in a pale nondescript face.

He was tall, thin, built like a million other young men who wore the uniform of Levis, shirt and lumber jacket.

He was obsessively tidy. Everything in his room was neat. Not that there was much to mess up: when he left Philadelphia he had taken nothing except a small carryall.

He worked in a seedy hotel in Soho. The afternoon shift – twelve noon until six p.m. He sat behind a desk and handed out room keys to a strange assortment of customers. Visitors to the city with an obvious lack of money, hookers, eccentrics, businessmen who didn't want to be seen on an afternoon tryst with their secretaries.

For the first six weeks he took a regular trip to the newstand in Times Square which carried the Philadelphia papers. Back in his room his eyes devoured the newsprint from front to back, missing nothing. When he was finished he neatly clipped out all the stories on the Friendship Street murders and studied them intently. Finally, when he was satisfied that he was missing no details of the investigation, he hid the news clips between the pages of a racing auto magazine which he then stuffed under his mattress.

Gradually the stories petered out. After all, there was nothing *that* sensational about the case. An ordinary middle aged couple. Mr. and Mrs. Willis Andrews. Who cared? Joey Kravetz. A tough street tramp who had been in and out of reform school since she was fourteen. Who cared?

THE POLICE WOULD LIKE TO INTERVIEW DEKE ANDREWS. THE ANDREWS' TWENTY-SIX YEAR OLD SON WHO HAS BEEN MISSING SINCE THE DAY OF THE CRIME.

How polite.

DETECTIVES ARE URGENTLY SEEKING DEKE ANDREWS, LONG HAIRED SON OF THE SLAUGHTERED COUPLE.

Less polite.

THIS MONSTER MUST BE FOUND.

A woman writer of course.

NO LEADS ON THE WHEREABOUTS OF DEKE ANDREWS. POLICE ARE BAFFLED.

He allowed himself a smile at *that* one.

New York was perfect. The streets had accepted him and swallowed him up just like one of its own. He could relax and go about his business.

And soon he would be ready to make his next move.

5

The Safeway supermarket on Santa Monica Boulevard was packed. Angel Hudson selected a cart and gave a little sigh as she glanced at the long lines waiting at each checkout.

A boy, busy packing groceries into strong brown bags, could not take his eyes off her. She had that effect on the male sex. Even gays couldn't resist checking her out.

Angel certainly was something. Nineteen years old. Five feet five inches of smooth creamy skin, long lashed aquamarine eyes, small straight nose, full pink lips, natural long blond hair, rounded breasts, a handspan waist, narrow rear, and endless legs. There was nothing trampy or obvious about her startling good looks.

38

As usual she wore very little make-up, and a simple outfit of pink sweater and baggy white overalls. It did not stop the stares.

Slowly she guided her cart down the crowded aisles, stopping occasionally to check out the price on certain items. Hmmm, she thought, Safeway or not everything sure costs a lot. All she had was thirty-five dollars, and that was supposed to keep her and Buddy going for a week. She smiled when she thought of him. She blushed when she thought of them in bed together that very morning. His hands everywhere . . . His tongue exploring hidden places . . .

Thinking about him gave her the shivers. He was so wonderful and worldly. So good looking. She shivered again. He was her husband and had been for two great and glorious days.

'Hi,' a voice said.

She glanced up at a muscled man in a red open-neck shirt and carefully pressed pants.

'Didn't we meet the other night at a party?' he questioned, edging round the side of her cart until he was standing quite close.

'I'm sorry,' she said quickly, 'but I only got into town yesterday.'

Now why was she apologizing? Buddy had told her about it a hundred and one times. *Don't go around saying sorry to everyone. You gotta learn to be more aggressive in life.*

'Well . . .' the man said, 'if you only got into town yesterday maybe I can buy you dinner tonight. Whaddya say to that?'

'I'm sor –' she began, then quickly stopped herself.

'I'm married,' she stated primly.

He laughed suggestively. '*I* don't mind if *you* don't.'

Why did they always have to pick on her? Ever since she could remember strange men had been sidling up and talking to her. On the street. At the movies. On the bus. She pushed the cart firmly down the aisle hoping to lose him, but he followed, mumbling one or the other of a hundred lines.

She stopped and fixed him with her devastating eyes. 'Please leave me alone,' she murmured softly. 'I told you, I'm married. My husband wouldn't like you talking to me. He wouldn't like it one little bit.'

She had not meant it as a threat. But it seemed to work, and the man retreated.

She had not lied. Buddy did hate other men looking at her. If he only knew how they approached her all the time he would go crazy. But it wasn't *her* fault was it? She gave them no come on. Never wore form-fitting clothes or short skirts. She kept herself to herself and could not remember ever having given any man an inch of encouragement. Buddy was the first man who had ever done more than kiss her goodnight. And that was only since their marriage. Instinctively she had known it was right to wait, and Buddy's appreciation on their wedding night had been worth all the slapped hands and frustrations of her past. How very lucky she was to have found him, he was a man in a million.

'Excuse me, miss,' mumbled a tall gangly boy in a torn baseball shirt, 'but I think you dropped these.'

She stared blankly at the box of crackers he held out. 'I'm sorry, they're not mine,' she apologized.

'No? I thought I saw them drop off your cart.'

'Sorry.'

He nervously scratched at a pimple. 'If I get in front of you in the line I can help you take all your junk out to your car.'

'No, thank you.' She moved quickly down the aisle. Safeway was teeming with them. Maybe next time Buddy would come with her.

Frances Cavendish leaned back in the chair behind her modern chrome desk and sucked greedily on a joint cunningly fitted into a roach holder. She held the rich smoke down in her lungs for a count of ten, then exhaled with a deep sigh of obvious satisfaction. She did not offer the contraption to Buddy Hudson, who slouched moodily on the other side of the desk, uncomfortable on a small straight-back chair.

'You've got your goddamn nerve walking in here,' she said.

'Huh?'

'Don't act like you don't know what I'm talking about. I got you that T.V. pilot, and with the help of that old crone you were shacked up with you blew the whole thing.'

'Hey, Frances. That was then. Now I need a job. I really do. I just got married.'

'Sorry, Buddy.' She waved her hand dismissively. 'But you must know how it is right now. Things are tight. I can't help you.'

She could help him if she wanted to. She was one of the most powerful casting agents in town.

'Hey – Frances,' he wheedled. 'You gonna tell me you haven't got *anything*? This is Buddy Boy you're rappin' with. I thought we had somethin' special.'

Frances picked up a pair of rhinestone trimmed glasses and

40

perched them on her long pointed nose. 'Didn't you just tell me you got married?'

'Yeah, I told you that.'

'Well, dear boy, I do think that makes a difference to our . . . relationship. Don't you?'

What relationship? He had escorted her to a few events. She had thrown a little work his way. It wasn't like he had ever balled her.

'Why?' he demanded sulkily, wishing he had never told her.

She glared at him. 'I haven't seen you for eight months. Then you just amble in here and casually announce you're married. What makes you think I should give *you* special treatment?'

He stood. 'So don't.'

She took off her glasses and narrowed flinty eyes. Buddy Hudson was the best looking male animal she had seen in months. It would be a shame to just let him walk out. 'I can send you up for a commercial,' she sighed.

'Shit! I don't want to do any more commercials. I've been in Hawaii for six months singing up a storm – they couldn't get enough of me there. What I want now is a classy guest shot on some television show. Little acting, little singing, I'll knock 'em on their fat cat asses.'

Frances picked up a pen and tapped it impatiently on her desk. 'You want to go for a commercial or not?'

He thought about his situation. Two hundred bucks to his name, a beat up old Pontiac, and a one room apartment off the Strip he had borrowed from a friend.

Some situation. And a wife of two days named Angel. Beautiful, soft, innocent, and all his. He had brought her back from Hawaii like a conquering hero. She thought he was a successful actor with jobs just lining up for him. Wouldn't do to disillusion her so early on in their married life.

'Yeah, I'll go,' he decided.

She scribbled something on a card and handed it to him. 'Four o'clock tomorrow, don't be late.'

He glanced at the card, then back at her. 'Frances,' he said, 'Aren't you at least going to give me a toke?'

Angel sang softly to herself as she unpacked the groceries. She could hardly believe how happy she was. So much had happened in such a short period of time. And everything had fallen into position perfectly.

To think – that only a year and a half earlier she had graduated from high school in Louisville, Kentucky, gotten a job as a reception-ist in a beauty salon, and one idle day entered a competition in a movie magazine. In her wildest dreams she had never imagined winning. But she had, and the prize was a thousand dollars and a week's paid trip to Hollywood with a companion.

Hollywood. *A magic place Angel had only ever read about.* Holly-wood. *A dream come true!*

Without hesitation she packed a bag and headed west with her best girlfriend, Sue-Ann. Taking off was no problem. Angel was a foster child in a large family, and the extra space in the small house they all shared was more than welcome.

A week in Hollywood at the Hyatt Hotel on the famous Sunset Boulevard. She and Sue-Ann barely had time to catch their breath. The magazine arranged for them to be photographed doing everything from exploring Disneyland to lunch with Burt Reynolds.

Burt Reynolds!! Angel thought she would faint. But he was very nice and made her laugh – even put his arms around her and Sue-Ann for a photo.

The week raced by, and when it was over she did not want to return to dull old Louisville. There were no real ties to pull her back. The family she lived with had never mistreated her, but she had always felt like an outsider, an intruder. Sometimes no more than just a maid. When she was growing, it had seemed natural to fetch and carry for everyone – but as she reached puberty and her beauty developed, it seemed she was resented more and more by the family.

Getting away had been on her mind for as long as she could remember, and this seemed like the perfect opportunity. 'I'm going to stay,' she told Sue-Ann, her eyes shining with the light of the con-verted. 'This is where I belong. I'm going to be an actress!'

Sue-Ann remonstrated with her friend, but to no avail. Angel had made up her mind. After all, every man she met in Hollywood had told her that she should be in the movies, so why not give it a try? She had the thousand dollar prize money, and if she was careful it should last her for several months at least.

First of all she needed somewhere to live, for she had no plans to waste money staying on at the hotel. The photographer gave her the phone number of a girl he knew who rented rooms. 'Call her,' he said, winking. 'An' don't forget, beautiful, if she's got no bed for you there's always a place in mine.'

She ignored his suggestive remark, called, and within an hour was installed in the back room of a large rambling house off Fairfax.

'Two minutes from May Co. an' a block from Farmers Market. How lucky can you get?' questioned the flashy redhead who rented out. 'You new in town, honey?'

She nodded. 'I'm going to be an actress.'

'Sure you are. An' the Pope got married yesterday.'

'What?'

'Forget it.'

Becoming an actress was not easy, but who had ever said it would be? First she found out that she needed photographs and an agent, and then Daphne, the redhead, told her, 'Ya gotta join some kinda stupid union. Sure ya wanna bother? There's easier ways of makin' a buck. A chick that looks like you . . .' She trailed off and stared.

Professional photographers cost a hundred dollars, although the photographer did suggest there were ways she could pay other than cash. She pretended she didn't know what he was talking about, but of course she did.

After visiting several agents she decided on a fatherly type with an office on Sunset. He seemed better than the younger ones who she instinctively knew would be trouble.

In six weeks he sent her on four interviews, none of them resulting in a job, but plenty of propositions. He then said he could get her the second lead in a porno movie, and she left his office in tears.

'Dirty old bastard,' Daphne sympathized. 'Tell you what, I'm gonna treat ya to a trip to Hawaii, all expenses paid.'

'What about your job?' Angel asked tentatively. Daphne had told her she was some kind of sales representative, always running off to appointments day and night.

'Screw the job. I need a vacation.'

Angel could hardly believe how lucky she was to have found a friend as nice as Daphne. What did it matter if she wore too much make-up and flashy clothes. She was a nice person. And anyway – the thought of visiting Hawaii was too tempting to turn down.

They arrived late at night after a turbulent flight. A twenty minute cab ride took them straight from the airport to the Hawaiian Village Hotel. Daphne, who had managed to consume quite a few drinks on the five hour journey, fell into a drunken sleep. Angel paid the cab fare and shook her awake, all the while staring around, her wide eyes taking in every new sight.

'Shit!' mumbled Daphne. 'We here already?'

Angel glanced at the cab driver to see if he had heard, but he stared impassively ahead.

They entered the lobby and approached the reception desk. 'You go in an' sit down while I register,' Daphne instructed.

She waited patiently, wishing that her friend didn't drink so much, maybe cut down on the swearing. Still . . . she wasn't in Louisville anymore . . . Daphne wasn't Sue-Ann. And it was so good to be out in the world and free.

'All set!' Daphne swooped down on her. 'Honey – I am one tired person, let's hit the old sack right away.'

The room was clean, with colour television, a view over the pool and a double bed. Angel hardly relished the thought of sharing. The heavy perfume Daphne wore failed to conceal the pungent body odour she exuded.

'Give the guy a tip,' Daphne ordered, indicating the bellboy who was placing their two suitcases on the floor.

Angel fished in her purse, thinking that her money was not lasting as long as she had hoped. Out of the thousand dollars she only had four hundred left. She gave the boy a dollar which didn't seem to thrill him.

By the time he was out of the room Daphne had stripped off her red dress and was heading for the bathroom clad only in a pair of brief purple panties.

Angel did not see how she could object to the double bed without feelings being hurt, so she gave a small sigh, opened up her suitcase and extracted the blue baby doll nightdress she had purchased at the May Co. Her one extravagance, but it was so pretty she had been unable to resist it.

Daphne emerged from the bathroom stark naked, and placed both hands on her hips while shimmying her large breasts. 'Not bad, huh? An' all mine, honey.'

Angel hurried into the bathroom where she showered, and pondered on the fact that maybe coming to Hawaii wasn't such a good idea after all.

Back in the bedroom all was quiet. Daphne was under the sheets and the lights were off. Angel crept into the other side of the bed, closed her eyes, and thought about her attempts at becoming an actress. She had to get a job to keep her afloat. Perhaps she could be a receptionist . . . in a film studio . . . or maybe Burt Reynolds needed a secretary . . . or Richard Gere . . . or . . .

At first, the hand creeping up her leg was just an irritation. She didn't realize what was happening until the hand dived between her thighs and suddenly Daphne was upon her, huge bosoms flopping in her face. 'Oh, no!' she gasped in horror. 'What are you DOING!'

'Well I ain't playin' tennis,' replied Daphne, trying to ease her fingers under the tight elastic of Angel's panties.

'Stop it! Stop it at once!' She kicked out.

'Oh. A playful chickie, huh? Tell you the truth, hon, I ain't averse to a few games myself.' The elastic tore, and Daphne's fingers were quick to touch the warm triangle of fluff.

'WILL YOU STOP IT!' screamed Angel, scrambling from the bed. 'What's the matter with you?'

'What's the matter with me? Why the heck do you think I brought you to Hawaii?'

'For . . . a . . . a . . . vacation,' she stammered shakily.

'For a fuck, sweetheart. For a little bit of soft pussy instead of hard cock. Makes a change, doncha know.'

Her hand flew to her mouth. 'Oh my God! I feel sick.'

'Go puke somewhere else,' blazed Daphne. 'You don't want to play – take your bag an' get the hell out of here.'

'But . . . but I've got nowhere to go.'

Daphne was not interested. 'Tough tit,' she spat.

Fifteen minutes later Angel stood forlornly in the lobby pleading with the surly desk clerk who told her repeatedly that there were no vacant rooms in the hotel.

Buddy Hudson, fresh from an energetic scene with an Australian tourist, could not help noticing the delectable blond. He checked out women automatically, and this one was something. When she turned away from the reservation desk he moved right in. 'Trouble?' he questioned sympathetically.

She gazed at him and quite literally felt her legs go weak. 'Oh!' she murmured.

'Oh – what? Trouble or no trouble?' He had to have this one. She was Christmas six months early.

'I . . . er . . . I can't get a room here.' She couldn't stop staring. Buddy Hudson was the most handsome man she had ever seen. A combination of her two favourite movie stars – Richard Gere and John Travolta. But better than both of them, with tight black curly hair, smoky ebony eyes, and a body that was both muscular and thin. She gazed up at him; he was over six feet tall, and his very closeness made her feel small and helpless.

'Hey – hey. That's not good. Didn't you make a reservation in advance? This is tourist seasonville.'

45

'I did . . . but . . .' Her wide eyes brimmed with tears. 'I just had the most horrible experience.'

This was going to be easy. 'Want to talk about it?'

'I couldn't!'

'Sure you could. Talking always helps. Come on – I'll buy you a drink.' He guided her to a nearby lounge, where the waitress greeted him by name. 'What'll it be?' he asked, wondering how long it would take to get her into bed.

'A fruit punch, please.'

'With a shot of rum to liven it up?'

'Plain.'

He looked surprised. 'You don't drink?'

She shook her head.

'Smoke?'

Again she shook her head.

He wondered if he dared . . . No . . . Why even make a joke of it – they all did.

'So . . .' he began, 'tell me what happened. Some jerk giving you a hard time?'

She didn't know why she trusted him, she just did. Soon she was confiding everything – from the moment she first set foot in Hollywood to her recent vile scene with Daphne. 'I feel so . . . dirty. Can you imagine a girl wanting to do something like that?'

Could he imagine? Oh boy – if he only had a buck for all the chicks he'd watched making it together. This little fox was either putting him on or she was a real innocent. 'I got a bed you can use,' he remarked casually.

Quickly she remembered he was a man. And men only wanted One Thing. 'No thank you.'

He didn't push. Just said mildly, 'You have to park it somewhere for tonight.'

'No I don't. I'm going to the airport and waiting for a plane to Los Angeles.'

'That's the dumbest thing I ever heard.'

'Why?'

'Because, sugar, you are here on one of the most beautiful islands in the world. And I am not letting you go anywhere until I have personally shown you around.'

'But –'

He placed a finger on her lips. 'No buts. I have a friend who owns a small hotel. We'll get you a room there.'

'But –'

'Rule one. Never argue with Buddy Boy.'

Three weeks sped by, and true to his word Buddy showed her the island. Not only did he give her a guided tour of Honolulu, but another friend of his who operated a tourist shuttle plane took them on day trips to Maui, Lanai and Molokai.

They explored white deserted beaches, coral reefs alive with exotic tropical fish, rain forests, and the dramatic Paradise Park.

Angel had never felt so excited and alive. Buddy created feelings in her she had not known existed. Installed in a cosy room at his friend's hotel, she waited anxiously each day for him to pick her up. He tried a few times to have her spend the night at his place, but each time she explained very carefully that she wasn't 'that kind of girl'.

He laughed when she said that. But his laughter did not weaken her resolve. Although secretly she had to admit that she did want him. She yearned for his hard strong body to possess her totally. When he kissed her goodnight it took every ounce of will power to push him away.

Buddy sang in a piano bar. 'I'm really an actor,' he explained. 'But I needed a rest – so I left L.A. – an' I've been down here a few months. I was working nonstop in Hollywood. Y'know – movies, television shows. You name it, I've been on it.'

'Really?' Her eyes widened.

'Sure. Didn't you recognize me when we first met?'

She shook her head. 'I don't watch much television . . .'

'Ha! An' I thought that's why you let me talk to you in the first place. I'm famous, kid!'

He allowed her, only once, in the place where he worked. She sat at the bar gazing lovingly at him while he warbled everything from 'My Way' to 'Chicago'.

'They like the old fashioned stuff,' he explained rather sheepishly. 'My real bag's more Billy Joel and rock. But I gotta make a buck.'

One day, lying on a quiet beach, he rolled over on top of her and began kissing her harder and faster than he ever had before. 'You know you're drivin' me crazy,' he muttered. 'No way can I go on like this.'

She could feel his hardness digging into her thigh, and instinctively her body pushed towards his.

'Oh baby!' he mumbled, burying his head in her golden hair. 'Oh baby . . . baby . . . baby . . . I got to have you. You understand what I'm sayin'? Got to.'

She wanted him as much as he wanted her. He was everything she

47

had ever dreamed of and more. He could be the family she had never had. Someone to care for . . . Someone who would look after her . . . Someone to belong to.

'We could get married,' she whispered timidly.

He backed off. Fast. Then later he reconsidered. So what was so terrible about marrying the most beautiful girl in the world? 'You got it, kid,' he told her, and a week later they were married. A simple ceremony. Buddy in a borrowed suit, and Angel in a white lace dress she purchased with the last of her money.

'You know what?' Buddy announced excitedly, the day after their wedding. 'We're headin' back to Hollywood. You and I kid – that's where we're both gonna make it so big they won't even know what's hit 'em!'

Dreamily Angel finished unpacking the groceries and hoped that Buddy would approve of what she was fixing for dinner. Hamburgers, green beans, baked potatoes and apple pie.

She smiled softly to herself and thought about *after* dinner. She and Buddy alone together . . . In bed together . . . making love together . . .

Thank you Daphne, for you changed my life and made me the happiest girl in the world!

Buddy was able to jazz Frances up to at least smiling before he left her office. She even let him have a couple of drags on her joint. Not enough to get him high – but who needed drugs with Angel in his life? Just looking at her gave him a shot of adrenaline – enough to take him right through the day with no trouble at all.

Who would have thought Buddy Hudson would ever get himself caught? Not him for sure.

Buddy Hudson. Answer to every girl's prayers. Stud. Hero. Superstar. Well jeez – if *he* didn't think positive who would? One of these days he'd make it . . . one of these days.

Buddy Hudson. Twenty-six years old. Brought up in San Diego by a mother who adored him, perhaps too much. She kept him by her side at all times and only relinquished her hold to allow him to attend school.

When he was twelve his father died, and although they were left in good financial shape his mother was distraught. 'You will have to look after mommy now,' she wailed. 'You must be my big big man.'

Young as he was her words frightened him. Her closeness was already oppressive, and now with his father gone it could only get worse.

It did. She insisted that he share her bed at night. 'I'm frightened,' was her excuse.

He hated the way she stifled him, and looked forward to school and a friend called Tony, who also had problems at home. The two of them fantasized about getting a little freedom. 'Why don't we make a break for it?' Tony suggested one day.

The idea appealed to Buddy. He was already fourteen, tall and well built, with a strong desire to get out into the world and see what was going on. 'Yeah,' he agreed. 'Let's do it.'

A few days later he borrowed twenty dollars from his mother's purse and during lunch recess he and Tony skipped out of school. They raced down the street laughing and yelling with relief.

'What shall we do?' Buddy asked.

Tony shrugged. 'I dunno. What'd'y' think we should do?'

Buddy shrugged. 'I dunno.'

Finally they decided on the beach and a movie. The beach was hot. The movie was 'The Thomas Crown Affair', and Buddy fell in love with Faye Dunaway, and decided that if Steve McQueen could be an actor, why couldn't he? The seeds of ambition were firmly planted.

They rolled out of the movie with no clear idea where to spend the night, and found themselves drifting down towards the harbour. Buddy thought about his mother alone in her big bed, and he wasn't sorry, just delighted that he had managed to escape.

They hung around outside a bar, bumming cigarettes from emerg-ing sailors, until eventually an older man in civilian clothes approached them. 'You want to go to a party?' he asked, his small eyes darting shiftily this way and that.

Buddy looked at Tony, and Tony looked at him, and they both nodded enthusiastically.

'Follow me,' said the man, walking down the street to a large foreign car.

The two boys jumped obediently into the back seat.

'I think it's a Bentley,' Tony whispered.

'More like a Rolls Royce,' Buddy whispered back.

Now that the man had the boys in his car, he ignored them, and drove silently and swiftly. After about ten minutes Buddy leaned forward and tapped him on the shoulder. 'Excuse me, mister, where exactly is this party?'

The man braked sharply. 'If you want to get out say so now. Nobody's forcing you to go anywhere. Just remember that.'

The words made Buddy uneasy, he nudged Tony. 'Let's split,' he whispered.

'No,' argued Tony. 'We got nowhere else to go.'

Very true. Suddenly Buddy wished he was home. Only he couldn't lose face and let Tony know that.

Another ten minutes or so and they pulled into a private driveway, then finally slid to a stop in front of a brightly lit mansion. The drive was full of other expensive cars.

'Whew!' Tony whistled. 'Some place!'

'Follow me,' said the man, leading them through the front door into a spacious hallway. 'What are your names?' he hissed.

'I'm Tony, he's Buddy,' Tony replied amiably. 'And we're both real hungry. Any food?'

'Of course. All in good time. This way.'

He threw open the double doors of a sunken living room filled with people. The room was abuzz with conversation and the clink of glasses. They stood in the doorway until they were noticed and the noise tapered off.

'Gentlemen,' their escort announced formally. 'I'd like you to meet Tony and Buddy.'

Every eye in the room fixed upon them and there was a deathly silence for only a moment. 'No sailors, Freddie?' An effeminate voice broke the hush, and laughter filled the room. A short butterball of a man in a bright orange kaftan detached himself from a group and approached them holding out a bejewelled hand. 'Welcome to my party, boys. What can I get you?'

Tony took the fat man's hand. 'Food!' he said, grinning, loving every minute of their adventure.

Buddy still felt uneasy. If he had wanted out before, now he felt doubly so. However he was drawn into the room along with Tony, realizing it was too late to make an escape. Besides, when he got a load of the table full of delicious food he wasn't sure that he still wanted to.

They were given drinks. Not hard liquor, but frothy concoctions in tall glasses that tasted more like milk shakes than anything else. Then they were served plates of rich food. Everyone fussed around them – not like they were a couple of kids – but nicely – asking their opinion on this and that – filling their glasses whenever they were half full – and giving them cigarettes.

Buddy felt pretty good after a while.

'Here, try this.' Butterball passed him a different kind of cigarette.

He managed only a short drag before Tony grabbed it from his hand and said, 'Is that grass? Let me try it.'

Butterball smiled; he had sharp, ferret-like teeth. 'So try it.'

Tony pursed his lips and drew deeply on the cigarette. Then he began to cough frantically.

Butterball laughed aloud, and even the man who had picked them up allowed himself a smirk.

Tony's eyes narrowed as he dragged on the cigarette again, this time managing not to choke, holding the smoke in his lungs for a while then exhaling triumphantly.

'You learn fast,' murmured Butterball.

'Sure I do,' boasted Tony. 'What else you got for me to try?'

Butterball's eyes gleamed. 'Are you big enough to sample a little cocaine?'

'I'm big enough to sample anything!'

By this time Buddy was feeling distinctly sick. 'Gotta go to the bathroom,' he mumbled, staggering from the room. Nobody took any notice. Tony was the centre of attention as he prepared to snort the white powder Butterball was lining up on a glass table.

Buddy found the can and took an endless pee. The relief was great, but he still felt ill. He wandered into the hall and spotted an open window right at the back. What he needed was a few big gulps of fresh air. He opened the window wide and leaned out. Coordination deserted him, and before he knew what was happening he lost his balance and fell, landing hard on a patch of grass.

He remembered nothing more until awakening in the early hours of the next morning, the daylight harsh in his eyes, his body stiff and cramped. He had no idea where he was. Panic swept through him. His head throbbed and the taste in his mouth was disgusting. Desperately he tried to think as he stood up in the unkempt garden and looked around.

Tony. Me and Tony. Running away. The movies. The harbour. Man in car. Faggots. Food. Drink.

My mother will kill me. For sure she will kill me.

He brushed down his clothes and made his way around the front of the house. There were no cars in the driveway. The place was deserted, and in the revealing light of day it looked run-down and dilapidated, not at all the magnificent mansion of the previous evening.

Buddy frowned. The front door was locked, but he was able to peer through a window and was amazed to see the few pieces of furniture in sight covered with dust sheets. The place looked like nobody had lived there in months.

He hung around for a bit, hoping that Tony would show up, all the while skirting round the house searching for a place of entry. But everything was securely locked. Tony had obviously split – and why not? He probably thought that Buddy had run out on him.

Suddenly leaving home did not seem like such a smart idea anymore. Not when you were on your own, cold, tired and hungry. His mother would kill him, but returning home did seem the only answer. He set off in what he hoped was the right direction.

The events of the next twenty-four hours still haunted him. Sometimes he would wake in the middle of the night bathed in a cold clammy sweat, and the memories would be there – as sharp as if it had all happened the day before.

Arriving home. His mother hysterical. The police . . . Questions . . .

Tony's body had been thrown from a car in the Bay Area at 5 a.m. Battered, sexually abused, and very very dead.

The cops pounced on him as if he had done it. He was taken to the police station and grilled continuously for seven straight hours, until his mother managed to drag him out of there with the help of the family lawyer.

He was taken home, given a sedative and slept a straight ten hours. Then the cops were back, requesting that he guide them to the house where the party had taken place. He was driven round in a squad car for hours, but he couldn't remember where it was.

'Are you sure there was a party?' questioned a suspicious detective. 'Are you certain there was a house?'

After three fruitless hours they drove him back to the police station where he was given book after book of mug shots to look through. He didn't recognize one face.

Finally the detective decided he should see the body. Together they went to a cold tiled room that smelled of formaldehyde and death. The ghastly smell made Buddy's nostrils twitch and his stomach churn uneasily.

The detective was casually matter-of-fact as he instructed a white-coated pathology assistant to show them the body.

A steel locker in the wall was pulled out, and there lay Tony, naked and dead. His lifeless body covered with purple bruises and weals.

Buddy stared, unable to believe that he was being made to look.

Then he started to cry, great racking sobs. 'I'm gonna throw up,' he mumbled. 'Get me out of here – please – get me away.'

The detective made no move. 'Take a good long look. That could've been you, boy. And don't you forget it.'

Buddy threw up all over the floor.

The detective gripped him by the arm. 'Let's go find that house. Maybe seeing your friend has jogged your memory.'

He was never able to locate the house, or identify any of the men at the party. Tony was buried, and after a flurry of outraged publicity the case faded from the headlines. Just another unsolved murder.

Only this particular unsolved murder changed Buddy's life. Whereas before, life with his mother had been smothering – now it was impossible. She did not leave him alone for a second, all the while smoothing his hair back, stroking his face, clinging to his hand.

He slept uneasily in her bed, keeping as far away as he could from her fussing petting hands.

She questioned him constantly. 'Did those men try to put their things near you?' 'Did they undress you?' 'You know it's not normal – two men together.'

How dumb did she think he was? He knew it wasn't normal. In fact he knew what was normal. He was beginning to eye the girls in class, and getting a hard-on just thinking about what he would like to do to them.

No chance, there was no escape from his mother. He couldn't even jerk off at home. He had to content himself with furtive sessions locked in the can at school with a faded Playboy centrefold for company.

By the time he reached fifteen he had his eye on a girl called Tina. He wanted to ask her for a date, but it was impossible. His mother allowed him no freedom, and when he complained, she just fixed him with a hurt expression, and mournfully said, 'Remember Tony?'

So it was down to grabbing what opportunities he could. Tina was not averse to his attentions. Buddy was certainly the best looking boy in school. They indulged in heavy petting sessions during lunch recess. Tina had pert breasts that he loved to feel, and in return she massaged him to orgasm on a pile of Kleenex. This all took place in the science lab, which was never used at that time of day.

'I think I love you, Buddy,' Tina sighed, after several months of this activity.

'I think I love you, too,' he dutifully replied, hoping that this meant she was finally going to let him do 'it'. He had her blouse and bra off,

and now he fiddled with the catch on her skirt while she gazed passionately into his eyes.

Her skirt dropped to the floor and quickly she said, 'I've never done this before. Have you?'

'No,' he replied truthfully, rapidly pulling down her panties before she changed her mind.

'Oh!' She shivered. 'Take your clothes off too.'

She didn't have to ask him twice. He was so excited he felt he might ejaculate there and then before he even got it in. He pulled down his pants and ripped off his shirt.

Neither of them heard the principal enter with two sets of parents he was showing around the school.

Many recriminations later, his mother arrived to collect him, her mouth set in a thin furious line. She had words with the principal, then drove Buddy home in silence.

Once home he escaped to his room. At least his mother would not want him in her bed tonight. He had never seen her so angry.

He undressed and climbed into the narrow bed he was so rarely allowed to use. His stomach ached and he thought about Tina, allowing his hands to travel beneath the covers and play with his erection.

The light was switched on so suddenly that his hands froze, as did his hard-on.

His mother stood in the doorway, clad in a long robe. Her cheeks flushed, her dark eyes glowing. 'So,' she murmured huskily, 'You wanted to see what a woman's body looked like, did you? Well see then.' With one gesture she shucked off her robe and stood before him naked.

His own mother! He was shocked and horrified, and even worse – aroused.

She walked towards the bed and ripped the covers down. His new erection could hardly be hidden. Lightly she began to caress it.

He was so confused. He wanted to cry or run. But instead he stayed perfectly still while she touched him. It was as if he had drifted out of his own body and was merely an onlooker watching the proceedings.

She climbed on top of him and guided his penis into a warm wetness. So warm . . . so . . . wet . . . so good. And he knew he was going to come any second, and it was going to be better than it had ever been before with any of the paper Playboy girls, or with Tina and a wad of Kleenex . . . And Ohhh . . . Ahhh . . .

'You'll never need anyone else but mommy now, will you, Buddy?

Will you?' she crooned softly, her voice full of gloating satisfaction.

He left in the early hours of the morning while she still slept. Only this time he was smart. He cleared her purse of two hundred dollars and took several pieces of expensive jewellery which she kept hidden.

This time he was really going. And no way was he ever coming back.

Outside Frances' office he extracted a wad of gum from his pocket and checked out a tall redhead walking into the building. An out of work actress, he could tell. They all had that same half-desperate look in their eyes as if they would do anything for a role. And most of them did.

He rolled the gum over his tongue, and walked slowly to the parking lot in back. Buddy had the perfect Hollywood stud walk – part Travolta in 'Saturday Night Fever' – and part Gere in 'American Gigolo'. He knew he looked great. He should – he worked hard to capture that lazy horny hip swaying thrust. He could have played the hell out of the guy in Gigolo. He had lived the part for Christ sakes. In the eleven years he had been on his own he had lived most parts.

'Hey – Buddy. How ya doin' man?' Quince, a black actor friend of his, slapped palms as they passed. 'Frances in a good mood today?'

Buddy shrugged. 'She's gettin' there – but I wouldn't do hand-stands.'

'When you get back, man?'

'A day or two ago.'

'So stay around – we'll share a cappuccino – I got a *wild* new fox nibblin' at my breakfast crunchies – one you gotta meet – a real peach. *And* she has a sister.'

'Some other time. I havta go see a guy about a T.V. series.'

'Sure, so like later. Give me a buzz and we'll get it together. Drop by Maverick's one night.'

'Yeah, I'd like that.'

They slapped palms once again and went their separate ways.

Buddy pulled up the collar on his leather jacket and headed for his car. Why hadn't he told Quince he was married? Why did he wish he hadn't told Frances? He wasn't regretting it was he?

Hell, no. But a guy had to promote a certain image, and *his* image was that of a sexy macho stud ready to do anything and go anywhere at a moment's notice.

Somehow a wife just didn't fit the picture.

He started the old car and tuned into a rock station. Angel was hardly a wife to be ashamed of. She was young, beautiful and *pure*.

Kind of a funny word – but how else could you describe a girl like Angel? Most of the stuff runnin' around Hollywood was into everything and everyone by the time they hit twenty. Angel was different – but how to keep her that way in a town crawling with slimy creeps?

Right now that wasn't the problem. The immediate problem was scoring some bucks. Angel thought he was a winner – and no way was he going to let her think otherwise. Even if it meant falling back into bad habits – only on a temporary basis of course.

Buddy put his foot hard down on the accelerator and headed towards Beverly Hills.

6

Millie Rosemont mumbled in her sleep, and threw her left arm restlessly across her husband.

Leon lay on his back and stared unseeingly at the ceiling. Carefully he moved his wife's arm and turned to look at her, willing her to wake up so that they could talk. She did not budge.

Silently he slid from the bed and padded into the kitchen where he opened the refrigerator and stared mournfully at the contents. Six eggs, a bowl of apples, some skim milk and a dish of cottage cheese. Some feast. But then he *was* supposed to be on a diet and Millie was only helping him keep to it.

Over a three month period he had put on twenty-four pounds. A steady two pounds a week. He felt big and ungainly, not to mention the fact that the waist on his pants had had to be let out three times, and his jackets and shirts were bursting at the seams.

It was Millie's fault. She was a sensational cook.

It was his fault. He ate like a pig – especially when he had something on his mind.

He took out the cottage cheese, a spoon from the drawer, and sat himself down at the kitchen table. There was no denying it. He *did* have something on his mind. The Friendship Street murders. Three people hacked to death in a small suburban house for no apparent reason. And one of those people was Joey Kravetz. Pathetic little Joey.

The newspapers had described her as 'beautiful teenage model'.

But what did they know? If a victim was under thirty and female she was automatically described as beautiful. It made better headlines.

Model, my ass. And he should know. He felt the anger rising in him. Anger combined with the sense of frustration he felt every time he thought of Joey and her bloody mutilated body. Joey, who was only a kid . . .

He remembered their first encounter.

'Lookin' for some games, mister?'

Leon could not believe he was being propositioned. He glanced around, convinced the baby-faced hooker in the black fake-leather mini-dress and ridiculous high wedges was talking to someone else.

The street was deserted.

'How old are you?' he asked incredulously.

'Old enough!' She winked cheekily, and he noticed a distinct cast to her left eye. She couldn't be more than fifteen, sixteen at the most.

'So – waadya say, cowboy?' She placed her hands on her hips and grinned at him. 'I can show ya paradise!'

'And I can show you my I.D. I'm a detective.'

The grin faded from her face. 'A cop? Aw shee . . . t.' She cocked her head to one side. 'You're not gonna pull me in are ya? I mean we was just talkin'. I didn't offer you nothin'.'

'Where do you live?'

She wasn't sure if he was accepting her original offer or planning to book her. 'I gotta go,' she whined.

'You live with your parents?'

'I ain't got no parents, man. I'm eighteen. I can do what I want.'

'And I can take you to the station and have you for soliciting if I want.'

She stared down the street and contemplated making a run for it. But he was a big guy and would probably catch her, so she stuck a finger in her mouth and chewed on the nail. 'Tell ya what. I'll give ya a freebee,' she said after a moment or two.

He wondered if he should take her in. Not that rounding up under-age hookers was his job. But Jesus! He was a cop. You had to have some sense of responsibility, and she was only a child.

'I think you'd better come with me,' he said wearily, and gripped her by the skinny arm.

'Motherfucker!' She kicked him hard on the shin, wrestled her arm free and ran.

He rubbed his ankle, watched her clatter wildly down the street, then limped to his car and sat thoughtfully behind the wheel. He would give the information to Juvenile, they'd pick her up in no time.

Angrily Leon spooned bland cottage cheese into his mouth. Joey. What a terrible waste.

In his mind he reviewed the case on the vanished Deke Andrews.

So many people interviewed. So many different opinions. Deke Andrews was remembered as smart, dumb, rude, polite, aggressive, a troublemaker, a loner . . .

The list went on and on, and no two people agreed.

Fact: He was a car nut.

Fact: He had shoulder length hair. Big deal – he probably cut that off the moment he ran.

Fact: He was sallow of complexion, six feet two inches tall, thin but strong.

Fact: He was not successful with women. Of the four girls tracked down he had dated, not one would admit to sleeping with him. Indeed, not one had even ventured on a second outing.

'Why?' Leon had questioned.

'Dunno.' Girlish shrugs. 'He was just sort of . . . weird.'

They all had variations on the same theme. So add weird to his list of outstanding qualities. A young apparently healthy male, and they could not find one girl he had screwed. Logical conclusion – he slept with hookers or was gay. So that must be where Joey came in . . . But why had he taken her home with him? And why had he indulged in such a passionate orgy of killing?

As the days turned into weeks and the weeks into months, Leon tried to get a picture in his mind of Deke. But there were so many contradictions it was impossible. Only the facts were clear. The Andrews family had moved into the house on Friendship Street over twenty years before. Their background was a mystery. They seemed to have sprung up from nowhere.

Deke went to junior high, graduated from high school, took a job in a garage, and stayed there until the murders. Then he vanished. Taking nothing but a carryall and the secret of what had precipitated his acts of violence.

Inevitably new cases came along and the Friendship Street murders became less important. The press stopped mentioning them because all at once they were old news.

At police headquarters the file was still open but it was no longer hot. Other cases came and went. But Leon was not prepared to let the case fade away and become just another dusty file. Most of all he was not prepared to forget about Joey.

Millie walked into the kitchen, her face swollen with sleep. She swooped on the dish of cottage cheese as though it was contraband. 'And what do you think you're doin', Leon Rosemont?' she demanded sternly.

Millie slept naked. For her trip to the kitchen she had not bothered to put clothes on her comely black body. Leon felt his first arousal in weeks. He grinned and rose from the table.

Her eyes were immediately drawn to his erection. 'My, oh, my!' she drawled. 'So *that's* what I gotta do to get you sexy. Just take me some cottage cheese to bed!'

He laughed with her, followed her into the bedroom, and was not embarrassed by the roll of fat around his middle as they began to make love. With Millie everything was natural, she was the warmest human being he had ever encountered.

He remembered the first time he had set eyes on her. She was a school teacher then, and she had brought a group of youngsters to the precinct for an outing. Some outing. Hookers screaming obscenities. A pickpocket or two getting booked. A few gang members with their heads busted open. And pimps and pushers and undercover cops and muggers and car thieves and junkies and rape victims.

Just a normal day on the job.

She was dark of skin and soft of voice. Her eyes were brown and kindly. Her lips wide and sensual . . . He was fifty years old and he had been divorced from his first wife, Helen, for years, so there was no reason why he shouldn't find out her number and call her. A month later they were married. And for three years they had been very happy indeed.

Millie sighed and rolled over. 'That was real gooood!'

'It was real fast too,' he apologized.

'Not my fault!'

True. What had happened to his control? Millie didn't seem disappointed, in no time at all her breathing was deep and even and she was asleep.

Leon lay there wide awake, his mind back on Deke Andrews. He was out there somewhere. Somewhere in the black night. Somewhere . . .

And he, Leon Rosemont, would have to find him. For Joey's sake.

7

'Str . . . eee . . . tch. That's it ladies. Put something into it. One more time. Come on now – str . . . eee . . . tch.'

Elaine thought she might have done herself permanent damage. She lay on her stomach in a large work-out studio with thirty other women, most of them in impeccable shape. Her right arm was behind her clutching desperately on to the ankle of her left leg. Every muscle in her body was on Air Force One alert. It felt terrible.

'Okay everyone. Let it go. Relax,' the instructor said. As Elaine slumped flat on her face she wondered if he was gay. He certainly enjoyed inflicting pain. She stared up at him from her supine position. He wore a yellow leotard, black leg warmers, and a striped scarf. His crotch bulged disconcertingly. 'Is he gay?' she whispered to Karen Lancaster, who lay beside her.

'I expect so,' Karen answered. 'All the pretty ones are nowadays.

'Okay,' said the instructor. 'Now I want you to join me in a little something called the Snake.'

'The one-eyed variety I hope,' murmured Karen wistfully.

Disco music blared out as thirty almost perfect bodies writhed across the floor on their stomachs.

Elaine joined in and inexplicably began to feel incredibly horny. All that pressure on the clit. And no action from Ross in God knows how long, although he was due back from location that very afternoon, and maybe . . . if she was very very lucky . . . and played the perfect wife . . .

I want to come she thought *right here and now*. She gazed at that impossible crotch and shuddered and wriggled to a quite satisfactory climax while the music blared and the slight smell of sweat filtered in amongst the heavy scent of Joy and Estee and Opium.

'Oh God!' she exclaimed.

'Sorry?' questioned Karen.

'Nothing,' she giggled, feeling very liberated.

'Okay ladies. That's it for today. Did you enjoy it?'

He had to be kidding. She would come every day. The double entendre almost made Elaine laugh aloud, and feeling very pleased with herself she got up and headed for the showers.

Ron Gordino's health and exercise class. The latest and the best. Bibi Sutton had discovered it. Where Bibi went others followed.

Elaine stripped off in a tiny cubicle, then, naked, stepped boldly into the communal shower. Very un-Beverly Hills. But right now very in. Anyone who was frightened to show everything they had at Ron Gordino's was immediately suspect. Nudity and letting it all hang out were *the* thing to do.

Perfumed soap oozed from a wall faucet at the press of a button. Elaine soaped herself thoroughly, her eyes darting this way and that checking out the other bodies on display. Karen had the largest nipples she had ever seen. Big brown buttons, like giant knobs on a transistor radio. Elaine decided that if she were a man she would probably find them quite repulsive.

'Have you heard about the new Neil Gray film?' Karen asked. She was tall, with a supple tanned body, thick copper coloured hair and carefully chiselled features. Her connections were the best, she knew everyone and everything – since her father was George Lancaster, a giant superstar who had retired five years previously to marry Pamela London, the third richest woman in America. He now lived in Palm Beach, and Karen visited him often. She was in her early thirties and twice divorced.

'No. What's he doing?' Elaine soaped under her arms, and tried to stop staring at her friend's awful nipples.

'A movie that his *wife* wrote. Can you imagine?'

For a moment Elaine was confused. 'Maralee?'

'No, not his ex-wife, silly. His *wife*. Montana. El big pain in the necko.'

'Oh. Her.' Elaine was silent for a moment while she digested this information. She always thought of Maralee as Neil Gray's wife although they had been divorced for years. Elaine had never met Montana, although of course she had heard enough about her.

'Neil sent the script to daddy in the hope that he would want to do it,' Karen continued. 'He told me it's very good. Of course nobody believes that Montana actually wrote it. Neil must have written it himself and decided to give her credit.'

'Is George interested?' Elaine asked curiously, wondering what Karen was leading up to.

'Of course not. No way would daddy do a movie – not even if it was guaranteed to be another "Gone with the Wind". He's *had* the picture biz, just adores doing nothing. Being married to Pamela London suits him fine. I mean they *own* Palm Beach.'

Together they stepped from the showers, wrapping themselves in giant fluffy bath sheets.

'The thing is,' Karen continued pointedly, 'that daddy says the part is perfect for Ross – you know he's always liked him.'

That was news to Elaine. Ross had only ever had bad things to say about George Lancaster, calling him everything from a ham actor to a hood. They hadn't even received an invitation to the Palm Beach wedding – one of *the* social events of the year. Karen had explained apologetically at the time – 'Can't invite too much show biz. Pamela's orders.' So how come everyone from Lucille Ball to Gregory Peck had been present? Elaine had burned with fury for weeks.

'Who *is* Ross's agent?' Karen inquired artlessly.

Elaine stared at her friend and wondered why she was taking this sudden interest in her husband's career. 'He's with Zack Schaeffer.'

Karen frowned. 'You know, I just can't understand why he isn't with Sadie La Salle. She really *is* the best.'

Elaine couldn't understand it either – but every time she brought the subject up, Ross muttered something about he and Sadie not getting along. At parties they studiously ignored each other, and he vetoed Elaine's suggestion of ever inviting the powerful Ms. De Salle to their home. It was a well known fact that Sadie had discovered Ross years and years ago – but apparently that meant nothing to either of them. It really infuriated Elaine, because Sadie La Salle *was*, as Karen said, the absolute best.

'I hear they're talking Tony Curtis or Kirk Douglas now,' Karen continued. 'Why don't you get Zack on it right away? I think it's called *Street People*. Oliver Easterne's producing. You know Oliver, don't you?'

Yes, she knew Oliver. He was What Makes Sammy Run reincarnated. A hot shot hustler who got lucky. Ross couldn't stand him either. And anyway, if George Lancaster thought Ross was so perfect, why hadn't *he* suggested him?

'Ross has got so much lined up . . .' she murmured vaguely. 'And if they're talking Curtis and Douglas they're hardly talking big time.'

Karen laughed softly. 'Come *on*, Elaine. Don't snow-job *me*. I know where every single body is buried in this town. Ross needs a good film, and this could be it.'

'Ninety-two . . . ninety-three . . . ninety-four . . .' The words shot out of Buddy's mouth as his arms propelled his body up and down, up and down. Push-ups. One hundred a day. Kept him in the greatest shape in town. '. . . Ninety-eight . . . ninety-nine . . . one hundred.' He leaped energetically off the floor, barely out of breath.

Angel clapped her hands in admiration. She watched him every day, it was the highlight of her morning – that was if they hadn't made love. Sweet love which every time took her on a roller coaster ride of joy. 'Buddy, I love you!' she sang out. 'I totally *love* you!'

'Hey – hey.' He grinned. 'What's with the outburst?'

'I just feel so happy!'

She ran to him and he opened up his arms to receive her. Angel liked to be cuddled more than anything else in the world. With Buddy it always turned into something more, but she didn't mind that either.

This time he pushed her gently away and stretched his arms high above his head. 'Gonna take a fast swim, then I've got me that important interview. Remember? I told you yesterday.'

She didn't remember. But maybe that was because he was always busy running here, there, and everywhere. They had been in Hollywood for two weeks and during the day she hardly ever saw him. 'Business,' he had explained. 'Y'know kid, I bin away. It'll take a few weeks before everything falls into position.'

She hoped it would fall into position soon. She could just see the movie magazines – *Mrs Buddy Hudson visited her husband on the set of his latest movie today, what a cute couple they make! Angel Hudson, an aspiring actress, says that Buddy and their home life together come first.*

She imagined a four page colour photo spread of them together. Jogging in matching track suits. Feeding each other ice cream. Laughing in a hot tub.

'Buddy?' She ran after him as he headed for the door. 'Do you think you'll be doing a movie soon?'

He stared at the upturned face, the wide eyes, the adoring expression. Maybe he had convinced her a little too thoroughly that he was hot shit in the movie world. But then he hadn't expected her to believe him so absolutely. 'Well . . . I sure hope so, babe. Like I told you, I *have* been away, an' this town's got a real short memory.'

'Oh.' Disappointment clouded her face.

'But you can bet on old Buddy Boy pullin' off somethin' real big an' juicy soon. Like I just turned down a guest shot on "Taxi". The part

63

wasn't big enough – I gotta come back with somethin' special. Right, sugar?'

'Right, Buddy.' She was glowing again.

He contemplated postponing his swim. Making love to Angel was like taking a ride to heaven. But then he thought – no – gotta get my act together – gotta get my muscles in shape – gotta swim off some of the anger and frustration that are beginning to creep into every pore of my body.

Back in town two stinking weeks and nothing. No goddamn action whichever way he turned. Commercial. Movies. Television. Zilch.

Six interviews.

Six turndowns.

He was Buddy Hudson. He had everything going for him. Why weren't they hanging out flags?

He ran down two flights of stairs to what was laughingly referred to as the pool area. There were twenty-two apartments, each of which housed at least two people. Every day forty-four bodies splashed and revelled in the slimy twenty foot pool which never seemed to get cleaned. The only good thing about the apartment was that it cost nothing – courtesy of Buddy's good friend Randy Felix, who was currently in Palm Springs shacked up with a wealthy widow and her daughter.

It was early so the pool was deserted. A thin film of oil formed a slick on top of the water. He dived straight in – if you stopped to think about it you were lost. Then he churned up and down like a frenetic dolphin confined in too small a space. When he hit it, man, he would get the biggest and the best pool in the whole of the city. Something with space, and cool clear water, and a diving board, and Italian tiles, and a filter that worked, and . . .

' 'Morning.' A girl stood by the side watching him. She had orange hair frizzed into tight little curls on top of her head, and she wore the smallest string bikini he had ever seen. It barely covered her large breasts, and merely skimmed her crotch.

He continued to swim.

She settled herself on a towel and began to oil her body.

Before Angel he would have hit on her. Immediately. He always had the best lookers, and this one – while being nowhere near Angel – *was* – in her own particular way – a very choice number.

'My name's Shelly,' she announced. 'Who're you?'

He hauled himself from the pool and began doing leg bends. 'Buddy. Buddy Hudson.'

'You live here alone?' she asked pointedly, unhooking the clasp of her bikini top and taking it off.

He couldn't help staring at her large firm breasts. 'No. I live here with my wife.'

She hooted with laughter. '*You're* married?'

What was so funny about that? 'Yeah. *I'm* married.' Furiously he worked on his legs – four more pulls on each thigh and then straight back into the pool for further punishment. He did the crawl for thirty lengths before emerging again.

Shelly lay on her back, legs spread and nicely oiled, tits pointing skyward like two polished aubergines. Dark shades covered her eyes, and a transistor radio was tuned to *KIIS F.M.*

Buddy picked up his towel and walked into the building. On his way upstairs he checked out the mailbox. Three bills for Randy. A leaflet urging all and sundry to *join Jesus*. And a brochure from an enthusiastic exterminator – *You got mice we deal with 'em nice*.

In the one room apartment Angel was busying herself with a vacuum. She switched off the machine when he entered and grinned. 'I borrowed it from the lady next door. She said I could use it anytime. Isn't that nice?'

'Sure is.' Angel was a nut. Why waste time vacuuming this dump? He pulled off his wet shorts and dropped them on the floor before walking to the closet they called a bathroom. There, he attempted to shower with a hand attachment that fitted onto the bathtaps – not an easy exercise.

When he emerged Angel was busy squeezing fresh juice for him behind the bar which doubled as a kitchen. The whole apartment, with no trouble at all, would fit neatly into two medium sized suitcases.

He opened the closet and selected black slacks, his one and only silk shirt, and a lightweight Yves Saint Laurent jacket. Fortunately, in Buddy's case, clothes did not make the man. Whatever he put on looked good and he knew it. This puzzled him. If he always looked so good how come he wasn't a star?

He dressed and gulped the juice Angel handed him. 'I'll be back around six or seven. What are you goin' to do today?'

'Go to the market I guess . . . Only I'll need some money . . .'

'Oh yeah, sure.' He was embarrassed. He had no goddamn money. He was down to his last hundred. Dragging some bills from his pocket, he gave her two tens. 'Don't spend it all at once.' Corny old clichéd joke. Sometimes he hated himself.

She smiled. 'I'll try not to.'

He grabbed her, ran his hands over her gorgeous body, kissed her on the mouth. 'Later, sugar.'

Pre-production was in full swing. Since *Street People* was to be shot mainly on location there was much to get organized. The availability of the crew Neil usually worked with was of prime importance, and so far everything was falling into position – no big problems. He was out early most days with his lighting cameraman and first assistant scouting for locations. Some directors employed location scouts, but he preferred to do it himself.

Montana was busy casting. She had settled into an office in Oliver Easterne's building on the Strip and gone straight to work. She could have got an agency to sift through the hundreds of possibles, or indeed hired a first rate casting director like Frances Cavendish, but she wanted to see everyone herself, then present her selections to Neil for his full approval. It was her movie, and she planned to see it stayed that way.

The excitement of actually launching into the pre-production period was heady. She knew she was lucky because she was married to Neil, and he loved her script and wanted to do it. But even if he had hated it . . . Well she was quite confident it was good enough to take to any studio or independent and get them interested. It was the best thing she had ever done, and she had no intention of employing false modesty. *Street People* was good because it was real. She had based it on scenes of life that were happening all around. Mostly she had based it on the characters she had observed while shooting her children's film on the streets of Los Angeles. Neil's enthusiasm was a real plus, but deep down she couldn't help wondering if he hadn't of grabbed the property – maybe – just maybe – she might have got the opportunity to direct it herself.

Bullshit. Since when did women get opportunities like that? Wise up kid and be grateful your old man's doing it so at least you get a fifty per cent say.

There were three star roles plus thirty-two speaking parts to be cast. Some of them were only one line, but they mattered. Montana didn't want to see actors who were in every dreary television show, she wanted new talent – and she was enjoying every minute of finding the perfect actor or actress for each role.

They came in their hundreds. Smiling, surly, eager. Old, young, pretty, ugly. All carried their portfolios filled with photos, lists of credits and résumés.

Agents assaulted her from all sides. The good and the bad.

'You wanna Marilyn Monroe type? I gotta girl that'll rouse every cock from here to the Valley!'

'This boy I'm sending you is James Dean. I'm telling you he's Dean – only better.'

'A young Brando . . .'

'An older Brooke Shields . . .'

'A sexy Julie Andrews . . .'

'A taller Dudley Moore . . .'

'An American Michael Caine . . .'

She was swamped with every type possible. But gradually she began to pick and choose, getting more excited with each find.

In the evenings she worked on the script – adding scenes, changing lines. Neil told her about the locations he had found, and she told him about some of the characters she had interviewed. Their personal lives got swept to one side while together they lived, breathed and ate *Street People*. It became the focus of both of their lives.

Occasionally they fought. The three main roles were not cast. Oliver Easterne wanted at least two bankable stars and Neil was hotly pursuing retired superstar, George Lancaster. 'If we get George,' he pointed out, 'the other two can be unknowns.'

'*If* we get the asshole,' Oliver agreed. To him all actors were assholes, be they stars or bit players. 'Which doesn't seem likely the way things are going.'

'I'll fly to Palm Beach this weekend,' Neil decided. 'He likes the script, I think I can convince him.'

'I hope so. Time's running tight. I have some ideas myself . . .'

Neil knew about Oliver's ideas. Half-assed star names that were wrong wrong wrong. He had no intention of even considering them.

Montana was not mad with enthusiasm about George Lancaster. 'He can't act,' she stated flatly.

'He will. With me.'

She was unconvinced, but realistic enough to know that certain concessions had to be made. 'What do you think? Should I come with you?'

Neil shook his head quickly. 'No. You've got enough to take care of here. I can handle George.'

She nodded, her mind filled with faces. 'There's a couple of actors I think we should test for the part of Vinnie.'

'*If* we land George Lancaster. Otherwise we're going to have to go with a name.'

'I don't know why.'

'Yes you do. It's called playing the box-office game.'

'I never did like playing games.'

'Learn.'

'Screw you,' she said amiably.

'Ah, if there was only time,' he replied.

She grinned. 'I'll make time, when you get back.'

Elaine's day.

After Ron Gordino's exercise class, a visit to The Nail Kiss of Life, then four hours at Elizabeth Arden having her legs waxed, her eyebrows shaped, a facial, and her hair washed and blow dried. She got home in time to change into green Norell lounging pyjamas before Ross arrived back from location. Even if she did say so herself she looked wonderful. 'You look divine!' she whispered to her bedroom mirror. *Eat your heart out, Etta the Elephant.*

She strolled into the living room and was about to fix herself a drink when glancing through the huge plate glass windows she was horrified to see him at it again. Pissing in her pool!

'Lina!' she yelled, striding to the glass doors and stepping outside. 'Lina!'

The boy lazily zipped up without – it seemed – a care in the world. 'Afternoon ma'am,' he drawled.

'You filthy pig!' she shouted. 'I saw what you did!'

He was now bending over the hose which gushed fresh water into the pool. 'Huh?'

'Don't huh *me*. You know what I mean.'

Lina appeared at that point, wiping her hands on an apron tied firmly round her waist and frowning. 'What ees it Señora? I try make dinner.'

Elaine pointed a perfectly manicured finger at the boy. 'I do not want him here again. You understand me, Lina? Not anymore.'

He continued to fiddle with the hose while Lina heaved a dramatic sigh. 'Miguel – he sick –' she began.

'I don't care about Miguel,' Elaine screamed. 'I don't care if he drops dead on the job. But I do not – and please understand me – I do not want this . . . this . . . person here *ever* again. You got that, Lina?'

Lina gave another dramatic sigh and raised her eyes to heaven. 'Sure,' she said. 'I got.'

'Good. Then get him out of here right now.' Elaine stalked back into the house and headed straight for the bar where she fixed herself a double shot of vodka with one token ice cube. Unbelievable! Help these days! Impossible!

An old pick-up truck flashed past from the back of the house just as a long black limousine pulled up at the front. Ross! Quickly Elaine checked out her appearance in the antiqued mirror behind the bar. She looked good. Wouldn't it be nice if he noticed for once?

He didn't. He strode into the house wearing mud caked boots over faded Levis, and a checked shirt with an old leather jacket. Lately Ross had taken to dressing young. It didn't suit him. He looked like an over-the-hill cowboy.

'Darling!' Dutifully she pecked at his cheek, and was rewarded with rough stubble.

'Hot damn!' he exclaimed. 'Am I glad to be out of *that* pisshole.' He flopped down on a white brocade sofa which Elaine had just had recovered at great expense and put his legs up, boots and all. 'I'm friggin' exhausted! Get me a drink – before I fuckin' faint!'

The movie star was home.

Buddy whistled as he ran down the stairs from the apartment. Angel with the trusting eyes. She never bugged him, complained about the apartment or their lack of money. She never questioned him when he came home, or insisted that he tell her what he was doing every minute of the day. She was perfect. Golden lady. One day he would swamp her with furs and jewels and stereos and cars. Whatever she wanted – it would be hers.

When? That was the question. When would it all happen for him? He had been in Hollywood ten years now . . . Ten years was a long time . . . a real long time . . .

Running away from his mother the second time was easy. Especially with two hundred dollars to help him on his way. Sixteen years old, wary as a fox, and determined not to be caught. He got out of San Diego as quickly as he could, jumping a bus to Los Angeles, then hitching his way down to the beach where he hung out sleeping rough, scrounging food, and making friends. There were a lot of kids in the same position as him. Runaways with nothing to do with their time except the five big Ss – Surf, Swim, Sunbathe, Sleep and Sex. With a few drugs thrown in whenever they could afford it. Buddy didn't hesitate, he got into sex in a big way. There was no lack of partners among the girls – even the boys – but that was definitely not his scene.

His first score was a big freckled girl who liked it rough. She loved to roll on the beach with sand penetrating every crack. He had her two or three times a day until she ran off with a fat man in a Cadillac who promised her Acapulco. Next came a little redhead whose speciality was 'sucking dick', as she called it. He didn't like that, it made him feel too vulnerable, like her sharp white teeth were going to clamp down and ruin his future. He moved on to a Swedish starlet who visited muscle beach to develop her pectorals. She taught him to drive her pale pink Thunderbird, and to give head. He enjoyed both.

He got himself a job slinging hamburgers at a beach hangout, and that gave him just enough money to rent a room. A friend showed him how to play the guitar, and he wasn't bad. He worked on his voice, getting together a repertoire of songs. Occasionally he landed himself a gig singing and strumming the guitar and that was a help financially.

The five big Ss remained constant. He was tanned all over, strong from surfing, muscled from working out. He had all the sex he ever wanted, plenty of sleep, and he never once thought of his mother. She was dead as far as he was concerned.

Buddy was a loner. He wanted it that way.

He palled up with a would-be actor named Randy Felix, and once in a while he'd hitch a ride into Hollywood and hang around the class Randy attended. Joy Byron's Method Acting School. Joy Byron was an old English broad with a voice like a hacksaw. She wore flowered dresses and carried a parasol at all times – even indoors. Her students adored her, and worshipped regularly twice a week in a disused warehouse on the wrong side of Wilshire. When Randy dropped out to pursue other interests, Buddy continued to go on his own. He loved every minute of the two hour classes, and soon he was performing everything from Stanley Kowalski in 'A Streetcar Named Desire' to Jay Gatsby in 'The Great Gatsby'.

Joy Byron said he was good, and she should know – for in her day she had acted with the very best. Olivier, Gielgud – all the English greats, or so she said, and Buddy was inclined to believe her.

As acting fever struck, so the beach lost its appeal. A move seemed logical, and Randy, who was sharing a house with two girls in West Hollywood, said there was always room for a fourth. Just before he hit twenty Buddy moved in.

The house was a dump, the girls were dykes, but living in Holly-

wood was living in Hollywood. Buddy felt at home in no time at all. Only problem. No money. No car. Getting by at the beach was one thing. Making out in town was another. Randy always seemed to be reasonably flush, so Buddy asked him how he did it.

'By gettin' paid for what you're givin' away for free,' Randy explained. 'I got me an agent takes twenty percent an' arranges everythin'. No hassle. No sweat. I sell dick – to ladies – it sure as hell beats shovellin' hot dogs!'

'You sell what?'

'Give it a try, Buddy. I get commission on every stud I bring in.'

They both started to laugh. 'Really?' Buddy asked between bouts of mirth. 'Really?'

Randy nodded. He was five feet nine inches tall, pleasant looking but nothing special. He had a large nose, small eyes and no back teeth. When he laughed this was very noticeable.

'Well I'll be a son of a bitch!' Buddy exclaimed. 'Who would believe it?'

Randy took Buddy to meet his agent, a black homosexual dressed from head to toe in tight white leather.

'No . . . er . . . male customers,' Buddy mumbled, hardly believing what he was getting himself into.

'No males?' sniffed the agent, affectionately known as Gladrags by his stable of active young studs. 'What are you – some kind of a weirdo freak?'

So began his life as a hustler.

The first time he wasn't sure if he could get it up. He met the woman at a designated time at an apartment Gladrags had arranged. She turned up twenty minutes late, a middle-aged lady in a severely cut business suit. 'You're new,' she remarked casually, as if she was familiar with every one of Gladrags' boys. 'I don't take my clothes off,' she announced, hitching her skirt around her waist, and removing sensible white panties. 'But I want you naked. Strip.' She lay down on the bed and watched him as he fumbled his way out of his clothes.

Jeez! He felt like he was en route to the dentist! No way could he get a hard-on until desperately he remembered Randy's advice – 'Close your eyes an' use your imagination.' Quickly he flashed onto a memory of a girl he had balled recently. Nineteen. Pretty. With a trick of licking his balls until he felt he could shoot his stuff twenty feet in the air.

It worked. Suddenly he was in business.

He never looked back. Servicing women for money was no prob-

lem. It paid the bills and enabled him to pursue an acting career. Joy Byron fixed him up with an agent, and he got some pictures together and began going on interviews. Almost immediately he landed a two liner in a 'Starsky and Hutch', followed by a small part in a Burt Reynolds block buster. He was on his way! He was going to be a star!

It didn't exactly work out that way. There followed a lean patch, during which time the 'Starsky and Hutch' episode aired and he was not in it. And the Burt Reynolds movie played and he was not in that either!

The humiliation of ending up on the cutting room floor twice was too much.

'Never mind,' Joy Byron consoled. 'Something else will come along.'

She was a funny old bird who had taken to inviting him to her house for 'extra coaching'. He was kind of flattered, and he certainly enjoyed acting out scenes from all the great plays with her, although sometimes, in the dusty living room of her Hollywood Hills house, when they were in the middle of a seene, she would move a little too close for comfort. He was servicing women for money regularly, but the thought of getting it on with Joy Byron was not to be relished. For a start she had to be at least seventy years old. And he respected her. She was a great actress. She was his teacher for crissakes.

One night she said to him, 'Buddy. I have a wonderful idea. The workshop will put on a special performance of "Streetcar". I will invite agents, casting directors, studio executives. I know these people, and if I invite them they will come. You – of course – will play Stanley Kowalski. A perfect showcase for you.'

'Hey . . . terrific . . .' he began.

She grabbed him before he could finish the sentence.

It wasn't that bad.

It wasn't that good.

He got to give up whoring. He moved into Joy's freaky house and she took care of all the bills.

He got to act day and night, night and day. Joy was always ready. He zipped through all the great playwrights. He zoomed through a stack of old screenplays. He emoted until he was blue in the face.

Joy Byron taught him plenty about the business. Everything from make-up to lighting and the best camera angles. She coached him in mime, and diction, and posture. She kept him very busy, and true to her word she starred him in a student production of 'Streetcar'.

Several important people actually did turn up. Frances Cavendish was one of them. The flinty-eyed casting agent was one of the best in town because she never missed an opportunity to view new talent.

Buddy looked sensational. Torn T-shirt. Skin tight jeans. Marlon Brando move over. He had seen the 1951 movie many times on television. He had studied every nuance and gesture of the great actor's performance. Now he had it down perfectly and he knew he was good. It did not surprise him when Frances Cavendish sent back a note for him to drop by and see her.

He waited a week. Did not want to appear too anxious. Then he sauntered into her office, perched on the side of her desk, and mumbled, *'I hear ya wanna make me a movie star.'*

She adjusted her glasses and stared at him. *'Shift your buns off my desk, sonny. They're casting a horror movie at Universal. I think you might be right. Get yourself over there pronto.'*

He got the part. Three days. No lines. There followed a series of similar bits. A week on a gangster movie. Two days on *'Police Woman'*. A shaving cream commercial. A two part *'Vegas'* – his best role yet. Finally – his shot.

'I think you're right for the lead in a new pilot,' Frances said, and actually smiled. *'This might be it, Buddy.'*

He was floating. The producers liked him. He ran home to Joy with a script and a stomach that wouldn't lie down. He was going to play the lead in a new pilot. He was going to be a star.

Joy Byron read the script and pronounced it *'Crapshit!'* She could be very salty for an old lady. *'We'll shape it into something worthwhile,'* she told him with a long theatrical sigh.

They worked long and hard. Joy gave him motivations, she told him exactly what to do and when to do it. She even accompanied him to the set to make sure he changed none of her instructions.

On the second day, directly after the producers had viewed the previous day's shooting, he was fired.

'So what?' snorted Joy Byron. *'I told you it was crapshit!'*

He left her house in the middle of the night while she slept. He was sick with disappointment and anger and frustration. When was Buddy Boy going to become a star?

He drifted right back into his old way of living. Only now he began to drink too much, and take too many drugs. A girlfriend introduced him to Maxie Sholto, an unsavoury agent who was into arranging Hollywood Parties – the kind where the hired help performed for an audience. At least he was getting seen. So what if it was with two *bimbos crawling all over him? He was on show. And the women at the parties loved him.*

One day he bumped into his friend, Randy. 'You're gonna be dog turd in this town if you don't watch it,' Randy warned.

Buddy was flying. 'I'm makin' big bucks. Y'want some of my action?'

'Where's your big bucks gettin' you? All I see is snow up your nose an' grass down your throat. Straighten out, or you'll be finished.'

He straightened out. Three nights later. In the middle of an orgy with come streaming down his face from a fat record producer, and a thin girl riding pony on his joint.

He caught his reflection in a mirror, and he also caught a camera in action which pissed him no end.

He threw the girl off him, smashed the camera, beat up the record producer, and stormed out of the place. He was Buddy Hudson. He was going to be a star, and nothing would stop him.

The next day he hopped a plane to Hawaii where he dried out, got himself a job singing in a piano bar, and met Angel.

So – Buddy thought to himself, as he climbed in his wreck of a car. What to do now? Returning to L.A. with new bride in tow all ready to set the town on fire was one thing. Reality was another. He needed money. And there was only one sure way he knew how to get it.

Neil Gray glanced around the VIP lounge. He nursed a large Jack Daniels on the rocks, his second.

Across the room sat Gina Germaine. Blonde, bubbly, bosoms and bum. Surrounded by admiring airline personnel tripping over each other to grant her every wish. He had greeted her briefly when she entered. Two people who knew each other only vaguely. Christ! But his balls were aching for her. He couldn't wait to be with her on the plane, maybe jam it to her in the toilet if she would let him . . .

If she would let him indeed! Gina Germaine would let him fuck her in Trader Vics on a Sunday night if he told her that's what he wanted.

God! Was he getting senile? Why this obsession with some blonde movie star? There was definitely something the matter with him. Had to be. Taking her to Palm Beach with him was sheer lunacy. The risk of getting found out . . .

The risk was giving him the best erection he'd had all year.

8

New York could turn you schizo. If you weren't already.

What mean streets. Dirt and grime and low down filthy reality. Rats. Cockroaches. The streets were crawling with them – the human kind too. A walk through the city could guarantee no end of meetings with the insane.

Deke kept himself to himself. He walked with a purposeful stride, his chin tucked down, his bleak eyes hooded and watchful.

Once two kids tried to jump him on the corner of 39th and Seventh Avenue. It was not yet dark, and people were plentiful on the street. No one came to his aid as he struggled with the two crazed teenagers, one of them armed with a knife.

Deke fought back. He thrust and lunged and clawed. Until he was able to grab the knife from his assailant and shove it into the boy's chest, surprise spilling out of the boy's stoned eyes as blood spilled out of his body.

The other attacker ran, and Deke strolled casually off while passersby scurried along the street, eyes studiously averted.

It gave him such a good feeling. A tremendous surge of power. It reminded him of Philadelphia . . . that night . . . that special night . . .

His step quickened as he remembered . . .

The machete he had bought from a pawnshop for twenty bucks because he liked the look of it. It had hung on the wall of his bedroom unused for two years, although occasionally he had taken it down and struck a pose in front of his dresser mirror. He had never imagined the day would come when he would use it for real.

He thought of Joey. Of her squat body, spiky hair, and wide red mouth.

Joey Kravetz . . .

'Hey – hey. You lookin' for some fun, buster?'

Deke attempted to walk past, but she blocked his way, planting herself firmly in his path. She cocked her head on one side and winked lasciviously. 'I don't wanna rip ya off, nothin' like that. I just wanna get in your pants an' give ya the hottest bounce y'had all year. Can y'dig it?'

He stared at her. She was almost pretty, but her nose was off centre, one eye had a slight cast, her lipstick was smudged over a red cavern of a mouth. 'How much?' he muttered.

'A buck a minute. Can't be fairer than that.' She squinted up at him, for he was much taller than her five feet three inches. 'Ya won't regret a dime of it, cowboy!'

Cowboy. He had never been called that before. It made him feel good. 'Okay,' he mumbled, knowing the event would take no longer than five minutes. 'Where?'

'I got me a little jive ass palace.' She grabbed him by the arm. 'Two blocks down, ya can tell me the story of y'life on the way. My name's Joey, what's yours?'

He had never met a girl like her before. Sure, plenty of hookers with sour mouths and empty eyes; and girls he had dated, who smiled politely and never let him so much as touch them. Joey was different. She seemed to want to be with him as they walked along the rain soaked streets.

Her 'palace' was a small room two flights up with a sink in the corner, a bed lounged on by a fat white cat, and one lamp draped with a singed pink chiffon scarf.

She shooed the cat off the bed, threw off her plastic raincoat, and said, 'Nice, huh? Sure beats my last dump.'

He stood hesitantly in the doorway and wondered if it would be as usual. Money out first. Then a furtive hump against a silent piece of meat.

Joey undid the side zip on her tight black mini skirt and wriggled out of it. Underneath she wore bikini panties with TUESDAY embroidered in red. It was Friday.

Deke groped in his pocket for some money.

'Put it away, y'don't know how long ya gonna stay,' she giggled. 'Sure y'don't wanna change the deal? Fifty bucks for as long as ya like?'

He shook his head negatively.

'Suit yourself, buster,' she said, pulling her sweater over orange spiky hair and flinging it on the floor.

She had very small breasts with cheaply rouged nipples. The color

76

had smudged, so had the mascara under her lazy eye.

She brought her fingers up and played with her nipples until they stood to attention. 'Now ain't that worth a buck an' a half,' she giggled. 'I got lotsa tricks like that, cowboy.'

He coughed dryly.

'You're really nice,' she said, continuing to play with her rouged nipples. 'I like you. I think you an' I could be friends – y'know – real close friends. You've got the kinda eyes I like, horny eyes. I could get off just lookin' into your eyes, cowboy – just lookin'.'

He stayed two hours. It cost him one hundred and twenty dollars and was worth every cent.

In the distance Deke could hear the familiar whine of police sirens. He quickened his pace. It was definitely time to move on. New York had been a good resting place, a city to get lost in while the murders faded away. Another day or so and he would be off. He had things to do, places to go.

9

So – the big movie star was home. Bitching and complaining about everything.

They were in bed, Ross propped up on four pillows, eyes firmly glued to the television, when Elaine decided the time was right to mention the movie Karen Lancaster had told her about. 'I think you should get Zack on it right away.'

'Ha! The great George Lancaster turns something down and *you* think I should call my agent,' sneered Ross. 'Jesus, Elaine! You really get to me sometimes.'

'If the part was offered to George it has to be good,' she insisted stubbornly.

'Bull*shit*! George made more crap than a laxative factory.' Irritably he changed the television channels with the remote control. 'And – George frigging Lancaster is fifteen frigging years older than me. Don't you forget *that*.'

'Twelve,' corrected Elaine. She knew everyone's age to the exact day.

77

Ross raised his ass from the bed and let forth a rampant fart.

Elaine was enraged. Oh, if his fans could only see him now! 'If you have to do that kindly do it in the bathroom,' she snapped.

In reply he farted again and switched channels.

'How come, before we were married, you always managed to control your bodily functions?' she asked coldly.

He mimicked her voice, 'How come, before we were married, you never nagged?'

'God! You're impossible!' She got out of their king-sized bed and pulled on a turquoise silk negligee.

'Where are you going?' he demanded.

'To the kitchen.'

'Get me some ice cream. Vanilla and chocolate, with some hot fudge sauce.'

'You're supposed to be on a diet.'

'I don't need a diet.'

'Everyone over the age of twenty-five needs a diet.'

He weakened. 'Get me the ice cream and I'll call Zack.'

'Promise?'

He grinned the famous Conti grin. 'When have I ever lied to you, sweetheart?'

Montana sat in her office and stared at the young actor sitting across the room. He was hitting on her and she knew it. She lowered her eyes and studied the list of credits he had handed her. The usual rota of crap television and bad movies.

'I never expected to walk into this office today and find someone like you behind that desk,' he said in a low husky voice.

He was hitting on her with his eyes again. A penetrating stare which she found most disconcerting, because in those eyes she could read stark desperation, and she understood the look only too well. 'It says here that you're twenty-two. I'm really looking for someone a little older,' she said briskly.

'How much older?' he countered.

She hesitated. Let him down easy. Rejection was never easy to dish out.

'Well . . . er . . . twenty-five, six.'

'I can look older. I'm really twenty-four.' He had a facial twitch which sprang into action spoiling his bland good looks.

'Fine,' she said, handing him back his résumé. 'I'll keep that in mind. Thanks for coming by.'

'Is that all?' He sounded surprised. 'Don't you want me to read or anything?'

'Not today.'

'Does that mean I'll be coming back?'

She smiled in what she hoped was a non-committal fashion. 'Thank you, Mr. Crunch.' *Crunch*. What kind of a name was that? 'We'll be in touch with your agent.'

He stood up and sauntered towards her. 'Can I see you sometime?' he asked, the desperate eyes and the twitch going full force.

She felt sorry for him and all the hundreds of other young actors just like him. 'Look,' she said patiently, 'don't sell yourself short.'

'Huh?'

'You're probably a very good actor, but not right for this movie – so stop pushing it.'

He reddened, bit down hard on his bottom lip, but still kept trying. 'You an' I could make some beautiful things happen. Give me a try?' he leered suggestively. 'I come highly recommended, y'know what I mean?'

She was getting annoyed. 'Why don't you just go. Okay?'

'Lady – you have no idea what you're missing,' he muttered.

Her patience snapped. 'Hey – I've got a feeling I know *exactly* what I'm missing.'

Reluctantly he slouched from the room.

She sighed. Hollywood. City of ambition. A town where success was the name of the game. If you had it you were top of the heap. If you didn't . . . goodbye Charlie – you were less than nothing.

Hollywood. To be an actor or an actress you really had to be a masochist. *That* was for sure.

Come to think of it being a writer was no picnic either. She recalled her first efforts with the original outline on her television series. Nobody had taken her seriously at first. She had done the rounds of agents and the so-called network executives. *Who are you? What are your credits? Baby, you got two strokes against you. One – you're from the East Coast. Two – you're a woman.*

Oh, really?

Wanna climb in the sack and discuss it?

She had never used Neil's influence to achieve anything. The television idea was good. Eventually it had sold. Then came the book on old-time Hollywood, and writing that had been bliss because she was her own boss and didn't have to answer to anyone. Doing the film on children was the biggest challenge of all. She had put it together herself. No small achievement. Especially for a woman, she thought cynically.

She buzzed for the next actor to be sent in, and lit up a cigarette, inhaling deeply. How was Neil doing in Palm Beach with the wonderful George Lancaster? Not that it bothered her either way. If they got him it would be good box office. If they didn't then they could go with a real actor – someone who would make the character of the old cop come alive. A far more exciting prospect.

She opened the script which lay on her desk and flicked through the pages. It could be a great movie. With Neil directing she was sure it would be.

So what was a guy supposed to do? Let his new bride starve? Because that's what was going to happen if he didn't score some bucks soon.

Buddy sat disconsolately behind the wheel of his car and thought it all out. Yet again. He had been doing so much thinking lately that his head felt like it wanted to bust right open and let all the crap out.

He was an actor. That was his trade. Couldn't land one job. So? What other job paid enough to keep him afloat, and still available to go on interviews? He wasn't about to park cars for a living. No way.

The answer was simple. No big deal when you really thought about it. Half an hour in bed with some faceless woman, a hundred in the pocket, free time to spend with Angel. Sex was like taking a piss. Get it out, do what you have to do, zipper up and vroom . . . long gone. And what Angel didn't know . . .

His mind was made up. He checked out his appearance in the rearview mirror, ruffled his hair and hooded his smokey black eyes. Satisfied with his appearance he leapt out of the car, and with his thrusting walk in overdrive, headed towards the men's store Gladrags owned on Santa Monica Boulevard. Six years before it had been a hole in the wall selling leather accessories. Since that time Gladrags had bought the buildings on either side and expanded. Now the store had glass windows which extended for a quarter of a block, and sold everything from Cerrutti suits to cashmere jock straps. Buddy was impressed. He wondered if he could get a discount.

Inside the store a perfumed transvestite hurried over to greet him.

'He-*llo*,' the lame clad creature gushed in a disturbingly masculine voice. 'And what can I do for *you*?'

Buddy took an involuntary step backwards. Gays. They always made him nervous.

'Your boss around?' he questioned.

Transvestite fluttered long false lashes. 'Do you mean Mr. Jackson?'

'Is that Gladrags?'

'I *beg* your pardon?'

'Black guy. Tall. Wears lots of leather.'

'*Sounds* like Mr. Jackson.'

'Tell him Buddy's here.'

'I would simply *love* to. But Mr. Jackson *never* comes in before one.' He put a manicured nail pensively to his chin. 'Perhaps you'd like to wait.'

'Hey,' snapped Buddy. 'I can't wait. I got things to do.'

'I'm *sure* you have.' Transvestite was in love. Amber eyes swam with promise of devotion.

'Where can I reach him now?'

'I really can't say.'

'Force yourself.'

'Oh, dear. You see, Mr. Jackson has strict rules about giving out his home address and phone number.'

Buddy narrowed his eyes tough guy style. 'An' I have strict rules about *always* getting what I want.'

Transvestite fluttered sensitive hands. 'What do *you* think I should do?'

Buddy winked. 'Give me the address and nobody will be any the wiser 'cept the two of us. Our secret. Right?'

Transvestite smiled nervously. 'If *you* say so.'

It was no wonder George Lancaster loved living in Palm Beach. In Beverly Hills or Palm Springs he was just another retired superstar. There were dozens of them around. Sinatra, Astaire, Kelly, Hope. You could trip over them every time you ventured out of the house or onto the golf course. In Palm Beach, George Lancaster reigned supreme. He was King. Or at least Prince Consort to his wife, Pamela London, the third richest woman in America.

Neil Gray sniffed around the two of them warily at a special luncheon in his honour. Pamela was a woman to be wary of. She was known for her sharp tongue and acid wit. She had been married four times, George was her fifth. 'A husband a decade,' she was fond of saying. 'None of them could keep it up longer than that. With the exception of George, of course.'

She was fifty-four years old. A large boned woman over six feet tall, with a wild mass of red frizzy hair.

George was an extremely well preserved sixty-two. He had been married twice before. The first time to a childhood sweetheart for thirty-two years, the result of that union being his daughter, Karen. And the second to a Hollywood bitch for nine months three days and two minutes exactly.

Pamela and George made an imposing couple. During five years of marriage they had forged an amicable animosity towards each other. Insults ruled the day, but togetherness was the name of the game.

'So,' Pamela said, cornflower blue eyes raking Neil. 'You want old George to get his big fat rump back to work. Is that it?'

Neil smiled and glanced down the other end of the long table where George was deep in conversation with a sun-baked cosmetic queen. Trust Pamela to seat him as far away as possible, she *knew* it was George he had come to see. 'If he wants to,' he said easily.

'If he wants to,' she sneered. 'If *I* want him to, you mean.'

Neil had known Pamela for years. At one time she had been married to a movie producer friend of his, lived in Beverly Hills, and they had moved in the same social circles. She didn't intimidate *him*. He kept smiling. 'George likes the script, he likes me. What would be so bad about taking a break from all this luxury? You could come along for the ride.'

She laughed hoarsely. 'You know how I *love* Beverly Hills. Little starlets showing everything they've got. *Dreadful* old men wearing gold chains and cracked suntans. Cheap people, Neil, darling. I *hate* cheap people!'

'Don't come then,' Neil said mildly. 'George could fly back here every Friday. We'll arrange a private plane.'

'I *have* a private plane,' Pamela laughed. 'Two in fact.'

'I know. But why use *your* plane when the production would supply whatever George requires?'

She raised an eyebrow. '*Whatever* he requires?'

'Name it.'

'Hmmm . . .' Pamela looked thoughtful.

Neil chalked up a small victory. The very rich loved the thought of getting something for nothing. 'Well?' he pressed.

'I'm thinking about it.'

'What'll it take for you to make up your mind?'

She indicated his glass of Perrier water. 'Why aren't you drinking?'

'Don't change the subject.'

'I hate a man who doesn't drink. It makes me uneasy.'

He summoned a hovering waiter. 'A double Jack Daniels on the rocks.' Then he turned back to Pamela. 'I wouldn't want you to feel uneasy.'

She grinned coquettishly. 'You *are* looking good, Neil. Maybe we *should* come to L.A. Do a bit of slumming.'

They were eating luncheon at the Palm Beach Country Club. An intimate luncheon for thirty guests, none of whom Neil knew, and most of them over the half century mark.

Suddenly he felt depressed surrounded by his contemporaries. He thought briefly of Montana and her exciting youth. He never felt the age difference when they were together. He felt it now surrounded by face lifts, expensive jewellery and liver-spotted hands. Then he remembered Gina Germaine waiting patiently at the hotel where they had checked into adjoining suites earlier in the day. She never made him feel old either. She made him feel young. Or at least she made his body feel young. His *cock* feel young.

'A cent for every dirty little thought that's clicking through your head,' Pamela said suddenly.

'What?' Neil was startled.

Pamela smiled. 'I always know when a man's thinking about sex.'

'Not me.'

She raised an eyebrow. 'No? What's different about you, Neil dear? Do you have cotton wool where you should have balls?'

He laughed. 'You're wasted here, Pamela. You should be writing steamy novelettes.'

'What makes you think I haven't tried it? I've tried almost everything else.' She leered at him. All the money in the world and her teeth were still yellow. 'Except you, Neil, dear. All these years and we've never taken a tumble together. You know we should make up for lost time.' She patted his knee intimately. 'And I always was a sucker for a British accent. So classy . . . so Richard Burton. In fact, I do believe you *look* a little like dear Richard. That same *ravaged* expression, that same –'

'Pamela.' He removed her hand. 'Stop making detours and let's get to the point. Do you, or do you not want George to make my film?'

'Goddamn!' screamed Ross, slamming down the phone. Agents. Fuck 'em and feed 'em to the fish. Goddamn parasites!

Hi, Ross . . . Yeah, Ross . . . Nothing doing, Ross.

What did they know? They knew nothing. They knew fuck all. They couldn't even wipe their ass without ripping off ten per cent of the toilet tissue.

All of his career he had brought everything to them. *Call Fox. Call Paramount. Call Wilder. Call Zanuck.* Jobs came to *him*. No agent had ever had to run his balls off on Ross Conti's behalf.

Now, after twenty-five years of dropping it in their laps, he wanted some action.

'What about the new Neil Gray film?' he had asked Zack Schaeffer. 'I hear it could be right for me.'

Don't know about it, Ross . . . I'll look into it, Ross . . . I'll call you back, Ross . . .

Screw him. *Why* didn't he know about it? It was his *job* to know about it. Sadie La Salle would know about it, and it was she who should be handling his career.

'Elaine!' he yelled.

Lina poked her head around the door. 'Meesus Conti go exercise class. You want coffee?'

He swore savagely under his breath. Elaine was never around when he needed her, only when he didn't.

'Yeah, coffee,' he growled.

Lina departed and he sat by the phone and sulked.

Sadie La Salle. She had started it all. Grudgingly he had to admit that without Sadie and her billboard it might never have happened for him.

So – how had he paid her back? He had run off with the first beautiful pair of tits that pointed in his direction, and signed with a big agency. No goodbye. No note. No phone call. Just a fast walk while he was out one day.

If all had gone according to plan Sadie La Salle should have just faded from his life never to be heard from again. And she did vanish – for a while. He didn't hear a thing about her as his career started to rise. And when he *did* start to hear her name mentioned it was nothing to get excited about. So she wanted to be an agent. Big deal. Without him she had no clients.

She found an unknown comic called Tom Brownie and built him into the biggest club act since Red Skelton. Then she nursed along a neurotic singer by the name of Melody Fame and turned *her* into the new Garland. Adam Sutton was struggling in B pictures when he joined the stable. Within two years his name was number one at the box office. George Lancaster defected from M.C.A. They all came running. Over the years she had built up the best client list in Hollywood.

Sadie La Salle. Short fat Sadie with the moustache.

Occasionally they ran into each other at parties and premieres. The moustache had gone, costly electrolysis had taken care of *that*. She had dropped thirty pounds and her clothes were expensive and well cut. A stylish bob replaced unruly black curls. She was no beauty but she was certainly an improvement.

He tried to be friendly. She gave him cold nods. He attempted conversations. She walked away.

In the early seventies he decided he needed her. Purely professionally of course. So he called her on the phone, got as far as her secretary, and suggested that Ms. La Salle might care to drop by and see him.

She never returned his call. It burned the shit out of him. What kind of a grudge was she carrying?

He cornered her at the next party they both attended. She was with a gay dress designer – rumour had it she was a dyke. Ross knew better than *that*.

'Sadie,' he breezed. 'I think you just got lucky. Guess what?' He flashed the famous Conti smile. 'I'm on the market for a new agent and it might just be you.'

She glared at him coldly. 'I'm not looking for any more clients, Ross.'

Hurt. Surprise. Fix her with the famous baby blues. 'It's been fifteen years, sweetheart. This is business.'

'Screw business,' she said tightly. 'If making commission on you gave me my one hot meal of the week I'd starve to death. Do we understand each other, Ross?'

Bitch! Dyke! Slimmed down cunt! He had not exchanged a word with her since.

Maybe it was time to try again . . . now that he was married to Elaine . . . and another ten years had gone by . . . Maybe . . .

'Meester Conti.' Lina stood solidly in the doorway, her legs like tree trunks emerging from the white uniform Elaine insisted she wear.

He turned off the sulks and managed a smile. Mustn't let the fans down. 'Yes, Lina, what is it?'

'Miguel sick. Okay I bring boy in?'

Why the hell was she bothering him? Domestic matters were Elaine's province. God knows he shelled out enough money to see that everything ran smoothly. 'What boy?' he questioned, pissed off because he had wanted Miguel to wash the Corniche.

'A good boy. Very nice. Okay I let him do pool?'

'Can he drive?'

'Sure he drive.'

'Fine. Get him over here. Have him get the Corniche out, wash it, and I want it ready by one o'clock.'

Lina nodded and gave one of her rare smiles.

'Where's my coffee?' Ross asked.

She shook her head stupidly. 'I forget.'

'So bring it.'

'Yes, me do that.'

She backed from the room as the phone began to ring. Ross snatched the receiver to his ear and barked a sharp, 'Hello.'

'Welcome back, baby,' whispered a low husky voice.

'Who is this?'

'My, what a short memory you have. Was our afternoon at the beach such a forgettable experience? I know it was a few weeks ago, but really Ross . . .'

He laughed. 'Karen!'

'The very same.'

'When can I see you?'

'You name a time and a place and yours truly will be there.'

'Your beach house. Three-thirty.'

'I'll be waiting.'

'I'll be coming.'

'Oh I know, I know.'

They both laughed.

Elaine was late for her tennis lesson, and her coach – a swarthy New Yorker with teeth like dazzling snow and a grip like a Samurai warrior – was not pleased. 'Ten minutes late, Mrs. C., is ten minutes lost.'

So what? she thought irritably. I'm the one that's paying. Or rather Ross is.

After three years of feebly hitting the ball over the net she had finally decided she must excel. It had nothing to do with the fact that Bibi Sutton had started to throw lavish tennis luncheons 'for the girls' at her Bel Air estate, and that Elaine had been invited once, performed like an amateur, and never been asked back.

She stood stiffly on one side of the court, her calf muscles killing her due to two days' hard work at Ron Gordino's exercise class. Going every day was just not on. Too punishing by far. She would cut it down to maybe three times a week. But what three days? That was the problem. What were the in days to go? When did Bibi Sutton attend? The ball wooshed past her racquet and she made a half-hearted swipe but missed it.

'Mrs. C.!' her coach complained.

She wished he wouldn't call her Mrs. C. It sounded altogether too familiar, and she was not one of those women who wished to be on intimate terms with her tennis coach. 'The name is Conti,' she said sharply.

'I know,' he replied, unabashed. 'Now, do you think you can concentrate, Mrs. C.?'

She glared at him. He had hairy legs with rigid thigh muscles which disappeared into crisp white shorts. She wondered how his cock was. Probably hairy and rigid and . . . She shook her head sharply. What was she thinking about his cock for? She couldn't stand him. Quickly she adopted an athletic stance and returned the oncoming ball gracefully.

'That's better!' he said.

Encouraged, she indulged in a passable volley, darting nimbly around the court.

Three quarters of an hour later it was over, and sweating profusely she hurried to the changing rooms where she took her third shower of the day. Ridiculous! Her skin would dry up like a prune. Must remember not to do the exercise class on the same day as her tennis lesson. She took a small black leather Cartier pad from her purse and wrote a cryptic *Tennis Gym No!* Then thoughtfully she added *ask Karen*. Karen would most certainly know the right days to attend Ron Gordino's class.

She dressed slowly, feeling a little tired. And she wondered if all those vitamin pills her nutritionist had recommended were doing her any good. Ross had sneered when he had caught her swallowing a dozen pills a day. But when she told him they gave you energy, stopped colds, prevented cancer, improved your skin, sharpened your eyesight . . . Well he had soon changed his mind. And now he took them too. Plus Ginseng, which was said to jazz up your sex drive. But it didn't seem to have done *him* any good. After three weeks away he had not so much as glanced in her direction. Fallen asleep like a dead camel and snored the night away.

She hoped he had called Zack Schaeffer about the Neil Gray film, if it had been offered to George Lancaster it *had* to be good. Oh, what a triumph to be back on top again. When you were on every guest list and the phone never stopped ringing and new designers begged you to accept their clothes as a gift and chauffeurs and bodyguards monitored your every protected move.

She thought resentfully of Ross. Why had he allowed the slide to happen? When was the moment, the hour, the day, he had fallen from the heights?

He aged, that's what happened. He drank too much, developed a gut, bags under his eyes, and his skin was leathered like an old ranch hand. She had begged him to return to the loving care of her former husband, the plastic surgeon. 'Forget it,' Ross had snapped. 'I don't want my face looking like a goddamn mask.'

Every month he had to pay out various amounts of alimony to his two previous wives. When he was making big money it was hardly noticeable. When the big money stopped it was a shocking drain.

The cutting down process had been painful. First the chauffeur, then the live-in housekeeper and her staff of two, next the gardeners and poolman. Now it was just Lina, who came in daily, except weekends. And Miguel, who was a combination gardener, poolman and chauffeur.

Elaine snorted with anger as she dressed briskly in a thin knit T-shirt dress from Giorgio's, and strappy high heeled sandals from Charles Jourdan. One thing she had refused to cut down on was her clothes. My God! If you couldn't dress properly in Beverly Hills you might as well crawl under a stone and vanish altogether! She had weathered it well though. It was not as if they were broke by any means. It was just that they had to be a little bit careful now that – as Ross's business manager had put it – 'The big money days are behind you, Ross.' Stupid fool. What did *he* know? Elaine would get Ross back on top if she had to kill doing it.

'Get back on top, Ross,' Karen Lancaster requested huskily.

He raised his head from between her thighs. 'I don't do this for everyone,' he asserted in startled tones. 'In fact, I can't remember the last time.'

'What do you want – an award? Get back on top.'

He obliged, pumping away with quite a bit of vigour.

Karen was a groaner. Her *oohs* and *aahs* and *go baby gos* got louder and louder.

The more noise she made, the faster Ross pumped, until they came together in a screechful climax.

He rolled off, said, 'Hot damn!' and waited for the praise.

Karen turned onto her stomach and played dead.

The sun slanted on the huge glass-walled room at an angle, playing across the enormous circular bed where they lay on top of a quilted satin bedspread.

Outside, the Pacific Ocean rolled lazily about its business, lapping the Malibu shoreline gently. It was a perfect clear day.

'Not bad,' he said at last, when it became obvious that she was not to be the first to speak. 'Not bad at all.' No reply. Lightly he patted her ass. No response. 'Are you asleep?' he asked incredulously.

'Gimme five mins,' she mumbled, rolling her body into a tight ball.

He rose from the bed and padded around the room.

Some room. A circular fantasy arranged around a central steaming Jacuzzi. On one side was the ocean, on the other a mass of greenery and a carport which now housed his gleaming gold Corniche and her sporty red Ferrari.

He found a space-age kitchen round the back, and extracted an ice cold can of Budweiser from the refrigerator.

Karen was definitely worth the trip to the beach. He had thought so the first time, but now he was sure. She had got him doing things he hadn't done in years.

Little Karen. Christ, he had known her since she was about six years old. George Lancaster had often brought her to the studio with him.

Little Karen. He had attended her first wedding to a real estate broker, read enough about her second to a spaced out composer, and spent many an evening in her company when she became one of Elaine's best friends.

Little Karen. A tiger in the sack.

They had bumped into each other outside Brentano's on Wilshire quite by accident the day before he left for location. 'You *must* come and see my new Ferrari Spyder,' she insisted. 'I only took delivery of it yesterday.'

She dragged him across the street to the American Savings carpark, where the attendant was taking special care of her latest acquisition.

'A present from daddy?' he asked casually, not taking much notice of the sleek red machine. He had never been a car buff.

'But of course! Come on Ross, take a ride with me. You're not in a hurry are you?'

Actually he was. He had a meeting with his accountant, but all of a sudden Karen was giving off signals, and he couldn't resist finding out if they meant what he thought they meant. He climbed into the low passenger seat and smelled fresh new leather.

'Nice, huh?' she said, settling herself on the driver's side. And then they were off, roaring down Wilshire at breakneck speed.

She was driving much too fast for the sedate three lane progression of Cadillacs, Mercedes, and Lincolns. But a delivery truck gave chase from a stoplight, and a kid drag raced her lane to lane. By the time they hit Westwood, Ross was enjoying every minute of the wild ride.

'You on for the beach?' she asked, fixing his eyes with a different unspoken question.

'Why not?' The meeting with his accountant could wait. Let his business manager take care of it. That's what he was paid to do wasn't it?

They made it to the door of her Malibu beach house in twenty minutes. Fifty-two seconds later they were rolling about on the thick pile rug groping at each other's clothes.

He mounted her like a stallion, ripping at her suede skirt and tearing through her brief panties.

She verbalized her enjoyment loudly.

They both had appointments in town to hurry back to, and the next day he had departed L.A. for the location.

He was glad she had called him upon his return. Karen was going to be more than just a passing diversion. Of that he was sure.

Gladrags resided in a penthouse apartment on Doheny Drive. He cohabited with a white interior designer by the name of Jason Swankle, and a hideous bulldog called Shag.

Buddy pressed the door buzzer impatiently. Now that he had decided to follow his former career he was hot to trot.

Jason answered the door. A plump dormouse of a man in a peacock blue jumpsuit festooned with gold jewellery. Shag accompanied him, took a perfunctory sniff at Buddy's leg, and mounted it as though it were the randiest bitch in the neighbourhood. 'Hey!' Buddy exclaimed, filled with horror. 'Get him off me!'

'Down boy. DOWN!' intoned Jason, tugging at Shag's diamante collar.

Buddy kicked out in disgust. 'Jeez!'

Shag dismounted and growled threateningly.

'And what can I do for you?' Jason inquired archly, placing one beringed plump hand on his waist, checking Buddy out, and liking what he saw.

'I'm looking for Gladra . . . uh . . . Mr. Jackson.'

'He's dressing. We're going to a wedding. Can *I* help?' Jason beamed, then winked. 'I'd certainly *like* to.'

Why did fags love him? 'It's business,' Buddy said swiftly. 'Private. I'll only take a minute of his time.'

Jason pursed fleshy lips. 'Marvin doesn't like conducting business at home. Is it about the shop?'

Marvin! Buddy nodded and attempted to edge through the front door.

Shag bared his teeth, and Jason made a decision. 'Oh, all right. Wait here and I'll get him.'

He waddled off on short stumpy legs and Buddy reflected that he and Gladrags must sure make a bizarre looking couple. Gladrags so tall and skinny and black; and Jason so rounded plump and white. Oh well . . . Everyone to their own kick.

Buddy whistled softly between clenched teeth and hoped that Gladrags might have something for him right away. It would be nice to go home to Angel bearing gifts. A new sweater maybe or . . .

'Who in the fuck are you?' It was Gladrags himself, skinnier than Buddy remembered, his black hair cornrowed and decorated with multi-coloured beads. 'And what in the fuck you want?'

Nothing like a warm welcome. 'Hey – my man – G.R. It's me – Buddy Boy. You gotta remember me.' He stretched out a friendly hand which Gladrags slapped sharply away. 'Come on,' Buddy persisted. 'I used to work for you, man. Randy Felix brought me in. I was one of your best.'

Gladrags sniffed deeply. 'One of my best what?'

Buddy checked out the corridor. 'Can I come in? Can we talk?' He attempted to move through the door. Shag growled ferociously. 'I . . . uh . . . I wanna get back in action. See – I need some bucks like yesterday, an' you were always pretty good at arranging things.'

'I ain't in that business no more,' Gladrags spat, sniffing again and beginning to close the door. 'An' even if I was – which I ain't – believe me, man, I sure *do* remember you. You was the weirdo could only get it up for the ladies. Right? *And* – if I remember correct, you dumped on me an' went inta business with that fat fucker Maxie Sholto. An' with *him* I understand if it moved ya screwed it. So if I *was* in that

91

business still, which as I said repeatedly I *ain't* – then even if you farted stars an' stripes, an' sported a flag on your pecker every time ya got the bone – I *still* wouldn't be interested in puttin' you together with anythin' human. Now get lost.' He slammed the door sharply.

'Shit!' muttered Buddy sharply. 'Goddamn *shit!*'

Angrily he turned and strode towards the elevator. It was his own dumb fault.

Jason Swankle caught up with him just as he was driving out of the underground garage. 'So glad I found you,' he puffed, running up to the car, dragging a reluctant Shag behind him.

Buddy glared. 'Why?'

'Because I'd like to help you. I think I *can* help you.'

'You're not my type,' snapped Buddy sarcastically.

'Take my card,' Jason insisted. 'And call me on my business number. Tomorrow.' He thrust a small white card through the open window. It fluttered onto the floor of the car as Buddy put his foot down and roared off into the late morning sun.

10

The small Italian restaurant with its checked tablecloths, excellent pasta and potent house wine was busy. Saturday night always brought out the crowds. Millie Rosemont was enjoying herself, but Leon felt uncomfortable and ill at ease. He had promised Millie faithfully that the one thing he would never do was bring his problems home, and he had kept that promise up until the time of the Friendship Street murders . . . Up until the time he was faced with Joey Kravetz's mutilated body . . .

He remembered their second encounter. It was long before he met Millie . . . long before . . .

It wasn't just raining, it was pouring the proverbial cats and dogs. Driving home late, his windshield wipers fighting the rain, Leon decided he was hungry after all. Only an hour previously he had phoned to cancel a dinner date with an attractive divorcee he had been seeing. She was nice enough, but deep down he found her boring.

On impulse he made a left into a Howard Johnsons and parked his car in a side lot. Then he hurried through the rain to a corner booth where he ordered himself a toasted chicken sandwich and some good hot coffee. Opening up the paper he studied the sports page.

The waitress brought his sandwich and coffee, and he settled back to relax after a long and tiring day.

'You sonuvabitch!' a voice screeched.

Startled, Leon looked up from his newspaper and stared at the angry, short girl standing by his table, her arms crossed over a grubby T-shirt, her legs encased in army surplus trousers which seemed several sizes too big.

'Don't remember me, huh?' she glared.

'Should I?' he asked at last.

'Should ya? Ha! Should ya? You can bet your fat butt ya should!'

He put down his paper. 'Now wait a minute. Just who do you think you're talking to?'

'You – cop!' she spat.

'Do I know you?' he asked angrily.

'Ya got my ass locked up in some girl's prison for a fuckin' year. You should know me,' she crowed triumphantly.

It was then he noticed the cast in her eye, and suddenly it all came back. She was the baby-faced hooker who had propositioned him one night, then kicked him on the leg when questioned about her age, and fled. He had called Grace Mann over on Juvenile, given her a general location and description, and left it in her capable hands. Grace had obviously come through.

'I thought you said you were eighteen,' he accused.

'So I lied – big deal. An' 'cos of you they come trackin' me, an' locked me up on some crappy farm with a bunch of babies. Thanks a lot, cowboy.'

He tried not to smile, she was so desperately angry, and he had no wish to inflame her further. 'It was for your own good,' he said.

'Screw you!' she replied, and unexpectedly sat down. 'My date never showed, so y'can buy me a coffee. I reckon ya owe me more than that anyway.' She wiped the back of her hand across her nose, and hungrily eyed his chicken sandwich.

'You want something to eat?' he asked generously. She was such a ragged looking creature, he felt sorry for her.

'Awright,' she agreed, as if she were doing him an enormous favour. 'Gimme the same as you.'

He signalled the waitress and gave her the order. She filled his coffee cup and hurried off to get a cup for the girl.

'What's your name?' Leon asked.

'Joey,' she sniffed. 'What's it to you?'

'I'm buying you a sandwich. I may as well know who you are.'

She glared at him suspiciously, muttered, 'Lousy cop,' and set upon her sandwich with ravenous ferocity when it arrived.

Leon watched her eat, observing her short bitten nails, grubby neck and spiky dyed orange hair. She was a mess, yet there was still something appealing about her. She's bringing out the father instinct in me, he thought with a wry smile.

'I take it they let you out of the girls' farm,' he remarked. 'I'm not buying food for a runaway I hope.'

'They let me out,' she said between mouthfuls. 'They had to when my sister finally came t'get me. 'Sides, I'm sixteen now, I can look after myself.'

'I'm sure you can.'

'You bet I can!' She threw him a sly look. 'Thanks t'you really.'

'How's that?'

'Well . . . If I hadn't of hit on you, an' you hadn't of sent the kiddie patrol after me, I might never have got myself connected with all those boss chicks at the farm. Y'know something? I met 'em all, an' I learned me plenty.'

He didn't know what she was talking about and he didn't much care to find out. It suddenly occurred to him that he shouldn't be sitting down with her anyway. He gestured for the check.

'Where ya goin'?' she demanded.

'Home,' he replied, then added sarcastically, 'that's if you don't mind, of course.'

'I thought you'd at least give me a lift,' she whined pathetically. 'Just look at it out there.'

He turned to stare out of the large windows. The rain still pounded down. 'What makes you think I'm going your way?'

'Look – if it's too much trouble just drop me at the bus station. I'm goin' to my sister, she lives outta the city an' I don't wanna miss my bus.'

He knew he should refuse her, but what the heck, he was off duty and she was only a kid.

'Get your coat,' he sighed.

'Don't have no coat.'

'In this weather?'

'Who knew it was goin' to piss?'

He paid the check, took his raincoat from the rack in the corner, was about to put it on, then changed his mind and threw it over her shoulders. 'Come on,' he said.

They ran for the car, Joey tagging behind, yelping as the full force of the torrential rain hit her.

'Come on,' Leon repeated, raising his voice as he opened the car door.

She hurled herself inside like an angry puppy. In spite of the protection of his raincoat she was soaked through.

He started the engine, and she found disco on the radio.

'Got a ciggie?' she asked.

'I gave it up,' he replied gruffly. 'And that's what you should do.'

'Sure,' she sneered. 'I mean I got so much goin' for me why should I need cigarettes?'

He glanced at her and turned the radio down. 'What time is your bus?'

She was silent for a moment, chewing on her thumb and wriggling on the seat.

'What time?' he repeated, slowing his speed as the rain increased.

'It don't matter what time,' she mumbled at last, ' 'cos there's no point in me catchin' it anyways.'

He frowned. 'I thought you wanted to be dropped at the bus station.'

'S'awright. I can sleep on one of them benches. I done it before.'

He was rapidly losing patience with her. Clicking off the radio he said, 'What are you talking about?'

'Well . . . Y'see my sister's gone off to Arizona to live on one of them communes. I was supposed to save some money an' go join her, but I had my money stolen.' She warmed to her story. 'These two black cats ripped me off, wanted to put me on the streets, pimp off me, but I got away from 'em, only thing is they got all the money I saved from workin'. Now I gotta start again.' She paused. 'You got any money to spare? I'll screw ya for ten bucks.'

Leon pulled the car over and stopped. 'Get out,' he said sharply.

'Waddya mean?' she whined.

'Out.'

'Why?'

'You know why.'

'I don't know what –'

'*Get out. Or do you want me to run you over to Juvenile? They'll find a bed for you.*'

'*Pig bastard!*' she spat, realizing he was serious.

He leaned across her and opened the passenger door. Heavy rain blew into the car.

Her voice quavered. '*You're throwin' me out in this? Why can't you take me to the bus station?*'

'*Because you're full of it, the bus station is out of my way, and you're a little liar. Now – out.*'

Reluctantly she stepped from the car into the pounding rain. He slammed the door shut and drove off.

She had her nerve. Doing it to him again. Propositioning him like he was some john who had to pay for it. Dumb stupid little hooker. Maybe he should have taken her to Juvenile, handed her in. Maybe that would have been kinder than dumping her on the street.

Jesus Christ! Now he was feeling guilty!

Well she was only sixteen, and it was the sort of night you wouldn't leave a cat out in.

But then, he reasoned, she wouldn't thank him for handing her in, and she could look after herself. She was a toughie. A street kid. Besides, she wasn't his responsibility.

Angrily he drove home, parked underground, and took the elevator to his apartment.

It wasn't until he was standing under a hot shower that he realized she still had his raincoat.

Millie leaned across the table and said, very softly, 'Honey, if I left, would you miss me?'

'Huh?' Startled, Leon returned to his surroundings.

Millie patted his hand comfortingly. 'Welcome back.'

'I was just thinking –'

'Oh, really?' Her sarcasm was thick. 'I would never have guessed.'

'I was just thinking,' he repeated carefully, 'about where we should spend our vacation this year. Have you thought about where you would like to go?'

'California,' she replied, without hesitation. Then, anxiously, 'We can afford it, can't we?'

'Sure we can.'

'I've always wanted to go to California,' she said, her eyes sparkling. 'Haven't you?'

Leon frowned. He could honestly say that he had never had even the faintest desire to visit the West Coast. As far as he was concerned California was a land of sunshine, oranges and freaks. 'I'll talk to a travel agent next week,' he promised.

She beamed. 'We have plenty of time, but it sure would be nice to get it all planned.'

He smiled reassuringly and wondered if Deke Andrews had had it all planned. Had he *planned* to viciously hack three people to death? Had he *planned* to leave the small house looking like an abattoir? Had he *planned* to calmly wash up, walk out and vanish?

The waiter appeared with two steaming plates of spaghetti and clam sauce. Leon felt his juices rising. Millie grinned and murmured something about the only sure way of turning him on nowadays was with a good hot plate of food.

He didn't reply. He wasn't up to playful banter about the growing infrequency of their sex life. It wasn't that he no longer desired Millie, it was just that he was so goddamn tired . . . And half the time when he got into bed and closed his eyes the images that he saw were not erotic, warm and sexual. They were of Deke Andrews. A photograph of him that had appeared in his senior class yearbook aged eighteen. 'He never changed much from that picture,' various witnesses had assured him. 'Just grew his hair some.'

The police artist had worked diligently on the photo, ageing it eight years and adding the longer hair. It had then been circulated across the country.

Leon knew the photo intimately. An ordinary boy with extraordinary eyes. Burning black deadly eyes. They haunted him. And so did the mutilated body of Joey Kravetz, her neck almost severed from her body so grotesque were her wounds . . .

'Eat up,' said Millie.

He stared at the plateful of spaghetti and felt distinctly nauseous. What was the matter with him? Had to get a hold of himself. Goddamn! He had lived through twenty years of gruesome murders and not one of them had ever affected him this way. He wound some spaghetti onto his fork and shoved it into his mouth.

'Good, huh?' questioned Millie.

Good, huh? mocked Deke Andrews in his head.

' 'Scuse me.' Leon pushed his chair away from the table and dropped his fork with a dull clatter. 'Call of nature, I'll be right back.'

Millie's eyebrows rose in surprise as he hurried from the room seeking refuge in the men's toilet. There, he rested his head against the cold tile wall and made a decision. He would open up the

Andrews file. He would apply to the Captain for permission, and if he didn't get it, he would work on the case in his spare time.

Suddenly he felt better.

11

Elaine Conti wore large tinted sunglasses, a wide brimmed hat, and a voluminous white linen coat. Casually she glanced around as she strolled through the make-up department of Bullocks, Westwood. Unobserved she pocketed a seventy dollar bottle of Opium perfume as she passed by a display table. Her eyes darted this way and that as she added a ceramic hand mirror and a lucite lipstick holder to the perfume already in her pocket.

By this time her heart was beating wildly, but her casual stroll never faltered. She drifted through to the sunglasses department and managed to pocket two sixty dollar pairs before taking the escalator down to the linens and notions. There she was accosted by a middle-aged saleslady in black and rhinestones who said, 'And what can I do for you today, madam?'

'Nothing, thank you,' Elaine replied. 'I'm just looking.'

'Do go ahead, please. I'll keep my eye on you should you find that you need me.'

Elaine swallowed aggravation, smiled, and beat a hasty retreat to men's casual clothes where she was able to add a silk Yves Saint Laurent tie to her collection of goodies.

She looked around and noted a male assistant checking her out. Her heart was really pounding now. It was enough. Slowly she sauntered towards the exit.

Leaving was always the moment of truth. What if a hand descended on her shoulder as she stepped outside? What if a voice said, 'Would you mind coming back inside for a moment?' What if she was *caught*?

Absolutely impossible. She was far too careful. She only took when she was sure no hidden eyes or cameras were watching. And she only took items priced at under a hundred dollars. Somehow she felt that she was safe.

Outside. On the street. No heavy hand on her shoulder.

She walked to the Mercedes which was parked at a meter on Westwood Boulevard, removed her linen coat, its pockets filled with ill-gotten gains, folded it carefully, and placed it in the trunk. Then she took off her hat and sunglasses and threw those in too.

She felt fantastic! What an incredible charge these illicit shopping sprees gave her. Better than an affair any day. Humming softly she climbed into the car.

Elaine had been successfully shoplifting for over a year. Once a week, regularly, she donned what she called 'her disguise' and hit a department store or a boutique. Department stores were safer, but the boutiques gave the biggest thrill of all. There you could *really* go to town, slipping a scarf, a silk knit sweater, or even a pair of shoes into your pocket right under some snappy little salesgirl's nose. Oh, the excitement! The kick! The shot of adrenaline that kept her vibrating for hours and hours. The greatest high of all!

It had started by accident really. She had been standing in Saks one day waiting for attention at the Clinique make-up counter. She needed face powder in a hurry, she was late for a lunch date, exhausted from a dance class (studying modern ballet had been the in thing to do then) and more than a little impatient and bad tempered. Suddenly, the easiest thing in the world had been to slip the box of powder – conveniently situated on the front of the counter – into her purse, and saunter quietly out of the store. She had quite expected to be stopped, and then coolly, calmly, she would just have explained that she was merely making a little protest, taking a stand against the gross rudeness of salesgirls who preferred conversation with each other to attending to a customer.

Would they have believed her?

She was Mrs. Ross Conti. Of course they would.

But she wasn't stopped. Not then. Not the next time. Nor the time after that.

What had started out as a protest soon changed into a habit. An unbreakable one.

'Buddy,' Angel whispered softly. 'Can I meet your agent?'

'What?' He frowned. They lay side by side on the narrow bed in Randy Felix's borrowed apartment watching a game show on a badly functioning black and white television.

She sat up, long blond hair falling around her perfect face, eyes shining with enthusiasm. 'I've been thinking,' she announced, 'it's silly – me sitting at home all day when I could be trying for a job too.

If I met your agent he could send *me* up for things. Wouldn't it be terrific if *I* got something?'

He spaced his words carefully. 'It's not a good idea.'

Now it was her turn to frown. 'Why?' she demanded plaintively. 'Why yes?'

'Because,' she replied quickly, 'things don't seem to be coming easily for you and I'd like to help. Before I went to Hawaii I had made up my mind that I wanted to be an actress.'

He breathed deeply, evenly. It had not been a good day. 'Are you saying you don't think I can look after you?'

Her eyes widened. 'Of course not. I know you'll always look after me. But we do need money, don't we?'

He was suddenly angry. 'Who says?'

She gestured helplessly around the cramped room. 'Well . . . this isn't our apartment. The car we have is falling to pieces, and you're so jumpy lately. Honestly, Buddy, I'm not complaining. I just want to help out.'

'Fuck!' He exploded, jumping off the bed, pulling tight Levis over French Y-fronts, and grabbing a shirt.

She looked alarmed. 'What's the matter?'

He snatched his wallet and keys from the top of the television. 'You want to hassle me? Make me feel like nothing? Do it on your own time, lady.'

Before she could even reply he slammed his way out of the apartment.

Angel was shocked. She had not expected such a violent reaction. In fact, what she *had* expected was a tender scene between the two of them which would have resulted in Buddy stating deep love and gratefulness that she was such an understanding and helpful wife.

Tears filled her eyes. What had gone wrong? What had she said that was so unacceptable? Weren't married couples supposed to stick together, tell each other everything, and have no secrets?

As the days passed, and Buddy became more irritable and no starring role or even a bit part materialized, she had slowly begun to realize that things were not exactly as he had told her they would be. Not that she minded. She had read enough fan magazines in her life to know that Getting There and Making It were not always a fast jog up the yellow brick road. Sometimes there were Pitfalls and Hold Ups. Buddy had been away, and now it would just take him a little time to get back up where he belonged. But while he was waiting why couldn't she have a chance too? She only wanted to help.

Tearfully she climbed off the bed and straightened the covers. Their first fight. How she longed for him to come running back and hold her in his arms, tell her everything was all right, make slow gentle love to her. She shivered, and hugged her arms around her slender body.

Buddy. If he didn't want her to work she'd never mention it again.

Buddy. She loved him so much. He was all she had, and she planned to stay with him forever.

'Have you ever considered a red hot prick up the ass?' asked an agitated masculine voice.

'Do me a favour and go jerk off on your own time.'

Montana replaced the receiver briskly. Obscene phone calls. How did the cretins get hold of the numbers in the first place? Did they scour the phone books looking for single female listings? Or did they lurk around the supermarkets and stores checking out customers and their charge cards? Who knew? Who really cared?

Energetically she leaped out of bed. A wave of well publicized violence was spreading fear throughout the hills of Hollywood, Beverly, and Holmby. People were into security gates, guard dogs, electronic alarm systems, and guns. Montana bothered with none of the precautions. She refused to live a well guarded life. If something happened it happened. Fate. What would be would be. If an obscene phone caller hoped to upset her day he had the wrong number.

Humming tunelessly she launched into a few yoga positions out by the pool. It was only eight a.m. A clear smogless day – and she had an insane desire to trash everything and drive out to the beach.

Why not?

Many reasons.

Twenty actors with appointments scheduled exactly fifteen minutes apart.

A meeting with the young dress designer she wanted to hire for the film.

A trip to the airport to surprise Neil on his return from Palm Beach.

For the first time she felt really good about living in L.A. She was glad that Neil had talked her into letting him buy the house a few months back. They had leased their New York apartment, packed up forty cartons of books, records and assorted possessions, and finally made L.A. more than just a hotel suite.

Neil loved California. She had always been a city kid . . . But she could change couldn't she? For Neil she could do a lot of things.

Five years together and still she loved him, probably more than in the beginning, because in the beginning it had been lust. She grinned at the thought. She, who had only ever climbed into bed with body beautifuls and youth. Then along came Neil Gray with his middle-aged spread, greying hair, and bloodshot eyes.

She had wanted him then. And she wanted him now. Just as much. He had given her more than body beautiful and youth. He had given her knowledge, and in the long run that's what life was really all about.

Working together was a new phase in their relationship, and so far it seemed to be a definite bonus. He cared about the movie just as much as she did, in fact that's all they ever seemed to talk about. Not that she was complaining – what more could she want?

She wondered if he had landed George Lancaster.

Even bigger question. How would she feel if he had?

Disappointed. The more she thought about it the more she hated the idea. But as Oliver Easterne constantly said in his highly unoriginal way – 'A star is a star is a star.'

Oliver was turning out to be even more of a major asshole than she had first thought.

She dressed quickly in a Calvin Klein jacket, chain-store jeans, a six dollar T-shirt, and two hundred dollar cowboy boots. The mix suited her, especially when she pulled her luxuriant black hair tightly from her face, and twisted it into a long braid.

Skipping breakfast, she slipped behind the wheel of her somewhat battered Volkswagen. Neil was always nagging her to buy a new car, but the V.W. suited her. It wasn't flash, she could drive around the city virtually unnoticed, and that's the way she liked it.

Actors. Twenty more today. Maybe one she wanted – one that was right – one that would walk into her office and bring a character she had created to life.

God! Putting this movie together was exciting. More exciting than anything she had done in her life before.

Movie making. It got in your blood. And she and Neil together – what a team!

Grinning quietly to herself she started the V.W. and set off to her office.

'Why can't you get me a copy of the goddamn script?' screamed Ross down the phone. 'Christ almighty, Zack, I'm not asking for a table at the last supper. All I want is a lousy script. Ninety frigging pages bound together. Sounds like a simple task to me.' He tapped the glass table beside the pool with angry fingers as he listened to the answer. The answer was that *Street People* appeared to be under lock and key. Nobody had a copy – but nobody.

Only George Lancaster and Tony Curtis and Kirk Douglas and Sadie La Salle and Christ knows who else. Probably half of fucking Hollywood.

He slammed the phone down in disgust. Here he was – a major star – chasing a frigging part in some half-assed frigging movie written by a woman no less and *he hadn't even seen the script*. What the fuck was the matter with him? Was he losing his smarts along with his hair?

The very thought sent him running to the pool house in a panic. What made him think he was losing his hair? He wasn't. No way. Well, maybe a little . . . nothing noticeable . . . nothing that combing it a different way couldn't take care of.

He studied his reflection in the mirrored poolhouse.

Ross Conti. Movie star. Still a good-looking son of a bitch. Only he and Paul Newman had kept it all together. The others had fallen to pieces – got fat, bald, had disastrous face lifts, wore bad toupees. Sinatra still looked good enough with his sewn on thatch. Still had a set of pipes that kept them creaming their panties when they heard his world weary tones. Satisfied, Ross returned poolside.

Elaine was framed in the glass entrance to the living room. Elaine. His wife. She didn't look bad for an old broad. One thing about her – she kept herself in good shape, didn't drink, screw around or make a fool of him.

'Honey,' he said warmly, 'I want you to do something for me.'

She looked him up and down. He was definitely developing a gut. Quite noticeable in the madras shorts he had chosen to wear. 'I'll do anything you want Ross, dear,' she said sweetly, 'as long as you promise me you'll start going to the gym again.'

He feigned surprise and patted his stomach. 'You think I need it?'

'Everyone over twenty-five needs it.'

'What is this everyone over twenty-five crap?'

'A fact of life, my darling. The older one gets the harder one has to work at looking good.'

'Bullshit.'

'Truth.'

'Bullshit.'

She gave an aggravated sigh. 'What is it you want me to do?'

'Oh, yeah.' He scratched his chin and squinted the famous blues. 'Call Maralee Gray. Get hold of a copy of Neil's new script, the one we were talking about.'

'Couldn't Zack get it for you?'

'Zack frigging Schaeffer couldn't pull milk from a cow if you handed him the tit!'

Elaine nodded. He was finally coming around to her way of thinking.

'I need Sadie La Salle,' Ross suddenly blurted.

He was *definitely* coming around to her way of thinking. 'Do you want me to see if I can arrange it?' she asked slowly.

He looked enthusiastic. 'You think you can?'

She smiled. 'You've always said I can do anything I set my mind to.'

'So I'm giving you the word. Set your mind to getting me Sadie La Salle and a copy of that damn script.'

Her smile widened. There was nothing Elaine liked better than a challenge. 'Ross, sweetheart – you're on!'

He smiled back. 'Elaine, sweetheart – my money's on you.'

Marital bliss at last.

'I bought you a present,' she murmured, handing him the Saint Laurent silk tie she had stolen earlier.

He was pleased. 'Always thinking of the star, huh?' he said with a big grin.

She nodded. 'Always, Ross. Always.'

Mavericks was crowded, the bar six deep, disco music blasting eardrums.

Buddy hadn't been there in a long while – before Hawaii – before the days of fat little Maxie Sholto. He shuddered when he thought of Maxie. Fortunately he had woken up to reality before it was too late. No more drugs and orgies for Buddy Boy. That scene was purely for life's losers. Hitting on Gladrags for work was one thing. Maxie Sholto was a whole different ballgame.

'Buddy! Good t'see you. Where y'bin hiding?'

He waved at the barman. 'Around,' he replied. 'Here and there. What's happening?'

'Same old story. Business is good. Didja hear about me on "Hill Street Blues"? I had lines, man, *lines*.'

Yeah? So why was he still behind the bar at Mavericks?

'That's great,' Buddy said. 'Is Quince around?'

'In the back.'

'Thanks.'

He made his way to the end of the crowded bar, across a jammed dance floor and edged along a line of booths looking for Quince.

He found him surrounded by girls. Three of them.

Quince. Tall. Black. Good looking. A good actor too. They had worked together at Joy Byron's.

'Hey, man.' They spoke in unison, and slapped palms.

'Sit,' Quince said. 'Join the party.'

Buddy squeezed on the end of the leather banquette while Quince indicated the girls one by one. 'This is my lady – Luann. Her sister, Chickie. And a good friend, Shelly.'

Luann was a gorgeous chocolate blond. Chickie was smaller, darker, with a set of teeth Farrah would kill for. Shelly was Shelly. The girl from the pool, looking good in a scant purple leotard and thin wrapover skirt.

'Hey –' he said. 'I know you.'

'Hey –' she replied. 'Buddy Hudson. Mister Married. Where's your old lady?'

'Buddy. Married. That'll be the day,' laughed Quince.

Shelly nodded. 'He's married.'

Quince raised an unbelieving eyebrow and grinned at Buddy. 'Tell 'em it ain't true, my man.'

Buddy scowled. His luck to run into Miss Bigmouth. It just wasn't his day. Or night. 'So I'm married, big deal,' he mumbled.

Quince began to laugh. 'I never thought the day would come when you would fall into *that* scene. What happened?' He hit his forehead with the palm of his hand. 'I know, I know. She's eighty-three, loaded, an' she has a *reaaal* bad heart. Am I hittin' it?'

Buddy's scowl deepened. He had run out on Angel to find a little relaxation. He didn't need this joke shit. 'Yeah, yeah, sure, you're right,' he said quickly. 'Only she's nearer ninety than eighty-three. More my speed, y'know?'

Quince guffawed loudly. 'That's my Buddy Boy! Always one eye on the main chance!'

'How about a little boogie?' requested Chickie, jigging about to the strains of a Donna Summer beat.

'Sorry,' Shelly intervened. 'I asked first.' She bumped against Buddy, forcing him to stand, then she slid from the booth, flung her arms around his neck and rotated her crotch against his on the edge of the packed dance floor.

'Eighty-three my ass,' she sneered. 'Twenty and goddamn spec-tacular. I've seen her out by the pool. Why you keepin' her a secret?'

He shrugged. 'No secret.'

'No shit? So where is she then?'

'What are you – a dyke?'

Shelly pushed her crotch sharply against his. 'If I *was* baby, I'd be scratchin' at your front door the moment you left with what *you* got stashed at home.'

He shoved her roughly away and went into his disco routine. He could give Travolta lessons – that's how smooth and sensuous and goddamn raunchy he was. *Allan Carr, walk in and see me now!*

Shelly matched him move for move, enjoying herself. She was good too.

He began to enjoy himself too. It was the first dancing he'd done in a long time, and when you had a partner who was with you all the way. Well . . . that was a real hot feeling.

They stopped when they'd had enough. When sweat coursed in little rivers down Shelly's bare arms and chest. 'Hmmm,' she said succinctly, 'you're good.'

'So are you,' he allowed.

They returned to the table. 'Should hope so. I'm a professional.'

'A professional what?'

She regarded him coolly. 'Dancer, asshole.' She turned to greet a new arrival who had moved in next to Chickie. 'Jer, babes, how'd it go tonight?'

Jer babes was a young good looking guy with nervous, shifty eyes. He shrugged. 'The same crap shoot. Y'know the scene.'

'Yeah,' she agreed sympathetically. 'Hey – have you two met?'

They shook heads negatively, summing each other up. 'Buddy Hudson – Jericho Crunch,' Shelly continued, the perfect hostess.

Buddy frowned. The loud music must be getting to him. Jericho Crunch! What kind of a name was that? Sounded like a religious Famous Amos!

Jericho's shifty eyes checked him over. 'You an actor?'

'What did you see me in?' Buddy asked quickly.

'Nothin'. I'm an actor too.'

'Yeah. What have you done?'

Jericho reeled off a few familiar television shows, then licked his lips and added, 'But I'm up for the big one. Think I'm gonna get it too.'

'What big one?' Buddy asked, immediately alert.

Jericho looked secretive. 'Nothin' I can talk about.'

'A television pilot?'

'Nope.'

'A commercial?'

'Nope.'

'So – what?'

'A movie. A real biggie.'

'A television film?'

'Nope. The real thing.'

'What's it called?'

Jericho narrowed his eyes. 'You think I'm gonna tell you so you can go runnin' after it too. No way. Besides, I'm almost set. I got the castin' bitch creamin' at the thought of usin' me,' he leered. 'Get the picture?'

Yes. Buddy got the picture. And the pisser was not about to give away a thing. He thought about Angel. She hadn't meant to nag. She had just caught him at a bad moment when all he had left in the world was forty-two bucks and no idea where to score. Unemployment was out. He had never wanted to get involved with forms and papers and all that crap. And he couldn't start now. 'Gotta split,' he said, rising from the table.

'Yeah,' laughed Quince. 'Time to run on home to old momma an' get out the bedpan, huh?'

'It's like this,' Buddy said patiently. 'If the Rolls ain't in the garage by two a.m. the Bentley gets lonely. You know what I'm sayin'?'

Quince hooted with laughter. Buddy pushed through the crowds, and took a deep breath as he hit the street.

Shelly followed him out. 'I need a lift home,' she stated.

He looked her over and decided she might be useful. 'Sure,' he said. 'My car's down the block.'

She walked beside him, smelling slightly of sweat and a heavy musk scent.

'What kind of dancing you do?' he asked.

'Artistic,' she replied.

'A stripper, huh?'

'One of the best.'

'Modest.'

'Screw you. I *am* one of the best and proud of it.'

They reached the car and he slid in the driver's seat springing the passenger lock for her.

'And you're an actor,' she stated, settling herself comfortably. 'I should have guessed.'

'One of the best,' he said quickly.

She laughed. 'Yeah. That's why you're driving this pile of crapola.'

'It gets me around. I'm not into image.'

'Can't afford to be, huh?'

'I'm gettin' by.'

She extracted a joint from her purse and lit up. 'I'll tell you somethin',' she said, offering him a toke which he declined because who needed to get stopped by the cops at this time of the morning? 'You'd make a terrific stripper. You got the body *an'* you got all the right moves.'

He laughed aloud. 'You have to be kidding.'

She was unamused. 'What's so funny? It pays good, an' just as many guys are doin' it today.'

'I'm an actor. I told you.'

'Doesn't mean you can't take off your clothes an' get paid for it.'

'I guess you think Sylvester Stallone did that kind of thing to get on?'

'Yeah. As a matter of fact he did – don't you read your gossip mags?'

'What about your friend – Brunch – Crunch – the great wall of Jericho. He take 'em off?'

'Undressed he's bad news. Sloped shoulders, knock knees, nothin' much in the bread bin. You dig?'

Silently Buddy nodded.

'He does a bit of waitering – Hollywood parties. Thinks he'll get discovered that way.'

The hell with it – Buddy reached for the joint and took a long satisfying pull, then casually he said, 'Maybe it worked for him. Like what's this movie he says he's all set for?'

'Oh, c'mon. You don't believe *that* do you? If Jer served a canape to Johnny Carson he'd tell everyone he was all set for The Tonight Show!'

'So there's no movie?'

'He went on an interview.'

'For what?'

She laughed softly. 'Wanna horn in on his action?'

Carefully he eased the car into a convenient parking space opposite their apartment house. 'It's a free country.'

'If you say so.'

'So what's the movie?'

'Come up for a snort. Coke always jogs my memory.'

He thought of Angel Beautiful. Innocent. Waiting.

Then he thought of forty-two lousy bucks. 'Sure. Why not?'

Gina Germaine had an agent, a manager, a secretary, a make-up artist, a hairdresser, an accountant, a business counsellor, an acting coach, and two ex-husbands to support. Sort of. They all depended on her for *something*.

She was thirty-three years old – twenty-nine to the press. Blonde – dyed, not natural. Pretty, with round, slightly protruding blue eyes, a retroussé nose, and a maneater mouth filled with sharp white perfect teeth. There were thousands of girls on the West Coast of America who were just as pretty as Gina Germaine. But her body made her something special. Long skinny legs, small ass, tiny twenty inch waist, and an enormous bosom. Thirty-nine firm fruity inches with huge pale chocolate nipples.

Gina Germaine became a star because of her amazing breasts. Featured in 'Playboy' at the age of nineteen, she was immediately discovered by Hollywood. 'Send for her at once,' demanded two studio heads, three corporate executives, and four enthusiastic agents.

She was already in town. Maxie Sholto, a canny hustler who knew a sensational pair of boobies when he saw them – had got there first. 'Let me represent you,' he said, his shifty smile going full force. 'Let me make you a star.'

The old-fashioned but meaningful words worked. Gina packed up a so-so modelling career in Houston, Texas, and flew with Maxie to Los Angeles, where he got her a few bit parts here and there. Nothing spectacular. Until one day she walked into a television executive's private office, sat on a high backed chair opposite him and casually spread her long skinny sexy legs just as Maxie had told her she should.

The executive's bloodshot eyes bulged with excitement. Gina Germaine was wearing a short white mini skirt with nothing underneath! No panty hose, no panties. Nothing!

She landed a role in a weekly television sitcom, and a weekly rendezvous with her television executive who expired two years later from a massive stroke. Gina was sorry to see him go. He was such a sweet old guy. But then again she really didn't need him any more. Television had made her a star, and Maxie had made her his wife.

Gina's television show lasted five years. Her marriage only a few months longer, but Maxie and she parted friends, and he was best man at her well publicized wedding to a macho actor whose main hobby was beating her up, so she divorced him too.

Her personal life was chaos, but her star continued to rise. A movie spinoff from her series had made big bucks at the box office. And she followed this with another money spinner. She was that rarity. A small screen star who could make it on the big screen. All at once she was hot. Every movie she did made money. She supported sagging superstars, playing straight lady to zany comedians, bubbled, wriggled and took her clothes off with monotonous regularity.

The public didn't think so. The public loved her. She was their Gina. A gorgeous package of golden flesh. A movie star whore with a heart of gold and tits to match. An old fashioned type movie star who evoked memories of Monroe and Mansfield.

'I want to be taken seriously,' she cooed on The Johnny Carson show one night. 'Y'know John, I want to do different kinds of films — something with a social message.'

Johnny had just looked to camera, his face a study in restraint, his expression said it all. The audience had roared with laughter and Gina was smart enough to shut up and return to sticking out her tits and indulging in playful flirts. Inside she was seething with frustration. Why shouldn't she do serious movies?

Two weeks later she met Neil Gray at a party. He was with his wife, but a little obstacle like a wife had never bothered Gina. What she wanted — she had. One of the advantages of being a film-star.

Neil Gray was serious with a capital S. He made important movies, meaningful movies. The kind of movies Gina knew that she should be doing.

She moved in quietly. Flattered him, hung onto his every word, made sure he got a good view of the amazing boobs when she leaned across him to reach for a cigarette, a drink, a scoop of dip. Three days later she called. 'I hope I'm not disturbing you,' she said in a throaty voice, knowing full well that if she was having her usual effect she was disturbing him a great deal. 'But I really do need some good advice, and you seem like just the person to help me.'

He was amused, intrigued. He knew 'some good advice' meant 'a good fuck'. They were both conversant with the language of Hollywood.

Lunch. Her house. A walled estate on San Ysidro Drive.

Salad Nicoise followed by solid fucking. Neither of them had the patience or the inclination to waste time.

A second rendezvous two weeks later. Same scenario.

They did not talk much, but Gina didn't mind. Once a man got lost in her beautiful boobs they always came back for more . . . and more and more . . . There would be plenty of time for talking.

She studied Montana at the dinner the Grays threw at the Bistro to announce their film. She was there with Chet Barnes. It sure startled the pants off Neil. But he needn't have worried, she was cool. She even chatted politely to Montana, told her about her own screenplay. Not that she had written it yet, but she was going to. So . . . Street People *was to be Neil's new film.*

The next day she called her agent, Sadie La Salle, and demanded a copy of the script.

'Nobody has seen it yet,' Sadie said briskly. 'Besides, I don't think it's your type of thing . . . From what I understand it's about two cops, an old one and a young one. And –'

'There must be women in it,' Gina interrupted tardily.

'Well . . . I expect so. But no star roles. I'm sure it's not a Gina Germaine vehicle.' She paused. 'Now tell me, dear, did you read "And Baby Makes . . ."?'

'No,' Gina snapped. 'I mean yes . . . and I hate it. Get me a copy of Neil's film Sadie, let me decide if it's a Gina Germaine vehicle or not.'

When Neil Gray phoned and suggested a weekend in Palm Beach Gina said yes without a moment's hesitation.

'Separate everything,' he warned. 'Rooms, travel, everything.'

'Sure,' she agreed.

'You might get bored, I'll have to spend time with Pamela and George.'

'I'll bring a book.'

She brought a book, but she never got to read it. She filched a copy of *Street People* from Neil's suitcase the second he left their adjoining suites, and read it in fifty-five minutes flat. Then she read it through again, concentrating on the part of Nikki. A buzz of excitement, a jolt of adrenaline.

NIKKI – EARLY TWENTIES – UNSPOILED BEAUTY – FANTASTIC BODY ALTHOUGH NOT OVERSTATED – NATURAL BLOND – CERTAIN INNOCENT QUALITY

I could play Nikki. I could. I could.

And it was a marvellous role. A catalyst between the two male parts. Daughter of one. Lover of the other.

I could play the crap out of a character like Nikki.

She was too old.

I've always looked younger than my age.

She was hardly unspoiled.

Good acting would take care of that.

Her fantastic body was more than a little overstated.

No shit? I'll diet. I'll bind the old boobies down. I'll fucking starve if necessary.

Innocent?

I can fake it.

She could hardly wait for Neil to get back. He looked tired and perplexed. She slid her arm around him and led him to bed.

'Pamela's a devious old bird,' he managed, as she started to unzip his pants.

'Really?' she questioned. 'Why?'

'Because –' he began, then groaned. She had him in her mouth and she was blowing him like her life depended on it – but then – in a way – it did.

Arriving back in Los Angeles Neil issued orders as they were leaving the plane. 'You'd better wait five minutes. I'll go ahead.'

Gina pouted. 'Ashamed of being seen with me?'

'Don't be ridiculous. We agreed to be . . . discreet.'

She sighed. 'Okay. But I will see you soon won't I?'

'Sooner than you think.'

He pecked her on the cheek and hurried on his way.

Most men were such bastards. But what did she care? She used *them*. No way did they use her. Her life was full of what she termed 'business fucks'. Men that could further her career, help her with her portfolio of shares (an impressive collection), assist her with real estate (three houses in Beverly Hills and an office block), and generally advise her on every matter from tax to abortion.

Gina always went to the best and never paid. Her current lovers included a Spanish real estate mogul. A Brazilian business whizz. A very rich Arab (he took care of her jewellery. That is he shopped 'Fred' and 'Tiffanys' every time he was in town). And the best lawyer, accountant and gynaecologist in Beverly Hills.

What she really wanted was a senator in her life, but she had yet to meet Teddy Kennedy whose fame attracted her the way plump skin attracts a hungry mosquito.

She looked upon Neil Gray as the next step in her career. He could treat her as badly as he wanted. For he would pay. One way or another. She would make sure of that.

Neil looked tired. Montana kissed him on both cheeks and said, 'Surprise! I thought we could talk on the way home.'

He glanced behind him. Thank God he had insisted on walking ahead of Gina. Quickly he grabbed Montana's arm and said, 'Wonderful, darling. You are just what I need after a weekend of Pamela and George.' Briskly he hurried her from the terminal.

'Well?' she questioned. 'I can't wait. Do we or do we not have the great George Lancaster?'

'You'll never believe this,' he said, hurriedly walking towards the open-doored limo where a chauffeur stood in uniformed attendance. 'But I still don't know.'

'Hey?' Buddy questioned. 'You really get off on that stuff?'

Shelly snorted a thin line of white powder from a mirrored table top through a folded banknote. 'Sure. Doesn't everybody?'

'Yeah. In Hollywood. I guess.' He prowled uneasily around her messy apartment. 'I used to be into it myself, but it got to be a drag.'

'A drag,' she repeated and grinned. 'You got broke and couldn't afford the habit. Right?'

'You know something?' He picked up a folder of photographs and flicked quickly through them. 'You have one smart mouth.'

She greedily snorted a touch more coke. 'So I've bin' told – *Mister* Married.'

'So?' he asked. 'Your memory got jogged yet?'

She stretched lazily. 'In a hurry?'

Yeah. He was in a hurry. He wanted to get back to Angel who he was sure was waiting up for him. 'No hurry.'

'Then relax! Take off your pants.' She yawned. 'If you like I'll give you a blow job that'll blow your mind.' She laughed. 'Get it?'

He sighed. 'Shelly, Shelly, who are you tryin' to turn on? There's only you an' me here, an' I think we got each other tagged.'

'You're right. But if ever you're in need . . . Like I give the best head in town. A hundred guys have told me. An' I'll tell you somethin' else, pal. I'm good because I enjoy it – *love* it.' She laughed again. 'Sure you don't want to give me a fast audition?'

'Quite sure, thank you.' There was something about her that

113

reminded him of himself before he met Angel. A real smart ass. Master of the fast line and the quick come on.

'Well . . .' She rose, and pulled at the tie on her wrapover skirt. 'I guess if you're sure.' The skirt fell to the floor, and very slowly she hooked her fingers into the top of her leotard and peeled it down.

'Hey,' he said quickly. 'Enough. You sound like a hooker.'

'Takes one to know one,' she taunted, stepping out of her leotard altogether.

He frowned. 'We met before?'

'Ah ha! You remembered.' She walked towards him, all stiletto heels and tanned nakedness.

He backed away. 'I'm going home.'

'Don't you wanna know where we met?'

'I'm not losin' sleep over it.'

'Ah . . . Buddy . . . Let me give you head. C'mon, huh? I'm askin' nicely.'

He had backed himself all the way to the door. Slipping the latch he let himself out. 'See you by the pool, kid. Don't catch cold.'

She waved her tongue at him obscenely. '*Street People* is the name of the movie Jer is up for. Oliver Easterne's the producer. Give it a shot.'

'Hey – *al*right. I will.' He took the stairs two at a time. Thirty seconds later he was fitting his key into the front door and calling out softly, 'Angel, babe. I'm home.'

'I just don't believe the bastard wouldn't give you a yes or a no. I mean the whole object of your trip was to get an answer.'

'I'm well aware of that,' Neil replied caustically.

He and Montana lounged on the top of their king size bed. She wore huge reading glasses and a man's shirt, her long legs stretched out before her, while her heavy black hair hung in a straight curtain to her waist.

Neil, in his pyjamas, looked tired and haggard. Two solid days of Gina Germaine would make anyone exhausted. Even a Warren Beatty or a Ryan O'Neal might feel the pace. Gina liked to fuck. Correction. Neil couldn't make up his mind whether she liked to fuck or fucked to be liked. Interesting problem. Not his. He wanted her for one thing and one thing only.

'Stars!' Montana exclaimed scornfully. 'They're all a giant pain.' She reached for a Salem and lit up. 'The real reason George

Lancaster won't commit is because he thinks if he says no you'll offer the part to someone else and his ego wouldn't like that.'

Neil scratched his chin. 'The problem is Pamela. She holds the balls in *that* household.'

'And is she squeezing them to say yes or no?'

'I don't think she's quite decided. She likes the idea of George doing a movie, but she doesn't like the idea of him running around Hollywood without her.'

'Ah,' Montana nodded knowingly. 'The lady is frightened of ambitious sixteen year old nymphets climbing on her old man's bones.'

Neil looked amused. 'You've never met Pamela, have you? The only thing that would frighten her is if the government threatened to take away her money.'

'Can't wait to meet her.'

'You'll like her.'

'Wanna bet?'

'I never risk my money with one of life's winners.'

A smile flickered across her face, and she pushed her reading glasses up into her hair. 'Such a charmer!'

'Of course.'

She reached out her arms. 'Come here, charmer.'

'I've got a headache.'

'Neil! That's supposed to be my excuse.'

'I really have,' he assured her.

She rose from the bed and padded towards the bathroom. 'I'll get you a painkiller,' she said sympathetically. A weekend in Palm Beach with George Lancaster and Pamela London can't have been all laughs. The poor bastard looked worn out. She hadn't really felt much like sex anyway – even though it had been a couple of weeks. Of course sex with Neil was still great, but they had been together long enough not to feel the need to do it every night, and right now work was the raging passion. Besides, getting a movie off the ground was never easy, and she sensed that he was more worried than he seemed.

She took two aspirin from a bottle, filled a glass with water and walked back into the bedroom. 'So,' she said, handing him the pills, 'we have to wait on his decision – is that it?'

He gulped the pills down quickly, not looking at her. There was no headache, but any more physical exertion after what he had been through with Gina was quite out of the question. 'George and Pamela will be here in two weeks' time. We'll get our answer then,' he said. Christ! He felt so goddamn guilty. He didn't need her sympathy to make him feel worse.

'Visiting royalty. What fun!' she said lightly.

'I promise, you'll like them both.'

She raised a cynical eyebrow. 'In a pig's ass I will.'

'Whatever you say, my dear, whatever you say.'

Angel was well aware of Buddy entering their apartment. Although it was almost three in the morning he made no effort to be quiet. He slammed the door, called out her name, and switched on all the lights.

She lay on her stomach in bed, silent and still. At first, when he had walked out on her, she had been anxious for him to return. But as the hours passed and he didn't even bother to call she had become hurt and angry. What was it about her that invited such behaviour? Why did she always end up being treated so badly? She had spent her life apologizing for just being around. With Buddy all that was supposed to change. He was her new beginning. The start of her own family.

Men: Hadn't her foster-mother always warned her?

'Angel?' he questioned softly.

Men: Never trust them.

'Are you awake, sweet stuff?' he asked more loudly.

Men: They have dirty habits and dirty minds.

He rubbed her back. 'Angel, babe?'

Men: They only want One Thing.

Slowly he slid his hands under the covers.

Men: If you give it to them they never respect you.

He pulled the covers off her immobile body. She was wearing her blue baby doll nightie with matching panties.

'You awake?' he whispered.

She remained silently on her stomach, her eyes squeezed tightly shut.

Buddy was undeterred. He hooked his fingers into the elastic of her panties and pulled them off.

She said nothing. Why should she? She was mad at him wasn't she?

He parted her legs and bent his head, his tongue darting into her warm wetness like a lethal cold snake.

Why was his tongue so cold? Why was she suddenly shaking with ecstasy? Why couldn't she stay mad at him?

116

'Ohhh . . . Buddy . . .' The words fluttered from her mouth like summer blossoms falling from a tree.

He raised his head long enough to say, 'You're not mad at me, babe, are you?'

She sighed very very softly and murmured, 'Turn the light out, Buddy. Please . . .'

He ripped off his pants. 'Why? You got somethin' to hide?' God but she made him horny! He spread her legs wider and replaced his eager tongue with something he had been saving up for her all night long.

12

Deke Andrews rode the subway out to Queens, and spent the morning checking out the used car lots along Queens Boulevard.

He finally found what he was looking for, a small brown van with tattered curtains on the back windows. It was five years old with plenty of mileage on the clock.

'How much?' he asked the shirt-sleeved dealer.

The dealer, a man with a bad case of B.O., summed his potential customer up. 'Price is on it,' he said finally.

'I know,' Deke replied, 'but you'll never get it.'

'Says who?'

'It's not worth it. Needs work.'

'How d'you know?'

'I can tell.'

'You ain't even driven it.'

'I can tell.'

The dealer spat a wad of chewing gum onto the ground. 'I can drop a hundred.'

'Three hundred.'

'That's my profit.'

'Cash.'

Curiosity got the better of the salesman. 'Don't you want to drive it?'

'I want to drive it out of here. Do we have a deal?'

The salesman nodded. He would have taken four hundred off if pushed. The engine was pure garbage.

Together they went into his office and did business.

Fifteen minutes later Deke drove away from the lot in the van.

He knew it was an inferior piece of machinery but he also knew that by the time he was finished with it the engine would sing. Deke had a way with cars.

Joey said, 'Do you have a car?'

Deke replied, 'No. I did have. I had a Mustang. It was –'

'Shee . . . it!'

'What?'

'I wanted to take a ride. Atlantic City maybe. Fun, huh? We could make out on the beach.'

'Make what?'

'Je . . . sus! Sometimes I don't believe you. We've bin seein' each other three weeks. Waddya think we're gonna make? Sand castles.'

'Sorry. I –'

'Don't say sorry. I hate it when you do that.'

'I could get a car.'

'How?'

'From the garage where I work.'

'When?'

'I don't know. I'd have to wait until one came in for repairs and was left overnight.'

'Shee . . . it!'

'What's the matter?'

'I wanna go for a drive tonight.'

'It's not possible.'

'Then I think I'll work. You'd better go home.'

'No! I'll get us a car.'

'Yeah? You sure, cowboy?'

'Yes. I'm sure.'

He drove the van slowly and carefully. Wouldn't do to get stopped. He drove out past Kennedy airport, turned off the main highway, and searched for a quiet side road. There, he parked and opened up the hood. The engine was no better and no worse than he had thought. A few days of hard work should do it.

Satisfied, he headed back for Queens, where he parked the van near the station and took the subway back to New York.

His room waited. A few impersonal square feet. A bed, a dresser, his scant possessions.

It took him only minutes to pack. And then, once more, he was on his way.

13

Lunch: The Bistro Gardens.

Cast: Elaine Conti. Maralee Gray. Karen Lancaster.

Menu: Salad, salad, salad. Nothing fattening. They were all on a permanent diet.

Subject: Gossip.

Karen to Maralee: 'You look absolutely sensational. Palm Springs must have agreed with you.'

Maralee smiling: 'It certainly did. I met this very interesting man called Randy Felix.'

Elaine: 'Did he live up to his name?'

Maralee: 'How would *I* know. It wasn't *that* sort of relationship.'

Karen, cynically: 'There *are* no other kinds of relationships.'

Maralee: 'Randy is into preserving our environment.'

Karen, sarcastic: 'Really?'

Elaine, down to earth: 'How old is he? And does he have money?'

Maralee, laughing: 'I don't know and I don't much care. I'm not planning to *marry* him.'

Elaine: 'What *are* you planning?'

Karen: 'She's planning to get into the poor kid's pants. When does he get into town?'

Maralee, affronted: 'He's not a kid. He's at least twenty-six or seven. And as a matter of fact he will be in L.A. shortly, he has his own apartment here.'

Karen and Elaine in unison: 'Sure.'

Maralee: 'God! You are a couple of bitches.'

Karen: 'Nothing wrong with getting laid.'

Maralee: 'I never said there was. And if I do decide to investigate "the poor kid's" pants, I'll certainly be sure to let you know, Karen, dear.'

119

Karen: 'Details! I want details! Like is he hung and does he give good head?'

'Karen!'

'Sorry, sorry. I'll shut up.'

The three women were firm friends. They moved in the same circles and had the same interests – clothes, money and sex. Also none of them had children, which created a bond. Karen – because she didn't want any. Maralee – because she had miscarried twice when married to Neil and had then given up. And Elaine because she could not conceive – a fact which had never bothered her or Ross.

'Oh! Will you look who just came in,' Karen said.

Three sets of eyes guarded by three sets of different expensive optics studied the entrance. There, suitably clad in a white silk Ungaro dress and jacket, with Cartier daytime diamonds, stood Bibi Sutton.

Now Bibi was fifty years old if she was a day. But in the twenty years she had been one of the so-called social lionesses of the Beverly Hills elite she had not aged a jot. Her skin was smooth roman olive, her hair a rich burnished copper, her figure voluptuous, without one inch of fat.

It was said she had been a journalist in her native France and had been sent to interview the American movie star Adam Sutton at his hotel in Paris. It had also been said that she was a highly paid call girl who had visited him every night in his suite at the George V. For free.

Who cared? It had happened years before – and whatever she *had* been, she was now a lady to be reckoned with.

Bibi Sutton set trends. She could make or break a designer, a restaurant, an artist, a caterer. If Bibi put the seal of approval on something or someone – then that business or person was made. She had clout, style and a forceful personality. Plus a French accent which even after twenty years sounded like Bardot on a bad day. She cultivated broken English, it was part of her charisma.

In comparison, Adam Sutton was a tall, quietly spoken man. A fine actor with two Oscars to prove it. Still a star at sixty-two, and an upstanding member of the Los Angeles community.

They had two children. Jennifer, eighteen, studying at a college in Boston. Charles, nineteen, away at Harvard. Rumour had it that there was another child born to Bibi before her marriage – the result of a torrid affair with George Lancaster. But Bibi had always denied the fact. 'A filthy lie,' she told the one journalist brave (or stupid) enough to ask her about it. And the rumour was laid to rest.

Bibi and Adam Sutton were Hollywood royalty. The perfect couple. Rich. Socially acceptable. Powerful.

'Hmmm . . .' murmured Karen. 'How I'd *love* to catch our Bibi with her pantyhose around her ankles.' She had always been somewhat amused at the thought of her father and Bibi locked in hot combat all those years ago.

Maralee licked her lips. 'And how I'd love to catch our Adam in bed one dark night. Preferably with me.'

Karen looked amazed. 'Adam Sutton! You must be joking. He has to be the most boring fuck in Beverly Hills.'

'Who would know?' Maralee retorted tartly.

'*I* wouldn't for one,' Karen replied. 'In fact I can't think of anyone who would. The man does not screw around.'

'How unusual,' Maralee said.

Elaine ignored them both. She was on her feet and heading full speed in Bibi's direction.

'Darling!!' Both together. Kissy, kissy on each other's cheeks. Lips not touching skin. 'How *are* you?' Still together. 'You look *wonderful.*'

The ritual was finished. 'Bibi,' Elaine said quickly. 'I'm thinking of having a little soirée on the twenty-fourth of this month. It's a Friday. Nothing vast. But it's been such ages since I've had time to get anything together. Ross has been so busy. My God – I don't have to tell *you* what it's like. Can you and Adam come?'

'Sweetie!' Bibi looked quite shocked. 'Eh! How I know? You think I know *anything* without my book? You call me. We looove to come if we free. Okay sweetie?'

'Yes, fine, I'll call you later,' Elaine said obediently. It would be unthinkable to plan a party on a date the Suttons could not attend. Quickly she returned to her table in the fashionable sunlit garden.

'Any luck?' demanded Karen, who knew every move.

'I have to call her later,' Elaine replied sulkily. 'She doesn't know a thing without her book.'

'Horseshit,' said Karen succinctly. 'She never commits to *any*thing unless she's certain there is nothing better going on that night. Years ago my father had a birthday party for her, and she bowed out at the last minute to go to some half-assed dinner for Khruschev. Daddy was *furious.*'

'I bet,' agreed Maralee. '*My* father had Adam doing two movies for him, and she *still* wouldn't invite daddy to her house because he never turned up at one of her special dinners once.'

Elaine stared at her two friends. Sometimes she got an uncomfortable insecure feeling when she was around them. They were so sure of themselves. And so they should be. They had both grown up in Beverly Hills with rich famous fathers behind them, always had money, and whoever they were married to would always be accepted. It was their birthright. Little Etta Grodinski from the Bronx had had to struggle for everything. Marrying a movie star, landing up in a Beverly Hills mansion, and becoming attractive clever Elaine Conti had been no easy job. Moodily she sipped her white wine.

Think yourself lucky. These women are your friends. They accept you. They like you. They tell you about their lives and loves, their clothes and make-up, their plastic surgeons and gynaecologists. You're one of them now. You are. Don't ever forget it.

Etta. Elaine. How carefully she hid her background. Her parents, still alive, had long ago moved from the Bronx to a pleasant house on Long Island. To this day she had never invited them to visit her in Beverly Hills. To this day they had never met Ross. She phoned them once a week, and sent them a monthly cheque. They were nice simple people. They would never be comfortable in her world.

You're ashamed of them, Elaine.

I'm not, I'm not.

'Look who Bibi's with,' exclaimed Karen.

All eyes swivelled to inspect Bibi's companion who had arrived late and was now hurrying across the crowded restaurant to join Bibi.

'It's only Wolfie Schweicker,' Maralee said dismissively.

'My God! For a moment I thought it was a man!' exclaimed Karen. 'He looks different. What *has* he done?'

'Lost about thirty pounds,' said Elaine, joining in.

'So he has,' marvelled Karen. 'He's positively slimline.'

Wolfgang Schweicker. Professional walker. The term used for any affluent, well connected man who escorted married ladies when their husbands were not available to accompany them to the various openings and galleries and restaurants that they simply *had* to be seen at. Nancy Reagan had hers. Wolfie was Bibi's equivalent. Once grossly fat, he had managed to slim down to merely chubby. He was round of face, short of leg, and expensively clad in the best Gucci had to offer. He was in his early fifties, and owned a very successful chain of designer bathrooms with franchises across America. Everyone adored Wolfie. He was so witty. But he belonged to Bibi Sutton and never strayed.

'Do you know,' Maralee said, tapping her perfect fingernails on the table top, 'I once invited Wolfie to a brunch. Without taking a breath he asked if Bibi and Adam were coming. I was married to Neil at the time, he *loathed* Bibi, and didn't care who knew it. Called her a socially miscast French cunt!' Maralee giggled at the memory. 'Anyway, I said no, and *he* said no. Can you imagine! Wouldn't even come to a tiny little *brunch* without her.'

The lunch passed in a flurry of gossip, innuendo, and general bitchery. Reputations, love affairs, talent and looks were casually pulled to pieces. Elaine asked for the check and charged it to American Express. Karen hurried off to her analyst, and Elaine and Maralee strolled outside to get their respective cars from an attentive parking valet.

Maralee raised her sunglasses, peered conspiratorially at her friend, and said, 'What do you think?'

Elaine cast a professional eye on Maralee's recent surgery. She had not been married to a plastic surgeon without learning a thing or two. 'Excellent,' she declared, after a thorough inspection. 'Really a first class job.'

Maralee was thrilled. 'Honestly?'

'Would I lie?'

'Of course you wouldn't!'

The parking valet drove up with Maralee's brand new Porsche Turbo Carrera. She grabbed every cent of alimony she could from Neil, but actually didn't need a dime. Her father had settled two trusts on her, both of which she had gained possession of. When Tyrone Sanderson died she stood to inherit another fortune. 'I'm going to Neiman Marcus,' she announced. 'Why don't you come?'

Elaine shook her head. 'I have to get home. Now that Ross is back my time's not my own.'

Maralee nodded understandingly and headed for her car.

'By the way,' Elaine placed a restraining hand on her friend's arm. 'There's something I'd like you to do for me.'

'Yes?'

'Look . . . I know you're not on the greatest of terms with Neil –'

'That's the understatement of the year!'

'But could you . . . would you . . .'

Maralee was getting impatient. 'What, Elaine?'

'I need a copy of *Street People*,' she blurted quickly. 'It's important. I need it immediately.'

Maralee raised her eyebrows. 'That piece of garbage!'

'Have you read it?'

'Do I need to? Montana *supposedly* wrote it. Doesn't that tell you enough?'

Elaine felt a flush spreading across her face. How she hated having to ask anyone for anything. 'Can you get it for me?'

Maralee gazed at her friend shrewdly. 'Don't tell me Ross is interested?'

Elaine shrugged in what she hoped was a noncommittal fashion. 'He likes to see everything.'

'Can't his agent get him a copy?'

'Apparently it's under wraps.'

'Probably because it's so bad,' Maralee sniffed. 'Oh, well – if you want it – it's yours. There's nothing in this town that *I* can't get my hands on.'

'Thanks, Maralee.'

'It's nothing.'

Lips brushed cheeks, once on each side, and they parted. Maralee roared off in her new Porsche, and Elaine climbed disconsolately into her four year old Mercedes. Soon . . . It would all change soon. The Contis would be back on top and she would never have to ask anyone a favour again.

'I just left your wife,' Karen husked over the phone.

'So?'

'I told her everything.'

There was a long pause while Ross digested this information. 'You did what?' he said at last.

Karen's voice was filled with emotion. 'Everything, Ross. About us. I think she'll probably kill you!' She could hold back her laughter no longer.

'Clever cunt.'

'You said it!'

'Where are you?'

'In my analyst's waiting room. I'm just about to tell him all about us.'

'Don't!'

'Why not? I'll tell you what he says. I promise.'

'Dammit, Karen, do not mention my name '

'What's in it for me if I don't?'

'The biggest dick *you've* ever seen.'

She chuckled felicitously. 'I wouldn't be too sure of that.'

124

'I'll call you tomorrow.'

'Not good enough. When?'

He wanted her, but he wanted the script of *Street People* more, and he did not plan to leave the house until he had it.

'I said I'll call you tomorrow.'

She was not prepared to be dismissed so easily. 'I understand it's going to be party time in the Conti household soon.'

'Yup.'

'Elaine spent the entire lunch yearning after Bibi Sutton.'

'Did she get her?'

'She got a maybe. You know Bibi.'

Ross understood the social mores of Beverly Hills. If Elaine could not get Bibi Sutton to their party she may as well not bother giving it. Maybe he would give Adam a call, pull the old pals act.

'I have to go,' Karen said abruptly. She wanted to be sure to get off the phone before he did.

'Don't you *dare* mention my name to your goddamn analyst,' he warned.

She hung up without another word. Ross returned to the lounger where he was carefully taking the sun and imagined the scene at the Bistro Gardens. Bibi playing hard to get, Elaine chasing, and Karen enjoying every fawning minute.

Karen. For one wild second he had actually believed her when she said she had told Elaine. The broad had a wicked sense of humour. Maybe he should dump her.

But why? She would never open her mouth to Elaine, and he certainly wanted more of her horny body and wonderfully erotic nipples. Oh those nipples!

More . . . Not immediately. But soon . . . when he'd seen the script of *Street People* . . . When Sadie La Salle was his agent . . . When he felt more . . . settled.

It seemed to Buddy that he had hardly closed his eyes when the phone woke him. 'Whoozatt?' he mumbled.

A burst of static, then, 'Buddy? You awake?'

'Call me in the mornin',' he said sleepily.

'It *is* morning,' replied his caller testily. 'It's eleven o'clock and about time you moved it.'

'Randy!' Slowly he opened an eye. 'How're you doin'?'

'Doin' all right. Doin' more than all right. I found me a *real* hot rich one.'

'Hey – that's good.' Buddy opened the other eye and groped around the bed looking for Angel. She was not there.

'Too right it's good,' said Randy briskly. 'And no way do I aim to blow the opportunity. Like so far I am Mr. Straight, an' she goes for me a lot – *and* with a great deal more input I think I can find myself *really* on the right track.'

'Good, good . . .' mumbled Buddy, hoping that the call had nothing to do with the apartment.

'I'm driving in tomorrow,' Randy said, 'and I'll need my apartment. I know it's short notice, but when I lent you the place we agreed it was only for a couple of weeks, an' well . . . you bin there a while. I'll be arriving around noon tomorrow.'

Buddy struggled for something to say. What *could* he say? *Hey, man. I got nowhere else to go. I got no money. I got a wife to support. I got* nothing. He couldn't say that. No way could he say that.

Pride. He had enough not to admit that in the time he'd been back he had not scored one lousy stinking job.

'We'll be long gone by then,' he said cheerfully. 'And thanks for the loan of the place, Rand. S'matter of fact we'll be movin' into Sunset Towers. Saw a place there only last week that's just right.'

'Sunset Towers, huh? Everything's goin' your way then?'

'It sure is.'

'Can't wait to meet your old lady.'

'We'll call you in the week an' get it together.'

He banged the phone down and leapt from the bed.

Shit! Shit! Shit!

He stormed the refrigerator, gulped orange juice from a carton, grabbed a handful of raisins, and bit into an apple.

Then he thought about what he could do.

Gladrags. No longer in business.

Maxie Sholto. Had to be a last resort.

Frances Cavendish. Call her at once about *Street People*.

Shelly. What did it take to become a male stripper?

He pulled on his shorts and automatically started in on some push-ups. Then he remembered Gladrags' roommate, the plump little fag with the horny dog. He had thrust his card at him and said, 'Call me.'

So why not? Find out the score.

Yeah. But where *was* the guy's card? What had he done with it? He tried to concentrate on his push-ups but it was useless. How could you concentrate on the body beautiful when you were about to find yourself out on the street?

Abruptly he jumped to his feet and punched out Frances Cavendish's number on the phone.

'Miz Cavendish is in a meeting. Can she call you back?' droned an unfamiliar voice.

'It's urgent,' Buddy snapped. 'Urgent business.'

'Oh. Well I'll see . . . Who shall I say is calling?'

'Robert Evans.'

Respect. 'Yes, Mr. Evans.'

A thirty second wait, then, 'Bobby, how are you? And what can I do for you?'

'Frances, this is Buddy Hudson, and don't get mad at me, this *is* urgent.'

'Jesus Christ!'

He spoke rapidly. 'Frances. There's a movie called *Street People*. There's a part in it for me. You want to create another star? Then just send me for the part, okay?'

Frances was more than exasperated. 'Not okay.'

'Why?'

'Because, dear boy, there is indeed a movie being cast of that name. But whether there is a role in it suitable for you, I do not know, because I have not seen the script. Indeed – very few people *have* seen the script. It's under wraps.'

'That's crap, Frances. You see everything.'

She made a sound like an angry horse. 'Very true, Buddy, dear. However, on this occasion all casting is being taken care of by the writer,' her voice filled with scorn, 'who obviously knows better than all of us poor old casting experts. I mean I have only been in the business thirty years, that's all. What could *I* possibly know?'

'Who is the writer?'

'Montana Gray, the director's wife. Does that tell you enough? Now get off this line, Buddy, and don't *ever* use a phony name to get through to me again. Do you understand?'

'I need a job, Frances.'

She sighed. 'You always *need* a job, but you never get any of the ones I send you for.'

'You got something for me? Next time'll be my shot. I know it.' He could feel her thinking and he willed her to come up with an interview.

'Are you interested in work as an extra?' she said at last.

127

Anger flooded through him. Extra work. He'd sooner leave town than stoop to that. 'No,' he said coldly.

'Sorry. Then I can't help you right now.'

How he hated the phone. First Randy, then Frances. Always bad news, negative happenings.

The sound of Angel's key in the door and what was he going to tell her?

She looked particularly beautiful, shining with a very special innocence.

'I'm sorry I wasn't here to fix your breakfast,' she murmured softly, going to him and putting her arms around his waist. 'I had to visit the doctor.'

His mind was racing. Montana Gray, wife of Neil Gray the director. Casting the movie themselves. An Oliver Easterne production Shelly had said. He gave Angel a gentle shove. 'Call information for me, babes. I need the number of Easterne Productions.'

She stared at him with a hurt expression. 'I said I had to go see the doctor, don't you want to know why?'

'Yeah, sure, 'course I do.' And then as an afterthought, 'Why didn't you tell me you were going?'

'I . . . I wasn't sure you'd be pleased.' She gazed at him, the happiness in her eyes mixed with a small amount of uncertainty. 'But now that it's confirmed . . .'

The horror of what she was about to say struck him like a lead bullet. 'Christ, babe. You're not –' He couldn't bring himself to finish the sentence.

She nodded and whispered the missing word. 'Pregnant.'

'Oh, no!'

'Oh, yes! Isn't it wonderful, Buddy? Isn't it absolutely wonderful?'

He didn't know what to say. A choking feeling overtook him. He wanted to push her away, but controlled himself.

'Hey – I gotta swim, I'm runnin' late. I'll be back.' He rushed from the apartment like a thief.

'Buddy –' she called out after him, but he didn't stop.

She closed her eyes for a moment, squeezed them tightly shut and determined not to cry. Oh boy . . . It sure wasn't like it was in the movies, but she had to stop feeling sorry for herself. If Buddy wasn't happy about the baby that was just too bad. *She* was thrilled. And eventually he would be too. She was sure of it. After all, he loved her, didn't he? And this would make them into a real family.

14

Captain Lacoste said, 'You want it, take it.' He indicated the thick file on his desk. 'But you know we've done everything we can. His description is across the country, his photo, his fingerprints. The next move is his.'

Leon said, 'I know that. I just feel there's something we're missing, and I want to go over the file again. I need to take my time over it.' He picked it up. There was nothing in it he didn't already know. He left the Captain's office and went straight outside to his car. It was raining . . .

Leon was annoyed about losing his raincoat. It was the genuine English article, purchased by a good friend at Burberry's in London, and brought back as a special birthday present. The thought of Joey-the-hooker parading around town in it burned him up.

He thought about getting in his car and going out to look for her, but after a long hot shower the idea of venturing once more into the filthy night did not appeal to him. So instead he put on his pyjamas, poured himself a substantial glass of brandy and settled down to watch an old western on television.

He must have fallen asleep in front of the set, because an urgent hammering woke him with a start. Half asleep he groped his way to the front door, glancing at his watch on the way and wondering who the hell was bothering him at two in the morning.

He threw open the door and was confronted with a sorry sight. Joey Kravetz stood there soaked to the skin. Her T-shirt stuck transparently to her body, her baggy trousers clung damply, her orange hair was flattened to her scalp, and driblets of water dripped off the end of her crooked snub nose.

'I brought back your raincoat,' she said forlornly handing it to him.

He was pleased to see his raincoat, not too pleased to see her. 'How did you know where I lived?'

She fished a crumpled envelope from his raincoat pocket. 'Your electric bill,' she stated, then imr.:ediately began to sneeze.

'I guess you'd better come in,' he growled reluctantly.

'Gee, thanks,' she sneered. 'Thought you'd never ask.' And then a grin spread across her face. 'Nice pyjamas. Reaal sexy. I like the peephole!'

He was mortified to find his fly gaping open. 'Just a minute,' he said stiffly, and hurried to the bathroom where he threw on a bathrobe. When he returned to the living room she was standing by the television set dripping all over his carpet.

'Look,' he said testily. 'I'll give you something to put on while your clothes dry. Then I'll call you a cab.'

'I don't have nowhere to go,' she whined.

'There must be somewhere.'

'No,' she said stubbornly.

'So we're back to dropping you at Juvenile then.'

Her attitude quickly changed. 'Aw, shit!' she snarled. 'You gotta record playin' in your mouth. Juvenile! Juvenile! Is that all y'can say?' A few more sneezes rendered her speechless.

'Will you go into the bathroom and get those wet clothes off before you catch pneumonia.'

She nodded obediently. He directed her to the bathroom, and tried to figure out what to do with her.

'Can I take a shower?' she called out.

'I suppose so,' he replied ungraciously. 'And throw me out your clothes. I'll try and get them dry.'

He went in the kitchen and switched on the electric kettle, then he picked up her clothes from the floor and placed them on a radiator. After that he brought her a baggy sweater and some old trousers from his closet, and dropped them outside the bathroom ready for her to put on.

How had he, Leon Rosemont, landed up with a sixteen year old hooker showering in his bathroom? Jesus H. Christ. This would make him a laughing-stock if anyone down at the precinct ever found out.

She emerged dry and clean, ridiculously swamped by his clothes. The water was boiling, so he poured some in a cup, added a tea bag, two sugar cubes, and handed it to her.

She sat herself down at the kitchen table and sipped it gratefully.

'And what exactly am I supposed to do with you?' he said.

'Let me sleep on your couch an' I'll be outta here first thing in the *mornin',' she replied, quick as a flash. 'Honest. I won't hassle ya or nothin', I'll be gone, man. Y'can lay bucks on it.'*

'I can't do that.'

'Why not?'

He thought for a moment. What else was there to do with her? The only alternative was to turn her in to Juvenile, and that meant getting dressed and dragging over to the station. It was still pouring down, the poor kid would get locked in a cell until morning, and the paper work alone . . .

He made a quick decision. The hell with it. Let her sleep on his couch, and in the morning he would take her to her friend just to make sure she was telling the truth.

Somewhere in the back of his head a warning voice said, 'Wrong,' but he ignored it, got spare blankets and a pillow from the hall closet and left her to it.

He closed his bedroom door, got into bed, read two chapters of a Joseph Wambaugh novel, and fell asleep.

The storm hit around three-thirty. Wild forks of lightning and deep rumbles of thunder. Leon slept. Nothing disturbed him. Joey woke immediately, hugged the blanket around her nakedness, and began to shiver. The brilliant flashes of lightning and the heavy thunder petrified her. She had had a bad experience as a kid. Storms panicked her.

She leaped from the couch and rushed into Leon's bedroom. He slept on his back, snoring, oblivious to everything.

Quietly she lifted the cover and crawled in beside him. He didn't stir. She snuggled close, and his bulk comforted her. He moved in his sleep, groaned, muttered something under his breath.

'You awake?' she whispered, fitting herself spoon-like into the curve of his back, her hands moving around to his chest.

He was still, his breathing heavy.

She searched his chest – thick with curly hair, until she located his nipples. Experience told her that men could get just as turned on by nipple-play as women. She found one, then the other, and the tips of her stubby little fingers went to work. His nipples soon hardened beneath her touch. She moved her hands down, found the opening in his pyjama pants, slid her hands within and grasped his swollen penis. Very gently she began to manipulate it up and down. Slow rhythmic motions that caused a low moan of pleasure to escape his lips, although he remained asleep.

She grinned, the storm forgotten while she concentrated on bringing him to a climax without waking him. 'You got a beautiful johnnie

there,' she whispered encouragingly in his ear. 'A real humdinger . . .
Come on, cowboy, give me what you got . . . give it all to mama . . .
Give me all that juicy jism . . .

Oh, she knew what they liked to hear alright. And it was so easy. He
came quickly, his sperm pulsating in long throbbing spurts onto the
sheets.

She snuggled closer to his back and drifted off to sleep. When she
woke, dawn was breaking and the storm was long gone. Leon snored
contentedly beside her. And why not? She had given him what he
wanted. What all men wanted. He may have come on with that phoney
fatherly concerned act . . . but he was only a man after all. He didn't
really give a damn what happened to her.

Carefully she wriggled from the bed and with one eye on his inert
form checked out his wallet lying on the dresser. Pay dirt. He was
carrying three hundred and nineteen bucks. Impulsively she grabbed
the money, collected her clothes from the kitchen, flung them on, and
silently crept from the apartment.

Millie Rosemont cursed the day Captain Lacoste had given Leon
permission to bring the Andrews file home. Every night, for two and
a half weeks, he had shut himself away in his cramped study, the
offending file laid out in sections on his desk. There he sat, for hours
on end, scribbling nothing much on his precious legal pad (she
checked the basket every morning and found page after page of
cryptic *Why? Where is he now? When will he strike again?*).

Millie decided the time had come to have it out. She entered his
study carrying a cup of coffee and a sandwich. 'Leon,' she said
sharply. 'May I speak to you for a moment?'

He removed his heavy reading glasses, rubbed the bridge of his
thick nose and looked up. 'If you can't I don't know who can.'

She placed his coffee and sandwich on the desk and stared at him
gravely. 'This case is becoming an obsession with you, and I don't
think I like it much.'

He regarded his wife sympathetically, and tried to see things her
way. It would be better if he could explain things to her. Tell her *why*
he felt so personally involved. But no . . . he couldn't do that . . . he
was ashamed, embarrassed . . . He stretched, feeling the strain in his
shoulders, the tightness around his neck. 'If you don't want me to
continue . . .'

She made a helpless gesture with her hands. 'It's not what *I* want or
don't want. It's what's best for you.'

'What's best for me,' he said slowly, 'is solving this case.'

'What do you mean – solving it?' she replied angrily. 'It's no secret who *did* the murders. You know the son did it. And you also know that he'll be picked up for something else. It always happens that way – you told me so yourself.'

He sipped the hot coffee. 'I want to know why, Millie. I *have* to know.'

'Didn't I tell you? It's an obsession with you. And not a very healthy one.' She looked at him for a long silent moment, then turned and left the room.

'Millie!' he called out after her. 'What did I *say*?'

No reply. She was mad at him.

He took another bite of sandwich, a sip of coffee, then picked up his pad. *Where was Deke Andrews born?* he wrote. *What hospital? What city? What date?*

It was probably unimportant. But still . . . Amongst the Andrews papers had been no documents that related to their lives before they had arrived in Philadelphia over twenty years before. No wedding licence, no birth certificates, no relatives' letters, no indication of *where* they had come from.

This bothered Leon. Why no record of their past? Were they running from something or someone? Had Deke found out something he shouldn't?

It was a thought.

In a neat script Leon wrote – *Get a computer check on Willis and Winifred Andrews.*

Why not? There was nothing to lose.

15

He looked the best he could – and that was something. The girl on reception double-taked and didn't even check out his name on the typed list she had before her. She directed him to the elevator with a glowing smile and a 'Lots of luck'.

Luck. He needed it.

Luck. His body craved it like a junkie craves drugs.

He pressed the elevator button. Floor twenty. Was twenty going to be the hot new number in his life?

There was a mirror on the side of the elevator and he monitored his appearance yet again.

You're lookin' good . . . you're lookin' good . . . you're lookin' good like a superstar should . . .

Keep thinking that way. Keep thinking up.

He stepped out of the elevator into a sea of people. They sat, they lounged against walls, they took up every inch of space, all sizes, shapes, and ages, and in the middle of the throng was a large lucite desk manned by a businesslike-looking blonde, and an elderly red-head. To Buddy, forty was elderly. Unless you were talking Jane Fonda or Raquel Welch.

He headed confidently towards the desk, and as he did so he quickly observed where the main action was. A panelled oak door. A small brass plaque. It read MONTANA GRAY.

Lady, you are in for a treat. Buddy Boy is here. Buddy Boy has come to star in your movie.

He went directly to the blonde. She had marvellous green eyes, a smooth skin, and a very bad nose job.

'Buddy Hudson,' he said confidently. 'Miz Gray's expecting me.'

The blonde smiled, popped on a pair of lavender reading glasses and consulted her list.

Knowing that she wasn't going to find his name on it, he added quickly, 'Bob Evans arranged my appointment personally.'

The blonde stopped reading. 'He did? With whom?'

'Uh, he spoke to Montana – Miz Gray. She said for me to come right over. I'm working on a special at NBC and I have,' he glanced at his watch, 'exactly forty-two minutes before my ass has to be back on the set.' Now for the smile that said *I think you are the most desirable female I have ever seen in the whole of my life and I would like to fuck your brains out because you are so totally and absolutely irresistibly gorgeous!* 'So,' he continued, 'I'd appreciate it if I could be next in. Not that I want to throw out your schedule or anything.'

The blonde had hardly led a sheltered life. She had been through many men and many scenes. She considered herself a tough nut to crack.

The smile never left her face. Buddy Hudson was something else! She knew instinctively that he desired her, and not just because she was the gateway to Montana Gray.

'I'll see what I can do,' she said, writing down his name.

His gaze was level, direct. 'I'd really appreciate that.'

*

The first thing that struck Buddy was that she wasn't his type. No way. Not at all.

She sat behind a big desk, cool and collected in a wide shouldered jacket and pinstripe shirt. Her jet hair was scraped back into a long braid and most of her face was obscured by huge, lightly tinted reading glasses. Her skin was olive toned and glowing. Her mouth wide and unrouged.

No sirree. She wasn't his type at all. Buddy Boy liked them soft and blonde, pretty and appealing. He liked them *girlish*.

She was busy writing something on a pad, and without looking up she indicated that he should sit. There was a leather chair opposite her desk for just such a purpose. He glared at it balefully. Who needed to sit? Where was the impact in that? First impressions were very important and when she looked up from her scribbling he wanted her to feel the full blast of his personality.

He hovered near the door ready for the walk towards the desk when he had her full concentration. The walk was important. It was part of him, the rolling thrusting strut. Jeez! He wasn't *nervous* was he? Buddy Boy was *never* nervous.

So what were the patches of damp under his arms? And why was his upper lip clouding with little beads of sweat?

Sonofabitch! Was she going to read all day? Up until now it had been a breeze. Who would have thought it would be that easy to lie his way in to see her? *And* get in ahead of a roomful of people who probably had appointments. He could thank the blonde with the bad nose job for that little piece of luck. *If all the blondes in Hollywood were laid end to end . . . Shit! They probably had been!*

He wished that he knew something about the role in the movie. Should he be aggressively sexual? Boyish? Charming? Dustin Hoffman with looks?

Goddamn it. All he knew was the title of the film and that she had written it and that her old man was going to direct it.

His stomach was knotting up. Tension. If he carried on this way he'd have ulcers before he was thirty.

Yeah. And why not? Randy was throwing them out of the apartment. He had no money, no job, and only hours before, Angel had calmly informed him she was pregnant.

Ulcers. Maybe they would kill him and do away with all the aggravation. He shuffled restlessly.

'I won't be a minute,' Montana said, without looking up.

I can wait. I mean why shouldn't I? I'm only another bum actor without a job. Why should anyone consider my feelings?

He had taken Angel's news calmly. She was so happy – somehow it had not seemed the right time to tell her that she'd have to get an abortion. No way could they afford a baby. He had acted like it was great news, the best. Then he had dressed in his one good outfit and moved ass. Fast.

Hitting on the Easterne offices had been a snap decision, and now he was here – and there *she* was – Miz Montana Gray. Not his type. No way. But quite a looker if you liked the strong ballsy type.

She stuck her pen in her mouth, pushed her reading glasses up into her hair, and hit him with laser beam tiger eyes. 'Buddy Hudson,' she said coolly. 'I don't remember Bob Evans calling me about you.'

She was no easy touch. He could see that. Try the honest approach and go for broke. He strutted toward her desk, and kind of threw himself into a chair, legs casually apart. 'He didn't.'

'He didn't,' she repeated patiently.

'Nope.'

'Then maybe you'd like to tell me why you're here?' Smoky ebony eyes met laser tigers and held.

'Because,' Buddy said slowly, with a touch of arrogance, 'you'd have been missing out if you hadn't seen me.' He favoured her with a long sexy stare.

She stifled impatience. 'I would?'

He was brimming with false confidence. 'Sure you would.'

She removed the tip of her pen from between her lips. 'Why don't we cut out the shit, Mr. Hudson?'

'Huh?'

'Let's cut out the I-am-the-most-desirable-sex-machine-that-ever-walked and let me get a look at the real you.'

He frowned. 'Hey–'

She smiled agreeably. 'Can't win 'em all.'

'I –'

'Do you have pictures? A résumé?'

'I didn't bring anything with me.'

'Why don't you just tell me what you've done then?' She poised her pen above the notepad on her desk.

Jeez! She was interested in his acting experience. Really interested!

'I . . . uh . . . I've done a "Starsky and Hutch". I was in "Smokey and the Bandit". Well, like I mean I was in it, but by the time it hit the screen I wasn't –'

'I think I get the picture.'

'Not that I wasn't good in it,' he added hurriedly. 'I mean – shit – I was *very* good, *too* good. Like it was a scene with Burt Reynolds and –'

'Yes. I understand.'

He stood up and paced excitedly in front of her desk forgetting image and impact for the moment. 'I studied at Joy Byron's school of acting y'know. Like I was one of her best students. I played Stanley Kowalski in "Streetcar". A special performance for talent scouts, agents, the whole schmeer. I was a smash, couple of studios wanted to sign me, but I had this singing gig in Hawaii I was already committed to – an' there was no way I would ever back out on a definite commitment.' He was speeding, his words tumbling out like an express train. 'I'm a professional all the way – you can bet on that.'

'I'm sure you are,' she murmured, watching him intently.

'Yeah . . . well . . . Like I came back from Hawaii straight into the recession. Ten thousand actors an' ten jobs, y'know?'

She nodded sympathetically. 'I think I've interviewed most of them.' The buzzer on her desk sounded and she said 'Yes' into the intercom.

'Mr. Gray on the line,' said the receptionist.

'Find out where he is, I'll call him back.'

Buddy returned to his seat in front of her desk and wondered if he'd said too much. What did she care if he was cut out of a lousy Burt Reynolds movie? What did she care about ten thousand actors hunting ten jobs?

'Is the "Starsky and Hutch" worth seeing?' she inquired crisply.

Honesty had suddenly become his best policy. 'I got cut out of that too. Y'see – Paul Michael Glaser –'

She laughed. What a laugh. Very sexy.

'I know, I know. Paul Michael Glaser couldn't cut the competition, right?'

He grinned. 'You got it.'

'Then there's no film we can see you on?'

He pushed his hand through his hair nervously. 'Nothin' worth lookin' at.' Buddy Boy. Mister Cool. Where was all this leading?

'I understand.' She paused. 'So . . . Maybe you'd like to read for me, and if I like your work we can arrange for you to test.'

He could hardly speak. 'Test?'

'If the reading works out. Here.' She handed him a script from her desk. 'Take this outside. Study it for a while, then when you're ready tell my receptionist and I'll see you again.'

He stood and grabbed the script. 'Hey – you're not gonna regret this. I'll be great.'

She nodded. 'I hope so.'

He hesitated by the door. 'Uh – which part?'

She laughed aloud. 'I bet you don't even know what the film's about.'

He regained a little of his strut. 'Who does? Every casting director in town is pissed 'cos they can't get their hands on it. If I walked out with this copy now I could probably make myself a few bucks.'

'And maybe lose the part of Vinnie.'

'Vinnie. Right on!' He bolted from her office clutching the script.

She watched him go. He had a quality she liked – plus devastating good looks and a certain vulnerability.

Yes. Buddy Hudson certainly had it. Now . . . If he could only act.

Elaine lay on a sunbed, quite naked apart from small plastic eye covers. She had abandoned the Sony earphones in favour of pure undiluted thought. How to have the best party in town? How to make it fun and exciting – the kind of party that people were talking about for days after?

The mix. That was the most important ingredient. However great the food, the decor, the music, it all came down to the mix. If the people weren't right then you may as well not bother.

Bibi and Adam Sutton came first of course. If you had them you were guaranteed acceptance from most of the other guests. Since bumping into Bibi at the Bistro Gardens Elaine had called her twice. Both times she had been blocked by Bibi's officious secretary who faithfully promised Mrs. Sutton would return her calls. So far she had not.

Elaine turned on her side and threw one arm up and back over her head. She had decided to obtain a light tan for her party, and the sun solarium was certainly better than sitting out in the real thing ruining your skin forever. She wished that Ross would stop baking himself to a deep mahogany, etching the lines even more deeply into his skin.

A sharp buzzing sound, and the full length machine automatically turned itself off. Thankfully she slipped from the clear plastic bed and studied herself in a full length wall mirror. Every inch of her gleamed radiantly. But there was no one to admire her gloriously glowing body, and Ross probably wouldn't even notice.

She frowned. Maybe it was about time she had some *fun*. But with whom? Her choice was limited if not downright nonexistent. After the dentist and the small time actor she had definitely decided affairs were not worth the bother. And the sex hadn't been up to much either.

You're spoiled, Elaine. After Ross, where would you turn? The Conti schlong is legendary.

She smiled at her reflection. Maybe if she got him the script, and Maralee *had* promised. And then maybe if she got Sadie La Salle to the party and she became his agent.

Good God! What kind of thinking was *that*? Did she have to get her husband in a good mood to lay her?

Well . . . it would certainly help.

Buddy bounced out of the Easterne production building on Sunset, and he was flying. The role of Vinnie was written for *him* – no doubt about it. He had given a dynamite reading, and the lady in the tinted glasses and cowboy boots – Montana Gray – she wasn't his type, but he had to admit that she was something else in the looks department – had said that he was impressive. Yeah – impressive had been the word she'd used. And then – more magic words – 'It looks like we're going to have to test you,' she had said calmly.

Hot shit! How could she stay so calm?

'Hey –' he had exclaimed, and then louder and wilder, 'Hey! Hey! Hey!' With a flourish he had grabbed her by the waist and whirled her round the room.

She extracted herself from his grasp and fled behind her desk, where, alarmed by his lack of control, she had started in on a whole speech about how it was only a test and she would be testing other actors and not to get too high on something that might only result in disappointment.

Didn't she know that testing for a major role in a major movie was the best thing that had ever happened to him in his whole goddamn life!

'Who is your agent?' she had asked.

Agent! Who had an agent?

'Uh, like I'm kinda between agents,' he had managed.

'I see. Let my secretary know where we can contact you, and you'll be hearing from us with a date.'

'When?'

'Maybe in a week or two.'

'Do I get to take a script with me so I can prepare?'

'My secretary will give you the pages I'd like you to work on.'

So he was walking tall. In spite of the fact that he still had no idea where he and Angel would be spending the night.

Goddamn Randy. Why couldn't he stay in Palm Springs with the mother and daughter act?

He needed a good agent. The fact that he was testing for Neil Gray's film should be enough to tempt *any* smart agent to sign him up – pronto. He would go to the biggies – William Morris, ICM, Sadie La Salle.

His old Pontiac sitting in a no-parking zone looked like a lump of rotting tin. The *first* thing he would do when he scored some big bucks would be to get himself proper wheels. A Caddy, a Merc, maybe even a Rolls. No, maybe not. A Rolls wasn't his image. Something sporty would suit him better. One of those Italian jobs or perhaps an imported Jaguar XJS. Now there was a car!

Jeez! He was finally on his way! He was going to be a star!

He opened up the door of the car, got in, and sat there silently buzzing with excitement.

Two hours later he was down again. Somehow he had gotten the idea that now that he was testing everything would change. His luck was on the rise and a good gambler always followed his luck. So, accordingly, he had presented himself at the William Morris Agency expecting action, and all he had got was a 'leave your name and number' from a secretary with about as much understanding as a slab of concrete. The same story at ICM. And at Sadie La Salle's office a mini skirted monster had told him to send in a photo, a biography, and a list of his credits. Didn't the dumb idiot recognize a new star when she saw one?

He left the office on Canon in a fury, and slumped into his car which had now collected a parking ticket. It was then that he noticed the small white card on the floor and quickly he picked it up. JASON SWANKLE was printed in raised type neatly on the centre of the card, and down in the left hand corner it read INTERIOR DESIGN PERSONAL SERVICE, and there was an address and a phone number.

Buddy kicked the old car into action. Well . . . What did he have to lose?

Not a lot.

*

It was madness of course. He was exhausted from a weekend in her company, but when Gina Germaine called, Neil Gray came running. He had looked at the whole situation very logically, decided she had to be dropped from his life, and then decided to *hump* her out of his system.

They made love on her whorish pink quilted bed. Then she went down on him in her whorish pink padded bathroom with the heart shaped tub in the centre of the fur rug.

Two orgasms left him dripping with sweat, his heart beating like a sledge hammer. 'Enough,' he managed to gasp when she started to play with his limp organ yet again.

'You could never be enough for me,' breathed Gina, wondering how far she could go with the dialogue. Not too far, Neil was smarter than most men, although once you got their pants off part of their brain seemed to disintegrate and you could say whatever you liked and they would believe it.

'I've got to go,' Neil said weakly. 'Preproduction on a movie is the most important time of all, *and* my lovely lady, *you* are causing me to neglect my responsibilities.'

'I understand,' she murmured sympthetically. 'But we do seem to have something special together, don't we? We make sparks fly.'

Why did women always have to make such a big deal out of simple fucking?

'Of course we do,' he agreed, thinking of Montana and feeling more than a twinge of guilt.

The afternoon sunshine filtered through the bathroom blinds, and he suddenly felt totally ridiculous lounging on the fur covered floor of Gina's over decorated bathroom. The pounding of his heart was slackening somewhat. Christ! A session with Gina Germaine was probably equivalent to a week's workout at the health club.

He stood up. 'I'll have a shower if I may.'

She was mildly turned on by his Richard Burton accent, but the real appeal was his talent. 'You may *have* whatever you like.' She stretched provocatively.

It *was* one of the most beautiful bodies in Hollywood. And she knew it. He stepped into the shower, turning the control knob until the water that hit his body was bracingly cold. When he emerged, Gina had slipped a lacy bra and French knickers over her nakedness. She held a large bath towel ready for him to dry himself with. 'Neil,' she murmured softly. 'I have a confession.'

141

'What?' Briskly he dried himself, feeling refreshed and ready to get back to work.

'Well . . .' She hesitated as if reluctant to proceed.

'What?' he repeated, reaching for his shorts.

'When we were in Palm Beach I sneaked a copy of *Street People* from your suitcase and read it.'

He was surprised. Gina had never struck him as a reader. 'You did?'

'I did.' Her voice became crisp and businesslike, all trace of hesitant dumbness gone. 'And Neil, I *loved* it. And I'll tell you something else, the role of Nikki is perfect for me – *so so* perfect.'

He was speechless. Nikki! The innocent unspoiled beauty. The untouched-by-life sweet young girl. Nikki! Was Gina making some kind of obscure joke?

'You see, Neil,' she continued earnestly. 'The whole of my career I've been typecast. Cunty dumb blondes with hearts of gold – and let me tell you something, that kind of part is not the real me.' She paused for breath, then plunged on, her huge bosom heaving with emotion. 'Neil,' she stated dramatically. 'The real me *is* Nikki. Everyone sees Gina Germaine, the big sexy film star. Underneath the dazzle lurks a vulnerable girl. A child of *life*!'

Where, for fuck's sake, was she getting her dialogue?

'I want to do your film,' she continued, her round blue eyes protruding alarmingly. 'I *have* to do your film. I'm right for it, I don't care what anyone says. *I know*.'

'Gina . . . I don't know what to say . . .' he managed, while he tried to think of what he *could* say. If he wasn't bedding her it would be easy – enough actresses had pitched him for a part and he had always dealt with the situation in an honest fashion – sometimes a brutal one. 'I know that you're a good actress –'

'That's a load of garbage,' she interrupted fiercely. 'You've never seen me *do* anything decent.'

'Yes I have,' he lied.

'And you're just about to tell me that I'm not right for Nikki?'

He chose his words carefully. 'What I *am* about to tell you is that you are too big a star to even consider a role like that.'

She was silent for a moment, staring at him with eyes full of resentment.

He reached for the rest of his clothes and began to dress. The sooner he was out of this conversation and out of her house the better.

'I think I should tell you that I am prepared to do a test for this part,' she said slowly. 'And if that doesn't convince you . . .'

He imagined Montana's expression if he told her that Gina Germaine wanted to test for the part of Nikki. The whole thing was nonsensical.

'Why don't I think about it?' he said soothingly.

'Why don't you think about the fact that I have a hidden video camera in my bedroom?' She had not been married to street smart Maxie Sholto for nothing.

'You have *what*?' he groaned.

'All I want to do is test,' she said sweetly. 'Then it'll be entirely up to you whether I'm right or not.'

'We're moving, sweet stuff,' Buddy said, entering the apartment and swinging Angel off her feet.

'Moving? I don't understand.' She looked puzzled.

'Yup.' He kissed her on the lips. 'Buddy Boy's gonna be a star an' we're movin' on.'

'Oh, Buddy! You got the part!'

'Well . . . kind of . . . Like they want me to test. But y'know, that's only a formality. I mean *everyone* tests – even Brando had to test before he got "The Godfather".'

'He did?'

He kissed her again. 'Sure. I told you – everyone does it.'

She smiled sweetly. 'I knew that something good would happen for us soon, and I was right.'

He patted her belly. 'Something good already happened, didn't it?'

She nodded happily. 'You're really pleased about the baby, aren't you?'

'Hey – of course I am.' And now that things were looking up – he was. Bye bye abortion. Hello baby. 'Why even ask?' he added, hugging her tightly.

She lowered her eyes. 'It's just that . . . well . . . this morning – when I told you . . . well . . .'

'I know. I kinda ran out of here. But I had a lot on my mind. You gotta understand me, babe, business first, then I can relax.'

'Oh, Buddy.' She snuggled close to him. 'I do love you.'

'Me too, sweet stuff, me too.'

'And we're going to be very happy, aren't we?'

'Happy. Rich. Famous. You name it.' He pushed her gently away.

'Hey – we really are moving. I forgot to tell you – Randy called and he needs the place.'

She was dismayed. 'When?'

'Would you believe tomorrow?'

'No –'

He held up an authoritative hand. 'Do not panic. I got us a place that is going to blow your little mind.'

'Where?'

'Questions, questions. We shall pack up, kiddo, and you will see for yourself.'

While Angel got their things together he decided to take a swim. It had been some day. A mixture of luck and shit. His adrenaline was racing full tilt. He needed to clear his head and relax. How one day could change your life. He was to be a father. He was to be a star. He had made contact with Jason Swankle and whether that was good or bad remained to be seen. But it had certainly turned out to be useful.

Jason Swankle's emporium was on Robertson Boulevard, an elegant glass fronted shop with spacious and luxurious offices in the back. Buddy had decided against calling first, a face to face confrontation was always best. Find out what he wanted, hopefully not his body. Buddy had never gone the gay route. Oh yeah – in his few wild months with Maxie Sholto he had been involved in plenty of far-out scenes, but always with females. Sometimes other men joined in with the girls, but they never went near Buddy. Oh no, he always made that clear up-front, however stoned he was. The closest had been the fat record producer on the night Buddy had freaked and smashed up a camera when he had discovered it filming the scene. He still shook with anger when he thought about it – which of course he tried not to – as with many other thoughts that slipped into his head – things he never wanted to think about again – but which refused to go away.

His friend Tony for example. Lying on a cold slab of concrete. Fourteen years old. Murdered by a bunch of fairies getting their rocks off.

Sometimes he saw the face of the man who had picked them up. A shifty face with small weasel eyes.

And the host of the party. Butterball. A plump babysoft man with a welcoming smile and the handshake of a dead fish.

Buddy saw them clearly every day – along with his mother. Naked. Smiling in triumph.

How he wished he could get rid of the images, just wash them away. But they were permanent, always with him. And he had no intention of adding any more nightmares.

'Can I do anything for you?' a sandy haired man in a light beige suit with matching moustache inquired as Buddy strode into Jason's shop. Only it wasn't a shop as such, it was more a showroom exhibiting exclusive Italian furniture and a few well placed antiques.

Buddy sprang Jason's card between thumb and forefinger, and waved it at the man. 'He wanted to see me,' he said.

'Mr. Swankle?'

'Well I ain't here to see Ronnie Reagan.'

The sandy haired man looked down his nose in disgust. How he hated these flashy macho types who acted like they owned the world just because they were so butch. This one stunk of raw sex, *and* he knew it, *and* what was even worse he *flaunted* it. 'I'll see if Mr. Swankle is available. Who shall I say wishes to see him?'

'Buddy Hudson. And *he* wants to see *me*.'

Sandy-hair retreated to the back of the store, while Buddy wandered around admiring the goods. There were leather couches, marble tables, carved lamps, and cut glass bowls filled with fresh roses. The place had class. Even he could see that.

Sandy-hair returned in minutes, his thin lips pursed disdainfully beneath his wispy moustache. 'Mr. Swankle will see you now.'

Jason Swankle's office was a large white room filled with greenery, flowered couches, and a huge marble slab of a table covered in drawings and designs. On the walls were a series of framed David Hockney boy-in-swimming-pool drawings.

Jason himself stood centre stage. He wore a pink safari suit with a pale green silk shirt and a pink rose pinned to his jacket.

Shag, the randy bulldog, slumbered on the thick pile rug making asthmatic breathing sounds. As soon as Buddy entered the room the dog woke, growled, and hurled itself at Buddy's leg, intent on carrying on where it had left off at their last meeting.

'Jesus Christ!' snapped Buddy, kicking the growling dog off. 'Can't you control this fuckin' animal?'

'Shag!' shrieked Jason. 'Down boy. AT ONCE.'

Reluctantly the dog obeyed, and slouched back to its place on the rug.

'So sorry,' said Jason with a friendly chuckle. 'I don't know why he always picks on you.'

'Nor do I,' complained Buddy, sensing at once that he could ask

Jason Swankle for anything he wanted and probably get it. Lovelight was shining out of the plump man's round blue eyes.

'Can I offer you a drink?' Jason fluttered, indicating a laden drinks trolley.

Buddy sat himself down on the edge of one of the flowered couches. 'Yeah. Why not. Vodka on ice. No mix.'

'Certainly. My pleasure.'

While Jason fixed his drink Buddy studied him carefully. He was a short, rounded man of about forty. He wore a bad hair piece, a fake tan, and the lavish jewelley that adorned his person was most definitely genuine. What was he doing with a freak like Gladrags? Silly question. What did he *think* they were doing – playing tennis?

As if reading his mind Jason said quickly, 'I do hope you have forgiven the way Marvin behaved to you the other day. He was *so* rude. It was inexcusable. I told him so, of course. He was very sorry.'

Oh sure! Marvin Gladrags Jackson sorry. That *would* be the day.

Buddy wondered how much Jason knew. Was he aware of the fact that his live-in friend had run a male call-boy service, and that he, Buddy, had been one of the boys?

Right on cue again Jason said, 'You see, you startled Marvin. His past is behind him now, he has *me* to look after him. I enlarged his premises,' delicate laugh at the double entendre, 'and now the clothes store is enough to keep him busy. He doesn't need to run that silly escort service any more, it's quite unnecessary.'

Escort service! Yeah!

'It's been a while, and you coming to our private residence and everything . . . It upset him.'

'I didn't mean to do that,' Buddy said, going along with the story. 'But I've been out of town an' I needed to score a fast buck, so I figured to look up old Gla – uh – Marvin, an' see if there was any action around. Y'know, tourist lady wanting to visit Disneyland – like that.'

'Believe me, I understand.' Jason handed him his drink in a mirrored glass and deliberately touched hands. Buddy snatched his away. 'That's why I came after you,' Jason added. 'I just hate to see Marvin behave that way. I thought that I might make it up to you.'

Here came the pitch. *Forget it. I don't need money that bad.* Buddy gulped his drink, the ice cold against his teeth.

'I wondered if you might be interested in doing me a favour,' Jason continued. 'For a fee, of course.'

'What favour?' Buddy asked guardedly.

Jason sat down on the flowered couch. 'I have these two ladies coming to town. Very wealthy, one is a widow and it appears her late husband left her a sizeable chunk of Texas.' He paused to allow that relevant information to sink in. Satisfied that it had, he continued, 'The other woman, a divorcee, has bought a mansion in Bel Air. On her last visit she handed it over to me to do with what I will.'

Buddy frowned. 'Huh?'

'Decorate, dear boy. Rebuild. Refurbish.'

'Oh . . . yeah.' So where was all this leading?

'Now you are probably wondering what this has to do with you, and how you can help me.'

The guy was telepathic. 'Yeah. I was wondering.' Buddy stood, drained the vodka, and moved across the room.

'Well you see,' continued Jason secretively. 'Two women, alone in a city where they have no friends, they need entertaining.'

'What kind of . . . entertaining?' Buddy asked suspiciously. He was going to be a star now. All thoughts of going back into business had vanished. The body was no longer for sale.

Jason let forth a maniacal giggle. 'Nothing . . . intimate. Nothing like that at all.' He rose from the couch and padded across the room so that he was once again in close proximity to Buddy. 'What I had in mind was for you to take the ladies out to dinner, the theatre, a club or two. For which, of course,' he added hastily, 'I will pay you handsomely.'

'How much?'

Jason threw his arms wide. '*You* tell me.'

Buddy thought quickly. Two old broads in town for a couple of days. No sex. Only taking them around a bit. It was a breeze. 'I don't come cheap,' he ventured.

'Nothing worth having is cheap,' sniffed Jason.

'I'd need a new suit . . .'

'Certainly.'

'And you'd take care of all expenses?'

'Naturally.'

'What about a car?'

'Would a chauffeured Cadillac be suitable?'

Does Streisand sing? This was turning out to be too good to be true. Where was the catch? He took a deep breath. 'Five hundred a day.'

Jason didn't even blink. 'Done.'

147

Shit! He'd sold himself too cheap. There had to be a catch. He couldn't help himself. 'So what's the scam?'

Jason beamed happily. 'No . . . scam. I just want these ladies to be happy, and if they are happy, then maybe the one who owns half of Texas will buy herself a simple three or four million dollar house to be near her friend, and *guess* who will get to fix it over? *Do* encourage her, Buddy, won't you, dear boy.'

Buddy grinned. Foxy little fucker.

'I'll tell them you are my nephew,' Jason decided, posturing around the room. 'And that you're an actor.'

'I am.'

Jason sniffed. 'Of *course* you are.'

'No, really. I am. Like I'm gonna be testing soon for Neil Gray's new movie.'

'How exciting!'

'Yeah, it would be, but I got problems . . .'

'Can I help?' Jason asked sympathetically, laying a friendly hand on his arm.

'I got a wife –'

'Oh dear! That's a *big* problem.'

'She's great,' Buddy said defensively, edging away so that the warm hand slipped from his arm. 'She's not the problem at all.' He stared thoughtfully at Jason while his mind was buzzing. 'You see, it's like this . . . We're staying in a friend's apartment, and he's comin' back tomorrow – unexpectedly. He only let me know a few hours ago, so what with everything I've had no chance to get another place together. I'd *like* to escort your two ladies . . .' he shrugged eloquently, 'but in the circumstances I guess I'll have to pass.'

Jason was not slow in catching a point. 'Because you have nowhere to live?'

Buddy nodded and helped himself to another drink. 'Right. I mean I'm gonna be too busy tryin' to find a place. You understand?'

'But what if I can assist you?' Jason asked quickly. 'Hey –' Buddy exclaimed. 'If you came up with something that'd solve my problem. I mean *you* help me . . . I help *you* . . . an' we're all happy. Right?'

'Just you and a wife?' Jason asked doubtfully, having second thoughts. 'No children or animals?'

'You gotta be puttin' me on.'

For a moment Jason remained undecided, but something about the handsome young man with the smoky black eyes and tousled hair had gotten to him. He wanted him in his life. Plus the fact that the two women were no story. They *were* coming to town. And they *would* appreciate an escort, especially an escort that looked like Buddy Hudson. It would mean another large mansion to decorate . . . more commissions on everything from the toilet seats to the onyx ashtrays.

Of course it meant taking a risk. What did he know about Buddy Hudson? And then there was a wife involved. Probably some Hollywood tramp . . . One of these days Buddy would wake up to the fact that boys have more fun . . . And wouldn't it be simply gorgeous if it was he, Jason Swankle, who could convince him of this?

Abruptly he cleared his throat. 'I've just finished work on a beach house,' he said. 'In the Malibu Colony. The owner is in Europe and won't be returning for three or four weeks. If you promise to be *very* careful . . . and I do mean *very*. No entertaining or parties or anything like that.'

Je . . . *sus*! It *was* his day. And what a day! A house on the beach for crissakes!

'Well . . .' Jason continued. 'I don't see any reason why you couldn't stay there, temporarily of course,' he added hastily.

Don't jump at it, Buddy. Cool it. Let *him* convince *you*.

'Jeez. Sounds good, but I don't know . . .'

'Oh, but you must. I insist!'

And that's how it had come down. Everything in position.

It was now six-thirty, and the pool was packed. No chance of doing his thirty lengths with the water crowded with tired bodies just back from a hard day's grind. Disgusted, he turned to go back inside and ran straight into Shelly. Her hair was piled high in tight gleaming curls and her muscular body wore only the smallest of bikinis. A beach towel was slung casually over her shoulders.

'Hey – Shelly! How y'doin'?'

She regarded him quizzically. 'Seems *you're* doin' okay. Where's the nervous wreck zoomed out my apartment last night?'

He laughed self-consciously. 'I guess I was uptight.'

'Uptight! Ha!'

'I'm glad I ran into you.'

She stretched a long leg in front of her and rotated her ankle. 'Whyssat?'

'Because I looked into that movie you told me about and I'm testing. Can you believe it?'

'Sure I believe it. Why not? Your Karma's on an up.'

He leaned forward and kissed her lightly on the cheek. 'Thanks, Shell, I'll say goodbye, we're movin' out of this dump.'

149

'When?'

'Right now.'

'Wow! One test an' you really take it to heart.'

'I'm gonna be a star, kid. I'll give you a part in one of my movies.'

She laughed lewdly. 'There's only one part of yours I want.'

He grinned. 'Cut it out, I'm a married man.'

'Yeah. Tell me that in six months.' She winked. 'Anyway, good luck, I'll see you around.' Without a backward glance she headed for the pool, dropped her towel, and executed a graceful dive between the mass of bodies.

In other circumstances . . . If there wasn't Angel . . .

What the hell was he thinking of? Angel was his life, his love. Abruptly he shook his head and took the stairs two at a time.

They were moving on. And things could only get better.

It took Neil several days before he could even bring himself to mention Gina Germaine in Montana's presence. The blond bitch was *blackmailing* him. He was caught in her cheap little trap, and he was going to have to give her a test or suffer the consequences.

They were in Oliver Easterne's opulent office, amusingly decorated with framed telegrams from various directors and stars swearing they would never work with him again. Oliver, a sandy haired man in his late forties, was busy cleaning his desk with a chamois leather. He had a fetish about cleanliness that bordered on the ridiculous. If anyone so much as smoked a cigarette in his office he immediately washed out the ashtray.

Montana had been discussing several actors she wanted to test for the role of Vinnie, and then the conversation automatically led on to the girls for Nikki.

'If we get George Lancaster, they can both be unknowns. If we don't – then we gotta go with names,' insisted Oliver.

'You're repeating yourself,' said Montana coldly. 'Christ, Oliver, don't you think we know that by now? Neil can't put a fucking gun to George's head, we'll just have to wait.'

Oliver ignored her. 'Do you think you'll hear from George soon?' he asked Neil.

'I'm sure I will,' Neil replied. 'But while we're on the subject of stars I did have this rather interesting thought on the girl.'

'Who?' questioned Montana, lighting up a cigarette which put Oliver in a nervous sweat.

'Don't drop any ash,' he muttered. 'The carpet's new.'

150

Neil cleared his throat, then casually said, 'Gina Germaine wouldn't be bad.'

Montana snorted derisively. 'You *have* to be kidding!'

'Scrub off the make-up –'

'Cut off the tits –'

'She's big box office,' interrupted Oliver.

'Who gives a shit?' snapped Montana angrily. 'I don't believe we're even discussing her.'

'Big, big box office,' mused Oliver.

'All I had in mind was running a test on her,' Neil said quickly.

Montana raised a scornful eyebrow. 'Oh *did* you. How come we've never discussed it?'

'She'd never test,' Oliver interjected excitedly. 'Would she, Neil? Waddyathink?'

'I think she would,' Neil replied stiffly, well aware of his wife's angry stare. He walked over to the bar and topped up his glass with bourbon. 'And *I* like the idea.'

'Christ!' muttered Montana in disgust. 'I just don't know how you can even *think* of that bosomy freak playing Nikki.'

'Listen,' said Oliver quickly. 'If she'll do it what's to lose?'

Deliberately Montana allowed her ash to fall on his precious carpet.

'Watch the rug!' screamed Oliver in anguish.

'I'm going home,' she announced coldly. 'You have your car, don't you Neil?'

He nodded.

'Then I'll see you later.' She swept out in a fury. Gina Germaine! God almighty! Gina Germaine! When had Neil come up with *that* idea. And why hadn't he discussed it with her before mentioning it to Oliver?

She was furious. *Street People* was supposed to be their special project – but gradually she was being edged out. How dare Neil treat her like an assistant! Since getting back from Palm Beach he'd been a total pain. Surly, short tempered, and drinking like the old days. And as for sex – forget it. She was too busy to take much notice of his moodiness. She had put it down to the fact that he hadn't got a definite commitment from George Lancaster, and had made allowances because of that.

Fuck him! He surely knew the stupidity of mentioning Gina Germaine to Oliver before checking with her. *Fuck him!*

In the underground garage the attendant bid her good evening.

'I'll take my husband's car,' she said shortly. 'Give Mr. Gray mine.'

'Yes ma'am.' He rushed to get the gleaming red Maserati, and Montana tipped him and climbed into Neil's favourite toy. He hated her little Volkswagen. Let him walk if he didn't like it.

16

'How about twenny for hot times?' the hooker drawled. She was a stockily built bleached blonde who had forgotten about the roots of her hair which sprouted black and coarse.

'Too much,' Deke muttered, glancing furtively up and down the dimly lit street.

'I 'kin give ya a ten buck special blow job,' she announced proudly, as if offering a discount in the supermarket.

His teeth clenched. 'I don't want that,' he hissed.

She adjusted a torn bra strap beneath a sweat stained T-shirt. 'Take it or leave it. Twenny a screw. Ten a blow. What's it t'be?'

He wanted to slap her stupid sluttish face and walk away. But he couldn't. He needed her. There had been no one since Joey, and he needed to be close to someone.

'Where?' he asked gruffly.

'Hotel roun' the corner.'

She set off, tottering uncomfortably on six inch heels. She crossed the street and headed for a darkened alley positioned between a greasy diner and a porno magazine shop.

Deke followed closely behind her, sniffing at the trail of sweat and cheap scent she left in her wake. He had arrived in Pittsburgh only hours before after driving steadily all the way from New York. His newly acquired van had not let him down. Drove smooth and clean the whole way. And so it should. He had worked hard to get it exactly right. He'd had to spend a little money on new parts, but then he had expected to.

They entered the alley, and the hooker began to whistle a tuneless rendition of the Beatles song, 'Eleanor Rigby'.

The alley was dark and filled with the stench of rotting garbage. Deke followed the whistling girl as she clattered along.

Hookers. Whores. Prostitutes.

Women.

All the same. All there for just one thing.

Greedy grabbing hands. Slack lustful bodies.

Joey had been different. Joey had never regarded him as just another john. Joey had truly cared about him. Joey had –

The first blow caught him on the side of the head and knocked him to the ground where he was kicked in the stomach by a steel-toed boot. The pain surprised him.

Desperately he tried to roll himself into a tight ball as vomit came rushing from his mouth, and with it a fast rising rage as vicious as the kicks that were aimed at his crumpled body.

'C'mon, get the motherfucker's money an' let's get outta here,' he heard the hooker say.

Then hands were roughly tearing at his lumber jacket, searching for a wallet, a stack of bills, anything.

They had caught him off guard just like his two assailants on the streets of New York. Only he had shown *them*, hadn't he. And these two would get the same treatment.

With a sudden urgent scream he lunged out, grabbing at legs, pulling and throwing off balance.

A shape fell on top of him and he heard a sharp curse, then muffled laughter before something exploded on the side of his head and everything faded to blackness.

The car impressed Joey. She grinned with delight when he turned up with it an hour after her request.

It was a black Camaro, and getting into it and hot wiring the engine had given him no trouble at all. He only hoped that the owner was staying home and not planning any night trips. If that was the case, then, if Joey didn't want to stay too long in Atlantic City, he would have it back in the same parking place long before morning, and no one would be any the wiser. Especially if he gassed it up before returning it.

'Crazee!' exclaimed Joey, looking the car over before climbing in. 'Clever cowboy!'

She made him feel ten feet tall. Who had ever called him clever before? Certainly none of the sour-faced girls he had dated. He knew what they thought of him, a couple had even gone so far as to tell him. 'You're boring, Deke. Sorry to say, but you're too dull for me.'

Joey was prettier and brighter. She saw him as he really was. She didn't see dull, she saw a quiet intelligence. She didn't see boring, she saw a man who was prepared to go out and hot wire a car for her.

She was a terrific girl.

She was a prostitute.

The two facts didn't gel.

The drive to Atlantic City was wild, with Joey giggling and shrieking and urging him to go faster and faster. When they arrived they didn't go to the beach, but to the brightly lit casinos, where Joey played the slots, her cheeks red with excitement as she fed quarter after quarter to the hungry machines.

Later, she wanted to stay. 'Book us a room,' she whispered. 'I wanna screw you in Atlantic City.'

He was worried about getting the car back before morning. And he hadn't told his parents he would be out all night. He didn't dare tell Joey his reasons not to stay, she would only laugh at him, and that's the one thing he hated more than anything.

People laughing at him . . .

'I don't want to stay,' he said finally.

'Don't then, but I will. I like it here,' she replied cheerfully. 'I can hitch a ride back tomorra.'

He didn't want to leave her, but there was no choice, so he bid her goodbye on the boardwalk at three in the morning, and the last he saw of her was her hip swaying walk as she headed back into one of the casinos.

She did not return to Philadelphia for six weeks. He was frantic. Twice he stole cars and drove back to Atlantic City looking for her, but she was never around.

He lived his life waiting for her to return, and when she did, white faced, with bloodshot black circled eyes, he shook her by the shoulders and demanded to know where she'd been.

'Fuck you, man,' she muttered. 'You don't own me. I can do what I like.'

'Not if you're my wife you can't,' he replied vehemently, wild with burning jealousy. 'I want to marry you, Joey. I want to look after you. I want us to be together always.'

She had endured six weeks of being abused by men. In fact she had endured a life of being abused by men. She was tired and sick and zonked out from too many uppers and downers. She was disgusted with life, her own life in particular.

Deke Andrews was a real weirdo, but he seemed to care for her.

'Okay bigshot,' she sighed wearily. 'Name the day.'

*

154

Voices. Far off.

A sick feeling. A sick *smell*.

He opened his eyes and a flashlight beam hit him in the face. An involuntary groan escaped his lips.

'It's all right. We got an ambulance comin',' the large cop standing over him announced.

His own vomit stained his clothes. He knew without looking that the money he carried in his inside pocket was gone.

'How many were there?' the cop asked.

Automatically he tested his arms, then his legs. Nothing seemed to be broken, although everything hurt. 'What?' he mumbled. There was dried blood on his lips, and he could make out a few idle onlookers in the gloom of the alley where he lay on the ground.

'How many?' the cop repeated.

Shakily he stood. 'I wasn't mugged,' he said. 'I got drunk . . . must have fallen. Don't need an ambulance, I'm fine.'

'Don't give me that shit!' the cop blurted. 'You've been ripped off an' I want to know who did it.'

'No sir. Not me.' He began to shuffle away. 'Just fell down drunk.'

'Goddamn it!' exclaimed the cop in exasperated fury. 'Next time I'll let you lie there.'

Deke kept walking. The sooner he was away from the cop the better. The van was parked several blocks away, the keys down the side of his boot along with the bulk of his money. Lucky that he knew the wisdom of never walking the streets with money in the expected place. The bastard pigs had only found the fifty dollars he kept in the zipped inside pocket of his lumber jacket. They had missed the big haul. Five hundred bucks in fifty dollar bills. Every cent he had made in New York while working shifts at the hotel, less the money he had paid out for the van.

He was filled with rage. At himself for falling into such a stupid trap. At the grabbing hooker. At her accomplice who probably thought he was so clever.

Deke Andrews was clever. *He* was the one who was getting away with murder . . .

He reached the van and viciously kicked at a tyre.

They would pay for it. He had heard them laughing just before he had passed out . . . laughing at him . . . laughter . . .

They would pay. There was plenty of time to take care of them before continuing on his journey.

17

Three days after Elaine asked her, Maralee, good friend that she was, came through with the script. She phoned Elaine early in the morning to tell her that it had not been easy.

Elaine was thrilled. Twenty minutes later she arrived at Maralee's sweeping house on Rodeo Drive where several Mexican gardeners worked on the perfect front lawn, and another Mexican answered the door.

'You should put up a notice, illegal immigrants' working hostel!' Elaine joked.

Maralee smiled. 'None of them speaks a word of English. It's wonderful. So peaceful.'

'I can imagine!' murmured Elaine, following her friend into the huge living room where a genuine Picasso hung above the marble fireplace, and a potpourri of original art decorated the walls. They sat on an ivory couch while a maid served coffee and peach danish.

'How are the party plans progressing?' Maralee inquired. 'Do we have an answer from dear Bibi?'

'No. I've left three messages, and she has not yet felt it necessary to call me back.'

'Hmmm . . .' Maralee looked thoughtful. 'What you need is bait. The party should be for someone. Andy Warhol, Diana Vreeland, a visiting New Yorker is always useful – Bibi adores that sort of thing. Now let's see . . . anyone you can think of?'

Elaine shrugged helplessly.

Maralee suddenly clapped her hands together. 'I've got it! Perfect!'

'Who?'

'Pamela London and George Lancaster. Karen told me they're coming in at the end of the month.'

Elaine liked the idea immediately. She knew it would guarantee an excellent turnout if she threw the party for them, but Ross might not like the idea, and she had only met Pamela London once, and briefly at that.

Still . . . Karen could sound them out . . . Important people always liked having parties thrown for them. God! It would cost a fortune, she'd never get away with fifty people as she had originally planned. *Think of it as an investment, Elaine.* What a coup it would be. Everyone would want to come. Absolutely everyone. It could be the hottest party of the year.

She felt excitement creeping over her body like a rash. She could see the columns now:

Jody Jacobs:

ELAINE AND ROSS CONTI HOSTED THE BEST PARTY BEVERLY HILLS ELITE HAS SEEN IN A LONG TIME LAST NIGHT . . .

Army Archerd:

ELAINE CONTI THE HOSTESS WHO KNOWS HOW TO PACK THE STARS WALL TO WALL . . .

Hank Grant:

PARTY QUEEN ELAINE!!

'I'll call Karen as soon as I get home,' she said excitedly.

'Good.' Maralee picked up a large manila envelope and handed it to her. 'Here'sthe script. Now that's two favours I've done for you, and I want one in return.'

Elaine held the envelope happily. She couldn't wait to give the script to Ross, contact Karen, and get things moving on the party.

'Name it. It's yours.'

Maralee tried to appear casual as she spoke, but two red spots lit up her cheeks and Elaine noticed that her eyes seemed unusually bright.

'Remember I was telling you about that man I met in Palm Springs . . .'

'Andy something?'

'Randy Felix.'

Elaine nodded.

'He's here, in town, and I thought it would be nice if the four of us had dinner.'

'Fine. When?'

Maralee looked flustered. 'It's not fine . . . I mean it is, but I don't know if he has any money . . . and I can't *ask* him . . . and well . . . I'm sure he'd love to meet Ross, and you're so good with people . . .'

'Why don't you have him checked out?'

'I don't want to do that.'

Elaine was sympathetic. 'You like him, is that it?'

Maralee grinned. 'Yes.'

'Good. So we'll meet him, and I'll let you know what I think.'

'I don't want another bad experience,' Maralee sighed.

Since her divorce from Neil, her track record with men was disastrous. Invariably she attracted the fortune hunters and penniless studs, with an occasional drunk thrown in for good measure. They spent her money, roughed her up, and daddy had to send in the heavies to get rid of them. She was totally weak when it came to men.

'How about La Scala, Friday night?' Elaine suggested.

Maralee nodded thankfully. 'Perfect. I'll arrange to have the check taken care of before-hand so that Randy won't be embarrassed.'

'Wouldn't hear of it. It's our treat.' Elaine stood and aimed a kiss at her friend's cheek. 'Now I must run. Thanks for everything. La Scala, Friday. See you there at seven-thirty.'

Everything happened so quickly. It was like Jason Swankle had taken over his life. The trip to Malibu, and Jason there to greet them. 'He's an old friend.' Buddy had explained to Angel, 'who owes me a favour.' She had bought that. No reason why she shouldn't. And if she'd had any doubts about anything, they were all swept away when she feasted her eyes on the house. What a place! Small, but prime beachfront and decorated like a futuristic fantasy. All white, chrome, and electronic, with insane speakers everywhere and quadraphonic stereo equipment that could bring tears to your eyes it was so great.

The house was on two floors, the lower floor a glass fronted living room overlooking the ocean, and the upper floor one big bedroom dominated by a water bed.

'Please,' Jason insisted. 'Be most careful.'

'We will Mr. Swankle,' Angel replied, wide-eyed and thrilled. 'I've always dreamed of a place like this and you can be sure we'll look after it as if it were our own.'

Jason was relieved. Buddy's wife was no Hollywood tramp as he had imagined. She was young and starry-eyed. Exceptionally pretty. But dull. He could accept her, she was no rival. He left, fully satisfied that lending them the house was not a rash move. And anyway, it was only for a few weeks.

Buddy and Angel settled in overnight. They spoke of Buddy's forthcoming test, read the few pages of script together, and later warmed frozen pizza in the microwave. Then they made long leisurely love on the waterbed.

'I love you, Buddy,' Angel told him many times. 'I love you *so so* much.'

He luxuriated in her adoration. He lay on the bed and imagined that the house was his, and that he was a star, and that no one, but no one, could take it away from him. Later he slept, and the nightmare faces came back to haunt him. But in the morning, when Jason's chauffeured car arrived, he was in good shape. He had jogged along the shoreline, swum in the icy surf, and eaten a solid breakfast of bacon and eggs.

He left Angel the keys of the Pontiac and fifty bucks. Jason had advanced him two hundred on his forthcoming date. The ladies were due in town in a couple of days, and Jason wanted to fit him out with some new threads before their arrival. He wasn't about to argue with *that*. He had thought that they would go to Gladrags' store, but this was not to be; when the car collected Jason, he instructed the driver to the most exclusive, expensive men's shop on Rodeo Drive, Bijan, where they spent three hours putting together two outfits.

Buddy could hardly believe his luck. All this for just taking out a couple of old broads?

'I get to keep the clothes, don't I?' he asked confidently.

'Of course,' Jason replied, beaming. 'Now. How about some lunch? Does Ma Maison appeal to you?'

Ma Maison appealed to him all right, but maybe being seen in such a restaurant with Jason Swankle was not the best idea in the world. The dude was an obvious queen, and everyone would think he was his boy . . . Shit! Not a good idea at all. He had seen the looks the salesmen had exchanged when he was trying on clothes and parading them for approval.

'No . . .' he hesitated. 'I really don't feel like heavy food. I'm into not eating too much.'

'But you could order something simple,' Jason insisted. 'The duck salad is quite divine!' He kissed his fingertips in fervent appreciation.

Buddy shook his head. 'I gotta get back to the beach, study my lines, y'know?'

Jason nodded understandingly. 'I'll send the driver for you at noon tomorrow, we'll have lunch then.'

'I don't think –'

'We simply must. I want to introduce you to Patrick, the owner of Ma Maison. When you take the ladies there for dinner I don't want you to walk in like a tourist.'

'Yeah, well –'

159

'Tomorrow,' Jason stated firmly.

There was no getting out of it.

Montana took Neil's Maserati, drove the hell out of it all the way to the beach, then zoomed along the Pacific Coast Highway, stopping only for a hamburger and a Coke. They were trying to edge her out. She knew it! She felt it! Bastards! *Street People* was her creation, and no way was she letting go.

George Lancaster . . . Gina Germaine . . . Did they want to make a piece of shit? The kind of movie Oliver was famous for. She had thought Neil had more style. She tuned the radio to a heavy rock station, smoked continually, and gradually calmed down.

What was she getting so excited about? So he wanted to test some busty dumb blonde. So what? Once he saw her on the screen playing Nikki he would know immediately how wrong she was for the part. So would Oliver.

Two major assholes. Men. Probably dazzled by Gina's outsize assets. She was making too big a deal over it. Getting pissed off because Neil hadn't mentioned it to her first. Well, she had four actors lined up to test for Vinnie, and she had no intention of asking his opinion until he viewed them up on the screen. Making movies meant taking risks. There was no way of knowing what would happen once an actor or actress got in front of the camera. It could be magic, it could be zilch. Maybe Gina – with the right clothes, hairstyle, direction . . . Unlikely, but maybe . . .

Let Neil and Oliver play their stupid Hollywood games. She was no idiot. She could play too if that's what they wanted.

She arrived home to find Neil asleep, with the television on. She didn't wake him.

The next morning they were scrupulously polite to each other, discussing locations over breakfast before departing for their day's activities.

'Oh, by the way,' Montana said casually, as she walked towards her car, 'If you *really* feel you have to test Gina Germaine – go ahead. Maybe she's got something that I haven't latched onto.'

'What do you mean by that?' he snapped defensively.

She frowned. 'Nothing earth shattering. But it would have been nice if you'd discussed it with me before telling Oliver.'

'I meant to,' he said weakly.

'By the way,' she continued, 'I've decided to direct the tests on the actors I've picked. You've no objections to that have you?'

He was relieved at the change of subject. 'I think it's an excellent idea.'

'Good. I want to set them up soon.'

'The sooner the better.'

She climbed into her car and drove off without another word.

Neil took a deep breath. It looked like everything was going to be all right. Test Gina. The test would stink. He would be off the hook.

Just who exactly did he think he was kidding?

Street People. What a property. What a *great part* for him.

Ross placed the script on the coffee table in the den. He shut his eyes and leaned back with a deep sigh. For a moment he sat silently. It was late and he was tired, but he was also exhilarated, his mind alive with ideas. It was one o'clock in the morning, and he had been reading solidly for two hours.

MAC. FIFTY YEARS OLD. A STREET COP FOR ALL OF HIS ADULT LIFE. CYNICAL AND TOUGH. BUT WITH A LOT OF COMPASSION AND HOPE FOR THE FUTURE. A WORLD WEARY MAN WITH OLD FASHIONED VALUES.

It was an Oscar nomination role, no doubt about that. Of course, it was not the sort of part that he had ever played before. A man of fifty. Forget it.

What the fuck do you mean – forget it? You are no longer the boy wonder. You are fifty, or at least you will be this year.

Would his public accept him in such a role?

What frigging public? They gave up stampeding your movies a long time ago. Now half of 'em see you in some old movie on television and they think you're dead for crissake.

He rose from the couch and went to the bar where he fixed himself a scotch on the rocks. *Street People.* It was strange knowing a woman had written it. She got inside a man's head. She put down thoughts and feelings that he had imagined only men knew about.

You're a definite chauvinist pig, you know that? Your ideas are corny and out of date. You'd better start thinking today – or you'll find yourself in an elephant's graveyard for old-time movie stars.

Jesus! He wanted the part. He wanted it so badly he could taste it.

Twenty-five years of movies.

Twenty-five years of shit.

He sipped his scotch, rolled the booze across his tongue, allowed it to trickle slowly down his throat.

He was calm, excited, nervous, confident. Christ! He didn't know *what* he was. He only knew that whatever it took he *had* to have that part. *Had to.*

But how to convince everyone? How to convince Oliver Easterne, Neil and Montana Gray?

Oliver was a hustler, a money-man. He wouldn't see talent if it climaxed all over his deal-making face.

Neil Gray was an overblown English egotist. Talented but a total pain.

Montana Gray he didn't even know.

Sadie La Salle, you asshole. She could get you the part. She weaves magic in this town. She has the power.

Yes. Sadie. She would *know* he was right for it. She would *know* he was capable of playing the hell out of it.

Had Elaine invited her to the party yet? Had she got a yes or no? He hurried into their bedroom.

Elaine slept soundly, her hair held back from her face with a white alice band. Her face itself liberally smeared with some kind of Royal Jelly which Ross had unkindly christened 'bees come'. She hid her eyes beneath a black sleep mask, and snored softly.

Ross stared down at her, he had given her a tough day, and he felt sorry now. But sometimes she bugged him with all her nagging and Beverly Hills bullshit. She had come rushing back from Maralee Gray's clutching the script as if it were stock in IBM. Thrusting it at him she said triumphantly, 'There you are. How's *that* for service?'

Perversely he tossed the manuscript to one side.

'Aren't you going to read it?'

'Later,' he said, enjoying her look of annoyed frustration.

He kept it up all day long, dying to read the damn thing, but stubbornly refusing to pick it up while Elaine was around.

They had dinner, watched a movie on television, and then she swept off to bed. He had fixed himself a drink, made himself comfortable, and started to read.

'Honey, wake up.' He shook her roughly.

She shrieked. 'Who is it? What? God!' Frantically she pulled off her sleep mask, blinked twice, then said, 'What the hell is it, Ross? You frightened the life out of me.'

'It's frigging marvellous, that's what it is,' he said excitedly.

'Are you drunk?'

'No. I am not drunk. I am very sober.' He sat down on the side of the bed. 'Have you called Sadie La Salle?'

She struggled to consult her bedside clock. 'It's one fifteen in the morning. Is that what you woke me up to find out?'

'It's important . . .'

'Goddamn it! Surely it could have waited until morning?'

He reached out and playfully rubbed his finger over her cheek. 'You're covered in bees come again.'

'I do wish you wouldn't say that.'

'Why? Does it make you horny?' As he said it he could feel the sap rising. Automatically he reached for her breasts.

'Ross –' Elaine began to object, then thought better of it. Just because she wasn't prepared did not mean she shouldn't grab the opportunity when it arose.

They went through their familiar ritual. Marital sex was like a favourite meal. Good but predictable. She had given up wishing that Ross would do something different. He had his routine and he stuck to it religiously.

No more than ten minutes passed before they both climaxed. Her first. Him second. He might have the biggest dick in Hollywood but it still only took ten minutes.

After, he lit cigarettes for them both and said, 'Good, huh.' He always said, 'Good, huh.' It wasn't a question, it was a statement.

She remembered the early days. The first time they made love. The months they were secretly seeing each other. The beginning of their marriage. Oh, what a lover Ross Conti had been then!

Ross drew deeply on his cigarette and thought of Karen Lancaster. He really should call her. She was such a little wildcat in the sack. Not like Elaine who lay there like she was doing him a big favour. She quite obviously didn't enjoy sex like she used to. She always made him feel that he was pushing himself on her and that he should get it over with as quickly as possible. If the truth were known he could honestly say that sex with his wife was dull, and it certainly wasn't *his* fault.

'Very good,' Elaine murmured. 'I was beginning to think you'd forgotten how.'

He ignored the barb. Ha! She should only know!

'I read the script,' he began. 'And I don't know if Montana Gray wrote it – didn't write it, whatever. It's going to make one hell of a movie.'

Her interest was aroused. 'It is?'

'No doubt about it.'

'And . . .' she paused. 'How about the part for you?'

163

'Perfect.'

'Really?'

'Well, not perfect for *me*, Ross Conti, but perfect for *me* as an actor. Do you understand what I'm saying?'

Did she understand? Who did he think he was talking to?

'So we *have* to get Sadie La Salle,' she said excitedly.

'It's our best shot.'

They were on each other's wave length at last. Elaine smiled. 'I'm having lunch with Karen tomorrow, she'll have an answer for me on whether I can throw the party for George and Pamela. If I can – then nobody will dare not to come – even Sadie La Salle.'

Ma Maison. Friday lunch. The small garden restaurant was crowded, the umbrellaed tables in close proximity, the aproned waiters running this way and that.

Buddy had decided to test out the pale tan Armani jacket, beige slacks and matching collarless silk shirt. The look was right, expensively casual.

'You need just a touch of gold,' Jason said, fussily toying with a thick gold chain that hung around his own neck.

'No, I don't,' Buddy replied quickly. There was nothing worse than California casual ruined by great chunks of flash jewellery. Gold chains on men always reminded him of the ageing swingers who cruised around Beverly Hills in their Mercedes and Porsches, with hair combed concealingly forward, and fat guts held tightly in.

Settled at their table in the corner, just the two of them, Buddy felt free to cast an interested eye around the fashionable restaurant. There were a lot of women lunching together. Tables of them. Chic. Stylish. Beautiful.

Jason suddenly felt it his duty to give him a run-down on every famous face in the place. 'You see that group of women over there, well the beautiful one with the dark hair is Mrs. Johnny Carson – the devastating Joanna. And at the next table is Louisa Moore – wife of Roger – she's *such* fun. And the couple in the corner –'

'Stephanie Powers and Robert Wagner,' Buddy interrupted.

'And next to them –'

'Dudley Moore.'

'Very good,' said Jason crisply, 'but I bet you don't know who *that* is.' He pointed out an exquisite black haired beauty deep in conversation with a man.

'I give up.'

'Shakira Caine. Married to Michael Caine of course. She's with Bobby Zarem – he made the slogan "I love New York" famous – wonderful P.R. and so amusing.'

'Do you know all these people?' Buddy asked, impressed in spite of himself.

'Not intimately, but many of them come to the store.'

'Hey – maybe you know an agent I can meet . . . Like a real hot one.'

'Let me see . . . I'm sure amongst my connections . . . Oh, you see that woman sitting down over there – that's George Lancaster's daughter, and on the other side of the room is David Tebet – he's the vice president of Johnny Carson Productions, and I see Jack Lemmon and . . .'

Buddy glanced restlessly around not really listening as Jason carried on. He had eyes, he could spot the stars for himself. Clint Eastwood sprawled at a centre table, his long legs impeding the waiters' fast trips around the room. And Sidney Poitier, Tom Selleck . . . there were celebrities everywhere.

Buddy felt good. Not that anyone had so much as glanced in his direction, but he was still *there*, still part of it.

'Do you like it here?' Jason asked, well aware of the fact that indeed he did.

Buddy shrugged. 'I've been here before y'know.'

'I'm sure you have.' Jason couldn't help allowing his eyes to linger on Buddy's restless countenance. The boy had such looks . . . such beauty . . . Ah . . . now if he bided his time . . . was patient . . . Ah . . .

Karen's green eyes gleamed. 'I promise you, I spoke to daddy *and* Pamela. They would both be delighted to be guests of honour at your party.'

'You're sure?' Elaine asked for the second time.

'Elaine. If I say something, you can bet it will happen.' She smiled and waved at Dudley Moore. 'Pamela would like you to phone her at ten o'clock tonight – Palm Beach time.'

'She would?'

'Don't look so dumbstruck, it's what you wanted, isn't it?'

'Of course –'

'So thanks to me you've got it. The hottest party in town. Just watch Bibi jump now!'

Maralee joined in the conversation. 'Who's doing the catering?'

Elaine had imagined she could use Lina and two of her Mexican friends, but things were different now. 'I hadn't really thought –'

'Better start thinking!' warned Karen. 'That salmon mousse Tita Cahn served last week was to die! I think she's made a new discovery. Why not give her a call?'

'Mortons could do the whole thing for you,' Maralee suggested. 'Or La Scala. I always feel more secure when one uses professionals.'

'Yes, but that's so safe,' argued Karen. 'Daddy adores oriental food. How about a Chinese feast?'

'Madame Wu's?' ventured Elaine, thinking about how much it was all going to cost, and how loud Ross was going to scream.

'Marvellous food,' said Maralee.

'Marvellous,' echoed Karen.

Buddy sipped the hot black espresso and wondered how long he was expected to sit there. Jason seemed quite settled as he toyed with a small glass of Sambuca.

'Uh . . . I guess I should be gettin' back to the beach,' he said at last. 'I'm expecting a call about the test, an' I want to go over the script again.'

Jason nodded. 'Is everything all right for you at the house?'

'Couldn't be better, Angel loves it.'

It annoyed Jason that at every given opportunity Buddy mentioned his wife. It was almost as if he was screaming – *I'm straight! I'm straight! And don't you forget it!*

Jason clicked his fingers for the check. Some of his most memorable experiences had been with so-called straights. When they came out of the closet they came out with a vengeance. 'Yes,' he murmured. 'Angel seems such a sweet girl.'

'She is,' Buddy assured him.

'Quite so. But I do think it best if we don't mention the fact that you're married to Mrs. Jaeger and her friend.'

'Sure.' Why bite the hand that was draping him in Armani?

'They'll be arriving tomorrow evening. Probably quite late,' Jason continued, squinting at the check. He withdrew a pigskin wallet from his jacket and extracted his trusty Master Charge card. 'I expect they'll be tired, so I'll have the driver meet them at the airport and deposit them at their hotel – the Beverly Hills of course – and I thought that on Sunday we'd all meet up for a perfectly wonderful brunch in the Polo Lounge. Won't that be fun?'

Buddy could have thought of another way to describe it. But he stayed silent and tried to look enthusiastic.

'Wear what you have on today,' Jason instructed. 'It suits you admirably.'

'Sure, thanks.' Impatiently Buddy glanced yet again at the tables around him. Clint Eastwood was long gone, but he spotted Allan Carr, Richard Gere and Rock Hudson. The famous producer and the two movie stars gave him a real buzz. Quickly he sneaked a look at his watch. Three o'clock in the afternoon. Shit! By the time he got back to the beach it would be four – too late to work on his tan. What a wasted day. Jason Swankle was a nice enough guy, but just who did he think he was kidding? Buddy *knew* the time would come when he would try to climb on his bones. Why else the beach house, the new clothes, and the money for dating two old women who any escort service could have taken care of for half the price?

The waiter returned the Master Charge card, and they rose to leave. Buddy strode quickly through the restaurant, leaving Jason to tag along behind. At the entrance he bumped straight into Randy Felix. They stared at each other in surprise, then delight.

'Hey –' Buddy exclaimed. 'What are *you* doin' here?'

'Meeting someone,' Randy grinned, and stepped back to look his friend over. 'And you're *lookin' good*!'

'Too right!'

They hugged quickly in an embarrassed masculine way, and parted just as Jason puffed up.

'Uh . . . this is a friend of mine – Randy Felix,' Buddy explained. 'Give me five minutes an' I'll see you out in the car.'

Jason pursed fleshy lips and nodded curtly at Randy. 'Just make sure you're not longer than five minutes,' he said possessively before leaving.

Randy stared quizzically at Jason's departing back. 'You changed sides, bro?'

'Come *on*. Who d'y'think you're talkin' to?'

'Just askin'. You never know nowadays.'

They both noticed the blonde waving. She had risen from her seat and was beckoning frantically. 'Over here, Randy,' she called, in case he missed her.

Randy waved back. 'The one I was telling you about,' he explained sotto voce. 'Maralee Gray, her father owns Sanderson Studios. Her ex is Neil Gray – the director. You like the set-up?'

'Like it – I want it!'

'Come meet her.'

Buddy was tempted. The mention of Neil Gray set bells ringing. But she was his ex-wife and probably had nothing to do with the movie. Besides, how would it look if Jason came waddling in to get him?

'Another time. Whyn't you buzz me later? I got plenty of news.'

They stopped a waiter for a pen and paper, and Buddy scribbled down his number at the beach. Then they slapped palms and went their separate ways.

'Who was that?' inquired Karen, when Randy was settled at their table and introduced to her and Elaine by a nervous Maralee.

'Who was what?' asked Randy, knowing immediately that Karen Lancaster was asking about Buddy. They *all* had the hots for Buddy. It was always the same.

'That gorgeous man you were talking to on your way in,' Karen persisted irritably.

'You mean Buddy.'

'Buddy?'

'Buddy Hudson. He's a friend of mine.'

'Gay?'

Randy licked his finger and exaggeratedly smoothed his eyebrow. 'If you say so, sweets!'

Maralee laughed nervously. 'Randy!' she admonished. 'Don't!'

Karen glared. She hated Maralee's new friend on sight. 'I have to go,' she drawled. 'Coming, Elaine?'

Actually Elaine was anxious to leave. She couldn't wait to get home and phone Bibi. But Maralee had begged her to meet Randy before their evening dinner date, and she could hardly say hello goodbye as soon as the poor man sat down.

'I'll stay a few minutes,' she explained apologetically.

'Suit yourself,' snapped Karen, and with an all-encompassing wave around the table she exited.

'You'll love Karen,' Maralee gushed, holding tightly on to Randy's hand, 'when you get to know her.'

He smiled and winked at Elaine. 'Can't wait!' he said cheerily.

She decided she couldn't stand him.

Angel spent the day dusting, polishing and vacuuming. The house at Malibu was really the most perfect place she had ever seen – straight out of a magazine, and she couldn't be more thrilled that they were lucky enough to be staying there.

She hummed softly as she went about her tasks, mopping the perfectly spotless kitchen floor, sponging the sparkling formica tops, pouring disinfectant down three unused toilets.

The beach was hazy all morning, but at twelve the sun broke through, and she slipped into a bikini and lay out on the patio deck overlooking the ocean. She took with her a pad and a pen, planning to write a letter to her foster family in Louisville. She had not heard from them at all, in spite of the fact that she had written several times. It was to be expected. They had never cared for her, her presence had merely been an extra source of income from the welfare people. But still . . . she wanted them to know about the baby. Maybe, just maybe, they would be pleased for her.

Dear Everyone,
Well I suppose you are wondering why I have not written for a while.
Well you see –

She paused for thought and gazed at two joggers running through the surf. They were holding hands and laughing. A dog ran behind them. Buddy was so jumpy lately . . . Perhaps now they were at the beach, settled into a beautiful house . . .

But for how long? And who was Jason Swankle? And why was he part of their lives all of a sudden?

She sighed, then abruptly screwed up the writing paper and threw it across the sand. Buddy was her family now. Louisville was her past. Buddy was her future even if he did not confide in her, and fed her a bunch of lies when she would have been quite prepared to face the truth.

For instance – where did he come up with the money to buy new *expensive* clothes? Why were they installed in this beautiful house? Who was paying for the chauffeured car that kept on arriving to pick him up? When she asked him all of these questions he had laughed, ruffled her hair and said, 'Don't you worry about it, babe. My old pal Jason owes me. He's just settlin' a debt.'

Angel wondered, if there was a debt to be settled, why didn't *she* get any new clothes? Not that she begrudged Buddy his outfits, but surely it would have been nice if she could have gotten something too? He hadn't even asked her to accompany him on his shopping spree, and she was hurt. Soon she would *have* to get new clothes – maternity clothes.

169

The thought caused a secret smile to play across her lips. She couldn't wait for her stomach to swell – confirming the fact that a person she and Buddy had created was growing inside her. All thoughts of being a movie star had faded. *Buddy* would be the star of the family, and she would be his loving wife. The fan magazines would feature photo lay-outs of them at home. Buddy so macho and good looking, and she in flowing dresses with flowers in her hair and lots of beautiful children at her feet. Earth mother. The thought pleased her. She smiled broadly. How long would it take for him to become a superstar? Two years? Three? Whenever. She would be ready.

The surf looked inviting, so she slipped off her white sandals and hurried down the steps to the sand. Then she ran towards the ocean, her long blond hair flying out behind her.

A man, sitting on the deck of a neighbouring house, watched her progress into the sea. He rose and walked to the edge of the deck, straining his eyes to get a better look at her as she plunged into the waves.

When she emerged he was still watching.

It took Bibi Sutton exactly eleven minutes to call back after Elaine had left a message with her secretary about the party being for George Lancaster and Pamela London.

'Sweetie!' she purred down the phone. 'I 'ave been so busy. You know 'ow it is.'

'Don't apologize,' Elaine said magnanimously. 'I know *exactly* what you mean.'

'Darling, you really 'ave party for Pamela and George?' Bibi always liked to check her facts before committing.

'I thought I told you it was for them,' Elaine replied innocently.

'No, no. Still. We come anyway, you know that.'

'Of course I do.' Elaine was enjoying herself. The worse star-fucks were the stars themselves.

' 'Ow many people you 'ave?' Bibi inquired.

'Nothing enormous. More an . . . intimate gathering. Close friends of George and Pamela's. Fifty, sixty. No more than that.'

'Ahhh . . .' Bibi sighed. 'This I like. An intimate gathering. Dressy I 'ope.'

'For the ladies, yes. I think the men are more comfortable casual,' Elaine replied firmly.

'So sensible, sweetie!' Bibi shrieked. 'I love it. *We* dress up. *They* wear boring sports clothes.'

Approval at last. Elaine glowed.

'Now,' Bibi continued, 'who do the food?'

Elaine hesitated for only a second. *Be positive. Don't let the bitch throw you.* 'I was thinking of using Madame Wu's.'

'No!'

'No?'

'I 'ave secret for you. A secret I tell only my good friends.'

Elaine waited.

Bibi paused dramatically. 'Sergio and Eugenio!' she announced triumphantly.

'I don't think I know them –'

'Sure you don't know them. Nobody knows them. They are *mine*. My *secret*.'

It was rumoured – though never proved – that Bibi got a kickback from every restaurant, caterer, store, etc., that she put her magic seal of approval on. Elaine wondered what Sergio and Eugenio would throw into the pot.

'Are they good?'

'Are they good! Ha!' Bibi laughed mirthlessly. 'Sweetie, would I recommend them if they not good?'

'Of course not, I –'

Bibi was in full flow. 'And I'ave another secret for you. The Zancussi trio. Italian love songs straight from Roma. You tent the garden?'

'I hadn't really –'

'You must! Now, let me give you some advice –'

The conversation continued for another ten minutes while Bibi honoured Elaine with her suggestions. And all the time Elaine was mentally counting the cost. Tented garden. Trio of musicians. Sergio and Eugenio. Valet parking. Floral arrangements. Two special bartenders to mix the latest drinks. Waiters. Kitchen staff. A new outfit.

To do it properly would cost a fortune. But properly it had to be done.

Bibi ended the conversation on an encouraging note. She invited Elaine to a lunch she was having the following Monday at her house. 'I 'ave the wonderful police come to speak about mace. We all get the permit,' Bibi explained brightly. 'What you think? Good idea, no?'

What did a woman like Bibi need a can of mace for? Her chauffeured Rolls never ventured out of Beverly Hills.

'Great idea,' gushed Elaine, hating herself for being such an ass licker.

Bibi Sutton calls – you run. I thought you hated her guts.

Shut ut, Etta.

Later, dinner at La Scala with Maralee, and her new boyfriend, Randy, was a disaster. How did Maralee find them? How did she know just where to look for the sharp-eyed hustlers who homed right in on her money and position. Elaine had taken an instant dislike to Randy at lunchtime, and her first reaction was strengthened upon their second meeting.

Ross was annoyed that they had to go in the first place. He and Maralee had never really hit it off. He tolerated her because she was his wife's best friend, but he didn't see why he had to tolerate her boring dumb stud boyfriends, *and* pay for dinner on top of everything else.

They ordered drinks, and Elaine spoke to Maralee, while Randy attempted to communicate with Ross. He called him 'sir' which made Ross scowl, and he said things like – 'You were my mother's favourite' and 'I've seen all your old movies on television.'

An asshole of the first order. Ross summoned the waiter and proceeded to down a series of scotch on the rocks.

Halfway through the evening Karen Lancaster arrived with Chet Barnes. She swooped down on their table like a predatory bird, Chet trailing behind.

'He-*llo* everyone,' she greeted, her eyes bright from a snort of pre-dinner cocaine – the Hollywood equivalent of a pep up pill.

Ross sat up straight at the sight of her perky nipples straining the material of a thin silk tank top, and wondered why he hadn't bothered to call her. He decided to rectify the situation first thing in the morning.

'Have you eaten?' Elaine inquired, thankful for the diversion.

'We're just about to.'

'Why don't you join us?' Elaine said quickly, giving Ross a sharp kick under the table.

He took his cue, fascinated by Karen's nipples through the flimsy material. 'Yes, come on, join us,' he encouraged.

Karen looked him straight in the eye and smiled sweetly. 'No thank you. Chet and I are into a heavy discussion about multiple orgasms and whether having a big dick helps a guy to be a good lover. We wouldn't want to put anyone off their dinner.'

Elaine laughed. 'You are unbelievable!'

Karen shot Ross a deadly look. 'See you all later.'

'Come and have coffee with us,' Elaine begged desperately.

'Maybe.' Karen smiled around the table, her eyes flicking past Randy Felix as if he didn't exist. Then she grabbed Chet's hand, and a waiter directed them to an intimate booth in the back.

'I didn't know Karen and Chet were having a thing,' Maralee said excitedly. 'How long has she been seeing *him*?'

Elaine shrugged. 'I can never keep up with her affairs.'

And a good thing too, Ross thought. He looked across the room. Karen was snuggling up to Chet, whispering in his ear, or was it her tongue in his ear?

All of a sudden he wanted her badly. He wanted her on her knees in front of him sucking his –

'Are you all right, Ross?' Elaine asked sharply.

'What?'

'You look most peculiar.'

'You mean I look frigging bored,' he muttered angrily. 'Why do you have to stick me with these evenings?'

'Shhh . . .'

Elaine need not have been concerned. Maralee wasn't listening anyway, she was gazing into Randy Felix's eyes as he told her a whole lot of lies about his past.

Every day, around five, Buddy called the Easterne office and spoke to Montana Gray's secretary. She was the blonde with the bad nose job, and she and Buddy indulged in long intense conversations. He was anxious to know exactly what was happening. Was there a date set for his test? What other actors were testing? Who seemed to present the most competition?

The blonde, whose name was Inga, confided in Buddy absolutely, and fully expected him to invite her out on a date. When he didn't she finally said, 'Look, it's difficult for me to give out all this information on the phone. Why don't you come by my apartment?'

He knew what *that* meant. 'I'm stuck out at the beach an' my car's in the shop,' he lied.

She was not to be put off. She had read her Cosmopolitan, and she knew her rights; if she wanted to get laid she was perfectly entitled to do the chasing. '*I* can drive down to see *you*,' she said firmly.

'Not a good idea. I'm stayin' with this neurotic guy who jumps on anything that moves. It's a bad scene here, you wouldn't like it.'

'Try me,' she said boldly.

'One of these days, kid.'

'Just name it, Buddy.'

'Look. Why don't I call you same time tomorrow?'

He got off the phone and prowled nervously around the house. Angel was in the kitchen fixing tuna salad for their dinner.

'Hey – why don't we go out to eat?' He grabbed her from behind and gave her a hug.

'Everything's nearly ready,' she said primly, extracting herself and continuing to chop cucumber.

'So what? I feel like showing you off.'

'Not tonight, Buddy. My hair needs washing, I've prepared dinner, and there's a Richard Gere film on television.'

What did she need Richard Gere for when she had him? That really pissed him. 'Okay. Okay.'

Wide eyed and unbearably beautiful, 'You don't mind, do you?'

'Naw, 'course I don't.'

He wandered out on the deck. Shit! Angel was beginning to sound like a wife. He would have thought she would have jumped at the chance of hitting the town with him. It wasn't like they had been living it up every night.

He felt uptight and restless. Jeez! You would think she would *understand* – what with the test coming up and everything.

They ate dinner with one eye on a space age television hanging from the ceiling. Then Angel yawned delicately and said, 'I'm sooo tired. Do you mind if I go to bed early?'

Yes. He minded. He needed to unwind, have a few blasts, relax.

'Sure babe, you go right ahead.'

She kissed him lightly and vanished upstairs.

He wished he had a joint to take the edge off.

He wished that he'd done the fucking test already.

He wished he was a star.

18

Joey Kravetz's sister was back in town. Louise Kravetz. Known as Lulu. Five years older than Joey. Arrested three times for prostitution, twice for drugs.

She arrived on a charter from Amsterdam on a Sunday morning, and Leon knew about it ten minutes after she cleared customs. He had his connections.

Ignoring Millie's objections, he jumped in his car and arrived at the run-down house where Lulu resided twenty minutes before she did. An angry black landlady let him into her room. It was a depressing array of musty clothes, dead plants, an old record player and stacks of worn rock albums. A thick film of dust covered everything.

In one corner stood an unmade bed. Over the other side there was a gas burner, with a few dirt encrusted dishes piled on top.

Leon positioned himself stiffly by the door ready to flash his I.D. and give the sister the bad news.

He wondered if she looked like Joey . . .

Leon awoke to the sound of an alarm ringing. Seven a.m. Without his alarm clock he could sleep forever.

He felt the dried stickiness around his crotch, and knew immediately what it was. A wet dream. Jesus H. Christ, he hadn't had a wet dream since he was sixteen years old!

Wet dream, my ass. Joey Kravetz jerking you off in the middle of the night while you played possum.

Christ. Had he really done that?

Yes, you did it and you loved it, and you were never that much asleep that you couldn't have woken fully and stopped her.

Shame crept over him. He, Leon Rosemont, and a sixteen year old hooker. It wasn't like he was desperate. He had regular sex – as much sex as he could use. Goddamn it! How could he have let her do it?

Shamefacedly he climbed out of bed, ripped off the offending pyjamas and covered himself with a bathrobe.

How could he face her?

How could he not?

He imagined the expression on her face. She would stare at him knowingly, triumphantly. You're just like all the rest.

But he wasn't. No way was he like the animals who prowled the streets. No damn way.

Angrily he marched into the living room. Get her up and out and give her twenty bucks to see her on her way.

That's right. Encourage her to keep on hooking. Pay her off and forget her. She's not your problem.

Oh yes she is. Sixteen years old and you should try and help her. Where's your sense of public duty?

175

Where had his goddamn sense of public duty been in the early hours of the morning?

The blanket and pillow he had given her were on the floor. The couch was empty.

He knew she had gone before he even checked out the kitchen and bathroom.

Lulu was taller than Joey, plump, like a stuffed chicken, her skin blotched red, and her eyes that sickly yellow colour that comes from too many drugs.

She was not alone. Accompanying her was a skinny nervous Chicano youth with matted wild hair and the same yellow eyes. They both had backpacks strapped to their shoulders, and the weight looked like it was just about to finish off the Chicano. Their landlady had obviously felt it best not to mention Leon's presence, because neither of them could have faked their looks of shocked surprise.

'Who the fuck are *you*?' Lulu shrieked. 'An' what you doin' in my room?'

Leon flashed his identification.

Lulu dropped her backpack, snatched his I.D. and studied it intently.

'Fuckin' pigs,' she finally muttered, throwing it back at him. 'I go away – they're hasslin' me. I come back – same thing.' She waved her fat arms in the air, revealing a tear in her Indian batik blouse. 'I'm clean, man. Search me.'

Lulu was an obvious charmer. However, the dialogue was getting her friend mighty nervous, and he began backing out the door without so much as a goodbye.

'Come back T.T.,' Lulu shrieked. 'You ain't runnin' out on me. Whatever they want, you're in it too.'

T.T. froze, sick yellow eyes darting around.

'I don't *want* anything,' Leon said quietly. 'I have something very distressing to tell you.'

'Distressing.' Lulu repeated the word blankly, as if she had never heard it before.

T.T. took his cue. 'Distressin',' he mumbled.

'It's about your sister, Joey,' Leon intoned gravely.

'What's the little tramp done now?' demanded Lulu, vigorously scratching a denim thigh. 'Got herself finished off?' She laughed wildly at her own humour.

'Exactly,' said Leon.

'Don't fuck with me, mister,' she snapped. 'Cop or not I don't think that's very funny.'

'Your sister, Joey, has been murdered,' Leon said formally.

The blotched face crumpled. Her friend's head jerked nervously.

'I'm sorry,' Leon said gently.

'Sorry!' Lulu shrieked, recovering rapidly from her grief. 'You motherfucker. What *you* know about bein' sorry? You pigs killed my little sister.'

T.T. said quickly, 'Hold it, Lou. Remember, *he's a cop.*'

'Sure,' yelled Lulu, out of control and quivering with fury. 'An' I'll fuckin' remember the times she got hassled by the cops. All the time, man, *all the time.* A blow job in the back of the squad car. A screw in an alleyway. One even dragged her back to his stinkin' apartment when she was only fifteen years old an' did her. Cops!' she snorted in disgust. 'She had no chance – an' you pigs never helped her. You *leaned* on her, man, every step of the fuckin' way.'

Leon stared at her angry face. *One even dragged her back to his stinkin' apartment when she was only fifteen years old an' did her.*

He coughed and attempted to say something, but all the while his mind was churning. *Deke Andrews. Deke Andrews. Got to catch him. Got to catch him for Joey's sake . . . for my sake . . .*

The guilt was impossible to live with.

19

Mrs. Norma Jaeger was not at all as Buddy had expected. Nor was Mrs. Celeste McQueen. No doubt about it – they were no longer spring chickens, but life – as the saying goes – was not yet over. And the jewellery the two of them were wearing had to be seen to be believed.

Mrs. Jaeger first. Hennaed red hair worn in a girlish frizz. The face hitting fifty if you looked close – but from a short distance – thirty-five – give or take a year or two. Subtle make-up, slightly too heavy on the amber eye-shadow. Figure very well preserved indeed, clad in a powder blue tracksuit. And round the neck a thick gold dog collar studded with several very large diamonds. A bracelet to match. And a gulls-egg diamond ring on her left hand which could lay a burglar out for a week and a half. No trouble.

Mrs. Celeste McQueen, a year or two older – an inch or two fatter. Streaked short hair, light suntan, freckles. White tennis dress and really impressive legs. Lots of turquoise and silver Indian jewellery, and a heart shaped diamond ring that rivalled her friend's in size.

Sunday noon, and they both gazed at Buddy expectantly as Jason executed introductions in the dimly lit Polo Lounge.

'Hey –' Buddy sing-songed, all charm. 'Good to make your acquaintance, ladies.' He slid into the leather booth next to Mrs. McQueen.

She patted him on the hand, fixed him with amused blue eyes, and said, 'Tell us that when we leave, sugar. Not when you just set your peepers on us.'

They all laughed.

'I've ordered for you,' Jason announced fussily. 'Champagne and orange juice. Smoked salmon with scrambled eggs.'

'Sounds good to me,' Buddy replied with an ingratiating smile.

What had he got himself into? What was he going to talk to them about? Light conversation had never been one of his smash acts.

'So, sugar,' Mrs McQueen said. 'Jason here tells us you're an aspiring movie-star. How exciting!'

Norma Jaeger leaned forward, green eyes glinting beneath the excess of amber shadow. 'I was reading an interview in "People" magazine,' she said excitedly, 'with this young actor from Knots Landing – or maybe it was Dallas, all those soaps seem the same to me. Anyway, it was *one* of those popular shows.'

'Get *on* with it,' Celeste McQueen said affectionately. 'It doesn't matter *what* show it was, just come to the point.'

'Shush, don't rush me,' smiled Norma, wagging a long manicured nail at her friend. 'You know I hate to be hurried along.'

'Oh, don't I just know it!' laughed Celeste.

Buddy did not miss the intimate looks they exchanged.

'Well, you see,' continued Norma, 'this actor who was being interviewed, *he* said that *he* thinks that nowadays actors get the casting couch treatment just like actresses used to.' She glanced wickedly at Celeste. 'Now what *I* want to know, Buddy, is – do you agree with that?'

'What she's *really* asking you, sugar,' grinned Celeste, 'is how far would *you* go to land a part?'

'No, no, what I'm *really* asking,' interjected Norma, 'is if you

178

would . . . well, you know what I mean . . . I don't have to spell it out.'

'You just did,' laughed Celeste.

'I did not!' objected Norma.

They smiled warmly at each other, not at all interested in Buddy's reply.

He wanted to laugh aloud. They were a couple of dykes! He had been fixed up to escort a couple of lesbos! Oh boy! And he had been worried they would be after his body. They couldn't care less about the Buddy Body Beautiful!

Their relationship was shifting into another gear and Montana did not quite know how to handle it. But she was sure of one thing – no way was she ever going to become the little woman at home. Not that she thought for a moment Neil would want her to. But what *did* he want?

He was drinking again. It was his problem. He was a big boy, if he couldn't handle it she was not about to slap his wrist. He was spending more and more time at the office – leaving early in the morning, coming home late. She had never believed in the where were you? Who were you with? bit.

She knew he was worried about casting the main parts, so she concentrated all of her energies on getting the rest of the cast right.

One day she got in the Volkswagen and drove downtown to the streets where it had all begun. She sat in the little car and gazed at the pasing faces. The hell with actors, why couldn't she use some of the real people?

One of the kids who had been in her short film swaggered by. He had grown in a year – a teenage macho with holes in his sneakers and a thatch of black hair. He didn't see her, he was busy blowing bubble-gum in the face of a blond-haired child with advanced breast development.

She was reminded of Gina Germaine for a moment. Neil was actually going ahead with the test. She couldn't believe it, but the smart thing was to accept it – for now anyway.

Ah . . . the power of big boobs. Gina had built an entire career on her attributes.

Montana watched as two middle-aged men passed the teenage couple. She knew exactly what they would do, and their actions did not disappoint her. They checked out the girl's breasts, looked towards each other, licked their lips and sniggered out some lewd remark which caused them both to roar with laughter. Just your average man-in-the-street letting each other know that women were merely tits and ass. Because unconsciously that's what they had been trained to think all their lives. It was standard behaviour. She had seen it a thousand times before. Sometimes she felt she could climb into a man's thoughts and actions with no trouble at all. In a group they were so predictable. But it was the unpredictable ones that had always attracted her.

She thought of Neil when she first met him. A bum wasting his considerable talents by boozing himself half to death. But an unpredictable bum, brilliantly clever, witty, well worth the challenge.

A hooker wandered by in polyester hot pants and stiletto heels. A bespectacled man scurried along behind her, getting up his courage for the transaction. Street People.

Writing the movie had come so easily. She was an observer with an uncanny ability to figure out exactly how men thought. She understood them, had sympathy for them. And watching the interaction on the street she had been able to create a marvellous story of real people.

Now. What was Neil going to do with it?

Was he going to blow it because the pressures were on again and he had to deliver. Or, was he going to come through, and make the film she knew he had in him.

He was strong.

She hoped he was strong enough.

All Elaine seemed to want to talk about was her goddamn party, and Bibi-Hot-Shit-Sutton.

'Christ, Elaine!' Ross snorted. 'Don't you know she used to be a hundred-buck-a-night hooker on the Champs-Elysées? I had her – George had her – we *all* took a ride. In fact, when she first came to Hollywood there was some big scandal about her being knocked up by George.'

'Nonsense.'

'They were very hot and heavy until his wife found out. Story goes Bibi went off to Tijuana for an abortion.'

'I don't believe it,' Elaine said primly. 'It's just Hollywood folklore.'

'It's *not* frigging Hollywood folklore. It's the truth for crissake, so stop licking her saggy ass.'

'She's in very good shape, Ross,' Elaine said crisply. 'There's

180

nothing saggy about Bibi's ass, it's *yours* that could do with a few sessions at the gym. *Especially* before the party.'

'You can never resist a dig can you?'

'And *you* can never accept the truth. Even when it's for your own good.'

'Don't be so frigging sanctimonious.' He stalked into his study and thought about phoning Karen. With Elaine in the house it was too dangerous by far.

He had taken the Corniche down to Nate 'n' Al's on Saturday morning, picked up lox, bagels and cream cheese, then he had stopped at a phone booth and dialled Karen's number. An answering service had picked up. He had no wish to reveal his name, so as a gag he said flippantly, 'Tell Miss Lancaster *Mr.* Elaine called and would like her to contact him about making another appointment.'

She had obviously not received the message, for it was now Sunday night, and not a word. Of course, she could have called and Elaine picked up. Then again, maybe she figured phoning on a weekend was not the smartest move in the world, and Karen was nothing if not smart.

Elaine was in the kitchen complaining about placing two frozen steaks on to broil. Lina did not come in on Sundays, even though she had tried to bribe her with double money. She really hated cooking, it played merry hell on her nails, and as for dish-washing – she left *that* to Lina, not even bothering to load the machine.

Ross wandered into the kitchen and began plucking radishes from the salad bowl. 'Who else is going to be at Bibi's kill and maim lunch tomorrow?' he asked casually.

'Learning to use mace is hardly kill and maim. It's a very useful and effective self-defence ploy.'

'Sure. Some cat with a magnum grabs you, and what do you do? Reach inside your purse, locate your cute little spray and say' – he affected a high squeaky female voice – 'Oh, do excuse me, sir. Would you just stand still for a tiny minute while I give you a quick whoosh of my mace. You don't mind, do you?'

Elaine was amused in spite of herself. 'I hope I never have to use it,' she said.

'Kick 'em in the balls an' run,' Ross advised. 'Forget about anything else.'

'What are you – an expert?'

'A man.'

She wanted to say – 'You could have fooled me.' But she didn't feel mean enough. Besides, as long as he didn't baulk too much at paying for the party – and costs were rising every minute. She peered at the steaks sizzling nicely. 'Garlic salt?' she questioned.

'No, I don't think so.'

'Going to get laid tomorrow?' she joked.

He tweaked her left breast. 'Tonight, if I'm lucky.'

Don't hold your breath, Elaine. Don't hold your breath.

Gina Germaine's voice was low and sexy on the phone. 'I didn't think my testing for your movie would end a beautiful relationship,' she purred.

Neil took a deep breath. He had arranged for her to test, which was what she had wanted. Now she wanted him to continue making it with her too?

'Gina, dear,' he said tersely. 'I'm trying to get a film off the ground. I hardly have time to go to the bathroom, let alone anything else.'

'All work and no play . . . I *miss* you Neil.'

God! But the blackmailing bitch had her nerve. 'I'm seeing you Wednesday, aren't I? You *are* going to turn up for the test you made such a fuss about?'

Injured actress. '*Of course* I am, Neil, sweets. And I'll be good, you'll be delighted with me, I –'

'I'll see you Wednesday.'

'Wait!' Her voice held a sharp command.

He sighed. 'What?'

'Come over later today,' she wheedled, changing tactics. 'I need to discuss the scene. I'd like you to help me.'

She was unbelievable. 'Gina,' he said shortly. 'I don't think you're listening to me. I am *very* busy. I –'

'We could watch our video,' she murmured. 'How does that grab you? Or would you prefer me to send a copy over to your house? I'm sure Montana would *love* seeing you on film. You look so virile and handsome and –'

What a first class *cunt*. 'I'll be there,' he snapped.

'I'll wear something sexy . . . Bye . . .'

He sat staring at the wall opposite his desk. Staring and seeing nothing. What was it they used to say in those old Laurel and Hardy movies . . . '*A fine mess you got us into Ollie. A fine mess.*'

*

Mrs. Jaeger and Mrs. McQueen wanted to play tennis after lunch, and since Buddy readily admitted he was no Connors or Borg, they did not ask him to join them.

Jason excused himself. 'I always spend Sundays with Marvin, otherwise he sulks.'

Marvin Gladrags Jackson a sulker? Never.

'However,' Jason continued, 'Mrs. Jaeger wants to visit her house later, so why don't I meet you there around five-thirty? I've reserved a table at Matteo's for dinner.'

Buddy nodded, thinking of Angel at the beach with nothing to do but lie in the sun and swim in the surf. How he envied her. He waited until Jason left, then he excused himself from the tennis-playing ladies and headed for a phone-booth. Angel answered on the second buzz.

'Why aren't you outside?' he demanded.

'I'm cleaning,' she explained.

'Cleaning *what* for crissakes? The place looks like a hospital as it is.'

Her tone was frosty. 'I am cleaning out the kitchen cabinets. Did you know the builders left them full of wood shavings?'

'Really?'

His sarcasm was lost on her. 'They certainly did,' she said, full of righteous indignation.

'Uh, listen. I won't be back for a while, maybe not 'til tonight.'

'But I thought we were going for a drive.'

'We'll do it tomorrow.'

She sighed.

'Tell you what, kid. Forget about cleanin', an' move that beautiful body of yours outside. That's an order, I want to see you tanned.'

'Do you think it's good for the baby?'

'Yeah, yeah, the best.'

'I'll get changed right now.'

He blew kisses down the phone, hung up, searched for more coins, then tried Montana Gray's secretary, Inga.

'Anythin' happenin'?' he asked without so much as a hello.

'On a Sunday?'

'Just checkin' in.'

'You want to come over?'

'I would, but I got my two aunts in town. I'm playin' the good nephew.'

'As long as it's not the good fairy.'

What did she mean by *that* smart-ass remark? He ended the

conversation and contemplated phoning Randy. Old pal Randy had been with some pretty heavy company at Ma Maison, maybe he should talk to him about Maralee Gray, see if she knew anything on *Street People*. He punched Randy's number, but there was no answer. Disappointed, he hung up.

Instead of heading straight for the tennis courts he detoured, checking out the activity, poolside. There were a lot of heavily tanned guys wearing mucho gold around their necks. And a lot of heavily tanned females wearing small bikinis, diamond stud earrings, and thin gold waist chains. They all looked the same.

He whistled softly as he strolled around. Quite a few of the women did a double-take. And one or two of the men. It didn't surprise him.

He recognized Josh Speed, an English rock star, and a couple of small-time-I'll-kiss-your-ass-if-you-kiss-mine actors.

Still whistling he returned to the tennis courts. Celeste and Norma were hard at it. Two ageing Chris Everts in full swing. They were good, and they obviously enjoyed the game. Buddy watched, following the ball as it zoomed back and forth. Jeez! He was hot. It was just the right kind of day to spend lazing around at the beach. But he had an assignment, and right now, Jason Swankle was the only crap-shoot in town.

'Game, set, and match!' crowed Norma triumphantly.

'Whew! You deserved it!' breathed Celeste.

They walked off the court, linking arms and smiling secretly at each other.

Buddy snapped to attention. 'What now, ladies?'

'A long icy shower,' said Norma.

'And a long cold drink,' added Celeste.

'Why don't I wait for you in the coffee shop?' he suggested. 'Then we can . . .' A shrug. 'Whatever . . .'

'How much is Jason paying you?' Norma asked, frizzy red hair glinting in the sun.

'Hey – it's a pleasure,' Buddy replied, surprised by her directness. 'I'm enjoying myself.'

Norma smiled. 'I thought you might want to enjoy yourself even more – for – shall we say double Jason's remuneration?'

He frowned. 'Come again?'

'And again and again and again. If we're lucky. And I'm sure we would all be very . . . compatible.' She paused, licked full lips and added, 'Don't you think?'

The message was beginning to seep through. A cosy little three-some.

'Uh . . . how much did you have in mind?' he questioned. May as well find out what they would be willing to pay. After all, it wasn't like he had never done it before.

Before Angel.

'I don't wish to bargain. You name it,' Norma said crisply.

Celeste nodded her agreement, and the two of them gazed at him expectantly.

He thought quickly. It wasn't like he was exactly rolling in the mighty dollar. This seemed like an opportunity not to be blown.

'Uh . . . I want a thousand bucks,' he mumbled, half expecting Norma to burst out laughing at what they both knew to be an exorbitant price.

She didn't. She grabbed his arm, linked up with Celeste on the other side, and drawled, 'What are we waiting for?'

Angel finished cleaning the kitchen before changing into a white swimsuit and heading outside. Truth was, she didn't enjoy lying in the sun that much. She found it boring.

She made her way carefully down the wooden steps at the side of the house, then over the sand towards the surf. The waves were gigantic, and further down the beach two bronzed teenagers played dangerous games with their surfboards. She watched them, fantasizing that it was she and Buddy frolicking in the great swell of the ocean. And then she remembered Hawaii, and Buddy so attentive and romantic and somehow . . . different. Hollywood seemed to have made him tense, unable to relax.

Slowly she wandered along the shoreline, the incoming surf tickling her bare feet. She gazed with awe at the luxurious beach houses, each one different from the next – but all in the two or three million dollar price range – or so the woman at the supermarket had confided.

'Excuse me,' a male voice said.

She turned around, startled. 'Yes?' Her aquamarine eyes caught the light from the sun and seemed enormous.

The man stared, struck by her innocent beauty. He cleared his throat. 'You don't know me,' he began hesitantly, 'but I've been watching you –'

*
185

a two bedroom bungalow. The air conditioning was going . . . ast, and the shades were pulled down. After the heat of the . . ernoon the place was freezing. Neither Norma Jaeger nor Celeste McQueen seemed to notice.

'Why don't you fix martinis,' Norma ordered, indicating a fully stocked bar, 'while we shower.'

'Right.' Buddy stood in the centre of the room and wondered why he felt nervous.

Nervous of banging two old broads? Buddy Hudson?

It had been a long time between professional engagements.

So what?

He set about fixing the drinks, poured himself a double vodka and gulped it down quickly. Too much alcohol slowed the action, but one fast blast always worked.

He wanted his thousand dollars first. Up front. On the table.

The sound of the shower filtered through the bedroom door. He picked up the two martinis and pushed the door open with his foot. The bed cover was folded neatly in half, and some money lay on the flowered pillowcases. Mrs. Jaeger read minds.

He put the glasses down and swooped. Ten one hundred dollar bills in mint condition. Yeah. Cheap Mrs. Jaeger was not. Quickly he stuffed the money in his jacket pocket.

So . . . what was the sequence of events? Mrs. J. first, followed by Mrs. M.? Or a double-header?

He threw off his jacket and unbuttoned his shirt to the waist. Unease rested over him like a shroud as he paced around the room.

What was Angel doing now? Probably cleaning out a closet or two. *That* brought a smile to his lips. My wife, the cleaner. Angel *had* changed. In Hawaii a free spirit – just like him. Now Miss Proper – scrubbing and making a big deal about every grain of sand he tracked into Jason's goddamn house.

'Ah-hah. I see you found the money.' Norma stood in the bathroom doorway, wrapped tightly in a terrycloth robe. 'Are you ready to shower now?'

Hey, hey. Didn't she think he was *clean*?

'Sure,' he replied. 'Why not?'

She walked into the bedroom, and he dodged past her into the bathroom, where he quickly stripped off his clothes.

A luke warm shower, scented soap, and then on with a thoughtfully supplied bathrobe. He glanced down at his dick. Softer than a well-cooked noodle. Psyche up time. Time to think sweet thoughts, flash onto erotic memories. *Time to get it on.* Confidently he swung into the bedroom.

Mrs. McQueen and Mrs. Jaeger were naked in each other's arms. A tangle of moaning flesh.

Was he supposed to join in? Watch? Wait?

The client always makes the choice. And for a thousand bucks these ladies could make any choice they wished.

He stood in the middle of the room awaiting instructions, feeling his hard-on deflate, feeling like a fool.

The women did not seem to be aware of his existence as they writhed and twisted on the large double bed, so he tried a subtle clearing of his throat, just to let them know he was around.

No reaction. Norma was intent on dive-bombing Celeste's muff, and heavy sighs and groans were signalling *somebody's* climax. Certainly not *his*. A climax was the last thing on his mind.

'Ahhhhh . . .'

'Come on, sweetie. Make it. Get there. *Come* on.'

They sounded like a drowning horse and a fast talking bookie. Buddy concealed a grin – not that they would have noticed if he had stripped right off and sung Jumpin' Jack Flash.

At last their bodies separated, and while Celeste lay gasping, Norma sat up and said triumphantly, 'Well, Buddy? And what did you think of *that*?'

What did she want? A review?

Gee, the action was a little slow in places, and the dialogue unoriginal, but it wasn't a bad performance. Norma Jaeger shone as the aggressor, while Celeste McQueen was suitably hysterical as the second lead.

'Uh . . . nice.'

She hooted with laughter. 'Just nice?'

He thought he should show a little enthusiasm. 'Vereeee horny.'

'Why don't you come join in?' Norma invited. Celeste was obviously a silent partner.

'I was just thinking the same thing,' he said lamely. Maybe he could fake it.

Fake an erection? What an ace trick *that* would be. Wow! No more money problems. Patent the scam and *watch* the big bucks roll. He could see the book title now. HOW TO GET A HARD-ON WHEN YOU'RE NOT IN THE MOOD FOR SEX. A *sure* best seller.

'Take off your robe first. I want to look at you. I love looking at beautiful young men's bodies.'

Oh, shit! He wanted out.

'You're not shy, are you?' she teased. 'Jason doesn't usually send me the shy ones.'

So that was it. Jason knew the set-up all along. All that garbage about just taking out a couple of lonely ladies was just that. Jason must have seen him coming.

Celeste surfaced, her streaked hair in disarray. She had hanging breasts that looked like they had seen plenty of action. 'Ummm.' She stretched. 'What's happening?'

She reminded him of San Diego and a fourteen year old boy . . . his mother standing in the doorway . . . slipping off her robe . . . big hanging breasts and musky thighs . . .

'I gotta go,' he mumbled. 'I *really* gotta go.'

'What?' Norma and Celeste both echoed their surprise.

'I have this appointment I forgot about –' He stumbled into the bathroom, threw off the bathrobe, struggled quickly into his clothes. 'Like there's this test I'm doin', an' I gotta pick up the new pages –'

He was at the door. His hand touched freedom as he grasped the handle.

'My money, Buddy.' Norma Jaeger's voice was ice.

'Oh, yeah . . . sure.' He reached into his jacket pocket, fingered the stack of crisp new bills, silently wished them goodbye. 'Here you go.' He threw them on the bed. They landed on Celeste's stomach.

Then he was out of there, running, running, taking deep gulps of fresh air, putting time and distance between himself and his past.

Accustomed as she was to men approaching her, Angel had never quite figured out a way to repel them without getting involved in some way. Conversation led to familiarity, and suddenly you *knew* a total stranger – whether you wanted to or not.

The man on the beach was different. Angel sensed it immediately. He didn't bother with the usual lines. He just came right out with – 'You don't know me, but I've been watching you. And let me tell you something – I could be the start of a whole new life for you.'

'Excuse me,' she said, backing away.

He pursued her. 'I don't want your body. I have no interest in anything personal.'

She backed away farther.

'Beautiful!' he exclaimed. 'Perfect!'

She looked around for someone to rescue her.

'We're neighbours,' he said, trying to calm her. 'I live in the house next to yours.'

'My husband is home,' she said nervously. 'He doesn't like me talking to men – he's very jealous – he's –'

'I don't give a damn about your husband!' he yelled, waving his arms in the air. '*Listen* to me, little girl, and listen carefully. I want to make you a movie star! If you can do to a camera what you do in person – then you're made. You understand me?' He paused dramatically. 'I want you in my movie.'

Her eyes widened. All her life she had dreamed of someone saying that to her. 'Who are you?' she gasped.

'Who am I?' He roared with laughter. 'Don't you read the trades? Didn't you see me on the cover of Newsweek last year?'

Silently she shook her head, awed by the frantic energy he gave off.

He narrowed his eyes and stared at her intently. 'You don't smoke do you? No, of course you don't.' He held his hands as if to frame her face. 'You – little lady, are going to be a star. I, Oliver Easterne, will make you one.'

20

PITTSBURGH, THURSDAY:
THE BODIES OF A MAN AND A WOMAN WERE DISCOVERED IN A DESERTED ALLEYWAY EARLY TODAY. THE WOMAN, A TWENTY YEAR OLD CONVICTED PROSTITUTE, HAD BEEN BADLY MUTILATED AND SLASHED. HER THROAT WAS CUT.

THE MAN, A THIRTY-FOUR YEAR OLD CUBAN NATIONAL AND KNOWN PIMP, WAS ATTACKED IN A SIMILAR FASHION. THE BLOWS RAINED UPON HIM WERE SO FEROCIOUS THAT HIS RIGHT ARM WAS SEVERED ABOVE THE ELBOW. IT IS BELIEVED THAT HIS ATTACKER LEFT HIM TO BLEED TO DEATH. POLICE ARE SEEKING WITNESSES.

The old brown panel van roared along the highway, leaving Pittsburgh far behind. And the radio, which had not worked at all when

Deke purchased the truck, now blared out from four hidden speakers. Rod Stewart. Passion.

In the bars and the cafes – Passion
In the streets and the alleys – Passion
Lot of pretending – Passion
Everybody's searching – Passion.

How true the words were, Deke thought. Everyone was getting it. But where was the passion in *his* life?

Hear it on the radio – Passion
Read it in the paper – Passion
Hear it in the churches – Passion
See it in the schoolyard – Passion.

Joey. She had given him passion. The only one who ever had . . .

Can't live without passion
Even the President needs passion
Everybody I know needs some passion
Some people die and kill for passion.

Joey. He had loved her, even though she was a whore, even though she was a liar, even though she was a whoring lying bitch bitch bitch . . .

Some people die and kill for passion.

The fact that Joey accepted his proposal of marriage surprised Deke. She said, 'Okay, bigshot, name the day.' And then added, 'An' I want a ring – an' if ya want me t'give up hookin' then you're gonna hafta hand me some bucks every week.' She collapsed with a weary sigh onto her unmade bed. 'An' when we gonna do it? Soon?' She nodded, as if asking herself the question. 'Yeah, soon,' she decided.

He stared at her blankly. Asking was one thing. Doing was another.

There were all sorts of things to consider. His mother, for one. He had only brought a girl home on one occasion – and that had been when he was much younger. She had made the girl perfectly welcome, then later, when they were alone, she had smiled wistfully and said, 'Not for you, son, is she? Not good enough.'

But then of course nothing was ever good enough for his mother. School marks, his job, his hobbies.

'Cars!' She would screw up her nose distastefully. 'We paid for your education so that you could lie around under cars all day. Is that it, son? Is that what we struggled for?'

She had never accepted his job at the garage. She would never accept Joey.

'Alright, soon,' he mumbled.

'When?' Joey demanded.

'I'll make some plans . . .'

'Where'll we live?' she flashed.

He was almost sorry that he had asked her. He had not expected to have to make such immediate decisions. *'I'll find a place.'*

'A house?'

The money he made at the garage wasn't that good. And then of course he had to give his mother a set amount. Before Joey, he had been able to put some away, but now he had only a few hundred dollars left in the bank.

'We'll see.'

She bounced off the bed, black circled eyes spiteful and menacing – the cast in her left eye emphasized by her tiredness. *'Listen, cowboy, don't do me no favours.'*

'I'm not,' he assured her anxiously.

'You bet you're not.' She stretched her arms above her head and yawned. *'I coulda got hitched hundreds of times if I'd wanted to. I even hadda cop crazy about me. How d'ya like that?'*

He didn't like it. Joey Kravetz was his. And anybody who tried to take her away from him was dead. Stone cold dead.

The van veered out of its lane, and an irate driver in a Cadillac gave Deke an obscene sign with his finger. Deke was incensed. Purposefully he changed lanes, came up real close behind the Cadillac, and began to beep his horn in short staccatto blasts.

Both vehicles were speeding, going way past the limit. But the Cadillac didn't give way, and Deke did not slow his pace.

Dangerously they raced along the two lane highway, the van only inches from the Cadillac's tail.

There were road works coming up, signals indicated that the two lane highway narrowed to one lane a mile ahead.

Deke pulled out and alongside the Cadillac. The driver, a middle-aged man, stared stonily ahead. He had decided that maybe he was dealing with a nut.

As they approached the road works the man slowed, ready to pull in behind the maniac in the van. But the maniac wouldn't let him, the maniac kept pace with his speed, blocking his entry onto the clear lane. Christ! The arrows indicated he must get over *now*. In a sudden burst of panic he put his foot down hard on the accelerator – there was no way a Cadillac couldn't outrun a faded old van. No way.

Except that inexplicably it couldn't. The van stayed alongside him all the way, pulling ahead just before the Cadillac smashed full speed into a heavy concrete mixer.

The middle-aged driver knew agonizing pain for only seconds, and then – nothing.

Deke arrived in Cincinnati three hours later. He was tired and very very hungry. It took him no time at all to find a diner where he had two orders of steak. After that he slept for five hours in the back of the van, and then, refreshed, he continued his journey west.

California was waiting for him, he had to hurry.

21

Bibi Sutton lived on a walled estate in Bel Air, with armed guards at the wrought iron gate, and specially trained German shepherd killer-dogs roaming the grounds. Nobody visited Bibi unannounced.

Elaine drove her Mercedes up to the gates and gave her name to a cowboy-hatted guard. He checked out a typewritten list. 'You know your way up to the main house, Ma'am?' he drawled.

'Yes, I do,' she replied, thinking how silly this whole rigmarole was. Everyone loved Adam Sutton. He was a legend – a John Wayne or a Gregory Peck. Who could possibly wish to do him harm?

Then she smiled. The security was for Bibi. Of course. Probably half of Beverly Hills wanted to slit her throat!

At one time the Sutton mansion had belonged to a silent movie star, Elaine could not quite remember which one. Maybe Barrymore or Valentino. It didn't matter, for Bibi had changed everything, and created a cool white roman villa with pillars, fountains, and marbled terraces. If she wasn't a professional movie star wife she could have taken a shot at interior design. She certainly knew what she was doing, even if it *had* cost a couple of million dollars.

A uniformed servant waited by the front steps to take Elaine's car, and a maid escorted her through marbled hallways to a sunlit terrace overlooking an olympic sized pool. There, Bibi held court.

Elaine's eyes darted round the assemblage. The upper-echelon ladies of Beverly Hills, Bel Air, and other suitably monied locations were out in full force. Saint Laurent, Dior, Blass, and de la Renta, rustled expensively on perfect bodies. And if they weren't perfect they made a damn good try. Electrolysis, body firming, cellulite control, vein removing, fat removing. All these things had taken place on one or the other of the bodies milling around. Tit renovation, teeth capping, snatch tightening, eyelid lifting, nose bobbing, ass raising. All these things and more.

'Sweetie!' Bibi bore down on her, a vision in a white summery Galanos. Very simple. After all it *was* only a lunch-party. 'So nice you come. I like your suit. I see it before, no?'

'No.'

'Ah, yes. I see it in Saks last week.'

At least she was aware of the fact that it was new. 'You look lovely,' Elaine enthused.

Bibi laughed gaily. 'This old thing – I throw it on.'

Elaine looked around for a drink, and an attentive waiter appeared at her elbow. He carried a choice on a silver tray. Champagne or Perrier. She quickly reached for a glass of champagne. There was only one way to get through *this* lunch, and it certainly wasn't sober.

The moment Elaine left the house, Ross reached for the phone. Karen picked up on the second buzz. She sounded politely cold. 'I have to go, Ross. I was just leaving for Bibi's lunch and I'm running late.'

'What's the matter, baby? Don't I turn you on anymore?'

'Can we discuss this some other time?'

'What's wrong with right now? I'm sitting here with a hard-on that would bring tears to your eyes.'

'So jerk off.'

'It's not the same, Karen. Not when I could be with you.' He paused for effect, then continued. 'Jesus, but you looked horny on Friday night. What were you doing with a schmuck like Chet Barnes?'

'Fucking him.'

'That's nice.'

'It was.'

'Does he still come before he gets it all the way in?'

She gasped. 'How did you know that?'

'This here town ain't nothin' but a village, lady.'

'You bum!'

He had her, he could hear it in his voice. 'How about lunch with me instead of Bibi?' he suggested.

'You're such a bastard. Why didn't you call me when you said you would?'

'I didn't think a little thing like that would bother a liberated lady like you.'

'I'm not some make-up girl or hairdresser you're throwing on to one side, you know,' she complained.

'Where shall we meet?' he asked confidently.

She sighed. She never had been one to turn down a better offer. 'The beach I suppose.'

'It's a long ride.'

She laughed huskily. 'I sure hope so!'

Montana summoned her secretary into the office with a sharp buzz on the intercom. 'Inga, I want all the actors I'm testing for the part of Vinnie available on Thursday.'

Inga nodded, itching to dial the good news to Buddy Hudson.

'Have them arrive at the studio at hourly intervals from seven a.m. on. They are to wear their own clothes – casual, suggest Levis and a shirt. Make-up and hair will be taken care of.'

Inga nodded again, making cryptic shorthand notes on her pad.

'There's four of them, right?' Montana checked.

'Yes,' Inga confirmed. 'Do you want them to arrive in any special order?'

'It makes no difference. They'll all have the same chance.' She pushed her glasses up into her hair. 'God! I'll be glad when every last role is cast on this movie. I seem to have spent the last year of my life interviewing actors and actresses.'

Inga wondered if it was a good time to throw some questions at her boss. 'Um . . . Is George Lancaster definitely doing it?'

'I wish I knew!' snapped Montana. 'The whole goddamn movie is cast except for the three most important roles. Wonderful, huh?'

Inga smiled politely. 'I understand Mr. Gray is testing Gina Germaine. Excuse me for saying so, but isn't she too *sexy* for the part?'

'Ha! Nice understatement, kid. Any coffee going around here?'

Inga retreated. Conversation with the boss over. She rushed to her desk and tried the number Buddy had given her at the beach. No reply. No service pick-up. Who had ever heard of an actor without an answering service? Somebody would have to get Buddy Hudson together. Maybe it would be her . . .

Oliver Easterne came bouncing into the office, interrupting her thoughts.

'Miz Gray around?' he asked, running a finger along the rim of her desk and inspecting it for dust.

'Yes she is. I'll tell her you're –'

Before she could even pick up the intercom he was past her and into the office.

Montana, looking through some photos at her desk, glanced up. 'Good morning, Oliver,' she said coolly. 'Don't bother to knock. Just come right in.'

He ignored her quiet sarcasm, polished off the seat of a leather chair with his pocket handkerchief and sat down. 'I have found us Nikki,' he announced.

'Oliver?' Montana questioned. 'Tell me, I'm curious. When you have sex do you disinfect your cock first?'

He stared at her, frowned, then laughed heartily. 'You got a cute sense of humour,' he allowed, 'for a woman.'

'Thank you,' she murmured mockingly. 'Your conversation never disappoints.'

He cracked his knuckles several times, then inspected his impeccable nails which were coated with clear nail polish. 'Don't you want to know who she is?'

'I do know. Gina Germaine. And the idea stinks.'

'No. I have found us a girl who makes Gina Germaine look like her fucking *mother*!'

She sighed, 'Have you told Neil this wonderful news?'

He leaned across the desk and lowered his voice. 'I wanted *you* to be the first to know.'

'Gee, thanks.'

'This girl I've found is sensational.'

'I thought you wanted Gina. I mean it was you who carried on about what a big star she was, and how great she would be for box office, wasn't it?'

'With George Lancaster who needs Gina Germaine?'

'George Lancaster is a maybe,' she reminded him wearily.

'He's a definite. I called him in Palm Beach last night and got a commitment. I'm having a meeting with Sadie La Salle this afternoon to firm up terms.'

'Does Neil know this?' she asked, feeling like a record stuck in the same old groove.

'Neil's the artistic side,' he said airily. 'I'm the business. *I* should have talked to George in the first place. Actors. *I* know how to treat 'em. Plus I'm paying him five mil and a piece of the action.'

Montana thought of the paltry sum she was receiving for the property. 'How nice,' she murmured drily. 'Don't you think you should tell Neil the good news?'

'He's out looking at locations. I'll see him when he gets back. In the meantime I came to tell *you* about this girl I've found.'

'Exactly where did you find her?'

'On the beach. She's my neighbour.'

Montana frowned. She was getting more and more disillusioned with the business side of making movies. First George Lancaster, news which didn't thrill her. Now a little nymphet Oliver had discovered roaming the beach. 'I've had it with the casting on this movie,' she said sharply. 'First Gina, then some bimbo you probably picked up. This is fucking amateur night, Oliver.'

He took no notice of her outburst. 'You'll see what I mean when you meet her. *She is Nikki.*' And with that he stood up, vigorously brushed the back of his pants, removed a dead flower from a vase on her desk, flicked it into the trash basket, and exited.

She took a long deep breath. Where was all this total control Neil had mentioned?

Late Sunday afternoon Buddy phoned the house at the beach. 'Pack up everything, get in the car, and come straight over to Randy's place. Leave the keys there, an' don't answer the phone. If Jason turns up don't talk to him about *anything*. Got it?'

'I don't unders –'

'Got it?'

'Yes.'

'Get moving. I want you out of there fast.'

Angel did as she was told, although her mind was alive with questions. She packed quickly. The phone rang once, but she ignored it. Jason did not turn up. Tearfully she realized it was goodbye to the house at the beach. Life with Buddy was certainly unpredictable.

He met her outside Randy Felix's apartment. She could smell liquor on his breath, and there was a wild excited look about him.

'I don't understand –' she began again.

He grabbed her in a hug. 'One day I'll explain it to you, babe.' And pulled her inside the apartment to meet Randy.

That was it as far as explanations went. Randy had a girl with him, Shelly. She seemed pleasant enough, although a little trampy to look at. They all sat around in the small apartment drinking cheap red wine and dragging on joints Shelly obligingly rolled. Angel did not indulge, and nobody seemed to mind, they were all too busy talking about themselves.

She sat in a corner, a slow steady anger building within. This was not the Buddy she had married. This was not the loving man she had met and fallen in love with – this jumpy, loud, stoned person.

Around twelve Shelly stood up and stretched. 'I gotta get me some sleep,' she yawned. 'I mean Sunday's my only day off, and I am *out-of-it*.'

Quick as a flash Buddy grabbed Angel by the hand and pulled her up too. 'You're sleepin' over at Shell's, sweet stuff,' he announced, like it was the most natural thing in the world. 'I'm gonna hit the sack on Randy's floor. Tomorrow I'll find us a place.'

She was dismayed. 'Buddy –' she began.

He squeezed her hand. 'Do it,' he muttered. 'It's the only game in town. She's a good kid, no hassles, she's not that way inclined.'

Angel stared at him coldly. His hair was tousled, his eyes bloodshot, sweat beaded his handsome features, and he smelled awful. 'What about my things?' she asked, feeling tired and disillusioned. 'Our suitcases are still out in the car.'

'Shell will set you up with anything you need, won't you, Shell?'

The curly headed girl nodded. 'And if you stop callin' me Shell, I'll even give her breakfast.'

Buddy grinned and swayed slightly. 'Thank *you*, Shelly,' he managed. 'I will remember you in my will.'

Shelly grinned back and patted his cheek affectionately. A move that did not go unnoticed by Angel.

'Let's go Angel-face,' Shelly said. 'You'll love my apartment, it's even smaller than this dump.' She waved vaguely at Randy, who was slumped on the middle of his bed. 'Nice to meet you, thanks for the vino.'

He waved back in an uncoordinated fashion. 'Nice to meet *you* – neighbour. Good grass. Next time I'll buy if you got any to sell.'

'Grass. Coke. Quacks. Name it. I'm your man.'

'Some man!' slurred Buddy.

Shelly grinned. ' 'Night all.'

Silently Angel followed her from the apartment, two flights up the outside staircase, tears stinging her eyes, anger stinging her tongue. It wasn't often she lost her temper, but when she did it was a surprise. The Madonna turned into a tiger.

197

They stopped outside Shelly's apartment while she groped for her key. Then she flung the door open and said, 'Enter paradise, Angel-face. The worst little flop-house in Hollywood!'

'More champagne, Mrs Conti?' the young waiter inquired.

Elaine nodded, and vaguely wondered how he knew her name.

Why shouldn't he? I'm famous too. I am a movie star's wife. A soon-to-be-back-on-top-and-screw-everyone movie star.

Christ! She was drunk and she knew it. Not sloppy drunk, fortu-nately, but on the edge . . .

Surreptitiously she tipped her champagne glass so that a thin steady trickle of the finest Dom Perignon hit the grass.

She sat on a white canvas director's chair along with thirty-six other women (she had done a head count after lunch). And along with the rest of them she was being bored to death by a muscular ex-detective who looked like a Kojak reject and spoke like an articulate boxer who had just found God. Only he had just found Mace, or so it seemed. And there was no detail too trivial for him to reveal about the goddamn stuff.

I want to pee, she decided, and shot a sideways glance at Maralee, whose expression was hidden behind tinted purple shades which matched her five hundred dollar Anne Klein jacket. Elaine knew it had cost exactly that for she had passed it by in her quest for the perfect outfit.

'I need to go to the bathroom,' she whispered.

'Who's stopping you?' Maralee whispered back.

She stood, caught Bibi's disapproving eye, mimed desperation, and hurried into the house.

A waitress, stuffing her mouth with expensive chocolates, jumped guiltily. Elaine swept past her to the pink and gold powder room. Idly she wondered about Karen. She had said she was coming to the lunch, so where was she?

Maybe a sudden flash of intuition had warned her that it was going to be the most boring luncheon of the year.

Elaine did what she had to do, checked out her appearance, and hurried back outside. Seated once again she reflected that by no means was the lunch a dead loss. The very fact that she had been invited in the first place was a plus. And a double plus was being able to say – ever so casually – to Sadie La Salle – 'I do hope you can come to the little party I'm putting together for George and Pamela Lancaster.'

Even Sadie La Salle could not afford to turn *that* invite down. She had nodded, said, 'Of course,' and even attempted a pleasant smile. Ross would be delighted. Once the woman was in his home she could hardly continue to ignore him.

Maralee gave a gentle snore. She had fallen asleep behind her shades. Quickly Elaine nudged her.

'Oh!' she started.

'And where were *you* last night?' Elaine whispered.

Maralee giggled. 'Recovering from Friday and Saturday night. Randy certainly lives up to his name!'

Elaine smiled and wondered if *she* should find herself a young boyfriend. Ironic really. Here she was married to the man with the biggest dick in Hollywood, and she was thinking about finding herself a young boyfriend. How on earth could anyone else measure up?

She almost laughed aloud.

'You ever thought about divorcing Elaine?' Karen inquired. She was astride him at the time, knees athletically gripping his hips, while tactile nipples rose and fell temptingly near his mouth.

He was so surprised that he failed to reply. As far as he was concerned, conversation while making it was a no no. He grunted.

'Well?' persisted Karen.

Her muscle tone was perfect. Why didn't she just keep her mouth shut? 'Divorce costs too much,' he gasped.

She manoeuvred her body on top of his and closed her legs.

He groaned in appreciation. This girl knew tricks even *he* hadn't tried. She was squeezing him with her muscles and driving him crazy.

'Would you divorce her if *I* wanted you to?'

He ignored the question. Gave himself up to the few precious moments before orgasm. 'Move,' he pleaded. 'I'm going to come.'

Her silent reply was to grip him even more firmly and rotate her body until she too was ready. As he exploded, so did she. Thrusting her extended nipples in his mouth, grabbing at his hair, squeezing her legs together so tightly that he felt the come was being suctioned out of him.

'Watch the hair!' he screamed desperately.

'Screw your goddamn hair!' she shrieked back.

They peaked together in a frenzy.

'Jesus H. Christ!' he gasped. 'You really are the best.'

Slowly she released him, leaned over to the bedside table and lit cigarettes for them both. 'You know how much money I have?' she asked.

He tingled all over. Hot damn, he felt about seventeen!

'How much?' he asked.

'Enough to pay Elaine off for a start. And when daddy goes, the sky's the limit!'

Wonderful talk. George Lancaster was only twelve years older than he was.

'What are you saying?'

She drew deeply on her cigarette. 'That you and I would make a good couple.'

He laughed half-heartedly, not at all impressed with the way the conversation was progressing. 'You and I are good together because we're *not* married.'

'You think so?'

'I know so.'

'We'll see . . .'

'We'll see what?' he asked alarmed.

'We'll just see, that's all,' she replied mysteriously. 'Why don't we swim?'

'In the ocean?'

'I don't see a pool around.'

'I haven't swum in the ocean for years.'

'Let's go then.' She jumped off the bed, rummaged in a drawer and came up with a pair of red shorts for him, and a one-piece cutaway suit for herself.

He slipped on the shorts, they were tight in the waist, even tighter between the legs. 'Ouch,' he complained.

'Never mind,' she crooned. 'Momma'll massage it all better in the Jacuzzi when we get back.'

'Why are you so good to me Karen?' he asked quizzically.

She grinned. ' 'Cos one good turn deserves another – and baby – your turns are *gooood*!'

They ran out of the house holding hands.

A lone photographer lying on his stomach under the wooden stilts of a nearby house adjusted his telephoto lens. Within five minutes he had shot two rolls of very interesting film indeed.

Angel hardly slept at all. The state of Shelly's rundown apartment shocked her. Clothes everywhere, dirty dishes, overflowing ashtrays, and cockroaches roaming the tiny kitchenette like it was their rightful home.

Shelly had indicated the unmade bed. 'Wanna share?' she questioned. 'I'm not fussy if you're not.'

Angel had already spotted a bulky armchair. 'I'll take that, if you don't mind,' she said quickly, memories of ex-landlady, Daphne, still fresh in her mind.

'Suit yourself, Angel-face,' shrugged Shelly, rummaging in a drawer. 'Want some coke?'

'I'm not thirsty, thank you.'

Shelly shot her a raised eyebrow look, which she ignored. Carefully she removed a scatter of clothes from the chair and placed them in a neat pile on the end of the bed. Sleep. Think. Work things out. She was upset and angry, there hadn't even been a chance to tell Buddy about her meeting with Oliver Easterne. A meeting that had left her breathless with excitement, his words ringing in her ears.

You, little lady, are going to be a star.

Naturally she had wanted to tell Buddy immediately, and he would have been as excited as she was. Now everything was spoiled. She would probably never get to see Oliver Easterne again.

Shelly threw over a grubby looking shawl as Angel settled into the chair. 'Sweet dreams, kiddo,' she said. 'If you should happen to be an early riser, move quietly. I don't like seeing daylight until at least eleven.'

Angel nodded. And then spent a miserable night trying to force her cramped body to sleep. By seven a.m. she was wide awake. Quietly she let herself out and went down to the pool.

As the morning progressed other residents appeared. Two girls in matching swimsuits who did a series of intricate gymnastics. An old bewigged lady leading a frazzled french poodle on a diaménta lead. A young schoolboy who had a secretive smoke under a palm tree.

Then came the serious sunbathers armed with towels and oils, nose covers and eye shields. Out of work actors all of them.

Angel sat quietly on a broken-down deck chair, her beautiful eyes tinged with worry and tiredness. She smoothed back her fine blond hair and tried to stifle a sudden rumbling in her stomach. She was hungry, starving in fact. She glanced at her watch. Only ten minutes before eleven. She would have thought that Buddy would have come looking for her by now.

•

Buddy surfaced slowly, the heavy pounding in his head signaling life. Only just. He groaned loudly.

Randy, unshaven and bleary-eyed, shakily poured two cups of black instant coffee and silently handed him one.

'Didn't we just go to sleep?' Buddy complained, burning his tongue with the steaming liquid and letting forth a string of expletives.

'Seems like it,' agreed Randy, scratching a sweaty armpit and peering at his Patek-Philippe gold watch – a present from Maralee. 'However – it is now two o'clock in the afternoon.'

'What day?' groaned Buddy.

'Monday,' Randy replied, groping for the phone. He dialled a number and asked to speak to Mrs. Maralee Gray.

Buddy staggered into the tiny bathroom. He knew he should call Angel at once, she had not looked pleased when he stuck her with Shelly. But shit, it was only for the night, today he would get something together.

He splashed cold water on his face and peered in the mirror. Buddy Boy was not looking his best. He had really laid one on, drugs, booze – the first time since Angel. But he had felt so depressed and frustrated after running out on the two women at the Beverly Hills Hotel. He needed to let go for once.

Thank God for friends. Randy, who had understood when he turned up at his apartment, and Shelly, who had agreed to put Angel up for the night. No problem.

The cold water revived him somewhat. He began to feel almost human. Randy was still on the phone talking intimately. Snowing Maralee Gray with bullshit charm.

Buddy pulled on his pants and signalled that he was going up to Shelly's.

Two sharp raps. Three. Angel at the door, a cleaning cloth in her hands, the smell of Lysol in the air.

Buddy threw up his arms in exasperation. 'What are you doing?'

Her voice cold, hurt. 'Cleaning up.'

'Cleaning up *what* for crissake?'

'Your friend, Shelly, lives like a pig. I'm repaying her for my night's board. It's the least I can do.'

He grabbed her arm. 'Don't be a silly girl. It's not necessary It's –'

With venom she shook his hand away. Anger that had been building all night exploded. 'Don't silly girl *me*, Buddy Hudson. Just

202

who do you think you are speaking to? A Barbie Doll?'

He was surprised by her outburst. 'Hey – baby – what's all this?'

Her eyes flashed dangerously. 'What is all *what*? Little Angel answering back? Little Angel showing feelings?' She threw the cloth angrily on the floor. 'I'm a *person*. I'm your *wife*. And I want to know just exactly what is going on, because if you don't care to tell me, I am packing up and getting out of here. You understand? Be truthful with me, Buddy, or I promise you, you'll never see me again.'

22

Lulu Kravetz did not even want to know where her sister was buried. Once she was informed of the murder and heard the details, she clammed up.

'I never knew no Deke Andrews,' she muttered. 'An' if you're so sure it's him, how come you don't catch the scum-bag?'

Logical enough. A simple statement. Why *didn't* they catch him?

Leon mumbled something about they were working on it, and Lulu threw him a look that needed no words.

'So, since you're not here to arrest me, or roust me for dope – can you split out of my life?' Restlessly she threw herself on top of the unmade bed and closed her eyes. 'I'm tired. man. I've been travellin' for fuckin' ever.'

He stared at the fat girl for a long silent moment. Did the murder of her sister mean that little to her?

Joey Kravetz. Nobody cared . . . Not one single person . . . Except maybe him . . .

'You going or not?' Lulu demanded.

'Yeah, man. You going or not?' repeated her Chicano friend, suddenly brave.

Slowly Leon nodded, and left. There was nothing to stay for.

Out on the street it was raining, a slow miserable drizzle. A bum slumped against the hood of his car. 'Move it!' Leon ordered fiercely, and the man staggered drunkenly off.

Why did he feel so depressed? Why did he feel like going to a bar and getting good and gloriously drunk. Hadn't done that in a long time.

Joey Kravetz . . . Joey Kravetz . . . Joey Kravetz . . .
Funny faced little hooker . . .

Relief was his first reaction. She had departed from his life without a murmur, and now he would not have to face her. He boiled water for a cup of coffee, and sat reflectively at the kitchen table. Should never have let her into his apartment in the first place. At his age he should have known better. She could have tried to blackmail him, screamed rape, anything . . .

He shuddered at his own stupidity, drained his coffee cup, and hurried to dress. It wasn't until he picked up his wallet that he realized his money was missing. Every last bill. He wasn't sure how much, but it was certainly more than three hundred dollars. Little Miss Kravetz had played him for a real sucker. She was probably still laughing.

He felt like the world's biggest fool. And then anger took over, and he thought about finding her and getting his money back. Just who exactly did she think she was ripping off?

His intentions were solid, but after a few days of cruising around streets where he thought she might hang out, a murder case came in, and his energies were otherwise engaged. Weeks turned into months, and the vision of the teenage hooker with three hundred plus of his hard-earned money faded. He had learned a valuable lesson, that was enough. Now all he wanted to do was forget the whole incident. Which he did. Until one night in Mackies Bar – a cop hang-out. He was there with several of his colleagues. They had cracked a big one. Arrested a forty-six year old man who had raped and murdered seven women over a two year period. The man had confessed after months of being their prime suspect. Celebrations were in full swing. Even Leon – not known for his partying – was feeling no pain.

He saw her before she glimpsed him. Who could miss the orange hair and squiffy eye? She was draped all over a young rookie, giggling and sticking her tongue in his bright pink ear.

Did she know she was in a cops' bar? Did she even care?

He waited until she went into the ladies room, a solitary door in the back, reached by walking along a dark deserted passageway. Ladies were not encouraged to frequent Mackies. Only the cop groupies survived.

Leon followed, positioned himself outside, waited until she emerged, then grabbed her and pinned her against the graffiti scarred wall, his breath heavy with too much alcohol. 'Remember me?'

204

'Oh. You,' she said cheerily, not at all surprised. 'How ya doin', cowboy?'

He wished he was sober and clear-headed. Drink had fogged his mind, even his tongue. 'You owe me money,' he slurred.

'Are you sure?' she questioned, blinking quickly while working out the best escape route.

'Yes, I'm sure,' he replied indignantly. 'Over three hundred bucks.'

'I think ya got the wrong girl, mister. Like I never hafta rip off anyone's bread. I make it – legit, y'know what I mean?' She grinned at him cheekily. 'For ten bucks I'll jerk y'off here. I just figured, in your apartment it's gotta cost ya more.'

His thoughts were tight but his mouth didn't follow through. 'Listen you –' he began slowly.

She ducked under his arms and was away. 'Fair's, fair,' she called out. 'Doncha think?'

By the time he got back to his friends she was gone.

He spent the rest of the evening trying to sober up, but two hours later when he got home, he was still in a bad way.

He must have slept for several hours before the need to relieve himself woke him. He felt like the bottom of a garbage can, and vowed immediately to give up drink forever.

He staggered to his feet, trying to ignore the shooting pains which attacked the back of his head like a thousand tiny needles. Then he saw her, curled on his couch, fast asleep, as comfortable and contented as a resident cat. Joey Kravetz.

For a moment he stared, too surprised to utter a word. Then he let out a sudden roar of rage – which did his head no good whatsoever. 'What are you doing here?'

She awoke quickly, rubbed her eyes, grinned. 'Glad t'see you're still alive.'

'What are you doing in my apartment?' he yelled. 'How did you get in?'

Like a cat she licked the tip of her index finger and cleaned under her eyes where shadow and mascara had mingled to give her the look of a forlorn clown. 'You left the key in the door. Some big-time cop!'

He quietened down. 'What do you want?'

She jumped off the couch, ridiculous in a fake leather white mini and over the knee boots. 'You'll never believe this, but I got me an attack of the guilts. You know – rippin' you off like I did when you was kind enough t'give me a place t'sleep an' all.' She peered at him intently. 'I got feelin's y'know, just like anyone else. An' I got to thinking –'

'After you saw me.'

'Yeah. After I saw you. I got t' thinkin' that even for a cop you're not so bad, an' like I should maybe say I'm sorry, an' pay ya back a few bucks.' She fumbled in a tattered purse and pulled out a ten dollar bill which she solemnly handed to him.

He stared at the money and at her, while his head throbbed and his eyes ached.

'You don't look so good,' she ventured. 'How about gettin' into bed an' discussin' this in the mornin'?'

'Christ!' he snapped. 'You're really full of it.'

She looked pained. 'I thought you'd be pleased . . .'

He pulled a disgusted face and marched into the bathroom.

Why was this run-down teenage hooker invading his life? What did she want from him?

He drank several glasses of tap water, and emerged to find that she had returned to her original place on his couch and appeared to be asleep again. It was four-fifteen in the morning, and he didn't have the strength or the heart to throw her out. Instead he double-locked the front door, then took his keys, wallet and gun to bed with him. He considered locking his bedroom door, but didn't.

Wearily he stripped off his clothes and climbed naked into bed. Deep down he knew that she would come to him. She was a kid, a hooker, a little nothing. Yet he knew that she would come – and worse – he wanted her to.

Mackies was crowded. It was at least a year since he'd been in. Nothing had changed.

He ordered a scotch and stood at the bar alone. Millie would be wondering what had happened to him. For once, let her wonder.

He downed the first shot and signalled for another. It was going to be a long hot weekend.

23

Thursday morning. At the studio. Washed and brushed. Nervous as an Arab in an Israeli bazaar. But looking good.

He gave his name to the guard on the gate and drove onto the lot like a star, even if he was only driving his old Pontiac.

His stomach felt queasy. He had *forced* hot coffee and a piece of burnt toast between his lips, then thrown up, dry empty heaves.

He had been a wreck ever since calling Inga, Tuesday afternoon, and getting a short sharp blast. 'Where have you been, Buddy Hudson? I have better things to do with my time than ruin my nails punching out a number that never answers.'

'What's up?' he had asked, adrenaline flooding his body because he knew what was up without her telling him.

'Your test. If you're still interested, that is. I never heard of a serious actor without an answering service. Honestly, I –'

'When?'

'Thursday.'

'Ohmigod!'

Now here he was. About to test for the chance of a lifetime. Jeez! No wonder he was nervous.

Buddy Hudson, this is your life. Can you hack it or can you not?

He parked his car, checked into reception, and was shown to a dressing room adjacent to Stage Three by a butch-looking girl in jeans, a Dodgers baseball jacket, and sneakers.

'Do you know where the make-up room is?' she asked him.

He wasn't about to admit that he didn't. Cool. Stay cool. Don't let anyone glimpse the nerves. 'Sure. Unless they've moved it.'

'Same place. Ground floor, you can't miss it. Be there in fifteen minutes. Wardrobe'll come by to check you out. Okay?'

'What time will I be . . . uh . . . what time's my . . . uh . . . test?'

'I guess they'll want you on the set 'bout eleven. If you're lucky they'll have you out of here before lunch. The break's at one.'

Two hours. Was that all it would take? He had imagined a day of close-ups and long shots. Shit! They were probably only shooting one set-up.

'See you later,' the girl said, and left.

He had wanted to question her, find out about the other actors testing. Too late now to do anything except sweat it out.

He stared at his reflection in the dressing-table mirror. *Lookin' good. Lookin' good. Lookin' just the way a movie star should.* No thanks to Angel. His dear sweet wife. His dear sweet *departed* wife. The love of his life had split. Gone. Run off. Just like that.

True he had dragged her away from the beach house and back to Hollywood without so much as an explanation. But what was there to explain? 'Hey, Angel, babe, I was supposed to screw these two old lesbo broads, only I couldn't get it up – didn't want to get it up – on

207

account of the fact that I love you. You see – Jason Swankle's a fag, an' he's after my body. So he hired me to keep these two ladies happy, and also to keep me in his life. That's why the beach house, the clothes, the chauffeured car . . .'

How could a girl like Angel ever understand a scene like that? She just wasn't into the trash and flash of life, and he didn't want her to be. Her innocence was one of the reasons he felt so strongly about her. There was no way he ever intended to tell her about his past. So . . . he had made a decision to keep her in the dark. It was the only way.

Somehow his decision had misfired. She wanted truth. He gave her lies. He had underestimated her anger. Placated her first outburst, soothed her with lies and kisses, and then collapsed out by the pool. By the time he felt human it was too late to start finding accommodation. 'Just one more night at Shell's, babe,' he pleaded. 'I'll get everything together tomorrow. Promise.'

She had gazed at him with those big eyes. Gazed at him long and hard. Only by that time he was into lighting up a little grass and getting high high high – because – goddamn it – since Sunday his mother was back to haunt him with a vengeance – and getting stoned seemed like some kind of an answer.

On Tuesday he slept late. It was almost three when he opened his eyes. Randy was long gone, and the small apartment was hot and stuffy. At least grass didn't give you a hangover, in fact it left you feeling quite mellow.

He knew that Angel was not going to be delighted with him, so he took his time showering and shaving. Then decided to check in with Inga, just in case. When he heard about the test he moved like a rocket. Couldn't wait to tell Angel. Only there was no one in at Shelly's, and he found himself pacing the sidewalk until five, when she came in alone.

'Where's Angel?' he demanded.

'I don't know,' Shelly shrugged. 'She was here when I came in last night, gone when I got up this morning.'

He knew at once she had walked. Even before he looked in the trunk of his car and found her suitcase gone. So here he was, ready to test, the most important day in his life. And where was Angel just when he needed her most?

*

'Why weren't you at Bibi's lunch, Karen?' Elaine asked, trying to avert her eyes from Ron Gordino's bunch-up – quite impressive in a Rudolf Nureyev way.

'I was laid up,' Karen gasped, stretching her left leg to its limit.

'What did you have?' puffed Elaine, desperately trying to emulate Karen's leg movement, but unable to complete the exercise.

'Some bug. I felt dreadful.'

'You look fine, now.'

'I'm known for my speedy recovery.'

'Need a little help here, Elaine?' Ron Gordino was bending to assist her, grabbing her ankle and *wheedling* the stretch out of her. He smelled of sweat and Brut after-shave.

'Ahhh . . .' gasped Elaine, enjoying the touch of his strong firm hands as they travelled from her ankle to her calf.

'Feel good?' he asked solicitously.

She nodded, flattered to be singled out for his personal attention. It was the first time it had happened to her, although she had often seen him bend to Bibi or Karen and *always* to the celebrities.

'Your muscles are real tight,' he drawled. 'Tense. Are you tense, Elaine?'

'Of course not.' She laughed nervously. 'Why on earth should I be tense?'

His hair was like dirty straw, long and coarse. She noticed a few stray hairs sprouting from his ears and wondered why he didn't do something about them.

His fingers dug into her calf muscles, causing her to wriggle uncomfortably. 'Come into my office after class, you need a massage.'

'I do?'

'Yup.' He raised his sinewy frame and ambled off.

'I think you just scored,' whispered Karen, hardly able to keep the amusement out of her voice.

'Not exactly my type,' replied Elaine crossly.

'Force yourself, darling. He's supposed to be an amazing lay.'

'I thought he was gay.'

'Bi.'

'How do you know?'

'*Never* ask me to reveal my source.'

The rest of the class passed quickly, and before she knew it, Elaine found herself lying face down on a massage table in Ron Gordino's office. His probing hands started at the base of her neck and worked their way down. She had experienced massages before, many times, but the way Ron Gordino operated was different. He sought out and found – with absolutely no trouble at all – every tight muscle in her body. His hands were so soothing that she nearly fell asleep under their touch. When he was finished he tapped her lightly on the ass. 'Better?' he drawled.

'Umm, yes.'

'Good. Next time I'll do it with oils. You'll love that.'

'I will?'

'For sure.'

She stood up and stretched. 'I feel so light, it's marvellous.'

He grinned. *My, what big teeth you have*, she thought.

'Understand you're having a party, Elaine.'

'Yes. For George Lancaster.'

'Nice.'

'I hope so. I think that's one of the reasons I'm so tense.'

'Could be. Pressure situation. You want to come by for a proper massage tomorrow?'

'What a good idea.' She wondered how much a personal massage with Ron Gordino cost. Probably a disgusting amount. Something else for Ross to complain about.

'Sure it is. We'll get you all lightened up in time for your party. In perfect shape.'

'Shall I settle with your receptionist or can it be added to my bill?'

He was affronted. 'I'm not going to *charge* you. Just invite me to your party and we'll call it quits.'

So that was it. He was not after her body – just her party. She didn't know whether to be flattered or insulted. At least it proved that her party was the hottest ticket in town! And that meant a lot more than any laid-back exercise instructor trying to get her in the sack.

'I'll put you on my list, Ron. You can count on that.'

'Thank you, Elaine.'

'Don't mention it.'

Oh, it was good to be hot again. So very very good.

Surprisingly enough Gina Germaine was not nearly as bad as Neil had thought she would be. Certainly no Fonda, but passable – if one ignored the monstrous bosom – which in spite of copious wrapping refused to lie down.

Viewing the test alone in the screening room he was quite pleased. At least it proved that he was not totally mad. Now he could show it to Montana and Oliver without embarrassment. Gina Germaine was not Nikki, but he had brought something out in her, a quality unseen before now. With him directing her in the right role . . .

He sat quietly in the screening room as the lights came up. Maybe it wouldn't be such a bad idea to have Gina in the movie he planned to do after *Street People*. He had bought a property over two years previously, and two young writers were working on it. With a few changes here and there it could be just the vehicle to launch a new Gina Germaine on an unsuspecting public . . .

Of course, the woman was a blackmailing bitch, and he was furious about the way she had behaved to get herself tested. But if he put her in the new movie he would have her in his power, and that should provide ample opportunity for getting his own back.

Childish but satisfying. He liked the idea.

Angel had absolutely no intention of returning to Louisville. How could she possibly go back a failure, and pregnant as well?

When she crept from Shelly's apartment early in the morning she had no idea where she would go or what she would do. She only knew that she had to get away from Buddy for a while, let him see that she meant business. He needed to be taught a lesson, day by day it was becoming increasingly obvious that he was interested only in himself. He *said* he loved her. But if he loved her how could he treat her in such a casual way?

Conversations with Shelly had not helped. 'You gotta understand a guy like Buddy, Angel-face. Basically he's a loner. Doesn't need anything or anyone. Gets off on just being himself.'

Advice from a girl like Shelly she could do without.

'I'm having a baby,' Angel informed her stiffly. 'So he'll just have to learn to be a family man.'

Shelly had snorted with laughter. 'Buddy? A family man? Angel-face, you are so way off track it's a joke. You'd better get yourself an abortion – and quick.'

Angel did not appreciate Shelly's snide amusement and unwelcome advice. She huddled in the chair that night and brooded about what to do. Then at seven-thirty in the morning she collected her suitcase from the car and trudged resolutely up the hill towards Sunset. Fifty-two dollars was all the money she had, but unlike Buddy she had no fear of taking an ordinary job.

After a while she passed a hairdressing salon with a card in the window advertising for a receptionist. There was a coffee-shop nearby, and she decided to wait until the salon opened and try for the job. She bought a couple of movie magazines, settled herself at a corner table, and for two hours absorbed herself in stories of the stars.

At ten o'clock she put away the magazine, paid her cheque, and retraced her steps to the salon.

A wild redhead with black ringed eyes and back-combed hair informed her the owner never appeared before twelve.

'Can I wait?' Angel asked.

Pencilled eyebrows shot up. 'You wanna wait two hours?'

'If that's all right.'

'Take a seat, it's your time.'

Angel did just that, leafing through various magazines and observing her surroundings. The entire place was white, with lots of plants. Loud rock music blared out of carefully placed speakers, and the hair stylists wore a unisex uniform of tight white jeans and tropical T-shirts.

Everything was quiet until eleven-thirty, when a stream of clients began to arrive. Women *and* men. Angel reflected that back in Louisville, men and women would not be caught dead in the same hairdressing establishment.

Around twelve-thirty an extremely tall, exceptionally thin man in his late thirties appeared. He wore a check shirt, faded pink boiler suit, and white tennis shoes. His hair was a rich halo of Shirley Temple yellow curls which surrounded an aquiline face. 'Morning darlings!' he sang out to all and sundry. 'Everyone happy?'

A plump woman, emerging from the dressing-room in a fern print robe, threw her arms around him and squealed with joy. 'Koko! That boy you gave me last week is a genius. He made me look positively Candy Bergen!'

'*Of* course he did, dreamheart. That's what we're here for – to please. That's what we're *all* here for. Isn't that right, Darlene?'

Darlene, the back-combed receptionist, did not crack a smile. She jabbed a three inch scarlet lacquered nail in Angel's direction. '*She's* been here since we opened. It's about the job. Give it to her for God's sake, because I'm warning you, Koko – I am *not* taking any more shit from Raymondo.'

Koko removed himself from the plump woman's grasp and scowled. 'I *know* your stance on this matter, Darlene. Not now, *please*.' He turned to Angel and gave her a sweeping glance. 'Well now, aren't we a pretty one. Just come along with me, dear, and let's talk experience.'

All she had to offer was a year's work in a small Louisville salon, but it was enough. Koko was obviously just as anxious for Darlene to leave as she was herself.

'I don't suppose you could start today?' he asked hopefully.

'I have to find an apartment,' Angel said.

'One room, cheap, close by?'

'Why, yes . . .'

'Your *lucky* day, dreamheart. I know of just the place. Darlene!' he screamed, his piercing voice rising above a raunchy James Brown.

'What?' she screamed back from her position behind the front desk.

'Such a lady!' tisked Koko. 'What a definite *joy* to see her go!'

'About that apartment –' Angel began tentatively.

'Ah, yes. One of my girls got married last week – poor fool. She wants to sub-let her place.'

'Where is it?'

'On Fountain. Are you interested?'

Within an hour she had viewed the apartment and taken it, talked Koko into giving her an advance on her salary, and started work.

Darlene gathered together her bits and pieces, shoved them in an army surplus bag, and departed the world of hairdressing with a pitying snort in Angel's direction.

'Lovely girl!' sang Koko. 'Never got along with a soul.'

Angel wasn't really listening. She was marveling at the fact that in such a short period of time she had found a job, money, and an apartment. It just proved it *could* be done.

So why hadn't Buddy done it?

She wondered if he was missing her yet. Her decision was not to contact him for at least a week. By that time he might just be ready to talk truth, and if he was – *then* they could start getting their lives back together. Not before. Angel had made up her mind.

Ross decided a work-out was not going to kill him. Elaine nagging on about his gut was beginning to have some effect. He had always been in great shape, never had to worry about a thing. Maybe now he *was* getting just a touch heavy around the middle.

So what? After all I'm nearly fifty for crissake. Can't stay frigging perfect for ever.

Besides, at his age they should want him for his acting ability, not his pristine pectorals.

Age. Fifty. Coming up fast. Racing towards him like an out of control groupie.

He thought about his life as he drove the Corniche along Santa Monica to the private health club he had once attended regularly. That had been in the days when he couldn't afford an inch of surplus flesh anywhere. The days when he had really been on top. King of the whole frigging heap. And willing to work at it.

A bitter smile twisted his lips. Where had all the gofers gone? The yes-men. His asshole buddies.

Oh, yeah. When he was king they were his best friends. The real estate moguls, bankers, rich men who handed out hospitality like peanut-butter cups because they wanted to be friends with a star. When the star faded so did the friendships. No more offers of private jets to fly him wherever he wanted to go, or parties in his honour. No more yachts and houses and islands to borrow whenever he wished. No more hot rich wives begging for his body. Or fanatic fans driving him crazy.

Fuck 'em. Ross Conti had learned a thing or two about people and the way they used each other. When he hit the magic circle again they could *all* go take a flying fart, unless *he* wanted otherwise, unless *he* cared to use *them*.

If the party was a success . . . If he got back with Sadie . . . If *Street People* became his . . .

The traffic on Santa Monica was heavy, and the stares were hitting him from all sides as he drove his Corniche slowly along the street. He was still a famous face in a city of famous faces – thanks to television which ran his old movies at least once a week. But what good was fame without the perks? Without the money to go along with it? *Fuck 'em all*.

He pulled up at a red light and considered the action on the street. Santa Monica had been taken over by the gay community. There were gay discos, open-pavement cafés, clothing stores, all catering more or less exclusively for gays. Personally Ross had never had any inclination in that direction, he had always been too fond of women. He thought of Karen and grinned. An oiled and muscled youth lounging by a bus stop took a tentative step towards the car. 'You going my way, mister?' he sing-songed through the open passenger window, one hand already reaching for the door.

Ross's grin turned quickly to a scowl. 'No, I'm not!' he snapped. 'And get away from my car.'

'Don't get excited.' The boy stepped back. 'If I'm not your style then that's cool.'

That's cool, is it? Angrily Ross gunned the car away from the light.

214

Did he look like a closet cruiser? A fine thing – getting hustled by a hustler in broad daylight. Didn't the stupid kid know who he was?

He made a sharp left turn and pulled into the parking lot. What he needed was some vigorous activity. The only vigorous activity he got nowadays was screwing Karen Lancaster. His countenance brightened again. Some broad! Maybe her talent was inherited. Old George had always had quite a reputation with the ladies. Like father . . . like daughter . . .

His grin firmly restored, Ross entered the health club.

'Cut!' Montana said sharply, turning to the first assistant. 'Let's take a ten minute break. I want a little rap with Buddy.'

She had already spoken to him six times. There had been six takes. He wasn't getting any better – in fact he was getting worse. But he was the best of the bunch. He had the look, and that's what really mattered. Where would Nicholson be without the sneer? Eastwood without the ice-cool stare? It was the look, and *then* came the acting ability. She could bring it out in him, she knew she could. She approached him warily. He was nervously muttering lines under his breath.

'Hey,' she murmured softly. 'You're not listening to me, are you? You're not taking in one single word I say.'

'I sure am,' he answered, wishing he were somewhere else.

'Just loosen up,' she crooned softly. 'It's a very simple piece of action if you relax, slow down, and take your time.'

'I can't get the words right. I can't –'

'Forget the words,' she soothed. 'I want you to give me the *essence* of the man . . . just go real real easy and give me Vinnie.'

He was shocked. 'Forget the words? You've got to be puttin' me on. I was up all night. I know every bit of dialogue. I mean I *really* know it.'

So why do you keep on blowing it? she wanted to ask. But she didn't, she put her arm around his shoulder and led him away from the set. 'Buddy,' she said softly, 'I know you can do this scene. I wouldn't have asked you to test if I wasn't sure you could do it.'

'Yeah?' He relaxed slightly.

'I don't need to waste your time, or mine. You're good. I can sense it. You're *very* good if you forget about the lines and just let yourself become Vinnie. If the words go – no big deal. Just stay in character and say anything you want. Don't blow the take. Let's get something in the can other than you saying oh shit!'

He nodded sheepishly. *Buddy Hudson gets his chance and oh shits himself out of a job!*

'I know what you want,' he assured her, taking a deep breath. 'Believe me, I got it now, really, you'll see.'

She smiled encouragingly and fixed him with her tiger eyes. 'We'll do another take, and this time you're going to be dynamite. Right?'

He licked dry lips and nodded. 'You got it.'

She kissed him lightly on the cheek before striding back behind the camera.

A make-up girl darted forward and powdered him down. 'Good luck,' she whispered.

A little luck in his life was *just* what he needed.

'You ready, Buddy?' Montana asked.

He nodded, bile rising in his throat, tenseness knotting his stomach.

'Remember. You *are* Vinnie. Okay. Action!'

Action. Walk into the scene from off camera. Glance in a mirror – instinctively he ruffled his hair. Phone cue. Pick up. Words. What were the fucking words? He wasn't going to screw up again was he?

The first line came out all right. Pause. Light a cigarette. *What came next?* Couldn't remember. Took her advice. Said his *own* words, made up the fucking dialogue, pretended he had Angel on the line and was sweet-talking her the way it used to be.

All of a sudden he forgot about the camera, the crew, blowing it. He made out like he was at home, confident, charming, good old Buddy Boy.

Montana watched him intently. He had taken her advice – at last. The lines went out the window and he was ad-libbing like a professional. He was doing his thing – and the magnetism was coming off him in waves. Christ! If the qualities he projected translated themselves onto film, he had it made.

'Cut!' she said jubilantly.

He almost didn't stop he was so into it.

'That's a print,' she said, walking over to him. 'Thank you, Buddy. You were great.'

'I was?'

'Exactly like I said you would be.'

'Hey –' His confidence was returning. 'I'm just gettin' started. How about once more?'

She shook her head. 'Two more actors waiting their turn and no more time. You wouldn't want them to miss their chance, would you?'

He grinned, full of adrenaline. 'Why not?'

She smiled and for a second they locked eyes, then she pulled her tinted reading glasses down from her hair and very businesslike extended her hand for a firm shake. 'You came through and I couldn't be happier. Goodbye Buddy, and good luck.'

Goodbye!! Was she out of her mind. 'Hey –' he gulped. 'When will I know?'

'We'll be in touch with your agent.'

He didn't *have* an agent, but it wouldn't look good to admit that sad fact. He'd just have to keep in constant touch with Inga.

'Yeah,' he said lamely. 'Like when?'

'When we decide,' she said firmly, conversation over. She turned and walked away humming to herself. She felt almost as high as he did. The charge of working with an actor and having it pan out was a kick indeed. She couldn't wait to see his test on screen and find out if she was right.

No wonder Neil became so immersed when he was shooting a movie. It was all in the director's hands – he or she created the magic. Oh, the satisfaction!

Buddy watched her retreat. It was fine for her, she had it made. But what about him?

The make-up girl approached. 'That last take was sensational,' she enthused. 'I wouldn't be a bit surprised if you got the part. You knocked *me* out.'

Now *that* was the kind of talk he liked to hear. Confidence flooded his veins. 'What makes you think that?' he asked.

'I just got a feeling.'

'You saw the other tests?'

'They weren't you.'

'You bet they weren't, but tell me about 'em anyway.' He took her by the arm. 'Let's go get some coffee.'

No harm in finding out about the competition . . . No harm at all.

24

How alike the outskirts of each city seemed. Huge giant freeways spewing off exits where squatted identical gas stations, motels, coffee shops.

To keep driving was all that mattered to Deke. Ohio, Indiana, Missouri, Oklahoma, slipped by almost unnoticed. The road became a mesmerizing force, beckoning him on, leading him mile by mile to his final destination.

Joey had led him on.

Joey had laughed at him.

He saw her often.

Bitch.

She was dead.

It was her own fault.

'I wanna meet your family an' make plans. I'm sick of bein' shoved around.' She stared at him hatefully. *'You hear what I'm sayin'?'*

He heard her clearly. She had been saying the same thing for weeks now, and he had been countering with a variety of feeble excuses.

'Ya think I'm not good 'nuff to meet them. Is that it? 'Cos if it is, y'can take your freakin' ring an' shove it where the sun don't shine.' She pulled the cheap garnet ring from her finger and flung it at him. *'I'm gonna meet 'em this week or we're through, buster.'*

He wanted to marry her. He hadn't changed his mind. But wouldn't it be better if they snuck off and did it? And then he could take her home, and they would be forced to accept her.

He had made this suggestion to her, but she would not hear of it. She wanted everything *'nice an' proper'* as she had put it. *'Just like normal folks.'* She had even gone so far as to buy a copy of Brides magazine and cut out a picture of a wedding dress.

'Don't they want to meet me?' she demanded sullenly. *'Aren't they waitin' to meet the girl their precious son is gonna marry?'*

*He did not dare to tell her that he had never so much as mentioned
her name to them. They would never approve of any girl he brought
home. And they especially would not approve of Joey with her flashy
clothes, heavy make-up, and spiky orange hair.*

*'Next week,' he promised lamely. He did love her. She satisfied his
flesh if that's what love was about.*

'You'd better mean it, buster,' she snarled like a wild alley cat.

*He meant it. But why did the thought of introducing her to his
parents create such a throbbing in his head? WHY WAS HE SO
AFRAID OF THEM?*

Memories came flooding back.

*He was six years old and playing mud-pies with a friend. His mother
appeared, face of darkness, voice an uncontrolled screech. 'You filthy
dirty boy! Those clothes were fresh on today. Get inside at once.'*

*She beat him until the sweat stood out in tiny beads all over her face,
and blood ran down the back of his legs. His father said nothing.*

*That was the first time, but there were many more occasions and
always for some minor matter like food uneaten, or a washcloth left on
the bathroom floor. When he was sixteen the beatings ceased as
unexpectedly as they had begun. Instead, the tongue lashed him. A
stream of verbal abuse more devastating than the physical damage.*

*He grew to believe her destroying words. After all, she was his
mother, as she never tired of telling him. She had given birth to him.
Painfully. 'You nearly killed me,' she often cried. 'I nearly died
bringing you into the world.' Guilt hung heavy. He had nearly killed
his mother, and that's why she punished him, and that's why he had to
accept it. She told him he was weak, dirty, useless, a parasite, a fool.
What girl would ever look at him? What employer would ever give him
work?*

*Yet she was full of contradictions. When he brought a girl home she
wasn't good enough for him. When he got a job it was never the right
job.*

Knock him down, build him up. Which was he to believe?

*Confusion and guilt were the two emotions he grew up with. Along
with a dark lingering fear which woke him most nights . . . And
sometimes sent him out on the street to do things . . . things he was
supposed to do.*

*He raped women. They were the enemy, and deserved to be
punished just as he deserved to be punished.*

*He was always careful, picking elderly victims who were too fright-
ened to fight back.*

*When he met Joey things changed. If his parents would only accept
her, everything would be all right . . .*

It was nearing dusk just outside of Amarillo, Texas, and Deke had
stopped to fill up with gas. As he rejoined the freeway he noticed a
girl hitching a ride. She was tanned, and carried a backpack. Her
outfit consisted of brief khaki shorts and a T-shirt emblazoned with
the words – JOGGERS DO IT IN THEIR SHOES.

He stopped. Didn't know why. Realized as soon as she was sitting
next to him that he had made a mistake.

She wanted to talk. 'What's your name, hon?' 'Where are you
heading?' 'What do you do?' 'How long you bin on the road?'

His surly grunts did not silence her. Ignoring the fact that he did
not answer, she chatted on about herself. She was a Southern girl, she
told him, married at sixteen, divorced at seventeen. A waitress for
two years, until one day she just decided to hit the road and travel the
country. 'Ah've had a real good time evah since,' she confided. 'No
stinkin' time clock to punch. Just free an' out for fun.' She edged
across the front seat. 'For a ten spot ah'll give you real sweet relief.
I'll even share a joint with you. How's that grab you?'

It didn't grab him. It infuriated him. They were all whores.

She took his silence as acceptance and patted him lovingly on the
knee. 'For an extra ten I'll relieve you with mah mouth, an' for five
more ah'll swallow it all down just like a good lil' old gal. Whaddya
think of *that*?'

He thought he would kill her. It was so easy to dispose of the slime.
Rid the world of bad people. Clear out all the whores and pimps and
PEOPLE WHO LAUGHED AT HIM.

But she hasn't laughed at you.

She will.

'Pull over at the next rest stop,' she said matter-of-factly. 'And
hon', you sure as sugar gonna *looove* mah southern comfort.' She
laughed.

There, you see.

He was satisfied. It was a sign that he should do what he had to do.
He would dispose of the whore. She had been sent to him for just
such a reason.

More and more he was beginning to realize that things didn't just
happen, they were worked out ahead of time, and certain human
beings were put on earth to keep order. He liked the phrase 'to keep
order'. The words were clean and precise.

220

'I am a Keeper Of The Order,' he said resolutely.

'Sorry?'

Mustn't let her *know*. Must not *warn* her ahead of time.

'Nothing,' he mumbled.

'C'mon, hon, find us a spot an' pull on ovah,' she said, wriggling close to him. 'Ah'm a lil' lady who *enjoys* her work. Hot damn! You an' I are in for some wild time!'

Hot damnation.

Another sign.

He put his foot down hard on the accelerator. The sooner it was done . . . The sooner he could get on with his real mission . . . The Keeper Of The Order had work to do in California.

He was getting closer all the time.

25

For three weeks Elaine had been having an affair. Her first one in two years. She had not meant to start anything as unsettling and time consuming – especially with her party plans progressing so well, and a great deal of organizing still left to do.

The party meant so much to Ross and herself, she really should not have allowed anything to distract her. But the best affairs are never planned, they just slide into your life like potent after dinner drinks, one leads to another, and before you know it you are deliciously tipsy.

Elaine's had started exactly like that. A private massage with Ron Gordino. 'Put on a towel,' he had drawled, 'and settle yourself on the table.' Casually he indicated his private bathroom, and she had slipped out of her leotard and wrapped the pink towel he had so thoughtfully supplied tightly around herself.

An affair? The farthest thing from her mind as she lay face down on his massage table and gave herself up to his strong probing hands.

He used scented oils, just as he had promised, and he worked her shoulders, her back, the base of her spine, firmly and sensuously. And as he worked he moved the towel lower and lower, until quite naturally he had whisked it away, revealing the lace panties she had prudently kept on.

'Elaine,' he complained. 'You're not supposed to wear anything for this kind of massage. These oils get real messy, an' I wouldn't want to ruin your fifty dollar panties.'

She was startled. How did he know they cost fifty dollars?

'That's all right,' she said quickly.

'No it's not, take 'em off. You're not shy are you?'

She hesitated for only a moment, and then decided she didn't want to seem unsophisticated. Little Etta from the Bronx.

'So let's go,' he said.

She nearly objected, but it seemed so silly, because he was only going to see her ass, and she had a very nice one, even Ross had confirmed that fact. Gingerly she reached back and wriggled awkwardly out of the offending garment.

He helped her, pulling them off with an easy authority. 'That's better,' he said, squeezing oil from a plastic bottle on to her now bare bottom.

She squirmed slightly – wondered if this was the service he gave Bibi Sutton – then surrendered to the deep circular motion of his kneading fingers. What a sensation! Instant turn on. Especially as the oil began to dribble down the division and Ron Gordino's fingers found a spot at the base of her spine that made her let forth an involuntary gasp of pleasure.

'Good, huh?' he drawled confidently.

'Very,' she replied, hardly daring to trust her voice.

'Turn over.'

Turn over? She was naked, vulnerable, tuned to a sexual pitch. Turn over, and what then? Sex? With an exercise instructor? Didn't she deserve better than that, even if he *was* the flavour of the month?

You had your dentist, Elaine. You had a two-bit actor. What are you, suddenly choosy?

She turned over. And so it all began.

Three or four times a week they met in his private office and he relieved her tensions along with his own. Conversation was limited, sexual acrobatics were not. Ron Gordino believed in stretching the body to its limit. Elaine was a willing pupil. For two years she had been sexually neglected, and suddenly she was like a desert survivor who craved as much water as she could get.

'You're a crazy lady, Elaine,' drawled Ron.

How right he was. Crazy to be involved with him, but enjoying every clandestine lustful moment.

Of course Karen noticed almost at once. 'What's going on with you and the Sheik of the exercise biz?' she inquired playfully. 'You spend more time in his office than he does.'

Karen was one of her best friends but a rule of survival in Hollywood was – 'Never trust anyone – *especially* best friends.'

'He gives great massage,' Elaine replied innocently. 'Remember my old back problem? I swear he's almost got it cured.'

'*What* old back problem?'

'I had a slipped disc – years ago. I've suffered with back aches ever since.'

Karen looked at her sceptically. 'Hmmm . . .'

The acceptance list for the party was shaping up nicely. Right at the top there was a definite yes from Sadie La Salle – for whom – although she did not know it – the party was being given. Elaine could not have been more delighted. If all went according to plan, life could be good again.

Things were already looking up.

Angel departing from his life without a trace did not thrill Buddy one little bit. In fact, it frightened the hell out of him. She might be twenty years old, but she was still a baby, and the streets of Hollywood were alive with pimps and hustlers who would be only too happy to get their slimy hands on a girl like Angel.

He shuddered at the thought and tried to believe that she had jumped a plane home. Although he knew it would be the last thing she'd do. He had Shelly phone Louisville anyway.

'Some woman says she's in Hollywood,' she stated, hanging up.

'Maybe she took a train, hasn't arrived yet,' he reasoned.

'Yeah. And maybe she's still here. Let's face it, kid, there *is* life in this town after Buddy Hudson.'

He ignored her. What did she know?

In his mind he played out a scenario. Angel, in Louisville, back with her foster family. Buddy, in Hollywood, signing a major deal to star in *Street People*. Then flying – first class of course – to Louisville. Being met by a limo – the kind that stretched for sixteen feet with television and a bar in the back. Driving to Angel's house where the chauffeur would open the door of the car, he would climb out, and Angel would come running to meet him . . . Beautiful Angel pregnant with his child . . . And let them all eat their hearts out . . .

'Any word on your test yet?' Shelly questioned.

Change of thought. Change of mood. He picked up the phone and dialled Inga's number. 'What's happening?' he asked anxiously.

'Buddy! This is the third time you've called me today. You only tested four days ago, and I've told you – I'll buzz you as soon as I know anything.'

Not good enough. Was Inga telling him everything she knew?

'How about dinner tonight?' he asked abruptly, deciding that a little personal attention might help.

Inga was startled, for weeks she had been trying to lure him into a date. 'You're on,' she said quickly, before he changed his mind. 'When and where?'

'I'll pick you up at your office. What time are you through?'

She wanted to say, 'No – make it later. I have to go home and get myself together.' But Buddy was mercurial and she didn't want him backing out. 'Five,' she said.

'Five,' he repeated. 'I'll be there,' with an eye to maybe bumping into Montana Gray, getting the true scam on what was happening.

He had forgotten Shelly was in the room. 'Goin' out on dates already?' she asked sassily. 'How quickly you guys forget.'

'Lend me fifty bucks?' he asked.

Shelly was outraged. 'I lent you fifty two days ago. Borrow from Randy – he's the one with the bread. I'm just a working girl who wants to get paid for your liberal use of my telephone as well as gettin' my fifty back.'

Buddy headed for the door. 'Don't worry about it.'

'Easy for you to talk – big man.'

'I think Elaine's playing doctor,' Karen Lancaster announced.

'What?' questioned Ross, lazily squeezing one of her incredible nipples between thumb and forefinger.

'Ouch!' she exclaimed mildly, rolling across her large circular bed to escape his touch.

'Come here, woman!' he demanded.

'Come get it, man!' she replied.

He crawled across the tangled sheets growling like a tiger, and fell on top of her, his tongue out and in action, his penis erect.

She laughed, loving every minute. 'You're becoming insatiable, Ross!'

'You're not exactly the Virgin Mary yourself.'

They made love noisily, knowing that their grunts and groans would disturb no one at the isolated beach house. And afterwards Karen said again, 'I think Elaine's playing doctor.'

And Ross repeated, 'What?'

And Karen said, 'She's screwing the hired help. She's got herself a lover-boy. She's having an *affair*.'

Ross snorted with amusement. 'You're nuts!' he exclaimed. 'Elaine doesn't even like sex at home, she's the last person who would go out looking for it.'

'Wanna bet?'

'You're way off base.'

'What's the matter, baby? Don't you like the thought of wifey getting it on with somebody else?'

Irritation crept into his voice. 'And who do you have picked out for Elaine's so-called lover?'

'Ron Gordino!' she announced triumphantly.

'Who the frig is Ron Gordino?'

'Ron Gordino is a twenty-eight year old, six feet two inch ex-lifeguard – now *the* body man in Beverly Hills. *Personally* recommended by Bibi Sutton.'

Ross began to laugh. 'Shit! That fairy!'

'Bi, darling. There's a big difference between gay and swinging both ways. Our Ron *definitely* swings every which way – *in*cluding loose – *I* can assure you of that. And right now he's giving Elaine everything you probably think she doesn't want at home. She's getting royally laid, Ross. Just take a look at her if you doubt it. She's positively glowing.'

'Elaine doesn't screw around,' he said shortly, racking his brains to remember when he'd last taken a good look at his wife.

Karen rose gracefully from the bed. 'Suit yourself,' she murmured sweetly. 'I've never met a man who truly believes his wife would cheat on him. Even though *he* may be jumping on anything that breathes.'

Elaine? Cheating?

Ridiculous.

Elaine was into the house, clothes, entertaining, doing the right thing. She didn't even *like* sex.

'Listen,' he said confidently. 'I *know* Elaine wouldn't do that to me.'

'*You're* doing it to *her*.'

'That's different.'

Karen pursed her lips and blew a short sharp raspberry. 'Chauvinist!'

'Cow!'

She selected a joint from a silver box, jumped back on the bed, and sat cross-legged while she lit up.

Ross watched her, his fingers aching to get back to work on her erotic nipples.

'Would you mind?' she inquired artlessly, dragging deeply, then passing the joint to him.

He took a satisfying long pull. 'Yes. I'd mind,' he said. And why shouldn't he? He paid the bills. He paid for her nails, her hair, her clothes, her *exercise* class. She was Mrs. Ross Conti. And if she *was* screwing around (although he sincerely doubted it) then wasn't that a direct attack on his masculinity?

'Why?' Karen demanded.

'Can we cut out the questions? Who gives a frig?'

'You. Obviously.'

He would have liked to have shut her up by turning her on her back and giving her a touch more action. But nearly fifty was nearly fifty, he'd need a crane to get it up again.

'How about making a bacon sandwich?' he suggested.

'Changing the subject?'

His patience snapped. 'You want to fix me a frigging sandwich or not?'

She bit back a sharp retort. The seed had been planted, it was enough.

It did not take long for Angel to become the darling of Koko's hairdressing salon. She sat behind the reception desk all wide eyes, smooth skin and soft blond hair falling loosely around her shoulders. What a change from the fiercely lacquered Darlene, high priestess of the bitchy comment.

'Who *is* she?' everyone asked Koko. 'And where did you find her? She's so sweet, and so polite.'

'Don't I know it,' Koko tisked, watching over her like an overpossessive pimp, terrified that she would be stolen from him by some marauding talent scout. It was the first time he could remember calm in the salon. No screaming hysterical women or bitter fights about over-booked appointments. Even Raymondo, the best stylist in the place, was calmed by Angel's presence. He kept a respectful distance, which for him meant not pinching her on the ass every time she passed.

Her beauty struck everyone, but up front she announced that she was happily married and that her husband was out of the country for a

226

while. Politely she declined all offers of social engagements – whether they be from staff or clients. She was friendly but aloof, revealing nothing about herself, but being quite prepared to listen to other people's problems for hours at a time.

Several times daily someone or other told her she should be a model or an actress, and she smiled and explained that she just wasn't interested. And with Buddy's baby growing inside her she honestly wasn't. Oliver Easterne and his wild promises were forgotten. Straightening out her life was more important.

She thought about Buddy a lot. He had let her down badly. Instinctively she knew that she must give him time if only to make him realize how important their relationship was.

In a way she felt very strong and proud of herself for what she was doing. Being alone wasn't easy, but it was better than being with Buddy and watching him destroy himself.

'You wanna go dancin' tonight?' Raymondo leered, passing by the reception desk for the tenth time that day.

Demurely she shook her head.

'No she doesn't,' snapped Koko, materializing from a private cubicle. 'Do you, dreamheart?'

She smiled softly. Koko's concern touched her. He fussed around her all the time. She turned to greet a fat woman in a voluminous caftan with frazzled yellow locks. 'Good morning, Mrs. Liderman, and how are you today?'

Mrs. Liderman beamed. 'Feeling the heat, and so is Frowie.' She scooped a miniature poodle from the floor and thrust it across the desk at Angel. 'Give baby a drinkie, there's a good girl.' Diamonds flashed on her fat hands.

'They'll cut off your fingers for those one day,' Koko sighed. 'I do wish you would be more careful, Mrs. L.'

The woman giggled coyly. 'I'd feel naked without my little sparklers.'

Koko mock sighed. 'Then for God's sake keep them on – do!'

Mrs. Liderman giggled even louder. Angel smiled politely, and the fat woman waddled off to be dealt with by Raymondo's capable hands.

'One of the richest old bags in L.A.,' Koko confided sotto voce. 'And she *still* looks like she buys off the rack at the May Company.'

'I like the May Company,' Angel protested.

'You would.' He sighed. 'Dreamheart, one of these days I shall simply *have* to educate you. With your looks, you too could end up

227

being one of the richest ladies in this town. But there is *so much* for you to learn.'

'What?'

'Everything.'

Gina Germaine padded barefoot across her thick white carpet and threw her arms tightly around Neil Gray's neck. You *really* liked my test, didn't you?'

He extracted himself from her grip. 'Yes.'

She was hungry for praise. 'Just yes?'

'You were very good.'

'What did Oliver and Montana say?' she asked anxiously. 'Am I Nikki, Neil? *Goddammit, am I Nikki*?'

He shook his head, said, 'No.' Held up a hand to silence her sudden anger, and explained his future plans for her.

She listened intently, twisting a lock of platinum blond hair between her fingers, biting her full lower lip, staring at him with protruding blue eyes.

The way he explained things it sounded good. No, she wasn't Nikki. He had far greater plans for her. A new movie. A showcase that would really establish her as a serious actress.

'Have you got a script?' she demanded excitedly when he had finished.

He smiled to himself. She had taken the bait. 'Enough of one to know that any actress in this town would mutilate to play the role.'

She licked her voluptuous lips, attempted to remain cool, but the need was in her voice as she asked, 'When will it start?'

'When *Street People* wraps.'

She stared at him even harder. Was he fooling her? Throwing out promises to escape from her trap? 'Why can't I do *Street People* first?' she demanded.

'Don't you understand a word I'm saying? That would ruin everything.'

A petulance crept into her voice. 'You're offering me pie in the sky.'

'I am offering you, my dear, the chance to stop playing dumb cunt of the year – to become a serious actress.' She looked thoughtful, so he took the opportunity to add, 'And I want the video tapes of us together. I have no intention of letting *you* run the show. You'll be putting yourself in my hands. I'm going to make you the hottest *actress* in town. When I've finished with you they'll all come running.'

228

'What guarantee do I have that you mean any of this?' she asked quickly. 'It all sounds good, but I'm no fool.'

'I never said you were. You see, my dear, I am prepared to sign a contract with you. Oliver Easterne will negotiate the deal with your agent, but don't be greedy, you need this film a lot more than I do.' He paused. 'And no press announcements. Nothing until I say so. Do you understand?'

She chewed on her lower lip and nodded.

'I want the tapes back the same day you sign the contract. No games, Gina. No copies. Because once we embark on this venture, I can make you . . . and then again . . . I can break you . . .'

'Let's go to bed, Neil,' she purred, his sudden forcefulness exciting her.

'Let's not,' he replied harshly. 'From now on our relationship is strictly business. You do understand that, Gina dear, don't you?'

Montana slipped off her cowboy boots and buzzed the projection booth. 'Run those tests through for me again, Jeff.'

'Comin' up Miz Gray.'

She settled back to watch the four actors she had directed one more time. Four actors. All different. All with something to offer. But it was Buddy Hudson who grabbed her attention and held her riveted. He was not the best actor by any means, but he had that special screen presence she had suspected all along, and *she* had brought it out in him.

Reflectively she sat in the dark and lit up a cigarette. What she really wanted to do was share her discovery with Neil. They should be together at a time like this, but when she had asked him to come and see the tests with her he had made some excuse about a meeting he had to attend. What meeting? She wasn't about to question him, and he had not bothered to elaborate.

A frown creased her forehead. Something was happening to their marriage. Something that she could not control, and did not like. Neil was drinking heavily again. They had no sex life. But the thing that *really* disturbed her was that they had always been so close, and now, suddenly, there seemed to be a huge void bridged only by the movie.

Her frown deepened. She wondered if it was just the pressure of working together for the first time, and decided yes, that was it. Pre-production was draining most of her energy, and Neil probably felt the same way. But somehow she knew there was more to it than that. Working together should be bringing them closer, not further apart. Angrily she ground out her cigarette. Maybe it was time for a long talk.

Buddy Hudson's image played on the screen. He really had it. Electric magnetism. Just as she had thought the day he bluffed his way into her office.

She wanted him for Vinnie. Her mind was made up. Now all she had to do was convince Oliver and Neil.

26

The computer check on the Andrews family finally came in. Leon Rosemont studied it intently. There was not a lot of information, but one discovery was the date of their marriage. 1946, Barstow, California. There was no information relating to Deke Andrews at all.

Leon wired off immediately for a copy of the wedding certificate. If he was to find any clues at all, then he might as well start at the beginning.

In the meantime it was Millie's birthday and she had planned a family party. She went wild in the kitchen making spare ribs, fried chicken, curried rice and her special black-eyed pea salad. For dessert he surprised her with a huge strawberry cake, and just in case he had forgotten she made chocolate fudge brownies which almost brought tears to his eyes.

He gorged himself, while her many nieces and nephews played The Jacksons on the stereo, and the grown ups kept pushing for James Brown. There was dancing and laughter and more good natured fun than he could remember in a long time.

One o'clock in the morning and they were alone, surrounded by stacks of dirty dishes.

'I'll wash – you dry,' Millie suggested.

'Why don't you wash *and* dry,' he countered.

'You lazy sonofagun!' she exclaimed, affection lighting her features. 'Just get that big fat butt in the kitchen right now!'

'Who does the dishes, an' your washin' an' all that garbage?' Joey demanded.

'I have a cleaning woman.'

'Yeah?' Reflectively she chewed on her thumb. 'I could do it if y'wanted. And wash your shirts. That oughtta save y'a buck or two.'

He did not want to save a buck or two. He wanted out of an unfortunate situation. They had been seeing each other – if that was the right phrase – for two months. And he had helped her a lot. Got her a job selling ice-cream at a movie theatre. Moved her into a decent rooming house. Given her a feeling of self-worth. And in return she had given him her youth, and a mighty fine hard-on. She made him feel twenty-two, and for a while that was nice. Now she was talking about doing his cleaning and washing, and he knew the time had come to close the chapter. It was only fair for both their sakes.

'Joey,' he said gently, deciding that now was as good a time as ever. 'Don't you sometimes think about having friends your own age?'

'Nope,' she replied blithely. 'After all, you're not exactly a granpop are you. You're about the same age as Paul Newman.' She had just seen 'Butch Cassidy and the Sundance Kid' twenty-eight times on account of the fact that it was playing at the cinema where she worked. And now every conversation was peppered with remarks about Paul Newman, whatever the subject.

'I think,' he said measuredly, 'now that we've got you back on the right track –'

'Right track, what am I? A fuckin' train?'

'You know what I mean,' he said evenly. 'And don't swear.'

'Okay then,' she announced, desperately trying to change the subject. 'I'll be cleanin' up for you – itsa favour. Like I don't wanna get paid – I was just kiddin' 'bout that part. Maybe you'd better give me a key.'

'Let's face facts, Joey, we've gone about as far as we can go. Now you have to start making a life for yourself which doesn't include me.'

'Why?' she demanded aggressively.

'Because it will work out better that way,' he explained patiently. 'You've got your life ahead of you. There's plenty of exciting things for you to do out there. A lot of new people for you to meet. And somewhere there's a nice young man –'

'Aw shee . . . it!' she exclaimed, disgust curling her lip. 'Exciting things to do, nice young man . . . what kinda dumbo d'ya think you're talking to here?' She glared at him, then added, 'I bin around y'know.'

'It's not right,' he continued stubbornly. 'It never has been, and I think you're smart enough to accept that. What do you want with an old man like me anyway?'

'Found yourself another little chickie y'kin get off on?' she jeered. 'Y'know, a real young one. Like I'm sixteen . . . Gettin' past it, huh?'

'Don't be so stupid.'

They argued back and forth for more than an hour. Joey did not want to leave. She screamed and yelled. Tried being sweet. Hurled insults. Even cried.

The more of an act she put on the more he realized that he was making the right decision. Finally at two o'clock in the morning, she left.

The following week was not easy. She phoned him constantly, begging and crying for them to get back together or shouting more insults. He couldn't take it, so he requested a six week vacation that was due to him, locked up his apartment, and took off for Florida. On his way to the airport, he dropped by the rooming house where Joey lived and paid her landlady six months' rent in advance.

Guilt money?

No. Just a parting gift to help her out.

He never saw her again.

Not until he saw her dead body lying slashed and mutilated on the floor of the house on Friendship Street.

Methodically Leon finished stacking the dishes, helped himself to a dish of ice cream and followed Millie upstairs.

She was at the dressing-table removing her make-up.

He wanted to confide in her, tell her about Joey . . . But he was so ashamed. He did not want to see the disgust in her eyes.

'Some party, huh?' Millie enthused.

He forced a smile, said, 'Sure was,' and wondered what would have happened if he had agreed to meet Joey one week before her death. She had called him right out of the blue. A three year silence, and then there she was on the phone, like they had only spoken yesterday.

'I gotta see ya, it's real important. I need your help.'

He did not respond. He changed his voice and stated that she had a wrong number. Millie was sitting across the room at the time.

Before he replaced the receiver he heard Joey say, 'Aw, shee . . . it, Leon. I know it's you.' But she hadn't called back.

One week later she was dead.

27

On the morning of the party Elaine awoke at seven. She left Ross snoring on his side of their bed and went into her bathroom. There, she inspected her face closely in a magnifying mirror, tweezed a few hairs below her eyebrows, carefully squeezed a minute whitehead, and marvelled at how clear and blemish-free her skin was. Some would say she had Aida Thibiant to thank. Aida gave facials to many stars – including Candice Bergen and Jacqueline Bisset – both of whom were coming to the party. But Elaine knew better. She knew who she should *really* thank. Ron Gordino. Lithe, athletic Ron, who she had really grown quite fond of in spite of herself.

Never get too familiar with the hired help, Elaine. Even if they are wonderful in bed.

Not that they had ever been to bed as such. Just massage table, couch and floor! Elaine allowed herself a fleeting smile before slipping off her silk nightgown and stepping beneath the icy needles of a cold shower.

Carefully she ticked off details of the party in her head. Everything was taken care of from table decoration to valet parking. She could not think of one thing she had forgotten. And soon an army of workers would be arriving to make it all perfect.

She towelled herself dry, and quickly applied a light make-up before slipping into a brown silk shirt and beige cotton pants. Then she walked over to the window and gazed out. It was going to be a perfect California day, the sun already high in the sky without a cloud in sight.

Ross snored loudly. Impatiently she shook him awake.

'What time is it?' he groaned.

'Early,' she replied. 'But I want you up.'

'I'm up all right,' he leered, indicating a healthy erection. 'What about a little head?'

'Don't be silly,' she said briskly. 'Have you forgotten it's party day?'

He groaned again. 'How could I forget? You've breathed and lived this frigging party for more weeks than I care to remember.'

'Get up,' she said firmly. 'Go to the gym or out to lunch or something, but please *do not* get in anyone's way today.'

'Whose way? It's my house,' he stated indignantly.

'Don't be difficult, Ross. This party *is* for you.'

'No, it's not,' he replied truculently. 'It's for George frigging Lancaster and Pamela frigging London. And it's costing me a fucking fortune which we can't afford.'

'It's for Sadie La Salle. Let's not lose sight of the *real* reason we're having it. Why don't we call it an investment in our future?'

He yawned loudly. 'It better be.'

'I'm going out,' she said, not prepared to put up with his complaints.

'Where to?' he asked, consulting his watch. 'It's not even eight o'clock yet.'

'I thought I told you last night. I'm having an early breakfast with Bibi at her house.'

'What for?'

'Do stop questioning me. We're going over the final list if you must know.'

'Why doesn't she come here?'

Elaine decided such a stupid question did not even deserve a reply. 'See you later,' she said. 'And don't forget to go to the bank and pick up some cash, we'll need a lot of twenties for tips.'

'Where are you going after Bibi's?'

Elaine swallowed her aggravation. Since when did Ross have to know every move she made? 'The hairdressers,' she snapped. 'Can I go now?'

'Feel free.'

She hurried into the kitchen. Lina had just arrived with two helpers. The three women were chattering excitedly in Spanish. It was the first time Elaine had seen Lina employ an expression other than surly resignation.

'*Buenos dias*, Señora Conti,' said the maid cheerfully.

'Good morning, Lina.'

'Theees my two amigos. Conceptia an' Maria.'

The other two women nodded and grinned. Probably wetbacks, Elaine decided, only too delighted to be working in such a beautiful

234

house. Well, it *would* be beautiful when they had finished scrubbing it from top to bottom.

'Do they speak English?' she demanded.

'Leetle,' said Lina. 'I 'splains everythings.'

'Good. I want this place spotless. The tent people will be here at eight o'clock. The flowers at nine. And there'll be other deliveries. I've left a list in the hall.'

Lina nodded encouragingly. 'No worry, Señora.'

'*You* answer the phone, Lina, and *take messages*. Write them down.' Hesitantly she used her only words of Spanish. '*Entiende ud*?'

'Sure. I understand good,' replied Lina, grinning proudly at her friends. 'You go. Everythin' fine.'

'I'll be back by twelve-thirty.'

Outside, safely in her Mercedes, she took a deep breath. The day had begun smoothly enough. Now if only everything went according to plan . . .

She started the car and set off. Thirty seconds later it occurred to her that she had not told Lina about the two ex-rock musicians arriving at twelve to set up their discotheque equipment. Ron Gordino had recommended them. 'You want the funkiest party of the year, then go with Ric and Phil,' he had stated. So it was the Zancussi Trio for the early part of the evening, and Ric and Phil for later on. God! Lina would never let them in with their wild long hair.

She spun the Mercedes into a U-turn and headed quickly back home.

Ross heard the front door slam and the rev of Elaine's Mercedes. For a moment he wondered if there was any truth in the things Karen had said about her having an affair. The very idea was laughable. She was Mrs. Ross Conti. She wouldn't dare screw around. He rolled lazily over and punched out Karen's number on the phone.

'What?' she mumbled sleepily.

'This is a dirty phone call.'

'Ross?'

'Who else do you get dirty phone calls from at this time in the morning?'

'You've woken me.'

He lightened his voice and did a passable imitation of Elaine. 'Have you forgotten it's party day!'

She laughed huskily.

'What are you wearing?' he asked.

'A red satin shortie nightie from Frederick's.'

'With crotchless panties?'

'And nippleless bra.'

'Jesus, Karen, you've just given me a giant hard-on.'

'I would hate to see it go to waste. Why don't you come on over?'

'I can't.'

'Why not? You know you want to suck on my tits.'

The thought of her erotic nipples in his mouth strengthened his desire. 'You're tempting me.'

'I know what turns you on. So why don't you climb into your jockeys, stick on some dark shades and let's chance it. I'll leave the name Edward Brown at the desk.'

He had never visited her at the fashionable Century City apartment where she lived. They had both decided it was too risky and stuck to the isolated beach house. But what was a risk or two between friends?

'I'm coming right over,' he decided.

'No. Wait till you get here.'

'Fun . . . eee.' He replaced the receiver and hurled himself under an ice cold shower. Then he was sorry, because without an erection he wasn't sure if he *did* want to visit Karen. He felt anxious. The thought of Sadie La Salle in his house was unnerving. What if she refused him as a client again?

Unthinkable. He'd turn the Conti charm on full force – dazzle her with it. She'd have no chance.

Quickly he dressed.

Elaine swept into the kitchen and was about to tell Lina about the two disco men when she spotted a light on the phone. Thinking it was for her she picked it up, and heard Ross say, 'Jesus, Karen, you've just given me a giant hard-on.' She listened silently to the rest of the conversation, hung up at the same time as Ross and hurried out the back door.

Once in her car she coasted down the driveway, started the engine and ripped off down the street barely screeching to a halt at the first stop sign.

She was being royally screwed by her best friend.

No. Correction. *Ross* was being royally screwed by her best friend.

Etta Grodinski from the Bronx.

Karen Lancaster from Beverly Hills.

A scream rose in her throat which she stifled, although many a therapist had told her to let it all out.

'That . . . that . . . cunt!' she hissed.

That cunt with those awful nipples.

'That cheating, stealing bitch!' she yelled out loud. 'Just who does she think she is?'

A man in the car beside her stared.

'What are you looking at?' she raged, and sent the Mercedes rocketing off down Sunset heading for Bel Air and Bibi. Because, whatever else, she wouldn't dream of letting Bibi Sutton down. A royal audience was a royal audience. And nothing would make her blow that.

Angel's silence had unnerved Buddy to such a degree that he hardly even cared anymore.

Not strictly true. He cared so much that to even think about it sent him into a total panic. So he blanked out on the subject of *Street People* and the role of Vinnie. He even stopped calling Inga seventeen times a day. He settled for once – in the morning at precisely eleven o'clock. Then he would inquire tersely, 'Any news?' and she would try to keep him on the phone because since their date she loved him madly – even though nothing had happened – no fault of hers. Once he heard the doom words – 'No news, but you're still being considered' – he just hung up. All he wanted to do was run.

And run he did. Literally. He bought himself a good pair of sneakers and covered Sunset from Doheny to Fairfax and back. Every morning.

It felt good channelling his excess energy that way. Stripped to a brief pair of white shorts he had never looked better. He was lean and tanned, his body like a sleek oiled machine.

Only Angel wasn't around to see it. She had dumped him like a sack of old garbage.

After two weeks of silence Shelly told him that Angel had called with a message. 'She doesn't want to see you again, she's had an abortion, met some guy, and you, Buddy Boy, are out of her life forever. She wanted me to be sure to tell you *forever.*'

He was shocked. He did not believe that Angel could be that harsh. 'Didn't you get her phone number? Or at least find out where she's living?' he demanded angrily.

'What am I – a message service?' Shelly retorted. 'I'm tellin' you, man. She just wanted out. O – U – T.'

He almost slept with Shelly that night. He was stoned. She was there, coming on to him strong as usual. She took off her clothes to the throb of Donna Summer and danced around in front of him. She did have a great body, but that's all it was – just another great body.

She sank to her knees in front of him, fiddled with the belt on his jeans.

She couldn't even excite him. The hurt of Angel running out and getting rid of his baby penetrated the grass and the coke. He just felt empty.

He didn't want anyone except Angel.

'You're crazy,' Shelly stormed. 'What are you – gay or something?'

Turn downs were not a great feature of her life.

He stayed at Randy's, hoping for the big break, and missing Angel.

Shelly did not hold a grudge for long. 'I'll get you one of these days,' she joked. 'Guess I've just gotta keep hangin' in, huh?'

Money he borrowed from them equally. Shelly was reasonably good natured about it, but Randy finally blew when he tried to hit him for yet another fifty.

'Come *on* man. I'm not a freakin' bank. I need every buck I got to keep this thing with Maralee going. If she thinks I don't have shit she'll run.'

He nodded, understanding only too well. Maralee Sanderson was Randy's shot at the big time, and after a lifetime of hustling maybe old Rand deserved a taste of the good life.

Reluctantly he could see he was going to have to get himself some sort of a job until he heard about the test. Having made that decision he put on his only clean silk shirt, persuaded Shelly to press his black gabardine pants, and finished off the outfit with his white Armani silk jacket – courtesy of Jason Swankle.

Once dressed he took himself off to see Frances Cavendish in the hope she would have something for him.

'Hey, Francie,' he breezed, walking into her office like he had only seen her the day before.

She leaned back in her brown leather chair and surveyed him carefully from head to toe. 'Well, well . . .' she said slowly. 'Look what the Santa Anas blew in off the street. I thought you were *dead*.'

He frowned. 'Huh?'

'An unseen actor is a *dead* actor in my book.'

'You're seein' me now.'

She squinted over her glasses. 'And looking quite fit I'm glad to say.'

'I bin running a lot.'

'It suits you.'

There was a long silence which she didn't seem inclined to break.

He cleared his throat. 'So what's happening, Francie?'

'For God's sake do *not* call me Francie.'

She had changed her rhinestone trimmed glasses for heavy horn-rims, and now she looked more mannish than ever with her close cropped grey hair and masculine style suit – too heavy for California by far, but one of her famous trademarks. She unlocked a side drawer in her desk and produced her other famous trademark – a somewhat battered roach-holder into which she fitted a joint. She lit up, dragged, then offered it across the desk. 'Still married?' she inquired brusquely.

Instinct gave him the right answer as he drew deeply on the cigarette. 'Nope.'

'Good. Marriage didn't suit you. I've got a job for you. A low budget horror epic for which you will be just right. Two weeks. Scale. You want it?'

He nodded, afraid to mention *Street People* in case he jinxed himself. 'When?' he asked.

'Universal. Next Monday.'

'Sounds good to me.'

'So it should.' She retrieved the roach and hung on to it. One drag was apparently all he was going to get. But one drag was better than none at all.

'Are you available tonight?' she asked abruptly.

In the past he had escorted Frances to a couple of boring award dinners, and an evening on the town with her eighty-six year old mother visiting from White Plains. He had no plans to do any more escort duty. On the other hand the picture at Universal probably hinged on whether he was free or not. 'Yeah, I'm available,' he decided.

'Good,' said Frances crisply. 'Ross Conti is having a party for George Lancaster and Pamela London. Pick me up at seven-fifteen promptly. You remember my address, don't you.'

It wasn't a question, more a statement. He nodded, delighted to be going to a big party – even if it was with Frances.

'Oh, and dear,' she added, 'wear something decent. Right now you look like one of those male hookers cruising the Polo Lounge.'

He tried not to scowl. What did she know anyway? If it was descriptions she wanted he could truthfully say she reminded him of a female Rodney Dangerfield.

Cheered by that thought he said, 'Seven-fifteen, then.' And made his exit.

Oliver Easterne absentmindedly emptied out the ashtray in which Montana's cigarette lay smouldering.

'Oliver!' she complained sharply. 'I was still smoking that.'

'What?'

'My cigarette!' She turned to Neil and made an expression of disbelief.

Neil was more interested in the glass of bourbon he was nursing.

Oliver scrabbled in the basket to put the offending cigarette out.

The three of them sat in Oliver's spotless office. It was eleven in the morning, and they were awaiting the arrival of George Lancaster. He was already an hour late.

Oliver and Neil both knew him well, but Montana had never met him. She was excited in a funny sort of a way – after all she had grown up with George Lancaster. He had always been there, a familiar face on the big screen and in the fan magazines. George Lancaster, John Wayne, Kirk Douglas. At thirteen she had nurtured a crush on all of them. Now things were somewhat different. She had written a movie, and George was all set to star in it. Unfortunately she did not consider him to be a very good actor, and the role of Mac in the film was so very important. But George Lancaster equalled big box office. And who could fight that fact of life?

Besides, with George starring, as Oliver said, they could use who they liked for the two other leading roles. And she liked Buddy Hudson. And so did Neil and Oliver after they saw the reaction of several secretaries she invited into the screening room when they ran his test.

'He may not be the greatest actor in the world – but he comes across like instant sex. He's pure Vinnie,' she explained.

Neil said, 'You don't have to convince me. I like him.'

Oliver agreed, while still fretting about the fact that he could not find the girl on the beach who he wanted for Nikki. She appeared to have vanished, and so after abandoning the idea of Gina, they had tested several other actresses for the role, and a couple of them were excellent. It was now a question of convincing Oliver to forget about his beach nymphet and make a decision.

The fact that George Lancaster had been signed was an extremely well kept secret. 'We want maximum press coverage,' Oliver kept on saying. 'When George hits town it's going to be an event. And when we call a press conference to make the announcement, it's world wide headlines.'

George had hit town late the previous evening. And Oliver was delighted. George Lancaster starring in his first movie for seven years. *Street People* – an Oliver Easterne Production. The suckers would be lining up to invest in his future projects.

A buzzer sounded on Oliver's desk and the flustered voice of his secretary announced, 'Mr. Lancaster is here.'

Before she could finish saying 'here' the door was flung open and George Lancaster made his entrance.

He was larger than life. Tall, bronzed, rugged. A true old-fashioned film star.

Oliver rushed into a welcoming speech. Neil didn't bother to get up. Montana stood, and waited for Oliver to stop crawling and introduce her. Naturally Oliver was too busy doing his Big Producer number to bother with introductions.

No slouch in the height stakes, standing near George Lancaster made Montana feel positively small. She waited until Oliver paused for breath, then she stuck her hand out and said, 'Hello. I'm Montana Gray.'

He almost ignored her, not quite. She got a fleeting handshake and a brief, 'I'm gasping for a cup of coffee, little lady.'

He thought she was an assistant, a secretary, just some female there to see to his every need! Oliver did nothing to correct this impression, he just kept right on talking.

'I'm Montana Gray,' she repeated. 'I wrote Street People.'

George favoured her with another quick look. 'You did? My, my, things are sure changing around here. I could still use that coffee, little lady.'

She did not believe it. No way. Who the fuck did this ageing macho man think he was?

'Then I suggest,' she said icily, 'that you have Oliver's secretary get it for you.'

Her iciness had absolutely no effect. He greeted Neil, told a few off-colour jokes, strode around the office with Oliver nervously dogging his every step.

The secretary, when she brought his coffee, was rewarded with a pat on the ass. 'Pretty lady,' he remarked to no one in particular.

241

Oliver outlined the plans for the following morning's press reception at the Beverly Hills Hotel.

'Yes, yes,' George sighed, bored with his own celebrity. 'We'll make every front page from here to Jipip.' He rose to leave. 'You're all coming to my party tonight?'

'Wouldn't miss it,' Oliver enthused.

'We'll be there,' Neil said.

George turned and gave Montana the benefit of his attention. 'And you too, little lady. You're coming, aren't you?'

'Every time I look at your picture Mr. Lancaster,' she murmured sarcastically.

His eyes froze for a moment. 'I don't like women that talk dirty,' he said, and then he was off, undeterred. George Lancaster was a superstar. And superstars didn't have to take crap from anyone.

There was a moment of silence after he left the room. Then Montana said, 'Thank you, gentlemen, for your support.'

'What?' Oliver said vaguely.

Neil swigged his bourbon.

She stared at them coldly. 'I'm going shopping,' she said. 'If you need any coffee why not give George a call.'

She swept out.

The salon was busy. In fact it was the busiest day Angel had seen. 'This is nothing, dreamheart,' confided Koko. Try Oscar night. Chaos! Pandemonium! Wonder . . . ful! I looove it. All the little dears out-bitching each other. And if you're not invited to Swifty's party you're dead!'

'Swifty?'

'Forget it, dreamheart. He'd *adore* you.'

'Why *are* we so busy today?'

'Ross Conti is throwing a big party for George Lancaster. You *have* heard of George Lancaster, haven't you?'

She nodded.

'Thank God for small mercies!'

Raymondo slid up to the desk, his jet hair slicked into a fifties swirl. 'Wanna go dancin' tonight, blondie?'

She shook her head.

'Wanna eat the best tacos in town?'

'Raymondo!' Koko screamed. 'Back to work if you please.'

Raymondo scowled. 'Bet you are a *natural* blond,' he muttered. 'Huh? Are you, pretty Angel?'

242

'Raymondo!' Koko's shriek forced him to move on, making way at the desk for a harassed Mrs. Liderman minus her precious dog.

'Where's Frowie?' Angel inquired solicitously.

Mrs. Liderman leaned confidentially across the desk, her eyes puffed and swollen. 'Dognapped!' she revealed tearfully. 'They took him two days ago and I'm waiting for the demand.'

'Who are "they"?' Angel asked, concern flooding her voice.

'I don't know,' quavered Mrs. Liderman, twisting a huge diamond solitaire ring on her finger. 'This town is full of crazies. It could be anyone.'

'Perhaps it's not dognapping,' Angel said reassuringly. 'Maybe Frowie's just wandered off. I wouldn't worry, Mrs. Liderman. I'm sure it will be all right.'

'Do you really think so, dear?'

'Oh, yes. I'm positive. Frowie will be back, you'll see.'

'You're such a lovely girl!' the fat woman sighed. 'A real comfort.'

'Thank you,' Angel replied modestly. 'Raymondo will be with you in a minute. If you'd like to take a seat . . .'

Koko waltzed over. 'What was *that* all about?' he asked, sotto voce.

She told him, then added, 'Nobody would kidnap her dog, would they?'

'Why not? This *is* Hollywood, dreamheart.'

The morning passed quickly, and by noon Angel was starving. She seemed to have developed a huge appetite and wondered if it had anything to do with being pregnant. Fortunately the swell of her stomach did not notice yet – not when she was dressed anyway. Eventually her secret would have to be revealed, but she was not in a hurry to tell anyone.

She thought about the baby all the time. And she tried not to think of Buddy at all. She had kept her promise to herself and not contacted him for two weeks. Then she had called Randy's apartment where there was no reply. She replaced the receiver and phoned Shelly. After all, it was only fair that she let Buddy know she was all right. Stoned or not he was probably concerned.

'Hi, this is Angel Hudson,' she announced when the phone was answered.

'Good for you,' slurred Shelly, still half asleep.

'Pardon?'

'Whaddya *want*?'

'I wondered if you would be kind enough to pass on a message to Buddy for me.'

'Spit it out, Angel-face.'

Hesitantly she began. 'I'd like you to tell him that I'm fine. I'm working at an interesting job, and I'll phone him at Randy's tomorrow, the same time.'

'Hmmm . . .' Shelly groped for a cigarette and tried to wake up properly. 'Still pregnant?'

'Yes I am,' Angel replied defiantly.

'You dumb bunny. Get rid of it, take my advice and el aborto.'

'I don't need your advice, thank you. The baby is Buddy's and my concern.'

'Oh, sure. But Buddy's bin' sleepin' in *my* bed lately, so that gives me some sort of a say.'

Angel could not keep the shock from her voice. 'What?'

'You heard. So why don't you grow up and face facts. Stop playing Daisy Mae an' get your shit together. Buddy doesn't care about you, he just cares about number one – himself, and I can dig that because it takes one to know one. So get rid of the kid, find yourself some real straight dude, an' hike your ass home. 'Cos Angel-pie, I'm tellin' you – Buddy's through with you. Capishe?'

Without uttering a word, Angel had replaced the receiver, her eyes filled with tears.

That had been weeks previously, and since that time she still hadn't decided what she should do. Divorce Buddy? She had no idea how to begin. He was no good, but she was still finding it hard to accept that sad fact of life.

Raymondo cruised by the desk as she was preparing to leave for lunch. 'Change your mind? Wanna hot date with me?'

'Leave the girl alone,' Koko scolded. 'Pick on someone your own size.'

'Nobody is *my* size!' Raymondo leered.

'Don't you wish,' retorted Koko tartly. 'Come dreamheart, I'll buy you a hero sandwich – everybody needs a hero in their life.'

Bibi Sutton was not getting the full focus of Elaine's attention and she knew it.

'Darling,' she said. 'Sweetie. Everything all right?'

Elaine nodded, forcing a bright smile to her lips. 'Of course it is. I'm just concerned about the party running smoothly.'

'How's Ross?' Bibi asked shrewdly.

Ross is a no-good cheating son of a bitch. 'He's fine,' she said flatly.

'You sure, sweetie?'

For a moment she nearly crumbled. How nice it would be to confide in someone, but she curbed herself just in time. To confide in Bibi would be like taking out a full page ad in the *Hollywood Reporter*.

'Of course I'm sure. Why?'

Bibi shrugged expensively clad shoulders. 'Nothing. People in this town so vicious. I take no notice . . .'

'What have you heard?' Elaine demanded, suddenly realizing that maybe the whole town already knew.

'You know sweetie, just nasty gossip . . .'

'What?' she insisted.

'That the movie Ross just finish not so good . . . I hear this from two or three people . . . Of course I no believe. This town, darling . . .'

Elaine almost gave a sigh of relief. So what if the movie stank? When he got *Street People* it would be a different story.

'Nobody's even *seen* the film,' she said calmly. 'It's still being edited. Who told you this?'

'It no important, darling.'

'Hmmm . . . I know what you mean about this town. Why, I heard the same thing about *Adam's* new movie. People are just *so* bitchy.'

Bibi was not used to being answered back. She wasn't quite sure how to handle Elaine this morning, she certainly wasn't her usual subservient self.

'Let me see the final list, sweetie. Then I must rush,' she said briskly.

Not to be outdone, Elaine replied, 'So must I. I had to squeeze you in this morning.'

'What you give up? Your exercise class?' Bibi inquired sweetly.

French cunt. She probably knew about Ron Gordino. And in view of what she had heard on the phone that morning Elaine didn't much care if the whole of Beverly Hills knew.

An exercise instructor, Elaine? Couldn't you at least have picked Robert Redford?

Shut up, Etta. What's wrong with an exercise instructor?

She handed over the final party list and Bibi checked it through like a computer expert. It *was* a great list, apart from the odd name here and there Pamela London had personally requested. Elaine could see that even Bibi was impressed.

She rose before she was dismissed. 'I have to rush. There's just so much to get organized.'

Bibi rose also. 'Sweetie. Tonight will be a night to remember.'

Elaine smiled vacantly. Was her erstwhile husband even now humping Karen Judas Lancaster's horrible body?

'I hope so, Bibi. I certainly hope so.'

Gaining entry to Karen Lancaster's high security apartment in the area known as Century City was no mean feat. Ross could remember when Century City was Twentieth Century-Fox Studios, and a sad day it was indeed when they sold off a goodly portion of their land and the real estate developers created Century City – a sea of concrete, glass and high-rises. He decided he wouldn't like to be around *this* section of town when the earthquake struck. No thank you very much.

'Who're you visiting?' the female guard at the gate demanded. She wore a permanent scowl and a tough looking uniform.

'Miss Lancaster. She's expecting me.' He wondered if the guard recognized him. He had taken the precaution of covering the famous Conti blues with a pair of Ray Charles shades. But there was always the famous dirty blond hair to contend with.

'What's your name?' the guard asked with an accusing stare. Obviously she was not a fan.

'Ross –' he began, before quickly remembering he was supposed to be incognito, and that Karen had left another name at the desk which for the life of him he could not remember.

'Er . . .'

'Yes?' snapped the guard.

'Mr. Ross.'

'Okay Mr. Ross. Please wait a minute.'

I've already waited more than a minute. What is this place anyway? Colditz?

The guard produced a pencil and pad, and walked around to the front of the Corniche where she took note of the licence plate. Then she slowly made her way around the back of the car and did the same thing.

Ross was not a patient man. He would have driven through, but a wooden barrier blocked his entry. 'Come on,' he muttered.

Deliberately moving as slowly as possible, she returned to her glass booth and dialled a number. After a long mutter on the phone she came back to the car. 'Do you know which way to go?'

'No,' he snapped.

'Proceed straight ahead. Stop at courtesy parking and a valet will take you to Miz Lancaster's apartment.'

She returned to her booth and raised the mechanical barrier. The Corniche shot through, narrowly missing an exiting Porsche.

'Ross!' screamed a blond female waving from the Porsche's window. 'See you tonight.'

He had no idea who she was, but whoever she was he would now have to think of an excuse for being there. Damn! He didn't even feel horny anymore.

The two Mexicans stationed at valet parking were fighting in Spanish. They ignored Ross, the Corniche, the baby blues and the dirty blond trademark hair.

Ross alighted from the car. 'This place is a frigging prison,' he screamed. 'Give me some attention.'

They forgot their fight and stared at him with looks of 'Who is this American fool?' Then one of them gestured to an open motorized buggy, while the other handed him a ticket and zoomed the Corniche away.

Ross indicated the buggy which resembled an open golf cart. '*I'm* supposed to get in *that*?'

'Si, Señor. Door to door service.'

'Shit!'

Elaine decided that she had to confide in *somebody*, otherwise she was just going to crack with fury. Outside the gates of the Sutton estate she slowed the Mercedes and tried to decide whether she should call Maralee, or just turn up at her front door. Since the country style sidewalks of Bel Air were hardly littered with phone booths she decided to take a chance and go right over. There was still half an hour of grace before she had to appear at the hairdressers where her stylist was waiting to create something sensational for the hostess of the week. That was the trouble with giving a big party in Beverly Hills – there was always someone around the corner waiting to top you. Why, only ten minutes earlier Bibi had murmured that she must throw a little soirée soon. Bibi's 'little soirées' made Oscar night seem like an evening at McDonalds.

Make the most of it, Elaine. Hostess of the week is better than a kick up the ass.

Fuck you, Etta. What do you know anyway?

What do I know? Ha! I know that I wouldn't sit back and let Karen

247

*Lancaster get away with screwing my husband. I'd bust her ass, and
damn the party. Have you forgotten New York Elaine? You're a street
kid, not some laid back Californian cooze.*

Three cars were parked in Maralee's driveway. And two gardeners
worked on the front lawn aimlessly hosing fallen leaves from one area
to another. Elaine parked behind a silver Jaguar, alighted from her
car, and rang the doorbell.

One of Maralee's army of Mexicans opened the door a crack and
stared at Elaine, the security chain firmly in place.

'*Buenos dias,*' said Elaine pleasantly, although she didn't feel
pleasant, she felt like screaming long and loud. 'Is Señora Gray up?'

'*Que, cual?*'

'Señora Gray,' Elaine repeated. 'Is she up?' Why couldn't Maralee
hire Mexicans who at least spoke English?

'No.'

Before Elaine could object the door was slammed shut. She was
speechless. Maralee definitely needed a talking to about the way her
help conducted themselves. The stupid woman hadn't even asked
who she was. She could have been someone important. She *was*
someone important.

Frustrated and angry she returned to the comfort of her pale blue
Mercedes and sat behind the wheel.

*Where to now, Elaine? The hairdressers where you get to put on a
wife of the star act? Or maybe Ron Gordino's for a decent fuck? Or
how about confronting Karen and Ross?*

Shut up, Etta. I'll do what I want.

What *did* she want?

She wanted to cry.

She wanted to yell and scream.

She wanted to kick out.

She wanted to have never picked up the phone and heard her
betrayal.

It was the most perfect day for a party. All around her immaculate
green lawns received attention, maids walked children to school, and
dogs did their duty beneath the palm trees. A police car cruised
slowly by, and a Sparkletts truck stopped two houses down.

Beverly Hills.

How she loved it. When you were up it was the greatest.

How she hated it. When you were down it was the worst.

At the hairdressers she was unusually quiet. When she was finished
she contemplated phoning Maralee, but then she thought no, I don't

need to tell anyone. I can handle it. I'm Elaine Conti. Not big-mouthed Etta Grodinski from the Bronx.

Screw Etta Grodinski.

Screw Ross Conti.

Screw Karen Lancaster.

Calmly she reclaimed her car from the parking lot and once more sat behind the wheel contemplating her next move. She *should* go home, time was pressing, yet she felt so safe and secure behind the wheel of the Mercedes, it was the onnly place she really wanted to be.

A man in a Cadillac bleeped his horn impatiently, and she found herself heading towards Wilshire. *I want to spend money, she thought. I want to spend every red cent that bastard hasn't got.*

She drew into the parking lot of Saks and entered the department store like a gladiator entering the arena. Within an hour she had charged eight thousand dollars worth of merchandise to be sent.

She left the store with a smile on her lips, and strolled down Wilshire to yet another large department store. Immediately she spotted an enamel bracelet she had to have. 'Charge it,' she told the salesgirl imperiously.

The girl took her charge card and since the amount was over a hundred dollars, went to the phone to check.

She returned full of apologies. 'I'm so sorry, but there appears to be a problem . . . If you would care to go up to our credit department I'm sure that it can be settled . . .'

'But I want this bracelet,' Elaine announced firmly.

The girl was embarrassed. 'I'm sorry . . .'

'You will be,' said Elaine, her voice rising sharply. 'Don't you know who I am?'

The girl gazed at her blankly. She saw a passably attractive woman with an elaborate hair-do. She certainly did not see a Goldie Hawn or a Faye Dunaway. Fortunately, another customer claimed her attention, and she moved quickly away from Elaine.

'Bitch!' Elaine said out loud. And then she felt sorry for calling the girl names. It wasn't her fault. It was Ross's fault. The bastard hadn't paid their last account.

For a moment she was uncertain what to do. Then, quite calmly, she realized there was only one thing *to* do. She glanced around her. The salesgirl was busy, other shoppers were going about their business. She was unobserved, free to do anything. Quick as a flash she scooped the bracelet from the counter where in her haste to get away the salesgirl had left it. Then, humming softly to herself, she headed for the exit.

Once outside she took a deep breath. And the adrenaline started to flow. *Now* she was ready to go home and look Ross in the eye without so much as a flicker to reveal she knew he was a no-good unfaithful *bum*.

What did she care anyway? *She* was Mrs. Ross Conti, not spoiled rich bitch Karen Lancaster whose only claim to fame was a famous daddy.

A firm hand on her arm stopped her progress along Wilshire. 'Excuse me, madam,' said a tall bespectacled woman. 'Would you mind returning to the store with me? The manager would like a word with you.'

Karen greeted him not clad in the red satin nightie, crotchless panties, and nippleless bra she had promised. Instead she wore a yellow track suit and a nasty scowl. She flung open the door and started to harangue him about the amount of time it had taken him to get there.

He marched inside the tribute to Architectural Digest and flung himself on a white leather couch. 'Will you shut up? It has just taken me twenty frigging minutes to get from the front entrance of this jail house to your front door.'

'Don't be ridiculous,' she stormed. 'You probably went back to sleep while I've been standing around waiting for you like some . . . some little groupie!'

He started to laugh. The thought of Karen Lancaster as a groupie was too absurd.

'Don't laugh!' she yelled. 'I could have had an extra hour's sleep!'

He stretched his arms above his head and groaned loudly. 'Nagging I can get at home. I came here for a fucking not an ear bashing.'

Her scowl deepened. 'I don't feel like it now.'

He got up and headed for the door. 'Take your bad mood out on someone else. *I* don't feel like it either.' He slammed the door behind him and buzzed for the elevator. Karen Lancaster in a track suit and a bad mood was not the way he wished to spend the morning. Impatiently he buzzed for the elevator again, letting forth a sneaky fart.

A middle-aged woman emerged from the apartment opposite and gave him a dirty look. She was clad in a multi-coloured robe, her hair full of shocking pink curlers.

'Yaes?' she said in a European accent, staring at him suspiciously.

'Yes What?' he snapped.

'Vat are you doing in my hallvay?' the woman said icily, sniffing the air with a look of disdain.

Ross raised his all concealing dark shades and glared. '*Your* hallway?'

She glared back. 'Yaes. *My* hallvay.'

'*And* Miss Lancaster's I presume.'

'Miss Lancaster did not give you key to the elevator. Since you do not have one I can only say you are trespassing in *my* hallway, and therefore I call security. At once.' She stepped smartly back into her apartment, slamming the door firmly behind her.

Ross did not believe it. You needed a key to get *out* of the place! This was better than San Quentin!

He hammered on Karen's front door.

She opened it on the chain. 'What?' she asked in a bored tone.

'Give me the key for the elevator. Let me out of this prison.'

'Why should I? You've ruined my morning.'

'I've ruined *your* morning.'

'I don't think I like screwing a married man. Your hours don't suit me.'

Through the crack in the door he couldn't help noticing that she had finally come through with the nippleless bra. An erotic nipple temptingly emerged from black and red lace.

'Hmmm . . .' he said, changing his mind about leaving. 'Aren't you even going to offer me a cup of coffee?'

Karen licked her index finger and lasciviously brought it down to her nipple. 'Maybe . . .' she said, making no move to release the chain.

He felt the return of his early morning hard-on. 'Come on, sweetheart,' he pleaded, enjoying her little game. 'I've got something for breakfast that you are going to *love*!'

'Something soft?'

'Not any more!'

'Something hot?'

'You bet your –'

Before he could finish his sentence a baby-faced security guard nervously wielding a pistol emerged from the elevator. 'Okay you –' he commanded Ross in a high-pitched voice. 'Up against the wall an' spread 'em.'

'What?' asked an outraged Ross, drowning out Karen's hysterical giggle.

'Don't think I won't use this thing,' twitched the guard. 'Do as I say or I'll shoot.'

The European woman in the pink hair curlers and the multi-coloured robe opened up the door of her apartment. 'Yaes,' she said firmly. 'That iss the intruder.'

'Holy shit!' exclaimed Ross.

'Spread 'em,' said the guard.

'What's the matter with all of you,' said Karen, releasing her security chain and stepping out into the hallway. 'Don't any of you recognize Ross Conti when you see him?

Three pair of eyes turned to stare at her simultaneously.

Karen Lancaster wore nothing but a nippleless bra and an amused smile.

28

It was early morning when Deke drove the van slowly into the small town of Barstow, California.

He was tired and unshaven, having driven non-stop from New Mexico. The very thought of being near his destination had sent him speeding along the arid desert roads, radio blaring, thoughts alive with the inspiring words – KEEPER OF THE ORDER.

He saw Joey often. Sitting in a passing car – her skirt hiked high above her thighs. Thumbing a lift roadside. Posing provocatively on billboards along the way.

He was not tempted to stop though. Oh, no. Not tempted one little bit. He knew better. Now.

California was not how he had imagined it would be. He had expected white palaces, blue seas, wide streets lined with palm trees. Instead he found dusty sidewalks and the same old gas stations and motels. The heat was acrid. It enveloped like a blanket and tried to suffocate.

Still. He had arrived.

Barstow, California.

He took a crumpled piece of paper with an address scribbled on it from the hiding place down the side of his boot and studied it intently.

For a moment the image of the girl's face in Amarillo danced before his eyes 'Why?' she had screamed in terror. 'Why me?'

The moment of her death was ecstasy. Her screaming stopped, and her body became slack and peaceful. He had felt so close to her then, because he alone had helped her . . . The knife was an instrument of God sent to do His work . . .

Upon her death she became Joey, and he was able to relieve himself of the passion that had been building in his body for so many months . . . The relief was glorious.

PASSION. EVEN THE PRESIDENT NEEDS PASSION.

A broken neon sign offered coffee and doughnuts. He steered the truck into an unkempt parking lot and alighted.

The place was deserted except for a lone counterman picking his nose and studying a sex magazine.

'Coffee,' Deke said, taking a faded plastic seat at the counter.

The man barely raised his eyes from the magazine, he merely yelled 'Coffee' to someone in back.

'And a doughnut,' Deke added.

'Doughnut,' yelled the man, not moving.

A line of ants had taken up residence around a grimy sugar container. Deke reached for a paper napkin and methodically squashed them.

'You ever see a naked broad with no legs?' the counterman asked, removing his finger from his nose and thrusting the open magazine across the counter.

Silently Deke regarded the pictures.

'Hot, huh?'

The girl in the pictures looked like Joey. The pictures were grossly obscene. Yes. He had done the right thing removing Joey from temptation. She was safe now. The Keeper Of The Order had performed his duty well.

'Waddya think?' asked the counterman, hoping for a discussion on the merits of sex with a legless woman.

Deke raised his cold black eyes from the magazine and stared. It wasn't right that Joey had posed for such pictures and that strange men could feast their eyes on her naked body. If he had time he would remove the scum, squash him dead, just as he had squashed the ants.

'They're all whores,' he said at last, realizing that the Keeper Of

253

The Order did not have time to deal with every stinking pervert who crossed his path.

The counterman laughed derisively. 'You're so right, pal. I couldn't've said it better myself. Hookers – every damn one!'

Damnation is closer than you know, Deke thought.

A fat girl emerged from the back, coffee in one hand, doughnut on a plate in the other. The counterman winked lewdly at Deke who ignored him. He drank the steaming coffee, wolfed down the greasy doughnut, then slammed some money down and left.

He was in California now, and nothing was going to stop him doing what he had to do.

29

A psychiatrist would say that it was a scream in the dark. An attention getting act performed by a person who desperately needed help. Elaine knew all the psychological garbage. She had not sat on an analyst's couch for a year without learning a thing or two. She had learned that seeing a shrink was expensive, time consuming, and ego boosting. Who wouldn't enjoy talking about themselves non-stop, an hour at a time, three times a week? It was one little luxury she had finally decided to do without.

These thoughts ran through her head as she sat in the manager's office and said – yet again – 'I am *outraged* that you could even have thought for one moment that I intended to . . . to *steal* that *tacky* bracelet. My husband is Ross Conti. If he so desired he could buy this whole store for me!'

'Yes. I understand that,' said the manager, not understanding at all. 'But you must see *our* point of view. You left here with the bracelet in your possession, and it was unpaid for.'

'A mistake,' she said haughtily. 'I misunderstood your salesperson. I thought she had charged it to my account.'

The store detective hovered by the door.

'I really must go,' Elaine said quickly. 'This whole incident is a gross error on your part.'

'I'm sorry, but we cannot allow you to go yet.'

Why had she been so *careless*? How *could* she have risked everything on the day of her party? What if it got in the *newspapers*?

'Why?' she demanded imperiously.

'Because,' said the manager, 'our policy is to prosecute.'

She leapt up in a panic, thinking of the publicity. 'Please!' she implored. 'You can't do that! I've told you who I am. Why can't we just forget it?'

He frowned. 'You've *told* us who you are. But that doesn't *prove* who you are.'

'I've shown you all my credit cards. Surely that's good enough?'

'No driving licence, no picture –'

'I never carry my licence,' she interrupted quickly.

'That's a shame . . .' He pursed his lips. If the woman was who she said she was, then the publicity would help neither of them. On the other hand, he couldn't just let her stroll casually out of the store merely because she claimed to be the wife of a film star. An idea came to him. 'If we could perhaps contact *Mr*. Conti, and he came to collect you then maybe we could forget about prosecuting. I'm sure, as you say, it was a genuine mistake.'

The female detective's lip curled in disgust.

'Yes,' said Elaine quickly, filled with relief. 'I know exactly where I can find him.'

Eventually they made love, because that had been the purpose of Ross's visit in the first place.

Karen kept laughing as he pumped solidly away. 'Did you *see* that woman's face?' she gasped. 'I mean *did you see it*?'

'I could hardly *help* seeing it,' he huffed.

'Ummm . . . let's change positions.' Skillfully she rolled around – keeping him firmly inside her – until she was on top.

He had noticed that Karen was not too thrilled by the missionary position. He liked it himself, it gave him somewhere to rest his bones when he needed a break.

'And that security creep!' she giggled. 'Can you imagine! If you had been a burglar he would've wet his pants!' She angled an erect nipple into his mouth and he sucked greedily. 'Niiiiice . . .' she sighed.

He felt the beginning of the rush. Not bad. He had given her ten minutes of solid action, she couldn't complain about *that*.

'Christ!' he groaned. 'Jesus H!'

The phone rang just before he hit. Valiantly they tried to continue, but the ringing was too intrusive.

Disengaging her nipple from his mouth Ross said, 'Well *answer* the frigging thing.'

She grabbed the receiver. 'Yes?'

Ross could not hear who it was, but from the way she pulled herself off him he knew it must be George Lancaster.

'Daddy!' she cooed in confirmation. 'Sorry . . . I mean George. How are you today?'

Ross watched his erection deflate. He felt like a horse blocked at the gate. Ten more seconds and he would have been a winner. Now he would just have to run the whole goddamn race again. If he had the strength. He looked pointedly at his watch. 'I've got to go to the bank,' he mouthed.

She nodded, covered the mouthpiece for a second. 'Okay. Go, and come back after,' and then she went back to her riveting conversation.

Enough was enough. Karen had given him more crap than he cared to handle for one day. He dressed, found the elevator key, and let himself out.

The morning had hardly been perfect. He hoped the day would improve as it progressed.

Karen spoke to her father for twenty-five minutes, and at the end of the conversation he invited her to a late lunch in the Polo Lounge.

'I'll be there,' she said breathlessly, conveniently forgetting that she had told Ross to return.

She ran a bubblebath, pinned her long hair up, and slid into the warm water. Daddy was back in town. And if he wanted her to she would spend every second with him. She might be thirty-two years old but she had her priorities straight.

The phone rang again and she picked up the bathroom extension. 'George?' she questioned hopefully. He didn't like her calling him daddy – said it made him feel too old.

'No. This is Elaine,' said the voice of her friend sounding uptight.

'Oh, hi.' She could hardly conceal her lack of enthusiasm. 'All set for the big night?'

'Yes,' said Elaine in a strained voice. 'Can I have a word with Ross?'

'Ross??' Surprise filled her voice.

'I know he's there, and I need to speak to him urgently.'

Karen laughed hollowly. 'Why would *Ross* be *here*?'

'*This is urgent. Put him on.*'

'I don't understand,' Karen said in a concerned tone. 'Are you all right?'

'He's not with you then?'

'*Of course* he's not here. I don't –'

Elaine hung up.

Karen was stunned. She stood up in the bath, bubbles sticking everywhere. How had Elaine known? Had Ross *told* her?

No. He wanted it kept a secret more than she did. Come to think of it she couldn't care less whether it was kept a secret or not. Having Ross Conti was the next best thing to having daddy. And since having daddy was a definite no-no . . .

She felt a brief feeling of remorse about Elaine, but that soon passed. Karen always got what she wanted, it had been that way since she was a little girl. And if someone got hurt along the way . . . Well . . . That's show biz – as daddy always said.

Elaine hung up the phone tight-lipped. 'It may take me a few minutes to locate my husband,' she said, wondering if perhaps she was having a nightmare and would wake up at any minute.

Then she called Lina, their bank, Ross's health club, Ma Maison, their business manager, Lina, the Polo Lounge, the suntanning salon, the Bistro, Lina, and finally Karen Lancaster again. Her phone did not answer, which convinced Elaine that even now they were rolling around on Karen's king size custom built bed having wild sex and laughing at poor Elaine.

'I'm having a big party tonight,' she said desperately to the manager. 'Is this really necessary?'

'Was it really necessary for you to take the bracelet?'

Suddenly she snapped. 'I hope you know what you're doing,' she screamed hysterically. 'I have important friends in *very* high places, and you are making a nasty mistake keeping me here.'

He had been on the verge of letting her go. After her series of phone calls there was no doubt that she was who she claimed to be. But he had never liked to be threatened, and just who did she think she was anyway?

'I'm sorry,' he said smoothly. 'You have a choice. The police or your husband. Whichever you prefer.'

As the Corniche glided away from Karen Lancaster's Century City apartment, so a shabby brown Datsun slid into the lane behind it.

The Datsun was driven by a man named Little S. Shitz. A name he had never been happy with, but one he had become used to over the years. The kids at school had dubbed him 'Little Shit'. His ex-wife had called him 'Big Shit'. And the people he came in contact with during the course of his work invariably ended up calling him every other name you could think of.

Little S. Shitz was a private detective – the kind you could hire for a hundred bucks a day as long as you paid in cash. And the sort of people who hired him *always* paid in cash. He was a weedy looking man in his late thirties, stoop shouldered, sharp nosed, with ferret-like eyes that continually darted this way and that. His thinning brown hair was plastered close to his scalp, and dandruff scattered on the collar of his scruffy brown shirt. He was not a class act. But he knew how to play dirty, and he specialized in divorce cases – the seamier the better. He was an expert at catching a cheating husband or wife. Many a motel door had felt the force of his shoulder as he burst in – flash camera in hand.

Little S. Shitz felt that he had lucked into the big-time with the Glynis Barnes divorce case. 'I want to know every move my husband makes,' she told him on her first visit to his one-roomed Hollywood office. 'I want times, dates, and *most important* – photographs of every woman he sees.'

He went to work at once. Following Chet Barnes was a pleasure and he soon settled into a daily routine which hardly ever took him out of Beverly Hills. He sat outside some of the best restaurants taking the occasional shot of Chet Barnes emerging with various women. Once a week Glynis Barnes arrived at his office bearing cash. She collected the photographic evidence, then departed with the words – 'Let's give it another week.'

One day a particular picture grabbed her attention. 'Do you know who this is?' she asked sharply, thrusting it at him.

He glanced briefly at a photo of Chet Barnes emerging from La Scala, his arm around a copper-haired woman in a tight dress. He shook his head while Glynis Barnes paced his small office muttering to herself.

'Have you seen him with her before?' she demanded. 'Did he spend the night at her place? What happened?'

Frankly he had no idea. Immediately after taking that picture he had quit and gone home. So he lied. 'Yeah, he spent the night. I thought you'd want me to stay until morning, so I did. Anything after twelve is double rate you know.'

'That doesn't matter,' she said. 'Now, this is what I want you to do . . .'

She told him the woman was Karen Lancaster. The name didn't mean anything to him until he put it together with George Lancaster and found out it was his daughter!

Glynis had suspected all along that her estranged husband had the hots for Karen. Now that she was sure, she wanted to prove to him what a tramp Karen was. 'I want her followed,' she said. 'And get me some *good* photos. Explicit. Watch her twenty-four hours a day. I don't care what it costs.'

He followed her to the beach house just a couple of days later. The photos he managed to get were hot. First he risked a roll of film through the glass front of her house while she rolled around on the bed with a man. Then he captured her and the boyfriend in the ocean.

It wasn't until later when he developed the photos that he realized the man was Ross Conti. And he had stills of him the like of which his fans had *never* seen!

He decided that handing the photos to Glynis Barnes would be crazy. Why settle for a few hundred when it could mean thousands?

He waited a week, then withdrew from the case much to Glynis Barnes's annoyance.

He waited a while longer, then enlarged some of his favourite shots and set about finding Ross Conti. It was easy. All he had to do was buy a cheapo map of the movie stars' homes, and the Contis were listed right there along with Tony Curtis and Johnny Carson.

Early one morning he parked opposite the Conti house and waited for the moment to be right.

Three maids arrived, giggling and chattering away in Spanish.

The milkman delivered twelve quarts of orange juice and six cartons of milk.

A woman left the house, climbed into a pale blue Mercedes, zipped out the drive, changed her mind, drove back to the house, then re-emerged and shot off again.

He bided his time until eventually he was rewarded with the sight of Ross Conti in his Corniche a mere twenty minutes later. He followed the car all the way to Karen Lancaster's apartment in Century City, and was delighted to think that the affair was still going strong.

Later, when Ross Conti drove out in the distinctive gold Corniche, Little S. Shitz was right there behind him.

*

259

Randy's apartment stank of Au Sauvage aftershave, Yves Saint Laurent deodorant and Jean Naté body splash.

'I hate all that crap,' Buddy said, busily doing one-armed press-ups.

Randy emerged from the bathroom clad only in brief jockeys. 'What crap?' he demanded.

'All that shit you're spraying yourself with. Doncha know that stuff can give you cancer?' He released his weight and lay flat on his stomach. 'Jeez, y'know I don't feel so good. I think it's breathin' in all these poison fumes.'

'You don't like it you know what you can do.'

Buddy got up off the floor and leaned weakly against the wall. 'I didn't sleep so good last night. I had a real bad dream – like it was vivid. I was –'

Randy held up a commanding hand. 'Don't tell me your dream. My own don't thrill me, so why should I want to know yours?'

Buddy went to the refrigerator. 'You've never got any food here,' he complained.

'Christ! You're worse than a wife! Why don't you go over to Shelly's an' excite her with your belly-aching?'

'That's the trouble. I excite her with more than my belly-aching. I'm not into another relationship. What Angel did to me was –'

'Cut it out,' said Randy sharply. 'I got a lot on my mind and I don't need your problems too. You wanted to sleep on my floor – I lent you my floor. You wanted to borrow some bucks – I lent you bucks. Now for this I don't need a running commentary on your lousy life.'

'Thanks. It's good to have friends.'

Randy had been in a bad mood ever since Buddy had mentioned that he too was going to the George Lancaster party. 'Stay away from me and Maralee,' Randy had warned, nervous of his past.

What did the schmuck think he was going to say. 'Hey – Maralee. Nice to meet you. Did you know that your boyfriend and I used to do a little hustling together?' Jeez! He wanted to forget about it just as much as Randy.

He had made his daily phone call to Inga, and got the usual – 'They're interested. They like you a lot. You're really a hot favourite.' How hot could he be when weeks were passing and nothing was happening? Maybe Inga was giving him sweet-bullshit. Maybe the role was already cast. Maybe he didn't have a hope . . .

'Angel!' He muttered her name under his breath. 'Why did you have to run out on me?'

Montana drove into Beverly Hills, but the thought of shopping for a new outfit to wear at George Lancaster's party failed to excite her. She was outraged by his arrogant and rude attitude. Just who exactly did he think he was? An over-the-hill ageing superstar, that's who. And as for Oliver and Neil, they had really let her down. Oliver, crawling like a modern day Uriah Heep, and Neil, nursing his bourbon like it was mother's milk.

She had tried to talk to Neil several times in the past few days, but he had dismissed her attempts at meaningful conversation with disruptive comments about the script, sidetracking her into heated discussions. All of a sudden she was fighting for scenes he wanted to cut. Scenes he had never objected to before. Important scenes.

She felt frustrated and out of control. What the hell was going on? Why was everything turning sour? *Street People* – her baby – was slowly being taken away. She had written the script and now it was as if the words no longer belonged to her. Okay so she had practically cast the film except for the leading roles – but so what? From now on it would be a George Lancaster movie and he was the kind of man she had always hated. Self-important, tough, assured in his mistaken knowledge that men are superior beings to women.

She decided not to go back to the office. The beach seemed like a much better idea, so she drove along Wilshire all the way to the ocean, where she parked the car and strode along the seashore, trying to calm down.

The waves were high enough to surf, and plenty of kids were indulging, their bronzed bodies flying over the water with speed and grace. She wished she had a swimsuit and a board – for that's just what she felt like doing. And why shouldn't she? On impulse she hurried back to the car and drove to a sports shop on Santa Monica. There, she purchased what she needed.

She hadn't surfed in years – certainly not since she had known Neil. Entering the swell of the ocean, at first she felt awkward and stupid – even – at twenty-nine – too old. But soon she was back in the swing of it, riding the waves just like the good old days – having a marvellous time.

She forgot about George, Oliver, the movie, and most of all Neil. Excitement swamped her as skills she had forgotten came into play.

How good it was to feel young again and to have nothing on your mind but the next wave.

How good it was to be in control.

*

261

'Can I talk to you a minute?' Little S. Shitz sidled up to Ross Conti outside Bijan on Rodeo Drive.

'Sure,' said Ross magnanimously, thinking the seedy looking man was a fan. 'What do you want to know? Did I *really* jump off the clifftop in "Prowler" myself or was it a stand-in? Don't worry, everyone asks me that, and I can tell you it was me. If you lend me a pen I'll sign your envelope. Who's it for – your sister?'

Little was speechless. You don't go up to a man to blackmail him and have him offer to autograph the envelope with the *blackmail* pictures inside it.

'You don't understand,' he stuttered. 'I have photographs.'

'Oh, you want me to sign your photos,' said Ross easily. He had always believed in being nice to his fans. Treat 'em good and they'll never stop flocking to your movies.

They stopped years ago, putz.

'Photographs you wouldn't want published,' he continued rapidly before this big-time movie star could confuse him further. 'Or your wife to see, or your mother, or your daughter, or your grand-daughter.'

Grand-daughter! Ross was incensed. How old did this scurvy prick think he was anyway?

'My mother is deceased. I do not have a daughter. I *certainly* do not have a grand-daughter – so why don't you take whatever you have in that envelope and stick it up your ass.' Ross spoke with dignity, then headed abruptly for his car parked in a red zone.

Little hurried after him. 'How would you – in bed with Karen Lancaster – look on the cover of the National Inquirer?' he asked, twitching nervously.

For one brief moment Ross's stride faltered, but then he thought – come on, what am I getting worried about? Who could possibly have photos of me and Karen?

Little S. Shitz fumbled in his envelope.

He produced an eight by ten black and white glossy of Karen and Ross in bed together.

Little S. Shitz had the goods.

'How much?' Ross asked wearily.

Karen entered the Polo Lounge with confidence, waved to Nino, the maître d'hôtel, and headed for the table George Lancaster always had when he was in town.

To her disappointment he was not yet there, so she sat herself down, ordered a Bloody Mary, then took an exquisite Fabergé compact from her purse and studied her chiselled features. Fortunately she had inherited her father's looks *and* his spirit – which she was pleased about because to her way of thinking her mother had been a weak woman, too weak by far to handle a daughter like Karen – *or* a husband like George, which was probably the reason he had sought out other women so consistently during the course of his marriage. When her mother died Karen got to spend a lot of time with George. For a dizzy six months they were inseparable. Then some ice-blond starlet stepped into the picture and blew everything. George, like a fool, married her. It lasted nine months and cost him plenty. In the meantime Karen married the first man she could – a real estate broker who had just sold her a house. Her marriage broke up two days after George's. But instead of moving back together as Karen had hoped, George went off to Palm Beach with some friends, met Pamela London, and as soon as his divorce was final, married her. Their wedding was *the* social event of the year. Karen got stoned and gave head to her date under a table. Two months later she married a spaced-out composer who spooned so much coke his nose gave way. When she realized George didn't care *who* she was married to she got a divorce, and since that time had been a single lady living alone in Beverly Hills. A single lady with a huge trust fund, a great apartment, a terrific house at the beach, three cars, four furs, and anything else her little heart desired.

George Lancaster made a rowdy entrance. People jumped to attention as he passed their tables, conversations stopped, flunkeys jumped to their feet and paid homage.

Karen stood as he approached. She wished she was a little girl again and could leap into his arms. Instead she settled for a quick hug.

'How's my girlie?' he boomed.

'You look wonderful da . . . um . . . George. Honestly, you look really *great*.'

'Naw . . . I'm gettin' old.'

'Come on. You – ne-ever.'

He grinned boyishly. 'Me and Reagan, kiddo. We're holdin' up pretty good for two old broncos.'

'Better not let *him* hear you say that.'

'Who, Ronnie? He wouldn't mind.'

'I love you, daddy,' she said, all of a sudden the little girl she wished she still was.

'Cut out the daddy, will ya? You know I can't stand it.'

She took a hurried gulp of her Bloody Mary, then brightly asked, 'How's Pamela?'

'For an' old broad she's not bad.' He laughed loudly. 'Did you hear the one about the Eskimo and the ice cubes?'

For fifteen minutes he told jokes, stopping only to josh with assorted staff and patrons who stopped by the table in a steady stream.

Karen munched her way through a delicious Neil McCarthy salad, downed two more Bloody Marys, wondered why the *hell* Elaine Conti had phoned *her* looking for Ross, and listened patiently to all of George's sexist jokes.

He didn't like women. Even Karen had to admit that.

Finally, he imparted the news of his commitment to *Street People*.

Karen had heard rumours – but she had dismissed them as just that. After all, how many times had George told her that there was no way he would ever do another film.

Her reactions were mixed. It would be glorious having George back in town. But what about Ross? *He* wanted *Street People*. He *needed* it.

'Oh, shit,' she mumbled under her breath.

'What?' boomed George.

'Nothing da . . . George. I was just wondering if you're sure it's the right part for you.'

'What's right? *I* don't become the role, the role becomes *me*. *That's* the secret of being a star in this town, and don't you ever forget it.'

By late afternoon Angel was exhausted. All she wanted to do was go home and collapse. The salon had been a madhouse all day, and everybody's tempers were frayed. The phone on the desk rang for about the hundredth time. Wearily she picked it up. 'Koko's. Can I help you?'

'Angel, dear?' gushed Mrs. Liderman.

'Yes.'

'I'm so glad I caught you. You'll *never* guess what. Frowie came home! And it's *all* thanks to you, dear, and your positive vibes.'

'I only said –'

'It doesn't matter *what* you said,' interrupted Mrs. Liderman. 'You sent out positive thought waves and that was enough to persuade my baby to come home to me. I'm *so* grateful.'

264

'What *is* going on?' hissed Koko.

Angel covered the mouthpiece and whispered, 'Mrs. L's dog came home, she seems to think I had something to do with it.'

'Good. Maybe she'll give you five hundred dollars.'

As if on cue Mrs. Liderman said, 'I have to reward you.'

And Angel said, 'Don't be silly.'

And Mrs. Liderman said, 'I'm sending my car to collect you. I'm taking you to a party tonight, you'll have a marvellous time. It's a very special party being thrown for my dear friend, Pamela London.'

Koko – who was now listening in, nodded enthusiastically, while Angel said, 'That's very kind of you Mrs. Liderman, but I don't think I can go.'

Koko snatched the phone from her grasp. 'Mrs. Liderman,' he cooed, 'Angel would *love* to go. Could your driver pick her up at her apartment? I'll give you the address.'

Angel shook her head helplessly while Koko arranged her life, and when he hung up she said, 'I'm not going. There is *no way* I'm going.'

'Dreamheart!' he exclaimed. 'Trust me. You *have* to go, there is no question about it. You simply have to learn that in life we do not always do what we want to do. Sometimes fate pushes us in other directions, and fate has said that tonight you *will* go to the ball.'

'What ball?'

'Haven't you ever heard of Cinderella? Oh, God! Must I teach you *every*thing?'

It was four o'clock in the afternoon. Elaine was calm. Her thoughts were clear and concise. After fourteen phone calls she had failed to locate Ross, and it was becoming increasingly obvious that she would be arrested.

She stared dreamily off into space.

Headlines.

WIFE OF STAR ARRESTED IN SHOPLIFTING BUST.

BEVERLY HILLS BABE BACK TO THE BRONX.

GEORGE LANCASTER SAYS, 'ELAINE WHO?'

Well, everyone would have a big laugh at her expense. She would be forced to leave town. The disgrace, the humiliation, the *embarrassment*.

Where was Ross Conti?

Where *was* the biggest lying, cheating shitheel in the world?

30

Leon Rosemont's investigation of the Andrews family yielded very little. There appeared to be no living relatives, and of the two witnesses listed on their marriage certificate, one was untraceable and the other dead.

It occurred to Leon that the only way he was going to find out any more about them was to go to Barstow and dig around. Millie had *said* she wanted to vacation in California. Somehow he didn't think she had Barstow in mind . . . But still . . . he could always make a side trip on a day when she was busy.

On impulse he went out and purchased two plane tickets to California and presented them to Millie with a flourish.

'We're going to take a month off,' he told her. 'The time is due me, and I figured we should do it properly. We'll hire a car and just drive around.'

'San Francisco?' she asked, her eyes gleaming.

He nodded.

'The Napa Valley? Arizona? *Hollywood*?'

He nodded again.

She threw her arms around his neck and hugged him. 'Honey,' she crooned, 'you are somethin' else.'

A week before they were due to leave he handed her four hundred dollars and told her to go buy some vacation clothes. She rushed off to the shopping mall as happy as if he had given her four thousand.

While she was gone he took the opportunity to secrete the Andrews file at the bottom of his suitcase. It wasn't strictly legal, but he had photo-copied all of the official documents, including the pictures . . .

There were fifteen still shots taken that morning in Friendship Street.

Fifteen photos of . . . murder.

266

31

At approximately four-fifteen Ross Conti strode angrily through the front door of his house. Chaos reigned. Strange people were everywhere.

'What in the hell is going on here?' he roared at Lina, who stood weeping in the doorway to the kitchen.

'Señor Conti,' she sobbed. 'Is impossible. I no take it. I quit.'

She clung to his arm and he shook her off while demanding, 'Where is Mrs. Conti?'

A wild-haired youth in tight jeans and a Hells-Angel studded jacket intervened. 'Hey-hey, man, you the boss man 'round here? I gotta get me more power – my amps just gonna blow I don't get me more juice.'

A middle-aged woman in a flowered pant suit thrust herself forward. 'Mr. Conti. *Please.* Your wife assured me that she had twenty matching vases which I need *des*perately if the miniature daisy arrangements are to be ready in time.'

A courtly Italian man carrying a violin case inquired in pained tones. 'Where is our room? The Zancussi Trio *always* has a room.'

'Christ!' exclaimed Ross. 'Lina. Where *is* my wife?'

Lina wiped her tears on the corner of her apron. 'She no come back. She leave everything to me. I quit.' She marched into the kitchen where her two friends stood in a huddle by the back door.

Ross followed her. The wild haired youth following him. The woman in the flowered pant suit and the pained Italian trailed behind.

Already in residence in the kitchen were two gays preparing raw vegetables at the sink. Two bartenders emptying out cardboard boxes of liquor. Another sad-eyed Italian, this one with an accordion. And a blond teeny-bopper in shorts and a cut-off top, Sony headphones clamped firmly to her ears.

Ross pursued Lina to the door, wondering bitterly if Little S. Shitz had shafted him, and already shown the pictures to Elaine. What else would explain her not being home on the day of their party?

'Did Mrs. Conti phone? Leave a message? Anything?' he asked desperately.

'She phone five times,' Lina said sourly. 'But she no come home.'

'Hey-hey-man. About my power?' sing-songed the wild haired youth.

'And my vases?' shrilled the pant suited woman.

'And a room for the Zancussi Trio?' sighed the melancholy Italian, determined not to be left out.

'Fuck off!' Ross screamed, losing control.

'Hey-hey-man, back down,' said the youth, holding up a steadying hand.

'Really!!' huffed the woman.

'Mama mia! Americanos!' The Italian shook his head sadly.

At that point the phone rang. Ross picked it up. 'Yes?' he yelled. And then listened in disgusted silence. A few moments later he slammed the phone down and without so much as a glance at any of the assorted injustice collectors stalked out of the house.

Oliver Easterne combed his sparse sandy hair first this way and then the other, but no amount of primping could conceal the fact that he was most definitely going bald. He had recently showered, but the effort of trying to organize his hair had caused pools of sweat to form under his arms.

The phone began to ring, but he did not bother to grab for it as he usually did. Let the staff get it. They could do *some*thing for the thousand bucks he shelled out every week.

Should he take another shower?

It might screw up his hair.

He could put on a hair net.

A sharp spasm across his stomach made him wince with pain. Bleeding ulcers, as if having thinning hair was not enough. And on top of everything else – haemorrhoids. At least they weren't bleeding. But they soon might be if he had any more aggravation with *Street People*.

Neil Gray was a pain in the neck – but then what director wasn't?

Montana Gray was a pain in the neck – but then what writer wasn't?

George Lancaster was a pain in the neck – but then what actor wasn't?

Oliver hated talent. But Oliver needed talent. Because all he was capable of doing was The Deal.

As a producer he was a legend in his own lifetime. Not as a great producer – but as a sensational dealmaker. Oh, the deals he had made! The scams he had pulled! The flops he had put up there on the silver screen.

Not that flops affected Oliver. Before the movie was even in production he had stashed away what he considered was rightfully his. The budget on an Oliver Eastern film always had that little extra bit – or a large bit – depending on what schmucks were putting up the money. And if the original budget didn't suit – well getting out two budgets wasn't against the law – not if you weren't caught it wasn't. And Oliver Easterne knew every trick there was to know.

He sniffed cautiously under one arm, and decided another shower was definitely going to be necessary.

On with the hairnet, off with the bathrobe.

Tonight, at the Contis' party, he would kiss ass. He would brown-nose his way from room to room. Montana, Neil, George, they would all feel the warmth of his sincerity. And he would enjoy doing it, because eventually he knew who would be top of the heap. Once the movie was made, it was his – and he could tell them all to go fuck themselves.

Total control for Neil and Montana my ass, he thought. They could whistle for it. He had tricks Houdini never knew!

Now, if he could only track down the girl from the beach . . . make her a star . . . sign her to a personal contract . . .

He spotted a dirty mark on the mirrored wall. Diligently he began to rub at it with a Kleenex. His stomach twinged again. Being a movie mogul was not all laughs.

They were in Angel's tiny apartment which smelled of Lysol and was impeccably clean and neat.

'I have nothing to wear,' she said stubbornly.

'Something simple . . .' Koko mused, rifling through her closet. 'Simple yet tasteful. Every bitch in town will be done up like Zsa Zsa at Christmas. I want you to stand out like a single rose at a bar mitzvah.'

'What's a bar mitzvah?'

He shot her a disbelieving look. 'Sometimes you go too far.' Then he pulled a black cotton ruffled skirt off a hanger, held it against her and said, 'Hmmmm . . . I like. What can we find to go with it?'

She shook her head. 'Koko . . . please . . . I don't even *know* Mrs. Liderman . . .'

'Dreamheart, don't expect to spend the evening with her. Every stud in Hollywood will take one look at you and –'

Angel was not conceited, yet she knew the effect she had on men. 'That's just it,' she wailed, 'they'll all be coming on to me with their phony lines. I'm *married*, Koko, I –'

Now it was his turn to interrupt. 'I never pry, Angel, dear. But I do know that married or not your husband has done something to you that has hurt you a great deal. You just want to shut yourself away and be miserable. Well, being miserable never helped anyone. I'm not telling you to go out and jump into bed with every would-be Warren Beatty that approaches you. All I'm saying is get out and enjoy the attention. You'll feel much better for it.'

She wondered how he knew so much. In just a few words he had managed to sum up her situation exactly. And he was probably right, getting out *would* be good for her. After all, it wasn't every day she got invited to a big Hollywood party.

'I'll go,' she said softly.

He was busy inspecting her blouses. 'What?' he asked vaguely.

'I said I'll go,' she repeated firmly.

A pleased smile spread across his aquiline features. 'Of course you will, dreamheart. There was never any doubt.'

Buddy had the apartment to himself while he prepared for the party. It was a bummer – having to escort Frances Cavendish. On the other hand it was a definite plus to be going at all.

He didn't know what to wear. Frances Cavendish's remark about his clothes had pissed him off. What did she know anyway? She'd probably never even heard of Armani. And wearing Armani was chic – any fool knew that.

With Randy safely out of the apartment he checked out his closet, found a shirt he liked, and tried it on. It was too narrow across the chest, so he discarded it.

He wondered if Montana Gray would be at the party, and if she was how should he come on? 'Hey – uh – listen, if I don't hear anything by Monday I'm gonna have to sign for a movie over at Universal.' Sounded good to him.

A sharp buzz at the door interrupted his train of thought.

Shelly stood on the threshold. 'Where have you been?' she demanded. 'I thought you were coming right back after seeing Frances Cavendish?' She walked uninvited into the apartment and threw herself down on the bed.

He could see she was stoned. Why had he ever gotten involved? He didn't want to go back to the kind of life he had lived before Hawaii, before Angel . . .

'I've got a job,' he said quietly. 'I'll be able to pay you back the money I owe you.'

'When?' she yelled.

'Soon.'

'Screw soon. I want it now. Why don't you go out an' score a few tricks? You don't remember *me*, Buddy, but I knew *you* when you were one of Gladrags' studs. We even worked together one time. How does it feel fucking old ladies for a living?'

He hit her across the face.

She laughed.

He grabbed her and half-pushed half-carried her to the door.

'Hustler!' she screamed. 'Hooker! *Pimp!*'

He gave her a final shove and shut the door on her hysterical yelling.

A sour feeling spread across his gut.

Stoned little tramp.

Stoned little tramp telling the truth.

Jesus. When was it going to happen for him? When was something in his life going to go right?

By the time Montana got back from the beach it was late afternoon. She felt exhilarated, like a kid who's played hooky from school. She didn't bother going to the office, instead she drove straight home, washed her long black hair and showered the sand and sea from her body. Then, wrapped in a white bathrobe, she called Inga to see what she had missed.

'Nothing much,' said her secretary. 'Mr. Gray called around three and said to tell you something came up and he'd meet you at the party tonight.'

'Where is he?'

'He didn't say.'

Now Neil didn't even bother coming home any more. She was tempted not to go to the party. But then she figured George Lancaster would think he'd scared her off, and if she was to make her presence felt it had to be right from the beginning. She didn't want

271

him to feel that he could do what he wanted with her script. She intended to be on the location every single day. Mr. Lancaster was just going to have to accept the fact that every woman did not fall at his feet in a faint.

She put an Al Green tape on the stereo and decided that her look for the party should be strong and noticeable. Something George Macho-Man Lancaster wouldn't forget in a hurry.

Ensconced in Bungalow Nine at the Beverly Hills Hotel, Pamela London lay on a folding massage table and enjoyed the firm masculine fingers manipulating her flesh.

'I heard you were good,' she said languidly. 'But you're *very* good.'

'Um . . . thanks, Mrs. Lancaster,' drawled Ron Gordino. 'I usually send one of my boys, but when Karen told me it was . . . um . . . for you, I decided to come myself.'

'Never send a boy to do a man's job!' said Pamela coyly.

'I wouldn't . . . um . . . dream of it Mrs. Lancaster.'

'Don't call me that. Miz London will do.'

How about Pamela? he thought. I'm sure as heck not calling you Mrs. Lancaster *or* Miz London at the party tonight. Elaine had come through with her promise and invited him.

She groaned as he dug his fingers into the spare tyre around her waist. She wasn't doing too badly for an old broad, she had to be at least fifty-five. But then, when you are the third richest woman in America you can afford to keep in shape.

He wondered what would happen if he gave her his 'special'. Would she, like all the other Beverly Hills matrons, fall for his special? Most of them were so easy . . . Get them on the table . . . out of their jewellery and clothes . . . take away the labels . . . A little pressure here – a little pressure there – and they were his.

Just as he was deciding whether to make a move or not George Lancaster breezed noisily in.

He ignored Ron, slapped Pamela resoundingly on her almost bare ass, and said, 'How's it going you old bat?'

She laughed hoarsely. 'Not so bad frog-face.'

'Getting all dolled up for the party.'

'I suppose we *do* have to go. I don't even know these Conti people.'

'So what? As long as they're paying. If we don't like it we can take a group on to Chasens.'

'Good idea.'

'Hey, you,' said George, acknowledging Ron Gordino at last. 'When you've finished with the heifer you can do me.'

Gina Germaine was perfumed, powdered and coiffeured to perfection. She was, however, not yet dressed for the party. She wore a flimsy negligee with black undergarments – a plunge bra, bikini panties, and sheer black stockings attached to a lacy garter belt.

Gina Germaine employed three live-in maids, but when the doorbell rang she answered it herself, having dismissed all three for the night.

'Hello, Neil,' she murmured softly. 'You look very elegant.'

He had changed at the office into a plum coloured smoking jacket, black silk turtle neck and black pants. He was all set for the party.

'Thank you,' he said curtly trying to ignore the fact that she was half naked. 'Do you have the tape?'

'I most certainly do,' she replied, all injured innocence. 'A deal is a deal is a deal, isn't it?'

She turned and led the way into an overdecorated pink living room.

'I can't stay, Gina. I don't want to be late. Just give me the tape.'

'How about a drinkie?' She handed him a bourbon mixed with ice in a crystal glass. 'Isn't this your pleasure?'

He accepted the drink automatically, forgetting the three or was it four he had already consumed since five o'clock.

'I'm so excited we've signed the contract,' she cooed. 'How long before we can – you know – let it slip out?'

He frowned. 'We cannot let it slip out. Not at all. To anyone. You do understand that, don't you?'

'It turns me on when you're forceful,' she purred.

'From now on my dear, we are just actor and director.'

'Actress,' she corrected.

'Actress,' he conceded. 'Where's the tape?'

'Come.' She took him by the hand, enveloping him in clouds of Tatyiana.

He hoped the sweet perfume wouldn't cling to his clothes.

'This is my games room,' she announced, leading him into a large room where every inch of wall space was covered with framed magazine covers of herself. The rest of the room housed everything from a pin-ball machine to the latest in video games. 'I love to play,' she added, somewhat unnecessarily.

'The tape, Gina.'

'Coming up.' She pressed a switch and before he could object there he was in living colour on her giant video screen. Bare assed and humping the second most popular blond in America. 'I figured you'd want to *see* it,' she explained sweetly. 'After all, you'd hardly want to take it home and run it for Montana, would you?'

Indeed he would not. He took a gulp of bourbon, sat down and considered the action on the screen from a professional point of view. Bad camera angle, you couldn't see her – Oh God, yes you could, she had moved around until those two great upstanding globes of flesh were filling the screen.

He felt the erection in his pants and silently cursed the inevitable.

On screen she heaved and panted while he slavered over her.

Off screen she threw off her negligee, stepped out of her panties and sat astride him.

One more time.

The last time.

He didn't know how right he was.

Sadie La Salle left her office two hours earlier than she usually did. Miko, her Japanese chauffeur, held open the door of her black Rolls Royce, and she sank gratefully into the luxurious leather seat and adjusted the air-conditioning to its highest point.

'Home, madam?' Miko inquired.

'Yes please.'

Home was in the exclusive Hills of Beverly. Home had a long winding driveway. Home was a mansion to rival those of the stars she represented. Home was never home without Ross Conti.

Damn! Damn! Damn! Twenty-six years since they were together, and still she thought about him.

Unseeingly she gazed out of the black tinted windows as the Rolls sped majestically along Rodeo Drive. Tonight she was going to his house. *The bastard*. Tonight she would see where he lived. She would make polite conversation with his wife. *Oh, how I hate you Ross Conti*. She would even talk to him.

Twenty-six years. She was a different person. Important, respected, some said even feared. She wore designer clothes, spent a full day a week at Elizabeth Arden, and wore jewellery from Cartier.

Oh sure she had seen him over the years. Hollywood. Such a small community. It was inevitable that they would be invited to the same parties and events. Once he had even suggested she handle him again. *Who did the son of a bitch think he was?* Did he imagine he could walk back into her life as a client and that she would just forget about the past? She had given him cold words and ignored him ever since.

The good times were always in her memory. She remembered every detail.

The first time she ever set eyes on Ross in Schwab's. Ohhh gorgeous, she had thought, and then when he had ambled over like a blond bronzed God and bummed a coffee she could not believe her luck.

The first time they made love. His hands on her breasts . . . His hardness deep inside her . . . His tongue buried between her legs . . .

The trip to New York to show him off on The Tonight Show. And the thrill when it all worked. Riding through Central Park in an open buggy. Admiring his billboard in Times Square. Eating hotdogs on Fifth Avenue.

And sex, sex, sex. Under the shower. In his dressing room at NBC. On the back seat of a cab. Pressed up against the wall of the hotel elevator. Ross was insatiable, and she loved it.

Twenty-six years later she could still feel his hands on her breasts. 'I'm a tit man,' he used to say. 'And baby, you've got the best.'

Until something better came along. Something that was packaged a lot more prettily than she was. And he just walked out of her life without a care in the world and not so much as a thank you.

The pain was still with her. The loss. The humiliating rage.

She stared sightlessly from the car as it glided across Sunset.

There had only been one other man since Ross and he didn't count. It wasn't for lack of opportunity. She was a star in her own way, and many a man had tried to pitch his way into her bed. She wasn't beautiful, not even pretty, but once she began to climb towards the pinnacle of success – Oh boy! Did they come running.

Very occasionally she went to bed with a woman. Sex with another female was not a threat, more a diversion. And Sadie called the shots. She liked that.

Her work became her passion. It was almost enough. Success can be very rewarding.

But now enough time had passed . . . too long in fact, and she wanted revenge for twenty-six years. And tonight she would have it.

At approximately four fifty-five Ross arrived at the department store.

At approximately ten minutes past five he left with Elaine by his side.

They both got into the Corniche tight-lipped and silent. Without a word being exchanged they endured the ride home.

Outside the house Elaine said coldly, 'It was all a mistake you know.' *You bastard, you think I stole the bracelet.*

Ross nodded. 'Anyone can make a mistake,' he said reasonably. *Stupid dumb broad. Do it if you must – but don't get caught.*

They entered the house. The wild-haired youth had blown a fuse. The pant suited woman was having hysterics. The sad-eyed Italians were trying to flirt with the pubescent teeny bopper who was dancing across the living room – oblivious to everything – earphones clamped firmly in place. The two gays were making faces as they prepared a gaucomole dip while observing the action. The two bartenders were lolling on a couch smoking grass; and Lina and her friends were stationed by the kitchen door ready to make a fast exit.

'Elaine, sweetheart,' said Ross. 'I'm going to take a shower. You wanted this party, and now it's all yours.'

32

Barstow, California, was hot. An oppressive heat with no cooling breeze to bring relief.

Deke checked into a cheap motel. He lay on a hard mattress in a small dusty room and gazed at the ceiling. A noisy fan whirred monotonously, while several flies buzzed around searching for escape. In the room next door a television blared, hardly drowning the sounds of a woman yelling in anger.

He had removed his boots, pants and shirt. On the table beside the bed he had placed his money, the hunting knife he always carried, and the piece of paper with the name and address written on it. The same paper that had been handed to him in Philadelphia while the three of them laughed . . . three pigs . . . laughing at him . . . laughing at The Keeper Of The Order.

Only he hadn't been The Keeper Of The Order then . . . No . . . Before striking out he was just plain Deke Andrews . . . A nobody . . . And their laughter had been a sign . . . Yes, a signal to control the vermin.

A shudder shook his body, and he drew his knees up to his stomach and hugged himself tightly. It would have been nice if Joey could have shared some of his triumphs . . .

Joey was wearing a red mini skirt, white plastic boots, a cheap pink blouse, and her usual alarming amount of smeared make-up.

Deke stared at her. To him she was beautiful, but he knew what his parents would think. They watched television constantly and called all women whores.

'Every one of those Hollywood starlets is a prostitute,' his mother would say.

'They sleep their way up the ladder,' his father would agree. But neither of them ever made any attempt to switch channels or turn off the set.

Deke never watched television with them. He preferred to be in his own room where he could lie on the bed and think about Joey and how he could safely bring her home.

There was much to consider. He wanted to marry her, but he didn't want to upset his mother.

All the time he tried to show her that he cared, but whatever he did was never good enough. 'One day you'll run off and leave your poor mother who went through such pain to have you,' she often told him. 'It'll kill me, you know.'

He always denied that he would.

'Maybe, maybe not,' she would say, adding craftily, 'If you stay, one day everything we have will be yours. Not much I know, the house, the car, your father has a nest-egg . . .' She always trailed off at that point, as if the nest-egg was too exciting to discuss.

He wondered how much there was. His father worked hard. Neither of them smoked or drank. Their only luxury was the colour television set.

Sometimes he lay in bed and fantasized about the two of them being killed in a car crash or a fire. Then everything would be his. The house, the car, the nest-egg . . . And nobody to nag him . . . make him feel small and unimportant and guilty . . .

Then Joey came into his life. For months he had kept her a secret. But eventually he had got up the courage to tell his mother. Or rather Joey forced his hand.

'I want to bring a . . . a . . . girl h . . . home,' he stammered one day.

Now he stared at Joey in her colourful outfit with her orange spiked hair. And he knew his mother would never approve.

'We ready, big boy?' she asked, cocking her head to one side.
He nodded.
She winked happily. *'Well then, it's up an' at 'em – ain't it?'*

'You dirty stinkin' piece a crap!' screamed the woman in the room next door.

There was the sound of flesh being struck, and a child began to wail.

Were they calling for him? Was he being summoned?

He sat up abruptly, reached for his knife, fingered the sharp blade.

Before he could decide what to do the noise ceased. The Keeper Of The Order could rest. He was not needed. Not for now, anyway . .

33

A line of cars snaked their way up the Contis' circular driveway where female and male valets wearing white T-shirts emblazoned with 'Superjock' waited to take control of the parade of Cadillacs, Lincolns, De Loreans, Rolls Royces, Porsches, Ferraris, Bentleys, Mercedes and Excaliburs.

Clustered at the bottom of the drive were six or seven paparazzi, cameras at the ready, eyes alert for the real celebrities – not the producers, money-men, super-agents and society flash. They wanted the real thing, the International Celebrity with the face that was recognizable from China to Chile.

They were rewarded by a smiling Burt Reynolds, followed closely by Rod Stewart and his striking wife, Alana. The paparazzi snapped happily away.

Inside the house all was under control. Elaine, fortified by two Valium and her new seventeen hundred dollar Galanos dress, greeted her guests as though she did not have a care in the world. She smiled, she hugged, she exchanged kisses and 'Don't you look wonderfuls' with everyone. She introduced people who had not met, she summoned waiters with a mere flick of her wrist, she was charming, witty, gracious, in command. Who would have ever

278

dreamt that only a short time before the first guest arrived she had been a raving screaming wreck?

Ross – the unfaithful swine – had vanished into the shower while she alone had attempted to create calm and organization from total chaos. She had done it. Etta from the Bronx had sprung into action. And now Elaine from Beverly Hills was taking the bows.

It had not been easy dealing with three recalcitrant maids, two stoned bartenders, a hysterical flower arranger, two temperamental members of the Zancussi Trio, and a hyped up ex-member of a rock group who gave great live disco, plus his zonked little girlfriend.

Elaine had sorted that lot out just in time – for more people had begun to arrive. The caterers. Security. Parking valets. The third member of the Zancussi Trio. The second member of the live disco twosome – another freak.

Finally, with only fifteen minutes to go before the party officially commenced, she had locked herself in her dressing room and forced herself to get ready in a hurry. She would have liked the luxury of more time – but it was amazing what one could do when one had to. She had emerged triumphant, ready to greet the first guest – Sammy Cahn who had promised to sing one of his famous parodies – this time on George Lancaster.

Now time had passed and the guests of honour had not yet arrived, nor had Sadie La Salle. But Bibi and Adam Sutton were making a spectacular entrance, trailed by the ever present Wolfie Schweicker. Bibi looked stunning in a black silk Adolfo dress, and breathtaking Cartier emeralds. Adam was handsome and dignified as usual. Elaine hurried forward to welcome them.

Koko had a way with make-up that enhanced even Angel's beauty.

'I didn't know you were so clever!' she exclaimed, gazing at her reflection in the mirror.

'With you – dreamheart – it's easy.'

She looked exquisite. He had pulled the front of her hair up and away from her face, leaving the rest to fall softly past her shoulders. He had flattered her with touches of gold scattered over her flawless skin. There was gold on her cheekbones, eyelids, even a touch on her lips. Her eyes he had emphasized with thick brown mascara on her long lashes, and pink and bronze shadow blended round the brow-bone. The effect was startling yet subtle.

She wore the black skirt he had chosen with a simple white off-the-shoulder blouse, and a white lace choker he had found.

'Hmmm . . .' He stood back to survey her. 'Divine!'

The buzzer rang. It was Mrs. Liderman's chauffeur.

'I'm so nervous,' she fluttered. 'Are you sure I should be going?'

He kissed her warmly on both cheeks. 'Have a wonderful time, dreamheart. Have a ball for *both* of us.'

'The hors d'oeuvres, Lina,' Elaine hissed through the kitchen door. 'They must come out faster. See to it.'

Lina nodded. She had not, as threatened, walked. Instead she and her friends had changed into clean black dresses and frilled white aprons, and were happily helping out. When Mrs. Conti was home things ran smoothly and Lina did not have to take responsibility for anything. That was the way she liked it. Besides, rumour had it that Erik Estrada was an expected guest, and the very sound of his name brought tears to her eyes.

Elaine kissed Bridget and David Hedison, waved at Dyan Cannon, squeezed Ryan O'Neal's hand, and moved in the direction of Sadie La Salle who had just walked through the door. Ross was nowhere in sight. Last seen talking to Adam Sutton and Roger Moore, he had now vanished.

'Damn!' she muttered. He was never around at the right moment. 'Hello, Sadie,' she gushed. 'Don't you look lovely. Do come in, I'm sure you must know absolutely everyone.'

'You're late, Buddy,' Frances Cavendish said crisply, answering the door of her Spanish hacienda, then slamming it shut behind her. 'Good grief! Is that your car?' She glanced at his ancient Pontiac parked in the street. 'We can't possibly arrive in *that*.'

'Why not?' he asked truculently.

'My God, dear. Isn't it obvious?'

'It's good enough for me, Francie.'

'Don't call me Francie,' she snapped. 'We'll take *my* car. Wait here, I'll get the keys.'

She marched back inside her house while he moodily marked time on the sidewalk.

She emerged shortly. She was wearing a wide-shouldered velvet pant suit that smelled faintly of mothballs, and for the occasion she had dug out her diamanté trimmed glasses.

He wondered if she had ever been married. Rumour had her listed as a dyke, but no little nymphet starlet had ever complained of her demanding a free pass to pussy-land.

She handed him the keys to what turned out to be a very large, very old Mercedes, and they set off.

'This is Angel,' announced Mrs. Liderman to anyone who would listen. 'She psyched my Frowie into coming back to me. Isn't that clever of her?'

'Your what?' inquired a tall thin man who looked like he had a perpetual bad smell under his nose.

'My Frowie. My poodle.'

Mrs. Liderman in purple taffeta was positively rattling with huge diamonds. They made Bibi Sutton's emeralds look ordinary.

'Who that woman?' Bibi demanded jealously.

'I don't know,' replied Elaine. 'She must be from Pamela's list.'

'And where *are* George and Pamela?' Bibi shook her head disparagingly. 'They come too late, sweetie. The guests of honour should arrive first.'

How well Elaine knew it, she did not need Bibi to tell her. 'They're on their way,' she said testily, hoping desperately that indeed they were.

Montana zoomed her Volkswagen up the driveway and waited while the silver stretch Cadillac limo in front of her disgorged its passengers. She couldn't have timed it better – or worse. George Lancaster and Pamela London were alighting from the Cadillac.

Well, she certainly wasn't going to skulk in her car waiting for them to get inside. Quickly she got out of the VW and walked over to Macho-man and Richo-wife.

'How's it going, George?' she asked heartily. 'I'm parched. Think you can get me a drink?'

The Zancussi Trio began to play tasteful background music at precisely eight o'clock. Ross, who had been doing a pretty good job of circulating, took the opportunity to sneak into the busy kitchen and stuff his mouth with canapes.

Elaine was not far behind. 'Where have you been?' she hissed. 'Pamela and George just arrived, and Sadie La Salle has been here twenty minutes. Is it too much trouble for you to put yourself out? Or do you just intend to stay in the kitchen all night?'

'I've been talking to the de Cordovas, the Lazars, and the Wilders.

What do you want from me – blood?' he said defensively.

'I want you to greet the guests of honour – if it's not too much trouble of course.'

They glared at each other. Both trying to concentrate on the party. Both seething with their own personal thoughts.

'Right,' said Ross at last. 'I'll go kiss ass. If you cruise the room, Elaine, maybe you can rip off a purse or two.'

'And this is Angel,' said Mrs. Liderman to Pamela London. 'She saved Frowie.'

'Christ, Essie,' sighed Pamela. 'You still got that god-awful canine – the one that peed all over my apartment in New York?'

'Frowie is thirteen years old,' Mrs. Liderman said proudly. 'In human years that's ninety-one. For ninety-one years of age she's like a young pup.'

Pamela inspected Angel. The girl was far too beautiful, although she didn't look like the usual predatory starlet. 'And how did you save Frowie?' she asked mildly. 'Because I don't know, dear, whether you should be rewarded or shot. That dog is a spoiled little pest who *ruined* one of my Persian rugs.'

'Pamela!' exclaimed Mrs. Liderman affectionately.

The two women hugged. They had known each other since college days, and since Essie Liderman was almost as rich as Pamela, their friendship had survived. The very rich are only really comfortable with the very rich. A fact of life that both ladies had learned, although Essie enjoyed spreading it around more than Pamela.

Angel was dazzled. By the house. The people. The atmosphere. *She*, Angel Hudson, was at a REAL HOLLYWOOD PARTY. And there were stars there. She spotted James Caan, and Elliott Gould, and Liza Minnelli, and Richard Gere. RICHARD GERE!! She could die now and feel perfectly satisfied.

If only Buddy were here to share it with her.

Buddy.

She frowned. He was not the man she had thought he was, nor the man she had married, and now she must forget him.

Essie and Pamela were reminiscing, oblivious to her presence. She looked around in awe.

'He-llo,' said an impressed male voice. 'And where have *I* been hiding all your life?'

'I should never have turned down "Raging Bull",' said the actor in the lizard skin boots. 'It was a key career mistake.'

'He pays me, I think it turns him on,' said the redhead in the mink-trimmed cape.

'I buy them dresses, take them to Acapulco – I have to give them head too?' asked an outraged stud.

Snatches of conversation as Montana made her way across the room to the bar. She looked incredibly striking. Six feet tall in white silk jodhpurs tucked into knee-high boots. A white silk blouse unbuttoned to the waist, and a long white leather vest fringed with Indian beads. Her jet hair was braided and decorated with beads and fringes. Around her neck she wore a solid silver choker studded with turquoise and thin silver hoops hung from her ears.

Neil was not yet at the party to appreciate her look. But Oliver Easterne looked twice when he saw her, and actually complimented her original style. Coming from Oliver she wasn't sure whether to be flattered or upset.

What a bunch of phonies, she thought, looking around. I had more fun at the beach today than they'll have in a lifetime.

She wasn't sure, but she thought she spotted Neil's ex-wife. Pretty, and blond. Groomed, and plasticized. The perfect Beverly Hills look.

Maralee must have felt Montana staring, for she turned and for a moment their eyes met.

'Sadie, I'm so glad you could come, it means a lot to me . . .' Direct stare. 'You know that, don't you?'

Sadie felt her stomach knot as it did whenever she saw him. 'Ross,' she said carefully. 'It's nice to be here.'

He pushed for a reaction. 'Just nice?'

She met his gaze steadily. 'I like your house.'

'Not bad, is it.' He leaned close. 'You know – *you* are looking sensational.'

'Thank you,' she said, edging away. She needed another drink before dealing with him.

'My little Sadie, you really made it didn't you?'

Oh God! He was as corny as ever. She backed away further, and with relief saw a friend approaching. 'Do you know Emile Riley?' she asked quickly.

'Yes, sure. Emile, nice to see you.'

'You too, Ross,' replied Emile. 'What a magnificent turn out.

Love the flower arrangements. I must congratulate Elaine, where is she?'

Sadie quickly took his arm. 'Let's go and find her. We'll see you later, Ross.'

Famous eyes still projecting. 'You can bet on that.'

He watched her cross the room. Powerful Sadie La Salle, the hottest agent in town. She had been his for a moment – he was sure of it. And the evening was only just beginning.

Karen appeared at his side. 'I want to talk to *you*.'

She wore gold lamé harem pyjamas which did nothing to conceal her amazing nipples through the thin silky material. He had a strong impulse to touch them, but controlled himself.

'Welcome to the house of Conti,' he said.

'Welcome my ass. Did you know Elaine phoned me today looking for *you*?'

'Me?'

'Yes, you.'

'Why me?'

'If I knew would I be asking?'

He frowned. 'Something's going on. Some asshole came up to me on Rodeo Drive today and thrust some pictures in my face.'

'What pictures?'

'Pictures of us. In bed.'

'Whaaaat?'

'Sweetie. Why you and Karen so close together? Naughty, naughty. I tell Elaine!' Bibi Sutton was joking of course, but they leapt apart like scalded cats.

Wolfie Schweicker was not far behind, resplendent in a velvet suit, ruffled shirt, and embroidered evening slippers. His hair, recently permed, framed a round face with small bitter eyes, a snub nose, fleshy lips and ferret-like teeth. Some said he resembled a feisty goldfish.

'It's a *very* good party, Ross. Bibi and I were just saying.'

'Thanks, Wolfie.'

'Not at all. Bibi and I always give praise where praise is due.'

'That's nice.' Ross couldn't stand the man. He wondered how mild mannered Adam Sutton even allowed him in the house.

Karen joined in the conversation. 'Great dress, Bibi.'

'Yes? You think? It nothing darling.'

'Nothing – my ass,' said Karen. 'It has to have set old Adam back at least two grand. If you got it, Bibi, flaunt it.'

'Darling, you so vulgar.'

'I'm my father's daughter – and I don't have to tell *you* what he's like, huh, Bibi?'

What was the quickest way to dump Frances Cavendish?

Good question.

Buddy pondered the problem as he checked out the party. Talk about hitting the action. He was moving with the stars, man. The place was jammed.

'If you're thinking of cruising the room, forget it,' said Frances acidly, as if reading his mind.

'Cruising. Who's cruising?' he said indignantly.

'Just a warning.'

'Am I allowed to go to the bathroom?'

'Now? We just got here.'

'What d'you want me to do – piss on my shoes?'

'Make it fast. I didn't bring you with me so that I could stand around on my own.'

He clicked his heels together. 'Yes, *ma'am.*'

'Hello, Elaine.'

'Hello, Ron.'

Why had she ever invited him. He looked quite out of place dressed.

'This is some . . . um . . . gathering,' he drawled.

'Thank you.'

'I'd sure like to meet Clint Eastwood.'

Who wouldn't? Only *she* wasn't going to take him by the hand and introduce him.

'Excuse me, Ron. I have a million things to do.'

'Stay loose, Elaine. Don't let the tension get to you. Did you take those vitamins I recommended?'

She nodded brusquely. He reminded her of a large shaggy dog. How come in the privacy of his office she had never noticed the moles all over his face, and the coarse straw coloured hair growing out of his ears and nose?

How could you have, Elaine?

Any cock in a storm!

'. . . she's like a Barbie doll – you wind her up and she buys new clothes . . .'

'. . . he'd fuck a bush if he thought it would invest . . .'

285

Buddy weaved his way through the room. He felt higher than he had in a long time. This was where he belonged, and this is where he would be – permanently – if only he got the part in *Street People*.

He smiled at Ann-Margret and she smiled back. He said, 'How-'r'you doin'?' to Michael Caine and got a friendly reply. Shit! Was he flying!

And then he saw her. Angel. *His* Angel. And he couldn't believe it, but she was there.

Oliver Easterne engaged in a stilted conversation with Montana. Their dislike of each other was mutual but the movie bound them together.

'Where's Neil?' Oliver asked, glancing at his watch.

'I thought *you* might know,' replied Montana. 'He had a meeting. He's supposed to see me here.'

Oliver was sweating, and he had a horrible feeling that he could smell it – in spite of two very thorough showers. 'Excuse me,' he said. 'I have to go to the men's room.'

He shut himself in the guest bathroom and ripped off his jacket and shirt. A quick sniff revealed the fact that he did indeed stink. Hastily he grabbed the cake of soap lying in a silver soap dish and lathered his offending arm-pits. Then he lowered his pants and swooped a soapy hand under his jockeys – just in case. He had not bothered to check the closed toilet and when Pamela London emerged they stared at each other in shock.

'What *are* you doing?' inquired Pamela in piercing tones. She had no idea who he was.

He failed to recognize the wife of the soon-to-be star of his movie. 'Fucking a goat,' he said swiftly. 'Why don't you mind your own business?'

'Angel?'

'Buddy?'

For one moment they nearly fell into each other's arms. Then Angel's face clouded over, remembering her phone conversation with Shelly. And Buddy scowled, remembering Angel's message via Shelly.

'What are you doing here?' they said in unison.

And the half-assed star of a television sit-com who had spent the previous half hour coming on to Angel put a proprietary hand on her arm and said, 'Everything all right, my lovely?'

286

My lovely!! Buddy wanted to smash his capped teeth right through the back of his obvious hairpiece.

'Fine, thank you,' she said politely.

'Uh, listen . . . maybe we can talk,' said Buddy quickly.

'I don't know . . .'

'What d'you mean – you don't know?'

'Well, I –'

'The lady means she doesn't know,' said Mr. Sit-com. 'So, why don't you check back later, sport?'

'Why don't *you* butt out, sport?'

'Now look here –'

They were interrupted by a half-naked Oliver Easterne pursued by a madder than hell Pamela London emerging from the guest bathroom.

'Don't you *dare* talk to me like that – you dirty little man!' yelled Pamela, wielding a hair brush.

'What's the matter with you – you menopausal old bag. Get away from me – you're fucking nuts!'

'What's going on?' boomed George Lancaster, breaking away from a group of sycophants.

'This pathetic man was jerking off while I was in the toilet,' announced Pamela in ringing tones.

'This *cunt* is crazy,' screamed Oliver in a fury.

'This *cunt* is my wife,' announced George Lancaster. 'Darling, have you met Oliver Easterne, my producer?'

34

There's no fool like an old fool . . .

Or a young fool . . .

Or a middle aged fool . . .

Clichés.

Gina Germaine was a cliché. She was also a hot, blond, sexy, big breasted WONDERFUL LAY.

I am lost in her juices, thought Neil Gray. I have no defence to this case.

What kind of fool am I?

Who can I turn to?

Why think of Newly/Bricusse songs at a time like this? A time when America's blonde of the year is sitting on my stiff organ, her private parts churning out an international message of lust.

Lustful thought.

The first woman I ever bedded was wearing black stockings and a suspender belt. Her name was Ethel and she hailed from Scotland. I was fifteen at the time and she was twenty-three. She had hairy legs and a predilection for cunnilingus.

Montana would never wear a garter belt as the Americans so charmingly called it. She would laugh in his face if he ever mentioned that it excited him.

Milky white thighs, enclosed, encased. A thick bush in the centre of the frame.

Oh God!

Gina shifted her weight, withdrew.

'I'm not ready,' he objected.

'I know,' she soothed. 'But I've got a surprise for you.'

'Not another hidden camera?' he groaned.

'Don't worry. This is our celebration, and I want to make it a night to remember.'

'The party –' he said thickly, watching Gina walk towards the door. He wanted her to come back and finish off what she had started. It was either that or someone would have to douse his ardour with a bucket of cold water.

'We'll go to the party,' she crooned. 'Eventually.'

He lay back in the chair and waited.

There's no fool like an old fool . . . a young fool . . . a middle aged fool . . .

The second woman he bedded was a Piccadilly prostitute. She charged him five pounds and gave him the clap. He was sixteen. She did not wear a suspender belt.

Suddenly there were two of them.

Gina. Voluptuous. Wanton. The all American sex goddess.

And beside her a slightly built Eurasian female. Dark olive skin, black hair that fell like a curtain to the top of her thighs, small breasts, and a tiny waist. She was quite naked apart from a white lace garter belt which emphasized her silky tangle of pubic hair. 'This is Thiou-Ling,' said Gina. 'My present for us. She speaks no English, but she understands. She has been trained in the art of making love since childhood. We shall celebrate our contract, Neil . . . And *then* we shall go to the party . . .'

288

35

'Your *what*?' said Oliver in horror, seeing his brilliant casting fade before his very eyes.

'Your *what*?' screamed Pamela. And then she started to laugh, great guffaws which shook her entire body. '*This* is Oliver Easterne,' she gasped between spasms of mirth. 'This . . . this . . . angry little man.'

George started to laugh too. 'Yes, you silly sow. Mustn't insult the producer, he's the one who pays us.'

She was choking with mirth. 'Oh, *he*'s the one!'

Oliver turned his fury and embarrassment into a sickly smile as he attempted to pull his pants up with a vestige of dignity. He knew when to eat shit. And how. 'Mrs. Lancaster,' he grovelled. 'Please forgive me. I had no idea . . . Mrs. Lancaster, it's such a pleasure to meet you at last. Mrs. Lancaster –'

'For God's sake call me Pamela. I think we know each other intimately enough, don't you?'

And with that she collapsed in a further paroxysm of uncontrollable laughter.

The furor with Pamela London and Oliver Easterne was over, but the sit-com star had not budged from Angel's side.

Buddy tried to ignore him. 'We have to talk,' he said urgently, putting his hand on her arm.

She shied from his touch. 'I . . . I don't think there is anything to say.'

'There's plenty to say.'

'Why don't you just back off, man,' said the sit-com star.

Angel saw the anger building in Buddy, and she quickly said, 'Please, don't cause trouble . . . Maybe we can talk later.'

What was she *doing* to him? What kind of a dumb game was she playing? She was his *wife*. He was her *husband*. 'Now,' he said flatly. He had things to say that couldn't wait.

The sit-com star said, 'Who *is* this creep?'

Before Angel could intervene Buddy swung a wild punch that glanced off the sit-com star's chin who, being a former stunt man, rolled with it and came back with a short tight poke to Buddy's stomach that pulverized him. He bent double with pain, and by the time he could stand straight, Angel and her gallant escort had vanished into another room.

Maralee Sanderson flicked her paged blond hair with annoyance. Elaine had warned her she would be inviting Neil and his wife. So where was Neil? And why was Montana strutting all over the place like a deranged Indian? The woman looked ridiculous in all her fringes and braids. How old was she anyway?

It beat Maralee how Neil could ever have married her. She was a freak. Too tall. Too wild-looking. Too everything.

Randy's hand crept up her thigh. She slapped it away like an aggravating fly. Randy was okay in bed – great in fact. But at a party like this he faded into the background. Didn't he *know* anyone? He lacked what her father called 'social strut'. It had never bothered her before, but tonight the way he refused to leave her side bugged her. Maybe Karen and Elaine were right . . . neither of them had said anything . . . but she could tell they didn't approve. You don't marry a man like Neil Gray one day, and go with a man like Randy Felix the next . . . Besides which, she was beginning to suspect that he had no money, and nobody was getting one red cent of her inheritance. No mistake about *that*.

'The biggest prick I ever knew had the smallest!' exclaimed a soignée middle aged woman in a chic black dress.

'If it cost him a nickel to shit he'd vomit,' said a fast talking producer.

'Every day she comes to my office, locks the door, gets under the desk and sucks my cock,' said the head of a studio.

Hollywood conversation. Ross had heard it all before. His mind was racing with thoughts of his own. Why had Elaine called Karen looking for him? Had she perhaps seen the pictures? Little S. Shitz wanted ten thousand dollars. If Elaine *had* seen the pictures then the prick could go whistle for it – which he'd probably have to do anyway. There was no way he could come up with ten thousand, he was over extended in every direction as it was. His business manager called him daily demanding a meeting. His business manager would shit himself when the bills for the party started pouring in.

He just had to hope that Sadie La Salle would save his ass and bring him back to the top where he belonged. She had done it once . . .

Oliver Easterne skirted the room looking for someone to talk to who had not witnessed his humiliation at the hands of George's drag queen wife. What a witch! Even *he* would find it hard sleeping with that, in spite of her millions. Although of course it was a well known fact that Oliver would do anything for money.

He had laughed with the red-headed cooze even though inside he was seething, his ulcer burning, and his haemorrhoids giving him trouble. He would get his own back though. When the movie was finished and there was more money in *his* pocket than in any of theirs.

Oliver had not been in the business as long as he had for nothing.

Dinner is served. And who sits where? For in Beverly Hills the placement is almost as important as the party itself.

Elaine had spent hours poring over the guest list deciding where to seat everyone. Twenty tables. Twelve people per table. Baccarat crystal. English bone china. Porthault napkins. Daisies, anemones, and freesia arranged in fine Waterford glass holders as a centrepiece to each table. The place cards were engraved – Elaine and Ross Conti at the top, and in fine calligraphy script the name of each guest underneath.

She had seated herself between George Lancaster and Adam Sutton. Ross, she had placed between Sadie La Salle and Pamela London.

After the Pamela/Oliver incident she had raced upstairs and gulped another Valium. By the time she came back down all was at peace. Oliver had apologized. And Pamela and George seemed to find the whole incident uproariously funny. And naturally – when George laughed, the whole world joined in. Elaine sighed with relief.

Ross watched Sadie approach his table, she certainly looked better in her fifties than she had in her twenties. She was almost slim, almost attractive. He wondered if she still cooked. What a cook! What a fuck! What tits! But she hadn't been right for his image . . .

She sat down.

291

'It's been a long time,' he said warmly. 'Too long, and you're looking sensational.'

She fixed him with soulful black eyes – her eyes always had been one of her best features. 'You told me that already, Ross.'

'So you look good enough to tell twice – big deal. After all, you and I – we go back forever, don't we?' He leaned confidentially towards her. 'Remember poor old Bernie Leftcovitz? And that night I turned up at your apartment when you were cooking him dinner?'

How could she ever forget? 'Bernie who?'

'Bernie Leftcovitz. You can't have forgotten schmucky Bernie. He was all set to hit you with a proposal. Come on, Sadie, it was the night you and I . . . the first time we . . .' He trailed off and grinned. 'Don't tell me you've forgotten *that*.'

She smiled thinly. 'You know this town – easy come, easy go.'

A waiter hovered with the wine.

'At last!' Pamela London said loudly, as if she had been sitting parched for hours instead of only five minutes. 'Show me the label, waiter, and if it's not a decent Cabernet Sauvignon you can take it back!'

'Aw – go sleep with your ego!' said a tall redhead to a cruising movie star. She turned to her friend. 'That guy's so out of it he needs a map to find his way home!'

'Don't tell me,' replied her friend. 'He's cheap too. Took me to the ball game and wouldn't even buy me a candy bar 'cos he didn't want to break a large bill!'

Oliver Easterne moved past them and bumped straight into Karen Lancaster. At the same moment he thought he spotted the girl from the beach on her way out to the tented patio with an older woman.

'Excuse me,' he said quickly.

'What's the matter?' Karen asked with a throaty chuckle. 'Got to go to the bathroom again?'

He ignored her and walked outside. The girl was sitting down at a table that included Pamela London. Much as he wanted to grab hold of her and make her a star he was not about to go over with that woman there.

Montana had no desire to join the other guests. She wasn't hungry, and she had already checked the place cards and found herself stuck between two people she didn't know. On top of that Neil had not yet put in an appearance which really infuriated her. What am I doing here? she thought. I may as well split because this is just not my ball game.

Then she saw Buddy Hudson hovering by the bar. He looked about as pissed off as she felt. Maybe she could bring a smile to his face. She went over and touched him lightly on the arm. 'Surprise. Are you having as much fun as I am?'

Buddy turned around and faced the wild looking female, all braided fringes and jet hair.

'Montana Gray,' she announced, noting his confusion. 'I look a little different out of working hours.'

He whistled softly, relieved that Frances hadn't tracked him down, and delighted to see Montana. 'You can say that again.'

'Friend of the bride or groom?'

'Huh?'

'I figure the Contis are the bride, because they're going to end up getting fucked – not to mention the check for all of this. And the Lancasters are the groom, because they don't give a good goddamn about anyone except themselves.'

He laughed, ready to forget the dull ache in his gut. 'I came with someone. I don't know any of them.'

'It's the best way.' She took a sip of the Pernod and water she was holding, grimaced and said, 'Hate the taste, love the effect.'

He was torn. Continue talking to Montana or try to find Angel. Instinct told him to stay with Montana – while heart told him to follow Angel.

'What's happenin'?' he asked automatically, expecting another bullshit 'we're still interested'.

'I was going to call you tomorrow, after George Lancaster's press conference.' She grinned. 'But since you're here . . .'

Oh shit! Was she going to say what he *thought* she was going to say? All of a sudden his throat was dry. 'Yes?'

'You're Vinnie, kiddo.'

For one wild moment he thought he might piss in his pants. 'Sweet Mick Jagger! Holy shit! I don't believe it!'

He was yelling, but what did it matter?

'Shhh . . .' Montana laughed, enjoying his excitement. 'I haven't appointed you President.'

He was flying high. 'As good as!'

'I'm glad you're pleased.'

'Give me a break – I'm out of my head!' He hugged her. 'You're *sure*? You're not jivin' me?'

293

'Would I lie?'

'Jeez! I can't believe it.'

'Believe it.'

'I . . . I gotta be dreaming.'

'Buddy! I never had you figured for a farm boy. Calm down. It's only a movie.'

'To you it's a movie. To me – it's my life.'

Oliver Easterne stories were buzzing from table to table amid much mirth. Angel did not understand the ones she heard – to her way of thinking he sounded sick. She recognized him as the man from the beach. She hoped he did not remember her.

All she could think about was Buddy. *I love you* – she wanted to say. But he had spoiled everything and there was no going back.

Only he looked so handsome tonight . . . And she was carrying his child . . . Perhaps they *should* talk in spite of everything. She felt bad about the sit-com star hitting him. But it was his own fault, he had struck out first.

She sighed, filled with confusion. She wanted Buddy. She didn't want him. Yet she still loved him . . .

'Are you all right?' Kindly Mrs. Liderman leaned across the table. 'You look a little pale.'

'I'm fine,' she replied politely. She should, in fact, be having a wonderful time, but Buddy had ruined everything.

A curly haired man in an immaculate white suit sitting on her left leaned across and said in a stoned voice, 'I gotta go work the room – you think it's easy bein' me? Who *are* you, dear?'

He was good looking. But not as good looking as Buddy.

'. . . use my apartment? Honey, I wouldn't let you use my Kleenex!'

'. . . You know what the bum says to me? He says – don't fuck on my property – you want to screw around do it on a bed someone else paid for . . .'

Elaine gazed around the room at her guests and smiled glassily at George Lancaster. 'Everyone seems to be having a good time, don't they?'

'They sure do. But why have I got an empty seat beside me?' he complained.

Elaine snapped to attention. 'I'm so sorry! Gina was supposed to be sitting there. Have you seen her?'

294

George leered. 'If I'd seen her I wouldn't forget it. She's the one with the big –'

'Quite,' Elaine said crisply, pushing her chair away from the table. 'Let me see if I can find her. She's probably still inside. I won't be a moment.'

'No problem little lady.'

She hurried into the house where a straggle of guests were still sitting around. She spotted Montana Gray and some man she didn't know chatting at the bar. Next to them were the Sean Connerys and the Roger Moores deep in conversation. Karen Lancaster and Sharon Richman emerged from the guest bathroom giggling and laughing.

Oh, Karen. I'm not finished with you. In fact, bitch, I haven't even started.

She went to the front door and checked with security. Gina Germaine had not yet arrived.

'Where *is* Neil?' asked Pamela London in a loud voice. 'I haven't seen him all night.'

Ross, who was trying to concentrate on Sadie La Salle, turned to the real guest of honour. She looked like she was wearing a bright red fright wig – why didn't someone tell her about her hair?

'He's around, isn't he?'

'I haven't seen him, and he's supposed to be sitting next to me.'

Christ, Ross thought. What kind of organization is this? Both guests of honour with an empty seat beside them. Can't Elaine get anything right?

As soon as Elaine left the table, Bibi slid into action and moved next to George.

'George, sweetie,' she sighed. 'This party nice – but no exclusive. I 'ave very special dinner for you and Pamela. Just a few friends. What you think?'

'I think you're holding up pretty good for an old broad.' He pinched her thigh. 'You're still a sexy piece.'

'George!' She pushed his hand away and tried to act insulted, but it didn't work. George Lancaster had known her since she was sixteen and walking the Champs-Elysées – something she hoped he had long since forgotten.

*

Montana put her finger to her lips and said, 'Not a word to anyone, Buddy. I shouldn't have told you until after the Lancaster story breaks.'

'I'm starring in your movie an' you're gonna tell me I can't mention it? *Come on* – I don't have that kind of control.'

'Learn it.'

'If I had a wife could I tell her?'

'Do you?'

He hesitated for a second, then realized now was not the time to start revealing truths. 'Do I look like the marryin' kind?'

She laughed. 'So why are you asking dumb questions?'

'I'm confused.'

'Un-confuse yourself. You've got to realize it's in your own best interest not to say a word. Hollywood law, kiddo – don't jinx yourself.'

'What happens next?'

'We call your agent.'

'I don't have one.'

'So get one.'

'How do I get an agent if I'm not supposed to say anything?'

'Agents are like priests – you can confide in them. I'll tell you what. *I'll* talk to Sadie La Salle, maybe set up an appointment for you tomorrow. How's that?'

'I think I love you.'

They both laughed.

In the distance he saw Frances Cavendish approaching, a furious expression on her face.

'Like I gotta split,' he said hastily. 'This . . . uh . . . person I'm supposed to be escorting tonight is comin' my way, an' I don't want to expose you to the language.'

Montana nodded gravely. 'I understand.' She liked him – instinctively she knew where he was coming from and that it hadn't been easy. She was pleased that he was going to get his chance.

He took her hand and squeezed it tightly. 'Thank you,' he said warmly. 'I think you saved my life.'

'Come on. Don't get dramatic on me – keep it for the cameras.'

Karen was burning. How come she was stuck at the shittiest table in the room with all the nothings and nobodies? How *dare* Elaine do that to her?

The final insult was Ron Gordino who just casually strolled over and sat himself down. *She was seated next to Ron Gordino – a fucking exercise instructor. What had she done to deserve this?*

I will kill Elaine Conti, she thought. No way is she going to humiliate me like this and get away with it. Better still, I will steal her husband away from her once and for all, and I'll have parties that *she* won't even be invited to.

Fat-ass Etta Grodinski. Oh yeah. I know all about your crappy beginnings. Your dear sweet unfaithful husband told me.

'Um . . . this is a great party,' drawled Ron Gordino.

'Tell me,' Karen said, smiling sweetly. 'How many times have you laid our hostess?'

36

Legs, arms, breasts. The whisper of mouths, the teasing of tongues, hot breath, saliva, taste and touch and tactile sensuality.

It was years since he'd been with two women. Maybe ten years. Paris. And they were sisters who fiercely resembled each other.

This was different. Two women from two separate cultures and they were transporting him to a plateau of ecstasy that he had thought was no longer his to visit.

Thiou-Ling was indeed an artist. Only she did not work with a palette of paints, instead she worked with scented oils and her feathery child-like fingers. She tended both Gina and Neil at once, touching first Gina's ripe nipples, then Neil's rampant penis which threatened to burst, the skin was stretched so tight.

She fussed and fretted over each of them, her long hair trailing on their skin like strands of fine silken thread.

After a while it was torture.

Exquisite torture.

He shoved the Eurasian girl away and mounted Gina, who wanted him as much as he wanted her. She was so wet and ready that he almost slipped out, but Thiou-Ling had not deserted them, she was there to help him enter the moist warmth of the second most popular blonde in America. She guided him into paradise. And he knew without a doubt that this was to be the most exciting sexual experience of his life.

Montana was long forgotten.
Street People was long forgotten.
The party was long forgotten.
He was entering Heaven.

37

At eleven o'clock precisely the Zancussi Trio faded out with a soulful rendition of the theme from *The Godfather*. Ric and Phil, their speakers in place, their long wild hair freaked out, moved into action. Kool and the Gang imploring everyone to 'Get Down On It' blasted out from seven hidden speakers.

'Shit!' Ross shot out of his chair. 'What a noise!'

A space had been cleared for dancing and Pamela thought he was offering. She leapt up too. 'Yes, Ross, let's show 'em how it's done!'

Six foot, red headed Pamela London dragged him onto the dance floor.

Sadie was only too pleased to have a short respite from the pressure of his charm. He had been coming on strong to her all night, and although she knew it was all a game, she couldn't help being affected. She felt uncomfortably aroused. He still had the power to excite her with words alone. How different it all could have been if he hadn't deserted her . . .

'Wanna dance?' Karen Lancaster demanded of Buddy Hudson.

He was sitting between her and Frances Cavendish, feeling confused. He *should* be feeling great. Instead he had one eye on Angel at a table across the room, and a nervous stomach that told him to keep a hold on himself until the contracts were signed.

Jeez! This was the best night of his life. It was also the worst. Who the fuck was Angel with?

He decided to go over and ask her to dance. Then he would get her in a quiet corner and say – 'Why did you get rid of our baby? Why did you leave me? Why can't we try again?'

'I said let's dance,' slurred Karen. She was high, her pupils huge. She and Shelly would make a great pair.

He wanted to say no, but with George Lancaster being her father

298

and all he thought it might be better to say yes, so he turned to Frances, who had just returned from smoking a joint in the guest toilet. 'Do you mind if I dance?' he asked.

'Do what you like,' Frances replied irritably. She was not pleased. He had hardly turned out to be the attentive escort she had envisaged. He could whistle for the Universal job. She would tell him when he took her home.

'Yeah, sure, let's go,' he told Karen, and they joined the third richest woman in the world – who couldn't dance – and Ross Conti – who couldn't dance – for a whirl around the floor.

Karen could Get Down On It with the best of them. She moved in such a fashion that her body went one way, and her bra-less breasts with their exotic nipples another.

'Hey –' exclaimed Buddy. He loved to dance, and among this group it was a pleasure.

Angel, baby, understand that this is purely business.

Karen moved nearer to Ross. 'Pamela, you old dog,' she slurred. 'Dint' know you were such a swinger. Here, Buddy, you dance with Pammy – I'm taking Ross.' Skilfully she moved between them, and Buddy found himself dancing opposite Pamela London which really blew his mind.

He grinned politely. She exhibited yellow horse teeth in response.

'Come on, Elaine, if they can do it so can we, old girl,' boomed George Lancaster, pulling her up.

Elaine forced a smile. She wasn't too fond of the 'old girl'. Karen had grabbed a vice-like hold on Ross, and was pushing her disgusting body up against his leg like a bitch on heat. The entire party was watching.

Put on a happy face, Elaine.

Screw you, Etta.

'I think I'm having an orgasm from your knee,' Karen husked drunkenly into his ear.

'Pull yourself together, everybody's watching,' he said tersely, keeping an alert eye on Sadie who was deep in conversation with Shakira and Michael Caine.

'So what?' slurred Karen.

'So cool it.'

'Cool it . . . cool it . . .' She raised her arms above her head and shimmied like a stripper.

'That's my girl!' shouted George, and he abandoned Elaine and moved over in front of his daughter.

Reluctantly Ross found himself partnering Elaine. At that particular moment the blonde in the Porsche who had waved to him that morning boogied on by. Now he recognized her as Sharon Richmond.

'And who were you visiting this morning?' she giggled. 'Caught you – didn't I?' she giggled again. 'Only joking, Elaine. I know for a fact that there are three practising dentists who live in *my* complex alone.'

Her date, sensing Ross's fury, yanked her away.

Elaine narrowed her eyes. 'You *bastard*!' she hissed.

In unison they left the dance floor.

'Jogging sucks!' said the curly-haired girl with an unlady-like hiccough.

'You know what I want?' mused her friend, a tastefully dressed brunette with a body like Bo Derek. 'I want a big star who'll do windows!'

Scintillating conversation, thought Montana.

Since Ric and Phil had taken over the music scene, and three hours of liquor had taken care of everyone's inhibitions, it was all happening. Only not for her. She might have been able to have a good time if Neil had put in an appearance. But his absence was beginning to worry her. Oliver didn't know where he was. She had tracked his secretary down and she didn't know either. All of a sudden thoughts were creeping into her mind about the way he drove his Maserati. Fast. Much too fast. Maybe he had had an accident.

As soon as Pamela left the table Oliver jumped to his feet and hurried over to Angel. 'It is you, isn't it?' he said, leaning over her chair.

She started. 'Sorry?'

'You're the girl from the beach. Don't tell me I'm mistaken, I know it's you.'

'Oh . . . yes . . .'

'I've had people trying to find you. Aren't you interested in becoming a star?'

'I . . . I . . .' She thought about Buddy's baby growing inside her, far more important than any quick shot at stardom. 'No,' she said.

'No?' he echoed in disbelief.

'No,' she repeated firmly.

300

'What's the matter? There something wrong with you? Nobody says *no* to becoming a movie star.'

'I do,' she said in a small voice.

'Sadie, we had such a great thing going between us. Where did we go wrong?'

We. He had the nerve to say *we*. What a selfish, self-obsessed egotist Ross Conti was.

So what else was new?

She waved at Warren Beatty and Jack Nicholson who were making a late entrance.

'Sometimes I wake in the middle of the night,' he continued, 'and I think to myself – why isn't Sadie lying here with me? Why isn't she next to me? With her soft warm body and her big fantastic tits . . .'

The man was actually still calling them tits. To her face. And he expected her to be flattered. Hadn't he heard of the women's movement and the sexual revolution? He was coming on to her as though she were a piece of ass that he could sweet-talk into the sack.

Poor Ross. He had learned nothing over the years.

He was going all the way. 'I want you, Sadie,' he whispered. 'I want you so badly that if you put your hand under the table you can feel just how much.'

'I wish to be escorted home,' said Frances Cavendish coldly.

'Now?'

'No. Tomorrow morning will do nicely.' She narrowed her flinty eyes. '*Now*, Buddy.'

'But the party is just gettin' going.'

'For us it's just ending.'

For one wild moment he contemplated telling her to get stuffed. After all, he had *Street People*. Who needed Frances Cavendish? But common sense prevailed, and he decided to drive her home, return to the party, corner Angel, and really talk things out.

'Let's go,' he said, pleased with his decision.

'I must say goodbye to the Contis.'

That's what he was counting on. While Frances thanked Elaine he skipped over to Angel's table, bent over her shoulder and said, 'I have to go somewhere, but I'll be back in twenty minutes, and I want us to talk – without any schmucks butting in. You at least owe me that, don't you?'

She frowned. 'I don't owe you anything. After what Shelly told me –'

'What did Shelly tell you?'

'That you and she . . .' She hesitated, unable to repeat what she had heard. 'Is it true?'

Goddamn Shelly. Had she been in contact with Angel again and not told him?

'What's going on, dear?' questioned the curly-haired man on her left, not so immaculate now, rather dishevelled and wild-looking. Angel ignored him, and pushed her chair away from the table. 'Okay, let's talk. Let's go somewhere quiet and –'

'Buddy. I'm waiting.' Frances Cavendish's commanding tone as she approached.

Shit. 'Twenty minutes,' he said desperately in a hoarse whisper. 'Just gotta run this old broad home. Like it's business, y'know?'

Sadly she nodded. He hadn't changed. What good would talking do?

'I'm telling you, Montana. She's right for it. Better than anyone we've tested,' Oliver said excitedly. 'I want *you* to talk to her. Maybe she'll listen to you. When –'

'What do you think can have happened to Neil? Should I call the police?' Montana interrupted anxiously.

'Are you nuts? I'm telling you about the perfect Nikki and you're talking police.'

'I'm worried about Neil.'

'He's a big boy.'

'Really?' Her sarcasm brushed off him like dandruff.

'Come on, forget about Neil – he can look after himself. I want you to talk some sense into this girl. Her name's Angel. Can you believe it? I think we should call her Angel Angeli – the press'll eat it up. Let's go, Montana, you can talk some *brains* into the kid. *Everyone* wants to be in the movies.'

302

38

He was climaxing. Thick salty spurts of life's essence.

And Thiou-Ling was breaking a small glass phial of Amyl Nitrate under his nose.

And he was coming and coming and coming . . .

Life's sweet wish. The never ending orgasm . . . Nirvana . . . Paradise . . . Bliss . . .

And then the pain. So sudden. So unexpected. A thunderbolt of agony that gripped him across the chest and down one side with an intensity that was killing.

'Oh good Christ,' he said. At least he thought he said it, but he didn't hear the words come out.

His cock was still hard, still pulsating, but the pleasure was no longer his, and no words would emerge to tell the world that he was slipping . . .

The two women did not realize that anything was the matter. His weight did not bother Gina, it merely enhanced her own moment of ecstasy. And then . . . when her moment was over . . .

'Neil?' she murmured. 'Neil, please move, you're crushing me.' Her voice rose. '*Neil.*' She tried to push him off her. 'Stop fooling around – it's not funny.'

He groaned. 'I . . . don't . . . feel . . . good . . .'

Oh, no. The English prick wasn't having a heart attack. Not on top of her. Not in her house. Oh, no!

She panicked and tried to throw him off, her vagina contracting in a most peculiar way. '*Get off me!*' she screeched.

The pain around his chest subsided and he attempted to withdraw from her clinging wetness.

Strangest sensation in the world. He couldn't pull out. His penis felt like it was caught in a vice.

'Gina, there's something wrong,' he mumbled weakly.

'Cut it out, Neil,' she snapped angrily.

Ah, but if only he could . . .

39

'One thing I'll always remember, and baby, *never* will I forget it. There has never been anyone else who did it for me the way you did. You feel the same, don't you?'

In a way Sadie wished he would stop. But then in another way she was enjoying every phony minute.

'Haven't you always felt that what we had was the best?' Ross persisted, wishing that Phil and Ric would turn their goddamn speakers down. Loud rock music was hardly conducive to stirring up a romance. And yet he felt he was doing pretty well. He hadn't got her to place her hand on his dick yet, but she was attentive all right. Lapping up every line of dialogue he came out with. 'Well?' He was determined to get an answer out of her. 'Has there been anyone better for you?'

She knew what he wanted. She decided to put him out of his misery. 'Do you want me to be your agent?'

'What?' He pretended to be shocked.

'I said how would you feel about me representing you again?'

'Sadie . . . I never really thought about it . . .'

'You thought about it a few years ago. Remember, at the Fox party?'

He laughed casually. He was not above getting in a dig. 'Yeah. I remember. You told me to take a hike – or something like that.'

'Actually I said if making commission on you gave me my one hot meal of the week I'd starve to death.' As if he didn't remember.

'You did?'

'I've mellowed since then.'

'I should hope so!'

'Well? Do you want to be my client or not?'

He pretended reluctance. 'I'm happy with the agent I have . . .'

'That's a shame. In that case –'

'No, no. I'm not *that* happy, and there *is* something I think you might be able to pull off for me.'

'Really?'

'Yes. It's –'

'Not now, Ross. Why don't you come to my office tomorrow. Does five o'clock suit you?'

It suited him. But was it right that he should have to go to her office like an aspiring client? Shouldn't it be lunch at Ma Maison or the Bistro Gardens? Shouldn't *she*, the agent, be pursuing *him*?

Cut it out. Who do you think you're kidding? The game is getting her back in your corner. Not playing footsie over chicken salad, and jerking off because a roomful of assholes can see that you're with Sadie La Salle.

'That'll be fine,' he said.

'Good,' she replied, getting up. 'Now you must excuse me, I have to spend some time with George.'

He watched her walk away.

It wasn't all that difficult getting you back, Sadie. You may be a toughie, but with me you're still cream cheese.

The heavy throb of disco turned slow, and the dancing space packed up with couples clinging closely together. A lone paparazzi had managed to break in and climb a tree where he perched precariously, desperately trying to get pictures before security yanked him down and out.

For a moment Ross thought about Little S. Shitz and the incriminating photos. Karen had plenty of money, maybe she would feel like buying the negatives . . .

He looked around. Everyone seemed to be having a terrific time. It was past twelve and no one was making any moves to go home. Hollywood was basically an early town, and past twelve was late. Elaine's party was a big success.

His thoughts rested on her for a moment. What had she been thinking of stealing a bracelet? Was she crazy? Hadn't she considered the consequences? It was back to the shrink time for Elaine. No doubt about that.

Where was she anyway? His eyes sought her out and found her dancing close with some superman clone. The throbbing beat of Donna Summer caressed them. Ross leaned across the table to Maralee. 'Who's Elaine dancing with?'

Maralee glanced over. 'Oh, that's Ron Gordino, our exercise instructor.'

Karen's words flashed across his brain. *I think Elaine's playing doctor.*

He peered intently at the entwined couple. Was it a trick of light or was the creep nibbling her ear?

Impossible. Elaine was his wife. She wouldn't dare screw around. Or would she?

'I think we should be going,' Mrs. Liderman said. 'Poor little Frowie will be wondering what's happened to his momma.'

Angel glanced helplessly around. Buddy had said he would be back in twenty minutes, but an hour had passed. It was quite obvious that he no longer cared . . . just as Shelly had said . . .

Her eyes clouded over, and she realized that once and for all she must forget him and be strong. 'I'm ready whenever you are,' she said resolutely.

'I don't have to ask if you've had a good time,' Mrs. Liderman said happily. 'I've been watching you, the centre of attention.'

Angel smiled wanly. She was being asked to appear in a movie, and the more she said no the more they seemed to want her. Oliver Easterne had even gone so far as to bring the woman over who *wrote* the film. 'Isn't she Nikki,' he had insisted. And the woman had narrowed her eyes and said, 'Maybe . . . If she can act.'

'But I'm not interested,' Angel had protested.

Interested or not Oliver Easterne had insisted that she call him the next day. She had finally agreed, although she had no intention of doing so.

Mrs. Liderman said, 'We won't say goodbye. I hate goodbyes. Besides I'm having lunch with Pamela tomorrow.'

Outside, Mrs. Liderman's chauffeur waited at attention by the door of her cream coloured Rolls Royce.

Angel sank back into luxury as the car glided smoothly down the driveway.

Had she been looking out the window she would have observed a harassed looking Buddy paying off a cab at the curb-side. He had just enough to cover the fare, although not enough to make it back to Randy's apartment. What a night! The new movie star in town was busted out. He raced back into the thick of the party anxious to find Angel. Methodically he went from room to room, checked the guest bathroom, the dancing throng, the outside tables. And he couldn't find her. His luck that the Pontiac had picked tonight to finally expire. Fortunately *after* he had dropped off an uptight Frances who

306

had told him on her doorstep that she did not think he was right for the picture at Universal after all. 'I made a mistake,' she said, expecting him to crumble.

'That's the way it goes,' he had replied cheerfully.

She was furious. Robbed of her spiteful moment of triumph.

He searched in vain for his beautiful Angel. The least she could have done was waited. He didn't even have an address or a phone number for her. How could he have let her get away again? What kind of a jerk was he?

And yet . . . She had got rid of his baby . . . She had done that without even speaking to him about it . . . *She* had walked on *him* . . .

He went to the bar and gulped down a Perrier water.

'Ah . . .' Karen Lancaster staggered over. 'There you are – the dancer. Let's go, killer. Let's show 'em steps'll make their eyes bulge!'

Montana felt foolish phoning the police. But she shut herself away in the Contis' bedroom and phoned the Beverly Hills station anyway. They had nothing to tell her, so she tried home again – but there was no reply, just as there had been no reply for the past two hours.

Neil's a big boy, he can look after himself, Oliver had said. Did Oliver perhaps know where he was?

She sat silently for a moment collecting her thoughts.

Yes. Oliver knew. He *had* to know. That's why he wasn't at all worried.

She sought him out.

'Okay, cut out the bullshit. Where is he?'

'What is it with you? I don't know.'

'You *know*. And if you don't tell me I'll cause one hell of a scene. You want that? Here? Tonight? In front of dear old George and your new good friend Pamela?'

'I never had you figured as the jealous wife.'

'Jealous wife. Ha! I just want to make sure that my old man's not lying in some hospital. Then I can split from this crummy party and get some sleep.' She paused and glared at him. 'I'm not like you, Oliver. I don't have to ass kiss my way around the room. *I* can go home. Now where is he?'

Oliver was suffering. His ulcer was sending out spasms of pain. His piles were pure anguish. And the scene with George Lancaster's vulgar rich wife was an intolerable embarrassment which would haunt him for at least two days.

On top of that he couldn't stand dealing with Montana. They had the screenplay. They no longer needed her. And why was he protecting Neil anyway? The schmuck couldn't even be bothered to put in an appearance at a party for the star of their movie.

'He had a meeting with Gina Germaine,' he said, savouring the moment. 'Who knows? Maybe it's still going on.'

She stared at him, tiger eyes cold as Siberia. 'Thank you,' she said icily.

He tried to meet her gaze, but he couldn't. 'My pleasure.'

'You know something, Oliver?' she said very loudly. 'You're a prick. And on top of that you stink – literally.' She strode angrily away while he surreptitiously tried to check out his armpits.

Pamela London, on her way to the powder room, caught him at it.

'Well!' she exclaimed, her strident voice carrying across the room. 'I've heard of kinky – but *you* are ridiculous!'

Dancing with Karen Lancaster was a kick he didn't need. She was drunk, *and* stoned. And she was using him to make Ross Conti jealous. He didn't want to be rude. After all – before Angel he would have loved meeting Karen. But now – so what? He wasn't Randy Felix, looking to hitch up with a rich one. He was his own man – and he had made himself a promise, whether things worked out with Angel or not he would never sell himself again. Self-respect and truth were the name of the game from now on.

Karen moved in close – her gyrations were being ignored by Ross and she didn't like that.

'Wass your name 'gain?' she slurred, pressing her sweaty body against his white Armani jacket.

'Buddy Hudson,' he said, pushing her gently away.

'Buddy, huh?' She fell against him, grabbing at his lapels for balance. 'Wanna be my buddy, Buddy?'

This flash of humour broke her up, and while she was laughing he spotted Randy and Maralee sitting at a half-empty table talking intently. He steered her over and deposited her on a chair.

'Karen,' Maralee exclaimed, pleased by the interruption. 'You look like a strong black coffee wouldn't do you any harm.'

'The hell with coffee,' slurred Karen. 'I know what *I* need.' She turned to Buddy. 'Sit down.'

He did so, studiously avoiding Randy's glare.

308

'Now . . . lemme see . . .' she continued. 'This is Maralee . . . an' her *friend* – I forgot his name . . .'

'Randy Felix,' said Maralee, toying nervously with a spoon.

'Now how could I forget a name like Randy.' She giggled. 'What-tayado sweetie-pie?'

Maralee frowned. 'Karen –' she began.

'So-rry. Mustn't ask what Randy does.' She grabbed a hovering waiter by the sleeve. 'Vodka. On the rocks. Now.' Absent-mindedly she did not let go of the waiter's jacket and Buddy painstakingly pried her fingers loose.

She looked at him gravely. 'This is Bud,' she announced. 'He's a dancer.'

'Hello,' said Maralee politely.

'Nice to meet you,' said Randy coldly.

Karen looked first at Buddy, then at Randy. 'Thought you two knew each other. Didn't I see you together at Ma Maison?'

'No,' snapped Randy.

Buddy did not want any hassles. He jumped up. 'You'll have to excuse me,' he said. 'I have a date here somewhere, and she's probably looking for me.'

'Sure,' said Karen vaguely. 'Better run find her. Give me a call sometime, Bud.'

'I'll do that.'

He made his escape with a sigh of relief.

George Lancaster was getting ready to make a speech. Montana decided it was definitely time to leave. Her mind was churning. Neil . . . with Gina . . .

Neil . . . screwing around . . .

Damn him.

Maybe it wasn't true.

Buddy Hudson caught up with her at the door. 'You going?'

'Uh-huh.'

'Can I bum a ride?'

'Where's your car?'

'It died on Sunset.'

'Where do you live?'

'Just off the Strip.'

'Come on.'

He was about to follow her as she strode out the front door, when

309

the sight of Wolfie Schweicker emerging from the guest bathroom pulled him up sharply.

Slimmer by far . . . hair different . . . But there was no mistaking those small mean eyes, that round face, the ferret-like teeth emerging from fleshy lips.

Butterball . . . the fat man at the party . . . twelve years ago . . . Tony's battered body lying on a slab in the morgue . . .

He shuddered, the memory too painful to contemplate.

Wolfie must have felt him staring because he glanced over, and, misjudging the intent stare for sexual interest, said, 'Hello.'

'Do you want a ride or not?' Montana reappeared at the door, her voice edgy.

Buddy dragged his eyes away from Butterball. He must be mistaken. It couldn't be the same man.

Why not?

He followed Montana outside. 'Who was that guy?' he asked urgently.

'What guy?'

'The one in the hall.'

She frowned, her thoughts elsewhere. 'Wolfie something – Schwartz or Schweiss – No Schweicker. He hangs around Bibi Sutton all the time.'

'Wolfie Schweicker . . .' Buddy repeated the name slowly. He never intended to forget it.

George Lancaster stood up, tapped the side of his champagne glass with a fork, and boomed, 'Let's have a little quiet for the star.'

The assorted gathering obliged.

'I'm going to make a speech here,' he announced.

There were a few good-natured groans and catcalls.

'Bo-ring!' Pamela cried loudly. Laughter filled the tented patio.

'Ignore the old sow,' George thundered. 'I should have put her out to pasture long ago!'

More laughter.

'Seriously though, folks,' George continued, 'it's a real pleasure to see all my old friends here tonight . . . some of them a little older than I remember . . .' Riotous laughter. 'But that's all right . . . What's a rug an' a set of false teeth between friends?'

Everyone fell about.

'You're probably all wondering what the Captain is doing back in

310

town. Why isn't he sitting on his ass in Palm Beach with his rich broad wife, huh? You really want to know that, don't you?'

'Get on with it,' shrilled Pamela, loving every minute.

'I'm making a comeback,' roared George. 'You know what that is – it's the thing Frank does once every year!'

'Right on!' someone yelled.

'I'm doing a movie for my friends Oliver Easterne and Neil Gray because Neil talked Pamela into what a swinging time she'd have here, and Oliver gave me an offer even *I* couldn't refuse. Also they couldn't get Burt –'

He droned on, but neither Elaine nor Ross were listening. They were exchanging shocked glances. George Lancaster doing *Street People*? *George Lancaster*, who – according to his loving daughter Karen – had turned it down months ago. And *they* were hosting a *party* for him. Spending a fortune they could ill afford – for what?

Elaine could not believe it. She wanted to just give up and crawl into bed.

Ross was even more stunned. He had *known* the part was his. Convinced himself that only he could truly play the role as it should be played. And with Sadie La Salle on his side . . . He could almost taste the bitter disappointment that flooded his body.

40

The American Airlines plane was crowded, but Millie didn't mind. It was the first time she had ever flown and her excitement was catching.

Leon was excited too. But for other reasons.

Timing was so strange. You waited and waited for something to happen, and nothing ever did. Then you went ahead and made your plans – and bingo . . .

Two reports had come up on the computer. The first a double murder in Pittsburgh. A whore and her pimp slashed to death. And the second a hitchhiker in Texas, stabbed twenty-eight times.

In both cases Deke Andrews had left his mark – his fingerprints.

Leon had wanted to cancel his vacation plans and investigate the new developments. But he couldn't do that to Millie. It would have been cruel.

A young detective by the name of Ernie Thompson was assigned to both Pittsburgh and Texas to check out the new findings. He would report in to Leon, wherever he was. It wasn't the most satisfactory of arrangements – obviously Leon would have preferred to make the trips himself – but in the circumstances it would just have to do.

'I can hardly believe we're on our way!' Millie squeezed his arm and kissed him on the cheek.

He responded to her affection. They were on their way all right. And they seemed to be heading in the same direction as Deke Andrews.

41

They were locked together. Gina Germaine, the second most popular blonde in America, and Neil Gray, respected and revered film director.

Gina, impaled like a fish, whimpered non-stop.

Neil merely groaned. Trapped by the object of his desire like a fly in the web of a praying mantis, he felt strangely unreal and weak. The pain that had gripped him before had subsided, but he was frightened by the intensity of it, and terrified of the situation he was now in. He was feverish and exhausted. Too tired to do anything but slump on top of Gina and wait for her to release him from her deadly female trap.

Thiou-Ling, no longer a sweet and docile Eurasian sex object, had done everything in her power to separate them – everything had included throwing cold water over their lower anatomy, wild tugs at Neil's nether regions, and vaseline liberally applied down there. Nothing had worked.

'Goddamn it, Gina,' snapped Thiou-Ling, who had suddenly developed a fierce New York street accent. 'Cut the fuckin' hysterics an' tell me what you want me to do.'

'Oh God,' Gina whimpered. 'What have I done to deserve this?' She wriggled around uncomfortably. Neil was hardly light. She felt like someone had jammed a cold cucumber inside of her and just left it there. She knew she would go mad if something wasn't done soon.

'Maybe I should call the paramedics,' Thiou-Ling suggested.

'Oh, for crissakes,' Gina groaned. 'We'd be the laughing stock of Hollywood. Try some more cold water. God! *Do something*!'

The small Volkswagen hit the road like a rocket. When it reached Sunset and Montana crossed over to Benedict Canyon instead of going towards Hollywood, Buddy said, 'Hey, uh, I think you forgot to turn.'

'No I didn't,' she said tonelessly. 'I just want to check something out. You don't mind do you?'

Who was he to mind? She was the one with the wheels.

The car zoomed up Benedict, swung right to Tower Road, an even sharper right on San Ysidro Drive, and finally slowed to a stop across the street from heavy iron gates.

Montana killed the ignition, shook a cigarette from a full pack, lit up, inhaled deeply, and said, 'I could do with a favour.'

He nodded obligingly. 'For you – anything.'

'Look – I feel kind of stupid asking you,' she said hesitantly.

He had no idea what she wanted and hoped it was nothing sexual. She was a beautiful woman . . . but he had to be needed for his talent not the action he could supply.

'What do you want me to do?'

She dragged on her cigarette and stared sightlessly out of the car window. 'Get past those gates, check out the driveway and garage of that house, and see if there's a red Maserati parked anywhere.'

He digested her request. How was he supposed to get past the gates? Climb them? And if he did, what if the owner mistook him for a burglar (highly likely at one in the morning) and *shot* him? After all, it was a well known fact that most of the residents of Beverly Hills were armed to the teeth ready for the revolution.

'Hey, listen –' he began.

'You don't have to,' she said flatly.

'Whose house is it anyway?' he asked, playing for time while he thought things out.

'Gina Germaine's.'

His luck. A movie star's house. She probably had armed guards sleeping on her doorstep.

'I'll do it,' he said reluctantly. After all, she had given him Vinnie, he had to give her *something* in return.

Oliver Easterne drove a gleaming English Bentley – vintage 1969 – a very good year for Bentleys. The car was immaculate, as it should be, for when not in use it was kept under pristine cloth wraps in the four car garage of the Bel Air house Oliver rented – three mansions to the right of Bibi and Adam Sutton's estate. The Bentley had been with him since birth. Straight from the factory to Oliver Easterne. An immaculate car for an immaculate man.

He reflected on his day. Pamela London had ruined it for him. And, of course, Montana. They were both too smart for their own good. If Montana and Neil broke up because of the information he had let slip – then fine. He for one would be delighted. She had her nerve talking to him the way she did. Calling him an ass-licker for all to hear. Didn't she know that it went with the job?

You produce. You ass-lick. There wasn't a producer in town who hadn't licked his share.

The early part of his day hadn't been bad. Signing Gina Germaine for Neil's new project was a plus. He looked forward to seeing Montana's face when she heard the news on *that* one.

Once home he showered, took a thick milky liquid for his ulcer, applied Preparation H to take care of the other end. He then put on fresh silk pyjamas, a hair net over his thinning locks, and climbed into bed thinking of Angel. Her unspoiled beauty and freshness were so right for Nikki. He had to convince her to do the role. She was just so perfect . . .

He fell asleep still thinking of golden haired Angel.

Buddy contemplated the heavy iron gates. They were spiked at the top, and at least ten feet high. 'Shit,' he mumbled, removing his white jacket, folding it, and placing it on the ground. He studied the gates again. They were surrounded on each side by an impenetrable sixteen foot hedge, and controlled electrically. The only way past was to climb.

He then noticed the signs, one on each side. The first read DANGER GUARD DOGS. The second WESTEC SECURITY ARMED RESPONSE.

'Oh, no,' he muttered. 'What am I *doin'* here?'

He visualized the scene. Buddy Hudson gets his chance and ends up being chewed by a Great Dane or – even worse – shot.

He hurried back to the car where Montana sat alone in the darkness.

'There's dogs and armed guards,' he stated indignantly.

'Don't take any notice of the signs. Everyone has them.'

Great. Thanks, Montana. It's not your ass out here.

He returned reluctantly to the front line and gingerly began to climb the gates. Fortunately the Art Deco design made them climbable, although going over the spikes at the top was a problem and he felt his pants tear which really pissed him. He muttered curses and made it over.

There was a steep driveway the other side, lit by evenly spaced green lights. He sprinted up it, keeping to the side, holding his breath, hoping to Christ that he didn't come face to face with an alert German Shepherd.

It came to her in a rush that Oliver was the only person who could help. If *he* couldn't keep his mouth shut, who could? The director of his movie. The star of his next production. Christ, it was *his* responsibility. What were producers for if not to get you out of a jam?

'Call Oliver Easterne,' she groaned to Thiou-Ling, who was now dressed and ready to make a fast exit.

'Who?' Thiou-Ling asked insolently.

'Do it!' screamed Gina. 'Don't question me!' She pushed at Neil's heavy body, she beat on his chest, she groaned again. His breathing was laboured. He had passed out which really infuriated her. *She* was the one stuck underneath him. He had been no help at all slumped on top of her like a massive hulk. 'Get a doctor,' he had gasped before losing consciousness. English fool. Did he honestly expect her to let a doctor see them like this? 'Oliver Easterne's number is in my book on the desk – try it – please. Hand me the phone when you get him. I think I'm going to die!'

'Save it for the screen, sister,' muttered Thiou-Ling.

'What?' gasped Gina.

'Forget it,' said Thiou-Ling, locating Oliver's number. 'I hope this dude is home because *I* have to split.'

'You have to what?' gasped Gina, outraged. 'You're in this with me all the way, you Chinese cunt.'

'I am not Chinese, I am Asian,' Thiou-Ling smiled inscrutably, and knew for a fact that the moment Oliver Easterne arrived she would leave. This kind of thing had a way of being bad for business, and with Thiou-Ling business always came first.

The phone shattered his pleasant dreams.

'Oliver!' gasped a hysterical Gina Germaine. 'I need you! Come quickly!'

Oliver Easterne dressed hurriedly, putting on a dark blue cashmere sweater, jeans with perfect creases, and Italian loafers. His hair was a little mussy though – he needed time for that.

Gina Germaine's hysterical phone call had unnerved him. Calls in the middle of the night were especially ominous, and this one would inevitably be no different from the rest. Unfortunately.

He drove quickly through the deserted Beverly Hills streets, gulping Maalox as he went, cursing and wondering – what now?

The Spanish style house at the end of the driveway was set in a square courtyard, and lights blazed from almost every window. Buddy didn't have to go searching for the red Maserati, it was parked right outside the front door for all to see. Keeping to the shadows he prepared to retreat.

One day he would own a house with guard dogs and an armed security guard. One day. Soon. Although he would make sure his dogs were on the loose ready to grab any poor slob that came climbing over *his* gates.

He skirted down the driveway, feeling for the damage in his pants – a ten inch tear at least. He mouthed a few more curses.

The whir of the electric gates opening startled the hell out of him and he stood stock still. Then the headlights of a car travelling full speed came roaring down the drive. Just in time he flung himself into the bushes landing on his right arm which sent out messages of serious agony. He groaned. The ground was wet from the constant attention of sprinklers, and he was rolling in mud.

He heard a dog bark and froze.

A petite gentle Asian girl answered the front door.

Oliver liked Orientals, they knew their place. 'Oliver Easterne,' he said respectfully. 'Ms. Germaine called me.'

'Where the fuck you been?' the not so gentle Asian girl said rudely. 'Follow me.'

Put out by this greeting he trailed her upstairs to the bedroom. There, the sight that met him was startling to say the least. Gina Germaine – American sex symbol supreme – spreadeagled like a beached great white. And lolling on top of her, his naked hairy ass on display, was Neil Gray.

'Holy shit!' exclaimed Oliver. 'You got me out of bed just to watch you two fuck? I seen it before you know – only with a better class of actor.'

316

'You *prick*!' screeched Gina, summoning all of her strength. '*Do* something, goddammit! You're the producer around here.'

42

'I'm looking for a woman,' Deke said tonelessly.

The plump female in the purple sweater and short black skirt, a small child straddling her hip, laughed and said, 'Ain't everyone?'

She stood in the doorway of her run-down house and waited expectantly for him to say something else.

'Mrs. Carrolle,' he said, fumbling for his piece of paper although he knew what was written on it only too well. 'C-A-R-R-O-L-L-E,' he repeated slowly, spelling it out.

The woman shook her head vaguely. 'Dunno.' The child's nose started to run, and she wiped it absentmindedly with the back of her hand. 'Dunno,' she said again.

'Who is it?' came a masculine voice, and a short squat man joined her at the door. 'Yes?' he barked. 'What do you want?'

Deke blocked the door with his foot. 'Who lived here before you?' he asked coldly.

Something about his eyes – so blank and steely – stopped the man from objecting. 'Some old witch.'

'Was her name Carrolle?'

'I don't know.' He tried to push the door closed, but Deke's foot held firm.

The woman said in a loud whisper, 'What's he want? Why don't he go away?'

'How can I find out who lived here before?' Deke asked, his black eyes burning with frustration.

'I guess y'could try the bum we lease this place from,' the man said, anxious to get Deke out of his doorway. 'He'll be able to tell ya. We don't know nuttin'.'

'Naw,' the woman agreed. 'We keep ourselves private.'

The man went inside and returned with a scribbled name and address on a torn off piece of newspaper. 'Y'kin tell the money-grabber he's bin' promisin' us a new roof for five years.'

Deke took the paper, removed his foot from the door, and set off down the street without another word.

'Fuckin' weirdo,' snapped the man, slamming his front door.

Deke walked quickly, staring straight ahead. Paper. Bits of paper. And all leading somewhere . . .

They sat side by side in a neighbourhood bar. Deke sipping plain Coca Cola, while Joey downed three rum and cokes in a row.

'It's gettin' late,' she said, crinkling her face. 'What time didja tell your folks we'd be there?'

'Anytime,' he replied. 'It doesn't matter.'

'Why?' she demanded. 'Ain't they all 'cited 'bout meetin' me?

'Sure they are,' he said dully, remembering his mother's words. She had stared at him as if sensing that this one was different. 'Bring her home if you must, and I'll tell you what I think of her.'

'Shall we come for dinner?' he had ventured.

'After dinner. I'm not cooking for some cheap tramp that I don't even know.'

'She's not a cheap tramp,' he had protested.

His mother had smiled thinly. 'If you picked her she's a tramp.'

'Let's go,' whined Joey. 'I'm tellin' ya cowboy, one more drink an' I'm gonna puke all over 'em.'

Deke looked at his watch. It was nine-thirty. 'I don't fell well,' he mumbled.

'Don'tcha go tryin' t'back out again. This is it.'

'I wasn't trying to back out,' he said indignantly.

'Sure,' she muttered. 'An' pigeons don't shit.'

He took a deep breath. 'We'll go now. Are you ready?'

From her purse she whipped out a grubby tin mirror and stared at her face. Then she foraged for a lipstick and applied even more. 'Wanna look nice for your ma,' she explained. 'Women notice things like make-up an' stuff. Didja tell her I was a model like I said?'

'I forgot.'

'Aw, shee . . it. She would've thought that was real classy. Sometimes you're so stupid.'

He gripped her wrist tightly. 'Don't say that.'

She pulled free. 'Okay, okay. You know I din't mean it.' Her voice became babyish. 'Gimme a smile, cowboy. I'm your little girlie.' Playfully she tweaked his ear. 'Girlie luvs big boy lots.'

He relaxed.

She was relieved. Didn't want another delay in getting to mom and

318

dad. She knew they would like her once they met her, it would all be so easy if they did. She needed a family, somewhere she belonged. Eighteen years old and burnt out. She had been on the streets since she was thirteen. It hadn't been easy but she had made out. She had hoped things would work with the cop. He was the first man who treated her kindly, and she would have done anything for him. She had phoned him to give him one last chance. He had pretended not to know who she was and hung up. Pig!

Leon, the cop. Like all the rest in the end. Fuck 'n run.

Then along came Deke, and she knew he was a screwball from the beginning. But she handled him carefully, quickly learning what knobs to push to make him work for her.

The possibility of family life thrilled her. Mrs. Deke Andrews with a mommy and daddy – his mommy and daddy, but they would grow to love her just like she was their own.

She sighed. Deke was better than nothing. Not bad looking if he would only cut his spooky shoulder length hair. His mother hated his hair, she had learned that much. Together they would make him cut it off. When they were married she would do a lot of things.

'Okey-doke, cowboy', she winked cheerily. 'This little girl is ready.'

He could not remember such heat. It was desert heat – all encompassing, suffocating.

He visited a barber shop and requested that they shave his scalp.

'You want I should take it all off?' asked the old man who owned the place.

Deke nodded.

'You got an infection? They got lotions take care of that.'

'Can you shave my head or not?'

'What are you? One of them religious persons?'

He nodded. It seemed the easiest way.

The old man performed his task, babbling on about this and that. Deke ignored him.

He liked his shaven scalp when it was done. It looked clean and fine. It looked like a beginning. Very fitting for The Keeper Of The Order.

He got directions for the new address he had written down. It was a one-storey office building on a quiet street. A secretary sat alone in reception picking at some carrot strips. Propped up on her desk was a copy of 'Us' magazine which she read intently. 'Everyone's out to lunch,' she told him, returning to an article on Tom Selleck.

Deke said, 'Maybe *you* can help me.'

Without looking up she said, 'Sorry. I'm only a temp.'

'You know where the files are, don't you? I want the file on Nita Carrolle. I need her new address.'

She glanced up briefly, didn't like the look of him. 'Why'n't you come back in an hour?'

He had no time to waste. 'Are you alone here?' he asked.

She was alone but she had no intention of telling this creep that. 'No, I'm not. So why don't you just go?'

He moved swiftly, knocking the magazine to the floor, pinioning her arms behind her.

'Show me the filing systems and I won't hurt you.' His voice was a lethal whisper.

She began to shake. He was a crazy, she should have known it immediately just from the look of him. 'You bald headed bastard,' she hissed, still shaking but determined not to break. 'I've been raped once and I'm not letting it happen again.' Her voice rose. 'You touch me and I'll *kill* you – you damned bastard.'

He was surprised at her reaction, but also strangely pleased.

He hadn't intended to do anything to her, but the message she put out was so strong and clear. She was *asking* for it.

Damnation.

Bastard.

Rape.

His knife was in his hand before he knew it. Her throat was so ready. After all . . . he was The Keeper Of The Order . . . There were certain things he *had* to do.

43

The last guests departed at five past two precisely. Ross's grin stayed in place until the front door shut behind them, and then he marched through the empty rooms to the bar where he sat morosely amidst the debris nursing a double scotch, waiting for Elaine to come and beg his forgiveness and offer her condolences.

He waited twenty minutes, and when she didn't show he sought her out, and found her in his dressing-room furiously throwing clothes into an open suitcase.

For a moment he stood watching, filled with confusion. Then the reality hit him and he roared. 'What the fuck are you doing?' Although it was quite obvious that she was preparing to throw him out.

'I . . . have . . . had . . . enough . . . Ross,' she said tightly, her face contorted with fury. 'How . . . dare . . . you. HOW . . . DARE . . . YOU. With . . . my . . . best . . . friend. You *bastard*.'

He had learned – at an early age – that whenever in doubt – deny it.

'I don't know *what* you are talking about,' he said, trying to sound outraged.

'Don't . . . give . . . me . . . that,' she spat, throwing silk shirts in on top of hand-lasted shoes. 'Save . . . your . . . acting . . . for . . . the movies.'

He had learned – at an early age – that the best form of defence was offence.

'*You* can talk. What about you and that overgrown surfer?'

She paused mid-throw, on an Yves Saint Laurent sweater. 'Don't you *dare* accuse *me* of anything. I have been a wonderful wife to you. An asset – as if you ever appreciated it.' She threw the sweater in his face and blazed, 'Karen Lancaster indeed. I thought you had more taste.'

He blew it. 'How could you think that? I married *you* didn't I?'

She slammed the suitcase shut, thrust it at him. 'Get out,' she hissed.

He wasn't thinking rationally otherwise he would never have gone.

'OUT!' she repeated.

'Don't worry, I'm going. I've had just about all I can take of your friggin' nagging.'

She escorted him to the door. 'Tomorrow I am phoning Marvin Mitchelson,' she announced grandly. 'By the time I am finished with you the only milk you'll be able to afford is from Karen Lancaster's tits!'

'Fuck you – you moaning bitch. At least she doesn't *steal* it!'

'OUT!' she screamed, and suddenly he was standing in his own driveway at two-thirty in the morning with nowhere to go.

By the time Buddy picked himself up and sprinted for the gates they were closed. In the distance he could still hear a dog barking, but the noise wasn't coming his way which was a relief. That's all he needed, some mad dog at his throat.

His arm throbbed painfully from the fall. Maybe it was broken. Who could he sue? Certainly not Gina Germaine.

Another thought. Could he play Vinnie with a broken arm?

Even more important. Could he get over the gates with a broken arm? He made an attempt, but failed dismally, managing only to rip his silk shirt.

'Montana,' he called urgently into the darkness.

She hurried across the street. 'What are you waiting for?'

'I've hurt my arm. I don't think I can make it back over.'

They stared at each other through the heavy gates.

'You'd better try,' she said at last. 'We can't hang around here much longer. Patrol cars cruise this area all the time.'

'Thanks,' he said bitterly.

'Come on,' she coaxed. 'You're in good shape. Scale it with one arm and *throw* yourself over.'

Since there seemed to be no other way he did as she suggested, landing on the cement with a thud and a grunt of pain. Two dogs began to bark in the house next door.

'Let's get out of here,' she said, hurrying over to the Volkswagen.

By the time he followed she had already started the little car and was raring to go. He hurled himself into the passenger seat and they took off.

Neither of them spoke for a minute, then she asked in a matter-of-fact voice, 'Was the Maserati there?'

'Yeah – it was there. Hey, listen, I'm not kiddin', I think I broke my arm.' He paused expecting words of sympathy, but she was silent. '*Shit!*' he exclaimed. 'I left my jacket on the ground outside. We'll have to go back.'

'I'm not going back.'

'C'*mon*, it's my best jacket. It's Armani. Besides, all my money's in the pocket.'

'I'll buy you a new jacket, and refund your money. How much?'

A dollar fifty. He was straightening out but need was need, and he could always pay her back when he was flush.

'Six hundred dollars,' he said, being careful to strike a balance between too much and too little.

Abruptly she stopped the Volkswagen just as they were about to hit Sunset. Oh Christ, she's going back, he thought.

She spun the car around and headed up Benedict again, making a sharp right on Lexington.

'I'm taking you to my house,' she said decisively. 'I can look at your arm and give you some money. All right?'

Who was he to object?

Sadie La Salle had a little ritual at bedtime. First she took a long scented bath. It relaxed her. Then she selected one of the many Sony Betamax video tapes that she kept neatly lined up on a shelf. She put the tape into her video, switched on the television and went to sleep every night with an old Ross Conti movie playing.

Tonight she chose one of her favourites. A big smash in 1958. Ross at the beginning of his career – young and careless – the baby blues and the blond locks and the sleek hard body. Not an ounce of excess then. Tonight she had noticed the beginning of a gut, and the eyes were not as bright, the hair not as blond, the skin leathery from too much living.

She wondered about the rest of him and shuddered with anticipation, although she hated herself for doing so.

Soon she would have him again. And she would use him as he had used her.

And this time *she* would do the walking.

No phone call. No letter. No explanation.

Nothing.

Ross Conti had *ruined* her life, and now, finally, she wanted him to pay for it. When *she* finished with him he would regret the day he met her.

On the television screen Ross smiled. Mister Irresistible.

Sadie settled back to watch the movie. She had seen it hundreds of times before.

Buddy prowled around the sparsely modern living room. The throb in his arm was easing, maybe it wasn't broken after all.

'Where's . . . uh . . . your old man?' he asked casually, a question which had been bugging him all night.

Montana was fiddling with the combination of a wall safe concealed behind a painting, and didn't look up.

'I mean . . . well like . . . shouldn't I meet him? Did he like my test? What did he say?'

She opened the safe, selected a bundle of notes from inside and began counting off hundred dollar bills. Then she handed him a wad.

'Twelve hundred dollars. That should cover your lost cash *and* the damage to your clothes.'

He could kiss her. Guilt overcame him all the same.

'And incidentally,' she added, 'I spoke to Sadie La Salle. She said for you to stop by her office at eleven o'clock tomorrow morning.'

His luck was getting better all the time. 'Hey, that's great.'

She reached for a cigarette on the table and lit up. 'It's nothing. Now – let's take a look at your arm.'

'I think I just fell on it the wrong way,' he said, flexing it out in front of him.

She insisted on looking anyway, feeling for broken bones with her long tapered fingers. 'You'll live,' she pronounced crisply.

Now he was feeling really bad. How could he possibly con money from her? He had more style than that. 'Uh . . . listen,' he began apologetically. 'I didn't really have six hundred bucks in my jacket. I was just kind of . . . uh . . . joking.'

She stared at him gravely. 'Do you need the money?'

He nodded.

She drew deeply on her cigarette. 'Call it a loan then. When you get your first paycheque I'll expect it back with interest.'

'*You* are one terrific lady.'

'Thanks,' she said drily. 'But don't tell me how great I am because right now I feel mean and vicious and not terrific at all.' She seemed immediately sorry to have revealed herself to him – even with so few words. 'Help yourself to a drink,' she said brusquely. 'I'll just go change, then I'll drop you home.'

'You don't have to bother. I can call a cab.'

'I promised you a ride home, and that's what you'll get. Anyway I feel like driving.'

She left the room and he looked around. The decor was comfortable and modern. The view of Hollywood spectacular. A silver framed picture of Neil Gray stood on a coffee table. On it was inscribed – TO MY DARLING M – WHO TAUGHT ME HOW TO LIVE AGAIN.

Montana breezed back into the room wearing skin tight faded Levis tucked into well worn cowboy boots and a plain white T-shirt. 'Come on, star,' she said, slamming the safe shut. 'Let's get you home – I don't want you appearing at Sadie's tomorrow with bags under your eyes. I gave you a build up as the best looking actor since Marlon in "Streetcar".'

One thing about Montana. She certainly knew how to say the right thing.

*

Valium had calmed her. She knew she was taking too many, but so what? It wasn't every day you were almost arrested, threw the hottest party in town, and threw your husband out on the same night.

Elaine nodded grimly. The bastard deserved it. If he wanted to walk a tight rope he had to be prepared to take a fall.

Come off it, Elaine. You would never have shoved him out if you thought there was a chance of him getting the movie.

Shut your fat face, Etta. You know from nothing.

I know that you've turned into a miserable Beverly Hills bitch. So he screwed Karen. Well you screwed Ron, didn't you?

It's not the same!

Says who?

Her past and her present. She wished the past would just vanish. Why did she have to be reminded of dumpy Etta Grodinski all the time?

Ross needed you tonight.

Ross doesn't know what the word means.

She thought she might cry. But then she thought about red swollen eyes on top of everything else and abandoned the idea.

Elaine Conti. Separated wife. What would she do? Who would she see? How would she manage?

Women's liberation had never interested her. Woman was there to look good and play hostess. Man was there to provide.

Bullshit.

I'm entitled to my opinion.

She prowled around the empty house, double checked the burglar alarm, wished that she had a cat – a dog – anything.

She didn't like being alone. Throwing Ross out had been a big mistake. He might be a son of a bitch, but at least he was *her* son of a bitch. Tomorrow she would get him back.

Montana felt sad as she drove Buddy down the hill. She was sad for herself, even more so for Neil. She had expected so much more of him. That he had decided to risk their life together for a fling with someone like Gina . . . What a waste. Because for a while they had had something really good. . . .

How could he be so goddamn stupid? Five terrific years down the drain. For what? Some big bosomed movie queen.

For a moment she was angry. How could he do it? How *could* he betray her trust?

Anger wouldn't help. He *had* done it. No inquests. Now her decision was whether to stay in Los Angeles until the film was complete, or make it easy on everyone and get out of town.

Hey – wait a minute, why should *I* go? She thought furiously. Why should *I* abandon a movie that has taken so much out of me, and leave it in the hands of Neil, and Oliver, and George to probably fuck up beyond recognition?

She made her plans. First thing was to move out – Neil could have the house, she didn't want one red cent of his money. She would take her clothes and records and books, *and* her car which she had paid for anyway. There was enough money in her bank account to last until she decided what she wanted to do next. Instinctively she knew that Neil would not let her go without a fight. He would make every excuse he could think of . . . Poor Neil . . . She was almost sorry for him.

Buddy's voice intruded. 'You're going the wrong way.'

'I am?' she said vaguely. 'I guess I've got a lot on my mind.'

He laughed. 'I'm glad my presence is really felt.'

She flashed tiger eyes at him and he thought how incredibly beautiful she was in a wild and sensual way. She was also troubled, and he had been so busy thinking about himself that he had not realized she had her problems too.

She slowed the car, looking for a place to turn.

'Uh . . . if you want to take a drive I'll come along,' he ventured.

She welcomed the thought of company. Without saying anything she put her foot down – sending the small car careening around the curves and twists of Sunset. 'Now's the time I wish I had a Ferrari,' she said softly.

He nodded, taking the time to figure out what was going on. Neil Gray. Not at the party. Gina Germaine not at the party. A red Maserati parked outside the blonde movie star's house. You didn't have to be Kojak to get the picture.

He leaned forward and pressed a tape into the cassette player. Stevie Wonder. *That Girl*. Good music all the way to the beach and the two of them wrapped in companionable silence.

Montana thought about being free again. She would miss Neil, but how surprisingly sweet the thought of freedom was . . .

Buddy thought about Angel, and getting the part in the movie, and being seen by the legendary Sadie La Salle . . . Then his face clouded over as he remembered the man at the party . . . Wolfie Schweicker . . . And the memories he could never shake . . .

326

She drove the car far along the Pacific Coast Highway, finally pulling onto a bluff overlooking the roaring dark ocean.

'You want to take a walk?' she asked.

'Why not?'

They left the car and made their way down a slope towards the beach. The tide was high, and they stopped while she pulled off her boots and he removed his shoes and socks.

'I used to live at the beach when I first came to L.A.,' he said. 'This is the best time. No one around.' He took a deep breath. 'You know what I miss? The smell.'

She smiled in the darkness. 'Up front you come on like stud of the year – and really you're not like that at all, are you? You're very caring and nice, and the combination comes across on the screen. It's a great mixture. Don't ever lose it.'

Nobody had ever called him caring and nice in his life. And yet . . . why not?

'Hey . . .' he mumbled, not knowing what to say.

She laughed softly. 'Let's walk, Buddy.'

The gold Corniche went first in the direction of Karen's Century City apartment, made an abrupt U-turn and came back towards Sadie La Salle's Bel Air house, then finally settled on the Beverly Hills Hotel – home of the stars.

Ross checked in with no difficulty although they were – as usual – booked to capacity.

'I'm a friend of the owner, Mrs. Slatkin,' he informed the night clerk, lest there was trouble with his reservation.

'No problem, Mr. Conti. For you there is always a room,' said the eager clerk.

'Good.' If Elaine wanted him out, that's where he would stay – out. She had proved herself to him tonight. Revealed herself as an unfeeling heartless bitch. She, above all people, had known what *Street People* meant to him. And she should have been there for him.

Never before had Buddy felt so at ease with a woman. Subconsciously women were the enemy. You either fought, outsmarted or conquered. But there was something different about Montana. He could actually talk to her, and talk he did, forgetting about her problems as for the first time in his life he unburdened himself. Walking along the dark seashore with the sound of the pounding surf, he found it almost easy. And once he started it was hard to stop. She

327

seemed genuinely interested in his life story – crummy as it was.

He began by telling her about his childhood – and once he started talking about San Diego it all came pouring out. Although he didn't tell her everything. He left out the two most important things. Tony's murder, and the night his mother came to his room . . .

He told her about arriving in L.A. young and broke and eager. His days at the beach, and Joy Byron's acting classes. Then about his Hollywood nights, the tricks he turned, the drugs, the disappointments, and the promises that never materialized. He got as far as Hawaii, and stopped. For some reason he didn't want to mention Angel. She was his secret. 'So I came back,' he finished off. 'And I heard about your movie . . . and . . . uh . . . here we are.'

She liked the way he called it her movie. He was about the only one who did. She knew that Neil would try to intimidate him, George Lancaster would walk all over him, and she wanted so much for him to succeed with the only chance he was likely to get.

It was almost sunrise by the time they got back to the car, and lone joggers were beginning to appear on the horizon.

She felt better having listened to his story. Listening meant not having to think about her own problems.

They sat in the car for a while silently watching the sun rise, then she said, 'How's your arm?'

'Hey – you know something? I forgot all about it.' He flexed it tentatively. 'Nothin'. How about that?'

'You know what I want to do,' she said huskily. 'I want to make love with you – because I like you and I think you like me – and it's something I need right now. No heavy relationships – just . . . togetherness.' She stared at him expectantly – wild tiger-eyes.

He hadn't really thought about sex with her.

It had been at the back of his mind since they left her house.

Oliver had a doctor who was expensive and discreet. One look at the unhappy couple and he summoned him instantly. For a fleeting moment it occurred to him that the paramedics would be faster. But, oh, the headlines. In that respect he and Gina thought along the same lines. On very rare occasions no press at all was the name of the game.

'I feel terrible,' she moaned. 'I'm sick, Oliver. You'd better help me.'

She didn't look sick to him. All giant tits and ass. Voluptuous

328

women had never appealed to him. He liked them understated, neat and very very clean.

He averted his eyes from Gina's rolling mammaries and concentrated on Neil. Now *he* looked sick. His complexion was greenish and his breathing laboured.

Oliver was not versed in first aid. He had no idea what to do. He certainly didn't want to *touch* them, the very thought digusted him. So, while he waited for the doctor to arrive he did what came naturally. He picked up the nearest ashtray and began to clean it.

They lay together on a water bed in an oceanside motel naked and relaxed. They had made love urgently and fast, and now it was Montana's turn to talk. She was giving him fragments of her life. Thoughts, opinions, ideas. She never once mentioned Neil.

Later they made love a second time, slowly and leisurely like two key athletes at play.

She was long limbed, sensual, and also aggressive – a trait which excited Buddy because he wasn't used to it and found he liked it.

She had a marvellous body, sleek and feline, with wide shoulders, high breasts, a narrow waist, and long legs. Her skin had the sheen and texture of dark olive oil and she was a wonderful lover. Skilfully she sought out the pressure points which really turned him on, massaging his neck, his chest, and slowly . . . slowly . . . further down until she was enclosing his hardness in her hands and bringing her lips down to caress him with her tongue.

He put his hands into her long jet hair and held her head steady as she teased him. He wanted to come in her mouth, but he also wanted to taste her. He withdrew and changed positions, burying his head between her legs.

Their pleasure was intense, the two of them expert and caring participants in a game they both enjoyed.

For Montana it was the release she needed. Five years . . . just Neil . . . She had almost forgotten the sharp thrill of a new body.

Silently they played out the scene.

Luxuriously they approached their climaxes.

Buddy had thought he was unique in that he never made a sound. But in Montana he had found a soul-mate. Just a long drawn-out sigh as she shuddered to a halt. And as he felt her vibrations so he came too.

It was nearly four in the morning. They fell asleep in each other's arms.

The sound of children playing on the beach woke them hours later. Sun streamed into the room, and for a moment Buddy could not remember where he was. Then it all came back to him, and automatically he groped for his watch.

Eight forty-nine, and Sadie La Salle at eleven. Time to get moving. Lightly he touched Montana on the shoulder.

She mumbled something and stretched like a leopard.

'It's nearly nine o'clock,' he said quickly. 'And I've got to get back and change my clothes before I go see Sadie La Salle at eleven. Can we make it in time?'

'Wow! You're a real romantic in the morning, aren't you?'

He grinned. 'Hey – what do you want from me? Business is business. I need an agent, don't I?'

She wrapped a sheet around her nakedness and said crisply, '*You're* telling *me*? I arranged the appointment. You use the bathroom first while I order us some coffee. Don't worry, I'll have you back at your apartment before ten.'

'You got it.' He hurried into the bathroom.

Montana picked up the bedside phone. 'Two coffees. Ditto orange juice,' she said, feeling surprisingly good. The sex had been excellent therapy. Maybe it was silly, but in a way she felt that she had evened up the score between her and Neil just a little.

She switched on the television, changed channels until the reassuring face of David Hartman greeted her. 'Good morning America,' she murmured softly. Several commercials dominated the screen. She wondered what Neil would have to say. He would lie of course. How depressing to have to go through it with him.

'*This is Angela Black with the news*,' said the beautiful newscaster on the screen.

Probably a former actress, Montana decided, not really listening as Ms. Black proceeded with the news. All bad. As if there was anything different about that.

'*Film director Neil Gray was rushed to hospital early today suffering from a massive coronary attack. A spokesman for Cedars of Lebanon Hospital said that he is in intensive care and in stable condition. In New York, Senator –*'

Blankly Montana clicked the set off. She could hardly think . . . Neil . . . a heart attack . . . massive coronary . . . intensive care . . .

Numbly she shook her head. Then, galvanized into action, she

330

began to dress while calling out urgently for Buddy.

'What's the matter?' He came bounding in from the bathroom dripping water.

'There's an emergency,' she said tightly. 'We've got to leave. Now.'

44

Ernie Thompson phoned Leon just when Millie was by his side, instamatic camera in hand, summery dress and white sandals complementing her deep bronze skin. They were about to set off on a bus tour around San Diego. How he longed to tell her to go without him, but she was having too good a time for him to burst her bubble.

'Give me your number, I'll have to call you back,' he told Ernie reluctantly.

'Who was that, hon?' Millie inquired, after he hung up.

'Nothing. Business.'

She arched an eyebrow but remained silent. When Leon was ready to tell her he would do so. She did not believe in prying.

They spent the day on and off the tour bus enjoying the sights of San Diego. Or at least Millie enjoyed. Leon merely plodded along behind her, wondering what news Ernie had, and planning how to get some time on his own.

From San Diego they were renting a car and driving to Los Angeles, stopping off at Catalina and Long Beach on the way. It was their last night in San Diego, and another couple they had met on the bus wanted them all to go to La Jolla for dinner. He resisted. She insisted. In Tijuana he had picked up a stomach bug, and he used this as an excuse, urging her to go without him.

'Leave you alone?' she protested. 'Never.'

'If you promise to be back before eleven I think I'll survive.'

She was tempted. La Jolla, or so she had been told, was a quaint little beach resort only twenty minutes away. Picturesque open air restaurants and little shops. Marvellous sea food. A place not to be missed.

'Well . . .' she hesitated. 'If you're sure that you don't mind my going without you . . .'

The moment she left he phoned Ernie. They spoke for twenty minutes, Leon questioning, repeating, absorbing every bit of information that came his way. He made notes on a scratch pad and requested that the typed up reports be sent on to him at the Holiday Inn in Los Angeles where he would be arriving in three days.

So, Deke Andrews had finally surfaced. In Pittsburgh and Texas. The bastard was out there somewhere . . . Leaving a trail . . .

Eventually he would be caught. When he was, Leon had every intention of being there.

45

Beverly Hills buzzed with the news of Neil Gray's heart attack. Coronaries were a hot subject around town. Everyone had their own opinion on how not to have one.

Gotta keep fit.

Gotta cut the cholesterol.

Gotta pop vitamins.

Gotta give up doing drugs.

Gotta jog, run, skip, jump, pump iron . . . Gotta EXERCISE!!

Oh, yes, and . . . Gotta fuck a lot (this from a twenty-three year old studio executive who didn't even know what a heart was!).

Juicy secrets have a hard time getting kept anywhere – especially in Hollywood – mecca of gossip.

'Did you hear he was with Gina Germaine?'

'Did you know they were taken into the hospital *joined* like a couple of mating dogs?'

'Did you hear they were snorting coke?'

'. . . smoking grass . . .'

'. . . popping ammis . . .'

'. . . gulping quacks . . .'

'. . . shooting speed . . .'

'He's a fag of course.'

'She's a dyke.'

'They were having an orgy.'

Oh gossip! Oh Hollywood!

332

What fun everyone had with rumour and insinuation and down-right dirt.

Montana rushed straight to the hospital in her jeans and T-shirt, her long black hair flying wildly behind her. The photographers were lined up and waiting, along with the press, television, and radio.

'Why weren't you with him?'

'Who was he with?'

'Where were you?'

'How come he wasn't at George Lancaster's party?'

'Any comment?'

'Can you say something for our viewers?'

She rushed past them and into the arms of one of Oliver Easterne's gofers, who escorted her upstairs to the great man himself.

'Where have you been?' were Oliver's first words. He stopped pacing the hospital corridor to stare at her accusingly. 'What do you think it looks like to the press? A man has a heart attack and his wife is on the missing list.'

She controlled her fiery reply. 'How is he?'

'Christ! How is he she asks. He's in intensive care, *that*'s how he is. He's been fighting to stay alive since he was brought in.'

She endeavoured to remain calm. 'What happened?'

He didn't know whether to tell her the truth or to lie. Montana was smart. She wouldn't be so easy to fool, and he himself had told her that Neil was with Gina earlier.

'Er . . .' He grabbed her by the arm. 'I got the use of a private room. Let's go talk.'

'I want to see Neil,' she said stubbornly.

'I don't think they're letting anyone in,' he muttered.

'I'm not anyone, Oliver,' she reminded him coldly. 'I'm his wife.'

'Why don't you talk to his doctor. It's not my decision.'

'I should bloody well hope not. If it was, we'd be in deep trouble.'

Elaine's phone rang early. She reached for it in her sleep, ready to receive the stream of compliments from people thanking her for a sensational party. Her groping hand sent a glass crashing to the ground and she opened her eyes with a start. She was not in her comfortable bed as imagined, but instead on a sofa in the living room surrounded by the aftermath of the party.

'Ross,' she said aloud, and then she groaned.

You threw him out you dumb bunny.

Don't remind me, thank you very much.

333

The phone was still ringing. She got up and approached it with caution. If it was Ross she had to be sure to say the right thing. He was a difficult bastard, it would take honey and coaxing to get him back. She lifted the receiver, not thrilled when she noticed it was only seven-thirty in the morning.

'Hello,' she said sweetly, in case it *was* Ross.

'Elaine!' sobbed Maralee. 'Something terrible has happened.'

Yes. To me. How did you know?

'What?' she snapped. It better be really terrible for Maralee to wake her at this hour of the morning.

'It's . . . it's Neil.'

'What's Neil?'

'He's had a heart attack. He's been rushed to the hospital. I must go to him. Will you come with me?'

Elaine was too shocked to reply for a moment. Anyone getting sick always shocked her. Somehow she expected everyone to stay healthy and live forever.

'Gosh . . . I'm sorry . . . it's awful . . .'

'Can you come with me?' Maralee pleaded tearfully.

'Not right now I can't. I've got . . . er . . . problems here.'

A very small disappointed, 'Oh.'

'But I'll tell you what,' Elaine rallied. 'I'll meet you later.'

'I'd appreciate it. I don't want to be alone at a time like this.'

You're never alone with your millions. Where's Randy? How is he taking this sudden ex-husband-love?

'Of course. I understand. What hospital?'

'Cedars.'

'I'll be there.'

She replaced the receiver, caught sight of her reflection in a mirror, and gasped with horror. Stale make-up ran riot over her face. She looked like a hag. How could she have possibly fallen asleep with her make-up on? God, she really must have been upset.

'And who *else* was there, dreamheart?' asked Koko. 'Was it divine? Did you have a fabulous time? Aren't you just *full* of the joys of spring today?'

Angel smiled wanly.

'Was Mrs. L. wearing lashings of diamonds?' Koko continued excitedly. 'Did she out-sparkle Pamela London? Is George Lancaster *gorgeous*? How about Richard Gere? Did he look divine? Who was *there*, darling one? Tell me all.'

Buddy was there, she wanted to say. I know I have to forget him, but I love him so much that it hurts. And he doesn't even care for me anymore. He made that obvious enough by not coming back . . .

'It was fantastic, Koko,' she said, summoning enthusiasm, because she knew how disappointed he would be if she didn't give a glowing report. 'Absolutely amazing. . . .'

After dropping Montana at the hospital Buddy raced back to Randy's. Montana had loaned him the Volkswagen which at least made him mobile again. He was worried about the movie. With Neil Gray in hospital it had to mean a delay. Just his luck.

He burst into the small apartment and was surprised to find Randy home – sprawled across the bed asleep. All he needed to do was change and get out of there fast. It wouldn't do to keep Sadie La Salle waiting. Problem. What to wear? Best jacket, pants, and shirt ruined. He opened the crowded closet, couldn't see a thing, raised the window shade.

Randy growled restlessly, 'Pull the goddamn shade down and get lost. I'm sleeping.'

A fine greeting. Quickly he shuffled through his things crushed at one end of the closet. He grabbed at his other Armani jacket. It was wrinkled and needed a trip to the dry cleaners, but it would have to do. The pants and shirt he chose were in the same condition. He swore softly and began to change.

Randy sat up and glared. 'Get your own fucking place, Buddy. I'm no charity, and man, I've had it with you.'

'Things didn't work out with Maralee, huh?' Buddy asked sympathetically.

Randy was not amused. 'Piss off and don't come back. Leave the key. And send me the fucking money you owe me.'

Buddy got his things and put them in a suitcase. He couldn't fault Randy. There *was* such a thing as overstaying your welcome.

A face to face confrontation with Neil's ex-wife was not exactly what Montana had expected. But she stayed cool, introduced herself with a brief handshake, and was humiliated to have to ask, 'Have you seen him?'

Maralee, stationed outside intensive care, shook blond curls negatively. 'No visitors,' she explained.

I'm his wife, Montana thought. I'll visit him whether they like it or not.

The doctor appeared. He was good-looking, fortyish, and groomed to within an inch of his life. Montana did not trust him on sight. Gucci shoes and thick gold chains beneath a starched white coat had a way of making her uneasy.

'Mrs. Gray?' he questioned smoothly, heading straight for Maralee.

'Yes,' gasped Maralee. She was one of those women who on stressful occasions adopt a breathy little-girl voice.

'*I'm* Mrs. Gray,' Montana said forcefully, stepping between them.

The doctor gave her a confused look. He plucked his eyebrows she noticed, and hid the dark circles under his eyes with just the tiniest dab of pancake.

Confusion gave way to a smile when he remembered that this was indeed Hollywood. 'Ah . . .' he sighed knowingly. 'You're *both* Mrs. Gray.'

'Top marks, doc,' snapped Montana. 'Is there somewhere we can talk privately?'

'You're the current Mrs. Gray?'

She withheld a sarcastic reply.

He led her into a private office. Maralee tried to follow, but she stopped her with a look.

'Mrs. Gray,' said the doctor, pressing his fingers together and gazing at her sincerely. 'Your husband is a very sick man.'

'I think I realize that, doctor. I would like to know exactly what happened.'

He picked up some papers from the desk and studied them intently. 'Have you spoken to Mr. Easterne yet?'

'Er . . . yes . . . I mean to . . . He hasn't told me anything. Did Oliver Easterne bring him in?'

The doctor hesitated a moment. 'Mr. Easterne called me . . . it was fortunate that he was with your husband at the time.'

But Oliver was at the party. Why would he leave the party and go and visit Neil? She frowned. Neil's Maserati parked outside Gina Germaine's house . . . and while she was waiting outside the gates for Buddy a car had arrived . . . travelling fast . . . on reflection it could well have been Oliver.

Neil must have had the heart attack while he was with Gina . . . *she* had summoned Oliver . . . and Oliver had sent for the doctor who was quite obviously supposed to keep the whole thing quiet.

'What brought his attack on?' she asked coldly.

He shrugged. 'Who knows, Mrs. Gray. Overwork, rich foods, stress –'

'Sex?'

He was no actor. Guilt clouded his handsome features. 'Maybe sex. Anything can trigger these –'

'With Gina Germaine?' she interrupted.

Now it was the doctor's turn to frown. Damn Oliver Easterne with his cover-up plans. The wife knew. And probably the whole hospital knew. It wasn't every day that emergency admitted a couple locked together who had to be surgically parted. Especially when one half of the couple was a movie star.

He sighed. 'You're obviously aware of the circumstances, Mrs. Gray. Unfortunate, but then we are all human, and I am sure that your main desire is to see Mr. Gray up and out of here.' He changed voices from understanding friend to businesslike doctor. 'He has suffered two attacks. The first before we brought him in, and the second after he and Miss Germaine were . . . er . . . separated.'

She wasn't sure that she had heard correctly.

'What?' she asked, feeling shivery and cold.

Carefully the doctor explained the procedure. 'Vaginismus. A severe contraction of the vagina causing Mr. Gray to be . . . er . . .'

She stopped listening. She felt sick. For Neil to have had a heart attack was bad enough . . . But the circumstances . . .

Vaguely she heard the doctor droning on.

' . . . dehabilitated and weak . . . unconscious . . . pulse and blood pressure nil . . . resuscitation brought good results . . . Intensive care . . . condition now stable . . . everything possible being done.'

She felt a weakness creeping over her body. A clammy feeling. Suddenly, with no warning, she slumped into a deep faint.

The faraway rustle of room service woke Ross Conti. Discreet sounds in the corridor outside his room, trays rattling, whispered Spanish. He stretched, cleared his throat, and reflected on the pleasures of sleeping alone. Then he reflected on George Lancaster's announcement, and scowled grimly. What a way to ruin a movie. George Lancaster couldn't act himself out of a French letter. Everyone knew that.

His scowl deepened, and he picked up the phone and ordered a large breakfast.

So Elaine wanted out did she? Well, if that's what she wanted she could damn well have it.

Elaine the nag. Elaine the ballbreaker. Elaine the *shop*lifter.

He was fed up with being told to do this – do that – go on a diet – get to the gym. You're fat. You're old. You're losing your hair.

He was *not* losing his hair. If anything *she* was losing *hers*. It came out in handfuls in her brush – he had seen it. Gleefully he reminded himself to tell her.

When? You won't be seeing her, schmuck.

He got up and emptied out his jumbled Vuitton suitcase. At least she had sent him on his way with decent luggage. Not that he gave a dog's turd. Labels didn't interest him, they never had. She was the one that lived her life by labels.

He yawned loudly. 'Don't *do* that,' Elaine would say. He farted – a trumpeter's salute. 'God Ross! You are utterly disgusting,' she would complain. Like she never farted. Come to think of it she probably never did. Now if only someone would come up with designer farts . . .

He laughed aloud. He would survive. Leaving home means never having to see the early morning bills . . .

Room service arrived with a cart laden with goodies. Freshly squeezed orange juice, hot coffee, corned beef hash with two eggs sunny-side up, buckwheat toast and a side order of hash browns. He fell upon it ravenously.

Should call Karen.

Didn't feel like it. Hadn't enjoyed her flashy behaviour at the party. She had no claim on him. Besides, if he was going to be free may as well enjoy it and play the field. Now that he was on the loose he could think of several women he would like to meet – Gina Germaine for one. She had boobs on her that would support an army of drowning soldiers for a week.

He smiled to himself and tried to forget the disappointment of losing the part and being thrown out of his house. At least he was seeing Sadie La Salle later in the day, and if anyone could save a sagging career she could.

It seemed that Neil had done the unthinkable. Montana had never thought he would fall into the obvious trap of an attention grabbing big breasted movie star – but he had turned out to be just another man. His betrayal stung, because she had expected so much more of

338

him. It hurt that he was weak . . . so weak he had almost killed himself.

She didn't hate him. Yet she didn't love him. She was numbed by his behaviour, and she knew for sure that whatever they'd had together was no longer there.

She made her plans. While he was in the hospital she would stay by him. But when he came out . . . well . . . As far as she was concerned there was no going back.

Eleven o'clock. Punctuality is next to stardom. Buddy felt confident in spite of his wrinkled clothes.

'Miz La Salle,' he said to the receptionist who was busy filing her nails.

'Who?' she staccatoed.

'Miz La Salle.'

This exasperated her. She was a girl of few words. 'Who *you*?' she snapped.

'Uh . . . Buddy Hudson.'

She consulted an appointment book, indicated a chair, said, 'Wait,' and relayed his name through an intercom.

Five minutes grew to ten. He checked out 'Time' magazine, 'Dramalogue' and the trades.

Ten grew to twenty. He thought briefly of Angel, reviewed his evening with Montana. She was a fantastic woman and he hoped that they would remain friends. The sex had been great, but it was just something they had both needed at that particular moment – nothing permanent. He knew she felt the same way.

The intercom buzzed.

'Go,' said the girl, pointing an eight inch lacquered nail in the direction of a corridor filled with offices.

He took a deep breath. Lately he was moving into the big time, and it was making him very nervous indeed. Buddy Boy could hold his own with the best of 'em. But suddenly it was all happening so fast . . .

A secretary in a red mini-skirt headed towards him. 'Buddy, welcome,' she smiled. 'Please come this way.'

She guided him to the end of the corridor, and flung open the door of an outer office where a man sat typing. He looked up and made a quick visual assessment of Buddy's assets.

'Hello,' he said. 'Sadie won't be a moment. Do take a seat.'

'This is Ferdie Cartright,' the secretary explained. 'Miz La Salle's personal assistant.' She smiled and departed.

Buddy sat down. Sweat was staining the underarms of his shirt. He hoped it wouldn't seep through to his jacket.

Ferdie finished typing with a flourish and pulled the paper from the machine. 'Done!' he exclaimed. 'Just a personal note from Sadie to Barbra.'

Buddy stared straight ahead and silently rehearsed his opening line. *'Miss La Salle.'* Correction. *'Miz La Salle. I have been dreaming of this day ever since I first set foot in Hollywood.'*

Corny bullshit!

'Sadie. You and I . . . we're meant to be together.'

Even worse.

'Sadie La Salle,' said with reverence. *'A legend in her own town.'*

Oh shit!

'Miz La Salle will see you now,' said Ferdie in response to three sharp buzzes.

Buddy leapt up. Cool blown in all directions. He followed Ferdie who led him through the door of the fabled inner office.

'Miz La Salle, may I present Buddy Hudson,' Ferdie said formally.

She sat behind a large antique desk stacked with scripts. A dark haired woman of middle age, with bobbed black hair and a non-descript face apart from huge liquid black eyes. Not attractive . . . not unattractive . . . There was something familiar about her which he couldn't quite place.

She was smoking a thin brown cigarillo which she waved at him to indicate he should sit.

Immediately Sadie saw what Montana meant. The boy didn't walk into her office, he sauntered with a special hip-swaying thrust which would be hard to miss. He had a great body – easy to see in the clothes he wore, and although he was dark she was reminded of the first time she ever saw Ross. Same walk. Same thrust. A direct sensuality that could leave you breathless. She had used it to propel Ross to stardom. What a challenge to do it again . . . Oh, she had created plenty of stars . . . But never in the same way . . .

How would Buddy look on billboards from coast to coast? The exact campaign all these years later. Faded Levi cut-offs and WHO IS BUDDY HUDSON?

The thought intrigued her.

He perched nervously on the edge of a chair, all opening gambits long forgotten. She was looking him over like he was prime beef and it was making him uncomfortable.

Finally she said, 'I'm glad you could come, Buddy. Montana Gray gave you glowing notices. I ran your test this morning and I agree with her.'

'You do?' He felt a buzz. His luck was on an up. Everything was falling into place. 'I'm glad,' he mumbled.

'You'll be more than glad by the time I've finished with you. You'd like to be a star, wouldn't you? And I think I'm the person that can do it for you.'

He could hardly believe what he was hearing, but then again he had been expecting it all his life.

Black eyes met black eyes.

'I'm ready,' he said.

'I know you are,' she replied.

46

Deke knew he had the living force of power flowing through his body. He had felt it growing within him for a long time . . . Now that his head was shaved the force was set free and he knew that he could do anything he wanted for the aura of power would protect him. He was invincible. He walked by himself in a world of scum. And he alone could give people liberty if he so wished.

Cutting a throat and watching the blood flow was an act of salvation. The Keeper Of The Order did not have to be careful anymore. He was untouchable.

Proof positive.

He had released the receptionist from her miserable existence. Cut her until the blood flowed and life vanished. Then he had washed in a nearby toilet, removed his stained shirt, squeezed the sticky blood out under the cold tap, put the wet shirt back on his body, and searched for the filing cabinet.

He did not hurry as he did all of this. He felt perfectly calm and secure.

He found what he was looking for, and tipped all the rest of the files from the steel cabinet to the floor. Then he set a match to the papers and watched the flames.

He walked unhurriedly to his van parked a block away. Joey would be proud of him.

Now he sat on the hard bed in his dreary motel room and flipped through the file searching for the information he required.

His mother said, 'So nice to meet you,' thin lips a prism of disapproval.

Joey enclosed the surprised woman in a clumsy hug, and deposited a jammy kiss on her cheek. 'Mama!' she blurted. 'That's what I'm gonna call you – I 'cided that first moment Dekey told me 'bout you.'

Winifred Andrews shoved the girl away with a certain amount of force and tried to recover her composure. She hated being touched. 'Don't call me that,' she said, her bony features a passionless mask. 'It is not correct for you to do so.'

'Yet!' added Joey, with a saucy wink.

Deke stood in the doorway to the tidy living room, every piece of furniture, every ornament polished and in its proper place. He didn't want to enter. He knew that things weren't going to work out, and that he was going to lose the one person who had ever meant anything to him.

'Wow!' Joey exclaimed. 'What a neat place ya got here. It's so . . . wow . . . like it's so homy. I love it!'

A nerve twitched beneath Winifred Andrews' left eye. She was an austere looking woman with grey hair and a pious expression. Her husband, Willis, was so drab and downtrodden it was possible to be in the same room and not even realize that he was present.

Joey had done exactly that. She had concentrated all of her energies on Mrs. Andrews, determined to be liked. 'Where's Mr. A?' she asked coyly. 'Is he as good lookin' as my Dekey?'

Winifred turned and glared at Deke, still hovering in the doorway. 'Introduce your . . . friend . . . to father.'

Reluctantly he entered the room and awkwardly performed the introduction.

'Ooooh, Mr. A. I never saw ya sittin' there,' Joey oozed pertness. 'Wow! You're a looker too! Can I lay a kiss on ya?'

She didn't wait for an answer, but bussed the colourless little man on both cheeks.

Willis shot a nervous look at his wife.

'Sit down,' Winifred said, her voice freezing 'It's Josephine, isn't it?'

'Yeah,' Joey replied. 'But my pals call me Joey. Like it's a nick-name, y'know?' She plumped herself down on a narrow brown sofa and beckoned Deke to sit next to her.

He did so reluctantly.

Silence.

Winifred broke it. 'You are very late, Deke. Why is that?'

'I told him we was late,' scolded Joey. 'I kept on telling the dumbo but he wouldn't listen to me.'

Deke was listening now. How dare she call him names in front of his mother. How dare she.

Winifred said, 'It's no good telling Deke anything. He never listens, just goes his own way, the wrong way, without a thought or feeling for anyone else.'

Joey nodded understandingly.

Winifred gave a long-suffering sigh. 'We've done everything for him. Sacrificed ourselves beyond reproach. Did he tell you that I nearly died giving birth to him?'

Joey shook spiky locks.

'Of course he didn't tell you,' Winifred continued. 'Why should he consider it important? It was I who almost died, not he.'

'Gee, that's a bummer,' interjected Joey, delighted at the way Mrs. Andrews was confiding in her.

'You might think that after what I went through I would have borne a considerate son, a boy who cared about his mother. But no. Deke has caused me nothing but pain and worry. He has . . .'

Deke could hear his mother's harsh accusing words pouring from her thin tight lips. He had heard them so many times before . . . All of his life . . .

Useless . . . good-for-nothing . . . weak . . . uncaring . . .

Joey was hanging on to every morsel, jammy lips parted, squiffy eye darting this way and that. She was nodding in agreement. SHE WAS SIDING WITH HIS MOTHER.

He felt horribly betrayed. They were making him nothing. Only, with Joey, he had been a big man. Her Cowboy, her Lover . . . HAD THE WHORE BEEN LYING TO HIM?

Very slowly rage began to envelop him. He would not allow his mother to destroy what he and Joey had.

Abruptly he stood up. 'We're going to be married,' he said.

Willis Andrews scuttled over to the television and switched it on as if his very action would avert the argument to come.

Winifred looked at Deke as one would regard a putrefying body.

Joey clapped her hands together like a child with a new toy. Then she said the wrong thing. 'Y'see Mrs. A. When we're married I'll straighten Dekey out. You an' I – we'll get him together.' She giggled inanely. 'We'll have him cut off that gross hair, an' buy some decent clothes.' Her eyes were shining. 'Mrs. A. I promise I'll make you a terrific daughter. You'll love me.' Hope oozed from every pore. 'Really y'will.'

Winifred Andrews gazed first at Joey then at Deke.

'Is this what you want, son?' she asked in disbelief. 'This . . . this . . . tramp?'

Joey's face clouded over.

Willis Andrews stared at the television.

'Yes,' said Deke.

Her thin lip curled. 'Did I hear you say yes?'

'She loves me and I want her.'

'Loves you. How could anyone love you?'

His head began to throb. 'She does.'

'Have you ever looked at her. She's trash.'

'Hey –' Joey began, but neither of them took any notice.

'She's kind to me . . . nice . . .'

'She's poor street trash. And still she's too good for you. Any woman is too good for you – you know that, don't you?'

Joey shrank into the old brown sofa, somewhere she must have overplayed her hand. Best to shut up until she could steer things back onto the right track.

Winifred continued to debase her son, her voice rigid and unbending as she heaped abuse upon him.

All of his life he had taken it. And never once defended himself or answered back. Even when they made him sell his car – his pride and joy. But with Joey sitting there, listening . . .

'I hate you,' he suddenly screamed. 'I wish you had died when you had me. I wish you'd fucking DIED. You've ruined my life.'

Winifred was stunned into only a brief moment of silence.

'You ungrateful parasite,' she seethed. 'Gutter language from gutter filth. We took you from nothing. Gave you a home and food and clothing. Even though you were not of our flesh. Your mother did not want you –'

'Winifred,' objected Willis.

'Be quiet,' she blazed. 'It's time he knew the truth.'

Deke shook his head. What was she talking about . . . he was confused . . .

'We bought you,' she said, her dull eyes almost alive. 'Like you would buy a dog. We chose you – the pick of the litter. Ha! Some pick.'

'What are you talking about –' he whined pitifully.

'One hundred and fifty dollars. A lot of money then.' Her face glowed triumphantly as though she had experienced some glorious relief. 'What do you have to say about that?'

He trembled. 'You're lying.'

'I am not.'

He yelled, 'Liar!'

'I am not,' she repeated stubbornly. She crossed the room to the desk she always kept locked and opened it. The only noise in the room came from the television set. Willis Andrews placed his head in his hands and mumbled incoherently.

Joey sat transfixed. What a bad trip this had turned out to be. Some loving family to welcome her with open arms.

Winifred produced a piece of paper and thrust it at him.

'Here,' she said. 'This is the name and address of the woman we bought you from in Barstow, California. A baby broker. God knows where she found the likes of you . . .'

He thought he was dying. His life flashed before him like a film. The beatings, the humiliations, the constant torture of being told he was no good . . .

And the guilt . . .

I NEARLY DIED HAVING YOU. YOU COULD'VE KILLED ME WHEN YOU WERE BORN.

All of his life the guilt.

For nothing?

She wasn't his real mother. Oh Lord no she wasn't . . .

The throbbing in his head, the haze around his eyes. He felt choked with frustration and fury.

Winifred Andrews. Stranger. Began to laugh mirthlessly.

IT'S NOT SO BAD . . . IT'S NOT SO BAD . . .

Joey joined in. A nervous reaction.

YES. IT IS BAD. YES. I MUST DO SOMETHING.

Willis laughed too. Or was he crying? No matter.

Three pigs. Three laughing faces. Teeth and eyes and hair. Three pigs.

The information was there in the file among the yellowed letters of complaint. Dry rot. Damp. Mice infestation. Mrs. Nita Carrolle had lived in the house from 1956 to 1973 whereupon she had moved to Las Vegas. Her forwarding address was typed neatly on a tattered white card.

Mrs. Nita Carrolle.

He hoped she was still alive. He desired the pleasure of killing her after he had found out the information he needed to survive.

47

Friday lunch at Ma Maison. Enter Gina Germaine. Every eye in the restaurant turned to stare. Silence. Only for a second. Then normal business resumed.

Gina joined Oliver Easterne at his regular table and spat venom. 'What *the fuck* are they looking at?'

'You, of course,' replied Oliver, dabbing at a mark on the table-cloth. 'You should be used to it by now. How many years have you been in the movies?'

'Long enough to know that in this restaurant – on a Friday – at lunchtime, *no*body stares. Racquel Welch could walk in naked and they wouldn't bat an eyelid.' Her eyes popped alarmingly. 'Everyone knows, Oliver, don't they? The word is out.'

He patted her hand reassuringly, and wondered how she could possibly think that she and Neil being rushed to the hospital – locked in combat so to speak – could be kept a secret. Everyone *was* talking. Big deal. If she was smart she would just brazen it out and enjoy the notoriety.

A week had passed. Neil Gray still languished in the hospital. The prognosis was not good. Oliver had not been idle. He wasn't about to let the film go down the drain just because Neil was out of action. Conveniently he had forgotten about the girl at the beach and reconsidered using Gina. A few discreet meetings had shown him the viability of the film starring George Lancaster *and* Gina Germaine. The two of them together spelled money in the bank. He had been offered a record breaking cable deal if he could deliver the goods. And that's just what he intended to do.

If Neil and Montana didn't like it – fuck 'em. They were hardly in a position to fight.

Gina summoned a waiter and ordered a Bloody Mary. She wore a white strapless dress which emphasized her magnificent breasts. Oliver did not find them magnificent at all, he found them disgusting. But as a showman he knew that you must give the public what they wanted, and one thing about Gina – the unwashed masses loved her and she was big big box office.

'Why the lunch, Oliver?' she asked pointedly.

'I'm reconsidering on you playing Nikki.'

'Oh!' She gave a little gasp. 'You are?'

'I always liked the idea, but Neil and Montana didn't think you were right. Frankly, I think you could do it.'

She purred softly. 'I always said you were a smart son of a bitch. Whenever anyone put you down I *always* stood up for you.' She fluttered long false eyelashes, and squeezed his hand. 'I'm very fond of you, Oliver.'

He quickly removed his hand. 'Thank you.'

'I mean it.'

'I'm sure you do.'

She fluffed out candy-floss white hair and lowered cornflower blue eyes. 'I'm really embarrassed about the other night. The whole thing was so . . . degrading.'

'Don't worry about it,' he consoled. 'Just think of your future.'

'Yes. I must.' She looked determined. 'The thing is I'm always so concerned about *other* people. For once in my life I must think about myself.' Deep sincerity entered her voice. 'I want to do *Street People* very much, but when will it start shooting? With Neil in the hospital and all . . .' she trailed off. 'What are your plans?'

He cleared his throat, waved at a few people. 'Well, Gina,' he began. 'Business is business, and as bad as I feel about Neil's . . . er . . . unfortunate illness . . . the show must go on as someone once said. I've got . . . ideas. Another director, maybe. Don't worry, just imagine the marquee.'

'Gina Germaine and George Lancaster,' she giggled.

Silently Oliver said it his way.

AN OLIVER EASTERNE FILM
AN OLIVER EASTERNE PRODUCTION
GEORGE LANCASTER AND GINA GERMAINE IN
STREET PEOPLE

'Right,' he said. 'I'll call Sadie after lunch.'

'What are you doing later? Why don't you come by my house for a drinkie?'

He shuddered. The very thought of going to bed with Gina gave him the horrors. 'I'll take you up on that invitation another time,' he said smoothly.

'Bet on it,' she flirted.

'I certainly will.'

Elaine's attempts to get Ross back under the marital roof were fruitless. First it took her two days to find him, and when she did track him down to the Beverly Hills Hotel he refused to return her calls.

She could not believe her stupidity in throwing him out. The big question was how to get him back without causing a public scene. That was the trouble with Beverly Hills, everyone knew your business.

The house looked like a flower shop. Yellow roses from Pamela and George – somewhat faded now. Orchids from Bibi and Adam. Tulips, lilies, palms and yucca plants . . . A never ending delivery of exotic blooms with short notes thanking the *wonderful* Contis for a *wonderful* party. Flower Fashions must have had a field day. Normally Elaine would have been thrilled. But without Ross she felt disoriented and empty. She had no one to talk to. Only Maralee, who was more interested in keeping her ridiculous vigil at the hospital.

'You're divorced from Neil,' Elaine had pointed out firmly.

'It makes no difference now,' Maralee had replied tearfully. 'I still love him and I want him to know that.'

Randy had been cast by the wayside and Maralee refused to talk about him. Occasionally Elaine stopped by the hospital to keep her company. But she didn't feel comfortable, especially when Montana appeared and strode around like she owned the place.

The bills were piling up. She stacked them by the front door ready to send on to Ross's business manager. Cash was running low, and she wondered what she was supposed to do about *that*. Not that she needed much, everything went on Visa or American Express. But Lina required cash, and it would be too embarrassing to admit to the maid that she had no money.

Oh, Ross. Why did you do it?

He didn't. You did.

A week after Ross's departure Ron Gordino turned up at her front door carrying a large hanging plant.

'Thought you might find a place for this,' he drawled.

Her eyes were drawn to the crotch of his jogging pants where his maleness made an impossible lump.

'Thank you,' she murmured. He looked better during the day than at night.

He hovered on her doorstep reluctant to leave, until finally she invited him in for a glass of iced tea. It was midday and Lina glared suspiciously as they sat out by the pool.

'Why haven't you . . . um . . . been in to see me?' Ron asked. 'You gotta keep in shape, Elaine. The body goes . . . everything else follows. Are you taking your vitamins?'

She nodded, quite touched by his concern. At least he *cared*.

'There's a rumour goin' around that you and . . . um . . . Ross have taken the road to splitsville.'

'Who told you that?'

'It's talk.'

'We're just taking a breathing space.'

'You look tense.'

'I'm fine.'

'You look like you need an . . . um . . . massage.'

'Not today, Ron.'

'Why not?'

'I'm not in the mood.'

He leaned across and lazily dug his thumbs into the base of her neck. 'One tense lady,' he drawled. 'You'll get facial lines.'

She sighed wearily. 'I've got facial lines.'

'Lie down.'

'I can't.'

'Why?'

She thought of Lina inside the house. 'It's impossible.'

'No sex, Elaine,' Ron drawled. 'I just want to . . . um . . . help you. You need it.'

Was she going to run her life for some Mexican maid. She *did* need it.

She led him into her bedroom and locked the door. Then she stripped down to her bra and panties and lay face down on the bed.

He went to work immediately – unkinking, smoothing, talented fingers relaxing her body.

'Turn over,' he instructed.

'No sex,' she protested weakly.

'Wouldn't . . . um . . . think of it, Elaine.'

He began to massage her feet, a sensation she particularly liked.

349

Then slowly he started up her leg – the ankle, the calf, the thigh. The inside of her thigh. Firm fingers kneading, massaging . . . Firm fingers pulling away the crotch of her panties and entering her with an authority she did not care to fight.

Oh, Ross. Come home now, all is forgiven.

Ohhhhh . . .

For one week Ross did not screw around. The Neil Gray-Gina Germaine incident had scared the shit out of him. Yes, sure, all macho men boasted about how they wouldn't mind going in the saddle. But the reality. Jesus H. Christ. Forget it. He couldn't imagine anything worse. And what kind of a snatch did Gina Germaine have anyway? A honeyed trap that no right thinking man would ever go near again. How fortunate that he had never met her. With *his* schlong it would have been trouble all the way.

Getting laid, for the moment, was out. Getting Sadie became a much more important item on his agenda.

He met with her at her office. She was ruthlessly businesslike. She kept her gay assistant in the room at all times, and went over his career with an acid tongue.

'You've made plenty of mistakes,' she said coolly.

Tell me about 'em.

Their meeting lasted an hour, and then she dismissed him with a brisk, 'I'm going to think about what we can do for you. No point in taking you on if we don't feel we can give you our best.'

He felt like a struggling starlet. Not that starlets struggled, they merely lay back, opened their legs, and welcomed America.

Hotel life was okay. Television. Room service. Monitored calls. No one to bug you. An occasional stroll around the pool. A random lunch in the coffee shop. A pre-dinner drink in the Polo Lounge.

He ignored Elaine's calls deciding to let her suffer a little. Elaine was no fool. She knew the score. Married to him she was a somebody – however much he had slipped. Without him she was a nobody. Beverly Hills law whether she liked it or not. Now, if she had a lot of money – which she didn't. Or maybe power – which she didn't – things might have been different. All she had was him, and she wouldn't be slow to realize it.

When Sadie didn't call he phoned her. 'Miz La Salle will get back to you as soon as possible,' was the response.

Miz La Salle took her time. In fact, four days later he called again and Miz La Salle finally saw fit to come to the phone.

'Sorry, Ross,' she said in that same businesslike tone as if the night of the party had never happened. 'It's been one of those weeks.'

'I've left Elaine,' he announced.

She didn't take a beat. 'I hope you have a good lawyer. Your alimony payments must be murder.'

He was aggravated by her lack of concern. 'I thought you were going to call.'

'I just told you – it's been one bitch of a week.'

'Yes I know. But it's important that you tell me. Are we a team again or not?'

Deliberately she paused far too long. Then she said, 'I'm going to Palm Springs this weekend. Maybe you'd like to meet me there and we can discuss it.'

He was perplexed. He knew a game when he saw one – he had played enough in his time. 'What about dinner tonight?' he countered.

'Love to, but I've got a screening.'

'Tomorrow night?'

'I'm afraid it's this weekend or nothing.' She paused, savouring the moment. 'What's the matter? Don't you *want* to spend the weekend with me?'

He had planned the seduction of Sadie. But on *his* terms. Now *she* was calling the shots.

'There's nothing I'd like better,' he said, attempting to change the course of things. 'In fact I'll pick you up and drive you there.'

'I'd love that,' she sighed wistfully. 'But I have other arrangements. I'll give you the address and why don't you just turn up around five on Saturday.'

He accepted her terms. Once he got her into the sack things would be different.

Guilt twisted Montana. And yet she knew that she had no reason to feel guilty. She stared at Neil in his hospital bed, still in intensive care, and she wanted to scream – 'It's your own fault.' But of course she didn't.

She passed the week in a daze, moving into a nearby room to be as close to him as possible. He lay like a stone, pale and wasted, as though the life had already drained from his body. There were tubes and drips and monitors to keep him alive. He couldn't speak, but she sensed that he knew exactly what was going on.

The doctor – whom she had christened Mister Gucci on account of

351

his label mania – said he was pleased with Neil's progress.

What progress? She wanted to get another opinion, but on checking out Mr. Gucci she found he had an excellent reputation.

Maralee was always there, blonde and tearful. Montana decided that she wasn't the bitch Neil had portrayed her as.

Oliver Easterne put in an occasional appearance, usually accompanied by several golfers. Speculation in the trades was rife about *Street People*, but Montana didn't even bother to read them.

One day Oliver cornered her and said, 'We should talk about the film.'

She couldn't believe that he wanted to discuss business at a time like this and she told him so.

'Don't be naive,' he snapped. 'I got commitments to fulfil. The delay is costing.'

'What do you intend to do?' she asked sarcastically. 'Make the movie without Neil?'

'Yes,' he snapped. 'And I got a lawyer says I have every right to do so – check out the sickness clause in his contract.'

She was outraged. 'You wouldn't do it.'

'Watch me. When it comes to a buck I'll do anything.'

Sadie La Salle issued orders. 'I am arranging a photo session for you, Buddy, with one of the best photographers on the coast, and I want you to look your absolute best. So, until you hear from me – plenty of early nights and sun. Can you manage that?'

He could manage a naked flash down Sunset Boulevard if that's what she wanted.

'Are you into drugs?' she asked crisply. 'Have you ever done porno? Nude photos? *Anything* I should know about before we get started? I don't want your past suddenly catching up with you – so please be truthful.'

He wasn't truthful. Didn't want to blow it before he had even begun. So he became Mister Clean and admitted to nothing except a few puffs of grass on occasion.

'What about family?' she asked. 'Any Billy Carters in the closet?'

He thought about his mother for one bitter moment, then shook his head.

'Are you married? Divorced? Gay? Bi?'

He admitted to being very straight with no marital attachments past or present. Angel would be a surprise. A pleasant one.

They discussed *Street People*, his test, and the fact that Montana Gray had assured him the part was his.

'There are no sure things in this business,' Sadie said. 'Learn that and remember it – however big you become.' She paused. 'Of course I'll talk to Oliver Easterne about you immediately. Although with Neil Gray still in hospital I expect he has other things on his mind. The film will probably be delayed, so let's not narrow our horizons.'

'I'm in your hands,' he shrugged. 'Whatever you think is best for me . . .'

'That's a smart attitude. Try and keep it.'

He left their first meeting truly believing for once that he *could* make it. If Sadie La Salle saw stardom then he hadn't been kidding himself all those years.

First priority was finding somewhere to live. He had money in his pocket – enough at least to settle on something decent for a change. He bought The Hollywood Reporter and checked out the real estate section.

After looking at a few places he settled on a furnished apartment on Wilshire near Westwood. No dump. It was costing, but there was a fully equipped gym in the basement, a large *clean* rooftop pool, and maid service.

He moved in and handed the maid twenty-five bucks to go through all his clothes, wash, mend and take to the cleaners. Twelve hundred bucks, courtesy of Montana Gray, had saved his life, and he resolved to pay it back with his first pay cheque.

A car was not an immediate problem, for Montana had said he could borrow the Volkswagen until she needed it. He tried to phone her at the hospital to tell her how sorry he was to hear about her old man, but she wasn't taking any calls. He left his new number so that she could claim her car when she was ready.

Angel, of course, was in his thoughts constantly. But maybe she would be more of a liability than an asset at this particular time, so he put her to the back of his mind for the moment. Sadie La Salle had said plenty of early nights and sun, so that's what he did, concentrating only on the body beautiful. By the time he presented himself for the photo session he wanted to be in even more sensational shape than ever.

Sadie did not leave him hanging. She called him as soon as she had spoken to Oliver Easterne and said it was as she had thought – no decisions were being made. He felt a twinge of anxiety. Why the hell did Neil Gray have to go and have a heart attack? What kind of timing was that?

'Your photo session is arranged for tomorrow,' she continued, seemingly unconcerned about the delay. 'A limo will collect you at nine o'clock in the morning. Be prepared to work hard.'

She wasn't kidding. At nine o'clock the limo arrived, and sitting in the back was Sadie herself.

He had been concentrating on his tan and his body. He looked in peak condition – like a runner just about to start the race.

'I'm pleased with you,' she said. 'You know how to take direction.'

He grinned. He could do with all the praise he could get. Then he wondered if she was going to come on to him. And hoped desperately that she wasn't.

She would. It was always that way when someone did something for you.

The session went well. Nine solid hours with just a short break for lunch. Seven people totally concentrating on him. A hairdresser, make-up artist, clothes stylist. The photographer, with his two assistants. And Sadie.

She had her say in everything. She conferred with all of them on every set-up. She knew what she wanted, and she didn't care to quit until she felt that they had captured it.

By the end of the day he was burnt out, but exhilarated all the same. If this was a taste of things to come he wanted more.

'When can I see the proofs?' he asked anxiously when Sadie dropped him off.

'Soon. I'll call you,' she promised.

The next day he was summoned to her office. When he entered the inner sanctum she was on the phone and waved for him to sit down.

He could hear a male voice shouting on the other end of the line. Sadie seemed unperturbed, she held the receiver away from her ear and listened patiently.

He glanced around the office. Framed photographs of superstars lined the walls . . . Where would she put *his* photo? Jeez! He could hardly believe all the good things that were happening for him.

'Don't worry, George,' she said soothingly into the phone. 'I'm meeting with Oliver again this evening. I'll have a start date for you without fail.'

More yelling echoed round the office.

'Later, George,' she said firmly. 'Trust me.' She hung up, reached into a silver box and lit up a long thin cigarillo.

'Can I see my photos?' he asked expectantly.

'They're not ready yet.'

'Oh.' He was becoming jittery. Why had she sent for him? Was it good news or bad?

She gazed at him speculatively. 'Well, Buddy, *Street People* is definitely yours. Fifteen thousand a week on a ten week schedule, and best of all your billing will be "introducing Buddy Hudson as Vinnie" on one line. The contracts are being typed now.'

He didn't say a word. He just sat there stunned.

'Is that all right with you?'

'Fifteen thousand dollars a week?' he managed.

'Would you prefer roubles?'

'Je . . . sus.'

'I'm glad you're pleased. It's nice to have one satisfied client.'

He didn't know what to say.

'Any other agent would have got you a quarter of that money,' she said bluntly. 'I want you to remember that in the future.'

'I'll never forget it,' he gulped.

'You'd be surprised how quickly you can,' she said succinctly. 'Within a year we'll be talking big bucks for your services and *that*'s the time you're likely to forget who started you off.'

She hadn't exactly started him off – he had Montana to thank for that. But he had no reason to doubt that it was she who had gotten him the big money – and for that he would be forever grateful.

Suddenly questions were falling from his lips. 'When can I get a script? Is Neil Gray directing? When do we start shooting?'

She answered briskly. 'No set date yet. But soon. I have a script being messengered over. Wardrobe will be contacting you later. The P.R. department want a current bio and photos – *don't* mention our photo session, that's very important – it's nothing to do with the movie – let's see it stays that way.' She had not yet told him of her plans to plaster him across America.

'I'm gonna be dynamite,' he said, gathering together his ego. 'I won't let anyone down.'

'I should hope not.'

'I really 'preciate the billing.'

'So you should.'

He stood up and prowled around the office wondering if now was the time to mention Angel.

No. Find her first. Start the movie. *Then* bring her onto the scene.

355

'I'm going to Palm Springs this weekend,' Sadie said casually. 'I have a house down there.'

He had known it would come.

'Do you know the Springs at all?' she asked.

Why was there always a price?

'Never been,' he mumbled warily.

'I'd like you to come on Sunday. It's only a short drive. You have a car don't you?'

He saw an escape route. 'It's kind of broken down on me.'

'Sounds like you need a new one. Why don't I arrange an advance for you. I have a very good business manager who will take excellent care of you.' She jotted down a name and number and handed it to him. 'Call him later today. I'll see that he knows who you are.'

'About Palm Springs –' he began.

'It's important that you come, Buddy. I have a surprise for you. Arrive sometime between ten and eleven on Sunday morning.'

He nodded reluctantly, and wondered how much of a star you had to be before you could quit putting out.

Oh shit. He hated the whole deal.

48

Millie had hordes of cousins in Los Angeles. She was happy to see them, and they were delighted by her presence, so when Leon said that he had to go to Barstow for the day on business, she did not object too strenuously.

He set off early in his Hertz rented car, hitting the Hollywood freeway before the early morning traffic.

Millie was enthralled by Hollywood. She loved everything – from sleazy Hollywood Boulevard with its star imprinted sidewalks – to the palm-tree lined streets of Beverly Hills.

Leon hated the place. It was too hot and unsettled. He felt it was a town in which anything could happen and usually did.

Driving along Sunset Boulevard one afternoon they observed a teenage hooker discussing terms with the driver of a sleek silver Mercedes. The girl looked barely fourteen. A baby face and pubescent body in black leather hot pants and a cut-away top. She reminded Leon of Joey and he looked quickly away.

'Did you see that?' Millie had demanded. 'My oh my – little girls soliciting in the streets. Why isn't anybody doing anything about it?'

He knew then that there would never come a time when he could confess about Joey. 'So how come you didn't help her?' Millie would cry indignantly. He would have no reply, just his shame.

Barstow was hot and dusty. He spent the day gathering information about Winifred and Willis Andrews – who came together in holy matrimony and then faded into the woodwork. The only lead was a retired doctor who Leon found from tracking an old medical record at Willis' place of work where *nobody* at all recalled him.

He phoned the doctor who sounded old and bad tempered.

'I don't know if I can help you, I've been retired twenty years.'

'Would you have a case history on Willis Andrews?' Leon asked hopefully.

The old doctor muttered something about having a basement filled with case histories of hundreds of patients.

'Can I come and look through them?' Leon requested. A grunt gave him permission.

The doctor lived an hour out of town, and as Leon drove through the arid desert he thought to himself – What am I doing out here in the middle of nowhere? What has any of this detective crap got to do with Joey Kravetz?

It was dark by the time he found the house. He was sweating and hungry but anxious for any information – however trivial.

A washed out looking woman answered the door.

'Excuse the mess,' she said, bringing him into a comfortable living room. 'But it's not often we get visitors. Da,' she called out, leading him to a basement door. 'That policeman's here.'

'Send him down,' yelled the old man.

Leon descended into the basement, a damp musty room stacked to the ceiling with rusting furniture, cardboard boxes, old bikes, and general junk. In the middle of it all sat the doctor. A gnarled nut of a man with a shock of wild silver hair and piercing grey eyes. Leon reckoned him to be a well preserved eighty at least. He was surrounded by old record books and scattered papers. More than a dozen boxes spilled documents and information onto the cold stone floor. At a glance Leon could see that it would take at least a week to sort through. He held out his hand and introduced himself.

The doctor gave him a bone crusher in return.

357

'How're we doing?' Leon asked.

'Now that's a good question,' said the old man, indicating the confusion.

Leon sighed. 'I don't suppose you remember anything about Willis Andrews?'

The old man chortled. 'Ah that my memory could tell me what I had for breakfast today.'

Three hours later he was riding the freeway back to Los Angeles with a promise from the doctor that he would telephone if he ever located the Andrews file. Not that it was important. He was chasing straws and knew it.

It was four in the morning by the time he got back to the hotel. Millie slept soundly. He climbed into bed beside her and she mumbled but did not surface.

He lay awake for an hour before sleep finally came.

49

Palm Springs and the temperature hitting one hundred and three degrees.

Sadie arrived Saturday at noon with her assistant, Ferdie Cartright. Ferdie had been with her for seven and a half years. He was forty years old, nattily dressed, sharp-tongued and extremely efficient.

The house she owned was on Sand Dunes Road in exclusive Rancho Mirage. Nothing fancy, just somewhere to get away to from time to time, or so Sadie liked to say.

Ferdie was delighted to accompany her, although she had made it quite clear that he was not to stay.

'Your house is divine,' he enthused, darting from room to room wishing he was there as an invited guest rather than just to help Sadie out setting up some surprise for Buddy Hudson. Frankly, Ferdie was somewhat taken aback by Sadie's sudden and all consuming interest in Mr. Hudson. Surely she liked ladies?

At her age wasn't it rather odd to switch?

In her position wasn't it rather crass to pick a young out-of-work actor?

Granted Buddy Hudson *was* gorgeous. But Hollywood was crammed with gorgeous.

He wondered if they had done the dirty deed yet – or if this weekend was to be the consummation. 'Ferdie,' Sadie called sharply. 'I appreciate the fact that you love my house. But do you think you can unload the car?'

He obliged. She was certainly going to a lot of trouble for Buddy Hudson. He sniffed disapprovingly, and hoped that she found him worth it. Although in his humble opinion the pretty ones were always a *vast* disappointment between the sheets.

Montana had always allowed Neil to take care of business. They shared a New York lawyer who was excellent at what he did, getting Neil top dollar and taking care of her interests adequately. She didn't know him well – a few business meetings, one dinner. After her conversation with Oliver she rushed straight to the phone. He was suitably sympathetic, made all the right noises, but then said something which stunned her. 'Of course, you must realize that Oliver Easterne owns the script of *Street People*. If Neil is unable to keep to the terms of the contract . . . well . . .'

She hung up the phone, furious. Paced around the room she was camping out in at the hospital and seethed. There had to be an answer . . . Oliver couldn't be allowed to do what he liked with her property. Correction. *His* property. She had sold it to the jerk.

Yes. But what about total control? What about the overall deal?

There was an answer, and it occurred to her slowly. Why couldn't *she* direct the film? Take over until Neil regained his health.

She shivered with anticipation. It was a far better idea than bringing in a new director, and if Oliver wanted to stick to the original schedule, she was ready. Nobody knew the property better than she did.

But could she do it?

Sure she could. It was something she'd been working towards all along. It wasn't her fault that Neil had suffered a heart attack and presented her with this perfect opportunity. Besides, she wouldn't be stabbing him in the back. When he recovered he would be able to just walk in and take over. Fired with enthusiasm she called Oliver and demanded a meeting. He agreed to lunch the next day in the Polo Lounge.

That evening Neil took a turn for the better and she knew immediately that she had made the right decision.

*

Surrounded by an abundance of greenery Elaine felt nothing but lonely. She had not realized quite how much her day to day existence depended on Ross. Oh sure she nagged and screamed at him, but he was the very centre of her life – like a spoiled only child. Everything she did was in some way connected to him. Excluding Ron Gordino of course. Whom she hated. With his hometown drawl. And sneaky fingers. And long thin cock.

She had been separated from Ross only three times during ten years of marriage. And they were enforced separations because he was on location and she had spent the entire time he was away doing things for him. Everything she did was for him – whether it was buying a new dress or having her legs waxed.

Realization hit hard. She actually loved the lazy, two-timing thoughtless son of a bitch.

She went to her shrink and told him.

'I know, Elaine,' he said smugly. 'That's what I've always tried to tell you.'

The phone stopped ringing as soon as the Beverly Hills grapevine went into action. Single women were not welcome at screenings and dinners and parties – not unless they were rich and famous in their own right. Elaine, on her own, posed a threat. One of the husbands might get itchy balls – and Elaine, in her position, was hardly likely to say no.

She discovered that she had no friends. Only fair weather acquaintances.

There was Maralee of course. Saint Maralee as the show biz community had bitchily named her since her vigil at Neil's bedside.

Then there was Karen.

Screw Karen and her outsize nipples. Elaine *hated* her with a passion. She only hoped, indeed prayed, that Ross was no longer seeing the bitch.

During the week Ron Gordino appeared at her front door again – this time with a loaf of whole grain bread and some farm fresh brown eggs.

She hid in her bedroom and told Lina to say she was out.

He gazed at her blue Mercedes parked in the drive, then finally ambled off and climbed into the ridiculous jeep he drove.

She began to drink. Never before noon. But white wine at lunchtime helped, and then maybe a tiny shot of vodka to see her through the afternoon. After six o'clock, with Lina safely out of the way, she consumed more wine, a vodka or two, and several rich liqueurs before sleep saved her.

Sometimes she forgot to eat. Soon she was a wreck.

On Saturday Ross had the Corniche washed and waxed. While this was being done he settled himself on a chaise out by the hotel pool and watched the world and the tourists go by. Several acquaintances waved in his direction, but nobody bothered him.

Understandable. He wasn't hot enough to be bothered. He wasn't even luke warm.

Idly he observed a blonde hooker doing her number on an out of town schmuck dripping with sweat and gold chains.

The blonde teetered past the man's cabana several times until he could not help but notice her. She was wearing a string bikini, spindle heeled white sandals, with every inch of her skinny body lubricated by a rich dark oil.

'Hello,' she cooed eventually. 'Do you mind if I glance at your copy of Variety?'

'Get lost, girlie,' the man said, not such an out of town schmuck after all.

'Excuse *me*,' snapped the hooker, and looked around for other prospects. She spied Ross watching her and threw him a tentative smile. He turned onto his stomach and pretended not to notice.

He must have fallen asleep in the hot sun, for the next thing he knew someone was dripping cold water on his back, and the unmistakable husky tones of Karen Lancaster were saying – 'You lousy bum. Walk out on your wife and I have to read about it in the trades. Charming!'

He groaned and turned over. 'What are you doing here?'

'I'm having lunch with daddy and Pamela. More to the point – what are *you* doing here?'

'I'm living here.'

'Nice of you to tell me.'

'I'm telling you now.'

'Big fucking deal,' she pouted. 'The least you could have done is call me. I mean correct me if I'm wrong, but I thought we had something special going.'

'You told Elaine about us.'

'I did not,' she objected strenuously. 'How can you even *think* that?'

'*Somebody* told her.'

'It wasn't me. She called looking for you the day of your party and I just acted amazed.'

'Maybe your acting's not so hot.'

'What's the big deal anyway? You were all set to leave her – so don't make her finding out about me an excuse.' She removed her mirrored shades and glared at him. 'Why did you move in here when you could have come straight to me?'

He could not think of a suitable reply. Karen Lancaster had no claims on him.

He was saved by the appearance of George Lancaster, Pamela London, and assorted entourage making their way to the Lancaster cabana where tables were set up for lunch.

'Ross!' boomed George.

'Ross!' echoed Pamela.

He should have known better. The pool at the Beverly Hills Hotel was hardly the place to come for a quiet sunbathe.

'Join us for lunch,' trilled Pamela, her angular body alive in an animal print muu-muu.

'Yes,' insisted George, resplendent in a white safari suit.

'I'd like that too,' husked Karen, replacing her mirrored shades.

It was just past twelve-thirty and he didn't have to be in Palm Springs until five. If he left by two it would give him more than enough time to make the drive. 'Why not?' he said, getting up and putting on his shirt.

Pamela linked her arm through his. 'I'm *so* sorry about you and Elaine,' she gushed warmly. 'But these things do happen.' She laughed hoarsely. 'I should know, I've had enough husbands!'

Saturday was always the busiest day. Koko rushed around like a madman organizing 'his ladies' as he liked to refer to the various females who frequented the salon. Raymondo leered and flirted as usual. Angel answered the phone, juggled appointments, phoned out for snacks, and generally organized everything.

'I don't know how I ever managed without you,' sighed Koko. 'Darlene was such a witch, getting her to order a tuna sandwich was like persuading Nancy Reagan to wear off the rack!'

Angel smiled wanly. Since the party she had not been feeling her best. She was not sleeping properly, and every morning she felt exhausted and sick.

Koko looked at her shrewdly. 'Are you feeling all right?'

Her beautiful eyes filled with tears. 'I'm fine.'

'Fine!' he scoffed. 'With a face on you like the end of the world.'

She dissolved into tears. 'I'm just so mixed up.'

The telephone rang. A frantic woman, hair in rollers, rushed up to the desk and yelled. 'Order me a taxi, I'm already ten minutes late.'

Raymondo screamed from the back of the salon, 'Next bitch pleeeaze!'

Koko enveloped Angel in a comforting hug. 'Your timing is off, lovely. Why don't we save the breakdown for this evening. Dinner at my house, and we'll play the truth game. Yes?'

'Yes,' she sobbed gratefully, realizing how much she needed to confide in someone. 'I'd like that very much.'

While Ross lunched out by the pool with the Lancasters, Oliver Easterne and Montana Gray respectively picked at their food in the Polo Lounge.

Oliver toyed with an omelette. Montana took random stabs at a spinach salad.

Both were busy with their own thoughts while trying to carry on a civilized conversation. Both hated each other. Both needed each other. Montana had realized it the day before. Oliver was only just beginning to accept the fact – thanks to Montana's persuasive dialogue. Relentlessly she carried on about how she was the only possible choice to direct the film until Neil was well enough to take over.

At first he had laughed in her face. What did she think he was – a crazy man? But as she set forth her case so she made sense.

She knew the property better than anyone.

She knew Neil's hand picked crew better than anyone.

She had cast the picture with the exception of George and Gina (he hadn't told her about Gina yet. He was saving that little morsel for dessert). She had discovered Buddy Hudson – who according to Sadie was going to be hotter than shit.

She had directed a movie before – true it was only a low-budget short – but she *had* won an award for it.

Best of all – she wanted it so much she would probably work for nothing. And of the three directors Oliver had already approached, two of them were asking for an arm and a leg – and the third his balls.

Montana directing the movie was not such a bad idea at all.

Of course he hadn't told her that. He was enjoying the fact that she was actually treating him with a little respect for a change. He would like to think that she was crawling – but she wasn't – not yet.

'I don't know . . .' he stalled. 'You're inexperienced. I doubt if George would accept you. My investors would probably laugh me out the door if I even suggested you.' He played his trump card. 'If *you* call me an asshole I can imagine what *they* would call me.'

She regarded him coolly through black tinted reading glasses. 'I apologize, Oliver. Sometimes I say things I should only think.'

'What's in Palm Springs that we should know about?' thundered George.

'It's just business,' Ross said, excusing himself from a dull lunch.

'I bet!' muttered Karen furiously.

'The only business *I* ever did in Palm Springs was with a golf ball or a tootsie,' leered George.

Ross smiled politely.

'You must visit us,' Pamela said loudly. 'If George's stupid movie doesn't start soon we're going home and good riddance to lotus land. This place is an absolute bore. Your party was the most fun.'

Ross felt a tingle, and it wasn't Karen's hand which had been grabbing at his balls under the table throughout lunch. 'Really?'

'Yes. I should call your wife. Nice woman.' She laughed, horse teeth flashing. 'Although I'm sure *you* don't think so.'

'When *does* the movie go?' he asked casually, standing up from the table.

'God knows. That peculiar Easterne man keeps on telling us yesterday. He's muttering about having to find a suitable director. I've told George, if it's not soon we're off.'

'When will you be back, Ross?' Karen asked tightly.

He wondered what Sadie had planned. Two days in bed, perhaps three. 'Tuesday or Wednesday.'

'Where are you staying?'

'My God, Karen, dear – you sound like the poor man's wife,' trilled Pamela.

Karen glared at her, while Ross exited fast. He strode briskly towards the hotel almost missing Oliver Easterne on his way out to the pool.

'Oliver!' he exclaimed, just in time. 'How are you?'

Can't the dumb schmuck see I'm the only actor for his lousy movie?

'Hi, Ross. How's it going?'

God save me from has-been movie stars in madras shorts.

'Great. Never felt better.'

Look at me. I look sensational. All I need is your frigging movie and I'm a star again.

'Good, good. See you around.'

They went their separate ways. Ross to prepare himself for Palm Springs and Sadie. Oliver to seek out his star and placate him.

Sadie dressed carefully, finally deciding that a white satin peignoir was perfectly suitable for what she had in mind.

It was a quarter to five, and she hoped that Ross would arrive on time. It was unlikely. Ross Conti had never been punctual in his life.

She peered at herself in the mirror and as usual was disappointed with what she saw. She had done her best, but nothing could ever change the fact that she was a plain looking woman, although she did have lovely eyes and thick glossy hair.

She switched on the stereo, placing a record on the turntable that had always been one of Ross's favourites. Stan Getz. Bossa Nova. Oh, the times they had danced around the room, laughing, joking, planning their future together . . .

Ross. She was going to have him again after twenty-six years. She felt the excitement between her legs and leaned her forehead against the coolness of the mirror.

What if she couldn't carry through her plan? What if she got caught up in the heat of the man . . . And Ross had so much heat . . .

She turned the music louder, checked the champagne chilling in a silver ice bucket, and waited for him to arrive.

Koko had never invited Angel to his house before. Sometimes after work he dropped her home, and occasionally he came in and chatted for a while, but she really didn't know that much about him.

She was surprised to discover that he did not live alone in the small stylish house he took her to in the Hollywood Hills. He introduced her to his friend, Adrian – a handsome man in his early thirties. Adrian did not rise to greet her, and for a moment she thought that he might be mad at Koko for bringing her there. But he seemed quite friendly and made polite conversation while Koko busied himself in the kitchen fixing *linguini al pesto*. It was not until dinner was ready, and Koko matter-of-factly transferred Adrian into a wheelchair, that she realized he was a paraplegic.

Adrian felt her stare and said, 'Vietnam,' without elaborating.

The *linguini* was delicious. So was the lemon mousse which followed.

'Koko's a whizz in the kitchen,' Adrian said, looking at his friend warmly.

'You're hardly in a position to object,' Koko retorted.

The two men's eyes met for a moment and Angel felt the love that flowed between them. She immediately thought of Buddy and how it had once been. Her eyes filled with tears.

'Now, now dreamheart,' Koko soothed. 'Don't go getting maudlin on us. I'll clear away the dishes and then we'll talk.'

Adrian discreetly vanished into the bedroom after dinner.

'He gets tired,' Koko explained.

'It's so awful . . .' she whispered.

'It's not awful at all,' he said sharply. 'It's life. And if Adrian can accept it then I don't know why the rest of us can't. Being paralysed is not a disease you know.' He shook his head angrily.

'I'm sorry,' she said.

He sighed. 'Don't be. It's just that it is . . . awful. But I can't allow myself to think that way.' He took a deep breath. 'Now, let's talk about you. That *is* why you're here, isn't it?'

She felt such a need to confide in Koko. He was warm, and kind, and somehow she knew her secrets would be safe with him. For a moment she hesitated.

'Come along, sweet girl, begin at the beginning,' he encouraged.

She started off tentatively, telling him about Louisville, her foster home, the way her surrogate family had treated her. Then winning the contest in the magazine, coming to Hollywood and all her hopes and dreams.

He listened without interruption as she told him about Daphne, Hawaii, and finally Buddy. Her face became alive and her eyes sparkled as she spoke of him.

'He's so marvellous, Koko.' Quickly she corrected herself. 'I mean he *was* so marvellous . . .'

She told him about the borrowed apartment, getting pregnant, shortage of money, then of Jason Swankle and the beach house.

He raised a cynical eyebrow when he heard of Buddy's shopping spree with Jason.

'When we left the beach nothing was right anymore,' she continued sadly. 'Randy and Shelly and the drugs . . . Buddy seemed like a different person . . . so one morning I just left . . . that was the day I came into the salon and met you.'

366

'And you haven't been in touch with him since?'

'Only sort of . . .' She mentioned the phone call with Shelly and the awful things Shelly had said. Then she finished off with the Contis' party and shrugged helplessly. 'I just don't know what to do anymore. Should I forget about Buddy? I mean it's silly to think about him all the time if he doesn't even care . . .' She began to cry.

Koko reached for her and rocked her back and forth in his arms. 'My poor baby,' he soothed. 'A regular modern day Cinders – and for God's sake don't say who!'

She loved the warmth of his arms, the softness of his sweater. Just the feeling of being held was so . . . comforting. He touched her eyes with a Kleenex. 'When you saw Buddy at the party did he *mention* the baby? Ask how you were or anything?'

Miserably she shook her head.

'Legally he has to support you and the child. What we need in the picture is a sharp lawyer.'

'Buddy doesn't have any money.'

'Then he will just have to go out and get himself a job like us ordinary folk,' Koko said matter-of-factly. 'It won't kill him you know.'

Stubbornly she shook her head. 'I don't want anything from him.'

'Now don't be so foolish . . .'

'I mean it.'

He looked perplexed. 'Shall we sleep on it? Tomorrow you might look at things differently.'

'I would *never* take his money.'

'Hmmm . . . In that case we'll just have to find you a rich husband won't we?'

'Koko!'

He put a finger to his lips. 'Don't worry, only joking.'

She managed a small smile. 'I should hope so.'

He gave her a hug. 'There, you're feeling better already, aren't you?'

She nodded. It was true. Somehow she was not alone anymore.

Ross made the drive in record time, flying down the freeway in his golden Corniche like frigging Charlton Heston in 'Ben Hur'. The news that George Lancaster might drop out spurred him on. Sadie was George's agent, she had her finger on the pulse. If George walked she would be the first to know and Ross Conti would be right there – ready and waiting.

He hummed to himself as he searched the parched streets for her address. Palm Springs was hot, and when he stopped at a gas station to ask directions the heat seeped in through the open window of the car like sticky molasses.

'You're Ross Conti,' said the old crone in the gas station as though she was telling him something he didn't already know.

'Yes,' he agreed amiably. 'I am.'

'Didn't like you in that film.'

'What film?'

'"Some Like It Hot".'

'I wasn't in "Some Like It Hot".'

She wagged an accusing finger at him. 'Oh yes you were.' She leaned closer to the window, all rotten teeth and knowing eyes. 'What was Marilyn Monroe *really* like?'

He drove off without replying. Being mistaken for Jack Lemmon or Tony Curtis was a first.

By the time he located Sadie's house it was five-thirty. He pulled into the curved driveway, parked outside the front door and honked the horn a couple of times just to let her know the star had arrived. Then he jumped out, opened up the trunk, and took out his suitcase.

By this time Sadie was at the door.

'Welcome,' she said, holding out a chilled glass of champagne.

He double-taked. She was wearing a night-dress. Talk about pushing the season.

He walked towards her, dumped the suitcase, took the proffered glass, and went to kiss her on the cheek.

She grabbed him in a vice-like embrace and stuck her tongue firmly down his throat nearly choking him.

He came up for air quite shocked. *He* was the one that was supposed to be making the moves.

'Let's go to bed,' she said throatily. 'I've waited long enough.' She clutched his hand and pulled him into the house, kicking the door shut behind him.

This wasn't the Sadie he remembered. She of the huge tits and reticent bed manners. Never once had she come on to him in all the time they were living together. But years had passed . . . and everyone had to grow up . . .

She dragged him into a cool bedroom. The drapes were closed and the hum from the air conditioner was drowned out by Stan Getz on the stereo. He took a quick gulp of champagne – which was fortunate

– because she took the glass away from him and set it down on a night stand.

'I want you now,' she said urgently, ripping at his clothes.

'Hang on a minute . . . wait . . . let me shower at least,' he protested.

'Now,' she said insistently, unbuttoning his shirt, dragging it from his shoulders, and going for his fly.

He knew he was not hard. In fact he knew that his schlong was probably curled up like a frightened rabbit.

'Just a minute,' he complained loudly. 'I can't perform on command.'

She stopped immediately. 'I thought it was what we both wanted,' she said coldly.

'Of course it is. But I just got here. It was a long drive . . . I feel dirty and tired. I don't want it to be like this.'

Christ! He sounded like a woman!

She managed to look disgusted and hurt all at the same time. 'I'm sorry,' she said. 'Perhaps I misunderstood.'

He was sorely confused. At the party she had been reasonably cool. In her office efficiently businesslike. Now this. He just hadn't been expecting her to come on so strong. She had thrown him completely off balance. He felt like a fool.

'Nice house,' he said lamely.

'The bathroom's through there.' She indicated a doorway. 'There's soap and towels, everything you need. Be my guest.'

He slunk into the bathroom feeling like he had done something wrong, but not sure what. He stayed under the shower for a safe ten minutes, hoping that by the time he emerged she would have cooled down.

No such luck. She waited for him on the bed, leaning against the padded headboard smoking a thin black cigarillo and sipping champagne.

He had dressed in his pants and shirt but that did not faze her.

'Come,' she patted the space beside her. 'It's been a long time. I can't help my impatience.'

He approached the bed warily. What did she want from him? He was prepared to give her his body, but couldn't she wait?

'Aren't you going to take your clothes off?' she inquired. Amused man talking to shy virgin.

Again he felt like a fool. He removed his shirt, stepped out of his pants, but kept his jockeys firmly in place covering the Conti jewels.

369

'That's better,' she said, holding out her arms in welcome.

He thought of her fantastic tits . . . they should get him going.

Close your eyes and think of Karen.

Why Karen? The thrill has gone.

Close your eyes anyway, schmuck.

Again she attacked him with her tongue, exploring his teeth, his gums, licking the roof of his mouth with sharp little stabs.

'Remember what you said at your party,' she whispered. 'About how great it was with us? And how it's never been that good for you with anyone else? Remember, Ross?'

Did he really say that?

Her tongue slid into his ear and for the first time he felt a stirring. The smell of her was bringing back warm sticky memories. Musky, womanly . . . Sadie's smell. He breathed deeply. Every woman gave off her own special aroma, and that's what was making him hot.

He reached for her breasts and disappointment flooded his body. They were gone! The best pair in Hollywood were now two hard little mounds, barely a handful.

'What happened to your tits?' he gasped.

'I had them fixed.'

'There was nothing wrong with them!'

'Yes there was.'

'I *loved* your tits.'

'I'm sorry. If I'd known you were coming back twenty-six years later I'd have hung onto them.'

He pressed her nipples, they felt like rubber. 'You made a big mistake,' he groaned.

'For God's sake!' she snapped angrily. 'Are we going to fuck or are we going to hold a funeral service for my tits?' She paused for a moment, then added, 'And I think you should know, Ross, that any man who doesn't wish to be labelled a dumb male chauvenist does not call them tits anymore.'

'Sadie, you've changed.'

'Goddammit! I should hope so.'

Buddy met with the business manager Sadie recommended. The man treated him like a somebody – why not? If he was going to be making fifteen thousand a week he was hardly a nothing anymore. It never occurred to him that this man looked after people who made millions and that he was merely doing Sadie a favour by agreeing to handle his affairs.

'Sadie tells me you need a car,' he said. 'I can get you an excellent deal on a brand new Mustang G.T. Are you interested?'

'I don't have the money . . . yet.'

'That's all right. It's all taken care of. When your cheques start coming through it'll be deducted. Tell me, what do you need in the way of cash for now?'

Sometimes Buddy felt that if he pinched himself he would wake up. It just didn't seem possible that everything was going right for a change. *Everything except Angel . . .*

He picked up the car Saturday afternoon. It was black with leather upholstery, and best of all four speakers and a tape deck. He drove straight to Tower Records where he purchased two hundred dollars worth of tapes. The Stones mostly. A lot of their early stuff. Then he drove around listening to 'Satisfaction', 'Jumpin' Jack Flash' and all the other golden oldies.

He thought about how he was going to find Angel. Obviously she had not run on home as he had hoped.

He frowned. Maybe he should take out an ad in the trades and hope that someone would show it to her. Only trouble was that Sadie would see it.

On Sunday morning he set off for Palm Springs earlier than necessary. The little car went like a pistol, and he arrived in the Springs at nine, an hour too early.

He stopped for breakfast and found that he had lost his appetite. Morosely he stared out of the window. He just wanted the whole scene over and done with.

Sunday morning Sadie awoke before Ross and hurried to the bathroom to repair the damage of the previous night's activity. She looked a mess. Black hair unruly and kinked. Every trace of clever make-up ground into her skin. Circles under her eyes, and the sharp cruel lines of age etched deep.

Her hand shook slightly as she applied fresh eyeshadow. The evening had gone as she had planned – up to a point. She had confused the hell out of Ross with her 'get your pants off' approach. He had been disconcerted and she had enjoyed every minute of his discomfort.

But then . . . eventually . . . he had her. In every way. And things were different. For a while.

She hated herself for being weak. She loathed the fact that he had been able to get to her with his unbeatable sexual prowess.

371

She shivered and wondered if she should still go ahead with her plan. It would be so easy to accept him back into her life. But then she knew what would happen. He would use her for as long as it suited him. And then he would leave her for some vacuous nothing with big boobs and a pretty face.

Ross Conti was not to be trusted. He had to be taught a lesson.

She dressed and returned to the bedroom. He was sprawled across the bed sleeping.

Staring at his slumbering form she realized with a furious pang that she still loved him – whatever love was. There had certainly never been anyone else in her life who made her feel the way he did. *Damn* the power of sex.

Angrily she marched into the kitchen. He was a selfish egotistical bastard. Nothing about him had changed except that he had gotten older.

A final snore. A quick start. And he was awake.

For a moment he was disoriented. Where was he? At home? Karen's? The Beverly Hills Hotel? Then it all came back to him. Sadie. Not so tough after all. A hard exterior. A sharp tongue. But once he gave her a little of his secret recipe . . .

He yawned, and grinned. She may have lost the tits, but she certainly had not lost the enthusiasm. He'd had her moaning and screaming – begging for it just like the old days.

He had always enjoyed getting Sadie into a frenzy. Once, he had taught her the words to use . . . made her say things which caused her to flush beet red all those years ago. She knew the words now – probably better than he did – but last night he had made her repeat every one of them ten times – and the game had made her gasp with long lost pleasure.

He was back in her life. And now they could both concentrate on his career.

A luxurious stretch and he looked forward to the day ahead.

Buddy paid his check and set off.

Maybe he wouldn't do it. Maybe he'd tell her the truth. Maybe she'd cancel out his contract, take back his car, whistle in the advance . . .

Shit! What's a fuck between friends?

Plenty.

Shit!

*

Ross grabbed her from behind, full of early morning confidence. 'Good morning, baby,' he crooned, grinding against her while reaching a hand inside her silk shirt.

She spun around fast, throwing him off. 'For God's sake get dressed. There's nothing that puts me off my breakfast more than a man with no clothes on. You look ridiculous.'

He was stunned. Where was the moaning, gasping, pleading lady of the night?

'Remember me? This is Ross baby.' He went to grab a tit. She slapped his hand away.

'May I suggest that Ross baby goes and gets dressed.'

He was semi-hard, ready to spring into action if necessary.

'I thought an early morning trip down memory lane . . .'

'You thought wrong.'

He hadn't quite figured her out yet. She was certainly doing a Jekyll and Hyde. But he could play games too, and tonight he'd *really* make her beg. He threw up his hands in a gesture of defeat. 'Okay, okay. I never forced a lady yet.' He aimed a kiss at her cheek, but she turned quickly away and he found himself kissing air. Somewhat puzzled he returned to the bedroom and put on his swimming shorts.

Today he wanted to straighten out a few things. One – *Street People*. Two – their relationship.

A little breakfast, a few hours' sun. Perhaps she would be in a better mood later. Right now she was probably feeling guilty because she had enjoyed the sex so much. Some women were like that, especially the older ones.

At exactly ten o'clock Buddy rang the bell of Sadie La Salle's Palm Springs house. He cracked his knuckles impatiently as he waited.

Sadie was in the kitchen. She called out to Ross who was still in the bedroom, 'Can you get the door for me?'

He emerged in a pair of striped madras shorts. 'Are you expecting anyone?'

'Can you get it or not?' she snapped impatiently.

He walked to the front door, threw it open, and came face to face with Buddy.

The two men stared at each other. Buddy recognized Ross Conti immediately and wondered if he had got the wrong house.

Ross recognized Buddy also, although he didn't know his name, he merely remembered him as one of Karen's partners when she was doing her drunken show-off dance at his party. 'Yes?' he said coldly.

He was never particularly friendly towards young good-looking studs
– they reminded him with a vengeance of his lost youth.

'Uh . . . Is this Sadie La Salle's house?'

'Yes.'

'Is she . . . uh . . . home?'

'Why?'

Sadie came up behind Ross, a welcoming smile lighting her
features. 'Buddy! I'm so glad you could make it.' She peered past
him. 'And I see you got your car. Are you pleased?'

'You gotta be kiddin'. It's great.'

'Come on in. Do you know Ross Conti?'

'Uh . . . Mr. Conti, sir. It's a pleasure.' He proffered his hand,
which Ross ignored.

'Ross. This is my new star to be,' Sadie said, savouring the
moment. 'Buddy Hudson. Remember the name, he's going to be big.
He's already been signed for one of the lead roles in *Street People*.'
She grabbed Buddy by the arm and led him inside. 'I have a surprise
for you which I know you're going to love. Ross, come with us. I
think this will also interest you.'

Ross wondered why she hadn't told him she was expecting company. And what was all this – 'my new star to be' crap? And 'Buddy
Hudson. Remember the name, he's going to be big.'

Once she had said the very same words about him. She had always
introduced him that way in the beginning – 'Ross Conti. Remember
the name, he's going to be big.'

He trailed them through the house, not pleased by this latest turn
of events.

She held on to Buddy's arm, a proprietary air about her that really
infuriated Ross. Something was wrong somewhere. It was *he* she
should be hanging on to after last night. He was surprised she could
even *walk* after last night.

They passed a glistening blue swimming pool and arrived outside
the guest house. With a flourish Sadie unlocked the door, sprang the
lights and the three of them entered a large white room, empty apart
from a billboard size poster covering one entire wall. Buddy was
there in living colour. Buddy with his curly black hair, smoky dark
eyes and little else except faded Levi shorts and a bronzed and perfect
body.

It was a sensational photograph. It was the same photograph Ross
had posed for all those years ago with his ruffled blonde hair, deep
blue eyes, and bronzed and perfect body.

Scrawled across the poster in bold red handwriting were the magic words – WHO IS BUDDY HUDSON?

'Je . . . sus!' exclaimed Buddy. 'It's sensational, but what's it for?'

'It's a surefire way to make you a star,' Sadie said. 'That poster will be on billboards from coast to coast.' She turned and looked Ross straight in the eye. 'I did it once before and I can do it again. All it takes is a little manipulation and an appreciative client.' She locked eyes with Ross until she was sure that he had received the message, then she linked arms with Buddy and said, 'Let's drive back to L.A. Palm Springs turned out to be a great big disappointment this weekend – one that I'll never repeat.'

50

Las Vegas welcomed Deke like the eye of the tiger. He drove at night through the black desert, and there suddenly – blazing in the distance – a million sparkling lights. Las Vegas. He had never seen anything like it in his life.

He drove into the city slowly, staring at the casinos, the flashing neon signs, and the people. Like ants they scurried all over the place. In and out, laughing, drunk, some clutching paper cups spilling quarters and silver dollars.

He remembered Atlantic City with Joey. She had loved to gamble, loved to stuff the silver shiny machines as though feeding an army of ravenous sharks.

He should have stopped her. The machines were evil. They ate money. Money was evil. People who played with money were cannibals. Blood sucking evil cannibals. Those people had taken Joey and devoured her.

He cruised around for a while getting the feel of the place, and all the time watching – with cold black expressionless eyes – the ants run in and out of their places of worship. Cannibal ants. Their God was money. They worshipped in the casinos. They had taken Joey as their sacrifice.

He was tired and needed sleep, food, and cold water to cleanse the dirt of living from his body.

A hundred cheap motels beckoned. They offered swimming pools, water beds, closed circuit porno movies, slot machines, and free breakfasts. Joey would have loved Las Vegas.

Sweet Joey. Where was she now? He missed her.

He frowned, unsure for a moment. Then he remembered. She was home with mother. She was safe.

He checked into a motel, but as tired as he was sleep eluded him.

Perhaps there was something he had to do before he was allowed the luxury of rest. After all, he was no ordinary man. He was The Keeper Of The Order. He had certain responsibilities . . . Perhaps there was something . . .

At three in the morning he prowled the downtown streets on foot. He needed sleep. His eyes were raw with the effort of keeping them open. But there *was* something for him to do . . . and he must wait for a sign . . .

The hooker spotted him long before he saw her. He was a weirdo all right with his shaven head and staring eyes, but business was way off and she had to score. Besides, what was weird nowadays? As long as she walked away with the money and he didn't beat up on her what did she care?

She followed him for a while before tapping his shoulder. 'Hiya, Cowboy. Lookin' for a good time?'

He spun around, red ringed eyes wild, and for a split second the hooker contemplated backing off. But then she figured – what the hell – he's only another dumb john.

'Joey?' he questioned.

'Who, me? You gotta be kiddin', I'm *all* woman. Wanna take a walk an' find out? Twenty greens'll buy plenny.'

Deke knew that he must go with her because she was Joey, and she was reaching out for his help. She had called him Cowboy. That was the signal.

He fumbled in the pocket of his shirt for money and counted out sixteen dollars in single bills.

'That all y'got?' she asked in disgust. Then she grabbed his arm in case he changed his mind. 'It'll do, I suppose,' she said as she hurried him down the street.

He went with her willingly.

A five minute walk took them away from the bright lights and into deserted dimly lit streets. She pulled him into a doorway and fiddled with the belt of her skirt. The material parted. She was naked underneath. Casually she leaned back against the wall and spread her legs.

'Seein' as ya can't quite reach twenny it's gonna have to be standin' up.'

She reached for his zipper.

He reached for his knife.

She was quicker than he was. She had him out of his pants before he knew it, and began to fondle him expertly.

He froze, the knife in his hand unmoving.

After a few seconds she said, 'Come on,' her voice an impatient complaint.

He did not move. Somewhere in the night a woman yelled drunken insults.

More manipulation. Then her voice again, 'Wassa*matter* with you? Got problems?'

He used his knife then, his real weapon, and release was sweet.

She screamed like an animal, while in the distance the drunken woman continued to yell.

When she slumped to the ground he was covered in blood. He took off his shirt and threw it on top of her.

'You can rest now, Joey,' he said in a low voice. 'When I've done what I have to do I will join you.'

51

The speed at which things were happening for him had Buddy dazzled. One moment he was just another actor hustling a break, the next he was Sadie La Salle's new discovery, and one of the stars of a hot new movie.

Thank Christ he was only Sadie's discovery. She hadn't come on to him at all – much to his relief. He had been sure that Palm Springs was to be the pitch, but no, she had shown him his poster, and then they drove back to L.A., he dropped her at her house, and that was that.

Sadie La Salle and Ross Conti. Kind of a mind-blowing combination. But on asking around he discovered that it wasn't so unlikely after all. According to Hollywood gossip Sadie had discovered Ross, made him into a star – whereupon he had promptly dumped her.

377

'I hope you liked your poster,' Ferdie sniffed archly, when Buddy stopped by the office on Monday. 'I had to drag it all the way down there, and now I've got to drag it all the way back.'

'I wish I looked like that!' Buddy joked.

Ferdie cracked a smile. 'And how was your weekend?' he couldn't help himself from asking.

'Hey – some weekend. Like no sooner did I get there than Sadie wanted me to drive her back to L.A. I never even got to sit in the sun.'

'You mean you didn't stay the night?' Ferdie asked.

'Nope.'

He was clearly astonished. 'Er, Sadie will be with you in a moment. She's on the phone to Oliver Easterne.'

'No problem.' Buddy prowled around the office, checking out the signed pictures of famous stars which decorated the walls. His eyes came to rest on a photo of the sit-com star who had been hanging around Angel at George Lancaster's party. 'You know this creep?' he demanded.

'I hardly hang pictures of *strangers*,' Ferdie replied crisply. 'He's with the agency. Sadie doesn't handle him personally of course. We have a television department.'

'Can you do me a favour?'

'It depends what it is. I do a lot for madam's favourite clients. But I do not supply drugs or members of the opposite sex.'

'Shit!' Buddy burst out laughing. 'If I needed *that* kind of a favour you'd be the last person I'd ask!'

'Thank you very much,' said Ferdie huffily.

'No offence. You see there's this girl I'm tryin' to find. She was at the Lancaster party – maybe with schmucko.' He pointed at the picture.

'What's her name?'

He could hardly say Angel Hudson could he?

'I never got her name. It might have been Angel. She's a very pretty blonde – beautiful in fact.'

'I'll see what I can do. Let's face it, there can't be many Angels in Hollywood!'

The day it was announced that Montana Gray was going to direct Street People George Lancaster walked. He didn't even stay around to fight. He and Pamela boarded her private plane and jetted off to Palm Beach with hardly a backward glance.

George Christy in the Hollywood Reporter quoted Pamela as

saying, 'Hollywood sucks,' but then Pamela had never been noted for her tact.

At first Oliver was furious. He saw his cable deal going right down the toilet. Then he started doing a touch of fast thinking, figured out the money he would save by *not* having George Lancaster, and decided it wasn't such a disaster after all. Gina's name alone would carry the film. And he'd gotten *her* for half her normal price – much to Sadie's disgust. Plus Buddy Hudson was getting monkey piss – and the amount he was paying Montana was a joke.

He had decided to build up the Buddy Hudson part – go for the young market. Much as he hated to give her credit, Montana had really produced a winner – the kid had potential.

Now all he had to do was come up with a stroke of creative casting for the newly vacated role of Mac – which he planned to have rewritten anyway – cut down and made less important.

Who needed another George Lancaster? Not Oliver. He wanted a reasonable actor with a half-assed name who would not ask for the moon.

Ross Conti sounded good to him when his agent, Zack Schaeffer, called with the suggestion. Not that he was the only game in town. A lot of anxious agents were calling offering clients, but Oliver liked the *smell* of Ross Conti. It was offbeat casting. Pretty Boy Conti playing a beat-up old cop, his first decent acting job ever – the magazines would love it. He could see the cover of 'People' now. Plus Ross was divorcing again, which would mean more good coverage. And the chemistry between Ross and Gina should be something . . . It was common knowledge that Ross was a tit man.

Put 'em together and what did you have?

A lot more good headlines that's what.

Yes. Oliver liked the aroma. He loved putting the final package together. Especially when everything was going his way.

Neil Gray was allowed to go home from the hospital three weeks after his heart attack. Only it wasn't home he went to – it was a rented house at the beach with a private nurse as his companion.

Montana arranged the whole thing. 'It'll be for the best,' she said.

'What about you?' he asked, feeling like a man dragged back from the brink of death – which in fact he was.

'I'll try and get down on weekends,' she said vaguely.

They had not talked about the cause of his heart attack. There had been no screaming fights, no accusations. But Neil knew that she was aware of the circumstances, and he was desperate to keep her.

'Promise?' he asked, hating the begging tone he heard creeping into his voice.

'I'll try. But with the movie and all . . .' she trailed off.

'Montana –' he began.

'I don't want to talk about it,' she said fiercely. 'Not until I'm ready.'

So he was banished to the beach with instructions to rest, and regain his health, while his wife took over his movie – starring Gina Germaine – which made the whole thing *really* bizarre.

He wanted to ask her why she had agreed to have Gina in the film, but he could not bring himself to mention the woman's name.

If he had she would have told him that the choice was not hers, and that if she wanted to direct the movie she had to go along with everything Oliver Easterne desired or he would hire another director.

'Take it or leave it,' Oliver had said, enjoying every minute. 'But remember – if you take it I don't expect any trouble from you. I'm in charge – the asshole rules – Okay?'

The *dumb* asshole. Because once shooting began she would be in control – everyone knew the director had the producer by the balls once they were rolling.

It was difficult to believe that Oliver had signed Gina. But it was done, and there was no other alternative but to go with it, so she summoned her to the studio for a meeting. Somehow or other she had decided to try and wring a creditable performance out of her.

'I was so upset to hear about Neil,' Gina gushed, all pop eyes, white hair, and impossible boobs.

Montana killed her with a look that said it all. Then she killed her with words. 'I want you to lose twenty pounds. Your hair is not natural enough, it'll have to be changed. And no specially made clothes. Off the rack. As for your make-up – no false lashes, lipgloss, or shading.'

Gina glared.

'I don't want to see Gina Germaine, movie star, up on the screen. You have to try and capture the simplicity of Nikki.'

Gina looked bored.

'Let's not kid each other,' Montana continued, determined to get things straight up front. 'I didn't want you for the part – you probably hate the fact that I'm directing. But basically we're both after the same thing – a good movie. So let's cut out the crap and work for the film. Can we shake on that?'

Gina looked surprised. 'Why not?' she decided, and the two women shook hands.

'He wants lunch with you today. Ma Maison,' said Zack Schaeffer. 'I think we might have a deal. Short money but it's something you should grab.'

The schmuck was telling *him* he should grab it. Who the hell had he been bugging about *Street People* for months? The moment he heard George Lancaster had defected Ross had contacted Zack and insisted that he call Oliver Easterne at once.

'I've called him, a million times,' complained Zack – who was more interested in chasing coke and girls than in getting his clients jobs.

'So call him again. Immediately.'

The timing was right. George's quitting hadn't even hit the newspapers yet. Karen had given him advance warning. She had finally come up with a call that interested him. Usually it was – 'Why haven't I seen you?' 'What's *wrong* with you?'

He did not know what was wrong with him. Since the episode in Palm Springs with Sadie he had been in a bad way. She had treated him like some kind of a sex object. She had *used* him to make her new stud jealous. And for once in his life he had been made to feel rejected and a fool. It wasn't a good feeling, damn her.

He shut himself in his room at the hotel and watched television day and night, calling for room service and not even bothering to shave.

His depression lasted several days and he didn't like it one little bit. It made him feel old and vulnerable, and to top everything off when his beard grew in it was grey. Christ! What with that and his tan fading he looked frigging ancient.

That was when he pulled himself together, just in time for Karen's call about George's imminent departure.

Elaine's messages mounted up daily. At first she had just left her name with a request that he call. Then the message slips that were put under his door became more personal – embarrassingly so. Did she want the world to know what was going on?

He had to do something about her. Go to his lawyer and talk about divorce. But when it came right down to it he wasn't sure if that was what he really wanted.

She should never have thrown him out. Let her suffer a while longer, then maybe he'd see . . .

*

381

Buddy had never been busier in his life. But he loved it. There were hair, make-up and clothes tests. Stills sessions. Meetings with the publicity people to get together a suitable biography. Came the evening he fell into bed exhausted. Friday was his first free day, and he decided to drop by and see both Shelly and Randy just in case they had heard from Angel. He also wanted to repay the money he had borrowed.

It was noon by the time he got to Randy's place. He pressed the bell for several minutes until eventually Shelly staggered to the door, clad only in an out-size T-shirt, red curls a tangled mess, sleep clouding her stoned eyes.

'Yeah?' she mumbled, not even registering that it was him.

'Hey – it's great to be remembered.'

She stared blankly until recognition dawned. 'Bud,' she slurred. 'S'nice t'see you, Bud.'

He followed her into the small apartment. Randy was sprawled naked and asleep across the bed. The place was more of a mess than usual – clothes and records everywhere, empty wine bottles, half-eaten pizzas, and on a table next to the bed a spilled bottle of quaaludes, a syringe and needle, and a tin box containing a small amount of cocaine.

Buddy took the scene in at a glance. 'I see you two found each other,' he said restlessly.

'Why not?' countered Shelly, yawning and running her hands through her tangled hair. 'Beats sleepin' alone.' She picked up a pair of jeans and swiped them at Randy's inert body. 'Wake up, we got us a visit from Bud.'

Randy mumbled, 'Piss off.'

'We had a heavy night,' she explained, gesturing vaguely towards the drug paraphernalia. 'In fact, we've had a heavy week. Don't time *fly* when you're havin' fun. Wanna blow?'

Buddy shook his head. Had he really been a part of this? No wonder Angel had run off.

'Look,' he said quickly. 'I just stopped by to pay you both the money I borrowed.' He reached for his bankroll.

She giggled hysterically. 'Whatcha do? Hold up Safeways? Randy! Wake up. Bud's here. An' he's got money.'

Randy sat up abruptly, wild-eyed. 'Goddamn it. Don't ever yell like that again. I hate it.'

'Toooo bad.' She turned her back on him, bent over, and waved her naked ass in his face.

He slapped it, hard.

Buddy felt claustrophobic. The whole scene was getting him down. He really didn't want to hang around.

'Where did you score?' Randy demanded. He looked like he was falling apart. Wild glassy eyes in a white drawn face.

'What's going on with you?' Buddy asked, indicating the syringe. 'Since when did you go that route?'

'Aw, cut out the phony concern. Just give us the bucks an' get outta here.'

For a moment Buddy felt that maybe he should get involved, at least try and talk to them. But then he thought – what am I? Crazy? They can both look after themselves.

'Here.' He peeled off some bills and handed them over. 'I guess this covers it.'

'Got yourself a job, Bud?' slurred Shelly.

'Yeah,' he replied. No way was he telling these two stoned zombies his news. 'Uh . . . listen. I've moved into a new place. If Angel calls I want you to be sure and give her my number.' He wrote it on a pad by the phone. 'And please – try and get her to tell you where she is. I've really gotta reach her.'

'She's ice cream, man,' mumbled Shelly, rubbing red ringed eyes. 'Melts under pressure.'

'So – I guess I'll see you two around,' Buddy said, backing towards the door.

'You sellin' it again?' demanded Shelly.

He didn't reply. He was out of there, running down the steps, jumping into his car, putting space between himself and the way things used to be.

'Adrian and I have discussed it, and we both agree that you should move in with us,' Koko said.

Angel began to protest.

'No objections,' he said firmly. 'Besides, I heard from the girl whose apartment you're leasing and she's coming back. So you see, it's all arranged.'

She wanted to put up a fight, assert her newfound independence. But the thought of moving in with Koko and Adrian was just too tempting to resist. They could be her family. Temporarily. Was that such a bad thing to want?

A few days later they loaded her possessions into his car and she moved into the little house in the hills.

At first she felt awkward and out of place, but Adrian was so cordial towards her, and Koko so kind, that she soon felt quite at home.

The baby was just beginning to show.

'Ah-ha!' Raymondo sneered one morning. 'You no wanna play han' ball wit the King. But you sure been playin' *some*where.'

'Go stuff a client,' said Koko tartly, hovering as usual.

'Sure glad *one* of us can,' snapped Raymondo in reply. 'That good for beezzness, y'know, man?'

'God save us from horny Puerto Ricans,' Koko muttered. He turned to Angel. 'I've found you a doctor. He'll look after you until the baby is born – in fact he'll even deliver the little monster.' He mock sighed. 'How we are going to deal with a baby in the house beats me.' He hugged her protectively. 'But not to worry – we'll manage. I'll probably adore every squealing minute!'

She squeezed his hand. 'I do love you, Koko. I'll always be grateful for everything you've done for me.'

He blushed beneath his halo of outlandish curls. '*Please* dreamheart – no mushy stuff. I can't take the emotional pressure. It's bad for my hormone level!'

Oliver liked playing with a hungry actor. Especially a famous one. Usually they had *him* by the balls, and usually they squeezed tighter than an angry dyke. With Ross Conti, Oliver held all the cards, and he loved it. In fact he double loved it, because he had insisted that Montana join them, and the very coupling of the names Gina Germaine and Ross Conti may well have caused her permanent damage.

'Christ, Oliver,' she said angrily when she heard. 'I can maybe understand why George Lancaster was so important to you – but why Ross Conti when there are so many really good actors around?'

Sitting at his usual table at Ma Maison, Oliver was in his element. Even his haemorrhoids had vanished – which only proved that aggravation did not agree with him – having it all his own way did.

Montana was edgy, not her usual cool together self.

Ross was on his best behaviour, and Oliver played with him like a spiteful cat.

'I think it's one of the best scripts I've ever read,' Ross said eagerly. 'It's got great pace and realism, and it's a terrific part for me.'

At least he likes it, Montana thought. An improvement on George who probably never even read it.

'Sadie called me this morning,' Oliver said, vigorously polishing his fork with a napkin. 'She seems to think Adam Sutton might be interested . . .'

Ross swallowed bile and said nothing. He knew what Oliver was doing and all he could do in return was sit it out.

'Of course, Adam's price is ridiculous,' Oliver continued, waving at Dani and Hal Needham. 'And Bibi on the set is enough to guarantee the poor bastard never works again. However . . . he *is* very popular, especially in Europe.' He finished polishing the fork and admired his handiwork. 'You know Ross, Zack is being very difficult. I'm aware that you have your price . . .' He shrugged. 'But I think I should tell you that this movie is over budget before we even begin.'

Ross began to sweat. He had talked to Zack before lunch, and what Oliver was offering was an insult. Did he expect to go even lower?

'Frankly,' Oliver said magnanimously, 'if we can meet on price the part is yours. If not . . .' He shrugged again. 'I must have a decision by four o'clock today.'

Montana rose. 'I know you'll excuse me,' she said. 'But I can't afford the luxury of long lunches these days. We start shooting in a week and I have a hundred things to do.'

'A week?' gulped Ross.

'Exactly,' she said, feeling sorry for him, liking him, thinking that perhaps he wasn't so wrong for the part after all. She waved briefly at Oliver. 'See you later,' she said, much to his annoyance, and was gone.

'I think she'll make a hell of a movie,' Oliver said grudgingly, 'even if she is a woman.'

'She wrote a marvellous script.'

'Yes. It's good,' Oliver was forced to admit. 'Of course I've had to make a few changes, nothing major.' He sipped a glass of Perrier and glanced around the restaurant. 'Isn't that your wife?'

Ross turned around in time to observe Elaine walking in with Maralee.

Christ! That's all he needed. He quickly straightened his chair and looked away in the hope that she would not spot him.

No such luck. She saw him the moment she entered, and once Maralee was settled at a table she came sailing over.

'Hello, Oliver,' she said, managing an ingratiating smile. 'Hello, Ross.' Hurt accusing eyes.

They both returned her greeting.

Awkward silence.

'Will you join me for coffee later, Ross? There's something I want to discuss.'

At least she had the good sense not to do a number in front of Oliver. 'Why not?' he said graciously, having no intention of doing so.

She gave a little nod. Quite humble for Elaine. 'Thank you.' She returned to Maralee without another word.

'I hear you two are separated,' Oliver said, as if it wasn't common knowledge.

'It's only a temporary thing,' Ross said airily. 'Nothing we can't work out.'

'Good. Wouldn't like to think you were on the loose around Gina . . .'

The way Oliver was talking it sounded like he already had the part. But then Oliver was about as trustworthy as a hungry piranha.

'How much truth is there in the Neil-Gina story?' Ross asked, mildly interested.

'Take what you've heard and treble it.'

'Really?'

'You've heard the phrase "grabbing cunt" – well that's what Gina is – literally.'

Both men guffawed – all guys together – relieved that Neil Gray was the schmuck that got caught and not them.

'I have a feeling we're goin' to work something out on this deal,' Oliver said. 'Only talk to your agent – I can't pull money out of my left sock. Be reasonable, and I think we can do business.'

Prick, Ross thought. What happened to all the money you no longer have to pay George Lancaster? Now, if Sadie was his agent . . .

But she wasn't. And to even think about her caused him extreme humiliation – an emotion he was not used to – and one he had no plans to encourage.

'He looks terrible,' Elaine fretted.

'He looks exactly the same to me,' Maralee replied. And she wanted to add – it's you who look terrible.

'His hair is too long, he's got bags under his eyes, and he's put on weight,' Elaine stated. 'He's neglecting himself.'

So are you, Maralee wanted to say. She had never – but never –

seen Elaine with chipped nail polish before. And talk about adding a pound or two – her friend looked positively jowly. As for her hair – was that a grey strand right at the front for all to see?

Maralee patted her own immaculate blond locks and reflected that whatever personal crisis she might be going through there was always time for grooming. Elaine was making a grave mistake letting herself go this way.

'I wonder what Ross is doing with Oliver,' Elaine mused.

'There's a rumour that he might replace George Lancaster,' Maralee said.

'Thanks so much for telling me,' Elaine snapped frostily.

'I only just heard, and I knew I was seeing you for lunch.' She paused, determined to get on to the subject *she* wished to discuss. 'Neil told me. I talk to him every day. He's making great progress you know.'

'Correct me if I'm wrong,' Elaine said irritably, one eye observing her errant husband's every move. 'But he *is* still with Montana, isn't he?'

'I suppose so . . . in a way . . . But I don't see it lasting much longer.'

Elaine could hardly conceal her surprise. 'And you want him back? After the way he dumped you?'

Maralee tossed her blond curls imperiously. '*You're* hardly in a position to talk about being dumped. Would *you* take Ross back?'

Elaine choked in anger. 'Ross *did not* dump me. I threw him out because of his affair with our dear friend, Karen. And while we are on the subject, *you* must have known what was going on. Why didn't you tell me?'

Maralee widened blue eyes, beautifully nipped and tucked so that you couldn't even tell they'd been fixed. '*I* didn't know.'

'Probably not. Too busy screwing Randy whatshiscock. Whatever happened to *him*? Didn't his bank balance match his hardon?'

Maralee quickly put on a pair of wrapover white sunglasses. 'I just don't know what's the matter with you. You certainly say things no *friend* should say.'

'If your friends don't say 'em, who will?' stated Elaine logically, grabbing at a passing waiter. 'Another Vodkatini,' she said. 'Make it two. I hate the pause between drinks.'

*

387

Ferdie caught Buddy in the middle of a push-up.

'You *must* get an answering service,' Ferdie scolded on the phone. 'Shall I arrange it?'

'Why not,' Buddy decided. If he was going to be a star, may as well start with the trimmings.

'I have a number on that girl you were looking for,' Ferdie said matter-of-factly. 'Her name *is* Angel. And she works at a hairdressing salon on the Strip.' He proceeded to give Buddy the number, and then he gave advice. 'You have to be careful who you date now, you know. Soon everything you do will be photographed and written about . . . Usually it's best to stick to dating actresses who know how to handle that sort of thing.'

Buddy grinned. Sometimes Ferdie sounded like a pale imitation of Sadie. She had already given him the same speech.

'Thanks, I'll remember that. Gotta split. I have Linda Evans waitin' in the hot tub!'

'Smart ass,' sassed Ferdie.

'Don't you know it!'

Buddy hung up and took a deep breath.

Angel. You are comin' back to me today!

He dialled the number Ferdie had given him and waited impatiently while it rang.

A male voice answered. 'Koko's.'

'Yeah . . . uh . . . I'd like to speak to Angel.'

A pause. 'Who is calling?'

'Tell her a friend.'

'I'm sure you are, but Angel is not available right now, so perhaps you would be kind enough to give me your name and number and I'll see she gets back to you.'

Fuck! Uptight creep.

'I'll call back later,' Buddy said, not pleased.

'Thank you,' Koko sing-songed.

Buddy put down the receiver and gazed into space. He should have gotten the address, climbed into his car and just driven over.

Then he could have grabbed Angel back into his life with no arguments.

But maybe she wouldn't come . . . The thought frightened him more than he cared to admit.

'Somebody telephoned you,' Koko said, when Angel returned from a visit to the doctor.

'Who?'

'He wouldn't leave a name.'

Buddy, she thought. Oh, please God, let it be Buddy.

'Will he call back?' she asked anxiously.

'If he doesn't it's his loss, isn't it dreamheart?'

One moment he was there, the next – gone. Elaine stared in helpless fury at Ross's empty table. She had only been in the ladies' room for a minute, and the bastard had taken that minute and made his escape.

'Did you see Ross go?' she snapped at Maralee.

'No.'

Elaine slumped into her chair. 'I *hate* this goddamn place,' she said. 'Full of fucking phonies – worried about this party and that one. And if you're not invited you stay in with the lights off so everyone thinks you're out of town.'

Maralee blinked. 'What?'

'Nothing,' Elaine said, her voice brittle. 'I'm beginning to sound like Ross.' She sighed. 'Let's have another drink.'

'I don't think so,' said Maralee disapprovingly. 'I have ballet class this afternoon.'

'Shit!' exclaimed Elaine belligerently. 'This place is full of it.'

At five to four exactly Ross Conti instructed Zack Schaeffer to call Oliver Easterne and accept his terms – whatever they were.

'If we drop your price it's going to be common knowledge this time tomorrow. It'll be a bitch bringing it up again.' Zack lowered his voice. 'You know, Ross, an actor is like a whore. She either fucks for fifty or five. You know what I'm saying?'

'I want this movie, Zack. And I'm the whore who'll do anything to get it. Call Oliver. Now.'

52

The doctor caught Leon early in the morning while he still slept.

'I wondered if you'd like to drop by and see me,' the old man said, as if he lived next door. 'I have the Andrews case history, and it's interesting stuff.'

'I can't do that,' Leon replied regretfully, edging away from Millie's inert body. 'Can you hold on a minute?'

He hurried into the bathroom and closed the door. Then he sat on the toilet and listened. It *was* interesting stuff. Once the doctor had found his file, he seemed to develop absolute recall.

'Willis Andrews was a quiet little man,' he remembered. 'Came to see me first because of migraine headaches. Wasn't migraine at all – it was his wife. Sexual problems . . . this didn't come out until he had visited me three or four times. You know, back then it wasn't like it is today, with sex discussed openly.'

'Quite,' agreed Leon.

'The problem with Mr. Andrews was that he could not maintain an erection,' continued the doctor. 'And this was causing friction at home. Mrs. Andrews, it seems, was most anxious to become pregnant.'

'Yes?'

'I counselled with the man. We talked of vitamins, diet, technique.' He paused, then added proudly, 'I was way ahead of my time you know.'

'I'm sure you were.'

'Yes indeed,' the old man chuckled. 'Sex was always one of my favourite subjects. I liked to help people with problems in that direction. It was a challenge.'

'Did you help Willis Andrews?'

'Alas, no. He was eager to be helped, but I remember thinking at the time after several consultations that maybe the problem did not lie with him. Maybe Mrs. Andrews was at fault . . .'

'Did you see her?'

'Unfortunately not. I suggested that it would be a good idea, but he became very agitated. In view of what happened later I wish that I had insisted.'

'What happened later?' Leon asked curiously.

'I clipped the piece from the newspaper and put it in his file.'

Leon persisted. 'What piece?'

'The Andrews couple adopted a child. A girl. There was an accident . . . the child was killed. They said that she fell down the stairs. The neighbours claimed the child was beaten to death . . . They were arrested, but somewhere along the line the charges were dropped. Not enough evidence, something like that. They left town of course. I could never understand the whole thing. Willis Andrews was not a violent man at all.'

Leon's mind was racing. Why did they adopt a child in the first place?

Could it be that because of Willis's problem they were unable to have a child of their own? In all of his checking Leon had been unable to come up with any information about Deke's birth. *Could it be that he was adopted too?*

Adrenaline coursed through his veins. He needed more information. Much more.

He needed to know who Deke Andrews really was.

53

The cast was set.

An Oliver Easterne Production; Street People; Starring Gina Germaine, Ross Conti, and introducing Buddy Hudson as Vinnie.

Produced by Oliver Easterne. Directed by Montana Gray.

Two weeks of interiors in the studio. Followed by eight weeks out on location.

A press party at the Westwood Marquis Hotel three days before shooting to introduce the cast to the media.

Montana could have strangled Gina Germaine. Blond hair puffed and backcombed to breaking point. A white dress that oozed over her curves, barely making it across the famous boobs.

'The idea,' Montana told her acidly, 'was to let the press know that this role is a big departure for you. How do you expect them to take you seriously when you look ready to open your act in Vegas?'

'Don't get touchy, sweetheart,' cooed Gina. 'I'm afraid you will find that I am *always* the centre of attention – what*ever* I wear.'

Obviously the woman was a total idiot who hadn't understood a word of their previous meeting.

'Listen,' Montana said quickly. 'I think we should talk.'

'Not now, sweetie,' Gina cooed dismissively, gesturing towards the waiting press and running her tongue over glistening lips.

'How about tomorrow morning?' Montana insisted.

'When I'm not working I *never* get up before twelve,' Gina scolded, as if everyone should know that.

'Lunch then.'

A reluctant sigh. 'Oh, alright.'

Montana then spotted Ross Conti. He looked positively hand-some. Whatever happened to the ageing actor she had lunched with at Ma Maison?

Three solid hours under a tanning lamp. Subtle bleach to cover the grey in the hair. A facial. A massage. A two day fast. Special eye drops to take the red out.

'Oh, no!' she muttered. What she had here was a couple of Hollywood movie stars determined to look their best and screw the movie. But they were going to have to deal with her, and she wasn't going to take it.

Only Buddy looked right. Nothing he did could conceal his animal sexuality. There was no mistaking the fact that he was going to walk right off with the film whether she managed to coax a performance out of him or not.

Gina did a long double-take when she met him. She appraised him the way an expert appraises fine gems.

While Gina was checking out Buddy, Ross zeroed in on her. She had a pair – the like of which he had not seen in a long time. Why couldn't he find a woman with Gina's tits, Karen's nipples, Sadie's business acumen, and Elaine's knack of looking after him??

He avoided Sadie at the party. He would never forgive her for treating him the way she had.

Still . . . the last laugh was his. He was staring in *Street People*, although he had been extremely pissed off when he saw the new script. His part was slashed to hell.

'Don't worry,' Montana had assured him. 'Ignore the cut version. We're shooting the original – only don't mention it to Oliver just yet.'

Sadie observed Ross with a mixture of regret and satisfaction. She knew she had hurt him – at least wounded his pride.

Her revenge was *nothing* compared to the way he had treated her. She should have demanded more.

Too late now – he was avoiding her. Shame. She could have gotten him twice the amount of money he had settled for.

Buddy sparkled. He was born to be in the limelight. A shining star. Well maybe not a star yet, but he was in orbit wasn't he? All set to soar.

A pretty black girl with a snub nose said, 'Hi, I'm Virgie from "Teen Topics".' She fumbled with a tape recorder. 'Can I ask you a few questions?'

He smiled. 'I'd love it.' Talking about himself was becoming a habit. Twenty-three pre-movie interviews in five days. Hardly time to go to the bathroom, let alone track down Angel. He had called her just the once. Time and space were needed to win her back.

Virgie's tape recorder clicked into action. 'Where were you born?' she asked.

Breathy little voice. Sweat beading her upper lip. Was she nervous? Talking to *him*?

'New York,' he lied. 'Hell's Kitchen. It was tough, but I made out.'

'When did you come to Hollywood?'

'Last year. I hitched my way from New York. When I got here I tried several jobs. Lifeguard, sports counsellor with kids, taxi driver. Things like that.' He paused. Dramatic effect. 'Sadie La Salle climbed into my cab one day and whammo! "Are you an actor?" she says. "Yes," I reply. "Then I want you to see Oliver Easterne at once," she says.'

Virgie's eyes widened. 'Gosh!'

'Hey – it was unreal. The next week I'm testing. Can you believe it?'

She faithfully recorded every word.

'Everything okay, Buddy?' asked Pusskins Malone, the chief P.R. man who had helped him make up his new biography.

Buddy made an affirmative circle with his thumb and forefinger.

'They want pictures of you with Gina. Excuse us, dear.'

The girl nodded. 'Thank you,' she said gratefully. 'I'll be watching for your film. Maybe we can do another piece when it comes out.'

'Sure. Why not?' Gracious star to the hilt. He *loved* it.

'Did you get a press kit, dear?' Pusskins asked. 'Pictures, bios – they're by the door. If you need anything else just give me a buzz.'

'I will.'

'Cute little thing,' he said, hurrying Buddy in the direction of Gina who was surrounded by a heavy throng of enthusiastic photographers. 'You met supercunt yet?'

'Haven't had the pleasure.'

Pusskins laughed cynically. 'Attila the Hun with tits!'

'Not my type.'

'Doesn't matter. Are you *her* type? 'Cos if you are – run for the hills!'

'Thanks, but I already heard the Neil Gray story.'

'He was lucky. Some guys have dived between those thighs and haven't been seen for a week!'

Gina greeted him with hungry eyes, a manufactured smile, and a great thrusting of boobs.

'Isn't he sexy, darlings?' she cooed to the photographers.

'Kiss him, Gina.'

'Hug him, Gina.'

'A little more cleavage, Gina.'

She grabbed Buddy in all the right poses.

He noticed that beneath the make-up and hair and flirtatious banter she was cold as an ice-chip.

The photographers clicked non-stop while she threw a few instructions his way. 'Smile.' 'Look sexy.' 'For chrissakes move, you're in my shadow.' 'What are you doing later?'

He thought of the old joke.

I wouldn't go near you with a ten foot pole.

Show me a pole with ten foot and who needs you.

Oliver strode over, beaming. 'What a couple! Inspired casting.'

Montana, conducting an interview with Vernon Scott of UPI, viewed the scene from afar and cringed. A fine send off for her movie.

Ross had been discovered by Virgie, and her anxious tape recorder was thrust in his face.

Sadie watched Gina and Buddy as they posed for the photographers. Now, if Ross was her client there would be no way he was not up there with them. Tomorrow these pictures would run nationwide and it would be *Street People*, Gina Germaine, and Buddy Hudson who were mentioned. Poor old Ross was left at the post. Again.

She felt sorry for him. Then she remembered and her expression hardened. The hell with Ross Conti. He was getting everything he deserved.

She turned away just as Pusskins grabbed Ross and hustled him over to the photographic throng.

'You owe me two weeks' money. Four hundred an' sixty dollars, Señora.' Lina stood stoically by the back door.

'Four hundred and sixty dollars,' Elaine repeated blankly.

'Two weeks. An' Miguel two hundred on Saturday.'

'You will be paid,' she said grandly.

How come when Lina talks money her English is perfect?

'When?' demanded Lina.

'Soon.'

'When soon?'

'Oh, leave me alone you stupid woman!'

She ran into her bedroom and slammed the door. Loyalty. That was a laugh. Lina had worked for her eight years. She had paid her regularly – through sickness and vacation. And now you would think she would be prepared to wait an extra day or two. Goddamn help. If Lina wasn't careful she would fire her and do the house herself.

You should have had children, Elaine. That way he could never have left you without money.

Leave me alone, Etta. Don't you think I know it?

She was lonely, rattling around the big house all by herself. Screw the money. Maybe it would have been nice to have children around. Grown ones preferably. She wouldn't go so far as to welcome diapers and toys and all that nursery stuff. But it had not been possible, so why was she even thinking about it? And Ross hadn't minded. In fact he was quite pleased. Typical actor. Didn't relish competition.

Pulling herself together she ventured out of the bedroom. Better make the peace with Lina. A stupid maid was better than no maid at all.

Little S. Shitz drove past the Conti house three times. He was hesitant about going in. He had never met Mrs. Conti, and wives could be very prickly when approached with pictures of their husbands in bed with other women. But after Ross Conti failed to turn up for their meeting, he decided she was his best bet.

A police car cruised slowly past, and the cop gave him a brief once-over. Little turned quickly into the Conti driveway and parked. He had read in the newspapers about the Contis separating. If Mrs. C. wanted evidence for her divorce he had it – in spades. And if she could pay – it was hers.

He got out of his car and approached the front door, observing that some people certainly knew how to live.

He rang the bell while chewing hungrily on his thumb-nail.

A surly Spanish maid answered the door, her face a thundercloud. '*Si*?' she spat rudely.

He pulled himself up to his full height, all five feet five inches, and handed her a battered business card.

'Give this to Mrs. Conti,' he said with all the authority he could muster. 'Tell her I have come regarding her husband.'

'Meester Conti no here. He go away – you come back 'nother time.' She began to close the door on him.

He used the foot ploy. Something he had learned from overdosing on Mickey Spillane books.

'Mover your goddamn foots,' yelled Lina.

'I want to see Mrs. Conti. *Mrs*. Conti,' he insisted. 'Give her my card.'

Lina glared at him suspiciously. 'Why you no *say* Meesus in place first?'

'I did.'

'You wait.'

She slammed the door with maniacal force, dislodging his foot and nearly crippling him for life. He jumped up and down filled with pain and rage. Whatever Elaine Conti was like she had to be better than her maid.

'Ah, Lina, there you are,' Elaine said sweetly. 'I wanted to apologize for my rudeness earlier.'

Lina scowled darkly and thrust the card in her face.

'What's this?'

'Man at door,' she muttered, and marched into the kitchen mumbling.

Elaine squinted at the card. She didn't have her contacts in, and the printing on the card was obscured by several dirty marks. She followed Lina into the kitchen. 'What does this man want?'

Lina shrugged disinterestedly. 'Don' know.' She busied herself at the sink.

Oh, God, it's a creditor. Ross has stopped paying the bills.

'Lina,' she wheedled. 'Would you please tell him I'm not at home.'

Lina banged a few dishes around and ignored her.

'Lina, dear. Please.'

The maid turned and glared at her. 'Man very rude. I no deal weeth him.'

Elaine stamped her foot. 'I *pay* you to deal with him.'

'You pay me nothing,' Lina crowed triumphantly.

Elaine stalked out of the kitchen. God! She could certainly deal with one lousy creditor herself, she didn't have to plead with the goddamn maid. How *dare* Lina behave in this fashion.

She marched to the front door and flung it open. 'Yes?' she shrieked. 'What do you want?'

Little took one look at Elaine Conti, wild-eyed in a peach negligee, and took two steps backwards, promptly tripping and nearly breaking his neck.

Elaine helped him to his feet, ever mindful of the fact that he was on her property and if he broke anything he could sue.

396

'I'm Little S. Shitz,' he gasped. 'Private investigator. And I have some photos that I think might be of interest to you.'

'What *are* you doing later?' Gina whispered in Buddy's ear.

The press reception was coming to an end. The bar had just been declared closed, and that usually meant a mass exodus.

'I don't know about you, but I'm studying my script,' he said.

She licked full glossed lips and smiled invitingly. 'Wanna go over lines together? Wanna screw a movie star?'

He feigned surprise. 'Hey – do you really think Ross Conti would let me?'

She frowned. 'If *you're* gay, sweetheart, then *I'm* Sadie La Salle's mother!'

'You said it.' He backed away, making a swift escape while there were still people around. Who would have thought that the day would come when he turned down a real life honest to goodness movie star. Hey-hey-hey – with age he was definitely getting smarter. He had *her* number the moment he set eyes on her, and he didn't even have the hots for her. What was the famous Paul Newman quote? Why have hamburger when you got steak at home.

Only he didn't have anything at home. And he should have Angel waiting for him.

He had to make a move. The longer he waited the more difficult it would be. Resolutely he searched out a phone booth. It was past six, but maybe she would still be there.

The same male voice answered. 'Koko's.'

'I want Angel,' Buddy said.

'Don't they all,' sing-songed the voice.

Buddy began a slow burn. 'Is she there or not?'

'Sorry, not. Can I give her a message?'

'Where can I reach her?'

'You can't.'

'But I need to talk to her.'

'Sorry. Any message or not?'

Reluctantly he left his name and number. 'See she gets it. It's urgent.'

Koko wrote the information down, and debated whether to give her the message. She was so settled and happy now. Did she really need the husband back in her life?

He thought perhaps not, so he folded the piece of paper and put it in his shirt pocket. He would discuss it with Adrian later, see what *he* thought. Adrian always made the right decisions.

Gina Germaine, miffed by Buddy's disinterest, switched her attentions to Oliver, much to his consternation.

'Your star is available for dinner at Chasen's,' she purred. 'Unless you'd prefer something cosier. We could always go back to my place and send out for Chinese.'

'Chasen's,' he said hastily. 'I've asked Ross.' Which was a lie, but one he would quickly amend. 'I was just about to invite you.'

Ross already had a dinner date with Pusskins Malone. The two men went back quite a way and enjoyed swapping stories of lurid pasts.

'You can bring Pusskins,' Oliver said reluctantly. Never one to spring for a large check.

Ross wanted to say no. But a rule of the game was be nice to the producer, so he said, 'Sure, we'll come.'

He did not know that Oliver planned to invite Sadie La Salle. Had he known that, wild buffalos wouldn't have dragged a yes out of him.

Oliver also decided to ask Montana and Buddy. Didn't want anyone feeling slighted. Besides, if he was going for a check, may as well go all the way. It would come off the budget anyway.

Somewhere between the lobby of the Westwood Marquis and the waiting limos the venue was changed from Chasen's to Morton's. A mistake as far as Ross was concerned, because the moment he entered the cool casualness of Morton's restaurant, Karen materialized in front of him.

'Why haven't I seen you?' she hissed, nipples on prominent display through a white silk shirt. 'If you're worried about Elaine I don't *mind* being named in the divorce.'

Without thinking he automatically reached out and touched an erect nipple. She let forth an animal groan. Several interested diners turned to stare. He realized what he was doing and dropped his hand quickly.

Pusskins came up behind. 'Karen, lovely. How are you?'

'Fine, thank you, Puss.' Her green eyes swivelled to take in Gina Germaine's entrance. 'Jesus!' she snorted, glaring at Ross. 'Are *you* with *that*?'

'It's a dinner laid on by Oliver,' he explained. 'Who are *you* with?'

'Some bore. I'll get rid of him and meet you in the parking lot as soon as you can shake your group. Give me a signal. Are we on?'

He dropped his eyes to her nipples. 'We're on.'

She walked off, wearing nothing beneath skin tight white silk pants.

'And she's loaded too,' groaned Pusskins. 'Some guys have all the luck.'

Gina shoved between the two of them and linked arms. 'Hi, everybody,' she giggled, aware of the fact that the entire restaurant was observing her entrance. 'This girl is *starving*. Anyone for din-din?'

The table was round. The seating thus.

Oliver. Gina on one side, Sadie the other. Beside Gina a truculent Ross, with Pusskins on his other side, and then Montana. Buddy was placed between Sadie and Montana, with Gina eyeing him hungrily across the table.

Conversation was stilted to say the least. Pusskins was the only one with anything to say. He regaled the somewhat uptight group with hilarious stories about the Cannes Film Festival, a celebrated actor and his even more celebrated toupee, and a few Monroe anecdotes.

Gina thrust out her formidable bosom determined to dominate the conversation. 'When I was in Vietnam entertaining the troops, some of the guys kept twelve year old hookers as *pets*. Can you imagine.' She paused, then added hurriedly, 'Of course, I was only a teenager myself.'

Ross shot a quick look at Sadie. Her strong dark eyes met his and did not waver. He tried to stare her out but could not make it. Bitch.

Buddy glanced around the restaurant restlessly. Much as he enjoyed being in such illustrious company he would sooner be home waiting for Angel's phone call. He excused himself from the table with a muttered, 'I gotta make a call.' Then he checked with his newly acquired answering service. 'Any messages?'

'One moment, Mr. Hudson.'

Angel had called him back! And he wasn't even home! He hoped she had left her number.

'Shelly phoned you,' said the message service lady. 'She wants you to return her call immediately. She said it was extremely urgent.' He took down the number and slumped with disappointment. He would have ignored Shelly's call but for the fact that maybe it had something to do with Angel, so he sprung another dime.

Shelly answered on the second ring, her voice flat, stoned, and frightened. 'You gotta get over here quick, Bud,' she mumbled. 'I think Randy's dead.'

54

'Mrs. Nita Carrolle?' Deke asked politely.

'Who wants her?' crowed the old woman suspiciously, glaring at Deke who stood on her doorstep, shaven head gleaming in the early morning sun.

'A friend in Barstow suggested that I stop by and see her.'

'Barstow!' she cackled. 'I never had no friends in Barstow, sonny-boy.'

'Are you Mrs. Carrolle, then?'

'I sure as fanny ain't Ava Gardner!' She placed one fat hand coyly on her hip. 'Who sent you? Charlie Nation I bet. He was hardly a friend – more of a son of a bitchin' louse.' She roared with laughter.

'I'm Charlie's son,' Deke lied.

'Charlie's son!' she screamed. 'Goddamn! C'mon in sonnyboy, tell me all about the bum. He still spend half his life at the track?'

It was that easy to enter Nita Carrolle's house where she lived with two yapping poodles, and a plethora of frills and flounces.

Nita Carrolle was fat. Her arms were fat. Her legs were fat. Her chins wobbled dangerously. And beneath a voluminous caftan lurked more fat.

She was also old. Seventy or eighty, it was hard to tell. Grotesque make-up covered her leathery skin, a slash of vermilion lipstick, beads of sticky mascara, green eyeshadow that lay like leaded paint in the cracks of her eyelids. Dyed yellow hair swirled around her head. There were pearls at her throat, diamonds in her ears, jangling bracelets on each fat wrist, and an assortment of fancy rings.

She steered him towards a stuffed velvet love-seat, inquiring warmly, 'How is the little worm? I ain't seen Charlie in years.'

'He passed away,' Deke said tonelessly.

She visibly sagged. 'Passed away,' she repeated blankly. 'Old Charlie? Sonnyboy, they'll never be a better louse on this earth.' She plucked a lace handkerchief from the folds of her caftan and blew her nose. 'The old biddy is still going strong though, I bet,' she said, when she'd recovered.

'Yes,' he replied.

'Givin' you a hard time, huh?' she asked sympathetically, blowing her nose again.

He nodded.

She pulled herself together. 'So – what you got for me? He always promised me his diamond pinky when he went. You bring it with you? Is that why you're here?'

'Do you live alone?' he asked politely.

'Just me an' the doggies. Why?'

'Because I want to stay for a while.'

'Y'can stay as long as y'like.' She shook her head sadly. 'Your daddy used to talk about you all the time. And your sister – what was her name?'

'I don't know.'

'Huh?'

He stared at her. Expressionless eyes in a pale face. His shaven head adding a sinister starkness.

She made a soft noise in her throat. A very small noise for such a fat person. 'You're not Charlie's son, are you?'

'No,' he replied calmly.

She gathered her strength and courage. 'Then who in hell are you?'

He reached for his knife in one easy motion, and tested the blade on the tip of his finger. A spot of blood appeared.

'That's what *you* are going to tell *me*,' he said calmly.

55

'I gotta split,' Buddy whispered in Sadie's ear.

'What are you talking about?' she demanded in a low voice. 'This may be a boring dinner but it is also an important one.'

'I know that,' he continued sotto voice. 'But this friend of mine is in trouble an' I have to help out.'

'In this business the only friend you have is yourself.'

He shrugged. 'They're not gonna throw me off the movie 'cos I didn't stay for dinner.'

He made his excuses and strode quickly from the restaurant.

Sadie frowned. His career hadn't even started yet, and already he was being difficult.

Gina pouted. She was not used to turn-downs. Buddy intrigued her.

Ross was pissed off. With Buddy's early exit it meant that he would have to stick around longer than he wanted.

Montana just wished that it was she making the early getaway.

Pusskins didn't care either way. As long as the booze flowed he was happy.

Elaine clicked the television remote control and stared at Merv Griffin. She adored Merv. He was so comforting and warm. Full of gossip and fun. Sometimes she felt closer to Merv than anyone in the whole world. He was always there, the same time every night. Reliable, dependable, and friendly.

Much as she loved Merv, tonight he could not hold her attention. The smell of Little S. Shitz was in her nostrils. Cheap aftershave, stale sweat, and sour hunger. The horrible little man's image danced before her eyes, and she leaned across the bed and reached for the large tumbler of vodka.

Ah! The clear sharp taste. So bittersweet and refreshing. She allowed a piece of ice to slip into her mouth, and sucked on it for a moment, enjoying the cold shock.

Little S. Shitz had certainly produced the goods. Pictures of darling Ross that would never grace the covers of 'Life' or 'Ladies Home Journal'. Even 'Playgirl' would baulk at using them. 'Too much cock,' they would say. Hmmm, Elaine thought with a wicked drunken smile, was there ever such a thing. . . .

She hiccupped in a most unladylike manner. One thing about living alone, you didn't have to look your best. You could cover yourself in bee's come from head to toe and there was no one around to complain. She slavered on some more of the face cream that Ross hated.

Little S. Shitz wanted ten thousand dollars.

She didn't even have enough cash to pay the maid.

'I must have an answer by the weekend,' he had said. 'I'll be back.'

It occurred to Elaine that she could summon the police, blackmail was an offence. They could lock the revolting little man away.

Only she was smart enough to realize that it didn't quite work that way. Some grubby lawyer would bail him out, the photos would become a *cause célèbre*, and everyone would know about Ross Conti and Karen Lancaster. She would become the laughing stock of Beverly Hills, not to mention the rest of the world.

With a rush of determination she picked up the phone.

'Maralee Gray here,' said her friend's dulcet tones.

Elaine took a deep breath. 'Maralee darling,' she said unevenly. 'Can you lend me ten thousand dollars?'

Shelly answered Buddy's insistent buzz by opening the door an inch and peering through the crack.

He pushed past her into the stuffy apartment.

'Am I glad you're here,' she said excitedly. 'I'm gettin' out.'

'Hey –' He grabbed her by the arm. '*You* are not going anywhere.' He took in Randy's inert body spread across the bed, and twisted her arm until she faced him. 'What *you* are going to do is sit right down and shut up.'

She did not argue, just slumped to the floor cradling her head in her hands. 'I told him it was too much,' she mumbled. 'I warned the crazy fuck – but he wouldn't listen to me. And I *know* about drugs, man. Jesus. I know. My old lady was a junkie.'

He ignored her and approached Randy's unclothed body. One arm dangled limply off the bed. Gingerly he lifted the wrist and felt for a pulse. There was none. He rolled Randy onto his back and stared at death.

For a moment he was in San Diego. The morgue. Tony. The smell of formaldehyde.

Vomit rose in his throat. He wanted to run.

Shelly began to snivel. 'Wasn't *my* fault. He wanted it. If he wanted it he shoulda bin able to handle it. Right?'

'What did you give him?'

She threw her arms up in despair. 'We were doin' a little of everything – goofing around – havin' good times.'

'Some good times,' he said grimly.

'Rand was depressed,' she said defensively. 'Since that rich bitch dumped him. When you blew in with the money we just went wild. I scored some ace coke, and Randy wanted to speedball . . .' she trailed off. 'It just all got to be too much.'

'Have you called a doctor?'

'Are you kiddin'. I'm gettin' *out*, man. I don't need no hassles with the cops.'

Buddy suddenly realized that he didn't either. He could just

403

imagine Sadie's face if he was involved in a drug bust. There was nothing he could do for Randy now.

'Let's go,' he decided. 'We'll call the paramedics from a phone booth.'

'Can I come with you?' she pleaded.

'Look – I don't –'

'Please, Bud. Please,' she begged. 'I can't be alone now. I'm really freaked by this whole scene. Just for tonight, that's all.'

He remembered the money she had loaned him. The bed that was always available whenever he had needed it.

'Come on,' he said reluctantly.

She clutched onto his arm. 'You're a pal,' she said thankfully.

'Yeah,' he replied cynically. 'A real prince.'

'Give her his number,' Adrian said.

'It's not that simple,' Koko argued. 'She's such a babe in the woods. This Buddy person is a user. In her condition, I don't think it's wise to put her in contact with him.'

Adrian spun his wheelchair around the kitchen. 'She can handle it. She's not as naive as you think.'

'She's vulnerable.'

Adrian laughed bitterly. 'Aren't we all?'

'Oh dear!' Koko exclaimed. 'You do still *like* her don't you? You're not upset about me bringing her to live with us?'

Adrian shook his head. 'I love her. You know that.'

'Good,' sighed Koko, relieved.

'But give her his number,' Adrian added. 'She's got her own life to lead.'

After dinner Koko did just that. 'I'm sorry, dreamheart. I forgot all about it,' he explained.

Angel tried to hide her delight, but she found it a hard job.

Koko wanted to ply her with warnings, but Adrian was watching him so he kept quiet.

A few minutes later she asked if she could make a call.

'Use our bedroom,' Adrian said. 'You'll be more private there.'

She glowed. 'Thank you.'

Koko gave a deep worried sigh.

'Cut it out,' scolded Adrian. 'You're like an old mother hen.'

'Just call me the mother, darling,' Koko retorted tartly. 'The old and the hen I can do without.'

They stopped at a call box and summoned the paramedics, then against his better judgement Buddy took Shelly to his new apartment. She was impressed. 'Je . . . sus!' she exclaimed. 'And what big mama is payin' *your* rent?'

He was too down to even bother to answer. Nobody had ever said Randy was the greatest guy in the world, but he had been a good friend, and Buddy felt a deep sadness, not only at Randy's death, but at the *way* he had died. Maybe it could have been him . . . Buddy Boy . . . If fate and Montana Gray hadn't taken a hand in his future.

He threw a blanket and a pillow on the couch in the living room. 'You can sleep here,' he said.

'I'd sooner sleep with you.'

'Let's get something straight up front. I don't want you in that way.'

He noticed that her pupils were dilated, her movements nervy and fast. She was still high on whatever cocktail had sent Randy over the edge.

'Why don't you sleep it off,' he said.

'Are you kiddin'. It's ten o'clock at night – I won't be able to sleep for hours. Not unless you give me somethin'.'

'What?'

'A few 'ludes will do it.'

'I'm fresh out.'

'You really became Mister Super-Straight didn't you?'

'I'm trying.'

She fished in her purse. 'I got a prescription – you want to run it by a pharmacy for me?'

'Is it forged?'

'The genuine article, man.'

He took the prescription from her, figuring it was the only way that either of them would get any sleep.

'I'll be fast,' he said. 'And don't answer the phone, let the service get it.'

As soon as he left she reached in her purse for a joint and lit up, letting the lazy smoke fill her lungs. She felt better immediately and started to look around the apartment, figuring that Buddy must have found himself a rich woman who had set him up for her convenience.

The telephone rang, and ignoring his instructions she reached for it.

A casual, 'Yeah?'

Angel's voice, breathy and sweet. 'Can I speak to Buddy Hudson please.'

She took a quick drag on her joint. 'Who wants him?'

'Angel.'

'He-*llo* Angel. This is your old friend, Shelly. How're you makin' out?'

Angel's voice faltered. 'Fine, thank you.' Why was Shelly there?

'Haven't run on back to the sweet old backwoods of Kentucky yet?' Shelly questioned.

'Is Buddy around?' Angel demanded, sounding stronger than she felt.

'Buddy is out. O.U.T. When he returns I shall tell him you phoned. And if you want my advice don't call again.' She paused to let her advice sink in. 'When it's over, Angel pie, it's over. And I can get real mad about sharing. Get my drift?'

Helplessness and anger engulfed Angel. She could not understand why Buddy was playing these cruel games. First, at the party, telling her he would be right back, and then not appearing at all. Now, asking her to call him, and having Shelly answer the phone. If he wanted Shelly he could damn well have her, because she had had enough. She slammed the receiver down with surprising force.

In the other room Koko and Adrian exchanged glances.

'Maybe you were right,' Adrian murmured. 'Perhaps she *shouldn't* have called him.'

Koko nodded wisely. 'I would say it is time to suggest a lawyer.'

Montana left the restaurant shortly after Buddy. She had to work with these people, she certainly didn't have to eat with them.

She drove home in Neil's Maserati. Somehow a fast car suited her mood. The Volkswagen was old times. The Maserati was her future. Speedy and sleek, capable of leaving everything in its wake. She felt really good. Apprehensive, but in control at last. She couldn't wait for the movie to start, although Gina was going to be trouble all the way if her behaviour tonight was any indication. Whatever had Neil been thinking of taking *that* to bed?

Gina Germaine. A golden cow. She hated Neil for his lack of taste. She could hardly bring herself to call him at the beach. The awful truth was she couldn't care less anymore. When the movie wrapped so would their marriage.

Secretly she hoped he would not be well enough to take over directing the movie. It was her baby now. She loved the power and

thrust of being in control. Momentarily Oliver was holding her back
. . . But once they started shooting – watch out asshole! Run for the
hills, dope!

She thought of Buddy and their one night of passion, scrupulously
never mentioned by either of them. He had arranged for the Volkswagen to be left outside her house, washed, the tank full, and the
keys in the mailbox. She was glad that he had turned out to be the sort
of man who understood that beautiful nights sometimes happened
between friends. And after that, they could still be good friends with
no inquests about how or why. She was looking forward to working
with him.

Gina was another matter. She was going to have to clear up a thing
or two at lunch. The woman might think she had got away with
screwing her husband, but she certainly wasn't going to screw her
movie too.

Once home she stripped off her clothes, threw on an old shirt,
searched for her tinted reading glasses, and sat down with the
shooting script. Right now the movie was all she cared about.

Watching a relationship develop between Gina and Ross was giving
Sadie heartburn or heartache. One of the two. She made her excuses
and left.

Pusskins Malone departed immediately after her. He had a date
with a cabaret singer who crooned the blues and gave great head. Not
at the same time, but near enough.

So then there were three. And Oliver was anxious to make tracks.
But at long last Gina and Ross seemed to have found each other, and
neither was interested in leaving.

Ross said, 'I think I'd like another Irish coffee.'

Gina said, 'And I'd like another Brandy Alexander.'

Oliver said, 'I know you two kids'll excuse me if I go home. I've
taken care of the check.'

As if either of them cared. Ross was staring down her neckline, and
she was wondering if the famous Conti dick was as large as rumour
had it.

Oliver rose. 'Good night.'

They barely glanced in his direction. He hurried out to the parking
lot and gave his ticket to an attendant. While he was waiting for his
car Karen materialized from the shadows.

'Where the hell is that scurvy prick?' she demanded.

Oliver could think of many who fitted that description.

'Who?' he asked mildly.

'Forget it.' She stomped off to her Ferrari and exited amid a cloud of angry exhaust fumes.

Inside the restaurant Gina husked, 'My place or yours?'

Ross could hardly imagine smuggling the very visible Ms. Germaine into the Beverly Hills Hotel. One look at her and the late night tourists would probably riot!

'Yours,' he said.

'Good,' she said.

Buddy handed the bottle of prescription quaaludes to Shelly, and asked, 'What kind of a doctor supplies you with these?'

'They started life as prescription drugs, man. Like for depression or relaxation – anti-stress – that kinda shit.'

She stretched, and the short tank top she was wearing pulled up and revealed inches of hard tanned stomach. 'I got one doctor thinks I'm *real* depressed. Another that'd hand me a slip for the big H if he thought I'd drop my pants for him.' She shrugged nonchalantly. 'And the third guy just likes the bread.' She nodded wisely. 'Always gotta keep a good supply of friendly doctors. Makes life a lot easier.'

He thought of Randy. Had it been easy for him? When the drugs hit . . . when the coke and grass and heroin all combined to blow him straight to heaven – or hell. Whatever.

The phone rang and he sprang for it, catching it on the second ring. 'Angel?' he blurted, so sure it was her.

'Who is Angel?' came Sadie's acid tones.

'Just a guy I know,' he answered, without taking a beat.

'I'm very mad,' she said angrily. 'And when I am mad I do not sleep – so rather than ruin my night's rest I decided to let you know what's on my mind.'

'Hey – Sadie. If it –'

'Just be quiet and listen. You came to me for representation. You arrived with your sexy strut and some half-cocked promise of a role in a movie.'

'Hey –'

'I took you on. Got you the film, special billing, excellent money. *I* am financing your billboard. *I* choose *you*, Buddy. And believe me there are plenty of other actors I could do exactly the same for.'

'Are you sayin' I don't appreciate it?' he interjected heatedly.

'I am saying that I do not like the way you behaved tonight. How *dare* you walk out in the middle of dinner. You *do not* treat people that way. Especially not me, any producer you are working for, or your director. When you are Al Pacino do it if you must. But let me tell you this – if you're going to be difficult I'll drop you now and cancel the billboard campaign. Do you want that? Better tell me now before it's too late.'

'I'm sorry, Sadie,' he said, suitably humble. 'It *was* an emergency. It won't happen again.'

'Just so long as we both know exactly where we stand,' she said crisply, and hung up.

'Tell me more about Sadie,' giggled Shelly. 'Is she Sadie Sadie married lady? Is she the one that set you up here?'

'Do me a favour, drop some more pills and go to sleep.' He headed towards the bedroom.

She was not anxious to see him go. 'Sure you don't feel like stoppin' by Mavericks? I feel so low.'

'*Sleep*, Shelly.'

He closed the door. Then he sat on the end of the bed and thought things out. If Sadie was pissed at him for running out on some dumb dinner how would she feel about him suddenly coming up with a wife?

Worse still. What if his *mother* materialized?

He never ever thought of her. Only in his nightmares did she come to him uninvited and unannounced.

Incest.

A filthy word.

His skin crawled every time he was forced to remember. His whole past was a mess. Names danced in front of his eyes. Maxie Sholto, Joy Byron, Gladrags, Jason Swankle, and a hundred faceless women who might see him on the screen and say – 'Wasn't that the stud I paid money to?'

The whole thing could blow up in his face if he wasn't careful. Yet how could he be careful now? What was done was done.

He hated living a lie. Wasn't truth supposed to be the name of the new game he was playing? How about coming clean with Angel for a start. If they were going to make a life together he owed her that at least. The more he thought about it the more he realized it was right.

A new beginning.

An unwelcome thought occurred to him. He should make the peace with his mother first. It had to be done before she came screaming recognition back into his life. Which could happen when all the publicity he was doing hit. As soon as his schedule allowed he would take a day and go to San Diego.

With that decided he felt better. Then he checked with his service to see if Angel had called. She hadn't.

Immediately he was depressed again. Why was he feeling so bad when finally everything was going so well?

He did press-ups until he was exhausted.

Then he slept.

On very rare occasions two people meet in bed who are totally compatible in every way – or so they both fondly imagine.

Gina Germaine and Ross Conti were just such a couple. She, all white-blond hair, sensual mouth and voluptuous breasts.

He, all leathery tan, blue blue eyes and enormous cock.

'Where have you been all my life?' he gasped, near orgasm, his rigid member clamped firmly between her heaving bosoms.

'I don't know,' she gasped, also on the point of divine release. 'But wherever it was, honey, I ain't going back.'

They exploded in a cacophony of moans, grunts, sighs and screams.

'Hot damn!' exclaimed Ross.

'Oh boy!' exclaimed Gina.

They had found each other with a vengeance.

56

Emmy-Lou Josus had been a maid for sixty of her eighty-two years. She had seen a thing or two in her time. Worked in a whorehouse in New Orleans, a cathouse in St. Louis, a bordello in San Francisco. She had observed fights, and stabbings, abortions and suicides. She had acted as a confidante to the girls, adviser to the johns. By the time she came to Las Vegas she figured she had more or less seen it all.

Emmy-Lou Josus was a tough little lady, nutcracker brown, with a few tufts of peroxide hair ribboned about her scalp. She muttered to herself most of the time. Incoherent ramblings of a past life filled with adventure. The ladies she worked for didn't seem to mind. Why should they mind as long as she vacuumed and dusted and walked the dogs and let the cats in or out and peeled the potatoes and took care of life's grand shit?

She mumbled happily as she let herself into Nita Carrolle's bijou house with her own key. Mrs. Carrolle was one of her favourites. She trusted Emmy-Lou. No locking up the booze when she was in *her* place.

The house smelled. Emmy-Lou sniffed and looked for the dogs to come running to greet her as they usually did. 'Doggie fellas,' she called out. 'Stinky fellas.'

She scratched her armpit and removed a faded wool jacked liberally decorated with moth-holes. Mrs. Carrolle had promised her something new. Maybe for Christmas. Or perhaps her birthday. She frowned. Couldn't remember when her birthday was. Couldn't remember much of anything nowadays.

She scratched under her arm again, sniffed the strange odour which filled the small house, and went into the kitchen. The dogs were on the table in the middle of the room, their throats slit.

For a moment Emmy-Lou stared. The white formica was covered in blood and she knew she was going to have to clean it. She didn't like blood. It got on your clothes and hands and the smell lingered and . . .

Silently she crossed herself. Mrs. Carrolle shouldn't have done it. It was a cruel thing to do. Emmy-Lou could not abide cruelty. Resolutely she set about cleaning up the mess.

She placed the dogs in black plastic garbage bags, scrubbed the heavily stained formica, mopped the floor, all the while muttering ferociously to herself.

When this was done she made a cup of hot sweet tea, sat down at the table and drank it broodingly.

Eventually she went into the living room armed with duster, mop, and vacuum. Maybe it wasn't such a bad thing Mrs. Carrolle had done. Maybe not so terrible. 'No more doggie shitty,' she giggled.

The words froze on her lips, and she knew for sure that she would never get the wool jacket Mrs. Carrolle had promised her.

57

Neil Gray stomped restlessly around his rented beach house. Nurse Miller sat in her usual place knitting. She was a thin, tight-lipped Scottish woman, and Neil was sick and tired of her dull company.

The doctor had given him a list of instructions: No drinking. No excessive exercise. No smoking. No fatty foods. No stress. No sex. In fact none of the things he enjoyed in life. He felt fine, wonderful in fact. Why should he continue to live his life like an invalid? The horror of the heart attack was behind him. He took his pills every day, and quite frankly believed he was fitter and stronger than he had been in years.

'How about a big juicy steak tonight, and a bottle of wine?' he suggested to Nurse Miller, who had abandoned her knitting, ready for her daily trip to the market.

'Now, now Mr. Gray,' she said, as if addressing a naughty child. 'We'll have none of that talk.'

'Ah, but we will Nurse Miller. I *fancy* steak and wine. Maybe even a cigar if they have anything smokable.'

'Quite out of the question. The doctor would never allow it.'

'The bloody doctor's not here, is he?'

She pursed her lips. 'I have been hired to look after you. And that is exactly what I intend to do to the best of my ability.'

She left for the market in her car, the only means of transport at the house. He had been delivered there by a chauffeur and Montana. The one and only time she had visited. Not that he blamed her. He had been caught in a situation that nightmares are made of. The question was – what to do now? He wasn't prepared to sit quietly at the beach while he lost his wife, his movie, and his sanity.

Impatiently he paced the room and glared out at the ocean. He hated the bloody sea. The noise alone was enough to drive him mad.

In due course Nurse Miller returned. She brought him the newspapers and the trades which he greedily devoured.

Inside the Herald Examiner there was a large photo of Gina Germaine and Buddy Hudson, accompanied by a short piece on the film. The picture was of Gina and Buddy, but the story was all Montana. He got a line or two. It seemed that he had graduated from being the celebrity in the family to just the sick husband.

He read the story through twice. It irritated him.

Then he stared at the photo of Gina – chief cause of all his troubles.

'Nurse Miller,' he shouted abruptly. 'Give me the keys to your car. I am going into town for an hour or two. Don't worry. I will not smoke, drink or have carnal knowledge of any female. You may rest assured that I shall behave perfectly.'

She confronted him immediately, her thin lips tight with disapproval. 'I cannot allow you to do that, Mr. Gray.'

He strode into the kitchen and plucked the keys from her purse. 'The choice, my dear woman, is mine, not yours.'

Her voice rose. 'Mr. Gray. If you insist on behaving like this I shall be forced to summon the doctor.' She hurried in front of him and blocked the doorway with her formidable self.

He shoved past her in a most ungentlemanly fashion. 'Frankly, Nurse Miller, I don't give a shit.'

Shelly was not easy to get rid of. She refused to wake with all of Buddy's pushing and shoving, so he was forced to leave her in his apartment while he went off to a business lunch with Pusskins Malone. He left large pieces of paper with 'DO NOT ANSWER' taped to both phones.

In the lobby of the Beverly Hills Hotel, Pusskins thrust two newspapers under his nose.

GINA GERMAINE AND NEW STAR BUDDY HUDSON.

They called him a star, and he hadn't done a thing!

'Can I get six copies of each?' he asked anxiously.

'You can get cancer if you want it bad enough,' replied Pusskins obscurely.

Lunch was in the Polo Lounge. A beautiful Mexican journalist with shiny black hair and a Miss Universe figure waited to interview him.

He had it down pat. Same questions. Same answers. Smile. Exert plenty of charm. He had yet to meet a heavyweight, although Pusskins assured him they existed.

The girl made shorthand notes while he gave her the same old

413

replies and let his mind drift. He wondered if there was anything in the paper about Randy. Probably not.

Sin. To die in Hollywood and be a nobody.

How about funeral arrangements? Who would take care of everything?

Second sin of the day. To die broke.

Pusskins snapped his fingers. 'Junior. Get with it,' he commanded. 'Michelle just asked you the same question twice. You got an answer for her or not?'

Buddy sprang to attention. Yeah. He had an answer for her. He had an answer for everything.

A piece of human garbage suitably nicknamed Rats Sorenson had started his long and non-illustrious career peddling nude pictures of his sister for twenty cents a throw. That was in the forties, when nude photos of females were something to get excited about. Realizing he had a talent for promoting, Rats soon progressed to selling photos of himself *and* his sister. By the time the fifties bloomed he was publishing, printing and distributing (under the counter of course) a crude attempt at a magazine subtly titled 'Twats That'. He made his fortune and swiftly produced a series of blue movies which also made money. In the sixties he decided to go legitimate. And he produced a glossy magazine about gardens which lasted for three issues and took every penny he possessed. By this time he was married to a sixteen year old nymphet who waited until the money went, then followed it. He caught her in a motel with a seventy year old married man and shot the old guy right between the eyes. For this he got a twenty-five year sentence. And with time off for good behaviour (he soon became the warden's favourite for reasons known only to himself and his cellmate – a blackmailer by the name of Little S. Shitz) he was set free on an unsuspecting world after fifteen years. Rats soon returned to the business he knew best, and made his second fortune. 'Twats That' reappeared – this time *on* the news stands and retitled 'Hard Pussy'. A waiting public embraced the magazine fondly.

But, of course, Rats wanted more. He married a seventeen year old go-go dancer, and accompanied her on weekly trips to the supermarket where he noticed a certain type of newspaper gain great prominence at the check-out stands. It started with the 'National Enquirer' which was swiftly followed by all kinds of imitators.

Rats wanted in. He decided to launch a newspaper which followed the same formula – but with an added ingredient. Hot, compromising *pictures* of celebrities – as hot as he could get 'em. Of course the supermarkets wouldn't carry *his* magazine, but that didn't worry him. People could buy it at their news stands.

Running into his old pal Little S. Shitz, turned out to be a fortunate coincidence for both of them. They collided outside Tony Romas restaurant deep in the heart of Beverly Hills.

Conversation revealed the fact that the new hot newsrag 'Truth & Fact' was owned, published and edited by none other than Rats himself.

'Have I got some pictures for you . . .' Little boasted. 'Not cheap, but worth every fat buck.'

The very next day business was done. Rats bought the entire Karen Lancaster-Ross Conti set of negatives and chose a rather tasteful shot of Ross just about to chew on a nipple for the cover. The real low-down dirty stuff he saved for the centre spread.

'I'm rushing it through for the next issue,' Rats said.

'Maybe I could have photo credit,' Little suggested tentatively. He never had been particularly smart.

Maralee turned down Elaine's request to loan her ten thousand dollars. In fact she was quite shocked that Elaine had summoned the nerve to ask her. She phoned Karen to complain, but Karen was most unfriendly, accusing her of siding with Elaine, and not calling her.

'I've been too concerned about Neil to contact anyone,' Maralee explained.

'But you hate the louse,' Karen said, perplexed.

'Hate is a word that is no longer a part of my vocabulary,' Maralee replied piously. 'Neil has changed. I think he's ready to get rid of whatshername and come back to me.'

'You can't be serious?'

'Absolutely.'

There was a short silence while they both digested Maralee's new personality. Then Karen remembered a small item she had read buried somewhere in the L.A. Times.

'What was your friend Randy's surname?'

'Felix. I introduced you to him enough times, the least you can do is remember his name. I know he's not famous, but - '

'He's dead,' Karen interrupted.

'What?'

'There's a piece in the paper. Someone called the police and they found him overdosed in some shitty one-room apartment in Hollywood. I thought you said he had money.'

Maralee was devastated. She had broken up with Randy, but still . . . How could such a thing happen? And what was he doing in a dump? According to him he had lived in a very nice apartment – 'It's only three bedrooms, but I find it comfortable,' he had told her. Of course she had never been there . . . Perhaps it was just as well . . .

'I must go to him,' she decided.

'What are you *talking* about? He's dead,' snorted Karen. 'The *police* are involved. They seem to think a woman was with him when he died, and they want to interview her.' A thought occurred to her. '*You* weren't doing drugs with him were you?'

'Don't be so ridiculous,' snapped Maralee. 'I don't even smoke marijuana.'

'Hmmm,' Karen sighed. 'You've no idea *what* you're missing.'

Maralee concluded the conversation and went into her bathroom to gaze at her blond prettiness in the mirror.

Why did she always pick losers? What was it about her that attracted the fortune hunters and the bums?

She thought of Neil. An older man. English, respected, a fine director.

Once he had been her husband and she had let him go. The time had come to win him back.

Neil hit the Pacific Coast Highway in Nurse Miller's pristine white Chevrolet. Now that he was out he had changed his mind about storming Oliver's offices and regaining control of his film. He wanted Montana more than he wanted the bloody movie, and she would certainly not appreciate him barging in and taking over. He decided to stop off, have a drink, return to the beach and call her. If he requested a meeting she could hardly turn him down, and then they could thrash everything out. A confrontation was long overdue.

He found a bar he knew and pulled into the parking lot.

A couple of decent brandies couldn't possibly hurt, they would probably do him more good than harm. Everyone knew brandy was a medicinal aid.

The first one was like nectar. And the second merely a complement to the first. His capacity was huge. In Paris he had thought nothing of killing a bottle a night. Of course that was years previously, but you never forget how to handle your liquor. Or your women.

He laughed hollowly at that, and ordered another drink.

416

'Move in,' suggested Gina, the morning after their night of passion. She was rushing to get ready for her lunch appointment with Montana.

Ross lay in bed watching her. He grinned lazily. One thing was for sure, he certainly didn't need asking twice. Her house was fabulous, her tits perfection – besides – the Beverly Hills Hotel was costing him an arm and a leg.

Montana arrived for lunch at El Padrino in the Beverly Wilshire Hotel on time. She looked around, ordered a pernod on ice, and sat back to wait. She knew for sure that Gina would make her wait.

True to form Gina made a typical movie star entrance thirty-five minutes later. She wore yellow silk slacks, a diaphanous blouse, huge white sunglasses, and a fluffy red fox jacket although it was seventy-five degrees out.

'Goddamn!' she exclaimed, flopping onto the banquet seat. 'Did I have a night! Ross Conti is everything they say – and more.' She giggled. 'Several inches more! Best lay I've had in a year!' She grabbed a passing waiter. 'Vodkatini. On the rocks. Lots of 'em.' She lifted her sunglasses and peered at Montana. 'So what's with the meeting? I coulda slept another two hours.'

Montana shook her head trying to hide deep aggravation. 'Gina,' she said slowly, as if talking to a recalcitrant child. 'I told you to lose twenty pounds, get your hair fixed, play down the sexy image. Didn't you understand me?'

Gina retreated behind her sunglasses and glanced restlessly around the dimly lit restaurant.

'Montana. Dear. You must realize I have a certain image to project. My public expects me to look . . . glamorous.'

'I don't give a good goddamn what your public expects. I, as your director, expect a hell of a lot more. And if I don't get it, you're out.'

'*I'm* out!' she laughed disbelievingly. 'Dear. Let us not forget who the *star* of this movie is.'

The waiter brought her drink and she almost downed it in one gulp.

Montana sipped her pernod and considered how best to deal with the situation. She felt surprisingly calm, because she knew she was going to win. Gina *would* toe the line. She didn't know how she was going to manage it, she just knew that she was.

She regarded the blonde woman coolly. 'O.K.,' she said. 'Fine. Have it your way. I guess I'll be busy enough taking care of Buddy, and I know Ross is going to be great. I think he may surprise everyone.'

Gina had not expected retreat so quickly, and it knocked her off balance. She shrugged her fox jacket off her shoulders – causing several nearby males to choke on their drinks. '*I'm* going to surprise a lot of people too,' she said petulantly.

'Sure you are,' agreed Montana. 'Voluptuous Gina Germaine does it again. Tits and ass wins the prize for non-performance of the year.'

'I resent that remark,' Gina snapped. 'Just because I screwed your husband don't think you can talk to me any way you like.'

Montana's eyes flashed dangerously, but she kept her temper.

Oh, Neil! With this? She was never worthy of you.

'Whatever you did with Neil is his affair, and your affair too. I never believed in putting on the shackles,' she said quietly.

Gina took off her sunglasses and narrowed her protruding blue eyes. 'You're really strange, you know that?'

Montana shrugged. 'I believe everybody has their freedom. Neil wanted you. He had you. Big deal. Look where he ended up.'

'God! That's not a very nice thing to say.'

'Why not? It's true.' She signalled for the waiter. 'Check please.'

'We haven't had lunch yet,' Gina objected.

'No point to it,' Montana said crisply. 'I wanted to talk to you about the role, try to help you with it. But I can see I'm wasting my time. You just want to play power games, and that's not my trip. I'm a working woman, Gina, not a Hollywood wife.'

'You're really a pistol.' A grudging admiration entered Gina's tone.

'Nope. Just a professional who wants to make the best movie I can. I told you that at our first meeting – I thought we had the same goal in mind, but obviously I was mistaken.' She accepted the check from the waiter and fished in her purse for a credit card. 'If you don't want to cooperate, I'm certainly not going to force you. I'll just concentrate on Buddy and Ross. They'll be so good that nobody'll notice *Miz* Germaine. And it's a shame because you could have been dynamite. It's all there, Gina. Hidden beneath the hair and the boobs and the make up.' She paused for a moment. 'You just need someone to work with you – someone who *cares* about what you're doing. I could bring it out in you, and you know it.'

'I don't work well with women.'

'Bullshit. When have you ever tried? You might find you enjoy the experience.'

A slow smile spread across Gina's face. 'Y'know something? You remind me of me!'

God forbid! Montana thought.

'Yeah,' enthused Gina. 'Fast with the mouth – and you got balls, kiddo. You can make it happen – I *bet* you can.'

'Does this mean you're going to listen to me?'

'Why not?' Gina said decisively. 'Yeah. Why not indeed? I've been listening to schmucks who wanted to get their rocks off all my life – so who knows? Working with you might make a change.' She leaned forward confidentially. 'I'll tell you something, Montana. Neil and me – it didn't mean a thing – just sort of a business arrangement.'

'I'm sure.'

'And you would be right to be sure because I am here to tell you that all men are unfaithful bums. *All* of them, honey. Never trust 'em as far as you can spit.' She nodded wisely. 'I *know*. I have been out on my own since I was fifteen years old, and let me tell you – it has not all been a pot of honey. How would you like to hear about some of the things I had to do to get where I am today?'

When Gina talked, she talked. Two hours later she was *still* talking. And Montana listened. Quietly.

Actors. Actresses. They were all the same. Give them a little sympathy, a little understanding, and they were yours.

When the movie rolled, Gina would be putty in her hands. And she would get a performance out of her the like of which her horny public had *never* seen before.

If Neil could do it so could she.

58

Leon went immediately to work. He made some vague excuse to Millie and returned to Barstow. There, he checked out police files, newspaper reports, and adoption agencies.

A day was not enough to do everything, so he took a room at the Desert Inn Hotel and called Millie. She was not happy. 'This is our vacation,' she reminded him flatly. 'You're not supposed to be working.'

'I know. But it's important. And I'll make it up to you – I promise.'

'Captain Lacoste phoned. He wants you to contact him.'

He was too caught up to notice the sullenness in her voice. 'Thanks. I'll probably be back tomorrow.'

'Don't rush,' she muttered coldly. But he had already broken the connection.

The captain had news that made Leon's skin crawl. Deke Andrews had struck again. This time in Las Vegas. The victim was an old hooker who cruised the downtown bars and casinos. 'He left enough signs to let us know it was him. Prints, saliva, semen. The same distinctive knife wounds. And his shirt. The police in Vegas have a couple of witnesses who may or may not have spotted him leaving the scene. We're sending his photo over the wire. Are you prepared to go there?'

Leon didn't hesitate. 'Of course. I want to be taken off vacation and declared officially on the case.'

'That's what I hoped you'd say. I'll contact Vegas and let them know you're on your way. They've promised full cooperation.'

Leon's mind was already racing. Why Las Vegas? Somehow he had thought that Deke was heading for Barstow. Just a hunch . . . Something . . . someone in Barstow . . . But what if Deke had *already* visited Barstow.

As soon as he got off the phone he decided to check out all local homicides over the last four weeks. And then he would head for Vegas – fast.

59

'Where is he?' demanded Maralee, blue eyes anxious and concerned.

'He *stole* my car,' stated Nurse Miller dourly. 'Assaulted me, and used foul language. I wish to tender my immediate notice.'

'Don't be so silly,' Maralee said vaguely. 'He's not allowed to drive.'

'I know that, Mrs. Gray. But I couldn't stop him. He was like a madman.'

Maralee could not control her disappointment. She almost

stamped her foot. 'I wanted him to be here. It's important. How *could* you let him go?'

'I expect two weeks' severance pay. And you are most fortunate that I am not planning to sue for bodily harm. If my car is not back here within the hour I am reporting it as a stolen vehicle to the police.'

Before long two or three drinks turned to four or five, and his heart began to thunder in his chest, but it didn't bother him. Nothing bothered him.

He was going to have it out with Montana. Tell her the whole story. Lay it on the line – as the Americans so charmingly put it. Come clean. Confess. Beg her forgiveness.

Only Montana wouldn't buy it. Montana, so clear-headed and cool. 'Fuck off, Neil,' she would say. 'I don't need your jerk-off excuses.' And she was so right, for that's all it would be . . . stupid excuses explaining several acts of lust for which he *had* no excuse.

He was going to order another drink, thought better of it, and walked unsteadily outside.

Shelly was still in residence when Buddy returned. She was stretched out on his couch painting her toenails bright scarlet.

'Hiya, star.' She picked up the Los Angeles Times and waved it at him. 'Why didn't you *tell* me?'

He shrugged, irritated that she hadn't made a nice quiet exit in his absence. 'We had other things on our mind. I was going to.'

'You and Gina Germaine. Wowee! Like it's big time, man.'

'Hey – listen. I got a lot of work to take care of. Why don't I drive you back to your place?' Before you move in, he wanted to add, but controlled himself.

'I don't have to go,' she said. 'I quit my job last week, and with Randy gone . . .' She held her leg in the air and admired her newly painted toes. 'Besides, I can help you. Read through your script with you. Then maybe we can drop by Mavericks and knock 'em all out. Just looove to see those green faces, wouldn't you?'

'It'll be better if I take you home,' he said bluntly.

'For you it'll be better –' she said glaring at him balefully. 'Why can't I stay?'

'Because I'm expecting Angel.'

'Like hell you are.'

'What makes you think I'm not?'

She jumped off the couch. 'Okay. Take me home big-shot. I can live without you.'

'What makes you think I'm not expecting Angel?' he repeated.

'Forget it,' she muttered.

'I don't want to forget it.'

'Well I suggest you do.' She grabbed her purse and slung it roughly over her shoulder. 'I'll get a cab – star. Wouldn't want to put you out.'

'Did Angel call? Did you answer my phone?' he asked furiously.

She reached the front door and turned, one hand on her hip, a sneer on her lips. 'That's for me to know and you to find out.'

She slammed the door on her way out.

He was already reaching for the phone.

When Maralee refused to loan Elaine ten thousand dollars it was just as well because Little S. Shitz failed to turn up for their second meeting which was okay because Elaine would never file for divorce anyway. If Ross wanted out, let *him* make all the moves.

Lina quit, but Elaine was able to cash a cheque at Ron Gordino's establishment (it would bounce – but so what?) and she bribed Lina back with a bonus.

A television actor in shorts and a UCLA T-shirt picked her up at the check-out counter of Hughes Market on Beverly, and she rather rashly invited him back to the house. Once he got a sniff of luxury he pounced.

She fought him off and sent him on his way.

He did not go quietly.

Lina quit again. She was a Catholic, and there was only so much she could take.

Elaine consumed four straight vodkas and passed out in front of her beloved Merv.

She missed the news flash which informed Los Angeles that Neil Gray had suffered another massive heart attack, collapsed and died in the parking lot of a Santa Monica drinking establishment.

60

Las Vegas behind him now, the glittering city in the desert fading into the distance as he spurred the van towards Los Angeles. He wanted to fly – to take off along the deserted road as he knew the van was capable of. But he did not do that. He kept within the speed limit. Had to be careful.

His mind was full of ugly images. Hate flowed through his veins. Yet he knew that Joey was watching over him. Kind, sweet Joey . . .

Where is the whore?

For a moment he couldn't remember and fury engulfed him.

The harlot was with another man.

The van screamed to a stop. He couldn't see anything, red flames engulfed him. Red . . . blood . . . Nita Carrolle's blood . . . Joey's blood . . .

It was alright. She was safe. He had saved her from sin . . .

He had stopped at one of the big hotels before leaving Vegas, and purchased black wraparound sunglasses – so dark that his eyes were not visible through the protective lenses.

He liked them. They were windows to the world outside, while he remained safely behind them, hidden and anonymous.

Joey would say he looked fine. She often complimented him. She was the only one who knew the true person behind Deke Andrews.

The thought of his name infuriated him.

'I am *not* Deke Andrews,' he screamed aloud.

Then he alighted from his truck and pissed across the empty highway.

He knew who his mother was.

He was going to Los Angeles to kill her.

61

Neil Gray's death was a shock. But Buddy felt sure that it would have no adverse effect on Street People. Everyone knew that Montana had taken over. The word was that the start date would be postponed by a week.

He realized that now was the time to make the San Diego trip and square things with his mother. But first he wanted Angel back. He had waited long enough. Reaching her, however, was no easy task. He called. She was never there. He called back. She was still not there. He requested her home phone number and was refused the information. Eventually he got in his car and cruised slowly past the salon hoping to spot her. Some guy with a halo of wild curls sat at the glass fronted reception desk.

Buddy parked the Mustang and sauntered in. 'Hey –' he said casually. 'Is Angel around?'

Koko knew without a doubt that this must be Buddy. The looks were dazzling. 'She no longer works here,' he said, playing with the zipper on his orange jumpsuit. It was no lie. He had decided that she should stay home until after the baby was born. She had protested of course, but he had finally convinced her that Adrian needed the company.

'Where can I find her?'

'I don't know.' Koko had never been the best of liars. He cracked his knuckles nervously.

Buddy slid his hand over the desk, a folded twenty conveniently placed. 'Where?'

Koko shoved the money away from him. 'Really!' he snorted. 'You've been seeing too many movies!'

Raymondo chose that moment to appear. His flashing brown eyes took in the scene. 'Koko! You is *bad* momma. You is sellin' it! On the premises, man!'

'Piss off,' iced Koko.

Whistling and cat-calling Raymondo did just that. But first a parting shot – 'Wait until I tell pretty Angel,' he sang. 'She no like!'

'Cut out the shit,' said Buddy angrily, leaning across the desk. 'I'm her husband. Where is she?'

'She wants a divorce.'

Buddy reached for the zipper on Koko's jumpsuit and pulled it up sharply until it dug into the flesh beneath his neck. 'Where . . . is . . . she?'

Brave was not one of Koko's attributes. He squealed in pain. 'She doesn't want to see you,' he gasped. 'Why don't you leave the poor girl alone?'

'And why don't *you* just butt on out?'

'Angel is my friend. And God knows she needs friends after the way *you've* treated her.' He wrenched himself free. 'If you don't leave the premises at once I shall call the police.'

Buddy picked up the phone and smashed it down on the desk. 'Go ahead. I have every right to look for my wife. And another thing – I'm gonna be here every day until you tell me where she is. You understand what I'm sayin'?'

Koko understood all right. But he wasn't prepared to reveal her whereabouts until he had checked with her. 'Very well,' he said tightly. 'I'll contact Angel and see what she says. If she refuses to see you will you stay away?'

'If she tells me so herself.'

'Tomorrow. The same time.'

'Six o'clock tonight, my friend. I'll be back.' He stalked out.

Koko agonized for a few minutes, then phoned Angel and told her the story. 'What do you want me to do?' he asked anxiously.

'I'll speak to him and tell him that I don't want to see him again,' she said firmly.

'*And* about the divorce,' Koko prompted.

'Yes,' she said, and at the time she meant it. But came six o'clock and Buddy on the phone and she was weakened by just the sound of his voice.

'Things are different,' he told her. 'It's all happening for me an' I want us to be together – y'know – like some kind of a new start. What d'you say?'

She hesitated. 'Buddy. It could never be the same between us. I've changed. I don't want to go back to the life we had.'

'Hey – aren't you listening to me? The past is behind us. We both did things we shouldn't have. Let's give it a fresh shot, babe.' He was

425

huddled over the phone, his voice a low husk, while Koko stood across from the desk with folded arms, pretending not to listen.

'Why don't you stay with Shelly?' Angel said desperately. 'She's your kind of girl. I'm not like her.'

He laughed. 'If you were like her I'd shoot myself!'

'You've been living with her since I left,' she accused. 'Twice she's told me to leave you alone. I just don't understand. What do you *want* from me?'

'Shelly told you to leave me alone?' he asked incredulously. 'She told you *that*?'

'I don't lie.'

'She's full of shit. I've been searching for you ever since you walked.'

'You moved in with her.'

'No way.'

Angel gave a little sigh. She wanted to believe him, but then again she was not fresh off the plane from Louisville anymore.

'I have to see you,' he urged. 'We've got to discuss this.' He huddled closer to the phone. 'I love you, babe. Only you. You gotta know that by now.'

'I'm confused, Buddy.'

'I'll un-confuse you.'

'I need time to think things out.'

'Think *what* out? I got a great apartment, a new car, I'm starring in a movie.'

'I know. I saw your picture in the paper. I'm very happy for you, Buddy.'

'Be happy for *us*. So much has happened, but I need *you* to share it. Without you it doesn't mean anything. Can you understand that?'

He realized as he spoke that it was the truth. Everything was going his way, but he had to have Angel to make it complete. When she came back to him he did not intend to keep it secret. He would tell the world, and if Sadie didn't like it – too bad. Angel was his wife, and he was proud of it. Together they would make a new start, and this time it would work.

'Give me a few days,' she said at last.

'What do you need a few days for?'

'I have to be sure that you mean what you say and that tomorrow you won't change your mind.'

Are you *kidding*?'

'I'm very serious,' she said gravely, and added, 'Are you still involved with drugs?'

'I'm so clean I don't even do grass.' He paused. 'Can I at least know where you are?'

'I'm staying with friends.'

'Where?'

'It doesn't matter. Why don't we speak tomorrow at this time.'

'You got it.'

'But please, *promise* me that you won't try and see me until I say so.'

'Scout's honour.'

She laughed softly. 'You were *never* a scout, Buddy.'

'I am now.'

She gave him her phone number which he committed to memory before they said their goodbyes.

Koko glared at him, bad vibes filling the air.

Buddy did not say a word. He walked from the salon without a backward glance.

As far as he was concerned it was just a matter of time before he had Angel back.

'Street People is cancelled,' Oliver said bluntly. 'Over. Finished. Kaput.'

Montana stared at him, not quite registering what he was saying. They were in his office, everything gleaming, polished, and meticulously clean. Neil Gray had been buried an hour before. A stately funeral, with a respectable turnout.

Montana had conducted herself with dignity.

Maralee had thrown herself across the coffin in screaming hysterics.

'What?' she said at last, unable to believe what she was hearing.

'The party's over.' He was quite enjoying the moment, even though she was a recently bereaved widow. 'This film has cost me a fortune with delays and everything. Now, with Neil's er . . . untimely death . . . I can pick up on insurance and cover my losses.'

'You can *what*?'

'Don't worry, you'll get paid.'

Her voice was controlled, but inside she was shaking. 'Let me get this straight. You're cancelling the film so you can collect the *insurance*?'

'Business smarts. Gotta have them if you expect to survive in this town.'

All the emotions she had been bottling up came spilling out in a diatribe of fury. 'You no-talent ass-licking crawling little *turd*. How can you *do* this?'

'You gotta stop holding back your thoughts, Montana. Get 'em out. Say what's on your mind.' He sniggered, enjoying himself. He had total power, and he revelled in it.

She recovered her composure quickly, determined not to give him the satisfaction of seeing her crumble. 'Oliver,' she said sensibly. 'Surely you must know what this film means to me? It's an important *good* film. It'll make money. A lot more than your goddamn insurance.'

'Every movie is a risk,' he said patiently. 'It can star Redford and Jane Fonda and nobody knows if the public'll go see it. This way I come out on top – it's a no risk situation.'

'You're really serious?'

'The movie is cancelled.'

She was too tired to fight him further. 'Is that all that interests you – making money?' she asked wearily.

'Let's put it this way – I am not in this business to get my cock sucked.'

'You're a real charmer.'

'I love you too.'

She left his office head held high, but spirit defeated. There were moments when she needed Neil desperately, and this was one of them. She marched into her office and slammed the door. Then she took a deep breath and tried to control the tears which threatened.

She did not need Neil. She had learned to get along without him. No good crying out in moments of stress. She had to be strong and deal with things herself.

Neil is dead, she thought, and it's his own damn fault. For a moment anger engulfed her. Once their love had been all consuming . . . then time passed and things changed.

He had deserted her.

But she was a survivor.

Finally she let the tears flow.

It felt good.

Sadie accepted the news calmly. It wasn't the first time and it would not be the last. The movie business was unpredictable to say the least.

Oliver told her over drinks in the Beverly Wilshire Hotel. He also informed her that he had found a director for the other project Neil had been working on – the one with Gina Germaine.

'We can start on pre-production immediately,' he said. 'Gina'll be happy. It's a much better part for her.'

'I didn't even know there was a completed script,' Sadie replied in surprise.

'There wasn't a few weeks ago. But ever since we signed the deal I've been behind it. Got a *great* script now – of course it needs a little work . . .'

'I'll have to read it,' she said shortly. 'The deal we signed was for Neil to direct. This is a different ballgame.'

'But one we can work out, huh Sadie?'

She refused to commit. 'We'll see,' she said, thoughtfully sipping Perrier water. 'Is there anything for Buddy Hudson in it? He's going to be a big star. You may as well get in at the beginning.'

'I think we can find something.'

'Something won't do. It's got to be right.'

'Read the material and see.'

'I'll do that.'

'Fast, please.'

'What a hustler you are, Oliver.'

'Just like you, Sadie.'

She couldn't argue with that.

Koko swept into the house later than usual. Angel was in the kitchen fixing southern fried chicken, while Adrian sat in front of the television watching male go-go dancers.

'Ah . . . sweet domesticity,' he snapped. 'While I work my buns off.'

Adrian clicked the remote and blanked the screen. 'What's eating you?'

'Nothing. I was only physically abused by dear Angel's macho husband today. Where *is* madame?'

'In the kitchen.'

'Ha! Hasn't she run off into his waiting arms yet?'

'What happened?' asked Adrian carefully.

'*You* should know. *You* were sitting here with her.'

'We can't hold on to her forever,' said Adrian mildly.

'For God's sake. Don't *you* go giving me lectures. I know. She's old enough to look after herself. But Adrian,' his eyes misted over.

429

'How can I explain this. She's such a *sweet* person. I want her to stay with us so that we can protect her.'

He had not heard Angel walk into the room. She stood quietly by the door. 'Thank you, Koko,' she murmured softly. 'But don't worry, whatever happens we'll still see each other, and we'll *always* be friends. I'll never forget how you've helped me.'

'You *are* going back to him then?'

Her hands fluttered towards the swell of the baby. 'I've got to give him another chance.'

'Ha!' he snorted. 'You'll regret it.'

Lying out by Gina's Italian tiled swimming pool watching two Japanese gardeners tend the exotic trees and blooms, while a maid served him iced tea, Ross decided that this was the life for him. All this luxury and activity, and he hadn't paid one goddamn red cent. Why hadn't he thought of it before? Find yourself a working woman, sit back and enjoy the advantages. After all – women had taken enough from him over the years – he deserved a little something in return.

Today was his birthday. He had finally reached the big five-o and it was not half as painful as he had thought it would be. Upon waking he had told Gina – he hadn't meant to – but what the hell – it wasn't every day you hit a milestone. And he could hardly hide his age – the film reference books had him coming and going. Fifty was hardly senile. Guys like Newman and Bronson had made passing the half-way mark a mere trifle.

'Why didn't you tell me before?' she exclaimed. 'We could have had a *huge* party.'

He did not want a 'huge party'. He had just suffered through one, although maybe it wouldn't be so bad with someone else footing the bills.

Gina gave him several birthday presents of the physical kind, leaving him exhausted but content. Then she dressed and left for lunch with Sadie.

He sat up, took a sip of iced tea and reached for the script. His lines were underlined in thick red pencil. He knew every one of them. A first – usually he just sauntered on the set and played it by ear. Things were different now. He had a great opportunity, and he did not intend to blow it.

*

Sentiment had never been one of Gina Germaine's attributes. She breezed through life caring only about what was good for her public image. When Neil Gray died she did not think – 'Poor Neil – what a terrible thing.' She thought – 'Thank Christ it didn't happen while he was in bed with me – I'd never have lived *that* down.'

She attended his funeral, a vision in black lace, and posed happily for photographers, Ross Conti by her side. The chemistry that she and Ross created together seemed to arouse great public interest.

Ah! And the chemistry in the privacy of her bedroom was more than right too. For a guy his age he sure had what it takes.

When Sadie told her that Street People was cancelled over lunch in the Bistro Gardens, she opened her mouth to yell.

Sadie silenced her immediately with the news that the other movie she and Neil had planned was an immediate go situation with a finished script, a new director, and Oliver Easterne in charge.

'I read it last night,' Sadie said briskly. 'It's a much better role for you. Trust me, dear.'

Gina always had trusted Sadie, her judgement was the best. She chewed on a lettuce leaf, then said something so totally out of character that Sadie almost spilled her glass of Perrier.

'I'll do it if there's a part for Ross.'

'What?' gasped Sadie.

'We're good together,' Gina explained nonchalantly. 'The press love us. We'll be dynamite on the screen. Fix it, you got the clout.'

'There's nothing for Ross in it,' said Sadie tightly.

'Have them write him in.'

Sadie stared at her lettuce munching client. Why had Ross moved in with this calculating blonde bombshell? She had wanted him for herself and now Gina had him. And worse . . . Gina – who wouldn't give a wooden leg to a cripple – wanted to help him. 'Do you know what you are suggesting?' she said.

'Sure I do.'

'You'd better think about it carefully. Writing Ross in could take weeks or even months. The film would be delayed and you should work at once. I'm sure you realize that.'

Gina gazed reflectively at her agent. One thing about Sadie, she always made sense – maybe it wasn't such a good idea. 'You're right. I guess I shouldn't wait. Send me over the script.'

Sadie patted her large Vuitton purse. 'I have it with me.'

'By the way,' Gina said. 'It's Ross's birthday – and I'm putting together a surprise party at the Bistro tonight. You'll come, oh, and tell Buddy.'

The last thing Sadie wanted to do was celebrate Ross's birthday, but business was business and Gina was a valued client.

'Wouldn't miss it, dear.'

Gina returned home at four o'clock laden with presents. A photographer from an Italian magazine accompanied her, and while she plied Ross with half of Gucci, the photographer captured every sentimental moment.

Ross was not aware of the fact that in exchange for exclusive photos the magazine had paid for all the expensive gifts.

He loved everything, although the photographer didn't thrill him – a stoned lounge lizard in tight white pants who kept on touching Gina's ass.

'Tonight we are dining at the Bistro,' she announced. 'With a couple of friends.'

'Who?'

She giggled mysteriously. 'Just you wait and see. I adore surprises, don't you?'

'Huh?' A look of stunned disbelief crossed Buddy's face.

Sadie said, 'There is no such thing as a sure thing in the film business.'

'But I got the part,' he said blankly.

'You certainly did.'

'They can't do this to me!' he yelled.

'Producers play God. They can do what they like.'

'Fuck 'em!' he screamed.

Ferdie popped his head around the door. 'Everything alright in here?'

'Perfectly fine, thank you,' Sadie replied.

Buddy was unaware of the interruption. He slumped into a chair, mumbling to himself.

Sadie picked up a gold pen and tapped it impatiently on her desk. 'Get a hold of yourself. This is but a small setback. You'll get fully paid, and you've had the benefit of quite a bit of publicity. Something *better* will come along.' She did not wish to reveal the fact that something already had. Timing was everything when dealing with a client.

'Jesus!' he moaned. 'Does Montana know?'

432

'Of course. It will be in the trades tomorrow. And Buddy – I was going to surprise you. Monday your billboard goes up across America, so pull yourself together and start feeling great again. This evening Gina is having a surprise birthday party for Ross – I want you there. You never know, by tonight, I might have good news for you. I am not known as the fastest agent in the west for nothing!'

He nodded with as much enthusiasm as he could muster – and wondered why every time he passed GO some smartass kicked him right in the balls with a cement foot.

Gina did not create her night-time appearance without a little help here and there. A professional South American make-up artist arrived at the mansion every evening promptly at six. He was preceded by a Hungarian masseuse, and followed by a French hairdresser.

What with the Japanese gardeners, the Philippine maids, and Gina's English secretary, the place was like a regular United Nations. Seven magnificent bedrooms, seven matching bathrooms, six enormous living rooms, staff quarters, and a hotel-size kitchen, yet Ross still had trouble finding a quiet spot for himself.

They did not treat him in the manner to which he was accustomed. This pissed him off. They treated him like 'the star's' boyfriend, blissfully unaware that he too was a star.

Gina appeared between make-up and hair. 'Did you call your agent today?' she asked crisply.

'Should I have?'

'Honey, everyone should speak to their agent at least twice a day.'

'Why?'

'Because you gotta keep a finger on the pulse.' Damn! she thought, he doesn't know the movie's been cancelled, and *I'm* not telling him. Why hasn't his schmucky agent called him?

'How about a finger on my pulse?' he leered.

'For an old guy you *suuure aaare* horny. But catch me before the make-up next time, huh?' She hurried from the room with an offhand, 'Call your agent.'

He was speechless. *Old guy*. She had to be kidding. She was no nubile nineteen year old herself.

He fixed himself a scotch on the rocks and admired himself in the mirrored bar. Old or not – he could still knock 'em dead. Ross Conti had a long way to go before they counted *him* out.

*

433

Elaine and Maralee resumed friendship. It was better to bore each other than not to bore at all.

Neither lady was looking her best, so they avoided Ma Maison, the Bistro Gardens, Jimmy's, and other fashionable places for lunch. Instead they stayed at each other's pools, taking ruinous for the skin sunbaths, and large glasses of various exotic alcoholic beverages. The ten thousand dollars Elaine had wished to borrow from her friend was discreetly forgotten.

Elaine talked of nothing but Ross.

Maralee talked of nothing but Neil.

Ron Gordino and Randy Felix were never mentioned. But in a town dedicated to who you were and how much money you had this was only to be expected.

Montana raged. She paced her house on the hill with the wonderful view and called Oliver Easterne every name she could think of – and a few more besides. She felt helpless, a feeling she was not used to and did not like.

The movie business.

You could shove it.

She had contacted her attorney in New York and demanded that he get the rights back to Street People. When he returned her call an hour later he informed her it was impossible.

'Nothing's impossible,' she stormed.

'I'll work on it. But what are you worried about anyway? You've been paid.'

She had always sensed that beneath the Savile Row suits lurked an insensitive fool. What did *money* matter?

Mental note. Change attorneys.

She tried to calm herself by sorting through Neil's desk. In a drawer she found a first draft of Street People – her handwriting scrawled across the title page. *To my darling husband from your darling wife – together we shall rise above the bullshit.*

Oh yeah? Where was Neil when she really needed him?

An idea formed in her mind, and for the first time in ages she managed a small smile. She would show Oliver Easterne something he wouldn't forget in a hurry. Something the whole fucking town wouldn't forget in a hurry.

Oh yeah.

Her smile widened as she remembered a little saying Neil had taught her. *Don't get angry – get even.*

She had a plan. It was crazy. But oh . . . the satisfaction! Neil would have loved it.

62

Once things started to happen they happened fast. Over the years Leon had discovered it was always that way. One break set the course. A hunch had told him that now Deke Andrews had resurfaced it would be hard for him to vanish again. Pittsburgh, Texas, and now Las Vegas. A trail of death. Two hookers, a pimp, a rootless hitchhiker. A pattern was beginning to emerge. Deke went after the low life . . . women were the enemy . . . women who sold their bodies . . .

These thoughts crossed Leon's mind as he raced his rented car across the desert towards Las Vegas. And another thought. Did Deke Andrews have anything to do with the murder and arson case that had taken place in Barstow only two days previously? No definite signs that he was there. The building had gone up like a tinder-box destroying all evidence. But an autopsy on the charred body of the secretary revealed she had been stabbed repeatedly – There was nothing to tie Deke Andrews to the case, but Leon just had a gut feeling, and over the years his gut feelings had been proved right more times than not.

As his car sped down the highway towards his destination he was unaware of the oncoming traffic headed west. Even if he had been he would have taken no notice of the shabby brown van speeding resolutely towards Los Angeles. The driver was Deke Andrews, his face a mask, black sunglasses concealing eyes of death.

Leon felt a chill for no particular reason. He reached forward and turned the air conditioning unit down.

The lights of Las Vegas twinkled a false welcome in the distance.

63

Normally last minute invitations were ignored by one and all. But Gina's secretary was a persuasive English girl with a honeyed voice and a smart brain. It also helped that nothing else was going on the night of Ross's birthday. No premieres, private screenings, parties or special events. So a perfectly respectable group arrived to celebrate in the upstairs room of the Bistro on Canon Drive.

Gina and Ross naturally made a late entrance. On the street outside lurked a group of paparazzi. Gina posed for them prettily, clinging on to Ross's arm.

Gently he tried to loosen her grip. She was wrinkling his jacket.

They entered the restaurant and proceeded upstairs where the group waited. Ross was really surprised by the turnout. He had expected maybe a dozen people but there were at least sixty.

Gina turned to him with a wide smile, her perfect teeth dazzling. 'Not bad, huh? And all arranged at the last minute.'

He surveyed the room and boasted, 'I'm a star again. I can lure 'em out anytime I want.'

'Sure you can. Only a little phone call from me helps you know.'

She hoped his agent had told him about *Street People* being cancelled. She had a horrible feeling the putz hadn't. If Ross knew he would be bitching and beefing from here to the beach.

Oh, well. It was not her problem. She refused to be the bearer of bad news. Let Oliver or someone give him the word. Then, when he came to her with the inevitable – 'Why didn't you tell me?' she would shrug and casually say, 'I *told* you to speak to your agent.' Then she would add, just so he could see how concerned and thoughtful she was, 'Besides, I didn't want to spoil your birthday.'

Buddy stood in the doorway and checked out the action. He saw fame, power, and money mingling easily together. And for a moment he felt that he belonged.

Not yet, Buddy Boy, not yet. Don't get carried away. Keep your cool.

He had offered to pick Sadie up and go with her, but she had declined. Now he searched for a familiar face.

Karen Lancaster sat at a table with a spiky-haired English rock star, Josh Speed, a caustic television comedian, and three assorted groupies.

Josh, the comedian, and Karen conversed excitedly, while the three groupies – all shaggy hair, skinny bodies, and eager eyes – listened hopefully.

Buddy wandered over. He didn't see anyone else he knew.

'Hey – Karen, how're you doin'?'

She gazed up at him, total non-recognition.

'Buddy,' he reminded her, slightly miffed. 'Buddy Hudson.'

Josh Speed and the comedian looked at each other, took a beat of three, and chorused, 'Buddy . . . Buddy Hudson.' Then they fell about laughing.

Karen, as stoned as they, joined in the laughter, followed quickly by the groupies.

The amusement slid from the comedian's face. 'What the fock you laughin' at?' he demanded of the youngest girl.

Her face froze. 'Nothing,' she whispered.

Buddy backed away. He wasn't sure why he was here. Sadie had said she might have some good news for him, and he trusted her to save him from falling back into obscurity.

He edged over to the bar and scored an orange juice. Earlier he had spoken to Angel. 'My movie's been cancelled,' he told her regretfully. 'But I got me this agent – Sadie La Salle – who is the best. And she says she'll find me something else. I still get paid – we're rich, babe.'

He was proud of the fact that he was being honest with her. And she seemed to appreciate it, for her voice filled with warmth, and he knew that any day now she would agree to come back.

Across the room, chatting to a talk show producer and his doll-like wife, Sadie noted Buddy's arrival. She watched him carefully. He handled himself well, and as he moved towards the bar she noticed the eyes of several women following him.

'What do you think of my new client?' she asked the wife, pointing out Buddy.

The woman – at least thirty years younger than her jovial husband

– stared longingly. 'Handsome,' she said at last, fingering a ruby and diamond necklace which swamped her pale swan neck.

'Yes,' agreed Sadie. 'He's going to be a big star.'

'Should we have him on the show?' questioned the producer.

'I'm sorry,' Sadie said regretfully. 'I've promised him to Carson first. But I'll give you second shot.'

'C'*mon*, Sadie. Don't give me that. We want him. First. Name a day.'

'Why don't we speak tomorrow?' she said, excusing herself and hurrying over to Buddy.

How easy it was to play the game – and win. When you knew all the rules.

She patted him on the shoulder. 'On time. Looking good. Drinking orange juice. You see – I told you it wasn't the end of the world.'

He grinned ruefully and shrugged. 'Guess I've learned to roll with the punches.'

'Well roll with this. There's a *very* strong chance that you are going to get the leading role in Gina's new film.'

He perked up. 'You're kidding.'

'Sadie La Salle does not kid.'

Jeez! Why hadn't he been nicer to Gina. Maybe she would bad-mouth him.

'When will I know? What kind of a part is it? Can I see the script?'

'The script is being rewritten. When it's ready you'll do a test with Gina, and if the sparks fly . . .'

He had known it was too good to be true. 'I've got to test again?' he groaned.

'Of course you do. But I have every confidence that you'll be wonderful. Don't you?'

Glumly he nodded.

'Smile, dear. Produce the charm. Tonight you are going to be exceptionally polite to Oliver Easterne – who – need I tell you – is the producer of the new vehicle. And even nicer to your fellow client, Gina Germaine.'

'I'll do my best.'

'I want better than that.'

'I don't think Gina likes me.'

'Make her like you. That shouldn't be too difficult for you.'

'You want me to fuck her?' he snapped angrily. ' 'Cos I don't fuck to work.'

'I never said you did. And don't speak to me like that.'

438

He glowered. 'Sorry.'

'Come. Let's start with Oliver.'

'Sweetie. So sorry to hear your film no more. They offer it Adam but he turn it down. No right for him. Perfect for you. Darling, I *so* sorry.'

Ross stared at Bibi Sutton blankly. He never understood a word she said.

'Sweetie. Elaine? She fine now? I hear she drinkie too much. She fine now though, yes?'

'You're looking magnificent as usual, Bibi,' he leaned forward and whispered in her ear. 'One of these days I'll catch you in the sack and screw the life out of you.'

She offered a coy smile. 'Naughty boy!'

Adam Sutton appeared at her elbow, nodded curtly at Ross, and said, 'The Lazers and the Wilders want us to sit with them.'

'Yes?' She glanced around to see if she could spot a better offer. 'In a minute, I come soon.'

Adam retreated. Ross leaned forward again. 'If you were between the sheets with me you would!'

'Ross! You bad boy!'

'Who's a bad boy?' Karen Lancaster thrust herself between them, all beige satin and erect nipples. She was accompanied by the rock star. 'This is Josh Speed,' she announced formally. 'He's in the middle of his American tour. This is his first Hollywood party and he's bored out of his skull, aren't you baby?'

He spoke perfect cockney. ''Ere, leave it out, gel. I'm lovin' every bleedin' minute.'

'He sounds like Mick Jagger,' Karen said knowledgeably. 'Only Mick fakes it. Josh is the real thing.'

'How George, sweetie?' asked Bibi.

Karen did not answer. She glared balefully at Ross. 'I'm glad your movie bottomed out,' she said spitefully.

'I wouldn't mind 'aving a bash in a fillum,' remarked Josh.

Karen grabbed his arm. 'How old are you?'

'Twenny-two.'

Bibi became bored with the conversation and moved away.

'Really? Ross is fifty you know. Today.' She laughed. 'Practically old enough to be your grandfather.'

They both sniggered.

Ross was unamused. Grandfather indeed. She was being ridiculous. And what did she mean about his movie bottoming out?

Before he had a chance to ask her she launched into an elaborate necking session with Josh. He was hardly going to stand there watching them exchange tongues. He looked around for Gina, and came eyeball to eyeball with Sadie on her way to the ladies room. They greeted each other stiffly and both moved quickly on.

Gina was deep in conversation with Oliver. Ross strolled over.

'Having fun?' she beamed.

His eyes dipped to her considerable cleavage. She certainly gave Dolly Parton a run for her money. 'I think I'll have more fun later,' he said, pinching her behind.

'You don't know how sorry I am,' Oliver said insincerely. 'But these things happen. I don't have to tell you that, Ross.'

'Excuse me,' Gina said hurriedly. 'I must say hello to Wolfie.'

'Sorry about what?' demanded Ross.

'You've been in the film business long enough to understand the way things are,' Oliver continued expansively. 'As long as you can take the money and run. Right?'

Three thoughts hit him.

Call your agent.

Sweetie. So sorry to hear your film no more.

I'm glad your movie bottomed out.

Christ. He didn't have to be a genius to figure things out.

'Oliver,' he said sharply. 'What the *frig* is going on?'

Buddy learned fast. Being nice to people usually meant listening to what they had to say, and not interrupting. He hung on to every word, tried to look interested, and watched their eyes constantly flick around the room. Twice he was deserted in mid-sentence when a better prospect came into view.

Adam Sutton granted him a few moments of his valuable time.

'I think you've got a great future ahead of you,' Adam said. 'With Sadie as your agent and –'

He never finished the sentence. Bibi beckoned and he ran.

Buddy saw Gina, took a deep breath and went over.

She greeted him coolly.

He exerted all the charm he could muster.

She thawed. 'Changed your mind about screwing a movie star?' she purred sexily.

He was saved from answering by her personal P.R. man who strode over, threw him a dismissive look, took her arm in a proprietary fashion, and said, 'Army Archerd wants to talk to you.'

Buddy cruised around the room again, smelling the money, anxious to be a part of it all, wanting to be recognized. Then he saw Wolfie Schweicker and stopped dead. The plump man was entertaining a small group with an obviously hilarious anecdote, for they were all falling about laughing.

Butterball. That's what Buddy had called him in his head. Butterball . . .

On second sight he was sure it was the man who had fed Tony cocaine the night of the fateful party.

He continued to stare. His black eyes chips of ice.

Wolfie felt the power of his stare and glanced over. His stomach tightened with sexual anticipation. 'Who *is* that?' he asked Bibi.

She threw a casual glance in Buddy's direction. 'Sadie's new discovery. Nobody important, darling. Why?'

'I saw him at George's party. I just wondered who he was.'

'Sweetie. Gina's dress. You think she make it herself?'

Wolfie tore his eyes away from Buddy and applied himself to keeping Bibi happy. He inspected Gina's outfit, a red dress which plunged to the waist. 'Hmm . . .' he said archly. 'Zody's with a touch of Frederick's of Hollywood, don't you think?'

And out of the giant cake sprang a nubile redheaded girl in a fluffy white bikini. She leapt on Ross's knee while everyone yelled and cheered and catcalled. Business conversations were suspended while the men inspected the near naked girl who began to sing 'Happy Birthday' as she wriggled around on Ross's lap. She was stacked, but not stacked enough to allow business discussions to be suspended for long.

Ross acted out his role. He was no slouch when it came to putting on the right face for the right occasion. He grinned, made all the correct noises. Blew out fifty candles while trying to dislodge the stoned ding-a-ling from his lap. And all the while he seethed.

Goddamn Gina Germaine. How dare she put him through this charade. How *dare* she do it to him when she knew – *had* to know – that the film was a no go situation.

Why hadn't the dumb broad told him? He could not wait to get her alone. Oh, how he seethed. But the easy-going smile remained in place. The blue eyes – a little crinkly around the edges but still knock-out – flirted their way around the room.

441

He was humiliated. Sadie would never have let something like this happen to him.

'I can score you some ace coke,' the girl on his knee whispered.

'Get lost.' He dislodged her by getting up.

'Speech,' someone yelled, and the request echoed round the room. In a pig's ass they'd get a speech.

Seeing Butterball soured the evening for Buddy.

He wanted out.

He wanted Angel.

'Is it all right for me to split?' he checked with Sadie.

'Yes,' she said. 'We'll speak on Monday. I'm going to Palm Springs tomorrow, but I'll be back in time to get something definite out of Oliver early in the week. Don't worry, everything's going to be fine.'

'I hope so.'

He drove home fast and dialled Angel's number.

'Yes?' answered a male voice.

She had told him she was living with two gay guys. 'Angel,' he demanded.

'She's asleep.'

He controlled the edginess in his voice. 'Do me a favour and wake her. This is important.'

'May I ask who's calling?'

'Buddy.'

An unfriendly, 'Just a minute.'

A long wait and then at last she was there. 'I can't go on like this,' he blurted urgently. 'I need you to be with me.'

'Are you high?' she asked accusingly.

'Stone cold straight, babes.'

'We made an agreement. Why are you calling me in the middle of the night?'

'Because we decided to be honest with each other. And if I'm honest then you have to know that I can't go another day without you.'

'Buddy –'

'I love you. We *should* be together.'

'I don't know –' she began hesitantly.

'Yes you *do* know, an' I'll tell you what's goin' on.' He took a deep breath. 'Like I have a mother I never mentioned –'

442

'You told me your parents died in a car accident', she interrupted accusingly.

'I *know* what I told you. But from now on it's the truth, right?'

'Yes.'

'My mother lives in San Diego. I haven't spoken to her in ten years.' He was silent a moment. 'I want to settle things, so I'm going to drive to see her early in the morning, and when I get back I need you to be waiting in my – our apartment. Will you do this for me, baby? Because you mean everything to me – and I don't want there to be any more lies between us.' He paused, willing her to say yes. 'C'mon, Angel. You know the time is right.'

Somebody up there liked him. For a change.

'Alright,' she whispered.

The love he had for her burned hot. From now on she came first. Without her everything else was nothing. Including the career he still wanted but refused to lie for.

'I'll arrange a limo to pick you up at five o'clock tomorrow afternoon, the maid'll let you in, and I'll be back around six or seven. If I'm going to be late I'll call.'

She gave him her address.

'Tomorrow,' he said. 'You won't ever regret it.'

'Bullfriggingshit!' screamed Ross.

'Smile, there's photographers outside the house gates,' an unfazed Gina replied.

'Who gives a flying fuck about frigging photographers?' he yelled, the veins in his neck standing out like telephone cords.

'*I* do.'

'Well FUCK YOU!'

'Maybe later. If you stop behaving like a horse's ass.'

'Up yours, lady!'

They had been screaming at each other ever since leaving the party.

'Did you know the film was down the tubes?' he had asked the moment they were alone.

'Yes, I knew. But it's not *my* job to tell you. I *said* for you to call your agent.'

'Too much trouble for you to mention it?'

'Is it *my* fault you have a dumb agent?'

The fight had started with name-calling and progressed to open warfare. Ross could not remember ever having been so angry.

Their limo was slowly approaching the gates of Gina's house. The photographers pressed forward. She had forgotten to mention to Ross that her personal public relations representative had alerted the wire services only half an hour before they left the Bistro, that Ms. Germaine was likely to announce her engagement to Ross Conti before the end of the evening. The press waited anxiously.

Gina realized that she might have picked the wrong moment for this particular publicity stunt.

'Oh, Jesus!' she exclaimed, pressing a button which operated the wall of glass between her and the chauffeur. 'Don't stop,' she instructed tersely.

'I'm afraid we have to Ms. Germaine. The remote control for the gate is not in the car.'

'*Why not!*' she hissed angrily.

He shrugged a 'how should I know, I was only hired for the evening' reply, and pulled the white stretch Cadillac limousine to an abrupt halt.

The photographers surged. Ross glowered.

Gina manufactured a quick smile and opened her window. 'Hi boys,' she said genially, trusting that her personality and Ross's sense of survival would get them past the gate. 'And to what do I owe this pleasure?'

They all spoke at once, asking the same question. Were she and Ross Conti planning a wedding?

'A wedding!' Ross screamed, his fury out of control. 'Number One – I am a married man. And Number Two – take note – ladies and gentlemen of the press. I wouldn't marry Gina Germaine if she were the last friggin' cunt in Hollywood!'

64

Night time on Hollywood Boulevard and the prostitutes and the pimps and pushers and the junkies and the muggers on parade.

Deke drove down the street slowly, his cold eyes taking in the scene.

At a red light two bored hookers sauntered over to the van.

'Interested in a threesome?' they asked in unison. ''Round the world, golden shower, name it.'

He shook his head negatively and rubbed the front of his dark glasses. Whores. The world was full of them.

'Come on,' one of them encouraged, putting a bony hand with six inch false nails on his arm.

'The sins of the flesh will kill you,' he warned, shaking her hand from him with such force that three of her false nails came off and fell on the floor of the van.

'Mothafucker!' she screeched in a fury, attempting to wrench his door open so that she could retrieve her precious nails.

He gunned the van into motion, and she fell back screaming obscenities.

Hollywood Boulevard. Gateway to the City of the Angels. Alive with vermin. Alive with the dregs of the earth. As The Keeper Of The Order it was his job to deal with this seething mass. He was sent to do such things . . . But first . . . A woman he must find. A whore mother . . . Joey would want him to deal with her first . . . She had told him so . . . Joey never left his side . . . She was a good girl . . . a sweet girl . . .

Los Angeles. City of the Angels.

Whoretown, U.S.A.

'Mother,' he said aloud. 'I know who you are. I will find you soon. I promise.'

'Good, cowboy,' said Joey. She sat beside him so bright and pretty, her skirt pulled demurely over her knees.

Familiar lights flashing 'MOTEL' attracted him.

'Are you tired, Joey?' he asked solicitously. 'Shall we stop?'

She had gone.

The whore had vanished.

He fingered the knife down the side of his boot. Next time he saw her he would slash the bitch to pieces.

65

Buddy could not sleep. After speaking to Angel he paced around his apartment excitedly. He had made a commitment and now he had to follow through. The thought of facing his mother was unwelcome . . . but the sooner it was over and done with . . .

No more lies.

Everything clean.

What about Sadie? The idea was to tell her before Monday when his billboard hit America.

He lay on his bed, fell asleep thinking about what to do, and woke early with an answer.

He did not have the nerve to wake Sadie with his outpourings of honesty at seven a.m. on Saturday morning, but he had no such qualms about stopping by Ferdie's before leaving for San Diego.

Ferdie was up and dressed – natty in a red cutaway T-shirt with matching shorts. He was suntanned, oiled and muscled, unlike the soberly suited man of office days. He seemed quite embarrassed to be caught out of character. Even more so when a tousle-haired youth of fourteen or fifteen appeared behind him at the front door demanding. 'Who *is* it?'

The boy wore a towel around his waist and nothing else.

'Get back in the kitchen,' Ferdie commanded, the tone of his voice brooking no argument.

'Glad you're up,' Buddy said breezily.

'Would it make any difference if I wasn't?'

'I had a choice – wake you or Sadie – I figured you were my best bet.'

'And how did you find out where I lived?'

'Looked you up in the phone book.'

'This *is* an emergency I presume?'

'Most definitely.'

Ferdie sighed with annoyance. 'You'd better come in I suppose.'

'Hey – don't make me feel so welcome.'

'What do you expect at seven in the morning? Flowers and a band?'

Buddy followed him into a spacious white apartment. A lone Andy Warhol silk screen of Marilyn Monroe took pride of place above the old fashioned mantle. Two burned out candles were placed beneath it.

He sat down without being invited and said, 'I can't stay long.'

Ferdie replied with crisp sarcasm, 'What a shame.'

The juvenile, now lurking in the kitchen, put on loud punk music just to let everyone know he was still around.

'God!' exclaimed Ferdie, then in a louder voice, 'Use the *head*-phones, Rocky.' He turned to Buddy. 'Well? Do tell. I'm dying to know what couldn't wait until Monday morning in the office.'

'I'm going to San Diego.'

'A short trip, or will you be taking up residence?'

'I have to be straight with Sadie.'

'Ahhh . . . I know.' Ferdie smirked knowingly. 'You're really a transvestite, and you couldn't bear to keep it a secret a *moment* longer. Is that your exciting news?'

'Cut the smart ass cracks. This is serious.' Buddy stood up and walked to the window. The view offered a swimming pool with two girls doing lengths while another one skipped rope by the side. 'Uh . . . there's a few things I never told Sadie about.'

'Like what?' asked Ferdie, intrigued at last.

'Like I'm married. I have a beautiful wife – and I don't want to hide the fact anymore.'

'Oh dear.'

'Is she gonna freak?'

'Let's put it this way – she is hardly going to dance on tabletops wild with delight.'

Buddy shrugged. 'That's the way it is.' He gazed at the view. 'I . . . uh . . . want you to tell her for me.'

'*Thank you.* You're *so* kind. But I must decline your generous offer. Tell her yourself on Monday.'

'I can't do that.'

'Why not?'

'Because she has to know today. The billboards will be up on Monday. I don't want to let it go any longer. It's just something that has to be done.'

Ferdie looked exasperated.

'Listen,' Buddy said persuasively, turning away from the window. 'You do this for me an' I gotta owe you one big favor. Right?'

'Maybe.'

'So *you* know an' *I* know that there's nothing like havin' stored favours in this town. Right again?'

Ferdie nodded reluctantly.

'Hey – who knows what's gonna happen to me,' Buddy continued expansively. 'I could become a big star or I could end up on the shit heap. It's all a role of the dice, huh?' He patted Ferdie firmly on the shoulder. 'But hey – if I make it big, a favor from me should be worth *somethin*'. Am I right?'

Ferdie sighed. He could never resist the lethal combination of pressure and charm. Besides, he wanted Buddy out of his apartment. 'Alright, alright, I'll do it. I don't mind *ruining* my day. Now what exactly am I to tell madame?'

'Tell her I got me this wife. Her name is Angel. And she's beautiful.'

'Oh, wonderful. Is that the one *I* found for you?'

'Don't worry – we were already married.'

'Then why did –' He stopped abruptly, as the juvenile wandered into the room, headphones clamped over ears, fingers snapping to the beat.

'Ferdie,' the boy whined. 'When we goin' to the picnic?'

'When you get dressed.'

The boy flicked the knot on his towel with studied insolence.

'For God's sake –' Ferdie began, and stopped when it was revealed that the juvenile wore a scant white bikini underneath.

Buddy was already at the door. 'Tell Sadie I'll be in the office first thing Monday.'

Ferdie followed him out. 'Don't worry, she'll be waiting.' He lowered his voice. 'Kindly do not discuss my personal life with anyone. *Especially* Sadie.'

Buddy winked. 'You got it. Hey – you know what, Ferd? Telling the truth is the best thing that's happened to me in years!'

'Yes,' said Ferdie drily. 'Especially when I get to do it for you.'

66

A letter. Special delivery. To Leon Rosemont in Las Vegas.

Dearest Leon,
We had a good time together.
Sometimes good times don't last.
This is sad . . .
But it is so . . .
Our vacation is over and I am going home – alone.
I shall always remember the good times.

Millie

He had received the letter earlier, read it through quickly, then stuffed it in his pocket. No time to deal with it . . . Everything happening fast . . .

Arriving in Las Vegas to investigate the murder of a hooker only to

448

be summoned to a house where Deke Andrews had most certainly spent time.

Killing time.

Leon felt his stomach turn as they photographed the body of the old woman – her face a morbid grimace of fear and death.

Carnage . . . blood . . . mutilation . . .

Deke Andrews' fingerprints everywhere. He had made no attempt to cover his tracks.

Scrawled across the bathroom mirror in smeared lipstick were the words – I AM THE KEEPER OF THE ORDER. WHORE MOTHER – I WILL FIND YOU. It was as if he felt he didn't have to be careful . . .

Leon spoke to the maid who found the body. She was hysterical. Hadn't seen anyone or anything, just kept on mumbling incoherently about a wool jacket.

Who was Nita Carrolle? Why had Deke broken his pattern, entered her house, and murdered her?

WHAT WAS THE CONNECTION?

Leon went to work, sifting through the remnants of a life.

He persevered through the night, and at seven-thirty on Saturday morning hit pay dirt. Hidden beneath piles of clothes in the basement he came across an old ledger. He studied the yellowing torn pages – some of which were missing. His original hunch was correct. Deke Andrews *was* adopted, but not by legitimate means. Nita Carrolle and her sister Noreen had run a babies for sale operation.

At last the puzzle began to make sense. Leon had the scent of Deke in his nostrils. There was much to do.

67

Elaine awoke to blinding sunlight. She had forgotten to close the drapes again and the early morning sun spilled into her bedroom. For a few moments she lay perfectly still, knowing full well that as soon as she moved her head would begin to throb as it did every morning lately.

She moved. Her head throbbed. She swore off drink forever. And knew for sure that the only way to get through the day was to add a slug of vodka to her breakfast orange juice.

449

Elaine Conti, you're a drunk.

Absolutely not, Etta. I can quit any time I want.

Who are you kidding? You need the booze. It kills the pain.

I'll stop tomorrow. Damn you, Etta. Just leave me alone.

She walked unsteadily into the bathroom and tried to recall what she had done the previous evening. She could not remember one single thing, even though she thought hard.

Maralee. Were they together?

No. Maralee had left for Europe with her father two days ago. Or was it longer? She honestly could not remember.

Better get your act together, Elaine.

Better leave me the fuck alone, Etta.

She wandered into the kitchen without even a passing glance in the mirror.

Elaine Conti. Tangled hair, streaked by the sun instead of from a bottle. Perfect white skin tanned for the first time in ten years. Figure slightly voluptuous – she had gained at least ten pounds. Instead of a lace nightgown – derigueur bedtime dress for ladies in Beverly Hills – she wore Ross's old pyjama top, the sleeves rolled high. For someone who should be looking lousy she looked pretty good. A little puffy around the eyes, but more attractive than the usual groomed to within an inch of her life Elaine Conti.

She was naturally unaware of this fact. She knew for sure that she looked terrible. But since she was seeing no one and no one was seeing her – what did it matter? Even Lina had deserted her.

The orange juice in the refrigerator appeared to have seen better days, but she poured half a glass anyway, and added a healthy blast of vodka – just to chase away the blues. Then she sat down and wondered how she was going to pass yet another long and lonely weekend.

Ross awoke shortly after Elaine. Only he had not had the luxury of a bed to spend the night in. The back seat of his yellow Corniche had done duty – and it was not the most comfortable place in the world, although better than sharing Gina Germaine's California Eastern King. Jesus Christ! Anything was better than that.

He kicked open the back door of the car, uncramped his body, painfully climbed out, and stretched long and hard.

A rat scampered across the garage floor. Beverly Hills was full of them. The four legged *and* the two legged kind.

Ross Conti. Movie star. Sleeping rough.

Not exactly planned, but since leaving Elaine nothing much had gone his way. Which was one of the reasons he had returned to the roost. Unfortunately too late at night to gain entry. The previous evening he had rung the doorbell for ten minutes and nobody had answered. His key was somewhere among his things at Gina's place. Too bad, but he wasn't going back.

When every dog in the neighborhood started to bark he had abandoned his attempt to get into his own home and driven the Corniche to the alley behind the house. There, he had used the remote control to gain entry to the garage, parked, and taken up his sleeping position on the back seat.

Christ! His back was now killing him, and at that particular moment in time taking a piss was the most important thing in his life.

He hoped that Lina was around to let him in. Didn't want to disturb Elaine's beauty sleep. He wanted her in a good mood for the return of her hero.

68

Deke had more information than he desired. It filled his brain like maggots swarming over the carcass of a dead cow. Eating at his sanity. Driving him mad.

Nita Carrolle.

Silent at first.

Until he punctured that fat flesh . . . And the words came spilling out like rich red blood . . .

She knew plenty. She was old, but her memory was sharp as an ice-pick. When he mentioned the names Winifred and Willis Andrews she faltered for a moment . . . but then she remembered. And she found papers to prove it.

He knew who his mother was.

He knew where she was.

Immediately he thought of Joey. At last they would be able to meet. Joey . . . so lovely . . . she could be a movie star . . . So much prettier than the trash that paraded the boulevards.

Next time he saw her he would tell her. She would love him for it. She would kiss him and hug him and call him cowboy again . . .

He missed her so badly.

If he took care of everything would she come back? He resolved to ask her.

Of course, The Keeper Of The Order could not beg.

Or pay.

Had he paid her? He frowned, unsure.

Maybe once.

SHE WAS NOTHING BUT A DIRTY WHORE.

Fury filled his head already bursting with the name of the woman who had brought him into this filthy world.

Nita Carrolle's words shattered like a zillion fragments.

' . . . *always knew who the mother was . . . my babies special . . . followed their lives if I could . . . never sold them cheap . . . nice girls who got in trouble . . . your mother's done so well . . . your mother . . . your mother.*

DAMN HIS MOTHER.

She left him. She gave him away. She abandoned him like garbage.

THE BITCH HAD NEVER EVEN WANTED HIM.

She would pay for every year of his life.

In blood.

Slowly.

69

'I'm leaving today,' Angel said quietly.

'I expect you are,' Koko replied crossly, spooning all-bran and raisins into his mouth while attempting to fix a cup of coffee.

Gently she took the cup from his hand.

He snatched it back. 'I'm quite capable of making my own coffee, thank you very much.'

She sighed. 'Why are you mad at me?'

'Mad? Who's mad? *I'm* certainly not.'

'Please don't be angry.' Tentatively she touched his arm. 'You're the one who has taught me to stand up for myself. Without you I would never have had the strength to give Buddy another chance.'

'Hah!' he snorted. 'I just hope you realize what you are doing.'

'I'm going back to my husband in the hope that things are going to work out and that my baby will have a father.'

'Adrian and I would have been perfectly wonderful fathers,' he sniffed.

'Will you settle for godfathers?'

'The Mario Puzo kind?'

'Who?'

'Oh goodness! You still don't know much do you?'

'I know enough, thanks to you. I'm not the same stupid girl who came crying into your salon looking for a job.'

'You were *never* stupid. Just unbearably sweet!'

They both giggled and embraced.

'I hate goodbyes,' he said gruffly.

'I'm not being picked up until five.'

'You know Saturday's our busiest day. I won't be back by then.'

'Can I bring Buddy over next week?'

'God! Do you have to?'

'Please.'

'We'll see.'

They hugged again, and he stroked her silken blond hair and held her to him very tightly. 'Be happy, dreamheart,' he whispered.

'I will,' she whispered back. 'I know I will.'

Montana refused to mourn for Neil. During the course of their marriage he had lost two good friends and both times he said the same thing. 'Never look back. Face whatever's coming to you head-on and let the bastards know that you know.' And then he had gotten uproariously drunk.

She knew that he would not want her to sit around and mope, so she didn't. Instead she set her plan to get her own back on Oliver in motion. It took a lot of organizing, but now it was all set and every time she thought about it a wide grin broke across her face. Monday morning was Oliver Easterne day and she could hardly wait!

In the meantime she packed up the rest of Neil's things, and then started on her own possessions.

Saturday morning she called Stephen Shapiro, a realtor she knew, and he came up to look at the house.

'Put it on the market at once,' she instructed. 'I'll leave it in your hands. I shall be flying to New York on Monday.'

Stephen seemed to think a price of two million dollars was not unrealistic. 'If we find the right buyer,' he added.

She deliberated over whether to call anybody and say goodbye. But then it occurred to her that all her real friends lived in New York. She only had acquaintances in Los Angeles. Would they care if she stayed or departed? Probably not.

She tried to reach Buddy Hudson, but his service picked up. She would try him again before she left, he deserved a proper explanation about the demise of the film, not the crap he was no doubt being fed.

Goodbye California . . . She would miss it in her own way. The ocean and the beach. The mountains and the parks. The very seduction of living in the sun. And of course, the view from the top of their hill. That very special spread of lights laid out like fairytale land.

Yes. She knew she would miss L.A., but as Neil would say . . . 'Never look back . . .'

Buddy had driven by his old home three times. The street and the house looked exactly the same. What had he expected? That everything would have been-replaced with multiple skyscrapers, and freeways, and that there was no way he could ever trace his mother again.

Nothing like that had happened. He had no excuse.

Maybe she didn't live there anymore.

Maybe she was dead.

He hoped.

And hated himself for hoping such a thing.

He did not feel well at all. Why couldn't he just walk over, ring the doorbell and get it over and done with?

Determinedly he started to leave the car, but as he did so the front door of his former home opened and a boy of about six emerged. Buddy paused while the boy ran over to a maroon station wagon, flung open the back door, and climbed inside. The front door of the house remained open, and Buddy waited, knowing for sure she would appear at any moment.

And so she did.

He ducked back into his car as guilty as the day he had left. He felt sixteen again. *She looked exactly the same.*

This really freaked him. Somehow he had expected – hoped – that ten years would have taken their toll. But even from a distance he could see that she had hardly changed. Her hairstyle was different, but that was it. Instead of hanging to her waist in rich curls, her auburn locks were trimmed to shoulder length, which made her look even younger than he remembered.

How old *was* she? He recalled asking her when he was about eight and she had replied primly, 'A lady never reveals her age. Always bear that in mind if you please.'

Eight years old and his own mother didn't even want to tell him how old she was.

She got into the station wagon and drove off in the opposite direction, leaving him in a hopeless state of deep frustration.

He decided hanging around outside the house waiting for her and the kid to come back was stupid. He had other things to do in San Diego, and the sooner he did everything and headed back for L.A. and Angel the better.

Wolfie Schweicker.

Wasn't it about time he told the police?

They confronted each other warily.

Elaine thought – My God – what do I look like?

Ross thought – My God – what does she look like?

They always had had a lot in common.

'Where's Lina?' he asked.

'She quit,' replied Elaine, aware for the first time in ages that her nails were chipped, her hair undone, her outfit unsuitable.

'That's my pyjama top,' he said accusingly.

'I know,' she replied. For some strange reason she felt quite lightheaded.

'Am I coming in?'

'Are you?'

'It's my home isn't it?'

She nodded. He was an unfaithful lying cheating bastard. She *should* tell him to go take a hike.

He was *her* unfaithful lying cheating husband. And he was back.

'Come in,' she said.

The famous blues twinkled. 'I thought you'd never ask.'

There wasn't much to pack. One suitcase and a carryall bag with all her bits and pieces in. Never again would she be able to travel so light. Soon there would be the baby to consider.

She looked in the bathroom mirror, turned sideways and regarded her bulge. What was Buddy going to say when he saw her? He hadn't even asked about the baby . . . not so much as a 'How are you feeling?'

Suppose Koko was right and going back to him was a big mistake?

She shook her head resolutely. He deserved a final chance. He sounded so different on the phone, so positive and sure about their future together. It was all going to work out, she just knew it.

Adrian knocked on the door of her room. 'Do you need any help?' he inquired solicitously.

'I'm all set,' she replied. 'By this time tomorrow you'll have forgotten I was ever here.'

He wheeled himself into the small spare room. 'I hope not.'

'I want to thank you for everything,' she blurted. 'Without you and Koko I don't know what I would –'

'Remember to keep in touch. Koko's very broody about you – don't disappoint him.'

They both laughed.

She brushed a strand of pale hair from her forehead and shivered with the anticipation of seeing Buddy again. He had said he was sending a car for her at five o'clock, but who could wait? She was ready to leave now.

'Hey – listen, man, I didn't *have* to come here,' Buddy said restlessly. 'I just figured – hey – y'know – like I'd be doin' you guys a favour.'

'A ten years later favour,' snapped the big detective. There were two of them in the interview room. The big man, and his partner – a silent black who stoically chewed gum and cleaned his nails with a toothpick.

'So what are you going to do about it?' Buddy asked impatiently. He had given them the information. Willingly. Nobody had dragged him in off the street.

'Just what do you expect us to do?' questioned the big cop. 'Put out a warrant on Wolfie whatever his name is because you walk in here an' tell us he killed your boyfriend ten years ago?'

'Why don't you look up the case?' Buddy persisted. 'Pull out your files. Understand what the hell I'm talkin' about.'

'You want the case re-opened?' asked the black cop wearily, speaking for the first time.

'Hey – listen, I'm not here to get a manicure,' Buddy snapped, outraged by their indifference.

'Means a lot of paperwork,' mused the black.

'Tough,' muttered Buddy sarcastically.

The big cop sighed. 'Leave your name an' address. We'll put it to the Captain. We need authority.'

Buddy shook his head in amazement. Being a good citizen was no easy job. Then he thought about the implications if the case *was* opened up. Publicity of that kind was not what he needed right now. Naively he had just assumed he could walk into the precinct, tell them about Wolfie Schweicker, and split. How dumb could you get?

Pretty dumb, Buddy Boy, pretty fucking dumb.

'I've changed my mind,' he said abruptly. 'I'll come back to-morrow.'

The detectives exchanged bored glances. Another weirdo with nothing better to do than waste their time.

'Yeah, you do that,' said the big cop with a liberal yawn. 'An' don't forget – we already caught the freeway strangler an' the joggin' killer, so think of something new to waste our time with, huh?'

Buddy left in disgust, got in his car, and headed back to his mother's house.

Sadie had planned to spend the weekend in Palm Springs, but when she awoke – late – she found she could not summon the energy to move. Seeing Ross with Gina had depressed her. Did he have no taste at all? Gina Germaine was a movie star, but she was also a tramp – sleeping with any man who might – in some way or another – further her career or her life. What she wanted from Ross was hard to guess at.

Sadie guessed anyway. And knew immediately she was right.

The legendary Conti schlong. What woman wouldn't be thrilled to wake up with *that* beside her?

Frustratedly she buzzed for her maid, and then remembered that she had given the maid and her husband the weekend off as she had expected to be in Palm Springs. No matter. She would enjoy being on her own for a change. No parties, screenings or business meetings. Just uninterrupted peace – something she did not manage to get very much of.

Ross.

She kept on thinking of him.

Ross.

She still loved him.

In spite of . . .

She reached for the phone and dialled Gina's private number.

The disgruntled voice of an American sex go   ss answered. 'Shit, Sadie,' Gina complained. 'Have you *seen* the papers?'

Sadie, as it happened, had not. 'What, dear?' she inquired sooth-ingly, knowing full well that Gina always had some complaint or another regarding the items which were written about her.

'You can take Ross Conti and shove him up your ass,' Gina fumed.

'What did he do?'

'Ha!' snorted Gina, incensed, even after a night to mull things over. 'Read all about it. I threw the bum out.'

'You did?'

'I sure did.'

'Where did he go?'

'Who gives a fast fuck?'

'I'm leaving for Palm Springs now,' Sadie said hurriedly. 'I'll call you on Monday.' She could not wait to get off the phone.

'That's a pity,' said Gina, her voice a disappointed whine. 'I thought you could come over, there's things I wanna discuss.'

'You wouldn't want me to forgo my one weekend of peace and quiet, would you?'

'Why not? You can go to the Springs any time.'

Selfish as always. 'I'm afraid I *have* to go. As I said, we'll talk on Monday.'

She put the phone down before Gina could bitch further.

So Ross had dumped the big movie star . . . And not a second too soon . . .

She thought for a minute, then called the Beverly Hills Hotel, the Beverly Wilshire, and the Bel Air. Ross was not registered at any of them. Could he perhaps have gone home? Back to the waiting arms of his wife? Sadie had no doubt that Elaine *was* waiting. In Hollywood, stars were *always* welcomed home, whatever they might have been up to. Hollywood wives were a breed unto themselves. Perfect, pretty women with a ticket to ride. That ticket being the famous husband.

She hesitated only a moment before trying his home number.

The phone interrupted their reunion. And what a reunion it was. Elaine spread-eagled on the thick pile rug while Ross pumped away above her like a shore hungry sailor.

He had taken her by surprise, strode into the house a conquering hero returned from battle.

'You look a mess,' he had said. 'And the house looks even worse.' Then he roared with laughter. 'What's been happening around here anyway?'

The embarrassment at being caught! He might at least have warned her he was coming home. She could have spent a day at

Elizabeth Arden, had professional cleaners in to deal with the house, bought fresh flowers . . .

Oh, why bother. He would just have to take her as he found her. He wasn't looking too sensational himself, plus he smelled like a sweaty horse.

They circled each other warily, then Ross blurted, 'I'll tell you something – you look damn sexy.' And he had pounced, surprising both of them. Silently they began to consummate their reunion on the living room floor.

Then the phone rang and automatically Elaine's arm reached for it while Ross growled, 'Forget it.'

Too late. Whoever was on the line was in the room with them. A disembodied voice echoing, 'Hello, hello . . .'

'Yes?' said Elaine impatiently.

'Ross Conti please.'

'Who's calling?'

'Sadie La Salle.'

'Sadie! How are *you*? This is Elaine.'

Ross's erection deflated. He grabbed the phone, spoke briefly, hung up and turned to Elaine with a satisfied smile.

'I think we're back in business,' he said. 'Miz La Salle requests the pleasure of my company at her house.'

'When?'

'Now.'

'You'd better get dressed.'

He fell back on top of her. 'Not until I've finished what we started.'

'Ross!'

'Let her wait . . .'

70

How long was he going to hang around? All day if necessary. He was not returning to L.A. without straightening things out. Laying ghosts they called it. Some ghost. His own mother.

Buddy chain smoked half an hour away, and at last the maroon station wagon reappeared.

No more sitting around waiting for the moment to be right. He stubbed out his cigarette and hurried from the car.

459

By the time he walked up the driveway the station wagon was parked with the back open and the kid was unloading brown supermarket bags. He looked up. 'Can I help you?'

'Sure,' Buddy replied. 'I want to see the lady of the house.'

'What about?' asked the boy, too precocious for his years.

'About none of your business.'

'Mommy,' he yelled. 'There's a man here being rude.'

Buddy double-taked on the kid just as his mother rushed from the house. Was this his *brother*?

She glanced from one to the other, not recognizing Buddy at first. But on second look she knew and a small gasp escaped her lips. 'Buddy,' she whispered. 'My God!'

She made no attempt to come towards him. Just stared as if she had seen a ghost.

'Who's Buddy?' demanded the boy.

'Go in the house, Brian,' she commanded.

'Don't want to,' he whined.

'Go!' Her skin was still olive smooth. Her hair burnished bronze. She had put on a few extra pounds, but other than that she had not changed. Brian dragged reluctantly indoors.

Buddy threw his arms wide, an expansive gesture, but not one that she responded to. 'Hey –' he said. 'I figured the time had come to make the peace.'

It was a hot clear day in Los Angeles. By ten-thirty in the morning the heat was already blistering and there was a general rush of cars heading for the beach.

The high temperature bothered Deke. He cut the sleeves from the black workshirt he wore, and hacked his jeans off at the knee. With his bald head, wraparound black sunglasses, boots and ragged outfit he looked bizarre. But in California anything goes, and when he strolled down Hollywood Boulevard muttering to himself nobody so much as second glanced him.

His head was filled with snakes. They enveloped him. They were round his neck, on his arms, legs, body, even in his mouth.

He spat on the sidewalk and watched the reptiles slither away.

A seedy doorway offered tattooes and he walked in. MOTHER took only a scant half hour to become a part of his life forever.

He was ready.

He walked to his old brown van parked on a side street and set off to do the necessary deed.

When the bell rang Sadie hurried to answer it. She didn't even bother checking who it was for she knew that it had to be Ross, and this time she wanted him for keeps.

She flung open the massive oak door in anticipation.

'Hello mother,' said the sinister figure in black. 'I'm home.'

book two

71

Sadie La Salle was twenty years old when she first came to Hollywood from Chicago in the fifties. It seemed the most unlikely place in the world for a girl who looked like Sadie to choose. Usually it was the beauties who flocked to tinsel town – long haired lovelies with smooth skin, and lissome bodies. Sadie was short, plump, ferociously dark, her hair a frizzy mass which grew not only on her head but everywhere else as well. Fortunately she had no desire to be an actress. She just wanted to get away from a stifling mother and live a life of her own. Hollywood seemed like a good idea at the time.

She arrived by Greyhound bus on a Monday morning, and by Tuesday afternoon she had an apartment and a job. Having worked for two years as a secretary in Chicago her references were glowing. Goldman, Forrest and Mead, a Beverly Hills law firm, took her on immediately. She started in the typing pool, but soon progressed to being Jeremy Mead's personal secretary. He was a tall gawky married man, tanned from golf, fit from tennis; with small brown eyes, an eagle's nose and thinning brown hair. It did not take Sadie long to become indispensable to him.

Work was fine. Her personal life was not. The only time men ever second glanced her was when they spied her extremely large breasts, and for a moment interest gleamed. If she was lucky enough to get asked out on a date it was always the same old story. A fast dinner in some secluded restaurant and then the great pounce. The third time this happened to her she decided that the dinner was not worth the struggle, and she gave up dating and took up going to the movies and reading. Both infinitely more exciting.

She developed a passion for books about Hollywood and the movie industry – storing every bit of information for future use. Eventually she wanted to do something concerned with films – although she didn't quite know what. While she waited to find out, she worked hard and *absorbed all the knowledge that came her way. Jeremy Mead had an interesting client list which included producers, directors and several famous actors. She studied their various contracts, finding out about percentages, the difference between gross and net profits, the intricacies of billing. She also learned to go over the small print with an eagle eye, and on several occasions she pointed out things to Mr. Mead that he had missed.*

He was pleased enough to invite her out to lunch, and since it was business she accepted.

Three glasses of wine was over her limit. A motel in Brentwood was certainly not a colleague's office – which is where he had said they had to go. He pounced. Of course. It was her overabundance of bosom that did it every time.

She allowed him certain liberties. After all, a girl couldn't stay a virgin forever.

He paid ten minutes faithful homage to her breasts, then with no further preliminaries, attempted to mount her. She stared at his small eyes, his hook nose, his thinning brown hair and decided that her virginity was far too precious a commodity to be surrendered to a man like Jeremy Mead. Besides, he was married.

She pushed him off. No easy job as by this time he was in full flight.

He complained hotly, but somehow his hardness became buried between her mammoth breasts, and a sudden orgasm left him red-faced and satisfied. He collapsed with a happy sigh while she locked herself in the bathroom and cried.

They drove back to the office in stony silence. Passion was over, and an uneasy business relationship took its place.

Two days later in Schwab's drugstore she spotted Ross Conti. And she knew for sure that if she was going to lose her virginity to anyone this blond bronzed Adonis, with eyes the colour of sapphires, and a smile to melt any girl's heart, would be the man.

She did not know how she did it, but she willed him to her side, and soon they were sipping coffee and chatting. Apart from his incredible looks he had an easy charm which was quite irresistible. He invited her to dinner (she paid, but it didn't matter) and when he made the inevitable pass she summoned every bit of will power she possessed and turned him down. She wanted Ross Conti, but she also wanted it to be more than just a quick one-nighter.

They became friends.

She cooked for him, listened to his problems, did his washing.

He confided in her, asked her advice, discussed his various girl-friends.

She bided her time while continuing to work for Jeremy Mead, who suggested two more lunches, both of which she declined.

One day she met a sad-eyed accountant by the name of Bernard Leftcovitz, and while Ross was out laying every female from the valley to the ocean, she began to date him.

Since Ross had a habit of telling her everything, she knew all about his latest passion – a married woman who wore Arpège perfume (and probably Frederick's of Hollywood underclothes). The woman's husband was a musician who travelled a lot, and one night when he was in San Diego, and Ross was spending the evening with his wife, Sadie decided to take action. It was simple for her to find out where the husband was playing, and whisper an anonymous phone message in his ear.

The stage was set. All she had to do was sit tight.

Bernard Leftcovitz ate dinner by candle light in her apartment when an outraged Ross burst in. He behaved badly, bitching about nearly being caught, talking about himself non-stop, glaring at Bernie just as Sadie had hoped. He outsat the unfortunate Mr. Leftcovitz, and then in a fit of possessiveness claimed his prize.

Oh yes. Ross Conti was certainly worth waiting for. Their lovemaking was all that she had ever dreamed of. She gave up her virginity thankfully.

And so began the most wonderful months of her life. She loved him. She would have done anything for him. And did.

Their relationship was one-sided, but it suited them both.

'I'll make you a star,' she told Ross when he despaired of his career ever taking off. 'I'll be your agent.'

He laughed, but she meant it, and what's more she knew she could do it. Suddenly everything she had been working towards made sense. She left her job, borrowed money, and with her brilliant billboard campaign forced Ross into orbit. The rest was easy.

They were halcyon days. New York. The Carson Show. A triumphant return to Los Angeles. Offers pouring in.

Negotiations. She had been born to make deals.

Sadie felt complete satisfaction for the first time in her life.

Ross left her on the day she planned to tell him she was pregnant. The doctor confirmed her suspicions at four o'clock in the afternoon, and she rushed straight from his office to buy champagne.

All the way home she rehearsed what she would say. 'I'm pregnant.

467

It won't change anything. I'll work right up until the birth. You'll be number one, Ross, always. Isn't it fantastic?'

She knew he might not be pleased. At first. After all it would mean marriage of course.

She parked the car, and hurried up to their apartment.

His closet was bare. His Sinatra records were missing. His bottles of 'Man-Tan' and 'Old Spice' and his toothbrush had vanished from the bathroom shelves.

The emptiness in the pit of her stomach was like a dull throbbing ache. Ross was gone.

She sat in a chair by the window and waited for him to contact her. She sat through the night, and half of the next day without moving.

Eventually the phone rang and a business-like female voice informed her that Mr. Conti had requested that all of his contracts and business papers were to be forwarded to the Lamont Lisle Agency who would be handling his affairs from now on.

Numbly she travelled to her office and gathered together all of his photos, contracts, press clippings and correspondence. It did not occur to her to fight. Never crossed her mind to hire a sharp lawyer and establish the rights she most definitely had over his career.

Ross Conti walked. And she allowed him to.

For a few weeks she did nothing at all except stare at the television like a zombie and eat. Then the bills started to come in, and a visit to the bank made her aware that Ross had cleared their mutual account of everything except a thousand dollars. She accepted this fact also. And thought about killing herself because as far as she was concerned there was nothing left to live for.

Jeremy Mead unwittingly saved her. He had lent her the money (albeit reluctantly) to launch Ross Conti's billboard campaign, and although she had since paid him back it irked him that she had never consummated their relationship. So when news of Ross's marriage to Wendy Warren hit the papers, he called immediately and invited himself over.

When he arrived he found her contemplating an overdose of sleeping pills which he talked her out of. An hour later they were in bed.

She felt nothing except the weight of his bony elbows, and when he left she sobbed long into the night, breaking the numbness that had enveloped her since Ross's departure.

In the morning she took a deep breath and decided to get on with her life. No man was going to destroy Sadie La Salle. She would show Ross Conti a thing or two by becoming rich, powerful, and successful without him. She did not know how – but somehow she would do it.

The first thing was to get an abortion. She was already four months pregnant, but because of her natural bulk it was hardly noticeable. She waited four weeks – then telephoned Jeremy Mead and requested a meeting. He came to her apartment thinking she could no longer resist his charms.

'I'm pregnant,' she said simply. 'It's yours.'

'Mine?' he spluttered. 'How do you know?'

'Because there hasn't been anyone else since you.'

He stared at dark fiery fat Sadie, and cursed the fact that he had not stuck to calm competent prepared blondes.

'Goddamn it,' he said angrily. 'Why weren't you careful?'

'Why weren't you?' she retorted, hating him almost as much as she hated Ross.

'You'll have to get an abortion,' he stated callously.

'I don't have the money.'

'I'll pay.'

'Thank you so much.'

Two days later he sent her round an envelope with the name and number of a doctor and an amount of money to take care of everything. The doctor was in Tijuana, Mexico.

She took a tourist bus there the next day, booked into a cheap hotel, then called the doctor who agreed to see her at his clinic at five-thirty.

His clinic turned out to be a small room in back of a souvenir shop. The only furniture being an old rattan desk and worn leather bench. He was a man of about fifty, with red rimmed eyes and a bad stutter. At least he was American.

'I'm pregnant,' she said quietly. 'I was told you could help me.'

'How p. .p. .pregnant?'

'Three months,' she lied.

He nodded, told her the price, and requested that she remove her clothes and lie on the bench.

She thought he was going to examine her and tell her to come back the next day to his hospital or wherever he took care of such matters, so she disrobed and lay down, prudently keeping on her bra.

'Take that o. . o. .off,' he commanded.

The small room was hot and dusty. A fly buzzed incessantly. Gritting her teeth she unclipped her bra.

The doctor's red rimmed eyes bulged. He licked his lips as he approached her. 'Open your legs.'

She shut her eyes and did as he bade.

His fingers were inside her immediately, roughly probing and searching. As she cried out he said sharply, 'Be quiet. I'm not hurting you.'

She wanted to get up, dress and leave. But what was the point? Ross's child was growing inside her and it had to be removed.

He finished his examination, pressed each breast roughly, and said, 'I can take care of it.'

'When?' she asked, sitting up.

'Now,' he said. 'If you've g. . g. .got the money with you.'

She was aghast. 'Here?'

He snorted. 'You g. .g. .girls are all the same. You get yourselves pregnant, want it terminated, then expect f. .f. .first class service. May I remind you that an abortion is illegal.'

'I know. But . . . here . . .' She gestured hopelessly around the dusty room.

'I've taken care of five hundred girls here,' he said dismissively. 'You w. .w. .want it or not?'

She was frightened, but want overcame fear. She lay back. 'Go ahead,' she said dully.

'The money first.'

She rose naked to get the money from her purse, and his red rimmed eyes followed her across the room.

'You need to lose some w. .w. .weight,' he said, when she lay down again. His hands passed lingeringly across her breasts. 'These m. .m. .must be heavy to carry around.'

'Let's just get on with it,' she muttered furiously.

An hour later she stumbled out to the street barely able to walk. He had probed and pierced and stabbed. But nothing had happened. Nothing except agonizing contractions and a steady flow of blood.

As time passed he had begun to sweat. His hands started to shake. His stutter became worse. Abruptly he threw down the steel instrument he was using. 'Go home,' he said. 'It's g. .g. .going to take more t. .t. .time with you. I've s. .s. .started it o. .o. .off. It'll h. .h. .happen spontaneously. There's n. .n. .nothing else I c. .c. .can do.'

'I don't understand,' she screamed weakly. 'I've paid you.'

He thrust a wad of cotton between her legs and quickly brought over her clothes, helping her to dress. 'It'll h. .h. .happen,' he assured her, pushing her out to the street. 'G. .g. .go h. .h. .home. It'll happen s. .s. .soon.'

Somehow she staggered back to the hotel, her contractions becom-

470

ing worse all the time. There she lay on the bed and watched the blood seep through the cotton pad bunched between her legs.

The pain was excruciating. When blood began to soak through to the bed, she realized hazily that she needed help. The doctor had not given her an abortion, the bastard had butchered her.

She attempted to get up and for one brief moment Ross's image danced in front of her eyes. Then she lost consciousness and slumped to the floor.

She drifted back to the real world days later, remembering nothing of the events following her collapse. Her eyes fluttered open and took in her surroundings. She was in a bed, a rubber tube attached to her arm. Her mouth was dry and parched, and she longed for a drink. A white screen enclosed the bed and the brightness hurt her eyes. She tried to gather her thoughts. Where was she? What had happened?

She must have drifted some more, for when she next awoke there was a face peering down at her. A middle-aged woman who gently said, 'Feeling better?'

'Can I have a drink,' she whispered.

'Certainly, dear.'

Vaguely she wondered why the woman was not in nurse's uniform. Surely she was in some sort of hospital? Then she remembered and when the woman returned with a paper cup of water she gasped, 'The baby? Am I still pregnant?'

The woman gazed at her silently for a moment, then nodded.

'Oh, no,' she groaned.

'It's God's way of telling you there are other ways . . .' the woman said mysteriously. 'Rest, dear. We will talk later.'

And later they did talk. Sadie found out that the woman's name was Noreen Carrolle. She was a former nurse. One day she had travelled to Tijuana with a girlfriend who needed an abortion. 'I did not approve nor disapprove,' Noreen said. 'It seemed a sensible decision. But my friend was treated like an animal, and later that night she died.'

Sadie listened carefully as Noreen told of how from that moment on she got what she claimed to be 'the calling'.

'I knew I could save other girls from the same fate,' she said simply. 'And that is what I have been doing ever since.'

'How did you find me?' Sadie asked curiously.

'The hotels know me. When a girl checks in alone they alert me. You acted so fast that I didn't have time to reach you before. But fortunately I found you in time, and even more fortunate your baby is safe.'

She shut her eyes, thought of Ross's baby safe inside her, and wanted to scream aloud with fury.

'Don't worry,' Noreen said quietly. 'I have an alternative plan. A happy solution for everyone concerned. Of course,' she added, 'I could have taken you to a hospital. The police would have been alerted, your family and the prospective father would certainly have been dragged into it. There might have been a prosecution.' She paused, watching for Sadie's reaction. 'Usually the girls like to keep this sort of thing to themselves, and I don't blame them.' She nodded knowingly. 'You see, I understand what happens. One night of passion . . . things get out of hand . . . no time to think about the consequences . . .'

She had Sadie's rapt attention. Carefully she outlined her plan. 'You'll have your baby, dear. You're too far gone to attempt another abortion anyway. I'll send you to my sister's place in Barstow where you can rest and regain your strength. When you give birth you'll be fitter than you've ever been and we'll take the baby off your hands. There are couples who long for a child . . . We arrange it without the fuss and bother of adoption. All those papers to fill out . . . it's dehumanizing. One simple document is all you have to sign . . .' Noreen smiled reassuringly. 'And my sister, Nita, and I will take care of everything.'

72

'I beg your pardon.' Sadie spaced her words carefully and spoke slowly.

Deke stared at her, his eyes glowing coals.

His eyes. Her eyes. Disturbingly familiar.

She felt a shiver run down her spine, and automatically began to close the door.

'Don't do that.' He blocked it with his foot. 'I'm home . . . Mother. Nita Carrolle sent me. It's been a long journey, but I'm here.'

The name Nita Carrolle made Sadie hesitate. 'I . . . I don't understand . . .' she said falteringly.

But she understood. Twenty-six years earlier she had given birth, and now part of her past stood before her.

'Push dear, push.'

'I am pushing. I am. I am.'

Tears streaked her face. A pause between contractions. Then the pain again, and her screams of agony. Long animal screams, while her hands tore at the roots of her hair. 'Help me, someone. Please help me.'

'Shut her up for God's sake.'

The mask descending over her face. The gas. Deep gulps. Relief. Drifting. Away from her body. Away from the pain.

Dully she stared at the familiar stranger. 'You'd better come in.'

Already she was thinking fast. Why was he here? What did he want? If he expected her to fall on him crying with pleasure he had another think coming. She had no maternal feelings. None whatsoever. Oh God! If it ever got out . . .

Maybe he wanted money. He looked like a freak. Do not admit anything. See what he knows.

How can he know anything? They promised me – those two women – they promised me nobody would ever know.

He followed her into the house. She led him through to the kitchen, glad that the servants were away for the weekend. At least she could deal with him alone.

'Sit down,' she said, recovering her composure. Purposefully she tried to sound casual. 'You know, I think you've made a mistake. Maybe you'd like to tell me who put you up to this?'

'I had a whore named Joey,' he said, covering his eyes with oblique wraparound sunglasses. 'She's not here now, but I loved her. You'll love her too.'

A shiver of fear. 'What?'

'Whores belong together.'

Her patience snapped. 'Who are you? What do you want?'

'I'm your son,' he replied calmly. 'You know that.'

'Oh, come on. Please. What makes you think such a ridiculous thing?'

'Nita Carrolle told me.'

'I don't know anyone of that name.'

He turned unexpectedly and struck her full force across the face. 'You lie, whoring bitch!' he screamed. 'I know the truth and you will tell me more.'

The force of his blow threw her to the floor and she lay there stunned, suddenly realizing her peril.

473

This was no long lost son. This was some sort of maniac. AND SHE HAD LET HIM INTO HER HOUSE.

Elaine brushed her hair vigorously. She could feel the tingle all the way down to her toes. There was nobody like Ross . . . nobody. He was the greatest lover in the world when he wanted to be.

She lined up her programme for the following week. The hairdressers, the nail clinic, the gym – no more Ron Gordino – who needed Ron Gordino? Maybe she would try Jane Fonda's Workout or Richard Simmons' Body Asylum. She hummed softly to herself. She would call Bibi and suggest lunch. Bibi would spread the news of Ross's return faster than The Hollywood Reporter.

And what about Ross's career? Sadie La Salle calling was an excellent sign, even if she had interrupted the best sex they had shared in years. The phone call had not fazed Ross. He could screw and talk at the same time, a feat not every actor could manage.

She felt so good. Ross had brought her to a majestic climax, then showered, and left for Sadie's house with a grin on his face. He was happy to be home. She was happy to have him. Together they would make it to the top again.

Angel took a cab and arrived at Buddy's apartment in the morning. She was sure he wouldn't mind.

'I ain't got no word to let anyone in,' grumbled the maid. Buddy's regular girl was out sick and she had omitted to inform her replacement of his message.

'But I'm Mrs. Hudson,' Angel protested. 'And Bud – er Mr. Hudson assured me he had left word with you.'

The maid sneered, ever so slightly. 'If'n you're his missus how come you ain't livin' here permanent?'

'I don't think that's any of your business.' Angel flushed, but stood her ground.

The maid's glance took in her swollen stomach. 'Okay,' she said grudgingly. 'You'd better come in. Ain't no skin off *my* ass if you rob the place.'

Angel re-entered Buddy's life. Not quite the way she had expected to, but she was back, and the anticipation of seeing him again made her breathless.

Ferdie knew that Sadie was going to Palm Springs for the weekend. He also knew that she wasn't planning on leaving until ten-thirty or eleven. He took pride in being aware of every move she made. Buddy's news *could* be given to her on the telephone, but *should* be given to her in person.

He vacillated for only a moment. It meant changing out of his beach clothes into a more suitable outfit. It meant explaining to Rocky that the picnic would have to be delayed, and Rocky would no doubt sulk . . .

Ferdie stamped his foot. A moment of unbridled aggravation. What was so important about Sadie knowing immediately anyway? God! If he had the news and she ever found out that he saved it for Monday. It *was* important, what with the billboard and everything . . .

Madame La Salle was *not* going to be pleased.

He stripped off his red T-shirt and shorts and hurried into the bedroom to change.

Ross felt surprisingly up. Things had a way of turning out for the best. An interlude away from Elaine had done them both good, and now he felt a togetherness that he thought had gone forever. Elaine was a fighter. She was no Beverly Hills bimbo. Sure she liked to spend money and live it up, but something he knew for sure – she would always be there when he needed her.

Sadie phoning – causing temporary coitus interruptus – had delighted both of them.

'She's changed her mind,' Elaine enthused. 'She must want to handle you.'

Ross had to agree. Why else the summons to her mansion on a Saturday morning?

He drove happily along Sunset, fit, tanned and fifty. Every career has its ups and downs. His was headed for an up, he could feel the good vibrations.

'Mother whore!' spat Deke. 'Harlot. Filth.'

He had tied her up, the threat of his knife ever present. Bound her tightly to a chair.

The fear of being cut prevented her from struggling. Ever since Tijuana, the doctor, and the unsuccessful abortion, she had been fearful of blood. In a way it was his fault . . . If he was her son . . . as he claimed to be . . .

The mask was pulled roughly away. The pain returned. And maybe death would have been more welcome as she felt herself torn. Scream-

ing was her only release. Different voices were everywhere.

'Shut her up.'

'You want every neighbour in the area to hear her.'

'What's taking so long?'

'It's a breech birth, goddamn it.'

The mask again. The sweet thunder in her ears and nose and throat like death inviting her to stay.

Drifting . . . drifting . . .

Sharp reality . . .

'It's a boy.'

'He's not breathing.'

'Christ!'

'Do something before it's too late.'

Smack.

Nothing.

'He won't make it.'

'Like hell he won't. We need the money.'

Smack.

'C'mon you little bastard!'

And crying.

Brief respite.

The surprise of another contraction. She knew it was the afterbirth, soon it would be over.

She sucked in her breath, let it all out in one long piercing yell that seemed to last forever.

Rough hands clamped the mask over her face again and she faded once more to welcome unconsciousness.

When she awoke it was over. She lay in bed clean and washed, only the dull throbbing ache between her legs reminded her of the ordeal. Noreen Carrolle stood next to her sister Nita. They both smiled. Two faces . . . one plain and kindly, the other over-made up and coarse.

'Your worries are behind you dear,' said Noreen.

'Yeah, no more screwin' around an' you're in good shape,' laughed Nita.

She drifted back to sleep.

She tried to keep her voice calm. Somewhere she had read when dealing with a psychotic that it was important to try and remain in control. Besides, she was no shrinking violet, she was Sadie La Salle. Grown men had been known to shiver in her presence.

She thought of her elaborate alarm system. Unfortunately it was turned off. But if she could only reach the panic button by the kitchen door a distress signal would go straight through to the police.

Deke stalked around the kitchen muttering to himself.

She wondered if she should try to get him talking. Personal contact. Another way of getting through.

If she *was* his mother, what could be more personal than that? And if she *was* that meant that Ross was his father. And even now Ross was on his way up to her house.

Deke stopped marching up and down and slumped to the floor in a sitting position, his back against the refrigerator.

'This is a big house,' he remarked.

In a strange way he reminded her of someone. She couldn't think who. He had her eyes. Oh God! He reminded her of herself, this bizarre disgusting stranger.

'I said you have a big house,' he repeated.

'Yes,' she agreed quickly.

'Joey would've liked it here.'

'Who is Joey?'

'My fiancée.'

She forced herself to sound as natural and friendly as possible. 'Where is she? Shall we call her and invite her over?'

He stood up. 'She's fucking men. That's what the whore does. She's like you, opens her legs for the world.' He said the words blankly, as if they meant nothing.

Sadie tried to change the subject, although her throat was so dry she could hardly talk. 'What's your name?'

He was pacing again. 'It doesn't matter.'

'Yes it does. What does Joey call you?'

'Joey?' He stopped and looked surprised. 'How do *you* know Joey?'

'Why don't you untie me and we can talk about her?'

'Talk about who?'

'Joey.'

'The whore bitch is dead.'

'I'm sorry.'

Deke resumed his pacing, lost in thought.

She eyed the panic button by the kitchen door, and wondered if there was any way she could get near enough to press it.

'This is a big house,' he said, repeating himself for the third time. 'I think I'll look around.'

'Yes, why don't you do that,' she said quickly.

He didn't hear her as he walked from the kitchen.

477

Laboriously she attempted to edge the chair towards the back door. It was no easy task. He had bound her with electrical cord, and it was cutting into her wrists and ankles. Nevertheless, painstakingly, she began to inch forward.

73

Leon Rosemont flew out from Las Vegas early Saturday morning. He felt a sense of urgency, but at the same time he knew that Deke Andrews was within his grasp . . . Maybe . . .

Ferdie drove his zippy white E-type Jaguar faster than the speed limit allowed. Next year a Mercedes. For sure. And the year after that – well maybe in two years – a Rolls.

Ferdie had goals. He aimed to attain every one of them. In the meantime he enjoyed the fast English sports car. It was a luxury he felt he deserved. Besides, his young boyfriends *loved* it.

He pushed one of Rocky's Rod Stewart cassettes into the tape machine and reflected on the boy's stupid behaviour. What a pain! Sulking and complaining all over the place. That was the trouble with the young ones, they acted like children.

'I wanna come with you,' Rocky had griped. 'I wanna meet the great Sadie La Salle.'

'Another time,' Ferdie replied firmly.

Another time. Another century. Never mix pleasure with business. A cliché. But a true one.

Then Rocky had burst into his 'You don't love me anymore' number and 'I'm splittin'.'

Ferdie had been forced to abandon everything and placate the boy. They ended up in bed. An exciting interlude that lasted far too long.

Anxiously he looked at his black Porsche watch. A Christmas present from Madame.

It was nearly eleven. He hoped that she hadn't left for Palm Springs yet.

The Rolls stalled at the corner of Canon Drive and Sunset, refusing to restart. Ross was furious.

When he had successfully worn the battery down to a mere click, he alighted from the car and gave it a resounding kick. A group of Mexican maids and children at the bus stop outside the Beverly Hills Hotel stamped and cheered. He gave them a mock bow and jogged across the street and up the driveway to the hotel.

'Car trouble,' he explained, handing the keys to the doorman. 'You buy a frigging Rolls you just don't expect it. It's on the corner of Canon.'

'I'll take care of it, Mr. Conti. Will you be in the Polo Lounge?'

A cup of coffee and a cigarette was tempting before meeting Sadie. 'The coffee shop,' he decided. 'It's nothing much, I think I just flooded the engine.'

'Don't worry, Mr. Conti. I'll have you paged when it's fixed.'

Ross entered the hotel.

The luxury of the house did not affect Deke as he walked from room to room. He stared blankly at expensive paintings and fine objets d'art. They meant nothing to him.

In her bedroom he stood before the four poster bed and slowly, deliberately, unzipped his jeans. He shut his eyes, thought of Joey, and did what he had to do.

In the corner there was a giant Panasonic television set. He stabbed the screen with his knife, methodically ripping it to pieces.

Joey would certainly love the place. He planned to send for her as soon as possible.

In the kitchen Sadie made slow progress. The cord around her ankles cut into her flesh, and every time she edged forward another inch it was all she could do to stop from crying out. She wanted to close her eyes and wake up from the horrifying nightmare.

Where was Ross? What a strange twist of fate that the intruder in her house might be their son. *Their love child.* Bitterness enveloped her. Their love child indeed. The hateful reminder of Ross's disinterest and desertion.

Why hadn't the baby aborted as it should have done?

She moved too fast and the chair hit the side of the kitchen table, teetered and fell – taking her down with it.

She cried out, then bit down hard on her lower lip hoping he hadn't heard.

She was trapped now. Tethered like some thing. Bile rose in her throat and she felt more alone and frightened than she had ever done in her entire life.

Deke continued his tour of the house. In her bathroom he emptied all the bottles of make-up and perfume and bath oils down the sink. Joey didn't need any of that artificial trash.

He removed his sunglasses and gazed at himself in the triple mirror over the vanity unit. The reflection he saw surprised him. He leaned closer to the mirror and rubbed his bald scalp – slowly at first – then faster . . . faster . . . faster . . .

He felt another erection grow in his pants, but he ignored it, didn't touch himself, couldn't touch himself. Must wait for . . .

'Joey,' he said. Then he began screaming wildly. 'JOEY. WHERE ARE YOU, WHORE? COME OUT WHEREVER YOU'RE HIDING, BITCH. I'M GOING TO KILL YOU, SLUT.'

He picked up a bronze figure and hurled it at the mirror.

The glass shattered into a thousand or more fragments.

Ferdie pulled into the driveway of Sadie's house. When was the woman going to put in security gates? Hers was practically the only house on the street without them.

He tut-tutted to himself. When he had enough money he would lock himself in a gilded cage immediately. Los Angeles was full of creeps and perverts and God knows what. Couldn't be too careful.

He hurried from his car and rang the front doorbell hoping that he hadn't missed her.

Trapped on the floor Sadie heard the buzz and relief flooded over her. Ross was here. At least she wasn't alone anymore.

Upstairs, Deke heard the bell ring too and reality intruded on his thoughts.

He remembered where he was.

He remembered his mother, his *real* mother.

He didn't want to lose her. Not after all he had gone through to find her.

He put down the thick black eye crayon he was playing with, loped quickly down the stairs, and rushed into the kitchen. For one blank moment he thought she had gone and he was filled with red hot fury. Then he saw her on the floor, tied and helpless.

'Who did this to you?' he demanded.

She stared at him in horror. He had blackened around his eyes as though drawing a cosmetic mask. High on his forehead he had written in smudgy letters WHORES DIE.

'Untie me,' she said rapidly. 'I'll see who's at the door. I can send them away. Hurry.'

He bent to do as she said. She held her breath, weak with the anticipation of escape. Ross would save her. Thank God he was here! Maybe if they could get to his car, lock the doors, drive quickly off . . .

He had unbound one ankle when the door buzzer sounded again. He stopped what he was doing and cocked his head to one side.

'Hurry!' she urged.

A look of disgust swept across his face. 'You think I'm stupid, don't you?'

'No . . . no . . . I –'

'If you laugh at me I'll kill you.'

'I'm not laughing at you.'

He slapped her across the face, snapping her head back hard. 'Don't ever laugh at me, whore.'

She could taste blood in her mouth. 'No,' she whispered. 'I wouldn't ever do that.'

'Stay here and be quiet,' he commanded.

Silently she nodded.

Ferdie's immediate instinct was to step sharply back at the sight of Deke. 'Who are *you*?' he questioned, shocked.

Before Deke could reply, Sadie began to scream.

Ferdie's reaction was unfortunately slow. He did nothing.

In one smooth action Deke stepped forward, knife in hand. He plunged it into the startled man, puncturing him through the heart. Ferdie's eyes bulged with a mixture of sorrow and surprise as Deke dragged him through the doorway and threw him down on the hall floor. He was dead before his head hit the tiles.

Deke kicked the door shut and went back into the kitchen.

Sadie's screams turned to a whimper when she saw him. His clothes were soaked in blood.

'Please,' she moaned. 'Don't hurt me.'

'You made a lot of noise,' he said mildly. 'You shouldn't have done that.'

She began to shriek wildly. 'What did you do to Ross? What did you *do* to him?'

481

'And the Lord giveth. And the Lord taketh away . . . Mother. You must realize, I am The Keeper Of The Order. A man of honour.'

Her voice rose even more hysterically. 'You killed him, didn't you? You goddamn *bastard*.'

'Am I a bastard . . . Mother?'

'If I'm your mother,' she screamed, 'then you just killed your own father.' Wild laughter fell from her lips. 'How do you feel about that . . . you . . . you fucking stupid moron.'

His eyes were insane with black anger as he walked towards her.

'Hi, Ross.' Montana slid onto the stool next to him in the coffee shop.

He glanced up from reading about himself and Gina in the morning paper. 'How are you?'

She shrugged. 'Okay I guess.'

He put the paper down. 'I was really distressed about Neil. I didn't get a chance to speak to you at the funeral.'

'Thank you.' She touched his arm lightly. 'I'm sorry about the movie.'

'Yes, well I'm sorrier than you are. That was one hell of a part you wrote. I really could have made an impact with a role like that.'

'I'm sure you could.'

He shrugged. 'Of course, with Oliver producing who knows what would have happened . . .'

She nodded her agreement.

'What'll you do now?' he asked.

'I'm going back to New York on Monday.' She sighed. 'I guess I'll miss the sunshine, but really I'm a city person. I figured a last breakfast in the coffee shop of the Beverly Hills Hotel was a fitting goodbye.' She glanced along the curved counter and laughed. 'I've gotten some of my best dialogue in this very room!'

He laughed with her.

'And how about you?' she inquired. 'What next?'

He smiled a crooked smile and projected with the famous blues. 'Something between Love Boat and death.'

'Huh?'

'An actor's joke.'

'Oh.' She ordered a double chocolate milkshake and an apple danish.

'Some breakfast,' he said admiringly.

'I've always been an eccentric eater.'

I bet she gives great head, he thought, and then scolded himself for having such a thought. Wasn't it possible to sit with a woman and not think about sex?

No.

Elaine did not like dipping her head to him. Maybe it was because he never returned the courtesy. He thought they might experiment. Together. It was never too late.

'I'm back with my wife,' he remarked.

'Good,' she replied with enthusiasm. 'I never did see you as just another of Gina's consorts.'

A bell boy arrived to inform him that his car was fixed. He tipped a couple of bucks and decided to stay for more coffee. Talking to Montana was no hardship. Besides – let Sadie wait. He didn't have to jump the moment she called, did he? He was still a star, wasn't he?

The voices in his head told him he had done the right thing. But he wasn't sure . . . Doubt crept over him like a dark hood as he moved from room to room in the big house. Restlessly he walked around muttering to himself. All rules of logic, time, and reason were suspended. He had travelled towards a goal and achieved it . . . But now what?

His head hurt. He felt disoriented. There was a throbbing in his temples, and the stroke of death surrounded him.

Where was Joey?

Out whoring of course. WHORE . . . WHORE . . . WHORE . . . She thought he was ugly. She thought he was a nobody.

She didn't want him anymore.

He screamed with anger and kicked open the door to Sadie's study. The scream died in his throat and he stood stock still, transfixed.

Oh, if Joey could see what he could see . . . Oh, yes . . . Oh, yes . . .

Tentatively he entered the room and approached the giant cardboard poster propped against the wall.

He reached forward to touch, to marvel.

It was him.

The picture was of him.

Buddy's mother gazed at him levelly. 'I thought you were dead,' she said, 'like your friend Tony.'

He laughed hollowly. For the first time he began to see things from her point of view, and whatever she had done to him he knew that he must have hurt her terribly. 'Still breathing,' he said, trying to make a joke out of it.

She nodded.

He shuffled his feet uncomfortably feeling like some young jerk. 'Can I come in?'

'No,' she replied flatly.

'Look,' he said, 'I've come back to make my peace with you. We both did things we shouldn't have – but what's that old saying – blood is thicker than water. Right?'

She glanced anxiously around, noted one neighbour watering her garden, another conversing with the postman. 'I suppose you *had* better come in,' she said reluctantly. 'But don't you say anything in front of Brian. Do you understand?'

He followed her inside the house and took a deep breath. It smelled the same – faint minglings of garlic, musky perfume and clean linen. Nostalgia enveloped him. He was prepared to forgive and forget if she was. One day he might even bring Angel here.

She led him into the formal living room, the one reserved for guests, and said, 'Sit down.'

On the black piano stood her collection of old silver photo frames. Grandma and Grandpa in sepia tinted Italy. Their beautiful daughter dressed in white, her hair braided to her waist. A wedding picture. The man in the photo not his father. Brian, at a younger age. No photos of him. No Buddy Boy once the light of her life.

She noticed him looking and said, 'I married again.'

He was shocked. Yet why should he be? She had her life to live too.

'Hey – that's great.' Sincerity was not in his tone. 'So I guess I got me a brother . . . I mean like a half brother. That's . . . uh . . . terrific.'

'No,' she said coldly. 'Brian is nothing whatsoever to do with you.'

He needed a family and a background again. 'I know you're mad. I should've contacted you – but I had to work things out my way. You've got to admit that what happened between us wasn't normal.' He paused, then continued insistently, 'Hey – you've got to accept *some* of the blame.'

Her eyes were ice chips. 'For what?'

His voice rose. 'Don't do this to me. You *know* what.'

'I wouldn't worry about it if I were you.'

'Look – I've worried about it for ten years. Now I just want to forget it.'

'Incest. Is that what you thought?'

Her callous way of saying that forbidden word shocked him. He'd had enough. He wanted out. Inexplicably he felt like crying – a sentiment he hadn't experienced in years. 'Why?' he managed.

'Because you are not my son, Buddy. You were adopted by us when you were four days old.'

He could not believe what he was hearing.

'It wasn't a legal adoption,' she continued calmly. 'We . . . bought you for a sum of money because we desperately wanted a son. I was told I could never have children . . .' She paused. 'But I gave birth to Brian, so you see – the doctors were wrong.'

He didn't know what to do or say. So many thoughts, such a mixed-up bag of emotions. And in a way – although it was a tremendous shock – relief almost. 'Who am I?' he asked at last.

'I was never told,' she said coldly, then added, 'I don't feel responsible for you, Buddy. You saw fit to leave me ten years ago. Let's just make believe you never came back.'

Elaine showered, then made an appointment at the hairdressers. She had tried tidying the house, but cleaning had never been her forte – so she phoned Lina and graciously requested her return.

'I have 'nother job, señora,' Lina said stoically.

'But I *need* you,' Elaine insisted as though there were some special bond between them. 'Mr. Conti is back, and you know how upset he'll be if you're not here.'

'Mebee I find you someone else.'

'Not good enough, Lina. He'll want you here, first thing Monday. Please don't let him down.'

She replaced the receiver firmly and made herself a cup of coffee. Fleetingly she was tempted to add a little shot of something, but the temptation passed as soon as she considered her new situation. Ross was back. She had standards to maintain.

She phoned Bibi. 'Guess what?' she announced dramatically, ignoring the fact that they hadn't spoken in weeks.

'What, sweetie?' inquired Bibi, barely disguising her aggravation at being caught.

'Ross and I are back together. I wanted you to be the first to know.'

'How you together?' Surprise spilled from her voice. 'Last night he together with Gina. I sorry, darling, you make a mistake.'

'Bibi,' said Elaine assertively, 'I am not a fool. Last night he may well have been with Gina, but this morning he came back to me. To stay.'

'You *sure*, sweetie?'

'Of course I'm sure.'

Bibi's voice warmed up. She thrived on exclusive gossip. 'So what happened with Gina?'

'How about lunch on Monday and I'll tell you all about it?'

'I busy Monday, but I think I change it. Yes, sweetie, for you I change it.'

'Wonderful. Jimmy's, one o'clock?'

'Jimmy's so boring, darling. I find new place, very nice. Chinese. My secretary call you early Monday with the address.'

'Perfect.' Elaine put the phone down and smiled. Lunch with Bibi. A fitting re-entry into the swing of things.

Angel waited until the maid left the premises, then she launched into action. Out came the Lysol, Ajax, and cleaning equipment. She tied her long blond hair away from her face and earnestly set about cleaning Buddy's apartment the way it *should* be cleaned. Thoroughly. Not a lick and a spit. When he came back she wanted everything perfect. And it would be.

Humming softly to herself she started in the bathroom.

Leon Rosemont arrived at the house in San Diego just as Buddy was leaving. Sometimes perfect timing occurs, and although Leon did not know it he was in exactly the right place at the right time. Five minutes later and he might have missed Buddy altogether.

They passed on the front steps.

'Excuse me,' said Leon sharply. 'Are you Buddy Hudson?'

486

Buddy was in no mood for conversation. The guy had cop written all over him. Shit! They had pulled the file and now they wanted to investigate the case. 'Yeah. But listen – I made a mistake this morning. I was blowin' steam, y'know?'

Leon looked at him strangely. 'What?'

'I got bombed last night,' he insisted. 'You can put the file away. *I* don't even know what I was talkin' about.'

Leon frowned. 'What *were* you talking about?'

'Hey – you *are* a cop?'

Ponderously Leon produced his identification. Buddy looked at it quickly. All he wanted to do was get back to Angel and let a little love into his life.

'Can we go inside and talk?' Leon asked.

Buddy indicated the house. 'In there? You gotta be kiddin'. I'm about as welcome in there as the clap.'

'It's urgent we talk. And I want your mother to hear what I have to say.'

'She's not my mother, man.'

'That's one of the things I want to talk about.'

And he took off his blood-soaked clothes and ran them through the washing machine.

And he removed the inky writing from his forehead and the blackness from around his eyes.

And naked, he knelt before his poster and touched the hardness he felt.

And climaxed, throbbing with ecstasy.

And wondered why the words WHO IS BUDDY HUDSON? defaced *his* poster.

'I've got to go,' Ross announced.

'I'm glad we had a chance to talk,' Montana said. 'Who knows . . . if I ever get the rights to *Street People* back . . . raise the finance . . .'

'You'll think of me.'

'Naturally.'

He alighted from his stool and kissed her on the cheek. 'You're one hell of a lady.'

She smiled ruefully. 'That's what Neil used to say.'

And it became clear. An impostor had taken his face, his image, his countenance, and PRETENDED TO BE HIM.

487

Rage swept over him.

WHO IS BUDDY HUDSON?

He went to her desk and picked up the leather bound address book.

WHO IS BUDDY HUDSON?

He flicked through the neatly typewritten pages searching for the letter H.

WHO IS BUDDY HUDSON?

There were many names listed under various cities. He ran his finger down the page marked Los Angeles.

WHO IS BUDDY HUDSON?

He snapped the book shut.

He knew where to find him.

'Nothing much wrong with it, Mr. Conti. As you said – the engine just flooded up a bit.'

Ross climbed into his Rolls and transferred a twenty into the doorman's palm. A middle-aged tourist recognized him and nudged her husband. The two of them stared.

Ross started the Rolls and moved out of the hotel driveway. After all these years it still pleased him to be recognized. In his rearview mirror he observed Karen Lancaster and her English rock star zoom up in Karen's bright red Ferrari. He figured he had had a lucky escape from *that* one. *And* from Gina Germaine. He had hardly been circumspect in his choice of women. Still . . . he had enjoyed himself, for a while anyway.

He wondered what Sadie wanted. Was she going to apologize for the way she had treated him? Or was she going to try and grab him back in the sack and then attempt to humiliate him all over again?

He did not wish to speculate. All he required from her were her business services, and if she had anything else in mind she would just have to forget it.

Clothes still damp, but they would do.

Outside a white Jaguar with the keys in.

He put on his black shades and slid behind the wheel.

Oh, mother.

Oh, Joey.

If you could see me now.

He turned the ignition, revving the engine until it roared like a tiger raring to pounce. Music blasted out from all four speakers. Rod Stewart. A fitting growl.

He steered the car down the long and winding driveway and stopped when he got to the street. His van was parked beside a ditch, partially concealed by a clump of trees. He reached inside for his carryall bag, then returned to the Jaguar. He took out a map of Los Angeles and studied it until he was satisfied he knew exactly where he was going.

The Jaguar had the power he desired. Together they ripped off down Angelo Drive fusing together in a blur of speed.

'Wolfie, are you up?'

'Always for you, Bibi. Although it is a trifle early for a Saturday morning . . .'

'Darling, it nearly twelve. What you do?'

'I'm in bed. Where is Adam?'

'Oh, Adam. He so boring. One day I leave him.'

'You're always saying that.'

'So what? I mean it.'

But they both knew she didn't. Who else would put up with Bibi and her deliciously bitchy tongue?

'Sweetie, guess what?'

'Tell me. Put me out of my misery.'

'Ross Conti, he leave Gina, he go back Elaine.'

'How do you know *that*?'

'I know everything first, darling.'

Ross was not a *bad* driver. But his attention wandered, he hogged the middle of the road, and drove too fast. He especially drove too fast as he and the Rolls progressed up winding Angelo Drive, a twisting street which meandered its way up into the hills, narrowing as it advanced.

Sadie's house was near the top. Normally two drivers heading towards each other would be aware of the fact that the street was dangerous, reduce speed, and keep a foot prudently near the brake.

Ross, racing up the treacherous road, did not do this.

Deke, speeding down, did not do it either.

By the time they saw each other coming it was too late.

75

Buddy drove back to Los Angeles in a daze. So much had happened in a very short period of time. He had gone to San Diego with one purpose in mind. To find his mother and make the peace.

So he found her, *and* the truth. That was soul destroying enough – but what happened next was so bizarre and quirky that he was still in shock.

Leon Rosemont. A cop. But not come about the Wolfie Schweicker identification as he had thought.

The two of them returned to the house and his mother (no, not his mother. Estelle . . . that's how he must think of her from now on) allowed them in only after Leon produced his identification and mentioned the name Nita Carrolle.

He thought of the words which once again changed his life. '. . . *brother . . . twin . . . murderer . . . will strike again . . . searching for mother . . . calls himself The Keeper Of The Order . . .*'

What an odd twist of fate. *Searching for mother*. Hell, it could become a national pastime.

He had asked questions. 'Who is my real mother? Where is she? Is she still alive?'

Detective Rosemont had shaken his head blankly and produced a yellowing piece of paper with the date marked on the top. The page was divided into two columns. One side listed Mr. and Mrs. Willis Andrews and a Barstow address. The other listed Estelle and Richard Hudson, and their San Diego address. Written beneath this in thick red pen across both columns was a notation – TWIN BOYS – one to each family – and on the appropriate sides were the prices paid. It seemed – at the time – that the Andrews family got themselves a bargain. The Hudsons had shelled out two thousand dollars – over fifteen hundred dollars more.

A scribbled notation on the bottom read 'see page sixty'.

'Page sixty was ripped out,' Leon explained. 'So the only connection was you, Mrs. Hudson. I tried to phone you – when I got no reply I thought it important enough to get on a plane and come here.' He paused. 'Who is the real mother?'

'I don't know,' she said coldly. 'It never interested me. Everything was taken care of – even a birth certificate with our names on was supplied.'

Buddy put his foot down hard and zoomed along the freeway. How could he lay this whole trip on Angel?

Hey – kid. You'll never guess. I got me this weirdo brother. Like he's . . . uh . . . my twin. And you know what? He goes around killin' people.

Angel would widen those big beautiful eyes and think he was taking drugs again. Shit! Talk about being in the wrong place at the wrong time. If he hadn't been there when Leon Rosemont turned up on her doorstep they never would have found him, and he wouldn't have had to hear all that garbage about some maniac twin out there somewhere.

But they would have found him because he had never bothered to change his name, and all at once he knew why. He had *wanted* to be found. *Wanted* his mother to care enough to come looking for him.

She never had.

Now he understood why.

Detective Rosemont said he would arrange a police guard for him back in Los Angeles. Buddy had said no, and quickly explained his situation. 'I'm just not connected to this whole story,' he ended flatly. 'An' I don't intend to be. There's no way this Deke character could ever track me.'

'Look at this,' Detective Rosemont said, and handed him a photograph.

Some long-haired jerk with staring eyes.

Some long-haired jerk with his features.

Different in a way . . . But chillingly the same. That's how the detective had recognised him.

It gave him real bad vibes. He had shoved the photo back at Leon abruptly. 'Looks nothin' like me,' he said roughly. 'I gotta head back for L.A. now.'

He had departed shortly after, reluctantly handing over his address and accepting a number to contact the detective should he need to.

Goodbye San Diego.

He drove down the highway, towards a fresh start, towards Angel . . .

Somewhere he had a mother . . .

It didn't matter. He was free now.

Sitting in a cab on his way to the airport Leon felt depressed. He had hoped that the Hudson family would be the key. But Richard Hudson was dead, and Estelle Hudson didn't know and didn't care. What kind of a woman adopted a baby and didn't even want to know who the natural mother was? The same kind of woman who *bought* a baby in the first place. He shook his head in disgust.

Questions . . . questions . . .

But where were the answers?

He desperately needed to know the identity of Deke's real mother . . . That's where Deke would go . . . If she was still alive . . . and a hunch told Leon that she was.

At the airport he went straight to a phone booth and called Captain Lacoste in Philadelphia. 'I'm on my way back to Vegas,' he said. 'There's nothing here.'

'Wait!' shouted the Captain. 'I just heard from Los Angeles. They think they got him. Get on the next plane.'

76

The moment of impact was so unexpected. A flash of white car, a staring face. Too late to do anything but jam on the brakes and wrench the wheel of the Rolls to the right.

The two cars collided. The crunch of bodywork crumbling, the shatter of glass, the unearthly noise.

Then silence except for the raspy raunch of Rod Stewart coming from the tape machine still functioning in the Jaguar.

> *In the bars and the cafes – Passion*
> *In the streets and the alleys – Passion*
> *Lots of pretending – Passion*
> *Everybody searching – Passion*

Angel finished cleaning the apartment around one o'clock. She walked from room to room admiring her work. Everything was gleaming and sparkling, just the way it should be. She felt the baby kick and stopped for a moment placing both hands on her stomach. It was a magical feeling. She wanted a boy, a miniature Buddy. Excitement swept over her at the very thought. They would call him Buddy Junior and he would grow up to be just like his father. Well . . . maybe not exactly the same . . .

She smiled softly, entered the bathroom, removed her clothes, and stepped under the shower.

Deke Andrews crawled from the wreck unhurt except for a cut on his forehead and a pain in his right leg. He should not have taken the white car. To steal was a sin. He was being punished.

But surely The Keeper Of The Order was above punishment?

He could hear Joey's laughter.

Oh whore of whores shut your painted mouth before I shut it for you.

'I thought ya could drive, *cow*boy,' she jeered.

He hated her with a

> *Passion*
> *Even the President needs passion*
> *Everybody I know needs some passion*
> *Some people die and kill for passion*

He realized he must move on. Get away from the two smashed cars. Dragging his leg behind him he started up the hill.

Not once did he even glance in the other car.

She put on a simple white shift, plain sandals, and fluffed her hair – allowing it to dry naturally. Koko had wanted to cut it all off, or at least style it. But she hadn't allowed him to. She knew that Buddy loved it exactly the way it was.

She applied scent behind her ears, on her arms, and between her breasts. Youth Dew by Estée Lauder. Koko had presented it to her. 'Better on you' dreamheart, than on some of the old bags who come in the salon. My God! If they saw a youth the only dew they'd get would be on their foreheads!'

She wanted Buddy and Koko to meet. Properly. Not as adversaries. And Adrian too, of course. Maybe she would throw a small dinner party. There was a nice little dining nook, space to seat everyone comfortably, and she could make all of Buddy's favourite foods.

So deep was she in thought that she did not hear the doorbell the

493

first time it rang. It was only on the second ring that she responded, and hoping that it was Buddy home early she ran to answer it.

'You're all right, gel,' said Josh Speed.

'I should be. I've been perfecting my act since I was thirteen,' replied Karen Lancaster drily.

'Thirteen, eh?'

They resumed athletic making out in a closed cabana located in a prime position beside the Beverly Hills Hotel pool. Courtesy of Josh's record company. The cabana not the fucking.

'Cor blimey!' screamed Josh suddenly. 'I'm comin' so fast it's like a bleedin' express train runnin' through me cock!'

'You're so poetic,' husked Karen, reaching her own peak.

He squeezed her nipples, always the main attraction. 'You ain't heard nothin' yet, gel. Later on I'll play yer some of me songs – that'll *really* get y'goin'.'

She rolled across the floor reaching for her abandoned swimsuit. 'Sounds good to me.'

He was not Ross Conti. But he would do.

'I won't be long,' Ferdie had said.

'I won't be long . . . I won't be long . . .' Rocky mimicked furiously three hours later as he stormed around the apartment. He had been looking forward to the beach picnic – sun, surf and new connections. He had not skipped off to Hollywood to spend his time waiting around for the likes of Ferdie. This little prince did a lot of things but he did not wait. Screw waiting.

He gathered together his things, stuffed them in a bag, then headed for the door.

For a moment Angel just stared, eyes huge and alarmed. 'Buddy?' she questioned unsurely as she backed into the apartment, shock etched across her face. 'Your hair . . . and you look so pale . . . My God! Buddy, what *happened*?'

WHO IS BUDDY HUDSON? *She* knew who he was. This Madonna with corn silk hair and the face of an angel.

Deke stepped inside, closing the door behind him.

She was Joey, of course. He had known all along he would find her. And she was pregnant. With his child.

The freeway allowed Buddy time to think, and the more he thought the more confused he became. In the end he put on the radio and lost himself in weather reports, rock music, commercials, and newscasts.

We can expect a beautiful high of eighty-five degrees today so get out those boogie boards and head for the beach . . .

Yeah. That's what he would like to do.

Stevie Wonder. 'Ribbon in the Sky'. Hot Chocolate. 'Chances'. Randy Crawford. 'Rio de Janeiro'. Music soothed him. Maybe he'd have to see a shrink, get his head together.

Shit! You ain't a movie star yet kid. Let's not go getting big ideas.

If being with Angel couldn't straighten him out nothing could. He'd be alright. He was a survivor . . .

Only he felt so alone . . .

Time on the freeway didn't mean anything. Like an endless conveyor belt cars proceeded to unknown destinations. A black Porsche zoomed by, doubling the speed limit.

He wondered what Monday would bring. Would Sadie have good news for him?

Sure she would. Think positive. Stardom was inevitable, he'd waited long enough. Especially with his billboard hitting America.

He hoped that Ferdie had kept his promise and told her about Angel. No more lies or false beginnings. He was going to make it on the truth – all the way to the top.

Santa Monica was too crowded for the likes of Rocky, the competition too fierce. He hung around for an hour but there was no action at all, and he did not like struggling to be noticed. Screw that game. At seventeen years of age he looked like an angelic fourteen year old and thought like a shrewd thirty-five year old. After only a brief six weeks in Los Angeles he felt that he knew his way around, and Santa Monica Boulevard was not the only game in town.

He put on his T-shirt, picked up his carry-bag, and headed up Doheny towards Sunset.

Gina Germaine swept into the Polo Lounge half an hour late for a luncheon appointment with a female journalist from a weekly news magazine. The way she looked at it the reporter was lucky to be getting her at all. How many other stars gave up their Saturdays to further the course of publicity? Not too many. And that is why *she* was at the top and others got stuck halfway up the ladder.

They treated her like royalty in the Polo Lounge. But then, of course, she *was* royalty – the Hollywood kind.

Gina was not in a good mood. She felt rejected. First by Ross Conti – who was a no-good has-been son-of-a-bitch anyway. And second by Sadie La Salle. Her friend. Her agent. And a woman who was too selfish to give up Palm Springs and spend the day with her.

Disloyal was a word that hovered in Gina's mind as she beamed a greeting at the woman journalist and launched straight into a ' . . . I'm a simple person really. All I want is a little cottage, a bunch of kids, and the right man in my life.'

'What about Ross Conti?'

Ice cold. *'Who?'*

Josh Speed wore bikini swimming briefs that left nothing to the imagination.

'Hmmm . . .' observed Karen, sharing a joint with him before emerging from the cabana. 'You certainly believe in letting it all hang out.'

'If yer got it, let 'em see it. I can make a groupie come from twenty yards!' He roared with laughter.

She smiled. Josh would be a riot with Pamela and George and their bunch of dinosaur friends.

They walked out of the cabana hand in hand. Instinctively they paused, aware of the fact that the tourists needed to feast their eyes. Then Josh yelled, 'First one in's a sissy,' and with arms and legs flailing wildly leapt into the pool.

Karen smiled indulgently. What a pleasant change to be with someone who knew how to have fun. She made her way more sedately to the deep end of the pool and executed a graceful dive.

'C'mere, sexy,' yelled Josh, scissoring her round the waist with his bony legs. ''Ere,' he whispered. 'Let me stick me big toe in yer drawers.'

'Not here, Josh,' she giggled huskily.

'Why not?' he demanded. 'Yer think this group a toffee noses never seen a big toe before?'

Elaine arrived at the Beverly Hills Hotel in good time for her two o'clock appointment at the beauty shop. She wore a pale blue silk shirt, white linen slacks and sunglasses.

'Mrs. Conti,' exclaimed the girl who usually did her hair. 'You look terrific! Have you been on vacation?'

She nodded vaguely. 'Sort of.'

'Hawaii?'

'Not exactly.'

'Wherever it was it's certainly done you the world of good. A tan really suits you.'

'It'll suit me even better when you do something with my hair.'

Oliver Easterne left a lunch meeting at Nate 'n' Al's, and hurried to a *late* lunch meeting at the Beverly Hills Hotel.

There was just not enough time in the day. But Oliver had developed his own philosophy. Never let a potential investor off the hook. Even if it meant choking to death.

Wolfie Schweicker was not in the habit of picking up boys. He had no need of doing so. His sexual appetite was not vast, and the once a month special parties that he and a select group of friends arranged were more than enough to take care of his every need. So when he spotted Rocky lounging against an RTD stop on Sunset the *last* thing he had in mind was to stop.

His silver Mercedes took the decision right out of his hands. The car slowed, the blond baby loped over, and before you could say Disneyland he was in the car.

Wolfie looked anxiously around to see if anyone had noticed. Apparently not. He drove quickly off.

How can I take the boy home? he thought. What will the servants think? He had *never* committed indiscretions under his own roof.

But what was the alternative? A motel? A baths? None of them the kind of places he frequented.

'Where we goin'?' the boy asked, as the Mercedes turned off Sunset and headed for the hills.

'My home,' Wolfie said crisply.

To hell with the servants.

News travelled like bush fire. Bad news faster than good.

The Beverly Hills Hotel was the perfect breeding ground for a rumour to get going. An accident on Angelo Drive was no big deal. But an accident involving Ross Conti in his Rolls was.

'He's hurt badly.'

'He's crippled for life.'

'He's dead.'

The story had its variations as the news passed from one mouth to another. How easy it was to embellish, distort and twist.

Gina Germaine was told by a red-faced publicist who hovered by her table like a nervous flamingo. She received the 'in serious condition' story.

'How terrible!' she fluttered, casting her eyes down, and allowing her lower lip to quiver appealingly.

'Shall we forget about the interview?' the journalist asked sympathetically.

Gina made a rapid recovery. Up came the eyes, and a wan smile took over the lips. 'No,' she said bravely. 'Ross would want me to keep going. I know that. He's a wonderful man.' Short pause. 'Now, what was I saying?'

Karen heard from a producer friend of her father's who took her to one side when she emerged from the pool and discreetly whispered in her ear that Ross Conti had been killed in a car smash. 'I think you should call George,' he said solemnly. 'He and Ross were always very close.'

Yes, but Ross and I were closer, Karen wanted to say, and she started to shiver uncontrollably.

Oliver heard the whisper in the Polo Lounge. Ross Conti was in intensive care. They didn't give him long to live. Thank Christ, Oliver thought, that I cancelled the movie. And then he had second thoughts. Maybe it wasn't such a smart move . . . look at the insurance he could have picked up!

Montana was still in the coffee shop when the news travelled from ear to ear. She had run into a journalist friend from New York, and they were catching up on old times. Badly injured was the story she got. 'Poor Ross . . .' she murmured. 'I just can't believe it . . .'

Elaine was not told at all. At first, anyway. A group huddled by the entrance to the beauty shop trying to decide who should impart the bad news. Finally her stylist volunteered and gingerly approached her as she sat reading 'Vogue' under a heat machine, her hair wrapped in a hundred tinfoil corkscrews.

'Mrs. Conti,' she whispered. 'Apparently there's been some sort of awful car accident up on Angelo.'

'Why are you telling *me*?' snapped Elaine.

But she knew why the girl was telling her, and she pushed the hood from above her and shakily stood up. Beneath her suntan she paled. 'It's Ross, isn't it?' she gasped. 'Oh no! It's Ross.'

78

When he touched her she knew. He held his hand – cold and clammy, to her cheek. She shrank away from him, her eyes wide with fear.

THIS MAN WAS NOT BUDDY.

In some horrible strange way he looked like a paler, thinner, ugly Buddy . . . but of course he wasn't, and how could she have ever thought that he was?

'Who are you?' she whispered.

'Who is Buddy Hudson?' he retorted calmly.

'My . . . my husband,' she said quickly. 'He'll . . . he'll be home . . . in a minute. He really will be. I promise you.'

Deke's black eyes grew angry. 'Joey. I do not want you to play your stupid mind games with me anymore. It upsets me.'

'I'm . . . I'm not Joey. I'm Angel.'

'I know that. I've always known that.' He reached forward to touch her face again.

'Don't!' she cried sharply, pushing his hand away.

He gripped her wrist. 'I have killed to reach here. I have done it once and I can do it again.'

Her hand flew to her mouth. 'Please. What do you want?'

'You, of course. I've always wanted you, Joey.'

'I'm not Joey,' she screamed.

But he was not listening.

Halfway to Los Angeles Buddy observed the black Porsche which had roared past him earlier pulled over to the side, a police car in evidence – lights flashing. Instinctively he reduced his speed. The last thing he needed in his life was more hassles with the police.

He checked out the time. It was two-thirty. Another hour and a half and he would be back at his apartment. At five, the limo would pick Angel up and bring her to him. He couldn't wait. They would talk . . . and make love . . . and talk some more . . . and make love . . .

He put his foot down hard, to hell with the cops.

The stewardess passed by with a cheery smile and a 'Can I get you a drink, sir?'.

Leon knew that he probably looked like he needed one. He was bleary eyed and unshaven, with wrinkled clothes, and the faint aroma of stale sweat. If Millie caught a glimpse of him she would have a fit.

He thought of Millie and dredged up a rueful smile. When she got mad she *really* went all the way.

'A drink, sir?' repeated the stewardess, slightly impatient.

'A club soda,' he replied.

He had not replied to her letter, and had no intention of doing so. What was the use of trying to explain? She would never understand. When it was over he would go home and she would take him back. It was as simple as that.

And maybe it would be over . . . soon.

He fell asleep before his club soda arrived and woke just as they were landing in Los Angeles.

She looked different, but that was as it should be. He had disposed of the old Joey, slashed away the squiffy eye, the jammy mouth and the brazen body. Now she was perfect. A Golden Angel Of Hope. True consort for The Keeper Of The Order.

But she was being difficult, and he could not allow that.

Trapped beneath him she struggled tearfully, so he decided to tie her just as he had tied his mother. This he did quickly, and marvelled at how calm they became when the cord restrained them. How quiet and beautiful.

He left her trussed on the floor while he examined the rest of the apartment. In the bedroom his image awaited him, covering an entire wall. He was not surprised.

WHO IS BUDDY HUDSON?

Was *he* Buddy Hudson? Or was Buddy Hudson Deke Andrews?

Confusion and anger mixed with the fury that welled up inside him. He took his knife from the side of his boot and ripped at the offending poster. Joey had done this.

ONCE A WHORE ALWAYS A WHORE.

'Are you still whoring?' he demanded, striding back to where Angel lay. 'Are you, Joey? *Are you?*' His eyes glared blackness as he leaned over her. He felt the swell of her stomach on his chest, and wondered if he should cut the baby free. Soon he would have to . . . But not now . . . Later . . .

'I've never been . . . a whore,' she whispered.

'You were *my* whore,' he replied slyly. 'You did things to me that only a whore would do.'

He touched her breasts and she began to cry.

Why was she crying? Wasn't she happy to see him? He had been through so much for her . . .

Marriage.

The thought struck him.

Joey wanted marriage.

They had discussed it so many times . . .

I wanna meet your mother. Whatsamatta, cowboy, ain't I good enough t'meet ya mother?

Abruptly he stopped touching her and rose to his feet. 'Alright,' he said. 'I agree with you. We've been together long enough. You shall meet my mother, Joey.'

'I'm not Joey,' she whimpered.

He ignored her denial, left her crying, and went back in the bedroom. There, he picked up a thick red marker and wrote a message across the tattered poster. Then he stood back, surveyed his work, and returned to his captive.

He bent over her and held the tip of his knife lightly against her stomach. 'I'm going to untie you now,' he said quietly. 'Do not cause me any trouble. If you make me angry you *will not meet my mother*. Do you understand me, Joey?' He put his knife away and began to loosen her bonds.

She was sobbing uncontrollably. 'Oh please God, somebody help me.'

'And God shall help The Keeper Of The Order,' he said piously. 'And I am he.'

501

79

Somehow Elaine got from the beauty shop to the front of the hotel – a ridiculous sight with tinfoil sprouting out all over her head.

Her stylist followed her. 'Mrs. Conti,' she implored. 'You can't drive. You mustn't.'

Elaine screamed for her car ignoring the concerned girl. She did not care what kind of a spectacle she made of herself. The only thing that mattered was getting to Ross.

'But you don't even know where they've taken him,' the girl wailed. 'Please wait. We'll phone the police. Mrs. Conti, you *can't* just rush off like this. You're too upset.'

Mrs. Conti could do what she liked. And did.

Disappointment. Frustration. Every negative emotion and more.

Leon stood in the noontime heat and watched the breakdown trucks remove the Rolls and the Jaguar – or what was left of them.

He gave a heavy disgusted sigh and spat on the sidewalk. He had hoped it was all going to be over. It wasn't.

The chase was getting him down. Especially when the message 'they've got him' turned out to be just Deke's carryall bag on the floor of the Jaguar – with his driver's licence to identify it. The bag was better than nothing, although it contained no leads. Leon had already gone through it thoroughly. The only items of interest were the newspaper clippings of the Philadelphia murders carefully preserved between the pages of a racing car magazine.

He was tired, rushing from city to city, not eating or sleeping.

But he wasn't too tired to go on. The chase was only just beginning.

Elaine turned left on Hartford Way and realized that she had no idea where they had taken Ross, so she drove home with the thought of getting on the phone and finding out.

A police car stood ominously in the driveway.

She felt the blood drain from her face and the heat vanish from the day. If Ross was dead she couldn't stand it. She loved him too much to lose him again just when she had him back.

What if he's crippled, Elaine?

I'd sooner that than death.

Suppose he can never work again? No more charge accounts, fancy restaurants or parties. No more Beverly Hills.

Get off my back, Etta. I love Ross. Nothing else matters.

'Mrs. Conti?' A cop jumped from the car as she pulled into the driveway.

Her heart stopped. 'Yes?'

'Mr. Conti's inside.'

She ran into the house.

Ross propped up the bar, a large tumbler of brandy in one hand. There was a small bandage across his forehead, and his left arm reclined in a sling. A second cop stood beside him jotting notes on a pad.

'Ross!' she yelled ecstatically.

'Sweetheart!' His famous blues crinkled with pleasure, then he started to laugh. 'What are *you* doing? Auditioning for "Star Wars"?'

Her hands flew to her tinfoil encased head. She looked dismayed.

'What the hell kind of a Hollywood wife are you?' he teased. 'If Bibi saw you running around like that she'd boot you out of the club!'

A slow grin spread over her face. 'Quite frankly – to quote my wonderful husband – who gives a flying fart!'

80

Heat. Smog. Sweat. Tiredness. Muscle cramps. A bad day. One Buddy wanted to forget as soon as possible. Wearily he parked in the underground space reserved for him, got out of the car, stretched and yawned. He'd had it. Physically. Emotionally. In every way.

It was four-fifteen exactly. In ten hours he had managed to totally fuck up his life – or straighten it out. He'd have to think about which. At least he'd gotten rid of the incest nightmare.

He paused in the coolness of the garage for a moment and decided that maybe he was lucky after all. No past. No shit. No nothing. Was that such a bad thing considering former events?

He rode the freight elevator up as the passenger one was busy. Seductive scent lingered in the air, it made a change from smelling garbage. Not that the building was kept in bad shape – there was a resident janitor on duty twenty-four hours a day. Some of the female tenants did not think that was enough. He had been asked to sign a residents' petition demanding a security guard in the basement parking area too. He sighed. What the hell. He wouldn't want Angel down there alone.

Angel. He ached to see her. Maybe he would cancel the limo and go and pick her up himself now that he was back early.

The scent stayed with him all the way to his apartment and when he opened up the door it was still there. His first thought was that the maid had been wearing it. But then he felt instinctively that Angel was there, and his heart quickened pace like some thirteen year old.

'Angel?' he called out. 'Hey – baby, where are you?'

He threw open the door to the bedroom and knew at once that something was horribly wrong.

Angel could hardly breathe, the back of the van was so filthy and stuffy, the heat unbearable, and the windows blacked out.

She clung to the side as the vehicle raced and jolted along, fearful for her baby as random pains stabbed at her insides.

She closed her eyes tightly and thought of Buddy, repeating his name to herself over and over like a mantra.

His poster hung in tattered shreds. But the eyes were intact – and written across them in heavy marker pen were the words:

THE FACE IS MINE
THE ANGEL IS MINE
WHO IS BUDDY HUDSON?
HE CEASES TO EXIST

THE KEEPER OF THE ORDER

Chillingly snatches of Detective Rosemont's conversation returned to him – . . . *brother . . . twin . . . murderer . . . calls himself The Keeper Of The Order . . .*

And Buddy could remember thinking – what bullshit – who cares – and it's nothing to do with me.

With a feeling of dread he had only to look around the apartment to know for sure that Angel had been there. On a table beside the bed was her alarm clock, next to it a small group of photo frames containing pictures of the two of them together. He wrenched open the closet and sure enough her clothes hung tidily beside his. In the bathroom her toothbrush, comb, assorted make-up . . .

There was no doubt she had been there. And if so . . . where was she now?

'Oh Jesus!' he groaned. 'Oh, no!'

Leon went to work, with the help of the Beverly Hills Police, the Department of Motor Vehicles and a comprehensive computer system. The Jaguar was registered to a Ferdie Cartright. There was no reply at his home. A neighbour reported she had seen him leave – in the car – alone – at approximately eleven in the morning.

Leon spoke to the woman. He was good with witnesses. People trusted him.

'Did you see Mr. Cartright in the company of this man?'

He produced two pictures of Deke. One the high school photo – and the other an artist's impression of how he would look today. Certain witnesses along the way had contributed to that look. Bald head, staring eyes, ragged clothes.

The woman studied them, squinting slightly. 'Mr. Cartright does have a lot of male visitors.' She leaned close as if imparting a state secret. 'He's gay you know. But please don't say you heard it from me.'

Leon nodded sombrely. 'Certainly not.'

'What's Mr. Cartright done anyway?'

'His car was in an accident. We're trying to locate him.'

'Is he all right?'

Leon swallowed impatience. 'That's what we're trying to find out. Please. Look at the photographs.'

The woman studied them again, screwing her face into contortions. 'I don't like the look of *that* one,' she said, pointing to the artist's impression of Deke.

'Was he here?' Leon asked urgently.

'Him? No, I'd remember him . . .' she trailed off. 'There's something about the other one . . .'

'Yes?'

'I'm not sure . . . it's not really like him at all . . .'

'Who?'

'This man who came by early this morning. Very good looking,' she laughed. 'This is going to sound crazy, but he was like an older, handsomer version of this one.'

She held up the year-book picture of Deke.

Leon felt a chill.

Buddy.

'You wouldn't remember what he was wearing, would you?'

'Black pants, a white shirt and a nice sports jacket – also black.' She roared with laughter. 'You're going to think I'm a dirty old lady glued to her window – but it's better than watching soap operas all day.'

'I'm sure it is,' agreed Leon, anxious to conclude the interview, already on his way to the door.

'I can remember thinking,' the woman called out. 'If this one's gay – what a dreadful *waste*!'

The detective in San Diego had given Buddy some numbers written on a piece of paper. But he had not been interested then, he had shoved the paper somewhere knowing full well he would never need to use it.

Feverishly he turned out his pockets – nothing. Then he vaguely remembered screwing up the piece of paper in the car and flicking it on the floor.

He raced from the apartment, into the elevator, down to the garage, scrabbled on the floor of his car.

HE COULDN'T FIND THE GODDAMN PIECE OF PAPER.

He turned out the glove compartment, dug around the seats, swore aloud in frustration. Then he hastened back upstairs.

The door to his apartment was open as he had left it. He hurried inside and stopped short. There was someone there.

Deke was taking her to meet mother. It was a good feeling. So different from the time before.

This time they would get along. They would smile and speak to each other. They would sing his praises instead of criticizing him and laughing.

'And the Lord shall sing the praises of the dead,' he said aloud. 'For only in death shall the soul be cleansed of evil and the devils released.'

He thought carefully.

Kill.

Kill mother.

Kill Joey.

Kill self.

WHO IS BUDDY HUDSON?

He didn't care anymore. He had the solution.

It felt good knowing exactly what to do.

And nobody would ever laugh at him again.

81

'What's your involvement with Ferdie Cartright?' Leon asked harshly, before Buddy could say a word.

'Hey –' Buddy grabbed his arm – not even curious about why he was there – just relieved that he was. 'Has Deke got Angel? Has that crazy sonofabitch taken my wife?'

'What are you talking about?'

'He was here!'

'How do you know?'

Buddy dragged him into the bedroom where he took in the ripped poster and the scrawled message.

'What does that shit mean?' Buddy demanded. 'Does it mean he's taken Angel?'

'Who is Angel?'

'My wife, goddammit. What are you going to do?'

'You'd better tell me everything you know.'

'Angel was supposed to meet me here at five. She came early for some reason, and now she's gone. I don't understand. How could he find me? *You're* the only one who knows my connection.'

'Who else has the poster?'

'Half of America. It goes on billboards coast to coast Monday.'

'Maybe that's the key.'

'What *fucking* key? Where's Angel?' Buddy screamed.

'We'll find your wife,' Leon said with more confidence than he felt. 'But I need information. Who is Ferdie Cartright?'

'What has *he* got to do with any of this?'

'Listen to me,' Leon said sharply. 'You visited him early this morning. Later his car was in an accident. By the time the police got there no one was in the wreck. But Deke Andrews' bag was in the car.' He paused. 'Talk to me, Buddy. Tell me what you know.'

'Ferdie works for my agent, Sadie La Salle. I stopped by to see him this morning. I wanted him to drop by Sadie's and give her a message for me.'

'Did he agree to do this?'

'Yes.'

'Was there anyone else there?'

'Some be-bop kid.'

'What was his name?'

'How the fuck would I know?' he exploded. 'Look, is any of this going to find my wife?'

'I hope so. Because it's all we've got.'

He was careful. You never could tell what forces would try to trap you. Even the air was dangerous. The heat. Enemies were always around.

This time Deke drove his van right up to Sadie's front door.

He walked around the grounds peering in windows.

The late afternoon sun was fading under low clouds. He hoped it would rain. He missed the rain. Water was a positive force. Heat came from hell.

Inside the house he could hear the telephone jangling, but nobody answered it.

He ran his right hand over the smoothness of his scalp. Then he took the keys he had stolen earlier from the pocket of his shirt and opened up the front door.

He had always known he would come back to mother.

Silence prevailed.

As it should.

She crouched in the back of the van and held back the screams which threatened to rip from her throat. The pain subsided, she unclenched her fists and breathed deeply. The van was almost airless causing her to choke on the thick dust. She was soaked in sweat and exhausted from the ride. At least they had stopped. Maybe he had gone away . . . left her . . .

Suppose she was trapped . . .

She struggled to the rear and began to hammer feebly on the double doors. 'Help me . . . Please . . . Please . . . somebody help me . . .'

*

How beautiful she was – his Golden Angel Of Hope. How different from the Joey he had first met.

She was sobbing as he helped her from the van. That was all right. Water . . . tears . . . all the same thing.

He half-dragged, half-carried her into the house. And knew that he desired her as he had never desired any woman on earth.

That was because she was truly his. He had guided her life, eliminated the evil from her body, cleansed her totally.

'Joey, sweet Joey,' he murmured, as he helped her up the stairs.

'I'M . . . NOT . . . JOEY,' she cried out desperately.

Immediately he was angry. Why did she want to make him angry?

Bitch.

Whore.

Prostitute.

Roughly he pulled her into Sadie's bedroom and pushed her on the bed. 'Don't say that,' he screamed. 'Don't *ever* deny who you are.'

He crouched over her and the hardness entered his body. There was nothing sinful about giving up his hardness to Joey. They were man and wife.

For a moment he couldn't remember where he was. Then the phone began to ring again, startling him into a frenzy. He leapt off the bed, grabbed the cord and yanked it violently from the wall.

WHERE IS MOTHER?

She would love Joey so pale and blonde and beautiful. Such a lady. But a whore too. Mustn't forget that.

ALL WOMEN ARE WHORES.

He stopped to think.

KILL.

KILL MOTHER.

KILL JOEY.

KILL SELF.

But first . . . the two women must meet . . . He owed them that.

Abruptly he tugged a sheet from the bed and tore it into strips. Then he bound her once again, spread-eagling her across the bed.

He was mad. She knew that. His black eyes glared insanely at the world.

Who was he? And why did he bear such a horrible sickening resemblance to Buddy?

Buddy was handsome.

This man was ugly. A monster.

509

The baby had stopped kicking. She felt a dull throbbing ache. He's killed my baby, she thought. And he's going to kill me too. Her flesh crawled. She would never see Buddy again.

'Mother. Mother. Wake up, this is important.'

Deke's face swam before her. His eyes so like her own . . . nothing of Ross . . .

Poor Ross . . .

Sadie tried to speak through the pain. Her jaw hung slackly. She could feel the jagged edge of broken teeth and her eyes were no more than slits. At least he hadn't used the knife . . . yet. How long had she been unconscious? It seemed like a long time. Why was he still here?

Maybe it was only a few minutes . . . She felt herself going again and tried to hang on . . . but the pain was so bad . . .

He was untying her from the chair. Maybe he was going to let her go . . . Maybe . . .

She slipped back into unconsciousness.

He said, 'Mother. You're being very stupid.' Then he screamed, 'MOTHER. WAKE UP.'

When she didn't he kicked her. Joey was waiting. It wasn't right to keep her waiting.

Things fell into position.

Ferdie Cartright worked for Sadie La Salle.

Sadie La Salle was Buddy's agent.

Ferdie goes to see Sadie.

She lives on Angelo Drive.

She has the poster.

Ferdie vanishes.

Sadie not in Palm Springs where she should be.

Phone does not answer at her house.

Phone is pulled from the socket.

'Let's go,' Leon said urgently.

It was slow work pulling Mother upstairs.

She was heavy, but he persevered. After all, a promise was a promise, and he couldn't let Joey down.

Angel heard him approaching. 'You've got to let me go,' she called out desperately. 'I'm losing my baby. PLEASE. PLEASE. LET ME GO.'

510

When he entered the room she froze and despair washed over her. He lugged the body of a woman.

She began to scream hysterically.

'Mother. This is Joey. Joey, say hello to Mother.'

It was a shame that Joey would not behave. He was forced to gag her and it really wasn't right that she had made him do that.

His head hurt. He remembered Philadelphia, so long ago and far away.

He looked at Mother, propped in a chair beside the bed. Then he looked at Joey bound and gagged.

The two women in his life.

The two *special* women.

It had taken so long to arrange this meeting. And did they appreciate it.

DID THEY?

Furiously he stripped off his clothes, removing his boots last.

He fingered his knife, tested the point, smiled a death-mask grimace.

Desire flowed through him. Bubbling through his bloodstream, filling his mind. His head hurt, his eyes hurt . . .

Joey was waiting. Her legs spread.

WHORE.

Joey was waiting for him and she would never laugh at him again.

ANGEL.

He lifted her skirt, used his knife to cut her panties away.

WHORE.

Her face was contorted, her eyes huge. She wanted him. The Golden Angel Of Hope *wanted* to merge with The Keeper Of The Order.

He straddled her, prepared for entry, raised his arm with the knife in readiness to strike simultaneously.

AND THEY SHALL BE JOINED.

Buddy grabbed him from behind, a desperate lunge that threw them both off balance and onto the floor. They struggled for a few seconds, then Deke made an inhuman sound in the back of his throat and slashed the knife towards Buddy's face. The knife carved across the palm of his hand and blood spurted freely.

Buddy didn't feel the agony, he just felt the fury, and the fury gave him strength. With his right hand he grabbed the wrist of Deke's knife hand and bent it back . . . slowly . . . slowly . . . forcing it . . .

For a brief moment their eyes fused. Black on black. Different and yet the same. 'WHO IS BUDDY HUDSON?' Deke screamed, and his wrist went suddenly limp, causing the knife to swoop down and slit his own throat.

It was all over by the time Leon lumbered into the room.

epilogue

epilogue

The Sadie La Salle break-in, Ferdie Cartright's murder, and subsequent events caused shock waves to hit Hollywood which *really*
reverberated when early Sunday morning Wolfie Schweicker was
found shot to death by an intruder in his own bedroom. People
panicked. Security was taken to new lengths. There was a run on
attack dogs, personal bodyguards, armoured limos, and shotguns.
Bibi Sutton started a trend by turning her bedroom into a fortress,
complete with electronically controlled steel gates on the windows
and a vault-like door.

Both Sadie La Salle and Angel Hudson were rushed straight to
emergency. Diligent doctors were able to prevent Angel from mis-
carrying. She was allowed home after a few days with instructions to
take it easy and rest.

Sadie was not so lucky. She had two cracked ribs, a fractured
cheekbone, broken nose and multiple contusions. She was also
suffering from shock and a total memory blank about what had
happened.

When Leon Rosemont questioned her he was unable to learn
anything. Angel had nothing to say either. Both women offered no
clues . . . they seemed locked in a conspiratorial silence.

Leon had his suspicions, but even if they were right, what difference did it make now?

Deke Andrews was dead. But the mystery lingered on . . .

Oliver Easterne followed the weekend events on various televisions
dotted around his house. He set off for the office early Monday
morning mulling over the idea of putting a writer on it immediately.

What a movie it would make! And if he could only sign Buddy
Hudson to play himself . . .

Seven a.m. precisely. And an eager parking attendant waited to take his car at the front of the building. No underground parking for Oliver Easterne.

The gleaming Bentley exchanged hands, and he hurried inside, stopping at the news stand to pick up the morning papers and three packets of breath mints. A morning ritual.

He jogged athletically up the stairs. Another morning ritual. He had no time for work-outs or gym. Running up stairs was the perfect cardio-vascular activity. Better than push-ups or skipping rope any day. By the time he reached the penthouse floor his heart was pounding at exactly the correct strenuous exercise rate.

He burst into the outer office full of the joys of screwing people on all sides. The big hustle. That's what life was all about, wasn't it?

His secretary did not appear until nine o'clock. This suited him fine, as it gave him time to shower and make his New York calls without interruptions. He opened the door to his office – a private sanctuary where he liked to sit behind his tooled leather desk, and admire the polished perfection of leather couches, fine rugs, and tasteful antiques.

He opened the door, sniffed suspiciously, then let forth a heart-rending cry of pure anguish. His desk was piled high with excrement.

He staggered back – a broken man.

Montana chose that moment to saunter through the outer office. ''Morning, Oliver. Just came by to pick up a few things from my desk.' She paused. 'My God! What's that *smell*?' She moved towards him. He stood like a statue carved in stone at the entrance to his office. She peered over his shoulder. 'Oliver!' she exclaimed. 'Your desk is full of . . . bullshit. Oh . . . my . . . God!' She could not control her laughter. 'Oh . . . Oliver!!! Who can have done this to you?'

He had never been a physical man. If there was any punching out to be done he had always hired someone else to do it. But a rage came over him of such magnitude that he could not control himself. He turned and charged towards her.

A mistake.

Casually she stepped to one side, causing him to trip and sprawl on the floor.

He yelled out in frustration.

'Oliver,' she said, exiting gracefully. 'You know something? I think you've finally got all the bullshit you could ever hope to handle!'

By noon the story swept Hollywood.

Rats Sorenson flooded the news stands with copies of 'Truth and Fact' the week after the Sadie La Salle headlines.

Ross Conti achieved greatness. Well . . . not exactly greatness. More a reputation for being the biggest cocksman since Erroll Flynn! There he was – in glorious colour on the front cover in all his natural glory. Accompanied by a very cooperative and very naked Karen Lancaster.

'It did for Ross what Cosmopolitan's centre spread had done for Burt Reynolds years before.'

Instant superstardom. Again.

Full thrust back into the centre of the limelight. Just like old times.

It helped that he had a smile on his face and an erection that caused the magazine to be withdrawn from the stands by several angry pressure groups screaming about the obscenity laws. When the delivery trucks turned face and set about collecting the outlawed copies – there were none left.

Ross Conti was a sell out.

Little S. Shitz did not receive a photo credit, but he did receive a handsome payment.

He celebrated in a Marina Del Rey singles bar, where he met a girlish redhead who gave him herpes and stole his car.

Elaine ruled the roost. She became the wife of the year. What sort of woman sat through the kind of indiscretions Ross Conti had committed – publicly – and came up smiling?

Journalists clamoured for her quotes. 'People' magazine devoted two pages to her – calling her warm, witty, and wise. Dear Merv had her on his show and discussed infidelity and understanding wives. *She was a celebrity in her own right.* The Contis were *the* hot couple in town. Bibi Sutton called *her.* They were invited to every opening, party, and event.

Together they enjoyed it. After ten years they had found each other and that's what really mattered.

Leon Rosemont returned to Philadelphia. Millie was not in their apartment upon his return. He waited weeks before contacting her. She was staying with her brother.

'Come home,' he said dully. 'It's over.'

'It'll never be over, Leon,' she replied, her voice tinged with regret. 'There'll always be another case . . . it's worse than there being another woman.'

Perhaps she was right. He was too weary to fight with her. Maybe he was born to be a loner. Often he thought about Joey. Her cheerful disposition and her crooked smile . . .

Buddy Hudson achieved everything he had ever desired in life and more. His heroic rescue of Angel and Sadie and his bizarre connection to Deke Andrews made world-wide headlines.

His billboard was a sensation.

He had Angel back.

Everyone wanted him. The big agents, the most important producers, network television executives, plus every magazine, talk show and newspaper in the country.

The mass attention was exciting in one way – terrifying in another.

He turned to Angel. His beautiful pregnant wife – more wonderful and warm than ever, but with an extra gentle strength which he welcomed.

'Don't do anything,' she said simply. 'Wait for Sadie. After all, she is your . . . agent.'

Her advice was sound. When Sadie emerged from the hospital she went back to work with a vengeance. And Buddy received top priority. She never mentioned Deke Andrews, Ferdie Cartright, or that fateful Saturday at her house. She never allowed anyone else to mention it either.

Gina Germaine had a run of disastrous publicity. It started with the reporter she had lunch with the day of Ross Conti's car accident. The girl wrote an assassination piece of the first order. Gina sulked for a week.

Then the Enquirer ran an exposé of her former life. T.V. Guide killed her in a cover story. And several supermarket rags took up the cause.

Gina fled to Paris, where she had breast reduction surgery in a desperate bid to be taken seriously, and fell in love with an ageing *cinéma vérité* French film director who promised her real acting roles and starred her in a low budget black comedy about a dumb blond American movie star. At last! She was being taken seriously as an actress. She cabled Oliver Easterne that it would be quite impossible for her to fulfil her commitment and return to America to star in his movie.

He hit her with a lawsuit.
She sent him a single word reply.
BULLSHIT.

Karen Lancaster left the country with her rock star. Daddy was unamused by her public indiscretion. Josh Speed found the whole thing hilarious.

She became groupie numero uno as she followed Josh around on his sell-out European tour. She enjoyed her new found celebrity for a while, and then the airplanes, hotels, different stadiums and parties parties parties became a boring routine.

She missed Beverly Hills. She missed Giorgio's and Lina Lee to shop in. She missed Ma Maison and the Bistro to lunch in. She missed Dominick's and Morton's to dine in.

She missed Bibi's wonderful Oscar night parties. And Sadie La Salle's star-studded casual dinners in her kitchen.

She missed valet parking, hot sun, tennis, the Polo Lounge. Hell – she missed *everything*.

It didn't take her long to persuade Josh that he *oughta be in pictures* and that she was just the lady with the right connections to arrange it.

He loved the idea. And he was no slouch in seeing the usefulness of being with a woman like Karen. When she discovered that she was pregnant a few weeks later they decided to get married.

Karen's eyes gleamed. 'We'll have the wedding of the decade!' she announced. 'We'll give Beverly Hills a show the likes of which will have 'em talking about it *forever!*'

Beverly Hills was abuzz. The Karen Lancaster-Josh Speed wedding was an event that if you weren't invited you may as well leave town.

Venue: Disneyland.
Dress: Whatever.

Sadie La Salle decided a beige lace suit was okay. She had lost a lot of weight, and with her new svelte figure could wear anything she wanted. She peered closely at her face in the mirror. Not a sign of the damage Deke had inflicted . . . Outwardly not a sign . . . but inwardly . . .

She thought about Buddy. So handsome and vibrant. And then she thought about Angel. The girl was a gem, sweet, kind and genuinely nice. Sadie adored her. And the feeling was mutual.

Angel was expecting her baby any day . . . Sadie smiled a secret smile. *I'm going to be a grandma* – she thought, *only nobody knows it but me*. Ross would have a fit if he knew.

Ross Conti. Grandpa.

Only he would *never* know. Because finally she had her revenge. And now she could forget him. In fact she already had. She had something else instead . . .

Buddy had told his story to Angel, and she in turn related it to Sadie. The two women became very close. They had a silent secret . . . something they never mentioned . . . but it bonded them together in a very special way.

One day, Sadie decided, she *would* tell Buddy. In the future . . . when the time was right . . .

Montana read about the forthcoming wedding in Liz Smith's column. Reading about Los Angeles reminded her of Oliver Easterne, and when she thought of him she grinned. That classic Monday morning in his office was one of the highlights of her life. It had not been easy to arrange, but oh – the lasting pleasure! Neil would have been proud of her!

In a funny way she missed L.A. There had been many good times, and now she was going back to direct Street People. Oliver had been forced to relinquish the rights in exchange for Neil's other project – the film that Gina Germaine was supposed to star in. He had not been happy, especially when Gina backed out. He was left with an empty package. No director. No star.

Montana had shed no tears on his behalf.

She went out and personally raised the finance to make Street People a go project again. And now she was in control. All the way.

She was proud of herself.

Pamela London and George Lancaster flew in from Palm Beach.

'I hate this tacky little village,' Pamela announced hoarsely to the waiting press.

'Come on, you big-mouthed cow,' George said amiably, shoving her towards their limousine. 'Move your fat ass.'

Marital bliss survived – with the help of an insult or two.

Bibi Sutton wore a white brocade mink-trimmed gown which had set Adam back four thousand dollars, and made her look like the fairy on top of the Christmas tree.

She was lost without Wolfie. Poor, dear Wolfie . . . who had listened to her constant stream of gossip, escorted her to all the places Adam refused to go, and always – *but always* – picked out her clothes.

Maralee Gray attended the wedding with the new love of her life. An ageing Jesus-freak who wore flowing white robes, sandals, and was hung like a prize-winning stallion.

She was ecstatic. What more could one ask out of life? Religion and sex.

How nice if he could have had money too . . . But so what . . . she was getting used to paying the bills.

Elaine wore pink.
Ross wore white.
What a couple!

Buddy wore Armani. Of course. Angel wore maternity. What else?

Koko fussed around her, making sure that every hair was in place and that her make-up was perfect.

Buddy grinned, 'Hey – Koko. You can't make her look any better than she already does.'

Koko shook his curls. 'I merely embellish the rose,' he said kissing her. 'Have a wonderful time dreamheart. And don't forget – I want to hear *all* about it. Call me when you get back.'

Angel nodded and smiled. 'Thanks for coming over. Give Adrian a kiss for me.'

Downstairs Sadie waited in a sleek silver limousine. She exchanged hugs with Angel, kissed Buddy on the cheek, and once again he marvelled at how great everything was. Sadie had accepted Angel. No hassles. Nothing. The two of them got along wonderfully.

He leaned back in the car and closed his eyes for a minute. It had all worked out . . . the bad memories were behind him now . . . Even Wolfie had got his . . . No more nightmares.

Success. Angel. He felt so lucky.

Halfway to Anaheim and the wedding Angel clutched his arm. 'Buddy,' she whispered. 'The baby . . . I think it's happening . . .'

He didn't panic. Stayed calm. Leaned forward and tapped the glass separating them from the driver. After all he was a star now. Had to act the part.

'Get this wreck to the hospital like yesterday!!' he yelled excitedly.

Sadie sat bolt upright and pressed towards Angel, taking her hand.

'You're going to be fine, darling. Don't worry. We'll be there in no time.'

Angel gave birth at four o'clock in the afternoon. It was not an easy delivery. Nobody had expected twins. The first one was a breech birth and for a moment it was touch and go.

Buddy, who was in the delivery room, picked up on the anxious vibrations as they struggled to get the baby to breathe. He felt fear grip him. Angel moaned as the second baby entered the world.

Twins.

Boys.

Just in time the first one let out a healthy yell.

Hollywood Husbands

To the wives who told me plenty . . .
And the husbands who told me more than
I ever wanted to know . . .

And special thanks to special friends
who tried to tell me nothing at all, but did
not succeed!

Somewhere in the Midwest . . .
Sometime in the seventies . . .

The nightmare began for the child when she was fourteen years old and alone in the house with her father. Her brothers and sisters were long gone. As soon as they were old enough to earn a living they left — quickly — and never came back to visit. Her mother was in the hospital, "women's problems", a neighbour had sighed. The child did not know what that meant, only that she missed her mother desperately, even though she had only been gone two days.

The little girl was an accident. Her mother often told her that. "You're a late accident," she would say, "an' too much work for me. I should be restin' now, not raisin' another kid." Whenever she spoke the words she would smile, hug her daughter, and add warmly, "I wouldn't do without you, my little one. Couldn't. You understand me, darlin'?"

Yes. She understood that she was loved by the frail woman in the carefully patched clothes who took in other people's washing and treated her husband like a king.

They lived in a run-down house on the outskirts of town. It was freezing in the winter and too hot in the summer. There were hungry roaches in the kitchen and giant rats that ran across the roof at night. The child grew up with fear in her heart, not because of the vermin, but because of the many times her father beat her mother, and the terrified screams that continued throughout the night. The screams were always followed by long, ominous silences, broken only by his grunting and groaning, and her mother's stifled sobs.

Her father was big, mean and shiftless, and she hated him. One day — like her brothers and sisters before her — she would leave, just sneak off in the early dawn as they had done. Only she had more exciting plans. She was going to go out in the world and make a success of her life, and when she had enough money she was going to send for her mother and look after her properly.

Her father yelled for his dinner. She fixed him a steaming plate of tripe and onions just as her mother had taught her. It wasn't satisfactory. "Slop!" he shouted, after he'd eaten most of it, belching loudly as she hurriedly removed the plate and replaced it with his fifth can of beer.

He looked her over, his eyes rheumy, his face slack. Then he slapped her backside and guffawed to himself. She scurried into the kitchen. All her life she had lived with him, and yet he frightened her more than any stranger. He was brutal and cruel. Many a time she had felt the sharp sting of his heavy hand across her face or shoulders or legs. He enjoyed inflicting what he considered his superior strength.

She washed the solitary dish in a bowl of water, and wondered how long her mother would be in the hospital. Not long, she hoped fervently. Maybe only another day or so.

Wiping her hands, she made her way through the cramped parlour where her father snored in front of a flickering black and white television. The buckle of his belt was undone, and his stomach bulged obscenely over a grimy tee-shirt, an empty beer can balanced on his chest.

She crept outside to the toilet. There was no indoor plumbing; a cracked basin filled with luke-warm water was the only means of washing. Sometimes she cleaned herself in the kitchen, but she wouldn't dare to do that with her father home. Lately he had taken to spying on her —creeping up when she was dressing and sneering at her newly developed curves.

Wearily she pulled off her blouse, stepped out of her shorts, and proceeded to splash water under her arms, across her chest, and between her legs.

She wished there was a mirror so that she could see what her new figure looked like. At school three of her friends and she had crowded together in a toilet and examined each other's developing buds. It wasn't the same as seeing her own body — she had no interest in looking at other girls' breasts.

Carefully she traced the swell of her small nipples, and sucked in her breath because it gave her such a funny feeling to touch herself.

So intent was she on examining her new body, that she failed to hear the clump of her father's footsteps as he approached the out-house. Without knocking he flung open the creaking door before she had time to cover herself. The buttons on his fly were open. "Gotta take a piss," he slurred. And then, as if working on a slow fuse, he added, "What you doin', girl, standin' around naked?"

"Just washin', pa," she replied, blushing beet-red as she frantically

2

reached for the towel she had brought in with her.

He was too quick for her. With a drunken lurch he stepped on the flimsy towel, and blocked the door with his bulk. "You bin seein' any boys?" he demanded. "You bin sleepin' around?"

"No." Desperately she pulled at the towel, trying to dislodge it from under his foot.

He staggered towards her, all beer breath and bloodshot eyes. "Are you sure, missy?"

"Yes, pa, I'm sure," she whispered, wanting to run and hide in her bed and die of embarrassment.

He watched her for a long moment. Then he touched himself and grunted loudly.

Her heart was pounding – signalling DANGER DANGER. She held her breath. Instinct told her she was caught in a trap.

He fiddled with his thing until it was completely visible, sticking through his trousers like an angry red weapon. "Ya see this?" he growled.

She stayed absolutely still and silent.

"Ya see this?" he repeated, his face as red as his weapon. "This is what ya gotta look out for." He stroked his erection. "This is what every boy ya ever meet is gonna want to stick ya with."

As he reached for her she began to scream. "No! No! No!" Her voice was shrill and unreal as if it belonged to someone else.

But there was no one to hear her. No one to care.

And then the nightmare really began.

PROLOGUE

Hollywood, California
February 1986

There were two major events taking place in Hollywood on a cool weekend in February 1986.

The first was a funeral.

The second, a wedding.

Some people felt obliged to attend both. Although, of course, they changed outfits for each occasion.

BOOK ONE

Hollywood, California
April 1985

Chapter 1

Jack Python walked through the lobby of the Beverly Hills Hotel with every eye upon him. He had money, charisma, a certain kind of power, razor-sharp wit and fame. It all showed.

He was six feet tall with virile good looks. Thick black hair worn just a tad too long, penetrating green eyes, a two-day stubble on a deep suntan, and a hard body. He was thirty-nine years old and he had the world by the balls.

Jack Python was one of the most famous talk show hosts in America.

"Hello, Jack," cooed a voluptuous woman sprayed into a mini tennis dress.

He smiled his killer smile – he had great teeth – and looked her over appreciatively, knowing eyes sweeping every curve. Standard greeting – "How's it going?"

She would have been happy to tell him, only he didn't break stride, just kept walking towards the Polo Lounge.

Several more people greeted him along the way. Two tourists paused to stare, and a very thin girl in a red tank top waved. Jack did not stop until he reached his destination. Table number one, a cosy leather booth directly facing the entrance of the Polo Lounge.

A man was already seated there. A man with a slightly manic look, clad in white sweats, black Porsche shades, and a Dodgers baseball cap. Jack slid in beside him. "Hiya, Howard," he said.

"Hiya, Jack," Howard Soloman replied with a wink. There was something about the perpetual motion of his features which gave him the crazed look. He was always mugging, crossing his eyes, sucking in his cheeks. In repose he was quite nice-looking – the face of a Jewish doctor who had strayed into the wrong business. However, his constant mugging gave the impression that he didn't want anyone to find out. "What was the action last night?" he asked, restlessly rimming the top of his glass with a nervous index finger.

"You've been to one screening at the Goosebergers' house – you've been to 'em all," Jack replied easily.

"Good movie?"

"Lousy movie."

"I coulda told you that," Howard said smugly.

"Why didn't you then?"

Howard took a gulp of hot coffee. "Adventure is finding out for yourself."

Jack laughed. "According to you *no* movie is any good unless it comes from your studio."

Howard licked his lips and rolled his eyes. "You'd better believe it."

"So invite me to one of your screenings."

"I always invite you," Howard replied indignantly. "Is it *my* fault you never show? Poppy's quite insulted."

"That's because Clarissa has very particular taste," Jack explained patiently. "Unless it's a film she's been offered and turned down, or unless she's actually *in* it, she has no desire to see it."

"Actresses!" spat Howard.

"Tell me about 'em," agreed Jack, ordering Perrier and two eggs over easy.

Saturday morning breakfast at the Polo Lounge had once been a ritual for Jack and Howard and Mannon Cable, the movie star, who had yet to appear. Now they were all too busy, and it was a rare occasion when they were able to sit down to breakfast together.

Howard headed Orpheus Studios, a recent appointment and one he relished. Heading a studio had always been his big ambition, and now he was there, King of the whole fucking heap – while it lasted. For Howard, like everyone else in Hollywood, realized that being a studio head was an extremely tenuous occupation, and the position of great and mighty power could be snatched away at any given moment by faceless corporate executives who ran the film industry like a bank. Being a studio head was the treacherous no man's land between high-powered agent and independent producer. The saving speech of every deposed studio head was: "I need more creativity. My talent is stifled here. Too much to do and too little time. We're parting amicably. I'm going into indie prod." In the industry, "indie prod" (independent production to the uninitiated) equals out on your ass. Canned. Can't cut it. Tough shit. Don't call us, we'll call you. And so . . . most indie prods faded into oblivion after one failed movie.

Howard Soloman knew this only too well, and it scared him. He had struggled too long and too hard to allow it to happen to him. The one consolation he could think of was that at least when you failed in Hollywood you failed up. Out at one studio – in at another. The old pals act reigned supreme. Also, he was lucky. Zachary K. Klinger – the multi-powerful magnate – owned Orpheus. And Zachary had hired him personally.

Tapping the tabletop with bitten-to-the-quick nails, Howard said, "Since Clarissa wasn't in the goddamn movie, I guess it was one she vetoed. Right?"

"Her decision made her very happy last night," Jack replied gravely. "*Terms of Endearment* it wasn't." He extracted a pair of heavy horn-rimmed glasses from his top pocket and put them on. He didn't need them to see, but as far as he was concerned they took the curse off his good looks. So did the two-day growth of stubble he carefully cultivated.

Jack did not realize that the glasses and the incipient beard made him all the more attractive to women. Ah . . . women . . . The story of his life. Who would have thought in seventh grade that shy, studious Jack Python would have developed into one of the great lovers of the century? He couldn't help the effect he had on women. One penetrating glance and they were his. No rock star had a better track record.

Not that Jack went out chasing. It had never been necessary. From the onset of puberty and his first conquest at fifteen, women had fallen across his path with monotonous regularity. Most of his life he had indulged shamelessly. One, two, three a week. Who counted? A brief marriage at twenty-five barely stopped him in his tracks. Only luck and a certain sixth sense had prevented him from catching various sexual diseases. Of course now, in the eighties, it was only prudent to be extra careful. Plus he felt a more serious image was in order, and for a year he had been desperately trying to live down his lover boy reputation. Hence his relationship with Clarissa Browning. Clarissa was a serious actress with a capital S. She had won an Oscar, and been nominated twice. No bimbette movie star she.

"I'd like to get Clarissa to do a film for Orpheus," Howard said, chewing on a bread roll.

"Have you anything in mind?"

"Whatever she wants. She's the star." Reaching for the butter he added, "Why don't you tell her to call me direct. If I operate through her schmuck agent nothing'll get done." He nodded, pleased with his own idea. "Clarissa can whisper in my ear what she wants to do, and *then* I'll do the dance of a thousand agents."

"Why don't *you* phone *her*?" Jack suggested.

Howard hadn't thought of anything as simple as that. "Would she mind?"

"I don't think for her. Give it a shot."

"That's not a bad idea . . ." His attention wandered. "Christ!" he exclaimed. "Willya look at that ass!"

Jack cast an appraising glance at a very impressive rear-end clad in tight white pants exiting the Polo Lounge. Recognizing the sway, he smiled to himself. Chica Hernandez – Queen of the Mexican Soaps. He would know that sway anywhere, although he didn't let on to Howard. Kiss and tell had never been his style. Let the tabloids guess their smutty little hearts out. Jack never spoke about his many conquests – even though it drove Howard and the other guys crazy. They wanted names and details, and all they got was a smile and a discreet silence.

Since the start of his year-long affair with Clarissa there wasn't much to tell. A couple of production assistants, an enthusiastic bit-part actress, a Eurasian model. All one-night stands. As far as he was concerned he had been scrupulously faithful. Well, with a woman like Clarissa Browning in your life you couldn't be too careful. Their romance was headlines, he had to watch his every move.

Jack Python was smart, charming, a concerned citizen interested in maybe pursuing a political career one day. (Hey – remember Reagan?) And although he understood women very well – or thought he did – he still believed (subliminally, of course) in the old double standard. It was okay for him to indulge in the occasional indiscretion – after all, a quick lay meant nothing to a man. But God forbid Clarissa ever did it.

Not that she would. Jack knew that for sure.

*

"Faster!" gasped Clarissa Browning fervently. "Come *on*. Faster!"

The young actor on top of her obliged. Although in shock,

12

he was managing to perform nevertheless. Well, he was twenty-three years old, and at twenty-three a hard-on is only a handshake away.

Clarissa Browning had done more than shake his hand. Shortly after their first meeting on the set of the film they were appearing in together, she had requested his presence in her dressing room. He went willingly. Clarissa was a star, and this was only his second movie.

She offered him a glass of white wine and a pep talk about his role. Even though it was only ten o'clock in the morning he accepted both gratefully. Then, in clipped tones, pushing strands of fine hair away from her delicate but interesting features, she said, "You do know, that on film reality is the core of everything."

He nodded respectfully.

"You play my lover," she said. Clarissa was twenty-nine years old with a long face, limpid eyes, a nose just saved from being too long, and a thin line of a mouth. In life she received no awards for beauty. However, she had proven more than once that her ordinary looks created incandescent magic in front of a camera.

"I'm looking forward to it," the young actor said enthusiastically.

"So am I," she replied evenly. "Realize, though, that anticipation is not enough. When we interact on screen it has to be real. We have to generate *excitement* and *passion* and *longing*." She paused. He coughed. "So," she continued matter-of-factly, "I believe in working our roles through *before* we get in front of the camera. That way we are never caught with our pants down – metaphorically speaking, of course."

He tried for a laugh and wondered why he was beginning to perspire.

"Let's make love and get it out of the way," she said, her intense brown eyes challenging his.

Who was he to argue? He forgot about his California blonde perfect girlfriend with thirty-six-inch boobs and the longest legs in town.

Clarissa reached over, unzipped his Levis, and they went to work. Even though he was somewhat shell-shocked that he was sticking it to Clarissa Browning. *The Clarissa Browning! Who would believe it?!*

When they were finished she said briskly, "Now we'll both be able to concentrate and make an excellent film. Just know your

13

lines backwards. Listen to our admirable director, and *become* the character you're playing. *Live* the role. I'll see you on the set."

Just like that, he was dismissed.

As the young actor left her dressing room, Clarissa reached for a thermos of vegetable juice and poured herself a small glass of the nourishing liquid. She sipped it thoughtfully. Interaction with her fellow actors, that's what real theatre was all about. Making love to the young man had put him at ease, given him the confidence he would need for the difficult role. He would no longer be in awe of her – Clarissa Browning – Oscar-winning actress. He would see her as a passionate woman – flesh and blood – and react accordingly. This was very important, although some people would think she was mad if she confided that she always made love to her on-screen lovers. It worked – and she had an Oscar to prove it.

Jack Python would throw a fit if he ever found out. Macho chauvinist. All-male stud. Did he honestly believe she didn't know about his little dalliances?

She laughed quietly to herself. Jack Python – the man with the wandering cock . . .

Ah well . . . as long as it didn't wander *too* far. Right now it suited her to have Jack as her permanent lover. Who knew what the future held. . . .

*

"I got a friggin' heart palpitation yesterday," Howard Soloman announced with a grim expression.

"What?" Jack wasn't quite sure he'd heard correctly.

"My friggin' heart," Howard continued in outraged tones, "started bouncin' around like a ping-pong ball."

Jack had long ago decided Howard was a hypochondriac. He changed the subject. "Where's Mannon?" he asked. "Is he coming?"

"Mannon would come very day of his life if he could," Howard said slyly.

"We all know that," Jack agreed.

Mannon Cable – movie star, director, producer, hot property (in Hollywood when you're hot you're hot, when you're not you may as well be dead) – made his entrance. As with Jack before him, every pair of eyes swivelled to get a better look. In fact Mannon actually stopped conversation. He was handsome. If you threw Clint Eastwood, Burt Reynolds and Paul Newman into a blender, you would come up with Mannon Cable. His eyes were cobalt blue; his skin sunkissed to a sexy leather brown; his hair a dark, dirty blond; his body powerful. Six feet four inches tall – "Every inch a winner," he would mock when he made frequent guest appearances on the Carson show.

He was forty-two years old – fit, fast, and right up there box-office-wise with Stallone and Eastwood. Mannon Cable was hitting a peak.

"Hey – I'm one hungry sonofabitch," he said, sliding into the booth. He grinned. He had the *I am a big movie star* grin down pat. He also had a great set of caps (lost the shine on his originals when he laboured as a stunt man for a couple of years) which enabled him to grin from here to eternity without any trouble at all. "What are y'all eating?"

"Eggs," replied Jack, stating the obvious.

"Looks like a couple of fried tits to me," laughed Mannon.

"Everything looks like tits to you," Jack replied. "You should see a shrink, you've got big problems."

Mannon roared. "The only big problem I've got is my dick. *You* should have such problems." He signalled to the waiter and proceeded to order an enormous breakfast.

Jack stared at Mannon and Howard. Sometimes he wondered why the three of them remained friends. They were all so different now. And yet, whenever he got to thinking about it, he knew why. The truth was that they were brothers under the skin, sharing their pasts. They had made it to the top together, and nobody could split them up – although many a wife and girlfriend had tried.

Howard had gone through three wives, and was currently on his fourth, the curvaceous Poppy. He had children everywhere. Mannon was still carrying a torch for his first wife, Whitney, and the new one, Melanie-Shanna, had not yet killed the flame. Jack had Clarissa, although deep down he knew she wasn't the right woman for him – a knowledge he refused to admit.

"I've got a great idea," Mannon said suddenly. "Why don't we fly down to Vegas next month? Just the three of us. We never get to see each other anymore. We could play the tables, raise hell, cause some trouble, just like old times. Whaddya say?"

"Without the wives?" Howard asked hopefully.

"You bet your *cojones* without the wives," Mannon said quickly. "We'll drop 'em off at Neiman's – they'll never even notice we're gone."

Mugging excitedly, Howard said, "I like the idea," forgetting that Poppy would singe his balls if he tried to go away without her. This one was a clinger, as opposed to the other three before her, who were strictly takers.

"How about it, Jack?" Mannon looked at his friend expectantly.

Jack had promised Clarissa a week in New York. Long walks through the Village. Off-Broadway theatre. Never-ending dinners with her strange, broke friends. Guess who would pick up the bill?

He hated walking, only liked movies, and her so-called friends were a pain in the ass.

"Yes," he said. "Set it up. Work permitting, you can definitely include me in."

Chapter 2

Jade Johnson was totally addicted to Bruce Springsteen. She had no desire to meet him, just lust from afar like a mildly randy fourteen-year-old. She put *Born in the U.S.A.* on her stereo and danced around her new apartment.

Jade Johnson was twenty-nine years old. She had shoulder-length shaggy copper hair, gold-flecked widely spaced brown eyes, a full and luscious mouth, and a strong square jaw which saved her from being merely beautiful, and made her face challenging and alert.

She was five feet ten inches tall, one hundred and thirty pounds, with very long legs, a lithe, supple body, broad shoulders, and an incredible swan-like neck.

Apart from being kind-hearted and a good friend when the need arose, she had an acerbic wit and a wild sense of humour. She was also smart, independent, and one of the highest-paid photographic and commercial models in the world.

The doorbell rang and she rushed to answer it, clad in blue jeans and an oversized sweatshirt.

It was the foreman of the delivery crew who had just stacked fifteen large packing cases in her hallway. "That's it, lady," he said, handing her a slip to sign. "All present an' correct. I hope you're satisfied."

Signing, she slipped him a fifty-dollar bill. "Buy a beer for you and the guys."

Pocketing the money appreciatively, the man thought about what a knockout broad this one was. Not only good-looking in her skin-tight jeans and sweatshirt, but generous too.

"Thanks," he said, and added with a smirk, "that commercial you got runnin' on TV sure is blistering!"

She grinned, displaying very white, even teeth, and a warm, sexy smile. "Glad you like it," she said, subtly edging him towards the door. Once they started on about her famous coffee commercial she knew the time was ripe to move them out, having learned, very early on in her career, to be friendly yet unreachable to her many unknown admirers. Once, at eighteen, she had been attacked and nearly raped by a crazed fan who had fallen in obsession with a swimsuit poster she had posed for. Only the intervention of a concerned neighbour had saved her.

The delivery man paused at the door. "Maybe ya gotta photo y'can sign for me," he said hopefully.

Out she projected silently. She was looking forward to being alone and beginning the great unpack. "I'll send you one," she said pleasantly.

"Scrawl, I love ya Big Ben," he leered. "That'll give the boys somethin' t' think about."

Big Ben! Was he kidding?

She waited patiently while he laboriously printed his address on a slip of paper. "Thanks again, Ben," she said, finally closing the front door on him.

Alone at last! In L.A. Who would have thought she would ever make the long trek west again? New York was her kind of town, always had been. California never beckoned. Well, once, when she was twenty and naively accepted the offer of a screen test. *Stupido.* She was no actress, and held no ambitions in that direction. But she was young and curious, and what the hell – a trip was a trip.

She had arrived to be met by a block-long limo with a youngish agent lounging on the back seat. He wore *multo* gold

17

chains with his open-to-the-limit silk shirt and carefully pressed designer jeans. He had a suntan, a mini-mogul cigar, a receding hairline, and an attitude. He offered her grass in the car and an invitation to dinner.

She turned down both, which caused frown lines to appear in his perfect suntan.

A suite at The Beverly Hills Hotel was reserved for her. Flowers and fruit abounded. She stayed five days, tested with a broody actor who tried to kill her close-ups, turned down several more invitations from the bronzed agent, returned to New York, and never heard another thing.

Several years later when she was really hot, Hollywood beckoned again. "Forget it," she told her New York modelling agent. "I'm going to be the best model in the business, *and* the highest paid. Who needs to travel the starlet route? Not this girl, baby."

And she was right. Jade Johnson *was* the best. And she was – due to the deal she had recently signed – the highest paid.

The deal was the reason she was once more in Los Angeles. Cloud Cosmetics made her an offer she couldn't refuse, and part of it was spending a year on the West Coast to make a series of million-dollar TV commercials. Normally she would never have considered leaving her beloved New York. However, she had just come out of a six-year relationship with a married man, and getting away seemed like an appealing prospect.

She wandered around the apartment kicking off her tennis shoes and unzipping her jeans as Springsteen belted out *Born in the U.S.A.* The sound of his raspy voice filled the room, and she was content. This was going to be a new beginning, the start of a whole different life. No more Jade Johnson – mistress. Oh no, sirree. That trip was over, *finito*. What a fool she had been. What a gullible idiot, falling for every cornball line he threw her way. She was hardly naive, and yet for six long years he had kept her captive with his tongue – in more ways than one.

She thought of him briefly. Mark Rand. An English Lord. An English asshole. A wild-life photographer of world-wide repute. They had met on assignment in Africa. She was doing leopard swimwear for *Vogue*, and he was shooting the photographs. He had curly hair, amused blue eyes, and fascinating conversation. It wasn't until a week of passion had passed that his fascinating conversation included mention of a wife, Lady Fiona Rand.

18

Jade remembered her fury. She had fallen for the oldest lines in the world . . . *My wife and I live together in name only . . . when the children are older . . .*

And Jade Johnson — smart, worldly, hardly a babe in the woods — listened to his corny bullshit and actually believed him! For six years she believed him. And she would have gone on doing so if Lady Fiona hadn't given birth to yet another little Rand heir, and Jade found out about it by accident while leafing through an English magazine.

The end had been acrimonious, her move to California swift.

Gazing around her new apartment she decided it was a great find. Situated on Wilshire near Westwood, she had leased it furnished, although there was no way she could think about getting through a year without her things around her. Books, records, her collection of china dogs, tapes of favourite movies, clothes, family pictures, and other personal possessions. Hence the delivery from New York a timely day after her own arrival, courtesy of TWA.

Contemplating the many cartons piled high in the hallway, she wondered if she could summon the energy to start on them now. With a sigh she realized she'd better. Grabbing a 7-Up from the kitchen she set to work.

Chapter 3

It was Silver Anderson's forty-seventh birthday, and she awoke with the thought that she was one year older foremost in her mind. She lay in bed for a full ten minutes ruminating on this fact, and then reluctantly she arose, first buzzing her houseman and ordering bran muffins, fresh orange juice, and lemon tea to be on her table in exactly fifty minutes. That was how long it took Silver to be ready to face the world. Rather quick considering the transformation that took place.

The woman who left the luxurious king-size bed was quite ordinary looking.

The woman who left the bedroom fifty minutes later was a television superstar.

Silver Anderson was ready for a *Vogue* photo session – the cover, of course, Silver only did cover stories. She was fully made up. Heavy base, dramatic eyes (she still wore false lashes, giving her a commanding but rather old-fashioned look). Her lips glistened with scarlet gloss, and her cheeks were sunken with shading. She wore heavy gold earrings, a white silk turban, and a pale beige leather outfit liberally studded with diamanté. It was only ten a.m. but Silver knew she owed it to her fans to always look like a star. She was five feet three inches tall, and had maintained her girlish figure. It took diet and exercise, and although it was a bitch keeping to the routine, the results made it worthwhile. From behind, with her tight ass and sassy strut, she could easily be mistaken for a twenty-year-old.

Sweeping downstairs, she ignored her Russian houseman, Vladimir, who was gay and couldn't care less *how* she treated him as long as she kept him in her employ. He dined out on his personal intimate Silver Anderson stories twice a week. To his friends *he* was the star, living vicariously through his mistress's exploits. Silver was *always* making headlines. She segued from men problems (two ex-husbands, dozens of boyfriends) to drink problems (thank you, Betty Ford, for making it legitimate) to feuds with directors, writers, producers – whoever was around to vent her anger on. Silver was very proud of saying, "I am a professional. And I *will not* be screwed around by unknowledgeable amateurs trying to step in my limelight. Let them remember just exactly who they are dealing with."

*

Silver Anderson first became a star at twelve. She was discovered singing and dancing in a school play by the talent agent father of one of her friends, who recommended her to the casting director of an important musical film. She auditioned, got the role, and went from there to ministardom singing like a bird in a series of hits. She certainly had a wonderful voice, full of power and extraordinary clarity. And so she should – her mother, Blanche (a failed singer herself), had made sure that her daughter had singing lessons from the age of five. Blanche often used to say to her, "I never made it. But you, my dear, will take the talent you inherited from me, and become the biggest star in the world."

Blanche had also insisted on dancing lessons and acting classes. As a result, when she was growing up, Silver never knew childhood, just vigorous training for the stardom her mother was convinced would one day be hers. When she was sixteen, the bottom fell out of musical comedy movies in Hollywood, and her agent suggested New York and the theatre.

"You're not going to New York," objected her father, George, a college professor and sometimes inventor of what her mother referred to as "useless devices". They lived in a large, rambling house in the Valley, bought with Silver's earnings, and he had no intention of uprooting.

"Daddy, I must!" Silver protested tearfully, as her mother had told her she should. "My career is at stake!" She overdramatized everything, even at sixteen.

Blanche agreed with her daughter. "We can't ruin her life, George. We must encourage her to soar!"

George stared mournfully at his domineering wife with the carrot-coloured hair and unfulfilled dreams. He knew there was no stopping her, so it was arranged that she would accompany Silver to New York for six months while he stayed at home with their son, Jack – at nine, seven years younger than his famous sister.

Both Silver and Blanche adored New York, and the feeling was mutual. Silver opened in a new show called Baby Gorgeous, *which ran for a phenomenal five years. During this time she married her first husband (tall, dark and weak), divorced him (he asked her for alimony), helped her mother to divorce George, and attended Blanche's remarriage to a twenty-six-year-old stage hand (her mother was thirty-eight at the time) and neither of them ever had any desire to go back to Los Angeles and the Valley. New York suited them just fine.*

"George and Jack are better off without us," Blanche reasoned. "You were born to be a star. And I was born to live in New York and enjoy myself."

That, she certainly did, what with her successful daughter and new younger husband.

After Baby Gorgeous *there was another smash show, a huge-selling record album, and sold-out cabaret appearances wherever Silver cared to appear.*

It took her ten years to go home. And then she didn't go home as such, she took a bungalow at The Beverly Hills Hotel with her current lover, a Scandinavian stud. And in between giving head and interviews she finally called her father. "Drive into Beverly Hills and I'll treat you and Jack to lunch tomorrow," she announced grandly, not letting on that Newsweek *were doing a cover story on her and needed to get some family pictures.*

George demurred; he had given up on Silver long ago. Just because she

21

was his daughter did not change the fact that she was selfish and egotistical, thinking only of herself. He held her responsible for breaking up his marriage, and he would never forgive her for that.

Jack was home from college. At nineteen he was handsome, smart, and curious to meet the sister he could hardly remember. "I'll go, dad," he said eagerly.

George agreed under protest. He wouldn't put it past Silver to try and lure Jack away from him too, a risk he would just have to take.

Jack went off to meet his famous sister in high spirits. He returned two hours later, a frown on his face and criticism on his lips. "She's fucking unreal!" he exclaimed. "She acts like the Queen of England."

George did not show his relief. "Don't swear," he admonished sternly. "Is this how they teach you to talk in college?"

"Dad! I'm nineteen, for crissake."

"Then I should think you know by now that swearing does not make you any more of a man."

"Okay. Okay. Sorry," Jack said quickly, and thought that next time he came home from college in Colorado, he would take his friend Howard Soloman up on his idea that they rent an apartment together in Hollywood. "It'll be an ace move," Howard enthused. Jack had said no. Next time he would say yes.

Silver thought her baby brother was a handsome dolt. He certainly had the family looks, although all the talent had obviously gone in her direction. One meeting was enough. She did not bother to call again, and it was another four years before they came face to face at the funeral in New York of Blanche, who had died of an untimely cancer.

Jack often wondered why he went. When his mother divorced his father she had divorced him too. He would never forget George's grim face when he sat him down one day and gave him the bad news. "Your mother won't be coming home," he'd said. "It's best this way."

As a kid, Jack could remember crying himself to sleep for many months, trying to figure out what bad thing he had done to make his mother desert him so brutally. In his teens he had considered contacting her, making her tell him. But he always put the dreaded visit off, and when she died it was too late, and he knew he must at least attend her funeral.

Silver was playing drama queen to the hilt. She was dressed in black fox furs and a pillbox hat with a veil. She clung to Blanche's husband, sympathy brimming from over-made-up eyes, while photographers bobbed and weaved around the graveside.

Silver failed to recognize her only brother. He tapped her on the arm to jog her memory. "Thank you for your good wishes," she murmured, and moved on to the next fan.

He could smell the liquor on her breath, and tried to understand. Three months later she married her former stepfather in Las Vegas vowing that this one was "forever". Ten months later there was an acrimonious divorce which caused nasty headlines.

It seemed that Silver always rode the wave of bad publicity and rose from the ashes smiling. The next year she bore a daughter, refused to name the father, and went off to live in Brazil with a very rich man (some said a plasticized Nazi war criminal) for two years. Then she returned to Broadway at the age of thirty-four and starred in two hit shows one after the other for a total of five years.

Meanwhile Jack was getting his life together. After college he shared an apartment in Hollywood with his friend Howard Soloman. Howard wanted to be an agent, mainly because he felt it opened the gateway to "unlimited pussy". He got himself a job at a big talent agency working in the mail room.

Jack wasn't sure what he wanted to do. Everyone said that with his looks he should be an actor — he shuddered at the thought. Writing interested him. Newspapers interested him. The journalistic world beckoned. He started to review movies and records for a small magazine, and to make his half of the rent he became a tour guide at a television studio. Within six months he was promoted to a researcher on a local talk show.

"You've got a way with people," said the head researcher, a woman who recognized raw talent when she saw it.

"Thank you," he replied, deftly avoiding her offer of a night of ecstasy in her Westwood condo.

He then proceeded to sleep his way through all the good-looking female guests on the show, while learning everything there was to know about television.

One day a young movie actor — one of the guests — grabbed Jack backstage. "Hey, man — you're fucking my girlfriend," the actor protested.

"I am?"

"You can bet your ass on it."

Jack couldn't figure out which one might be the actor's girlfriend so without naming any names he gave a blanket sorry.

"So you goddamn well should be," huffed the actor. "She won't let me get beyond first base. What's she like in the sack?"

Conversation led to the nearest bar, and Mannon Cable — newly discovered and busted out — became the third roommate to Jack and Howard. They called themselves the Three Comers — a reference to their career goals rather than their colourful sex-lives. Howard was a walking hard-on. Mannon had looks and humour to lure them between the sheets. Jack had everything.

One thing Jack never advertised was his famous sister. Howard knew, but kept it to himself. Mannon found out, and thought it was a hoot. "Why the secret?" he asked.

Jack shrugged. "I hardly know her. Who needs the connection?"

Fortunately, Silver, at the start of her career, had chosen to use her mother's maiden name, which was Anderson. Jack preferred the more dramatic family surname – Python.

And so the Three Comers' careers rose.

Howard by the age of twenty-six became a fully fledged agent, and at twenty-eight he was hot. Along the way he got married, took out a mortgage on a too-expensive house in Laurel Canyon, purchased his first Mercedes, and gave great meeting.

Mannon hit the road to big stardom via a centrefold in a popular woman's magazine. He out-Reynolded Burt Reynolds, starred in several sure-fire hits, bought the requisite beach house and cream Rolls-Royce, and supported a constant stream of beautiful ditsy girlfriends.

Jack went off to Arizona and worked on a local television news station. After two years he was hosting everything they had to offer. He got an anchor position in Chicago, then Houston. He tried his hand at everything from serious news to fluff pieces, covering politics, film festivals, murders, movies, child molestation. You name it – he knew something about it. In Houston they gave him his own show, The Python Beat. He out-rated everyone and everything in the vicinity. His fan mail was legion. By the time he hit New York to host a nightly network show, Silver was on her way to Hollywood to star in a movie version of one of her Broadway hits. He often wondered if she would make contact to congratulate him. After all, like it or not, they were brother and sister, and maybe they could forget the past and start again.

He never heard a word from her.

The movie Silver starred in bombed. It wasn't just an ordinary bomb, it was a mega-explosion, a nuclear disaster, wiping out all connected with it. Silver fled to Europe, humiliated. Everyone seemed to blame her. As far as she was concerned she was the best thing in it.

She went through what she now delicately referred to as her "nervous breakdown" period. Actually it was a serious flirtation with booze and drugs which very nearly ended her life – let alone her plummeting career.

That's when Jack heard from her. Well, not from her exactly, he got a call from London, and a ten-year-old girl named Heaven. "Are you

24

my uncle?" she demanded. "Can I come and stay with you? Mama's sick. They've taken her away."

Jack cancelled a week's interviews and took the Concorde to London. He found Heaven living with a transvestite in Chelsea. Silver was locked up in a mental institution.

"She tried to take her own life, poor dear," the transvestite whispered. "Can you imagine what it must be like when the looks go, and the talent. I did what I thought was best. Oh, and by the way, she owes me two thousand pounds. I'd like cash, please."

Jack took care of everything. He paid the bills, arranged for Silver's transfer to a private nursing home, hired twenty-four-hour nurses and the best psychiatrists.

When he visited his sister she stared at him blankly. Without makeup she looked like a pale white shadow, but her eyes burned with heat. "How's George?" she asked. Forty years old and she was finally asking after her father — the father she had abandoned at sixteen.

"He's doing okay," Jack replied. "I'm taking Heaven to stay with him. If that's all right with you."

"Yes," she replied listlessly, her tapered fingers plucking at a loose strand of hair. "I'm finished, you know," she continued matter-of-factly. "All washed up. In Hollywood they can't see real talent for shit. All they want is twenty-year-olds with big boobs. I'll never come back."

Jack felt uncomfortable with this pale, wan woman who spoke with such bitterness. This was not the Silver Anderson he had watched throughout the years. In a way it was a relief to know he was out from under her shadow — although the shadow had only existed in his eyes.

"Hey —" he tried to give her confidence. "You're still a beautiful woman. And you'll always be a big star."

"Thanks!" Her tone was full of sarcasm. "Words of encouragement from baby Jack. God! When you were still in diapers I was a star. I don't need you to tell me."

She made no comment on his career. Jack Python. Man of the hour. His own network show.

Settling everything, financial and otherwise, he flew back to California with Heaven. "You'll camp out at your grandpa's house," he told the child. "He's quite a character. And when your mother is better she'll send for you."

"No she won't," replied Heaven, wise beyond her years. She was small, with pinched features and enormous amber eyes.

"Yes she will," he countered.

"Bet?" questioned Heaven.

"Sure. You're on, kid."

Heaven won her bet. In London, Silver recovered and never did send for her daughter.

Jack was disgusted. He talked to the head honchos at his network and asked for his show to be moved to Los Angeles. They agreed, and he was delighted. At least Heaven would have someone around — apart from her grandfather — who genuinely cared for her.

Silver resurfaced on the English stage in a new production of Pal Joey, which brought her excellent reviews and a resurgence of fame. English fame. She loved being back in the spotlight and basked in the light. But it was only English light, and that wasn't enough. England was a small pond and she wanted America. With that thought in mind she acquired a new agent in Hollywood, Quinne Lattimore, and badgered him to do something about it.

Quinne did not think they were going to create any fires. Silver Anderson was hardly hot news — she had been around too long and stepped on too many toes to set the town alight. He suggested her name for a few projects and heard everything from "She's too old" to "The broad's a lush." And then along came the unexpected offer of a role in Palm Springs, a daytime soap. Normally Quinne would have rejected the project immediately. Silver wanted to come back, but hardly on daytime television playing an ageing torch singer. However, when City Television came in with an offer that was too tempting to ignore, he called her in London and said, "I think this might be the showcase to get you here, so that the people who matter can see you."

"I'm not doing a soap," she steamed.

"It's a six-week guest spot," Quinne interrupted. "Top dollar, unlimited budget for wardrobe, and you get to keep the clothes, approve the script, and anything else we want to throw at them. They're anxious."

"So they should be," she sniffed. "A soap indeed!"

"Sleep on it," he suggested.

"Why should I?" she argued.

"Because it's the only ballgame in the park."

Silver did Palm Springs. She was fabulous. The show's ratings rocketed. The producers made her an offer she couldn't refuse, to stay on. And Silver Anderson became the hottest actress on daytime television.

For three years now she had reigned supreme. She was bigger than she'd ever been, and revelled in every minute of her success.

*

A black stretch limo waited outside the front door of Silver's mansion high up in Bel Air. Inside the limo sat her publicist,

Nora Carvell, a fifty-nine-year-old lesbian with knowing eyes and a gravelly voice (who else could possibly put up with Silver?), and her personal assistant – a tall, jumpy young man who had held the job for two weeks and was about to get fired.

"Good morning, everyone," Silver beamed.

There was an imperceptible sigh of relief. Silver was in a good mood – thank God for that!

Chapter 4

When Mannon Cable got up to go to the john, Howard Soloman leaned anxiously towards Jack Python and said, "You're never gonna believe this, but I ran into Whitney at a party last night, and I swear she's got the hots for me."

Jack started to laugh. Whitney Valentine Cable was Mannon's ex-wife, a stunning-looking actress for whom Mannon still carried a torch. "Whitney," Jack said slowly, "has the hots? For *you*?" He continued laughing.

"For crissakes," Howard said irritably. "What's so funny about *that*?"

"Because you and Whitney hated each other when you were Mannon's agent. Christ! If I had a nickel for all the times you bitched about her, and likewise she about you."

"A hard dick an' a soft pussy creep up on people in a variety of ways," Howard said wisely.

Jack almost choked. "I love it when you wax poetic."

"Fuck you."

"When I'm at a loose end I'll think of you first."

Howard belched, not so discreetly. "I'm tellin' you, *she* came on to *me*. The next move is mine an' I'm gonna make it."

"You'll make it when Mannon's six feet under," Jack warned. "You move on Whitney and he'll have your balls for breakfast."

"What's the big friggin' deal?" Howard waved his arms

excitedly in the air. "They've been divorced for nearly two years. Mannon's married to Melanie what's-her-name. And Whitney hasn't exactly acted like a virgin since they split."

"You're talking like a dumb asshole," Jack said, bored with the conversation. "Has it ever occurred to you that Whitney suddenly getting the hots for your body coincides very nicely with your primo position at Orpheus?"

"Are you saying –" Howard began indignantly. He stopped abruptly as Mannon slid back into the booth.

"I've been thinking," Mannon said expansively. "Somebody should do a movie about middle-aged broads who follow movie stars into the can. I just got trailed by a real prize. She bird-dogged me into the goddamn john and asked for my autograph while I'm in the middle of taking a leak! Can you believe it?"

Jack could easily believe it. The same thing had happened to him a week before at a fashionable restaurant. Fame. It was the one part of his life he did not enjoy. Sister Silver revelled in it. You couldn't pick up a magazine without seeing her face staring at you. Her come-back was phenomenal, and yet fortunately it hadn't affected him. In the public's mind they had two very separate identities. Like Warren Beatty and Shirley MacLaine, the fact that they were brother and sister rarely came up.

Today was Silver's birthday. He hadn't spoken to her in months. The only conversations they did have concerned Heaven, who was now sixteen years old. When Silver first came back to America, the expectation was that the child would leave her grandfather's house and return to live with her mother. However, one week in Silver's company put paid to *that* plan, and Heaven returned to her grandfather, who had continued to bring her up ever since. It pissed Jack off. George was getting older and needed a little peace and quiet in his life. Heaven was turning into a wild child and Silver was the last one to care. She wouldn't even reveal who Heaven's father was.

"What d'you think, Howard?" Mannon demanded. "How about doing a movie called *Old Groupies* or *How I Learned to Take a Piss in Public*? Is the idea grabbing you?"

"I think you *should* do a film for Orpheus," Howard said seriously. "Name the deal and it's yours."

"C'mon. *You* know better than anyone that I don't even have a minute to scratch my ass."

Swooping on another roll, Howard said, "Let's get something

in the works. When you're free we want you. Remember, Orpheus is first in line."

"What is this, calling-in-favour time?"

Howard nodded vigorously. "Yeah."

"In that case," Jack joined in, "when are you going to do my show? You've promised for God knows how long. What is this unswerving loyalty to Carson?"

Throwing up his hands, Mannon grinned. "I'm in demand! I love it!"

He had been in demand for over fifteen years now, and he was still enjoying every minute, not to mention the public's adoration and the millions of dollars he made.

Mannon had everything he wanted. Except Whitney. She had left him just when he needed her most, and he was taking his time getting over her. His new wife, Melanie-Shanna, had not solved any problems. She was a recent Miss Texas Sunshine, pretty and sweet, but Whitney she wasn't, and marrying her had been a grave mistake. If it wasn't for alimony and community property, he would have dumped her a week after the wedding. Like a jerk he hadn't gotten her to sign a pre-nuptial agreement limiting her demands. However, his lawyers were working on it, and as soon as he got the all-clear he was going for a divorce. Naturally, Melanie-Shanna knew nothing of his plans. It wouldn't do to forewarn her. Let her think everything was perfect until D-Day – and then bye-bye, pretty little beauty queen.

He must have been insane marrying her. It was a revenge strike aimed at Whitney, who had moved in with his ex-friend, a Malibu stud named Chuck Nielson. The guy couldn't even act, and only appeared in the movies Mannon turned down. Fortunately their affair was shaky, and now Mannon (as soon as he could arrange a divorce) planned to win her back.

"I can't do your show," he said gravely. "You're too serious."

"Serious!" Jack shook his head. "I guess you missed me and Ms. Midler last week."

"Great tits!" interjected Howard.

"Great talent," scolded Jack.

"*And* great tits," added Mannon.

Jack couldn't help laughing. "You two!" he said. "Tits 'n' ass. The story of your lives."

"And you never think about it, right?" Howard and Mannon said as one.

"Only when I'm horny," Jack replied, and the three friends laughed.

*

Whitney Valentine Cable had a spectacular body and a striking face. Her eyes were a dreamy aquamarine, her nose straight and freckled, her mouth drooped at the corners until she smiled, and when she did, Whitney Valentine Cable had the biggest, the best and the whitest smile in Hollywood.

Her hair was blonde and long and fluffy. Grown men fantasized about her hair. And grown women copied whatever style she chose to wear her luxuriant tresses in.

She was a personality and a star, but sad to report, Whitney Valentine Cable could not act.

This did not seem to matter very much, for in the five years she had pursued an acting career she had ridden the crest of mild popularity. Countless magazine covers helped. And a year-long television sit-com, followed by a string of exploitation movies featuring her in various scanty outfits. Whitney had worn everything from three strategically placed fig leaves, to a mink peek-a-boo ball gown. She had *never* shown EVERYTHING. Oh no. Gorgeous as she was, Whitney knew the good sense in keeping *something* hidden. So the great unwashed public had never spied upon her luscious nipples or her silken furry bush. Even though *Playboy* and similar magazines had begged, pleaded, even cried for her to reveal all – offering vast sums of money for the privilege.

It was never enough. If Whitney was going to show off the goods it would be for a million dollars or not at all. And that offer hadn't materialized yet.

*

Whitney Valentine made the trek to Hollywood the easy way. Working as a hairdresser in a small town outside of Fort Worth, she was as eager as the rest of the town to watch the location shoot of a genuine Hollywood film taking place. She visited the outdoor set with her girlfriend on a Saturday afternoon, and immediately caught the eye of Mannon Cable, the macho star of the movie.

It was not exactly love at first sight for Mannon. More If it moves – nail it. And delectable Whitney was the most nailable girl he'd seen all week. She was eighteen and innocent, or so she said when he tried to initiate her into the joys of going to bed with a movie star.

30

Whitney was not happy living in a small town. She wanted out, and Mannon Cable seemed the perfect exit visa. Holding back, instinct told her, was the only way to get him. And she was right. He called her everything from a dumb broad to a prick-tease, but six weeks later he married her, and when the movie finished shooting he brought her to Beverly Hills as his bride.

For five years Whitney played the model wife. Cooking, shopping, taking care of their Malibu ranch house, posing for photo layouts with her famous husband, and generally behaving like the woman every man wished was his.

And then, one hot Malibu Sunday, with the jacuzzi going full force, and the waft of barbecue in the air, Mannon's friend and agent, Howard Soloman, whispered in her ear that there was a role in a television pilot for which she would be perfect if only she were an actress.

Excitement lit up her face. "Put me up for it, Howard," she begged. "Oh, please! You must!"

"Mannon'll kill me," he groaned.

"And so will I if you don't," she hissed.

Secretly she tested for the role.

Secretly she got the job.

When all was revealed to Mannon he was furious. "You stupid asshole," he yelled at Howard. "The last thing I need is a starlet for a wife."

"It's what she wants," Howard argued lamely.

"Well, you're no longer my agent, I can tell you that," Mannon screamed, then turned his wrath on Whitney.

"I want to work," she told him calmly. "I'm bored."

"Bored!" He was outraged. "You're married to me, for crissake. How can you possibly be bored?"

"You're always working," she complained. "I have nothing to do all day. I'm lonely."

"So how about starting a family? We've talked about it enough times. You know it's what I want."

"And I want to do something with my life before I settle down and have babies. Please, Mannon, you've got to understand that this is what I need."

Reluctantly he agreed that she could take a shot at it. Whitney was the only woman he wanted to spend his life with, and if she required a few months messing around in show biz, let her do it. She'd soon find out what a crap-shoot it all was.

The first thing she did was dye her light brown hair blonde. And *then she decided to call herself Whitney Valentine — adding the Cable to please Mannon (it also pleased the press department of her television show, but that's another story).*

And so began her climb to stardom. It wasn't difficult. The sit-com was a hit, she had all the right requirements in abundance, plus a very famous husband, and the publicity mill took it from there.

Five years and five hundred magazine covers later she was a star — just as she'd wanted. And she and Mannon were history. She hadn't planned to divorce him, but he was jealous of her success, and there was nothing she could do about that. They had been divorced for eighteen months. The moment the decree was final Mannon had married some Texas beauty queen. Whitney could not help feeling hurt, for it was she who had instigated the divorce, not Mannon, who had declared undying love right up until the moment he married again. For a while she was tempted to do the same with the guy she was living with — Chuck Nielson, an ex-friend of Mannon's. But Chuck was great when he was straight, and insane when drugged out. Besides, she was enjoying her new-found freedom.

*

As she sipped a glass of iced tea beside her kidney-shaped swimming pool in the garden of her house on Loma Vista, Whitney thought about Howard Soloman. Who would ever have imagined that one day he would be running Orpheus Studios? When he was Mannon's agent she couldn't stand him. And when he launched *her* career she tolerated him, until he left agenting to form his own production company. A few powerful jobs later he was head of the studio. She was impressed.

Extending a delicate foot, she admired the pearly glow of the polish on her pedicured toenails. Howard Soloman. One of Mannon's best friends. Funny, vulgar, street-smart Howard.

She shivered uncomfortably. Even thinking about going to bed with Howard was crazy; she had known him for too many years — *and* all three of his wives, including Poppy, the present one. And yet, last night at the Fields' party, Howard and she got to talking — quietly, in a corner, with no one else around — and something had happened. He understood her. He understood her career needs. And sometimes that could be the most important part of any relationship.

Chapter 5

Springsteen belted, and Jade felt good. She had unpacked three boxes and already the apartment seemed more like home. The doorbell buzzed and she peered through the spy-hole – an old New York habit. "Who is it?" she called out.

"Pizza."

"I didn't order any."

"You've *always* got an order of pizza on the way."

"Corey!" She flung open the door. "What a sneak! You told me you couldn't get here until next week."

"For you, sis, I worked magic."

He placed the box of pizza on the floor and hugged his sister. There was no family resemblance. Corey was shorter than Jade, and several years younger. He was pleasant looking, with uniform features and none of his sister's mesmerizing charisma.

"This is *so* great!" she exclaimed.

"Me or the pizza?"

"The pizza, what else? Let's eat. I'm starving! It's double mushroom, I hope?"

"And cheese and bologna and meatballs and peppers. Does that suit you?"

"Oh, Corey, baby – *you* suit me. It's fantastic to see your silly smiling face."

He grinned. "Likewise, pretty sis. It's been too long."

"I know."

He picked up the box of pizza. "Am I coming in?" he asked jokingly. "Or are we eating out in the hall?"

"Sorry! C'mon. In. Now. Food. And all the news. Right?"

"You got it." He followed her into the ultra-modern kitchen and placed the box on a counter top.

Jade reached for plates and a knife. "How's Marita and the Johnson heir?"

Corey looked around. "This is a really nice place," he said admiringly.

"Better than my rabbit hole in New York, huh?" she teased.

"Bigger."

"What do you want to drink? Shall we live dangerously and open a bottle of wine?"

He consulted his watch. "It's only twelve-thirty."

"Y'know, sometimes I think you never moved to the big city."

He glanced out of the window. "Sometimes I wish I hadn't." Turning towards her he added, "Have you spoken to mom and dad lately?"

She handed him a bottle of white wine and an opener. "I'm going to call tomorrow. I always call on Sunday. If I change the routine they get panic-stricken and think God knows what. Why?" her tone became anxious. "There's nothing wrong, is there?"

He wrestled with the wine. "They're fine. I spoke to mom yesterday."

"Good." She busied herself with dividing the pizza into two huge pieces.

Uncomfortably he said, "It's just that I figured if you'd spoken to them you would've heard."

She fixed him with a sharp look. He had something to say and she wasn't sure she wanted to hear it. "What's on your mind?"

"Marita and I split up."

"Oh, shit!"

Shrugging defensively he said, "It's no big deal."

"Yes it is," she replied grimly. "You have a child. That makes it a *very* big deal."

He glared. "No lectures. Not unless you want me to talk about *your* situation."

"I'm *out* of my situation," she said pointedly, a determined set to her jaw.

Sensing a weakness he pounced. "You've wasted six years of your life with a married guy, so if you're planning to give *me* advice I'm not interested."

Anger filtered across her face. "Don't get uptight with me," she snapped. "What *you* do and what *I* do are two different things."

As soon as she'd said it she wished she hadn't. All his life Corey had played second to her. She was the successful one in the family. He'd never made it. She was at the top of her profession. He had a mediocre job with a public relations firm in San Francisco. He hadn't even left home until he met and married Marita – who was Hawaiian – and moved with her to California four years ago.

"I'm sorry," she said quietly. "I guess I'm upset. Marita and you seemed so terrific together. What happened?"

He made a gesture of defeat. "I don't know."

Jade found she had lost her appetite. Her brother's happiness was important to her and his news was a bombshell. She couldn't wait to get on the phone to her mother and discuss it.

"I wanted to tell you myself," he said, getting up and restlessly pacing the kitchen. "Mom and dad know, but that's about it."

"Is it irrevocable?"

"'Fraid so. I'm moving to L.A. I've got a transfer from the San Francisco office."

"At last some good news. You can move in with me."

Shaking his head he said, "I've got a place. I'm sharing a house with a friend."

The scene became clear. Corey was involved with another woman. Hopefully, when his hard-on wore off he would hurry back to Marita and the baby.

"Can I give you some advice?" she ventured.

"No, thank you. Look, sis, I've got to run. There's a lot of stuff I have to organize."

"You only just got here," she protested.

Kissing her forehead he said, "We'll be living in the same town. We haven't done that since we were kids. It'll be just like old times, won't it?"

The shine was off her day, but she nodded anyway.

"I'll call you," he said, "as soon as I'm settled."

The moment he left she phoned her mother, who knew no more than she did, and was very upset about the situation.

"Has anyone spoken to Marita?" she asked.

"Corey says she's gone back to Hawaii with the baby to stay with her family," her mother said.

"Not permanently, I hope?"

"I don't know."

As soon as she hung up, she felt an urge to talk to Mark.

They had been apart for five weeks and she still had withdrawal symptoms. For six years they had shared each other's lives. Except he had led a separate life of his own in England, one she was supposed to know nothing about.

Bastard.

That didn't mean she couldn't miss him if she wanted to.

Without thinking she wolfed down the rest of the pizza, an act she immediately regretted. Mark would have laughed at her. Sometimes, when she went on eating binges, he called her the Fat American. Hardly a title suited to her slim curves. When they had fights – and it had not been a peaceful six years – she called him the Uptight Englishman. They used to joke about writing a sit-com with the two nicknames combined. "It'd be a smash!" Jade would laugh.

"Only with you in it," he'd reply.

They always used to go on trips together. She enjoyed his world as much as he was fascinated by hers. Twice a year she had accompanied him to Africa on his photographic safaris, and she would certainly miss the breathtaking beauty of waking up in the wilderness with the most incredible dawn skies and the sounds of nature all around.

Mark Rand.

He was part of her past.

She had to stop thinking about him.

Chapter 6

Wes Money shared a birthday with Silver Anderson, only he didn't know it, and even if he had he wouldn't have cared. He was thirty-three years old and getting nowhere fast. The trouble with Wes was that he had no direction in life. Having tried a little bit of everything, he had failed to succeed at anything.

*

Wes Money was born in a slum area of London to a sometime hooker and her part-time pimp. Childhood was not exactly made in Disneyland; growing up was a tough game, and Wes learned early on in life to play it fast and dirty. When he was twelve, his mother found herself a rich American (or at least she thought he was at the time), married him, and moved to New York. Wes thought he had died and gone to heaven. He was getting laid at thirteen (all the little high school girls just loved his cockney accent), getting arrested at fifteen (shoplifting — nothing lethal), and getting out at sixteen. He did not say goodbye to his mother — she probably never even noticed he was gone. By the time he split, she had divorced her husband and returned to her old ways. Hooking suited her better than cooking.

Wes moved in with a buxom stripper who thought he was twenty. He did a little pimping of his own, but his heart wasn't in it, and a small amount of drug dealing led him to the fringes of the rock business, and what he thought at the time was his true love — music. He discovered he could sing, unearthing a low throaty growl which lent itself to the heavy-metal sounds popular in the seventies. After toiling as a roadie for a year with a group called In the Lewd, his chance came when the lead singer came down with an acute case of the clap. Without hesitation Wes stepped into his shoes if not his pants.

Ecstasy followed. He was twenty-two and singing with a group. Fourteen-year-old virgins threw themselves at him. He met Mick Jagger and Etta James. He was going to be famous!

In the Lewd disbanded after ten months. They hadn't even gotten a record deal. Wes was pissed off, although he quite expected other groups to be lining up to sign him.

Nothing happened. Absolutely nothing. So he moved to Miami in search of the sun, and took a job as a bartender in a night club where he met a Swedish divorcee of forty-two, with money, steel thighs, and no sense of humour. She kept him for three years, which was all right with him, especially as he was making it with her maid, a well-stacked Puerto Rican girl.

Both relationships ended when the Swedish woman decided to get married again, and the bridegroom-to-be was not him.

Reluctantly he went back to tending bar at one of the big hotels. A suitable job for someone who couldn't make up his mind what to do next.

Vicki entered his life when the last thing he was looking for was a woman with no money. Vicki was twenty and perfect. There was no way they couldn't team up. Love was a new experience for him, and it made him uneasy. Vicki was a dancer in one of the lavish hotel shows, and unfortunately she made even less money than he did. They lived together in a tiny ocean-front apartment, and before long Vicki was making ominous mumblings about marriage.

A picket fence, unpaid bills, and babies was not the future he saw for himself, so he cheated on Vicki with her best friend, and made sure she found out. Then he left town and returned to New York, where he soon realized it was too cold for him —but not before doing a small part in a porno video for a fast thousand bucks cash.

The money brought him a one-way ticket to Los Angeles, where he rented a two-room run-down house in Venice —on the boardwalk — and worked as an extra in a few movies. After a while he got bored hanging around film sets, and drifted back to tending bar at a variety of Hollywood hang-outs.

One day he woke up and he was thirty-three.

*

Luckily Wes was not in his own bed, as he would have been so depressed he might have killed himself. He groped for a cigarette and looked around, while a thousand needles jabbed relentlessly at his temples. He had no idea where he was.

A half-full glass of scotch stood on the bedside table next to a pink telephone and a frilled Kleenex holder. There was also a cheap plastic alarm clock, and an ashtray shaped like an owl, overflowing with old cigarette butts.

Well, he obviously hadn't hit pay dirt. For years he had been looking for another Swede. Being kept by a woman was the kind of cushy lifestyle that appealed to him.

Yawning loudly he sat up. A stuffed ginger cat stared down at him from a shelf. "Good morning," he said amiably.

Was it his imagination, or did the cat wink?

Shit! Too many late nights and hard women.

The bedroom was small and hot. No air conditioning. He had definitely lucked out.

"Anyone home?" he called, and his hostess made her entrance. She was a plump blonde with teased hair, caked makeup, and silicone breasts displayed through a polyester negligee.

"I thought ja'd never wake up," she said. "Y'can put it away quicker than my old man, an' *that's* goin' some."

He could swear that he'd never set eyes on her in his life. And he must have been very drunk to have honoured her with the pleasure of his cock. "Do I know you?" he asked.

She eyed him appreciatively. "At least y'can get it up, which

38

is more'n *he* could when he ran out on me. You'd be amazed at the number of fagolas around today."

"Really?" He dragged on his cigarette and pretended to be surprised.

"I ain't kiddin' you, hon." She fluffed out her hair and gave him a long, lingering look. "I gotta be at work in half an hour . . . What the heck, I've time if you have."

He would sooner have walked on hot coals all the way back to New York. This drinking of his had to stop.

She began to divest herself of the negligee. Underneath she wore a red garter belt, red patterned stockings and nothing else. Her bush – wiry and black – grew all the way to China. He was surprised she didn't back-comb and style it.

"Nothing I'd like better," he said, lifting the sheet and peering down at his penis – rigid, but only with the need to take a piss.

"Looks good t' me," she leered.

"Just checking," he said.

"What for?"

"I've got this ongoing case of herpes. The doc says it's only catching when it flares up. However, in the interest of not passing anything on, I like to keep an eye on it."

She froze. "You *low*-life!" Quickly she struggled back into her negligee, rolls of fat shaking indignantly. "Get out of my bed and take a powder."

"It's not communicable now," he protested.

"Just get lost, scumbag."

She turned her back while he pulled on his pants and shirt. He left her house without another word being exchanged, and was surprised to find himself in the Valley. *How* had he made it to the Valley in the condition he must have been in?

Fortunately his car was parked outside. An old Lincoln won in a poker game. He did have his moments.

Stopping at a coffee shop on Ventura Boulevard, he went straight to the men's room. In the mirror above a cracked basin he wished himself a happy birthday. On the wall somebody had scrawled MY MOTHER MADE ME A HOMOSEXUAL and underneath someone else had written IF I GIVE HER THE WOOL WILL SHE MAKE ME ONE TOO?

Leaning closer to the mirror he saw the marks of time and too much booze. Right now, unshaven, with a hangover and bleary eyes, he didn't look too good. But he washed up nicely, and when he had lived with the Swede he had been positively good-looking. Of course, manicures and facials and massages and new expensive clothes helped anyone look good. Life with the Swede was quite a few years ago though. He missed her steely thighs, *and* her money.

Anyway, he could still get most women if he put his mind to it. He had longish brown hair and regular features marred only by a broken nose (acquired in a bar-room brawl), and a small inch-long scar beneath his left eyebrow (the result of an argument with Vicki when they split). His eyes were the colour of fresh seaweed, and while he didn't exercise or any of that crap, his five feet eleven inches was in pretty good shape – give or take a few extra pounds.

He knew how to please the ladies too. Sober or drunk he could still make 'em sing Streisand.

After coffee and a couple of sugar-packed doughnuts he set off home, almost stopping for a teenage hitchhiker in red shorts – only changing his mind when he realized he was playing Russian roulette with his sex life. There were all sorts of things to consider nowadays: herpes, which he didn't have – not to mention AIDS, which did not mean a shot of pencillin and goodbye Charlie. AIDS meant death. Slow and lingering.

Shuddering, he decided he definitely had to clean up his act. No more lost-weekend nights. In future he had to *know* who he was sleeping with.

Outside his house lurked a local prostitute. Once, when he was really busted, he had let her use his bedroom for a week. She entertained forty-two men and the place had smelled like a doss house toilet. Never again.

"Hiya, Wes," she trilled. "I brought you a present."

He was touched. The local hooker had remembered his birthday.

No such luck. It was a packet of cocaine he had ordered for an acquaintance.

"How much?" he asked.

Money was exchanged for goods, and he realized funds were alarmingly low. Even though he could sell the coke at twice the price, it was time to find another job.

Inside his house nothing had changed. Dirty clothes, dirty ashtrays, dirty sheets – the usual mess. Idly he wondered if he could hire the hooker for maid service. Probably not. She would think it was beneath her.

Punching on his phone answering machine he waited for the

message that would tell him he was wanted for another group. Singing was his life – only he hadn't done any in years.

"Listen, pal," said the voice of his friend Rocky. "You gotta do me a big favour. Tonight there's this party up in Bel Air at some TV star's place. Silver Anderson. Me and Stuart were supposed to take care of the bar, only the stupid sonofabitch broke his arm jumpin' out of a movin' car. Don't ask me why. Sixty bucks for a coupla hours. You can't let me down. Okay, pal?"

It was his birthday. He had nothing else to do.

Chapter 7

Jack Python drove a dark racing-green Ferrari. He did not like anyone else behind the wheel, and as most of the parking valets in town were aware of his idiosyncrasy they were quite happy for him to park it himself.

Leaving The Beverly Hills Hotel, he walked briskly to his car, trailed by a couple of tourists from Minnesota who, camera in hand, hoped to get his picture. Before they could summon the courage to ask, he roared off into the hazy afternoon sunshine.

He was supposed to play tennis, but breakfast with Howard and Mannon had sapped his energy and he didn't feel like it, so he cancelled the appointment on his car telephone, making it for the next morning. Then he tried Clarissa at the studio, only to be informed that she was on the set and unavailable.

"I know who you are!" a girl in a white convertible at a stoplight yelled.

His smile of acknowledgment was uncomfortable. He honestly did not enjoy public recognition – unlike Mannon, who revelled in it, or Howard, who craved it. When Howard was first made the head of Orpheus, his finest moment was getting the front round table at Morton's restaurant, wiping out two movie stars and a very important producer.

41

The Three Comers. Well, they sure had come a long way. Three guys with big ambitions sharing one small apartment. And they'd all made it to the top. He was proud of their achievements.

He drove slowly to his penthouse in the Beverly Wilshire Hotel, preferring the looseness of hotel life to the responsibility of his own apartment or house. It gave him a nice sense of freedom.

Clarissa rented a home on Benedict Canyon, and he spent a lot of time there. Lately he had been thinking of leasing a place at the beach for the summer. Not in the Malibu Colony, that was too full of recognizable faces. More like Point Dume or Trancas. The idea really appealed to him. Maybe he'd just take the summer off and become a beach bum. He also thought it would be good for Heaven, who might like to come and stay with him for the summer.

Clarissa wasn't thrilled at the prospect. She was a city person, more comfortable with dust and smells and bustle. She was always complaining about Los Angeles as opposed to New York. And she hated the beach.

They had met in New York at a fund-raising party for a Democratic Senator, who he later found out she was sleeping with. Their meeting was no big deal, apart from the fact that she dumped the Senator and ended up in *his* bed. After that they saw each other intermittently for a couple of months, always pursued by frantic paparazzi.

When Clarissa appeared on his show it was considered a big deal, a first, because she didn't do television talk shows. Struggling through an hour with her he understood why. She was a difficult guest, and he was sorry he'd asked. *Face to Face with Python* depended on a lively exchange of interesting conversation between Jack and his guest of the hour. He wanted people to feel that after they'd watched his show they walked away from their television set with a new knowledge and understanding of the person in the hot seat. With Clarissa they found out nothing. She was a brilliant actress, and a lousy interview.

Face to Face with Python had been running with consistently excellent ratings for six years. The show aired once a week on Thursday nights, which left him plenty of time to pursue other activities. He had formed his own television production company five years before, and oversaw the making of docudramas with something important to say.

Jack had an image problem. He was too good-looking to be

taken as seriously as he would like. And his womanizing reputation was hard to live down. But he was trying.

*

Howard Soloman drove a gold Mercedes 500 SEC. He stood,
or rather fidgeted, beneath the portico of The Beverly Hills Hotel
and waited for the valet to bring it round.

To his eternal disgust Howard was on the short side for a
man. He barely made five feet six inches, although when he
wore his specially made European shoes with the hidden lifts he
could sometimes add another four inches, making him a respectable five feet ten inches. In his weekend uniform of sweat
pants and Adidas jogging shoes, lifts were not possible. Yet.
Howard had asked his shoemaker in London to work on it.

Howard was also – at only thirty-nine – losing his hair. It had
started to thin alarmingly years before, and prudently he had
added a custom-designed hairpiece before people began to
notice. The hairpiece was good, the only drawback being that it
made him sweat. Once, on a weekend in Las Vegas, he had
taken a girl to his hotel room. He had removed his clothes,
shoes, and then his hairpiece, because it was so damned hot and
she looked like a certain maniac who would pull crazily at his
hair in moments of passion.

She had stared at him in amazement. *"Shee . . . it!"* she exclaimed. "I came up here with a nice lookin' guy, an' I end up
with a bald midget!"

Which, of course, had swiftly ended *that* night of sexual high
jinks.

The only time Howard removed his hairpiece now was in the
privacy of his own home with only his wife and visiting children
to mock him.

There had been four wives – one of them current, three of
them ex. And there were five children. Nobody could ever say
that Howard Soloman didn't have what it took. He was a
walking hormone!

Wife number one was a black activist who moonlighted as an
"artistic dancer". In spite of Jack begging him not to, he married
her when he was nineteen and she was forty. It was not a lasting
marriage. They both decided it was a mistake, and after forty-
eight hours of fucking their brains out they got an annulment.

Wife number two was somebody else's wife when he met her.
She was pretty and sweet – nothing to get into a lather over.

43

Howard railroaded her into divorcing her husband. Then he married her, fathered three children by her, and divorced her – all in the space of five years. She was exhausted by the time it was over, and now lived in Pacific Palisades with the kids and a new husband.

Wife number three was an incredibly tall, sophisticated, Brazilian ball-breaker. She generously gave him a child and two years of her life, and then hit him for so much alimony he thought he might never recover from the shock.

Wife number four was Poppy, his former secretary. They had been married for three years and had a daughter named Roselight. Their daughter was the reason they married in the first place. Poppy did not believe in abortion, so when she became pregnant she put the screws to him and he married her. Well, what else could a nice Jewish boy do?

Poppy made the Brazilian ball-breaker look like the good fairy.

"Howard!" A hand clapped him on the shoulder. "You old son of a gun! I haven't seen you in too long."

Howard recognized Orville Gooseberger, the producer. He wished he had on his lifts: Orville was tall enough to make him feel uncomfortable. The only tall people he wasn't uncomfortable with were women. That feeling of dominance was a turn-on. Once, he had made a very tall woman stand open-legged on a table while he went up on her. He got quite horny just thinking about it. It was definitely a scene to be repeated, only not with Poppy, who was short. And besides, there was no way he'd suggest an act like that to her -- she thought he was perverted as it was.

"You know, Howard," Orville boomed, "we have to do a project together. It's about time."

Why hadn't it been time *before* Howard was head of Orpheus?

"Why?" said Howard.

"What?" said Orville.

Ah, the hell with it. Orville was an ace producer, *and* he brought his pictures in on time *and* within budget, which is more than you could say for most of the assholes running around calling themselves producers.

"We'll take a meeting," Howard said expansively, using Hollywoodese.

"Lunch?" Orville suggested. "Perhaps here. On Monday or Tuesday?"

"I gotta check my book," Howard said. "Call the office on

44

Monday. My girl knows every move I make better than I do."

He realized he could see right up Orville's nose and the view was not pleasant.

The parking valet zoomed up with his Mercedes. Howard slipped him a ten, impressed with his own generosity, and slid behind the wheel, inhaling the smell of the rich leather which never failed to please him. There was nothing like having money. No thrill in the world. Even naked ladies standing on table tops with their legs spread.

★

Mannon Cable drove a blue Rolls-Royce. The Roller, he called it.

He did not leave the hotel at the same time as Jack and Howard, because he had to pick up Melanie-Shanna in the hotel beauty shop.

She was not ready when he arrived, which infuriated him. Major movie stars were not supposed to cool their heels while ex-beauty queen wives primped and fussed.

Whitney had never spent hours in the beauty shop. She was naturally beautiful, and how could he have ever let her go?

The final split, when it came, was clean-cut. They had been fighting for months, mostly over her career, which had taken off with alarming speed – thanks to Howard Soloman, who Mannon barely spoke to for a while, until he got out of agenting and left Whitney alone. She had become an enormous television star and the demands on her time were insatiable. Mannon had just finished a difficult movie and needed to get away. "Let's go to the south of France," he'd suggested.

"I can't," Whitney replied. "I've got fittings, interviews. Oh, and I promised to do the Bob Hope special. *And* the photo spread for *Life* magazine is being scheduled now."

"I can remember when *I* came first," he'd said angrily.

She had turned on him, all hair and teeth and pent-up frustration. "And *I* can remember when I wanted you to."

"Jesus! I took you out of hick town to be my wife, not some trumped-up starlet. I've giving you a choice, Whitney. It's me or your career."

He never weighed his words before saying them. In retrospect he wished he had, for they were both too stubborn to retreat.

"You want me to choose?" she'd said, very slowly.

"Goddammit. *Yes*."

"Then I'll take my career, thank you very much." Her eyes, filled with hurt and anger, challenged him to back down.

He didn't. He packed a suitcase and left the house.

A week later she started divorce proceedings.

One thing about Whitney, she was scrupulously fair. No Hollywood Wife she. There were no demands. She didn't want alimony or a settlement. She kept half the money from their house when it was sold, and that was it.

"I don't believe your luck!" Howard had exclaimed.

"I'd still be married if it wasn't for you," Mannon growled.

He had never stopped wanting her back.

Chapter 8

The photo session was going well. Lionel Richie tapes flooded the studio, and Silver, watched by a large entourage, put the photographer through his paces.

He was a famous Italian photographer, a star in his own right. Only Silver remembered when he'd photographed her *before* superstardom, and had treated her like shit. He'd also made her look like shit, which wasn't surprising considering he'd only shot one roll of film, and any idiot knew you never got anything worthwhile until the third roll at least. He'd also forced her to use his own makeup and hair people. A bad mistake.

Now *she* was in charge, and enjoying every minute.

"Antonio, dear," she said, stopping the click of his shutter. "Do you know that today is my birthday?"

Antonio threw up his hands as if she had just declared World War III. '*Bellissima!* You don't have the birthday. You have the celebration!"

"Exactly." She smiled sweetly. "So where's the caviar and champagne?"

Antonio looked concerned. "You want some, *cara?*"

"I'd love some, Antonio, dear. And if you are *very* good, I'll invite you to my party later."

He beckoned one of his assistants. "Champagne and caviar for Signorina Anderson. *Pronto. Pronto.*"

The assistant, a girl dressed like a boy, held out her hand. "I'll need money," she said, wondering how much he would come up with. His stinginess was notorious.

A scowl flitted across Antonio's small but perfectly formed fifty-five-year-old features. He reached into the back pocket of his impeccably cut trousers and reluctantly pulled out a hundred-dollar bill.

Silver laughed loudly. "My God, Antonio, you're as tight as your own ass! The poor girl will need more than that. Let me see –" she played to her entourage – "there must be at least ten of us. We'll want three bottles of Cristal, and a nice big jar of fish eggs. Give her your credit card."

Give her yours, bitch! Antonio wanted to snarl. Only he didn't. He knew she was getting her own back for the last session, and in a way he didn't blame her. One had to admire Silver Anderson's success. A few years ago she was washed up, completely finished. And now she was sizzling, at what – forty-three? Four? Nobody knew her exact age. She was up there somewhere and that's all that mattered. In a town comprised mostly of big-bosomed twenty-two-year-olds, her achievement was certainly something.

He produced his MasterCard with a flourish. Let Silver see that the great Antonio accepted defeat with style.

She stretched languorously. "How about a break?" she suggested in a low, husky voice, standing up before finishing the sentence, uninterested in whether Antonio cared to break or not.

"My idea too, *bellissima*," he said quickly.

Strolling behind the camera she playfully peeked through the viewfinder. "Hmmm," she said. "Let me see the Polaroids again."

Dutifully her hairdresser Fernando, her makeup artist Yves, *and* the stylist for the shoot sprang forward – each waving an instant photo for her inspection.

She gazed at the pictures of herself like an uninvolved critic.

"Your hair looks *mah*vellous," raved Fernando, who wore his own spiky locks in a currently fashionable purple Mohawk.

She touched her long wavy wig. "I'm not sure it's dramatic enough."

"Ah, but it is! It is!" he protested. "Very *you*."

47

"I like the short wig better."

"We can change it."

Shaking her head she said, "I don't know . . . I'm not sure. What do *you* think, Nora? Isn't this style a little too young for me?"

Nora Carvell, a cigarette butt attached to her lower lip, squinted from her seat on the sidelines. "Cut the crap, Silver. You know you're the youngest lookin' broad over forty in this town. Y'can wear anything an' get away with it."

Nora had worked with Silver as her publicist for three years. One of the reasons they continued to get along was that Nora always spoke her mind and never kissed ass. Surrounded by sycophants, Silver respected and enjoyed Nora's honesty. It was good to have someone around who wasn't afraid of opening up her mouth.

Silver giggled. It was true. She looked early thirties, not a day over. All the husbands and lovers, fights and booze had left nary a mark. She was sensational for her age. Any age, in fact.

"You're right," she agreed, holding the Polaroid at a distance and squinting slightly. She needed glasses, but vanity would not permit it.

The rest of the shoot progressed without incident. Above all else Silver was a professional. So professional, in fact, that when the champagne and caviar arrived she touched neither, opting instead for a plain glass of Evian water.

Antonio was furious as he observed her entourage scoff the lot.

"I've changed my mind," she said sweetly, when offered a glass of Cristal and a tasty cracker with a mound of imported caviar on it. "Mustn't smudge my makeup. Besides, I don't want to feel hungover for my party tonight."

*

"You think it's easy?" the young girl with the multi-coloured punk hair demanded of the eighteen-year-old boy lounging against the side of an old Ford Mustang smoking a joint. "I am in like a very negative position," the girl continued, snatching the roach away from him and taking a healthy drag. "Like first of all I'm *me*. An' then people find out all the garbage, an' then I'm Silver Anderson's daughter, or Jack Python's niece. Sometimes I'm even George fucking Python's grand-daughter – ever since he invented that stupid pool-cleaner." She looked

48

outraged. "Get this action, Eddie. I'm over at a girlfriend's house the other day totally sitting around bullshitting, and her father comes in the room — her *father*. So she says, 'Daddy, I want you to meet Heaven.' And *he* says, 'Aren't you George Python's grand-daughter? He's saved my weekends with his machine.' I mean, I ask you. With a name like Heaven there's no escape."

"Y'could change your name," Eddie mumbled, retrieving the joint from her multi-coloured fingernails.

Heaven widened startlingly amber eyes. "Why should I?" she demanded. "It's *my* name. My identity. It's like the only *positive* thing in my life."

"Y'got me," Eddie said.

"*And* my music," she added.

"Our music," he corrected.

"*I* write the songs," she pointed out. "And I sing 'em."

"Yeah, an' who would you be singin' 'em *with* if me an' the guys didn't back you?"

She wasn't going to hurt his feelings, only she knew that the group meant nothing. *She* was the star when they appeared at local events, not Eddie and his group.

She yawned loudly and executed a little dance in the front yard of Eddie's house.

He watched her through slitted eyes. She was a difficult girl to figure, most of the time she kept him confused. He liked her a lot, even if she *was* totally screwed up because of all her famous relatives. "Wanna go for a drive?" he asked. "Get a hamburger?"

"No, thank you," she replied, picking at the material of her jagged denim micro skirt.

"What *do* you wanna do, then?"

"I thought you said your parents were away this weekend."

"They are."

"So why can't we go in your house an' fix something? I won't eat you."

"I wish you would," he leered, shifting his weight from the side of the car.

"Eddie," she sighed, tipping her head to one side. "I thought you'd *never* ask."

He wondered if she was teasing him as he felt the start of something big build up in his pants. Heaven had been flirting with him from the day they met three months ago, only every time he made a move she shoved him off. "C'mon," he said quickly. "In the house. I'll show you who's asking."

She followed him inside. His sisters were out and the small neat house was very cool and quiet.

"I wanna see your room," she said.

Hastily he thought about whether there was anything around to embarrass him. He decided it was all clear. She would just have to understand about the life-size poster of Daryl Hannah on his wall.

His room was overloaded with stuff and very untidy.

"Slob!" she exclaimed. "Like I mean you totally get off on disgusting mess."

Grabbing her from behind he rubbed his hands across her small breasts – bra-less beneath a baggy tee-shirt.

She didn't push him away as usual; instead she stood very still allowing him the feel he had been waiting months for.

His hard-on chafed for escape as he slid his hands underneath the flimsy tee-shirt and reached bare tit.

Still she didn't object.

He fingered the tips of her nipples and groaned, waiting for her to stop him.

She turned around and faced him. "Do you wanna do it?" she asked, her eyes unusually bright.

Did he *want* to? There was *smoke* coming out of his ears as he tried to appear casual. On the surface he was Mister Cool, but in reality he was nervous as hell.

"Do you?" she persisted, amber eyes staring into his.

"Yeah," he managed.

"So do I," she said, slowly pulling her tee-shirt over her head.

★

"You invited Heaven tonight, didn't you?" Nora asked in the limo on the way back to the house.

Silver gazed out of the tinted side window. "As a matter of fact, no," she replied coolly.

Nora grunted her disapproval, which caused Silver to come up with a list of reasons why she had not invited her only child to her birthday party. They ranged from "There'll be nobody else her age there" – which was a lie, because two of the actors from *Palm Springs* were under twenty, and they would certainly be there – to "She hates parties." Which was something Silver could not possibly guess, as she knew nothing of her daughter's

50

likes and dislikes. In fact, since being back in America, she had managed to see Heaven as little as possible. "It wouldn't be wise for me to disrupt her life," she told anyone who asked. And then she would add with a conspiratorial laugh and a knowing wink, "Besides, I'm hardly a mother figure, am I?"

The truth was that having a teenage daughter did not suit Silver one bit. It made her feel her age, and anything that made her feel that was banished from her life.

Nora projected silent disapproval.

"Why?" Silver asked at last. "Do you think I *should* have?"

"Given that you've invited a hundred and fifty of your closest friends, and more than a smattering of the press, I don't think it's such a terrible idea. After all, she'll be reading about it in every gossip column in town, so maybe you should give *her* the choice of attending or not. There's still time to ask her."

"God!" Silver sighed dramatically. "As if I don't have enough problems!"

Chapter 9

Unpacking boxes had lost its thrill. Corey's visit had upset Jade and she found that she could no longer concentrate. In frustration she sat down and consulted the L.A. pages of her phone book. Several of the friends listed belonged to Mark, so she left them alone, and tried a fellow model and ex-roommate, black and exotic Beverly D'Amo. Beverly had moved to Los Angeles two years ago to pursue an acting career, and was now, according to her answering service, in Peru, and not expected back for a while. Disappointed, Jade called another model friend from New York. The girl kept her on the phone for thirty-five minutes complaining about an errant husband. Next, she spoke to a married girlfriend; this one was in the throes of a messy divorce. Man trouble was obviously catching.

A more fun group seemed to be the way to go, so she telephoned Antonio – the photographer, an amusing friend once you got over his *I am a star photographer* trip. They had worked together often and enjoyed many a great night out in New York when he visited.

"I'm here," she announced. "And the good news is that I'm a free agent, so let's get together. Preferably tonight."

"Bellissima!" he crooned. 'My *bella* Jade. What *dee*-lightful pleasure to hear your voice."

"You too, baby. How's Dix?"

"Dead!" was the dramatic retort.

"Another one hits the dust, huh?" She was not surprised. Antonio had a new boyfriend every month, and according to him they all let him down.

"He was *Eeenglish*," Antonio snorted, as if that explained everything.

"Well . . ." she said. "That makes two of us with dead boyfriends. I gave Mark back to his wife."

"Bene. He was *Eeenglish*. Tonight I take you to the birthday part of the true beetch."

"Anyone I know?"

"Seelver Anderson. The woman *kill* when she see you. Dress up, *bella*."

Hanging up the phone she decided a big Hollywood party in the company of the waspish Antonio was just what she needed. Usually the word *party* produced an instant excuse. Mark shied away from them – probably because he did not wish to risk being photographed with her.

What *had* he told his wife? They had often been caught by stray paparazzi leaving Elaine's restaurant in New York, or attending the opening of a new art gallery. Knowing Mark, he no doubt passed her off as a casual acquaintance, and aristocratic Lady Fiona must have believed every lying word. Mark and his clever lies. God!

Pouring a glass of wine, she allowed herself the pleasure of reliving the denouement.

*

Lord Mark Rand returned from a photographic trip, his thin features flushed with enjoyment, his brown wavy hair untidy –like a little boy's. He was almost fifty, but looked no more than thirty-five. The plan was that he spend six days in New York with her, and then return to London. Usually he divided his time between England and America, with numerous foreign assignments in between.

Dropping various camera cases, he put both arms around her. "Hello, lovely lady. Are you ready to give home and comfort to an extremely tired Englishman?"

Six years was just about to be part of her past. She didn't want to rush it. "You smell like a camel," she remarked, wrinkling her nose.

Laughing, he said, "Bathe me. Cover me with sweet oils. Massage my tired body and I shall be yours forever."

What a corny English asshole. Why had it never bothered her before?

He walked into the crowded living room of her Village apartment. Quite a few times he had suggested she move uptown to a more expensive place. "You can afford it," he would complain. "Why stay here?" Never once had he offered to share the rent. Not that she needed his money, she did very nicely on her own. Still . . . the offer would have shown commitment.

It never bothered her until they split.

"How was the trip?" she asked.

"God, it was unbelievable!" he said enthusiastically. "Sunsets the like of which even I have never seen before."

"And the girls?" She referred to the three models he had been photographing for an upmarket nude calendar layout.

"Young. Boring. And stupid."

"Did you sleep with them?"

Raising an eyebrow he looked at her quizzically. "What a strange question."

"Do you sleep with your wife?"

Frowning, he said, "What is the matter with you? You know I don't. We've discussed it many times."

She stared at him. "I want you to tell me again."

Shaking his head he chanted, "I did not sleep with my three dopey little model girls. And I do not sleep with my wife." He paused. "Does that satisfy you?"

"How long is it since you have slept with her?"

"Jade —" an edge crept into his voice — "I'm tired and I'm very hungry. It's been an arduous journey and I would like to relax."

"How long, Mark?"

She was giving him one last chance to be truthful and tell her everything.

"Fiona and I have not slept together since I met you," he snapped. "You know that perfectly well, and I resent being questioned in this way."

Her eyes glittered dangerously. "Not even once?"

He returned her gaze unblinkingly. "Not even twice." Removing his jacket he added, "Now, please may I have a scotch and soda. A hot bath. And the unadulterated pleasure of your beautiful body. In that order."

It was over, but why not prolong it? Make him suffer, as he had done to her.

"Certainly, sir," she said lightly. "One large scotch with a dash of soda coming up. And I'll get your bath ready."

He relaxed. "What a girl!"

What an English asshole!

In the bathroom she turned on the water to fill the tub — only the hot. Then she went into the kitchen and poured Kentucky bourbon into a plastic glass — Mark hated plastic glasses almost as much as he hated bourbon — and added two cubes of ice — which he couldn't stand.

Whistling, and looking ridiculous in baggy boxer shorts, Mark strolled into the bathroom. She followed him with his drink.

Stripping off his shorts he stepped into the steaming tub. "Jesus Christ!" he screamed, hopping out immediately. "It's scalding hot!"

"Sorry," she murmured, handing him his drink.

He took a healthy sip and almost gagged. "This is bourbon," he said accusingly. "You know I hate bourbon."

"Oh, dear." She stared at him without feeling. He was not the most attractive sight in the world standing in her bathroom, naked. His legs were too skinny, and bright red feet and calves from the boiling hot bath water did not help matters. He had a limp penis, a slight paunch, and a chest matted with gingery hair flecked with grey.

This was exactly how she wanted to remember him.

"There appears to be something on your mind," he said at last. Apparently he was not completely insensitive to her feelings.

Reaching into her pocket she pulled out the crumpled clipping of Lady Fiona cradling the latest little Lord or whatever it was.

Keeping his cool, he glanced at it. "Oh," he said calmly. "That's a printing error. Damned silly mistake. This is a picture of Fiona with my brother's child."

He must think she was an idiot. And why not, indeed? She had behaved like one for six years.

"I checked," she said coldly. "This is your son."

He stretched for a towel and tied it around his waist, his eyes refusing to meet hers. "How did you do that?" he asked, a tad nervously.

"It's all right," she said flatly. "I didn't call Fiona and ask her. You're perfectly safe to go home."

"Now, listen," he said, pulling himself together. "This whole baby thing was an accident, pure and simple." Warming to his theme he added, "I didn't tell you about it because I didn't want to upset you."

Staring at him scornfully she said, "An accident, Mark?"

"Let us go and sit down and I'll explain it to you over a drink."

He attempted to pass her. She blocked the bathroom door.

"Explain it to me now," she said icily. "I can't wait to hear."

He cleared his throat and gathered his thoughts. "It's quite true that since being with you I have not slept with Fiona," he began.

"What does that make the baby — an immaculate conception?" she interrupted sarcastically.

He continued, seemingly unperturbed, not to be stopped from telling his story. "A while ago I returned from a trip. Fiona was depressed. Her favourite uncle had died, and she had been thrown from her horse on a hunting trip, which bruised her self-esteem more than anything else."

Watching him make up the story as he spoke was pure theatre. He was the best instant liar she had ever seen.

"Yes?" She wanted more.

He tightened the towel around his waist. "It was her birthday. She drank too much champagne. When we went to bed that night she was crying, and came to me for comfort. I didn't have the heart to reject her. It was only once in six years, and the result was Archibald."

"Archibald!"

"It was her uncle's name," he said sheepishly. "She wanted to remember him."

Jade began to laugh uncontrollably.

"I'm sorry, darling," he said, believing all was forgiven.

She managed to control herself enough to say, "Take off the towel."

"What?"

Touching her fingertips to his nipples, she brushed them lightly. "I said, take off the towel. Or do you want me to do it for you?"

"Do it for me," he replied, feeling the swell of relief followed by a generous erection.

She pulled the knot on the towel and it fell away from his body. "My, my," she said admiringly. "Look what you brought me back."

Relaxing, he leaned against the tiled sink.

With practised moves she stroked his chest, then his belly, and as she reached lower she sank to her knees and teased his excitement with her tongue.

He leaned back even further and surrendered to the sensual caress of her luscious mouth, his enjoyment mounting as she increased her rhythm.

Just as his pleasure was reaching lift-off, she bit down roughly with scissor-sharp teeth.

He yelled in agony.

Calmly she released him, and stood up. Catching him off balance and unprepared, she pushed him into the scalding water of the bath-tub.

"You bloody maniac!" he screamed.

"You goddamn liar!" she replied. "Her birthday, indeed! That line is older than George Burns!"

Marching to the bathroom door she turned for one final look. He was struggling from the burning tub like a hyper fish. With satisfaction she noticed the faint trace of teeth marks on his rapidly shrinking penis. "Goodbye, Mark," she said. "I'm going to dinner. When I come back I want you and all your worldly shit out of my life forever."

He was gone when she returned three hours later.

Once she split from him she found out he had been cheating on her all over town. Why hadn't anyone told her? The general excuse was that it didn't seem proper while they were together.

She felt duped. Getting out of town was the best tonic she could think of.

*

Sipping her wine, Jade went to the closet and chose a suitable outfit for the night's activities.

A party with Antonio. It might be fun, it might not.

Whatever. It was better than sitting home.

Chapter 10

"Lighten up," Wes Money said. He was speaking to his landlady, Reba Winogratsky, who had arrived unexpectedly to collect two months' overdue rent. "I'll have it for you next month."

"Wesley, Wesley!" she sighed despairingly. "One of these days I'm gonna have to throw you out."

With an appealing look he said, "You wouldn't do that to me, Reba, would you?"

She ran her tongue slowly across her top teeth. "I might."

He tried to ascertain whether she was in line for a screwing, decided that if she ever turned up alone she would be. Today she had what appeared to be her son with her – a fat boy of about ten with a sulky expression. They had arrived in a new Mercedes which she quickly explained belonged to a friend. He didn't believe her. The car was hers and she didn't want anyone to know lest they struggled even more about paying her exorbitant rent demands. She wore a tight halter top, shorts, and stiletto heels. Her legs were waxed and so was her moustache. She was no beauty. From her left shoulder hung a huge leather purse. She was obviously out on a rent-collecting binge.

"Can I offer you a cup of coffee?" he asked politely. If the kid wasn't with her he would have offered her more than that. Last time she turned up it had been with a Mexican maid who cleaned the kitchen floor while they argued over a rent increase.

"Come up with some cash soon or you're just gonna have to go," Reba decided.

"I will."

"I hope you mean it, Wesley. You owe me two months, an' next Saturday I'm sendin' the collector."

"Who's the collector?" he asked, alarmed.

"Better you should never find out," she replied, absent-mindedly scratching her crotch.

I could cure that itch for you, he wanted to say, but curbed the impulse.

She ran a finger across a table top, leaving a fresh and shiny trail through the dust. Then she peered into the cramped kitchen, which was stacked with filthy dishes and half-eaten food. "The way you keep this place is an open invitation to rats," she remarked, without too much concern.

"Can we go?" whined the fat kid.

"Clean up your act, Wesley, an' get me my money."

He followed her to the door. "Yes, *ma'am*."

She gave him an appraising stare. "Y'know, you're not bad lookin' if you took better care of yourself. You've got a kinda Nick Nolte quality."

Nick who? "Thanks," he said. "I'm working on it."

"Get a job," she scolded.

He decided to impress her. "Tonight I'll be at Silver Anderson's house helping her out. She's havin' a party."

"*The* Silver Anderson?"

"No. Silver Anderson who works as a checker at Vons Market," he said sarcastically.

"Huh?"

"Of course *the* Silver Anderson."

"Really?" She didn't quite believe him, but she gave it a shot anyway. "Get Timmy here" – she patted the fat boy on the head – "an autographed picture, an' I'll knock ten bucks off the money you owe."

"If I can."

"Good." She took the boy's hand and clicked her way across the wooden porch out onto the boardwalk.

Hazy sunshine caught Wes's attention as he watched her go. A pretty Chinese girl skate-boarded by. He thought he might grab a few rays and liven up his complexion. Somehow, in his busy schedule of screwing, boozing and partying he never found time for the sun.

His nextdoor neighbour emerged from her house at the same time. She had moved in six weeks ago, shortly after the previous tenant overdosed on heroin and was carried off in a body bag. He'd never seen her before, but sometimes he'd had to hammer on the dividing wall in the middle of the night (when he was home) for her to turn down the godawful classical music she liked to play. It figured. She looked like a school teacher: brown hair in a bun, baggy clothes, and John Lennon glasses. She appeared to be surprisingly young, probably only early twenties.

"Hello, neighbour." He waved a friendly greeting.

She pretended not to notice, and set off along the boardwalk. Snob. She was no doubt pissed off he'd banged on the wall. He followed her because he had nothing better to do.

She turned up a side street and climbed into an ancient Volkswagen. Bored, he headed in the other direction, across the sand, down to the sea. It was a mild day and the ocean was calm. He liked it better when the surf was up, and the waves came belting in. He loved it when it rained. And a storm was a special treat.

He sat down on the sand, and the next thing he knew he must have nodded off for a couple of hours, because when he awoke, water was lapping his feet. Nearby, a lone dog sat on the sand staring at him.

Wes was not partial to animals. An old girlfriend had once kept a monkey. It pissed and crapped everywhere, and for a grand finale jerked off whenever they made love. No more pets after that.

He consulted his copy of a Cartier tank watch. Fifty bucks from a travelling Iranian. It lost five minutes a day and sometimes stopped altogether. He ascertained it was late afternoon and hauled himself up. Rocky would be getting panicky. Better put him out of his misery.

Chapter 11

Poppy Soloman was getting dressed, and when Poppy got ready for a party – watch out!

Howard repaired to his own bathroom, locked the door, and had his second snort of the day. Cocaine. A little habit he had been indulging in for a few months now.

Carefully he laid out the white powder on a special mirror-topped tray, coaxed it into two neat lines, and with the help of a straw, snorted it into his nostrils. One long, deep breath and the rush was incredible. Better than sex. Better than anything. Howard felt like he could own the world. He *did* own the world. He owned a fucking studio, for Christ's sake. Well, not exactly owned it, ran it. The same thing. It gave him the power he wanted, only to really enjoy the power he needed an occasional snort. Nothing habit-forming, mind you. Howard knew when enough was enough, and duly limited himself. Once in the morning to get off on the right foot. And once in the evening *only* if they were going out or entertaining at home. Since they went out or entertained every night, he regularly snorted twice a day. Not such a terrible thing. Some actors, producers and studio people couldn't get through a meeting without visiting the john three times.

Howard considered himself a very conservative user, one who could certainly never get hooked. Stopping was no problem. But why stop something that made you feel so goddamn good?

Howard had concerns. Once you reached the top, where else was there to go but down? And the pressure was on.

A huge conglomerate owned Orpheus Studios, headed by Zachary K. Klinger, a major powerhouse. Zachary K. liked Howard – in fact it was he who had chosen him for the top position. But that was now. What if Howard was unable to deliver? Zachary K. wanted box office giants in whammo grossing movies. He wanted Howard to turn the failing fortunes of Orpheus around, and he wanted him to do it fast. Maybe too fast.

Picking a movie that's going to soar is like singling out a puppy from a large litter. You could end up choosing the runt – whatever its pedigree.

Howard sweated every time he had to make a decision. But now, with the coke to fortify him, he decided that in the few months he had been at the helm he had done a marvellous job. His first move had been to pick up a couple of sleepers for distribution – which meant he took two small independently produced movies, and had Orpheus distribute them as they were short of product. The results were sensational. Both films went through the roof. Howard was a hero.

Now all he had to do was oversee some hits of his own. Just make absolutely sure that every new picture he gave the green light to was a potential smash.

The following month Zachary K. was coming to town to check up on progress. Not that he didn't get a daily report from one of his spies. Howard knew for a fact that there were at least two stationed in key jobs.

He wasn't going to let it bother him. Nothing bothered him. Look what he had done with his life. He was a genius, for crissakes.

*

Howard Soloman was born when he was sixteen, and his mother divorced his father, fled from Philadelphia to Colorado, and shortly after, married Temple Soloman. He couldn't wait to change his name from Jessie Howard Judah Lipski to the much more simple Howard Soloman. What an escape! His natural father was a rabbi, a cruel, hard man who treated both his wife and son as if they had been put on this earth solely to do his bidding, and he made sure that their lives were pure misery. When Howard – or Jessie as he was then – reached his teenage years he begged his mother to get out. "I'm going," he told her, "an' you'd better come with me."

She didn't take much persuading, and one dark night they fled to New York, and from there to Colorado, where an old school friend of his mother's put them up. It was like getting out of prison, and when his mother married Temple Soloman six months later, it was as if God had smiled on them for doing it. Temple was an easy-going mild-mannered man. He was the senior partner in a clothing manufacturing business, and while he wasn't exactly rolling in it, he had enough money to buy Howard a second-hand car and send him to college.

Howard felt like a Russian who finally saw America and all it had to offer. He was alive and free. And so was his mother. The early years were just a bad dream.

As a teenager Howard was plump and plagued with acne, until he discovered girls. Once that happened his weight soon dropped, and the acne vanished overnight. Temple sat him down one day and gave him a lecture. "Always use a johnny," he said, snapping a Durex in front of his stepson's face. "And give the girl a good time too." Big wink. "Only don't get anyone pregnant."

Howard thought about Temple's remarks. What did he mean by "give the girl a good time"? Wasn't she having a good time just by being in his company?

The next time he had a young lady in the back of his shined up old Buick he asked her casually as he humped away, "Hey – you havin' a good time?"

"You're heavy," she whined. "Why is your back so hairy – it's . . . ugh! My mother will kill me if she ever finds out I'm doing this."

So much for conversation. He almost lost his erection. God forbid!

It took Howard's first wife, the fierce black activist whom he married when he was nineteen, to teach him the joys of getting a woman off too. "Just go for the button an' liiiiift-off, babee!" she instructed while clasping him around the back of the neck with ebony legs he thought might strangle him.

Hitting the button on his third attempt, he realized there was a difference. Instead of the female being a reluctant participant in the act of sex, she turned into a stark raving maniac! Why hadn't Temple mentioned buttons to him! Look at all the time he had wasted!

One day Howard read a book about Howard Hughes. He liked it so much he reread it three times. Temple had told him – early on in their relationship –that he was the heir to the manufacturing business of which Temple was the senior partner. "When you graduate," his stepfather had said, "I'll teach you everything I know. You're like my own son, and when the time comes I'll hand the business over to you."

Howard was grateful, but not at all sure he wanted to stay in Colorado and make ladies' dresses. He had bigger plans. He wanted to be like Howard Hughes. He saw Hollywood in his future. *"What's it like?"* he asked his friend Jack Python, as they struggled through a business administration course together. *"You're from L.A. Is Hollywood really something?"*

Jack shrugged. *"I live in the Valley. I don't go over the hill much."*
"What hill?"

"The Valley is separated from Hollywood and Beverly Hills by several large canyons. You drive over Benedict Canyon or Coldwater or Laurel."

"And? What's it like when you get there?" Howard asked impatiently.

"Streets. Palm trees. Tourists. It's no big deal."

"Well, I'm going there. Summer vacation I'm getting a job and renting an apartment. Why don't we take a place together?"

Jack shook his head. A year later he changed his mind, and when they graduated they moved into a two-bedroom apartment just off Hollywood Boulevard. No luxury abode, but it was functional and convenient.

By that time Howard had already spent the previous summer in Los Angeles, and returning he felt like a veteran. He knew where to get the cheapest hamburger, the fastest dry cleaning, the best place to hang out for the price of one cup of coffee — and where to find the prettiest girls. He had already been married (though it was annulled), worked at one of the studios in the mail room, and had his first case of the clap (unfortunately not his last). Temple Soloman had been disappointed but understanding of his need to try his luck in Hollywood. *"What do you want to do there?"* he had asked.

"Be an agent," Howard blurted in reply. And the seed was sown. Why not be an agent? With his conversational skills he could be the greatest.

So he changed positions, and instead of going back to his old job at — yes — Orpheus Studios — he started in the mail room of S.M.I. Specialized Management Incorporated. And from there, history was made.

It had taken him seventeen years to get to the very top.

*

"Howard!"

He could hear Poppy calling. Clearing up his coke paraphernalia, he unlocked the bathroom door.

"Howard," she sighed, in the little-girl voice she had recently affected. "What do you think?"

She twirled for him.

Poppy was five feet two inches tall, rounded and perky looking. She had very long blonde curls, slightly protruding blue eyes, and a self-satisfied permanent smile which went nicely with her retroussé nose. She also had new tits – thanks to a man she referred to reverently as "plastic surgeon to the stars". She wore a turquoise frilled, strapless dress, and many real diamonds. Her new tits protruded nicely.

"You likee my dress?" she asked.

He wanted to say no. He wanted to say that she looked like a short, tiered Christmas cake. He wanted to say, cut your hair, lose fifteen pounds and put on a plain black dress. He wanted to say – *Bring back the old tits, I liked them better*.

"Dynamite!" he exclaimed, wondering if Whitney would be at the party.

She smiled happily. "I knew you'd like it."

When she was his secretary she had worn neat tailored suits and plain, well-cut dresses. She had kept her hair up and featured little jewellery. Now she looked like a walking advertisement for a fancy jewellery store.

She held up a bracelet-laden wrist. "You likee?"

He inspected multiple diamonds. "Very nice."

"Very nice!" she squealed, grabbing him in a hug. "You're the most generous man in the world!"

Wasn't he just! Even his accountant – a seasoned veteran of Hollywood marriages – was beginning to blanch at the constant stream of bills. "Can't you keep her home at least *one* day a week?" he'd complained. "The woman is a walking charge card!"

Howard saw no way of stopping her, short of breaking both her legs.

"Get dressed, Howie," Poppy said. "It's party time. We don't want to be late, do we?"

It was the first time she had been ready before him in five years of marriage. He was too busy thinking about Whitney to wonder why.

Chapter 12

"I invited her," Nora Carvell said.

Silver felt a small stab of annoyance. Who needed a teenage daughter to remind her of the creeping years? "Is she coming?" was her casual response as she stripped off her clothes in the privacy of her bedroom and pulled on a silk robe.

Nora lit a fresh cigarette from the smouldering butt attached firmly to her lower lip. "She said she'll try."

What Heaven had actually said was a sarcastic "Why doesn't she wait until it's all over to ask me? Don't count on me bein' there. As if she gives a shit." For her years Heaven was quite eloquent.

"Why don't you try to get along with your mother?" Nora had rasped. "You haven't even sent her a card."

Heaven's laughter rang out. "She's *never* sent one to me. In fact I'm lucky to get a cheque three weeks later when *you* remind her."

Nora couldn't deny the truth. "Try and make it tonight," she urged before hanging up.

There was nothing she would like better than to see mother and daughter get along. A lot of people – including Heaven – thought Silver was a bitch. Nora saw another side of her. She saw a successful woman alone in the world with no real friends. She saw an ambitious woman who had been hurt and used by men. She saw a woman who had alienated her family yet needed them desperately.

"God!" Silver exclaimed. "She'll try, indeed! You would think she would run barefoot over hot coals to attend my party."

Nora said, "I'm going home to change, I'll be back in an hour."

"Fine," Silver responded, as she tried to decide whether to refresh the heavy makeup she had worn for the Antonio photo session, or take it all off and start again.

She compromised. Left the dramatic eye makeup intact, and cleansed her skin with cotton pads soaked in witch-hazel.

The cold lotion on her face was delightfully soothing. She walked over to her luxurious king-size bed and pulled down the purple satin cover. Pratesi sheets awaited. A welcome lie-down for fifteen minutes was just what she needed.

Her bedroom was peaceful and cool. Pale lilac silk walls complemented the deep purple of the carpet. Mirrors abounded.

Lying back on the bed she tried to empty her mind, but tonight it was impossible. All she could think about was Heaven's father, and what a bastard he had been.

*

Silver Anderson met "The Businessman", as she always referred to him, when she was thirty-one and he was fifty-two. He was extremely rich, very powerful, and naturally — married. Silver was starring on Broadway at the time. She was also divorcing her ex-stepfather and rekindling an affair with her co-star.

"The Businessman" walked into her life at a party and took over. He was a big man in every way: tall, portly, with heavy features and hooded eyes. Some whispered that his early connections included organized crime. Some whispered that he had the ear of the President. Some whispered that the late Marilyn Monroe was once a girlfriend.

His wife was a social lioness. Small and petite, forever clad in designer clothes, groomed to within an inch of her life, she ruled their three homes with an elegant iron fist.

"We never fuck," was one of the first things he revealed. Silver had heard that before, from every married man who ever cheated on his wife.

"What do you do?" she asked sweetly.

"We socialize," he replied gruffly, and presented her with a hundred-thousand-dollar diamond necklace from Cartier.

"The Businessman" was a very demanding man when he found the time. His sexual appetite was voracious, and Silver, who was no slouch in the sexual stakes herself, found him hard to keep up with. He was rough and crude, but God he was exciting!

Silver fell in love with a married man twenty-one years her senior, and she fell hard. On the one hand he treated her like a whore. On the other he showered her with expensive gifts — the diamond necklace was just the beginning.

One day he arrived at the penthouse apartment they used as a meeting place, with two other women. A seductive-looking redhead, and a soigné black girl with the style of a fashion model. Instinctively Silver knew they were hookers. High-class ones, and very costly, but hookers all the same.

Angrily she cornered him in the kitchen after he had fixed them all drinks. "What's going on?"

"Nothing, if you don't want it to," he replied blandly.

She knew it was what he wanted and her stomach churned. Silver Anderson had been around, but never that much.

They returned to the living room and polite chat. The two girls were good, they knew their stuff. "Isn't it a little hot in here?" one of them murmured, taking off her light silk jacket.

"Very hot," the other agreed, stretching out her legs and removing her shoes and stockings.

Silver felt "The Businessman" tense beside her on the couch.

The black girl stood up and smiled seductively. "You don't mind, do you?" she asked, unwrapping her crossover dress. Underneath she wore a scarlet lace G-string and that was all. Her breasts were pointed and polished like the finest onyx.

The redhead stood too. "I love to take off my clothes," she said softly. "I need to feel nothing between me and nature." She stretched, allowing her full breasts to fall free of her blouse.

The penthouse apartment was hardly the great outdoors, but Silver got the drift.

Idly the two girls began to touch each other. Fingers caressing breasts and other, more secret places. Tongues warm and soft. The secret places exposed for all to see.

"The Businessman's" breathing was laboured. Beneath his trousers Silver saw the proof of his excitement. Without moving from the couch, and without taking his eyes off the two call-girls, he urged Silver to lift her skirt.

She had tried to remain unaffected by what was going on — an impossible task. And to her shame she knew she would do anything he asked. So while the womem writhed together on the floor, Silver Anderson lifted her skirt, removed her panties, spread her legs, and allowed "The Businessman" to mount her and take his ride of perverted passion.

When it was over she felt dirty and humiliated. She was Silver Anderson, not some cheap tramp to be taken and used in front of whores. She was furious with him, and angry at herself for succumbing so easily.

The next day he sent her a ruby as big as an egg and a note. We'll do it again soon. Like hell they would. She refused to see him in spite of his bombardments of gifts and flowers.

Six weeks later she realized she was pregnant.

The first thing she did was consult her gynaecologist. "I don't want this baby," she told him flatly.

He was a charming man with grey hair and a crinkly smile. "Why not, my dear? You're in excellent health."

"I know that," she said irritably, searching for a suitable reason. "I'm not married." That would shut him up.

He laughed. Charmingly. "Silver, Silver," he sighed, placing the tips of his fingers together and rocking back and forth behind his desk. "You're a very famous woman. What does it matter whether you're married or not? You'll have a beautiful baby with none of the inconveniences of a husband in the house." He chuckled at his own wisdom. "You'll make single motherhood fashionable."

She liked the idea. Silver Anderson, a pioneer for women! Also the thought of an abortion terrified her. Eventually she decided to go ahead and have the baby.

By the time she gave birth, "The Businessman" was gone from her life. She had threatened him with exposure to his wife if he didn't leave her alone. He had no idea the baby was his.

The press went crazy in their quest to find out who the father was, but Silver remained silent. Three months after Heaven was born she moved to Rio with a Brazilian polo player. Heaven was left in New York with a nanny.

As Silver watched the child grow, she regretted giving birth. Every time she looked at Heaven, she was reminded of "The Businessman" and her unforgettable night of degradation.

Heaven had never asked who her father was. Jack did once, when he came to London to pick up the child. "He doesn't exist," she'd said coldly.

Unfortunately he did.

*

Silver sighed and stretched. Opening her eyes she stared at the silk draped ceiling above her bed. If Heaven appeared tonight she was not going to be pleased. *Damn* Nora for asking the girl, and bringing back all the bad memories.

The Baccarat clock on the bedside table told her it was time to start getting ready for her party. She wished she could sleep for ten hours. When was the last time she'd done that? Work . . . Work . . . Work . . . Parties . . . Parties . . . Parties . . .

Ah, well . . . for great fame you paid a price . . .

It was worth it.

Almost.

Chapter 13

Mannon Cable worked out in his private gym before getting ready for the party. He didn't really want to go, he was not fond of parties. This was a favour for Nora Carvell. She had phoned a week before and asked him to attend. Nora was an old friend, and one of the few people in Hollywood he would do anything for. Well, not quite anything – however, if she wanted a favour, she was on. At the beginning of his career she was the one person who was always there for him. The crusty old publicist was in his corner from day one. He recalled walking into her office on the lot the day he signed for his first important movie. Fifteen years ago to be exact.

*

Mannon Cable was twenty-seven years old and the best-looking hunk ever to cross Nora Carvell's path when he walked into her office. Not that she was interested. She preferred girls, always would. Only Mannon didn't know that, so when he first set eyes on the middle-aged woman with the cropped hair and the permanent cigarette dangling from her lips, he went into his number. Sexy walk. Macho scowl. Cobalt blue eyes scorching everything in sight.

"Take a seat," Nora snapped. "And tell me your life history. Then we'll make something up." She shuffled some papers around on her desk. "Have you been over to the stills department yet?"

"Nope." He shook his head.

She squinted at his sun-kissed good looks, trying to decide how to sell this new piece of beefcake. "Go ahead. Shoot."

He told her about being born in Montana, coming to Los Angeles at nineteen. Studying at various acting classes, working as a waiter, an extra, a gas pump attendant, a repossessor of cars, and a stunt man.

"Married?" she asked.

"Nope," he replied.

"Homosexual?" she persisted.

He shifted uncomfortably. *"Are you kidding?"*

Pencil poised, she checked him out for signs of lying. *"I'm not gonna make it public knowledge, sonny. I just have to know these things so I can protect you."*

"I am not a queer," he said stiffly.

She scribbled on a piece of paper and said, *"Come back tomorrow. I'll have you all figured out."*

He returned the next day to be handed a typed sheet of imaginative accomplishments. He was a football hero, an English honours major, who had been injured in a football game and told that he would never walk again. For two years he had lain in a hospital bed unable to move, until — miracle of miracles — blind faith pulled him through and he came to Hollywood and was discovered for this very movie he was about to make.

"This is all lies," he protested.

She shrugged. *"So I bent the truth a little. Big deal."*

"I don't like it."

Inhaling cigarette smoke she said, *"You don't havta like it, sonny, just remember it."*

He shook his head. *"No way."*

"It's studio policy. Bio info's gotta grab 'em. Whaddya think's gonna grab 'em about your background?" *A cloud of smoke enveloped her and she began to cough.* *"Are you sure you're not a fag? Y'live with two other guys. What's the deal?"*

"Get fucked," he steamed, and walked out.

After that they became good friends. It was Nora's idea that he do the Burt Reynolds spoof centrefold. He did it with a big, shit-eating grin and a large picture of a strutting cock (the barnyard variety) covering his strutting cock (the Mannon Cable variety). It caused quite a stir, and everyone knew who Mannon Cable was after that.

When Nora left the studio a few years later she came to work for him as his personal publicist. Eventually she went off to live in Italy with her companion of many years, and when her lover died she came back to America and took a job at City Television. Her first assignment was Silver Anderson. She had worked with her ever since.

*

Mannon finished a series of gruelling press-ups, and threw a towelling robe over his shorts. When he was married to Whitney, parties were a rare event. Whitney was content to stay at home on the ranch, just the two of them. She liked to ride their horses, walk on the beach, and join him in fixing a barbecue. Until she started her dumb career and fucked everything up. Now the Malibu ranch was sold, the horses too. Home was a formal mansion on Sunset Boulevard, and he wasn't happy.

Melanie-Shanna waited in the games room, which featured a pool table, full western bar, and his collection of guns on the walls.

When Mannon had showered and dressed he joined her.

"Hi, honey," she greeted him quietly. "Feeling good?"

"Yeah, great."

He didn't know what it was about Melanie-Shanna – it wasn't her fault, she just aggravated the hell out of him. Maybe it was because *she* was his wife and Whitney wasn't. They had met when he went to Houston to make a movie. While he was there, recovering from Whitney's walk-out and her subsequent affair with Chuck Nielson, he had judged a beauty contest. Melanie-Shanna, with her mane of auburn hair, her clean, long-limbed body, and her sweet smile, was the natural winner. He had taken her out to dinner a few times. Then he had taken her *in* to dinner. One thing led to another and he made love to her on the floor of his sumptuous suite. She was only twenty years old when they married a week later. Whitney was nearly thirty. Let her eat her heart out.

Basically Mannon married Melanie-Shanna to make Whitney jealous. It didn't work. And it left him in the crapper with a young wife and no pre-nuptial agreement. To make matters even worse, Melanie-Shanna adored him.

"Can I fix you a drink, honey?" she asked.

"Why do you always have to tag *honey* onto the end of every sentence?" he said aggressively.

"Sorry, hon – er, dear. I'm not aware that I do."

"Well, *be* aware," he warned. "It makes you sound like a cheap dance hostess."

She turned away so that he couldn't see her large eyes fill with tears. What was she doing wrong? For months he had hardly had a good word to say to her. When they first met he had been so loving and kind, truly the man of her dreams. He hadn't known that for years she'd had his picture tacked on her wall after seeing him in *Sweet Revenge*. Mannon Cable had always been her favourite movie star.

Now she was Mrs Mannon Cable, and it wasn't making either of them happy.

Quietly she poured scotch into a glass, added ice cubes and handed it to him.

He swallowed the drink in two gulps. "I suppose we'd better go," he said dourly, walking to the door. "And I'm warning you, I don't want to stay late."

"Neither do I," she said, following him out. Tonight she wanted to come home early. Because tonight she was going to tell him they were expecting a baby.

Chapter 14

"Wanna go party?" Heaven asked Eddie on the phone.

He laughed, low-down and dirty. "I thought we had our own party this afternoon."

"Some party," she giggled.

"A blast, right?"

"A *big* blast."

"You wanna repeat it?"

She paused. "I have another sort of party in mind."

"Aw . . ." Eddie said. "I hate those open parties. They're always full of kids, an' I hate not gettin' in the house, an' being treated like garbage, an' —"

"This is a *proper* party," she interrupted. "Like a *Beverly Hills* party, with movie stars and fancy food and probably some dumb band."

"Food?" Eddie questioned. "Real food?"

"I guess."

"Who invited us?" he asked suspiciously.

"Nobody invited *you*," she responded tartly. "Only *I* can take you," she taunted. "That's if *I* want to, an' if your car'll get us over the hill."

"Whose party is it?"

"My mother finally remembered I'm alive."

"Silver Anderson?"

"I'm not related to Linda Evans, you geek."

There was a short silence while Eddie digested this information. Finally he said, "What'ud I have to wear?"

"Anything you like," she replied blithely. She herself planned to cause a sensation in her red leather micro-dress, and the longshoreman's overcoat which she had just bought at Flip on Melrose with money from her singing gigs.

"Do y'*wanna* go?" Eddie inquired, remembering how she felt about her famous mother.

"I dunno," she replied, unsure for a moment. "I don't see why I *shouldn't*. I *am* her daughter."

"Uh . . . let's do it then," he said.

"Oh . . . I don't know." She changed her mind quickly.

"Aw, c'mon, H. Get on the track 'n' stick to it."

"Maybe I will. I'll call you back."

She hung up on him before he could argue. She enjoyed playing games with Eddie. Especially *now*. Anyway, she couldn't make up her mind whether she wanted to go to her mother's dumb party or not. On the one hand it might be a real blast to spy on the Hollywood set first-hand. On the other – who would Silver have there? Certainly not Rob Lowe and Sean Penn. More like a bunch of doddering old farts.

As if to make up her mind, her grandfather, George, appeared at the door of her room. He was a tall, thin man, with a shock of thick white hair and a preoccupied expression always in place on his deeply lined face. He didn't look like Silver, and no way resembled Uncle Jack. He had a sort of nutty professor air about him. Heaven liked him a lot. For a grandfather he was ace. And he left her alone. *Most* important.

"Are you home for dinner, dear?" he asked, fiddling with his glasses which hung from a blue cord around his neck.

"I think I'm going out, pops."

"Good, good," he said absent-mindedly. "Then I can let Mrs Gunter go."

Anything to let Mrs Gunter go. She was their housekeeper/cook/busybody, and she drove Heaven nuts.

"I'm not bothering with dinner myself," George added vaguely. "I shall be in my workroom all night." His eyes fixed on a half-naked poster of Sting tacked to her closet. "Where are you going?" he asked.

"Out with Eddie," she replied, deciding the hell with it – she *would* go to her mother's party. Why shouldn't she? "We're playing a gig."

"Twelve o'clock curfew," George reminded.

"Sure, pops," she agreed. She could walk in at four in the morning and he wouldn't know it. Once he was in his workroom nothing disturbed him. Usually he carried on through the night, losing all track of time.

She didn't mention Silver's party. It would only upset him, and he might try to dissuade her from going. George and his famous daughter did not speak. It had been that way for thirty years.

Oh well ... Heaven didn't blame him ... Maybe she shouldn't talk to her mother either. Silver treated her as if she hardly existed. Never called. Never asked anything about her life when they did get together. Usually it was a twice-yearly dinner at La Scala with Nora in attendance. The woman was a bitch.

Big fucking deal. Who cared?

She did.

Chapter 15

Clarissa Browning rented a secluded house on Benedict Canyon. She leased it from a young director who had gone to work in Europe for a year. The house was dark and old, surrounded by tall trees and untended grounds. Clarissa liked the coldness of the house, the bathrooms that were over fifty years old, the dark wood panelling everywhere, and the general gloom.

Even the swimming pool was not of the usual California variety. There was no jacuzzi. No floating pool furniture. It was always filled with leaves, as the filter rarely worked. And it was always ice cold, as the heater *never* worked. At night coyotes howled, and other small, wild animals scurried across the old tile roof. Sometimes snakes slithered into the pool and drowned.

Clarissa enjoyed lighting a log fire in the bedroom and reading from her extensive collection of classics. She liked to bundle up in a long flannel nightie with a hot mug of cocoa for company, and pretend she was back east.

Arriving home from the studio early Saturday evening she was pleased to see Jack Python's dark green Ferrari parked out front. He had his own key to come and go whenever he pleased. It suited her. Clarissa never brought her homework to the house.

He was in the bedroom watching television. Or was he watching? On closer inspection she discovered he was asleep.

Silently she observed him for a moment – so still . . . so quiet. Usually Jack was always on the move. The green eyes probing, finding out things. The hard body ready, poised. The sharp mind, clickety clickety click.

He excited her. He always excited her.

The first time they met she had thought – *Handsome son of a bitch with a hard cock and not much else.* She had changed her mind soon enough. He had a hard cock all right, but that wasn't all. Jack Python had energy and curiosity and a steel trap of a mind. He was a fast thinker with words to back up his thoughts. He was not just a pretty face.

They slept together immediately, in spite of friends warning her that Jack Python came and ran. Not with Clarissa Browning he didn't. She had no intention of becoming just another name on his long list.

Patiently she attempted to get to know him. It wasn't easy. Charming and warm and intelligent as he was, Jack never allowed anyone to get close. Clarissa understood. She was the same way herself.

She moved to California to do a movie, and when he eventually got around to calling, she played his game, and refused to see him. It soon became clear that Jack did not like rejection.

When they finally saw each other it was understood they were an item. They had been an item for over a year now. It suited both of them.

Clarissa scrubbed off her studio makeup, removed her clothes, and stood over the sleeping figure of her lover. She forgot about the young actor at the studio that morning. Merely business. Jack Python was pleasure. Such pure exquisite pleasure . . .

She shuddered in anticipation of what was to come. In bed he was a master. He had an uncanny knack of knowing her every need, combined with the most impressive staying power.

"Just a trick," he said one day, when she asked him how he did it.

"Tell me!" she persisted.

"Just call it mind over matter," he grinned.

Her presence was not waking him. She clicked off the hated television. (Hated by her, loved by him. "How can you not watch *Hill Street*?" he demanded every Thursday night at ten o'clock.) The sudden silence disturbed him, and he rolled over, still asleep and still dressed in his usual weekend clothes of Levis and a sweater.

She unzipped his jeans with her teeth.

He woke up and groped for her.

Pushing his hands away she rolled his Levis down. He wore no undershorts. He never did. She bent her head to his sudden interest.

"I surrender," he said, throwing his arms to the side.

"I knew you would," she murmured.

Later they shared a cigarette and discussed their plans for the evening. There were several possibilities. A screening of a new Mel Brooks film. "I'm too tired to laugh," Clarissa demurred. An industry dinner honouring an old actor. "Why?" Jack questioned. "He was a no-talent when he was young. What's the trick in growing old?" And dinner with Clarissa's agent at Spago. "He's a lunch," she decided.

"What do you feel like doing?" he asked, clicking on the television. "Want me to send out for Chinese?"

Clarissa flicked the television off. "What about going to your sister's party?"

"Huh?" He was surprised. "How do you know about Silver's party?"

"I was invited."

"You don't know her."

"Maybe I should."

"Why?"

"Because she's your sister, and I've never met any of your family. Not your father, or your niece. I think Silver Anderson is an interesting woman, and I'm intrigued to meet her."

"Shit!" Jack said, jumping from the bed and pacing around the darkened bedroom.

"Are we nervous of being in her company?" Clarissa chided. "Does she make you feel inferior?"

"You talk such crap sometimes."

"Yes? My psychiatrist says that to conquer fears you simply have to face them."

"You pay two hundred bucks an hour for advice you can get out of a Chinese fortune cookie?"

"He's helped me a lot."

"Hey – I'm not going to get into a fight over this. Silver doesn't make me nervous. She doesn't make me anything."

"Then we'll go?"

"If that's how you want to spend your Saturday night."

"It is."

He wasn't going to fight it. Clarissa was a stubborn woman, and if she wanted to do something they usually ended up doing it.

He did not believe in fighting. He believed in exiting. Quietly. If it ever got to be too much.

Chapter 16

Silver Anderson's party was being paid for by City Television. Silver was notoriously tight with a buck, and there was no way *she* was shelling out thirty or forty thousand dollars – even if it *was* for her, and she could certainly afford it.

City was planning a big celebration for the cast of *Palm Springs* before the summer hiatus, when Nora suggested it might be a better idea to make it a party to celebrate Silver's birthday. "Do I have something for you!" she told them. "Glamour. Style. Stars. A media event with sensational coverage." They fell in love with the idea immediately, and once she had them hooked all she had to do was convince Silver.

It wasn't difficult. Not when Silver discovered City Television was paying. "I'll have the party," she agreed. "And when it's all over and done with I want my entire house re-carpeted. A little gift. They can afford it." A dramatic pause.

"Oh, and by the way, Nora, forty-*five* is my official age this year. Not a moment older."

Nora didn't want to get into *that* one. She reckoned City Television would certainly pay for the carpeting of Silver's house. Where else could they get this kind of world-wide publicity for such a steal? And the coverage would be sensational. No problem. For Nora Carvell knew plenty about publicity. Television was taken care of, and then there were photographers from *U.S.A. Today*, *People*, *Newsweek*, and a personal photographer who would capture shots to be sent out world-wide on all the wire services. The paparazzi would be outside, flanking a red carpet and crash barriers to the house. Along with several of Beverly Hills finest, who would take care of the vigorous security.

Nora had personally supervised the guest list, inviting a hand-picked group of important industry people, and a mix of very famous actors, actresses, sports stars and assorted V.I.P.s from other fields.

Dressed in a plum velvet suit with clumsy pearl jewellery not complementing her short, untidy grey hair, she rushed back to Silver's house early. Swamped in Ma Griffe scent and cigarette smoke she parked in the back next to Wes Money, who was just alighting from his old Lincoln.

"Who're you?" she asked tartly, ever wary of uninvited spies from the *National Enquirer* or *True Life Scandal*.

"I'm bar. Who're *you*?"

"I'm publicity. Pass the word. Anyone calling the supermarket rags with overheard gossip will not be working in this town again. Got it?"

Wes nodded. The old broad had just come up with a great idea for scoring extra bucks. She hurried off, and he took a leisurely stroll down a garden path to the back door, which led him into an overcrowded, very large kitchen.

"I'm bar," he said to an elderly Chinese women who stone-walled him with a glare. "Bar?" he said to a big-bosomed girl in a white uniform.

She gestured vaguely towards a door.

He walked through into the house proper. Some house. Marble floors. Overstuffed couches. A series of luxurious rooms all leading into other luxurious rooms. And finally a glass wall overlooking a black-bottomed swimming pool, at the end of which was a curved black marble bar.

A frantic Rocky waved to him. "Hey, man, thank Christ you're here," he said, busily unloading boxes of booze. "What took you so long?"

"I had to find it, didn't I?" Wes complained. "Fucking Bel Air is like one of those mazes in an amusement park. You told me Bellagio. It goes on for fucking ever in every direction. You're lucky I'm here at all."

"You really crack me up," said Rocky, who looked like a poor man's Sylvester Stallone – hence the name. "Only *you* could get your ass lost in Bel Air."

"And only *you* give out shit directions," Wes responded. "I wasted gas driving up and down."

"Do me a favour – get to work," Rocky said, shoving a heavy box of wine in his direction. "We've only got an hour before blast-off." He lowered his voice. "There's a mixed box I've put together, it's over there." He gestured. "Get it out to your car whenever seems like a good time. I'll come by tomorrow to split it."

"Why *my* car?" Wes asked peevishly.

"'Cos it's *me* they'll be watching."

Sure. If anyone was to be caught stealing booze it was good old Wes Money.

Screw Rocky. He must think he was some schmuck. But so what? He'd do it. Life was a risk, and in a kind of perverse way he enjoyed taking 'em.

*

Silver discarded five outfits before deciding on chiffon purple harem pants, a floating top embroidered with gold, and a long Cleopatra wig. She looked exotic, like an Egyptian queen. Especially when she added solid gold slave bracelets, giant hoop earrings, and several huge diamond rings.

She hadn't touched a drink in months, but she certainly wasn't an alcoholic, and she quite fancied a glass of ice cold Cristal to put her in the mood for the evening's activities. Decisively she picked up the intercom and buzzed the kitchen.

Her houseman, Vladimir, elbowed the Chinese woman out of the way to answer his mistress's call. The woman almost fell, and cursed in Chinese about rude American pigs. Vladimir, who spoke a little Chinese (thanks to a five-year live-in relationship with a Chinese waiter who unfortunately fell off Santa Monica pier and drowned) ignored her insults and cooed into the phone.

"Yes, madame?" His English was almost impeccable except for his mispronunciation of *w* as *v*. "Vat can I get for you?"

"Champagne, Vladimir. Very cold. Very soon."

"Yes, madame." He grabbed Wes, who was passing by on his way to the back door with the box of contraband carefully prepared by Rocky. "You!" he said sharply.

"Who, me?" replied Wes innocently, thinking – *Oh fuck, now I'm caught.*

"Champagne. For Madame. *Pronto.*" (The *pronto* came from an Italian waiter who shared his affections for two nights and screamed *pronto, pronto* every time he came, which was often.)

"Madame who?" asked Wes patiently, thinking the Russian queen probably meant Madame Wong who was glaring at both of them, and what had *she* done to deserve champagne?

"Madame Silver," said Vladimir, raising a scornful eyebrow at this cretin's ignorance. "Cristal. In a Baccarat glass. And make sure it's icy. Hurry, hurry!"

"I'll be right back," Wes said cheerfully, realizing the game was not yet up. He hurried out to his car with the box and loaded it into his trunk.

When he returned to the kitchen, Vladimir screamed, "Vere is it?"

"What?"

"The champagne for Madame."

"Oh. That. Just gettin' it."

"Now!" Vladimir leaped excitedly in the air. In his youth he had trained as a ballet dancer – long before he defected to the West and freedom.

Wes mock saluted. "Yes *sir, Kapitan.* One glass of bubbly comin' right up."

★

The 1965 Mustang spluttered to a full stop halfway up Coldwater Canyon.

"Like I don't believe this!" Heaven screeched.

"Jesus!" groaned Eddie.

"This can't be happening," she yelled, jumping from the car.

"Jesus!" repeated Eddie, following her. "It was runnin' fine when I picked you up."

"Like what are you gonna do?" she demanded, venom in her voice.

"What are *we* gonna do," he corrected.

79

"It's *your* fault," she pointed out. "It's *your* dumb car." She kicked the side of the old Mustang with a sharp booted toe.

"Don't do that!" he objected.

"I will if I want," she replied in a childish sing-song, and for good measure she gave the car another solid kick.

He was incensed. "Cut it out. What's the matter with you?"

"I'm pissed off," she said. "I'm *really* pissed off."

"You think *I'm* dancin'?"

They glared at each other. Heaven, with her spiky multi-coloured locks. Eddie, with his black hair greased back in true sixties style.

"This is like the bummer of all time," she announced flatly.

Eddie headed for the hood of the car. "Don't worry 'bout a thing. I'll fix it," he said, less hopeful than he sounded.

With an exasperated sigh she sank down on the grass verge muttering, "Yeah. You an' who else?"

*

Silver did not like being kept waiting. When she wanted something she wanted it *now*. Ten minutes had elapsed since her request for champagne, and her taste buds were on full alert. With a snort of annoyance she buzzed the kitchen a second time, and Vladimir, who was knee deep in Chinese caterers, grabbed the phone.

"Are you keeping me waiting, Vladimir?" she asked icily.

"*Never*, madame."

"Then *why* are you still in the kitchen?"

"The bartender is on his vay up to you at this very minute, madame," Vladimir lied.

"I should hope so." She replaced the receiver with a crash.

Vladimir muttered ominous words of Russian under his breath. Reverting to his mother language relieved him when he was about to undergo a stress attack. "Bar!" he screamed loudly.

Five minutes later Wes was found. Vladimir equipped him with a silver tray, a Baccarat glass brimming with chilled Cristal, and dispatched him upstairs to face Madame's wrath. Vladimir knew when to make himself scarce.

Whistling a Beatles' song as he negotiated the sweeping staircase, Wes reflected on the vagaries of life. That very morning he had woken up in a little house in the Valley with a cheap dyed blonde. Now he was heading – tray in hand –

towards the bedroom of one of the biggest television stars in America, who lived in a frigging mansion! Pity he wouldn't be sharing *her* bed. Although he would sooner it was Whitney Valentine Cable. Now *there* was a real stunner. Not that he watched television much — just sports and late movies if he was in the mood. In fact, he wasn't quite sure what Silver Anderson looked like. All he had was a vague memory of a big dark woman staring out at him from countless magazine covers.

Wes was in for a surprise. Silver Anderson was dark all right, with her long jet hair and almond-shaped heavily outlined eyes. But big she wasn't. She was small and slender, almost petite. And beautiful in a dramatic and compelling way. He eyeballed her as she flung open the door of her bedroom as soon as he finished knocking.

She gave him an icy stare, and said coldly, "Exactly *how* long does it take to pour *one* glass of champagne and bring it up *one* flight of stairs?"

Walking past her into the purple wonderland of a bedroom, he looked for a place to put the tray. "Search me," he said cheerily. "Next time I'll put a stopwatch on it."

"I beg your pardon?" she said, hardly believing his cheek.

He spotted a mirrored dressing table and figured that was as good a place as any to dump the tray. As he placed it down, their eyes met in the mirror, and for a split second they held each other's gaze.

Silver saw an unruly attractive man, with a certain restlessness about him and a don't-give-a-damn attitude.

Wes saw a good-looking, if slightly older woman — and with unusual sensitivity for him, he sensed a mixture of need and loneliness coming off her in waves. The combination, with her mature beauty, was quite appealing.

Sexual chemistry was strong in the air.

He knew there was a moment to be seized, only it wasn't *his* place to seize it. *She* had to be the one, and if she didn't make a move *he* certainly wasn't going to set himself up for rejection by some big-time television star. It was probably all his imagination anyway.

He gave her an opening shot, just to play the odds. "Can I get you anything else?" he asked, his words loaded with innuendo.

Silver was no fool. The last thing she needed was some deadbeat bartender hitting on her. She iced him off with her eyes and a cold "No."

The moment was over. Leaving the star's bedroom he returned downstairs.

Vladimir pounced on him. "Vas Madame happy?" he asked anxiously.

"Yeah," replied Wes easily. "Why?" The Russian queen had obviously expected him to get torn off a strip. Tough tit. He was unscathed.

Or was he?

Chapter 17

Rule One: Smile for the photographers.

Rule Two: Be charming for the television cameras.

Rule Three: Always leave a good impression among the staff. They are the people who made you famous in the first place, so never forget them.

Whitney Valentine Cable knew all the rules by heart. And so she should. They were *her* rules, and she abided by them religiously.

She alighted from Chuck Nielson's red Porsche, and allowed the paparazzi to capture the widest smile in America. Chuck, who was boyishly handsome although he would never see thirty-five again, joined her, and the two of them posed.

The paparazzi clicked desperately. This was a hot picture, and one the entire world would want to see. The previous year Whitney Valentine Cable and Chuck Nielson had been an item – an on/off affair of epic proportions, complete with public fights and equally public reconciliations. Then they split, and Chuck stole the French actress wife of an English director – which made wonderful copy; while Whitney dated a series of different men – which also made wonderful copy. Now it appeared they were back together. A paparazzi's dream! Second only to Whitney reuniting with Mannon Cable.

Slowly the two of them moved inside, and Jeanne Wolf for *Entertainment Tonight* greeted them effusively.

Meanwhile, Howard and Poppy Soloman drew up in a very long, very flashy limousine. Howard failed to see why he should drive himself at night when he could use a studio limo any time he pleased.

The paparazzi failed to spring to attention, which aggravated Howard and devastated Poppy.

A lone flash captured their consternation. And then all the photographers surged forward to focus on Michael Caine and his beautiful wife, Shakira.

Howard and Poppy entered the house, and the first person they saw was Whitney, sensational in a white strapless dress. Hollywood kisses were exchanged. Howard inhaled her scent and wondered if she wanted him as much as he wanted her.

"I've been thinking about a project you'd be just right for," he blurted, with a manic twitch.

Her gaze was direct and interested. "Have you, Howard?"

"Are we speaking of the Weissman script?" Poppy joined in.

He turned to her with a frown. What the fuck was she talking about? "What Weissman script?"

She clung to his arm. Poppy Soloman had decided that as the wife of a studio head she must make it her business not to get left out of anything. "The script on your desk, darling. I read it yesterday. Whitney would be *wonderful* as the girl. It's such *off* casting." She planted a wifely kiss on his cheek. "You're brilliant to think of her."

He was brilliant and he didn't know it! His comment to Whitney had just been a ploy to talk to her later. He had no project she was right for. Now he had the Weissman script. He'd better have someone read it for him fast and find out if there *was* anything for Whitney in it.

Howard did not read scripts. It was too time-consuming. He had three readers whose opinions he trusted, and they analysed every story and gave him a succinct two-page synopsis. Poppy was not one of them. He wouldn't trust Poppy's opinion of Army Archerd's column in *Variety*, let alone a script!

"Yeah, Whit," he said quickly. "I wanna have a word with you about it later."

Whitney smiled. She hadn't been wrong about Howard; he was interested in her as an actress *and* as a woman. Perfect.

Chuck Nielson appeared at her side with two glasses of orange juice; neither of them drank alcohol – one of the few things they had in common.

Howard was disturbed to see her back in his company. Chuck Nielson was a low-life and trouble. He specialized in stealing other men's wives, and he couldn't get himself arrested as far as starring in a movie was concerned. Nobody wanted to hire him. In the past he'd starred in a couple of hits. But that was five years ago, and in Hollywood memories are notoriously short.

The two men greeted each other affectionately – macho slaps on the back and mild insults. Poppy brightened considerably. She still thought Chuck was a star, which just showed how much *she* knew.

While she spoke animatedly to Chuck, Howard threw Whitney a low aside. "What are you doing back with *him*?"

She shrugged. She probably had the most beautiful shoulders in the world. "Desperation," she whispered. "I couldn't get a date for tonight and I didn't want to miss seeing you."

Howard's ego pumped. Whether the Weissman script was right or not he would make sure it was rewritten to accommodate the fabulous Miss Whitney Valentine Cable. And when she starred in the movie for Orpheus Studios he would also make sure she dropped the Cable. Who needed to be reminded of Mannon every time he heard her name?

*

Outside the gates of Silver Anderson's estate, Mannon and Melanie-Shanna were fighting as they sat – captive prisoners in his blue Rolls-Royce – trapped in a line of expensive cars waiting to gain entry to the party. They were at least eight cars away from the uniformed guard at the gate, and Mannon was steaming.

"If we'd left home on time," he said angrily, "we wouldn't be caught in this mob scene."

"*I* was ready," Melanie-Shanna protested, not prepared to take the blame for everything.

"Then why didn't you make sure that *I* was?" he shouted.

She shut up. She had learned with Mannon that sometimes silence was the only way to handle his frequent temper tantrums. To the outside world being married to a superstar seemed like a dream. But the reality was far different. Sure there were advantages. Money. Position. And sharing the bed of a man millions of females wanted to sleep with.

There were plenty of disadvantages too. No privacy. No

peace. The ever-present army of people to tend to his every need. The relentless come-on from every single woman he ever met. The bad moods only *she* witnessed. The insecurities – an affliction suffered by every actor, be he superstar or bit player.

Mannon was right at the peak of his career now. Melanie-Shanna shuddered to think what he would be like should his star ever dim. She hoped he would be thrilled when she told him about the baby.

She wasn't sure he would be.

*

And so they came.

A legendary movie star with a rugged profile, foreign wife, and dead career.

A younger movie star (but only by a decade or two) with a starlet girlfriend, and a nearly dead career.

A cheating producer and his socialite wife.

A cheating wife with her gay husband.

A young hot actor with an even hotter coke habit.

A pretty young actress who only liked other pretty young actresses.

Nora was pleased by the turn-out. Everything was proceeding without a hitch. The only slight hiccough was Silver's non-appearance. A late entrance wasn't a major tragedy, only Nora wished the star would get her act together. Several times she had popped upstairs to check that all was well. Silver, dressed and ready, sat by a large picture window in the bedroom gazing out at the magnificent view, smoking a cigarette. Los Angeles at night, as seen from high in the hills, was a fairyland of twinkling lights – Silver seemed mesmerized.

At nine o'clock – the party started at eight – Nora trekked upstairs again.

"Who's here?" Silver asked anxiously.

"Everyone," Nora replied. "You can come down now."

"In a minute. Don't rush me."

Nora decided it was time to put the pressure on. "*Now*," she said pointedly. "Otherwise they'll start going home."

Silver sighed, and arose obediently. Moving over to a full-length mirror she inspected the image.

"Perfect," flattered Nora.

Silver took a deep breath. "I should hope so. I work hard enough to create it."

One last, lingering glance and she walked towards the door.

Silver Anderson was having a birthday party. She didn't want to miss it.

Chapter 18

"Are you sure you want to do this?" Jack asked quizzically as his Ferrari negotiated the winding curves of Bel Air.

"Yes," Clarissa replied curtly. "Why wouldn't I?"

He felt he was being tested and he wasn't sure he liked it. "Because," he replied slowly, "parties have never been your favourite way to spend an evening. Especially not big glitzy bashes filled with press."

She smoothed down the skirt of her tailored brown gaberdine suit. "I didn't say this was my favourite way to spend an evening." She spoke in a measured tone. "I said I was interested in meeting your sister. I'm sure you must understand my curiosity."

No. He didn't understand at all.

"You've never really explained why you don't get along," she persisted.

And I have no intention of doing so now, he thought.

"We're different people," he said shortly.

"I know *that*."

"So if you know it, let's drop the subject."

"As you wish."

They drove the rest of the way in silence.

★

When Jade partied she threw herself into the spirit of the evening. She knew that a night spent in Antonio's company was not exactly a cultural event. It was more a blast, an experience, a let-it-all-hang-out-and-get-down! So she dressed accordingly in tight black satin pants tucked into matching boots. A long black shirt cinched at her twenty-two-inch waist with a wide belt. Fake jewellery galore from Butler & Wilson in London: gifts from Mark – he had a surprising knack for picking out just the right pieces. In retrospect she thought that maybe another woman had chosen them. Who knew? He no doubt had mistresses everywhere; she had just been his New York connection.

Piling her shaggy copper hair on top of her head, she secured it with a couple of pins, deftly arranging strands to fall artfully free. Then she applied tawny makeup, and emphasized her widely spaced gold-flecked eyes with brown shadow and thick kohl pencil. Plenty of lip gloss over a gold-toned lipstick, and she was ready when Antonio and three of his friends came piling into her apartment laden with flowers, record albums, bottles of wine and an assortment of gourmet Chinese tidbits picked up at Chinn Chinn on Sunset Boulevard.

"I thought we were going out," she said, as they proceeded to make themselves at home.

"We are, we are, precious," insisted Antonio, instructing his minions. One to the kitchen to warm the snacks in the microwave. One to the bar to open the wine. And a third to arrange the profusion of glorious flowers.

She began to laugh. "This is an invasion," she protested.

"A welcome." Antonio showed off his neat, precise little grin. "To Los Angeles, *bellissima*."

"Won't we be late for the party?"

He pursed his lips. "Who cares? Nothing happens until *Antonio* arrives!"

His companions all nodded their agreement as they fussed around.

Antonio kissed the tips of his fingers. "You look a dream, *cara*. A death in the family it suit you."

"You're *bad*, Antonio."

"But of course!"

"*Very* bad."

"Naturally!"

*

Nora greeted Mannon with a warm hug. "*You* are a prince," she whispered.

"No, I'm a putz," he responded. "Have you any idea how long I've been sitting in my goddamn car waiting to get in here?"

"I'm sorry."

"So am I."

She summoned a waiter. "What'll you have?"

"Scotch. You'd better make it a double."

Melanie-Shanna stood silently by his side. Nobody asked *her* what she would like to drink. Nobody cared, as long as Mister Superstar was taken care of.

"I'd like a glass of white wine," she told the waiter quietly.

Mannon was still complaining. Nora listened attentively, then teased him and flattered him, and gradually Melanie-Shanna felt him relax. Until Whitney, his ex-wife, appeared, and Melanie-Shanna felt herself go hot and cold, for they had never met.

"Christ!" Mannon muttered to Nora. "What's *she* doing here?"

"I didn't know you two weren't talking," Nora said.

"We're talking," he replied gruffly, although he wasn't sure if they were or not. The last time he'd seen her she had been distinctly cool. In fact, she had brushed him off completely. Well . . . understandable, really. He had just had a piece published in *People* where he called her a career-mad starlet, and Chuck Nielson a washed-up beach bum.

Thank Christ she was no longer with *him*. And as these thoughts crossed his mind, Chuck materialized beside her, and the very idea of *his* Whitney with Chuck Nielson *again* drove Mannon wild with fury.

"Fuck!" he mumbled under his breath.

"What?" asked Melanie-Shanna.

"Nothing," came the surly reply.

They were on a collision course. There was no way they could avoid coming face to face.

Mannon steeled himself for confrontation.

*

"I'm going," Heaven said impatiently, rising from the grass verge and brushing dead leaves and debris from her long overcoat.

"Whattya gonna do — fly?" demanded Eddie, as he fiddled with the engine of the Mustang, getting nowhere fast.

"I'll thumb a ride," she announced, now determined to get to her mother's party.

"You can't do that, it's not safe."

"Ohhh! Listen to daddy!" she mocked. "I *can* look after myself, y'know."

He straightened up. "Yeah — you get a ride from one of those mass murderer freaks an' you'll *really* be able t'look after your-self."

"Oh, *sure*. Every one of these cars goin' by is just *crammed* with serial killers waitin' to grab little ole me!"

"Cut the crap," he said angrily. "You're not takin' any rides on your own. I'll leave the Mustang here an' come with you."

"About time!" she huffed.

*

Working the party kept Wes busy. Whatever Rocky was paying him wasn't enough. He grabbed a couple of beers behind the scenes, but basically he was sober. Well, he had to be, didn't he? There was a lot of action going down.

First of all Rocky was operating a lucrative sideline selling coke to a number of studio hot shots. And once the word got around, business was brisk. Rocky brought him in on a com-mission basis, and between the two of them they scammed the party pretty good.

Behind the bar out by the swimming pool, Wes didn't get a lot of opportunity to observe Silver Anderson. But he saw her make a dramatic entrance at nine o'clock, and the assorted press went crazy.

"Is she married?" he asked.

"Naw," Rocky drawled. "The fag in the kitchen tells me she has a different boyfriend every week."

"Who's the one this week?"

Rocky belched. "What the fuck do y'think I am – a gossip hack?"

They both stopped talking to observe Whitney Valentine Cable as she undulated past.

"Now *there's* a broad." Rocky smacked his thick lips with relish. "I could stick it to that one any way, any day."

"Yeah," agreed Wes.

Later he sold a gram of coke to Chuck Nielson. He felt like asking him about his gorgeous girlfriend, only he didn't. Wes knew how far to go and with whom.

*

Nora couldn't believe her luck when Jack Python arrived with Clarissa Browning. All she had to do was get him with Silver for a picture, and the front pages of the world's press would be hers. The brother and sister had never been photographed together.

She greeted Jack effusively and tried to guide him in the right direction.

He shook her off with his customary charm. "Why don't you take Clarissa to meet Silver, she can't wait."

"What about you, Jack? Aren't you going to wish your sister a happy birthday?"

"Maybe later, Nora." He gave Clarissa a gentle push in the right direction. "Off you go. That's what you came here for, isn't it?"

Spotting Howard, he strolled over.

"You're the *last* person I expected to see here," Howard said in surprise.

"Me too," Jack agreed. "Hopefully I won't be staying."

*

"Hello, Mannon," Whitney said in her silky voice, her mouth downturned, no dazzling smile in sight.

"Whitney." He nodded curtly. "Chuck."

Once, the three of them had been close friends. They had lived in neighbouring beach houses and spent all their time together. In fact Mannon could remember going on location and asking Chuck to look after Whitney for him. Ha! What a laugh! Chuck had looked after her all right: he was probably trying to get her in his well-used bed even then.

"How're they hangin', pal?" asked Chuck.

The bum was stoned as usual. Whitney loathed drugs. Why was she with him again?

"Have you met my wife?" Mannon asked tightly, and introduced Melanie-Shanna, who realized immediately this was an uncomfortable reunion.

"Melanie," said Chuck, swaying slightly. "What an unexpected pleasure. You're lovely. But then my old buddy always did have great taste."

"Thank you."

Mannon gripped her by the arm. What was she thanking the creep for?

Whitney began to edge away. She looked stunning. She always did. Melanie-Shanna was pretty, but every woman paled in comparison to Whitney.

Chuck, sensing Whitney wanted to split, dutifully followed her. "Nice seein' ya, pal," he said to Mannon. "And I liked meeting *you*." He gave Melanie-Shanna a burning look. "Come and visit us at the beach sometime."

"Goddamn moron," muttered Mannon, watching them move off.

"He seems pleasant enough," Melanie-Shanna said, knowing, even as she spoke, that it was the wrong thing to say.

"Jesus!" Mannon rolled his eyes. "When will you learn!"

*

Silver enjoyed playing star hostess. She circulated and smiled and flirted. She posed with the cast from *Palm Springs*. She gave witty quotes to George Christy from the *Hollywood Reporter*. She chatted to friends and acquaintances. Eventually she instructed Nora to get rid of the press. Their constant questions and the bright lights of the television crews stationed by the door – they weren't allowed beyond that – were beginning to annoy her.

"I want them to get a picture of you and Jack," Nora fretted.

"Who?"

"Your brother."

"Oh God! What's *he* doing here?"

"He's with Clarissa Browning."

"Hmmm . . . Her taste must be slipping."

When it came to family Silver was not a warm and wonderful person. Once Nora had asked her about it. "We're not close," Silver had admitted. That could be the understatement of the year.

Nora had been observing Jack Python. He always made absolutely sure there was a roomful of people between him and his sister. Obviously he had no intention of getting anywhere near her.

*

"Can we have lunch?" Howard asked Whitney. His palms were slippery with sweat as he watched her contemplate her reply.

"Is this about the movie you want me to do?"

"The film and uh . . . other things."

"What other things, Howard?" she teased, and her down-turned mouth broke into a wide smile.

"Don't get me hot, baby. I think you and I have been heading in this direction for some time."

"I *can* have lunch," she decided sweetly. "I'll bring my agent."

"Your agent my ass."

"Does that mean his presence is not required?"

"When?" he asked urgently.

"Let me call you."

Howard glanced outside. Poppy had Chuck Nielson pinned against the bar. "What are you doing with that stoned Nielson schmuck again?" he asked, leaning closer to her smooth outdoor beauty.

"He's convenient."

"He's also crazy."

"I can handle him."

"I hope so."

Nora cut in. "Do you mind, Howard? Whitney dear, the press will kill for a photo of you with Silver. *Newsweek* wants it for their 'Newsmakers' page."

"Sure," Whitney said pleasantly, kissing Howard on the cheek. "Be patient," she whispered. "I'll call you on Monday."

*

Mannon said, "What were you talking to Whitney about?"

"Orpheus wants her," Howard replied. It wasn't a complete lie. According to Poppy there was a suitable script, and besides – *he* was Orpheus and *he* wanted her. To hell with his twenty-year friendship with Mannon.

*

Heaven and Eddie got a ride down the Canyon with a couple in a station wagon who were going into Hollywood to see their first porno movie. They were a young couple, and tried to persuade the teenagers to accompany them.

"Forget it," Heaven said when they hit Sunset, having encouraged them all the way.

Outside The Beverly Hills Hotel, by the bus stop, they hitched a lift with two girls heading for a party at the beach. They got off at the West Gate into Bel Air, and walked for twenty minutes before they flagged a security patrol car. The two guards listened to their story and took them up into the hills, letting them off right outside the gates to Silver's mansion.

"Some place!" exclaimed Eddie, as Heaven informed the sceptical guard who she was.

"Yeah," she agreed. "I guess it's okay."

"Why don't you live here?" Eddie asked as they traipsed up the driveway to the house – having got the go-ahead from the guard.

"I dunno," she said vaguely. "I like it where I am."

She didn't care to mention that her mother had never suggested she move in. Not that she wanted to.

"Jeez!" said Eddie. "I'd be here like a rocket!"

As they neared the house they could hear music playing and the clink of cutlery and glasses.

"I guess dinner is served," Heaven joked. "Silver is into all that formal crap."

"Are you sure we're dressed okay?" Eddie asked, anxiously tugging at his black leather studded jacket.

"Whadda we care?" Heaven said defiantly. "She's lucky I'm here."

They entered the house. Two photographers walked by them on their way out. They did a double-take, but Heaven was used to that. She wasn't exactly Sally Prom. With her spiky multi-coloured hair, heavily streaked makeup and outlandish outfit, she looked like a cross between Twisted Sister, Rod Stewart and Cher.

She was wearing her red micro-dress with a huge overcoat. The dress was cut out in strategic places, exposing much bare flesh. On her feet were lace-up black boots covering zebra-striped tights. Cheap plastic jewellery jangled from her person like baubles from a Christmas tree. One ear — pierced four times — held four different earrings.

"Holy shit!" Eddie exclaimed as they stopped and took stock of their surroundings. "This place is a freakin' palace!"

"Yeah," Heaven said confidently. "And I'm the visiting princess!"

Chapter 19

Jade, Antonio and friends demolished four bottles of red wine and all of the delicious Chinese tidbits before leaving for the party at ten. Antonio's companions were an animated group. One makeup artist with a pageboy bob and oriental eyes. One hair stylist with the thinnest body Jade had ever seen. And one U.S.C. film student, who was obviously Antonio's latest love.

The student, who had only consumed one glass of wine, drove Antonio's Cadillac Seville. They entered Bel Air by the West Gate, and immediately got lost. There were loud shrieks of "This way! That way!" Contradicted with "*Down* the hill, not up. We're going around in circles."

Jade had no idea where she was, it was all foreign territory to her.

Al Jarreau blared from the car stereo as they drove up and down the hills.

They found the house by accident an hour later.

The guard at the gate glared suspiciously into the car.

"Spray perfume, darling," Antonio stage-whispered. "Otherwise he get stoned just breathing our air!"

Jade obliged with a quick spritz of Opium. The Cadillac was alive with the fumes of the joint Antonio's friends had been enjoying.

"Thank you!" squealed the makeup artist.

The guard consulted his guest list, found Antonio's name, and waved them on.

*

When Heaven and Eddie swaggered into the party, Jack had just persuaded Clarissa to leave. Coming across his errant niece on her way in stopped him abruptly. "I don't believe this!" he said.

"Uncle Jack. What are *you* doing here?"

"God knows. More important, why are *you* here?"

"Beats me," she shrugged. "It seemed like a good idea at the time!" She giggled. "This is Eddie. Y'know, I told you about him. I sing with his group."

Jack shook hands formally with the dark-haired boy, and duly introduced Clarissa to them both.

Heaven was impressed. She had heard about Jack's affair with the famous actress, yet she had never met her.

Clarissa was amused by the girl. "So *you're* Heaven," she said, looking her over. "A most unusual name."

"Yup. That's me."

"I like your hair."

"Thanks."

"And your coat."

"Got it at this brilliant place on Melrose."

"You must take me there."

"God! *Me* take *you*!"

Clarissa nodded. "If you're free sometime, we'll go shopping and have lunch."

"Wow! If *I'm* free!"

"Does Silver know you're coming?" Jack interrupted.

"Like I guess so. Nora invited me."

Jack wondered why Nora would do that. He could hardly imagine Silver begging that her daughter be present. She had never taken any notice of Heaven before, why would she start now? Maybe, on her birthday, she'd had a change of heart. Wouldn't *that* be something?

"We're going," he said. "Try and have a good time – although somehow I don't think this is quite your scene."

Heaven pulled on the sleeve of his jacket. "Uncle Jack. Eddie's car broke down comin' over the canyon. How'll we get back to the Valley?"

She was exasperating, but he loved her anyway. "Is that my problem?"

She giggled. "It is now." One thing about Uncle Jack she knew for sure – he was always there for her, which is more than she could say for her mother.

He groped in his pocket and produced some bills. Peeling off a couple of fifties he said, "Have Nora call a cab when you're ready to leave." He peered at his watch. "And don't make it too long. Your curfew's still twelve, isn't it?"

"Yup."

"Don't break it."

"Nope."

"And if you do something normal with your hair we'll take you out to dinner one night."

"What's normal?" she asked innocently.

He touched her cheek affectionately. "*You're* certainly not. I love you anyway, kid." He nodded at Eddie, and said curtly, "Look after her, or you'll have *me* to reckon with."

"Yes sir!" replied Eddie, standing to attention.

"Isn't he the best?" Heaven said as she watched him go. "And you know something – she's nice too. Like not big-time or any of that film star crap. Don't you agree?"

Eddie wasn't listening. His eyes were popping. He was star-tripping and loving every minute.

*

"How do you like my niece?" Jack asked, putting his arm

95

protectively around Clarissa's shoulder as he guided her towards the front door.

"I think she's a lost little girl."

"She needs her mother," Jack said tightly. "Only she's never going to get her. Silver lives only for herself."

"Maybe she has to," Clarissa replied. "She's created the image – every day she must fuel the fire."

"What a wise lady," he said, "for an actress!"

He handed his parking ticket to an attentive valet who leaped forward. "Coming right up, Mr Python."

"And you are a rude man, Mr Python," Clarissa mocked.

He studied her long pale face and the intense eyes. "Let me take you home and show you just how rude I can be, *Miz* Browning."

She nodded and allowed the anticipation to begin.

The parking valets were not expecting any new arrivals. They were busy jockeying the cars for departing guests when Antonio and his group drove up.

"Is everyone leaving?" Antonio asked, jumping from the car and flapping his hands.

"No sir," replied a surfer type. "Just a few people."

"Dahlings!" Antonio spotted Jack and Clarissa.

They broke away from each other and greeted the famous photographer. He was – as usual – surrounded by a group of eccentric misfits who came piling out of his car. Among them was a great-looking girl Jack knew he had seen somewhere before. He did a classic double-take, and immediately wished he hadn't, for Clarissa missed nothing.

The girl was tall and slim, with direct, challenging eyes, a sensual body, and a tumble of copper hair piled on top of her head. Her eyes flicked right past his intent gaze as if he didn't exist. Jack was used to more attention than that.

"Your car, Mr Python," said the parking valet, holding open the door.

"*Divine* to see you both," sighed Antonio. "And such a *surprise!*"

Jack climbed into his Ferrari, revved the engine, and shot off a little too fast.

Clarissa rested her hand on his thigh. "Home," she said coolly. "And get that bimbo off your mind. You are no longer stud of the year. Remember?"

How well she knew him.

*

"Let's get out of here," Mannon said.

"Any time you want," Melanie-Shanna responded obediently, anxious to be alone with him so she could tell him their good news.

Mannon had endured more than enough of viewing his ex-wife across a crowded party. He wanted her back so badly he could taste it, and he was in no mood to watch her with the likes of Chuck Nielson.

He planned to call his lawyer first thing in the morning and hammer out a settlement to offer Melanie-Shanna. He wanted to be fair about it — she was a sweet kid, but not for him. Things had to be done at once, even if it did cost him. And then he would be free to concentrate on getting Whitney back.

★

Nora saw Heaven first. At least, she assumed it must be Heaven, for who else could possibly turn up looking like that? She hurried over, almost speechless, and for Nora that was something. "I hardly recognized you," she said.

Heaven grinned cheekily and turned in a circle, her long overcoat trailing behind her. "I'm an original!" she said proudly. "So's Eddie."

Eddie nodded, hungry eyes still scanning the room.

"I can see that," Nora remarked dryly. She hadn't seen Heaven in over a year. The child had certainly changed. Silver would be horrified.

"Eddie an' I, we've got our own group," Heaven confided. "He plays the guitar. I sing an' write all our stuff. We've got a couple of other guys involved — like a drummer an' a second guitar. If you'd given me the word we could've played here tonight."

"Not quite suitable," Nora said quickly. "Have you seen your . . . er . . . Silver?"

"Nope." Heaven ran her hands through her spiked hair, pulling at it to make sure it stood at attention.

"I'll take you over," Nora volunteered. She knew it had to be done, and she was the one to do it.

"Sure," Heaven said casually. "C'mon, Eddie."

The two of them followed Nora across the room, and outside to the tented patio where Silver held court at a table for ten. She was in the middle of telling a joke, and the other people at the table listened with rapt attention — waiting for the punch line. "I don't recognize Elvis," Silver concluded, barely controlling her own laughter. "But the one in the middle is Willie Nelson!"

The entire table broke up.

Nora took the opportunity to grab her attention. "Look who's here," she said.

Silver turned graciously, ready to greet yet another power broker or fellow star. When she saw Heaven she visibly blanched. "God God!" she said. "What have you *done* to yourself? You look *dreadful!*"

Only Nora observed the flash of pain which flitted quickly across the girl's face. And then a rebellious expression took over, the amber eyes hardened, and Heaven blurted, "Gee, mom, nothing changes. You're still as old-fashioned as ever."

Silver didn't like *that*. She stood up from the table to prevent her guests from hearing any more, and said in a low voice, "And you're as rude as ever, I see."

"I guess it runs in the family, mommy dearest," Heaven replied defiantly.

"Don't call me that," Silver hissed, and glared at Nora as if to say — *I told you so*.

Nora shrugged. "C'mon kids," she said, "I'll get you some food."

Eddie was not to be shifted so quickly. He stuck his hand in Silver's direction and said in an awe-struck voice, "Miss Anderson, I love your work, you are the very best."

This was news to Heaven, who shot him a filthy look. Eddie. *Her* Eddie. Her confidant and friend. And as of that very afternoon — her lover. He was behaving like a star-struck fan. And to her mother of all people! Outrage enveloped her.

Eddie stood there with a stupid sloppy grin on his face, while Silver bestowed the royal handshake, and even managed a charming smile.

"Garbage city," Heaven muttered to herself, and began to edge away.

"Aren't you going to wish your mother a happy birthday?" Nora said pointedly.

"Oh yeah — Happy birthday, mom." She raced for the bar, leaving Eddie behind — what a geek!

*

By chance, Howard had purchased a small glassine envelope of what he was assured was first-rate Peruvian cocaine. A young actor he knew assured him. And since Howard's connection at the studio (a rather flaky female production executive) was not altogether reliable — there were days when she never even bothered to turn up – he decided to accept the actor's offer of a "great deal". Little did Howard know he was paying twice the amount the actor had given to one of the barmen. He made the buy discreetly, underneath a palm tree out by the pool. "This isn't for me," he explained to the actor, who couldn't have cared less. "It's for a friend."

He felt secure with the coke stashed on his person. So secure, in fact, that he saw no reason why he shouldn't have a small snort on the premises – just to rev himself up.

Finding an empty toilet in the pool house, he laid out a suitable amount of the white powder. It wasn't that he needed it or anything like that, he just felt like testing out his new source – making sure it was primo.

*

"Give me a vodka martini," Heaven said to the barman. She had no idea what a vodka martini was, but it sounded like a sophisticated enough choice.

Rocky checked her out. She looked like she could be a customer. He was carrying Quaaludes and other assorted goodies apart from cocaine. As he fixed her drink he mumbled, "Y'can score anythin' else y'like if you've got the honey."

"What?"

"Honey – money."

She wanted to giggle. Silver, with all her fancy trappings, had ended up with a dealer behind her bar!

"I'm not in the mood for buying," she said haughtily. And then she remembered the money Uncle Jack had handed her, and thought – *Why not?* It certainly wouldn't cost a hundred dollars to get a cab back to the Valley.

"I'll change my mind. Do you have any joints?"

"How many?"

Shrugging vaguely she said, "Three or four."

"Ya look like a rock star, an' ya buy like a kid."

Heaven propped her arms on the bar. "Do you *really* think I look like a rock star?" she asked eagerly.

Rocky, adopting the Stallone stance, said, "Yo, pretty lady."

She gave him a second look. He was of medium height and muscular, with drooping eyes, a funny crooked nose, and a shock of longish black hair. He was an older man, he must be at least thirty, but so what? Eddie was behaving like a jerk-off. He had joined the court of Silver, and a quick glance across the room confirmed that he was *still* hanging onto her mother's every stupid word. "Thanks," she said. "I *am* a singer, only I can never get anyone to listen to my tapes."

"Poor pretty lady," Rocky crooned sympathetically. Lately he liked them younger and younger. This one looked positively illegal. If he wasn't so stoned he would go for her now. "I have a friend in the record biz," he added, thinking he could save her for another time.

"You do?" she asked hopefully.

"Oh yeah yeah yeah, I sure do. He's a good buddy. Maybe I can fix it for him to er . . . hear your tapes."

Her amber eyes sparkled. "Really?"

"If I can do – I will do." He winked suggestively.

"Two brandies," demanded a fat man in a too-tight cummerbund and rented tux.

"Comin' up," said Rocky agreeably. He scribbled his number on a paper napkin and slipped it to her. "Give me a call. Maybe I'll be your manager. I'm the kinda guy can make things happen."

She took the napkin and stuffed it in her pocket. He was probably full of crap. Most people, she had discovered early on in life, were full of crap.

*

Antonio and his group fussed around Jade, keeping her a part of their own private circle. "You're a new face in town," Antonio warned. "So, *cara*, we protect you."

"Come *on*," she laughed. "I'm the *last* person who needs protecting. I'm from New York – remember?"

"This is a place filled with beautiful women, but you, *bellissima*, are special."

Jade couldn't help smiling. Antonio the flatterer. He got some of his best pictures that way.

"Okay, okay. I guess I'm surrounded," she sighed grudgingly. "Only I want a running commentary on everyone and everything. For a start – who's that?" She pointed out Heaven, lounging defiantly against the bar hanging onto her vodka martini.

"Who indeed?" echoed Antonio, peering over. "*Another* new face, and one that's not been lifted either."

"She looks completely out of place," Jade remarked. She had already observed that the party was filled with impeccably groomed and well-coiffed women in expensive designer clothes.

"True," agreed Antonio. "And so young. José!" He snapped his fingers at the makeup artist with the careful pageboy bob and oriental eyes. "Bring the young lady over. She has the peculiar style. Maybe I photograph her."

José sprang to his feet.

Jade smiled. "Still collecting strays," she mused.

"It makes the life exciting," agreed Antonio.

Jade looked around the tented patio filled with tables. Dinner was over, and now the party guests table-hopped and danced to the strident disco music. Antonio had commandeered his own table, and he proceeded to point people out as they boogied past. He had a line of gossip on everyone. "*She* take the heroin." "*He* a bigamist." "*She* in the porno films." "*He* only like two women."

"Stop!" Jade held up her hand sternly. "I don't want to know any of this."

"Why?" inquired Antonio, quite hurt by her lack of interest. "Is true."

"I don't care."

"You *should* know these things now you live here, *cara*," he said huffily.

"Why?"

"Why . . . she ask me why . . .?" He trailed off as José brought Heaven to their table.

The girl was indeed an original. Very pretty. And young. Glowingly, vibrantly *young*.

*

Silver wanted the evening to end. Fortunately people were beginning to depart. She couldn't be more pleased. She had a strong desire to strangle Nora. Did the stupid woman honestly expect her to be thrilled and delighted by Jack's presence? Not to mention Heaven, who arrived late looking like a reject from a rock concert.

She had struggled long and hard to regain the title Silver Anderson – Superstar. And tonight was to have been her crowning triumph. Now everything was ruined by her daughter and her brother. Just the very sight of them put her in a bad mood, and what the hell did Nora think she was gaining by inviting them?

Poppy Soloman tapped her on the shoulder to say goodbye. "We *must* have lunch," Poppy gushed.

"I'm far too busy for lunch," Silver dismissed her crisply. Then, remembering that Poppy was married to Howard Soloman, and Howard *was* the head of Orpheus, she added, "Perhaps dinner." There was no reason, now she was a major television star again, that she couldn't return triumphantly to the big screen.

"I'll *give* a dinner for you," Poppy promised.

"What a nice idea." Silver warmed to the plump blonde with the pink and white complexion. They had hardly spoken before, although both realized the advantages of a dinner party in Silver Anderson's honour.

"I'll have *my* secretary call *your* secretary," Poppy said, well versed in Hollywood protocol.

"Do that," replied Silver graciously, and moved on to the next departing guest.

Chapter 20

Wes had back-ache. He surveyed the stragglers at the party and wished they would all go the fuck home. He was tired and fed-up, not even slightly bombed, while Rocky was stoned out of his head.

Rocky was a dangerous friend to have. He was heading for big trouble, and Wes had no intention of being dragged along for the ride. Selling a small amount of cocaine on the side was one thing, but as soon as Rocky realized he had more customers than he could handle, he made a call and dispatched Wes to the front gate to accept a fresh delivery. Some black dude in a white stretch limo arrived all set to join the party.

"No *way*," Wes told him. "It's a private event."

"C'mon, man, you look like y'can get me inside," the occupant of the limo coaxed. "There'll be somethin' sweet 'n' extra for you. I just *looove* that Silver Lady. She's got *reeeeeal* style."

"Sorry," Wes said firmly, accepting delivery and hurrying back up the drive before the guard at the gate became suspicious.

Rocky was way gone even then, and while he developed his lucrative sideline, Wes got to fix everything from a Marguerita to a frozen strawberry daiquiri. And he was pissed off. Rocky was making all the money while *he* was doing all the work. Fuck it! Rocky was treating him like a paid lackey, not a loyal friend who was kindly helping out.

Wes did not like fixing drinks for rich jerk-offs in dinner jackets and their ladies – if that was the right description. Most of the women had tight mouths, and anyone who knew a thing or two about the female sex knew if their mouths were tight their pussies were too. Waiting to get laid. The guys were so busy with their big deals and their drug habits, they didn't have time to service their old ladies. And usually the broad wasn't old *or* a lady.

Wes knew these things. He had worked enough bars around town and listened to enough stories.

Working a bar in a club was a whole different ball game. There, he was his own boss. He had attitude and authority – even a little bit of power. Working bar at a party it seemed he was just hired help. A servant. At everyone's beck and call.

Wes decided no more favours. He was nobody's errand boy.

*

"And so," Heaven continued, "like Eddie formed this group, an' I sing an' write the songs. And we're really, *really*, totally brilliant!"

"What do you call yourselves?" asked Jade.

"The Rats," Eddie joined in. Boy, was he having a good time! Not only had he got to meet Silver Anderson, now he was sitting talking to this fantastic model whom he'd seen on television in the sexiest freakin' commercial ever! What did it matter that Heaven was ignoring him – he was on a roll!

"The Rats!" Jade repeated with distaste.

"No *bene*, dahling," interrupted Antonio – ignoring Eddie and concentrating on Heaven. "You must have a name – people they love – they remember."

"Heaven and the Boys," Jade suggested.

"No! No! No! I have it!" exclaimed Antonio. "*Heavenly Bodies!* What a name! *Heavenly Bodies.* It must be. Antonio, he say so."

"I don't know . . ." Heaven cocked her head on one side, enjoying all the attention.

"What about *me*?" interjected Eddie. "I can't be in a group called Heavenly Bodies. It sounds like we're all freakin' dead! We're called the Rats. And we're not changin' our name. Nobody's complained before."

Antonio dismissed him with a wave of his elegantly manicured hand. "Tonight things they change," he stated. "I, Antonio, have decided to help this young lady to succeed." He smiled benevolently at Heaven. "The same as her mama, she too will be the big star."

"Wow, and you haven't even heard me sing," Heaven protested, thrilled by this unexpected turn of events, yet also frightened lest she didn't live up to this funny little man's expectations.

"Ah, but I don't need to," Antonio said with a Cheshire Cat smile. "When Antonio decide to photograph someone, that someone become the star. Antonio *smell* talent!"

*

Vladimir's kitchen was almost clear. The Chinese caterers had departed, and only a few waiters and the two barmen remained, servicing the last guests who seemed reluctant to leave, even though Madame Silver had retired upstairs at least half an hour ago.

Vladimir had his eye on the waiters *and* the barmen. The end of any party was a dangerous time. That was when bottles of liquor, bar implements, and cartons of cigarettes always seemed to mysteriously vanish. Vladimir checked everyone at the back door as they prepared to leave. He double-checked a waiter who vaguely resembled Rob Lowe. He sent out signals, and the young man responded.

"Vould you care for a night hat in my apartment?" Vladimir tempted.

"Sure," the waiter responded.

"Good, good." Vladimir was excited. He had been eyeing the boy all night. "Valk across the courtyard to the garage. Vait for me." He gave a winning smile, and shooed him on his way.

Silver Anderson's instructions were explicit: "No entertaining on my premises." Surely she did not consider *his* apartment above the garage her premises?

"Hey, chief." Wes smiled his way through the kitchen. "I'm taking off."

Vladimir eagle-eyed him. He seemed contraband-less.

Wes eased himself out the back door. Most of the fags who

ran these rich houses didn't know their ass from a hole in the ground. This Russian dude was checking him over because it was the end of the evening, and yet at the beginning of the evening he had calmly walked past him with a full box of booze and not a question asked. Stupid.

Rocky was stupid too. Somewhere along the way Wes had made a couple of scores of his own with the new supply of cocaine, and Rocky hadn't even noticed. When he woke up in the morning maybe he'd realize — maybe not. That's what happened when you snorted your own business.

Getting into his car Wes took a long deep breath. He was tired. Exhausted. Tomorrow was another day. A Sunday. He planned to sleep it through.

Chapter 21

The morning after the party . . .

Silver Anderson stirred at noon, adjusted her royal-blue sleep mask, and returned to a wonderful dream about herself.

Jack Python was up at seven. Swam twenty lengths in Clarissa's pool, then drove to his hotel and worked on ideas for his upcoming series of shows.

Clarissa Browning waited until she heard his car leave, and then arose and spent a solitary day absorbing her latest role. She enjoyed being alone.

Howard Soloman surfaced. Felt lousy. Snorted coke. And played three sets of punishing tennis with a movie star, another studio head, and a female executive they all wanted to fuck.

Poppy Soloman covered her face in rejuvenating creams, submitted to a thorough massage from a sadistic woman with a genteel voice and cruel hands, and spent the remainder of the day gossiping on the phone.

Jade Johnson, got up at ten. Dressed in sweats. Went to a

coffee shop, had breakfast (prune juice and a danish), bought the papers and a selection of magazines, and spent the day by herself.

Mannon Cable left his bed at eight. Called his lawyer at eight-fifteen and had a lengthy discussion about how to get rid of Melanie-Shanna.

Melanie-Shanna Cable left her bed at nine, marched into the kitchen where Mannon was on the phone, and announced that she was pregnant.

The rest of their day was spent in long discussions.

Whitney Valentine Cable woke up on Chuck Nielson's water bed in his Malibu beach house. They made love – which he was very good at. Afterwards they managed to consume a large breakfast, then they swam in the ocean and lazily sunbathed.

Wes Money was disturbed by the phone at eleven o'clock. "Get lost, whoever you are," he mumbled into the receiver. It was a woman. Naturally. Why did they find him so goddamn irresistible?

He was forced to say she could come over. Which she did. And he was sorry, because he was too tired to get it up, and she was determined to have at least three orgasms.

They parted company on bad terms, and he went straight back to sleep.

Heaven floated through the day planning what totally brilliant outfit she could wow the great Antonio with when she turned up for the photo session he had promised her.

Vladimir got rid of the young waiter early in the morning, and spent the rest of the day agonizing over his latest conquest. How could he continue to be so indiscriminate when dreaded disease roamed the streets?

Later, dressed in red, he cruised Santa Monica, and took home a sixteen-year-old runaway who did unspeakable things with his queen-size tongue.

Silver Anderson would have a fit if she knew what went on above her garage.

Fortunately she didn't.

Another lazy Sunday drifted by.

Somewhere in the Midwest . . .
Sometime in the seventies . . .

The girl put up with the unwelcome attentions of her father for almost two years. After his initial attack she learned to stay out of his way as much as possible, and with her mother home from the hospital it was not so easy for him to get to her.

But he managed. In spite of her fear and pain. He grabbed her whenever he could, and forced himself on her.

She was too ashamed to tell anyone, for she blamed herself for tempting him, and withdrew into a shell, unwilling to make friends or mix with the other children at the local school she attended. Whenever she could she avoided school altogether. There was a place in the woods she could hide, a large oak tree with a hollow in its trunk she could squeeze into. For hours she would stay there, curled in a ball, her arms wrapped around her knees, her thoughts tumbling around in her head.

She loved her mother. She didn't want to hurt her.

She hated her father. She would gladly kill him.

When she was almost fifteen she got her first period. The blood confused and shocked her. It was just like the first night when he'd mounted and thrust into her. Now the blood was back again. Bad blood. A sign she was unclean.

When her father found out he mumbled drunkenly, "We gotta be careful. Can't getcha in the family way. Can't do that."

But he wasn't careful, and it was only when her stomach began to swell that she realized with horror that a baby was beginning to grow inside her.

She didn't know who to turn to or what to do. Her mother was sick again, and back in the hospital. Her father found himself a lady friend and brought her to the house. The woman was big, with huge, floppy breasts and a raucous laugh.

The girl cowered in her bed and listened to their animal sounds.

When her mother died, the woman moved in permanently. That same night, at three in the morning, they came for her, the two of them. They were drunk and mean-spirited, out to have some fun.

The woman watched while the man stripped the cover from his daughter's bed, and the thin nightdress from her young body.

The girl began to scream, but the sound of her anguished cries was cut off when he covered her mouth with the palm of his hand. With a grunt he fell on top of her and roughly began to thrust with brutal strength, while the woman crowed her encouragement and urged him on.

The girl felt waves of nausea. She pushed his heavy body away and begged him to stop. His weight was crushing her so she could hardly breathe. He was hurting her.

When the pains started she knew with an ominous feeling of dread that something was wrong. In vain she continued to struggle. It did her no good.

When he was through the woman took her turn, using anything that amused her to torment the girl.

And at last it was over. The two of them staggered off, too drunk to care.

Silently, in unbelievable pain, the girl staggered to the outhouse. Her body was racked with contractions, as thick trails of blood trickled down her thighs.

Squatting on the floor, all alone, she witnessed the birth of her baby. Only it wasn't a baby, it was a four-month-old foetus, and when the girl felt strong enough to walk, she wrapped it in a towel, took it to her favourite tree, and buried it in the earth.

After that there was only one thing left to do.

She was calm as she collected a can of gasoline from beneath the kitchen sink, and poured it around the perimeter of the small wooden house.

Lighting the first match was easy. . . .

BOOK TWO

Hollywood, California
June 1985

Chapter 22

"What do you want out of life, Miss Anderson?" the English journalist asked. She was a middle-aged woman with brittle looks and dyed yellow hair. She was a failed actress, a failed singer, and a failed writer of novels. Finally she had made her mark with a weekly page in a London daily newspaper, and was now known for her vitriolic dislike of successful actresses, singers, and novelists. She attacked them in print whenever she could.

Silver summoned up a meaningful look. "Happiness," she said wistfully. "After thirty years in this business I think I deserve it, don't you?"

The journalist, who went by the unfortunate name of Cyndi Lou Planter, and looked like a man in drag, leaned closer to the famous star to see if she could spot any signs of a face lift or an eye job. Alas, nothing, except a mask of smooth, expertly applied makeup. Later, when she wrote her piece she would say:

> Silver Anderson exists beneath a two-inch layer of Max Factor. While relentlessly pursuing a thirty-year career she searches for happiness. Maybe if she scraped off some of her makeup she'd have a better chance of finding it.

"You certainly *do* deserve it," Cyndi Lou Planter gushed. The poison oozed from her pen, not her lips. She was too much of a coward to insult anyone to their face.

"Thank you." Silver smiled graciously. "That's very kind of you."

Where the hell is Nora? she thought. This Planter woman with her phoney smile and dull, unoriginal questions was getting on her nerves. Apart from anything else she had body odour, and the room was beginning to stink.

Nora! Silently she summoned her publicist.

Magically Nora appeared. Cyndi Lou Planter's hour was up, and Nora knew how to get rid of them better than anyone.

Silver rose and offered the journalist a friendly handshake. She was aware that the woman was a bitch, in print and out. So what? Someone had once said *As long as they spell your name right*. Yes. And possibly Ms. Planter could just about manage that.

Silver retired to her bedroom while Nora got rid of the journalist. She was the last in a day of interviews for England. *Palm Springs* was to be shown on television there, and they wanted immediate impact. The English company that had bought the series had asked Silver to fly to London for a week. She wasn't sure if she wanted to. England conjured up mixed memories. It was the scene of her lowest point in life, and although she had made a miraculous comeback, she was not sure if she ever wanted to return. Hence the parade of journalists through her house.

Nora bustled into the room. "Done!" she announced triumphantly.

"Thank God!" replied Silver, stretching with relief. "Nobody can ever say I don't work hard for my money."

Nora had to agree. Silver never stopped. Her energy level was quite incredible. Mere twenty-year-olds would kill for her dynamic vigour.

"Tonight's the opening of that new restaurant you promised Fernando you'd attend," Nora reminded. "Do you need me to come with you?"

"Dennis is taking me," Silver said with a sigh.

Dennis Denby was the latest in a long line of escorts. He was thirty years old, blandly good-looking, the son of a well-known producer and his socialite wife. Dennis, who ran his own advertising agency, was quite amusing and very ambitious. He was also reasonably adequate in bed. However, he did have one major drawback. From the age of twenty-one, Dennis had systematically bedded every married woman over thirty-five in Hollywood. It seemed to be an obsession with him, and Silver was not sure she liked being on the end of a very long assembly line.

They had been dating for several weeks, and he was certainly a personable escort. The problem was she found she couldn't really take him seriously.

"I thought you'd be bored with him by now," Nora remarked intuitively.

Silver laughed. "When the plate is empty you pick up the crumbs." With a knowing nod she added, "Especially when one is hungry."

Nora squinted with amusement. Silver Anderson's sexual appetite was legendary, dating back to times when it wasn't fashionable for a woman to demand equal rights in bed. Silver had always defied convention when it came to the male sex. If she ever wrote her autobiography it would be a regular *Who's Who* of famous and attractive men – although she was proud of claiming never to have slept with anyone to further her career.

"Who am I to say how hungry you are?" Nora remarked cynically. "But licking the plate is a bit much!"

Silver laughed wickedly. "It's not the plate I lick!"

Nora was the only one who could criticize and get away with it. Silver enjoyed the feisty honesty of her publicist, whom she also regarded as a good friend.

Growing up in show business, Silver had never had time to make friends. Hundreds of acquaintances, and now that she was a star again – thousands. None of them cared about her as a person; all they were interested in was getting close enough to bask in the stardust – hoping that a little of it would rub off on them. Dennis Denby was a perfect example. He *adored* going out with her. He revelled in the attention, the photographers, the fans.

He didn't love her. That was okay, she didn't love him either. They were both using each other for their own purposes.

Silver tried to remember the last time she was in love, and couldn't. It was years since she'd experienced the exhilarating flush of being with someone just because . . .

She was forty-seven years old. Too experienced, too wise, too famous.

*

Wes Money did not know how he ever got into the position of having to take Reba Winogratsky, his landlady, out on a date. *Just luck, I guess,* he thought, as he struggled into his only suit, and tried to hide the frays around the collar of his one white shirt.

Last week, Reba had turned up alone. No Mexican maid or fat son in tow. She had collected the back rent he owed, prowled around the house, and then sprawled on his couch and confided what a bastard her husband was. It seems she had caught him in bed with his secretary, and all hell broke loose.

"I am taking that scurvy son of a bitch for every dime he ever made," she announced. "I am gettin' me the best shit-hot lawyer in America!"

"Good idea," Wes responded, wishing she'd remove her waxed legs and vindictive expression from his couch.

"The man's a cockroach!" she declared. "Lower than a cockroach!" And angry tears rolled down her over-rouged cheeks.

Naturally, good old Wes Money had to console her. And somehow that consoling had ended up with him on top of her investigating the private parts of his landlady, who drove a new Mercedes, only wanted cash, and called her husband a scurvy son of a bitch cockroach.

He wouldn't have minded, but he didn't even get a rent rebate. Just an invitation to the opening of a new restaurant she had invested in. Reba, he discovered, had a passion for cash and sex. In that order.

He should never have started with her. Too late now.

She arrived, dressed for the occasion in a tighter than tight green lurex dress, hooker ankle-strap stiletto heels, and a silver mink jacket. Her dyed red hair was teased into a bird's-nest, and her leathery face and flinty eyes were inexpertly loaded with the best Elizabeth Arden had to offer. She smelled of Blue Grass.

"Hello, sailor," she said, with a crooked leer, and he detected an excess of whiskey on her breath.

"Hello, Reba," he replied, and wondered how he was going to extract himself from *this* one and still run a month late on his rent.

Chapter 23

The studio audience buzzed with anticipation. Jack Python was back in stride, and they loved him. Unlike Carson and Letterman and Merv, he did not sit behind a desk; he operated from a square table for two, just him and his guest – a probing, hour-long confrontation. Unlike Donahue he did not roam through his audience with the hypnotizing speed of a tornado. He took it easy, sometimes loosening his tie (he always wore one) or taking off his jacket. He made his guests feel comfortable. So comfortable, in fact, that sometimes (most times) they forgot about the eager, intent audience, and the intrusive cameras, and chatted as if it was just Jack they were talking to.

He drew them out gradually, carefully. And because he only had one guest a week, he was able to read every piece of research, and decide which questions he wanted to ask. No researchers pointed Jack Python in the direction they wanted him to go. He did it his way.

Today he talked to a bespectacled film-maker who rarely did interviews. The man was a genius, an autocrat and an egomaniac. Layer by layer Jack exposed him, and the reasons he was the way he was became clear.

The audience hardly dared to breathe. They devoured the one-to-one conversation. Jack Python brought them truth, and they respected him for it. He was the perfect American combination: brains and looks. All the Kennedy brothers had possessed it, and Jack Python had been told that if he wanted it, a political future lay ahead. With his amazing popularity and keen awareness he was a prime candidate for an electoral position. He had already been approached by a group with the money to back him should he ever express a desire to run for the Senate.

"That's crazy!" he'd said at first. But when they explained

where his popularity could get him, he hadn't been so sceptical. Hence his all-out effort to clean up his act with the ladies, just in case he wanted to give it a shot.

The show was nearly over. Jack observed "wind up" signals from his producer, and he gently cut off his guest, who was revealing more than he'd come out with in almost ten years of analysis.

Spontaneously the audience began to applaud. A genuine wave of real appreciation. The applause signs hadn't even been raised.

Jack thanked his guest, who was determined to keep talking. They shook hands. Camera one panned back and the lights lowered. As the credits ran, the two men were shown in silhouette.

The show was over.

Jack wanted to get up and race for the shower, only it was never that easy. Extracting himself from the guests was the most difficult part. For an hour he had been their sympathetic, interested, questioning friend, drawing things out that they might never have talked about before – especially not in public. Now it was finished, and with few exceptions they always seemed to need to keep talking.

The women were the worst. Most of them wanted to end the conversation in bed, and once upon a time so be it. Usually he was very careful, and his only slip with a guest, since being with Clarissa, was with a small, rounded movie actress who had such a puppy-dog desire to be loved that he hadn't had the heart to say no. She apologized throughout their lovemaking for everything about herself. Then she fixed him a dish of nourishing lentil soup, and sent him back to Clarissa with the promise that she would never tell.

Fortunately she kept her word, and was now married to a dog trainer. It seemed a suitable match.

Jack's producer, Aldrich Pane, came to the rescue as usual, giving Jack the signal to vanish while he brought the guest down from the Python high.

Jack didn't hesitate. Straight to his dressing room, under the shower, a release of all thoughts.

Half an hour later he was dressed, refreshed, and sitting in the control room watching a tape of the live programme. Aldrich usually joined him, and they had their own private wake if the show was bad, and a celebration if it really took off.

The most important element was the guest. If the guest worked, the show did. If the guest was a dud, everything collapsed.

Tonight was a gem, which pleased both men. It meant an excellent rating for the week. Usually they were somewhere in the top ten.

"Betcha we'll be in the big five," Aldrich said, beaming happily.

Jack agreed. Finding the right guest to carry an hour was never easy, and when it worked as well as it had done tonight it was a good feeling. Especially when he was right, which had just been proven. None of the production team had wanted the reclusive, bespectacled film-maker: they had all claimed he wouldn't talk. What a joke! It had been difficult to shut him up.

"I'll see you tomorrow," Jack said, striding out to his car.

Aldrich waved goodbye. They made a good team. Aldrich had all the patience Jack lacked, and Jack was the driving force. When *Face to Face with Python* went on the air, Jack had insisted on bringing Aldrich in as producer. They had worked together on *The Python Beat* in Houston, and Jack knew he was the right choice. Aldrich moved with his wife and children to Los Angeles, and years later the weekly hour-long programme was hotter than ever.

Driving back into Beverly Hills on the freeway, Jack pushed a tape into the deck and listened to his personal assistant, Aretha, reading off some of his mail. She had the most delightful sing-song voice, and a smile to match. He had found Aretha when he was working in Chicago. At the time she was making coffee around the studio and not much else. Jack spotted potential, and wangled her a job as production assistant. When L.A. happened, he called and asked if she was interested in being his right hand. "Jack, honey, I'd be anything for you," she enthused, and caught the next plane out. She was black, weighed two hundred and twenty pounds, and everyone loved her. Including Jack. He called Aldrich and Aretha his two A's, and swore he'd never get through the day without them.

The traffic was heavier than usual, and by the time he reached Hollywood he was wiped out. He called Clarissa on the car phone and told her he was running late. "Did you watch me?" he asked, anxious for her opinion if not her praise.

"Why should I watch you?" she said, quite seriously. "I'm seeing you soon."

One of the things he hated about Clarissa was that she took no interest whatsoever in his work. She *knew* he liked her to watch. Was it a conscious effort to annoy him that she never did?

"Listen, I'm kind of tired," he said. "I'm going to sleep at the hotel tonight."

Her voice sharpened a fraction. "If you want."

"Yeah. I'm not much company."

"Very well."

There was no *I'll miss you — I'll massage your back — I'll look after you.*

Was *that* what attracted him to Clarissa? Her aloofness. Her undemonstrative attitude. Or did he just like being with her because she was an Oscar-winning actress and not some Hollywood bimbette?

He shook his head. Ecstatically in love he wasn't. The truth was he never had been. He was thirty-nine years old with everything going for him. He had experienced one short marriage which had scared him to death, and legions of women. And yet he just didn't know.

Love.

It probably didn't even exist.

Chapter 24

"Good evening," said Dennis Denby.

"Good evening," sneered Vladimir.

Dennis raised a quizzical eyebrow. "May I come in?"

Vladimir allowed him to do so reluctantly. Vladimir was very possessive about Madame Anderson, and this one did not strike him as one of Madame's better escorts. Vladimir had preferred last month's, a caustic New York man-about-town who cracked incessant jokes, and tipped handsomely.

Dennis Denby walked into the library and began to pour himself a drink.

Following him accusingly, Vladimir edged him out of the way. "My job," he said, taking over. Not that he wanted to make Dennis Denby a drink, but his familiar way in Madame's home infuriated Vladimir.

Dennis walked to the nearest mirror and inspected himself. He was nice looking, if somewhat slight. Beverly Hills born and bred he had manners, style, and a rakish way of dressing. Tonight he wore a canary-yellow jacket over a pin-stripe shirt, and black silk Italian trousers with patent leather shoes. On anyone else the outfit might have looked odd, but Dennis managed to carry it off with great aplomb.

"Will you let Miss Anderson know I'm here," he said to Vladimir as the houseman handed him his drink.

Vladimir wondered if Dennis Denby travelled both roads, and decided he did. Poor Madame. She probably didn't suspect. Maybe he should drop a gentle hint – although Madame's escorts barely lasted longer than a month, so this one's time was almost up. "I vas just going to do so," Vladimir said, the sneer fixed firmly on his face.

Dennis decided to say something to Silver about her houseman. The man had an attitude problem. Trust Silver to employ a Russian.

*

Reba insisted on driving.

"I see you've still got your friend's Mercedes," Wes remarked dryly.

Reba extracted a piece of gum from the glove compartment and stuck it in her mouth. "I'll let you in on a little secret, Wesley," she said confidentially. "This car belongs to my husband. I didn't wanna tell anyone, cos – well ... y'know, what with me goin' around collectin' rent an' all. But yup, it's the scurvy bastard's set of wheels, an' now, goddamn it, it's mine." She chewed gum and went red in the face. "Just let the shithead try t'get it back from me an' I'll crush his balls in the blender."

Wes went pale at the thought. "Has he moved out?"

"You betcha ass he has."

"So you're alone?"

She shot him a suspicious look as the powerful car careened down Pico away from the beach. "No, Wesley, I am not alone. I have a son and a maid and a German Shepherd. I am *certainly* not alone. And the last thing I need is a roommate."

"I wasn't offering," he said quickly.

She continued to chew gum. "Maybe, maybe not. I know I'm a catch – what with all the alimony I'll be gettin' an' everything. Not to mention the car an' the house." She paused reflectively. "I'll be very . . . sought after."

"I'm sure you will," he said. *And not by me.*

Taking one hand off the wheel she patted his knee. "That's not to say I don't like you. Only I can't reduce your rent – I need the money – so don't even ask."

"I didn't."

"I'm tellin' you just in case."

He decided to develop Herpes. Again. Preferably tomorrow. To change the subject he said, "What does your old man do, anyway?"

The car roared down Pico. Silence for only a moment. "He's in the Mob," Reba said, adding spitefully, "an' any time the cops want me t'sing – I'm ready."

Wes almost choked. A moonlight flit was definitely in order.

*

The great car discussion went on outside Silver's house. Should they take Dennis's car, a snappy Porsche? Or would Silver's white Rolls-Royce be more suitable? They decided on the Rolls, with Dennis driving.

Silver wore a red Adolfo suit with a beige lace blouse. Tasteful rubies adorned her ears and throat, and for a change of look she featured a chic short wig.

"I wish you'd told me you were wearing yellow," she said, a trifle irritably.

"We don't clash," observed Dennis. "We complement."

"Hmmm . . ." She narrowed her eyes. "Yellow photographs better than red. Are we getting used to seeing ourself on the cover of the *National Enquirer*?"

Dennis laughed self-consciously. She was right, he *had* given some consideration to the way his outfit would photograph. The paparazzi adored and worshipped Silver Anderson. Every time she appeared anywhere they whipped themselves into a frenzy. If he was beside her he certainly wished to stand out, not fade into the background like most of her previous escorts.

The restaurant they were going to was called the Garden of Delight, and it was owned by the lover of Fernando, Silver's hairdresser, and two lesbian friends of his. Silver had agreed to appear as a favour. She knew her being there on opening night would guarantee the place maximum publicity and possible success.

Ah . . . power . . . She did so enjoy it.

*

"There's a rumour," Reba confided, "that Silver Anderson's gonna turn up tonight."

Wes didn't believe it for a moment. Why would Silver Anderson honour a gay hang-out like the Garden of Delight with her presence? He eyed the crush in the pink and white candy-striped room. "I doubt it," he said.

"Anyway," Reba said accusingly, shrugging off her mink jacket, "I thought you was gonna get me her autographed picture for my little boy."

"Next time."

Reba flung her mink jacket at him as if he were her personal maid. "You don't even know her," she remarked scornfully. "Check that in, an' be sure t'get a ticket. I don't wanna lose it *thankyouverymuch*."

He fought his way through fag city to the door, where a girl in black leather accepted the jacket and handed him a numbered claim-check. "Silver Anderson's coming here tonight," she confided excitedly. "Don't you just *a-dore* her in *Palm Springs*?"

"Never miss it," he lied, and considered ducking out. Why was everyone telling *him* about Silver Anderson? As if he cared. Although he *had* been in her bedroom, and if this group knew there'd be mass heart failure.

By the time he got back to Reba she was guzzling cheap pink champagne while talking to an undersized man with a huge buoyant quiff of silver hair and matching eyebrows. "Boyce," she said, a perfect Miss Manners. "Meet Wesley."

"*Looove* your frayed collar," Boyce trilled, "*Very Miami Vice.*"

"*Looove* your hair," Wes responded, quick as a flash. "*Very* Grecian Formula."

Boyce tossed his head like a frisky pony, and turned away.

"Don't be rude," Reba whispered furiously. "He lives with Silver Anderson's hairdresser."

Wes slapped his forehead in mock horror. "Oh! Jesus Christ! Why didn't you tell me before?"

Reba's mouth tightened into a thin scarlet line.

*

Smile fixed firmly in place, Dennis on her arm, Silver navigated her way through the crowds towards the bar.

The sea of people parted. She was the Queen. They were quite prepared to pay humble homage.

The photographers fought hard for their shots, elbowing and kicking everyone out of their way as they surrounded the star.

"Gangway. Gangway, *please!*" yelled Boyce, who had met Silver once before and was so overcome by her proximity he thought he might faint. He looked desperately around for Fernando, his roommate.

"This place is impossible," Dennis whispered in her ear. "Shall I phone Spago for a table?"

Smiling at her adoring fans, she acknowledged them with a regal wave.

"Silver!" a very young man in a diaphanous caftan screamed. "You're beautiful! We love you! We worship you!"

"Yes, do," she hissed to Dennis. "One drink and we're out of here."

Fernando materialized and all but threw himself at her feet. "You came!"

"Of course I did, darling. You know I wouldn't let you down. I must warn you though, I can only stay ten minutes."

"You're such a loyal person." Fernando's eyes filled with tears of joy. He had produced Silver Anderson, and now – however long she stayed – he would be a hero.

Dennis slipped away to call Spago and warn them of Silver's imminent arrival. The crowd pressed around her. The photographers continued to fight and struggle.

"Gangway!" Boyce pleaded desperately. "Miss Anderson is getting crushed. *Please!*"

Silver's smile became a touch tight around the edges. She didn't notice any security, and Fernando and Boyce were hardly a pair to make one feel secure.

"Silver! Silver! Silver!" The opening night mob swayed with joy as they pressed closer and closer. Over the din the paparazzi's curses flew through the air.

"Don't worry," Fernando said in a panicky voice. "Once we get you to the bar you'll be safe."

Safe? *Safe!* Wasn't she safe now?

Silver began to steam. She was too kind-hearted, that was her trouble. And why hadn't Fernando been *prepared* for her appearance?

A bizarre face straight out of a Fellini movie bobbed in front of her. She couldn't make out if it was a man or a woman. The voice was distinctly deep as it murmured, "You beautiful bitch-goddess. Sing for me! I beg you!"

And then the pushing and the shoving and the quest to get close to her and touch her became seriously dangerous. Fernando's yells of panic filled the air, and a fight started with one of the photographers and a group clad in chains and leather.

Silver felt a clutch of fear. She was going to be loved to death! Oh God! Where was Dennis? And why was she here?

*

Wes smelled trouble before it took place. When you worked bar you knew how to gauge a room. You always had one eye on the something that could happen, and the other on the nearest exit.

"Shit!" he muttered to no one in particular. He was caught up in the crush himself, Reba was nowhere in sight, and when the fight started he knew this was not the place to be. Bad enough for him, because when blows got traded he always managed to catch one. Even worse for Silver Anderson, who was well and truly trapped unless somebody did something fast.

With a weary sigh and a quick scan of the crush he realized he was the only one *capable* of doing anything. The poor woman was on her way to getting trampled underfoot.

"Shit!" he repeated, and moved into action. "L.A.P.D." he shouted authoritatively, causing a minor lull, and giving him enough time to grab Silver's arm and mutter hoarsely, "If you want to get out of here *fast*, come with me and don't waste time asking questions."

He had to hand it to her. She was with him from word one, as he propelled her through the seething mob towards the back exit, giving nobody any time to do anything about it.

They hit the back exit door, and burst out into the parking lot.

"Where's your car?" he asked urgently.

Wordlessly she pointed at the white Rolls parked at the front. He bundled her into the passenger seat, grabbed the keys from a bemused attendant, leaped in himself, and they were on the move just as the crowd and the fight and a hysterical Fernando came pouring out of the door after them.

Chapter 25

For weeks Heaven had been placing phone calls to the great Antonio. Okay, she knew he was a world-famous photographer and all, but *he* had approached *her* at Silver's party, she hadn't asked *him* to do anything. *He* was the one with all the brilliant ideas – telling her she was *young* and *now* and had such a *fabulous look* and he simply *had* to photograph her.

Bull.

Shit.

Another phoney – and she had met enough of *those* along the way. Only this one wasn't going to get off the hook so easily. He had made her a promise, and she was going to see he kept it, however long it took.

Since the party, Eddie had been a complete minus. He was embarrassed because she'd caught him with star-worship in his eyes as he rubber-necked all over the place. And he was pissed off because Antonio hadn't asked *him* to pose. Now he was trying to be Mister Cool again, and he couldn't wait to crow about Antonio not calling her back. "I guess you're not the new Madonna after all," he sneered.

"He's only going to photograph me, not sign me to a record deal," she snapped.

"Yeah. When?"

"Soon."

"You said that last week."

"So?"

He was also pissed off because she wouldn't sleep with him again. Once was enough. She hadn't enjoyed it *that* much, and who needed the hassle of worrying about getting pregnant? At least she wasn't a virgin anymore. No one could tease her about *that*.

One day she hopped into George's car, a slow-moving Chevrolet, and drove over the Canyon to Antonio's studio on Beverly Boulevard. She skipped school to do so. School was a drag anyway; she often took a day off and hung out at the movies or one of the big shopping malls. Once, she had driven over the hill into Hollywood and spent the entire day in Tower Records on Sunset. What a treat! Until two dorks tried to sell her drugs and get her to go to a motel with them. "Bug off," she had told them, which made them pursue her even more.

Heaven liked to think she knew how to look after herself. Living with Silver from birth to ten (give or take the times she was dumped with nannies or left with a strange assortment of her mother's "friends") had certainly made her grow up fast. Most of the times she was with Silver were the lean times – and Heaven remembered them well. She also remembered the pills and the drugs and the booze and the men. Oh, how she remembered the men. Practically every week she acquired a new "uncle".

And then came the really bad days just before Silver's breakdown. There were no men then, nobody to help them when they were evicted from a cheap London hotel for not paying the bill. Thank goodness for Benjii. He was definitely weird on account of the fact that he couldn't make up his mind whether he wanted to be a man or a woman, but he was *very* kindhearted, and took them both in without a murmur.

It was Benjii who told her she had a well-known uncle in America. He helped her locate him, and Uncle Jack came rushing over to rescue her. Life changed after that. With Silver she had lived all over the place and learned to look after herself. Uncle Jack took her to her grandfather's in California, and all of a sudden she was living in a proper house with proper mealtimes and a housekeeper to wash her clothes and make her bed. There was also a school to attend every day. It was all very strange, and took a lot of getting used to. Grandfather George was okay – but it was obvious to everyone that he lived in a world of his own. Uncle Jack was a hunk. He attempted to spend time with her – only it was never enough. Realizing he was very busy, she tried to understand.

Silver never reclaimed her. Heaven could have bet on *that*.

The old Chevrolet chugged grudgingly over the Canyon, slowing everything down behind it. She was only supposed to drive the car to school and back, and she fervently hoped it wouldn't behave like Eddie's Mustang and break down. Uncle Jack had promised her a car for her seventeenth birthday. Who could wait that long? She'd better get her act together and start scoring money of her own. Antonio was the key. If he photographed her then she'd be known, and maybe one of the creeps at the record companies she'd been sending her tapes to would actually *listen* to them.

Unfortunately, Antonio was not at his studio. "He's out on a location shoot," a bored receptionist told her. "You should really call first before coming here."

"I *have* called," Heaven pointed out. "Ten times!"

"Make it eleven," said the receptionist. "Antonio is a very busy man."

Heaven returned to the Valley, dejected but not deterred. She would get to him. Eventually. And when she did, things were going to happen.

Chapter 26

A thousand thoughts went through Silver's head. This man driving her Rolls could be a murderer, a kidnapper, a fan (God forbid!) . . .

She glanced at him sideways. He had an interesting profile, masculine and rugged. And the air of authority he had shown when rescuing her from the crush and spiriting her outside was quite . . . hmmm . . . dare she think it? Horny.

"May I ask exactly who you are?" she demanded haughtily.

"Just call me Robin Hood," he replied.

"Robin Hood stole from the rich and gave to the poor. Is that what *you* intend to do?"

He lightened his foot on the accelerator. "Oh, that's nice," he said. "Really nice. You do a good deed and get kicked in the balls."

She thought she detected the slight trace of a rough English accent. Maybe he was a reporter. She gave him a penetrating look. There was something vaguely familiar about him. "I'd like to know who you are," she repeated crisply. "And exactly where you think you are taking me."

He glanced at her. She liked his eyes – they were knowledgeable eyes, *horny* eyes.

"Listen, lady," he said. "You looked like you might be in a small spot of trouble – like getting crushed to death – y'know what I mean?"

"Maybe," she allowed.

"So I thought I'd do the Good Samaritan bit an' get you out of there." He swerved the powerful car over to the side of the road. "I can always take you back if you like."

"That won't be necessary," she said quickly.

He set the car in motion again. "In that case I'll take you home – an' maybe you'll give me cab fare to get back to my date, who is probably screamin' thief on account of the fact that I ran off with the keys to her car, *and* the ticket for her mink jacket."

"Did you leave your wallet behind along with your girlfriend?" she inquired tartly.

"Naw. I never carry a wallet."

"Where *do* you keep your money?"

"Wherever it'll do me the most good."

She began to laugh. "Who *are* you?" she asked for the third time.

"Just call me Wes," he replied. "An' don't bother with the introductions 'cos I already know who you are."

"*Really?*" Her sarcastic tone was lost on him. "In that case you are one up on me. I'm famous, you're obviously not. What do you do ... Wes?"

He was enjoying himself for a change. Having a conversation with a woman for a change. Christ, she smelled good. "What perfume are you wearing?" he asked.

"Giorgio. Do you like it?"

"If I don't get asphyxiated by the fumes."

She laughed again. "What *do* you do?"

The Rolls was a dream to drive. He felt quite at home behind the wheel. "A little bit of this, a little bit of that."

She hoped he wasn't an actor.

He read her mind. "I'm not an actor."

"How did you know what I was thinking?"

"It figures." He turned on Fairfax, and headed up towards Sunset.

"I presume you know where I live," she said acidly.

"Yeah, only you'll have to direct me once we get into Bel Air. I always get lost."

"Exactly *how* do you know where I live?" she persisted.

"I bought a stars' map. You were on it."

"Nonsense."

He shot her another glance. She looked different from the night of her party. Then it struck him. "You've cut your hair," he remarked.

His face was definitely familiar. "Do I know you?"

"Not exactly."

"Are you a fan?"

"Are you kidding?"

She was perplexed. Here she was, hurtling through the night in her car exchanging light banter with a complete stranger (although a familiar one), and she wasn't the least bit apprehensive. In fact, she was enjoying herself. "I suppose I should thank you," she said. "It could have been a nasty situation."

"I can see the headlines now," he said. "Five hundred faggots on top of Silver Anderson. Star gives in to the pressure."

She couldn't help being amused. "The gay population does not like being called faggots," she chided. "It's not a very nice expression."

"Excuse *me*."

She tried to decide what to do. Should she allow this refreshingly unimpressed man to drive her home? Or should she have him pull over to the side and get the hell out of her car? She was quite capable of driving herself. And maybe she *should* go back for Dennis. Poor Dennis. He must be frantic.

*

Sometimes Vladimir invaded Madame's bedroom when he knew she was safely out for the evening. The maids, her secretary, her new assistant, and Nora Carvell had all gone home.

Vladimir danced into Madame's private domain and ran the water in her luxurious jacuzzi tub. He stripped off his clothes, went into her dressing room and selected a short curly wig which he placed on top of his wheat-coloured hair. Next he played with a selection of her cosmetics and created a face for himself. When he was finished he had conjured up a great illusion. From a distance he had the Silver Anderson "look" down pat.

*

"Tell me," Silver asked. "Where *have* we met before?"

"I was at your party," Wes replied truthfully.

"Oh, of course." She decided she must have noticed him across a crowded room and had been attracted to him even then. Because there was no denying it, she *did* find him extremely attractive. Dennis Denby was a baby in bed. This one looked like a man. "Who were you there with?"

"Rocky."

Ah . . . he must have been with the Sylvester Stallone group. She relaxed. "Well, Wes. Since we're old friends, you can take me home and I'll give you a drink. I think it's the least I can do. Without your quick action I don't know what would have happened."

He heard a definite invitation in her voice. *Don't tell me I've scored again*, he thought. Only this time it was *bingo* all the way home.

Chapter 27

"Show me a strong woman an' I'll show you a dyke," Howard said to a room full of his key executives — two of them women. They exchanged looks of fury, but neither of them spoke up. It was difficult enough holding down a top job without making waves. Everybody knew Howard Soloman was coked up half the time; it was best to ignore his sexist remarks.

"I don't think she's a dyke," the moon-faced head of production said. "I think she just needs to get laid!"

Guffaws all round. They were talking about the Swedish star of an Orpheus film currently shooting in Brazil. She was causing

129

a lot of problems, and because of her the movie was behind schedule.

Howard stood up, indicating that the meeting was over. "Listen," he said expansively. "If she doesn't get her act together soon I'll just have to go down there an' shove my cock in her mouth – that'll shut her up once and for all!"

More guffaws. More frozen looks between the women.

"I'm only joking, girls," Howard said affably, patting one of them on the behind.

He waited until his office cleared then buzzed his secretary. "Any calls?"

"Orville Gooseberger about the lunch date you've postponed three times. Mannon Cable – he mentioned Las Vegas last weekend and said you would know what he was talking about. And Burt Reynolds's agent."

"Okay. Okay. Hold all calls again until I tell you."

"Yes, Mr Soloman."

Howard went into his private bathroom and locked the door. Removing his stash of cocaine from its hiding place, he laid a small amount on a square-cut flat mirror. With a shaking hand he snorted first one nostril and then the other. Christ! Zachary K. Klinger was coming to town and he was a wreck. Only temporarily, though. Two minutes later and he was back in control, feeling like he could kick ass from here to Boston and back. Picking up the phone next to his john, he summoned his secretary. "Book me a table at Morton's for tomorrow night. Eight people. Make sure it's the front table. Tell 'em I'm bringing Zachary Klinger with me."

"Yes, Mr Soloman."

"And phone Fred, the jewellery store on Rodeo, and ask Lucy to pick out something nice for my wife. In fact tell her to pick out a couple of pieces, and maybe she can stop by the office tomorrow."

"When tomorrow, Mr Soloman? You're busy all day."

"Schedule something. It's important."

"Yes, Mr Soloman."

"Did you get that script over to Whitney Valentine?"

"Yes, Mr Soloman."

"When?"

"This morning, Mr Soloman. Just as you requested."

Hanging up, he opened the medicine cabinet and swallowed some Maalox. Goddamn production meetings, they always upset his stomach. He didn't know why, because he was born to run a studio – nothing fazed him – even the Swedish cunt in Brazil who was costing him fortunes.

Taking a deep breath, he pressed the button on his private line and called Whitney. Nothing had taken place between them yet. They had experienced one lunch and that was it. Sometimes, he decided, the waiting was even better than the happening.

Nobody answered Whitney's private line, which meant she was out. He imagined her riding along the beach on her horse, hair flying, long limbs gleaming. Or maybe she was swimming in the ocean. No luxurious pools for Whitney – she was an outdoor girl.

Now, if he wished to locate Poppy, he would know *exactly* where to look. The Bistro Garden. She lunched there almost every day at her own special table, holding court among her circle of designer-clad friends. And later – Saks, Magnin's, Lina Lee, Gucci. She could be tracked down easily at any of those establishments.

Poppy had once told him that being the wife of a studio head was not easy. There were charities to belong to, people to impress, and rigid standards to uphold.

Poppy's commandments were: Thou shalt not be –

> *Too fat*
> *Poorly dressed*
> *Badly seated in a restaurant*
> or
> *Ignored by those who matter*

The list of Those Who Matter changed weekly depending on a variety of things.

Poppy always managed to know.

Howard had no desire to locate his wife. He would see her later for dinner. He would make love to her if he felt like it, or if just imagining what Whitney was like in the sack got him hot enough.

Zachary K. Klinger was coming to town, and he had to be ready for him.

*

Mannon Cable had always wanted to be a father, so when Melanie-Shanna hit him with the news that she was pregnant, he was delighted. For about sixty seconds. And then the implications set in. How *could* he have a baby with Melanie-Shanna?

131

Whitney was the love of his life, and Whitney was the only woman he wanted as mother of his children.

"Are you sure?" he'd demanded.

She had looked at him strangely. "Yes, I'm very sure. The doctor has confirmed it."

He didn't know what to say. For once in his life he was speechless. How could he mention divorce now? And an abortion was out of the question. Mannon had very strong views on that subject.

"Aren't you pleased?" she asked.

"Yeah," he replied, desperately trying to summon up the right degree of enthusiasm. "Thrilled."

The next day he met with his lawyer and asked for advice.

"Well," his lawyer had said. "If you don't want her to get rid of the kid, you're stuck. You'll have to wait out her pregnancy, and then stay around until the baby is a few months old at least. If you leave her before that the publicity will slaughter you."

Glumly Mannon had to agree. He could see the headlines: MANNON CABLE AND STRANGE LOVE TRIANGLE! SUPERSTAR DUMPS PREGNANT WIFE FOR WHITNEY!

Oh yeah. The tabloids would have a grand jerk-off at his expense.

There were also Whitney's feelings to consider. How was *she* going to react to this latest turn of events? It wasn't exactly going to make her think he was pining away for her. They hadn't spoken for a while. He had planned that the next time they did he would be a free man.

"Financially this is quite a blow," his lawyer had said grimly. "Are you *sure* you don't want her to have an abortion?"

He was sure.

They took a trip to New York, where he had to finish dubbing his last film. Melanie-Shanna was full of plans. "We'll decorate the second guest room," she said. "Yellow will be the perfect colour. Or blue?" She couldn't make up her mind. "What do you think, Mannon? Yellow or blue?"

He shook his head, not wanting to get involved. The further away he stayed from this pregnancy and the resulting baby, the better.

Chapter 28

Once inside her house, Silver was able to get a better look at Wes, and she liked what she saw. He was tall — she preferred big men. His hair was longish, brownish, not styled and sprayed like a lot of men around today. His eyes were extraordinary — sludge with touches of a murky seaweed green. He was distinctly masculine, and she felt the juices rising like they hadn't risen in a while. Certainly not for Dennis Denby, who was about as exciting and unpredictable as bacon and eggs for breakfast.

"Fix yourself a drink," she said, giving him an encouraging push towards the bar in the den. "I'll be right back."

"Can I make you something?" he asked politely.

"Vodka," she said over her shoulder as she mounted the grand front staircase. "Lemon twist, no ice."

Ah, maybe she'd remembered he was a barman. It certainly sounded like she did.

Choosing a Baccarat glass, he poured in an inch of vodka, added another one for good measure, and picked a slice of lemon from a small silver dish, expertly skewering it to the side of the glass. For himself he poured a cold beer. Best to make sure everything was primed and ready to go.

Luxuriating in the centre of Silver Anderson's large jacuzzi tub, Vladimir presented a strange and wonderful sight. He sat ramrod straight, naked, bewigged, and fully made-up, while the water bubbled and jetted around him. Clamped around his head were the headphones of a small Sony Walkman. The music reaching his ears was an early Silver Anderson album, and he sang along, mimicking her voice to perfection.

So intent was he that he failed to notice Silver enter her own

133

bathroom and stand transfixed. "What *the hell* is going on here?" she said in complete amazement.

He did not hear her.

She stepped forward and ripped the headphones from him, flinging them across the room.

"Madame!" he shrieked in horror, and stood up.

"Vladimir?" She couldn't believe what she was seeing.

Uttering a stream of Russian curses he tried to cover his most personal items with his hands. The effort was ineffectual, as Vladimir was hung like the proverbial bull.

"God!" Silver flung him a towel and said icily, "Get out of my bath and *cover* yourself."

"Madame! Madame!" he wailed. "Vill you forgive me for this? Vat can I ever do to beg your forgiveness?"

"You can take off my wig for a start. And get *out*."

Vladimir was almost weeping. "Is Madame firing me?"

Silver caught sight of herself in one of the many mirrors and was immediately distracted. She had come upstairs to prepare herself for what she hoped might be a rather interesting evening – not to argue with her obviously deranged houseman. "We'll discuss it tomorrow," she said coldly. "Kindly get this bathroom cleaned up. Now! And then go to your quarters and stay there."

He hung his head in shame as she swept out.

*

Wes was disappointed to note that she had not changed when she returned to the bar. He had hoped for the filmy black negligee, sheer stockings, garter belt (*Down boy, down – not yet – don't blow it*) and high-heeled mules. Instead she was still wearing her fashionable red suit and unrevealing lace blouse.

"Whew!" she said, uncharacteristically flushed. "I just had the most *bizarre* experience. Hand me my drink. I need it."

He gave her the glass of vodka and waited for an explanation.

Flopping down on the couch she sipped the clear alcohol. "Vladimir, my houseman, is crazed!" she announced. "Quite obviously certifiable."

Wes remembered her houseman well – a bossy Bolshoi with an eye for the waiters. "What happened?" he asked expectantly.

She kicked off her shoes and savoured the moment. "He was in *my* bath. Wearing one of *my* wigs. A lot of *my* makeup. Singing one of *my* songs in *my* voice!"

Wes started to laugh. "What?"

She couldn't help smiling. "You heard."

"Was he dressed?"

"Unfortunately not."

They both began to laugh.

"He looked ridiculous," she spluttered. "And when he stood up in the bath with the bubbles all over him –"

"And the makeup and the hair?" Wes joined in.

"Yes. Yes. It's a sight I'll never forget."

He was as caught up as she was in just imagining Vladimir – the star of such a scene.

"What did you *do*?" he roared.

"I was too amazed to do anything!" she retorted. "Oh God! It was so . . . so . . . *funny*!"

Her laughter was catching – he couldn't stop either. This was not the cool bitch-goddess the newspapers and magazines wrote about with such awe – this was a warm and amusing *woman*.

"I guess he'll be looking for another job tomorrow," Wes said at last.

"Not necessarily," she replied. "I might just keep him around for the *entertainment* value!"

More laughter, interrupted by the persistent buzz of the front gate.

Silver frowned. "I don't know who this can be. Will you answer it for me?" She picked up the intercom phone and handed it to him.

"Silver Anderson's residence," he said smoothly.

"Dennis Denby," said an aggravated voice.

He covered the mouthpiece with the palm of his hand. "Dennis Denby," he repeated.

"Oh, no! I suppose you'd better buzz him in."

He gave her a little eye contact. "Do I have to?"

She responded nicely. "I think we'd better, don't you?"

All of a sudden it was *we*. He wasn't being dismissed.

Dutifully he pressed the intercom while she slipped her shoes back on. And a minute later, a red-faced Dennis Denby arrived at the front door. He clutched Silver, glared at Wes, and said, "Thank God you're all right!"

She disentangled herself from his grabbing hands. "I'm perfectly fine, Dennis." She indicated Wes. "Thanks to Mr —"

"Money," Wes supplied obligingly.

Silver raised an amused eyebrow.

"It's an old English name," Wes explained airily.

"Most unusual," she remarked.

"Yeah . . . well . . . most things about me are unusual."

She smiled. "They are?"

"So I've been told." The woman had dynamite eyes – kind of probing and sexy. And Wes knew he wasn't misreading the message in them.

Dennis couldn't help noticing the interaction going on between them, and he asserted himself immediately. "Well, it was very obliging of Mr er . . . Money to bring you home. Although it really wasn't necessary. Everything was under control."

"Whose control, Dennis?" Silver inquired caustically. "Were *you* controlling the crowd when I was about to get crushed to death?"

"Don't exaggerate, dear," Dennis said in a condescending tone.

He had made two fatal mistakes. One was calling her dear – a patronizing term she hated, although she often used it herself. And two was doubting her ability to judge a situation. "You really are stupid, Dennis, *dear*," she said. "You honestly had no idea what was going on, did you?"

"I was calling Spago," he explained, oblivious to her insult. He looked at his watch. "And there's a table waiting for us now." Turning to Wes he added, "So . . . Mr Money. If you'll excuse us."

"Mr Money will *not* excuse us," Silver said crisply. "Because we – you and I, Dennis, *dear* – are not going anywhere. In fact" – she took him by the arm and led him out of the room – "you are going home, and *I* am finishing my drink with Mr Money, who *did* have the presence of mind to see what was going on, and got me the hell out of there before I was bloody trampled underfoot!"

"Silver!" Dennis protested. "Why are you mad at me?"

"I am not mad," she replied, propelling him towards the front door. "I am merely bored."

He rallied desperately. "You can't stay alone in the house with this . . . this *person*. Who is he? What do you know about him?"

"That he has balls, Dennis, *dear*. Which is more than I can say for you! Goodnight!"

She closed the front door on his objections, and returned to the den.

Wes faced her. "Uh huh," he said, "we've had the crazy Russian and the uptight boyfriend. What next?"

She smiled, slowly, seductively. The smile America loved to hate. "I think something'll come up, don't you?"

Who was he to argue?

Chapter 29

Jade fell into the rhythm of Los Angeles easily. She had thought she would hate it, but after a month in the city she decided she loved it. There was so much to do, and gorgeous weather to do it in.

With her books, records and possessions around her, the apartment soon felt like home, and the only downer was Corey. He was weird – something was going on in his life and he obviously had no intention of sharing it with her. She had only seen him a couple of times. "I'm real busy," was his explanation. "What with the new job and settling in and everything."

He might be settling in but she didn't even know where or with whom. When she questioned him he was evasive. "Am I ever going to see where you live?" she asked him pointedly one day.

"Sure," he replied cheerily. "Very soon."

Whenever she mentioned Marita, he clammed up. "What about little Corey Junior?" she asked, referring to her eighteen-month-old nephew.

"He's in Hawaii."

"When are we going to see him?"

"Soon."

Everything was "soon". And Corey was a pain. She called and complained to her mother. "He's going through a bad time," her mother said sympathetically. "Leave him alone, he'll come to you eventually."

So she did. And he didn't.

The good news was that Cloud Cosmetics had hired Antonio

to do the photographs for the print ad campaign. A top video director, Shane Dickson, was to shoot the commercials, and she had been busy with hair, clothes, and makeup tests. The look had to be perfect.

Working with Antonio was always a joy. Not only did they have fun, but his photographs were a stunning visual treat. He combined the style of Norman Parkinson with the gloss of Scavullo and the sharpness and originality of Annie Leibovitz.

Jade found herself hanging out with him and his artistic group of friends more and more. They went to great restaurants, fun parties, and usually ended up on Friday and Saturday nights eating and dancing the night away at Tramp — a private club.

Getting out was excellent therapy. For years Mark Rand's contract had been exclusive. Now she was a free agent again.

She tried not to think about Mark. Every time he came creeping into her thoughts she blanked him out. The affair was well and truly over. *Finito*.

Good.

On her travels around town with Antonio and his friends several propositions of a sexual nature came her way. A sallow-faced producer with bad teeth and hollow eyes made her an offer she could easily refuse. A permanently stoned Puerto Rican told her she was the sexiest woman he'd ever seen. A French hustler in baggy jeans and designer sweatshirt informed her he knew everyone and could make her a star.

Men. She had had enough for a while. And then she met Shane Dickson, and she thought — *Well, maybe not* quite *enough* . . . She needed *someone* to take her mind off Mark.

Shane Dickson was short, surly, dark-haired and bearded. She liked the fact that he didn't fall all over her like most men did. For a while they circled around each other. He conducted her tests with a detached, professional air. He wanted a certain look for the series of commercials, and he didn't plan to shoot one foot of film until he got it.

Eventually he asked her out to dinner so they could talk about what they were trying to achieve. He took her to Nucleus Nuance on Melrose, and spoke about commercials being the true art form of the cinema. "In a two-hour movie you have time to screw up, get back on track, screw up again. In a commercial or a video you're going for gold in two minutes flat. There's no room for mistakes."

"Are you married?" she asked. Her skin was tingling, every nerve alert. It had been a long time between men, and she needed to feel wanted again.

"Yes," he replied, reaching for her hand across the table. "But my wife and I are separated. She just doesn't understand me."

Were men actually still using that line? She couldn't believe it.

He invited her back to his apartment – an invitation she declined. One married man in her life was enough.

And then, late one afternoon when she'd just returned from an all-day shoot and wanted nothing more than food and sleep, Mark phoned. "I'm in town," he said. "As a matter of fact, right now I'm standing in the lobby of your building. I have to talk to you, Jade. May I come up?"

Chapter 30

Whoever said all cats are alike in the dark must have been deaf, dumb, and blind. From her low moans of ecstasy to her litany of husky requests (Silver was not backward in telling him what she enjoyed), and her expensively perfumed flesh – everything was different. Try driving a Bentley after a succession of worn-down Toyotas.

Wes shifted position, allowing Silver to mount *him*. She had the tight, compact body of a teenager. Taut breasts, firm thighs (not rock hard like his Swede) and a flat stomach. She enjoyed sex with a gusto he was unused to. Reba lay on her back like a skewered fish. Other women talked dirty just for effect. When Silver said, "Fuck me hard, Wes," she meant it. And he did it. And they both got off on it.

She lowered a hard-nippled breast to his mouth while riding him fast. He sucked obligingly. She even tasted different.

He felt the ultimate trip beginning. Thoughts flashed through his head — it had all happened so quickly.

Exit Dennis.

Conversation.

Nothing heavy.

"Let's go upstairs."

Her invitation.

His acceptance.

Once in the bedroom he went for the clinch.

She returned his kiss with teeth and probing tongue and an encouraging stroke of the frothing hound. "I'll be right back," she had said.

This was hardly the time to tell her he was a busted-out some-time barman who lived in a run-down house in Venice and got it on with a variety of unattractive but very grateful women.

When she came back into the bedroom she looked quite different. Gone was the short thick hair — a wig, he realized — and in its place was her own shoulder-length dark hair. She had also removed her heavy false eyelashes, and now she appeared younger and softer. She wore a silk kimono.

"This is the real Silver Anderson," she'd said without a trace of embarrassment. "I hope you're not disappointed."

Disappointed? He was pleasantly surprised. Taking her hand he'd guided it to where it would do her the most good. "Do I feel like a disappointed man?"

She'd laughed, low-down and dirty. "You feel like a man — that's enough for me."

And they set sail.

He climaxed with a ball-busting jolt which shuddered through his body like a fast-moving express train. "Jesus H. Christ!" he groaned.

She was tight, holding him a steady captive. "What's *he* got to do with it?" she asked breathlessly.

*

Humiliated, Vladimir cleaned up Silver's bathroom and fled from the house to his private retreat above the garage. How could he have been so careless? He shook his head. No, no, not careless, just caught. Usually when Madame went out she was gone for at least three hours. This time she had returned within the hour.

Too bad, Vladimir. You should have been more careful.

He was sure that she would fire him. The next morning there would be a curt dismissal from her personal assistant, and a severance cheque from her accountant's office.

He was mortified. How he wished he could close his eyes, then open them and find the whole episode no more than a bad dream.

Before Silver, he had worked for a gay television producer who lived high in the Hollywood Hills. And before that, a retired couple who presented ideal domesticity to the world, and behind closed doors entertained their gay and lesbian lovers at non-stop weekend orgies.

Ah, Vladimir knew plenty. As a houseman he was privy to an Aladdin's cave of secrets. Only what could he do with them? And who would believe him?

Silver Anderson was going to miss him, he was positive of that. For three years he had served her faithfully. He knew her likes and dislikes. He gauged her moods and never disturbed her solitude. He protected her privacy, made sure her house was in impeccable order, and was discreet about her men friends.

Opening his closet he peered mournfully at his clothes. He possessed two suits, a brown one and a blue. Several shirts, a few sports clothes, and a black rubber diving suit. Not that he indulged in underwater pursuits – the rubber suit was a gift from a former friend – a six-feet-four black jock, who *loved* playing water sports. Vladimir had lived with him for two months somewhere between the gay producer and the ideal Hollywood couple. He preferred living alone in his own part of the fabulous mansions he serviced.

Lovingly he fingered the material of a floor-length purple beaded dress nestling in the back of the closet. One day Silver had given him a trunk-load of old clothes to be picked up by a charity organization. Upon perusing the contents, he had come across the dress. Naturally he kept it. Why not? It fitted him perfectly.

He pulled a suitcase from beneath the bed, and in a desultory fashion began to pack. When he was fired he would depart swiftly in a dignified manner. After all, by birth he was a Russian, and he had his pride.

*

Wes leaned across a sleeping Silver to reach his pants, dumped unceremoniously on the floor, and from the back pocket he recovered a crumpled pack of Camels, and lit up. Dragging reflectively on the cigarette, he wondered what was going to happen next. Laying the Big Star was one thing – mission accomplished – although it hadn't really been a mission – more a mutual attraction which led to great sex. So what was the next play to be? He was hardly in a position to entertain her at Chasen's, and somehow grabbing a bite at Kentucky Fried Chicken did not appear to be her scene.

Wes had a problem. He had just made love to a very famous lady indeed, and if she'd enjoyed it half as much as she seemed to, then they were on for more than a ten-cent ride.

What was he going to tell her? The truth? Or lie just a little.

He blew smoke rings towards the ceiling, and studied Silver Anderson in repose. She looked good, the old broad – and he'd had 'em at all ages. Some women after sex looked like they had just gone seven rounds with Joe Frazier – especially the over-thirty-fives. Well, Silver Anderson was certainly no juvenile, but she sure held up in the trenches.

As if she sensed his eyes upon her, she opened hers. For a moment he thought she was going to say "Who are you?"

She didn't. She gave him a long, appraising stare, stretched in a very feline way, and stepped from the bed nude and proud of it.

He could tell she reckoned her body was something special the way she strutted to the mirrored bathroom door. Who was he to argue?

Taking another drag of lung-cancer-inducing smoke, he got out of bed and followed her.

Chapter 31

The production meeting was well underway. Once a month Jack and his team met specifically to discuss suitable guests for the upcoming shows. There was a bulletin board with suggestions, ideas, and a list of what Aldrich called "the current hot hundred". The list was comprised of personalities from every field: politics, theatre, music, sports, movies, publishing, and so on. Since the show only aired for twenty-six weeks a year, there were only twenty-six guests required, and the struggle by publicists to get their clients a spot was competitive and vicious. Bribes were often offered. Bribes were always turned down. *Face to Face with Python* could sell a movie or a book or an event quicker than any other show on television. The bookings were done four weeks in advance, allowing Jack plenty of time to study the material on each guest.

"Why can't we have Mannon Cable?" Aretha demanded. Nobody was surprised: she demanded it every month because she knew Jack and Mannon were close friends.

"Not again," Jack groaned. "I've told you enough times, he always turns me down."

"Bet he wouldn't if *I* got hold of him," Aretha joked in her sing-song voice. "Poppa! That man'ud have the best time he ever had in his whole damn life!" She beamed happily at the thought. "Yessirree!!"

"I'll tell him," Jack dead-panned.

"You *always* say that," Aretha chided. "How come he appears on Carson all the time, and *you* can't get him?"

"Because I don't really want him," Jack replied lightly. "We know each other too well and too long. It wouldn't work."

"Yes it would," she sang. "Stand back an' watch our ratings *riiiiiiise!*"

"Let's get serious," Aldrich interrupted. "Eddie Murphy is a definite yes. Diane Keaton won't commit. We can get April Crawford if we want her. And do we go for Fonda or not?"

"We're getting too show-bizzy," Jack complained. "There has to be balance between entertainment and information. Put April Crawford on hold. Fonda's overexposed right now. How about Mailer? There's that new biography on him; it's interesting. I did a three-minute segment with him in Chicago years ago – now might be the right time to talk to him again."

"I'd sooner see Prince," sighed Aretha. "What a guy! A touch petite for me – heck, I can overcome *that*! He has such adorable buns!"

Aldrich ignored her. "I'll get one of the researchers onto Norman Mailer," he said. "See what he's up to."

"Do that." Jack pushed away from the conference table. "We can talk again on Monday. Right now I've got to see a man about a house."

Both Aretha and Aldrich raised eyebrows and voices and chorused as one, "A *house*?"

He grinned. "Don't worry, nothing serious. I thought it might be relaxing to take a summer rental at the beach."

"Very relaxing," murmured Aretha sarcastically. "All those steamy teenage bodies parading up and down your front lawn and frolicking in your pond!"

"Trancas," Jack said. "Away from the madding crowd."

*

It took him an hour to drive there from the television studio. And that was on a quiet Friday afternoon without much traffic. By the time he found the turn-off, parked his Ferrari, and walked down a series of stone steps hewn into the side of a mini-cliff, he wasn't so sure this was such a sensational idea.

When he entered the house he changed his mind.

The rental agent let him in. She was a divorced woman in her forties who had dressed for the occasion in a jersey suit too tight for her spreading curves. Half a bottle of Estée wafted from her excited body. It wasn't every day she got to show a house to Jack Python.

She greeted him effusively. He was twice as handsome off the little screen as on. His direct green eyes sent her into an absolute tizzy.

"Are you alone?" she asked, when she'd recovered her composure.

"Yes," he replied. "Why? Shouldn't I be?"

"No, no, it's just that . . ." She trailed off. Most celebrities travelled with an entourage of yes-people, and she was surprised that Jack Python obviously preferred solo. "Do come in," she gushed, remembering her manners. "The owners are out for the day. They're leaving for Europe in three weeks, and they wanted me to assure you that all their personal items – clothes, etcetera, will be packed and put in storage. Right now the house has a lived-in feel. However, I'm sure you understand. Actually, I always think –"

Jack moved past her into a glorious circular glass-walled living room. Outside was a huge deck, with steps leading down to a deserted cove, and the Pacific Ocean in all its glory.

For a man who had never been house-hungry he fell in love instantly.

The rental agent launched into her hard-sell routine, completely wasted on Jack, who wasn't listening as he strode to the glass walls and discovered they folded back to create a completely open environment.

He walked out onto the deck. It was a clear, windy day with high rollers and a very blue sky.

"This location is absolutely private," the realtor said, following him outside. "As a matter of fact I've been here several times, and I've never seen another soul."

He noticed a sunken hot-tub, a barbecue pit, and table tennis all set up.

"No tennis court?" he joked.

"Actually," the woman said anxiously, "the owners are considering building one." She laughed nervously. "Not before their trip though."

He gazed out at the blue sea. The waves and the soothing sound of the surf were almost hypnotizing. "How long will they rent it for?" he asked.

"It's a six-month rental," she replied. "With an option to buy if they decide to stay in Europe."

"I'll take it," he said decisively.

"Mr Python, you haven't even looked around."

"I've seen everything I need to see."

"You're a very impetuous man, and a clever one. This is the best house in Trancas. I've already got two couples thinking about it – their cheques are only phone calls away."

"And mine" – he slid his chequebook from his jacket pocket – "will be with you any second. The house is rented."

Driving back to Beverly Hills he felt elated. His first house! Only a summer rental, but he had a feeling he might go for the buy if the couple stayed in Europe and decided to sell.

Driving directly to the Beverly Wilshire, he showered and changed clothes. Clarissa had finished her movie and taken off for New York. She had wanted him to accompany her. He had made "too much work" noises, so she had gone without him.

Before leaving there had been a confrontation, something he had been unconsciously avoiding for months. They had attended a screening at the Academy, and stopped by the party at Tramp afterwards. The paparazzi trailed them with gusto. Unfortunately there were three of his former girlfriends present, all well-known females who greeted him warmly, while the paparazzi struggled to capture every moment.

"I can't stand this," Clarissa said angrily. "The trouble with you, Jack, is that you attract too much attention."

"*Me?* How about *you? You're* the one with the Oscar on your shelf."

"I don't court publicity."

"Neither do I."

"Nonsense. You love every moment of it. You revel in it."

"That's absolute bullshit and you know it."

They were in the car, driving back to her house. It was raining, and the streets were slick.

"I've been thinking," she said slowly.

"What?"

"I want to get married."

The Ferrari hit a puddle of water and skidded. A car coming towards them sounded its horn. It took all his concentration to get the Ferrari under control.

Clarissa was unfazed. "I'd like a baby," she said.

He swallowed hard. Marriage was bad enough, but now she wanted a baby too!

Measuring his words carefully he said, "We've never discussed this."

"I know," she replied flatly. "I think you should consider that we've been together over a year. Either our relationship is going somewhere, or we may as well end it."

"Are you giving me an ultimatum?" he asked tightly.

146

Her long face was ghostly pale in the night light. "I am saying we can't drift along anymore. I want a commitment."

He was stunned. Miss Independent all of a sudden wanted a commitment!

"I've never considered marriage," he said truthfully.

"I'm well aware of that," she replied. "Neither of us has. We're both loners –"

"You've never complained," he interrupted.

"I'm not complaining now," she said evenly. "I'm merely suggesting a change." Turning away from him she stared out of the side window at the relentless rain. "Between us we have no family. I think I want to start planting roots."

He stifled an insane impulse to laugh. She sounded like she was planning a garden!

"*I* have a family," he protested. "My father, and Heaven."

"Your father lives in a world of his own, you've often told me that. As for your niece . . ." She shrugged. "You pay her no attention."

"They're still family."

"That's not what I'm talking about, and you know it." She lapsed into silence for a moment, and then said quietly, "I'm not asking you to make up your mind right now. Tomorrow I leave for New York. I won't come back until you tell me what you've decided."

One thing about Clarissa, she didn't mince words.

He had no idea what he was going to do. With Clarissa in the East he was enjoying his freedom. Good behaviour had gone on far too long. He needed a break – and a weekend with Mannon and Howard in Las Vegas was just the way to celebrate.

Chapter 32

Howard had use of the company jet. He saw no reason why it couldn't take him to Vegas and back, and *then* go to New York and pick up Zachary Klinger, who was coming out to the Coast to torment him. The man was driving him crazy. He had already cancelled two proposed visits at the last minute. Zachary K. Klinger, Howard realized, liked to keep people on their toes.

When Mannon suggested Las Vegas, Howard jumped. He needed the break. Oh, how he needed it! A weekend away from Poppy was better than ten days at the Golden Door.

Poppy was not so thrilled. "Baby Roselight and I will come with you," she said firmly.

"No way," Howard countered. "Your luggage will ground the plane!"

"Don't you *want* us?" she pouted.

"I do, sweetheart," he lied. "Only you'll be bored, and I just won't have the time to spend with you."

"Why not?"

"Because it's a business trip, puff-pie. I keep on telling you that."

"What sort of business do people get to do in Las Vegas that they can't do in L.A.?" she asked suspiciously.

"How many times must I explain it to you?" Swallowing his aggravation he told her – yet again – why he and Mannon were going. He had concocted a highly original story about an old and infamous gambler who lived just outside of Vegas and refused to travel. Mannon wanted to meet him with a view to filming his life story. For Orpheus, of course. Poppy knew Howard had been trying forever to get Mannon to commit to a project for Orpheus. She bought the story. Finally.

"I'll miss you," she said tearfully, as if he were going for two months instead of two days.

"Me too, sugar-lips."

"What'll I *do* all day?"

"Spend money."

She seemed to like that suggestion, and cheered up considerably, enabling him to escape from the house without further hassle.

He snorted coke in the back of the limo on the way to Burbank airport, and by the time he boarded the company jet he was in fighting shape.

★

"Have a safe flight," Melanie-Shanna said softly.

Mannon had to admit that when it came to choosing women he certainly had an eye. He didn't know if it was Melanie-Shanna's pregnancy or what, but she looked a picture of glowing health as she bade him goodbye from the door of their Sunset Boulevard mansion.

For a moment he forgot Whitney. "What'll you get up to this weekend?" he asked, the first time he had bothered to inquire.

"I don't know – this and that. I thought I might go nursery shopping."

"Good idea." He kissed her on the cheek.

She responded by turning her face towards him and kissing him on the mouth.

He savoured her cherry-fresh breath, then pushed her gently away. "Don't make me miss the plane," he joked.

"I thought planes waited for big stars like you," she said wryly.

Her eyes needed him – their message was loud and clear. He hesitated: it was weeks since they'd made love – now that she was pregnant it just didn't seem right. "Gotta go, kid," he said decisively. "Have fun."

She watched him stride towards the stretch limousine, climb inside, and vanish from sight.

Her movie star husband was off for the weekend and she would miss him. She would also spend most of her time worrying about what he was up to. When it came to movie stars women had no shame. The unspoken message was always there. *I'm available if you want me.*

Melanie-Shanna walked back into the house and hoped that he didn't.

The phone was ringing. Before she could reach it their Mexican housekeeper picked up.

"For you, missus," the woman said.

Melanie-Shanna took the phone and wondered who it was. She didn't encourage friendships, preferring to be available for Mannon at all times. When he first brought her to Hollywood, the Beverly Hills wives had rallied round — inviting her to this luncheon, that charity event, this celebrity fashion show. She declined all invitations politely, and eventually they left her alone.

"Hello," she said tentatively.

"Hi, sweetie," said the unmistakable voice of Poppy Soloman. "Now I *will not* take no for an answer. The husbands have deserted us, and you and I are going to have lunch at the Bistro Garden tomorrow, followed by a *tiny* little stroll down Rodeo."

"Oh, Poppy, I don't think —"

"I told you, dear, I am not allowing *any* excuses. We're having lunch, and that's that."

★

"Welcome aboard," greeted Howard.

Mannon grinned, all thoughts of Melanie-Shanna and her appealing freshness forgotten. "It's a pleasure to be flying with you, Mr Soloman."

"May the trip last all weekend," said Howard. "Do I need a touch of R & R!"

"Who doesn't?" agreed Mannon, flopping into a leather armchair.

The interior of the jet was decorated like a luxurious conference room — all leather and brass, with polished tables and a curving bar. There were two attractive stewardesses — an Australian girl, and an English redhead. They both wore tight beige gaberdine skirts with matching belted jackets, and a little insignia on the right-hand breast pocket that read KLINGER, INC.

"Can I get you anything, Mr Cable?" asked the Australian.

"What did you have in mind?" Standard responses came easily to Mannon. He loved double entendres.

"Vodka. Scotch. Rum. Perrier. Soda. 7-Up. Coca—"

"Hold it!" he laughed. "A scotch on the rocks'll do me fine."

She smiled — "Yes, sir" — and walked away.

Mannon watched her ass. Beneath the pristine gaberdine lay great promise.

"Where's Jack?" Howard asked.

Mannon stretched. "I don't know. Is he late?"

Howard checked his watch. "A few minutes, he's probably on his way. He had to go see a house or something."

"A house?"

"Yeah – you know. One of those buildings with four walls an' a window."

The Australian stewardess delivered Mannon's drink with a linen napkin and a silver dish full of nuts. Curbing an impulse to pinch her ass he asked, "What's Jack looking at a house for? He's not going legit, is he?"

Howard pulled a face. "Whadda *I* know?"

"Universal is pitching a script for me to do with Clarissa," Mannon said casually. "I'm not sure she'd be a laugh a minute to work with. What do *you* think?"

"I think you should do a film for Orpheus," Howard said self-righteously. "Jesus! Don't you have a loyal bone in your body?"

"Come up with something, friend, and I'll consider it."

"You fuckin' actors," spat Howard. "When you're on the way up you'll grovel for a walk-on. When you make it you're impossible assholes. And when you're stars you're so full of shit it comes pourin' out every time you open your goddamn mouths! Don't forget, I remember you when – *friend*."

Mannon laughed. "And I remember *you*."

Jack kept them waiting twenty minutes, and then he came bounding up the outside steps into the plane. "Traffic," he said, before anyone could complain.

"What's all this crap about a *house*?" Mannon asked.

"I saw it. I liked it. I rented it."

"Let's get this show on the road," Howard said impatiently. "We've waited long enough to make this weekend. If we don't get our ass in gear we're gonna spend it sittin' on the goddamn plane!" He picked up the intercom and spoke to the pilot. "All aboard. Let's fly!"

Chapter 33

They circled each other like suspicious tigers. Jade hadn't wanted to see him, yet when Mark announced he was downstairs in the lobby, it seemed too petty to say he couldn't come up. So she let him. And here he was. Mark Rand. English asshole.

She had wanted to remember him as he was in her bathroom the last time they met, but it was not to be. Mark looked good. Very good. He was wearing an impeccably cut blue blazer, a Turnbull & Asser white shirt open at the neck, a thin lizardskin belt, and blue slacks with a knife-cut crease. His brown hair was appealingly ruffled, and he had a slight tan.

"It's so *good* to see you," he said enthusiastically, wandering around the apartment inspecting her books and paintings and ornaments.

She had not had time to plan for this meeting, and wasn't quite sure how to handle it.

"You moved so swiftly," he continued. "When I came back to talk to you, you were gone – just like that."

"When *did* you come back, Mark?" she asked, curious to know how long it had taken him.

"After we ... er ... had our fight, I returned to England." He paused at a table set with her collection of glass decanters and bottles of liquor. "Do you mind if I pour myself a drink?"

"Go ahead," she said coldly, not about to do it for him. "Please make it a short one, I have an appointment."

He looked at her with honest eyes. "I promise not to keep you, Jade. I'll say what I have to say and be on my way."

His crisp English accent was a turn-on – it always had been. She stared at him warily as he poured scotch into a glass and added a touch of soda.

"May I get something for you?" he asked politely.

"No, thank you," she replied, equally formal.

"Well . . ." He sipped his drink. "When I returned, you were gone. No forwarding address, everyone sworn to secrecy about your whereabouts." He allowed himself a tiny smile of triumph at his own cleverness. "But I found you."

"I can tell," she remarked, concentrating on his crooked teeth in the hope they would take her mind off the rest of him. She felt uncomfortably warm.

"I heard about the contract with Cloud Cosmetics. Quite a coup. Congratulations."

"Thank you."

His grey eyes sought out hers. "I miss you very much, Jade." His English accent dripped sincerity.

Oh damn! Why didn't she just admit it? He was a lying, cheating sonofabitch, but she missed him too.

Her jaw tightened in a determined thrust. She had to get rid of him before she did something she would regret.

"When we parted I flew straight to London," he continued. "On the plane over I thought about everything and I was deeply ashamed of the way I'd tried to deceive you."

"If this is an apology I accept it," she said, jumping up from the couch. "The thing is, Mark, I've got a date, and if I don't get ready . . ." She trailed off, waiting for him to take the hint.

"I'm divorcing Fiona," he announced dramatically. "I have already consulted my lawyer, and we are proceeding immediately."

It was a bombshell. For six years she had heard nothing but *when the children are older*. What caused *this* sudden change of heart?

"I realize asking you to forgive me is not enough," he said gravely. "I can't expect you to resume our relationship the way it was. This is my pipe of peace. When I'm divorced, I would like you to be my wife."

She was speechless. This was the last thing she'd expected.

Laughing self-consciously he said, "I know this is a surprise, and I don't expect you to make an immediate decision. I just want to be sure that you realize how very important you are to me, and that I love you very, very much."

Oh God! Mark, full of sincerity with his crooked English teeth, tousled hair, and "little boy lost" stance, drove her crazy.

Come clean, Johnson. You're infatuated with this guy. You want to jump his bones. Why hold back?

153

She took a deep breath. "This is a little too much for me to digest in one sitting," she said, striving for a light-hearted approach. "Why don't we talk tomorrow when I've had a chance to . . . uh . . . think this over?"

He nodded, and raised a quizzical eyebrow. "This *is* a proposal, Jade. I have come to you hat in hand, so to speak. Please don't punish me for the past, let's think about the future. *Our* future," he added pointedly.

She walked him to the door.

"I'm staying at the L'Hermitage," he said. "Maybe you might care to visit me later, after your . . . date."

"I'll call you," she said.

He held her shoulders and gazed into her eyes. "I know I've been foolish. I'll never risk losing you again. Am I forgiven?"

She *wanted* to forgive him, only something held her back. She wasn't going to be sweet, wonderful *trusting* Jade anymore. She was going to check his story out before she committed herself.

He leaned close to her. He smelled of peppermint breath spray and Hermès aftershave. "Cancel your date," he said urgently. "We've been apart too long. I want to touch you . . . stroke your glorious body. I want to make love to you, Jade. You must feel the same way." Pulling her to him he began to kiss her.

For a moment she allowed his insistent lips to press against hers, his familiar tongue to invade her mouth. Hard against her thigh she felt the pressure of his desire. She wanted to say — *The hell with everything, Mark is back, and I'm glad.*

But she didn't. She had her pride. He wasn't going to walk into her life just like that and take over.

With supreme willpower she disengaged herself. "Please, Mark, go back to your hotel. We'll see each other tomorrow."

He was disappointed, but determined to behave like a gentleman. "For breakfast?"

"Lunch."

"Where shall we meet?"

"I'll come to your hotel."

"Who's your date with, Jade? You know I'm an extremely jealous man." He smiled when he said it, but she knew he was in agony. Mark was unreasonably possessive.

"Just a friend," she said lightly.

"Why can't you cancel it?"

"Don't push me."

"I miss you."

"Tomorrow."

She closed the front door on him. Her head was spinning. For six *years* she had waited for this moment. Now that it was here she wasn't sure *what* she wanted . . .

She paced restlessly around her apartment. There was no date arriving to take her out. Shane had wanted to see her, but she had begged off, claiming exhaustion. On impulse she called Antonio. He had mentioned something about going away for the weekend. She wouldn't mind going with him. Anything to get away from Mark while she thought things out.

Antonio was still at his studio.

"Where are you off to?" she asked.

"Las Vegas, *bella*. You want to come?"

She didn't hesitate. "Definitely."

Chapter 34

The ride back to reality took Wes twenty minutes. That's how long it was between Silver Anderson's Bel Air mansion and his run-down house on the Venice boardwalk. Silver had loaned him what she referred to as her "spare car". It was a snappy red Mercedes Sports 350 SL. A classic model. "Nobody uses it," she had said airily when seeing him off the morning after their night of passion. "Why don't you return it around eight tonight, and we'll have dinner at the house?"

She certainly wasn't backward in coming forward. He liked the fact that she didn't leave him hanging. She was obviously used to calling the shots, and enjoyed doing so.

"I'm not sure I'm free for dinner," he'd said lazily.

Her eyes challenged his. "Make yourself free."

"I just did."

He gave her his phone number at her request, and took off in the red Mercedes. What a trip! He had a feeling he had fallen into one peachy scene. Only how to proceed? When she found out he was nothing more than a broke barman she was not exactly going to be thrilled to death. Right now she had no idea who he was or what he did. And how to keep it that way?

Parking her Mercedes in a side street he walked briskly to his house. Silver obviously trusted him. She had lent him her car, hadn't she? If she thought he was a bum she wouldn't have done that. Although what did a car mean to Silver Anderson? Probably nothing. She was insured if he did a quick vanishing trick. All rich people were insured. And she was probably loaded.

He felt a building excitement. Maybe he'd just lucked into a whole different lifestyle.

There was a note tacked to his front door. It was short and to the point:

PAY UP OR GET OUT BY NOON TOMORROW.

Reba, venting her fury at being dumped last night. He wondered if she'd recovered her precious mink jacket for which he still had the claim check. Poor old Reba, she must be boiling.

"Is this your dog?"

Wes turned to confront his nextdoor neighbour, the uptight female who played classical records all night and drove him crazy with the noise. She was a skinny little thing, plain, with her scraped-back hair and granny glasses. She wore no makeup and looked about twelve in her baggy pants and tee-shirt. He had tried to talk to her several times – well it was only neighbourly to be friendly, wasn't it? Every time he made an attempt she had ignored him.

"You should be ashamed of yourself," she continued hotly, not waiting to find out if it was his dog or not. "The poor animal sat outside your door howling all night. That is, until *I* took it in. He had a nasty cut on his front paw which I cleaned and bandaged as best I could. You'd better take him to a vet."

Wes checked out the dog sitting patiently beside the girl. It was the same dog that had been following him around for a while – ever since picking him up on the beach one day. It was a mutt, a mongrel with stupid trusting eyes, and he'd thrown it a few bones once in a while – just to get it off his back. "It's not *my* dog," he denied vehemently. "Never set eyes on it before in my life." He had no intention of acquiring any vet bills.

"Liar!" she accused. "I've seen this dog with you on many occasions."

"How many?"

"What?"

"Okay, okay. So it's followed me around sometimes, but it's not my dog. You can have it. It's a stray."

The girl was busting with fury. "You bum! How can you give your dog away? How can you be so . . . so . . . *uncaring*?"

He caught sight of her nipples – erect under the skimpy tee-shirt. If you did the old secretary trick – took off the glasses and let the hair loose – she might be quite pretty. "Who, *me*? You're the one with the crappy loud music all night long so that nobody gets any sleep."

Glaring at him she said, "The last thing *you* do is sleep. You're never home."

"Have you been spying on me?"

"I've got better things to do with my time."

The dog whined pathetically, and lifted its bandaged paw.

She calmed down. "Look," she said. "I took a day off work to wait for you. I thought it was your dog; you say it's not. Why don't we get together on this and take it to the vet?"

"Go ahead. I'm not stoppin' you." He indicated the note on his door. "I have problems of my own to take care of."

She glanced at the note then back at him. "Oh, you can handle our dragon landlady, I've seen you do it before."

"It seems you know a lot more about me than I do about you."

"I'm observant."

"So I've observed."

She didn't crack a smile. But she did remove her glasses, and he noticed that her eyes were ever so slightly crossed, giving her a rather appealing look. She was extremely young. And on closer inspection quite pretty, as he'd suspected. She made him feel ancient. He watched her twirl her glasses in child-size hands.

"If I take the dog to the vet will you pay half?" she asked tentatively. "And if we keep it, then maybe we can split the cost of its food."

"Something tells me you're not exactly flush," he remarked.

She fidgeted. "Not exactly."

"I wasn't really thinkin' of getting a dog."

"Half a dog," she corrected.

Shit! Why was he such a sucker? "Okay, okay," he said, giving in.

Her face registered relief.

"What's your name?" he asked. "I suppose that now we're partners in a dog I should know."

"Unity."

"Wes." He held out a friendly hand. "And what'll we call the mutt?"

The shadow of a smile flitted across her face. "I think we should."

"Should what?"

"Call our dog Mutt. It suits him perfectly."

He laughed – she was a funny little thing, but quite spunky. "You're on. While I live here we'll share the do– Mutt. Right?"

She nodded. Little did she know he would be moving out at any moment.

*

Silver greeted everyone on the set with unusual friendliness. Purring her way into the makeup chair, she leaned her head back, closed her eyes and murmured, "Make me divine!"

"Hmmm," commented Raoul, her makeup artist. "*Somebody* had a wonderful time last night, and it wasn't me."

She giggled girlishly. "Do I look haggard?"

"Quite the opposite actually."

Another giggle. "Great sex is better than sleep any day."

"Mr Denby living up to his reputation, is he?"

"You've *got* to be joking."

"Not a new one?"

"A real man."

"Oooh, I *love* real men!"

"Don't we all. And there aren't too many of them around."

"*Tell* me about it."

By noon, news of Silver Anderson's new lover had swept the sound stage. Everyone wanted to know who it was, only after her initial chat with Raoul she wasn't talking.

"I'm *so* sorry about last night," Fernando fretted, as he fussed with her hair. "It was an absolute *mob* scene. Boyce was awfully upset."

"I survived," Silver said dryly.

"So I heard!" Fernando pushed for information. "Anyone we know?"

"Ouch!" She pulled away from his teasing brush. "More care if you please."

"Sorry!"

"So you should be."

She stared at her reflection in the mirror as Fernando darted around her like an exotic plumed cockatoo. Wes Money. An unusual name. An unusual man. He wasn't in awe of her, not one bit. She adored that. Not like Dennis Denby, who was a waste of time.

Wes Money. What did he do? Where was he from? Was he married? Divorced? Did he have kids?

Last night was not a fact-finding mission. It was a night of hot sex, lustful sex. She smiled at the memories, still so very recent.

In the morning there was no time for talk, she had an early call and had to rush. Tonight she would find out about him.

Nora turned up for lunch. "I think I missed a page in your book," she said acidly.

Silver blinked. "What are you talking about?"

"Cut the crap. Who is he? And what does he want?"

Silver picked daintily at a chef's salad. "Does nothing escape you? Are there no secrets anymore?"

"Once Raoul knows, you may as well take out a full-page ad in *Variety*. Everyone is aware you got *schtupped* last night. And the big question is, by whom? Because it's common knowledge poor old Dennis didn't get lucky."

Silver smiled. She adored the attention and speculation her love life received. "Let them all keep guessing," she said. "I met a new man, with the emphasis on *man*!"

"Big cock, huh?"

"Nora!"

"Don't act shocked with me. I've seen a few in my time – before I changed tracks, of course."

"His name is Wes Money."

"And does he have any?"

"*I* don't know."

"Shall I give him the Dun & Bradstreet treatment?"

"I'm not planning to *marry* the man."

"Is he an actor?"

"Don't be ridiculous."

Nora chain-lit a cigarette. "What'll I tell the news hounds?"

"Nothing."

"They'll drive you crazy."

"There's nothing unusual about *that*."

Indulging in a coughing fit, Nora said, "You love it, doncha?"

Silver beamed. "I've been all the way to the bottom. And now I'm right back at the very top. Why *shouldn't* I love it?"

Chapter 35

The Forum Hotel accommodated Jack, Howard and Mannon in great style. They were given the Presidental six-room suite, which sprawled across the top floor of the hotel replete with terraced bedrooms, a sunken living room, an eight-seater jacuzzi, and a small screening room.

"I like it," Howard announced. "I want to run the studio from here and never leave."

Mannon threw himself down on an oversize fur-covered couch. "Not bad," he agreed. "If we don't have enough beds, this'll do!"

Jack wondered why he was there. In the plane, all the way to Vegas, Howard and Mannon had talked nothing but women. One might think they were a couple of out-of-towners on their first night away from their wives. Howard Soloman – the head of Orpheus Studios. And Mannon Cable – superstar. And all they had on their minds was getting laid.

Jack knew for sure he'd outgrown them long ago, and it didn't bother him one bit. What *did* bother him was that he'd agreed to come on this weekend. It was his own fault. He should have know what to expect.

Howard was bounding around like a tennis ball. "I love it!" he kept on exclaiming. "This is sensational! No phone calls. No wives. No pain." The phone rang and Howard automatically grabbed it. "Yeah?"

Jack thought of Clarissa. He wondered how she was. He wasn't sure if he missed her or not.

Howard spoke rapidly and hung up with a smile on his face. "That was Dino Fonicetti," he said. "He and Susanna wanna throw a party for us tonight. Whaddya say?"

Dino Fonicetti was the son of Joseph Fonicetti, who owned the Forum Hotel. He was married to Susanna, daughter of Carlos Brent – the legendary singer.

"Sure," said Mannon at the same time as Jack said, "No."

"What's with the no?" Howard yelled excitedly. "We came here to party, didn't we?"

"*I* came here for a break," Jack said determinedly.

"I can recall when the only break *you* cared about was between some bimbo's legs!" Howard laughed at his own humour. "You don't wanna party, don't do it. Mannon an' I will show 'em. Right, Mannon buddy?"

Mannon nodded agreeably.

Jack wondered what would happen if Mannon ever suspected that Howard planned to hit on Whitney. He wouldn't be so amiable then. "I'm going to take a walk," he said. "Maybe I'll lay fifty bucks on black, lose, and go to bed. I've put in a heavy day."

"So what was *I* doin'? Lyin' in the sun?" demanded Howard indignantly. "My day was a crap-shoot from start to finish. However, *I* am ready to roll – all the way."

"Have a good time," smiled Jack.

"Yeah," said Howard. "We'll tell you what you missed in the mornin'. Y'can cry in your orange juice!"

*

From the moment they set off, Jade had her doubts about why she had wanted to accompany them. Antonio had a new boy-friend, a dapper interior designer whom he couldn't keep his hands off. And along for the ride was a sulky male model with a waist-length mane of hair. Jade wasn't sure who *he* belonged to, but he was Danish and didn't speak any English, so she didn't let it bother her. After all, he wasn't *her* responsibility.

Las Vegas was not her kind of town – she knew it the moment they arrived. Gambling had never interested her, and the heat on the streets was suffocating. The hotels were all glittering gambling palaces, the people tourists, and the noise of whirling slot-machines non-stop. She hoped Antonio wouldn't be insulted if she hopped on a plane back to L.A. early in the morning.

Yeah. Just in time to keep your lunch date with Mark. Who are you kidding?

Antonio had arranged rooms in a hotel called the Forum. Talk about bad taste. The place was a salute to it! In her room she found a vibrating bed, thick-pile gold carpets, a mirrored ceiling, and porno movies on the closed circuit television.

"Later we party," Antonio advised. "My friends, Dino and Susanna, they have the hot party."

Jade almost yawned in his face. Exhaustion had set in. Two days in bed, sleeping, might be the perfect way to spend the weekend. "I may pass on that," she said.

"You may not!" exclaimed Antonio. "You come here for fun. *Bene*. Fun you shall have!"

*

"Good evening, Mr Python."

"Hiya, Jack!"

"Hello, Jack Python."

"I know you."

"God! You're better lookin' off than on!"

The greetings and comments surrounded him until he felt he was drowning in a sea of flattery.

"Do you like Bette Midler?"

"Is Meryl Streep tall?"

"Does Dustin Hoffman smoke?"

"What's Ann Margret really like?"

The questions came at him from all sides, until a fixed smile slid into place on his face and stayed there as he searched for the nearest exit.

"Hi. I'm Cheryl. Wanna have a nice time?"

"Try my room, 703, in ten minutes."

"I'd really like to sleep with you. I'm a big fan."

"Wanna get it on, TV star?"

The women were not shy. They were aggressive with their come-ons. A tiny blonde, with huge boobs hardly concealed in a shiny blue cocktail dress, trailed him relentlessly. Finally he had to turn on her and say, "Listen. Don't follow me. I *am not* interested. Okay?"

"Who d'y think you *are*?" she shouted belligerently.

"I know who *I* am," he muttered, and pushed through swing

doors to the peace and quiet of the vast swimming pool.

The outside area was deserted. It was past ten, and the sun-bathers and swimmers were long gone. He gazed up at the sky. The stars were out with a vengeance. Tomorrow was going to be a scorcher. Mannon had said something about taking a boat out on Lake Mead.

What was he doing here? In theory it sounded great – a weekend with the guys. But he'd already realized he wasn't one of them anymore. He had other things on his mind, and getting drunk and getting laid just for the sake of it had lost its appeal. Maybe he should alert Aretha to send him a fast telegram saying his presence was urgently required back in Los Angeles. Not such a bad idea.

*

"Hiya, beautiful."

"Want a drink?"

"How about dinner?"

"Do you live around here?"

"Mama! Mama! I died an' went to pussy heaven!"

Jade ignored the remarks. She was used to getting attention. New York had taught her how to deal with it. Just ignore the suckers and they'll soon go away.

However, in Las Vegas they did seem a touch more persistent.

She whirled on one man who made a particularly obscene remark. "Dream on, asshole!"

"Right between your legs, baby!"

She hurried away. Taking a walk around the casino to get the feel of the place was not such a good idea. In Vegas, a woman alone at night obviously spelled available. She followed the SWIMMING POOL sign, and walked outside.

*

"I love giving head," the expensive hooker in the filmy chiffon dress whispered into Howard Soloman's ear. "It's my favourite sexual act. How about you?"

Howard, who had no idea the woman was a hooker, nodded happily. "If you wanna give it, who am I to stop you?"

The woman smiled. Her teeth weren't great, but the rest of her was verging on perfect. Long legs, big bosom, long hair. "I like a man who folds easily," she said, leaning all over him. "And you're *sooo* attractive. Exactly my type."

Howard felt the old one-eyed snake stir. This broad was something else. She had been coming on to him from the moment she sat down next to him at Dino and Susanna's party. "You're not an actress, are you?" he asked suspiciously.

"No," she replied with a scornful toss of her head – although if the truth were known she was a better actress than most of the flibberty little bits of fluff she saw on television. "I'm in real estate," she added. "What do *you* do?"

Was she putting him on? Perhaps. Perhaps not. After all, he wasn't a famous *face*. "I'm a businessman," he said guardedly. Better she didn't know too much about him.

"I *looove* a man who handles things," she purred. Her expensively manicured hand moved onto his thigh. "Why don't we go somewhere private?"

Howard agreed readily. He didn't find time to play around in Hollywood. Oh sure, he could always use the never-ending supply of actresses looking for a part – but he didn't like the thought of a woman sleeping with him just because of what he could do for her career. And if you got laid in Hollywood, the whole town knew about it the next day. A lot of men simply didn't care, they just went for it and the hell with the consequences. One well-known producer regularly checked into The Beverly Hills Hotel for an afternoon tryst with his various paramours. Once, his wife was attending a charity function in the Coterie Restaurant, but that didn't fazè the producer; he still checked in with a top-heavy redhead, and waved a greeting to his wife's friends at the same time. That was called *chutzpah*.

Howard didn't have the nerve – Poppy would kill him. "Excuse me a minute," he said. "I'll be right back."

Dino Fonicetti was talking to a group of people. Howard drew him to one side and indicated the woman. "Do you know her?" he asked.

Dino looked across the room. Did he know her? Oh, yeah, he knew her, she was the perfect sexual partner for some of his more important guests at the hotel, and he paid her handsomely to entertain them. "Yes. She's very nice. Very respectable. Not a spinner."

"Spinner?" This was a phrase even Howard hadn't heard.

Dino chuckled. "You know, a spinner. A broad who spins from one guy to the next."

Howard laughed too.

"You're not leaving, are you?" Dino asked.

Howard winked. "I'll be right back." He indicated Mannon, who was playing poker with a tableful of high-rollers. "Tell him I'll see him later, or in the morning."

Dino nodded understandingly.

★

"Don't we know each other?" Jack asked.

Jade, sitting on the edge of the diving board, sighed with annoyance. She'd had it with the never-ending pick-up factor. *"Go away."*

"Huh?"

"You heard."

She hadn't even looked at him. He persisted. "Hey – I'm not trying to hit on you. I remember you from . . . uh . . . Silver Anderson's party. My name's Jack Python."

She didn't exactly jump, more a slow turn. She knew who he was all right.

He decided maybe Vegas wasn't such a dead loss after all. He'd been watching her for ten minutes, and he recalled her leaving Silver's party very well. She had been with Antonio's group.

"We never met," she said, recognizing him immediately.

"You *were* there," he stated.

"So was half of Hollywood," she pointed out.

"Can we have a drink and discuss it?"

She began to laugh. *"Mr.* Python. Have you any idea how many times I've been asked that tonight? I'm *surprised* at you. Couldn't you have come up with a more original approach?"

Smiling the Python killer-smile, he said, "Tell me an original approach and I'll use it."

"How about . . . what's a nice girl like you doing in a sleazy city like this?"

He nodded. "That's good. It's got impact. Let me try it." He took three steps away from her and then strode briskly back. "Excuse me – Miss?"

She played the game. "Ms., if you don't mind."

"Uh . . . Ms.?"

"Yes?"

"What's a nice girl like you –"

"Woman," she interrupted.

"Woman?"

"Girl is a patronizing term."

"Come on – *you* told me what to say."

"Just checking to see if you're smart enough to change it."

"Hey – watch the insults!"

Getting up, she said, "Don't sweat it, Mr, Python. I can't have a drink with you anyway." She took the sting off her words with a dazzling smile. "I do enjoy your show, only my mother warned me never to talk to strangers, and let's face it, you may be famous, but you're still a stranger."

She walked briskly away before he could answer, and vanished into the hotel.

Once inside she stopped to think. What was a man like Jack Python doing picking up girls – women – out by the pool of the Forum Hotel at ten-thirty at night? He was dangerously good-looking. Too dangerous for her. She had enough involvements right now, and certainly did not need a one-night stand with a man who had a stud reputation. Besides, she had made a strict rule to always steer clear of well-known men – they had egos the size of Atlanta. And that's the last thing she needed.

*

"Take it off, Howard," crooned the woman.

"What off?" gasped Howard. He was marooned among her long legs and big breasts and mass of hair, naked as a bare-assed baby, and just as happy.

"Take off the rug, it's inhibiting you."

"What rug?" he asked indignantly.

"*This* rug!" she said with a triumphant tug at his prize thatch of hair. She whirled it in the air and threw it on the floor.

"Shit!" he exploded.

She bounced on the bed, large breasts jiggling. "I get off on bald men," she explained. "It's sexy. Let's do sixty-nine."

"I'm *not* bald."

"Gettin' there."

"Thank you *very* much."

"Let's do sixty-nine."

"No."

"Why?"

"Because . . ."

"What? You don't like to eat pussy?"

He didn't answer.

She shrugged, and her large breasts heaved. "Your loss," she said, thinking of the female lover she would get it on with later.

*

Mannon Cable won fifty thousand dollars. The party was going strong. He shook the women off like aggravating bugs, and retired to the suite – alone. Jack was in the living room fixing a drink. The door to Howard's bedroom was firmly closed.

"You know something?" Mannon said, "I think I'm getting too old for catting around."

"Want a shot?" Jack asked, pouring himself a scotch.

"Brandy."

"Coming up."

"This place is loaded with hookers. Who did Howard end up with?"

Jack found a bottle of Courvoisier. "I never made the party. I took a walk instead."

Mannon clicked the television on and ruminated. "I've got a beautiful wife, and a beautiful ex-wife. I came here to get laid, but quite frankly – who needs it?"

"You're asking *me*?" Jack said, handing him his brandy. "Let's take the plane back tomorrow."

"What about Howard?"

"What *about* him? He's over twenty-one. I think he'll make out."

Mannon held the brandy glass between his hands and swirled the amber liquid. "It's strange, isn't it? Once we would have given our right arms for this kind of set-up. Now we've got it, who wants it? Who needs it?"

Jack laughed. "Howard."

"Yeah. You can take a kid out of Colorado –"

"But you can never take Colorado out of a kid!" Jack finished Mannon's sentence, and as he did so Jade's coffee commercial appeared on television. "Hey –" he exclaimed. "*That's* where I know her from."

"Who?"

"The girl on television."

They both stared at the set. Jade in a supermarket, buying a jar of coffee. She wore shorts and a tee-shirt and looked like every man's fantasy of the girl next door with her hair piled on top of her head. Next shot. Jade at home – drinking the coffee. Dissolve ... She's dreaming ... Jade on a Caribbean beach swaying from the sea in a white bikini, her body tanned and supple, her copper hair long, tangled and wild. She strides from the sea, an Amazon princess. What a body! The camera pans in for a close-up of her face. What a face! *"My place or yours?"* she asks with a long and challenging look straight at the camera. Fade out.

Jack was mesmerized by the commercial. "I think I'm in lust," he dead-panned. "Have you any idea who she is?"

"I thought *you* knew," Mannon said.

"I *want* to know. She's here in the hotel — I just saw her."

Mannon was amused. "Is this love at first commercial? Should we alert Clarissa?"

"Aw . . . get lost!"

Howard emerged from his bedroom and staggered in, hairpiece in hand. He wore a white hotel bathrobe and looked like a beaten man. Two prominent love bites decorated his neck. "Drink," he requested hoarsely.

Jack handed him the bottle of scotch.

"Cigarette," he mumbled.

Mannon handed him a half-full pack of Marlboros.

Howard took a deep breath. "I think I'm having a wonderful time," he said, his voice heavy with exhaustion. "She's got a pussy like a vacuum cleaner. Wake me if I'm not dead in the morning."

And with that he reeled off.

"Viva Las Vegas," said Jack dryly.

Chapter 36

Reba turned up at noon. She let herself in with her pass key, and stood, arms akimbo, a furious expression on her heavily made-up face, at the end of the bed where Wes lay snoring.

He did not stir, in spite of her malevolent glare, which could have cracked paint.

She kicked the end of the bed. "You *shithead!*" she shrieked.

He opened one eye and smelled trouble. Best to face it head on. Sitting up quickly he said, "Jesus! Am I glad to see *you*. I couldn't figure out what happened last night. Once I got Silver Anderson home I came racing back to find you, but you'd gone." He stared accusingly. "Why did you leave without me?"

She opened her mouth like a surprised fish. This was not what she'd expected to hear at all.

"Reba, Reba," he continued, warming to his theme. "You *ran out* on me. I was stranded. I had to stay at a friend's house, and get the bus back this morning."

Frowning, she tapped extremely long fingernails on the end of the bed. "*I* didn't know you were comin' back," she said. "I thought you'd run off an' dumped *me*."

He managed to look hurt. "You thought that?"

"That's what it looked like, didn't it?" she answered defensively.

"It may have looked that way, only surely you know me better? I had your car keys, the claim check for your jacket. I *broke my neck* gettin' back." He paused, careful not to lay it on too thick. "How *did* you get home?"

"I always carry a spare set of keys for the car," she admitted.

He stretched out and yawned. "I'm just glad you're okay. That mob scene was a joke. I had to get the poor bitch out of there before things got out of control."

Reba sat on the end of the bed. "I guess I owe you an apology," she said lamely. "I didn't believe you even knew Silver Anderson."

"I told you I knew her. We're old friends."

She perked up. "I'd love to meet her."

He dodged that one. "So would half the world."

"Maybe we could all have dinner," she suggested hopefully.

Reaching for a cigarette he said, "Maybe." He threw her a stern look. "What was the welcoming note on my door when I got back this morning? What kind of crap was *that*?"

"Oh." She looked embarrassed. "You *do* owe me, Wesley."

"And I'm gonna pay you. Next week. I don't appreciate being threatened with eviction."

She licked her scarlet lips flirtatiously. "Would I do that to you?"

He played along – after all, he didn't want to find himself out on the street, did he? "I don't know *what* you'd do to me, given half the chance."

Laughing lasciviously, she edged along the bed. "Wanna find out, Wesley?"

"I can't, darlin'," he said, quickly. "I gotta see a man about a job. Y'want your rent, don't you?"

She stood up. "It's not that I'm pushin' you, Wesley. Only now that I'm about to be a single woman, I can't let my finances lag behind."

"I quite understand," he said gravely.

Pursing her lips she said, "Well, next time there's some sort of an event —"

"You'll ask me."

She preened coquettishly. "I'll have to see."

"Yours truly will be waitin'."

Her voice took on a businesslike tone as she prepared to leave. "Please telephone me as soon as you get my money."

"I don't have your number. You want to give it to me?"

She thought about that one — and decided against it. "Don't worry, I'll drop by next week."

"Can't wait," he said, with a friendly wink.

As soon as she left he reached for the Yellow Pages and called up the nearest locksmith. There was no way Reba Winogratsky was going to come and go as she pleased in *his* house. Who the hell did she think she was, letting herself in and standing over him while he slept, like a wronged wife?

Screw *her*.

It was over.

*

"Your behaviour was quite reprehensible," Nora said sternly. "However, after a day of thought, Miss Anderson has decided to keep you on." Dragging on her cigarette she added, "Why, I don't know."

Vladimir, head bowed, allowed relief to flush his cheeks. "Madame Silver is very kind," he murmured.

"She sure is," agreed Nora. "I hope you appreciate it."

"I do."

"You'd better."

"I do, I do." He backed gratefully out of the room.

"You're on parole," Nora called after him. "So watch it, sonny!"

He didn't reply.

Nora buzzed the bedroom. "All done," she said.

"Thank God!" replied Silver. "I do *so* hate scenes."

"Are you coming down, or shall I come up?"

"Neither, Nora dear. I'm going to soak in a long hot bubble bath. Wes will be here at eight. Thanks for doing the dirty work. I'll see you at the studio."

"Don't you want me to stick around and meet the new Boy Wonder?"

"Not necessary," Silver replied crisply. "And he is *not* a boy, Nora. He is a man."

"How old?"

"I haven't asked him."

"Fifty? Sixty?"

"Don't be ridiculous."

"Nineteen? Twenty?"

"Cradle snatching is hardly my style."

"Give me a clue."

"Good*night*, Nora."

Talk about being dismissed! Nora gathered her purse, and a stack of photographs Silver had autographed. She was tired after a long day. How come Silver never got tired? With a shake of her head she set off to her apartment in West Hollywood and a quiet TV dinner.

Upstairs, Silver relaxed in a Calèche-scented tub. A Frank Sinatra tape serenaded her. She loved Frank. He was a survivor, just as she was. He would be a performer until he dropped, and so would she.

*

Getting dressed was a problem. He couldn't wear the same suit again, and it was his only suit. He couldn't wear his one white shirt either, it didn't smell too fresh.

Wes inspected his closet. A depressing experience. He possessed two pairs of worn jeans, a pair of black gaberdine pants with a dodgy zipper, two blue shirts – both with frayed collars to match his white one – several unexciting sweaters, a leather bomber jacket and one sports jacket with old-fashioned large lapels. A fashion plate he wasn't. Usually he just stuck anything on and didn't give it a second thought.

A date with Silver Anderson required second thoughts.

He checked the time. It was a quarter to seven, and she had told him to be at her house by eight. She had also said they were staying in, which meant tonight he didn't have to sweat it. Tonight the jeans would pass muster, and maybe a blue shirt (if he could only hide either the missing button on one, or the gravy stain on the other) and his well-worn leather jacket. Of course, tomorrow was another matter. If indeed there was a tomorrow.

He showered, found a small shaker of Jean Naté talcum a

girlfriend had left behind, and liberally tossed the powder over his body. Underwear presented no problem because he never wore it.

A quick shave, on with the chosen outfit, and he was ready.

*

Silver could not make up her mind what to wear. Should she be casual? Dressy? A cross between the two? Finally, after discarding several outfits, she settled for black silk jersey floppy pants, and a black sweater with Joan Crawford shoulders. She doused herself with scent, and wore her dark hair drawn tightly back.

When she was satisfied with her appearance, she swept downstairs and surprised Vladimir in the kitchen.

He jumped to attention. "Yes, madame. Vas there something you needed?" Her visits to the kitchen were not a frequent occurrence.

She tried to forget she had seen him naked, in all his Russian glory. Oh God, banish the very thought! "Yes, Vladimir. I'd like a glass of Cristal. And I'd like you to set the dining room table for two – use the best cutlery and china. Then I want you to phone Trader Vic's and order dinner for two. Have them deliver it, and when it arrives lay out the dishes on the hotplate in the dining room, and go to your apartment. In other words – get out until the morning. I don't want you hanging around."

"Not even to clear up, madame?"

"Didn't you *hear* me, Vladimir?"

"Yes, madame."

She left him to organize everything while she selected more Sinatra to put on the elaborate stereo system, and lowered the lights – all the better to flatter her complexion.

It had been a long while since she'd felt like this about a man. Wes Money had her juices flowing. She couldn't wait to see him.

*

Just as he was leaving there was a knock at his front door. He hoped it wasn't Reba – he wouldn't put it past her to return.

"Yeah?" he called out.

The lock was safely changed, so at least there was no way she could come marching in.

"Are you busy?"

172

He recognized his neighbour's voice. *Don't tell me she's going to drive me crazy too*, he thought.

"I'm just on my way out," he shouted back.

Silence. She must have taken the hint. He turned off the television in the bedroom, grabbed the keys of Silver's Mercedes from the dresser, and set off.

Leaning against the wall outside was Unity with their newly acquired dog. "Hi," she said.

"Hello," he replied.

She had let her hair down. It was soft and brown, and curled around her heart-shaped face. She was getting prettier every visit.

"I took Mutt to the vet," she said.

"That's nice."

"Don't you want to know what he said?"

"What did he say?"

"He looked at his paw, cleaned it, and put another bandage on."

"Is that all?"

"Yes."

"Great. You'd already done that, hadn't you?"

"Yes, but we had to make sure."

"How much?"

"Your half comes out to nine dollars."

"You mean he charged you eighteen bucks just to look at the dog's *paw*?"

"And a flea bath."

"What's with the flea bath? I never agreed to that."

"He had to have it. The poor dog was crawling."

Wes shook his head. He was down to about fifty bucks, and now he had to shell out nine of them because the dumb dog had fleas. Jesus! If there was an award for sucker of the year he'd win it for sure.

Reluctantly he dug into his bankroll, peeled off a five, and four grubby one-dollar bills.

She accepted the money before springing the next bombshell. "I bought him a collar and lead," she announced.

"You're a generous little thing, aren't you?"

"I guess you don't want to pay half?"

"Look," he said patiently. "I am broke. Busted out. I would like to help you, but nine bucks for a dog is about as far as I'm prepared to go."

"What about its food?"

"Jesus!"

"You promised you'd pay half."

"How much?"

"Your split is a dollar fifty-seven. I got a bag of Gravy Train
– I think it will last the week."

"If it doesn't," he said fiercely, groping for more money, "the
mutt goes hungry."

She accepted two more dollars from him, and began to search
for change.

"Forget it," he said grudgingly. "Put it towards the collar
and lead."

"That'll give you a five percent share," she said gravely.

He couldn't help laughing. The dog began to bark. Gingerly
he patted it on the head.

"Did you work things out with our dragon landlady?" she
asked.

He nodded.

"I told you it would be easy for you."

"Yeah, well y'just have to know how to handle her."

"And I expect you do."

Was she giving him a jab? He couldn't tell. God, she was
young. Too young to even know how to jab.

"How old are you?" he couldn't help asking.

"Older than I look," she replied mysteriously.

Since she looked about twelve that didn't help much. "Lucky
you. I'm about ten years *younger* than I look."

She almost smiled. He couldn't tell what was going on behind
her John Lennon specs. "Well, I gotta get goin'," he said. "See
you."

He strode briskly away, leaving her standing outside his front
door, a rather forlorn little figure. Didn't she have any friends?

What did he care whether she did or not?

Come on, Wesley, Get your ass in gear. The star is waiting.

Chapter 37

In the Bistro Garden, an elegant Beverly Hills restaurant, the hum of conversation was muted as the rich and famous checked each other out. Poppy Soloman had a table in the tree-shaded garden. She had invited two other women apart from Melanie-Shanna, and while she waited for her guests to arrive, she sipped Perrier with a slice of lime, and inspected the other diners.

There was a well-known producer – well known for his shop-lifting proclivities.

There was his wife – an English rose from whom the bloom had long since faded.

There was a young screen writer – whose main claim to fame was his perpetual state of inebriation.

There was a teenage actress who had slept her way *down* the ladder.

Scattered among them were the stars, the true royalty of Hollywood. Poppy counted two retired greats, and a semi-retired almost-great. She also spotted Chuck Nielson with his agent. They exchanged waves.

Melanie-Shanna arrived before the other two women. She was flushed and full of apologies. "Am I late? I'm so sorry. I do hope I haven't kept you waiting."

Poppy tossed back her long blonde hair. Her thick tresses were her best feature, and she always made sure her hair was clean and shining and smelled of deliciously expensive shampoos and conditioners. "You're not late," she said, consulting a diamond-studded watch. "As a matter of fact, you're exactly on time."

"Thank goodness!" sighed Melanie-Shanna.

Poppy summoned the waiter with an authoritative gesture. "What would you like, dear?"

She quickly looked to see what Poppy was drinking. "The same as you, please."

"No, no. You must have something alcoholic. I'll join you in a minute." Poppy clicked her fingers at the waiter. "Bring Mrs. Cable a Mimosa."

Melanie-Shanna hesitated for only a second, then asked, "What's a Mimosa?"

"Champagne and orange juice," Poppy replied patronizingly, as if everyone should know. Before she married Howard, and got herself an education, she'd had no idea either.

Melanie-Shanna looked apologetic again. "Mannon doesn't like me to drink."

"A Mimosa is hardly a drink. You'll love it." Poppy stared critically at her luncheon guest. The girl was pretty enough in a very Texan sort of way. She had wonderful hair and skin, widely spaced eyes, and a body men watched. However, she was not Whitney – who apart from being dazzling was also a big star. Things like that made a difference. Poppy wondered where Mannon had found this one. It seemed every time he went on location to Texas he came back with a wife. "You know, dear," she said, "we've never really had an opportunity to *talk* before. I want to hear *all* about how you and Mannon met."

Melanie-Shanna shrugged. "The papers were full of our story. I thought everyone knew."

"Not *me*," said Poppy. "I never have *time* to read the newspapers, what with my charity work, catering to Howard, and watching Roselight. She's such an *active* little girl, just like her daddy. You must come over and see her one day."

"I'd like that."

The waiter placed a Mimosa in front of Melanie-Shanna. She sipped it delicately, and wished she hadn't come. Ladies' lunches always made her feel uncomfortable, as if she had a run in her tights or chipped nails.

"Good," Poppy said brightly. "Here are the girls."

The "girls" were two women of indeterminate age, although both would never see fifty again. Ida White was the fourth wife of super-agent Zeppo. She was put together with cement to hide the joins, and had pale skin, dramatically white hair pulled back in a tight chignon, an Yves Saint Laurent ensemble, and a blank stare. Rumour had it that Ida was permanently stoned, preferring the land of la-la to life with her womanizing husband.

Zeppo was an infamous Hollywood character known for his sharp tongue and two-inch cock, which – at one time or another – he had offered to every actress in the Western world.

The second woman was the wife of Orville Gooseberger, the producer. She was big and matronly, with the requisite facelift, frosted hair, and a very loud voice. Her name was Carmel, and her husband was even larger and louder than she.

"Does everyone know each other?" trilled Poppy, in between accepting hair-crushing kisses and cries of "You look *wonderful!*" from each of the women.

"Melanie, dear," continued Poppy (she loved playing hostess, it made her feel so important and busy) "this is Ida – you know, Zeppo White's wife. And I'm sure you've met Carmel Gooseberger. Her husband's the producer." Poppy made sure she gave everyone billing. "Girls," she said happily, "we have *finally* managed to get Mannon's wife *out*. Can you imagine? She never goes *anywhere*. We simply *have* to befriend her."

"I knew Mannon when he was getting under a hundred a picture," boomed Carmel.

The stoned Ida rallied. "He was adorable then. So ... so witty ..."

"And quite a ladies' man, I hear," giggled Poppy. "I'm too young to remember, but the rumours! Oh dear me!"

Melanie-Shanna smiled politely. She knew about Mannon's past reputation – they didn't have to stick her nose in it. After all, it was a long time ago, before Whitney. She swallowed hard when she thought of her predecessor. Last week she had gone to Mannon's bedside drawer, searching for aspirin. And there, face up, was a framed photograph of Whitney and him together. Just the two of them, in muted colour, standing with their arms around each other, a faraway look in their eyes.

Her immediate reaction was to smash the frame to the ground and rip up the picture. She *hated* Whitney Valentine Cable. If Whitney wasn't around, Mannon would be hers. For in her heart of hearts she knew he still belonged to his ex-wife.

The waiter delivered drinks to the table, and Poppy raised her glass of Perrier. "Now that we're all here," she said gaily, "I'd like to propose a toast."

Ida picked up her double vodka. Carmel lifted white wine. Melanie-Shanna reached for her second Mimosa.

"To us," announced Poppy. "Just because we deserve it!"

The ladies drank.

"And to Melanie." Poppy was on a roll, and wasn't about to quit. "Because we want her to feel she's one of us."

They made an incongruous quartet. Melanie-Shanna, so young and pretty, and obviously painfully out of place; Poppy, designer-labelled to the eyebrows, but not quite chic – her hair style put paid to that; Ida, totally out of it; and Carmel, old enough to be Melanie-Shanna's and Poppy's mother.

"I nearly fucked Mannon once," recalled Ida, a faraway look in her eye.

"Shush!" said Poppy warningly. "Melanie doesn't want to hear about *that*."

"Zeppo was his agent," Ida continued, oblivious. "We were all on location. I wasn't married to Zeppo then, but he was after me all right!"

"Zeppo was after everything that drew breath," Carmel remarked loudly.

"So was Orville," retorted Ida, with a spark of clarity. "I can remember when no actresses would step into his office because he insisted they give him a blow job under the desk."

"Really?" Poppy gasped.

"The Screen Actors Guild had to step in," Ida added. Her thoughts drifted. "I nearly fucked Mannon once."

"Well, you *didn't*," roared Carmel, "so *do* get off the subject."

Poppy giggled. She adored these two Hollywood old-timers – one never knew what was going to come out of their mouths next. And in their own way they were important women. At least their husbands were important, which made them important by association.

There is a certain kind of woman in Hollywood who believes that because she is married to a famous/rich/powerful man everyone loves her, and she is one of the queens of Hollywood.

Sure everyone loves her, while the marriage lasts. When the divorce comes – forget it. Suddenly the invitations cease and the loyal friends vanish. Sad but true. The friends stick with the famous/rich/powerful husbands. Some friends.

Ida and Carmel were two such women. Fortunately for them their marriages had lasted, sparing them the humiliation of being cast aside.

Chuck Nielson, sitting across the restaurant, had one eye on Melanie-Shanna and one eye on his agent, Quinne Lattimore. His concentration wavered between the two.

"Chuck, are you *listening* to me," Quinne asked irritably.

"Yeah," Chuck replied. "Only I gotta take a leak. I'll be right back."

He had noticed Mannon's wife rise to go to the ladies' room, and he was conveniently there when she came out. "Hello, pretty lady," he said.

She looked startled and flushed and exceptionally fuckable.

"Chuck Nielson," he reminded.

"Yes, I know."

"When are you coming to visit me at the beach?"

"What?"

"The beach. Malibu. Remember? I invited you down."

"Oh, yes."

"Don't go wild with excitement."

"We'd love to come."

He raised an eyebrow. "We?"

"Mannon and I."

Chuck grinned boyishly. "You don't have to bring him, y'know."

She edged away.

He stopped her with a hand on her arm. Whitney was giving him a hard time and he needed to teach her a lesson, bring her into line. She was too independent by far. If he started an affair with Mannon's new wife it would drive Whitney crazy.

"Take my number," he urged, handing her ı packet of matches with the number scrawled inside. "Call me."

Melanie-Shanna smiled vaguely; she didn't know what else to do. Mannon would be furious if he found out about this. "Excuse me," she said, pulling free.

"Call me," Chuck repeated, as she hurried back to her table.

"Well," Poppy said, savouring every word. "I see our local beach stud has you in his line of fire. How incestuous!"

"He was just inviting Mannon and me to his house in Malibu," Melanie-Shanna explained lamely.

Poppy grinned knowingly. "I bet he was!"

"*Really.*"

"That man is a rutting dog," Carmel announced. "Orville had him in a film once. He laid every woman on the set, including his co-star."

"And who might that be?" Poppy asked anxiously, never one to miss out on good gossip.

"I don't know. One of those flat-chested little popsies with

179

goo-goo eyes. They all look the same to me. She married a vet or a dog trainer or something – I can't remember which."

Poppy's eyes gleamed. "You must know some *outrageous* stories."

Ida knocked over her glass of vodka and pretended not to notice. "*I* know the best stories," she said in her strangely flat voice. "*I* know everything."

"You should write a book," Poppy gushed.

"I will," Ida said vaguely, "when I find the time."

Chapter 38

They were headed in one direction all night. Bed.

The champagne was cold.

The food delicious.

The conversation light.

Sex was on both their minds.

After dinner Silver suggested that they have brandies upstairs.

Wes grabbed a bottle of Courvoisier and two glasses, and followed her up the winding staircase.

It wasn't long before they were rolling around on her California King without a care in the world.

Silver Anderson, in bed, did not have any inhibitions. From experience Wes knew that after thirty, most women (he could only think of one exception – a tall thin porno star who swallowed men whole) had the most incredible hang-ups about their bodies. *Am I too thin? Fat? Floppy? Have I got stretch marks? Do my breasts sag?* God almighty! They carried on and on and on.

None of that from Silver Anderson. She wasn't twenty-two, and didn't give a damn. She had a compact, sinewy body, with firm breasts and hard nipples. Her bush was a little sparse, which was the only disappointment as far as he was concerned – he liked them with an abundance of hair down there. It didn't matter, though, and it certainly made it easier when going down on her. He didn't end up with a mouthful of annoying little pubic hairs which were impossible to get rid of.

Silver *loved* getting head. She didn't mind giving it either. Some women thought they were doing you the favour of all time. Not Silver. She got down and boogied with a good solid beat.

Tonight she gave him another ball-busting climax, and after a few minutes' recovery time he began to repay the compliment. Only he was in no hurry, and she didn't object.

He laid her out, put pillows under her ass, spread her legs, and went to work. Eating pussy was not one of his favourite things, but he tackled the task gamely. Tongue probing, pushing, exploring. Going for the gold, and finding it.

She responded nicely, with just the right amount of moans and groans.

Usually he didn't offer this service. In fact he could only remember doing it to two women before: his steel-thighed Swede, and the one love of his life – Vicki. Well, you had to keep *something* special, didn't you? He wouldn't have gone down on Reba Winogratsky for a thousand big ones. Maybe two thousand, but that was a lot of bucks.

Silver climaxed with abandon, thrusting her pelvis towards him until he was almost suffocated by her juices. He felt the throb, and knew it was a job well done.

He rolled away from her and dived into the bathroom, where he took a mugful of tap water and swished it around his mouth. Then he peed, and returned to the bedroom.

Silver was sitting up in the rumpled bed with the sheet tight to her chest. She had a smile of pure satisfaction on her face.

He grinned at her. No need for words as he bounded into bed beside her, reached for cigarettes for both of them, lit up, and handed her one.

They puffed silently, perfectly in tune. And when she was finished with her cigarette she reached for his balls under the covers, and kneaded them gently.

Not again! he thought. And rose to the occasion.

This was better than conversation any day!

Chapter 39

The yacht on Lake Mead was a rather grand affair with two
decks and a uniformed crew. It belonged to Joseph Fonicetti,
but he hardly used it, so his son, Dino, usually commandeered it
at weekends.

This particular weekend Dino and his wife, Susanna, were
hosting a luncheon with a somewhat disparate group of guests.

There was Howard Soloman, extremely hung over, with red-
rimmed eyes, and a turtleneck to cover his scars of battle.

There was Mannon Cable, with his cobalt blue eyes, dirty
blond hair, and sly, self-deprecating humour.

There was Jack Python, looking uncomfortable.

And three of Susanna's girlfriends. Two divorced, and one
still searching for a victim. On a scale of ten, they ranged from
a three to a six and a half.

There was Dee Dee Dionne, a beautiful black chanteuse, who
was Carlos Brent's current lady friend. She wore dark glasses
and sat watchfully in the background.

There was Carlos Brent himself. He was Susanna's father, and
a true legend in his own lifetime.

And Carlos Brent's assorted entourage.

There was Antonio, with his decorator boyfriend, and long-
haired Danish friend.

And there was Jade Johnson.

Quite a group.

Jack had only stayed to see Carlos Brent. He wanted him for
his show, and going through intermediaries was never satisfactory. When he spotted Jade, he knew fate had a hand in
things somewhere along the line, and he was glad. Quickly
noting who she was with, he detected no competition. Clarissa
was in New York. He deserved a break, didn't he?

Without hesitation he started to move towards her, only to be short-stopped by Antonio, who wanted to show off their acquaintanceship.

Jade smiled at him across the deck. A good sign. At least he wasn't losing the Python touch.

"Who is she?" he asked Antonio, pointing her out.

"You don't know Jade?" the photographer said in surprise. "How can that be?"

"Who is she?" Jack repeated.

The hunting look in his eye was duly observed by the wily Italian, and his *bella* Jade could do worse than Jack Python.

"She is Jade Johnson. The most famous model of all. Forget Jerry Hall, Cheryl Tiegs and Christie Brinkly. *This* is the one."

Jack felt like an idiot. Of course. He knew her name. *And* her image. Only she managed to look different in everything she did.

Putting on his glasses, he rubbed the stubble around his chin. Jade Johnson. A famous lady in her own field. She must think he was a grade A schmuck going for a quick pick-up. No wonder she hadn't responded.

Jade Johnson. He had heard her name a hundred times. Shaking his head he smiled to himself. She presented a challenge. It had been far too long between challenges.

Susanna Brent's girlfriends could not believe their good fortune. They were three Beverly Hills princesses with tight asses and hungry eyes. Susanna had invited them to Vegas for a reunion of sorts – they had graduated from high school together over twelve years before. "Maybe you'll find some hot guys in Vegas," Susanna had promised temptingly. Hot guys were one thing – but Mannon Cable and Jack Python, both within reaching distance! They were in heat!

Naturally, it was Howard who did the chasing. Howard, sweating in his turtleneck sweater, dropping names, *and* his pants if they would let him. On this weekend away from home ground he had gone pussy crazy!

Susanna's trio of girlfriends were not interested. None of them wanted to be actresses. The term *studio head* did not impress them. And Howard, with his insane mugging and overpowering approach, scored a zero.

Mannon began telling jokes, and soon drew an attentive audience. Carlos Brent strolled over and started to top each one

183

of Mannon's stories with a better one of his own. The two men enjoyed each other's celebrity.

Jack edged over to Jade, who was leaning over the rail studying the cool green water.

"Searching for sharks?" he asked casually.

She straightened up and faced him. Up close, in the strong daylight, she was staggeringly good-looking. Her very lightly tanned skin was soft and luminous, her gold-flecked eyes fascinatingly direct. The best thing about her, though, was her strong square jawline – which took the edge off perfection and made her vulnerable, strong, and just a touch aggressive, all at the same time.

He curbed a wild impulse to reach out and touch.

She pushed a hand through a tumble of shaggy copper hair and looked around at Dino and Susanna's guests. "If I was searching for sharks, I'm sure there are better places to look than in the water. Yes?"

He liked the way she said "yes" at the end of a sentence.

"You see that man over there." She indicated Howard, who had now moved on to Carlos Brent's girlfriend and was promising her stardom.

"What about him?" Jack asked curiously.

"When I first came out to Hollywood – I guess it must be ten years ago. Anyway, he was an agent then, chic in his gold chains and perfect suntan. God, he gave me a real hard time. Chased me around the couch in my hotel suite, and badgered me day and night to go out with him. Antonio tells me he's the head of a studio now. I'm in shock. The man is a moron! Do you know him?"

Jack considered his reply carefully. It was not going to do him much good if he admitted he was spending the weekend with Howard the moron. And he had to agree that if you didn't know Howard, he *could* come across as an asshole. Choosing to shift focus he said, "What were you doing in Hollywood then?"

"A screen test. The usual bullshit. Ten minutes in town was enough to convince me that I didn't want it. I like to be in control of *my* life."

A woman who thought along the same lines as he did. He liked her style. "Hey – I'm sorry for not knowing who you were last night," he said apologetically.

"It's not required knowledge," she joked. "A good model sells a product, not herself."

"And you're the best, I hear."

"Who told you that?" She paused. "Ah . . . let me see, could it be the great Antonio by any chance?"

"God, you're quick!"

"Only when I'm running away from Howard whatshisname! Or maybe we should just call him Moron Numero Uno." She tilted her head. "Do you think I'm being too cruel?"

"He's not such a bad guy once you get to know him."

"Ah ha! So you do know him."

"Guilty, I'm afraid."

She thought he had the sexiest eyes she had ever seen. They were an incredible green, with a deep intensity she could easily get lost in. "I hardly ever watch your show," she blurted foolishly, just so he wouldn't think she was impressed.

He regarded her with cool amusement. "I didn't ask you, but go on, make me feel bad."

"I didn't mean to do that –"

"Oh yes you did."

She laughed. "I didn't. Really."

Their eyes met and stayed locked together just that moment too long.

She felt a jolt of electricity and so did he. Neither of them could ignore it.

"What are you doing tonight?" he asked.

She didn't hesitate – sometimes she liked to take risks. "We're having dinner, aren't we?"

He liked a direct woman.

He liked everything about her.

Chapter 40

Immediate problem: make a score. He had to pay Reba, and support his half-share in a dog, and eventually he was going to have to take Silver out, although *in* suited him just fine, and he wasn't pushing.

Another night of unadulterated lust. And very nice too. Somewhere along the way she had asked him what business he was in. Casually he had replied, "Liquor." She hadn't pushed it. Probably thought he owned Seagrams!

Now he was driving back to Venice in her 350 SL, early a.m., and feeling no pain.

She likes me! She likes me! he thought, feeling like Sally Field when she gave her Oscar acceptance speech.

If he played it right he could be moving in any day now. He strongly suspected that Silver quite fancied the idea of having a man about the house. She had dropped a few not so subtle hints about the way everyone took advantage of her, and how nice it would be to have someone she could trust to look after her affairs. This, after two nights of passion. Things were looking good.

However, it did not solve the pressing problem of scoring bucks.

Usually, when he needed money, he went to work. Tending bar on a good week – with a touch of petty larceny on the side – he could pull in eight or nine hundred. Just the kind of money he needed now. Only he couldn't take time off right at the beginning, she wasn't *that* hooked. His only alternative was Rocky, who could probably point him in the direction of something seriously illegal. He didn't have much choice.

Taped to his front door was an envelope. Not Reba again!

He ripped it open and read the childish scrawl, bad spelling and all.

MUTT AND I THAWT YOU CAN COME
TO EAT WITH US TONITE. I WILL
COOKE. 7 OCKLOCK. LOVE FROM
UNITY.

What brought that on? He couldn't go. Silver had already booked him.

Happiness was being in demand.

*

"Poppy Soloman called," Nora said, in between bouts of coughing. "She wants to have a dinner for you. She said you'd discussed it."

"You sound terrible," Silver scolded. "Aren't you planning to *do* something about that cough?"

" 'Twasn't the cough that carried me off, 'twas the coffin they carried me off in!" joked Nora, with a macabre grimace.

"*Most* amusing," said an unamused Silver.

They were in her dressing room at the studio. It was the lunch break, and Silver rested on a couch, her legs up, her head supported by two large pillows. "I'm exhausted!" she announced. "Pass me my vitamins, for God's sake."

Nora duly obliged. Silver gulped the mixed vitamins down by the handful. Then she yawned, a long-drawn-out self-satisfied yawn.

"I presume last night was another winner," Nora said acidly.

Silver closed her eyes. "Mmmmmm . . ."

"When do I get to meet Mister Wonderful?"

"Soon."

"When?"

"How about Poppy Soloman's dinner?"

"I don't think she's planning on inviting *me*."

"Tell her you're part of the deal. You know I like to have you around."

"I get overtime for attending dinners," Nora rasped.

"Good. Charge it to the studio."

"Don't think I won't."

A knock on the door announced lunch. A tray for Silver. Grated carrots, sliced peppers, raw broccoli, and thinly sliced cucumbers on a plate.

She looked at it with distaste. "What I wouldn't give for a big fat juicy hamburger!" she sighed with longing.

"Shall I order you one?" Nora asked.

"Are you mad?"

*

Rocky knew just the trouble Wes could get into. He had heard there was a very special collection to be made which would pay big. "I don't wanna have anythin' t'do with it," Rocky said. "There's warring factions out in the hills of Laurel Canyon. It's not serenity city, but if you wanna score fast, I'll give you the man to call."

If Rocky didn't care to be involved it had to be heavy, and usually Wes liked to steer clear of any whiff of trouble. He went for it, though – there didn't seem to be much choice if he wanted fast bucks.

*

"I'm going back to the office," Nora said. "Are you cozying with Stud of the Year tonight?"

"I see no reason to quit while I'm on a winning streak, do you?"

The older woman shook her head. "Where do you get the energy? Sex every night. Work every day. And interviews in your spare time. Which reminds me, I want to go over next week's schedule with you. *Bazaar* wants you for the cover, and –"

Silver waved her away. "Not now, Nora. I'm hardly in the mood."

If Silver didn't want to talk covers, she must be *really* hooked. "Later?"

"I shall be busy later. *Very* busy."

*

The deal was this. A certain bad-boy rock star and his fifteen-year-old girlfriend were holed up in a remote house high in the hills of Laurel Canyon. They owed. And they owed big.

"These people don' wanna pay," explained the black dude to whom Wes had refused entry to Silver's party. He was a short man, with a toothy grin and huge white-framed sunglasses. "You wanna go get the green stuff. We grateful. We pay big."

The meet was taking place in the back of the man's limo at the bottom of the multi-storey parking lot in the Santa Monica shopping mall. They were separated from the driver by a thick tinted glass window.

When Wes had called, the man had suggested they get together at once, and arranged the rendezvous, which Wes just managed to arrive at by noon.

"What's the big fuss?" he asked; there didn't seem to be anything complicated about picking up some money.

"You wan' the truth, I give it to you," the black man said. "This boy a bad one. He beat up on my las' delivery man. He steal my coke. He keep my money."

"Yeah?"

"This not good scene fo' me. *No trouble* is my motto. I don' wan' no connection to this bad boy. None at all."

"You're tellin' me he's not going to greet me with a kiss and a fistful of dollars. Right?"

"Maybe. Maybe not. I don' pay no thousan' for nothin' easy."

"I figured that."

"This famous bad boy — he collect guns. His sweetie-box — she only fifteen. We don' want no duckin' an' divin' with this couple. So we sen' you in for pick up. You fuck up — no connection."

"And what makes you think he'll hand over the money to me?" Wes asked cynically.

"He say he will now. He ready." Taking a silk handkerchief out of his top pocket, he wiped his face. "You carry a piece?"

"Whoa!" Wes said quickly. "I'm not gettin' into any of *that*."

The man made a face. "I don' care personally. Jus' for your own protection. You want the job? You carry a piece. Insurance, thas all."

Staying silent, Wes thought it out. On the one hand it seemed fairly straightforward. On the other it stank stronger than a dead catfish.

"I don't get it," he said at last. "Why would you pay a thousand for this pick-up?"

"Don' give me no D.A. questions. You do it or no?"

So it wasn't the smartest move in the world; even Rocky had turned *this* one down. But he had luck on his side. Wes Money always made out — somehow.

"I'll do it," he decided.

"Tonight."

"Not tonight."

"Nine o'clock on the stroke, or no deal."

Shit! He could call Silver and tell her he'd be late. Better still, he could turn this offer down and ask *her* for money. Just a loan. Nothing serious.

Sure. And it would be goodbye Wesley without a second thought.

"Money up front," he said.

"No problem."

Now he was more suspicious than ever. What kind of a schmuck parted with money *before* the deed was done?

The man handed him a small snub-nosed revolver, and a crisp packet of new hundred-dollar bills.

"Aren't you worried I'll tango out of town with this?" Wes joked.

"You'd be motherfuckin' crazy to do that to me," the man said, removing his shades and staring.

"Wouldn't think of it," Wes said quickly.

The man passed him a slip of paper with an address written on it. "Nine o'clock. They be expectin' you. Then you bring package to me here. I be waitin'."

Wes nodded. And with gut instinct he knew he was making a wrong move.

Chapter 41

A strong blast of the white powder into each nostril made Howard Soloman feel like a real man. He was on a roll. Vegas was the best time he'd had in a while.

Leaning back against the cool marble of the bathroom wall he allowed the full drug-induced sensation to take over his body. By the time he was ready to rejoin the party he was fucking invincible!

He determined to tell Mannon Cable where his loyalties lay. How dare he refuse to do a film for Orpheus. Shithead actor. Stars or not they were all shitheads. Mannon was his friend. You made certain moves for friends. And goddammit, signing a deal with Orpheus should be one of them.

Conveniently he forgot he was hellbent on getting Mannon's

ex-wife into the old sackeroney. Exquisite Whitney. He got hard just thinking about her. Which made him think of Poppy, for whom he had a permanent soft-on!

Howard laughed aloud, leaned over the basin, and splashed cold water on his face.

He was at another party, a Saturday night after-the-show bash for Carlos Brent.

Carlos hadn't done a movie in ten years, and Howard planned to nail him. Okay, so Carlos Brent had made a few flops in his time – singing was his forte, not straight drama. Howard's brilliant idea was to offer him a *musical*! Shit! What an idea! The kind of musical they used to make way back in the forties with John Payne and Betty Grable. Nostalgia time. Everyone would love it!

Howard was at a loss to figure out why nobody had thought of it before. The idea screamed BOX OFFICE! He would get a young hot-shot director/writer. One of those boy geniuses just waiting for a big budget. And an experienced producer to keep a steady eye on things. Orville Gooseberger would be ideal. And Whitney Valentine for the female lead!

Howard was so excited he had to take a quick pee before rejoining the party.

He had just come up with the project of the year!

*

"I hate some of your movies, they're so masculine. And you play a real macho sexist pig!" So spoke one of Susanna Fonicetti's girlfriends, hoping this negative approach would impress Mannon Cable so much that he would whisk her off to his hotel suite for further discussion.

He blinked his impossibly blue eyes and winked. "Let me tell you something, darlin'. You're absolutely right."

"On the other hand," she added quickly, "in some of your films you really are quite wonderful. The quintessential golden-haired hero riding in from the west."

"You gotta make up your mind, sweetheart," Mannon drawled. "What am I? The macho sexist pig? Or the golden fuckin' hero?"

"You're both," she stated dramatically, convinced that he thought she was the most intelligent woman who ever drew breath. "And you're magnificent!"

"And *you're* full of it, sweetheart. Excuse me." He ambled off in search of Carlos. Swapping dirty stories was a lot more fun than swapping conversation with the ding-bats floating around Vegas.

For once in his life Mannon did not feel horny. He felt homesick. Away from home he was on show. *Come see the movie star. Watch him walk, talk, eat. Try and get him to fuck.*

Damn it, he was fed-up with the attention. He felt like he was in a sideshow – only *he* was the main attraction.

"Are you all right, Mannon?" Susanna Fonicetti, née Brent, appeared at his side. She was the typical Beverly Hills daughter of a great superstar. Hollywood kids turned out one of two ways. They either dropped out completely, or went with the lifestyle all the way. Susanna had gone all the way. She was the seed of Hollywood royalty and she knew it. Oh, how she knew it!

"I'm fine, darlin'," he said, with a big grin. "Where's your daddy?"

Susanna giggled. "The way you say that makes me feel about fourteen!"

"You don't look much older."

"Flatterer!"

She took him by the hand and led him to a corner table where Carlos held court. The entourage scattered, giving Mannon room to sit down.

"Did you hear the one about the Porsche and the rabbit?" he asked Carlos.

Carlos roared. "Did I *hear* it. *I* made it up, for crissake!"

*

The candlelight in the small Italian restaurant cast a warm glow. The conversation too, for Jack found Jade to be an informed talker and attentive listener. They covered everything from Reagan's politics to idle gossip. And also ate a hearty meal which consisted of thinly sliced mozzarella cheese and tomatoes to start with. And delicious medallions of veal, accompanied by a side order of pasta in a delicate cream sauce.

"Dessert?" Jack asked, when the trolley came around.

Jade grinned. "Why not?"

The waiter pointed out the various delights, and she picked chocolate chip cheesecake.

"I'm a chocolate freak," she admitted guiltily. "Complete with withdrawal symptoms and all."

He laughed. "I can relate to that. Ice cream is my downfall. Show me a carton of Häagen Dazs and I'm anybody's!"

The waiter kissed his fingertips. "We have the best ice cream," he announced. "Made on the premises. We have vanilla, cherry, rum, banana, strawberry —"

Jack stopped him. "You've hooked *me*," he said. "Bring a dish of banana."

"With hot chocolate sauce?"

"The works."

"Nuts?"

"Everything!"

"And two cappucini?"

"I think I'll live dangerously and have a plain coffee with Amaretto on the side," Jade said.

"Make that two." Jack smiled across the small table at her. "I knew you'd make me live dangerously — one way or the other."

She smiled back. "Is an Amaretto all it takes?"

"That and a back rub." He regarded her closely. This was the most enjoyable evening he'd had with a woman in a long time. He hadn't realized quite how serious Clarissa was. She would slit her throat rather than eat a meal like this. Not only was she a vegetarian, she also wouldn't touch sugar or alcohol, which made culinary activities somewhat boring.

"I hope you're having a good time," he said, meaning every word.

"I'm having a lovely time. You're great company." And indeed he was. Even if he hadn't been, just looking at him was a treat. Those eyes. Those penetrating green eyes. And the way he smiled, and his jet black hair which hit the back of his collar in exactly the right place. She had seen a lot of good-looking guys in her time, mostly models, and mostly gay. Jack Python was different. He was amusing and smart, with a cynical edge. And he was making her forget Mark Rand with a vengeance.

The coffee and Amaretto arrived, along with Jack's ice cream. She leaned across the table and stole some of his chocolate sauce. "Mmmm . . ." she murmured, licking her lips. *"Fan-tas-tic!"*

"Are you involved with anyone?" he asked abruptly.

She paused before answering, because she wasn't quite sure if she was or not. Mark Rand wanted to be back in her life. She hadn't said yes or no, just run for cover. She was supposed to be thinking things over — and yet here she was, having a perfectly wonderful evening. What kind of answer could she give him? It wasn't that simple.

"I don't know," she said softly.

He stared at her quizzically. "You don't know?"

She picked up her glass of Amaretto and tipped it into her coffee. "Uh . . . it's complicated. I *was* involved, *very* involved. Now I'm not so sure."

"Anything you want to talk about?"

"I don't think so."

They lapsed into silence.

"And you?" she said, breaking the pause in conversation.

Okay. What did he tell her? That he was supposed to be considering getting married. That would go down well.

"I guess I sort of see Clarissa Browning," he said guardedly. "We've been together over a year. She's in New York at the moment."

She sipped her coffee. This wasn't exactly fresh news; Antonio had filled her in before the date. "Oh," she said, and added as an afterthought, "She's a magnificent actress."

"That she is," he agreed. And they looked at each other, and the look could burn bridges.

"I want to sleep with you," he said.

She was completely lost in his eyes. "I know."

"Well?"

"I don't think we're the perfect couple – what with our commitments and all."

He stared at her intently. "Do you want me as much as I want you?"

The "yes" slipped from between her lips before she could help herself.

Chapter 42

Okay, Wes knew it was some kind of set-up, only he couldn't figure out the angle.

He called Rocky and questioned him.

"Don't involve me," Rocky said. "I only gave ya the connection to help out. My advice is watch your balls, an' tread carefully at all times."

That made him feel very secure.

Next he called Silver at the studio.

A raspy voice answered the phone with a not too friendly "Silver Anderson's dressing room. What do you want?"

"I'd like to talk to the lady herself."

"She's on the set. Who is this?"

"Wes Money. It's important."

"I'll have to take a message."

Shit! He had really wanted to explain things to her personally.

"Go ahead – shoot," said the raspy voice.

"Can you tell her somethin' came up – business-wise – and I'll be running late tonight. I'll try to be with her by ten-thirty."

"Got it."

"Say I'm sorry, it's unavoidable."

"Right."

"Tell her if I could have changed it I would."

"What is this – a continuing saga? I'm taking a message not writing a book!"

"Sorry. Oh, the name is Wes Money. M-O-N –"

"I know how to spell money."

"Thanks."

"I'll give her the message."

He rubbed the bridge of his nose. Funny thing, whenever he was uptight or tense his nose always gave him trouble. Usually he got a dull ache right by the break.

He had sealed the thousand dollars in an envelope, and now he had to decide where to hide it until this job was done. There was no safe place – break-ins were common along the boardwalk.

He waited until he heard Unity return from work, and knocked on her door.

She was fastening an apron around her tiny waist as she opened up. "You're too early," she admonished. "Dinner won't be ready for an hour. I'm fixing stew."

He loved stew! It was his favourite meal. In fact it was the *only* meal his mother had ever cooked.

"I can't make it over for dinner," he said regretfully, remembering her note.

She didn't look him in the eye. "That's okay," she said, and he sensed her disappointment.

"You didn't give me much notice, did you?" he complained.

"I asked you. You can't come. I understand," she said flatly.

"Remember me next time," he urged.

"Sure," she replied unenthusiastically.

The dog appeared and wagged its tail. Wes leaned over and patted it. "How's the paw?" He glanced around her side of the house. Same rented furniture, dismal prints on the walls, cramped little kitchen. Reba's taste was up her ass. "What kind of job do you do?" he asked.

She was busy peeling carrots. "I'm a waitress in a bar."

"No kiddin'! I work bar on occasion."

"Yes?" she said, completely uninterested. "Where?"

"Around. I pick and choose. How about you?"

"Hollywood Boulevard. Tito's."

"I don't know it."

"You don't want to."

He pulled the envelope of money from the pocket of his leather jacket and hoped he could trust her. Since he had no choice he asked her anyway. "Can you look after this for me? Just for a couple of hours?"

"What is it?" she asked suspiciously.

"My life savings," he replied sarcastically. "What else?"

Smoothing down her apron she glared at him, her slightly crossed eyes giving her a vulnerable look.

"Seriously," he said. "There's some important documents I can't leave in the house. So if you wouldn't mind ..." He trailed off.

"I'm going to sleep early," she said, taking the envelope from him. "If you're any later than ten you'll have to pick it up in the morning before I go to work."

"What time's that?"

"Tomorrow my shift is eleven till three. I'll be leaving here at nine-fifteen."

"Perfect." Silver usually booted him out at seven, when she left for the studio. He could collect his money at eight a.m. if he got held up tonight. "I'd appreciate it if you could do me this favour," he said.

She nodded, put the envelope on the side, and continued peeling carrots.

"Okay," he said, backing towards the door. "Enjoy dinner. Oh, and Unity?"

"Yes?"

"Do me another favour. Don't let the envelope out of your sight."

★

"Your boyfriend phoned," Nora said. "He sounds a real charmer."

"What did he want?" Silver asked, trying to conceal her sudden interest.

"Your body. He says you're the best lay he's ever had!"

"Thank you, Nora. I already know that. What did he *really* want?"

"He's running late. Cannot be with you until after ten tonight."

"Damn!"

"What?"

"I hate being kept waiting. You know that."

Nora lit up her forty-fifth cigarette of the day. "He said it was business."

"What kind of business does he have to do at night?"

Nora shrugged her shoulders. "Ask *him*, not *me* – I'm only the message taker."

"I'll do that." She swooped into a large Gucci tote bag for her telephone book and handed it to Nora. "Get him for me, will you?"

Nora backed up. "I'm here to look after your publicity not your lovers. Where's your assistant?"

"For Christ's sake, Nora. Each one is worse than the last. I fired the last one, you know that."

Grumbling, Nora looked up Wes Money's number. "I should be getting double pay. I'm doing two jobs."

"I'll buy you a present," Silver said graciously.

"Make it a condo in Miami. I think I'll retire."

Nora punched out the number, and waited. An answering machine picked up. She passed the phone to Silver.

"This is Wes. I'm out. I'll be back. Leave your name, number and time of call. Go for it . . . NOW!"

Perfect timing. The bleep sounded immediately.

"Wes." She hated machines, she felt so stupid speaking into them. "Er . . . *Why* are you running late? It's really *most* inconvenient. Phone me at home before you come over."

"That'll tell 'im," remarked Nora sarcastically.

"Kindly shut up, dear," said Silver grandly, and swept back to the set.

★

Wes took Sunset all the way in from the beach. He drove Silver's Mercedes, and stayed in the right-hand lane and under the speed limit. It wouldn't do to get stopped while he was carrying. He sweated at the very thought.

Jeez! What had he got himself into, and why?

He knew enough to realize if you carried you'd better be prepared to use. And he had no intention of doing that. In and out. That was his plan. If the guy gave him any trouble he would back gently off and split fast.

Laurel Canyon wound its way off Sunset into the hills, and meandered all the way over to the Valley. The house Wes was looking for was located halfway up, along with several other homes on a private road. The numbers were listed on a row of mailboxes, and a sign read PRIVATE PROPERTY. STAY OFF. ARMED PATROL. BEWARE OF DOG.

Talk about a warm welcome!

It was dark up in the hills and he had to shine a flashlight outside the car window to be sure he was at the right place.

Turning up the side road, he drove slowly, looking for the correct number. When he found it he idled past, just to get the lie of the land. There was one more house after it, and then the hills grew wild and steep.

He turned his car around with difficulty, all the while planning, thinking. He didn't want to drive up to the front door, park the car, and present himself just like that – a sitting target if things went wrong. He had to be in a position to make a fast getaway if the need arose – which he hoped it wouldn't, but you could never be too careful.

He drove two houses down. Each home had its own private driveway snaking up into the hills. None of the residences was visible from the private road. They all seemed to have these long, winding paths to negotiate.

On impulse, he drove up the wrong one. It was not your manicured Beverly Hills type driveway. This was pure country, with overhanging trees, and a lot of wild bush.

He reached a ranch-style residence with several cars parked outside. Switching off his lights, he turned his car around, and headed back to the main private road. Halfway there, he pulled

198

the Mercedes tight into the side, killed the ignition, and got out. Pocketing the keys he checked his watch. It was five of nine. The man had said to collect at nine o'clock prompt. He was running on time.

On foot he moved swiftly, having had the good sense to wear comfortable sneakers.

Down the path, up the private road, until he reached the right number, and yet another sign warning of armed patrol and dogs.

Feeling a shudder of apprehension, he made his way up the steep incline towards collection point. Shit! This whole cloak-and-dagger bit was like something out of a James Bond movie!

The house, when he reached it, was silent. Only one light shone in an upstairs room. A silver Maserati, a black Jeep, and an old blue station wagon were dotted around outside. A coyote howled somewhere in the hills.

With trepidation, he approached the front door. *This is a piece of pussy*, he thought.

The hairs on the back of his neck told him it wasn't.

He groped for the gun. It nestled in his pocket like a security blanket. Not that he would ever use it. As the man had said, just insurance in case of trouble.

What trouble?

Confidently he rang the bell. It was nine o'clock exactly.

Silence. Nothing. Nobody answered.

He rang again.

Repeat performance.

Stepping back he glanced up at the lighted window. No sign of movement there.

Shit!

Drawn like a magnet he reached forward and tried the front door.

It opened. Just like that. Deep down he had known it would.

Inner voices screamed – *Don't go in, schmuck! Get your ass in gear and vamoose!*

Far off in the distance he heard police sirens. They harmonized with the mournful howling of the lone coyote.

As he entered the house he thought about Silver. Her throaty laugh, expensive skin, hot, throbbing –

Jesus! He had known it was a set-up.

Sprawled halfway down the stairs was the body of a man. Blood dripped from him like a faucet, forming a pool on the hall carpet. He had been shot in the head.

Drawn unwillingly, Wes stepped farther into the house, chills coursing through his body.

Face down, half in and half out of a room, lay the body of a female – a fan of yellow hair spread out and spotted with blood.

He felt the bile rise to his throat, and as he turned to run he glimpsed a shadow with a raised arm, and a lead pipe heading in his direction.

"Oh, *Jesus Christ – no –*" he began to say, raising his right arm to protect himself.

It was too late.

Blackness descended.

Wes Money was temporarily out of the game.

Chapter 43

Somewhere between the restaurant and the hotel, Jade changed her mind. Deeply attracted as she was to Jack Python, one-night stands were not her style, never had been. Besides, there were too many complications. She hadn't made up her mind about Mark. And Jack had admitted he was deeply involved with Clarissa Browning. Nothing was ever easy.

When she told him, he took it with a philosophical shrug. "I guess our timing is off, huh?"

She touched her hand to his cheek lightly. Somehow she felt they were intimate strangers. "Something like that," she said softly.

He understood perfectly. And they parted good friends with no mention of further meetings.

The next day, on the flight back to Los Angeles, Antonio was dying to know everything.

She was noncommittal. "We had dinner. We talked. He's a terrific guy."

"*And, bella?* You make love with him?"

"It's none of your business," she said firmly.

Antonio sulked. He hated being left out of anything.

She thought about Jack Python quite a bit on the way home. And then she thought about Mark. And she realized it wasn't over. Not yet anyway.

Mark had left several messages with her answering service. There was also a call from her brother, Corey, which made a pleasant change. She telephoned him first.

"What's up, bro?" she asked cheerfully.

"Nothing." He sounded wistful. "I was thinking about you. Thought I might take you out to lunch."

She glanced at the time. It was almost six on Sunday evening. "A little late for lunch," she said lightly. "How about dinner?"

"Can't do it. I'm all tied up."

You're always tied up, she wanted to say. *Don't you remember how close we used to be?*

"Where are you going?" she asked, a trifle stiffly.

"There's this party . . . business."

Sometimes he really pissed her off. If *she* was going to a party and knew he was alone, she'd ask him to go with her. But no such offer was forthcoming.

"You know something? I still haven't seen your house *or* met your housemate," she said, and before he could answer she continued with, "Look, I know you think I don't approve. And I have to admit that I *was* upset when you told me about you and Marita splitting. However, I love you, and whatever you do . . . well . . . it's your life. When can I meet her?"

"Who?"

"Your housemate, densehead!"

A long pause. He obviously wasn't insane about the idea.

Too bad. She had waited long enough. She might as well get a look at the woman who had broken up her brother's marriage.

"I'll tell you what," she said. "Why don't I take you both out to dinner next week? My treat. How about Friday night?"

He was silent.

"Can I get an answer around here please?" she persisted.

"Let me check. I'll call you tomorrow," he finally said.

Anyone would think she was inviting him to a funeral!

"Promise?"

"I promise."

Hanging up, she put a little Bruce on the stereo. Springsteen always cheered her up; he could do no wrong.

Then she realized she was going to have to do something about Mark, and reached for the phone again.

"Lord Mark Rand checked out at noon," said the hotel operator.

"Are you *sure*?"

"Quite sure, madame."

"Did he leave a number where he can be reached?"

"One moment please. I'll find out for you."

He certainly hadn't hung around waiting for her. What enthusiasm. What tenacity. What a bastard!

You're being unreasonable, Johnson. You were the one who took off.

The operator came back on the line. "No referral number."

"Thank you." She put down the phone, and wondered where he was now. She'd played games with him. He was merely returning the compliment. English asshole. He knew she hated playing games.

★

Jack couldn't fault Jade for changing her mind. After all, it was a woman's prerogative, and he had always tried to be a gentleman about such things. Only it didn't alter the fact that he still wanted her. And when Jack Python wanted, he usually got.

He returned to the empty suite, and placed a call to Clarissa in New York. She was staying with a girlfriend in the Village. Not for Clarissa the large hotel suite or penthouse apartment. "I enjoy living among ordinary people," she had told him. "Nobody takes any notice of me in the Village. I can wander around and not be bothered."

Sure she could. Because nobody recognized Clarissa off the screen.

She answered the phone herself.

"Hi, babe," he said. "I was just sitting here thinking about you."

Her voice sounded muffled. "Who is this?"

Christ! You go with a woman for over a year and she doesn't even recognize your voice!

"Phil Donahue," he said dryly.

"Oh, God. Jack. It's two-thirty in the morning here. Where *are* you?"

"You'll never believe this."

"Try me."

"Las Vegas."

"Are you drunk?"

"When have you ever seen me drunk?"

"You must be if you're in Las Vegas."

"I am sober. And missing you. I'm calling to say hello."

"You *are* drunk. And you've woken me. Really, Jack, you can be very thoughtless at times. A broken night's sleep disturbs my bio-rhythms."

"Spoken like a true Californian."

"What?"

"Nothing."

"I'm going to *try* to get back to sleep. Call me tomorrow if you want."

Hey – give the lady the prize for Ms. Romantic of the year.

He poured himself a brandy. Thoughtfully he sipped it, took a cold shower, and went to bed.

Some nights you just couldn't win.

*

Failing in the pursuit of the prettiest of Susanna's three friends, Howard settled for a short redhead with enormous silicone boobs and a silly smile. When he got her back to the suite and undressed her, even *he* was turned off by her two jutting great globules of flesh. They felt like movable cement before it hardens, and looked like a couple of giant melons with a cherry on top of each.

"I'm fighting a cold," he announced, with a phoney sneeze. "You'd better go home."

"Let me fight it with you," she begged. "I've got the cure of the century!"

"No," he insisted. "I feel sick. I think I've got a temperature."

Dressing reluctantly, she confided she was working on a screenplay with a friend. "Can I send it to you?" she asked hopefully.

Trapped again. "Yeah, of course."

As soon as she left he tracked down the woman from the night before. An answering machine picked up, but she called him back five minutes later.

"Come over," he said. "Let's continue what we almost didn't finish."

She hesitated. "I'm busy."

"What could make you un-busy?"

She decided he could take the truth. "I get a thousand bucks a night. Last night was on the house – the hotel picked up the tab. How about it, sport? I take American Express."

He was outraged. "Are you a pro?"

"No. I'm Mary Poppins. Can't you tell? Do you want me to come over or not?"

He slammed down the phone. Howard Soloman didn't sleep with hookers. Howard Soloman had never paid for it in his life!

God damn Dino Fonicetti. Who did he think he was dealing with?

★

Mannon went back to Carlos Brent's magnificent house after the party. The entourage trailed them, plus they picked up a few strays along the way.

Carlos took him on a tour of the mansion, which had sixteen bedrooms, a full recording studio, two Olympic-sized swimming pools, and its own golf course.

"This is just my little ole hang-out," Carlos boasted. "My *real* home is in Palm Springs. I'd like you and your lovely wife to come and stay with me for the weekend sometime soon."

"Sounds good to me," Mannon said agreeably.

"I've seen that wife of yours on television. She's some gal!"

When was Melanie-Shanna on TV?

"Whitney Valentine Cable," mused Carlos. "What a pretty lady!"

Mannon scowled. "We're divorced," he said.

Carlos looked amazed. "Any man who lets *that* filly go, has *got* to be *insane!*"

Mannon nodded. There were some statements you just couldn't fight.

★

The Klinger plane took off from Las Vegas earlier than expected. All three passengers were aboard, and anxious to get back to L.A.

Chapter 44

There was a blue haze somewhere in his head. And a pain of ferocious intensity. And when Wes opened his eyes he had no idea where the fuck he was.

Oh shit. He had to quit with the one-night stands. Waking up in strange women's beds was getting to be a drag.

Only he wasn't in a bed. He was on the floor. And clasped in his right hand was a gun. And . . . oh shit . . the blue haze lifted, and he knew he was in big trouble.

Trying to coordinate his body with his mind, he made an effort to rise, first dropping the gun to the floor.

He was in the entry hall of the Laurel Canyon house, and his companions were the same two bodies that had been there before.

Vomit threatened, and he staggered into a nearby toilet and threw up. Blood trickled into his eye from a gash on his head, and he realized a rapid exit was in order. For some unknown reason he had been set up, and he did not care to wait around to find out why.

A fast look at his watch told him only seven minutes had elapsed since he'd arrived at the house, which meant he must have a skull made of fucking concrete.

There was an eerie stillness. A loud silence screaming GET OUT.

Still feeling disoriented and sick he picked up the gun. It had his prints on. Whoever hit him over the head had wanted it that way.

Was it the murder weapon?

Probably.

We want no connection with this bad boy an' his sweetie-box.

Sure. No connection. Murder the two of 'em, then send the

schmuck in to take the blame. Schmuck gets caught red-handed and the man walks away with no connection.

Fuck!

They had bought him for a thousand dollars. The perfect patsy. Who was going to believe Wes Money's side of the story?

His heart was beating so fast and so loud he hardly dared to move in case it exploded. Grimly he tried to remember every murder mystery he'd ever seen. *Prints. Get rid of all the prints.*

He shoved the gun into his pokcet. It was no good trying to clean it now. The gun was important evidence, and he had to dispose of it properly, to be absolutely sure it could never be connected with him.

Frantically he raced into the toilet again, grabbed a handful of tissues, and cleaned anything he might have touched.

GET OUT! GET OUT! GET OUT!

The front door was still ajar. He made sure he wiped the handle. And the buzzer. And – *shit!* He heard the sound of a car approaching, and threw himself bodily into the shrubbery.

His heartbeat alone was enough to give him away.

Within seconds a police car appeared at full speed and screeched to a stop outside the open front door. Wes could make out two officers inside, neither of whom seemed ready to leave the safety of their vehicle.

It figured.

Set the schmuck up.

Send in the cops.

Schmuck discovered with murder weapon in hand. What would it matter that he had been beaten unconscious? He was holding the fucking murder weapon, for crissake. Book him and throw away the key!

With a supreme effort he tried to breathe slowly, evenly. Once they ventured inside the house, the whole area would be alive with cops. He had to get out fast.

Random thoughts raced through his head. If only he could get rid of the gun it would be a big help. But how could he risk it?

Sweat mingled with the blood dripping into his eye as he slowly crawled along the damp earth, hidden by the thick trees and bushes which tangled with his face and hair and body – scratching and tearing at his skin.

Wes Money had never been a religious man. Only now it seemed quite apt to say his prayers, and he did so with fervour.

One of the cops got out of the car. He was big and burly, the way policemen are supposed to be. He said something to his partner, but Wes couldn't hear what it was. Fortunately he was on his way, putting distance between himself and discovery.

The other cop got out of the car, and the two of them had a short discussion before drawing their weapons and approaching the front door of the house. They had their backs to him.

With perfect timing he judged it was safe for him to rise, slide into the shadows, and jog sharply away from the scene of the crime.

He ran down the driveway as if the devil were pursuing him. Along the private road. Up the other driveway where he had prudently parked the Mercedes. A feverish grope for the keys. Into the car. Start the ignition. *Not too fast. Don't attract attention.*

His breathing was laboured, and his throat felt like he'd just vacated a burning building. A sharp stitch dug into his side, and his head hurt like hell. He hadn't realized he was in such lousy shape.

Slowly he coasted down the driveway to the private road, only just stopping himself from flooring the gas pedal. When he hit Laurel Canyon he made a sharp right turn, and allowed himself to breathe. Clumsily he took the gun from his pocket and stuffed it under the passenger seat. There was other traffic going down the hill, and he slid in between a Honda and a Jeep. Again he allowed himself to breathe.

Halfway down, coming from Sunset, were two police cars, one behind the other. With sirens screaming and red lights flashing, they roared up the hill.

Along with the other vehicles, he pulled the Mercedes over to the side and allowed them clear passage. Breathing heavily he took a Kleenex from the glove compartment and mopped his head. The blood was drying now, congealing in a mass.

He wanted to throw up again, but he didn't dare.

He was safe. Temporarily.

Only what the fuck did he do now?

*

Angrily Silver glanced at the clock again. It was past nine. She was not used to being kept waiting, and certainly not by the likes of Wes Money.

In a sudden fury she called Dennis Denby.

He was home. She would have been most surprised if he wasn't.

"That table at Spago, Dennis," she purred. "Is it ready and waiting?"

Dennis, who had been trying to contact her ever since the gay restaurant débâcle, did not hesitate. "For you, Silver, beauty, anything is possible."

"Pick me up in fifteen minutes," she commanded.

He was one minute late, which was admirable considering he'd had to get rid of a lady friend (the forty-five-year-old raven-haired wife of a director who was secretly into boys), call Spago and request an immediate table. Not easy, but for Silver Anderson they complied. And dress. He wore a white sports jacket from Bijan, Italian trousers, and a light pink cashmere sweater.

"You've forgiven me!" he exclaimed, kissing her hand, a gesture he had seen George Hamilton employ with great success.

"I was never mad." She looked elegantly casual in a suede jacket and pants, her own hair scraped back, a full studio makeup still in place.

"You never returned my calls," he pointed out.

"Dennis, dear, you must realize that I don't even have time to go to the bathroom!"

He understood. Silver was a very busy woman.

On the small hill outside the fashionable Spago, photographers and fans stood in a huddle waiting for a celebrity arrival. Since the celebrities always used the back entrance, the chances of catching a good shot were remote.

Silver chose to have Dennis drive her Rolls. The fans gathered at the entrance to the parking lot and called to her longingly. She gave them a queenly wave, and swept into the restaurant the back way with Dennis trotting obediently behind her.

Before reaching their table – ready and waiting – they went through a parade of smiles and kisses and fond greetings. Spago, with its laid-back atmosphere, mind-blowing pizzas and in-credible array of desserts, was celebrity hang-out numero uno. And Wolfgang Puck – the chef and owner – along with his darkly dramatic wife, Barbara, made sure everyone felt com-fortable and at home.

"I absolutely *adore* the glorious flower arrangements here," Silver remarked, when safely seated.

"So do I," agreed Dennis.

"And it's such a *fun* place."

"I agree," agreed Dennis.

When did he ever not? He was her yes-man. She could do with him whatever she wanted.

Not so Wes Money. There was something about him . . . an unknown quality . . . a lurking danger.

She shivered excitedly. And he was not used goods either. Well, not by anyone *she* knew. It was quite possible that half the women in the restaurant had romped in the hay with Dennis.

Tonight she would teach Wes a lesson. Let him know exactly *who* he was dealing with. She had left explicit instructions with Vladimir that if Mr Money called, he was to inform him that she was out, and to phone back the next day. Alternatively, if he arrived at the house, Vladimir was to send him on his way.

Let Wes know she was not *completely* at his beck and call just because he had a hard cock and a persuasive tongue.

She smiled at the thought of both pieces of his anatomy.

"What are you smiling at?" Dennis asked anxiously.

She picked up a piece of bread, looked at it longingly, and put it down again. "Nothing that would interest you, Dennis, dear. Shall we order? I'm famished."

*

The men's room in a gas station on Sunset supplied Wes with an image which frightened the shit out of him. He was wild-eyed, wild-haired, with scratches all over his face. His clothes were dirty and torn, and there was a nasty spongy spot on the top of his head where he had been hit.

Better than being dead, with a bullet through his skull.

He felt the bile rise again, only this time he could supply nothing but dry heaves.

Quickly he cleaned up as best he could. The result was not Paul Newman. Face it – he looked fucked.

Searching through his pockets for a pack of cigarettes he came up with two unexpected items. A large glassine envelope filled with a white powder that looked suspiciously like cocaine. And a wad of used thousand-dollar bills totalling twenty-two thousand.

Shit! Part of the set-up. They had wanted him pegged as a dealer.

Swearing viciously, he stuffed everything back in his pocket. Just in time, as two Mexicans entered the can, unzipped, and began to relieve themselves.

He hurried out of there, and went over to a pay phone. His

first thought was to call Rocky. Just how much did his good friend know?

For a moment he played with the quarter. Should he? Shouldn't he?

A hooker drifted by in orange fishnet stockings and little else. "Wanna visit love city?" she drawled.

He ignored her. Maybe it wasn't such a smart move to contact Rocky. After all, *he* was the one responsible for getting him into this mess in the first place.

And then he thought about going home. Was it safe?

Sure it was safe. What could they do to him now?

They could come searching for their money, that's what. It was hardly loose change. They could come to reclaim their cocaine — there must be at least fifteen hundred bucks' worth.

He had no intention of parting with either. This money he had *really* earned. *And* the thousand stashed with Unity.

No, going home tonight was not the best idea in the world.

He thought of alternatives. And then he thought of Silver Anderson. Nobody would come looking for him at her house. With Silver he'd be safe.

Chapter 45

"We're having a dinner for Silver Anderson," Poppy announced, as she brushed her long hair in front of her dressing table mirror.

Howard, who had returned from Vegas earlier in the day, and was sitting up in bed surrounded by papers, documents, and unanswered memos, looked at her as if she had gone berserk. "Why? You hardly know her."

Poppy continued to brush her luxuriant blonde tresses. "Politics, sweet-buns. There may come a day when you want her in one of your movies. A touch of social intercourse never did anyone any harm."

"Willya talk English, for crissake?"

She leaned closer to the mirror and inspected her pampered skin. "I'm going to give the dinner in the back room at Chasen's. Who would you like me to invite?"

Knowing Poppy, she already had the guest list planned. "I don't care. How many people you got in mind?"

"Eight couples. I'd like your input on this, Howard."

A dinner party for Silver Anderson. Cross brother Jack off the list for a start. Mannon would be okay, but if they invited Mannon he couldn't invite Whitney, and he really wanted to see her.

"I don't know. You're the social queen. You'll come up with a good group."

Just the answer she had been hoping for. She put down her hairbrush and dipped her fingers into a pot of expensive cream, which she then proceeded to massage gently around her eyes. "Well," she said, "with us, and Silver and her escort − I do hope it's Dennis, he's so charming − that makes two couples. And then I thought the Whites, and the Goosebergers. Maybe Oliver Easterne, and Mannon and Melanie, and −"

"I'd sooner you invited Whitney," Howard interrupted. "I'm still thinking of using her for that script you suggested."

Poppy finished patting in the cream. "Whitney is still seeing Chuck Nielson," she informed him. "You know you don't like him. And I've already mentioned the dinner to Melanie. I can't very well *dis*-invite her. I suppose having Mannon *and* Whitney is out of the question, isn't it?" She turned around and looked questioningly at him.

He pulled the collar of his pyjama top up. Cleverly he had concealed his Las Vegas love bites with a stick of makeup he had found on Poppy's dressing table. He could hardly wear a turtleneck to bed. "No way," he said shortly.

"Oh, dear . . ." Her little-girl voice wavered. "I hope I haven't made a boo-boo."

He hated it when she came out with baby talk. "So we'll give another dinner," he said magnanimously. "Big deal. You can plan a special night for Mannon and whatever her name is."

Poppy thought about it, and decided it wasn't such a bad idea at all. She could gain a reputation for throwing chic little dinners − maybe once a week − and everyone would fight to be included.

"Delicious!" she exclaimed, jumping up and hurrying to his

side. She knelt on the bed, completely messing up his profusion of papers. "Who's a clever boy, then?"

He peered down the décolletage of her rose pink peignoir. Perkily waiting were a perfect pair of 36B tits. *His* tits. He had paid for them. They were nothing like the Vegas redhead's monstrosities. They were lively and upright. Not too big and not too small. Just right, in fact. Before having them done, Poppy had consulted him on his preferences. "A perfect handful," he had said, and she had obliged.

"I'm in the mood, Howie," she whispered coyly.

I'm not, he wanted to reply. Only he didn't. He bundled his papers to the side, switched off the light, and reached for one of his possessions. A perky 36B possession.

*

"I had lunch with Poppy Soloman yesterday," Melanie-Shanna informed Mannon.

He paused, mid press-up, and said, "What did you do that for?"

"She invited me."

"Oh yeah, and what did she want?"

"Just to be friendly."

"Sure!"

"No, really."

"Everything Poppy Soloman does has a purpose."

"If there *was* a particular reason for inviting me, it never came up."

"It will."

"What do you mean?"

"You'll see."

He resumed a punishing set of press-ups, and then moved over to his Nautilus machine, where he proceeded to work on his arms.

Melanie-Shanna watched him pensively. He was so handsome, and she loved him so much. And yet every day – in spite of her pregnancy – he drew further and further away from her. Nothing she could say for sure, just a feeling.

"Was Vegas fun?" she asked brightly.

"Hell, no. I hated it."

Then why did you go?

She couldn't ask him. Mannon did what he pleased, and she never questioned.

"I went shopping with Poppy after lunch," she volunteered.

He had lost interest. "Good," he said vaguely.

"She took me to Giorgio, and I opened a charge."

"Glad to hear it."

She wondered how glad he would be when he found out she had spent several thousand dollars. Poppy had encouraged her. "Spend his money, for God's sake!" she had urged. "What do you think he *makes* it for?"

So, for the first time in her marriage, Melanie-Shanna had spent without asking.

Mannon heaved and grunted as he worked up a sweat. His muscles rippled.

"Poppy's invited us to a dinner she's having for Silver Anderson," Melanie-Shanna said.

"Poppy this and Poppy that. I thought you hated lunch and shopping and all that phoney crapola."

"It wasn't phoney. I enjoyed it. I met some very interesting women."

"Who?" he demanded disbelievingly.

"Ida White . . . Carmel Gooseberger."

Mannon burst out laughing. "Those two old mares! Jesus, kid, you're really mixing with racy company. Those broads are so jaded they wouldn't blink an eyelid if Reagan streaked across Rodeo and lit a fart!"

Melanie-Shanna pursed her lips. Sometimes Mannon treated her like an idiot, and it was beginning to gall. Everything she did he sneered at and criticized, and she'd had enough. At lunch the women had been discussing a recent scandalous divorce. The wife was demanding *and* getting half of everything the billionaire husband possessed. Poppy had winked gaily. "California law. So fair. I *love* it!" And then she had leaned conspiratorially towards Melanie-Shanna. "You didn't sign a pre-nup, did you?"

"What's that?"

Poppy had laughed loudly, and explained it to her.

Now Melanie-Shanna realized her strength, and if Mannon didn't change his attitude, she was certainly going to change hers, and stop him treating her like a doormat.

Chapter 46

"Madame Anderson is out," Vladimir said firmly, on the speaker to the front gate.

"I know that," Wes replied evenly. "But I have her car, and she asked me to return it."

"Ah . . ." sighed Vladimir.

"Ah . . ." copied Wes.

A pause, while Vladimir considered what to do. Madame hadn't mentioned her car. She would obviously want it back. Vladimir was also curious to see the man who had ousted the awful Dennis Denby from her bed. Pressing the buzzer to open the gate, he marched to the front door. When Wes drew up in the zippy red Mercedes, Vladimir was ready.

Wes pulled the car to a stop and jumped out. "Evenin', mate," he said to the houseman, attempting to push past him and enter the house.

Vladimir pulled himself up to his full height of five feet nine inches, and blocked the way. He was shocked at the man's unruly appearance.

"Excuse me, *sir*," he said grandly. "Madame Anderson left instructions that you are to telephone her tomorrow. Tonight she is out."

"Is she now?" Wes sized up the situation. An unthreatening gay butler. No problem. "I guess I'll just have to wait for her. She won't mind."

With no further ceremony he shoved past Vladimir, who was outraged, and headed for the library, and the bar, where he proceeded to pour himself a much-needed drink.

Vladimir stomped in after him, his authority questioned, his face turning a dull red. "Vat do you think you are doing?' he demanded. "You can't come in here vithout Madame Silver's permission."

Wes took a long gulp of straight scotch. It hit his belly with a warm spreading sensation. He threw the houseman a threatening glare. "Who says?"

"*I* say." Vladimir peered at the invading stranger. There was something disturbingly familiar about him. "I am in charge. You vill please leave."

Wes flopped into an armchair. Frankly, he didn't need this crap. He was all washed out. "I ain't goin' nowhere, sunshine. Don't get your balls in an uproar. Just lie back an' enjoy it."

"Vat?" steamed Vladimir.

"Relax. Hang loose. Go with the flow."

Vladimir felt a migraine creeping up on him. He would get the blame for this. He knew it. Madame Silver was going to be furious and she would fire him, the firing he had nearly got after the bathroom incident. He didn't know what to do. Physical action was definitely out of the question. This man looked positively *violent*. Definitely rough trade.

Running his hands through his wheat-coloured hair, he tried to decide how to deal with this uncomfortable situation.

Wes leaned back in the chair and closed his eyes. "I feel like shit," he mumbled. "If you're smart you'll just leave me alone. Stay out of my way an' everything'll be cool. I'll fix it with your boss. Don't sweat it." He was drifting into a light sleep, and he had no strength left to fight it.

Vladimir stared.

And stared again.

His memory was trying hard, but he couldn't quite come up with where he had encountered this unruly person before.

Almost . . . almost . . .

The knowledge eluded him.

*

"So, Dennis?" Silver said belligerently. "Why do you accept defeat like a bull with no balls?" She had demolished half a bottle of champagne, picked at a lobster salad, tasted dessert (the apple pie and caramel sauce was to die for!) and was now in an argumentative mood.

"*Moi?*" asked Dennis, a slight lilt to his voice.

"Do you swing both ways?" she asked suspiciously. She had never thought that of Dennis before, but tonight there was an air about him.

He reacted strongly. Too strongly?

"Are you drunk?" he shouted. "How *dare* you. How can you

– of *all* people – accuse me of having homosexual tendencies? Surely you know me better than that?"

"Calm down, Dennis," she said soothingly. "Some of my best friends are gay. It's just that I do not wish to sleep with them."

"I'm extremely insulted," he said sternly. "How would you like it if I asked *you* the same question?"

Her eyes drifted around the restaurant. Dennis Denby bored her. Everything about him was bland. His face, his clothes, his conversation. "Let's change the subject," she said mildly.

"Why?" He glared at her spitefully. "Have I hit upon something? Do you swing both ways?"

Icicles could have formed on her smile. "Get the check. You're taking me home. And if we're both terribly fortunate, we'll never have to see each other again."

*

Vladimir did not dare disturb Madame Silver at the restaurant. He did the next best thing, and disturbed Nora at her apartment.

"What do you want?" she asked irritably, interrupted in the middle of *Cagney and Lacey* and a chicken sandwich.

Vladimir explained his predicament.

Nora was torn. She was enjoying the programme, and her chicken sandwich was delicious. However, the idea of getting a peek at Silver's new boyfriend was certainly tempting.

"Are you telling me the guy just walked in the house and fell asleep?" she asked incredulously.

"Madame Silver vill blame me," Vladimir said mournfully.

What the hell . . . She clicked off the television, clicked on the tape machine, and with a large bite of her chicken sandwich under her belt, set off.

Vladimir greeted her at the door.

"Is he still asleep?" was her first question.

"Yes," hissed Vladimir, still furious at this gross intrusion by such an uncouth-looking man. At least Dennis Denby was well dressed and seemed prosperous. *This* one appeared to have crawled off the street. Sometimes Vladimir thought Madame Silver employed exceptionally bad taste.

Nora hurried inside, making her way straight to the library. The sight of Wes, sprawled out snoring peacefully, brought her to a full stop.

"Is this the specimen?" she said loudly.

Vladimir, hot on her heels, nodded. "Vill you get rid of him before Madame returns?" he requested hopefully.

Wes, oblivious to the conversation going on around him, slept on.

Nora stepped closer. This big, distinctly masculine, grubby-looking character was not what she'd expected at all. This guy looked like he'd been digging ditches, and that wasn't Silver's style. Or was it?

She adjusted her glasses and blew cigarette smoke in his direction. " 'Scuse me," she said in her smoke-encrusted voice. "This is not a hotel."

He opened one sludge-coloured eye and peered up at her. " 'Ello, darlin'," he said, reverting to his childhood English cockney. "Wanna give me a back-rub?"

Vladimir clicked his tongue in disgust.

Wes yawned and stretched, throwing his arms wide. "I know *you* would," he said to Vladimir. "Only I'm not givin' *you* the chance."

Nora frowned. He was not your standard Beverly Hills bachelor by any means. Nor your Hollywood stud. She had a feeling she had seen him somewhere before. "Have you and I met?" she demanded.

He stretched again, very slowly. Then he stared at the two of them – Silver's butler and the old publicity broad. He had a hunch they were of a mind to throw him out.

"Where's Silver?" he asked, playing for time. "She told me to meet her here, an' now she's on the missin' list."

"*When* did she tell you to meet her?" said Nora.

"Last time I spoke to her."

"And when was that?"

Jeez! He needed this scene. He stared the dyke down. "I don't think that's any of your business."

"*Everything* Silver Anderson does is my business," she replied tartly. "And I suggest you shift your fat ass before Miss Anderson comes home and finds you here."

It was the "fat ass" he took exception to. Who did the old bag think she was dealing with? What right did *she* have to throw him out? The only person who could do that was Silver.

"Go whistle up Liberace's ass," he said insolently.

Nora was startled. "What?"

"You heard."

"Unless you get out of here *now*, Mr . . . Money," Nora said

217

slowly, emphasizing every word, "I shall call the police, and they will evict you in a proper manner."

He stood up. "Y'can do what y'want. Silver invited me. An' here I stay until *she* tells me to get out."

"You're giving me no choice," Nora said sternly.

He was unmoved. "Go ahead. The *Enquirer*'ll love it."

"Yes. I suppose that's the sort of scumball you are. Anything for the money. Am I getting your number?"

"You're gettin' on my tits, old lady. I don't appreciate bein' threatened when I'm an invited guest."

Vladimir watched the heated exchange like a spectator at Wimbledon. He loved every minute of it! Wait until they heard about this one down at Rage. Better than Dennis Denby any day.

"Mr Money," said Nora, very, very slowly. "Are you going to leave quietly, or am I going to telephone the police?"

"Why don't you call Silver an' save us all a lot of bother?" he suggested.

The idea *had* crossed her mind – although she would sooner see him dragged off in chains. Instant hate had taken place.

"If you insist," she said stiffly. Turning to Vladimir, she instructed him to call the restaurant where Silver was dining.

Meanwhile, Wes picked up his glass and strolled over to the bar. He needed a refill. He was handling this much more calmly than he felt. His stomach was churning, his head still aching. What if Silver *did* tell him to get lost? And the last thing he needed was the cops.

He poured a steady stream of scotch into his glass. His legs felt like two hollow pipes. If he drank all night there was no way he could get the slightest buzz on. Pleasure was out.

Then three things happened all at once. Vladimir held the phone aloft and announced, "Madame is on her way home."

Silver herself burst into the room, flushed and slightly tipsy, with Dennis one step behind.

And Nora, with a sudden start of recognition as she watched Wes pour his drink, stared at him closely and exclaimed, "*Now* I know where I've seen you before. The night of Silver's party – you were one of the barmen!"

"Yes, yes!" agreed Vladimir, almost jumping up and down with excitement. "I remember too!"

Silver looked at Wes.

Wes looked at Silver.

There was a dramatic silence.

Chapter 47

"I'm renting a house at the beach for the summer," Jack said.

Heaven, who had been gazing idly out the window of his Ferrari, jumped to attention. "A beach house! Wow! Is it near Muscle Beach?"

He laughed. "No. It is not near Muscle Beach. It's in Trancas. And it's remote and quiet and – well, *I* love it."

What kind of a place was *remote* and *quiet*? – somewhere dull. Why couldn't Uncle Jack rent right in the heart of Malibu where all the interesting people were?

"I want you to come and stay," he said. "Maybe bring a girlfriend if you like."

She fidgeted on the hot leather seat. "It sounds awfully . . ." Searching for the right word she came up with ". . . lonely."

"Not at all. There's shops and restaurants just a short drive away. And I want you to stay when *I'm* there. We'll keep each other company."

God! She had seven girlfriends who would adore to keep Uncle Jack company. For an older man he sure had fans. "What about Clarissa?" she asked. "Will she be there?"

"I don't know," he replied honestly. There were decisions to be made, and he wasn't in the mood to make them.

"Hey, Uncle Jack, I think I'll love it!' she decided. "When can I come? And for how long?"

"All summer if you want."

"What about grandpa?"

He smiled. "I don't think he'll notice, do you?"

She smiled back. They both understood about George.

Sometimes she felt very close to her uncle. Tonight was one of those times. He had called late Sunday afternoon and said, "I just got back from Vegas, and I feel like grabbing a Chinese feast. Do you know anyone with the same urge?"

"Me! Me!" she had replied, standing Eddie up, but who cared?

"I'll pick you up in an hour."

True to his word he was there within the hour, and drove at breakneck speed to Madame Wu's on Wilshire, where he had pre-ordered a great Chinese meal. Now he was taking her home, and she wished he wasn't. She would give anything to live with him permanently.

"How's your music going?" he asked casually. They had covered school, home life and boyfriends at the restaurant.

"Okay," she replied listlessly. Frankly it was going nowhere. Just the occasional school party gig, and nothing else. "I've sent my tapes to all the record companies. All they do is send them back with a shitty form letter." She gazed at him hopefully. "I wish you'd come and *see* me next time I perform."

He nodded, knowing full well he had promised many times before, only something always came up. He made a mental note to definitely do it. Heaven was important to him, and he was going to have to make more time for her now she was growing up.

"You've never even listened to one of my tapes," she added reproachfully.

"Why don't you give me one? I'll play it on the drive home."

"Promise?"

"Would I lie?"

She didn't think so, but he had certainly never gone out of his way to take an interest in what she did.

George was locked away in his workroom when they arrived home.

"I won't disturb him," Jack said. "I'll call him about you coming to stay with me."

"Promise?"

He kissed her lightly on the cheek. "What is it with you tonight? Don't you believe *anything* I say?"

She laughed self-consciously. "Just making sure."

He was gone before she could find a tape to give him.

Halfway across the Canyon, listening to a soulful Billie Holiday on the car radio, Jack realized he'd forgotten to get Heaven's tape. Not that he really wanted to hear it. What if she sounded awful? He wasn't about to take the responsibility of telling her. Maybe she sounded like Silver. God forbid! His sister's voice did not thrill him. It reminded him of his mother, and the way she had deserted him when he was a kid. The same way Silver had deserted Heaven.

His thoughts moved on to Clarissa, still in New York. Did he miss her? He still couldn't decide.

Then he thought about Jade Johnson, and what might have been if she hadn't changed her mind so swiftly. One night of great sex. Maybe more . . .

How could there be more until things were resolved with Clarissa?

He shook his head, turned the addictive Miss Holiday up loud and clear, and headed for the hotel suite he called home.

Chapter 48

Wes did not like confrontations. Never had. Especially when he wasn't looking his best, and he knew the image he presented was pure shit.

Silver stared him down. She was angry — little glints of light caught the reflection in her eyes and bounced right off him. But she was cool. Didn't give in to pressure, handled the whole thing with style.

"Hello, Wes," she said calmly, and turning to Nora she added, "I didn't know we had a late meeting?"

Nora knew her moods as well as anyone, and prepared for flight.

Silver then iced Vladimir with a glare. "What are *you* doing here? I didn't ring."

"Madame Silver —" Vladimir began valiantly. "This man is an intruder. I —"

"Good*night*, Vladimir. You may go to your quarters. I won't be needing you again tonight."

He slunk from the room.

Nora cleared her throat. "I guess I'll be going home."

"Good," said Silver shortly.

"Vladimir called me," Nora began to explain. "He thought there was a problem . . ."

Silver waved a dismissive hand in her direction. "Remind me to add a security bonus to your pay-cheque."

Nora was affronted. She had only been trying to help. "I'll tell City Television," she rasped. "*They* pay me, not you."

Picking up her purse she followed Vladimir from the room. Silver Anderson was treading on dangerous ground. No wonder she had wanted to keep Wes Money to herself; the man was nothing but a cheap hustler – a barman! And when word got out – and it was only a matter of time before it did – the whole town would be laughing.

Dennis Denby stepped forward, determined to assert himself. "Who exactly *is* this man, Silver?"

She'd forgotten he was behind her, trailing her like an eager puppy dog. "Dennis, *dear*," she said graciously. "I know I invited you in, but now I'm inviting you *out*. Please be understanding about this. I promise I'll telephone you tomorrow." As she spoke, she edged him from the room.

"What's going on?" he whined. "I thought we had something together."

Kissing him lightly on the cheek, she continued to edge him towards the front door. "Whoever said we didn't?"

Reluctantly he allowed himself to be shepherded out. "Is anything going on between you and that man?" was his final plaintive cry.

"Don't be so silly," she said firmly, closing the door on him.

She paused in the hall before returning to the library and Wes, trying to gather her thoughts. Nora's words had not escaped her attention. *Silver's party . . . one of the barmen.* And Vladimir's excited confirmation.

Goddammit! Why hadn't he told her?

And if he had?

She shook her head – if he had she would have sent him on his way without a second glance.

Marching into the library she confronted her latest lover. Hands on hips she raked him over with a very cool expression indeed. "Well?" she demanded icily.

Slowly, deliberately, without rising, he lit a cigarette. "I'm getting really fed up with bein' treated like a piece of shit around here," he said.

"*You're* fed up!" she raged, pacing up and down in front of him. "How the *hell* do you think *I* feel?"

"About what?"

"God! Don't pretend there's nothing happening."

He blew smoke in her direction and stood up. "I think I'll go," he said. "I've heard of warm welcomes, but this is ridiculous."

Taking in his dishevelled appearance she snapped, "You look like a tramp."

"Sorry about that, *Madame* Silver," he said sarcastically. "I wasn't plannin' on gettin' beat up before I came to see you."

She regarded him warily. Even in the state he was in there was something about him. A masculine, strong quality.

She knew she should tell him to get out – out of her house *and* out of her life.

Why?

Just because he was a barman? Who said that Silver Anderson had to follow rules? She could do whatever she pleased.

"I wish you'd been honest with me up-front," she said edgily.

"Why?"

"Because then I wouldn't have had to be humiliated in front of the people who work for me."

"*Are* you humiliated?"

"Yes, I am."

He tested the water. "*How* humiliated?"

She heard the humour in his tone and was not amused. "Fuck you, Wes Money," she said, stalking to the bar.

"Promises! Promises!"- Beating her to the bar, he positioned himself behind it. "And what can I get for Madame? A glass of her favourite bubbly? A vodka martini? Or let me suggest one of my specialities – a strawberry daiquiri with just a hint of Bénédictine? Oh, and I give great nuts!"

He had her with that one. She couldn't conceal the glimmer of a smile.

"You look terrible," she said crossly.

"I had a hard night."

"A shower will help."

"Is that an invitation?"

"You know, I really do not appreciate you just turning up here uninvited."

"You *did* invite me."

"And you cancelled."

"Postponed."

"I don't like being kept waiting."

"Sometimes it's worth it."

"When?"

"Shall we put it to the test?"

Later, much later, after hot sex and a cool shower, while Silver slept, Wes crept downstairs and switched on the television in the kitchen. He opened the fridge and dug into a plate of cold cuts while searching for a news channel with the remote control.

When he found one he almost choked. The murders were a big item. A pretty blonde news reader told the story:

> "Heavy-metal singing star Churnell Lufthansa, and his fifteen-year-old girlfriend, Gunilla Saks, were found shot to death in a remote Laurel Canyon hideaway late last night. No murder weapon was found. The police have no suspects at this time. Churnell Lufthansa climbed to fame in the late sixties with his band the Ram Bam Wams. He was known for –"

Abruptly he switched off, hardly wanting to hear the details, as long as *his* name wasn't included, and he didn't see how it could be.

Quickly he picked up the phone and punched out Rocky's number. Several rings, and then Rocky's unmistakable pugilistic voice.

"Where the fuck are ya, man?" Rocky demanded.

Wes spoke carefully. How did Rocky know he wasn't at his house? He hadn't said anything. "I'm home," he said guardedly.

"Naw!"

"Why wouldn't I be?"

"Because they're fuckin' loo –" Rocky stopped.

"Lookin' for me?" Wes finished the sentence for him.

"I guess." Rocky's voice was sulky. He didn't want to have this conversation.

"What's the scam, my friend?" Wes asked, knowing he wasn't going to get a straight answer.

"Ya dumb fuckhead!" Rocky exploded. "Waddya havta ice 'em for?"

"Huh?"

"Ya heard me, birdbrain."

"Shit!" Wes said disbelievingly. "You don't think *I* did it, do you?"

"Word is out that not only did ya do it, but y'ran off with fifty thou in cash, an' plenty of the white stuff."

"That's bullshit!"

"It's on the street. They're lookin' for ya."

"Where?"

"Everywhere."

"Who's they?"

"The big boys."

"*Shit!*"

"So . . . where are ya?"

Rocky's attempt at casual was pathetic. Not only were they looking for him, but there was probably a price on his head. One that Rocky wouldn't mind collecting.

"Arizona," he said quickly. "I came here for my health."

"And you'd better stay there." Rocky paused, then all in a rush said, "Hey – what's ya number? I'll call ya if I hear anything."

"Don't call me, I'll call you."

Thoughtfully he replaced the receiver. If he'd gone home tonight there was a likelihood he would have joined Churnell Lufthansa and Gunilla Saks in the Garden of Eden. And he wasn't ready to start fertilizing tomatoes. No way.

He opened up the fridge again and took out a cold beer, wiping the top before putting it to his lips because someone had once told him dogs peed on the side of cans.

Okay. What was he going to do?

Alternatives.

New York. He had a few friends scattered around.

Too goddamn cold.

Not as cold as ten foot under.

Florida and Vicki.

There was no going back. She was probably fat and married now, with two kids and the picket fence she had always dreamed about.

Okay. He had no family. *So what the fuck was he going to do?*

Silver entered the kitchen silently. She glided on high-heeled mules, a peach robe wrapped around her nakedness. "Hmmm . . ." she murmured. "And what do we have here, a compulsive eater?"

Automatically he reached for the curve of her ass and

scrunched a handful. "You're hot stuff," he said, charm on automatic pilot.

"So I've been told."

"Yeah? Who told you that?"

"Half of America."

"Crazy people."

"Don't be so rude!"

"Maniacs!"

"Watch it, barman."

"No. *You* watch it."

Pulling her close to his chair he parted her robe. Then he pressed his mouth to her thatch and inserted his tongue.

Obligingly she spread her legs, allowing him free access.

Eating Silver Anderson was no hardship. Half the turn-on was the realization that he was tonguing one of the most famous women in America.

She arched her pelvis back with great agility, enjoying every minute of his expert attention.

After a very satisfying orgasm she smiled and said, "A first, Mr Money. Nobody's ever done that to me while I was standing."

"You've led a sheltered life," he remarked, helping himself to a piece of Sara Lee chocolate cake from the freezer.

"You'll break your teeth," she warned.

He flopped into a chair. "Listen – if your pussy didn't do it – chocolate cake's a breeze!"

"You crud!"

She could be very girlish, old Silver Anderson. He found himself laughing with her. And then she was on her knees giving him a little lip.

Whew! If anyone had told him he could get it up again tonight he would have said they were crazy! But up it came. Eager as a housewife at a swap meet.

She knew her stuff. He nearly zoomed through the fucking ceiling! And he certainly forgot all his troubles.

Temporarily.

When it was over she smiled at him. "You're keeping me up," she said succinctly.

He grinned. "Who's keeping *who* up?"

"You're a bad influence. I need my sleep. I'm not nineteen, you know."

"Jeez! You must be kiddin'!"

"Fun*nee*. I'll look like a hag on the set tomorrow."

"*You* could never look anything but beautiful."

"Flatterer."

"And you love it."

"I can't deny it, barman."

"Wanna get married?" He blurted it out before really thinking what he was suggesting.

She raised an amused eyebrow. "I *beg* your pardon?"

He might as well go all the way. "I thought we could hop a plane to Vegas an' just do it."

She wrapped her peach robe tightly around her and began to laugh. "Why on *earth* would I marry *you*?"

Everything fell on top of him. He was too tired to take any more crap. "Yeah," he said bitterly. "Why would y'wanna marry me? I'm all right to screw the ass off — but marriage? You're right, rich lady — I'm just a bum. I'll take your money and scam out of your life quicker than a wino with ten bucks. *Fuck* it!"

Getting up from the table he paced around the room completely naked. Turning on her angrily he said, "I've never asked anyone to marry me in my life. And waddya do? Huh? *Huh?* You laugh in my face like I'm some kind of pet fuckin' joke! Well, let me tell you this — I don't *want* your money, I'm not *interested* in your fame. I just kinda thought we'd have a good time together. You enjoy me. I enjoy you. Why not go all the way?"

She was caught off guard. This was the last thing she'd expected. Wes was furious, like a big caged animal. And he looked so funny as he marched up and down her kitchen with his highly impressive credentials swaying in the breeze.

Marriage. Hmmm . . . Each time she did it, it was a terrible mistake.

Marriage. Hmmm . . . It might be kind of fun. And front page news, of course.

Wes grabbed another can of beer from the fridge, and pressed it open so violently that a fine spray flew all over the floor.

"I don't know a thing about you," she pointed out reasonably.

"I'll tell you whatever y'need to know."

"How *kind* of you."

He ignored her sarcasm. "I'm free, white, and over twenty-one. I'm also broke, and in a spot of trouble with some characters who think I owe them money – only I don't. There are no strings attached to me. I've got no social diseases. I won't be your go-fer, but I'll look after you and watch out for your interests. I'm no fuckin' genius, but I'm street smart and sharp – y'can learn a lot from me."

She went on to say something. He held up his hand and stopped her. "I don't want anything you've got. Not your house, your cars, your money. I'll sign any goddamn paper your lawyer puts in front of me."

"If you're broke, perhaps you can give me some kind of indication about what you intend to live on?" she asked acidly.

He swigged from the can of beer. "I don't mind you payin' the bills. I got no macho problem about *that*."

She began to laugh. "What a relief!"

Walking over to her, he grabbed her around the waist, and pulled her towards him. "I think we'd be a pretty steamy combination, don't you?"

"I've got everything to lose and nothing to gain," she protested feebly.

He rubbed the scar above his left eyebrow with one hand, and cupped her tight ass with the other. "Yes you have. You got me. And y'know somethin', rich lady?"

It was ridiculous, but she felt the heat of desire creeping up on her again. Her voice was husky. "What?"

"I'll make you the happiest broad in Hollywood."

Somewhere in the Midwest . . .
Sometime in the seventies . . .

The girl grieved for her father and his lady friend in a proper manner. She was taken in by a neighbouring farmer's family, while the entire community speculated on who could have committed such a hideous crime — setting a man's house on fire and incinerating everyone and everything in it.

"They said he was crisp as a burnt chicken," the girl heard the woman of the house confide to a friend. Good, she thought. I hope he suffered. I hope he died a thousand deaths.

Nobody suspected her of the crime. In fact, for the first time in her life she received love and sympathy from most of the people around her.

The farmer and his wife had four children of their own, and it was understood right from the start that her stay with them was only temporary. She shared a room with the two daughters and kept to herself. The sisters — one seventeen and one almost eighteen — regarded her as an unwelcome intruder. Although she was younger than them and in a lower grade at school, they knew her reputation as a loner, and thought she was odd. Their names were Jessica-May and Sally, and they thought and talked about nothing but boys.

"I think Jimmy Steuban's cute," Jessica-May would say.

"I like Gorman," Sally would join in. And then they would discuss the pros and cons of both boys for hours at a time.

Occasionally they would both stare at the girl and demand belligerently, "Who do you like?" When she didn't answer they would dissolve into fits of giggles and whisper among themselves.

The farmer's wife was a kind woman. Her husband was a brusque man with bright red hair and matching beard. Their two sons, ten and twelve, were little rascals, up to tricks day and night. The girl settled into family life, and waited for the sheriff to find one of her brothers or sisters to take her in. She had no regrets about what she had done. Her father and his painted whore deserved it.

Money in the farmer's household was short, and it wasn't long before the girl was asked to contribute to the family income by getting a job. She worked weekends as a box girl in the town's only supermarket. Her sixteenth birthday came and went. She didn't tell anyone. There was nobody who really cared.

At night, in the room she shared with the two sisters, she would lie in bed and gaze at the ceiling for hours on end wondering what was to become of her. She had no intention of staying in the town, and secretly she started saving the tips she got at work. With her sixteenth birthday behind her, her body began to fill out at last. Her breasts grew, and her waist narrowed. Suddenly she looked like a woman, and the boys at school took a lot more notice of her than they ever had before. One boy in particular, Jimmy Steuban, started to follow her everywhere. He was seventeen, with black hair and an athletic build. The girl tried to ignore him, because she knew Jessica-May liked him. But he was very persistent — always asking her for a date, and hanging around outside her place of work.

One night she let him walk her home. He grabbed her in the bushes near the farmhouse and tried to kiss her. She screamed so hard he ran like a frightened moose.

But he didn't give up, and against her better instincts she started to like him back, and before long they were girlfriend and boyfriend. Jessica-May was furious. Every day she pleaded with her mother to get rid of the unwanted boarder.

"She has nowhere to go," the kindly woman pointed out. "No kin that anyone can find. We're God-fearing people. We must keep her till she's at least seventeen."

Jessica-May got angrier, and did everything she could to make life difficult for the girl. She put dead mice and cockroaches in her bed, messed up her school books, cut the buttons off her clothes, and generally bad-mouthed her. She elicited the help of her sister, Sally, who joined in gladly. Both of them wanted to see the back of her.

Jimmy Steuban was her only solace. He treated her nicely. Took her to the movies and on picnics, and talked to her as though she was a decent human being. When he finally tried to make love to her, she found that she couldn't say no. So she allowed him, one cold night in the back of his father's rusty old Ford, to remove her blouse and then her flimsy bra. He touched her breasts reverently, and spoke of how much he loved her. Then he lifted her skirt, pulled down her panties, and thrust his manhood into her.

230

She was rigid with fear and anxiety, expecting it to be like it was with her father. Only somehow, with Jimmy, it was different, and she found herself relaxing and responding with more feeling than she'd ever had in her life.

"You're terrific!" he gasped. "I really love you!"

She really loved him too. And over the next few months they made love and plans on a regular basis. "What if I get pregnant?" she asked him nervously one night, although deep down she was sure that she couldn't, after what had happened.

"I'll marry you," he said gallantly. "We'll live in a castle, and I'll be your prince!"

Six weeks later she discovered she was pregnant. She told Jimmy, who told his father. Two days after that Jimmy was sent out of town, and she never heard from him again.

Jessica-May and Sally crowed the news from the rooftops. Shortly after, she was sent to a home for unwed mothers fifty miles away. The home was run by nuns —strict, unsmiling women, who demanded respect and obedience at all times. The sixty pregnant girls had to rise at five a.m., do two hours of penance on their knees in a freezing cold chapel with a concrete floor, and then housework until noon, when they were given a plate of soup, a piece of stale bread, and a cup of milk. The afternoon was study time, because most of the girls were under eighteen. Bed was seven p.m., and once every two weeks a florid-faced, bull-necked doctor arrived to examine them. The doctor had his own examining room in the house. Some of the inmates christened it the torture chamber.

The girl dreaded his visits. She never slept the night before his always punctual arrival. He drove a dusty sedan, and was usually accompanied by a sour-faced nurse, who preferred to spend her time drinking cups of herb tea with the nuns. The doctor didn't seem to mind. As girl after girl presented herself to him he always said the same thing. "Clothes off. On the table. Legs in the stirrups."

He never looked at their faces or knew their names. He called them by numbers, and when one of them was carted off to the hospital and gave birth, he crossed her off his list, and added a different name in front of the number.

The girl drew number seven. It wasn't her lucky number. She had never been to a gynaecologist, nor even heard of them — but a fat redhead confided that this was not the way it was supposed to be.

First the doctor drew thin rubber gloves onto his bony hands. Then he dipped his index finger into a jar of Vaseline, and plunged straight into whoever was on his table. He stayed inside a good five minutes, sometimes ten, probing, pushing, hurting – for he was never careful. Sometimes he bent his head down, grabbed a torch, and peered inside for a very long time. Once he arrived with a hat that looked like a miner's, a flashlight perched on the top. This contraption enabled him to look and feel at the same time. Occasionally he forgot to put on his gloves. The worst times were when he inserted a wooden speculum and forced the labia wide. The girl had to stop herself from screaming because it hurt so much, and when she mentioned it he'd said, "Don't be such a stupid child. You let your boyfriend get inside and have a good time. If you hadn't, you wouldn't be in this mess today."

The breast exam came next. A long session of fondling, pinching and squeezing.

Businesslike, when he was finished, he would say, "Off the table, let me look at you." And whoever was in the room would have to endure a lecherous once-over from the rheumy-eyed doctor. Once a month he took a Polaroid picture. "For my files," he always said.

"Dirty old man, he should be struck off or whatever they do to filthy old perverts," said one eighteen-year-old. But everyone found out that complaining got them nowhere. The nuns thought the good doctor was a saint, and would hear no ill of him.

The girl endured her pregnancy as she had endured the rest of her life. She kept to herself and remained silent.

"Fuckin' stuck-up bitch!" said a skinny brunette. "Think you're too bloody good fer us, doncha?"

She didn't think. She knew. One day she was going to leave her humble beginnings far behind and make something of herself.

When her baby was born, shortly after her seventeenth birthday, it was put up for immediate adoption. She suckled the infant for a mere six days, and then it was taken from her.

"Sign this," said a big nurse with pop-eyes and a hairy chin.

"I don't th –"

"You have no choice."

She signed, and was sent from the hospital to a foster home. While there, she learned that Jimmy Steuban had gotten Jessica-May pregnant and that they were to be married immediately. No exile for Jessica-May – far from it. The wedding was a lively affair, with four bridesmaids and a two-tier cake. The girl read a report in the local paper. And there was a picture of the happy couple. Jessica-May wore a white dress her mother had sewed for her. And Jimmy Steuban looked fine – if slightly uncomfortable – in a rented tuxedo.

The girl waited until she was eighteen before doing anything about it. She waited quietly and patiently. Then one night, when the moon was full and shining like a beacon, she borrowed her foster brother's bicycle, stole a can of gasoline from the local gas station, and rode seven miles to the tiny house where Jessica-May and Jimmy Steuban lived with their new baby.

Quietly, methodically, she shook the gasoline around the house. Lighting the first match was easy . . .

BOOK THREE

Hollywood, California
August 1985

Chapter 49

Poppy Soloman had changed her outfit five times. She was in a panic and simply could not make up her mind. Should she wear the Valentino? The Chanel? The Saint Laurent?

She stamped her foot and let out a blood-curdling yell of frustration.

Howard came running into her dressing room from his bathroom. He wore boxer shorts, his usual manic expression, no toupee, and a dribble of white powder between his nose and his upper lip. "What the fuck happened?" he shouted excitedly.

Poppy, clad in nothing more than sheer beige panty-hose and a magnificent diamond necklace, her long blonde hair swept up in an elaborate style, pouted. "Baby can't decide what to wear!" she wailed.

"Jesus *Christ*!" he roared. "I thought you were being murdered!" He waved lethal-looking scissors in the air. "I nearly cut my friggin' balls off!"

"What were you doing with scissors near your balls?" she asked curiously.

"Trimmin' the grass," he replied sarcastically. "What do you *think* I was doing?"

Poppy sighed. She was in no mood for one of Howard's silly outbursts. "You've got to help me, sweet-buns." She picked up a deep pink Bill Blass creation from the floor. "Tell me *truthfully* which dress you like best."

"Pick the most expensive," he said sourly.

"I don't keep the receipts in my head," she replied tartly. "Now, please be sensible and cooperate. Otherwise we'll be late."

"You can't be late for your own dinner party," he pointed out.

237

"Exactly!" she agreed.

Twenty-five minutes later, after he'd had to endure a mini fashion parade, the choice was made. An exquisite Oscar de la Renta short silk jacket in a kaleidoscope pattern of shimmering beads over a black velvet long dress. It had cost him nearly six thousand bucks, and she'd never worn it!

"Thank you, honeybunch." She gave him a hug, and then noticed that he was still in his undershorts. "Get dressed, Howard!" she exclaimed crossly. "If you make us late I'll kill you!"

Muttering ominously, he locked himself securely in his bathroom. Poppy could drive a man nuts! This dinner party had changed dates, venues, and guest lists ten times. Now it was all set. An intimate little sit-down for seventy-five people, and it was tonight. Although why *they* should be the ones giving an exclusive wedding dinner in the upstairs room at the Bistro for Silver Anderson and her mystery bridegroom, was beyond him. He hardly *knew* Silver, and she and Poppy were certainly not close. Of course, he had realized two minutes into his marriage that Poppy combined the most ferocious qualities of a social climber and a star fuck. Personally he didn't give a rat's ass. Whatever made her happy.

Reaching for his rug he plopped it in place, securing the two clips that held it in position, then combing his own hair over the join.

The buzzer on the telephone next to his toilet signalled. He picked up the receiver and snapped a no-nonsense "Yes?"

"Mr Klinger for you, Mr Soloman," said the housekeeper.

Why was Zachary K. Klinger calling him at home on a Saturday night? The man was an erratic prick. Seven times he had threatened to fly out to the Coast for a meeting, and seven times he had cancelled. Good. Howard didn't need him. He was doing very nicely without Zachary K. Klinger looking over his shoulder. Orpheus was in good shape. Three movies in production, and three more just about ready for preproduction, including Howard's brilliant idea – the old-fashioned musical starring Carlos Brent, with Orville Gooseberger producing, and Whitney Valentine even now reading the script, a remake of an original classic.

"Hiya, Zachary," he said, in the friendliest tone he could muster, waiting for the latest cancellation. Zachary was supposed to be arriving on Monday.

"I'm surprising you, Howard," Zachary said. He spoke in a

sinister whisper, sounding very much like Marlon Brando in *The Godfather*.

"I know, I know," Howard replied easily. "You can't make the meeting on Monday. It's okay, Zach." He used the nickname with confidence. "We all understand. Everything's buzzin' along without you."

"I'm here," Zachary announced with no preamble. "I'd like to meet tonight."

"You're here?" Howard repeated hoarsely. "Really?"

"Flew in fifteen minutes ago."

"You did?" Howard felt sweat break out all over his body. He didn't need this kind of surprise. Months of farting around, and now the asshole had to appear on the night of Poppy's big dinner for Silver Anderson. "Jesus, Zach. I wish you'd given me some warning."

"Why?" Zachary asked mildly.

Howard knew the unruffled voice was a front, concealing unbridled fury. When Zachary K. Klinger wanted something, a person didn't argue. The stories about him were legendary.

"Uh . . . my wife, Poppy, she's giving this uh . . . black-tie dinner. It's for Silver Anderson." He laughed nervously. "Broads! If I backed out of this one she'd be at Marvin Mitchelson's before breakfast!"

"No problem at all," said Zachary understandingly.

Howard breathed again.

"Fortunately, I always keep a tuxedo on both coasts," Zachary continued. "Which means I'll be able to join you. What time? And where?"

For a split second Howard was speechless. *What time? And where?* Poppy had spent three days seating this dinner. *Three fucking days!* Zachary K. Klinger's appearance was going to throw her into a tizz she might never recover from. And he, Howard Soloman, would feel her wrath for weeks, months, maybe even years!

"This is great news, Zach," he managed. "Will you be coming alone?"

"Yes."

"Fine, fine. It's at the Bistro. Eight o'clock. Black tie, but you already know that, don't you?"

"Yes, I do." A pause. "And, Howard?"

"What, Zach?"

"I don't like being called Zach. My name is Zachary, or Mr Klinger. Make your choice and stick with it."

The line went dead in Howard's hand. *"Shit!"* he screamed. Poppy would never give him head again!

★

Nervously Heaven peeked at the third contact sheet handed to her by one of Antonio's assistants. She could not believe that the image she saw in stark black and white was herself. The photographs were staggering.

"You like?" asked the assistant, a butch-looking female.

"Sensational!" breathed Heaven. "Is this really me!"

"Yeah. Antonio's hot stuff with a camera. As long as he has someone to work with — an' you've got it."

"Do you think so?" Heaven asked modestly.

"Just look at the pix. You give out attitude. The camera can play with you and have a good time."

She gazed reverently at the contacts. It was true. The success of the photographs was *not* just due to Antonio. Her personality shone through her eyes and gave the pictures real life. With a little help from a makeup artist, a hairdresser, and an incredible stylist. They had all done their bit.

She was glad she'd persevered and not given up on Antonio's promise to photograph her. It had taken some doing, but she had finally got herself in front of his camera — and the results were brilliant! She was sure he'd enjoyed the session as much as she had. He'd played loud rock music, and encouraged her to move to the beat and have fun.

When signing the release she had made one stipulation — she had asked him to make sure that wherever he placed the photos, there was no mention of Silver Anderson being her mother.

"Bene," he had said, and that was that. She trusted him.

Wow! Silver would freak out when she saw these pictures!

"What's he going to do with them?" she asked Antonio's assistant.

The girl said, "No idea. Feel relieved that he likes them. He's *very* particular."

"Can I order some?"

"You *are* joking, aren't you? Antonio *never* gives out prints. Sorry."

Heaven wondered if she could steal a contact sheet. What was the point of *doing* the pictures if she couldn't get hold of any?

"Well" — the assistant relented a bit — "I'll ask him what plans he has. Call me in a couple of weeks."

240

Reluctantly she left the studio half excited and half let down. At least it was a *positive* move. How many other girls of sixteen got to pose for the great Antonio? And how many other girls got to spend the summer at the beach with their famous uncle? She was elated about *that*, even though Jack's house was definitely in the wrong direction. Santa Monica was where all the action was. Still ... it was probably a brilliant house and she couldn't wait to see it. It was dynamite of him to invite her – she knew how busy he was.

Her mother hadn't even called to find out what she was doing for the summer.

Her mother ...

Sometimes she wondered who her father was, and if she had known him would he have cared about her? Or would he be just like Silver?

She was frightened to ask his identity. Anonymity was better than more rejection.

Stopping at the big Rexall drugstore on the corner of La Cienega and Beverly, she stocked up on suntan oils, and began to feel excited. At six o'clock that evening Uncle Jack was picking her up, and her summer at the beach would begin. As Jack had predicted, Grandfather George had hardly reacted at all. In fact, he had seemed quite pleased. Now she could look forward to six weeks of total freedom! Ah, if only she could get her career going everything would be perfect.

Driving over the hill she thought about Eddie. He was such a dork. She didn't like his guitar playing anymore, and she didn't like him. Perhaps this was the break they both needed.

The rambling house was empty when she got home. Her grandfather was in his workroom, and the housekeeper was out. She called a couple of girlfriends, found out nothing new, and began to pack.

What to take for six weeks at the beach? Bikinis, shorts, tank tops, tee-shirts and pants. She came across her long army coat hanging in the closet. A few months ago it was her favourite garment, but after Silver's party she'd never worn it again. Dragging it out she slipped it on. Hey – this was a definite *look* –why had she abandoned it?

Because it reminded her of dear mother. Her caring mother who recently got married for the *third* time, and did not even bother to inform her. Like the rest of America she had read about Silver Anderson's latest wedding in the newspapers.

She spun in front of the mirror, and the huge coat encircled her. Hardly right for the beach. Too hot.

She thrust her hands in the deep pockets and came up with a crumpled napkin. Written on it was ROCKY and a phone number.

For a moment she gazed at it blankly. Rocky? And then she remembered. The dude from Silver's party. The one behind the bar with a friend in the record biz. She had forgotten about him, what with meeting Antonio and the quest to get him to do the promised photos.

On impulse she dialled the number.

No answer.

Carefully she folded the napkin and stuffed it in the side of her suitcase. Rocky. She would give him a call and see if he *did* have a friend in the music industry. After all, she was going to be seventeen soon. She wasn't getting any younger.

Chapter 50

Wrapped in a soft leather Donna Karan dress, Jade arrived at the Ivy restaurant before her brother. She couldn't believe he hadn't changed the date as he had been consistently doing for weeks now. Since dinner never seemed to work out, she had finally pinned him down to a lunch. She was pleased, but also apprehensive. What if she hated his new girlfriend? What if the girlfriend hated her?

A Bloody Mary seemed like a good idea. She ordered one and sat back. A man at a nearby table smiled. She nodded distantly. Because her face was so familiar people always thought they knew her. Commercials did that for you. Wait until the Cloud Cosmetics campaign hit an unsuspecting public. It was going to be an all-out push to make Cloud bigger than Revlon and Estée Lauder put together. And *her* image was going to be on every television commercial, in every print ad, featured on the cover of every brochure – there would even be billboards across the country.

Cloud Cosmetics was already a famous and successful international company. Now the name Jade Johnson would be synonymous with Cloud. For she was not only the face to launch the new products, she was also the personality to sell them. There was a cross-country tour planned, personal appearances, and a host of other things. Mark would never have allowed her to sign such a deal. "It's too public," he would have proclaimed. "Hang onto your privacy, it's one of your most precious possessions."

And thinking of Mark, she realized that if he'd wanted to pique her interest, he'd certainly done a good job. But then he always *had* been a *clever* English asshole.

Since turning up at her apartment and the subsequent phone calls, she had not heard a word from him.

Isn't that what you wanted, Johnson? You ran off to Vegas fast enough.

She wasn't certain. Maybe he *was* divorcing Lady Fiona. Maybe he *had* changed.

Sure.

"Jade?"

She glanced up and exclaimed, "Beverly! I don't *believe* it!" Pushing away from the table she leaped to her feet and hugged her old friend Beverly D'Amo.

Beverly was a very tall, black, exotically beautiful model turned actress. She had jet hair hanging in a thick plait past her waist, and cheekbones that could cut glass.

"Believe it, J.J.!" yelled Beverly. "What the fuck you doin' here, girl?"

Several people turned to stare. Beverly's language never *had* been lady-like.

"I called you," Jade said. "Your answering service told me you were in Peru or somewhere."

"I was doing a movie, babee. A real-life DRAMA! She*it*! I got the runs the moment I arrived, an' spent most of my time visiting the can. Two minutes on the screen and two months in the crapper!"

Jade smiled. "Nothing changes. Still the same old Bad Beverly."

"Yeah. This may be hot-shot city, babe, but the *Brrr*onx is in my blood."

"You left the Bronx when you were fifteen," Jade pointed out.

"So ... I can have my roots, can't I?"

Grinning, Jade said, "Why don't you just sit down, shut up, and order a drink."

Beverly grimaced. "I can't. I'm having lunch with my agent. A power lunch, my dear. We have my *career* to discuss, you know." She waved across the room.

Jade shook her head. "You're so full of it! But I still love you. Can we have dinner?"

"Not tonight we can't. Tonight I am attending a very chic little dinner party for Silver Anderson. Just seventy-five of her *very* closest dearest friends!"

"And you're one of them, I presume."

Beverly let loose a wild, high-pitched Eddie Murphy type laugh. "Don't even *know* the bitch! But hey, J.J., I'm a party animal, you remember that, don't you?"

How could she ever forget? She had started modelling with Beverly, and for a while they were known as the Terror Team, because of all the practical jokes they played. Jade had nothing but warm memories of the wild and wonderful Ms. D'Amo. "How about tomorrow night?" she suggested.

"Babee, you're on. We'll go cruising. Where's His Lordship?"

"Dead."

"He deserves worse."

"Oh. So you knew about him too?"

"*Everyone* knew about him. His prick stood at attention whenever you left the room."

"Thanks for telling me."

"We'll talk tomorrow. I've got gossip comin' out my ears!"

"Can't wait."

"Call me in the morning. See ya!"

Jade watched Beverly slink across the room and settle at a table, her loud laughter ringing across the small, intimate restaurant.

Sipping her drink she waited patiently – brother Corey and friend were late. Signalling the waiter she ordered another Bloody Mary.

Corey walked in twenty minutes later, with what she had learned to recognize as his guilty face. When they were kids he employed it every time he did something naughty.

"What's up, bro?" she asked, determined not to comment on his tardy entrance and spoil their lunch.

His greeting was strained as he glanced anxiously around the restaurant. A pretty blonde girl approached their table, and Jade steeled herself for the introduction.

The girl walked briskly past. Behind her was a very handsome young man, slight of build, with dark curly hair, and a dimpled chin.

Corey put his hand possessively on the young man's arm. "Norman," he said in a strained voice, "I'd like you to meet my sister, Jade."

Norman had an open smile, and a gold Rolex on his wrist. He extended a friendly hand and introduced himself. "Norman Gooseberger," he said pleasantly. "Delighted to meet you. I'm the mystery roommate. I'm sorry it's taken so long for us to get together — but *you know* your brother."

She had thought she did. Suddenly she wasn't sure at all — for it was quite obvious that Corey and Norman were much more than mere roommates.

Chapter 51

They entered the Bistro like couple of the year. Which, of course, they were. Silver Anderson and her new husband, Wes Money.

The photographers skulking around the entrance went beserk when they drew up in a sleek limousine. Silver wore a shimmering long gown of gold and a big smile. Wes wore a recently purchased tuxedo and a white silk shirt with diamond and gold studs — a wedding present from Silver.

He was unused to the sudden rush of photographers, and nearly tripped. Grabbing Silver firmly by the arm he pulled her inside, his expression grim.

"What's the matter?" she asked, with an amused smile.

"Those people are animals," he complained. "Don't pose for 'em, it just encourages the sleaze-bags."

"Charming! What a delightfully *visual* word."

"Believe me, it sure describes *this* group."

She adjusted the top of her dress before ascending the staircase to the upstairs room where the party was taking place. "Get used to it, darling," she said casually. "Wherever Silver Anderson goes, the press follows. Sometimes it's fun, most times it's not. I just bare my teeth and take it in my stride."

"*I* don't," he said grimly.

"You soon will."

"Care to put money on it?"

"We'll see."

They had been married for exactly five weeks. The wedding had taken place in Las Vegas. Quick, quiet, and very secret. So secret, in fact, that the press had no smell of anything going on, and Silver, unrecognizable in a long blonde wig and dark glasses, had completely fooled the old couple in the wedding chapel. Only later, when checking the register, had they noticed her name. By the time the wire-services and television crews were alerted, Silver and her new bridegroom had flown to a remote hideaway house in Hawaii, loaned to them by the executive producer of *Palm Springs*. There they stayed for several delicious weeks, shut off from the outside world, quite content to just relax and get to know each other. What they actually did most of the time was make love. A lot. As Silver later remarked to Nora in a confiding moment, "It was the perfect honeymoon. Sex, sleep, sex, food, and sex, sex, sex!"

Nora, as usual, marvelled at the woman's energy.

Once Silver made the decision that, yes, she *would* marry Wes, everything fell into place like a perfectly planned chess game. She told only Nora, her lawyer, and the producer of *Palm Springs*. Together they eased the way for a publicity-free union. Not easy, but possible. Especially as Wes had never been publicly connected to her, and nobody knew who he was anyway.

Naturally they all tried to talk her out of it. She listened to one minute of *Who is he? You know nothing about him. He could be after your money*, etcetera. Then she told them, very politely, to kindly butt out of her personal life. Which they did. Albeit reluctantly.

Prudently she did have her lawyer draw up a document excluding Wes from sharing her wealth. He signed it quite happily.

"Do you have any family you wish to tell?" she had asked him shortly before the ceremony.

He'd shaken his head. "Nope. I come to you free and clear of any mothers, fathers, sisters, brothers, children or ex-wives."

"Hmmm . . . You also come to me free and clear of any worldly goods."

"I've got a few things – nothin' I'm in the mood to collect right now. I can get 'em when we come back."

Their timing was perfect. One more day's work, and then Silver was on hiatus from her television show for three months. She had been considering doing a Movie of the Week – fortunately nothing was signed.

Several days after he proposed, they did the deed, and Silver Anderson became Mrs Wes Money. Actually, Wes Money became Mr Silver Anderson, because that's the way it goes in Hollywood. The famous name is the one everyone knows. So limo drivers and doormen and porters all referred to him as Mr Anderson. What did he care? He was safe. He was no longer a nobody – overnight, Wes Money had become a somebody.

Now they were back in L.A., still comparative strangers, although he *did* know her favourite food was golden caviar – which he hated. Her favourite booze, champagne – which gave him ferocious hangovers. And her favourite sexual position – anything, anytime, anywhere.

The whole scenario was like some kind of wild fantasy. He kept on thinking he was going to wake up and find himself lying on the floor in the hall of the Laurel Canyon house with the cops right outside and the murder weapon clutched in his hand.

Jesus! Every time he thought of that little nightmare he got the chills. But he had outsmarted them all the way down the line. First – he had escaped before discovery. Second – he had married well. They couldn't try to pin anything on him now, he was no longer Joe Schmuck. And let them whistle for their money. As far as he was concerned they could all eat shit. He had nearly been tricked into oblivion, and they could damn well pay for it. The money and cocaine were stashed in a safe-deposit box at the bank. It was his insurance in case Silver ever threw him out.

"Poppy, darling — this is Wes," Silver said, between cheek kisses which missed by half a mile. "I want *you* to be the first to meet him."

Wes took in a short blonde with silicone tits (he could always tell), fabulous real diamonds (he could always tell) and a self-satisfied smile.

"So *you're* the mystery man!" she exclaimed in a breathy voice. "How *exciting!*"

He nearly choked on her perfume.

"*Do* meet my husband, Howard Soloman." She pulled at the sleeve of a short man with obvious shoe lifts and a rug. "Howard, poppet. Say hello to Wes."

Howard Soloman winked at him, just as Silver said, "Congratulate me, Howard. I've done it again!"

"Congratulations, kiddo," Howard said amiably. An out-of-control muscle twitched on his cheek. "Nice to meet you, Les."

"Wes."

A lone female photographer stepped forward and took their picture.

"C'*mon*," said Wes forcefully. "No pictures."

"Don't worry" — Poppy dimpled nicely — "it's only George's girl."

"Who's George's girl?" he muttered to Silver.

"George Christy, darling. He writes the wonderful back page in the *Hollywood Reporter*."

"They allow photographers into these things?"

"Only the key ones. Oh look, there's Dudley. He's so wonderful. I adore him. Did you see him in *Ten*? Such a *funny* man."

For the next-half hour it was "spot the stars". It seemed everyone from Johnny Carson to Kirk Douglas had turned out to inspect Silver's latest husband.

Wes tried to maintain an aura of cool as he said hello to Jacqueline Bisset, Whitney Valentine Cable and Angie Dickinson. Three women he had lusted after forever.

And then came the men. He actually got to meet Carlos Brent. He had grown up *fucking* to the records of the legendary Carlos Brent. What a night *this* was going to be!

*

Poppy took the news of Zachary K. Klinger as an extra guest extremely well. She moved Howard's place card from his seat of honour beside Silver, and cleverly replaced him with Zachary.

Then she switched place cards with Whitney Valentine Cable, and put herself the other side of the new guest. Howard and Whitney she relocated on table number two. Had it been anyone else but Zachary K. Klinger she would have screamed for days. As it was she felt quite elated. Getting Zachary K. Klinger was a hostess's coup.

Meanwhile, it was past eight-thirty, and Zachary had failed to put in an appearance.

"Where is he?" she hissed at Howard. "I'm going to have to seat everyone in fifteen minutes."

"Go ahead, he'll be here." Howard spoke in a carefree manner, but oh . . . was he going to get it if Zachary didn't show.

He eyed Whitney, who was standing across the room, positively glowing in a strapless lime-green dress. He was purposely staying away from her until dinner when he would be sitting next to her. Maybe by this time she had read the script and wanted to do it. How could she *not* want to do it with Carlos Brent starring and Orville Gooseberger producing? The lady was going to move into heavyweight country, and *he* was responsible. He hoped she would be suitably grateful.

Mannon Cable made an entrance. Late, of course. The bigger the star, the later the entrance. Once the guest list passed thirty people, Poppy had decided it was perfectly proper to invite Whitney *and* Mannon. "After all," she had said, with a great deal of logic, "if one stopped inviting people because they were once married to other guests . . . well, in Hollywood, you'd end up with no one!"

Very true.

Mannon waved at Howard. Howard waved back. If he *did* have an affair with Whitney, and Mannon found out . . .

It didn't bear thinking about.

*

Zachary K. Klinger greeted his driver curtly, and stepped into the back of a maroon Rolls-Royce. The Rolls, although several years old, was in pristine condition. Zachary rarely visited California, but believed in keeping a car and chauffeur in every major city across the world. He was rich enough to have dozens of cars wherever he wished. In fact, his riches enabled him to do whatever he damn well pleased for the rest of his life.

Sighing, he leaned back against the plush leather upholstery. Money. It could buy him anything and almost anyone. Except . . .

249

with nagging realization he knew the old cliché was true –
money could not buy the happiness he so fervently desired.

*

"Enjoying it?" Silver gave Wes a sly smile. She was loving
every minute of the attention.

He nodded. To tell the truth, he was quite bemused. All
these people, all these well-known faces. He knew for a fact that
if he wasn't Mr Silver Anderson, they wouldn't give him the
time of day. Rich folks lived life different. They only wanted to
mix with other rich folks. Wes knew this. He had stood behind
enough bars in enough fashionable establishments to observe the
way things were.

Famous people were exactly the same. Show a star another
star and they'd break bones to be together. Unless they were
deadly rivals, in which case icy politeness ruled.

Jeez! If this lot only knew who Wes Money *really* was.

Fortunately, the supermarket rags had managed to find out
nothing. He was a complete mystery man.

Nora had released a statement on Silver's behalf. It was short
and to the point:

SILVER ANDERSON, STAR OF *PALM SPRINGS*, MARRIED
RECENTLY FOR THE THIRD TIME. HER NEW HUSBAND, WESLEY
MONEY JUNIOR, IS A BUSINESSMAN.

Wes had exploded when the announcement appeared. "What
the *fuck* is this *junior* crap?" he'd demanded.

"Nora's idea," Silver had replied. "And I must admit, it does
give you *some* sort of background."

"You want a background, you should've married Teddy
Kennedy!"

She had smiled. "Just a touch too plump. I do so *hate* love
rolls, don't you?"

He had to admire Silver. She didn't give a damn about anything or anybody. She was a tough, gutsy broad who did what
she wanted, and to hell with criticism.

"My life hasn't always been easy," she had informed him one
balmy night on their lust-filled honeymoon. "Four years ago I
had a nervous breakdown. I thought it was all over."

"Yeah?" He wasn't interested in talking pasts. He couldn't
imagine Silver anywhere but at the top. And once they were

married he couldn't imagine himself being anywhere except by her side.

This was not love. This was good times.

Poppy fussed among her guests as they began to sit down at their various tables. She wanted Howard. She wanted his blood. Zachary K. Klinger had failed to show.

Just as she was about to start screaming – discreetly, of course – Zachary K. Klinger walked through the door. She recognized him at once, and wasted no time in hurrying over. "Mr Klinger," she gushed. "This is *such* a pleasure! I am delighted you made it."

"Who are you?" he asked, in his sinister rasp.

"Why, I'm Poppy Soloman." She smiled sweetly. "Your hostess."

He looked her over. He was a big, well-preserved man in his late sixties, with exaggerated strong features – and behind his steel-rimmed glasses, cold, opaque eyes. He made her feel immediately uncomfortable.

"Why don't I find Howard for you," she suggested.

"Yes. Why don't you?" he said, taking a cigar from his breast pocket and lighting up.

How rude, she thought, *and before dinner, too*. Perhaps she had made a mistake seating him next to Silver; the man obviously had no manners.

She grabbed Mannon, on his way back from the men's room. "Have you seen Howard?" she asked anxiously. And then, as an afterthought, because she was nervous, she introduced him to Zachary. The two men had never met. They shook hands and tried to out-grip each other.

"Howard's in the john," Mannon informed her.

"Can you get him for me?" she pleaded.

"I'll find him myself," Zachary said, staring piercingly at Mannon. "We'll talk later. I want you for Orpheus. When you hear what I have to offer, you'll jump."

"I never jump," said Mannon easily – his ease belied by his mouth, which set into a thin line.

"Never known an actor who didn't," said Zachary, with all the confidence of a man used to getting his own way.

"Well, I guess you're looking at him," replied Mannon.

"I don't think so." Zachary set off to find Howard.

Mannon was not pleased. "What a jerk," he said derisively.

"I'm certain he's not," Poppy said quickly, not quite sure why she was defending a man she had taken an instant dislike to.

"Grow up, Poppy. These guys that come walking into a business they know nothing about are all uniform jerks. You can take everything they know about the film industry and shove it up Howard's ass – *and* you'll have room for an agent or two."

"Mannon!"

"Believe me. I've been around."

He stalked off to his table, which unfortunately was the same one Zachary would be sitting at.

*

Locked safely in a booth in the men's room, Howard snorted the magic white powder. With a sigh of deep pleasure he felt the effect almost immediately. Nothing like it. Instant head honcho of the jungle. King Kong with concrete balls! Infuckingvincible!

He sailed out of the booth and bumped straight into Zachary K. Klinger.

"Mr K. You made it!" he exclaimed.

"Was there any doubt in your mind?"

"Never. *Ne-ver.*"

"When I say I'll be somewhere, I'm there."

"Sure you are." *When it suits you.* Howard walked over to the sink and began to wash his hands.

"I just talked to Mannon Cable," Zachary said, in his heavy whisper.

"Good."

"I want him for Orpheus."

Glancing in the mirror Howard noticed a dusting of white powder beneath his nose. Quickly he wiped it away. "I've tried to get him. The trouble is he's always tied up on some other project."

"I want him," Zachary repeated.

Howard wondered if old Zach ever cracked a smile. Probably not.

"I'll give it another shot," he said.

"You'll do more than that," Zachary retorted sharply.

"What?"

"I have a proposal. When he hears it, he'll be ours."

"Don't get too excited. Mannon's a lot pickier than everyone seems to think."

"Money talks."

"To some people."

"To everyone."

"Like I said — we'll give it another try."

As he walked towards the door, Zachary blocked him. "I don't believe in tries. I believe in certainties. I want Mannon Cable and *I will have him.*"

"If you say so." *Shit,* Howard thought. *The old guy thinks he's Harry Cohn and this is the 1950s. No way, José.*

*

"Well?" Silver whispered, reaching for Wes's thigh under the table. "Are we having a good time?"

He didn't go overboard on this new, semi-patronizing attitude she was adopting. Benevolent keeper, showing her new pet off to the crowd.

"It's all a crap shoot, Silver, and you know it."

Giggling girlishly she said, "Don't I just! Some of the women can't keep their eyes off you. They're all *dying* to know where I found you."

"You didn't *find* me anywhere. Let's get it straight, I rescued you from a bunch of fags who were out to rip you to shreds. Remember?"

"How could I *ever* forget. The thing I liked about you — even then — was your forcefulness."

"Silver, dahling!" Carmel Gooseberger descended on them, a nightmare in huge yellow frou-frous. "Is *this* the bridegroom?"

"Yes," said Silver. "Wes, meet Carmel Gooseberger."

He shook the large woman's hand.

"I know, I know," boomed Carmel, in an extremely loud voice. "Wesley Money, Junior. I think I know your father."

Wes looked alarmed. "You do?" he asked, remembering a shifty-eyed English pimp whom he hadn't seen since he was eight, and a pot-bellied American stepfather who had only been in his life for five minutes.

"Yes," nodded Carmel. "It's the San Francisco Moneys, isn't it?"

Silver kicked him under the table.

"Sure is," he agreed.

"What a family! Ah yes, I remember them well. It was quite a few years ago. Orville and I had just started going out together, and I was in San Francisco on location — I used to be an actress, you know."

Silver leaned forward glowing with amusement. "Go on, Carmel. Confess. You had an affair with Wes's father."

Carmel laughed in a loud and bawdy fashion. "If I did, dahling, you're the *last* person I'd tell."

"What won't you tell Silver?" Carlos Brent flashed a smile as he sat down at the table, accompanied by Dee Dee Dionne.

"Carmel claims to have slept with Wes's father. She was cheating on Orville at the time." Silver spoke with obvious relish.

"I reckon Carmel humped every good-looking cat in this town before Orville found her an' took her in off the street," Carlos said, with a big grin. "Am I right, gorgeous?"

"Stop!" roared Carmel, loving every minute of it. "You're so *bad*, Carlos."

"You can't fool us, sweetie," he joked. "I got in line once, but the line was so long I didn't have the strength to wait!"

"You're ruining my reputation," shrieked Carmel, patting her frosted hair, frou-frous heaving above a mammoth bosom.

"*What* reputation?" cracked Carlos.

The wisecracks continued as the table filled up. Mannon and Melanie-Shanna came over, and Orville Gooseberger, who had an even louder voice than his wife.

Silver was in fine form. Glittering like a Queen. Accepting compliments and congratulations as her due. Many years before, she and Carlos Brent had indulged in a short and passionate affair. Someone had tipped the press off that they were going to get married, and Carlos had blown a fuse – thinking Silver was the culprit. They had parted acrimoniously. Now, years later, she felt very secure with her hot career, and her horny new husband.

Poppy hovered, waiting for Zachary to emerge from the men's room so she could guide him to his seat. Howard was settled at his own table, with Whitney on one side and Ida White on the other. Ida was looking particularly glassy-eyed. Poppy hoped she'd last through the dinner. Ida had been known to go to the ladies' room at parties and fall into a blissful, drug-induced sleep. No one was sure what she was on, but whatever it was it certainly kept her floating, her head calmly above water – only just.

Zachary appeared, and Poppy grabbed him. "You're at my table," she cooed, and then proceeded to name-drop. "You're sitting with Carlos Brent, Mannon Cable, Silver Anderson – you do know this party is for her?" Without waiting for a reply she rushed on with, "Oh, and Orville Gooseberger. *Quelle* character! Quite a group for one table, don't you think?"

"Am I next to Silver Anderson?" he asked curtly.

"As a matter of fact, that's *exactly* where I've seated you."

Zachary nodded his approval.

Proudly, Poppy led him across the room. Several people tried to greet him, but Zachary gave the word *ignore* new meaning.

They reached the number one table, and Poppy began to introduce her most important guest.

Silver had a glass of champagne halfway to her lips when she looked up and saw Zachary.

The colour drained from her face.

Zachary K. Klinger was "The Businessman" from her past.

Zachary K. Klinger was Heaven's father, although he didn't know it.

Zachary K. Klinger was the hate of her life.

Chapter 52

"It's amazing!" Heaven exclaimed for the tenth time. "I totally, like, *love* it!"

She was referring to the beach house, which she had explored several times.

Jack loosened his tie and removed his jacket. He had been in a meeting with his accountant all afternoon and felt a strong need to flake out.

"And my room is just brilliant!" she continued. "It overlooks the beach and the ocean. I can just sit at my window all day and stare!"

"Sounds good to me. Do you want to stare in the fridge and see what the maid got in for us? I left a note for her to stock up at the market."

"I'm *starving*!"

"You're always starving! Whenever I see you I get this feeling you don't eat between my visits."

"I don't."

"You're a funny one."

She giggled happily. "I'll check out the food situation. Do not go away!"

As she rushed into the kitchen, he wondered what he had gotten himself into. Who would ever have thought he'd be living in a house *and* looking after a kid. Jack Python – surrogate father!

He kind of liked it.

Clarissa was still in New York. Because she had time between films, she had decided to do an obscure off-Broadway play for a limited run. They spoke on the phone every few days, but it was definitely a relationship that had gone off the boil. He knew she was waiting to see what he planned to do about her ultimatum. And quite frankly, the more he thought about marriage, the more he loathed the whole idea. Who needed it?

Silver had just married again. Silver could do what she damn well liked. He cared about *her* the way *she* cared about Heaven. Zilch feelings.

"I found potato salad, coleslaw, chicken and ham," Heaven announced triumphantly.

"Or we could go out," he suggested.

"Let's stay in."

"You don't have to twist *my* arm."

Much later, after food and unpacking and calling all her friends – including Eddie – Heaven fell into a happy sleep while Jack prowled around the house. He wasn't at all tired. Grabbing a sweater he decided to take a walk along the beach.

The dull realization hit him that he had to go to New York and settle things with Clarissa. They were either on or off. He *definitely* did not want marriage. She did. Either she was prepared to go on with the relationship the way it was, or it was over.

Decision made, he felt better. He would tell Heaven to have a girlfriend stay with her, and as soon as that was arranged, he'd take the next flight into New York. The show was on a six-week break, so it was the perfect time to sort things out.

In a way he hoped Clarissa would tell him it *was* over. Being with her was not exactly a laugh a minute. She was a broody, intense woman, simmering with secrets. She never revealed herself to him. There was always that guarded quality as if there were an unseen wall between them. The only time she really laid herself wide open was on the screen.

If he was really truthful with himself he would admit that the real appeal of Clarissa was her enormous talent.

He jogged back to the house and watched a late night movie. Lana Turner in her prime. A sexy, ballsy broad. They didn't make 'em like that anymore.

By one a.m. he began to fade, his eyes closed, and he drifted off to sleep.

Tomorrow he would work things out.

*

Back in the city, in her apartment on Wilshire, Jade sat alone on the terrace with a pack of Camels, a glass of wine, and a small dish of yoghurt-coated pretzels. She had *A Star is Born* on her stereo – the Streisand/Kristofferson version of the movie was one of her favourites.

The lights of Los Angeles were laid out like a glittering patchwork quilt. She never tired of watching them sparkle. *Hmmm*, she thought, *I'm turning into a loner. I like my own company a lot more than the party circuit.*

Well, that's what happened when there was no one in particular she wanted to be with. Besides, she enjoyed her own company, and never felt lonely. Ever since she was a child she had been self-sufficient and able to entertain herself. Whereas Corey had always needed friends over.

Corey –

My brother –

Is gay.

Subconsiously she had tried to stop herself from thinking about it all day. After lunch, which turned out to be a stilted affair, she had bolted from the restaurant fast. Without thinking, she'd gotten in her car and headed for the nearest shopping mall, which happened to be the Beverly Center. Once there, she had toured the shops with a dedication bordering on the obsessive.

One leather jacket, two pairs of Levis, a silk shirt, three pairs of stiletto-heeled shoes, four hard-cover books, an assortment of makeup, and a heavy glass ashtray later, she had driven home, where she showered, watched a tape of *Hill Street Blues*, and mindlessly ate a can of cold baked beans, a bar of chocolate and an orange. She smoked three cigarettes – a habit she had given up six years ago – and now she was sitting on her terrace *finally* thinking about Corey.

The revelation was an enormous shock. Not that he'd said anything. It hadn't been necessary. Just watching him with Norman Gooseberger the picture had become excruciatingly clear, and she knew immediately why her brother had been avoiding her.

Desperately she had tried to act normally, but it was difficult when all she wanted to do was scream at him – *Why? Why? Why?*

Polite conversation took place. *Have you seen this movie? Been to that restaurant? Tried this hotel?*

Norman seemed nice enough. His father was Orville Gooseberger, the well-known film producer, and his mother – to quote him – *gives great charity*.

"How did you two meet?" she'd found herself asking.

And Norman replied. Corey had nothing to say. It seemed they had worked together in the San Francisco branch of Briskinn & Bower, the big publicity firm. When Norman was transferred back to Los Angeles, he'd asked his father – who owned a chunk of B & B – to arrange for Corey to be transferred too.

She didn't want to know any more, hardly caring to hear the details.

Now, sitting quietly on her terrace, she began to wonder. Had Corey always been gay? Or did Norman bring it out in him?

She remembered how when he was a teenager he had always been inordinately shy around girls. One day her mother had voiced a mild doubt, swiftly forgotten, because the very next week he had started steady dating a girl named Gloria, with big breasts and sturdy legs. Were he and Gloria making out? She had asked him once, but he never replied. And then she had taken off for New York and her career, and only saw him on her occasional visits home.

When he met Marita, the entire family had been delighted, once they got over the shock of her being Hawaiian. Their wedding was old-fashioned and lovely, and they both seemed very happy. A year later, when the baby was born, everyone felt Corey was settled for life.

Now *this* bombshell. Her mother would have a nervous breakdown.

She reached for another cigarette. Some of her best friends were gay.

Jesus Christ, Johnson. What kind of a bigoted thought is that?

She hated herself for it, but she couldn't control the shock and disappointment she felt. And she was angry too.

Why hadn't he told her?

Because, asshole, he knew you'd react just like this.

Shut up.

It's true!

Guilt crept up on her. Was Corey doing it to spite her? Beautiful, successful Jade Johnson. Always the centre of attention. Always the star of the family. Was Corey striking back in the only way he could think of?

Drawing deeply on her cigarette, she realized *she* was the one who would have to tell their mother.

Why?

Because she has to know.

Why?

Oh, fuck off!

The phone interrupted her argument with herself. Since the answering machine was still on she let it pick up. First the message, then the bleep, followed by the unmistakable tones of Lord Mark Rand. English jerk-off artist.

"Jade?" he asked. "Are you there?"

When she said nothing he left his message, sounding embarrassed, as most people are when faced with speaking to a machine.

"Er . . . I'm in town."

Obviously.

"Please telephone me at L'Ermitage."

Oh, great! A repeat performance.

"This is Mark."

As if I don't know.

"Er . . . call me. Please."

He hung up.

She sighed. She wasn't ready for him. Not now.

Yes she was. She just wanted to curl up in his arms and shut out the world.

With a sigh of resignation, she reached for the phone.

Chapter 53

Silver managed a frosty smile. She was outraged, furious, *incensed*. What was Zachary doing at *her* wedding dinner? Who *the hell* had invited him?

She had gone over the list of guests several times, making sure there were no enemies included. Poppy had been most obliging, crossing off a ridiculous actress made of silicone, and a glassy-eyed producer who everyone knew was certifiably insane, but put up with anyway because he continued to produce movies, even though none of them ever made any money.

"I don't think we should invite riff-raff," Silver had remarked mildly, and the two offenders' names were struck through with a heavy felt-tip pen.

Now Zachary K. Klinger was present. And not only was he present, he was sitting down beside her.

The smile was fixed on her face like a frozen mask. *Poppy Soloman knows! Poppy Soloman did this on purpose! I'll get the bitch for this!*

"Good evening, Silver," Zachary said.

"*Zachary!* How *lovely* to see you. What a surprise! I'd like you to meet my husband, Wes Money, Junior."

"Will you cut out the Junior," Wes muttered irritably.

Zachary ignored him, concentrating only on Silver. "Congratulations on your success," he said.

"Thank you," she replied, anxious to excuse herself and rush to the ladies' room just to make absolutely certain she looked her best. Not that she cared what Zachary thought. It was just that after sixteen years one didn't want to be caught looking anything but perfect.

"You haven't changed," he said.

Nor had he, only she wasn't about to flatter him. His hair was completely grey, and there were more lines on his face, that was all. He had never been handsome, but he radiated power, and it was that which had attracted her to him in the first place.

When they first met, he was an important and extremely rich man. Since their last encounter he had become a legendary business tycoon and billionaire.

"Well!" Poppy exclaimed, as a delicate avocado and papaya salad was served. "Isn't this *fun!*"

★

"When are you goin' to dump the bozo?" Howard asked, with a knowing wink.

Whitney flashed her famous teeth. "Don't be bad, Howard. Chuck is an excellent actor, and extremely misunderstood."

"The guy is a stoned beach bum who is not worthy of you."

He liked that. The "not worthy of you" exhibited a great deal of class.

Whitney held her smile steady. "I'm not planning to *marry* him."

Howard wanted to say – *Just hump his ass off, huh?* But that wasn't classy, not classy at all. And above all he wanted her to regard him as a man of style.

"Have you read the script?" he asked.

She nodded, all teeth and hair and sparkling aquamarine eyes. "Yes, I have."

"And?"

"Zeppo has asked me not to discuss it with you."

"What?" He was outraged. "Since when has Zeppo been your agent?"

"Do I hear my name?" Zeppo White asked. He was sitting next to Beverly D'Amo, who was keeping him royally entertained with stories of her exploits in Peru.

Whitney widened her eyes. "I was just telling Howard that you're my agent now."

"How'd he take it?" snapped Zeppo, blinking rapidly several times. He was a small nut of a man, with a shock of bright orange hair, alarmingly styled in some kind of crazed pompadour. His reputation was fierce.

"I don't know," smiled Whitney. "How *did* you take it, Howard?"

"When you get bitten by a snake, you look around for someone to suck out the poison."

She continued to smile. "Yes?"

"And if I'm very lucky, you'll suck it for me, won't you, Whitney?" Not too classy, but funny all the same.

She laughed. Zeppo laughed. Beverly laughed. Ida White looked vague, but laughed anyway.

"I wouldn't put all your money on it if I was you, Howard," teased Whitney.

"Dirty talk! I love it!" exclaimed Beverly. "I thought you warned me to behave myself tonight, Zeppo."

"I wouldn't ask you to do the impossible, kiddo," Zeppo replied with a jaunty wink.

*

"Did you know that my wife died several months ago?" Zachary said, staring intently at Silver.

She sipped champagne, refusing to return his gaze. What did he want from her? Was she supposed to say she was sorry? Silver Anderson was not a hypocrite and refused to act like one.

"This means I'm free at last," he said pointedly.

She thought she might laugh in his face. Free. Sixteen years later. So what?

"How nice for you," she replied coolly.

He continued to stare at her, waiting for a more positive reaction. Didn't she understand what he was telling her? Finally they could be together, for over the years Silver was the only woman he had thought about and always wanted.

She was the perfect match for him. The Queen to sit beside him on his throne. Now that his wife was dead there was nothing to prevent their union.

"I have an interesting proposition for you," he said.

She appeared bored. "Really?"

"Perhaps you can meet me at my hotel tomorrow."

"I don't think so."

"It's to your advantage."

"I *don't* think so."

"A business meeting. That's all."

Arrogant bastard. Did he really imagine he could walk back into her life and take over? "I would hardly suspect it to be anything else," she said icily.

He lowered his voice, so only she could hear his harsh whisper, determined to get to her. "Don't flatter yourself, Silver. You're too old for me now."

His words stung like a sharp slap. How dare he talk to her like that. HOW DARE HE!

Lowering her voice to match his, she said, "You were *always* too old for *me*, Zachary."

He laughed without humour, remembering her weak spot. "Dear Silver, you never could take criticism, could you?"

Unable to control herself, she said, "Shove it, Zachary *dear*, right up your decrepit *old* ass."

*

"How're you doin'?"

Melanie-Shanna, on her way out of the ladies' room, jumped. Chuck Nielson loomed in front of her, stoned eyes and boyish grin.

Pulling herself together she asked him evenly, "Do you follow me every time I go to the bathroom?"

"Only when I know you want me to."

His come-on was out in the open. Usually it worked. Tonight it didn't.

"You're on the wrong track, *Mr* Nielson," she said. "And if you don't get off it, I'll tell my husband."

"Hey – hey – hey! Back off, beautiful. I'm only makin' polite, not grabbing your gorgeous body."

She looked him straight in the eye. "Don't. Okay?"

He threw up his hands. "You got it, babe."

She hurried past him, back to her place at the table next to Mannon. It crossed her mind that maybe she *should* tell Mannon, if only to see what he would do. Then she thought, no, why cause unnecessary trouble, she could deal with it herself. All her life she had been dealing with it . . .

*

For the first time in Silver's company, Wes was bored. Mixing with the movers and shakers from the other side of the bar was not the trip he had imagined it to be. Here he was, surrounded by the rich and famous, and once he got to talking to them, he realized they were just as boring as the rest of the population.

Carlos Brent was no great wit. Orville Gooseberger talked too much and too loud. Ditto the wife; *nobody* could shut her up. Mannon Cable was broodingly quiet, and Melanie-Shanna Cable – although a knock-out to look at – didn't open up her mouth all night.

Which left Dee Dee Dionne, who was quite charming; Zachary K. Klinger, who monopolized Silver from the moment he sat down; and their hostess, Poppy Soloman – a supercharged bundle of nerves.

Without exception, everyone had one eye on the door to see if anyone they should know about was exiting or entering. Wes caught on fast. He'd be mid-sentence and their eyes glazed over while their attention wandered. It could make a person feel very insecure. Especially as nobody seemed to give a flying fart what anyone else had to say.

Silver seemed well taken care of with Zachary Klinger whispering away in her ear, so after the entrée Wes excused himself, and took a walk around, mentally counting the stars. He hadn't met Whitney Valentine Cable, and since she was the best-looking female in the room, he thought it might make life worthwhile. He caught himself staring as he hovered near her table.

She smiled at him, brilliant white teeth flashing.

He walked over and proffered his hand. "Wes Money."

What a smile she had!

"I know. Congratulations."

"Thanks."

"Have you met Chuck Nielson?"

Yeah. He had met good old Chuck when he'd sold him cocaine at Silver's party. Only he was just a barman then, and who remembered barmen? Certainly not anyone at *this* dinner.

"Hey, man." Chuck gave him a bone-crushing handshake. "You an' Silver are gonna make each other very, very . . ." He trailed off and looked to Whitney for help.

"Happy," she said, her dazzling smile still going strong.

Ida White leaned back in her chair and placed a thin, blue-veined hand on his arm. "I hope you're going to be good to Silver," she remarked, nodding her own confirmation. "We all love her, you know. She's one of us. If you can –"

"She's a pro," interrupted Zeppo, spitting out each word like machine-gun bullets. "The important thing in Hollywood is to always act like a professional, and Silver does that better than anyone. Except perhaps Elizabeth Taylor, Shirley Maclaine . . . there's still a few of 'em left. Anyway, Silver has class."

"Yes," agreed Wes. "She sure does."

"The woman's a star," Zeppo added. "One of the last of the truly *great* stars. You see 'em running around in tee-shirts and sloppy clothes with straggly hair. All the young actresses today look like somebody's maid."

"Thank you!" interjected Whitney.

"Not you," Zeppo barked. "You look okay, kiddo."

"And how about me?" demanded Beverly.

"You're an original, but you can all learn from Silver," Zeppo continued, warming to his theme. "Star quality! She had it the first time I saw her nearly thirty years ago. And she's *still* got it."

For the next fifteen minutes he continued to sing her praises. Chuck got up from the table. "Wanna smoke?" he asked Wes. Wes nodded, and they headed for the door.

"Let's take a walk, it's hot in here," Chuck suggested.

They went down the stairs and out to the street, where Chuck lit up a joint, drew deeply, and handed it over.

Wes did not wish to look unappreciative, so he took a drag, then passed it back.

"This is grade A shit," Chuck stated proudly.

"Yeah," Wes agreed. He'd had better, but what did a permanently stoned, out-of-work movie actor know?

"Zeppo White's a fucking bore," Chuck remarked sourly.

"What does he do?" Wes asked.

Chuck turned on him in surprise. "Are you shittin' me, man?"

He shrugged. "I'm not in the business."

"Yeah, well Zeppo would have a cardiac arrest if he thought there was someone around who's never heard of him."

"I'm that someone."

Chuck began to laugh. "He's an agent. He's *the* agent, or at least he thinks he is."

"Is he *your* agent?"

"I wish. But Zeppo only wants 'em when they're ridin' high. Right now he's Whitney's agent. An' don't think the little turd hasn't tried to fuck her, because he has."

Wes couldn't conceal his surprise. "Zeppo White has fucked Whitney Valentine Cable?"

"Naw . . . just tried to. Bad enough."

"He must be at least *seventy*."

"So? You think it stops poppin' when you pass sixty-five?"

*

"I wish you'd leave me alone." Silver's voice was tightly coiled. "What are you doing here anyway?"

"I told you," Zachary replied patiently. "It's been sixteen years and I've never forgotten you. Now that I'm free, I want you back."

She snorted with laughter. "How flattering!" And then she added sarcastically, "But I thought I was too *old* for you, Zachary. And you're *certainly* too old for me."

Ignoring her sarcasm he said, "I want you, Silver. This time for keeps."

She could not believe the nerve of the man. Not to mention the conceit. "It may have escaped your notice," she said coldly, "but this is my *wedding* dinner. I just got married."

"And how much do you think it will cost me to get him out of your life? He looks like he comes cheap."

"You *bastard*! As far as you're concerned money buys everyone, doesn't it? You always thought that."

"Shall we put it to the test?" he asked mildly.

With an exasperated sigh she got up from the table. Wes was nowhere in sight, which infuriated her. She swept off to the ladies' room.

Poppy, who was not completely insensitive to atmosphere, jumped up and followed her.

*

Mannon noticed Chuck was on the missing list and took the opportunity to stop by the next table and greet his ex-wife.

"Hello, Mannon," Whitney said guardedly.

"You're looking well," he replied, equally guarded.

"So are you."

They hadn't spoken in months. It made the situation awkward, but Mannon plunged in anyway, although he was sure half the people at the table were trying to overhear, especially Zeppo, who never liked to miss a thing.

"There's something I want to talk to you about."

She played with the base of her wine glass. "What?"

"I can't go into it here."

"Why not?"

He indicated the rest of the table. "Why do you *think* not?"

"Hello, Mannon," said Ida White, catching his eye.

"Mannon, my boy," greeted Zeppo. "I hear you're considering the role Reynolds turned down." He wagged a warning finger. "You shouldn't do it. No way."

"I'm not planning to."

"Good, good."

In the distance Mannon saw Chuck. His fist itched to connect with the slimy creep's jaw.

Whitney sensed trouble and quickly said, "It was nice seeing you." She turned away in the hope that he would leave.

Chuck approached the table. He looked good until you put him next to Mannon, and then you realized he was just a poor copy.

"Hey — it's my ole buddy," he exclaimed. "How're ya doin'?"

Mannon did not consider them friends, although they had once been close. He did not even consider that he had to be civilized to the prick, so he ignored him.

Chuck took this as an insult. "What the fuck's the matter with *you*?" he demanded belligerently. "Don't come sniffin' around Whitney if y'can't even say hello t'me."

Mannon began to walk away.

Chuck went to stop him with an angry hand on his shoulder.

"Oh, no," sighed Whitney. She knew what was going to happen, and there was nothing she could do to stop it.

Mannon spun around, removed Chuck's hand and shoved him hard.

Chuck kept his balance and automatically struck out. A punch which Mannon countered with style and grace, while his right fist did just what it had been wanting to do all night, and smashed into Chuck's jaw.

★

"I've made a boo-boo, haven't I?" asked Poppy.

Silver, busy applying a liberal amount of lip gloss as she peered in the mirror, said, "I don't know what you're talking about."

"Zachary," persisted Poppy. "I shouldn't have put him next to you."

Silver thought about her reply. It was unlikely anyone knew about her affair with Zachary. Sixteen years was a long time, and they had been very discreet because of his marriage. Obviously she had misjudged Poppy. Seating Zachary beside her was probably supposed to be an honour – he *was* the most influential man in the room.

"Don't worry about it," she said dismissively.

Poppy confirmed what she was thinking. "I had no idea you two even *knew* each other."

"Oh, we're old adversaries," Silver said vaguely. And then, realizing she should tread carefully, she added, "I've always found men like Zachary Klinger to be ego-inflated bores."

"I agree," said Poppy, patting her elaborate upswept hairstyle. "I can't stand him. He's so pompous. I should have given him to Howard's table, they deserve him."

"Quite!" agreed Silver.

"Maybe he'll leave soon," Poppy said hopefully.

"If he doesn't, *I* shall."

Poppy saw her entire evening falling to pieces. "You can't do that," she said in an alarmed voice. "You're the guest of honour."

Silver licked her lips, squinted slightly, and took a step backwards to admire the overall effect of her makeup repairs. "Yes I can, Poppy," she said sweetly. "And I will."

Before Poppy could plead and beg, which she was fully prepared to do – *anything* to save her party – Melanie-Shanna came rushing into the ladies' room, tears streaking her pretty face. "I hate her!" she shrieked. "I hate that woman!"

"What woman?" Silver and Poppy chorused as one.

"That bitch – Whitney Valentine. She's *ruining* my life!"

Poppy had never perceived Melanie-Shanna as anything but a docile little mouse. The anger she was exhibiting was a revelation. Not such a quiet one after all.

"What has Whitney done?" inquired Silver, only mildly interested in gossip unless it was directly related to her.

Before Melanie-Shanna could reply, Ida White and Carmel Gooseberger barged through the door, both talking at once.

"Poppy!" Carmel boomed excitedly. "Don't you know there's a *fight* going on?"

"Blood!" exclaimed Ida in her deep, flat voice. "Everywhere!"

It was getting too crowded for Silver; she edged her way towards the door.

"A fight?" wailed Poppy. "At *my* party."

"It's that bitch's fault," yelled Melanie-Shanna. "That *fucking bitch*! I'd like to break every bone in her body!"

Chapter 54

Regrets were immediate:

Ms. Jade Johnson regrets. Making love with the English asshole one more time was a grave mistake.

She stared at him, asleep in her bed. He lay on his back with his mouth slightly open, a whispery snore escaping from between his lips.

It was seven o'clock in the morning and she was awake and alert, already reviewing the activities of the night before.

Why had she called him?

Because it seemed like a good idea at the time.

Naturally he'd been delighted to hear from her, and arrived at her apartment in what seemed like minutes, although half an hour probably elapsed.

She had turned off all the lights and decorated the place with small votive candles. Springsteen made beautiful background on the stereo. A bottle of chilled Russian vodka and two shot glasses stood on a table by the bed. She greeted him in an oversize black tee-shirt and nothing else except Opium scent.

He started to talk the moment he walked through the door.

She wasn't after conversation. Silencing him with a finger to his lips, she drew him towards the bedroom.

It didn't take long for him to get the message.

The sex was okay. It was not sensational. If she wanted to be *really* truthful it was pretty damned ordinary. What were the words of that old song? *The thrill is gone. The thrill is gone. I can feel it in your arms, see it in your eyes . . . the thrill is gone.*

Shutting the bedroom door behind her, she padded on bare feet into the kitchen, and switched the kettle on.

At least she knew. It was over. As far as she was concerned there were no doubts about *that*.

*

"I've got to take a quick trip to New York," Jack informed Heaven. "Can you arrange for a girlfriend to stay here with you?"

"When?"

"As soon as possible."

She thought about who she could invite, and rejected every possibility. Some of the girls at school were okay, but she really didn't have much in common with any of them. Eddie was her best friend, only since Silver's dumb party, where he had trailed after her mother like some moronic fan, she had gone right off him.

"I'll get someone over," she promised. "Just tell me when you're going."

"How about tomorrow?"

She nodded. "Terrific." And she thought – *I'll stay here alone, I don't mind.*

"Good, that's settled. I'll only be away for a couple of days."

She rather liked the idea of being by herself. Maybe she *would* have Eddie down and they could do some rehearsing. Lately their gigs together were pure garbage. Either he'd lost his touch or she was just bored with screaming out rock and roll.

Uncle Jack had *still* not heard any of her tapes. It pissed her off. But . . . he was an okay dude – at least he *cared* about her, which was more than she could say for her mother.

One day, when she was rich and famous and no longer treated like a dumb kid, she was going to confront Silver Dearest, and ask her plenty.

Like – *Who is my father?*

Like – *Why don't you give a damn about me?*

Like – *Why did you shove me out of your life as if I didn't matter?*

Anger and frustration welled up inside her. What kind of crap was it not to know the identity of your own father?

*

Mark emerged from the bedroom at nine-fifteen, tousled charm on full wattage.

Jade sat in the kitchen, clad in jeans and a shirt, legs on the table, watching *A.M. Los Angeles* on television. She had a cup of black coffee by her side, and a cigarette (her new favourite habit) smouldering in an ashtray. She was thinking about Corey. Their lunch had been an uncomfortable experience for both of them, and now that she'd had time to mull things over, she knew she had to call him.

"Good morning, lovely lady," Mark said, bending to kiss her, clad only in a pink bath towel knotted tightly around his waist, a look not suited to his skinny physique. He had spindly arms.

"Hi." She tried a friendly smile. It wasn't going to work – she never *had* been able to hide her feelings.

"What's the matter?" he asked, immediately sensitive to her restless mood.

Fixing him with a look, she said, "It's over, Mark. This time it's *really* over."

He preferred not to deal with her statement. "Why are you smoking?" he asked sternly. "You gave it up years ago."

"How's Fiona?" she asked. "Is *she* upset about the divorce?"

Mark considered her question. He was smart; he never liked to get himself caught in any traps. "She's had an extremely bad case of the flu," he explained seriously. "It dragged on. Almost turned into pneumonia."

"Most unfortunate."

"Yes, very. Naturally, I wasn't able to broach the subject of divorce."

"Naturally."

He gave a deep sigh. "Is that why you're cross with me?"

He was so English and refined. *Cross with me*. How quaint!

"I had no idea Fiona wasn't aware of your divorce plans," she said truthfully.

"Ah, but I'm going to tell her on my next trip home."

"Will that be soon?"

"Very."

"Not on my account, I hope."

He sat down beside her, and as he did so the towel parted, and she couldn't help noticing his aristocratic balls blowing in the wind.

"I *am* going to tell her, Jade, darling. And you and I *are* going to be married."

"There's only one small snag."

"What's that, sweetheart?"

"It's *finito*, Mark. Last night was the proof."

Tapping his fingers on the table, he was unsure of how to handle her. "You didn't have an orgasm, did you?" he asked at last.

Typical! Change the subject. He was so full of shit.

"The sex was great," she lied. "Don't you see? It makes no difference. We're history."

"Never," he insisted adamantly.

"Believe it." She was equally adamant.

"When Fiona and I are divorced you'll feel differently," he said confidently.

"*No*, Mark."

"*Yes*, Jade."

There seemed no point in continuing the argument. She didn't have to. Mark Rand was *definitely* history.

Chapter 55

Wes scooted from the house before anyone was up. He had told Silver the night before that he might go out early, and she had said, "Whatever you do, don't wake me. I need plenty of sleep to recover from *this* débâcle."

He was forced to admit that it had turned out to be *some* party – what with Mannon Cable and Chuck Nielson getting it on like they were the star players in a bar-room brawl. And Poppy Soloman having hysterics. And when the main event was over, Whitney Valentine and Melanie-Shanna Cable had indulged in a most unladylike screaming match. Wes couldn't help noticing that when Whitney Valentine got angry her tits swelled like a couple of melons, and her nipples headed straight for the entire male population's eyeballs.

So this was Hollywood high society. Not quite as boring as he had thought.

Naturally, he had gotten involved. Well, he had to, didn't he? Nobody else was doing anything about the battle of the movie stars, and Mannon Cable was beating the bejesus out of his new friend, Chuck Nielson, who was too stoned to defend himself. There was blood pouring from his nose, and he was reeling all over the place, while Mannon seemed intent on beating him to a pulp.

"For God's sake, somebody *do* something," Whitney had pleaded. That's when Wes moved into action, with the help of a waiter or two. They pulled Mannon off with difficulty as Chuck sprawled groaning on the ground.

By this time Poppy had emerged from the ladies' room to view the demise of her wonderful party, and was yelling furiously at a bemused Howard Soloman. But the real surprise was Melanie-Shanna Cable, who hadn't said a word all night.

She followed Poppy from the ladies' room, walked straight over to Whitney Valentine and shouted, "Leave my husband alone, you sex-crazed bitch! He's not yours anymore. Just remember that, or you'll be sorry!"

Whereupon Whitney had responded with a pithy "Fuck you, cunt! Don't you *dare* speak to me like that."

And they almost came to blows, only Mannon grabbed Melanie-Shanna and practically carried her off without a backward glance.

"Makes *Dynasty* look positively tame," crowed Carmel Gooseberger, loving every minute.

The party – as the saying goes – turned out to be a blast.

Silver was strangely quiet on the drive home, which surprised Wes. Usually she liked discussing every moment of the excitement.

"What's the matter?" he asked.

"I'm exhausted," she responded.

I'm exhausted was her favourite expression – she used it constantly. It hadn't taken him long to learn that she was only exhausted when it suited her.

No longer confined to the Mercedes, he took Silver's Rolls on his morning trip. He had decided to visit his former home, pack up his possessions, and officially move out. By this time it had to be safe. He was Mr Silver Anderson now. He was untouchable.

*

As soon as Wes left the house, Silver awoke. She had hardly slept all night, and felt dreadful. Reaching for the phone, unmindful of the early hour, she contacted Nora.

"Guess what?" she stated dramatically.

"He ran off with all your money," yawned Nora.

"Don't be facetious."

"How was the party?" Nora was miffed she hadn't been invited, but wise in the ways of Beverly Hills hostesses, she knew that *some* hostesses refused to accommodate the star's entourage. And as Silver's P.R., that's what she was regarded as. If Silver had *really* wanted her there she would have been included, but obviously that was not the case. Since Wes Money's entrance into her life, Nora's presence was no longer required at every event.

"I'm sure you'll read all about it," Silver said dryly.

"Does that mean you can't be bothered to tell me?"

"It means, my dear, that *my* party ended up being a fist fight

between Mannon and Chuck. And a verbal battle between Whitney and Mannon's present wife – who's *not* the mild-mannered creature she appears to be."

"No kidding?"

"The *real* shock of the evening was my dinner companion."

"Who was it, the Ayatollah?"

Silver laughed ruefully. "Just as bad. Zachary Klinger."

Nora knew when she was needed. "I'll be right over," she said.

★

Parking Silver's Rolls in a side street, Wes reflected that it might have been a mistake driving it into the seedier reaches of Venice. What if it got damaged?

No big deal. Silver would just buy another one. He had to learn to think rich. All his life he'd counted dimes, now he could relax and stop worrying. He was married to a wealthy woman! Hey – shout it out!

He walked briskly along the boardwalk towards his old house. It was a bright Californian day, early, but already hot, and a few serious skate-boarders were in action – girls in tight shorts and minuscule tank tops, and a few guys wearing even less. They were in pursuit of the perfect tan, and what better way to get it?

Wes could think of a better way. Lying out beside Silver's luxurious swimming pool with Vladimir serving him piña coladas, and a portable colour television at his elbow.

It seemed funny, approaching his old house. Actually, it gave him a shudder or two. He had no desire to resume his former lifestyle; the present one suited him just fine.

He groped for his front door key, fitted it in the lock, and was surprised to find it didn't work.

Sonofabitch! Somebody had changed the lock.

Why was he surprised? Reba Winogratsky wanted her rent. She wasn't going to allow him to walk in and cart off his stuff without paying. Good old Reba!

He knocked on Unity's door. Once he picked up the thousand bucks she was holding for him he would have to pay a good chunk of it straight over to Reba. Well, that was the breaks. It wasn't like he needed it desperately.

Nobody answered, so he knocked again.

A drag queen flung the door wide. A six-foot drag queen with crew-cut hair, and the remnants of last night's makeup smeared across his face. He wore a flowered bedspread and dusty pink toe-nail polish on inordinately large feet. "What the hell

do you —" The voice changed. He liked what he saw. "Hel-*lo*. Are you visiting or staying?"

"Looking for Unity."

"Sounds *divine*. Is it a new religious cult?"

"What?"

"Do I have to join?"

"Unity. She lives here."

The drag queen batted sturdy false eyelashes that had lasted through the night. "You remind me of my first lover," he said coyly. "*Très* butch."

Wes sighed. Fags loved him. He brought out their animal instincts — or so he'd been told on more than one occasion. Patiently he said, "I'm looking for a girl called Unity. She lives here, or used to. Where is she?"

"Oh. *Her*. I think she did a moonlight disappearing act and stuck the landlady for the rent. This place looked like a *prison* when I moved in. Brown peeling paint and —"

"Do you know where she went?"

The drag queen shrugged. "Search me." A ribald laugh.

"Please!"

"Have you got a phone I can use?"

"Ring my bell any time! Only how do I know you're not going to rob and rape me?"

Wes levelled him with a steely stare. "You'll just have to live in hope."

*

Over coffee, Silver and Nora discussed the ramifications of Zachary K. Klinger being in town.

"He makes me sick!" Silver exclaimed. "Sitting next to him was a terrible ordeal — I don't know how I did it."

"Does Wes know about you and Zachary?" Nora asked.

"Certainly not. Nobody knows. Only you."

Nora, the perennial cigarette stuck to her lower lip, nodded. "If I were you I'd leave it that way."

Silver got up and paced the room. She was clad in a pale lilac tracksuit, with her hair pulled back and no makeup. Nora was constantly amazed at how good she looked unadorned. If she wasn't so vain, and cared to tackle a non-glamorous role, she would probably surprise a lot of people.

"The good news is that Zachary knows nothing about Heaven," Silver said, as if to reassure herself.

Nora decided to step onto dangerous territory. "Why is that

such good news? Surely the child asks you who her father is?"

"She never asks. And if she does, I'll tell her it's none of her business," Silver snapped unreasonably.

Nora sniffed her disapproval. They'd had this discussion before, and Silver always firmly maintained that it was her privilege to keep the knowledge of who Heaven's father was to herself.

"I fail to see what you gain by *not* telling her Zachary Klinger is her father. The man's a billionaire with no children. You're denying her the right to inherit an enormous fortune."

"He humiliated me," Silver said stubbornly. "I will *never* give him the satisfaction of knowing that *my* humiliation resulted in *his* becoming a father."

Sometimes Nora wished she had not been made privy to Silver's big secret. She was the only person to know the truth, and it was a burden – for she understood only too well that it was completely unethical *not* to inform Heaven. With a heavy sigh she reached for the coffee pot.

Outside the room, Vladimir strained to hear every word. Ever since the threat of dismissal when Silver discovered him in her bath, he had decided to take out a little insurance. His six-figure policy was a thick notebook filled with gossip about his famous employer. He noted her moods, phone conversations, purchases, clothes, and he had a whole section on her new husband – the ex-bartender. Now he had the most interesting and explosive material of all. Zachary K. Klinger was Heaven's father! This information must be worth a small fortune! And Vladimir knew exactly how to get it.

Chapter 56

Breakfast at the Beverly Hills Hotel at eight o'clock in the morning was not exactly the ideal way for Howard Soloman to start his day. But breakfast it was, at Zachary K. Klinger's command.

Howard awoke late, threw himself in the shower, cut himself shaving, dressed too quickly, and with a fast snort of cocaine to see him on his way hurried from the house.

Fortunately, Poppy still slept. She had kept him up half the night talking, and he couldn't take a repeat performance. Personally he had enjoyed every minute of Mannon beating the shit out of that slime-bucket Chuck Nielson. Poppy had been destroyed. "It *ruined* my party," she moaned all night long.

"It *made* your goddamn party," Howard had assured her. "People'll be talkin' about it for weeks."

The parking valet at The Beverly Hills Hotel took his car, and he rushed inside aware that he was ten minutes late, and if he knew old Zach like he thought he did the old bastard was bound to be a stickler for punctuality.

Zachary sat in the Loggia, the garden part of the Polo Lounge, and acceptable to be seen in only for breakfast and Sunday lunch. The big man's salute to California was no tie. He wore a grey suit and white shirt. Howard had thrown on a white sports jacket over a loose-knit sweater and dark pants — all the better to conceal the lifts in his shoes.

"You're late," Zachary greeted him.

"Traffic," Howard replied airily.

"Isn't your house close by?"

What is this, a fucking inquisition? "How'd you sleep, Zach . . . er . . . Zachary?"

"As well as can be expected."

A waitress appeared with coffee and began to pour him a cup.

"Ah," Howard said, making a face. "Nothin' like the old caffeine to get you off to a racin' start. Right, Zachary?"

"It's bad for your heart."

"It is?"

"My doctor only allows me to drink decaffeinated products."

"Really?" Howard took a sip and burnt his tongue. Maybe the goddamn caffeine was responsible for the wild heart palpitations he had been getting on and off for the past few months. He was certainly due for a complete physical. "Do you get a check-up once a year?" he asked curiously.

"Every three months," Zachary replied.

Howard noticed the older man was drinking a glass of water with a slice of lemon, and on the plate in front of him was a plain bran muffin. "I gotta re-think my eating habits," he announced as the waitress handed him a menu. Without bothering to look he ordered scrambled eggs with smoked salmon, and hash browns on the side.

His eyes hurt. Maybe he needed glasses. Had to go see the optician too. He hoped he remembered to tell all these things to his secretary. She was a lovely girl with a milky complexion and dangerous lips. Once Poppy saw her she would be fired like all the rest. Poppy liked his secretaries to resemble Hulk Hogan on a bad day.

"How long are you staying in L.A.?" he asked, hoping the answer would be five minutes.

Zachary extracted a very long Cuban cigar from a thin leather case, and lovingly caressed it. "It depends on *you*," he said.

Howard made a gesture of compliance. "I'm all yours. Although it would have been better to take this meeting in my office, where I've got all the facts and figures."

"I already have that information."

Howard didn't want to get into *that* one. He knew that Zachary had spies everywhere. What did he care? As long as the studio was making money, everyone should be happy.

"Then you've heard about my plans for *Romance*, with Carlos Brent starring and Orville Gooseberger producing? It's gonna be a big one, Zach, uh, Zachary. It's gonna make us millions."

"I read the script."

Howard was surprised. Even *he* hadn't read the script. He liked to concentrate on story outlines, and this one was sensational, better than the original. "Great, huh?"

"Expensive."

"It takes money to make money."

"I know that."

The waitress delivered Howard's food. As she set it before him, Zachary lit his cigar, and the expensive fumes drifted lazily over Howard's plate. He needed this. Didn't the old fucker have any manners?

"Bad for you," Howard said, indicating the cigar and trying to make a joke of it. "Worse than caffeine. What does your doc say about *that*."

"I listen to my doctor when it suits me to listen to him," Zachary replied reasonably. "I pay him to tell me so much, and when I've heard enough I make my own decisions. I carry that policy through in every one of my business dealings."

Howard sensed a zinger was on its way, and he wasn't wrong. "An example." Zachary paused. "I pay you a great deal of money to run Orpheus for me. But ultimately, *I* make the final decisions. I do what *I* want, when I want."

"Sounds good to me." Howard winked, falsely jovial. "As long as we agree."

Zachary didn't crack a smile. He smoked his cigar, and watched two girls in tennis clothes settle at a nearby table. Howard enjoyed girl-watching, but Zachary stared at them with such intensity that even *he* became embarrassed.

"I want Silver Anderson for the female lead in *Romance*," Zachary said, still staring at the two girls. "I want Mannon Cable for the reporter in *The Murder*, and Whitney Valentine Cable for his sidekick. And I want Clarissa Browning to do a cameo as the victim."

Howard began to laugh. "What is this? Some kind of *joke*?"

"I haven't finished," Zachary said coldly. "You will offer them each exactly double the money they made on their last project. And if they have participation deals, you will double their points." He paused, and dragged his eyes away from the two girls, who had noticed his relentless stare, and were fidgeting uncomfortably. "No negotiations. These offers are to be made to their agents immediately – in writing."

Howard felt the muscles in the back of his neck turn to steel, and a dull flush of anger suffuse his face. "You're not serious?" he asked tightly.

"Yes. Very serious," Zachary replied, perfectly sanely. "Why? Don't you feel that having Mannon Cable, Silver Anderson, Clarissa Browning and Whitney Valentine Cable is good for Orpheus?"

"Well, sure," Howard replied, trying to figure out how to handle this maniac who knew fuck all about the movie business. Humour him, that was the way to go. "Only I don't think Clarissa Browning would ever consider doing a cameo."

"You think not? I disagree. A week's work at double the price of her last film. She won her Oscar four years ago, and hasn't been in a moneymaker since. She'll do it."

"Mannon won't," Howard argued sourly.

"Yes he will. The money will lure him. *And* the opportunity to work with Miss Browning."

Howard decided there was no point in mentioning Whitney – she would do whatever came along – but Howard wasn't sitting still for Silver Anderson. "About Silver. She's too old," he stated brutally.

"And how old is Carlos Brent?" Zachary replied, with a great deal of logic.

"I dunno — fifty-five, six."

"He's sixty-three. Silver Anderson is in her forties. They'll suit each other admirably."

"She's a daytime television star," Howard objected vehemently.

"She's a *star*. That's all that matters. And *I* want her." Zachary blew cigar smoke in Howard's face, and rose from the table. "I'll expect you back here at four o'clock, in my bungalow, with the letters of intent to go to each artist's agent. I wish to look them over before they're delivered." He stared at the two girls in tennis garb once more, then back at Howard, who sat helplessly surrounded by cigar smoke and congealing eggs. "Excellent party last night," he said casually. "Have someone at the studio send your wife flowers from me."

With that he walked off, leaving Howard a seething, infuriated wreck.

Chapter 57

Once Wes revealed that he was the tenant from next door and needed to contact their landlady so he could get into his house and pack up his belongings, the drag queen — whose name was Travis — realized exactly who he was and fawned accordingly. "You're married to Silver Anderson," he said reverently, allowing his flowered bedspread to slip off one shoulder.

"Yup," agreed Wes, reaching for the telephone and calling Reba.

"Wesley?" Her voice was a mixture of surprise and disbelief. "Stay where you are. I'll be there in twenty minutes."

Travis made him a cup of overly strong black coffee served in a mug with MAKE MY DAY OH PLEASE MR EASTWOOD! emblazoned on the side. Then he stared at him with an awestruck expression and asked breathlessly, "What's Silver Anderson *really* like?"

Wes parried questions until Reba's arrival. She was accompanied by a male, baby-faced streak of lightning, wearing blue jeans with a worn patch at the crotch, and a string vest. He looked like an eighteen-year-old hooker plucked straight from the cruising end of Santa Monica Boulevard. Travis fell instantly in lust.

"Oh, Wesley, Wesley, Wesley," Reba greeted him, with her usual hungry expression. "You moved right up, didn't you? Surprised us all, I can tell you."

"I surprised myself too," he admitted truthfully.

"You promised me a picture," she reminded him reproachfully.

"Oooh . . . *I* want a picture," interrupted Travis. "Signed if you please. To Travis. With love and admiration, Silver Anderson."

"Can I get a picture, too?" the street hustler mumbled.

"Shut up," said Reba sharply. "I'm payin' you to be my bodyguard, not to horn in on my conversations."

Wes raised a quizzical eyebrow. "Bodyguard?"

"You think you're the only one who's important?" she sniffed. "I'm havin' problems with my divorce. I need protection."

Her protection and Travis were falling in love, exchanging long looks of serious intent to commit a sexual act.

"Why did you change my locks?" Wes asked.

"You'll see," she replied mysteriously. "C'mon."

He bade Travis goodbye.

"Don't forget my picture," Travis reminded him with a pout. "And remember – any time you want to bring Silver over, she's *always* welcome" – a flirtatious tilt of the chin – "and so are you . . ."

Wes concealed a grin at the thought of Silver anywhere near this neighbourhood.

He followed Reba next door. She produced a bunch of keys and gained entry, then stood back and allowed him to walk in first. Understandable. The place was a wreck, and she wanted him to get the full impact. Someone had gone over his house with a thorough and not too gentle hand.

"What were they lookin' for, Wesley?" she asked, picking up a small lamp that seemed to have survived the search and placing it back on a table.

"How would *I* know?" he replied irritably. "I only live here."

"Lived," she corrected, producing a large notebook from her purse. "I suppose you've already moved to Beverly Hills or Bel Air, or wherever Silver Anderson resides."

"You got it."

"Nice of you to contact me before," she said reproachfully.

"I'm here, aren't I?"

She began ticking off items in her notebook. "You owe me three months' rent. Breakage on several items —"

"*I* didn't break anything," he objected.

"Whoever came in did."

"Am I supposed to be responsible for burglars?"

She pursed her lips. "Yes."

"You can whistle for it, Reba."

"Don't act like a cheapskate. You're responsible for everything that happens in this house while you're the tenant. It's the law, you know."

He kicked at a bunch of clothes strewn on the floor, then bent to pick up scattered photographs from his short career as a singer. The room stank of stale cigarettes and dirty clothes, a far cry from Silver's Bel Air palace. He wanted to get out as fast as possible, and with that thought in mind he grabbed an old duffel bag and began stuffing in anything salvageable.

Reba leaned against the wall watching him. She had left her "protection" outside. "You were never the perfect tenant," she said, with a sly smile, "but you an' I — we always understood each other, didn't we, Wesley?"

"I guess," he agreed.

"An' we had good sex, didn't we?"

He knew better than to argue with *that* one. "The best," he replied warily.

She licked her lips, coated with jammy scarlet lipstick. "Is that what Silver sees in you?" she asked. "Is it the sex?"

He shrugged non-committally, and speeded up his packing.

Reba cleared her throat and suggestively fingered the top button of her blouse. "I wouldn't say no to one last fling, Wesley," she announced. "Would you?"

"C'mon," he chided. "I'm a married man."

Ignoring that piece of information she began to unbutton. "You an' I, we were always special together."

Yeah, he thought, *about as special as a corn-beef sandwich.*

She nearly had her blouse off, revealing a pink Frederick's of Hollywood push-up bra. He held up a warning hand. "Enough, Reba."

"Don't enough *me*, Wesley. You know you're horny. And I'm better than your fancy movie star any day."

It occurred to him that he didn't have to be nice to her anymore. He did not need Reba Winogratsky. She was his past. Just as the run-down house was, and hustling petty scams to make a buck, and working bar. He was a free man!

With a feeling of triumph he reached into his pocket and took out a stack of bills — he had visited his safe-deposit box the day before and taken out enough cash to pay her just in case Unity wasn't around with his thousand bucks. Good thinking. "How much do I owe you?" he asked, businesslike and brisk.

She paused before unclipping her Frederick's special. "I'll tell you when we've finished."

Shaking his head he said, "No you won't, darlin'. Because we ain't even gonna start. I owe you money, that's all. The rest is not for sale."

*

Mannon regarded Melanie-Shanna warily as she entered the breakfast room. She looked calm enough in a flowing house-dress, her auburn hair tied sedately back.

She sat down opposite him at the table, and reached for a piece of toast.

" 'Morning," he said.

She mumbled a reply.

Mannon regarded her quizzically. He'd had no idea he'd married such a wild-woman. Last night she'd surprised the hell out of him, and everyone else in the vicinity of her whip-lash tongue. He'd had to practically drag her out of the Bistro before she went for Whitney's throat. The two of them were all set for a cat-fight.

Driving home, she'd let him have it, mouthing off about Whitney full-throttle. The force of her fury really turned him on, and once they reached the privacy of their bedroom he had silenced her with the best lovemaking of their marriage. It had been several weeks since he'd touched her, and now he wondered why. Whitney was making it with Chuck. Why shouldn't he enjoy himself with his wife? Even if he *was* planning on divorcing her.

"How do you feel?" he asked.

"Fine," she replied, eyes downcast.

The housekeeper waddled in with a plate of home-made pancakes — Mannon's favourites. He looked over at Melanie-Shanna. "Did you tell her to make these?"

"No."

It seemed quite obvious she was not in a talkative mood. Last night she had accused him of still being in love with Whitney. True. But he wasn't about to admit it. He'd denied it vehemently.

Mannon was between movies. He had just finished shooting a tough, lean Western. And his next film was not due to start for several months. For the first few weeks he always enjoyed the rest, and then he got stir-crazy if the break lasted too long.

He could work non-stop if he wanted to. His ego did not require that kind of boost. It was important to be prudent, and he chose his future projects with a great deal of care. He was right at the peak of his career, and that's exactly where he planned to stay.

This morning he felt pretty damn good. The thud of his fist connecting with Chuck Nielson's dumb-ox features had delighted him. What a victory to knock the asshole on his butt in front of a roomful of the industry. Especially in front of Whitney.

Chuck Nielson was an unprincipled prick. He deserved it. You didn't screw another man's wife and get away with it — especially when that other man was your ex-best friend.

"What are you going to do today?" he asked.

Melanie-Shanna refused to look at him. She stared out of the French doors at a vast expanse of lawn, leading to a kidney-shaped swimming pool. "I don't know," she said.

"Well." He rose. "I'm playing tennis, so I'll see you later."

She waited until he had left the room before untensing her muscles. It took a great deal of effort even to be civil to him. He had allowed her to make a fool of herself in front of everyone last night, and every time she thought of her behaviour she cringed,

Mannon Cable. Big movie star. Big lover. So what? When he made love to her last night she *knew* for sure he was thinking of Whitney. And she hated him for it. *Really* hated him.

*

The telephone began ringing in the Soloman household from eight-thirty on. First Roselight's nanny took care of the calls, and then Poppy's own personal secretary, who arrived at nine-thirty.

Poppy did not emerge from her bedroom until noon. She kissed her little daughter, who was playing with a Cabbage Patch doll, one of twelve Roselight had received the previous Christmas from Howard's business associates, and proceeded into her pastel office, where her secretary sat watching *As the World Turns* on a portable Sony television.

"Don't I give you enough to do?" Poppy asked tartly.

"So sorry, Mrs Soloman," said the woman, turning the television off with a guilty start and replacing it on Poppy's side of the huge ornate double desk.

Poppy liked to be referred to as Mrs Soloman – English style. Not for her the free and easy first-name camaraderie of American workers. She and Howard had spent their honeymoon in London at the Savoy Hotel, and she had never got over the dignity and respect of it all. She was Mrs Soloman'd all over town, and loved evey minute of it.

"Messages?" she said irritably, not in a good mood at all.

"Mrs White called at eight-thirty. Mrs Gooseberger at nine. Army Archerd at ten – he'd like you to return his call."

Poppy listened, trying to decide who to call back first. There were seven more messages, including columnist Liz Smith in New York. Who to talk to? Liz or Army? Better see what Carmel had to say. Poppy dreaded the older woman's pronouncement of "Disaster of the Year".

Carmel Gooseberger did not say "Disaster of the Year" at all. Carmel Gooseberger said, "Poppy! Darling! One of the best parties I've ever been to. I adored every minute. Did you *hear* Mannon's wife? My God, I never realized she could *speak*, let alone come out with words even Orville never uses! And did you *see* Silver and Zachary Klinger? I don't know if I was the only one to notice but –"

An hour later Poppy got off the phone. From the big mouth of Carmel Gooseberger to the hills of Beverly, Bel Air and anyplace else where you couldn't buy a house for less than a million bucks – her party was a hit! A smash! A rip-roaring success!

She phoned Howard to give him the good news, but he was in a meeting. Shame. Last night she had really steamed into him, claiming everything was his fault. Poor Howard. Sometimes she knew she was too rough on him, only a little aggravation did him good, kept him alert. And he needed to be alert with that snake Zachary Klinger in town.

She wondered if Howard might feel like buying her a cabochon ruby and gold necklace she'd had her eye on in that divine new jewellery store Tallarico.

Ten minutes later she decided he would. After all, a hit party created *great* public relations, and she deserved a prize.

Without further ado she slipped into a simple Karl Lagerfeld suit, and Christian Dior sunglasses.

On her way out of the house she noted twelve flower arrangements lined up in a row, awaiting her inspection before being placed in the perfect spot. She plucked the small white envelope from the most extravagant basket, ripped it open and read it quickly.

> You give great party. Can you join
> us for dinner Saturday?
> Silver and Wes

Poppy felt a small glow of pleasure. *Yes, thank you, Silver. Howard and I will be delighted to join you.*

Smiling with satisfaction, she hurried out to her car.

Chapter 58

Howard hit the office like a mini-tornado after the meeting with Zachary. He shut himself in his private bathroom, telling his secretary, "No calls. I don't care if it's the friggin' President!"

She knew when to leave him alone, and went back to reading a riveting article on herpes.

Howard took off his jacket and rinsed his face with cold water. His heart was racing, and so was his mind.

JUST WHO THE FUCK DID ZACHARY KLINGER THINK HE WAS DEALING WITH?

Howard Soloman.

He was Howard Soloman.

He was nobody's office boy, and he refused to be treated like one.

What was this "I want" shit, "pay 'em double" crap? Was Zachary Klinger serious?

Yeah, unfortunately the dumb bastard was. And Howard Soloman was supposed to follow through.

Well, screw that. Howard Soloman did not jump rope for anybody.

He sat on the closed toilet seat, head in hands, and tried to think clearly.

Zachary Klinger paid him a vast amount of money to run Orpheus, and in the year he had been in power he had done exceptionally well. When Zachary brought him in, the studio was in deep shit. The asshole before him had been running up astronomical overheads with no product. Howard had stepped in, and within months made it an efficient operating company. He had pared overheads to the minimum, cut off the blood-suckers and go-fers on the payroll, and bought money-making outside product for distribution. Not to mention getting three pictures into production, and at least two dozen development deals.

So he didn't have major superstars or world-renowned actors working for the studio. Big frigging deal. He had pictures that were going to make money. And wasn't that the whole idea?

Now Zachary Klinger flies in and wants to play Father Christmas. *Pay 'em double. Give 'em points.*

Howard had to turn this to his advantage or get out. There was no choice, otherwise he could end up looking like paid schmuck of the year.

★

Chuck Nielson had a black eye and a split lip. "I'll sue that sonofabitch!" he yelled when he awoke in Whitney's bed.

"Up and out," she said, matter-of-factly. "Today I've got two interviews, and a meeting with my new publicity people. I don't think you should be here."

"What new people?" he demanded disagreeably. "And why *shouldn't* I be here?"

She hated it when he questioned her. After all, they weren't married, and she saw no reason why she had to answer all his never-ending queries. The trouble with Chuck was that his once very successful career had ground to an inexplicable and sudden halt, and it was driving him crazy. It was also driving her crazy. She was definitely considering Zeppo White's advice. "Get rid of him, kiddo. He's an albatross around your neck. Dump the putz."

It had to be done. And the sooner she did it, the better she would feel. But it wasn't going to be easy. Chuck was like a big, excitable puppy one minute, and a jealous, aggressive nut the next.

287

He was jealous of her career – which was about to take off again nicely, thanks to Zeppo.

He was jealous of Mannon.

In fact, he was insanely jealous of everyone and everything around her.

Fortunately, they did not live together as such. She spent time at his home on the beach. He stayed the occasional night at her house on Loma Vista. She wasn't locked into anything. Thank God!

"You shouldn't be here," she said patiently, "because it will be boring for you."

"Yeah, you're right," he admitted. "Who's the new P.R.? And why? I thought you were happy with the one you've got."

"I am. Zeppo wants me to have a new image, so I'm going to Briskinn & Bower."

"What new image?"

"More serious."

He hooted with laughter. "Serious? *You?*" he sneered derisively.

Her mouth drooped with displeasure. Chuck had no confidence in her ability as an actress. He hadn't actually said so, but she knew it, and it irked her.

Zeppo was right. The time had come to disassociate herself from Chuck Nielson.

*

The cocaine blazed a trail. A trail of clear, clean thoughts. A lucid path through the machinations of Zachary K. Klinger.

Howard released himself from his bathroom a new man. He was moving into turnaround. Taking a crazy situation and making it work for him.

He buzzed his secretary.

She entered his office looking like a ripe kumquat, all quivering lips and an ample bosom encased in angora. "Yes, Mr. Soloman?"

How come Poppy had let this one through the net? And then he remembered that his regular girl was on vacation – this morsel was only a temporary replacement.

"Get me a list of the agents for Silver Anderson, Mannon Cable, and Clarissa Browning." No need to ask about Whitney: she was represented by Zeppo White – a legend in his own eyes.

"Yes, Mr Soloman."

"Are you an actress?" he couldn't help asking.

She nodded.

Well, act on this, he wanted to say. He had a hard-on. Must be the challenge of outwitting Zachary.

Taking a packet of toothpicks from his desk drawer, he broke one in half and vigorously attacked his gums. Add dentist to his medical requirement list. He was sure he had a loose crown and a cavity. Who had the time to go?

The secretary got him the list within minutes. He studied it carefully.

Clarissa Browning was with Artists, a large corporate outfit. Her representative was Cyrill Mace, a shrewd, no-nonsense type of man.

Mannon Cable paid his ten percent to Sadie La Salle. Ah, Sadie . . . the queen of the lady agents. She was always a pleasure to deal with.

Silver Anderson employed Quinne Lattimore. Small potatoes.

It was just past ten o'clock. He summoned his secretary again. "Get me Sadie La Salle," he commanded. "And after that I want to speak to Cyrill Mace, Zeppo White and Quinne Lattimore, in that order. I'm not accepting any incoming calls – including my wife – in fact, any of my wives."

The secretary nodded. "Yes, Mr Soloman," she said obediently.

*

"I think" – Whitney's striking face was very serious – "that the public perceives me as altogether too frivolous."

"Why do you say that?" asked Bernie Briskinn, the senior partner at Briskinn & Bower. He was old Hollywood, with a moon face, thick lips, and a black patch covering one eye. Rumour had it he had lost his eye in a skirmish with Humphrey Bogart over a woman.

Whitney gestured impatiently. "I've shown too much, too many times."

"Ever done *Playboy*?" Bernie asked anxiously. He was nearing seventy, but still interested.

Norman Gooseberger cut in. "I think Whitney means that she's travelled the scanty-outfit-decorative-role path as opposed to . . . uh . . . nude shots."

Whitney's face lit up as she smiled at the dark-haired young man who was so obviously on the ball. "Exactly," she said. "I wouldn't dream of posing nude. I never have."

Bernie Briskinn looked disappointed.

"I understand the problems you have to overcome." Norman said, taking over the interview. "And I'm sure Briskinn & Bower can satisfy you in every way."

"Yes?" breathed Whitney.

"Certainly," replied Norman, with confidence.

"Oh, that's wonderful!" she sighed.

Bernie Briskinn sucked on his false teeth. He was merely a figurehead, but never failed to attend first meetings with beautiful actresses.

"How do we begin?" Whitney asked eagerly.

Norman was quick to reply. "First of all we drop the Cable from your name. It always reminds people of your former husband, and there's no need for that now. And then we cut the hair."

"What?" Her voice filled with panic.

"The hair is going to keep you exactly where you are today. So it's goodbye Cable and goodbye hair."

"How about breast reduction surgery?" she asked sarcastically.

"Not necessary," Norman replied with a cheerful grin.

Bernie chimed in. "Thank God for that!" he said.

Norman was hitting his stride. "You have your own identity," he said enthusiastically. "And before we're through with you that identity will be as a strong and beautiful *actress*. Right now, with all due respect, you are viewed as a lightweight. When Briskinn & Bower have finished with you – well ... dare I say it? Producers will think of you at the same time they think of Jessica and Clarissa and Sally."

Whitney glowed. "Really?"

"Don't forget, Jessica Lange started out sitting in King Kong's paw, and Sally Field was Gidget. If it can be done for them ..." Norman trailed off as if he were personally responsible.

Whitney was visibly excited. Bernie Briskinn nodded approvingly. Orville's boy was a winner. He had the gift of conviction, and in the P.R. business conviction was better than gold. Bernie was glad he'd hired him at Orville's insistence five years ago. Relatives usually turned out to be duds. This one was a winner. "We'll talk price with Zeppo," he said. "Norman will handle your account himself. He's one of our best. And I'm always available. Any time you want me. Any time at all ..." He sucked on his false teeth again and buried a fart in her white couch. "Welcome to Briskinn & Bower, Whitney, dear. You won't be disappointed."

*

In the space of two hours Howard was whistling. Not quite *Dixie*, but he had done a certain amount of creative manoeuvring, and saved his ass from mooning Hollywood.

Sadie and Zeppo were easy to deal with. They understood power, money, and deals. They understood "jerk me off a little and I'll do the same for you". Offering them a deal on the one hand, and a kickback to him under the table on the other, made sense to both of them. Sadie seemed to think she could convince Mannon as long as the script of *The Murder* was halfway decent. Zeppo said of Whitney, "She'll lick your balls, Howard."

He should be so lucky.

"As part of the deal I want to be there when you tell her," he insisted.

"We'll do it together," Zeppo promised — and called him back with the news that they could do it at six o'clock, when Whitney was free.

With Cyrill Mace he played it straight. No creative moves with Cyrill. Just an out-and-out straight-up offer.

"Send over the script, and the offer in writing," Cyrill said. "Are you feeling all right, Howard?"

"Generous and well," Howard replied. "I need an answer within twenty-four hours, otherwise the offer is withdrawn."

"A week."

"No way."

"Clarissa's in New York. It'll take a day to get the script to her. Then she's got to read it."

"For this kind of money she doesn't have to read. She's ten minutes on the screen, for crissake. I'll give you forty-eight hours."

"Three days."

"You got it."

Howard phoned Jack for extra insurance, telling him the deal, and urging him to talk Clarissa into it. When Jack informed him he was on his way to New York, Howard knew the timing was perfect, and messengered a copy of the script over for him to deliver personally.

Which left Quinne Lattimore — an honest, middle-of-the-road agent, with about as much fire as a stagnant pond. Howard trod carefully with Quinne. It was the honest sons-of-bitches who tripped you up every time. City Television, he had found out, were paying Silver Anderson far less than she deserved. Quinne had negotiated a contract that, quite frankly, stank. Howard decided to double the amount she received for six weeks' work on *Palm Springs*, and try to get her on her hiatus. It was still play money, although it caused Quinne to almost choke with excitement.

By the time the offers were all written up, Howard felt confident about the structure of the deals. He had what was on paper, and he had his special arrangements with Sadie and Zeppo. They would both throw back half of their commission on the money above the established price their clients would receive. It suited everyone. Mannon and Whitney would have raised their going price by double the amount. Sadie and Zeppo could look forward to larger commissions in the future. And Howard got the stars *and* an added bonus. The kickback money was destined straight for his numbered Swiss bank account.

It wasn't stealing from Orpheus. It was creative operating – Hollywood style.

Chapter 59

The moment Jack left the beach house, Heaven sprang into action. She had already invited Eddie, who was on his way. It seemed the perfect time to call the guy from Silver's party, the one with all the contacts in the record business. She had tried him several times before with no luck. He had a stupid answering machine with some dumb voice on it. She refused to talk to answering machines.

"Yeah?"

At last! He actually picked up the phone himself.

"Rocky?" she asked tentatively.

"Who wants him?"

"Uh . . . is he there?"

"Do you have a name?"

"Heaven. But . . . uh . . . he probably won't remember my name. Tell him we met at Silver Anderson's party a few months ago. He asked me to call him. It's . . . uh . . . it's like business."

A long pause. Then, "Hey, *I* remember you. The baby fox in the long coat. Y'wanna be a singer. Right, chicken?"

"Am I speaking to Rocky?"

"The one an' only."

"Why didn't you say so?"

"Back off, baby. I don' havta say nothin' to no one. What's the deal?"

"You told me you had connections," she said stiffly.

"Are y'on a buyin' spree?"

"You said," she repeated slowly, "that you might be able to help me with my career. You know, your friend in the record business . . . you wanted him to hear my tapes."

The dime slid into the slot. Rocky remembered. She was a pretty one. And young – just the way he liked 'em.

"How come it took ya so long t'call me?" he asked.

"I've been busy. School . . . y'know."

"Yeah. I get the action."

A silence.

"Can you help?" she asked impatiently. "I've got my tapes, and Antonio has taken some brilliant pictures of me. You said you're the kind of guy can make things happen. Can you, or not?"

"Don' challenge the great Rocky, baby fox. He can do anythin'."

"Then let's get going. I'm ready."

★

"Mr Python. How nice to see you again."

Jack checked out the stewardess. Nice legs. Nice ass. Nice smile. He was feeling uncomfortably horny. Clarissa had been away too long, and apart from the night he nearly connected with Jade Johnson in Las Vegas, there had been no one. Jack Python had been boringly faithful. Talk about changing one's way of life!

He felt good about the fact that he *could* do it. It certainly proved he had willpower.

"Can I get you anything?" asked the stewardess.

He remembered flying with her several months before. She had inviting eyes.

"I'd like a Jack Daniels."

She smiled. "I'd like a Jack Python."

"Huh?"

"Just joking, Mr Python."

But she wasn't, and they both knew it.

There was a rainstorm pummelling New York when they landed. A representative from the travel agency met him at the airport, spiriting him to a black limousine waiting curbside.

He had not told Clarissa he was coming. All his life the element of surprise had worked in his favour. He wanted her unprepared reaction to his sudden visit.

*

Eddie was fully impressed. He tried not to look it, but he was. And how!

Heaven couldn't help grinning to herself. Let him eat his heart out. Eddie was no longer number one on her hit parade.

He did look good though, with his black leather jacket, tight jeans and slicked-back hair. Real fifties. He carried an overnight bag and his guitar. "I hadda leave your number with my mom," he announced reluctantly. "I told her there's a whole group of us stayin' over. She'd freak out if she thought it was just you an' me. Y'know what moms are like."

"As a matter of fact, I don't," Heaven said pointedly. "And aren't you a little *old* for your mom to be keeping such a close watch on you?"

"I guess I gotta put up with it until college," he complained.

All her friends took it for granted they were going to college. She had no intention of doing so. Why waste another three years of her life being ordered around by dumb teachers?

She was thrilled she'd finally made contact with Rocky. At least it was a start. He might be all talk, and then again he really *might* have connections in the record industry. It was worth a shot.

She had asked him over. He'd said he would try and make it. She couldn't wait!

Eddie stripped down to shorts and a tank top. He was tall and lanky, with an athlete's body. Most of the girls at school thought he was the babe of all time. Heaven couldn't care less.

They sat out on the circular deck with a portable tape machine and a couple of beers. Eddie nursed his precious guitar, and Heaven held a sheaf of papers to her bare stomach. She wore a bikini and a Bruce Springsteen bandanna. The papers were scribbled all over with the lyrics of her latest songs.

Eddie strummed a few chords, and she began to hum.

"Uh ... I've got a couple of slow songs I wanna try," she said, after a few moments.

He groaned. Eddie only liked rock and roll. He didn't understand anything else.

"Just ease me along with a little background," she pleaded. "And then I've got some other stuff you'll love."

She started to sing, a low sound at first, as she wasn't used to hearing herself without a rip-roaring background, and it seemed strange.

> Baby –
> I never told you how I felt before –
> Because . . .
> Baby –
> You always make me wait for you –
> Because . . .
> Baby –
> Don't you know I love you
> Don't you know I want you
> Don't you know I need you
> Because . . .
> Baby –

Her voice strengthened and began to soar. She sounded like a cross between Carly Simon and a less sophisticated Annie Lennox from the Eurythmics. She combined innocence and knowingness, and her voice had a wonderful husky quality.

She did not sound anything at all like Silver Anderson, although it was obvious she had inherited her mother's talent.

Even Eddie was forced to admit reluctantly that she was good. "I hate the song, but you're singin' fine," he said, bursting into a lively rendition of *Blue Suede Shoes* on his guitar.

She didn't mind that Eddie couldn't appreciate her slow songs. *She* knew they were right.

"One more time," she said forcefully. "I want to tape it, and I want it to be perfect."

★

There was a young actor in the off-Broadway production Clarissa was appearing in who played her lover. Naturally, she had felt an immediate urge to put him at his ease – even though he was living with one of her best friends. "What Carole doesn't know, will not hurt her. And we need this closeness for our performances," Clarissa explained logically.

He struggled weakly, gave in, and found it was so good for his performance that doing it every night seemed only fair to the audience. Clarissa agreed.

When Jack arrived at the theatre he was informed that Ms. Browning could not be disturbed before the show. It was a strict rule.

"I think I'm an exception," he said confidently.

When he entered her small dressing room with a pass key and the script of *The Murder*, he found Clarissa bent double over her dressing table, and a skinny bare-assed actor servicing her doggy-style.

His eyes met hers in the dressing table mirror. Her deeply intense gaze was completely devoid of any emotion.

Without a word he threw down the script and left.

Chapter 60

"Quinne's dropping by." Silver stretched and smiled as she lay out by the pool. "He says he has something important to tell me."

"Quinne's your –"

"Agent." She finished the sentence for him.

"Is he good?" Wes asked, reaching for an open can of Coca-Cola.

"I wouldn't be with him if he wasn't, would I?"

Shrugging easily he replied, "I know fuck-all about the film business, but isn't Zeppo White supposed to be the best agent around?"

"Ah . . . Zeppo." Silver popped a white grape in her mouth and savoured the taste. "When I was planning my comeback in America, Zeppo White would not even answer my phone calls."

"I bet he's sorry now."

"*Naturellement.* All the big agents are sorry. Quinne was there for me and I'll never forget it. He was the only one who knew I could do it."

"Does he renegotiate your contract every season?"

Giving him a penetrating look, she plucked another grape from the glass dish. "For someone who knows nothing about the biz, you've certainly picked up a phrase or two . . ."

"I was talking to Chuck Nielson. He was thinking of signing with Quinne."

"And did he?"

Wes shook his head. "He said going with Quinne Lattimore is like admitting defeat."

"Hmmm . . . for someone like Chuck it probably is. Once you fall from Sadie La Salle's favour . . ."

"Who's she?"

"The hottest *female* agent in town. I was with her once, long ago and far away. And before you ask, she *also* didn't answer my calls when I was desperate."

"Desperation breeds contempt."

"You're telling me! *I* lived through it." She sat up and reached for a huge straw hat. Her eyes were already covered by black wraparound sunglasses. She did not believe in allowing too much sun to reach her face. It dried the skin, causing premature lines and wrinkles.

Her body, in a strapless pink swimsuit, cut high on the thighs, was beginning to tan nicely.

"A weekend in the Springs might be nice," she murmured. "Now that I'm a free woman we must take advantage of it. Once I go back to work, the schedule is pure murder."

"You work very hard, then."

"Like a dog!" she exclaimed, obviously loving every minute of the pressure.

"Why?"

She stretched a smooth leg out in front of her. "To make the bucks, darling. To keep us in the style you are soon going to become *very*, *very* accustomed to."

Laughing, he caught hold of her slim ankle. "I'm used to it already."

She twisted towards him. "I know. Luxury *is* irresistible, isn't it?"

He allowed his fingers to tip-toe up her leg, pausing on her inner thigh, where he began slow stroking.

"I like it," she said, her voice husky.

His fingers crept between the flesh of her leg and the elastic of her swimsuit.

She sighed with pleasure.

Just as he was about to go for the gold, Vladimir appeared.

Vladimir had developed a habit of ignoring him whenever possible. The Russian houseman had decided he knew exactly who Wes Money was. A con man, a hustler, and a paid stud – in that order.

"The phone, madame," Vladimir said, handing her the instrument. "It's Miss Carvell."

She reached for the receiver. "Nora. What are you up to?"

"Fending off investigative reporters," Nora replied grumpily. "Everyone wants to know more about Wes. If we don't give 'em something, they'll *really* start digging."

"Let them," Silver said defiantly. She turned to Wes. "Do you have anything horrible to hide, darling?"

He indicated the telling bulge in his brief swimsuit. "Only this."

She laughed delicately.

Vladimir, standing in the background, glared.

Wes gave him a look. "We don't need anything," he said. "You can go."

"I'm vaiting for the telephone," Vladimir replied stiffly. "I only bother Madame vith calls she vishes to receive."

Wes glanced at Silver, who was busy chatting to Nora. "Piss off, Vlad," he said in a low voice. "When we want you I'll give you a shout. Until you hear me calling – stay in the kitchen, or wherever you hang out, and don't bother us. Have you got that?"

Vladimir blushed a deep scarlet. "I obey Madame's vishes –" he began.

"You obey *mine*, or you're out on your ass," Wes interrupted sharply.

Vladimir backed off, vanishing into the house without another word.

Wes concentrated on Silver. "Hang up," he said.

"I'm speaking to Nora –"

He started to stroke her thigh again. "I *said* hang up."

298

She giggled girlishly. "Nora, I have to go now, a minor emergency. I'll call you back."

His fingers began serious exploratory work.

She lay back in the hot sunlight and spread her legs, murmuring, "Easy access."

"C'mon." He pulled her to her feet. "Show me how to switch the jacuzzi on."

"I don't want to get my hair wet," she objected.

"I don't think I care."

"Wes! You're incorrigible!"

Is that what they call it? he thought with a grin.

She threw two levers, and the jacuzzi bubbled to life.

He took her by the hand and led her down the steps into the steaming water. She still had on her hat and sunglasses, but he didn't care. He was suddenly as randy as a dog after a bitch in heat. Making it in a jacuzzi was a fantasy he had not yet realized.

She sat on the marble seat and began to complain. "This is *not* a good idea. My hair . . . my skin . . . this water is too harsh . . . I . . ."

He silenced her with a kiss, and at the same time he took off her hat and threw it away, while his other hand pulled the top of her swimsuit down and played with a nipple.

She stopped objecting and leaned back.

With both hands he peeled her swimsuit all the way down and off, crushed her breasts together, and tongued both nipples lightly.

"Mmm . . ." she sighed.

Slipping out of his shorts, he manoeuvred her legs until they were wrapped firmly around his waist. And then, without hesitation, he plunged straight in, fighting the water every inch of the way.

"I love it," she gasped. "More, more, give me more!"

The strong jets of water were everywhere. Very slowly he withdrew, and holding her legs apart he positioned her in front of one of the jets.

"*Oh . . . my . . . God!*" she shouted. "*Ohhhh . . . goddamm*it!"

Instant orgasm. Which excited the hell out of him, and he immediately went back for more, catching her in the throes, making her come again and again, and finally letting go himself with a triumphant yell. At which point they both sank under the bubbling water.

Silver was some sport, which really surprised him. She surfaced choking and coughing, her hair plastered to her head, her wraparound sunglasses askew. "You sonofabitch!" she exclaimed, spluttering with laughter. "It just gets better all the time."

He had to agree. And he wanted to pinch himself to see if he woke up. He'd gotten luckier than he'd ever dreamed possible.

"Towel," she commanded.

Quickly he hopped out of the jacuzzi and grabbed a large striped beach towel which he held open for her to step into.

"Thank you," she said formally. "You're very kind."

"And you're some hot broad."

"So eloquent!"

"So full of it!"

Jumping back into the jacuzzi he groped for their swimsuits.

Vladimir, lurking behind a curtain in the living room, watched everything, and as he saw them approaching the house he scurried off to the kitchen and made copious notes. When he was ready to sell his story, he was going to make an absolute fortune!

Chapter 61

Vaguely it occurred to Howard Soloman that snorting cocaine was becoming more than just a habit. He did not feel comfortable unless he knew the soothing white powder was within easy reach.

I can afford it, he thought. *It's certainly no worse than alcohol and much less anti-social.*

The only problem was he couldn't get through the day without it. No problem really – because he didn't have to.

Over the months he had developed several new sources of supply, so he did not need to depend on anyone in particular

It was an expensive habit, but God – it was worth every hard-earned dollar.

The day passed smoothly, thanks to his quick thinking and clever way of dealing with Zachary's cockamamie orders. By four-thirty he had all the offers in writing, and a runner standing by to deliver them to the forewarned agents.

He drove over to Zachary's bungalow at The Beverly Hills Hotel, and sat there cockily while the old man scanned them one by one.

I'm the highest-paid messenger boy in history, he reflected, with a private smile.

Zachary paused when he came to the offer for Silver. "Why so little?" he asked.

"It's double the amount she received for six weeks on her soap. That's more than fair, isn't it?"

"It's pennies compared to the others."

"We're talking big bucks with the others. Quinne'll kiss our ass from here to Australia. And so will Silver, if she's smart. They're not exactly rushing her to do movies, y'know. Sure, she's big on television, but that means cow dung. Look at Tom Selleck. The guy was hotter than she is today. Three movies later and nothin' happened. When they can get it for free, they don't want to pay for it."

"We'll see," said Zachary.

"I hope you're right," Howard remarked cheerfully. His throat was parched. Sitting here for twenty minutes and no offer of refreshments. The old guy was either tight or rude. Probably a combination of both. "Do you mind if I order a drink?"

Placing the written offers in a neat pile, Zachary stood up. "I'm going out," he said brusquely. "Feel free to use the Polo Lounge if you want a drink."

"Good idea. I'll do that." *Take your job and shove it all the way up your constipated asshole, prickface.*

"Before you go, Howard. Two requests."

"Yes?" *Cheap motherfucker.*

"Since I've decided to stay over, I'm free for dinner tonight. May I join you?"

"Absolutely. Wouldn't have it any other way." *Oh, Christ. Poppy will be really thrilled.*

"And please arrange companionship."

Howard looked blank. "Companionship?"

"Two high-class ladies. Discreet, and under thirty." A

meaningful break, then, "And they should both have clean bills of health, dated today."

His own stuttering took Howard by surprise, along with the request. "Er . . . c-c-certainly. I'll g-get right on it."

Fuck! Paid messenger was one thing. But pimp, too? Maybe it *was* time to start looking around.

* * *

"This is the big leagues, kid," Zeppo White said, edging closer to his beautiful client. "I told you I could do it for you."

"What? *What?*" Whitney begged.

"Not a word until Howard gets here. I promised."

"Ha! An agent's promise is like a Bloody Mary without the vodka. It doesn't mean a thing. *And* you know it."

Zeppo displayed a row of flawless false teeth. When he removed them he could give a woman more pleasure than she'd had in her entire life. "Patience, kiddo. Howard can be a mean one."

"Nobody's mean to *you*, Zeppo," she coaxed. "You're too important."

"Flattery'll do it every time," he said, and just as he was about to tell her, Howard arrived.

Whitney tried to compose herself. It had been an exciting day, what with her meeting with the new publicity firm, and now Zeppo White *and* Howard Soloman arriving at her house with something good to tell her.

She knew what it was. They were finally going to confirm that she had the role in *Romance*. Although the script had been sent to her, it was no sure thing. Word was out that Orville Gooseberger wanted an actress who could sing. Well, she could learn, couldn't she?

Howard appeared even more manic than usual. He had stopped in the Polo Lounge and consumed a large piece of chocolate cake (lunch) and two glasses of warm milk (he feared an ulcer.) He had also spoken to the head of publicity at Orpheus. "Get me two hookers for a V.I.P. The expensive stuff. I need 'em tonight, an' they both have to bring doctor's certificates dated today." A pause. "Yeah, yeah. I know it's oddball. Tell 'em to add the doctor's charges to the bill."

That was easy. Now came the difficult part. A phone call to his wife. "Poppy, honey?"

"Our party was a smash, Howard! Rave reviews! What time will you be home?"

302

"One more meeting and I'm on my way."

"Roselight wanna kiss big daddy daddy nighty-night," Poppy baby-talked.

Whew! She must be in a sensational mood. "What are we doing tonight?" he asked.

"Dinner at Mortons with the Whites. I'm going to bask!"

"Add three more."

Her tone changed. "Who?"

"Zachary Klinger and his date, and her . . . friend."

Ominous silence.

"C'mon, Poppy sweetie, it's business." He hated it when she forced him into what she referred to as "poppins talk".

More silence.

Shit!

"You can stop by Cartier tomorrow," he suggested.

A guilty giggle. "I was in Tallarico today."

Trust his wife. She knew exactly when to strike.

Whitney looked quite edible, as usual. She had a healthy glow about her, an outdoor radiance coupled with an indoor sexuality.

"Drink?" she inquired breathlessly.

"Water," Howard replied.

She ran to the kitchen and got it for him. Whitney did not surround herself with servants. It made a refreshing change. Most of the women he knew were all terrified of breaking a nail.

Zeppo beamed. "Well, kiddo," he announced. "I'm gonna let Howard tell you – it's *his* studio."

"I've got *Romance*, haven't I?" she pleaded.

"Better," said Zeppo. "You've –"

Howard cut him off at the pass. "Orpheus wants you for the starring role in a sensational new film, *The Murder*. I may as well tell you up front – we're after Mannon as your co-star, and Clarissa Browning for a cameo as the victim."

"Clarissa Browning!" Whitney whispered reverently.

"Hey – we're not talking *Friday the Thirteenth part fifteen*. This is class," said Howard proudly.

She glanced over at Zeppo as if she did not quite believe him. "Is this true?"

"You're damn right it is. And I got you double money, kiddo."

Howard watched her nipples carefully. They were hardening

303

before his very eyes. He urgently required the chance to see them unadorned, and decided then and there to add a nude scene to the script.

"Will Mannon *do* a film with me?" she asked both of them.

"The offer is out. I think he'll say yes," Howard replied.

"You bet your bananas," agreed Zeppo.

Whitney smiled, and thought of her humble beginnings.

She was about to achieve more than she'd ever dreamed possible.

Chapter 62

Mortons, a fashionable West Hollywood restaurant located on the corner of Melrose and Robertson, was crowded with Hollywood's movers and shakers. Beverly D'Amo steamed in like she owned the place, exchanging kisses with the maître d', while waving greetings to everyone in sight.

"You sure made yourself at home in *this* city," Jade remarked.

"Girl, I make myself at home just about every place I go. It's the only way to operate. Especially here."

They were given a table at the front, which, according to Beverly, was the only place to sit. "The back of this restaurant is Siberia," she warned. "Land of the under-achievers. Don't even *glance* in that direction."

Jade laughed. She had never understood people's fixation with getting good tables in restaurants.

"You're lookin' hot, babe," Beverly announced. "I wanna hear all about the dead Englishman, an' the Cloud deal. Rumour has it that you've moved into megabucks country. True or false?"

"True, I guess," Jade admitted modestly.

"Fanfuckintastic!"

"How about you?"

Beverly grinned. "I'm gonna be a movie star. Doncha love it?"

"I think it's great, if that's what turns you on."

"Sure does. I've already made two films – nothing *memorable*. But this week I changed agents an' signed with Zeppo White. He's gonna do it for me. He's a wild character and horny as a sailor, an' I love him! He's a real goer. You've got to meet him, you'll love him too!"

"I doubt it."

"Huh?"

"Hollywood men do not turn me on. They *are* what they *drive*, and they all look like Porsches to me!"

Beverly hooted with mirth. "I don't mean you'll want to *fuck* him. He's like a cute little dog. You'll enjoy watching him get feisty. And apparently he gives great dinner – parties that is."

Beverly paused to swap kisses with a good-looking man in a white sweater and matching pants. From his smooth suntan to his white shoes he was perfection. The woman with him was older and crusty. She dug him in the small of the back to hurry him along. She was not interested in being introduced to a couple of devastatingly beautiful models.

"Penn Sullivan. He's in my acting class," Beverly said knowledgeably as the couple moved off. "And the old broad with him is Frances Cavendish, a casting agent. I bet she'll be casting around in *his* pants tonight!"

"Do you know *everyone* in town?"

"Only the ones who matter."

Jade felt good being with Beverly. A little of the New York excitement rubbed off; she enjoyed swapping stories and hearing all about their old friends. Beverly seemed to know what everyone was doing, and with whom. It certainly took her mind off Mark. He had been difficult to get rid of. And Corey – she knew she had to call him and let him know that however he wished to live his life was his business and perfectly all right with her. After twenty-four hours of worrying, she had finally realized that whatever he did was okay. It was *his* life.

"Now here comes a man I'd like to meet," said Beverly, her voice filled with admiration. "Mister Big. Zachary K. Klinger. He owns Orpheus Studios, you know."

They both watched the large man settle at the front round table with a skinny redhead and a cool blonde.

"I can't believe there's actually someone you haven't met!" Jade said teasingly.

"I'll meet him before the end of the evening," Beverly replied confidently. "I nearly did last night at the wedding party for Silver Anderson. He was at the next table, and just as I was going over, Mannon Cable and Chuck Nielson started to have this amazing fight!"

"You're kidding?"

"Haven't you heard?"

"Beverly, I am not – repeat, *not* – remotely interested in the movie business. Why would I hear?"

"Because, my dear, you have to know what's goin' on."

"Why?"

"Good question."

Beverly continued to chat, but her focus of attention had shifted. Her eyes were now on Zachary Klinger. She wanted him to notice her, and it wasn't long before he did. In fact, he noticed both of them. They were hardly low-key. Beverly was clad in a red body-suit with a purple Claude Montana leather jacket and boots, her jet hair scraped back into one long plait. Jade's shaggy copper hair framed her direct, challenging face. She wore a black jeans jacket over a short knit dress, and lots of silver jewellery.

Most men in the restaurant were trying to cool it, pretending not to notice them. However, there were a record number of trips to the men's room just to check them out.

Zachary stared.

Beverly, who was facing him, stared back.

"A little eye contact?" Jade teased.

"I bet I can get him hard at fifty paces!"

"Trouble is, you'll never know."

"Don't lay money on it."

"Beverly, he's *old*."

"So's Reagan. And I'd jump into bed with him too, if he asked me. I'm into power, girl. It really creams me up."

"You're impossible!"

"I'm truthful." She leaned forward. "The two bimbos with him look like hookers, and – hold everything – here come the rest of his party."

Poppy and Howard Soloman walked in, followed by Ida and Zeppo White.

Beverly was on her feet in a flash. "Zeppo!" she shouted. "It's me. Your new star, babee!"

Zeppo paused, undecided as to whether he should kiss

Zachary's ass, or greet Beverly D'Amo. He chose Zachary. One of the first lessons you learned in Hollywood was whose ass to kiss first.

"Just a minute, kiddo," he said with a distracted wave, hurrying to pay homage to Zachary.

"Who are those two women?" Zachary demanded, ignoring Howard and Poppy, who were both busy apologizing for being late.

"That's Beverly D'Amo," Zeppo said. "Lovely girl. Good actress. She's expensive, but if Orpheus has something for her I'm prepared to talk a deal."

"And the other one?"

"I don't know. Do you want me to find out?"

"Later. Sit down. I'm ready to order."

Across the room Beverly sank back into her chair and watched the action from afar. "Shit!" she exclaimed.

"What's the matter?" Jade asked.

"The little mouse is not coming over. He'll pay for that."

Sipping her wine Jade said, "Don't you think you're taking this all a bit too seriously?"

"Hell, no! Hollywood is a combat zone. And baby – *I* fight to win!"

Poppy's bright eyes darted around the restaurant. She wore her new cabochon ruby and gold necklace like a badge of honour. Howard loved it. He hadn't seen the price-tag yet.

"Thank you for the gorgeous flowers, Zachary," she gushed. "So *thoughtful* of you. I'm *mad* for orchids. How did you know?"

He gazed at her blankly.

Go on, light up a cigar, you ill-mannered pig, she thought. The least he could do was tell her how wonderful her party was.

She glanced around the room again with a feeling of pride. Mrs Howard Soloman. Hostess supreme. Nobody knew what a struggle it had been to get where she was today.

Nobody knew how hard it had been . . .

Chapter 63

At night the pounding of the waves thundered on the beach. Heaven decided she never wanted to be without that sound again.

"How long is your uncle gonna be away?" Eddie asked, comfortably stretched out on the deck listening to an old Elvis album, a can of beer nearby.

She shrugged. "I dunno. He's gonna phone tomorrow. A few days, I guess."

"We should throw a party," he suggested.

She had to admit the thought *had* occurred to her. "Who'll pay?" she asked.

"We'll make it a bottle party. Everyone brings their own."

Hesitantly she said, "Gee, I don't know . . ."

"We could have it out here on the deck an' on the beach. Nobody would havta go in the house." Digging in the pocket of his shorts he produced a sorry-looking joint. "Whaddya say?"

"When?"

"It's too late to get it together tonight. How about tomorrow?"

She was angry that Rocky hadn't shown. Dumb geek. He was probably a loser anyway. "Yeah, let's do it!" she agreed, knowing full well that Uncle Jack would be pissed off if he ever found out.

"Right on! Let's go for it!" exclaimed Eddie. "We'll get the group down, an' some of the other dudes. We can tell the Fish to pick up pizzas. It'll be a full blast!"

"Like no more than fifty," Heaven warned. "And *not* in the house."

"No way," Eddie said adamantly.

*

Jack Python was drunk. Uproariously, rip-roaringly drunk. And he did not care. In fact, he felt great as he sat at a back table in Elaine's and held court. At least he wasn't sloppy drunk, he was talkative and very funny.

Elaine herself watched from afar, as she kept an eye on all her famous clientele to make sure none of them was bothered. Ocasionally she came and sat, tossing back a drink or two and missing nothing.

Jack shared a table with a couple of writers, ace publicist Bobby Zarem, a publisher, and a wicked-tongued socialite. Elaine's mixed group. She enjoyed shaking up her famous singles at a large round table.

Getting drunk, Jack decided, was not the act of a desperately unhappy man. It was an act of celebration. He was out of a relationship he had been reluctantly hanging on to because it was good for his image.

Well, screw his image. And screw Clarissa Browning. Jack Python was back on the field.

He couldn't help laughing.

"What's so funny?" asked the socialite. She had red hair worn in a bun, sharp cheekbones, and dazzling diamonds.

"Just thinking," he explained, reflecting on the irony of it all. *He* was the one with the supposed stud reputation. Clarissa had told him how all her friends warned her he would never be faithful. And *she* was the one screwing around. Unbelievable!

"Thinking about what?" she persisted, determined to attract his interest.

He looked her over, slowly, lazily. She was old money, an heiress to a billion-dollar fortune.

He lowered his voice so only she could hear his reply. "I'm thinking about how I'd like to fuck you."

Billion-dollar heiresses did not have to play games. "What are we waiting for?"

And so, later on, he ended up in the socialite's bed in a Park Avenue penthouse, with the scream of police sirens outside, and the clink of diamonds inside. "I never take them off," she announced with a restless smile.

She was an insatiable woman, but that was Jack's speciality. Once he got on for the ride he never quit until the lady asked him to.

Later, when he awoke, he had a relentless hangover, and a

strong desire to be elsewhere. The woman slept beside him. Red hair, naked white skin, and gleaming diamonds at her ears, wrists, and throat.

Not wanting to wake her, he dressed hurriedly, and let himself out of her sumptuous apartment.

Early morning light filtered through the tall buildings as he walked briskly to the Helmsley Palace Hotel, where he had a suite.

The desk clerk in the private tower section greeted him warmly, as did the pretty elevator operator.

He rode up to the forty-eighth floor thinking of the lucky escape he'd had. If he hadn't flown to New York and caught Clarissa cheating on him, he might never have known. And he had actually given serious consideration to marriage!

Christ! One mistake in his life was more than enough.

"I love your show, Mr Python," smiled the elevator operator.

"Thank you." He smiled back, his hangover receding.

In the privacy of his suite he clicked on the televison, stripped off his clothes, and allowed a cold shower to wash away the faint aroma of Private Collection.

Jack Python was back where he belonged. Single and up for grabs.

*

Found out and unrepentant, Clarissa studied the script of *The Murder*, along with an incredible financial offer, which was really quite ridiculous and very tempting.

She read the script twice. Carefully.

And then she called Cyrill, collect. Clarissa had never been known for her loose purse strings.

"Well?" asked her agent anxiously. "I know it's garbage. However, for five days' work, at that price . . . Clarissa, I have to leave it entirely up to you."

"It's not garbage," she replied crisply. "Not at all. It's a very interesting and provocative thriller, with a fine relationship between the two main characters, and a strong line of humour."

He sounded relieved and surprised at the same time. "Does this mean you want to do it?"

"I most certainly do. Only listen to me carefully, Cyrill. I will not play the victim. I desire the leading role. It's *exactly* the kind of part I've been searching for."

Chapter 64

"Hello," Wes said. "Make yourself comfortable – Silver'll be down in a minute."

"Thank you," said Quinne Lattimore, a stocky man in his fifties, with a florid complexion. He regarded Wes warily. Like all Silver's friends and acquaintances he viewed the new husband with deep suspicion. Who was he? Where had he come from? And what was he after?

"Silver tells me you've got good news," Wes said amiably.

"Excellent," replied Quinne, full of confidence. "I have something to tell Silver that will make her a very happy woman indeed."

Wes drifted over to the bar. Vladimir had already served an English tea, but he felt like something a touch stronger, so he poured himself a hefty scotch, added a couple of ice cubes, and turned to check out the agent.

The man did not look big-time. The man looked comfortable but not affluent. He didn't give off any energy, and he certainly didn't have killer eyes.

Wes remembered his own short career as a singer. The group he was with had an agent who made big promises and never came through. More-successful groups had agents with energy. The big boys had agents with killer eyes. Wes always remembered the look. Zeppo White had it written all over him.

Chuck Nielson had warned him, "Lattimore's nowhere city. Silver can be with whoever she wants. You should get her to change."

Silver made her entrance a few minutes later – hair swept up, makeup perfect, simple lounging pyjamas in gold lurex. She enjoyed creating impressions. Even in her own house, with only her agent for an audience.

"Quinne, darling!" She kissed him on each cheek, European style.

"You look gorgeous as usual," he said. Quinne had always had a little bit of a hidden crush on her.

"I feel outrageously *wonderful*." She reached out her hand for Wes. "It's marriage, you know, it agrees with me. I adore it!"

Quinne chortled uncomfortably.

"Pour me a glass of champagne, darling," she said to Wes, and then lowering her eyes coquettishly she added, "I think I deserve it, don't you?"

He moved into the role of barman easily. It didn't bother him.

Quinne took Silver's arm and led her over to the couch. "Sensational news," he announced, puffed with pride. "Orpheus wants you to co-star with Carlos Brent in *Romance*. It's a definite offer, and wait until you hear what they're going to pay us!"

Silver, who had quite resigned herself to being a television star, and did not consider movies — because they did not consider her — shrieked with delight. "I can't believe it! When did this happen?"

Wes poured the champagne and kept a steady ear on the conversation.

"Today," Quinne said happily. "Out of the blue. Shooting starts in ten days, and the schedule fits right into your *Palm Springs* break."

"I'm *thrilled*!" she exclaimed. "When can I see a script?"

Ambling over, Wes handed her a glass of cold champagne. She looked up at him, glowing with delight. "Did you hear, darling? They want me for a movie!"

"Why shouldn't they? You're a star, aren't you?"

"A *television* star," Quinne said pointedly.

"The biggest female television star in America," Wes replied, equally pointed. "I'm surprised this hasn't happened before. What movies have you suggested her for? It'd be interesting to know exactly who's turned her down and why."

Quinne began to stutter about movies never being their goal, and timing, and how great this deal was.

Silver went to say something, and Wes silenced her with a look. He knew he had the agent on the defensive.

"Were you out hustling this deal, or did it just turn up on your desk?" he asked.

Quinne was a truthful man. It was probably his downfall as

far as his relationship with Silver Anderson was concerned. "I didn't exactly chase after them. I must admit they came to me."

Wes just looked at Silver as if to say – *This is an agent? Agents are supposed to be out there selling. Getting more money for their clients. Hustling. Hustling. Hustling.*

Quinne Lattimore was useless – and by the time he left the house twenty minutes later, they both knew it.

After he'd gone, there was a meaningful silence. Silver walked over the large terrace windows, opened them, and walked outside.

Wes followed her.

"Quinne's been very good to me," she said.

"Do you pay him commission?"

"What kind of question is that? You know I do."

"Then he's been well compensated, hasn't he?"

"What are you suggesting?"

"That we move on up." He put his arm around her. "You're a huge star, baby. You belong with Zeppo White. He can do things for you that Quinne Lattimore can't."

It was the first time since the death of her mother that somebody was telling her what to do, making decisions, and really caring. "Do you think so?" she asked tremulously.

"I *know* so. And I don't want you to worry. I'll take over. Tomorrow I'll go see Zeppo. We'll hand the movie deal over to him, and make a generous settlement with Quinne. You can bet your ass Zeppo'll get you better terms. And then I want Zeppo to check out your contracts with City Television. I don't know what they're payin' you, but whatever it is, I bet it ain't enough."

"Will you really take over everything?" she asked hopefully.

"Why not? I've got nothing else to do."

"The accountants and the lawyers and all the boring stuff I hate, hate, hate?"

He rather liked the idea of being in charge. "Everything, Silver. You just act. I'll look after every single thing." He paused and hugged her tightly. "After all, if you can't trust me, who *can* you trust?"

Chapter 65

The ambience at Le Dôme, on Sunset, appealed to Mannon. The restaurant attracted a mixed clientele of music people, producers, agents, and entertainers. The tables were not on top of each other, and in the back the restaurant divided into several sections so you could always hide if you so desired.

Mannon strode through the bar to Sadie La Salle's table. Sadie was a powerhouse agent. Short, dark, with one hand poised forever near the jugular. A scandal had rocked her life a couple of years before when two murders took place at her mansion. Sadie had survived the storm, and gone on to bigger and better deals.

She regarded Mannon with a critical eye. "You're still the best-looking sonofabitch in this town," she announced, downing a shot of straight vodka. "How would you like to walk away with eight million buckeroonies for one lousy movie?"

He smiled. "If anyone can get me that kind of money, Sadie, it'll be you."

She picked up a script sitting on the chair next to her. "Here's the words. That's the price. It's for Orpheus and they're anxious."

Taking the script from her he said, "Are we talking on the level here?"

"Do I tango with midgets?"

"Sounds good to me."

"Read it. They're going for Clarissa Browning —"

"If Clarissa does it, I'm in," he interrupted quickly.

"Wait, there's more."

"What?"

"They want Clarissa for a cameo, and Whitney for the lead."

He couldn't conceal his surprise. "*My* Whitney?"

"I thought she wasn't anymore."

314

He leafed through the pages, giving himself time to think. He was being asked to star in a movie with Whitney, for double the money he had received on his last project. So why was he even hesitating?

Because . . . he had always been opposed to Whitney's acting career.

Because . . . Whitney couldn't act.

Because . . . why should he pay half of eight million dollars to Melanie-Shanna when he was planning to divorce her?

"Listen," Sadie said. "You know I never try to influence you in any way, but I've read the script, and it's not bad at all." She paused, and signalled the waiter to get her another vodka. "Plus, this is going to raise your price to new heights. I'm not saying we'll always get this kind of money, but we're in a whole new ball park. And I think I like it."

"The money is acceptable."

She raised an eyebrow. "*Sooooo* glad!"

"I've got to think about it though."

"You have to *think* about eight million bucks? What's the problem?"

"Personal."

She skewered him with a look. "Personal like you married some Texas bimbette on the rebound an' now you want out? Or personal like being close to Whitney is gonna get your hormones workin' overtime?"

He laughed. She knew him so well.

Sadie placed a soothing hand on his arm. "Here's my advice. Take the money an' run. It's 'fuck you' money. I'm tellin' you, the script's okay. It's not *Officer and a Gentleman* but it plays. Whitney will be able to manage it." She shrugged. "And if you don't want to do it, that's okay too. I'm your agent, I can only advise you."

Mannon nodded. Eight million bucks and he was hesitating! Jesus! Had he come a long way!

*

The beach party started at nine o'clock, with a straggle of Eddie and Heaven's friends who toured the house saying "Holy shit!" and "This place is *it*, man."

They were impressed, but only for a short while, then out came the crates of beer and the boxes of pizza, and the grass and the Quaaludes.

Heaven enjoyed being the focus of attention. It was *her* party, and she strutted around taking full advantage, all thoughts of keeping them out of the house forgotten. As the evening progressed, more and more people started to arrive. The word was out. There was an open party going on, and everyone wanted to be part of the action.

Eddie got the group together, and they played a set of Elvis Presley's oldies – with Heaven doing the vocals. When she first got into singing she really loved the loud stuff – as far as she was concerned the louder the better. Anything to be totally different from her mother. Silver's voice was powerful and strong. In her time she had been compared to Streisand and Garland. Today, after years of misuse, her voice was thicker, more smoky. But Silver had always remained a traditional singer, excelling at show-tunes and material written by the masters – Sammy Cahn, Cole Porter, and the other great popular song writers of the forties and fifties.

Heaven was certainly different. She skidded out of a ballsy rendition of *Jailhouse Rock* and took a rest.

The party was growing. Young people seemed to have a bush language all their own – news of the party had them arriving from as far away as Pasadena and Hancock Park.

Heaven thought that maybe they should put a brake on it, and cornered Eddie to tell him.

He was stoned, and had a line going with a Pali High senior who looked like a female version of David Lee Roth.

She knew why he was coming on to the girl. He was trying to make her jealous, only she couldn't care less. One thing she had learned from her mother: never expect anything from anyone – that way you can never be let down. Silver taught her that when she was six or seven, and the lesson stuck.

"We gotta push this blast out onto the beach," she warned Eddie.

He regarded her lazily, with blank eyes and slack lips. The excitement of playing for an appreciative and rowdy audience had worn off; now he just wanted to guzzle beer and get laid. "Everyone's havin' a good time," he said, pulling Miss David Lee Roth closer.

A loud crash signalled the demise of a crystal lamp.

"Shit!" Heaven snapped. "Move 'em outside, Eddie, or I'm callin' the party off."

"Whaddya think *I* am, Superman? They ain't goinna take any notice of me."

She wanted to pull his long, dirty black hair and kick him in the crotch. He was the one who had talked her into having this party, and now he was backing off from the responsibility. Goddamn geek! She'd had it with him.

The place was being wrecked before her very eyes. Several guys were playing a makeshift game of baseball with empty beer cans, couples were lolling all over the couches with greasy pizza and burning cigarettes, someone had broken the lock on the cupboard in the bar and was passing out bottles of scotch and vodka, drugs were being used openly all over the place, and a buxom blonde girl was taking it all off to shrieks of delight from the assorted gathering.

Heaven remembered London, six years earlier. She was ten and she'd been around. Silver and she were staying with a woman called Benjii. Only Benjii wasn't a woman, she was really a man. Actually, at the time, Heaven couldn't decide *what* Benjii was – she only knew that Benjii took them in when they ran from a London hotel in the middle of the night because mama – as Heaven called Silver then – couldn't pay the bill.

For two months they put up with Benjii and his parties and his strange friends. Until one night mama just freaked. She ran out on to the little balcony which overlooked the King's Road in Chelsea, ripped off all her clothes, and screamed and screamed. "I'm jumping! Don't try to stop me. I'm jumping!" And stark-naked, she attempted to climb from the shaky balustrade, while a petrified Benjii held her desperately around the waist and shouted hysterically for Heaven to phone the police.

Which she did. Calmly. Until they took her mother away.

After that she curled herself into a tight ball and sat in the corner sucking her thumb, listening to Benjii on the phone telling everyone what had happened.

Heaven felt numb them. She felt numb now.

A feeling of *déjà vu* overcame her. She was in a situation she couldn't control, and all she wanted to do was find a corner and hide.

*

Jack took the last flight out of New York to Los Angeles. He thought about hanging around, taking in some meetings, doing a little business. But Heaven was alone in the beach house, so he figured he'd give her a nice surprise. Besides, he had made love to one of the richest women in New York, and where did he go from there?

Sitting on the plane leafing through a magazine, he came across an advertisement for Cloud Cosmetics. Jade Johnson stared out at him. She was stunning, and not in a Whitney Valentine or movie-starish way. She was pictured leaning against an old brick wall, clad in faded, skin-tight jeans and a washed-out denim shirt casually unbuttoned to the waist. Her breasts were hidden, but if you looked closely you could make out slightly erect nipples through the material, and the faint shadow of cleavage. Clasping her waist was a silver-buckled belt, worn low. And cowboy boots covered her feet.

She looked straight at the camera with a direct and challenging stare. Wide-apart eyes, straight nose, sensual mouth, and aggressive square-cut chin. Her copper hair, shaggy and shoulder length, tumbled around her face.

The copy was simple:

Smart women
wear Cloud

Jesus! How had he ever let her slip by? Their dinner together in Vegas remained a memorable occasion.

Jade Johnson.

He was free now.

He only hoped that she was too.

Chapter 66

"Mr White wondered if you ladies would care to join his table," the waiter said.

"No, thank you," replied Jade swiftly, as Beverly snapped a quick "Yes, please!"

The waiter, an unemployed actor, winked at Jade as if she were some out-of-town hick. "Zeppo White. The *agent*," he said knowingly.

"*My* agent," Beverly interrupted possessively.

The waiter was deeply impressed, and wouldn't have minded a lengthy conversation about how one got the infamous Zeppo White to represent you.

Beverly ignored him. "C'mon," she pleaded. "This is business."

"I don't want to sit with a group of people I don't know," Jade objected.

"I'll introduce you."

"Big fucking deal."

They glared at each other. Back, when they shared an apartment over ten years ago, they had always fought. Both spoke their minds and never dodged a confrontation.

"I'm asking nicely," Beverly said. "Like I'm saying *please* and *will you* and this means *a lot* to me."

"Why don't *you* join them, and I'll go home? I've got an early call in the morning. I really don't mind."

"Hell, no."

"Why not?"

"Because if you can't help me out on this, then you're not the friend I thought you were."

"Shit, Beverly. Don't give me that line."

"*Plllleeease?*"

With a sigh of resignation Jade said, "Okay, I'll do it. But it's against my principles to watch you play kissy ass with the rich and powerful."

Beverly grinned triumphantly. "Observe a true professional in action." She rose from the table shrugging off her Montana jacket, causing a man nearby to almost choke on his drink. She was ebony-coiled perfection – beside her even Grace Jones seemed understated.

She undulated over to Zeppo's table, where waiters struggled to fit in two more chairs.

"Beverly, kiddo." Zeppo leaped to his feet, his bright orange hair standing on end.

"Zeppo, babe! Say hello to my best best friend Jade Johnson."

He clasped her hand. "Jade, it's a pleasure. You ever thought of doing movies?"

She smiled politely. "Never."

"Lauren did it ... Marisa ... Kim Basinger. You'd be a natural."

"Thank you, Mr White, but I'm not interested."

"Call me Zeppo. All my friends do. And my enemies!" He honked with amusement.

Meanwhile, Beverly lost no time in zeroing in on Zachary. "Mr Klinger," she purred. "I'm a fan. That article about you in *Forbes* last month was a dazzler. By the way" – she extended a friendly hand – "my name is Beverly D'Amo."

Poppy kicked Howard under the table. It was bad enough to be saddled with Zachary and what appeared to be two hookers, but now this black freak, although Poppy had to admit she admired Jade Johnson, whom she had seen on numerous *Vogue* and *Bazaar* covers.

Howard was busy slipping and sliding down memory lane. Beverly D'Amo reminded him of his first wife, the fierce activist to whom he had been married for a fast forty-eight hours. What a panther in the old sackerooney! Je-*sus*!

The two expensive call-girls exchanged bored glances. They had seen it all and done it all. Nothing surprised them. They knew for sure that later the black woman would be joining them for a delicate trot around Zachary Klinger's sexual fantasies.

"Goddamn *hot* in here," remarked Ida White crossly. "And noisy."

Everyone ignored her, including Zeppo, whose hand was busily creeping up Beverly's thigh under the table. She shook it off like an annoying gnat, and questioned Zachary about the stock market.

What an operator! thought Jade. *Nothing changes.* Once, on a cover shoot in Tennessee, Beverly had slept with a local department store owner, his son, *and* his son-in-law. On separate occasions, of course, just because the photographer had bet her a hundred bucks she couldn't do it. Beverly loved to achieve the impossible.

Howard Soloman stared at Jade. "Haven't we met before?"

She nodded, and took a deep breath. "About ten years ago," she said. "I came out for a screen test. You were a studio exec or an agent or something."

Shaking his head sympathetically, he said, "Didn't work out, huh?"

"Howard!" Poppy scolded. "Jade Johnson is one of the top models in the country."

Howard was unimpressed. As far as he was concerned everyone wanted to be a movie star. It was the great American dream.

"Excuse my husband," Poppy said with an ingratiating smile. "He doesn't understand. I'm crazy for the new Cloud ad. Antonio is a *wonderful* photographer. Does he ever – you know – photograph *real* people?"

By the time Jade made her escape an hour later, Poppy was her new best friend.

"I have to be up *so* early," she said as she excused herself.

"Call me," Zeppo said insistently. "I can do things for you."

"Call me," Howard said, "if you ever change your mind about the movies."

"Call me," Poppy said, "we'll have lunch."

"Call me," Beverly said, with a huge wink, "tomorrow for sure."

She rushed out to the parking lot, where Penn Sullivan, the actor Beverly had greeted earlier, and Frances Cavendish, the casting agent, argued hotly while waiting for their car.

Jade caught ". . . I'm not just a piece of fucking beefsteak" out of his mouth, and ". . . If *I* say it's right, *you'll* do it" out of hers.

The two of them got into an old Mercedes, still fighting, and roared off into the night.

Jade found herself alone again.

Naturally.

★

"Sit next to me," Zachary Klinger instructed, when Beverly arrived at his bungalow a few minutes after him. She had left her car with a valet at the front of the hotel. He travelled by chauffeured limousine.

"I'm more comfortable over here," she said, settling into a couch across from him. "Where are your girlfriends? Did you drop them home?"

"I want you next to me," he repeated.

"He who wants might never get," she joked.

"Don't play with me, Miss D'Amo. Tell me what *you* want, and let us not indulge in childish and time-consuming games."

"I want to be a big, big star, Mr Klinger. Bigger than even *you* can imagine."

"Then sit beside me, and we shall see."

"Promises don't interest me."

"What does?"

"Action. Do something for me, and *then* I'll do something for you."

"Agreed. But I need something tonight."

"No can do. You shouldn't have sent your girlfriends home. Between 'em they looked like they could do *plenty* for you."

"And they will. Only you must sit next to me and watch. I won't touch you. They won't touch you. Unless you ask . . ."

A definite weirdo. Berverly complied – she had absolutely nothing to lose, and plenty to gain.

*

"I'm tired," Poppy complained.

She was tired. Ha! She sat on her fanny all day, and only moved it out of the house to buy jewellery and have lunch with her cronies.

"I've had a very tough day," Howard said. "*I'm* frigging exhausted."

Poppy giggled. "Are we both too tired to play naughty?"

"Sorry, sweetheart, tonight I'd need Arnold Schwarzenegger to lift it for me."

She giggled again. "You're so funny!"

"I try to please."

"Oh, babykins, you do!"

What had he done right for a change?

They were approaching their house, and he pressed the automatic gate opener, pulling the car to a halt while the massive iron gates swung open.

"Howard?" Poppy asked plaintively. "Do you love me?"

"What kind of a question is that? You know I do." He hated it when things got sloppy.

They were in their own driveway now. "Pull the car over to the side," she whispered. "Park, Howard. Pretend we're in high school."

"What?"

"*Do* it."

Reluctantly he obeyed. Poppy was a woman you didn't fight with, not unless you wanted to be up all night.

As soon as he stopped the car she was on him, burrowing into his lap like a hungry rabbit.

"What are you *doing*?" he blustered, as she went for his zipper.

"The thing you like best in the whole wide world, Howie." She reached his shorts, and triumphantly pulled his limp, exhausted penis out into the moonlit front seat.

"Poppy –"

"Be quiet. You know you love it."

Enclosing him with her mouth, she gave him her special kiss-of-life technique. The same technique she had used the first time they became more than just boss and secretary. Somehow she had gotten under his desk and displayed her special talent. Three months later they were married.

"Poppy!" he groaned, as she did the impossible and summoned a dead person back to life.

For the first time in a long while he did not think of Whitney as he fell asleep later that night.

Chapter 67

Rocky had the Sylvester Stallone walk. He had honed his imitation until it was perfection. Slight swagger, macho steps, a forward thrust. He could, if he wanted to, have made a living as a celebrity look-alike. But hey – as far as he was concerned Sylvester copied *him*.

The drive to Trancas was a bitch, and a couple of times he almost turned his Jeep around and headed back to civilization. The Pacific Coast Highway drove him nuts. He always got this insane urge to cross the line and play chicken with the oncoming traffic. It bothered him that one night he might just get stoned enough to do it, and end up in the slammer for sure. Again.

Funny, he'd been living on the edge all his life, and the only thing he'd been put away for was reckless and drunken driving. Six months' hard time just because this old couple broke down on the freeway and *he* was the jerk who had to run into them. If it hadn't been him, *someone* would have hit 'em.

Heaven. A foxy little piece. With her own beach house. Probably some shack, but hey – check it out.

When he found the turn-off there were cars crowding the shoulder of the road, and a lot of noise and loud music coming from the house, which was situated beyond a series of stone steps.

Party time, he said to himself. There was nothing Rocky liked better than to party.

★

Stewardesses always came on to Jack; it was automatic. The one on the flight back was outrageously pretty, a blonde Californian peach.

"How long have you been doing this?" he asked.

"Six weeks," she replied. "It's hard on the legs, but I'm *really* enjoying it. I get to meet so many interesting people." She paused and twinkled, all shiny-bright and eager. "Like you, Mr Python."

"Call me Jack."

"Give me your number and I will," she said boldly.

He reckoned she would last another six weeks on the job before she was either discovered and became an actress, or lured off to get married. She was that pretty.

"What will you do when we get to L.A.?" he asked.

She laughed ruefully. "Flake out."

He had a strong desire to take her to bed. She was so different from the socialite, and very appealing in a one-night-stand kind of way.

Strapped in his seat, with a scotch on the rocks and Jade's picture shut safely in the magazine, he tried to make up his mind whether to come on to her or not.

Christ! he thought, as the 747 prepared to land. *I've been almost faithful for eighteen months. And for what? To catch Clarissa with her talented ass in the air servicing some macho actor. The hell with it.*

He rang the buzzer and the stewardess came running.

"I'll buy you dinner if you're available," he said.

★

Heaven didn't care anymore. She would make up a story for Uncle Jack. Like she invited a couple of people over, and a whole crowd gate-crashed. Which wasn't such a lie, it was the truth.

The trashing of the house was almost complete. Couples were now making out in both bedrooms, and strangers surged everywhere. Someone had turned on the jacuzzi, which was packed with naked bodies.

324

She couldn't see Eddie. She hated Eddie. She would never speak to him again for allowing this to happen.

*

Roaming around, Rocky figured he had fallen into teenage heaven. Baby pussy was knee deep, and he was in love with all the little foxes with their tight fannies and perky tits.

Rocky partied a lot, but usually the parties were full of hard-faced women who pretended to be actresses or models but usually turned out to be hookers on the side. He had lived with a few – more than a few, in fact. Good bodies – money-trap minds. Any money he made was strictly for himself. He had a decent apartment, and a third-hand Merc, which he used when he wasn't in the Jeep. The Jeep was strictly for business purposes only. Like tonight, for instance. He had worked bar at a big party and walked away with three thou in drug sales, *and* a case of the best scotch.

He had not walked away with Silver Anderson – who wasn't even there.

When he thought about his so-called friend Wes Money, and what he had gotten away with, he could hardly believe the jerk's dumb-ass luck. And *he*, Rocky the man, was responsible, for it was he who had taken Wes to Silver Anderson's house in the first place. And not so much as a "thank you" for his trouble. No dinner invite. No "Come by the house." No nothin'.

Some people.

Some people were dogshit.

Rocky glowered. And flexed his not inconsiderable muscles. And said, "Yo there, fox-trap," to a fifteen-year-old, who moved away fast.

Conveniently, Rocky forgot it was he who had set his good friend Wes up the Laurel Canyon trap. Not that he'd known the extent of the scam, but he *had* known it was something heavy, and if he'd been a true friend he would never have given Wes the number to call.

Grabbing the attention of a tall lunatic in Levi cut-offs, he asked, "You seen Heaven, man?"

The boy jumped excitedly. "A few of the dudes got Ecstasy. What's this Heaven shit?"

It occurred to Rocky he was wasting precious time. He

had the perfect opportunity to go for sales. Business looked like it could be brisk.

*

The stewardess had peach-fuzz-smooth skin, a glorious mound of apricot pubic hair, and an obliging disposition. Making love to her was like taking a trip through a small-town candy-store.

They were in Jack's suite at the Beverly Wilshire, and it was past midnight. After the event he just wanted to get rid of her.

And then he got an attack of the guilts. She was genuinely nice, and tried so hard to please.

She was also a fan, which he couldn't help being irritated by.

"What's it like being Jack Python?" she asked in an awe-struck voice.

What *was* it like?

"Very public," he said at last, which seemed to satisfy her.

"I bet you've met everybody."

"Not quite."

"I bet you've met Paul Newman."

"Yes," he admitted.

"I always buy his salad dressing," she said reverently. "It's excellent. Have you tried it?"

Time to extract himself.

Definitely time.

He was out of practice, and couldn't quite remember how to go about it.

She gave him the perfect cue by sitting up in bed and stretching – bouncy tits glowing with health. "I'm hungry," she said. "Aren't you?"

He was out of bed in seconds. "I've got a great idea."

"What?"

He reached for his pants and pulled them on. "Where do you live?"

"Santa Monica. Eleventh Street. I don't have to be home until later . . ." She gazed at him expectantly.

"Get dressed," he said cheerfully. "We'll go over to Hughes and buy everything in the market. Then I'm going to drive you to your place, and you're going to cook me the best breakfast I ever had."

"I am?" she asked uncertainly, disappointed because room service seemed like a much better plan.

"You *can* cook, can't you?"

"Sort of."

"Let's go!"

*

Making money with the kids was better than raking it in from their rich mommies and daddies. And they knew what they wanted too – a few uppers, downers, ludes, grass, coke. Especially Ecstasy – the new designer drug. Like their Calvin Klein and Guess jeans, they wanted only the best. And Rocky found that quite a few of the little foxes were prepared to barter for their goods.

He was just thinking about taking one grateful teenager for a walk along the beach, when he spotted Heaven, curled up in a corner, ignoring the wild action like it wasn't even happening. With a growl of recognition, he pounced. "I made it!"

She regarded him with huge amber eyes, and dragged herself back to reality. "Like a day late," she muttered.

"Din't wanna miss the party," he said breezily. "This is some heavy place. You got an old man keepin' you or what?"

"I live here alone," she mumbled. She certainly didn't owe *him* any explanations.

He was impressed. "Yeah?"

She stared at him warily. "Have you *really* got a friend in the record business?"

He scratched his armpit. "Yeah. Wanna warble somethin'?"

"If you clear all these total creeps out of my house, I'll play you my tape. Can you get rid of them?"

He looked affronted that she would even consider he might not be able to. "Yer askin' Rocky," he said boastfully. "I've bounced 'em out of bigger parties than this."

*

Jack purchased two hundred dollars' worth of groceries in the market while the blonde stewardess kept on exclaiming, "You're *crazy*. Who's going to *eat* all this stuff?"

"Let me enjoy myself," he insisted. "I never get to do this."

Filling the Ferrari with paper sacks, he drove to her apartment, a modest place she shared with two other stewardesses.

"Shhhh!" she giggled, as he filled the tiny counter space in her kitchen. "It's three o'clock in the morning!"

"I'd better go," he said, when he'd delivered everything.

"No, no. I'm going to cook for you, remember? That was why we went to the market."

He kissed her button nose. "I'm not hungry anymore. And I've got a teenage niece alone in my beach house. I've got to be going."

In a way she was relieved. Explaining Jack Python to her roommates at three in the morning was not a simple task.

Understandingly she nodded, and asked very softly, "Will I ever see you again?"

He wasn't about to lie to her. "Tonight was special." Only a white lie. "The truth is, I'm just coming out of a long relationship, and I don't want to make any promises I might not keep." He touched her cheek. "So . . . pretty lady, don't wait for the phone to ring, because right now I'm not the most reliable guy in the world."

"I appreciate your honesty . . . Jack," she said earnestly. "Take my number anyway – you never know when you might feel like shopping!"

He grinned.

"And thanks for the groceries," she added.

He left feeling good. It was nice to be able to walk away with a clear conscience.

*

He was doing it! Rocky was clearing them out in clusters. Telling them the party was over and brooking no argument.

Eddie was the only one to give him trouble.

Heaven turned away when Rocky forced him over to a quiet corner and had a word in his ear.

Eddie left shortly after, his face red, his guitar under his arm. *Bye-bye Eddie.*

She was going to tell Uncle Jack she wanted to transfer from her high school. Better still, stay out altogether and become a professional singer – with concerts, and gold records, and personal appearances – the whole deal.

As the last stragglers left she turned to Rocky in the debris of a once perfect house.

"Sit down," she said, determined that *someone* was going to hear her tapes. "And listen."

*

Driving along the Pacific Coast Highway, Jack broke the speed limit with reckless abandon. He let the Ferrari rip, tearing up the road with a cool forcefulness.

The dawn light was breaking, casting a pale glow along the coastline. Traffic was light and he enjoyed the effortless drive. New York seemed like a dream. In. Out. It was almost as if he'd never been there.

Humming softly to himself he arrived at the Trancas house in record time.

*

"This is not bad," Rocky said grudgingly. "Kinda catchy."

She had played him the slow tape of her new song; now she decided to try him with some good old rock and roll.

She put on the fast stuff and waited for his reaction.

While she was busy watching Rocky, lolling in a leather chair smoking a recreational joint, Jack walked in.

Rocky noticed him first. "Hey –" he began, starting to sit up. "Aren't you –"

"What the *fuck* is going on here?" Jack asked coldly.

Somewhere in the Midwest . . .
Sometime in the seventies . . .

*The girl ran from her foster home. She ran at night and she ran fast,
having first stolen three hundred dollars from a savings stash she had
discovered hidden behind a sack of flour in the kitchen.*

*She was still only a teenager, but she looked older than her years
and attractive, in spite of cheap clothes and amateurish makeup.*

*It did not take her long to find a job in the city she ran to. Working
behind the toiletry counter of a five-and-dime-store gave her enough
money to rent a room, and just about scrape by.*

*The manager of the store liked her. He was a short man with a
bulbous nose and two fingers missing from his left hand. Middle-aged
and married, he watched her constantly. She hadn't been working there
two weeks when he trapped her in the back room and stuck his hand —
the one with the missing fingers — up her skirt.*

*She shoved him off and told him he was a pig. Her angry words
only seemed to excite him more, and he continued to chase after her.*

*The girl tried to ignore him, but he was persistent, and never seemed
to leave her alone.*

*One day his wife came to the store. The woman was even shorter
than her husband and quite fat. A fine black moustache decorated her
upper lip.*

*The manager behaved himself that day, which was a relief. Only
the next day he was twice as bothersome, and the girl found herself
complaining to the driver of one of the delivery trucks.*

*"I know how y'can deal with him," the young driver said. "Meet
me after work an' I'll tell yer."*

*She met him. And one thing led to another, and before long she
found herself going out with the driver, who was called Cheech, and
seemed decent enough, although he had a bad case of acne and never
bathed.*

Of course he wanted One Thing. The girl knew by now that all men wanted One Thing. And she also knew what could happen when you gave in, so she vigorously rejected his advances.

Cheech was not used to being turned down. In spite of the acne and the body odour, girls loved him. He was a real loverboy. Cheech always made out. "I can't see you no more if'n ya don' give me no lovin'," he warned her.

"Okay," she replied.

"Okay what?" He was startled by her cool attitude.

"Don't see me."

The girl puzzled Cheech. She must be . . . what was the word he'd heard Jane Fonda use in some movie?

Frigid — yeah, frigid, that was it.

They stopped seeing each other.

One day the store manager came into the ladies' room while she was sitting on the toilet. "Get out!" she screamed.

It was after six, and the other staff had gone home for the night.

"You don't fool me," the short man said. "You want it. I've seen you looking at me with your hot eyes."

He was on her before she could pull up her pants.

For a moment she was caught off balance as he lunged for her, shoving his fat hand between her legs.

She saw that his penis was out, protruding from his trousers like a fat white slug.

With all her strength she jammed her knee up, catching him in the balls.

"Aaiieee!" he screeched, doubling over.

She ran from the store and never returned.

Two weeks later Cheech turned up at her rooming house. "Why didn't yer tell me you was leavin'?" he asked.

"Why should I?" she replied.

Grabbing her around the waist he said the words she had been waiting to hear. The words that would protect her from the world forever. "Let's get hitched."

They were married two days later in a civil ceremony. She told him she was nineteen and an orphan. They were well suited, for his only relative was an older brother whose house they moved into.

Cheech wanted sex five minutes after they walked through the front door, and she obliged, because now she was his wife she could hardly keep on saying no.

He pulled her into the small room they were to share and lifted her skirt. Then, pushing her down on the narrow bed, he went to work, grunting all the time.

331

"Yer not a virgin," he said, after a minute.

"I never said I was."

"Fuck me!" he screamed angrily. "Yer not a fuckin' virgin. Yer tricked me, bitch!"

He slapped her hard, and continued to cuss and scream.

Cheech never recovered from what he referred to as her "trickery and lies". But his anger did not stop him from thrusting himself upon her every night, and sometimes in the morning too.

His brother was a surly fellow, with a common-law wife who came and went when it suited her. She worked as an exotic dancer, and refused to do a thing around the house, so the girl found herself cleaning and washing, shopping and cooking for everyone. Including Cheech's brother's friend Bryan, who stayed over on Friday nights after their beer and poker binges. Bryan was a huge man. Six feet two inches tall, and three hundred pounds wide. He had long hair, matched by an unruly beard, and a permanent sneer.

The girl soon realized that marrying Cheech was a mistake; however, it was better than being alone. She suffered in silence, accepting her fate as inevitable. At least she had a husband, and that was something.

It was on a Friday night, shortly before Christmas, that she sensed danger in the air. Cheech came home drunk, waving a half-full bottle of scotch — a seasonal present from his employer. His brother arrived shortly after, angry because his common-law wife had phoned him at work to inform him she had met another man and was never coming back. By the time Bryan got there, both Cheech and his brother were drunk. It didn't take Bryan long to catch up.

The girl hovered in the kitchen nervously. She served them a meal of fried steak and potatoes, and then got out of their way by shutting herself in the small room she shared with Cheech.

Outside, the three of them were laughing bawdily and shouting at each other. Soon she knew that Cheech would come in and crawl all over her. At least he was quick, and when he was finished she could shut her eyes and seek solace in sleep.

Sure enough, no more than twenty minutes later, he staggered in, drunkenly mumbling under his breath.

She steeled herself to accept his advances as he lunged on top of her. No preliminaries for Cheech — he went right for the goal, chafing against her dryness.

"There's somethin' wrong with ya," he grunted disgustedly. "Yer got no juice."

Silence.

"*I'm* talkin' to ya," he screamed, slapping her across the face, as he had taken to doing a lot lately.

She tried to sit up, but he pushed her roughly back on the narrow bed. "Yer'll go when I say so."

He slapped her again, and once more thrust into her.

With a weary sigh she let go and relaxed. The sooner it was over the sooner he would leave her alone.

Alcohol had slowed him down, and he could not maintain an erection. With a steady stream of curses he fell off her. "It's yer fault," he muttered angrily.

His brother pounded on the door. "What's goin' on in there?" he shouted in a slurred voice. "Thought we was goin' t'a bar."

"I'm comin'," yelled Cheech irritably, standing up and zipping his fly. "You've given me a belly ache, bitch. Yer nothin' but a prick-tease."

He stormed out, and she thought it was over.

Five minutes later his brother entered the room. "Why'ja havta upset Cheech?" he whined.

"I didn't do anything," she said softly.

"He's not so bad to ya, is he?" the brother asked, sitting on the side of the narrow bed.

"No," she lied.

"He feeds ya, puts clothes on ya."

"Yes."

His big hand swooped over and enclosed her left breast.

Shrinking back against the wall she whispered, "Please don't touch me."

Whiskey breath enveloped her. "I gotta do it. I gotta see if yer normal. Cheech says ya ain't."

His fleshy mouth descended on hers, while his hands worked on dragging her legs apart.

She began to struggle as she felt the full weight of him. And then she started to scream with fury and frustration as he plunged inside her.

"Cheech's right. Yer a dumb bitch," he slurred, pinning her arms to the side with a show of macho strength.

"And you're a dumb bastard," she responded gamely, in spite of the pain he was inflicting.

"Doncha call me names, cunt." He hit her twice, across the face, quieting her futile struggle. And then he finished what he had started with an animal growl of satisfaction.

When he got off her she touched her mouth and discovered blood seeping from the corner. She explored with her tongue and felt a loose tooth. Her breasts were sore, and both eyes were swollen and blackened. It was another nightmare. There had been too many in her short life.

Shakily she attempted to sit up. Before she could, Bryan entered the room. They stared at each other warily. Bryan was drunk; if he had been sober she might have been able to talk him out of what he was about to do.

"No!" She shook her head as he approached her. "No! Please, no!"

He didn't say a single word as his huge bulk crushed her beneath him.

She must have passed out, for when she came to she was lying in the back of Cheech's panel truck, and she could hear the three of them in the front, talking.

"We'll throw her right in the middle of the city dump." She recognized Cheech's voice.

"Naw" — his brother talking — "the river's better."

"Ya stupid fuckers," snarled Bryan. "We coulda got a prostie for twenny bucks."

"You fuckin' did it," accused Cheech. "Ya fuckin' smothered her to death."

If she had known fear before, it was nothing compared to now. Her skin crawled with clammy horror as she realized that, when she lost consciousness, in their drunken state they must have thought she was dead, and that they had killed her. And now they were disposing of her body.

Shivering uncontrollably she decided not to put them out of their misery.

Twenty minutes later the truck ground to a halt. The three of them were still arguing among themselves, deciding on alibis and explanations in case anyone asked awkward questions.

Cheech finally did his own summing up. "She was just a nobody — who's gonna notice she's not around anymore?"

Grunts of agreement as they manhandled her body from the truck and flung it into a deep pit of garbage.

As she fell she knew the revenge she would take.

And six weeks later she did.

Lighting the first match was easy . . .

BOOK FOUR

Hollywood, California
November 1985

Chapter 68

"Andermon Productions," Unity said into the white telephone. "Just one moment, please."

She tapped on the glass window of the pool house, attracting Wes's attention as he lounged outside catching the winter sun — which in California is sometimes just as hot as the summer.

"Who?" he mouthed.

"Mr Samuels. Revolution Pictures."

He made the effort and ambled into the pool house office to take the call.

In three months, Wes Money had learned a lot. He had taken over Silver's career with a vengeance, and although Zeppo White was her official agent, Wes himself was her personal manager, and went over every deal with a street-sharp eye.

"Harry, baby." He had learned the lingo right away. "Have you rethought our deal?"

Harry obviously had, for they spoke for five minutes, and ended with a luncheon date.

"Put me down for a twelve-thirty at the Palm on Wednesday," he told Unity, hanging up.

Opening a large leather appointment book she scrawled in the arrangement.

He leaned over her desk. "How're y'doin'?"

"Okay," she replied primly.

She certainly looked okay. A lot better than when he'd tracked her down to that sleazy bar she was working at. Shit! Was she in lousy shape then.

One morning, a couple of months ago, he had woken up and suddenly remembered her telling him that she worked at Tito's, a bar on Hollywood Boulevard. And it was like *bingo*! He thought he might amble over, collect his thousand bucks she was holding for him, and see how she was doing. Maybe he'd even get his dog back.

He hung around until Silver took off to appear in a charity fashion show, and then he was out of there. Silver had wanted him to come and watch her. "No way," he'd said. "Women in clothes bore me."

"You're such a macho man!" She had smiled affectionately, not really minding at all as long as he was waiting when she got home.

He drove the Roller to Hollywood, cruising along the seedy boulevard searching for Tito's.

He found it conveniently located between a porno movie theatre and a sex aid shop. Nice neighbourhood.

The thought of leaving the Rolls-Royce on a meter made him nervous, so he drove to the nearest parking lot, where he tipped the Mexican attendant ten bucks to keep a special watch on it. The Mexican thought he was crazy and rolled his eyes.

"You gonna do it, or shall I take my money back?" Wes asked threateningly.

"Sure, me do," sneered the attendant.

"You'd better," he warned. "If I come back and there's one single scratch on this car, I'll slice your balls an shove 'em in an enchilada."

He walked briskly to Tito's, by-passing the porno shop although he was tempted to pop in and buy Silver a gift. She would love something rude. Maybe a peek-a-boo bra for her, and a jar of Tiger Balm for him. Tiger Balm was an aphrodisiac cream that supposedly got it up and kept it there. He remembered using it once when he was sixteen and going with a twenty-year-old raver who was very demanding. Locking himself in the bathroom, he had rubbed the cream on his cock. Ten strokes later and he came all over the floor. So much for Tiger Balm!

Wes had been in seedy bars in his time, but this one was a real lulu. The barman looked like he'd just been released from Attica. The customers – all six of them – looked like his cell-mates. And a crusty old cashier, hunched over an ancient cash register, appeared to resemble Mae West's grandmother – long platinum wig and all.

"Five bucks floor show fee," she wheezed as he walked in.

"What floor show?"

"You wanna peek, ya gotta pay."

338

Fishing out a ten, he waited for change that was not forth-coming.

"Two drinks minimum," the old hag said, hitching at a faded scarlet dress covering withered breasts.

Over by the bar the escapee from Attica watched him sus-piciously.

He slid onto a bar stool and asked for a beer. In strange locations he found it was always advisable to order something that couldn't be watered down.

A tough-faced woman with badly dyed yellow hair and black fishnet stockings peeking from a fake leather mini-skirt appeared from nowhere and sat beside him. She fished a cigarette from her purse, stuck it in her mouth, and turned to him with what she obviously thought was a provocative ex-pression.

"Light?"

"What?"

"I wanna match fer my ciggie."

Even at his lowest point he would never have second-glanced this one. Obligingly he took out his solid gold Gucci lighter – another present from Silver – and allowed the woman to suck on her cigarette until it glowed.

"I'm looking for a girl called Unity," he said. "I understand she works here."

"Who says?"

"She told me she works here."

"When?"

"A short while ago. Does she?"

The woman shrugged. "Don' ask me."

Leaning across the bar he summoned the barman. "You got a girl called Unity here?"

"Who's askin?"

"Shit!" he said forcefully. "I feel like I'm in a friggin' James Bond movie. Does she work here or not?"

The barman pointed to a door in the back. "Second booth."

Taking a swig of beer, he eased himself off the stool and made his way through the door, which led into a dark, foul-smelling hallway. Along the wall were three closely spaced peephole windows, each one covered with heavy black-out shades. A man crouched in front of the last window along, obviously indulging in an activity most people did in private. Trying to ignore him, Wes paused in front of what he presumed to be booth two. A slot signalled the deposit of two dollars before the shade lifted. He put in the money and watched the action.

Unity appeared on the other side of the glass. He hardly recognized her, for this was a different Unity. Her pinched little face was covered with makeup, the Lennon specs were gone, and she had on a straw-coloured Tina Turner wig which made her look ridiculous.

She wore a red shiny skirt, white plastic boots, and a tight tee-shirt.

Lethargically she began to take it all off, revealing a leopard G-string and minuscule bra on a painfully skinny body.

He tried to attract her attention to let her know it was him, and that she didn't have to do this. But the glass was obviously one-way and she couldn't see him.

"Goddammit!" he muttered as she stripped off everything.

The black shade – on a two-minute timer – snapped shut.

Stalking outside, he grabbed the barman's attention. "I don't want to watch her," he said angrily. "I need to talk to her."

"Who?"

"Unity, for crissake."

"She gets off at three."

"I have to speak to her *now*."

The barman cleared phlegm from his throat and spat on the floor behind him. "It'll cost ya."

"Everything costs in this joint. Are y'sure you don't charge to take a piss?"

After a short discussion they came to a financial arrangement, and the barman went off to get her.

Unity. His uptight little neighbour. He had thought she was a waitress, not some peep-show hooker.

She came out a few minutes later, sulky looking, with a long woollen sweater covering her "ready to strip" outfit.

"Remember me?" he asked.

She stared at him, her expression a mixture of surprise and insolence. Before he could utter a word she blurted, "I spent the money. I didn't think I'd see you again. And after the way they beat up on me, I reckon I deserved it."

"You spent *my money*?" he asked, outraged. He might have given it to her, but the thought that she'd spent it without asking infuriated him.

"I had to get out, didn't I? What was I supposed to do, wait for 'em to come back?"

"Wait for *who* to come back?"

"Your drug friends. You should have warned me it was drug money."

"It wasn't."

"Don't give me that. I may look stupid, but I'm not."

"I'm tellin' you, it was *not* drug money."

She shrugged. "I don't care either way. I spent it, an' there's nothing you can do about it." She continued to stare at him, daring him to do something.

Shaking his head he said, "You're a fucking thief."

"And what are *you* – a boy scout?"

"Jesus *Christ*!"

"Can I go now? I've got to make a living, you know."

"Some living. Taking it off for a bunch of jerk-off artists."

"Maybe I should deal dope instead. Pays more, doesn't it?"

They glared at each other.

"Where's Mutt?" he demanded.

"I've got him."

"I want him."

"No way."

"I can give him a good home now."

"Bully for you. He's stayin' with me."

What a pain in the ass she was with her semi-cross eyes and stupid crazy wig. She'd stolen his money, wouldn't give him back his dog, and apparently suffered no guilt about ripping off his thousand bucks.

"What are you workin' in a toilet like this for?"

"Because it pays my rent."

"I'll give you fifty bucks for Mutt."

"Mister Generous," she sneered.

"He's half mine anyway," he stated self-righteously. For some insane reason he had a burning desire to recover the dog they had once shared.

"Sue me."

Maybe it was the wig, or the place, but Unity was like a completely different person. It occurred to him that she might be high. "What are you on?" he asked.

"Fuck *you*."

Grabbing her arm, he rolled up the sleeve of her sweater

341

before she could stop him. And sure enough he found what he was looking for – a thin line of recent track marks.

She snatched her arm away with a jerk of fury. "Whyn't you piss off out of here?"

"When did y'start *this* charmin' little habit?"

"None of your goddamn business."

"I guess my thousand bucks financed you."

Staring at him arrogantly, she said, "You could say it started me off. When your *friends* came in an' beat the shit out of me, forcin' me to move on, I figured why not? I had the money for once."

He felt immediately responsible. And although he didn't do anything about her that day, he went back twice to see her, finally suggesting that she give up her present lifestyle and come to work for him as a secretary.

"*You* need a secretary!" She hooted with mirth. "What for?"

"Because I married well. My wife is Silver Anderson."

"No shit? And I've been dating Don Johnson!"

She took some convincing, but he was very persuasive. There was something waif-like and appealing about Unity – and he wanted to use a little of his good luck to try and get her back on the right track. He offered her a drying out period in a drug rehab clinic, and then the job.

"We'll have to tell Silver you're my cousin. I don't want to go into long explanations."

Three weeks ago she had started work. The old Unity. Quiet and serious looking, with her John Lennon shades, makeup-less heart-shaped face, and pulled-back light brown hair.

It seemed to be working out well.

*

"It's a wrap," the first assistant announced, after the director had called "Cut" on the set of *Romance*.

Silver swept off to her dressing room, trailed by her entourage of Nora – who now worked for her exclusively – Fernando, her hairdresser; Raoul, her makeup artist; and Iggi, her personal stylist and dresser.

Being a movie star again meant great luxury. Compared to the daily grind of episodic television it was absolute ecstasy. Silver adored every moment.

She had an expensively furnished and large dressing room three times the size of the rat-hole City Television had given her for emoting three days a week on *Palm Springs*. A rat-hole she would no longer have to languish in, thanks to the swift, no-nonsense negotiating clout of the admirable Zeppo White. Thank God she had listened to Wes, and returned to the all-encompassing power of Zeppo. Quinne Lattimore had been distraught – naturally. But as Wes so forcibly (she was crazy about his forcefulness) pointed out – business was business. And since she had never signed a formal contract with Quinne, she was free and clear.

Goodbye, Quinne.

Hello, Zeppo.

Wes took care of the details.

Zeppo had taken one look at her contract with City Television and thrown a fit. "Slave labour!" he tut-tutted. "Shouldn't be allowed. Whoever had you sign this should be shot!"

He knew perfectly well who allowed her to sign it. Quinne Lattimore. She felt sorry for him at first, but when Zeppo and Wes explained to her how she had been taken advantage of – money and perks-wise – she didn't feel so sorry any-more.

Wes sat her down one day and gave her a lecture. "You're a beautiful woman."

She preened.

"And a great actress and a wonderful singer."

This was getting better. She loved compliments, especially from Wes, on whom she grew more dependent each day.

"But you're not getting any younger."

Her smile turned to frost. She hated mention of her age. Forty-seven was only three years away from fifty. And fifty was only ten years away from sixty. And . . . oh God, she felt quite faint.

"What are you trying to say?" she asked icily.

Catching her vibes, he jested around before getting to the main point. "You'll *always* be the sexiest broad on the block – no doubt about *that*. But I don't want you bustin' your ass in a few years' time. I want you to be able to sit back an' say fuck 'em – I don't think I'll work this year. And to be able to do that we've got to rake in the big money now. Quinne held you back a couple of years. With Zeppo we've gotta go for it. An' we gotta go for it *now*."

She recovered her composure. He was right. It might be quite a change to sit back and do nothing – when it suited *her*. "I agree," she said.

"The thing is," he went on, "don't freak out, but Zeppo is trying to break your contract with City Television."

She was aghast. Appearing on *Palm Springs* three days a week was certainly hard work, but without it what would she do? *Romance* was not going to take forever, and she had nothing else lined up.

"I enjoy doing *Palm Springs*," she said quickly. "And if Zeppo negotiates more money . . ."

"*Palm Springs* got you back, made you a star again. Now you don't need it anymore. Zeppo can keep you as busy as you want to be. He's already talkin' about an hour special with NBC. An' he's talkin' mega-bucks. There's a recording deal in the works. Commercials, endorsements. Christ, Silver, do you realize the money we can make?"

"Are you *sure*?" she asked tentatively. She suffered from every performer's lack of confidence when it came to viewing her own future.

"Yeah, I'm sure, otherwise I wouldn't be talkin' this way. Zeppo wants to explain everything to you himself – I figured I'd run it by you first."

That conversation had taken place three months ago. And in those three months, everything Wes and Zeppo promised had happened. Right now she was in the midst of shooting *Romance*. True to his word, Zeppo had got her out of her contract with City Television. How he did it she had no idea. But the great thing was that she was to guest on *Palm Springs* four times a year – at her own convenience. And for that four weeks she was to receive the same amount of money they had been paying her for a full year.

Unbelievable!

Wes was more than right. Moving to Zeppo was the second-best thing she'd done in her entire life. The first was marrying Wes. Contrary to everyone's belief that he was going to grab all her cash and run, he had turned out to be a canny operator – who was making sure she made even more bucks. And he looked after all her interests too. Banking, investments, tax, accounting. She still paid so-called professionals to do it, but Wes watched and interfered and made sure they did it right, and didn't steal from her.

Oh, the relief of having a real man around the house. She didn't care what his background was. She trusted him, and that was enough for her.

They had their fights of course, real screaming matches. The making up was worth every delicious spiteful insult. Wes was the lover she'd been searching for all her life. A powerful animal in the sack. A real man.

Recently he'd come up with a cousin, and a mangy dog. She wasn't exactly thrilled that he'd installed them in the house. The girl was a nonentity, the dog an aggravation.

Wes insisted they both stay. "She's my only family," he said firmly. "Put her in one of the maids' rooms, they're empty anyway."

How could she argue? He was doing so much for her, and as it turned out Unity was quite useful to have around. She kept to herself and didn't bother anyone.

The dog was another story. Silver wished it would fall in the pool and drown! She hated dogs at the best of times – especially pedigree-less mongrels.

When *Romance* was completed it was all go on her television special. And then she had an album of old show tunes to cut, and a commercial for Savvy perfume.

The money was rolling in. Right now Silver was content. Except for the matter of Zachary K. Klinger, who quite blatantly refused to leave her alone. He was pursuing her relentlessly, and his unwelcome attentions were beginning to unnerve her.

So far she had managed to keep it from Wes, although it wasn't easy. She was inundated with red roses daily – fortunately they arrived at the studio, where he also sent her expensive pieces of jewellery which she always had Nora return.

Occasionally he even visited the set. After all, it was an Orpheus picture, and he owned Orpheus.

Studiously she managed never to be alone with him. But she knew Zachary. When he wanted something or someone he never gave up. And he wanted her.

Toying with the idea of telling Wes, she finally decided against it. There was nothing he could do, and pitting Wes against Zachary Klinger would be like placing a small rowboat in front of an ocean liner.

She would just have to wait it out, and hope that Zachary faded quietly back into her past where he belonged.

Chapter 69

Jade Johnson was everywhere. Or rather her face was. She stared down from two giant billboards on Sunset. She was in every magazine. Her image – larger than life – decorated all the Cloud make-up departments in every one of the better stores. Her series of television commercials – daring, amusing, depicting her as a true woman of the eighties – had created quite an impact wherever they were shown.

In a short period of time she was better known than she had been in her entire career. And for the first time she was seriously considering taking it one step further. Orpheus Studios and Howard Soloman kept on making her offers she was finding hard to refuse. The more she said no, the more they said yes. Going so far as to promise she could debut in the story of her choice. And proposing a very lucrative deal indeed.

While she wasn't an actress, Jade also wasn't a fool, and she knew that opportunities like this only came once in a lifetime. She had read a book called *Married Alive*, whose central character was a young fashion designer who falls in love with a married man. It was a comedy – reminiscent in a way of *A Touch of Class* – one of her favourite movies of all time. Saying yes – if the book's film rights were still available – seemed like a tempting prospect.

Beverly D'Amo urged her to get together with Zeppo White. "You have to be with the right agent," she insisted. "Look at what he's done for me."

Beverly was currently shooting *Romance* with Carlos Brent and Silver Anderson. After that she was due to go to work on *The Murder* in a featured role.

Jade nodded. She agreed that the right representation was important, and with that thought in mind she arranged a lunch with Zeppo at The Palm on Santa Monica.

When she walked in he leaped to his feet. "You've taken your time, kiddo," he said.

"I always take my time," she replied coolly.

He cackled. Beautiful women turned him on. Especially beautiful women with razor-sharp minds of their own.

"So . . . you wanna be a movie star," he mused.

Shaking her head she said, "No, Mr White. I want to make enough money to buy myself an island, so that when the bullshit gets a little too thick on the ground, I can just take off and do whatever I want."

He cackled again. "I like it! I like you! Tell me what the thieves are offering you, an' I'll get you double."

She nodded. "For ten percent I shall expect you to do just that."

*

All things considered, Beverly D'Amo was quite happy with the way her career was progressing. Two movies and plenty more on the horizon if she continued to please Zachary Klinger. And there was no reason why she couldn't do so. He was easy to please – kinky – but what the hell – she had met a few in her time.

Zachary's particular kink was making it with her while two ladies of the night watched attentively. Of course, first she and Zachary had to eyeball the two hookers, which could get a little tedious if you weren't into that action. But Zachary loved it, and who was she to spoil his pleasure?

Beverly had never thought the day would come when she had to screw to get ahead of the game. After two and a half years in Hollywood, getting exactly nowhere, she had decided to go for it. And there was nobody bigger than Zachary K. Klinger. He was the top man.

They had an agreement. She would put out for him. And he would put out for her. Fair enough.

The only drag was he expected her to find the professionals. Easy it was not. He required new ones each time, and they always had to bring along a clean bill of health. Not that he ever touched them. Never went near them.

Beverly was seriously thinking of having a whole bunch of phoney doctors' letters dummied up. He would never know the difference, and it would surely make her job a lot easier.

The first time she slept with him he demanded a doctor's certificate from *her*. Goddammit. She nearly told him to shove the deal. Who needed the humiliation?

347

When he purchased the huge house on Carolwood Drive in Bel Air, he invited her to move in with him. She liked that – it showed that in his own peculiar way he cared. Another man in his position might not be so anxious to set up house with a black woman. Zachary didn't give a damn. In a funny way she loved him for it.

She had her own bedroom, her own maid, and her own Rolls-Royce. When he entertained – which admittedly wasn't often – she played the official hostess part. What with the work and the status, it was a role she could live with.

A very different role from the one she had played while growing up.

*

Rodeo Drive was quiet when Jade slipped into Lina Lee after lunch and did some serious shopping. She spent three thousand dollars on clothes, and wondered guiltily if she was going Hollywood.

It's my money, she thought defiantly. *It's not like I'm spending some poor guy's hard-earned dollars.*

She loved clothes, and recently she had needed a new outfit every day, what with personal appearances and television talk shows. In New York she used to get a lot of stuff given to her, just so she would wear it and everyone would say, "Where did you get *that*?"

The spending spree was a celebration. She had instructed Zeppo White to represent her in her negotiations with Orpheus. If all fell into position she *would* do a movie. It would be crazytime not to.

"Jade?"

Turning, she did not recognize the short blonde woman in a peach jumpsuit and large dark glasses. Beside the woman stood a tiny child, identically dressed.

"Poppy," the woman reminded. "Poppy Soloman. You were supposed to call me. Lunch. Remember?"

"Oh, yes. How nice to see you," she said graciously, quickly trying to recall where they had met.

"And this is Roselight Soloman," Poppy continued. "Isn't she adorable? Everyone says she looks just like me. But I can see a touch of Howard in her, can't you?"

Ah! Mrs Howard Soloman. They had met at Mortons, the night Beverly was bird-dogging Zachary Klinger.

"She's lovely," Jade said kindly. The child wasn't lovely at all. She was on the plump side – just like mommy – with a petulant, screwed-up little face. "How old is she?"

"She'll be four in two weeks." Poppy paused, then added airily, "We're taking over Disneyland."

"How . . . original."

"I think it will be different, don't you?"

"Uh . . . certainly different."

"Children so easily get bored these days," Poppy confided. "Last year it was a tent and clowns and donkeys in the garden. This year she'll expect more."

"Absolutely," Jade agreed, looking for an escape.

"Now," said Poppy firmly. "While I've got you here, I absolutely *refuse* to take no for an answer. I *insist* upon giving a lunch for you. What day can you manage? Just name it, I'm all yours."

"I'm not sure when I'm free . . ."

"Monday?"

"No."

"Tuesday?"

"No."

"How about Wednesday?"

"Wednesday, let me see . . . ah . . ."

"Wednesday it is," Poppy said firmly. "Twelve-forty-five at the Bistro Garden. No excuses. I'll invite a few close chums. Is there anyone in particular you'd like?"

'Er . . . Beverly D'Amo."

Poppy gave a bitchy laugh. "She's quite a lady, isn't she? Although I guess *lady* isn't *quite* the right word."

Jade jumped in. "What is?" she demanded.

"Me wanna pee pee," interrupted Roselight.

"Be quiet," said Poppy sharply.

"What is?" repeated Jade.

"Character," smiled Poppy, recovering fast from her almost gaffe. "A charming, original *character*. And *such* a funny comedienne. Howard *raves* about the dailies on *Romance*. He says she's like a beautiful Whoopi Goldberg."

Jade relaxed. "I have to go," she said.

"Me too," agreed Poppy. "Busy, busy, busy. There's never enough time in the day is there? I'll see you on Wednesday."

A sudden noise startled both of them.

Roselight had peed in her pants, and the result was trickling to the ground.

Jade laughed all the way home. Poppy Soloman's face was a picture postcard of undisguised horror.

★

"Where's your sister?" Norman Gooseberger asked.

"She'll be here in eight minutes exactly," Corey replied, consulting his watch. "Jade runs ten minutes late on everything. No more, no less."

"Unlike baby brother," Norman said with a smile. "Always punctual, always correct."

"Not always," replied Corey.

Their eyes met and locked and did an intimate little dance all their own.

"Do you know," said Norman, "that this is the longest time I've ever been faithful?"

"Really?" replied Corey.

"Really."

They continued to stare at each other. A long stare where plenty was said, yet no words were spoken.

For the first time in his life, Corey felt completely at ease with himself. For years he had been forced to live a lie; now finally, with Norman, he was free to be himself. Norman had no hang-ups about being gay. "I knew it when I was fourteen," he had confided to Corey. "And a year later I told my parents. They freaked at first, but after a while they got used to it."

Corey had nodded. There was no way he could tell *his* parents. How could he? All they ever talked about was Jade, and how wonderful and successful she was. It wasn't easy being the under-achiever in a family used to excellence.

Jade entered the restaurant, causing the customary stares and comments. She kissed Corey on both cheeks, and then did the same to Norman. After her initial shock, she had accepted her brother's homosexuality with good grace. After all, if she were to suddenly change tracks she certainly wouldn't expect him to judge her.

"I met with Zeppo White at lunch today," she announced. "And I've decided to let him go ahead and negotiate with Orpheus for me."

Norman clapped his hands. "Bravo!" he said. "You'll be our new client. B & B signed the Orpheus account last week."

She smiled. "Not so fast, there's a lot to be worked out."

"You *should* be with us anyway," he commented.

"I know. I spoke to the Cloud people this week, and told them I wanted B & B to take over the publicity on the campaign."

"That's great!" he exclaimed.

"Great," Corey echoed, although he wasn't sure that he wanted Jade working with Norman. She had this habit of taking over on friendships — she didn't mean to do it, somehow it just happened. He loved his sister very much, only he was tired of always being in her shadow.

Dinner passed, gossip was exchanged. Jade told her Poppy Soloman story, and had Norman in hysterics.

Norman had a few stories of his own about Whitney Valentine and Chuck Nielson. "They battle non-stop," he confided. "He is *soooo* jealous of her, and she is career crazy. They're the Hollywood couple I always dreamed of representing. They break up — regularly — every ten days. *True Life Scandal* would go out of existence without them!"

Corey tried to come up with some gossip of his own. And then he thought, why even try? Norman had all the controversial and famous clients. He was stuck with Deacon the Dog, and a sixty-two–year-old male star of a television sit-com. Exciting stuff.

"How's your love life?" Norman asked boldly.

"Extremely dull," she replied matter-of-factly. Since her break-up with Mark no one had come along to pique her interest. And unlike her friend Beverly, she never slept with guys just for the hell of it. There *had* been a time when she was twenty-two that she remembered with mixed feelings. Her wild period she called it. She hadn't counted, but a lot of guys passed through her life then. Enough for her to realize that sex and nothing else was never enough. The sex was only important if it included a relationship.

"Aren't you seeing *any*body?" Norman persisted.

"I've got a lot of friends."

"We'll have to find you a winner."

Laughingly she said, "Thanks, but I'm not looking."

Driving home that night, Norman was full of how great she was. Corey had heard it so many times — he didn't need to hear it from Norman too.

They ended up arguing over something inconsequential, and Corey slept on the couch.

*

Two days later Jade and Norman lunched alone. It was a

business lunch: Norman had a promotional plan he wished to present to her.

She went over his ideas carefully, and liked what he had in mind. "You know I can't do anything without Cloud's approval," she said. "Not until my contract with them is up."

"I think you'll find that everything I'm suggesting will more than please them. It's all publicity for the product. Let's face it, you *are* the product."

She made a face. "Thanks a lot!"

"I mean the product is *you*."

"I'm not sure I like that either."

He had the blackest, curliest hair she had ever seen, and a most appealing smile. She found herself wondering if he had always been gay.

"How's Corey getting on?" she asked briskly.

"Fine. He's happy." A meaningful pause. "*I* make him happy."

"I'm sure you do," she responded quickly. Discussing their relationship still made her feel vaguely uncomfortable.

"When are you coming by the house?" he asked.

She had been avoiding it. Somehow she wasn't quite ready to see them at home together.

"Soon."

"Promise?"

"Absolutely."

After lunch she went straight to her apartment, changed into a bikini, and lay out by the pool for an hour. There was nobody around — the building was half full, and most of the tenants only used the pool on weekends.

As she re-entered her apartment the phone was ringing. Hurrying inside, she grabbed it.

"Yes?"

"Miz Johnson?"

"Yes."

"My name is Aretha Stolley. I'm calling on behalf of *Face to Face with Python* — you know, the Jack Python show?"

"Yes?"

"We'd be honoured to have you on as a guest, and Mr Python suggested I contact you directly. He always feels it's much simpler than going through agents and managers, etcetera."

"*Does* he?"

"He sure does. And I must say I agree with him. At least this way we get a direct yes or no. Usually a yes. *Very* few no's."

Jade remembered Jack Python with a taste of anticipation. Lord Mark Rand was not only dead, he was now buried.

"Tell Mr Python," she said slowly, "to call me himself." She paused. "And tell him . . . to do it soon."

Chapter 70

Aretha hung up and squawked with mirth. She put on a low, sexy voice and did a lively imitation. "Tell Mr Python," she said huskily, "to call me himself. And tell the randy sonofabitch to do it soon!"

"*Whaaat?*" said her secretary.

Aretha laughed. "I think our Jack just got lucky – yet *again!*"

"Who with this time?"

"The usual. A beautiful, stacked, *famous* lady. Are there *any* he's missed?"

Her secretary shrugged. "Don't ask me."

Aretha sailed into the production meeting with a big smile plastered across her face. She was enjoying Jack's freedom more than he was. Every week there was a different romance going on – it sure kept life interesting. Since his break-up with old sourpuss – as Aretha had nicknamed Clarissa Browning – he was back in action with a bullet.

"I called Jade Johnson," she told him.

He rubbed his unshaven chin. "And?"

"*And*, she would like to hear from you personally."

He tried not to show any particular interest. "Why's that?"

"How should *I* know? Maybe she wants to jump on your decrepit old bones. I'm paid to *do* – not *ask*."

Casually he shuffled some papers. "Does she want to appear on the show?"

"You've got to call her and find out for yourself."

"Who are we talking about?" Aldrich, his producer, joined in.

"Jade Johnson," Aretha replied, with a wink.

"We don't need another Clarissa Browning fiasco," Aldrich warned. "Are you sure she can hold a conversation, let alone one hour of prime-time television?"

"What is this?" Jack said shortly. "I don't pick duds. She'll be just fine."

He had no idea whether she would be a good guest or not. Somehow it didn't matter. He wanted to see her again. For the last few months her image had haunted him. Everywhere he looked, there she was. Beautiful. Challenging. Direct.

And yet he hadn't called her. He couldn't explain why. Perhaps it was because he needed space between Clarissa and his next serious relationship.

When the production meeting was over he shut himself in his office and stared at the phone for a while. Tonight he was taking out Kellie Sidney, a blonde, smart, divorced film star, who produced her own movies which made mega-bucks, and yet she still looked like a fresh-faced cheerleader.

The night before he had been with a slinky, dark-haired singer, who gave "sleek" new meaning.

Tomorrow night was the French actress with inviting eyes and smoky voice.

He was certainly occupied – if that was the appropriate word.

All this occupation . . . all these different bodies . . . and yet no one seemed to satisfy him. He felt restless and hemmed in. What he really needed was someone to fly with.

He picked up the phone and went for it.

"Jade Johnson?"

"Yes."

"This is Jack Python."

She sounded politely friendly. "Well . . . hi. How are you?"

"It's been a long time."

"Quite a while."

"Las Vegas, wasn't it?"

"Right."

Silence.

Long silence.

Christ! He felt like some schmuck about to request a date.

"Hey . . . uh . . . my assistant called you about doing the show, didn't she?" he asked.

"That's right, she phoned today."

"So all I need is a simple yes or no, and we can start working out schedules."

"The thing is . . ." She paused. "The thing is, I love your show. I always watch it —"

"I'm pleased to hear *that*."

"But . . . uh . . . I don't think I'd be the kind of guest you're . . . uh . . . looking for."

He was taken aback. "Why not?"

She hesitated before plunging ahead. "I just don't know what I can talk about for an hour. I guess I'm a well-known face, but I'm sure the public really doesn't know who I am. And what's more, I shouldn't think they care."

"Very modest."

"Very truthful."

"Listen, *I* want you on the show. I think you'll be great. Can you do it for me?"

"Why? So you can watch me make a fool of myself?"

"Sure. Let's all have a good laugh at your expense," he teased.

"No, thank you."

"I refuse to take no for an answer. Will you at least think about it?"

"Hmm . . . maybe . . ."

"And what can I do to help you come to the right decision?"

She could think of a lot of things he could do. Only she wasn't about to make the first move.

"Call me next week."

The moment was right to ask her out. *Are you still involved?* he could say casually. *I'm not, and I'd like to see you.*

"Fine, I'll call you next week. It was really nice speaking to you again."

"You too."

He replaced the receiver and could have kicked himself. He was a forty-year-old adult male with a certain reputation, and he couldn't even ask her out! He was behaving like fourteen not forty. *"Shit!"* he said loudly.

Aretha put her smiling face around the door. "What's up? Is she doin' it?"

"Were you listening?"

"No way."

"She's thinking about it."

"Big frigadoon deal!"

"Aretha."

355

"Yes, boss?"

"Piss off."

★

She could have sworn he was going to ask her out. Jack Python, with the dangerous green eyes and killer smile. Jack Python, who every day was pictured somewhere or other with a beautiful woman attached to his arm.

How about dinner? she had expected him to say.

No, she would have replied.

Jade Johnson had never considered herself to be one of the pack. She didn't want to be added to his ever-lengthening list.

Still . . . he could at least have asked.

There was only so much work one could bury oneself in. Beverly kept on fixing her up with likely candidates, and she felt no click with any of them. "Please stop," she had told her after the last one – a skinny lizard of a man with dull conversation and several billion dollars.

"But he's rich rich," Beverly insisted. "Almost as rich as Zachary."

"Who cares?" replied Jade.

She loved Beverly, but lately all her friend seemed to think about was money. Zachary K. Klinger was not the greatest influence in the world. She couldn't warm to him, and she sensed that he was uncomfortable with women. Especially strong, independent ones.

Beverly would not hear one word against him. "You don't understand Zachary," she informed Jade crossly.

"Yes I do."

Shane Dickson, the director of her Cloud commercials, was the only man she thought about getting involved with. Since his divorce he'd become quite persistent. He wasn't perfect, but he was available.

That evening she was dining with him at Spago, so she dressed accordingly. White pants tucked into boots, and a loosely belted oversized white cashmere sweater.

When he picked her up at a quarter to eight she was ready.

★

At five to eight, Jack Python arrived at Kellie Sidney's house on Sunset Plaza Drive. She wasn't ready. Kellie always ran late.

The house was filled with dogs and children. Kellie's three-

356

year-old son had two friends over. And the dogs were a Labrador, an Alsatian and a golden cocker spaniel. A cheerful maid cooked up a storm in the huge open-plan kitchen, and televisions blared in every room. Domesticity ruled.

Jack wondered if he'd ever fit into a scene like this. It had been difficult enough keeping an eye on Heaven during the couple of months she had spent at the beach with him. He hated to admit it, but when she returned to the Valley and George, he had been relieved.

What really pissed him off was that the entire time Heaven had been his responsibility her dear and caring mother, Silver, had not called once. The woman was unbelievable.

Kellie greeted him half dressed, with rollers in her hair. She gave him a distracted wave. "I'll be two minutes," she promised. The beaming cook poured him a tumbler of scotch, and he reflected further on Silver's coldness towards her only child. Like everyone else he had often wondered who Heaven's father was. It seemed extremely callous of Silver not to at least tell her daughter. He had no respect for her because of it.

Half an hour later Kellie appeared, wholesomely pretty in a pale blue dress and dangly earrings. Word had it that she was a tough businesswoman when she got involved in producing her own movies. You would never have guessed it from her carefree appearance.

"Where are we going?" she asked, petting the dogs, kissing the children and issuing instructions to the maid — all at the same time.

Obviously she'd forgotten that when he made the date she had requested Spago, "Because I *adore* their smoked salmon pizza," she'd said.

He jogged her memory. "Spago."

She smiled happily. "*Perfect* choice. I *adore* their smoked salmon pizza!"

*

Shane had just signed a contract to direct his first feature film. He was in a celebratory mood, ordering champagne — which always left Jade with a ferocious hangover — and talking excitedly about his future. A former New Yorker, he had a certain street-smart sexuality. He looked like Al Pacino. And like Al Pacino, he was short. It was a minor turn-off as far as she was concerned. Because she was so tall, she liked men of at least equal stature. Shane was several inches shorter than she, and up until now it had put her off getting involved with him, although he kept trying.

Tonight, maybe she would change her mind. All work and no play . . . And he *was* an attractive man, although he *did* talk about himself a lot. He had just completed two years of psychoanalysis, and now thought he could cure the mental ills of the world.

She glanced idly around the noisy restaurant as he described a meeting he'd just had with his recent ex-wife — a waspy Bostonian whom he should never have married in the first place.

"You know something?" he said eagerly. "For once I didn't want to slap her."

"How civilized of you," she remarked dryly.

"No. You don't understand. For me that's a major breakthrough. We are talking *major* here."

"Are *we*?"

"Yes. I can look straight into the bitch's eyes, and *not want to go for her throat*."

"Amazing."

"Damn right."

He kept talking and she kept on glancing around the celebrity-filled restaurant. Johnny Carson over here. John Travolta over there. Elizabeth Taylor and George Hamilton making a grand entrance.

She wondered if Shane would talk about his ex-wife in bed. Or even if he would talk at all.

And then she wondered if it was true — the rumours about short men being over compensated in other areas . . .

"What are you grinning about?" he demanded. "I'm pouring my guts out to you here, and you think it's *funny*?"

"Sorry! I just remembered something Antonio did in the studio yesterday. He's *such* a character!"

"Yeah, right. So let me get back to what I was telling you . . ."

She tuned out. Sometimes he was suffocatingly boring. Attractive, but boring. Attractive, but short . . .

Jack Python entered the restaurant.

Jack Python with Kellie Sidney.

She sat up straight and watched him as he paused at the reservation desk to jest with the girl there, and was then led immediately to his window table. A table that put him directly across from her.

He didn't see her at first as he leaned over and said something intimate to Kellie, who laughed. And then, just as he was about to order drinks, he noticed her and did one of those classic double-takes.

"Hey –" He smiled and waved.

She smiled back. "Hello."

Both Kellie and Shane turned around to see who their respective dinner dates were waving to. As it happened they knew each other, and exchanged greetings of their own. And then Kellie effected introductions. "Shane Dickson, Jack Python."

And Jack said, "Kellie Sidney, Jade Johnson."

And everyone came out with banal compliments before turning back to their own conversations.

"I always wanted to meet him," Shane said. "Interesting guy. Where do you know him from?"

"I met him with Antonio," she replied vaguely.

Kellie said, "She's stunning. Where did you meet her?"

"Las Vegas, I think. One of Carlos Brent's parties. Who's the guy?"

"Shane's a director from New York."

"Movies?"

"Commercials. Although I hear he's getting offers. He directs the Cloud commercials. They're wonderful – very original, have you seen them?"

"No," he lied.

"The camera work is superb. I wouldn't mind looking like she does in my next movie."

I bet, he thought. *Only pretty as you are, my sweet – no chance.*

Dinner was interesting. Shane and Kellie, back to back, had no idea of the electricity sparking between the tables. Jade tried to concentrate on her date – an impossible task with Jack Python so close. While Jack tried to give Kellie his undivided attention, as surreptitiously he watched Ms. Johnson's every move.

She couldn't eat.

"You said you were starving," Shane remarked.

She gulped more champagne – to hell with the hangover, it was needed. "Just thirsty, I guess," she said lamely.

Jack ordered smoked salmon pizza, and was relieved to see Kellie finish every piece. She was telling studio stories. Horror tales of male executives' attitudes to female movie stars who took control of their own destinies.

"I wish you'd mentioned this on the show," he said. She had been his guest three weeks before.

"I'll come back again," she said sweetly. "When I have another movie to plug."

He glanced up and met Jade's gaze head-on. They had been conscientiously trying not to stare at each other all night. This time neither of them looked away.

She felt the burn right down to the soles of her feet, and knew that Shane Dickson had just lucked out.

Chapter 71

The frigging asshole bought a mansion and moved himself out to Beverly Hills. Howard Soloman nearly had a heart attack. It was bad enough having Zachary K. Klinger driving him loco from New York – but right on his own frigging doorstep? Jesus H. Christ. Somebody up there was not looking out for him.

"It's not so terrible," Poppy tried to console him.

"How would *you* like it?" he demanded. "I'm supposed to be running a studio, not waitin' to wipe Zachary's ass every time he goes to the john."

"Does he really interfere that much?" she asked.

"Yes," he replied sourly. Actually, it wasn't that bad. Zachary's main concerns were the two movies he considered to be *his*. *Romance* and *The Murder*. The rest of the product he left alone – allowing Howard more or less *carte blanche*.

Howard had gone development crazy. Out of pique, he was spending the studio's money at an alarming rate. Buying properties, commissioning screenplays, purchasing best-selling novels, and giving the green light to a slew of producers, writers and directors with passable ideas.

Fuck it. He didn't give a damn. There were other studios to run. Orpheus was not the be-all and end-all.

Howard Soloman had a yen to move on.

And on the set of *Romance*, the two stars had fallen out, causing a certain frostiness all round.

Silver Anderson said it was Carlos Brent's fault.

Carlos Brent said it was Silver Anderson's.

"The man is an egomaniac," Silver said.

"The old broad is a pain in the tonsils," Carlos said.

"His voice is gone," from Silver.

"She can't sing anymore," from Carlos.

"Box office arsenic," announced Silver.

"They'll only watch her on television," announced Carlos.

Orville Gooseberger tried to patch things up. They both told him to go play with himself.

Zachary arrived on the set most days to observe the filming. Silver complained to Orville, "He makes me uncomfortable."

Orville shrugged. This one he could do nothing about. The man owned the studio.

Silver said she had a sore throat and claimed she couldn't work. Each week the film crept more and more over budget.

Meanwhile, on location in Arizona, where *The Murder* was shooting, a new romance was blossoming. It startled everybody, including Whitney Valentine, who like everyone else stood on the sidelines and watched.

Mannon Cable and Clarissa Browning came together as if they had been waiting for this moment all their lives.

One love scene in front of the camera, and they disappeared for an entire weekend.

Whitney was shocked. For some time now she had sensed Mannon was getting ready to ask her back into his life, and in spite of his pregnant wife and her own involvement with Chuck, she had considered the possibility of saying yes. She had even gone as far as discussing it with Norman Gooseberger. He not only handled her publicity, but had become a friend, whose advice she listened to.

"Take him back if he asks you," Norman had urged. "Chuck's a destructive influence. He's no good, and he drags you down with him."

Agreeing, she waited for Mannon to make his move.

He didn't. He started his ridiculous affair with Clarissa Browning, and everyone wondered what she had that was so special.

First Jack Python.

Now Mannon Cable.

Two of the best-looking men in Hollywood.

And while Clarissa was undoubtedly a magnificent talent, she would certainly never win any prizes in the beauty stakes. Plus her charm was non-existent. Most of her co-workers couldn't stand her. She was critical, demanding and tight with every cent, never so much as buying the crew a drink if she happened to be in the hotel bar when they were all present.

On screen she was magic. It was as simple as that. Her acting was flawless, and because of her, Mannon accomplished a lot more than his usual macho strut and self-deprecating sly glances to the camera. He was giving a very fine performance.

Whitney felt betrayed. Not only had Clarissa Browning taken her role, she had taken her man too.

The bitch would pay. Whitney knew how to make people pay . . .

Chapter 72

It was Jack's idea they all join up for coffee and dessert, and Kellie was amenable. "Ask your friend," he suggested.

She turned around and nudged Shane, who was surprised and pleased. "Is it okay with you?" he checked with Jade.

"Sure," she replied, trying to keep her tone casual.

They got up and moved to Jack's table, where Kellie immediately patted the empty chair beside her. "Sit here," she said to Shane enthusiastically, "and tell me *all* about the camera operator you used on the Cloud commercials. I *love* his work."

"*He* is a *she*," he replied. "A very talented lady."

"*Really?* I'm wild about working with women. My goodness – if females can't support each other I just don't know who will. Do you?"

As Kellie chattered away, Jack turned to Jade and said very quietly, "Hello."

"Hello," she replied, immediately getting lost in his green eyes.

There was no need to say anything more, for they both knew where they were heading.

Under the table she felt the pressure of his thigh against hers.

"Have you thought about whether you'll do the show or not?" he asked.

Laughing softly she said, "Give me a break, I've got other things on my mind."

Kellie leaned forward and peered across the table at her. "You must tell me, who does your makeup?" she asked eagerly.

"I usually do it myself."

"How *clever* of you. I'm hopeless with shading. Fortunately, I have this wonderful Algerian boy who always takes care of me for photo sessions – and then . . ."

Jade did not hear a word the blonde actress was saying. All she knew was that she was in the throes of a wild sexual heat, and she did not care *how* many women Jack Python was photographed with. She only knew she wanted him. And she wanted him now.

Abruptly she rose from the table. "Excuse me," she murmured. "Just going to the ladies' room."

Her legs were weak, her throat dry.

Get a hold of yourself, Johnson, she cautioned. *He's only another guy.*

Both restrooms were occupied, so she leaned against the wall by the pay phone and attempted to pull herself together. It had been a long time since she'd felt this way.

"Hello." He was beside her.

Weakly, she managed, "We've got to stop meeting like this."

He thought she was heartbreakingly beautiful, and he had an insane desire to touch her face and body; bury himself in her hair; kiss her eyes and her mouth and her breasts and everything else she possessed. She had him under a spell, and he couldn't remember when he'd felt like this before.

"What's going on with you and the guy?" he asked urgently.

Shaking her head, she murmured, "Nothing." And after a slight pause, "How about you and Kellie?"

"She means nothing to me," he replied truthfully.

Suddenly he couldn't hold back any longer. Pinning her against the wall with his hands each side of her shoulders he kissed her long and hard. A forceful, penetrating kiss, which she didn't try to block, but responded to, just as he knew she would.

After a few moments he pulled back and said, "We're getting out of here."

"We can't do that."

"We can do whatever we want to."

Ida White emerged from one of the restrooms and smiled glassily. "Good evening. Jack, dear." She was stoned as usual. Oblivious to everything.

He waited until she had wandered off before whispering to Jade, "Come with me. Don't say a word." Taking her hand, he led her through the crowded restaurant to the back entrance.

"We can't just leave them sitting there, waiting for us," she protested weakly.

"It's not our problem. I've picked up both checks, and left a message with the waiter that you got sick and I had to escort you home."

"They'll never believe it."

"Who cares?"

His Ferrari was waiting, engine running, an attentive valet ready to usher them into the car.

She got in and leaned back against the plush leather. "This is crazy behaviour," she said, tingling with anticipation.

"Crazy," he agreed.

"And exciting."

"You got it."

The car surged forward, scattering photographers and fans. He drove down the short hill, waited impatiently at a red light, and took off like a rocket all the way to his hotel.

"Why here?" she asked, as he helped her from the car.

"Because it's where I live."

"Good evening, Mr Python," said the doorman.

"No apartment? No house?" she persisted.

"This is home."

"Good evening, Mr Python," said the desk clerk as they walked past.

"No family? No roots?"

"Has anyone ever told you that you ask too many questions?"

"Frequently."

"Good evening, Mr Python," said the elevator operator.

They rushed into his suite like impatient lovers – which any minute they were to become. And as soon as the door closed they fell on each other with indecent haste – removing clothes with a no-nonsense speed bordering on the obsessive.

"Christ! You're beautiful!" he breathed.

She trailed her fingers down his chest. "And you're just as beautiful."

There was no conversation after that as he took her with a powerful urgency. It was something he had to do before he could even begin to think straight.

And it was like that for her too. They were both holding back, and their mutual release was fast and sweet – earth-shattering and very, very necessary.

Now they could relax and enjoy the sinful pleasures of discovering each other's body. Which is exactly what they did, slowly and luxuriously.

Leading her into the bedroom he laid her on the bed, and began – with exquisite restraint – to carefully explore every inch of her smooth, taut body.

She responded by touching his skin with the tips of her fingers, tactilely feather-stroking his chest, until his further pleasure became only too obvious.

"I'm glad to see you're a man of action," she murmured happily.

"For you – anything!"

"Just because you want me on your show . . ."

Tantalizingly he started to kiss her neck, moving down at a leisurely pace, relishing the piquant taste of everything about her.

She enclosed his hardness with her hands and teased his unquenchable desire, until the slow, erotic pace of things turned once again into fervent, reckless lovemaking.

And after the second time they fell asleep, wrapped in each other's arms, peaceful and voluptuously content.

Chapter 73

"Wow!" sighed Heaven. "It's like *totally* killer!"

Rocky nodded his agreement. He felt pretty confident standing in the recording studio listening to the final mix of her record. She had people swarming all over her – the producer, the sound engineer, a couple of record company executives – but he felt confident because *he* was the one who had set the whole gig up, and *he* was the one with a signed management contract in his pocket, giving him a hefty fifty-one percent of her. And it was signed by her grandfather – who happened to be her legal guardian, even though he lived in cloud-cuckoo-land. She had told the old guy it was something important to do with school – dragged in the housekeeper and a television repairman as witnesses – and he had signed away without even reading it.

Rocky had warned her – up front – that unless she got the contract signed, he wasn't doing a thing.

Well . . . once he realized who she was he'd had to protect himself, hadn't he? She was the under-age, unwanted daughter of – guess who? Silver Anderson. Sweet coincidence.

When Jack Python had walked into the beach house that night, three months ago, Rocky had thought the television king was her *boyfriend*. It soon became clear he was her uncle, and a very pissed off uncle at that. He had wasted no time in throwing Rocky out. Hey – it wasn't the first time.

Rocky had driven off into the night with no thought of ever seeing the kid again.

Two days later she called him. Out of curiosity he arranged a meet at Charmer's Market, in Venice.

When she arrived he sat her down, brought her a cup of coffee, and got the full scam.

She was Silver Anderson's kid. How could he resist?

First of all he came up with the legal papers giving him fifty-one percent of any deals. And once it was safely signed, he got hold of the guy he knew at College Records.

His contact was a major buyer, who was really only interested in scoring the best dope to supply to the recording company's biggest stars.

"I've gotta girl I wancha t'hear," Rocky told him. "She sings the ass off Madonna."

The man sighed wearily. "So does my niece, my janitor's daughter, my bookie's girlfriend, an' the checkout flim at Safeway. *This* is what I need from you." He then gave Rocky a hefty order for cocaine and Quaaludes.

Rocky filled the order, and shoved Heaven's tape at him. "She's Silver Anderson's kid," he said. "Pass this on to someone who can listen. If anythin' happens there'll be a cut for you."

A week later the man came back to him. "What does she look like?"

"A sixteen-year-old prick-tease. We're talkin' juicy."

"Get me over a picture. No snaps. Something professional."

"It's done."

Rocky had to wait for her to call him. He was bad news at the beach house – Uncle Jack had put up a few rules.

When she finally phoned he asked her about photographs.

"Antonio – you know, the famous photographer – has like these incredible shots," she said. "Only I can't get hold of them."

"Leave it t'me," Rocky said. "Just give me his address."

The next day he sauntered into Antonio's studio, displaying greased-up muscles and a crooked smile.

"Hiya, beauty," he said to the receptionist, who was all L.A. style – with punked hair, orange makeup, and sixties geometric clothes.

She stared at him. The last time she'd seen anyone who looked like Rocky was on a television programme called *Hollywood Close Up* – when they did a segment on Sylvester Stallone.

"Can I help you?" she asked.

"Baby – y'can help me all ya want. I'm yours!"

He ended up swapping a full ounce of prime coke for one twelve-by-fourteen glossy print of Heaven, which he had to admit was a dynamite photo.

"Don't you *dare* ever say where you got this," the receptionist warned. "It's appearing in *Bazaar* soon, and Antonio will kill me if he finds out I did this."

Rocky touched his lips with his index finger. "Your secret — my secret. I live by the code of silence."

Without showing the picture to Heaven, he delivered it to his contact, who must have handed it directly to the right person, for the next day Rocky got the call he'd been waiting for — "Bring her in."

So he did. And after that it all happened.

Now, here they were, months later, with a very hot record all set to hit the airwaves.

Hey — he'd had a hunch his break was on the way.

Heaven was it. And he owned fifty-one per cent of her.

*

She accepted everyone's compliments with a warm glow, hardly believing that it was finally happening for her. All she needed was the record to be a hit. And it would be. She *knew* it. Even though it wasn't exactly the record *she* would have made. For a start it wasn't a song that she'd written, and the arrangement was too upbeat — she would have preferred a slower tempo. And the title of the song — *Gonna Eatcha Tonight!* — was kind of gross. The lyrics were certainly bound to cause *mucho* controversy, which wasn't such a bad thing.

The hook went:

> I'm a Maneater . . . yes I am . . .
> Maneater . . . sure I am . . .
> Maneater . . . and baby —
> I'm gonna eatcha tonight!

Real sophisticated stuff. But she had given it her all. And it sure sounded good!

Sneaking a glance at Rocky she decided he looked pleased, and so he should, for he had half of her action, which as far as she was concerned he deserved. Without Rocky, none of this would have happened.

When Uncle Jack had walked into the aftermath of that bummed-out party, he had vented his wrath on poor Rocky — who was really innocent of any blame. After kicking him out of the house he had turned on her. "I don't want you *ever* seeing that creep again. Do you understand me?"

"Why?" she had asked defiantly.

"*Why?* Are you asking me *why?*"

She had never seen him so angry.

"I'll give you a list of reasons why." He continued in a tightly controlled voice. "One – he's a lowlife. Two – you're a child and he's almost old enough to be your father. Three – he's –" He stopped, exasperated. "What am I explaining this to you for? I trusted you and you let me down. In future you'll listen to me, and *when* I say you'll do something, you'll do it. No questions."

What a summer to look forward to! She was better off with her distracted grandfather.

As it happened, all turned out okay. After a few days Jack cooled down, and things returned to normal.

Secretly she contacted Rocky, and after the hassle of traipsing over to the Valley and getting George to sign the contract Rocky produced, it was all go.

Now she actually had a record ready to come out, and it was the most exciting day of her life!

Unfortunately there was nobody she could share it with. Only Rocky, for he was the only one who knew about it.

Soon, everyone would know. College Records planned a big party to launch her upon an unsuspecting world.

"They'd kinda like it if your mother came," Rocky had told her a couple of days ago.

"NO WAY!" she'd exploded. "Like I don't want any trading on *her* name or Jack's name. I really mean it."

"Forget it," he'd said easily. And promptly told the publicity department to drop the information into any column that would run it.

Hey – the kid was a kid – she'd soon learn. Use whatever you have.

Rocky loved the idea that he might soon become a successful personal manager. Jeez! What a kick. Just like Wes Money he could move into the big time without a backward glance. And taking a ride with the same family too. What a double kick! Wes got the old broad, and he got the kid. Not that he'd made a move on her – yet. There was plenty of time for that. Plenty.

Chapter 74

"Have you noticed the way he watches me?" Silver asked Nora edgily, as they sat in her dressing room eating a light lunch.

Nora picked an olive out of her salad and put it to one side. "They should only allow those things in drinks," she grumbled.

"Listen to me when I'm speaking to you," Silver said authoritatively. "Zachary Klinger can't take his eyes off me."

"I'd be flattered if I was you."

"You are *not* me – thank God! And stop being so flippant."

Nora crunched on a lettuce leaf. "The man had an affair with you. He's never forgotten it. That's not such a crime, is it?"

"You don't *know* Zachary. When he wants something, he *always* gets it. He was like that when I was with him before, and he wasn't as powerful then as he is now."

"So?"

"He makes me nervous."

Nora swallowed a laugh. The thought of Silver Anderson nervous about anything was too ridiculous to contemplate. Silver ate people for breakfast, and spat them out half-digested. On this film she had already seen to it that three crew members were fired because she didn't like their "attitude".

"You'll get a reputation for being difficult," Nora had warned her.

"Professional," Silver had corrected. "There *is* a difference, you know."

Silver thought everyone on the film loved her. Some of them did. Some of them didn't. Right now the crew was split into three camps – Silver's, Carlos Brent's, and Orville Gooseberger's. The poor director didn't have a chance. He just shot the script and hoped for the best.

That afternoon there was a heavy love scene scheduled between Silver and Carlos.

Nora watched her pop a piece of raw garlic in her mouth and suck on it. "What *are* you doing?" she asked, as if she didn't know.

"It's *so* good for the blood," Silver replied innocently.

"Breathe it over Zachary," Nora remarked. "*That'll* get rid of him forever."

"You're not taking this seriously," Silver scolded. "What if he decides to . . . do something to Wes?"

This time Nora *did* laugh aloud. "I'd like to see any*one* do any*thing* to Mr Money that he doesn't want done. Your husband can look after himself. Of that I'm sure." She pushed the salad away and reached for a cigarette. "And talking of family, how long is it since you've seen Heaven? It's her birthday next week, you know."

"She's not a child," Silver responded sharply. "The phone works both ways. She could have congratulated me on my marriage."

"Did you invite her?"

Abruptly Silver stood up. "Are you trying to aggravate me? Is that it? Sometimes, Nora dear, you're a real pain."

Nora drew deeply on her cigarette. The mystery of Silver and her daughter continued to confound her. Whatever the circumstances of the child's birth, flesh was flesh, and Silver *had* kept Heaven with her until she was ten. "Shall I send her a present from you?" she inquired.

"Do what you like."

Nora decided to mention it to Wes. Maybe *he* could persuade Silver to change her attitude. Now that they had been married for a few months, Nora found she was changing her opinion of him. He had certainly done wonders for his wife's career. And so far all her hard-earned cash was still intact.

Wes Money – the mystery man – could turn out to be a surprise winner after all.

*

The eruption took place the moment they clung together in romantic bliss.

"Goddammit!" screamed Carlos Brent. "The fucking bitch has got a mouthful of fucking garlic!"

"Language! Language!" chided Silver, infuriating her co-star even more.

371

Orville, hovering on the set as was his habit, leaped into the fray. "Carlos. I'm sure you're mistaken."

"Mistaken, for crissake. You can smell the fucking bitch from here to Palm Springs!"

Zachary K. Klinger stepped out of the shadows. "I hardly think that's a gentlemanly way to address Miss Anderson," he said menacingly.

"Go fuck yourself," snapped Carlos. "Who gives a shit *what* you think?"

Zachary, who was only a few years older than Carlos Brent, but at least four inches taller and fifty pounds heavier, hauled off and hit him straight on the chin.

Carlos staggered and fell.

An amazed silence took over the set.

Silver broke it with a small, triumphant laugh. "Well," she said succinctly. "I guess that takes care of shooting for today. Can we all go home, please, Orville, dear?"

*

"Where are you from?" Wes asked curiously.

"Why do you want to know?" Unity replied.

He sat on a corner of her desk in wet swim-shorts. "Is it a secret?"

"Virginia," she replied shortly.

"I've never been there," he said, sizing her up and deciding that whatever her reasons she was lying. "Do you still have family living there?"

"No family," she said shortly. "They all got it in a train wreck. I came to California with a man. He left me. End of life story."

"Pretty exciting stuff."

"Yeah. Do you think they'll buy it for the movies?" she said sarcastically. "It'd be a natural for Sissy Spacek. She plays all the losers, doesn't she?"

Regarding her warily he wondered what was going to happen to her. This time he'd been around to give her a helping hand. It wasn't always going to be that way.

Outside, in the garden, Vladimir tried to see what was going on in the pool house. Ever since Madame's husband had brought that girl home, saying she was his cousin, Vladimir had harboured a deep suspicion. *He* thought they might be lovers. *He* thought they could be planning to *murder* Madame and run off with all her money.

This was America.

Anything could happen.

Chapter 75

Jack awoke with a sudden jolt, automatically groped for his watch, and realized it was only four in the morning and he was not alone. Jade was asleep beside him. She lay on her side, her arms stretched languorously above her head, the sheet tangled around her waist.

The window shade was up, and a misty dawn filtered through the windows casting a faint morning light.

Leaning back against the headboard he watched her intently as she lay motionless. God! She was so beautiful and desirable. There was something about her that really reached out to him. And it wasn't just a sexual attraction, although the sex was incredible. Instinctively he knew Jade Johnson was destined to be much more than just a great time in bed. He had known it the first time he saw her.

Stirring in her sleep, she shifted slightly.

"Hey," he said, very softly. "Are you awake?"

"Mmmm . . ." she murmured, still fast asleep.

Gently he reached out and touched her breasts, lightly caressing her nipples.

"Mmmm . . . ." she sighed again.

Caught up in the sharp burn of desire, he felt as if he hadn't been with a woman in months, and yet, only a few hours ago, they had made love twice with hardly a pause for breath.

Christ! He, who usually had such admirable control, was ready for lift-off almost immediately.

Sliding down beside her, he let his hands roam her body, as his insistent hardness pressed up against her cool, smooth skin.

She was asleep – but she felt him.

She was asleep – but she wanted him.

How little she knew of Jack Python, and yet already he was an addiction. Her eyelids fluttered – almost awake... almost.

He teased her breasts with his tongue – slowly – surely – small strokes destined to stimulate and excite her.

What was it about this man? Arousal was immediate.

Stretching luxuriously she whispered, "Is it morning?"

"I guess if you usually have breakfast around four a.m. we can consider this morning."

"Oh, no! Why are you waking me?"

His laugh was husky contentment. "Take an educated guess, beautiful lady,"

She felt a deep flood of pleasure, and opened up to allow this intimate stranger to transport her to the edge of ecstasy.

He was filled with pure energy as they began the incredible ride.

Almost immediately she was swept away, her breathing constricted, a rush of voluptuous sensuality waiting to explode.

Usually he could wait. It was a trick, a game. Making love was an art.

And yet, with Jade, he couldn't even consider waiting. They were so in tune, and conscious of each other's every need.

He rode her with a compelling exquisite certainty. They were heading in the same direction... Breathing the same intoxicating air...

"Ohhh... God! This... is... *sooo*... fantastic..."

A sudden jolting rush.

A simultaneous shudder of satisfaction.

And then a slow, dreamy drift back to sleep, once again wrapped contentedly in each other's arms. Two soulmates who had finally found each other.

*

"Good morning." Jade ventured onto the set, fully made up with her hair done, ready to shoot the second batch of Cloud commercials. She'd had two hours' sleep, but it didn't matter. Everything about her was alive and glowing.

Shane Dickson threw her a stony look. "Feeling better?" he asked sarcastically.

"I'm sorry about rushing off last night," she said apologetically. "I couldn't help it."

Shane was a picture of jealous fury. "Was he as good as his reputation?" he asked bitterly.

She ignored the question.

"I'm surprised at *you*," he said incredulously. "Miss Commitment and Caring. According to Kellie – who was completely humiliated by the entire incident – Jack Python sticks it into anything that doesn't struggle."

She refused to be baited into a conversation about Jack. Maybe she was dreaming, but as far as she was concerned, from now on he belonged to her, and she belonged to him.

Not that they'd discussed it. In fact they hadn't discussed anything at all. Just savoured the unlimited pleasures of each other's body. In the early morning she'd had to leave while he still slept. A cab took her home to change, and then a car picked her up and delivered her to the studio, where she'd sat dreamily in the makeup room thinking about him.

She smiled. A big, satisfied smile which irritated Shane even more.

"Wipe that dumb grin off your face," he said brusquely. "Today we're shooting the dream sequence."

She didn't feel at all like working. She just felt like smiling and singing and looning about.

Was it like this with the English asshole at first?

She couldn't remember. In fact she couldn't remember one damn thing about Lord Mark Rand, except that he was married, and a liar.

*

She was gone.

He groped for her cool velvet body and found that she was no longer there.

Jack got up and investigated. She was not in the bathroom. Her clothes, left trailing across the living room floor last night, were missing. The lady – as the saying goes – had vanished.

Disappointment flooded over him. And then he found her note in the kitchen, propped against the toaster, and the moment he read it he felt great.

> Good morning. Thank you for putting a smile on my face that will probably stay there until I die! If I was with you now I'd make you toast, or maybe I'd just make you . . .

Gone to work to shoot a commercial. I'll be home after seven. If you want me to, I'll cook for you.

JADE

He was doing his show later, and the guest was an interesting and controversial senator. Last night, after dinner with Kellie, he had planned to read a lengthy bio on the man. Now he couldn't even concentrate on getting dressed, let alone anything else.

Throwing on clothes, he headed for the studio, where he immediately instructed Aretha to send six dozen yellow roses to Jade Johnson.

"Is this persuasion or thanks?" Aretha asked jauntily.

"Don't be so inquisitive."

"Any message along with the flowers?"

"Just say 'And you cook too?' Have them put a question mark *and* an exclamation point."

Aretha rolled her eyes knowingly. "My, oh my! I guess that answers the question!"

"Oh, and have somebody call that French actress we had on – you know who I mean."

"Big bazoombas and a frog in her throat?"

"You got it. In fact, do me a favour and call her yourself. Lie a lot on my behalf. Tell her I can't make dinner tonight."

Aldrich hurried into the office looking harried, his usual expression on the day of a show. "Have you read all the material?" he asked anxiously.

"Honey," sighed Aretha, "the only thing *this* man read last night was the stars in his lady's eyes!"

*

"It's not going to work," Shane said shortly. "Can't you at least try?"

"I *am* trying," Jade replied patiently. He had been on her case all day.

"You're supposed to look ethereal and dreamy. Why are you grinning like a fucking Cheshire Cat?"

They both knew only too well why she was grinning, and it wasn't helping matters.

"Imagine something serious," he said sternly. "Like getting AIDS or the clap. That's what happens when you sleep with a person who fucks like he's on an assembly line."

The smile disappeared from her face. "That's an uncalled-for, *dumb* remark."

"Think about it," he repeated vehemently. "I'm only telling you what everybody in this town already knows."

"No. *You* think about *this*," she said furiously. "*I'm* the star of this commercial. *You're* the director. You can be replaced – *I* can't."

She hadn't planned on being quite so forthright, but he'd been asking for it all day.

After her outburst, they finally got some work done, and she was able to get out of there just after six. Instructing her driver to stop at the Irvine Ranch Market in the Beverly Center, she bought thin slices of veal, potatoes and vegetables, butter pecan ice cream, a rich chocolate cake, and two bottles of wine.

Gathering an armful of fresh flowers, she rushed home, where she was surprised by an apartment full of glorious yellow roses, placed in vases by her cleaning lady – and Jack's voice on her answering machine. Listening to his message three times, she glowed with delight.

How was it possible to be *this* crazy *this* fast?

She didn't know and she didn't care.

I'm doing the show today, said his voice on the machine. *And after that I can't think of anything I'd like more than you cooking for me. A pause. Yes, as a matter of fact I can. Let's forget about food. I'll see you later.*

He had a great voice. A great everything else.

She put Springsteen on the stereo, and without a trace of tiredness began to unpack the groceries.

Chapter 76

"I gotta fly to Arizona," Howard announced disgustedly.

"Why?" Poppy demanded.

"Because Whitney Valentine is trying out for cunt of the year."

Poppy pursed her lips. "You know I don't like that word, Howard."

"Sometimes there's just no substitute."

"Try and find one," she said sternly.

"Back off, Poppy. I'm not in the mood for your 'holier than thou' number."

One thing about Poppy, she knew exactly how far she could go, and when he told her to back off she did so at once.

"I've had a day that was pure murder from beginning to end," he grumbled, and proceeded to tell her about the Silver/Carlos/Zachary incident on the set.

Her eyes widened. "Zachary Klinger actually *hit* Carlos Brent?"

"Punched him right out."

"What's going to happen?"

"Guess who spent the afternoon sorting it out?"

"You, of course."

"Right on. Silver started it all. Another cunt."

"Howard!"

He held up a restraining hand. "Okay, okay, no more cunts."

"Is everyone speaking?"

"Barely. Carlos is threatening to walk – and he can do it – you know the kind of temper *he* has. The good thing is that he needs us more than we need him. What other studio is gonna give a burnt-out bum like him the lead in a twenty-million-dollar movie?"

"Oh, Howard," Poppy exclaimed, little-girl voice in full swing. "You're so clever!"

Poppy knew how to trowel on the flattery just when it was needed.

"Anyway," he continued, "we had to stop shooting for the rest of the day, and hopefully, by tomorrow, all will be calm."

"Shouldn't you be here to make sure?"

"You bet your ass I should. But we've got bigger problems on *The Murder*. If I don't get down there and get Whitney's ass back in gear, *that* production's gonna have to stop. She's only playing a cameo role, but all her stuff takes place on the location shoot in Arizona."

"And what's she doing?"

"Pretending to be sick, which is bull. She's pissed off because Mannon and Clarissa are steamin' up the screen."

"Isn't Chuck with her?"

"He was. And yesterday they had another fight and he took off. That's when the – uh – that's when she supposedly got sick and took to her bed."

"It's so unfair," Poppy wailed. "All these problems, and only *you* to solve them."

"I'll do it," he said bravely, thinking this might be the perfect opportunity to fling a fast fuck into Whitney. God knows, he'd waited long enough.

"Shall I pack you an overnight bag?" Poppy asked, the concerned wife.

"You'd better. I shouldn't be gone for more than twenty-four hours."

He was on the company plane shortly afterwards.

Poppy, left to her own devices, called Carmel to find out Orville's version of the story. Then she reported the entire event to Ida, who already knew, and couldn't have cared less anyway.

"Don't forget my lunch tomorrow for Jade Johnson," she reminded everyone. "The Bistro Garden, at twelve-thirty."

She tried to decide whether to call Melanie-Shanna or not. *No*, she thought. Very soon Melanie-Shanna could be the *ex* Mrs Mannon Cable, and there was nothing more boring than having to pretend to be friends with an ex-wife. Once the husband was no longer around, what was the point?

On the other hand, shouldn't someone *tell* Melanie-Shanna about Mannon and Clarissa? After all, it was only fair that she should know. If Howard was dropping his pants elsewhere,

Poppy would most *certainly* want to be alerted. *And* the poor girl was about to give birth any minute, so maybe Mannon wouldn't dump her, and she would remain Mrs Cable.

Poppy sighed. Ah, decisions, decisions. Her manicured hand reached for the phone.

*

Dirk Price, the director/writer of *The Murder*, met Howard at the airport in Arizona. He was a long-haired, twenty-eight-year-old graduate of UCLA Film School, and had made two other movies, both of them teen-oriented (naked virgins, horny boys and the trashing of public property) and both of them enormous money-makers. This was his first venture into grown-up territory, and the dailies – flown to Howard in Hollywood every day – were quite impressive. Especially Mannon's performance: he was really marvellous, surprising everyone. Clarissa, of course, was incandescent as usual. And Whitney looked sensational and acted like she'd just got out of drama school.

"I want to replace her," were the first words out of Dirk's mouth. "She's ruining my film."

"*Our* film," Howard corrected. "And we have a contract to honour."

"She's not honouring *her* part of it," Dirk said heatedly. "I had to shoot around her all day, and it's going to put us over budget."

"That's why I'm here. I'll talk to her."

"Why can't we just pay her off?" Dirk demanded. His long hair was tied back in a ponytail, and he wore one diamond stud earring.

"Because," Howard replied patiently, feeling about eighty-five years old, "we can't. It's as simple as that."

"Fuck!" snapped Dirk.

Howard patted his toupee to make sure all was in place. Dirk had a receding hairline. What good was all that hair at the back going to do him when there was nothing left up front?

They had booked him a room in the same hotel as Whitney, and he showered and changed clothes before going to visit her.

The door of her suite was opened by her stand-in, who also doubled as her secretary. "Mr Soloman," the woman said. "Thank goodness you're here. Whitney has been expecting you."

She waited, sitting cross-legged in the middle of her bed. She wore a pale pink tracksuit, pastel running shoes, and a petulant expression. Her trademark hair was tamed in two schoolgirlish braids, and her face was devoid of makeup, although with her healthy tan that didn't matter.

He felt a message from Father Christmas, and hoped that it wasn't obvious in the light grey pants he had slipped on with a casual sweater.

"Howard!" she wailed. "They're trying to crucify me!"

"Who?" he asked patiently, sitting on the edge of the bed.

"All of them!" Her aquamarine eyes filled with true tears.

Ah . . . if she could only act *on* the screen like she could *off* it.

"Tell me everything, baby," he soothed.

Lower lip quivering, she came out with a litany of complaints. The director didn't want her; Clarissa was a bitch; the crew weren't friendly; Mannon was a bastard; everyone was ganging up against her.

"After all, Howard," she finished off indignantly, "I accepted a cameo role in this movie, when I *should* have been playing the lead."

"I know," he agreed sympathetically. "And you won't regret it. This role will open up all the doors you ever wanted. You're obliterating Clarissa in the dailies. It's *your* film."

She brightened considerably. "Really?"

"Would I lie?"

"You know I trust you."

Trust me with this, he wanted to say, as his hard-on chafed uncomfortably in place.

"Listen, baby," he said. "Don't be your own worst enemy. Get your fanny back on the set tomorrow – *pronto!* You're makin' Clarissa a very happy woman by not showing up for work. She figures *this* way she'll be able to squeeze you out." He paused, getting ready to nail a point. "And if you don't . . . jeez, Whit, the lawyers are gonna move into action, an' there'll be nothing I can do. I'd hate to see you ruin your career with one dumb move."

She stared at him thoughtfully, mouth downturned and expression intent.

And then – like the sun appearing from behind a cloud – she smiled. Whitney Valentine had the most dazzling smile in the world. A lot of teeth and very patriotic.

"You're damn right, Howard. And I love you for being so honest." Crawling across the bed she kissed him.

The kiss was aimed at his cheek, only he managed to move

quickly enough for it to land on his mouth. Grabbing her in a bear hug, he gave her the famous Howard Soloman smackerooney. In high school his kisses were the stuff legends were made of.

She gave a little struggle – not too hard – and then he had her! She was responding. And there it was, a long, passionate, real soul kiss.

Pushing him away at last she sighed, "Oh, Howard, we shouldn't be doing this, you're married."

"In name only," he said, faster than the speed of sound. "Since we had Roselight, Poppy can't have sex. The doctors say it's psychological. We're working on it. Meanwhile I'm still a man, Whitney. And a lonely one."

"Surely not lonely? You have so many opportunities . . ." She trailed off.

"I've thought about this moment for years," he said excitedly. "You, me . . . Nobody else around . . ."

She didn't believe his story about Poppy for a minute; however, an affair with Howard would certainly secure her position on the set, *and* infuriate Mannon – who might not care about her anymore, but would no doubt be affected if she and another of his ex-best friends got together.

"Later," she promised in a low whisper. "After dinner. Just you . . . and me . . ."

Chapter 77

"Get that *horrible* dog away from me," Silver screamed. "For God's sake, Wes, it's filthy!"

"He's not," he argued, ruffling Mutt's fur.

"And I suppose you're going to tell me it doesn't have fleas either?"

"Naw. Except this one!" He plucked an imaginary insect from Mutt's shaggy coat and waved it at her.

She shrieked hysterically, while he doubled up laughing. "Only joking," he confessed.

Glaring at him she hissed, "You stupid bastard. I don't know *how* I ended up marrying someone with the mentality of a ten-year-old."

"Easy. You married me for my money."

"Oh, so *that's* what it was."

"And my charm."

"Why didn't *I* think of that?"

"And my big dick."

"I've seen bigger," she sniffed.

"Yeah?"

"Absolutely."

"Well, cop a look at *this*, lady."

Soon they were playing games on her king-size bed, while Mutt raced excitedly up and down the carpet, barking.

"Get . . . rid . . . of . . . it," she warned insistently.

"Now?"

"*Right* now."

"Are you sure you want me to stop?"

"*Right now, Wes.* I am *not* joking."

With a grunt of resignation he rolled off the bed, grabbed the dog by the scruff of its neck, and gently shoved it out of the room.

"I *never* want to see that animal in here again," she said, watching him intently as he walked back towards the bed. She never tired of checking out his body. He was so masculine. His strength impressed her, and his complete lack of ego when it came to his looks. An actor would kill to get near a mirror first. Wes couldn't care less. He had a natural animal sexuality, and she loved it, and he knew it, which made them both very happy.

So he was younger than her. She really didn't give a damn. It was the ridiculous newspapers and gossip columns who made it into some sort of big deal. She was hardly snatching him from the cradle. Carlos Brent was sixty something, and his current girlfriend, Dee Dee Dionne, was in her early thirties. There was at least thirty years between them and nobody said a word.

Wes climbed into bed and clicked the television on with the remote control.

Silver took it from him and switched it off. "We were in the middle of something," she reminded.

He looked surprised. "We were?"

"Yes."

"Jeez .. I got me a mother of a headache . . ."

She threw a magazine at him. "Don't start with me."

Grinning, he said, "I thought that's exactly what you wanted."

*

Downstairs, Vladimir prepared dinner, while Unity, out in the pool house office, fielded phone calls. They were coming in fast and strong: Orville Gooseberger to speak to Wes; Zachary Klinger for Silver; three calls from Zeppo White for Wes; Poppy Soloman for Silver; Nora for either Wes or Silver.

However urgent any of them said it was, Unity had strict instructions never to disturb the happy couple while they were upstairs in the bedroom. Dutifully she took messages, and promised everyone their calls would be returned in due course.

At six o'clock she decided she was finished for the day, and turned on the answering machine. This job was no big deal. Sure, she was grateful to Wes for helping at a time when she needed it — but the loneliness of living in the huge mansion with nobody to talk to was beginning to get to her. Queen Silver and ever-faithful Wes. Who needed it?

She wandered into the kitchen, where Vladimir ignored her as usual. He had hardly spoken more than three full sentences to her since her arrival.

"What are you making?" she asked.

"Chinese chicken salad," he replied resentfully. He hated having Unity around all the time, certain that she spied on him, making it difficult for him to smuggle in his transient lovers. Even in his own apartment above the garage he had no privacy. She had knocked on his door the other day for some inane reason. "It's my time off," he had shouted through the closed door. "Vill you *never* please disturb me here again."

The Italian waiter he was servicing at that particular moment became paranoid that it was his wife searching for him, and was unable to get it up. Vladimir was livid.

"Can I taste it?" Unity asked. "It looks delicious."

"There's not enough," Vladimir replied waspishly. "The cold spaghetti in the fridge is for you."

Mutt came bouncing into the kitchen, wagging his stubby tail.

She bent to fuss the little dog.

384

"No animals in the kitchen vhile I'm preparing food," snapped Vladimir.

"I wish you could be halfway polite," she snapped back, surprising both of them. Up until now she had acted like a timid mouse and not complained about anything.

He recovered at once. "Vat vill you do? Report me to your . . . *cousin*?" he sneered.

Her face reddened. "I'm not a spy," she retorted hotly.

He was glad to hear *that*. But he made no comment, continuing to cut and slice and chop.

"Listen to me," she said sharply. "The truth is I hardly know my cousin. He's just helping me out because I was in trouble."

Finally she had Vladimir's interest. "Vat kind of trouble?" he asked curiously. "Vere you pregnant?"

"No." She shook her head. "Nothing like that. It was . . . drugs."

Vladimir perked up even more. Laying his work knife aside, he put a sympathetic arm around her shoulders. "Vhy don't you tell me all about it?"

*

Wes left Silver to bathe and dress, and loped downstairs. He couldn't smell anything cooking, which was a disappointment. Vladimir, in spite of his numerous faults, was at least a knockout cook – the one reason Wes hadn't dismissed him the moment he moved in.

Flinging open the door to the kitchen he was startled to find Unity and the gay Russian sitting at a table engaged in intimate conversation. He was startled. Up until now the two of them had managed to stay out of each other's way, which suited him just fine. He didn't want Unity revealing anything – especially about his past.

"What's going on? Where's dinner?" he asked.

Vladimir was on his feet in a second. "Is Madame ready to eat?" he inquired solicitously.

"Yeah, she's ready," Wes replied. "What is it?"

"Chinese chicken salad," Vladimir replied, scurrying back to his chopping board.

"Chinese chicken *what*?"

"Salad."

"You mean it isn't hot?"

"No."

"Shit!"

"Madame requested it personally. She mentioned that in her opinion you could lose a pound or two." Vladimir knew he had scored a point and enjoyed Wes's discomfort.

"Did she?" Wes stalked from the kitchen, followed by Unity, who relayed his messages to him. "Put them on my desk in the study," he said shortly. "I'll return the calls after dinner."

"Mr White said it was urgent. So did Mr Gooseberger."

"Okay, okay."

Settling himself in the study he placed a call to Orville. The producer had never telephoned him before, and he was curious to know what it was about.

"Did Silver tell you what she did today?" shouted Orville.

"No," Wes replied.

"You mean you don't know?"

"Spit it out, Orville. I never liked *Twenty Questions*."

"We had to close the set down this afternoon. Silver had a chunk of garlic hidden in her mouth when she kissed Carlos. He went berserk and insulted her, and Zachary came to her defence. Carlos then insulted *him*, and Zachary knocked Carlos out."

Wes did not believe what he was hearing. All this had taken place and she hadn't mentioned a word.

"Go on," he said flatly.

"Well," Orville continued, "between Zeppo, me and Howard Soloman, I think we got everyone calmed down. However, tomorrow is another day, and I don't trust your wife. For some reason she's got a knife at Carlos's throat. I think she'd like him to walk off the picture. The gossip on the set is she thinks he's too old for the part, and wants a younger co-star."

"Yeah?"

"I don't have to explain to *you* what it would mean to this production if Carlos Brent walks. You're a businessman, you understand these things."

"I sure do."

"So .. Howard, Zeppo and I thought it might be a good idea for you to accompany her to the set tomorrow and whenever you can, to keep an eye on things. If you'll excuse my French — when you've got a difficult woman on your hands, the one who controls her is the one who's *fucking* her. In my experience it always works."

Wes laughed without humour. "Yeah. I get your point. I'll try an' be there."

386

Orville thanked him effusively and hung up – whereupon Wes had an almost identical conversation with Zeppo White, who was slightly cruder than the old producer, but made exactly the same point.

By the time he was finished with the two of them, he was furious. Why hadn't she told him? What was he? The houseboy? The lackey to screw in the afternoon when she had nothing better to do? Didn't she have any respect for him?

Striding angrily into the hall, he picked up the keys of the Rolls and yelled, "Vladimir!"

The flaxen-haired Russian appeared at the door of the kitchen.

"Tell *Madame* that I *will not* be home for the Chinese chicken salad. And tell her that I won't be back until later – *much* later. If at all."

With that he stalked out of the house.

Chapter 78

" 'Ellooo, Jacques." The French actress with the inviting eyes and smoky voice was in the Green Room when he put his head around the door a few minutes before showtime. Tantalizingly she undulated across the room, kissing him on both cheeks with Gallic style, drenching him in a powerful musk scent. She was dressed all in scarlet.

Senator Peter Richmond, his guest for the evening, jumped up and followed her over. "Jack." His handshake was hearty. "Good to see you again. I'm looking forward to crossing swords with you tonight. Only be gentle – it's my first time – with you, that is," he added with a twinkle.

Searching desperately for Aretha, Jack tried to figure out what was going on. Signals were crossed somewhere along the line. Aretha was supposed to have cancelled his date with Danielle

387

Vadeeme, and unless she was here to be with the very married Senator Richmond he was in trouble.

He gave them both the benefit of a friendly smile. "It's my pleasure to have you here, Senator."

"I flew in specially." The Senator winked. "And Miss Vadeeme here has invited me to join you both for dinner. I keep on telling her the last thing you want is me along, but she absolutely insists. At least I'll have something to look forward to while I endure a full hour's torture!"

"With time out for commercials," Jack said, automatic charm on full pilot, thinking how he would strangle Aretha when he found her, although murder was probably too gentle a punishment.

Meanwhile, what was he supposed to do about Jade? He could hardly ask her along. And yet all he wanted was to be with her.

"Five minutes, Mr Python," yelled Genie, the assistant floor manager.

Senator Richmond's researcher hurried to his side.

Danielle leaned close to Jack. "Later, chéri," she whispered seductively. "We get reeed of Meester Senator, an then we make the – how you say – beeeauteefool looove."

He had no desire to make anything again, unless it was with Jade. Christ! How did he ever get caught in this trap?

"Where's Aretha?" he asked Genie, as he followed her to the studio ready to confront his expectant audience.

"In the booth, I guess," she replied.

"Goddammit!"

"Something wrong?"

"Get a message to Aretha and tell her to call Jade Johnson. Have her say I can't make it, I'm going to be held up at the studio, and I'll contact her later. I want that taken care of at once."

"Yes sir!"

*

Jade changed into jeans and a sweater. Then she changed the sweater three times. Then she changed the jeans for tracksuit pants, hated the way they bagged, and changed back into jeans.

First, she had scrubbed off her studio makeup, applying a much more subtle look, and had washed her hair, leaving it to dry naturally – framing her face with a wild tumble of shaggy curls.

High on pure energy, she went to work in the kitchen, marinating the veal in lemon, slicing potatoes, chopping parsley, stringing *mange-tout*.

Next she soaked strawberries in Grand Marnier, and whipped sour cream with brown sugar.

Not bothering to set the table, she laid place-mats on the coffee table in front of the television, just in case he felt like watching *Hill Street Blues*. And if he didn't, she put Sade on the stereo.

After opening a bottle of cold white wine, she switched on the television, just in time for the beginning of his show. *Face to Face with Python*.

Happily she settled down to watch.

*

The Senator was affable and slippery, a true politician who answered all questions with bland good nature, at the same time getting in every point he wished to make.

Jack found him an interesting study. How could one man talk such a crock, and *still* manage to come across as disarmingly nice? Senator Richmond succeeded. And for once Jack let him get away with it — his mind elsewhere.

"That was one prize of a sluggish hour!" a frustrated Aldrich complained after the event. "You gave him the chair. For Christ's sake, Jack, it was the Peter Richmond show."

"Where's Aretha?" Jack asked tightly, ignoring the criticism.

"I said —"

"I *heard* what you said. I'm not in the mood to discuss it."

He found Aretha in the office. When she saw him coming she gestured helplessly. "I know, I know. I'm sorry. What can I tell you?"

"You can tell me what the fuck happened."

"I *did* telephone Danielle earlier. She wasn't in, so I spoke to some foreign person who seemed to understand the message I left."

"Which was?"

"That you had to cancel dinner. I even spelled your name, just to make sure."

Shaking his head he paced around the office. "Now not only do I have to take *her* to dinner, I'm stuck with the goddamn Senator too. You're incompetent, you know that?" He snatched a cigarette from her desk. "What did Jade say?"

"Uh . . . Jade," she said blankly.

"Don't tell me you screwed that up, too?"

Aretha looked vague. "Was I supposed to do something?"

"Jesus Christ!" Now he was really angry. "Haven't you phoned her yet?"

Frowning, she said, "Stop screaming at me please."

Taking a deep breath he said patiently, "I told Genie to pass you a message in the control booth to call Jade and tell her I can't make it tonight. Did you do that?"

"Oh yeah, yeah."

"How did she sound?"

"Calm."

He gave a resigned sigh. "Book me a table for three at Chasen's."

"You got it."

As soon as he walked out of the room she grabbed her phone book. Genie had passed on no such message, and Aretha knew that as soon as Jack heard the news he would fire the girl. Genie was new and enthusiastic, and Aretha didn't want to see that happen.

Covering up for her, she made the call. It was nearly nine-thirty.

*

Putting down the phone, Jade couldn't help feeling a wave of disappointment. Why hadn't he called himself? Why had he waited until nearly nine-thirty to have someone phone and cancel for him?

"Jack has to have dinner with the Senator," his assistant had explained.

If that was so, why hadn't he asked her to accompany them?

Maybe she was expecting too much. After all, she knew her own feelings, but to Jack Python perhaps she *was* just another one-night stand.

Anger flushed her face. He had a reputation, Shane had warned her – why hadn't she listened? The roses were probably standard practice. And she had acted like a gullible idiot.

Well, there was no way she was going to sit around and cry. Corey had called yesterday and invited her to a private party for Petrii, the New York dress designer.

Antonio had also left a message on her machine insisting she be there. And that's exactly what she intended to do.

*

It didn't take a genius to figure out that the very married Senator had eyes for the provocative French actress. With a little creative match-making, Jack decided he could be out of Chasen's in an hour, and if Jade still wanted to see him . . .

He thought about her as Danielle droned on in her monotonous smoky voice, and the Senator's eyes feasted hungrily on her cleavage. There was something wonderfully different about Jade. Beautiful and exciting as she was, those attributes were not the main attraction. She was a free spirit. He'd sensed it the first time he saw her, and now that they'd embarked on a relationship he wanted to get to know her properly. In fact, he couldn't wait . . .

Glancing impatiently at his watch, he decided he could slide off and phone her without being missed. "Excuse me," he said politely.

As if they'd notice.

*

The doorman summoned a cab, and she was on her way, having quickly changed into a short black leather dress worn with masses of silver jewellery.

"Chasen's," she told the Iranian driver, who took off as if he was being pursued by half the L.A.P.D.

In the cab she lit a cigarette, had one drag, then stubbed it out. Opening up her purse she took out her compact and carefully checked her makeup. She noted – with a buzz of annoyance – that she had that look about her. The glow of really great love-making. Ah . . . if only someone could bottle it, they'd make the fortune of all time.

God *damn* Jack Python. Why had he walked into her life?

The cab driver began to talk, while executing his death-defying dash along Wilshire. "Where you from, lady?"

"New York," she muttered, not wishing to engage one second of his concentration.

"I thought so. You look New York. I got two brothers live there. One – he marry this beautiful girl. The other, he . . ."

She stopped listening, wishing that she'd taken her car instead of subjecting herself to the driver's family history.

*

There was no answer in Jade's apartment. Her machine wasn't on, so he couldn't even leave a message.

She's probably gone out, he thought. After all, he couldn't expect her to just sit around waiting for his call. Now, if he

391

could only get rid of the Senator and Danielle at a reasonable hour, he might drop by her apartment and wait for her.

The thought cheered him. He wasn't prepared to be patient.

As soon as he returned to the table, Senator Richmond jumped up. "I have an early appointment tomorrow morning," he said, by way of explanation.

"You do?"

"Seven-thirty."

Danielle extended her hand. "*Au revoir*, Senator."

"Goodnight, Miss . . . uh . . . Vadeeme. It was a real pleasure."

"*My* pleeeasurrre, Senator."

Jack looked from one to the other. What was going on here? He had thought they were all set.

The Senator made a fast exit, leaving him stuck with Danielle.

Snaking her hand along the back of his neck she moved closer. "He want me to sleep with heem," she whispered huskily. "I promise to veesit hees hotel later." With a mysterious smile she added, "What I do, Jacques?"

Without a doubt she expected him to tell her no way. And normally he would have done so, but now things were different, and all he desired was to get rid of her.

"Hey . . . Danielle," he said sensibly. "A promise is a promise."

Disbelief crossed her face. Danielle Vadeeme was used to men getting down on their knees. "You sonofabeetch!" she exclaimed in surprise.

"I may be a sonofabitch, but I'm a truthful one," he said, lightening his words with a killer smile.

Staring at him knowingly she said, "What happen, Jacques? You fall for someone?"

Nodding, he was almost embarrassed to admit such a weakness.

With a Gallic shrug she said, "Then why you weeth me, *chéri*?"

"Circumstances."

"Ah, Jacques. You *sooo Américain*." And she patted him on the hand matter-of-factly. "We go. I veesit the Senator. And you . . ." Another shrug.

Miss Vadeeme was a very understanding lady.

*

Naturally the cab driver did not have change for the fifty Jade offered him. It just wasn't her night.

"I'll get it broken," she said irritably, walking into Chasen's and stopping at the front desk for change.

The driver followed, obviously thinking she was going to vanish out the back. He was still babbling on about thieves and robbers and the dangers of carrying more than twenty dollars in change.

She broke the fifty and gave him his money, whereupon he left with a grunt.

Turning to go in, she was stopped by a hand on her arm. "Jade?" said an unfamiliar voice.

She turned and looked into the eyes of a complete stranger.

Seeing she didn't recognize him, he introduced himself. "Hi, I'm Penn Sullivan. We met with Beverly D'Amo a few months ago at Mortons. I was with Frances Cavendish – the casting agent. It was a business dinner."

Looking faintly amused she said, "It was?" Then she remembered him. Beverly had said he was an actor. "I hope it did you some good," she added, also remembering the terse exchange between him and the elderly casting woman in the parking lot.

Brushing his hand through a wiry mass of hair he said, "I'm working. It beats waiting tables – which I did for *three* years in this town."

He couldn't be more than early-twenties, and he was undeniably attractive.

"I'm going to the Petrii party. Are you having dinner here?" he asked.

"I'm here for the Petrii party too," she said.

"Alone?" he asked, definitely coming on.

*

Jack helped Danielle from the table. As Howard would put it – the old French broad had come up trumps. Maybe as a favour he would introduce her to Howard, get him to put her in one of his films. In France she was a huge star, but in America she had yet to break through in a meaningful way. After all, she was behaving like a lady, and he admired her style.

Putting a friendly arm around her shoulders, he began to walk her towards the entrance.

*

Just as Jade was about to repel Penn Sullivan's very obvious

393

come-on, Jack and Danielle strolled into the vestibule of the restaurant. They seemed entranced with each other. His arm was around the French actress's bare shoulders, and she was gazing up at him lovingly. As they appeared, she murmured "*Merci, chéri*," and stood on tip-toe to kiss him on the cheek.

Jade was momentarily stunned. What a bastard! She could hardly believe her own eyes!

Hardly taking a beat, she recovered her composure and turned to Penn. "Let's go party," she said boldly, attaching herself to his arm.

"Great!" he replied, happily surprised.

At which point Jack spotted her. "Hey —" he began. "What are *you* doing here? I was just —"

She smiled, but her eyes were cold steel. "Jack Python," she said, keeping her tone light. "How *nice* to see you. Have you met my good friend Penn Sullivan?"

He had no desire to meet the handsome, young actor. And what the fuck was she doing with him anyway?

Christ! It didn't take Jade Johnson long to get over a broken date — and he had thought she was different.

Chapter 79

It was an extraordinarily balmy night. Howard could feel the sweat forming under his hairpiece before he even left the hotel. He was trying out a new glue and it worked really well, only perspiration wrecked it, and he couldn't afford any mishaps on this night of nights.

After visiting Whitney, he had taken a trip to the location, where Mannon and Clarissa were sequestered in her motor home. It took ten minutes of knocking loudly on the door before it was opened.

Wonderful! Howard thought. Especially during the times they might be needed on the set immediately.

"We call them twenty minutes early," Dirk had confided. "That way we get them there on time."

Mannon emerged eventually, rumpled and smiling. "Howard! This is a surprise. What are you doing here?"

"Trying to see that we get a film made," Howard said grimly. "Remember? That's why we're *all* here."

Grinning, Mannon said, "Am I giving a performance or *what*?"

"Yup," Howard agreed. "The dailies are something."

"Something? Is that all you have to say? Clarissa thinks if we keep up this energy, and the studio does its job when it comes to nomination time – well, she reckons we're *both* on for the ride."

"Nobody would like that better than me. I'd also like to see Whitney happy."

The sound of her name wiped the smile from Mannon's face. "I hate to be the one to say this – but that lady is strictly amateur night. She shouldn't be in this film. We need a real actress in the role."

From 'love of his life' she had gone to 'that lady'. Clarissa must have some heavy influence.

"The thing is," Howard said patiently, "she is in the film. We have a contract. And it would be nice if she got a little support."

"Fire her," Mannon said callously. "I don't care."

Howard – who never gave much thought to anyone's morals, including his own – was shocked. "This is *Whitney* we're talkin' about."

"I know."

"Well, goddammit, two months ago you would've kissed my ass to get her back. Now you want her thrown off the picture?"

"Listen, Howard," Mannon lowered his voice to a confidential whisper. "Clarissa knows what she's talking about, and she says Whitney is dragging the movie down. Dirk agrees. And the crew, everyone."

"So you'd like me to fire her?" Howard asked tightly.

"Right."

"Fuck you. Your contract gives you plenty of power, but you and Clarissa are not runnin' the friggin' studio – an' until you are, *I* decide who gets the axe. And *I* still have some loyalty to old friends."

Clarissa appeared at the door beside Mannon. "Howard," she greeted him curtly.

"Clarissa," he replied, just as curt.

"We only want what's good for the film."

He would never understand her success. What was it that took place between her and a camera?

"I know that," he said. "And I want *you* to know *this*. Whitney stays. I'm flying in a special acting coach for her. She'll improve. She'll be okay."

"If you say so," Clarissa said stiffly.

It occurred to Howard that neither one of them was about to invite him inside. Actors! Actresses! Stars! Phoney, insecure assholes who woke up one morning and got lucky. What made them think they were all so special?

"You're both doing a sensational job," he said, with insincere friendliness. "Keep it up, an' try to go easy on the kid."

"Hardly a kid," murmured Clarissa bitchily.

"Yeah . . . well . . ." He stared at his good friend Mannon, and went for the jugular. "Poppy's seen Melanie a few times. She says she looks healthy enough for someone who's about to drop a baby any second. Do you want me to relay a message?"

Mannon provided a quick flash of guilt. "No," he said. "I speak to her all the time."

Howard did not approve of the way Mannon was treating his pregnant wife. Shrugging, he said, "Gotta go kick ass. See ya."

What he actually had to do was arrange for an acting coach to be flown in at once. And then break the news to Whitney.

She took it better than he expected, glad of the support.

The only acting coach the studio had been able to arrange at such short notice was Joy Byron, an eccentric old Englishwoman who presided over Joy Byron's Method Acting School in Hollywood. Her main claim to fame was that she had discovered Buddy Hudson – currently *the* hot new star. Joy was thrilled to be asked, and arrived on the next plane.

Now Howard had to take them both to dinner, plus Whitney's secretary – who apparently accompanied her everywhere on location. *And* her publicist, Norman Gooseberger, who had also flown in that day.

Howard wasn't worried about dinner. Getting through that would be a breeze. It was *after* he kept on thinking about. Finally, he and Whitney would be alone together. She, so beautiful and vibrant. He, so . . . what?

He was short.

Nearly bald.

He had a paunch.

And more pubic hair than she had probably ever seen in her entire life.

He snorted too much cocaine before leaving the hotel, and gulped a couple of Valium. What a combination! The coke to bring him up, and the Valium to calm him down.

Biting his nails, he allowed a limo to deliver him to his fate.

*

Howard's snide comments about "loyalty" and "old friends" really pissed Mannon off. Whitney was an actress. She had a job to do, and if she couldn't deliver, then she *should* be out. Clarissa had explained that to him. In fact, Clarissa had explained a lot of things to him – especially about acting, and that's why he was giving such a great performance.

For over fifteen years he had played movie star. Now, with Clarissa's help, maybe he'd get a little critical acceptance as a damn good actor. And why should he feel guilty about trying to bump Whitney from the film when she deserved it? Screw Howard and his smartass remarks.

The trouble with Howard was they had known each other too long, and instead of Howard treating him with the deference a star of his stature deserved, he talked to him as if they were equals.

"You don't have to be nice to him," Clarissa pointed out. "He's nothing more than a coked-out buffoon. Zachary Klinger's messenger."

"You think he's on something?"

"Don't be naive. The whole town knows."

Mannon digested this information in silence. Back in the sixties, when he had shared an appartment with Howard and Jack, they had all experimented with various drugs. Jack and he got into smoking grass for a while. Howard was the straight one. He tried everything once, and never came back for seconds. "Addles the brain," he had said. Now *this* little revelation.

"Cocaine?" Mannon asked.

"Exactly."

"Jesus!"

He wondered if Jack knew, or even cared. Lately the three of them saw less and less of each other. Really they had nothing in common anymore.

He hated knowing Clarissa had been with Jack. For almost a year, too. It took all his control to stop himself from asking what his good friend was like in bed, and if he was better.

Clarissa would never say. She was secretive about past loves. He had to curb a strong desire to kill all of them. Clarissa was an unusual woman. He had never been with anyone remotely like her.

If someone had said to him before the start of the movie that he was going to fall in love with Clarissa Browning, he would have told them they were stark, raving crazy.

It had all happened so fast. He had knocked on the door of her hotel suite the first night they arrived on location, just to say hello and be friendly. Four hours later he was still there, discussing script changes, characterizations, and the film in general.

"We fall in love in this movie," she had said. "We make love."

"We sure do!" he had joked in his usual light-hearted way.

"When we interact on screen it has to be real," Clarissa continued seriously. "We have to generate *excitement* and *passion* and *longing*."

"Just try me, baby!"

"Do you know what I believe in, Mannon?" she had asked him gravely.

"What?"

"That we should work our roles through *before* we get in front of the camera."

"Really?"

She'd stared at him intensely. "Let's make love."

He had no idea this was a line she used with all her co-stars, and he fell for it immediately, immensely flattered such a serious actress would want to go to bed with him.

Lying back, he had enjoyed every moment of her fiery passion. After that they were an inseparable team.

The newspapers got wind of it — blind column items appeared daily. He knew he had to tell Melanie-Shanna, but as usual he kept on putting it off. She was expecting their baby any day, and he was only too aware what an uncaring louse he would look if he walked out on her now. His timing was off. "Wait six months," his lawyers had told him.

Clarissa never mentioned his wife. She behaved as if he didn't have one. He managed to phone Melanie-Shanna every few days. She sounded fine, and in spite of his passionate affair with Clarissa he was looking forward to becoming a father for the first time.

Mannon Cable wanted it all. And he saw no good reason why he couldn't have it.

*

The dinner was a bore. Howard never had been good at playing Entourage. For that's what the people around Whitney were. Norman, an adoring fan; her secretary, a willing slave; Joy Byron, a wacky, off-centre flatterer. Every one of them spent the entire evening buttering Whitney up, while Howard fidgeted uncomfortably.

"Let's get *outta* here," he muttered over coffee. "Say goodbye to the go-fers, an' let's split."

Whitney yawned. "I'm *sooo* tired," she announced.

"You need plenty of sleep when you're working," Joy Byron said crisply. "Peace, calm, work, and rest."

"Yes, Whitney," Norman joined in quickly. "We're being selfish, keeping you up. Why don't I take you back to your hotel?"

"*I'll* take her," said the secretary possessively.

"Perhaps you would like to go through a scene or two before sleeping?" Joy suggested.

Howard managed to kick Whitney under the table. A kick that said, "Get rid of them," as sure as if he had spoken the words.

"Um, I have some business to discuss with Mr Soloman. So why don't you all take my car to the hotel, and I'll be back later."

Within five minutes they were alone in the restaurant.

"Thanks," Howard said.

She looked at him serenely. "You're welcome."

His eyes dropped to her breasts, their magnificent outline clearly visible beneath the pale pink angora sweater she wore.

"I've been waiting for this night for years," he said, his voice thick with desire.

"Are we being fair to Poppy?"

Clutching her hand he came up with "Think of it as an act of mercy." Frantically waving for the check he said, "Let's get out of here."

Hand in hand they walked outside to his waiting limo. He was as excited as he'd ever been, and on the way to the hotel he thought about how it would be.

Good. That's how it would be.

Sensational.

Fucking sensational.

Sensational fucking!

With a practised move he pressed the button, raising the dark glass separating them from the driver. And then he grabbed her, his hands reaching for her fabulous breasts beneath the soft angora.

"Howard! Not here!"

Silencing her objections with his lips, he plunged his hand beneath her bra, and popped a tit.

Oh, Jesus! He thought he was going to come in his pants. This was better than high school!

Bending his head, he sucked on the rosy nipple bursting from the rim of white lace.

"Not in the *car*," she protested.

Her struggles were in vain as he sprawled all over her.

"HOWARD! WE'RE HERE!"

The limo pulled up outside the hotel. Quickly he leaped off her, as she hurriedly pulled her sweater down.

There was a nuclear explosion waiting to go off in his pants. He hoped he could make it upstairs.

The driver opened the door and they climbed out.

"My suite or yours?" he asked, bursting with expectation as they entered the hotel.

Before she could reply, Chuck Nielson came bounding eagerly out from behind a potted palm. He carried flowers in one hand, and a huge stuffed toy panda in the other.

"Baby!" he yelled. "I'm sorry. I love you. I'm a bum. What can I tell you?"

Howard's hard-on deflated like a pricked balloon.

Chapter 80

Drawing into the parking lot behind the Bistro Garden, Jade wondered what she was doing. Surely she could have thought of *some* excuse to extract herself from Poppy Soloman's lunch?

She *had* tried, phoning Poppy at ten in the morning. "I don't think —" she'd started to say.

"I hope you're not even considering telling me you can't make lunch," Poppy interrupted. "You *are* the guest of honour. And I *have* gone to a great deal of trouble." A pause. "Of course, if you're dying . . ."

"No, I'm fine," she'd said, coward that she was. "I'll be there."

"*Won*derful. Your friend Beverly is coming. Melanie-Shanna Cable, Ida White, and Carmel Gooseberger. We'll have a good time."

"Great."

It wasn't enough that Jack Python had turned out to be just another cheating liar. Now she had to get stuck at some ladies-only lunch she was dreading. Well, at least Beverly would be there.

The day was a Californian blisterer. A freak November blazing sky, and the temperature way up in the eighties.

Last night she had ended up drinking too much and staying out far too late with a group that included Corey, Antonio, and Penn Sullivan. A strange combination but they all seemed to get along surprisingly well. Norman Gooseberger had flown off to Arizona to visit Whitney. "I don't see why I should sit around while he's out of town," Corey had said defiantly.

"No," she'd shrugged. "Nobody should sit around waiting for anybody."

And then she had proceeded to get good and drunk.

Corey brought her home at three in the morning. He guided her to bed, and camped out on the couch. In the morning they shared coffee and a companionship that had been missing far too long.

"Are you happy?" she had asked him.

"Getting there," he'd replied. "How about you?"

The phone had saved her from answering. A business call about her upcoming trip to New York for a special Cloud promotion party. She was glad to be rescued. There seemed no need to burden Corey with her problems.

*

It was easy to get rid of Danielle. Jack just dropped her off at Senator Richmond's hotel, bade her goodbye, and she was history.

Considering that Jade was out on the town without a

moment's pause, gazing into the eyes of her next conquest, he should have kept Danielle, taken her to *his* hotel, and vented some of his frustration and disappointment.

He was more than disappointed. He could have sworn that he and Jade Johnson were on for a beautiful, long, crazy ride.

Wrong.

Another one hits the dust.

She couldn't even wait *one* day. What an operator!

And yet . . . he remembered her note – all about how it was impossible to wipe the smile off her face, and did he want her to cook for him.

Sweet.

Phoney.

Shit!

He went to bed and slept badly. In the morning he was woken by Heaven on the phone. She sounded suspiciously cheerful, and suspiciously guilty.

"What's up?" he asked. "Do you need money?" He saw to it that she received a healthy allowance, only most months she seemed to run out of funds.

"Nope."

That was a surprise. "Don't tell me you've heard from your mother?"

"Get serious, Uncle Jack."

"You can drop the uncle. Aren't you going to be seventeen next week? I think plain Jack'll do just fine." He groped for his watch and realized it was only seven-forty-five. Too early for idle conversation.

"I'm seventeen the day after tomorrow," she corrected.

Damn Aretha. He'd told her to remind him – now it looked like he'd forgotten. "I know that," he said quickly. "Just testing to make sure *you* remembered."

"Very funny." A short silence. "I'm dropping out of school."

Struggling to sit up, he said, "You're doing *what*?"

"Don't freak out. It's okay – really. I've got something exciting to do – it's not like a job exactly –"

"Can we discuss this over lunch?"

"Why?"

Why. The kid asked him why. He was in no mood to play the father figure, but it seemed unavoidable.

"Meet me at Hamburger Hamlet on Sunset at twelve o'clock. Be there," he said sternly.

"I don't see why I have to . . ."

"I said be there." He hung up abruptly.

*

Poppy Soloman adored her ladies' lunches. They gave her an ideal opportunity to star in her own productions.

She dressed up accordingly, and wore important pieces from her ever-growing collection of fine jewellery. Sometimes she had her hair and makeup done by a professional. It was nice to look one's best, especially when most women were super-critical – usually behind her back.

Howard had phoned early in the morning. Poor Howard. He could hardly survive without her. "I've got a stomachache," he'd complained. "I feel lousy."

"Get on a plane and come home," she'd said sensibly.

"I will, as soon as Whitney gets her ass back on the set."

"Hurry, pusskins, Poppy misses you."

She knew he loved it when she babied him. There was no doubt about it, she could take care of him better than his other three wives put together.

Sighing, she consulted her watch. It was nearly twelve-thirty, and her guests would soon be arriving. She always liked to be there first so she could decide on the seating and position herself in a key spot.

The garden restaurant was already abuzz with activity. She waved to several acquaintances, and blew kisses to a favoured few. Poppy Soloman was a force in so-called Hollywood society. As the wife of a studio head she expected and received deferential treatment wherever she went.

How different from her first months in Hollywood, when she worked as a lowly secretary . . . How very different . . .

"Don't even tell me I'm the first! Jeez! And you look so lonely sittin' there all by yourself. Hi – I'm Beverly D'Amo. What a pleasure to *finally* get to have lunch with you."

Poppy looked up at the extremely tall, exotic black woman. Beverly certainly was striking.

"Sit *here*," she said, indicating the chair next to her. "I'm delighted you could come today."

Beverly rolled her eyes and winked wickedly. "Girl, I *come* whenever the opportunity presents itself! Doesn't everyone?"

Poppy was saved from answering by the appearance of Jade

Johnson, clad all in white and looking spectacular. "I'm not late, am I?" she asked breathlessly.

"Not at all," replied Poppy, patting the chair the other side of her and saying, "Please sit here."

"Hiya, J. J.," Beverly greeted Jade. "Who's the guy? Seems to me you're sending out those special signals."

"Huh?"

"You heard."

"I don't know *what* you're talking about."

"Babee, it's *me*. C'mon, tell."

"Champagne, everyone?" interrupted Poppy.

"Why not?" replied Beverly. She grinned at the waiter. "Make mine a Mimosa. Fresh orange juice, the best bubbly, an' a little shaved ice."

Poppy could see that if she wasn't careful, Beverly would take over her entire lunch. Quickly she asserted herself, making her position clear up front. "Beverly," she said sweetly, "Howard speaks *so* well of you. He's *very* impressed with your performance in *Romance*. Even though it's only a small role he says you have great potential, and he hopes to use you again soon." Actresses had to be put in their place. Firmly.

Beverly's grin widened. She, too, could play power games. "No shit? The little guy said that about me? Hey – I'm *really* flattered. I guess that must be why old Zach's promised me the lead in my next flickeroony."

Before anyone could say anything else the odd couple arrived – Ida and Carmel. Poppy busied herself with introductions, placing Carmel next to Jade, and Ida beside Beverly. There was one chair left for Melanie-Shanna, who was late.

"Didn't I see you at Spago with Jack Python?" Ida said, peering myopically across the table at Jade, her striking white hair shimmering in the sunlight.

"Uh . . . yes, I guess so."

"Ah *ha!*" yelled Beverly triumphantly. "Jack Python, huh?"

"A rutting dog," boomed Carmel. "He's had more women in this town than Silver's had men."

"Silver?" echoed Beverly. "As in Anderson?"

"They're brother and sister, you know," said Poppy. "It's not a well-publicized fact."

"I never knew that," said Beverly. "They don't look anything alike."

"Of course, she'd much older than he is," Carmel confided

404

knowledgeably. "Silver and I go *way* back."

"She had Orville once, didn't she?" remarked Ida.

"No, she didn't," replied Carmel crossly. "I wish you'd stop suggesting that Orville has had every woman in this town."

"Probably one of the few he missed," chortled Ida, surprisingly lively for once.

Carmel glared at her.

"It sounds like brother and sister have covered the waterfront," observed Beverly. "And *I* wouldn't mind covering *him* any day of the week. How was he, Jade? All tight pants, teeth an' talk? Or is there gold in them there hills?"

Shrugging vaguely Jade said, "I've no idea. We were just . . . uh . . . talking business."

Beverly raised a quizzical eyebrow. "Business?"

Sometimes Beverly got completely on her nerves. "Yes, business," she said shortly. "He wants me to appear on his show."

Noting her guest of honour's discomfort, Poppy switched subjects. "And what is everyone's opinion of the new *Mr* Silver Anderson?" she asked.

"A sly one," Ida said without hesitation.

"Who is he? Where does he come from?" Poppy mused. "That's what *I* wonder."

"Orville says he's quite sharp," interrupted Carmel.

"Must be," Ida said. "He got her to marry him, didn't he?"

"Has she ever had anything *lifted*?" Poppy asked curiously. "She looks so wonderful – for her age."

"There are more plastic surgeons in Los Angeles than anywhere else in the world," Beverly announced authoritatively. "My gyno told me. Amazing what they'll come out with when they're eyeballin' one's snatch!"

"I wonder where Melanie is," fussed Poppy. She had called her the day before, dropped a big hint about Mannon and Clarissa, then invited her for lunch. "I hate people who think they can walk in half an hour late. It's so rude."

"Does she know about hubby dearest?" inquired Carmel, lighting a long thin cigarillo.

"I really have no idea," replied Poppy innocently. "Isn't the wife always supposed to be the last to find out?"

Jade felt lost in a sea of idle gossip. She abhorred the casual way they were picking everyone over. Jack Python probably *was* a rutting dog, but she didn't want to hear about it from this group.

"Like I think you gotta let me do this," Heaven said earnestly. "And if it doesn't work out, I'l go back to school, college, the whole bit. Uncle Jack, you gotta understand – if I *don't* do it, I could like totally miss out on the greatest opportunity of my life."

"You should have told me at the beginning," he said sharply. "Before you signed contracts, and made a record, and committed yourself."

"You would've stopped me," she countered.

He had to admit she was right. "So what you're telling me is that you want to drop out of school for a year, and pursue a singing career. Is that correct?"

"That's it."

"And what if this record of yours flops?"

Pouting, she said, "Thanks!"

"Hey – don't get carried away, young lady, it could happen." Picking at her hamburger, she said, "Not to me, I've had enough bummed-out scenes in my life."

Staring at his pretty, forlorn niece, he wondered what was in store for her. She had come to him with a whole scenario, and he knew if he stepped in and said no, she would hate him forever. Why hadn't his father asked him about it? How could George just go ahead and sign contracts without knowing a thing about the business? Goddammit. If he'd spent more time with her she might have come to him *before* the event.

"I don't know," he said unsurely.

"Yes you do," she wheedled.

"What about Silver?"

"What *about* her?"

"I guess if you're going to drop out of school, someone should tell her."

"Why? Do you like honestly believe she cares?"

Once again he had to admit she was right.

Pushing her plate away, she went on, "It's settled then? You agree?"

"Would it make any difference if I didn't?"

With a guilty laugh she said, "I guess not."

"Show business is a tough number to conquer."

"Easy sucks. I'm into struggling."

"When do I get to hear your record?"

"The record company's having a party for me. Sort of like to introduce me to disc jockeys and the newspaper people. I want you to come. Only, Uncle Jack, promise not to get mad at me?

The thing is, I just don't want to advertise the fact we're related. Okay?"

He began to laugh. "Ashamed of me?"

Giggling, she said, "You got it in one!"

"Once again I suggest you drop the uncle – it does kind of give things away."

"Thanks, Unc – I mean – Jack."

"You're welcome." He called for the check. "When is this party anyway?"

"On my birthday."

"Give me a time and a place. I'll be there."

*

As soon as the waiter suggested coffee, Jade was out of there. She had heard enough about face-lifts, and who was sleeping with whom, and designers, and servant problems, and character assassinations.

Beverly left with her, and they both burst into hysterical laughter as they hit the parking lot and handed over their respective tickets.

"*Shee-it!*" exclaimed Beverly. "Heavy duty."

"Bor-*ing*," Jade said. "I never intend to get trapped at one of those lunches again."

"Right on. Poppy Soloman is somethin' else," agreed Beverly.

"You can say that again."

The parking valet drove up in a maroon, impeccably polished Rolls-Royce – licence plate KLINGER I.

"I see the beat goes on," Jade remarked dryly.

"Sure does. Why don't you come back to our simple little mansion and we can *really* spill our guts? Leave your car here – I'll get one of the slaves to pick it up later."

Jade hesitated. She felt like confiding in someone, but on the very few occasions she had been in Zachary Klinger's company he made her uncomfortable.

Reading her mind, Beverly said, "It's all clear on the Bel Air front. Big Daddy's at the studio – I think he's hoping to get another pop at Carlos Brent!"

"Is it true he actually hit him?"

"Whacked old Carlos out, an' proud of it."

"Why would he do that?"

Beverly tipped the valet and got in the car. "I think he's got a secret crush on Silver Anderson. How hysterical can things get?"

*

And at the studio, Zachary Klinger stood silently in the background and watched.

He had more than a secret crush on Silver. He had an all-consuming passion. And very soon he would win her back.

One way or the other she would be his again, and nobody was going to stand in his way.

Chapter 81

"You're a first-class cooze," Carlos Brent muttered.

"And you're a broken-down old swinger," Silver replied coolly.

"Pulling that stunt with the garlic yesterday. What kind of crap was that?"

"I had this mad urge to see Zachary Klinger knock you down."

"Yeah, you would." Grabbing her in an affectionate hug he added, "You're not such a bad old broad. I guess I'll have to put up with you."

"Are we ready to shoot?" the director called nervously, wary of his stars coming to blows after yesterday's débâcle.

"Whenever you are," Silver replied sweetly, extracting herself from Carlos's embrace, and strolling in front of the camera.

Following her, Carlos walked with the jaunty swagger of great fame.

Silver had to admit that he was still an extremely attractive man, in spite of the hair transplant and extra pounds which filled out his once gaunt frame. And he was an American legend. Which is more than she could say for Wes Money – who wasn't even American, let alone a legend.

She was furious with Wes. How *dare* he walk out on her last night. How *dare* he do such a thing.

And – even worse – he had not returned home. When she left for the studio in the morning, the bastard was still missing.

She had not married Wes Money for him to walk out on her. Oh, no. Absolutely not.

And she had no intention of letting him get away with such behaviour.

Vladimir had been quite triumphant about the whole episode. When she drifted downstairs last night with a faint smile and a languorous air, Vladimir was waiting to greet her. "Mr Money vill not be dining vith you tonight," he said smugly.

"And why is that?"

"Mr Money vent out for the night, madame. He instructed me to tell you he vill not be back until later."

"Where's he gone?"

Vladimir professed ignorance.

She tried to find out from Unity if *she* knew the reason for Wes's sudden departure. Unity didn't know, and what's more she didn't seem to care.

Silver felt uncomfortable with the girl: there was something about her she didn't like — a cold, unspoken insolence. "Did Wes speak to anyone since coming downstairs?" she had asked.

Unity shrugged. "I think he returned a couple of calls."

"To whom?" Uneasily it occurred to her that maybe there was another woman in his life. After all, he was hardly keeping it zipped in his pants when she found him. He was probably embroiled in affairs with cheap women all over the place.

"Orville Gooseberger left an urgent message to return his call, and so did Zeppo White," Unity said flatly.

The picture became clear. Orville and Zeppo telling tales. And Wes becoming miffed because *she* hadn't told him.

With a sigh of annoyance she had tackled a solitary dinner, and waited for the return of her husband.

As far as she was concerned, she hadn't been keeping any secrets. Why *should* she feel obliged to report everything to him?

Deep down she knew that she hadn't told him because he would have said she behaved childishly. Screw him. Silver Anderson didn't have to answer to *anyone*. She hated criticism, and wasn't about to hear it from her own husband.

When he failed to come home, her anger grew. Just who exactly did Mr Money think he was dealing with?

On the way to the studio that morning she had decided to teach him a lesson. One he wasn't likely to forget in a hurry.

The first thing she did was send a note of apology to Carlos, and then she sat back and waited for his reaction.

It was predictable: she knew Carlos of old.

After their mild exchange of insults on the set, he invited her to his dressing room for lunch.

She hadn't had Carlos in twenty years. Why wait any longer?

*

After storming from the house, Wes headed straight for the nearest bar, where he downed a couple of fast scotches and took stock of the situation.

As he began to calm down he realized what Silver had done – or rather not done – was no big deal. She merely needed a little reminder that *he* was the boss of the household, and as such deserved some respect. By not telling him about the furor on the set she could have made him look like a prize jerk to Orville and Zeppo. Fortunately, he was a quick thinker, and had saved the situation by pretending he knew all about it when he spoke to the two of them on the phone.

It was about time Silver realized she couldn't treat him as her latest resident stud and nothing else. If he stayed out late the lesson should be well learned. After all, it wasn't like he was risking anything – they were married now, and there was nothing she could do about it.

He didn't like the bar he had chosen. It was dimly lit and stuffy, filled with an assortment of secretaries trying to score, and men in three-piece suits. Deciding more familiar haunts would suit him better, he drove down to Venice, to a bar/restaurant he used to hang out at. The place was not Chasen's, nor even Spago. It was rough and noisy, with a loud juke box, and an assortment of hookers and drug dealers hanging round the bar.

This was your life, Wes Money, he said to himself – and he knew immediately how difficult it would be ever to go back.

*

One thing about Carlos, age had not slowed his sexual prowess. Once a cocksman, always. And Silver enjoyed the visit from an old friend.

A revenge fuck. Fast and furious. Ha! She would make sure Wes found out about it.

"You're one hell of a sexy old broad," Carlos said with a chuckle, as he pulled up his pants. "Why'd we ever break up?"

"A matter of ego," she said crisply, adjusting her clothing.

410

"Yours. It threatened to engulf both of us." Rising, she went straight to the mirror and inspected her makeup to make sure nothing was disturbed. "And kindly don't call *me* old. You're at least twenty years ahead of me. If *I'm* old, what does that make you?"

"Men don't get older, only better," he said boastfully.

"Stuff it, Carlos dear."

"I thought I just did!"

Feeling strangely unsatisfied, and a tiny bit guilty, she decided that maybe she wouldn't tell Wes after all.

Then she remembered he'd been out all night.

The hell with *him*.

*

He saw a few friends, only they didn't seem so friendly. Brief exchanges stilted conversation.

"What's the matter with everyone?" he asked his ex-local hooker.

Looking battered and worn, like an old used car, she mumbled, "Ya ain't one of us anymore, Wes." She ran a hand through yellow hair with black roots. "Ya rich now, an' famous."

"*I'm* not famous," he said. "My wife is."

Staring at him curiously she asked, "What's she like?"

"Great," he replied, and found that he meant it. Silver could be surprisingly great when she dropped the "big star" act.

The sad-looking hooker wagged a finger at him. "Ya got a break. A real lucky break."

"I know," he replied truthfully.

She scurried off, even though he wanted to buy her a drink. "Gotta get back t'work," she explained.

By the time she left he was deeply depressed, and he decided Silver had been punished enough. He was going home to Bel Air, where he belonged.

Outside, in the back parking lot, two men walked slowly towards him.

He smelled trouble before it happened, went to defend himself, and was felled by a heavy blunt instrument.

Oh, Christ, not again, he thought, just before drifting uneasily into the land of nod.

Chapter 82

Bazaar hit the stands in the morning, and Heaven hit an un-suspecting public the next day with what was destined to become the hottest single of the year.

Her combination seventeenth birthday and *Gonna Eatcha Tonight!* promotion party turned out to be a blast, covered by *Entertainment Tonight* and a host of other media, as there was nothing else going on that night. It took place at Tramp, the private club. Giant blow-ups of her Antonio pictures covered the walls, while white and gold balloons inscribed *Heaven* and *Gonna Eatcha Tonight!* decorated the ceilings.

Heaven glimmered and glittered her way through the party — an irresistible mixture of innocence and seduction in a white lace body stocking worn with a black leather micro-skirt, lace-up gold boots, festoons of diamanté jewellery, and a trailing gold trenchcoat.

Lindi, the publicity girl from College Records, had taken her on a shopping spree down Melrose, and the result was slightly bizarre, very individual and stylishly effective. "We're calling it the Heaven look," Lindi told a group of hungry journalists — always on the alert for a new trend. "This kid'll make Madonna look like a non-starter. Just wait until you hear her."

Speaking to the press was a completely new experience. She knew her mother had complained about it all her life, but Heaven couldn't see what was so bad, talking about herself non-stop. Pushing her hands through her multi-coloured hair, she answered questions on clothes, style, fashion, school and background.

"I spent my childhood in Europe with my parents," she half lied. "And now I live with my grandfather in the Valley."

"There's a rumour going around that you're Silver

Anderson's daughter," said a fat woman in a peasant blouse, with jangles of beads around her plump neck.

Heaven glared at her. "Really?" she said. "I guess I'll be Cyndi Lauper's *sister* next!"

Everyone laughed, and Lindi spirited her away to get ready for the debut of her record.

"You know," Lindi said sympathetically, "we're never going to be able to keep it under wraps."

"What?"

"That you *are* Silver Anderson's daughter. I know you want it kept a secret, but that's not easy when your manager is going around telling everyone."

She was aghast. "Rocky?"

"'Fraid so."

"I could *kill* him."

Lindi shrugged philosophically. "It *will* get out eventually, one way or another. So we may as well scoop it now, then at least it's behind us."

"Why?" she asked stubbornly.

"Because if the media thinks you're trying to hide something, they'll *really* go all out. We don't have to announce it – it's just best you don't deny it. Okay?"

She nodded resignedly. Deep down she had known it was an impossible secret to keep.

The debut of her record was planned for eight o'clock, and she was supposed to mime to it. Shaking with nerves she changed into a slinky leopard catsuit, and then slipped on a long black leather coat worn open. The Heaven look.

Several of the College Records executives crowded round her, wishing her good luck. Rocky appeared at her side, mumbling *his* encouragement.

This was it. This was the opportunity she had been waiting for.

She heard the opening beat of the record, and tensed up.

Lindi gave her a little push, propelling her in front of the disc jockey stand, where a spotlight hit her in the eyes.

Oh, no! She wanted to throw up! Everyone was staring at her expectantly. Waiting, watching, expecting great things!

And then, as the music enveloped her, she began to move her lips, stiffly at first, intimidated by the crowd and the lights. This wasn't like performing at some high school dance with Eddie in attendance. This was it. This was the big time.

Get loose, she told herself. *Lighten up.*

Miraculously something clicked, and she was suddenly gloriously, *wonderfully* into the music.

> I met a guy who's big and strong –
> his muscles make me quiver
> I look at him – he looks at me –
> Oh, wow, he makes me shiver.
> There's one thing I will do to him –
> because I know he wants it
> I get real near – with message clear
> I whisper low – all systems go
> I'm a Maneater . . . yes I am . . .
> Maneater . . . sure I am . . .
> Maneater . . . and baby –
> I'm gonna eatcha tonight!

By the time she finished her adrenalin was really pumping and she felt sensational. The crowd of guests gave her a rapturous reception. And Uncle Jack told her how proud he was of her.

"You were *fantastic*," Lindi whispered, grabbing her arm as soon as Jack left. "Come with me, the photographers want a shot of you and Penn Sullivan."

Heaven tried to hide her excitement. Penn Sullivan! The actor! He was *gorgeous*!

Things were *certainly* looking up.

Somewhere in New York . . .
Sometime in the seventies . . .

The girl arrived in New York on a freezing Saturday afternoon. Clad in a thin cotton dress and a cheap nylon jacket, with one small suitcase clutched in her hand, she stood in the Port Authority bus terminal and wondered where to go.

New York had seemed like such an exciting idea when she first hatched her plan to travel to the big city. Now, as she ventured out onto West Forty-second Street, she wasn't so sure.

The street was filthy, full of garbage and dirt. A crazed bag lady hurried by – pushing a shopping cart full of brown paper bags and newspapers. A skinny black man in a pink jacket with matching eyes hey-babied her. Two punks eyed her suitcase, contemplating grab and run. They'd be very disappointed if they did, for their entire haul would consist of two old sweaters, some worn underwear, a pair of jeans, scuffed sneakers, and two packets of Oreo cookies.

Those were all her worldly possessions. And in the pocket of her nylon jacket she had eighty-four dollars in assorted bills.

That was it.

A police car screamed by, just as a sharp-nosed white man in a sheepskin coat approached her. "Hiya, sweetie."

Ignoring him, she began to walk quickly along the street.

Companionably he fell into step beside her. "You look like ya need a friend," he said.

"I'm okay," she replied, shivering as a blast of icy wind penetrated her light clothing.

"Where ya from?"

"California," she lied.

"Yeah? I was there once. Got me a tan and a blon cutie."

She stopped and turned towards him. "What do u want?" she demanded bluntly.

415

"Jest bein' friendly," he replied, taken aback.

"What do you want?" she repeated.

"Sex," he said hopefully. "I'll give ya ten bucks, an' tell ya where t'get connected."

"Connected?"

"Y'know, I'll meetcha the right people. Ya need a job, doncha? An' someplace ter park yer butt."

Sighing wearily she said, "Get lost."

He pulled up the collar of his warm sheepskin coat. "Ya turnin' me down?"

"That's right."

"Well, fuck you," he spat. "See how far you'll get without my help."

"Go away."

He walked off, muttering to himself.

Waiting until he was out of sight, she leaned against the wall and clumsily opened her suitcase. Removing both her sweaters, she took off the nylon jacket and struggled into them, feeling warmer at once. Then she put her jacket back on, asked directions to Herald Square, and set off, walking briskly until she reached Macy's, the famous department store she had read about. It was supposedly one of the biggest stores in the world — occupying a full square block of space.

Inside, the activity was frantic, shoppers mingled with tourists, everyone rushing back and forth anxious to spend their money.

Approaching a bored-looking redhead stationed behind one of the cosmetics counters, she asked, "Can you help me? Who do I see to get a job here?"

The redhead stared. "You're going job hunting with a suitcase?" she questioned. "No chance."

"No chance of what?"

"No chance of them hiring you."

"Why?"

"For a start, you look like you just got off the bus."

"I did."

The woman laughed derisively. "Holy cow! I suppose you're broke, with nowhere to live, and probably knocked up."

"Two out of three. Any suggestions?"

"I hope it's the right two. Get a room at the Y overnight, and then catch the next bus home."

The girl did neither. She had made up her mind that in New York things were going to be different, and one way or another she was going to rise from her crummy beginnings and make a success of her life. No job and no place to stay were minor setbacks. She was a survivor.

Hadn't she proved it? Failing to land a job at Macy's, she was able to get a room at the YWCA, where she deposited her suitcase, and then took a walk to Times Square. She looked around, finally noticing a DISHWASHER NEEDED *sign in the window of* Red's Deli, *a huge, noisy restaurant.*

One thing she knew — she was never going to succumb to the easy money she could make selling her body. Even dishwashing was better than that.

Washing dishes non-stop on a seven-hour shift was back-breaking work. The girl threw herself into it, in spite of the hostility of the other three dishwashers — all male. Even at such a low level of employment, men resented a female's intrusion. They made sure she got the dirtiest work of all. The huge frying pans covered in hard grease. The garbage pails to clean out. She was even allotted the cockroach run — cleaning out the lower cupboards once a day, and getting rid of the mice and rat droppings before the health inspector appeared. Working hard, she kept to herself, discouraging the friendliness of several of the waiters and short-order cooks. The girl knew that relationships could get her into trouble.

She never felt guilty about what she had done in the past — for all her victims deserved it. But she didn't want to keep on having to punish people . . . and running . . . running . . .

There was one waiter called Eli. He was black, gay, and unfailingly cheerful. He talked to her whether she wanted him to or not.

"Woody Allen's sitting at table four," he confided. "And yesterday Liza Minnelli was in — she just loves our apple strudel. It's not fair that you don't get to see anybody. Why don't you ask for a job as a waitress? Stella's quitting, there'll be a vacancy. How about grabbing it?"

"Does it pay more?"

"Yes. Yes. Yes!"

She took his advice and asked for the job. And she got it.

"Good," Eli said, "now you can come and live with me. I am in desperate need of someone to split my rent."

His kindness made her suspicious. Nobody had ever been kind to her unless they wanted something in return. Warily she moved into his cramped Greenwich Village apartment, paying half the rent, and waiting patiently to see what he was after.

"I'm an actor," Eli confided. "And a dancer, and a singer. What are your ambitions?"

Just to survive, she nearly said. Only Eli wouldn't understand. Nobody would. The tragedy of her life was her secret, and she would never reveal it to anyone.

BOOK FIVE

Hollywood, California
December 1985

Chapter 83

A shout of annoyance from the general direction of Silver's bathroom indicated she was not ready to leave the house. Wes cast an eye at the clock. They were running late for the wrap party of *Romance*. Nothing new about *that*. Silver ran late for everything. She and Elizabeth Taylor held the record for tardy arrivals.

Yawning, he sat on the edge of the bed and clicked on the television. He'd been ready to go for forty-five minutes.

Another scream. "Damn!" Silver yelled, emerging from the bathroom. "I look like a hag!"

She was clad in a beige suede gaucho outfit which didn't suit her. The shoulders were too wide, the skirt too long, and the waist too cinched. It was an outfit suitable for a twenty-two-year-old six-foot model.

"What do you think?" she demanded belligerently, knowing full well it wasn't right.

"Great," he said mildly.

"Liar!" she shouted, and marched into her dressing room, slamming the door.

Slipping off his shoes, he put his legs up on the bed. He could bet on at least another half-hour before she was ready. It didn't bother him. He felt perfectly safe and secure lying on the bed waiting for her. The trip back to his past six weeks ago had straightened out any desire he might have had to go wandering. Getting beaten up in a seedy parking lot and dragged off to meet with some fat drug pimp was not exactly his idea of a wonderful time.

He recalled the evening with distaste. The *whole* fucking evening, for they hadn't released him until the next day.

He was sure somebody had squealed on him when he went

visiting his old haunts. And he had a hunch it was his pathetic hooker friend. Not that he blamed her – anything for a buck – although it would be interesting to find out what the going price for fingering him was.

It was fortunate he possessed a concrete skull. The mother-fuckers had hit him with something heavy, dragged him into the back of a car, and taken him to visit the black dude with the shit-eating grin and big white sunglasses.

This time the meet was in a deserted warehouse. When he regained consciousness, he found he was slumped on a dusty concrete floor, his hands and feet bound with wire.

For a moment real fear had taken over. Mr Silver Anderson was going to end his days alone and unloved – just as he had begun them.

His heart jumped about like an out-of-control tennis ball, and he almost relieved himself in his pants.

STAY CALM a voice screamed in his head. THEY CAN'T DO ANYTHING TO YOU – YOU'RE A SOMEBODY NOW.

"What you think, man?" The black man prodded him with his foot. "You think we be dumb-ass fuckers? You think we gonna wait forever for our money?"

He'd groaned, and quickly tried to collect his wits.

"You owe us, white boy, an' we ready to collect."

"I owe you fuck all," he managed. "You set me up."

"We want our money," the man said. "We be fair. You pay us the twenny-two thou an' we forget about drugs you steal."

Struggling to free himself he said, "I don't fucking believe this!"

"You think fast 'bout payin' money you owe."

A swift kick caught him in the lower abdomen, landing dangerously close to his balls, making him gag with pain.

"Think carefully. I be back tomorra."

They left him, trussed like a chicken, all night long. In the morning a henchman returned to set him free. "Ya bring the money t' the same parkin' lot Tuesday nite, eight o'clock."

By the time he got the circulation going in his wrists and ankles, made his way back to the car, and drove to the house, Silver had departed for the studio. When she arrived home later that night to find him stretched out on the couch with an ice-pack on his forehead, she was furious.

"Hangover? Serves you right," she had snapped coldly.

"I got mugged," he objected.

Sarcasm flowed. "What a *shame*."

"How about some sympathy?"

"Whistle for it."

She had swept upstairs and ignored him for several days.

Obviously, everything was okay on the set, for both Orville and Zeppo phoned to thank him. "I don't know what you said to her," Orville chuckled. "Or *did* to her. But she and Carlos are behaving like best friends."

Concealing his surprise, he had accepted the congratulations as if they were his due. "I told you everything would be all right," he said magnanimously. "Any time you want her pulled back into line, just call on me."

Orville and Zeppo loved him. It took a while before Silver did again. She liked getting her own way – without exception. He had challenged her, and she did not enjoy the experience.

Slowly he charmed his way back into her good graces. Sex. Silver needed it, wanted it, hated to be without it. But they had both learned a lesson from their brief estrangement.

Meanwhile, he had no intention of paying back the twenty-two thousand dollars. Fuck 'em. They had planted the money on him, and as far as he was concerned it barely compensated for the screwed up Laurel Canyon caper. Besides, it was his "fuck you" money. He had it stashed in a safe-deposit box at the First Interstate Bank – minus the rent he had paid Reba – and he did not plan to go anywhere near it. There was nothing they could do. He was back in Bel Air, safe and protected by the new security system he had persuaded Silver to install. For insurance he took the gun – another souvenir of Laurel Canyon – out of hiding, and carried it for protection. No way was he getting caught again. Wes Money was back in the big time.

At last Silver appeared, clad in a gold jacket worn over a short black dress. "*Do* come on," she sighed impatiently. "Aren't you ready?"

Ha! *She* was berating *him*. He had been ready for over an hour. Lately her mood had been lousy. He knew the reason. And the reason had a name. Heaven. Silver's well-kept secret daughter was an emerging rock star, and it was driving her crazy.

*

Sound stage six at Orpheus Studios was set up for a party. There were balloons, round tables with pink cloths, a small combo playing music from the film, an open bar, and a buffet table covered with food. The party was crowded, but not with stars. A wrap party was a thank you from the producers to the cast and crew, and usually they were allowed to bring their respective mates.

The stars generally put in an appearance. Always late. Certainly brief.

Neither Silver nor Carlos had shown. However, Howard Soloman was there, a bejewelled Poppy in close attendance. She distributed largesse and sweetness. Poppy considered it excellent public relations to be nice to the "little people". "After all," she told Howard earnestly, "I was once one myself."

Yeah, he remembered only too well the days when Poppy was his secretary. It hadn't taken her long to change roles.

Since getting back from Arizona, and his aborted affair with Whitney, Howard had been on a downhill slide. He was doing more coke than ever, spending the studio's money rashly, and indulging in even more scams where the gains went straight into his own pocket.

Paranoia reigned supreme – he thought that everyone was talking about him. And for the first time in his life he was off sex.

Once that happened, Poppy noticed. "Howie, baby, is anything wrong?"

"Work pressure."

"Poor sweetie. We need a vacation. Shall I book a suite at the Kahala in Hawaii?"

"I'll let you know."

Going away was not the answer. He didn't want to be stuck in confined quarters with Poppy, where she could find out about his habit. He had finally admitted to himself that it *was* a habit. Not an unbreakable one. He could stop any time he wanted.

The problem was – he didn't want to.

*

Carlos Brent made his entrance first – walking with the same swagger as in his youth. He travelled with two bodyguards, a secretary, a personal publicist, and his long-suffering girlfriend, Dee Dee Dionne.

His attendants hovered around him like anxious butterflies.

Shortly after, Silver arrived, with Wes and Nora. "I hate these things," she muttered to Nora. "All this smiling makes my face muscles ache." She waved to the lighting cameraman – always an actress's best friend – and graciously stopped by his table to meet his wife.

Now that the film was finished shooting she was feeling slight tingles of apprehension. Had she done the right thing leaving *Palm Springs*? A television soap gave her constant exposure to a more than fickle public. Would that same public go to see her in *Romance*? Would they watch her upcoming television special? Would they still *love* and *adore* her?

She wasn't ready for rejection. Silver *needed* adulation, just as Howard needed his cocaine.

And Zeppo White was not Quinne Lattimore. Quinne used to be available for her calls day and night. She could summon him to attend to minor problems any time she wanted. Zeppo was another matter. As a star agent he refused to jump, and that annoyed her.

"I'm not sure Zeppo is the right agent for me," she'd complained to Wes.

Looking at her quizzically he'd said, "Zeppo is the tops. From now on it's only the best for you."

She was harbouring guilty feelings about cheating on Wes with Carlos. What if he ever found out?

Of course, he never would. How could he? And if he did, she would merely deny it. Nora was the only one who knew. Well, Nora was privy to all her secrets – why should this one be any different?

"Can I beg a favour from you?" the lighting cameraman's wife asked.

Silver smiled generously. The woman probably wanted an autographed photo – everyone did.

"Certainly."

"It's not for me."

Of course not. It never is.

"It's for our grand-daughter."

Grand-daughter! Her fans were getting younger every day!

Still smiling, she noticed Wes talking to Carlos and wondered what they were discussing.

Hey – did you know I fucked your wife the other day?

Really? I hope you enjoyed it.

Yeah, why not? She's a good old broad.

"Little Marybethe will be thrilled to pieces if I can promise her an autographed picture of your daughter, Heaven. And if she can sign it – to Marybethe – M-A-R-Y-B-E-T-H-E."

Silver's smile was fixed on her face like a concrete mask, while shivers of annoyance mixed with jealousy mixed with disbelief ran up and down her spine.

Goddammit! What the hell had she ever done to deserve *this*?

Chapter 84

Getting away was the best tonic Jade could think of. Only it seemed that every time she made a trip, she was running from a bad relationship. Los Angeles to escape from Mark. Now back to New York to forget Jack Python. Although she could hardly call *him* a relationship. More like a night of passion with a professional stud. Making conquests was obviously his hobby.

How *could* she have been so gullible? It wasn't as though she hadn't been around.

In New York she tried to put the entire incident behind her, and threw herself into seeing old friends. There were lunches at the Russian Tea Room, Mortimer's, and Le Cirque. Evenings at the Hard Rock Café, Twenty-One, and Elaine's – depending on her mood. And crazy shopping trips to the three great B's – Bendel's, Bergdorf's, and Bloomingdale's.

Walking the streets she breathed the freezing city air and had a wonderful time doing it. Then she visited her parents in Connecticut for a long, blissful, promotion-free weekend.

When she'd signed the Cloud deal, she had not fully realized the extent to which they expected her to sell their product. After complaining to her modelling agent, she was shown a copy of her contract, and there it was in black and white – *Ms. Johnson will undertake eight weeks of personal appearances during a twelve-month period.*

Ms. Johnson had signed.

Ms. Johnson had to do.

She was certainly incredibly well compensated. The Cloud deal had set her up for life. Now she could venture into movies on her terms, or not at all.

Zeppo White called to inform her that Howard Soloman had

purchased the film rights to *Married Alive*, and that a top screen-writer was tailoring the script to accommodate her.

"I got you the sweetest deal in the world," he crowed. "Everything you asked for an' more. I'm couriering the contract to you overnight. Get it back to me right away, kiddo."

"How's L.A.?" she asked, shivering in the borrowed apartment of a friend.

"Hot. Christmas is coming. I'm havin' my turkey out by the pool. How about you?"

"I'll spend Christmas with my family and be back right after the holidays."

"Looking forward to it. Ida wants to throw a party for you."

She was all partied out. The Cloud Gala, held at the top of the World Trade building, had been a lavish affair attended by a mix of New York's movers and shakers, plus press, and the most avid stylesetters.

Men had hit on her from all directions. A plump politician with an indecipherable accent. A Broadway star who liked to score. A former consort of Silver Anderson's. And a tall, thin dress designer who swung both ways.

She'd declined every offer, having decided – quite firmly – that men were out, career was in.

Christmas was only a few days away, and when it was over she planned to return to Los Angeles and shoot the final batch of Cloud commercials and photographs. Actually she was looking forward to it. After nine months of living on the Coast she'd gotten used to the L.A. pace, the beautiful weather, and friendly people. She even missed her apartment, and thought she might buy a couple of cats when she returned. If the movie deal panned out she entertained the thought of renting a house – maybe at the beach.

Christmas shopping in New York was frantic. The stores were packed. Choosing presents was fun – paying for them a nightmare. And Jade found that everywhere she went she was recognized. Losing her freedom was quite a blow.

Finally, all shopped out, she was ready for a family Christmas. Corey was flying in from the Coast, and when the holidays were over they planned to travel back to L.A. together.

The day before she was all set to leave for Connecticut, Mark Rand re-entered her life with a vengeance.

He was divorced, and ready for commitment.

"We need decisions, Jack," Aretha said, in her best persuasive voice. "Otherwise we are going to be producing shows with just li'l ole you sitting all on your lonesome in front of the camera."

"I told you," Jack said stubbornly. "I want Jade Johnson on the show."

"And I told *you*," Aretha replied patiently, "she is in New York, and will not be back until after Christmas."

"I'd like to have a definite commitment from her people that she'll do the programme the week she returns."

Sighing, Aretha fluffed out her hair. "I'll do my best. Ever since Norman Gooseberger took off from Briskinn & Bower, it's a bitch getting them to return a call – let alone anything else. They're all a bunch of deadheads over there. Our show is hotter than Carson, an' those assholes can't even put their finger in the dial."

"Get her," Jack said sternly.

"I'm *workin'* on it. Meanwhile, the Carlos Brent booking looks like a definite. And we're still working on Zachary Klinger."

"Sounds good."

As he walked from the office, Aretha made a face behind his back. He'd been a real pain in the ass for weeks now. Usually he was such a sweetheart, but when he had something on his mind – watch out! Somehow foxy Jade Johnson had gotten under his skin. Aretha couldn't figure how or why, she just knew he was hot to confront her. If Jack wished to destroy someone, he did it in front of a camera, and *Ms*. Johnson was his next proposed victim.

She placed another call to Briskinn & Bower, this time asking for Bernie Briskinn. Aretha had found that if you couldn't get what you wanted from the employees – go to the boss. It always worked.

*

Jack hit the freeway in his Ferrari, already late for a meeting with Heaven and his business manager. Suddenly his little schoolgirl niece was an earner – heading for big bucks, and he wanted to make sure her money was well protected and invested correctly.

What a shock he'd had the day of her launch party. Expecting some minor hype which would fizzle out to nothing, he'd walked into a major event.

Heaven was all set for stardom, and when he heard her record he flipped. She had a sensational voice. Without a doubt he knew she possessed that very special quality which would propel her right to the top. She was going to be a star. Just like her mother.

At first he was assailed by so many different emotions. She was too young to get caught up in the crap. And then he felt an almost parental pride that she was good, a winner, for Jack was a winner himself, and he knew what it was like to have to struggle for achievement.

How was Silver going to feel? It would be interesting to observe her public reaction if the kid actually *did* make it.

After Heaven had lip-sync'ed her song, he made his way over, pushing through the crowds of congratulators.

"Hey – I'm one proud uncle," he whispered, aware she didn't want anyone making the family connection.

"Really?" She glowed with triumph and delight.

"Call me tomorrow. I know you're busy now, so I'm taking off."

She nodded excitedly, amber eyes gleaming.

Lindi moved in. "I'm getting questions about why Jack Python is here," she said, smiling at him. "Hi, I'm Lindi Foxworthe. In charge of P.R."

"And I'm making a fast exit," he said, kissing Heaven on the cheek, and slipping her a small gift-wrapped package. "Happy birthday, sweet seventeen."

He hadn't seen her since, although they spoke on the phone often. As soon as her record took off he had suggested this meeting with his business manager.

"I *have* a manager," she'd said, which was news to him.

"Who?"

"Remember Rocky?"

Sure – he wasn't likely to forget Rocky. And how'd she ever got caught up with *that* creep, when he'd issued specific instructions she wasn't ever to see him again?

Goddammit! He wasn't her father. He was her uncle. She would be eighteen in a year, and how could he prevent her from doing what she wanted? At least when she reached eighteen he could stop worrying.

"Bring all the contracts George signed on your behalf and meet me at my business manager's office in Century City, Thursday at two-thirty," he instructed.

She was there, and so was Rocky – a walking nightmare in a white suit, black shirt, white tie, and two-toned shoes.

"Hiya, man," Rocky greeted him, friendly as an over-boisterous puppy.

Jack ignored him, checked out the contracts with his business manager, and was shocked to discover that Rocky owned fifty-one percent of her blossoming career.

"Why didn't you show these to me *before* you got George to sign them?" he steamed.

"Because," she shrugged, "you're always so busy. Anyway," she added saucily, "you might've not let me do it."

Indicating Rocky he said, "This Stallone clone owns fifty-one per cent of you. Does that seem right?"

"Hey, man," objected Rocky, adjusting his cuffs, "I *got* her the gig with College. Without me she'd be just another little girl tryin' to make it."

"Back off," warned Jack. "These contracts are going right over to my lawyer's office."

"They're legal," Rocky scowled. He didn't appreciate being treated like a nothing.

"We'll see."

"Stop!" announced Heaven. "I'm perfectly happy with Rocky getting his cut. Lay off him, or I'm going home."

Could it be his imagination, or was there the faint shadow of Silver emerging? Was this budding young rock star going to turn out to be just like mommy?

The least he could do was see that the money she earned was well looked after. Then she was on her own, if that's the way she wanted it.

*

Heaven skipped out of the meeting, a disgruntled Rocky trailing her. "Your uncle treats me like a real shitheel," he complained. "I bin good t'ya. Haven't I?"

"Yep."

"So what's his problem?"

"I guess he just wants to see that I'm okay. He's my only family, y'know."

"No shit? You gotta grandfather, *and* a mother. S'more than I've ever had."

"You must have had a *mother*."

"Naw. I got dumped on the steps of a church when I was born. Nice, huh?"

Staring at him earnestly, she said, "I didn't know that, Rocky. It's like really awful."

"What can I tell ya – I survived," he mumbled.

They walked towards her car, a bright red Chrysler convertible – Uncle Jack's birthday present. The gift-wrapped package he'd handed her at the launch party had contained the keys. How thrilled and surprised she'd been. What a hot car!

"Mebbe I should get *me* a business manager," Rocky mused. "Handle all *my* loot."

Sliding behind the wheel she said, "Why don't you?"

"HEAVEN! HEAVEN!" Two teenage girls ran over to the car. "Oooh, you're so pretty! Can we touch you? Can you write your name on our hands? Oooh!!"

"Get *outta* here," Rocky growled, jumping into the passenger seat.

Not quite sure whether he meant the girls or her, she started the car and zoomed off. Being recognized was such a blast! She loved it more each time.

As they drove along, Rocky threw her a sidelong glance. Sweet, sweet baby flesh. And he hadn't laid a finger on her, although the prospect was tempting.

He knew he was in on a pass – one false move and maybe her uncle *would* start checking with his big-shot lawyers. Everything was legal ... but if Jack wanted him out of the picture ...

Hey – he had no urge to go back to dealing drugs. It was a dangerous occupation and he'd had about enough. This kid was going all the way. And he was going all the way with her. Meanwhile, she was still living with her grandfather. He had to get her out of there, set her up in her own place. And to make things *really* tight – how about if he *married* her? Then Uncle Jack could go take a hike.

The thought appealed.

"Listen, babe," he said lightly. "Ya wanna go t'a party tonight?"

Rocky had never asked her out socially; it was always business. "I don't know ..." she replied guardedly. "Whose party?"

"Friend of mine at the beach. You've bin cooped up writin' that theme song for *The Murder* all week. It'll be a trip t'get outta the house."

"I guess ..." she said hesitantly, wishing it was Penn Sullivan asking her out. Meeting him at her record launch party had been a real thrill. Unfortunately it was true – since her success it was all work work work, and no time for play. Eddie had telephoned on a couple of occasions, and she hadn't even had time to return his calls. Getting the plum assignment to write the theme song for *The Murder* was probably more exciting than *Gonna Eatcha Tonight!* climbing the charts faster than anyone expected. It was currently at number four with a bullet on the *Billboard* chart – which meant it was still rising.

"You're gonna be number one!" everyone at College Records assured her. And then they had asked her if she would like to write and perform the theme song for *The Murder*.

Would she? wow!

Originally Orpheus had wanted Cyndi Lauper or Madonna. An executive at College Records had taken a meeting with Howard Soloman and convinced him that Heaven was the hottest and youngest meteor on the horizon.

The Murder was still filming, behind schedule, in Puerta Vallarta. Heaven had been shown a rough cut of the dailies, and even she knew the finished product was going to be a smash. Clarissa Browning was staggering; Whitney Valentine looked breathtaking; and Mannon Cable gave a wonderful performance. It wasn't a youth picture, but she loved every scintillating minute –for it combined all the elements of exciting moviegoing.

"You like?" Howard Soloman asked, having snuck into the screening room while she was watching.

"Brilliant!" she enthused.

"Write us something tricky," he requested with a wink.

"I will, Mr Soloman, I will!"

And she had. As far as she was concerned it was the best song she'd ever written.

Grandfather George was in his workroom when she returned home, which meant that he wouldn't emerge for the rest of the night.

She had dropped Rocky off at his Hollywood apartment. "Pick me up at ten," he'd said.

"Ten!" she'd exclaimed. "What time does this party start?"

"Babe – no party worth goin' to starts before eleven."

"If I can get out."

"If ya can get out!" He'd laughed derisively. "We gotta start thinking 'bout movin' you to a place of your own."

The seed was planted. He had to pull Heaven away from any sign of family. She was going to be a rock star. What kind of a rock star lived in the *Valley* with her *grandfather*?

Yeah, Rocky decided. Tonight was the night his sweet little piece of baby flesh was going to grow up all the way.

Chapter 85

Puerta Vallarta was hot in more ways than one. If the days were steamy while the cast and crew toiled away shooting the final scenes of *The Murder*, then the nights were even more so.

Everyone was on edge. They all knew the film was special. They all wanted to be finished with it before Christmas, and get home to their families.

Between Arizona and Puerta Vallarta there was only a three-day break. Clarissa had said to Mannon, "What shall we do?"

"Honey," he'd replied apologetically, "I've got to go see Melanie-Shanna and my baby. There's no way I can't."

On the day Poppy Soloman had thrown a lunch for Jade Johnson, Melanie-Shanna had given birth. Somehow, bearing Mannon Cable's son had seemed a more pressing engagement. Mannon had wanted to fly to L.A. as soon as he heard, but Clarissa stopped him.

"For the first time in your career you are giving a fine performance," she had told him. "If you break your concentration now it will spoil everything. Trust me."

He trusted her. Clarissa was like no other woman he'd been with in his life. Her intensity had him caught in a web he really didn't want to escape from. With Clarissa Browning he was not a macho superstar with startlingly blue eyes and a way with the ladies. He was a *real* man, with honest feelings. And he was a damn good actor.

Strutting, sexy, good-humoured Mannon Cable had taken a walk. Clarissa taught him to centre his feelings and care about himself more.

"You're much too nice to people," she'd said. "They walk all over you, and treat you like a fool."

He hadn't realized that. So he withdrew a little, became more aloof, stopped being so unassuming and good-natured.

"And you eat like a wild animal," she informed him. "No more red meat, sugar, salt, alcohol."

"Hey —" he'd objected.

"Trust me," she'd said patiently. It was her favourite expression.

He'd trusted her, and he knew it was working, because he'd never felt so physically healthy in his life.

There was no way she could stop him from visiting his son. Wasn't he entitled to be excited about becoming a father for the first time? Even if he *did* plan on divorcing Melanie-Shanna, as soon as his lawyer gave him the go-ahead. So, in spite of Clarissa's objections, he flew to Los Angeles. She wasn't pleased.

"What'll *you* do?" he'd asked her, before leaving.

"Don't worry about me. Please," she'd said icily.

"I don't want you to be angry."

"I'm not."

He knew she was, but he figured he could straighten everything out once he got to Puerta Vallarta.

Clarissa had formed an alliance with Norman Gooseberger. He had arrived in Arizona to take care of Whitney Valentine, but once Clarissa ascertained he was very good at what he did, she decided she wanted him for herself. Placing a direct call to Howard Soloman, she demanded Norman's exclusive services for the remainder of the picture.

Howard was bemused. "You refuse to do publicity," he pointed out. "Why would you want Norman?"

She did not reply that she had a whim to take him away from Whitney. She just said one word — "Because."

Howard understood *Because* when it was spoken by a star. "He's yours," he said resignedly, wondering how Whitney would take the news.

Howard phoned Norman personally to give him the good news. "I've cleared it with Bernie," he said. "Just do whatever she wants, and stay close."

Norman was thrilled. Clarissa Browning was his idol. He regarded her as one of the finest actresses of her generation — she ranked alongside Meryl Streep and Vanessa Redgrave as far as he was concerned.

Corey was not so thrilled. Norman had left for the weekend,

and now could be away for weeks. "You mean you're not coming back?" he asked anxiously.

"Don't sweat it," Norman replied. "I'll fix it so you get a few days in Puerta Vallarta. Meantime, pack me a suitcase and get it out on the next plane."

Clarissa and Norman spent the three-day break between locations redefining Norman's sexual urges.

"You're not *really* gay," she teased him, the night Mannon and the crew took off. They were in her suite, lying on the bed fully dressed, downing lethal concoctions of grapefruit juice, vodka and gin.

He nodded affirmatively. Not many people discussed his sexual preferences.

"Come *on*," Clarissa said lazily. "How do you *know*?"

His voice sounded surprisingly dry. "It's always been that way."

"Always?"

Another nod.

"You mean you've never had a woman?" She trailed delicate fingers across his cheek.

Shaking his head he remembered his mother's loud voice when she discovered *Penthouse* magazine hidden under his pillow. He was thirteen at the time. "Filth!" Carmel had boomed. "Pornography! You want to grow up just like your father, humping every open-legged starlet you see?"

No. He didn't want to be like Orville. He'd heard the fights in the huge mansion the three of them inhabited with four Filipino servants. He'd seen the anger and hurt they inflicted on each other. So one day, when an older boy at Beverly Hills High made a suggestion to him, it seemed like a safe alternative. If he wasn't to be just like Orville, he had to strike out in the other direction. And the other direction turned out to be extremely pleasurable.

Dropping out of school at seventeen, he went to New York, and enjoyed himself in the fast lane of the gay culture for several years. His parents, although horrified when they first found out he was what Orville called "a faggot" and Carmel termed "queer", were only too delighted that he chose to do his growing up out of sight. They gave him financial support, and the feeling they'd be happier if he stayed away.

When he decided to take a job and start shaping his life, Orville arranged a position for him in the San Francisco offices

435

of Briskinn & Bower. He turned out to be excellent at what he did. P.R. was his vocation.

After meeting Corey, he felt the time had come to go home, and without delay he bought a house in the Hollywood Hills with some trust money he'd inherited. Setting up housekeeping with Corey was a real challenge. Norman was a grasshopper – he liked the thrill of many different sexual partners. So far he had managed – only just – to remain faithful to Corey.

"You don't know what you're missing," Clarissa said softly, allowing her fingers to creep down to the buttons of his shirt.

Laughing uneasily he tried to figure out what she wanted. Clarissa Browning was a star, an Oscar-winning actress. She had Mannon Cable – what could she possibly want from him?

"You're very handsome, Norman," she said, lightly touching his exposed nipples. "It seems to me such a waste . . ."

"What is?" His voice cracked. He knew exactly what she meant. In spite of himself he felt a hardness in his pants. *My God! She's actually turning me on!* he thought.

"You know what," she replied huskily. "Don't you ever wonder about a woman's body? Oh, I know you can look at pictures if you so desire. But pictures can't tell you about touch and taste and smell, can they?"

As she spoke she continued to massage his nipples, and by the time she began to unbutton her blouse he knew he was ready to do whatever she asked. The excitement of the unknown was pounding through his body. Norman Gooseberger was twenty-six years old, and he had never had sex with a woman.

"Take off your clothes," she commanded.

With trembling hands he started to do just that.

Clarissa opened her blouse as she watched him. She wore no bra, and her breasts were small, with sharply extended nipples. As he stripped off, her eyes never left him. Distractedly she touched herself.

Now he was naked, and she was still dressed. His hard-on dominated the room.

"Very nice," she murmured. "I want you to straddle me and touch it to my breasts."

He could hardly breathe as he obeyed her request.

"Easy," she said, taking his erection in her hands and rubbing it back and forth, the tip playing against her erect nipples. "Just take it slow and easy."

How could he? All he wanted to do was come, and there was no way he could control it any longer.

"Clarissa – I'm going to –" Before he could get the word out, it happened. A throbbing, pulsating explosion.

And as his semen pumped all over her, she smiled – a secret smile. "We'll make a man of you yet, won't we, Norman?"

*

The first thing Mannon did when he arrived back in Los Angeles from the Arizona location was to instruct his driver to stop at a hamburger joint and get him two double burgers with everything on. This health kick Clarissa had him on was all very well, but he needed a break. Fuck it, he was doing his best – she couldn't expect miracles.

Munching the burgers in the limo on the way to his house, he felt one hundred percent better.

Arriving home, he marched inside, the conquering hero returning from the wars of location to see his son.

There was no one to greet him. "Where is everyone?" he hollered.

The Mexican housekeeper appeared. "Meesus Cable, she out."

"And the baby?"

"He out."

Wonderful. He'd rushed home specially, and everyone was out. What a welcome!

Not only were they out, but they did not return for another two hours. By this time he was furious.

"Where have you been?" he demanded, as Melanie-Shanna entered the house. Behind her stood a uniformed nurse carrying his three-week-old son, Jason. Not waiting for an answer, he rushed over to the nurse and inspected her small charge. "Jesus!" he exclaimed. "He looks just like me!"

Later that night, after he'd spent plenty of time staring at his son and heir, and consumed a hearty roast beef dinner and a couple of scotches, he took a second look at Melanie-Shanna. He had to admit it – she was gorgeous. Of course, Clarissa had taught him that gorgeous wasn't everything, and he missed her already, but Melanie-Shanna *was* still his wife, and maybe – until he broke the divorce news – he would be wise to pay her a little attention.

They had just got into bed when he reached for her. "How're you doing, pretty?"

Edging away from his touch she replied, "Fine, thank you."

"You fine – me fine – baby fine. It's good to be home."

"For how long?"

He detected hostility in her voice. Was it possible she'd heard about Clarissa and him? *Deny it. Deny it* and then *Deny it.*

"Only three days, but the rest of the location'll pass faster than you can buy yourself a present at Cartier."

"I want a divorce, Mannon."

What? What did she say? Was he losing his hearing? *I want a diamond necklace* he could understand. *I want an emerald ring* was easy. But *I want a divorce?* Come *on.* That was *his* line. And he wasn't ready to say it. Not yet, anyway.

"Huh?"

"I said" – her voice was clear and calm – "I want a divorce."

"Are you goddamn *crazy?*"

"No. I'm perfectly sane."

"Why?"

"You know why."

"Have you heard things about me and Clarissa?"

No reply.

"*Have* you?"

No reply.

"You've been listening to that cunt Poppy Soloman, haven't you? Well, I'm here to tell you it's lies – *all* goddamn lies."

"I've seen a lawyer."

"You've *what?*"

"He insisted I shouldn't allow you back in the house, but I said you're entitled to spend at least one night with your son."

Fury overcame him. "WHO IS THIS FUCKING SONOFABITCH? I'LL KILL THE MOTHERFUCKER!"

"I want you out, Mannon. I'm divorcing you, and nothing you say will stop me."

He had ranted and screamed, raved and roared. And eventually he'd had to leave for Puerta Vallarta. But not before meeting with *his* lawyer, who told him it was the best thing that could possibly happen. "*She's* throwing *you* out. Can't you see how much better that looks?"

No. He couldn't see it at all. He was very angry.

Clarissa welcomed him back with a wintry smile and a new constant companion – Norman Gooseberger, who followed her everywhere like an obedient and adoring dog.

"If he wasn't a fag I'd say he had the hots for you," Mannon remarked one day.

"Maybe he's *not* gay," she replied mysteriously.

"Ha ha! What a joker."

And so the filming continued, and Mannon tried to forget about Melanie-Shanna and her unfair behaviour.

Clarissa helped him slip back into his role. He was soon as spellbound by her as ever.

Chapter 86

Christmas shopping was an ordeal Silver was glad she didn't have to put up with more than once a year. Under sufferance, Wes agreed to go with her, if only to park the Rolls as they went from Neiman Marcus to Saks, and then across the street to Rodeo Drive. It was a California Christmas, the fancy street decorations and the bright sunshine forming an incongruous alliance.

"At least Rodeo is civilized," Silver remarked, throwing off benevolent waves of good cheer to all who recognized her. She was in rather a good mood, thanks to the way she had handled the Zachary Klinger situation.

Zeppo had called her. "We'll have a lunch, kiddo. Just you an' me."

"As long as you promise not to jump on me, Zeppo dear."

Cackling with amusement he'd said, "Don't think I can't."

"I wouldn't *dream* of thinking *any* such thing. I know you are perfectly capable – you scoundrel, you!"

Zeppo White thrived on flattery, and Silver knew how to pile it on.

Something told her she should make a special effort, so Fernando was summoned to do her hair, and Raoul for her makeup. She chose to wear a devastatingly glamorous Yves Saint Laurent suit.

Arriving at The Beverly Hills Hotel, for lunch in the Polo Lounge, she looked every inch the star.

"Greetings, Miss Anderson," said the maitre d'. "How lovely to see you again."

"Thank you, Pasquale," she said imperiously, and swept to booth one, where Zeppo waited.

Standing up, he said, "Gorgeous, kiddo. Ravishing."

"How kind of you."

"Kind − bullshit. You're the last of the great stars, and don't you ever forget it."

"I'll try not to," she said modestly.

"What a gal!"

During the meal − lightly grilled sole for her, a rare steak for him − they discussed her future career. Zeppo had plenty to talk about, but not one *firm* offer for her to do another movie. Oh yes, there were guest spots on *Palm Springs*, the NBC special, and talk of a record album, but where were the starring film roles he had promised?

"People gotta see what happens with *Romance*," he explained. "When that goes through the ceiling − we name our price."

"You're sure of that?"

"Do dogs crap in Central Park?"

"*So* eloquent."

"So what? As long as you get the game plan." He shifted uncomfortably.

She had a feeling he wanted to say something but wasn't quite sure how to go about it. Unusual for Zeppo.

And then Zachary Klinger walked in, and she knew why she'd taken such care with her appearance. A confrontation was inevitable. Zeppo, the unscrupulous little turd, had arranged it.

"Silver," Zachary greeted her formally.

"Zachary," she replied with cool aplomb.

"Do you mind if I join you?"

Before she could say − *Yes, I do mind very much*, Zeppo was on his feet. With feigned amazement he peered at his oversize watch. "It's two o'clock. Jesus, kiddo, I'm running late. I'm leaving you in excellent hands − the best. This man is a king!"

"Goodbye, Zeppo." She didn't care to listen to his ass-kissing speech. Enough was enough.

Zeppo raced off, and Zachary sat down. There was a long silence. Finally he said, "Tell me, Silver, what is it going to cost me to get you back?"

She glanced edgily around the restaurant. "Too much for even *you* to afford."

"I own Orpheus, you know."

"I'm well aware of that."

"I could make you the most famous woman in the world."

A hint of sarcasm entered her voice. "I'm not doing *too* badly as it is, thank you very much."

"If I don't wish to put *Romance* out, I don't have to. What will *that* do for your career? Everyone will think the film is so bad it can't be released."

Narrowing her eyes she said, "Just try it."

Taking a Dunhill cigar holder from his pocket, he extracted a fat Cuban cigar and lit up, blowing a steady stream of smoke in her direction. "Maybe you'll force me to."

She refused to be intimidated by this man. He had used her. Why did he have to come back after all these years and expect her to fall into his arms?

"Maybe," she said coolly.

He began to laugh. "I always admired your spirit, it always excited me."

"Let this excite you," she said evenly. "I am married. *And* I am in love with my husband. So kindly leave me alone with your disgusting threats and blackmail."

"You're married to a bum," he stated.

"My choice, and I like it." Swiftly she rose.

Putting a restraining hand on her arm he said, "I can spend millions to promote *Romance*, or I can let it languish on a shelf. One night of your company might persuade me to spend the money. Think about it."

"Good*bye*, Zachary."

"I'll be waiting for your call."

Well, she hadn't called him, she had contacted Carlos Brent instead. In his own peculiar way, Carlos had as much power as Zachary Klinger. It was rumoured he was connected – politically and otherwise.

"Carlos, dear," she'd said, glad they were friends again. "What would you do if you found out Orpheus might not release *Romance* because of some *whim* of Zachary Klinger's?"

He'd laughed. "Don't even think about it. *Romance* will be the hit of the year, *I'll* make sure of that."

She wasn't worrying. And she was pleased with the way she'd dealt with Zachary.

They walked into Giorgio, Silver and Wes. He sat at the private bar in the middle of the store while she tried on everything in sight.

"I thought we were *Christmas* shopping for *other* people," he said pointedly.

"Ah, yes," she replied, choosing a beaded handbag for Nora, plus an assortment of Giorgio scent. Then she decided she had to have the most delicious gold beaded Fabrice gown she had ever seen. It was six thousand dollars. "Come and see it, darling," she called to him. "I'll wear it on New Year's Eve."

Strolling over, he said, "What do I care? It's your money. Enjoy it."

He went back to the bar, and was just settling into a nice cold beer, when a familiar voice exclaimed, "Wesley!" And Reba Winogratsky, his former landlady, was all over him with unwelcome wet kisses and a hug or two.

Extracting himself – she was like an over-made-up spider – he gave her a lukewarm greeting.

"Wesley! Wesley! Wesley!" she sighed, with a knowing shake of her head and an affectionate wink. "Look what happened to my Wesley."

Her Wesley?

"How's it going, Reba?" he asked, with more enthusiasm than he felt.

"All the better for seein' you." She spotted Silver emerging from a dressing room and gave an orgasmic yelp. "Introduce me, Wesley. Oh my God! Do I look all right?"

Reba, in a creased beige linen suit – the skirt too short – with bare scorched legs and feet encased in stiletto heels, did not look all right. She looked like a cheap tramp, in spite of the extra-large diamond ring he spotted winking and blinking on her finger.

Noticing his focus of attention, she waved her hand in front of him. "I'm back with my old man – a reconcili-present."

"Nice," he said.

"Intro*duce* me," she hissed again.

Silver strolled over, ignored Reba, and took Wes possessively by the arm. "We can move on, darling. I'm all through here."

"Er . . . this is Reba," he said awkwardly. "She wants to meet you."

Silver gave her the distant but charming smile reserved for

fans. "Hello," she said – and then promptly ignored her again.

Reba sprang into action. "I *looove* you in *Palm Springs*," she gushed. "And I'm so thrilled you and Wesley have gotten married."

"Thank you," Silver replied coolly.

"Wesley an' I are old friends," Reba continued, tripping over her words as she peered at Silver closely to see if she'd had a face-lift. "You *could* say that we shared a house."

Silver voice was pure acid. "How *cosy*."

"Reba was my landlady," Wes explained hurriedly, lest she get the wrong impression.

"And more!" Reba said with a saucy wink. "I was separated from my beloved at the time. And of course, Wesley hadn't met you. And –"

Silver's eyes glittered dangerously as she interrupted Reba in full swing. "*Do* excuse us, we're running late." With a stony expression she swept towards the entrance of the store.

Wes shrugged as he went to follow her. "Bye-bye, Reba."

"What's the matter?" she asked spitefully, blocking his way. "Aren't I good enough to talk to movie stars?"

"Sure you are," he replied easily, trying to dodge past her. "Only we've got a lot of ground to cover today."

A thin smile spread across her face, cracking her carelessly applied makeup. "Pay the money you owe, Wesley. The big boys are impatient. I wouldn't screw with them if I was you. It's gettin' dangerous."

Chapter 87

The New Year's Eve invitations were sent out three days before Christmas, arriving in most homes on Christmas Eve.

Beautifully embossed, and printed on white cards with festive red lettering, they read:

443

Zachary K. Klinger
requests
the pleasure of your company
for a
New Year's Eve cruise
on
December 31
1985

Within hours it was known to be the hottest event of the year, and if you hadn't received an invitation – forget it! Leave town. Crawl under a stone. Kill yourself!

Only fifty invitations were sent out. Zachary had decided that only fifty couples would get lucky. One hundred choice people to see the New Year in with him.

Since Zachary Klinger was one of the richest men in the world, plus he owned a Hollywood movie studio, nobody could afford to turn his invitation down. Zachary had decided that at the party he would announce plans for Orpheus to film a remake of the classic *All About Eve*. The coveted Bette Davis role was a part Silver would kill for. He should have known blackmail wouldn't work, but she was an actress after all, and if the bait was right, maybe he could win her back that way. It was worth a try. And a magnificent party was a small price to pay to gain her attention.

Beverly D'Amo had a great time checking out the guest list with Zachary's fleet of efficient secretaries. She made sure Jade and Corey were included, and then, with a wicked grin, double-checked to ascertain whether Jack Python's name was on the list. It was. Frankly, she saw no harm in getting the two of them together again. After the things Jade had told her she figured they must really be something as a duo. Not that Jade had revealed any gory details – sexual descriptions were not her style. However, by listening to what she *hadn't* said, Beverly knew instinctively they should give each other another chance. There was nothing she would like better than to see her friend settled with the right guy.

"Why are you having this party?" she asked Zachary.

"The start of the New Year should be celebrated in a proper way. I'll make this celebration memorable," he replied.

"I bet you will," she murmured, already aware of some of his plans to make it an event to be remembered. Belly-dancers, break-dancers, a Brazilian trio, disco music, fireworks. And all on a spectacular cruise between Long Beach – where the party guests would join the yacht, courtesy of a fleet of limos – to Laguna and back.

Beverly found that living with Zachary – in spite of his age – was an adventure. And the only part of the adventure she couldn't stomach was his predilection for having sex while hookers watched. God – how she hated it! At first she had thought of it as one of life's more bizarre experiences, shutting her eyes, gritting her teeth, and going with the flow. Now the whole sordid scene disgusted her.

She had moved in with Zachary to advance her career – no use in kidding herself on *that* score. Unfortunately she had fallen in love with him.

Not with his money.

Not with his power.

Beverly D'Amo loved Zachary K. Klinger – the man.

God help her.

Chapter 88

There was only one more day and night left before the cast and crew of *The Murder* left Puerta Vallarta and winged their way back to Los Angeles just in time for Christmas.

As a location it had not been an easy one. The oppressive heat made everything a constant effort. And when it wasn't hot and muggy, it rained – putting the film even more behind schedule. Plus most of the cast and crew suffered at one time or other with what one wag had christened 'the Mexican Hot Trot'.

Clarissa was one of the fortunate few. She ate only fresh vegetables, fish and fruit, flown in daily from L.A. and because of this had not succumbed to the dreaded runs.

Mannon was okay while he stuck to her regime, but a couple

of days before leaving he cheated with an enchilada and a few tequilas with the crew, and lived to regret it.

"It's your own fault," Clarissa said bluntly.

Sometimes he thought she didn't have a sympathetic bone in her body.

He made it through the day's filming, and then lay groaning on his bed all night.

Clarissa did not visit him.

Clarissa was conspicuous by her absence.

"You know, you're a real cold-hearted bitch," he complained to her the next day.

"I am not a nurse," she replied. "If you hadn't filled yourself with junk food, you wouldn't be sick."

True. But still . . . she *could* show a little sympathy.

They had decided that when they returned to Los Angeles, he would move in with her. He hoped he was making the correct decision. Melanie-Shanna fussed the hell out of him if he had so much as a cold. And Whitney always had, too. But then how could he expect Clarissa to behave like other women? Indeed, he wouldn't want her to. She was different, a true artist, and her blazing talent was her main attraction.

He felt a little better the next day, but by the evening his stomach was churning again, and he didn't care to risk being anywhere except close to his bathroom.

Clarissa visited him later. Her fine hair was twisted in a knot and threaded with gardenias. She wore a white off-the-shoulder dress instead of her usual uniform of baggy slacks and a shirt.

"You're all dressed up," he remarked.

"It's the last night. I'm going dancing."

"Who with?"

"Norman."

He should have guessed. Norman Gooseberger. Her faithful slave.

"Have fun."

"I'll try."

"See you in the morning."

Restlessly he lay in bed thinking. Tomorrow was the start of his new life. *The Murder* was the start of his new career.

And yet he couldn't help worrying about the son he was leaving behind.

Jason.

The boy looked just like him.

Was he making the right move?

Yes. Clarissa was his woman now. She combined class and talent. She would bring him up to a new level.

When he awoke several hours later, he was bathed in sweat and had an awesome erection. Best of all, his stomach felt calm. In fact, he was in good shape. The pills the makeup girl had given him had obviously worked. "Take these," she'd said. "You'll wake up singing."

Getting out of bed he showered, waited for his erection to subside, and when it didn't, decided to pay Clarissa a visit, sure she would enjoy it.

Fortunately, they were on the same floor in the hotel, just a few doors apart. Naked under a white towelling bathrobe, he padded barefooted down the corridor, humming softly to himself. Fitting the spare key to her room in the door, he entered quietly.

She was asleep – the room was in darkness. Faintly he could hear the steady rhythm of her breathing.

Slipping off his robe he slid into bed beside her.

She had her back towards him, and he nestled up against it, willing his hard-on to wake her. Or if she didn't want to wake, he would be quite happy to accommodate her while she slept. Cupping her ass with his hands, he prepared to slip in through the back entrance.

Several things happened at once.

Mannon encountered balls.

Norman Gooseberger let out a yell.

And from the other side of the bed Clarissa mumbled a sleepy "What's going on?"

"Jesus Christ!" shouted Mannon, with a rush of realization, leaping from the bed.

Norman sat up equally startled, just in time for Mannon's fist to connect with his jaw.

There was a sickening splintering sound.

Howling with fury, Mannon dragged Norman from the bed, hitting him again and again.

Desperately putting up his hands to defend himself, Norman began to scream with pain. His jaw was hanging as if unhinged, and he knew it was broken.

"You fucking phoney faggot!" Mannon roared. "You cock-sucking ass-licking little *prick!*"

He continued to beat up on Norman, who slumped unconscious under the vicious rain of blows.

447

Clarissa went wild, first trying to grab Mannon's arms and then kicking him on the legs. She couldn't stop him. He was out of control with anger.

Spinning around, he whacked her across the face. "You cheating *bitch*! How dare you cheat on me."

"Fuck you!" she began to scream. "Who do you think you are? Leave him alone, you *monster*. LEAVE HIM ALONE! YOU'RE KILLING HIM, FOR GOD'S SAKE!"

Chapter 89

Christmas morning.

Jack Python took a trip over to the Valley for lunch with Heaven and his father. George appeared to be even more vague and preoccupied than ever. The old man attended lunch, prepared by the housekeeper, then rushed off to his workroom, muttering about a new braking device he was working on.

Heaven waited until George was safely out of the way, and made an announcement. "I'm movin' out," she said. "Rocky found me a great apartment – like with security an' all that stuff."

If she was looking for a fight from Jack, she wasn't going to get it. He didn't blame her.

They exchanged presents, then she went off to see Rocky, and Jack drove over to Kellie Sidney's house, where there were children and dogs and family and food.

Being on his own, Christmas was not Jack's favourite time. Last Christmas he had spent with Clarissa in New York, and hated every minute. He had heard the rumours about her affair with Mannon. What a strange combination! It was difficult to imagine those two together.

Briefly he thought about Jade Johnson, and wished that it had worked out.

It hadn't.

No good thinking of her.

* * *

Rocky greeted Heaven, ushered her into his high-rise Hollywood apartment (cheaply furnished and functional) – and then ushered her into his bed.

She was lonely, but not that lonely.

* * *

Howard Soloman flew back from fixing things in Puerta Vallarta a nervous wreck. How come, when anything bad happened, the first person they called on was him? What was he? The original fixer?

The director of *The Murder*, Dirk Price, had telephoned him in the middle of the night in a total panic. "Mannon's beaten up Clarissa and almost *killed* someone," he screamed hysterically down the phone wires.

"Calm down," Howard responded, already climbing from his comfortable bed. "No police. No hospitals. Use the unit doctor, an' keep everything under wraps until I get there. I'm on my way to the airport now."

"How can I do that?" whined Dirk.

Howard toughened up. "If you ever want to work again, you'll find a way," he warned, and then as an afterthought added, "Who did Mannon nearly kill?"

"Norman Gooseberger."

"Holy shit!"

It had taken clout, but he had fixed it. Norman Gooseberger was in a private nursing home in Mexico City with twenty-four-hour guards to keep out any snoopers. He had suffered a broken jaw, a broken nose, kidney damage, and various cuts and lacerations. His condition was stable.

Clarissa was back in her rented house on Benedict Canyon. She was bruised and shaken, with a black eye Marvin Hagler would have been proud of inflicting.

Mannon had insisted on returning to Melanie-Shanna.

Keeping it out of the newspapers was a nightmare. Finally, Howard huddled with the unit publicist, and they released a short statement.

ON LOCATION IN PUERTA VALLARTA, MEXICO, STARS OF *THE MURDER*, CLARISSA BROWNING AND MANNON CABLE WERE

INVOLVED IN A CAR ACCIDENT. BOTH SUFFERED MINOR BRUISES.
NORMAN GOOSEBERGER, PUBLICIST TO MS. BROWNING, WAS
ALSO HURT.

End of statement.

It took an hour before the rumours swept Hollywood like a tidal wave.

The most difficult part was telling Norman's parents. Howard called them from Puerta Vallarta and gave them the same story as the press release.

"What's the truth?" Orville asked bluntly.

"Not an attractive scenario," Howard replied. "We'll talk when I return. Meanwhile, Norman's fine. All taken care of."

"Should we fly in?"

"Not necessary."

So they didn't.

When Howard returned from Mexico, Poppy grilled him as if she was the F.B.I.

He didn't crack – Poppy had a mouth like the Grand Canyon.

*

Mark Rand accompanied Jade to Connecticut for the Christmas festivities. He was a new Mark Rand – attentive, concerned, caring. He was also divorced.

"I did it for you, sweetheart," he told her in his fine English accent. "Life was very dull without you. You *do* know we belong together, always. And now we can get married."

She was confused. Mark was the man she had lived with and loved for six long years. Theirs had never been a perfect relationship, but she couldn't deny they had experienced a lot of very good times indeed. And when Mark wanted to be, he was the most charming man in the world. He charmed her mother *and* her father.

"Isn't it about time you two got married?" her father asked. "You've waited long enough."

"Just think," her mother whispered excitedly. "When you marry, you'll have a *real* title, you'll be Lady Jade!"

Fortunately, her parents were old-fashioned enough to put them in separate bedrooms. Jade was relieved because, much to Mark's chagrin, she was not ready to leap back into bed with him as though their ten-month break had never happened.

"I want us to get married at once," he informed her.

Was it what *she* wanted?

Hell, she'd wanted it for six years – why not now?

Jack Python. His name kept on intruding into her thoughts.

Damn Jack Python. He was one night of great sex.

That was it.

Period.

In yesterday's newspapers there was a picture of him with Kellie Sidney at a film premiere.

How nice.

She hoped the two of them would be very unhappy.

"We'll get married in California," she promised Mark. "On New Year's Day."

"You'll never regret it, sweetheart," he replied with heartfelt sincerity. "I'll make up for all the time we've wasted."

Since arriving from California, Corey had seemed fidgety and nervous.

"What's up, bro?" she asked.

"It's Norman," he said. "Everything was going so well between us, until he went off to work on *The Murder*."

"There's nothing wrong with that, is there? It's his job, and you know he's the best at what he does."

"I know," Corey confessed miserably. "And at first he phoned me every day. But since he became Clarissa Browning's personal P.R., I haven't heard from him in weeks. He was supposed to be back in L.A. by now. I keep on calling the house, and there's no reply."

"Try his parents," she suggested. "It's Christmas Day – I bet he's over at their place."

"Will you do it for me?" he begged.

Sighing, she said, "Give me the number."

Orville answered the phone, and wanted to know exactly who she was and why she was calling.

"My name is Jade Johnson," she said. "I'm a friend of Norman's, and a client. Can I speak to him?"

"Norman's not here," Orville said, lowering his voice. "He had a car accident in Mexico, he won't be back for a while."

"I'm sorry to hear that. It's nothing serious, is it? Is he all right?"

"Perfectly all right. He's . . . er . . . recuperating. Somewhere, I'm not sure where."

"I'd like to send flowers."

"They'll have to wait until he gets back. I have no address for him."

When she put down the phone, Corey was frantic to know what had happened. She relayed Orville's conversation.

He nodded, dully accepting the fact that Norman had no doubt found someone else.

Jade felt so sorry for her brother. She wished there was something she could do, only somehow words didn't seem enough. "Are you okay?" she asked full of concern.

He attempted a wry smile – didn't quite make it and gestured helplessly. "I changed my life for Norman," he said.

"No." She shook her head. "You didn't change *just* for Norman. You changed because it was what you *wanted* to do."

He realized the truth in what she was saying and nodded again. "You're right. Living a lie was killing me."

"And now you're free."

"I guess I am."

She squeezed his hand. "You know what Beverly always says – miss one taxi – there's a dozen more around the block."

"I'm not looking."

"You will."

He couldn't help smiling. "Love ya, sis."

"You too, baby brother."

★

Melanie-Shanna baked the turkey herself. And she fixed sweet potatoes, broccoli, corn bread, fresh peas, and a thick country gravy to go with it.

"Sen . . . *sational!*" Mannon praised, holding his plate out for seconds.

Piling more food on his plate, she wondered at the sudden difference in her errant husband. He had arrived back from Puerta Vallarta a changed man. The first words out of his mouth were "I don't want a divorce. I love you. I love the baby. That movie made me crazy. WE ARE NOT GETTING DIVORCED. I want to sell this goddamn mansion and buy a place in Mandeville Canyon – near the beach. We'll have room to keep horses and dogs. And I want us to have six more children. What d'you say?"

At first she had refused even to entertain the idea. But Mannon could be devilishly persuasive – not to mention charming, and eventually she succumbed. After all, she loved the man.

"That place was a nightmare," he told her. "Next time I go on location you're coming with me. You and the baby. No more lonely nights."

He'd hugged her so tight she thought she might break in two.

"What happened, Mannon?" she asked very quietly.

"Nothing," he said. A pause. "Nothing I want to talk about . . . not yet anyway."

*

Nora was at Silver's Christmas lunch, along with Fernando, his friend Boyce, her makeup artist Raoul, and her ex-agent Quinne Lattimore – who had recently separated from his wife of twenty-eight years.

"I can't *bear* to think of anyone alone at Christmas," Silver confided to Wes.

"Yeah," he agreed, thinking of all the Christmases he had spent alone and broke, usually ending up in bed with a woman as lonely as he.

Happiness was Silver speaking to him again. After bumping into Reba at Giorgio, she had flipped out – throwing a total jealous fit.

Who was that woman?
Have you slept with her?
My God, Wes. Where is your taste?
Or should I call you Wesley?
Wesley, indeed!
Was she hot in bed?
She looks like a prostitute.
An old prostitute.
A cheap hooker.
How could you?
When?
Recently?
Since we've been together?
I hate you!

A jealous Silver was a new Silver. Despite her acid tongue, he was glad she cared. So glad, in fact, that with a gesture of defiance he marched into the First Interstate Bank, requested his safe-deposit box, and took out the money he had stashed there. Screw the perpetrators of the Laurel Canyon scam. He was not returning one red cent. He had earned every dime.

And screw Reba Winogratsky too. What did she know anyway?

With the money in his pocket he strolled calmly into Tiffany's, the jewellery store, and announced his requirements. "I want a necklace for around nineteen thou," he said casually. "Tax included. Show me what you got."

The result was a ruby heart, embedded in pavé diamonds, on a diamond-studded gold chain. He hadn't given it to her yet. The moment had to be just right.

"Delicious turkey," Fernando said, dabbing his lips with a napkin.

"Delicious," echoed Boyce, his quiff of silver hair bobbing agreement.

"Did you cook it, Silver darling?" teased Raoul.

"*Naturellement, mon chéri!* Don't you all know how handy I am toiling over a hot stove?"

Everyone laughed.

In the kitchen Vladimir and Unity faced each other across the table and solemnly raised their shot glasses of the finest Russian vodka in a toast.

"To freedom," Vladimir said, downing the colourless liquid in one fast gulp.

"To money," Unity said.

They smiled at each other like conspirators. Which they were. *True Life Scandal* was paying them one hundred and twenty-five thousand dollars for the *real* story of Silver Anderson, Wes Money and Heaven. It was to be serialized over three weeks, and the first instalment was due to hit the stands on the Monday after New Year's.

By that time, Unity and Vladimir would be long gone.

Somewhere in New York . . .
Sometime in the seventies . . .

The girl found that living with Eli was the beginning of her life. He was the most unfailingly cheerful and good-natured person she had ever met, and after a while she couldn't help responding to his kindness.

"Where are you from?"

"I don't want to talk about it."

"What do you wanna do?"

"Being a waitress is fine."

"No, it's not."

"Why?"

"Because we are all put onto this earth to do something amazing with our lives. Make a goal, an' go for it!"

She didn't have any goals. Just living was enough.

Eli wouldn't allow her to drift. He insisted she accompany him to his singing classes and dancing lessons. One day he took her to his drama group, and she watched enthralled as he acted out a role in Macbeth.

"It's Shakespeare," he told her.

"What's Shakespeare?"

"Are you kiddin' me, girl?"

On her birthday he bombarded her with books on great playwrights, and text of their best work. "You gotta be more than just a pretty face," he told her.

She was captivated by the realistic scenes of great pathos and drama. Occasionally Eli brought a friend home. She hated it when this happened, and if it was early enough she would go out and walk the streets rather than listen to the unwelcome sounds of their lovemaking.

One day he brought a friend home to stay. "This is Luke," he said, and she shivered with certain knowledge of bad things to come.

Luke was a burly, British blond with bulging muscles and a permanent sneer. He never dressed in anything but crotch-hugging Levis and torn tee-shirts.

"Luke thinks he's Marlon Brando," Eli joked.

"Don't fockin' laugh at me — yer spade fairy," Luke spat.

Eli winced and took it.

Luke didn't work. He sat on the roof all day, concentrating on his suntan and guzzling beer.

The girl did not understand what Eli saw in him. She knew it was only sexual, and hoped the attraction would soon pass.

At night she heard them together and buried her head beneath the covers, desperately trying to shut out the disturbing sounds.

Luke soon became violent. After several weeks he began to take Eli's money, and go out on drinking binges.

He tried to steal money from her one day, but she turned on him with such ferocity that he never went near her again.

She slept with a knife under her pillow, and was ever watchful.

"Get rid of the fockin' bitch," she heard him tell Eli.

"She stays," Eli replied, standing up to him for once.

"She goes or I go."

"So be it," replied Eli bravely.

To her enormous relief, Luke departed.

"I don't know what happens to me," Eli confessed. *"When it comes to the Lukes of this world I just can't control myself."*

They talked late into the night, and for the first time, falteringly, she began to confide in Eli, as he was confiding in her. They shared a closeness that was very special.

Sometime in the early morning, Luke returned. The girl was roused by stifled noises. Luke was not alone, he had two friends with him. They were taking turns holding Eli down and using him.

She felt the fear leap into her throat as she remembered that time — not so long ago — when she had been abused in the same way. Leaping from her bed, she brandished her knife in the air, shouting, "Stop it! Go away! Get out! STOP IT!"

They took their time before leaving, finishing what they'd set out to do.

The ambulance arrived too late.

Eli bled to death from internal injuries on the way to Emergency.

Several weeks later the girl tracked Luke down to a seedy walk-up he was sharing with a male prostitute in a condemned building. She waited until the prostitute was out plying his trade, and then she torched the building.

Lighting the first match was easy . . .

BOOK SIX

Hollywood, California
New Year's Eve
December 31
1985

Chapter 90

"Our limousine awaits," Mark said, with a twist of irony. "I do love you Americans – you do things with such panache. The driver tells me there are forty-nine identical white limos with fully stocked bars and a supply of the best caviar, to transport Zachary Klinger's illustrious guests to his waiting yacht. You'd think he might want to double up, save a bob or two. I wouldn't have minded more of the incredible Zeppo White, and that strange zombie-like lady he's married to."

Jade stifled a laugh. "Don't be so rude."

'You must admit, they do make strange bedfellows."

"Well . . ."

Taking her hand he said, "Speaking as a premier photographer of wild and beautiful creatures, you, my dear, are the most beautiful of all."

"Thank you."

"Surpassing even a pregnant leopard I recently had the privilege of observing."

"You're such a flatterer."

"Part of my English charm."

"And *sooo* modest."

"One tries one's best."

She had to admit that being with Mark again was pleasurable. He made her laugh with his dry sense of humour. And she was almost convinced that marrying him was the right thing to do.

It better be. They had taken out the licence, had the requisite blood tests, and tomorrow was the big day.

Beverly had freaked out when she'd told her. "*Whaaat?* You an' the English asshole? This girl does *not* believe it."

"Now that I'm marrying him, Bev, let's drop the asshole bit, huh? I don't think it's really appropriate, do you?"

"Whatever you say. I'm easy."

When Beverly realized that Jade was seriously getting married, she offered the use of Zachary's mansion for the ceremony, sure he wouldn't mind.

"No guests," Jade warned. "We just want to do it quietly, and then take off for a couple of days in Carmel before I have to shoot the final batch of commercials."

"Try this for fit. The two of you. Corey. Me. A sunlit garden – if the goddamn weather doesn't change – and a nice friendly preacher. Zachary's flying off to New York right after the party. How does the scenario grab you?"

"Perfect!"

"It's arranged."

Mark had liked the idea when she told him. "I can't wait, my darling," he'd said.

She knew why. She still hadn't slept with him, and he couldn't stand that she was making him wait.

"Aren't I worth waiting for?" she'd teased him.

"Jade. This is ridiculous. We lived together for six years. Why are you doing this?"

"Because it's romantic. Besides, it's such a short time, and it'll make our wedding night really special."

For Zachary's New Year's Eve cruise she had chosen to wear a black cashmere Ralph Lauren sweater, sleeveless, with one shoulder completely bare; white silk pants; a bronze buckled belt; and a whirl of delicately thin bronze bracelets around her upper arm. Hoop earrings, and slave bangles on each wrist, completed her look. On her engagement finger was the antique sapphire and diamond ring Mark had presented her with on Christmas day.

"Let's go," she said, with a dazzling smile. "I promised Corey we'd pick him up on the way."

Mark was ready.

*

Poppy was in gold. From the ornament in her hair to the shoes on her feet, everything was gold, including her nails.

Howard took one look and decided she should be frozen in time, reduced in size, and placed on somebody's mantel – next to an Oscar.

He did not feel well. After snorting cocaine all day, gulping a few Quaaludes, and a Valium or two, he felt like shit.

Once, cocaine was the answer to everything. A couple of toots and he was King Kong. More, and he was ready to take over the world.

Now the rush didn't last. It brought him up, and sank him back down almost immediately. And his nose was killing him. Every time he snorted, the pain was like a thousand tiny needles jabbing the sensitive membrane in his nostrils.

Of course, he knew there were other methods of doing it. If he wasn't so queasy about needles, he could inject himself with the magic potion.

He'd tried it once and nearly passed out. Besides, injecting drugs? Wasn't that getting a little desperate? He was no junkie.

"Honeybunch, have you set the tape machine?" Poppy asked. "I don't want to miss Zachary on the Python show."

"If I know old Zach," Howard said, with a manic twitch, "he'll have a screening room on the boat, and we'll all have to sit and watch. Talk about a captive audience! That's probably why he's having the party on his yacht in the first place. Nobody can escape."

Poppy adjusted a huge gold earring. "*I* think it's a *wonderful* way to spend New Year's Eve. I'm bored with normal parties."

"As long as you don't get seasick."

"Oooh. It's not going to be *rough*, is it?"

"Just kidding."

On their way out to the car, Roselight's nanny came running after them. "Mr Soloman," she called, "there's a call for you from Mexico City. The operator says it's urgent."

*

"I can't imagine like *why* they invited *me*," Heaven said, excitedly gobbling caviar as the white stretch limousine transported her and Rocky to Long Beach, and Zachary K. Klinger's exclusive party.

"'Cos you're a star," Rocky said confidently. "An' don' forget who did it for ya."

"Maybe Uncle Jack suggested they ask me," she mused.

"Naw. Why'd he do that?"

"It's New Year's Eve. He always tries to see me then."

"Yeah?"

"Yes."

"Forget about ya Uncle Jack," Rocky said, flicking on the built-in television. "You're a big girl now – ya got *me*."

*

461

"I must have been unhinged to even *think* about letting you get away from me," Mannon said, his arm around Melanie-Shanna as they entered the limousine.

"I was sure it was what you wanted," she replied softly. "You were so cold towards me. I could never do or say the right thing. And when I got pregnant it was like you couldn't care less."

"I guess the idea of becoming a father made me nervous."

"It wasn't exactly easy for *me*. Especially with your attitude . . ." She hesitated. "And Whitney . . ."

He hadn't thought of Whitney in months. One thing Clarissa had cured him of was his obsession with his ex-wife. And now he was cured of Clarissa too. Christ! When he remembered that night in Puerta Vallarta he was so ashamed. Beating that boy, half killing him. The memory was a nightmare. Thank God for Howard, who kept the whole deal out of the press, and spirited him out of there.

The fucking pills the stupid makeup girl had given him had made him crazy. Not to mention Clarissa. Thinking of her now, he shuddered. The woman was a fling, an interlude, and an unfaithful liar.

He couldn't care less if he never set eyes on her again.

*

They'd taped *Face to Face with Python* early, ready for viewing later that evening, and it was a smash. Zachary K. Klinger was the kind of guest Jack wished he had on every week – forceful, opinionated, jagged, and sharp as a stiletto.

"What a show!" Aldrich congratulated him. "Dynamite! Especially when you got him talking about his personal life, and his sorrow at never having kids. Jesus, Jack – it's compulsive viewing."

Jack agreed. He knew it was a sensational show, and he also knew it presented an in-depth portrait of a man who had everything – and yet yearned for what he thought he was missing. Great insightful television. It wasn't often he could say that.

Zachary had been pleased too. Considering he never consented to do interviews, it was a real coup for the Python Show to get him.

"I'll see you at my party," Zachary said as he departed, accompanied by several assistants. "I understand you're bringing Senator Richmond with you. I'm delighted. I haven't seen him for a while. I had no idea he was out here."

Jack didn't say — *He's visiting Danielle.* He merely nodded, and wondered how he had become the beard for Peter Richmond.

They were all going to the party together: Jack with Kellie Sidney, the Senator with Danielle Vadeeme.

Peter Richmond had phoned him and asked, "Are you attending Zachary Klinger's party?"

When he'd said yes, the Senator had inveigled an invitation for himself and the French actress. "Danielle wants to go," he'd explained. "If we come with you it will appear *you're* with her."

"I'm taking Kellie," Jack had explained.

"With your reputation," Peter guffawed, "everyone will naturally assume you're with the two of them. I have to be careful. I *am* a married man, you know."

On the cheat.

Weren't most of them?

Sometimes Jack found it useful to store favours, so he'd agreed.

Kellie kept him waiting as usual. He was used to it now, as the dogs crawled all over him, and her three-year-old son greeted him with a sticky hug. Kellie walked the tight-rope between movie-star, mom, and producer with careless style.

"Ooops!" she exclaimed, rushing into the living room clad in a sexy long dress. "Odd earrings!"

"And shoes," he pointed out.

"No?"

"Take a look."

Glancing down at her feet, she clapped a hand over her mouth. "What a putz!"

"But a lovable one."

She grinned at him. "Thanks!"

It had taken effort on his part, getting connected with Kellie again. After the Spago incident, when he had slipped away with Jade Johnson, she had not been inclined to see him again. It had taken roses and persuasion, for out of all the women he'd dated since Clarissa (excluding Jade, of course — *she* was something else) Kellie was the nicest. And he admired her strong sense of family.

"I can't wait to meet the Senator," Kellie said. "I hear he's quite a boy in Washington."

"So I believe."

"Politicians are *very* highly sexed."

"How do you know?"

She giggled. "I never said I was a virgin when we met!"

* * *

Up in Benedict Canyon, Clarissa let the driver wait as she finished getting ready. She wore a navy blue pants suit and a white sweater. Nothing fancy for Clarissa Browning. She didn't need the phoney glitter of Hollywood.

Leaning close to her mirror, she traced the outline of a faint black eye – a souvenir of Mannon Cable. The violent bastard.

Earlier, she had called the private nursing home in Mexico to ask after Norman. They refused to give out information on the phone, even though she had a private number to contact.

She brooded about Puerta Vallarta and what had taken place there. Mannon Cable should have been properly punished for behaving like a maniac, but no – Howard Soloman had arrived with his warnings and threats. "If you let out one word of this," he had told her, "your career will be over, finished. Just like that."

Hollywood folk.

They had their own laws.

Hollywood folk.

Sometimes she loathed the whole pack of them.

* * *

Beverly D'Amo was rushing from the house on her way to Long Beach to meet Zachary when the messenger arrived, carrying a brown manila envelope marked:

EXTREMELY URGENT

PRIVATE PAPERS

Attention of: ZACHARY K. KLINGER

Hand-delivered envelopes arrived for Zachary every day – often marked URGENT. But extremely urgent?

She decided she'd better bring it with her. Not that he would want to be bothered in the middle of his party – only with Zachary, one never knew. And if she *didn't* take it he'd probably ask if it had arrived, and then berate her for *not* bringing it.

Couldn't win.

She tossed it on the back seat of the limo and promptly forgot it for the moment.

* * *

"Happy New Year, Vladimir. And you too, Unity, dear," Silver said graciously, thinking to herself what an absolutely bizarre couple they made – her gay Russian houseman, and Wes's little cousin. They seemed to have formed some peculiar kind of liaison "Are you going out?"

"Yes, madame," Vladimir replied courteously. *We are going out and never coming back.* With sixty-five thousand dollars apiece, finding somewhere to go should present no problem.

"Perhaps you'd like your picture taken with me," Silver said with a winning smile. "Wes – get your camera."

She knew she had never looked better. Wes Money was like a rejuvenating tonic. Her skin was smooth and clear with the flush of regular sex, her body trimmer than ever. And the six-thousand-dollar Fabrice dress she had invested in was spectacular. Not to mention Wes's surprise gift – a stunning diamond and ruby heart necklace. She'd been quite taken aback when he presented her with it on Christmas night. "Tell me," she'd whispered later, "did *I* pay for it?"

"No, you didn't," he'd replied, insulted.

"Well, where did you get the money?" she'd asked, perplexed.

"My life's savings," he'd replied jauntily. "Consider it well spent. Now I really *am* busted out."

How touched she was by his generous gesture. "I've been thinking, we should put you on the payroll," she'd said. "After all, you've been handling all my affairs. Does ten percent of my earnings seem fair? We can have my lawyer draw up contracts."

He'd laughed. "While we're together what's yours is mine. Right? Let's leave it that way."

Time and time again he had proved that he wasn't after her money. Thank God she'd chosen him, and not that dreadful, power-hungry, social-climbing Dennis Denby.

Wes picked up his new Nikon camera – a Christmas gift from Silver, along with a metallic silver Ferrari ("Every time you look at it, darling, you'll think of me!"), a Sony video camera, and a virtual closetful of new clothes.

"Come here, Vladimir," she called. "And Unity, dear, would you like to be in the picture too?"

Vladimir threw Unity a commanding glare. This photograph would be worth another few thousand! What luck!

Silver stood between Vladimir and a reluctant Unity, her arms around each of them, a perfect smile in perfect place. Pictures with the staff were part of the game. Oh, how they loved it!

Vladimir would be able to show the snap to all of his friends and boast endlessly of his famous employer.

"Perhaps Madame vould like a photograph of herself and Mr Ves together?" Vladimir suggested respectfully.

"What a good idea," she said, beaming. "Oh, and Vladimir, you may sleep in tomorrow. No sense in you getting up at six as usual. Shall we say nine o'clock?"

"Thank you, madame." Selfish woman. She wouldn't leave *her* bed until at least noon. Besides, New Year's Day was supposed to be a holiday.

Why should he care? He would be long gone. Hawaii was his first planned stop. Hawaii, with a tall and tanned ex-stripper, who sang like Sinatra, and gave great toe massage.

Snap.

"Another one," Silver said.

Snap.

"Just one more." She snuggled closer to Wes.

Snap.

"That's enough," said Wes. "We can't be late, they'll sail without us."

Silver raised an amused eyebrow. "You *are* joking?"

"Mr Ves," Vladimir said humbly. "Just one vith you and your cousin."

Wes didn't need a picture with Unity – she'd turned out to be a miserable cow, not at all grateful for his help. Serious thought was going into how to get rid of her – without the whole story being revealed.

It seemed simpler to pose and get out of there. Vladimir took the picture, and Wes took the camera from him. "Shall we bring it with us?" he asked Silver.

Laughing delicately, she said, "Darling, this is the most important and exclusive party of the year. If *you* want to look like a Japanese tourist, bring it by all means."

And on that line she exited. Ever the star. And ready to party.

466

Chapter 91

Everyone was aboard. Music played, champagne flowed, and the white yacht – christened *Klinger II* – set sail from Long Beach on time. Zachary's main yacht – *Klinger I* – stayed permanently on the Mediterranean coast. But *Klinger II* was no slouch in the luxury stakes. A large sleek vessel, it accommodated Zachary's party with ease. The hundred guests mingled happily, giving off a certain air of triumph. They were the lucky ones, the chosen few. This would be a party to remember.

The heated main deck was festooned with fairy lights, flashing and winking in the dark night sky. Small, intimate tables surrounded a dance floor, while a trio of musicians played appealing Brazilian sounds.

"Kiddo!" Zeppo stood up and waved to Jade, beckoning her over to his table. "Join Ida and me."

"Shall we?" she whispered to Mark.

"Certainly," he replied. "The man is a riot!"

"Okay with you?" she checked with Corey.

"I think I'll just wander around," he said.

"Are you sure?"

"I'll feel more comfortable doing that."

Leaving his sister and her bridegroom-to-be, he made his way into a magnificent dining room, where white-coated waiters were putting the finishing touches to a sumptuous buffet of lobster, cold salmon, oysters and numerous salads.

Corey was in a deep depression. Norman leaving Los Angeles was bad enough. But not to even call, to just drop him without a word over Christmas and New Year's, was unforgivable. He had left his wife and child for Norman, completely changed his way of living, and now his whole world had crumbled.

"Looks good enough to eat, doesn't it?"

467

"Huh?" Corey glanced over at the speaker, a skinny blond waiter with bright sharp eyes and a thin mouth.

"I guess, if we're lucky, we'll get the leftovers."

"Yes," Corey agreed vaguely.

"Are you in the biz?"

Slowly Corey realized the waiter was coming on to him. Jesus! he thought. Don't tell me it's beginning to show. One glance and they *know*.

"I'm married," he said quickly.

"No law against *that*," the waiter replied with an encouraging wink. "*I* don't care if you don't."

Retribution. A suitable punishment for Norman. They had sworn to each other that they wouldn't play around. AIDS was the Russian Roulette of the eighties, and only a fool would risk promiscuity.

*

The butterflies were churning as Heaven accepted compliments from all and sundry.

You're an original!

Love your record!

My daughter worships you!

My son wants to know if you have a poster out?

She was being fêted by every old fogey in town!

And none of them was mentioning her mother!

A blast.

A mega-blast.

"I'm famous," she informed Rocky.

"Told ya I'd do it for ya," he boasted.

Swirling her fake leopardskin coat around her, she revealed a cut-out lace body suit underneath, and a lot of bare midriff. "They like what I do!" she squealed.

"Hey – hey – hey – why shouldn't they?"

Bobbing her head confidently, she said, "You're right. Why shouldn't they? I'm almost a star, and I *loooove* it!"

Rocky grinned. He loved it too. Only he couldn't let a party like this go to waste. There were big spenders aboard. Studio heads and movie stars. He was almost bailing out of dealing drugs. Almost . . . not quite. There were some opportunities he just couldn't let slip by.

"I gotta go t' the john," he said quickly. "Don't go away."

Where did he think she was going? She was having the time of her life. She'd already greeted Uncle Jack, successfully avoided her mother, and now she was enjoying all this newfound attention.

"Hello, again."

She turned, ready to accept another compliment, and found herself facing Penn Sullivan.

Oh God! She felt sick, nervous and hesitant all at the same time. Penn Sullivan! He was totally gorgeous!

"Uh . . . hi," she mumbled, sounding like a stupid idiot.

"Having fun?"

"Are you?" she managed.

"Well, now that I've seen Heaven . . ."

Was it her imagination or was he coming on to her?

"Do you know something?" he asked.

"What?" she gulped.

"We're the youngest people on board. Somehow, I think we got railroaded into the wrong party."

She couldn't care less *what* they'd got railroaded into. Penn Sullivan was utterly amazing!

*

"When are you visiting Washington? I'd like very much to be your official guide," Senator Peter Richmond said to Kellie Sidney. He was a Kennedy clone, with a John Lindsay profile, and – one of these days – a fair shot at the main chance.

"I wasn't planning a trip in the near future," she said brightly.

"You're missing a lot of fun," he replied, double entendre at full mast.

"I'm sure I am." She looked at Jack to save her, but he was allowing her no mercy, forcing her to handle the randy Senator all on her own.

Whitney Valentine, undulating past, rescued her. The Senator took one lecherous look at the quivering Ms. Valentine – sheathed in body-hugging silk jersey with nipples on show – and was on his feet in a flash.

Jack almost laughed aloud. Washington meets Hollywood. What a *perfect* combination. Real power and real glamour. He remembered the Kennedy scandals and Marilyn Monroe. The entire country had shivered on the edge of ecstasy for months.

Unfortunately, Danielle Vadeeme had failed to materialize. Earlier, when Jack and Kellie had arrived to pick them up, the Senator was alone. "Food poisoning," he'd explained. "Danielle insisted I mustn't let you down."

Now he was hot to boogie. With whoever cooperated.

"Hasn't the man ever seen a woman before?" Kellie whispered, as they both watched him go to work on Whitney, who seemed to take him quite seriously.

*

Zachary held court in his library. The large yacht featured several entertaining areas, and the guests could wander around as they pleased.

Poppy Soloman sat as close to Zachary as possible. She was worried about Howard. He had been behaving very strangely lately. In the car on the way to the party he was like a zombie, and he wouldn't even tell her what the urgent phone call from Mexico was all about.

"What's the matter?" she'd asked.

"Migraine."

After that he'd refused to speak, in spite of valiant efforts on her part.

"I've been meaning to ask you something," she said to Zachary in her breathy, little-girl voice. "You do know that Howard lives, eats, and breathes Orpheus? The studio is his life."

"I've always appreciated loyalty," Zachary replied, puffing on his cigar. "I pay well for it."

"I'm sure you do. And you can't get anyone more loyal than my Howie."

Zachary couldn't be bothered with people who didn't get right to the point. "What are you getting at?" he asked brusquely.

"He needs a vacation, he really does," she sighed.

"I'm not stopping him," Zachary pointed out.

"I know," she said, very seriously, realizing that if Howard caught her having this conversation he would be furious. "But he refuses to take one. And unless you force him, he'll just keep going until he drops."

Zachary nodded. He was quite impressed by her concern. Poppy had never struck him as a caring wife until now.

"I'll see he takes a vacation," he promised. "I'll order him to. Will that suit you?"

"Thank you," she said gratefully, already planning Paris, Rome, maybe even London — the shops were great in London.

*

Meanwhile, Clarissa had cornered Howard on one of the upper decks.

"I phoned the nursing home earlier," she said sharply. "They refused to give me any information about Norman. You know perfectly well they're supposed to tell me how he is. Have you changed the instructions and forgotten to leave my name?"

"Uh . . . things are a little different."

"Different? What are you *talking* about?"

He looked around to see if they were being overheard. "It's not a matter for discussion tonight."

"*What* isn't?" Aggravation filled her voice.

"Tomorrow, Clarissa. I'll come by your house in the morning."

"I don't need you in my house, Howard. I want to know what's going on, and I want to know *now*."

Howard muttered something she didn't hear. "What?" she snapped, making him repeat it.

"He's dead," he mumbled.

Mesmerized, she watched a muscle twitch wildly by his right eye, while a cold, clammy feeling swept over her, a mixture of fear and hate. "Dead?" she echoed dully.

Taking a deep gulp of night air, and wiping the sweat from his brow, he said, "'Fraid so."

Chapter 92

He knew she was aboard – Beverly had told him. Only Jack Python had her number now, and he wasn't about to fall a second time.

Casually he strolled around the yacht looking for her. He had told Kellie he was going to the men's room, and she seemed quite happy chatting to an amenably stoned Chuck Nielson.

When he spotted her, he thought – *Ha! So she's beautiful. So what?* And like a magnet he was drawn towards the table where she sat with the Whites and a sandy-haired man.

"Hello, Zeppo. Ida, how are you?"

Zeppo jumped to his feet. "Jack, my boy. The report on tonight's show is fabulous."

Zeppo always knew everything — sometimes before it happened.

"Thanks. Zachary's putting it on later, are you going to watch?" He could smell her scent; it reminded him of no one else.

"Wouldn't miss it, kiddo," enthused Zeppo. "Do you know Jade Johnson?"

"Yes, he does," interrupted Ida knowingly.

"We've met," Jack replied, staring straight at her.

"And her fiancé, Lord Mark Rand."

Her *what*?

"Congratulations," he said, almost too quickly. "I didn't know you were engaged. When's the wedding?"

"Tomorrow," she said calmly. "How are you?"

"Fine, great, I couldn't be better."

Her eyes were wide and flecked with little pieces of gold coin. He knew what her hair felt like, soft and silky. And he could remember in an instant how incredible it was to be in bed with her.

She was engaged, *goddammit*. She was about to marry someone else.

"I saw the show you did with Lord Snowdon," Mark said. "A very interesting piece of journalism. You asked all the right questions." Turning to Jade he added, "Didn't we see it together, darling?"

Together? The show with Snowdon was three years ago. This must be the English jerk she'd mentioned. The English jerk she'd said was out of her life.

"I don't remember," she murmured vaguely.

The Brazilian trio were playing *The Girl from Ipanema*.

> Tall and tan and young and lovely
> The girl from Ipanema goes walking
> And when she passes each one she passes goes
> Ahhh . . .

"Do you mind if I steal a dance with Jade?" Jack asked abruptly.

"It's up to the lady herself," Mark replied with a hearty chuckle. "She always makes her own decisions."

"Shall we?" He held her gaze with his deadly green eyes.

Oh God! Why did she feel like this whenever she saw him? *I*

472

swear I'm regressing, she thought. *I'm sixteen, and standing next to the football hero at my first prom.*

She wasn't about to let the professional stud think he'd got to her. "Sure," she replied casually, wondering why her voice sounded like an idiot's squeak.

They moved to the dance floor, held each other at arm's length for a beat or two, and then – as if by mutual consent – he pulled her closer to him, and she felt her flesh burn where his hand rested on her bare shoulder.

"Hello," he whispered, as if nothing had happened.

*

"*Adore* your dress," Silver said to Dee Dee Dionne.

"Adore *yours*," Dee Dee replied. "Fabrice?"

"But of course."

"Shit! I hate it when broads gab on about clothes," Carlos said loudly. Zachary and he had forgotten about their fight, and were now talking again, hence his appearance at the party.

"It's just our way," soothed Dee Dee.

"Broads are good for fuckin', suckin' an' shoppin'. Give 'em anything else t'do, an' they're lost souls." Carlos roared with laughter at his own humour, expecting Wes to do the same.

Wes didn't. He wasn't entourage material, and Silver loved him for it.

Carlos was three-quarters of the way through a bottle of Jack Daniels, and feeling no pain. "Wassamatter?" he slurred. "Not funny?"

"No," Silver said curtly, remembering why their affair – so many years ago – had broken up. When Carlos got into heavy drinking he became a pig. "Vulgar and *very* unamusing."

Ignoring her, he nudged Wes. "Ever had a black chick suck your dick?"

Dee Dee's mouth tightened with disapproval and embarrassment.

"Black chicks are the best," Carlos continued. "*The . . . very . . . best.*"

"Come on, darling, let's go get some food," Silver said quickly.

"'Course, our little Silvy here doesn't want to hear that," Carlos sniggered. "'Cos our little Silvy thinks *she's* the best cocksucker in town. She th –"

Wes hauled back and punched him right in the mouth.

Carlos slid to the ground like a pole-axed bear.

It was over in seconds.

Summoning a couple of waiters, Wes said, "Carry Mr Brent downstairs an' put him to bed, he's not feelin' well."

The waiters exchanged glances, then proceeded to pick up the fallen superstar and cart him off, a concerned Dee Dee in attendance.

"You shouldn't have done that," Silver said, her eyes bright with admiration.

"Why not? He insulted you."

"Darling, he was drunk."

"Yup. An' that's the only way to deal with 'em. When I was working bar I used to do it all the time. He won't even remember when he wakes up."

"Someone will tell him. And Carlos Brent is not a nice man to have as an enemy."

"You think I care? Listen, Silver, I may be a peasant, but where I come from – if someone insults a lady, they're askin' for it. 'Specially if that lady just happens to be my wife."

Inexplicably she felt like crying. Nobody had ever defended her before – except Zachary, and he didn't count.

*

The news was brought to Zachary by a minion.

"Put him in my stateroom," he said generously.

"Yes, Mr Klinger."

"What happened?" Beverly asked.

"A little fracas. Carlos seems to have a penchant for inviting a right hook."

"That man is one rude sonofabitch."

"We're fortunate he left his bodyguards on shore. A brawl was hardly my plan for this evening."

"Maybe he'll sue you," Beverly said flippantly.

"He didn't sue when *I* hit him. Why should he do so now?"

"It's your boat."

"Perhaps I'll go see him."

Beverly stopped him with a hand on his arm. "What *is* it with Silver Anderson? She's not exactly Brooke Shields, and yet every time there's a fight, she's involved."

Zachary paused to think of the right answer. "She's a true star," he said at last. "She excites loyalty."

*

"Has anyone ever told you that you are —"

"Whatever you're going to say — don't. Okay?"

"Why?"

"Because I can't stand bullshit. You've drowned me in it once, and I don't need a repeat performance. Shall we sit down?"

"No." He had her in a tight hold, and he couldn't help noticing that she didn't attempt to break it. "Are you seriously getting married?"

"Yes, I seriously am."

"Why?"

"I don't really imagine it's any of your business, do you?"

"As a matter of fact I think you owe me an explanation."

Now she did struggle, but only slightly. "*I owe you* an explanation?" she asked incredulously.

"We had a great time, didn't we?"

"Oh, sure. One *helluva* night. Only that wasn't enough for loverboy Python, huh? It was on to the next victim, with hardly a pause for a coffee break."

"What are you talking about?"

"Forget it."

"I don't want to forget it."

"Well, *I* do."

"You hardly waited around, did you?"

"What?"

"You heard."

"Will you quit holding me so tightly. I want to sit down."

"No you don't."

"Yes I do."

"No — you *don't*."

"You're a bastard."

"You know something? I think I'm going to forgive you."

Her voice was icy. Her body uncomfortably warm. "For what?"

"For standing me up."

"Standing *you* up. You stood *me* up, with that French jam tart."

"If you mean Danielle, she was with the Senator."

Caustic sarcasm. "Sure."

"And who was the guy *you* were walking into Chasen's with? Some half-baked actor, huh? I credited you with better taste."

"I guess you would have been happier if I'd sat at home thinking about what a wonderful time we had together, and hoping that one of these days you'd call me again. You know — when you had nothing better to do." She paused, her voice alive with indignation. "I actually *cooked a meal for you*. Your slave phoned me at nine-thirty. If you couldn't see me, why didn't *you* call me earlier? Or are you too big a star to pick up the phone yourself?"

"Aretha phoned you before the show at eight o'clock and told you I was tied up at the studio, and that I'd contact you later. You couldn't even wait, could you? Out on the town without missing a beat."

"Don't tell *me* what time she called and what the message was. It was after nine-thirty. And there was *no mention* of you contacting me later."

"Hey, lady — when you're angry I think I love you even more."

"Can I break in?" Mark smiled smoothly as he pried them apart, but there were daggers of anger in his eyes.

Jack half considered saying — *No — you can't*. And grabbing her back. But it was already too late. She was in Mark's arms. He was whirling her around the dance floor as the fairy lights twinkled, and the yacht headed on its way to Laguna and the New Year.

*

Carlos Brent sprawled snoring in the middle of Zachary's bed in the master stateroom. Dee Dee Dionne sat in a nearby chair, her ebony features calm and composed, like a beautiful carved statue.

As Zachary walked into the room he wondered why she put up with the ageing superstar. She was a talented singer, with a certain amount of stardom of her own — she didn't need Carlos Brent.

"How is he?" Zachary asked.

"Sleeping it off," she replied. "He won't even remember. He was very drunk."

"Has he ever considered A.A.?"

"Carlos? Never." Faint amusement lit her face. "He enjoys drinking. It never upsets *him*, only other people."

"How do you manage?"

She smiled wanly. "Oh . . . I manage. When you love someone you always do."

Zachary felt like an intruder in his own room. With a blustering cough he walked into his bathroom. Propped against the mirror was an envelope addressed to him marked EXTREMELY URGENT.

Nice of whoever had delivered it to hand it straight over. Staff. They were never good enough.

Without hesitation he ripped it open. He was in need of a pause before rejoining his party, which seemed to be going extremely well, in spite of the fact that Silver was successfully avoiding him.

At first all he saw was a magazine, one of those cheap supermarket rags which everyone claimed never to read, yet knew the contents off by heart. Attached to it was the white card of one of his personal assistants in New York, with a handwritten note:

> *A contact got an advance copy of this over to me today, and I'm couriering it straight to you rather than discussing it on the phone. It hits the stands on Monday. Please advise if you wish to take action.*

The magazine was called *True Life Scandal*. And the headline proclaimed in huge black print:

FATHER OF SILVER ANDERSON'S SECRET LOVE CHILD REVEALED!!
BILLIONAIRE ZACHARY K: KLINGER IS HEAVEN'S DADDY!!

And underneath, in smaller type:

VLADIMIR KIRKOFF AND UNITY SMITH REVEAL THE SENSATIONAL TRUE-LIFE DRAMA OF SILVER ANDERSON'S LIFE! READ ALL ABOUT THE FORMER BARTENDER AND DRUG DEALER SHE MARRIED! HOW SHE HATES HER DAUGHTER — SEVENTEEN-YEAR-OLD ROCK STAR SENSATION HEAVEN! AND DESPISES HER FORMER LOVER — HOLLYWOOD TYCOON AND BILLIONAIRE ZACHARY K. KLINGER!

READ THE SECRETS!
READ THEM HERE!
Revealed by the two people who know her BETTER THAN ANYONE ELSE!
Full story on PAGE TEN.

Zachary blinked rapidly a few times. Then he took off his steel-rimmed glasses and stared blankly in the mirror above his black onyx sink.

If this garbage was true he had a daughter. A seventeen-year-old daughter. And for seventeen years Silver had kept them apart.

Damn the woman.

Damn the bitch.

She'd got away with everything all her life. Forget the announcement he'd planned as the party's climax. If this was true, he would personally see to it that she paid, and paid in full.

Chapter 93

"I wouldn't have expected it of you," Mark said, an annoying, supercilious curl to his lip, as they sat down.

"Huh?" In her mind she was still dancing with Jack, caught up in his arms, listening to his voice.

"You and the leg-over merchant."

"I beg your pardon?"

"Leg-over merchant, my dear, is a quaint old English expression meaning a man who likes to put it about."

"Put *what* about?" she asked, irritated by his superior attitude.

"For Christ's sake, Jade. A *stud*. You do know what that is, don't you?"

"Fuck you, Rand, what are you trying to say?"

He went very red in the face, a sure sign that he was angry. "Oh, tough talk. The liberated woman. Bravo, darling. Was he enough for you in bed? Is that why I haven't had the pleasure?"

Was she *really* marrying him in the morning? Had she *honestly* made that decision?

The Whites returned to the table after a quick whirl around the dance floor.

"Invigorating!" exclaimed Zeppo.

"Boring!" muttered Ida.

Jade arose. "Excuse me," she said politely. "I'm going to find Corey."

Leaving an angry Mark sitting with the Whites, she took off.

*

"You're not eating, Howie," Poppy complained. "The lobster is delicious."

"If I've told you once I've told you fifteen times – I *am not* hungry, so stop shoving food at me. Just back off."

"Grouchy, grouchy! Maybe the belly-dancers will cheer you up. I hear there's *three* of them. Hand picked by Zachary, and *gorgeous*!"

The sick ache in his stomach would not quit. If he was smart he would have cancelled out on this whole deal, flown off to Mexico, and found out what the fuck had happened.

Norman had been getting along fine, they'd told him that yesterday – the asshole doctors he'd hired.

Correction. They weren't assholes. They were the best.

He'd paid plenty to keep the situation under wraps. He'd lied to all and sundry, and in a matter of weeks Norman Gooseberger was supposed to stroll back into town fit and well, with a brand new position as head of publicity at Orpheus.

Dammit! What went wrong?

The kid was dead. Massive internal haemorrhaging, he'd been told.

Technically Mannon had killed him. Oh, Jesus!

Carmel and Orville were somewhere at the party. Who was going to tell them? And what would happen when they found out? Were they going to just sit back and take it in the good old Hollywood tradition of keeping silent to protect the guilty?

Clarissa was wrecked. Maybe he should have waited to reveal the news to her, but he'd had to share it with someone, and she was sworn to secrecy.

"Mannon has to be punished," she'd said, white with grief.

"No," he'd replied. "The knowledge alone is gonna be with him forever. That's punishment enough."

"I don't understand. Justice must be done."

"You're sounding like a movie. It's too fucking late for justice. I've told you before – the scandal and publicity will ruin *both* your careers, and kill *The Murder* stone cold. You want that? For what?"

"Yes. I want that."

"Get serious, Clarissa. Bigger stars than you have been dragged down by a lot less. Imagine yourself in court, telling *your* side of the story. Jeez! They'd crucify you. In France the blame would be *all* yours. Don't forget, if Mannon hadn't caught you in the sack with another guy none of this would have happened. You were involved in a hot and heavy affair with Mannon. Everyone knew about it. One word of the truth and it's over for you. I'll *personally* see to that, along with Zachary Klinger and most of the other people aboard this yacht tonight. You'll end up doing art movies in Siberia. Is that what you want?"

"It's all so sick."

"And I guess you in bed with a confirmed fag is normal?"

She'd pulled her jacket close around her and shivered in the breeze, while all around them the party went on, unaware of their personal drama.

He'd reached over to touch her, a small gesture of sympathy to show he wasn't completely heartless.

She drew away as if he had communicable herpes.

"You'll get over it, Clarissa. Hey – *we all* liked Norman. I'll fly in tomorrow and take care of everything. He's going to suffer a burst appendix. I hope to Christ he's still got one."

"You'll be an accessory to murder," she'd said slowly.

"No, I'll be helping everyone out – *including* you."

He'd left her alone on the deck – a solitary figure. She'd be all right. Clarissa wasn't some dozy-headed starlet – she had guts. She'd survive.

"Hello, Howard and Poppy." Whitney wafted into sight wearing a dress that would give any healthy male a hard-on for life.

"So *lovely* to see you," enthused Poppy.

"Have you met Senator Richmond?" Whitney asked, taking his hand and pulling him forward.

"*The* Senator Peter Richmond?" Poppy said triumphantly. She was never at a loss for a name – especially an important one. "No, we've never met, but I'm *delighted*. Are you visiting? Is your wife with you? We'd *love* to give a dinner for you. Something small and intimate, say fifty or sixty people?"

*

The belly-dancers appeared with dessert: nubile young women, clad in full Eastern garb – their smooth, round stomachs on display as they undulated from area to area, pulsating and fluctuating their agile hips.

Chuck Nielson tried to grab one as she slid by, her eyes bright with promise above the veiled part of her face.

"C'mere, baby," he crowed, pulling at the flimsy chiffon twirling between her legs.

"Get lost, pox face," she muttered out of the corner of her mouth, skilfully moving on.

Only Beverly and Zachary knew the true identity of his exotic belly-dancers. They were all hookers, trained especially for tonight's performance. It amused Zachary to entertain his guests with the unexpected.

After the belly-dancers came the break-dancers – six talented black youths.

"They're *sooo* jazzed," Heaven exclaimed excitedly.

"Yeah," agreed Rocky, although he couldn't see what all the fuss was about. He preferred the belly-dancers himself. Now they were something else!

*

Below decks, in the powder room, Melanie-Shanna found herself washing her hands next to Whitney Valentine. They hadn't seen each other since the famous fight between Mannon and Chuck upstairs at the Bistro.

Whitney hitched the top of her clinging dress a touch higher. "Hello, Melanie. How are you?"

"Oh – hi, Whitney, I didn't see you."

Nobody could miss Whitney Valentine in all her glory. She had a body capable of reducing grown men to tears.

"Congrats on the baby," Whitney said. "I'm sure it's made Mannon very happy, he always wanted kids."

"Thank you."

Whitney glossed her lips and fluffed out her hair. "I'm so glad you two stayed together. Believe me, Clarissa Browning is a grade A cunt. She would have made him nothing but miserable."

Melanie-Shanna, busily applying lipstick, nodded her agreement. "It's all worked out," she said quietly. "We're over Puerta Vallarta and his affair with her. He's happy being back with me and the baby. He says Clarissa was just a bad nightmare."

"Good," Whitney said firmly. "Let's be friends, huh?"

Melanie-Shanna could hardly see that happening, but at least she finally felt secure with his ex-wife. Whitney didn't want Mannon, and he didn't want her anymore. "How's Chuck?" she asked. "Are you two still together?"

"On and off." Whitney shrugged. "Tonight more off than on. He's such an asshole when he drugs out – like right now." She leaned confidentially towards her new friend. "I have met *the* most attractive and interesting older man. His name is Peter Richmond. *Senator* Peter Richmond. And I think he likes me."

"Isn't he married?" Melanie-Shanna asked, putting away her lipstick and closing her purse.

"In name only. When you're in politics getting divorced is a definite no-no. Anyway – he says –"

They left the powder room chatting amicably.

Clarissa waited a beat of ten before emerging from a locked toilet.

*

"So you're not talkin'?" Wes asked.

"I never *said* we weren't speaking," Silver replied, an argumentative edge to her voice.

"She's sitting right over there, an' you haven't said one word to each other. What's the deal? You don't talk to your brother and father. And now I find out you don't even talk to your kid."

"I think she should come over to *me*, don't you?"

"I think you're full of crap."

Silver put on her haughtiest tone. "And what exactly do you mean by *that* remark?"

"Just what it sounds like. She's your *daughter*, for crissake – not some deadly rival. Loosen up an' at least say hello."

"Keep your nose *out* of it, if you please. It's not your business."

"You're being unreasonable. An' if *you* don't wanna say hello, *I* will."

Glaring at him angrily, she said, "Don't you dare!"

"Why shouldn't I? I'm her stepfather. I'm goin' right over an' introducing myself."

Silver was unaware of the conversation he'd had with Nora concerning her relationship with Heaven.

"Why doesn't she want to have anythin' to do with the kid?" he'd asked.

Nora had shaken her head. "Some kind of guilt about the girl's father."

"Who was that?"

"Nobody knows."

482

"Come *on*. You know."

"No, I don't."

"Yes you do."

"I *don't*."

"Swear on your life."

"If you could forge some sort of relationship between the two of them it would be nice. See what you can do, Wes. You're the only one I've ever seen her listen to."

Silver picked up her champagne and drained the glass. "If you go over to her, I will not speak to you for the rest of the night."

"That'll make a whole bunch of us you're not talkin' to."

"I mean it, Wes."

"We'll see."

"I said I *mean* it."

He stood up. "I'll be back in a minute."

★

Jade couldn't find Corey. She wandered from area to area, bumping into Poppy along the way, an unfriendly Howard, and finally getting stuck with Chuck Nielson, who introduced himself and then wouldn't leave her alone.

"You're somethin'," he kept on mumbling. "An' I'm just a bum."

He offered her a joint.

She turned him down.

He offered her cocaine.

She turned him down.

He offered her his body.

She laughed.

"Don' *laugh* at me," he said, roughly grabbing her.

"Leave the lady alone." Jack was there, dangerous green eyes and killer smile.

Chuck backed off without a word.

"Do you know what we are?" Jack asked, his voice caressing her.

She shook her head.

"We're unfinished business. And there is no way I am letting you marry that jerk tomorrow. No way at all."

Chapter 94

Clarissa left the powder room, her pale face impassive. She ignored the activity around her – giggling women dressed to the hilt, two belly-dancers hurrying to their makeshift dressing room, waiters rushing back and forth.

She headed down the corridor, away from the noise of the party, entering the part of the large yacht where the staterooms were located.

She was approaching Zachary Klinger's private suite when a uniformed security guard stopped her.

"Can I help you, Ms. Browning?"

"You startled me!"

"I'm sorry."

"I suppose you're just doing your job."

He grinned happily – after a night of solitary boredom he was finally meeting a star. "Sure am!"

"I bet you're an actor," she said.

"How'd you know that?"

"We all had to moonlight at one time or another."

"You too?"

She smiled. "Me too. What have you done?"

"A few television shows. It doesn't pay the rent. I've been doubling with this job for three years."

"You'll get a break."

"D'you think so?"

"It happens."

"From your lips . . ."

"Can you do me a favour?"

By this time he was ready to do anything she asked. "Name it."

"One of my future projects takes place on a yacht."

"No, really?"

"It's true."

"Is there a role for me?" he asked boldly.

"You never know . . ."

He'd heard stories about Clarissa Browning being aloof and difficult to work with. This woman standing before him was so nice and natural. Friendly too, not at all a big movie-star phoney.

"There's just a little information I need," she said lightly. "Perhaps you can give me a quick tour. Nobody will miss you, will they?"

"I'm not supposed to leave my post."

"It doesn't matter."

"But, for you –"

She smiled. "Thank you."

Chapter 95

"Mr Klinger wants to meet you."

"He does?" Heaven's eyes were wide saucers of surprise. "Why?" She was still recovering from her exciting encounter with Penn Sullivan, who Rocky had frozen out with a baleful glare. "Catch you later," Penn had said as he left, giving her hope for the future.

Beverly grinned. "I guess he gets off on your music. C'mon, girl, he's waiting."

"Me too?" asked Rocky hopefully.

"Nope. But hang around, big boy – if Central Casting ever sees you, you've got a job for life!"

As she spirited Heaven off, Wes appeared. "What are *you* doin' here?" he demanded of Rocky.

"Hey – hey – hey. The big time only suitable for *Mister* Anderson? I found the kid, y'know. I like – discovered her."

Wes couldn't conceal his amazement. *"You?"*

"Yeah, *me*. Ya think I'm not good enough or somethin'? I'm makin' it too." Rocky smoothed down the lapels of his rented white tuxedo, his muscles bulging. "An' while we're talkin', the word is out you're cat food if you don' pay back the money ya owe."

"I don't owe *one fuckin' dollar*," Wes said angrily. "I was set up – you know that better than anyone. A fine friend *you* turned out to be."

"I told ya t'be careful," Rocky said sulkily.

"I was. An' that's why I'm here today. An' they ain't gettin' back *one thin dime* of the bucks they planted on me. Fuck 'em. Let's see what they can do about it."

"Blow you away," Rocky muttered.

"Just let 'em try. I'm ready."

*

"I can get into Los Angeles once a month," Senator Richmond said, devouring Whitney's delectable flesh with ravenous eyes. "No problem."

"Why would you want to?" she asked demurely, her breasts rising and falling, nearly escaping from the confines of her sprayed-on dress.

"Because I've met you," he said with deep sincerity. "And you're special."

Lowering her eyes she murmured, "What a lovely compliment."

"Why don't we go downstairs to one of the staterooms where we can talk properly?" he suggested. "There's so many people here, so many interruptions. I'd really like to get to know you better."

"Well . . . I don't want to miss the fireworks display. I understand it's going to be spectacular. I've always loved fireworks, haven't you?"

"My passion," he said, glancing at his watch. "They're not due to go off until midnight. We have an hour."

*

There was something about being on a boat, confined for hours on end, that Mannon didn't like. It gave him a trapped feeling, which indeed he was. Everywhere he went there were the same familiar faces with the same predictable questions.

486

What film are you doing next?
Who's producing?
Who's directing?
Who's your co-star?

Quite frankly, he'd had the movie business for the time being. He needed to take a long vacation with Melanie-Shanna and the baby. He needed to go someplace where they didn't even know what a movie *was*.

In the distance he saw Howard approaching. Manic Howard Soloman, whose outrageous coke habit was the talk of the town.

"Can we have a word together privately?" Howard requested.

"What do you suggest we do – jump off the deck and swim alongside?" Mannon said sarcastically.

Howard didn't crack a smile. "It's a serious matter."

"I'll be back in a moment, sweetheart," Mannon said to Melanie-Shanna.

Howard walked with him to a quiet spot along the main deck. "Bad news," he said soberly. "I'm gonna give it to you straight. Norman Gooseberger died tonight."

"What?"

"Complications. An internal haemorrhage. I don't know . . ."

"Jesus Christ! Does this mean *I'm* responsible?"

"Technically – yes. In the real world – no. I'm taking care of it. Paying off the right people. It'll be fixed."

"And I'll be forever in your debt. Is that what you're trying to say?"

Howard shrugged philosophically. "Hey – that's what friends are for."

Angrily Mannon stared down at the dark, cold water rushing by. "I let you talk me into a cover-up," he said bitterly. "You promised me everything was going to be all right."

"Listen, sport, I'm not God. *I* didn't kill the poor bastard – *you* did. You wanna come out in the open now? Is that it? You wanna play Truth and Consequences an' let the media rip you to shreds? Be my guest."

Mannon leaned over the side and began to sob.

Embarrassed, Howard turned away.

*

"Nice to meet you, Heaven."

"You too, Mr Klinger."

He peered at her intently, searching for a clue. She was pretty in spite of her outlandish makeup, hair and clothes. But he couldn't spot any striking resemblance.

"I understand your record is doing extremely well."

"Zoomin' up there. Like it's number two with a bullet. Which means by next week it could be –" she paused to draw a huge expectant breath. "Number one!"

"I hope so."

"Yeah! What a blast!"

"Heaven."

"Yes, Mr Klinger."

"I have some information that I think you should know."

"Yes, sir?" She waited expectantly, quite awed to be in the presence of such an important and powerful man.

"Er . . . there seems to be a possibility – only a possibility, mind you – that I might be your father."

Chapter 96

The breeze was cool on her face. She knew what she was doing, and she had no regrets. They all deserved it. Every one of them.

IT'S TOO LATE FOR JUSTICE.

Really, Howard. Is that what you think?

BELIEVE ME, CLARISSA BROWNING IS A GRADE A CUNT.

Thank you, Whitney. It takes one to know one.

YOU'LL END UP DOING ART MOVIES IN SIBERIA.

Better than ever having to do anything for you again, Howard.

HE SAYS CLARISSA WAS A BAD NIGHTMARE.

Did Mannon say that? Poor Mannon, he doesn't know what a nightmare is. Yet.

ONE WORD OF THE TRUTH AND IT'S OVER FOR YOU.

And you, Howard. And all your Hollywood friends.

SHE WOULD HAVE MADE HIM NOTHING BUT MISERABLE.

You should know, Whitney. You tried for long enough. Now you'll never make anyone miserable again.

I'LL PERSONALLY SEE TO IT, ALONG WITH ZACHARY KLINGER AND MOST OF THE OTHER PEOPLE ABOARD THIS YACHT TONIGHT.

Will you, Howard. Will you?

Lighting the first match was easy . . .

EPILOGUE

February 1986
Seven weeks later

There were two major events taking place in Hollywood on a cool weekend in February 1986.

The first was a funeral.

The second, a wedding.

Some people felt obliged to attend both. Although, of course, they changed outfits for each occasion.

★

Compared to what took place on *Klinger II*, the night of December 31, 1985, the impact of *True Life Scandal* hitting the stands a few days later was considerably diminished. Who cared about Silver Anderson's indiscretions, when an entire yacht – filled with Hollywood celebrities – had been blown sky high the night of Zachary Klinger's exclusive New Year's Eve party.

No movie could beat *this* story. A desperate struggle for survival in the cold night sea, while explosions rocked the luxurious yacht, raging fires spread from one end of the boat to the other – and an insane fireworks display gone wrong shot rockets and stars, blazing wheels and jumping crackers, into the dark sky.

This was the most headline-making drama possible, with the most expensive cast ever assembled. Every ingredient was there. And the world couldn't get enough.

The horrific accident was quite obviously sabotage. Investigators sifting through the debris of the gutted vessel found traces of rags soaked in gasoline near each of the firework displays, and elsewhere on the boat.

The tragedy was not caused by one fire, but by a series of them, set by a person or persons unknown to cause the maximum amount of damage. Obviously, by sparking the fireworks – resulting in explosions and chaos – mass mayhem and panic took place. Fortunately, the lifeboats had been successfully launched, otherwise the tragedy could have been infinitely more serious.

Now, seven weeks later, things were finally quietening down. And today, after the wedding and the funeral, maybe the focus would shift from Hollywood and people could resume their normal lives.

The funeral was due to take place at eleven o'clock, the wedding at three in the afternoon. There was plenty of time to attend both.

*

Poppy Soloman, draped in black Saint Laurent, glanced anxiously at Howard standing next to her at the Forest Lawn cemetery. He looked all right, a touch pale. It was taking some getting used to – seeing him without his hairpiece – but at least he was well again.

Howard had suffered a heart attack the night of the accident. Huddled in the lifeboat, he had suddenly clutched his chest and started to groan. By the time they were picked up by rescue teams, he was unconscious. She had thought he was dead.

The last few weeks had not been easy. He had been rushed straight to the hospital, and Poppy found herself alone – unprepared and frightened.

His doctors had been embarrassingly frank with her, talking about his cocaine problem as if she knew all about it.

She'd had no idea he took drugs. Oh, the shame!

When Howard recovered, he told her he was stepping down as head of Orpheus.

Poppy saw her whole world crumbling. "Why?" she wailed.

He'd looked at her for a long time, and finally said, "If it doesn't suit you, Poppy, we can separate. I don't need the pressures any more."

She'd thought about what he'd said, and then she'd thought about life without him. True, she loved being the wife of a studio head, but that wasn't the only reason she was with Howard. She loved her husband. It was as simple as that.

*

Nearby, Melanie-Shanna and Mannon held hands. It had been a terrible few weeks. Mannon had insisted on standing up and

494

taking full responsibility for Norman Gooseberger's death, only nobody wished to prosecute him. "An unfortunate accident," said the Mexican police. "There is no case." And that was that.

He had behaved like a hero the night of the yacht disaster. Along with Jack Python and Senator Richmond he had helped to launch the lifeboats, and after seeing that Melanie-Shanna was safely aboard, bodily thrown frightened, screaming women into them. After that he had dived repeatedly into the sea to rescue survivors with horrible burns who had flung themselves into the water. Carmel Gooseberger was one of the people he saved. Somehow that made him feel better.

There had been five fatalities. Four bodies discovered within days.

Funerals for Chuck Nielson, a security guard, and two waiters had taken place almost immediately. The Chuck Nielson funeral had been a lavish affair, with many touching speeches from producers and directors who had refused to employ him for the last year and a half of his life. The only genuine gesture was from Whitney Valentine, who laid a single red rose on his coffin and wept discreetly.

And now the fifth victim was being buried – Hollywood-style. The body had washed up on shore, and been found by a beachcomber only a few days ago.

*

Senator Peter Richmond attended the latest funeral as a mark of respect. Never underestimate the glamour connection between politics and Hollywood. The public loved it.

Besides, the funeral gave him an excuse to visit Whitney Valentine. She stood nearby, her blonde hair shrouded by a black lace veil, her brilliant eyes shielded by opaque dark glasses. Next to her stood Kellie Sidney, and then Zeppo White. Ida had been the unfortunate recipient of an exploding firework in her face. She was lucky not to have lost the sight in her left eye. Currently she was undergoing extensive plastic surgery.

Orville and Carmel were also present, with heads bowed. The tragic death of their only son had quieted them both down. They lived, shrouded in their own guilt.

*

Jack Python stood at the back, his handsome face impassive, well aware of the gangs of waiting photographers, the ghoulish crowds, and the television cameras.

Hollywood was burying one of its own. A true luminary. And the world was watching.

Clarissa Browning was certainly getting a star's send-off.

*

Meanwhile, at Zachary Klinger's Holmby Hills mansion, preparations for a wedding were underway. Caterers' trucks stood in the driveway, last-minute flowers were being delivered, security guards patrolled the grounds, and a nervous future bride stared at her reflection in a full-length mirror. "I don't know why I let you talk me into this," she said, in a verging-on-the-edge-of-panic voice.

"Because you'll love it!" Beverly replied confidently. "And as Zachary says – this town needs a beautiful wedding. A new beginning. And, girl – there ain't *no*body more beautiful than you!"

"I wanted a small, quiet ceremony," Jade said, adjusting the zig-zag skirt of her exquisite white silk wedding gown. "You and Mark tricked me into this."

"Honey, you were in the hospital – *somebody* had to make the arrangements. And when Corey called your parents and invited them, it just seemed right to make it an *occasion*. Mark loves the idea – I'm tellin' you, girl, he'll go Hollywood in no time at all! I hear that Zeppo's bachelor rip for him last night was something else."

"Good."

"You're a disappointment to me, Jade, y'know that?"

"Why?"

"*We* should have done somethin' last night. Gone to Chippendale's and watched the guys take it all off. Or had our *own* party."

"Sorry. Next time I get married I'll try not to disappoint you."

They both giggled.

"Hey, did anything happen with you and Jack Python?" Beverly asked curiously. "I always had a feeling you two might get together again."

"Whatever gave you that impression?"

Beverly smiled. "Vibes."

"A fine conversation when I'm just about to marry Mark."

"You two were dancing at the party, the night of the disaster."

496

"I don't remember."

"Yeah, well . . . I guess I gotta go check everything out. Do you need anything? A stiff drink? A stiff prick? Anything! A bride's last request will always be met."

"Springsteen."

"Bruce?"

"Is there another one?"

"Hey – I've heard of last requests, but this guy might be just a *little* hard to get hold of. Now – if you'd only given me time . . ."

"His music, schmuck! Do you have any records or tapes?"

"Oh. His music. Easy!" Beverly dived into a stack of albums piled next to an elaborate stereo system and produced a special re-mix twelve-inch version of *Cover Me*. Pulling out the record, she handed Jade the album. "Horny, huh?"

There was a picture of Springsteen sitting on the door of a white convertible, legs apart, wearing jeans, scuffed boots, a wide leather belt, striped sleeveless tee-shirt, and a bandanna round his head.

"It's his music that turns me on," Jade said.

"Yeah? You'd say goodbye on a rainy night, huh? *Sure* you would. Eyeball those muscles an' tell me that." With a ribald laugh, she left the bride alone.

Springsteen's voice came across loud and clear, flooding the room.

Jade closed her eyes. She was lucky to be alive, she knew that – enough people had told her. Apparently, when the yacht started to blow apart, she must have been hit by falling debris and knocked unconscious. Someone had helped her into a lifeboat, and eventually she was taken to hospital, where she lay in a coma for a week. Waking up one morning she felt fine, and remembered absolutely nothing about the entire experience. Her last recollection was getting ready to go to the party. "I remember you saying something about forty-nine identical white limousines, and that's it – complete blank-out, until I woke up in the hospital," she told Mark.

"You're fortunate, my darling – it wasn't a pleasant time."

He'd sprained an ankle, but other than that was unscathed.

They were both lucky. And Corey too, although he'd suffered a few minor burns helping to get people into the lifeboats, including a young waiter who'd had a leg blown off below the knee.

Naturally, she and Mark had postponed their wedding. And the next thing she knew she had allowed herself to be talked into this circus. Pretty stupid for someone who liked things private. But too late to do anything about it now.

*

"You okay?"

"Of course."

"Y'look friggin' fantastic for an old broad."

"Darling, I know he's your hero, but *do* try to stop sounding like Carlos Brent on a bad day."

Wes laughed. "Just jokin'!"

"Oh, goody. I do so *adore* your sense of humour."

Bantering back and forth was just their way. Since the *True Life Scandal* revelations, Silver and Wes had become closer than ever. He had blown his stack about her recent dressing room affair with Carlos, and she had not been thrilled about his supposed drug-dealing activities – he'd denied everything. But all in all, they weathered the bad times, relieved to be alive after the night of horror on Zachary's yacht from which they'd both escaped without injury, thanks to Wes's quick thinking. He had hustled Silver into a lifeboat, and at her insistence gone back and found Heaven, bringing her to safety too.

Suddenly, with chaos all around, a reunion had taken place. Mother and daughter were together again. Temporarily.

After the appearance of *True Life Scandal* on the news-stands, Silver had been forced to admit reluctantly that Zachary Klinger was indeed Heaven's father. And with both Wes and Nora urging her on, she had met with Heaven privately, and falteringly tried to explain why she'd kept it a secret. Of course, she hadn't told her the real truth – she'd just said that he was a married man at the time, and she'd done what she thought was best.

To Silver's annoyance, Heaven and Zachary forged an immediate and wonderful relationship. Heaven moved into the Klinger mansion – and to make matters even more aggravating, her record went to number one.

Wes couldn't understand her pique. "She's your own *daughter*. You should be goddamn proud. I thought everything was okay between you now."

Silver wasn't proud she was jealous. She just couldn't help it. Now they'd promised Zeppo White to go with him to Jade

498

Johnson's wedding, and there was no getting out of seeing Zachary and Heaven together — a sight Silver dreaded.

*

Corey visited Jade just as Springsteen faded.

"Dad's on his way up," he said. "How are you feeling?"

"Like I'm entering prison with no hope of a reprieve!"

"I told mom to stay downstairs — she'll only make you cry."

"How do *you* feel?" Since Norman's death he had become even more quiet and withdrawn.

"I'm quitting the publicity business," he said. "It's not for me. I think I'll be better away from the atmosphere."

She took his hand, "I think you're right, and remember, Corey, whatever you do, I'm always here for you."

A knock on the door announced their father. Oh God! Father of the bride. She was really doing this.

She felt hot and cold, dizzy and sick.

She was getting *married*!

HELP!

*

As Wes drew out of their driveway, with Silver sitting beside him in the Rolls-Royce, a black sedan appeared from nowhere and cut in front of him, forcing him to brake abruptly.

"Sonofabitch!" he yelled angrily, leaning on the horn.

"Don't get excited," soothed Silver, taking out a compact and checking her appearance yet again.

The sedan came to a stop, blocking the narrow street up in the hills of Bel Air.

Without thinking, Wes got out of the car and started to walk towards the other vehicle, swearing.

The gunshots took him completely by surprise.

*

"And do you, Jade Johnson, take this man, Mark Rand, to be your lawful wedded husband?"

Yes, I do.

No, I don't.

She stared at the preacher in the magnificent grounds of Zachary Klinger's opulent estate. He was a Californian preacher. Blond streaked hair, blue eyes, and a suntan.

A helicopter hovered overhead, causing an unpleasant breeze.

499

". . . forty-nine identical white limos with fully stocked bars and a supply of the best caviar, to transport Zachary Klinger's illustrious guests to his waiting yacht . . ."

SHE COULD REMEMBER!

Picking up Corey, the ride to Long Beach, boarding the yacht, and joining the Whites.

SHE COULD REMEMBER!

The preacher cleared his throat, a gentle reminder that they were waiting for her reply.

She turned to Mark. He nodded encouragingly.

Tall and tan and young and lovely

The girl from Ipanema goes walking

Jack Python.

Jack Python with the deadly green eyes and the killer smile. Was he really going to let her go through with this?

Impatiently the preacher cleared his throat again and decided to repeat himself. "Do you, Jade Johnson, take this man, Mark Rand, to be your lawful wedded husband?"

"Are you seriously getting married?"

If you don't stop me I am.

"You know something? When you're angry I think I love you even more."

Well then, where are you when I need you?

The noise of the helicopter was getting louder.

"Answer," hissed Mark, becoming red in the face.

She remembered him saying – *"Was he enough for you in bed? Is that why I haven't had the pleasure?"*

Yes. Right, Mark. On both counts.

Instinctively she looked up, just in time to see the helicopter swoop down and lower a rope ladder.

Thank God! Rescue was at hand.

Without a second thought she gathered up the flimsy skirt of her white silk dress, kicked off her shoes, and made a dash for the ladder, freedom, and most of all – Jack Python.

"Holy *shit*!" yelled Beverly, with a hoot of crazed laughter, as Jade scrambled up the precarious rope stairway. "One thing about Johnson – she always *was* a wild one!"

And the helicopter rose like a bird, and whirled off into the future.

NINE MONTHS LATER

Zeppo White gave up agenting, and became the new head of Orpheus Studios.

His wife, Ida, recovered from her burns, and as the result of extensive plastic surgery looked twenty years younger.

Zeppo continued to chase nubile females who lusted after an acting career.

Ida gave up drugs, and took to very young men instead.

Zeppo made her a producer. She never produced anything, but gave endless auditions.

They remained locked in marriage.

*

Whitney Valentine posed nude for a prestigious men's magazine, and was paid a record amount of money. A million bucks for revealing paradise. Her movie career took off like a rocket, and she became the highest-paid bad actress in the world.

Senator Peter Richmond flew in from Washington once a month to visit her, and after a few months swore faithfully he would leave his wife and marry her.

He never did.

*

Vladimir Kirkoff stayed in Hawaii, living off his revelations of life with a star. He liked the climate. He liked the people. And most of all he liked the huge, bronzed surfers with their wicked grins and penchant for thrills.

Vladimir never forgot Silver. He kept her picture in a silver frame with a single orchid beside it. If Madame ever called, he would be there.

*

Unity Smith was picked up by the police in Amarillo, Texas, working in a peep-show bar. She had spent her money from *True Life Scandal* on drugs and a hustler with lean hips and a way with the ladies. He dumped her when the money ran out.

She was recognized from her picture in the cheap tabloid.

Unity Smith's real name was Unity Serranno, and she was wanted in the state of New York for the cold-blooded murder of a young couple during the course of an armed robbery in 1983.

Her husband and partner in crime helped finger her. He was doing time for the same murders, and when he saw her photograph in *True Life Scandal* he whined to the police – "This is her – how come she's runnin' around free while I'm locked up? *She's* the one pulled the damn trigger."

Unity Serranno was taken back to the state of New York and sentenced to life imprisonment.

*

Mannon Cable bought a home in Carmel. A large, rambling, comfortable ranch house, perched high on a bluff, overlooking the ocean.

He was acclaimed for his fine work in *The Murder*, and the quality of the material sent to him improved considerably.

"I'm taking a year off to enjoy my family," he told his agent, Sadie La Salle.

"Work comes first," she admonished. "I've got a script for you that Redford would kill for."

"Bye-bye, Sadie. See you in a year."

Melanie-Shanna became pregnant again. She glowed with health and happiness. Every day Mannon woke up and thanked God for his son, Jason, and his wonderful wife, whom he finally appreciated.

For the first time in his life Mannon Cable let go. And it made him a very secure and contented man indeed.

*

Carlos Brent married Dee Dee Dionne in a lavish ceremony in Las Vegas. It was his fifth wedding, and he bought the bride a magnificent diamond necklace as a betrothal present.

His daughter, Susanna, was incensed. "You see that bitch," she told anyone who would listen. "That bitch is walking around with *my* inheritance hanging round *her* neck!"

*

Orville Gooseberger retired from the movie business and moved to Palm Springs with his wife.

Palm Springs was too quiet for Carmel. They divorced after thirty years of marriage, and he remarried – a twenty-one-year-old mud wrestler.

Carmel moved to Houston, Texas, and found herself an oilman. She, too, remarried. Unfortunately her new husband expired six weeks after the wedding, leaving her most of Houston.

Orville divorced his mud wrestler, got back together with Carmel, and they returned to Hollywood where they both belonged.

*

Howard Soloman went into "indie prod" – independent production – and gave up cocaine with the help of a fine organization called Cocaine Anonymous.

He genuinely loved the movie business, and had no intention of ever getting out. But the pressures of running a studio were not something he missed. Now he was his own boss, the pace of his life was a little less frantic: there was time to take the occasional trip, no need to go out every night, and if he wanted to spend a day at home just lazing around the pool – he did so.

Poppy adjusted. She was very adaptable when she had to be.

And, of course, she still gave great parties.

*

Corey Johnson gave up his P.R. job at Briskinn & Bower and moved back to San Francisco. It took him a long time to get over Norman, but eventually he met a successful writer called Ted, who invited him to move in. He did so, and six months later Ted died of AIDS. For a while Corey was numb with grief – he had nursed Ted through the last helpless months, and Ted had left him his house and a reasonable monthly allowance. The doctors told him he had not contracted the disease.

After much thought, he decided to use Ted's house as a hospice. He opened it up as a haven for AIDS victims who had nowhere else to go, and helped them through the final difficult days, allowing them to die in dignity and peace, with someone nearby who cared.

*

Wes Money almost died. He took two bullets, one dangerously close to the heart.

Silver Anderson, who without any thought for her own safety had left the car and rushed to his assistance, was also shot.

As the black sedan raced off, leaving them both on the ground wounded, she had managed to memorize the licence plate as the car sped away. And then she crawled to the Rolls and phoned for help.

More Hollywood dramas! The press was ecstatic! Silver Anderson alone could keep their circulation rising!

They were rushed to the hospital. Wes was operated on immediately for the removal of two bullets, and Silver was treated for minor lacerations – a bullet had merely grazed her shoulder. "You can go home tomorrow, Miss Anderson," she was told.

Silver never stepped from the hospital until Wes was out of intensive care and off the danger list. When he drifted back into the real world, she was there beside him, her hair a mess, no makeup, dressed in a crumpled tracksuit. "How dare you!" were the first words out of her mouth. "If you think you're leaving *me*, Mr Money – you can think again! I *need* you, barman. And don't you ever forget it!"

She postponed her NBC special to nurse him back to health, personally cooking him greasy chicken soup and burnt scrambled eggs.

"Silver," he begged her weakly. "If you ever want me to recover, you'd better quit with the cooking!"

Thanks to Silver's diligence, the black sedan was traced to a known drug kingpin, Sol Winogratsky. Within hours he was picked up and charged with attempted murder.

*

Nora Carvell decided she was getting too old for all the excitement and that it was time to retire. She gave up smoking and went to live with her sister in Florida.

Before leaving Hollywood she was delighted to be present at a reconciliation lunch between Silver and her daughter, Heaven. The two of them finally seemed to be getting along.

*

Reba Winogratsky took over her husband's business while he was doing time for an attempted murder rap he should never have gotten involved with in the first place. It was all the fault of that stupid magazine *True Life Scandal*. Printing that she'd had an affair with Wes Money. Really!

Like a fool she had left the magazine on the floor in the can, and Sol had read it on one of his marathon craps.

"Is this the same motherfucker who ran off with my money?" he screamed.

How many Wes Moneys married to Silver Anderson did he think there were?

"Yes, Sol."

"An' you *fucked* him?"

"Yes, Sol. We were separated at the time. You were *schtupping* the female bodybuilder with the big biceps. Remember?"

Sol had a hot temper. It was his undoing.

*

Heaven adored living with her father, even though it was unbelievable to realize she was Zachary Klinger's daughter. He was such an important man, so rich and powerful. At first she was in complete awe of him, but gradually – with the help of Beverly – the two of them began to get to know each other.

And things with her mother were looking up. Since the shooting incident, while not exactly close, they were in regular contact, and it pleased Heaven a lot. At last she felt she was part of a real family.

And her record went to number one. What a blast! But best of all, she and Pen Sullivan had become an item – as they say in Hollywood.

At twenty-three, Penn was old enough to look after her, and young enough to understand.

They really enjoyed being with each other.

When Zachary K. Klinger suffered a mild stroke, his daughter and Beverly were by his side, a close-knit family unit.

It was the relationship Heaven had yearned for all her life.

*

Rocky was cast adrift right after the great yacht disaster. Zachary K. Klinger bought his part of Heaven's contract for a princely sum, and banished him from her life.

Heaven didn't care – she hardly seemed to notice.

Rocky bought a Porsche, a closetful of new clothes, and a penthouse in Marina Del Rey.

He met an Amazon woman with Nordic bones and a voice

like the crunch of gravel on a wet day.

"Gonna make ya a rock star, babe," he promised her.

He was still trying.

*

Lord Mark Rand stayed in Hollywood and directed a film for Zeppo White and Orpheus. Zeppo was under the misguided impression that anyone with a title could do no wrong.

Mark's directorial debut was the flop of the year. Fortunately for him he was still invited to lots of parties. After all, he was a Lord, and Hollywood was crammed with social-fucks.

*

Jack Python assisted at the birth of his first child with all the aplomb of a seasoned veteran. He held the baby immediately after the doctor, placing it lovingly on Jade's stomach. "It's a boy," he said for the sixth time since his son had entered the world.

"A boy," she murmured happily. "Looks just like daddy, I hope."

"Take a peek."

She raised her head. "Gorgeous! All that hair!"

"I think we should get married," he said seriously.

"Why?"

"Because."

"Because what?"

"Because I love you, *goddammit!*" he said, exasperated.

"Let's stay single," she suggested.

"Why?"

"Because."

"Because what?"

She smiled. "Because I love you, *goddammit!*"